THE
AMERICAN
PEOPLE

THE AMERICAN PEOPLE

VOLUME 2: THE BRUTALITY OF FACT

LARRY KRAMER

FARRAR, STRAUS AND GIROUX   NEW YORK

Farrar, Straus and Giroux
120 Broadway, New York 10271

Copyright © 2020 by Larry Kramer
All rights reserved
Printed in the United States of America
First edition, 2020

Library of Congress Control Number: 2019028473
ISBN: 978-0-374-10413-9

Designed by Jonathan D. Lippincott

Our books may be purchased in bulk for promotional, educational, or business use. Please contact
your local bookseller or the Macmillan Corporate and Premium Sales Department at 1–800-221-7945,
extension 5442, or by e-mail at MacmillanSpecialMarkets@macmillan.com.

www.fsgbooks.com
www.twitter.com/fsgbooks • www.facebook.com/fsgbooks

1   3   5   7   9   10   8   6   4   2

Once again, for David Webster

The goal of every serious artist is to rework reality by artificial means to create a new vision of the world intensely more truthful than anything ever seen before, the brutality of fact.

—FRANCIS BACON

AUTHOR'S NOTE

Volume 1 of *The American People* took us up to postwar America. It ends rather abruptly because Your Roving Historian was taken to the hospital to die. He didn't and is now able to continue. He prays that you don't leave now. So many others have and will.

PART I

Your Roving Historian welcomes you back. Let us continue to follow our bouncing ball.

•

This is your virus speaking. I, too, am glad you've come back to learn more about my taking over the world. Your author considers anger "a healthy and productive motivating force." Thank goodness he talks too much and accomplishes so little and words are cheap. My English is much better now, don't you think? My anger is also what is motivating me. And I am, as you would say, "getting my own back."

DAVID JERUSALEM GOES TO WORK AT MR. HOOVER'S HOMOSEXUAL WHOREHOUSE

Mr. Hoover started his whorehouse to trap male spies and gather information "to save America." It's called the Club. He says he started it because a Senator McCarthy and a Mr. Sam Sport were criticizing him for not doing his job. I recognize Dickie Fratragelli from Partekla and other guys on staff here look familiar too. There are thirty-seven of us. We're required to wear jackets and ties and keep ourselves clean and smelling nice. There are boys from farms, and Indians and Negroes, and from foreign countries. Each of us has our own room and shower. Showers are popular because if you can get your customer hard again after sex that's another ten bucks.

The Club gets a lot of business. I do everything without much feeling. I ask some of our guys if they really feel, and some say yes and some say sometimes and some say no, but they all give me a funny look for asking, as if they've never thought about it.

I think about feeling a lot. I think a lot about how am I going to survive my survival. After that camp they held me in when I came back from Germany, what am I meant to learn in this next chapter? And Mr. Hoover suggested I start my next chapter here. What am I supposed to learn?

Each guy has been chosen for something special he can do. The Indian kids can take it up the ass for hours, and they're particularly affectionate. I'm no good at either. Dickie said we don't have to do what we don't want to do. It's the scars on my back that make me "special." Some customers run their hands and lips over them. They want me because of my scars. When they want to know where I got them, I'm told to say, "From Mr. Hitler," and see if that brings forth any interesting information from them. But sometimes my scars make a man start to hit me, at first slapping my back softly, but then working up to more, which I don't want or like. That's when I'm told to call in Sammy or Charlie.

Dr. Horse doesn't like such weakness. "You must at least try everything," he says. "If it doesn't get you excited, take another Dridge Ampule." That is how I get erections a lot of the time. They make you forget the outside world.

We tell Dr. Horse all we can after each customer. What we could find out about his work, and his life outside of work, and how he felt about anything we could get him to talk about in "casual conversation." Dickie, who took lessons on how to do this at Partekla, was great at this. He could get guys to tell him their entire life. "In the end, they're all sort of boring and not all that different," he said. They don't sound like spies to me. "You let us be the judge of that," Dr. Horse says. He takes notes on what we tell him. We get an extra bonus if we can get the guy's phone number or address.

I recognize Dr. Horse from Partekla too. He's very handsome and a cutup, goosing guys and telling jokes. He's called Dr. Horse because "I'm hung like one." But he isn't. He's regular size. Being in charge, he's older than the rest of us. He has silver white hair but his body is hard like a younger man's. He works out every day with weights. He has lots of young customers.

There's a lot of laughter. The guys here all think this is fun and don't mind if their cocks or asses are sore from twelve customers a day. Borff and Sammy have competitions at Sunday breakfast to see who can get bigger and shoot farther. Everyone's punchy from being up all night. Someone runs into the kitchen to bring back a big bowl and a measuring cup, and someone turns on the radio, which only has loud church organs. Clyde often comes to watch and see how much gism we can shoot into the bowl. One Sunday morning everyone got erections and started playing with each other, which isn't allowed. A kid named Tiger who'd just arrived stuck his hand in Clyde's crotch, trying to be friendly. Clyde's cock wasn't hard, and so Tiger started massaging it for him. There was immediate silence. Tiger was fired, and Borff says it's only a matter of time before he's found dead in the park. Sammy says that's because Tiger found out Clyde has a small one.

Guys are always disappearing, like in Germany and in Idaho, and now here.

One day, Dr. Horse called us all together to "vaccinate you against disease." He said, "You boys are interacting with a great many men in a great variety of different ways and we all know that the body is a great big harbor of all kinds of nasty dirty things. So this shot will protect you. We consider ourselves very lucky that because of all our wonderful work in Idaho we have this shot to protect us." Then he laughed as he patted his dick.

Mr. Hoover assured me that we were protected by something. Of course I was forbidden to say anywhere that he was our "employer," or had anything to do with us, which made no sense what with Clyde coming around to be so social.

I fucked with man after man in that whorehouse and now I assume I gave them whatever it was I had been given. Have men died because of what I've done with them? Will I die from what was done to me? I don't know why I'm so sure of it now, but I am.

I don't know what got me through Mungel and Partekla, and now here. I'm not certain about everything that happened to me there. I am like some sponge. How do I squeeze it all out of me or vomit it out and clean myself up or what?

Will there ever be a time when I know anything but sorrow, pain, and loneliness and death? I'm not sure why Mr. Hoover thought that working here would teach me what I want to know.

Grodzo had taught me at Mungel that not everyone reacts the same way to the same illness or what he called "bodily intrusions." And that being exposed to something can sometimes make you not get it and stay healthy. And that Philip and Rivka gave me good genes. Dr. Omicidio will tell Fred that in the early days what some of us got was maybe weaker and not as strong as what was in the guys who died later. And that that's why the plague didn't really get going for another twenty years.

It would be a while before I figured out that Mr. Hoover knew all along about Amos Standing, who worked for Hitler, and how Amos loved my father so much he wanted to live with him for the rest of their lives. And he knew that Philip didn't want to stay in Berlin with Amos Standing, but to come back to America because he was feeling guilty about leaving my mother and brothers, and so he promised he'd return to get me. Amos just in case made a deal with Mr. Hoover. I was the deal. Mr. Hoover talked to Mr. Hitler and I was safe. And once upon a time I'd been told I was going away to school in Boston! When I asked Mr. Hoover what he wanted me for he said he found me "a most interesting case." I was cute and made him smile.

Mr. Hoover said he saw me playing with Skipper across the street from his house when I was five years old. Funny how some people stay in your lives. I have a couple of customers who are of particular interest to him. He asks me lots of questions about them. One is someone named Boris Greeting. "He is potentially a very dangerous man," Mr. Hoover tells me. "One reason I opened this place is for people like him and other high-level men to have somewhere where they feel safe to come to." He also wants to know what I do with a man whose name I will learn is James Jesus, who is evidently also very interesting and "in charge of our country's spies." "Well, he is very what here is called 'nelly,' and likes to put on women's underwear and for me to fuck him, which I can only do when I take a Dridgie," I tell him, which makes him laugh.

Borff and Sammy and Dale have been taken to the hospital. Vaughan is off duty until his ruptured anus heals, which it may not. Hare has disappeared. They will find Tiger dead.

Dr. Horse says, "You will live forever." Dr. Horse now gives us vaccinations every week. "This is miracle stuff I'm giving you! You'll never get sick. You are lucky you're here to get this." He calls it a "booster shot."

DR. SISTER GRACE

What the fuck? I have blood from here in Washington, I have blood from Partekla, I have blood from Mungel, I have blood from San Francisco and St. Louis and from Chicago and many other American cities. I have contaminated ancient shit from the Table family discovered by Nesta Trout. Grodzo has obtained tests from Max Planck Institute scientists that he says I must see. Von Lutz and Brinestalker and Nostrill have given me names of hundreds of homosexuals. I have no frigging idea what anyone expects me to do with them.

A SON'S CRY FOR HELP

Momma, if anyone comes to your house and asks about Ralph it's me they're talking about but you must pretend not to know anything about me. I'm being followed, Momma, and I'm afraid. I wanted you to know I'm still alive. I hid in a delivery truck all the way to Boise. I'll stay in touch as best I can. I love you, Mamma. I am sorry I left you. But you and Poppy didn't understand.

FROM THE COVENANTS OF THE DISCIPLES OF LOVEJOY

We keep the departments small so that the structure of each, and of each to each, and of each to the whole, remains stable. Each is headed by someone with enough influence and contacts to keep his site intact, operational, and productive. There is no doubt all our policies reflect what our fellow Lovejoys wish to do and have done. Our fellow Lovejoy, Senator Vurd, constantly reminds us that this particular essential task was identified long ago: to remove them from all areas of life. He has also suggested partnering with the Catholic Church, which disdains us but hates queers as much as we do. So he has arranged with the Vatican to share generously in our campaign to rid us all of this scourge.

What we are doing is the will of God. Homosexuality is a crime and a sin. Thus our honest and noble and healthy hatred is quite naturally an established moral imperative, not only for us but for all God-fearing peoples.

We call it the Grand Elimination.

INTERVIEW 102.3497PJ

Subject: Twenty-year-old male. Was in Partekla before St. Purdah's. Both parents missing, possibly deceased.

> I cry all night but they don't believe me. I have no idea why I can't go out into the world. They tell me I'm not ready. Why is a nun taking care of me? All the doors are locked. Who's paying for me to be here? How can I get out of here? I think I was happy once.

Patient takes his life the day after above interview wherein he had signed over all his worldly goods. He had several hundred dollars and a gold and diamond ring. He hangs himself with his sheets, the method most often used.

—PJ

FROM DAME LADY HERMIA BLEDD-WRENCH'S
HISTORY OF EVIL

BLOOD IS VERY COMPLICATED

I am digesting and redacting this evil history as quickly as I am uncovering it.

Dr. Grodzo was among the many Nazi scientists covertly hired "to advise" The American People. He had much to share, for he was an original planner of the Mungel experiments, which, judging from the young David Jerusalem's horrid report, indicates an imagination unparalleled in this new field of "incarceratory treatments."

"I am here to observe, to learn, to sniff around" ("*herum schnuffeln*"). "In Germany I shot my load" ("*verdamte gekaufen*"). The Ivy Lee office, through Amos Standing, facilitated Grodzo's transfer. I was surprised to learn that Grace was appointed his "supervising overseer." It seems that as a boy Grodzo's father knew Grace's father when he was murdering women in the Black Forest. Dear Cousin Grace never told me about any of this! Boris Greeting is his "corporate sponsor," and it is unclear how he got in on this act.

It was Brinestalker's idea, this importation of enemy scientists, and he evidently sold it quite easily to Hoover. Brinestalker father and son had been much in touch with German scientists for many years. I knew little about this Hoover but the little I commence to learn is uncomfortable. "You don't understand, Dame Lady Hermia," my contact on this Hoover chap said to me, "Washington is all about power and one obtains it quite often by messing in matters that no one else wants to. So you pick up all the pieces of paper off the floor that no one wants to pick up. Then they're yours. People are increasingly terrified of Hoover, including at the White House." One gathers he's picked up many pieces of paper from many floors.

Since 1924, J. Edgar Hoover had been head of the FBI. The Federal Bureau of Investigation has been around under one name or another since that other Roosevelt, Theodore, started it in 1908. In 1927 Edgar sees the photograph of and hires one Clyde Tolson, whom he will appoint as assistant director in 1930. They are both young and rather handsome. Clyde is very solemn-faced. From the beginning they are obviously inseparable. Some believe Clyde had the brains. David Jerusalem will tell us otherwise. Hoover will run his kingdom until he dies in his office in 1972. Clyde will die in 1975. From 1924 until 1972 is a very long time for any single individual to acquire so much power. Hoover found ways to make himself untouchable and irreplaceable, indeed invincible, until he was virtually a king. I know you people are not familiar with kings and what they can do with power. You should be. No president could get rid of him. The files he collected on tens of thousands of people were sufficient as to pose enormous threats and Hoover wielded this information mercilessly.

There is no question they were bound together, Hoover and Tolson. Scholars are reluctant to call their relationship a homosexual one, God knows why.

It would appear that Boris Greeting, after the war, has a few things he wants studied in "human trials." The Greeting vaults had revealed many concoctions acquired over the years of its history. He has blood samples from all over the world. Neither NITS nor COD is set up for human trials, leaving Partekla as the only place for a "fast track." Human trials, fast track, this is science fiction talk, Dr. Frankenstein talk. Your American Congress is not about to fund human guinea pigs. So it has not been informed about Partekla, which has a secret budget from . . . where? I wonder if someone exceptionally prescient set up Partekla in the first place, knowing . . . what? That another war might be coming and you are not prepared? Is this a Cold War tool? Get there before the Commies? I had in fact been considering Partekla as a germ warfare factory of some sort. Every country had one and still does. But Grace had her own ideas to investigate, with no other place to do so legally. She is thinking that the blood and vaginal discharges of women could be revelatory, particularly after contact with men. She is exceptionally clever. Hookers usually are. What are smart ambitious scientists to do when they are bursting with the conviction that what, come-hell-or-high-water, they must test would save humanity? She reminds me of the iconoclastic work done by our joint ancestor Lord Guelph at his laboratory at St. Simon's on the Wharf. I am discovering that Cousin Grace has my growing approval. I wrote to tell her so, and we have been meeting and talking quietly here in Washington at her monastic residence-cum-laboratory. (It was a very touching reunion, after so many years. Age can do that for one.) For her, Partekla is a dream come true. But she is right to keep her mouth shut for the nonce and until she has something to show.

An awful lot of ex-Nazis, and many not so ex-, take up permanent residence on your safer shores after the war, and, we are discovering, before it, and, we are discovering, during it as well. It is the policy of your State Department that it's better to have the important ones here than there. Much research must *always* be done on blood. "Blood is *sehr* important." Grodzo agrees with Grace.

Who is really paying for this Partekla place?

I find that there have been grants from NAFTRA, NonComp, PERK, and PUCS (all new government agencies set up by who knows whom to do who knows what), which are now allowed to support specific nonspecific scientific research programs. Corporate gifts from Vidalia Farms, from International Frats, from Nasie-Ever-More, from GreetingBaxxterDridge, among numerous others, do the same. If one were paranoid one could see that some sort of takeover is revving up, some sort of infiltration by aliens from another planet. What in God's name is PERK, or PUCS?

The first batch of questionable blood arrives in Lot 21098xcv458trn/abed\ frish Vat 69, from GreetingBaxxterDridge Pharmaceuticals. It is sourced "from twenty-seven 'donors.'"

Grodzo evidently doesn't like what he sees.

What's interesting to him is not from whom the blood comes but from how many it comes. Indeed, twenty thousand donors per lot of pooled plasma are required to concoct a batch of what will shortly be marketed by Greeting as . . . I must remember the name of this drug: Factor VIII. Twenty thousand donors needed per batch. No wonder things get so out of hand.

"This is not so good," Grodzo writes, "as I look through my microscope at a coil of rants. No, no, no! What I see in here. Bad!"

He writes a letter expressing his concerns to GreetingBaxxterDridge Pharmaceuticals, which had sent the blood to Grace for testing for (she told them) a potential cure for the mismitosis she suffers from. She had developed several profitable products for them in the past, such as Vel, a hormone-measuring technique that won her the Nobel Prize.

"Your blood is not so clean. Your blood should be more clean. You have in your blood a number of Grade 987231032l impurities (see attached list). It is my strong recommendation that before you put your blood into further testings all of said Grade 987231032l impurities (see attached list) are removed from your blood."

For an old Nazi, Grodzo seems to be harboring awfully good American instincts. Grace advises him to keep his mouth shut. *"Aber dieses Blut ist immer noch Scheisse,"* Grodzo protests, meaning, "But this blood is still shit."

"So is everyone in Washington" is Grace's knowledgeable reply.

Also noting that the blood is shit is Dr. Rebby Itsenfelder, a young gay doctor from South Africa at NITS on a fellowship. He cannot believe his eyes. This blood from GreetingBaxxterDridge is not only Scheisse, it's triple Scheisse. Are these people serious? He tells Monserrat Krank, with whom he'd done cancer research at Cambridge (for a few years they thought they'd discovered its cure), and who, more important, is very rich. How did Rebby see this blood? Grodzo is also at NITS. Blood is so complicated.

In due course, A. W. Napp, the executive in charge of "New Blood" at GreetingBaxxterDridge, replies:

"Our blood is clean enough. We have followed the guidelines promulgated by the Federal Government on 17 Sept 1928. It is not necessary to obtain your approval. We sought it only as a courtesy to Dr. Sister Grace Hooker, and at the same time to show to you and others what important work we are doing. Please be advised that we have received approval from Dr. R. S. Napp (no relation) of FADS for continued development of our product pursuant to its sale to the public."

Neither a Napp at GreetingBaxxterDridge nor a Napp at the Department of Food and Drug Supervision can I locate on any personnel list of this era.

"Our product"? What product?

Blood is very complicated.

A DREAM COME TRUE?

FRED: Indeed, for many who knew about it, Partekla was a dream come true, a veritable ground zero for the killing fields, to utilize current palaver, imposing itself insidiously on our daily life. Can we not begin to sense, to smell, as Hermia does, how all the little bitty pieces of paper are coalescing into the evil that is this postwar world? The notion of "for the sake of humanity," which our Florence Nightingale and your Clara Barton fought so valiantly to introduce into all matters of health, is not taking root.

Yes, blood is very, *very* complicated. It cannot be stated enough.

•

I have learned many tricks to survive. I keep hoping a brilliant person will appear with a discovery we all can live with. It has troubled me that we are all traveling different journeys that do not allow that to happen. More than ever I now see it is either me or you.

I thought I could infect the world during this past Great War, and then live forever. I killed many but evidently not enough.

I will not fail this time.

THE COEUR D'ALENE *RATTLESNAKE*

The Coeur d'Alene *Rattlesnake* reports, "Dazed young men are wandering about the North West, bruised and speechless. Their bodies are covered with black and blue marks and scabs. They drift off into the distance. Good luck to them. We did not want them here but we nevertheless wish them well."

DR. ISRAEL JERUSALEM WRITES IN HIS LAB AT ISIDORE SCHMUCK

I am reminded of Kristallnacht in Germany. This was the first big sign from the government of Hitler that Jews were not wanted in any way. Partekla reminds me of this. Someone is saying that homosexuals are not wanted in America in any way. I have a patient who works for that Hoover in a top-secret job. He confides in me that 3,500 young homosexual men have been imprisoned at Partekla—*at least*—and that few of them survived. I tried to discuss this with Grace but she would not talk about it. Indeed, she became hysterical. "How dare you imply I know details about something so awful! How dare you, Israel, not trust me after all we've shared with each other!" I hope she will calm down so we return to our work, which was beginning to prove interesting. I am seeing more new infecteds no one knows what to do with or what is wrong with. They are infected with strange things. I believe I have seen such before.

The war is over but it is not over! It is really never over. Where is the congressional hearing about any of this?

At the center of all history there is always a terrible secret. I am too familiar with this feeling of warning.

TWO OF OUR LEADING CHARACTERS MEET EACH OTHER

They'd seen each other many years ago when perhaps they looked sufficiently different to keep them from remembering each other now in the Masturbov Gardens drugstore.

"Do you remember me?" Daniel, now twenty-one, asks Fred, now all of fifteen, who is staring down at a turquoise Estabrook fountain pen in a display case. "Isn't it beautiful? I use ink the same color. I write everything in turquoise ink. It's my color."

Fred looks up at him and answers. "It's my color too! But you must have it!"

"No, no, I use a Parker Fifty-one. You must have it!"

"I haven't got enough money yet, but I will after I babysit a few more times." Then, "You remember me?" Fred asks.

"Of course I remember you. Grace Hooker babysat us a couple of times together when our parents went out to the same blood thing. Our moms know each other from their work."

"Pudgy Waffle!" Fred exclaims. "I wonder what's happened to her." He looks at the pen again, and then back at Daniel. "He said it was the last one ever."

"Here, let's put a deposit on it, so they'll hold it until you can get the rest." Daniel summons the clerk and hands him a dollar bill. "We'd like to place this deposit on this beautiful turquoise Estabrook fountain pen that you say is the last one. So you can hold it for Mr. . . . ."

"Mr. Fred Lemish," Fred tells the clerk. He's disappointed that Daniel doesn't remember his name. He corrects the salesman's spelling. "One M. I promise I'll pay you back. Do you still live in Masturbov Gardens?"

"Yes, but I'm away at college now. I go to Yaddah. I'm going to be a doctor. Would you like to go for a walk in the park across the street?"

"What were you reading so seriously? I saw you there before."

"Come to the park and we'll sit down and you can read it."

Homosexuals in government, 1950
Congressional Record
Volume 96
Part 4
81st Congress 2nd Session
March 29–April 24, 1950
(pages 4527–4528)
ON THE FLOOR OF THE HOUSE OF
REPRESENTATIVES:

Mr. Arthur L. MILLER of Nebraska. Mr. Chairman, I realize that I am discussing a very delicate subject. You must know what a homosexual is. I would like to strip the fetid, stinking flesh off of this skeleton of homosexuality and tell my colleagues in this House some of the facts about them. But I cannot expose all the putrid facts, as it would offend your sensibilities. Make no mistake several thousand, according to police records, are now employed by the Federal Government. It is amazing that in our Capital City of Washington we are plagued with such a large group of those individuals. Washington attracts many lovely folks. These are not they.

In the Eightieth Congress I was the author of a sex pervert bill that passed this Congress and is now a law. It can confine some of these people to St. Purdah's Hospital for treatment. We learned two years ago that there were around four thousand homosexuals in the District. The Police Department the other day said there were now between five and six thousand in Washington who are active and that 75 percent are in Government employment. There are places in Washington where they gather for the purpose of sex orgies, where they worship at the cesspool and fleshpots of iniquity.

You will find odd words in the vocabulary of the homosexual. There are many types such as the necrophilia, fetishism, pygmalionism, fellatios, cunnilinguist, sodomatic, pederasty, sapphism, sadism, and masochist. There are many methods of practices among the homosexuals. Some of those people have been in the State Department, and some of them are now in other departments. These people are likely to be known to each other.

I ask you to bear in mind how many of these homosexuals have had a part in shaping our foreign policy. How many have been in sensitive positions and subject to blackmail. If all the facts are known, homosexuals have been used by the Communists. I believe many of them are Communists.

I believe there is physical danger to anyone exposing the details and nastiness of homosexuality, because these people are dangerous. They will go to any limit. These homosexuals have strong emotions. They are not to be trusted and when blackmail threatens they are a dangerous group.

They are now not knowingly kept in government service. They have been locked up in a place called Partekla.

Upon their release they must not be employed in Government. I trust both sides of the aisle will support my amendment that will prohibit them from so being.

Daniel watches as the young Fred slowly and intently reads the pages with bowed head. "Do you understand it?" Daniel asks. "Do you know people like this?"

"Do you?"

"The people I know are mostly nicer," Daniel answers, as he adds to himself, "Yeah. Like Uncle Hyman."

"Our neighbor across the hall disappeared last week. He and his friend were gone. They took all their belongings in the nighttime. We didn't hear a thing. They'd left their door wide open. Mr. Nelson was teaching me how to type. I've bought a Royal portable typewriter from my babysitting."

Now Daniel remembers Fred's sad and lonely eyes, with which he identifies.

"So you know what a homosexual is?" Daniel asks.

"Yes."

"Do you have feelings for other boys?"

"Yes. I want a friend. A boy friend. Do you have one?"

"No."

"So you have feelings for other boys too."

"Oh, yes."

Fred confesses. "Have you had them for as long as you can remember?"

Daniel smiles and nods. "For as long as I can remember." Then he stands up. "Excuse me, young Lemish. I must get going."

"When will I see you again?"

"Oh, we'll meet again. We're bound to."

"But when? I don't want to let you go!" He grabs for Daniel's arm.

"When the time is right. When you get your lovely turquoise Estabrook pen will you write to me? Your mother and my mother can find me."

And then Daniel is gone. He cannot bear to look at young Lemish and his eyes and his bowed head a moment longer for fear it will break his heart. He reminds him of his young self who had also wanted a special fountain pen to write with to a boyfriend.

And young Lemish longs to see Daniel Jerusalem naked. Now he knows they both belong to a people the House of Representatives doesn't want to see at all.

LONG LIVE THE QUEEN!

"A fucking virus is a fucking virus if we're at the fucking right place at the fucking right time."

"Yes, yes, I learned this from the Iwacky! Please, why necessary are so many fucks?"

"Because there are so many fucks is what this is all about!"

"You know this for certain?"

"I am Dr. Sister Grace Hooker! I am the Queen of Blood. You are Dr. Israel Jerusalem. I have studied under a stronger microscope the samples that you sent me. We're going to get another fucking Nobel Prize!"

Then she asked him: "Tell me again. What did you win your Nobel Prize for, so long ago?"

"The cause of an ancient disease."

"And with what proof?"

"My Iwacky boys eat each other."

"Exactly."

"You have lost much weight."

"I have had much stress. We will be in touch. I must go somewhere far away at present."

TWO OF DORIS HARDWARE'S WHORES

Today's girl is Jinx Seeley. When Mordy Masturbov hears her name on the phone from Clothilde, who does the bookings for his mother's Hardware House, he doesn't recognize it. Mordy has his own first home away from home. A very large and elegant house, built by one of Abe's companies in one of his big-deal neighborhoods near Isidore Schmuck. Mordy is just over twenty. He'd decided to start *Sexopolis*. Instead of going to college, he just tells Abe he's launching a big enterprise and Abe's sufficiently intrigued to let him off the hook. After all, he never went to college himself. Claudia helps Mordy decorate. He's still in love with her. A lot of good it does him. He knows she's working for his mother. He'd been writing articles about her for *Sexopolis* before it was even in print. He figures loving Claudia was all the pre-on-the-job training in the romance area that he needed to get. So he started *Sexopolis*. From its very first issue it's been a roaring success.

When Jinx arrives she turns out to be unexpectedly perky and amusing, qualities unfamiliar to him.

"My name is Jinx Seeley and my parents are Mr. and Mrs. Horace Plotkin and my real name is Rebekkah Regina and my aunt and uncle are the Chesterfields, he's the famous rabbi and I believe she's dead. I lived for a while in India. Seeley is for the soul I didn't find there. Jinx is for the mess I've made. You sure are younger than the usual. Where's the bedroom?"

Can my cock handle funny?

She walks around the house. "It's like George Washington at Mount Vernon." She gawks and studies and admires and occasionally sighs. "I know how much *that's* worth!" She's impressed. She walks through the foyer and into the dining room with its enormous table peopled by dozens of stern high-backed chairs ("for some dinner party you won't invite me to"), and then back to what she calls "the main lobby," and again, without invitation, she goes up the curving staircase to the floor above. Mordy follows, not knowing quite what to say.

"You're a very charming act," he says finally. "You have a very charming act," he repeats, trying to keep up with her.

"Is it? I'm glad this hugeness is yours. It's right and proper that a man of your prominence should have this house all on your own. You're so young, though. You certainly are a prodigy. That's a new word I just learned. Do you know what it means?"

Is she putting him on? He has little sense of humor, Claudia has told him on more than one occasion, and he seems unable to do much about it. He never remembers jokes; he usually fucks up the punch line of those that he tries to tell. "It's not about jokes," Claudia said when he asked how to right his deficiency, "it's about lightening up," which he understands even less: he isn't heavy, he's very light on his feet, he's a good dancer, he can swim a hundred yards in no time. "Forget it," she finally said when she realized he didn't get it. Which of course he picked up on. He doesn't like this feeling. How do you get a sense of humor? Does he even want one? He sort of likes being stern and unsmiling. Shouldn't a powerful editor/publisher be both?

By the time he enters his bedroom she's already yanking off her clothes. The bedspread is still on. This she rips off, making him feel that the order of things is slipping out of his control. In this baronial room—his lair, with the huge phallic mahogany bedposts, the thick black carpet, the gaping fireplace that could receive a pig, the canopy of drapery protecting the bed like a bulletproof vest—in this room, there she is, inattentive to him, not paying him one fucking bit of attention as she neatly folds her clothes and places them on a small armchair that she talks to. "So thoughtful of you to be here just for my undies and the undies of those who still wear undies and who come here to take off their undies." She's still smiling and being perky. "I genuinely do like this house," patting her palms together pleasurably, like a flapping seal or a kid in a sandbox. She is now completely naked, which he sees pleases her: she's comfortable in and with her body, which he isn't. He'll call his article "My Adventures with Jinx."

"You're a Jewish girl?"

"You're Jewish too."

"I haven't had much experience with Jewish girls."

"Most Jewish men haven't."

"It's been my experience that Jewish girls are rarely hookers. And Jewish girls are never so relaxed naked as you," he says, sitting on the edge of his bed and bending to untie his laces.

Now commences, as always, his consciousness of what he considers his deficiencies: the slight roll of fat that bulges a bit as he bends down, the looseness of all of him because he hates physical exercise, loathes the outdoors; the strange patches of his red body hair that display little regard for symmetry (a right shoulder with a smaller blotch than the other, a left nipple sprouting, the other bare, the chest with little settlements, rare villages in the desert, his pale white legs, and the effusive tuft around his penis that sprouts upward and cascades forward). He displeases himself aesthetically. He'd waited so long for his body hair; why, when it finally came, did it arrive in such a disorderly fashion? Claudia told him if he didn't like it to take a scissors and trim it, or take a razor and shave it off, or visit an electrolysist, or make an appointment at Elizabeth Arden for a waxing. Or forget it. He will observe it. He'll write about it. This problem must be others' too. He is always composing new feature stories as he lives them. Perhaps men's bodies should be styled as much as women's. Is there an Elizabeth Arden for men?

He grabs for Jinx before she can study him like she's studied everything else. She smells nice. She feels nice. She wraps her arms around his back and her legs around his waist and she feels like a big soft beach ball he's carrying. She is nicely pale, not brazenly white like he is. Her body looks like it belongs to another time, like a flapper's perhaps, fragile yet sturdy: breasts small but proportionate to the rest of her; arms flighty and sparrowlike in their dartings and never-restings, her palms running up and down his back, touching his face gently as she looks into his eyes; legs thin but strong, like those of runway models who stride forth best foot forward. Her neck is amazing: very long, as if her head, from which she observes so much, needs a special perch from which to gaze and swivel. Suddenly she stands up on the bed and regally looks down at him.

"Are you ready to be master of all you survey?" she says at length.

He'd wondered whether he should be haughty and masterful, or if this would make him look as silly as he felt, his fleshy midsection rolling over the elastic waist of his underpants, his pouch of genitals still docile, inert, like a kid's pawful of silly putty still waiting for a stick to protrude from it, a flag on the top of Mount Everest. Men's underpants are in no way as seductive as women's underpants. He'd been meaning to have sexy ones designed so his readers could buy them. Hell, this isn't the way his seductions usually transpire. He drops them both to the mattress and sticks his finger in her crotch.

"Don't believe much in foreplay, huh? Just off with the rags and smack-dab into it?"

He rolls off her. He's certain it has never looked more shriveled. He's angry with her. It's her fault.

"I guess we're off to a bad start," she says. "Let's not tell your mother." From the foot of the bed she hauls up an afghan comforter of intricate pattern and soft heather colors. When he keeps lying there, looking a bit silly, a bit fragile, a bit petulant, no, a lot petulant, his skin even whiter from the goose bumps some sudden chilliness brings to him, she tucks him under the comforter. "I hope you're not thinking of bringing out any exotic drugs to get you going. I don't do drugs or alcohol or whips or chains or Dridgies. I'm a naturally healthy and happy woman."

He wonders why, emotionally and physically, he is immobile. Why can't he speak? He is not supposed to feel for this woman. He should have jumped her by now, should have entered her by now. He might even have had her in and out and finished by now. (No, that wouldn't make a good story.) But he has to fuck them all, don't you see, or they'll go out there and say, Mordy Masturbov's a lousy lay. (His readers would identify with *that*.) If he does it quickly he can say, You're my third of the day. That way they can't say, Mordy . . .

"Are you going to climb into Momma and let's fuck?"

He lies on top of her quietly. He puts his hand over her mouth, hoping she'll understand it just means for her to shut up. He lets her fragrance seep into him. He gets hard. He climbs into her.

What am I feeling, what am I feeling? is always the thought that runs through his head as he pumps and pumps, as he kisses, caresses, embraces, pinches, licks, sucks, fondles, strokes, and, if he thinks it's desired, hits, strikes, clobbers, perhaps even ties and binds. He may be young but he'd read all the books Abe left for him. This one wants to kiss and kiss and she emits her sighs of pleasure when he does so, all over her, top and bottom, bottom to top. Kisses are easy for him, and they excite him. He stays harder when kissing. He seems to be enjoying this Jinx Seeley more than some others, but all of them, even Jinx Seeley, remain faceless if his eyes are closed, which they usually are. He says to himself, If I remember her next week, if she pops back into my memory with a good feeling next week, then I'll know that she's something a bit more meaningful.

They never pop back to him.

Dr. Ludens suggests it might be because he knows nothing about them, that he should engage them in personal conversation. "On the contrary," Mordy protests, "I know everything about them." He only sees Dr. Ludens to please his mother, who's worried he's too young for what he's doing.

"Okay, you did it," this jinx woman says when they both reach orgasm simultaneously. "Just like it's supposed to be done. Very textbook. Every guy should do it so good."

"It's usual to be polite and say, 'Thanks, that was great.'"

"Who says it wasn't great?"

"You're saying it. Your tone is saying it. You are sounding very facetious."

"I don't know what that word means. It was great, it was great, it was *great*. It just wasn't very personal. Tell your psychiatrist it's not because you don't know anything about me. It's because you don't give anything of yourself."

"How do you know I go to a psychiatrist?"

"Oh, please."

"Please what?"

"It's the latest thing since the war's been over. Rich guys got nothing better to do except talk about themselves. And come to hookers like me, of course. I have clients who go every week, or do it by phone. From what I can tell, docs all say the same thing: the problem is that you don't know anything about the women you're with. Men are in trouble, dear. The war's over but you still don't know what you've won."

"I'm not in trouble."

"Of course you are. And so you should be. Isn't that why you want to teach the whole world how to fuck better?"

He wants to ask her right this moment to sign on to *Sexopolis* as a columnist. She would appeal to younger readers.

She then proceeds, like some clairvoyant, some astrologer who announces truths, to tell him things that of course he knows and of course would be known by any Perceptive Other who has just fucked with him for forty-five minutes. Still, it frightens him that he could be so nakedly known by another who has merely seen him with his clothes off.

"Your cock is like a piece of wood, very hard, but brother, if you had any feeling in it throughout all that we did, I'd be surprised. You never have a lick of trouble getting it up and keeping it up, but that's as far as it goes. Don't ask me how I know so much about you, how closed and constipated you are, how selfish you are with sharing your insides. Hookers know everything. I'm going to go now. You plumb tuckered me out. Most of the guys are easier to earn the money with. Although now I can splurge on a couple of pieces of pie for dinner. One thing about being a hooker: it saves going on a diet."

He nods and gets up and finds himself giving both of them robes and leading her downstairs to a handsome but obviously little-used kitchen where he sits her down on a stool and lays out many kinds of pie and cake and ice cream.

"Pigging out!" she screams, raising one hand above her head and pinching her nose with the other as if jumping in a pool's deep end. Both do appear to be having a rather good time of it.

"I guess I'll have to go on a diet for a few days," she says ruefully.

"We can work it off again."

"I don't think so," she says seriously. "I don't want another hammering from that piece of wood. You hurt. Nice little Jewish girls don't like to get hurt, especially by nice little Jewish boys. Gentile boys is another matter."

She's putting on her clothes, the undies and the soft green dress that ties around her waist, when he pulls her into an adjoining room that is his office, with its Regency mahogany desk and throne of a chair, and next to it, sitting on a Roman column under a glass cover, his very own stock ticker, ticking away. He opens the top drawer of his desk and pulls out a ledger, proudly unfurling its pages of columns and rows with a proprietary smile, as if to say, Look at all I have. Jinx looks on with complete detachment, saying nothing as he actually caresses the glass covering his rapidly accumulating wealth.

"Don't," she says softly. Perhaps he doesn't hear her.

"This is what really counts." His finger locates the column. "Total value of assets owned by Mordecai Masturbov as of this date—"

"Please don't." She covers her ears and goes back to the bedroom. Mordy cries out after her, "If that's how you feel you can go fuck yourself!" But he follows her, his feet follow her, and as she finishes fixing her face and hair in the mirror he stands in the doorway blocking her exit. "Have dinner with me, honey?"

"I'm not your honey. I'm your afternoon fuck. That's all I want to be. I don't want to know about all your money. I don't want you trying to impress me as if I have to be bought, which I do, but on an entirely different level. If you follow me."

"Yes, you do have to be bought. You'd leave me in a minute if I don't pay for you."

"And you'd send me away in a minute if I didn't look and act the way I do. That's our barter and our bargain. Nothing new. Old as time." She reaches up and runs her hand down the side of his cheek. He refuses to look in her eyes, and she takes her hand away. For a second she feels sorry for him. He still is so very young. Not that she isn't. He grabs her hand and puts it back against his cheek and pulls her clumsily to him. "I don't seem to want you to leave. When we made love, I didn't let myself go, I watched myself, watched to see how hard I got, my eyes all the time peeking to see how you reacted to every single thing I did, hoping your breasts and your . . . everything would drive the emptiness from my body."

"You didn't look at me one second."

This throws him. "I most certainly did. I saw you. I saw you . . ."

She isn't going to let herself cry at his confession. She isn't certain if it's real or a speech concocted for any old broad he wants to stay with a little longer. But she knows that's *her* problem.

She pulls herself away and says, "I'm sorry, Mr. Mordecai Masturbov."

As always after sex, when the women leave him, while his cock recovers from its soreness (it's always blazingly sore, as if its feelings come to life only postcoitus), he feels abandoned and alone and discarded. Sex has ballooned more and more into such a huge part of his life. He goes each morning to Dr. Ludens. Mordy trumpets sexual freedom and *Sexopolis* to her, and to anyone who will listen.

•

Claudia and Jinx talk about how they feel safer at Doris's than anywhere. Some of the other girls think they're nuts. Some feel terrified of men. Some feel terrified of so many men. Some fear that one of them will go crazy in the middle of sex and kill them. Or one of their powerful clients will have them murdered to shut them up. This is Washington, remember. Some of them are worried they'll get infected with something that doesn't show up on their monthly blood tests. Some talk about going away, as a group, to live somewhere in the sun. When they make enough money. Which will be never. They make good money, but they spend good money. There's usually someone or something to send the money to or spend it on. Some of the girls think everything's just fine. So what if some of the other girls think they're nuts. Jinx wishes Claudia would open up more when they talk. They're both still so young to be in a place like this forever, but that's how it seems to be playing out.

No, Claudia isn't good at talking with the other girls. She knows that however she sees things, no one else will understand. A pattern is emerging. She memorized the Kierkegaard maxim "anxiety is the dizziness of freedom," which Nutra, the black whore recently hit by a truck and instantly killed, had hanging in a frame over her bed in needlepoint. Claudia has difficulty correlating "freedom" with the fantasies that are requested of her—whippings, penetrations, even slashes that might bleed, being bound and left alone, oh so many acts of humiliation that evidently bring pleasure to the beneficiary. What about to her? She had thought she had never cared. Stephen tells her it's okay to have fantasies, and okay to act them out, but she worries—she seems to have become a worrier—that she will come to love some man who performs them too adeptly. This perplexes her. She had come into this place to get away from the world and her new world is turning out to be more complicated.

She is aware that it was only days, nights, after her arrival at Doris's that these questions came to be more her friends than any friend. She doesn't understand these thoughts, and there's no Daniel to tell them to. There hasn't been for some time. Often she wants to call him, but she doesn't. He knows where she is. Why doesn't he call her?

She thinks of unloading onto Doris. Doris would understand. But Doris is on this kick that what they're doing is legal and should be recognized as such. Most of the girls look at Doris as if *she's* going nuts. Anyway, Doris would say something like "just be careful you don't fall in love."

A gentleman caller is downstairs. An international tycoon of something or other who likes to get pissed on. Claudia always keeps her clients waiting. She'll douche until she's so empty that she'll ache in there, a void. Water will drip down the insides of her legs as he rings her bell, and she'll make him lick her dry. It sounds so silly that she giggles.

It is interesting that she thought she would be safe here.

Claudia still thinks she will be safe, after she's stayed here long enough.

So, too, does Jinx.

That's why they've sort of bonded.

·   •

A man walks into a clinic in Ahashueras, Kitonka, South West Africa. There is much bloodshed going on in this German territory. People are murdering each other, more and more.

This man wants someone to take some blood from him because he hurts. He believes this will take away his pain. It is an old custom in his tribe. You did it in your early America. He says he hurts because everyone in his family was eaten by another family. And they all have eaten many monkeys. This I think you did not do in America, at least as I remember. The nurse takes his blood. He walks away. The nurse gives the blood to that lady with one arm I worry about.

What is she doing here?

RICKETS

In Ahashueras, at this same moment in time, a Western-backed study of rickets is under way. Some children have bones so soft that they can't stand. The study is financed by the Baxxter-Bissbee-Box Corporation (known as BBB or Threebee), a leading manufacturer of diapers and baby foods and owned anonymously by Greeting-Dridge. Dr. Francine Punic is in charge of this study. She believes that what's going on has something to do with one of her primates.

SEXOPOLIS!

After the first issue of *Sexopolis* had sold fifty thousand copies Mordy found himself constantly seeking newer methods, newer versions for his libidinous outpourings. He writes about what he thinks are acts required for maximum enjoyment, and then he expands his notes into feature stories. He tries all his ideas out for himself, with one girl after another, as in some Betty Crocker bake-off, to find out which ones are winners.

Years before, Mordy had been walking in Miami Beach, where Doris had taken him and Abe for a treat. All these tanned men of all ages walking by want something, he realized. They need something. Just as he needed Claudia. They don't get it. Just like him, again. Even with tans and even in Miami Beach they don't get it. Even after all their years of hard work and all their millions they don't get it. There are some things they just don't know how to get. He will serve them all as well as himself. It's then that he decided he wouldn't go to college and that the time was closer for his launch.

Now that *Sexopolis* is out there more and more he feels men watching over his shoulder. They're always waiting for him. They want him, Mordecai Masturbov, to tell them how to get what they can't get. In hundreds and soon thousands of letters they tell him they're hanging on his every orgasm, his every quiver of pleasure in that wooden cock of his. We want to know! they say to him. Tell us more! I've somehow survived the world and I want to learn before it's too late! Mordy's wartime experiences had been more pacific. He'd been too young to serve so he doesn't talk about it. *Sexopolis* is what he talks about. It's his gift to "my fellow returning warriors."

And so every month he writes editorials for "my men." Hang on! Be patient! Believe! Read my magazine! Tell your friends to read my magazine! I will not desert you! You will not be lonely for much longer. Every month *Sexopolis* sells more copies and Mordy teaches them more acts to perform.

Now he has everything he dreamed of. And when you print 153 million copies a month worldwide, which he'll be doing in not too many years, you should realize that you've touched a nerve.

At first it is mailed in brown paper envelopes. Then it brazenly dares to appear on newsstands. You can even open it up at newsstands and look at exposed female genitalia, staring right at you, and some men can actually get an erection standing at newsstands staring right back. That's right: from coast to coast men browsing at newsstands can get erections staring right back.

Sexopolis will change the sexual mores of the heterosexual world. As Jinx had tipped him off, winning wars frees up a lot of fellows with a lot of time. At first various censorship restrictions and government edicts and religious denunciations will be troublesome, but they will drop by the wayside after (most often) being kicked in the balls by one Sam Sport with his young sidekick, Dereck Dumster. Heterosexual men who want to fuck are emerging as a powerful force for getting what they want, this sexual freedom to which *Sexopolis* is leading them. It will be harder and harder to argue with 153 million erections, worldwide, of course.

Block by block his grandfather and his father had bought up whole neighborhoods to become Washington's biggest landholder. For now it's all in trust until Abe dies, which he very well may do—*Sexopolis* may kill him. He'd thought that Doris's house would do it. That his son Mordy is his mother's son only adds to Abe's heartbreak. Enough already, dear God, my no-longer friend.

MASTURBOV GARDENS

Masturbov Gardens is now twenty years old. The little bushes are now ugly trees, pissed on by too many dogs. Abe walks around it every day. Accountants and old ladies who check invoices and dun people for back payments look after the properties he owns. The trusted Nate Bulb rules their roost. Abe doesn't much like Masturbov Gardens. It isn't pretty. He owns an awful lot of pretty. But here there are no ghosts. This place is honest. He set out to build good value for good people, and he did. For him Masturbov Gardens is the most neutral place on earth, as safe as the cardigan sweater he never changes, once vaguely stained, now more visibly so, like the clothes of absent-minded aging people.

Abe. Doris. Each becomes richer as the days pass. They talk to each other five times a day, like brother and sister, like best friends, like trusted advisers and confidants. She never relays the details of her activities because she knows they bother him. They do. He invests her money. From the amounts she gives him he knows more than he wants to know.

•

I was in Romania and Libya at the turn of the century. I was a big success. They were just such ugly and filthy places to live. I realized that America was the place to be. I would clean you out once and for all. I would make America even greater! Isn't that what all your presidents are always promising? Out with the old filth! In with the new clean slate!

NAMING NAMES

They're naming names, again. One has only to read the newspaper files of these days, or the many volumes written about Naming Names by such scholars of this act and era as Victor Navasky in his book of that very title, to comprehend the enormity of the bombs being hurled at the social fabric. Presumed Communists and homosexuals named publicly, out loud, are expelled from the once safe harbor offered by American democracy and its rights of privacy supposedly guaranteed by a Constitution and a Bill of Rights. Suddenly freedom for many is gone. It's been removed. It's no longer there. New laws are written and enacted before anyone sees them. "Communists" and "homosexuals" are actually put in prison, unless they have money and buy their way to Canada or abroad. Of all the people that "they" go after, it's the Hollywood writers and moviemakers that now get it the worst. A second-rate actor named Peter Ruester is president of a union many belong to. He and Sam Sport are buddies. By mistake Ruester's wife-to-be had been blacklisted. That's when Peter Ruester learns firsthand to be buddies with whoever's where the power is.

O'Trackney Vurd, an obscure senator, is obscure no longer. He is endlessly addressing too-willing audiences such as a national convention of women's clubs at the Greenbriar in West Virginia, decorated by the legendary Dorothy Draper in her signature massive green fronds and brown coconut trees, in front of which Vurd waves a piece of paper he claims lists the names of 505 homosexual "agents" employed inside the State Department. He joins the no longer obscure Senator Joseph McCarthy, who makes a speech in 1950 in this very same location, brandishing "205 Communists in the White House" for Vurd's 505 homosexuals. The president of Yaddah invites Vurd to speak at Yaddah as a "Visiting Scholar," and it gives him an honorary degree. When Eisenhower is elected president, one of his first acts is to fire all the fairies.

Some of those named as Communists fight back. Some actually go to prison for refusing to testify against themselves. Some even confess. All now become blacklisted and both unemployed and unemployable. Ruester doesn't do anything to find his besmirched actors, directors, and writers work. He thinks whatever they did was all their fault.

No one talks officially for homosexuals, and homosexuals don't talk about or for themselves.

WHO IS THIS FUCKED-UP MAN?

Smart, rich, handsome, old Boston family, Harvard, Harvard Law, "a bachelor's bachelor; as Eisenhower's National Security Adviser no man in the

Government, with the possible exception of the President, knows so many of the nation's strategic secrets" (*The New York Truth*).

Robert Cutler is a gay man who for eight years sat atop the national security bureaucracy at a time when people like him were being purged from government service.

Ike's campaign slogan, "Let's Clean House," alluded not only to corruption and sedition but also to an executive order mandating security background checks for federal employees. It was Bobby Cutler who added to the list of Unacceptables those guilty of "sexual perversion."

Per Executive Order 10450, signed by Ike on April 27, 1953, thousands of Bobby's fellow gay government compatriots lost their jobs, pushed out by one of their very own, a traitor to all the gays he knew both in government and socially.

To have such power as Eisenhower's personal assistant and close friend shows a man of great intelligence.

But that this man himself is passionately, obsessively, and unrequitedly in love with one young man after another shows one truly fucked-up homosexual. His diaries of his many years of looking for love have recently been discovered. They are painful. They are pathetic. They are infuriating.

Yes indeed. Robert "Bobby" Cutler was one fucked-up homosexual.

PROFESSOR GEORGE CHAUNCEY, YADDAH UNIVERSITY

"Congress specifically prohibits homosexuals as well as Communists from entering the country. A generation of foreign visitors applying for tourist visas has to sign statements swearing they belonged to neither one of these threatening groups, and a generation of lesbian and gay male immigrants must hide their identities from the authorities. Yes, the real-life consequences of heterosexual definitions of national identity do not stop here. Even homosexuals who were American citizens find themselves virtually stripped of their citizenship, including their rights to free speech and assembly. The federal government purges them from the civil service and bans the gay press from the mails. Local police departments raid gay bars and other meeting places, shut down newsstands daring to carry gay papers, and arrest thousands of gay men and women every year for cruising, dancing together, or simply gathering openly in restaurants, and even private homes. Lesbians and gay men are regularly depicted as treacherous outsiders who threaten both the nation's security and its children."

YOU ARE NOW OFFICIALLY SICK!

The American Psychiatric Association declares officially that homosexuality is a mental disorder and includes it as such in its newest edition of its DSM, or *Diagnostic and Statistical Manual of Mental Disorders*. This falls in line with previous decisions that declared oral-genital sex as deviant and masturbation evidence of out-of-control behavior.

THE MAJOR IN LOVE

I fell in love with him and I shouldn't have. That's why we've stayed here so long. He feels the same about me. He said he doesn't know where to go or what to do, just like me. He broke my heart. He doesn't talk much, just like me, just like many soldiers in combat, I tell him. He's told me plenty of his own war stories, though, and they were pretty awful, just like mine. When he told me his I actually started to cry. So it was as if we bonded. I'm waiting for reassignment, which makes us both sad. He has this way of letting me hold him in my arms like he fits there and he curls up in me. It just drives me nuts. He has these scars. His back is all scarred. At first he wouldn't tell me how he got them. He just wouldn't. I know from combat that they come from something pretty strong. And at first he wouldn't let me touch them. It was pretty hard to fuck not touching his back but we got there soon enough. When he saw that I accepted him scars and all he bawled his eyes out. That's when I knew I was in love with him. I've never been in love with a guy. I just went to the Club to get it off with guys. I didn't go very often until I met David. Now I go too much. I'm going to get in trouble when they find out. And they are going to find out, the MPs. I tease him that I'll have to kidnap him. We start playing with that idea, like where would we go? Where would I take him? I think of exotic places like the battlefields I fought on, which I would like to see again. Most of them were in the South Pacific. Bataan. Corregidor. Iwo Jima. They must be getting pretty enough again. My telling him my war stories makes him cry too. He says we were both used for awful things. I tried to cheer him up by telling him how gay the army really was. "Every foreign posting I was stationed at all over the world, half of all the soldiers were gay." He said, "If you had such a gay army why didn't you fight back?" I never knew I could feel this way about another man. I tell him about my wife and my kids somewhere with a new father. I tell him about growing up in Austin, Texas. I don't know what I'm going to do with the little fucker. He has my heart all right. I'm now a major in the United States Army. The army has been my whole life. There is no other work I know how to do or want to do. I can't have him and have my army too. I think about all this but I don't tell him about it. I am way far ahead of him in my feelings. I know that. Funny thing is, I'm not scared of it. I'm not scared of the military police hauling me in. It's pretty scary that I'm not scared!

I let him read all this. One day I just take it to the Club and give it to him. "What's this?" he says.

"It's a letter I wrote to myself. And I guess to you."

"You want me to read it?"

"Yes. Yes, I do." There. I said it out loud. I wasn't so sure I could say it when it came right down to it. I can tell by the way I hear myself say it that I mean it. It's a good feeling. I wait for him to read it. He has his back to me. After a while I see his body shaking. I take him in my arms. He collapses into me. I have to turn him around to look in those eyes. They're closed. "Open your eyes," I say to him. He shakes his head no. But he kisses me.

DAVID STARTS OUT FOR FREEDOM

I leave the Club. I've been here too long. It isn't easy. I know I have to leave now, but how can I without telling Mr. Hoover? I try writing him letters of explanation. None of them sound right. Just writing them makes me realize what a prisoner I've been choosing to be. I'm afraid he won't let me go. But if he's been tied up with Amos and my father, maybe he won't come after me.

Sammy had died. It took him a couple of years. He was followed by Charlie, who was followed by Dickie, who was always falling in love with his old rich clients. They found Matthew and some others dead somewhere.

Then my major died, Mike Starr. I figured I'd killed him. That's when I decided to get out of here. I wanted to have a little breakdown somewhere quiet.

I didn't make it. I was about to climb out my window when Clyde knocked on my door and said Mr. Hoover wanted to see me.

"I assume Major Starr's death means you want to leave me," Mr. Hoover said.

"Yes. I want to learn. I want to see the world."

"You've seen a good bit of the world already, haven't you?" He was staring at me in a way that made me feel uncomfortable. I had not had this feeling with him before.

I try to put it into words. "Yes, and it makes me wonder why we do the things we do. We talked about this when you suggested I'd learn a lot working at the Club. Why don't we just love each other? Why do we do it in the dark? Why do we have to hide? Why are we punished for trying to love each other? Do you think there are answers?"

He was silent and I worried for my boldness before he answered, "I should be interested in them myself."

I waited for him to go on, but when he didn't I said, "Many guys are getting sick now. They turn purple and choke to death."

"Why do you think that is?"

"We've had so many shots and vaccinations. Maybe one of them is making us sick. Or all of them put together."

"Then shouldn't you be dead?"

I waited a long time before I answered.

"I am."

He actually gave me a little nod.

I ask it again. "Why are we being punished so much for trying to love each other?"

This time I thought I had gone too far. But he said, "All people do it in the dark." Then he pulled himself up a bit, shaking his head as if to clear it. "Did you write me a report? You're required to submit a severance report. You've had sex with a lot of men."

"Not so many. I wasn't very popular."

"So I noticed in the ledgers."

"Then why did you keep me on so long?"

"I figured you'd let me know when you wanted to leave. But tell me what you've learned here."

He waited for me to compose my answer in my head. "I've learned that there are a great many of us, but we try to be invisible. I think we could be a big army if we'd all join. What do you think?" I added, "If you don't mind my asking."

He smiled. The first thought I had was, he is going to let me live. Until this moment I had not thought that he wouldn't. But him knowing about Mike Starr being dead frightened me, the extent and reach of his knowledge.

"I think your future is going to be very interesting." Then he stood up as if to say the meeting was over. "You have become a very handsome and intelligent and capable young man. Your experience here has matured you. I put my money on the right horse, ensuring that you could stay alive and flourish. Make good use of your gifts. You haven't turned out so badly for all your particular adventures."

He offered me his hand to shake. It was cold and sweaty. He held on to mine. "I wish things had been different for you. For me. For us. You will understand when you grow older. Give my regards to your father. His work for our country has been outstanding."

"In what way? What does he do for you?"

"I will leave that for your father to tell you."

I suddenly found myself asking, "Would you send me to college?"

"That can be arranged. Our government at least owes you that. I'd suggest something in San Francisco. A lot is starting to happen there. You can finally send me a report."

•

You do not know about my history. All you are interested in is your own history. So you can all feel important.

FRED LEMISH TRIES TO COMMIT SUICIDE

I went to Yaddah. Six months later I tried to kill myself. Life has not been good so far and I don't see it getting any better.

Henry was the first person I met the day we both arrived for freshman year. We got there early because we both had parents who believed in getting there the minute the gates opened. Registration was a three-day affair, and almost everyone else had sense enough to wait until the end to show up. But there we were, deposited on the steps of Hooker Hall first thing on the first morning, wondering if anyone else was coming to Yaddah this year. My parents left, I'm sure because they couldn't wait to get rid of me, although Algonqua cried and Lester teared up. "I lived in Hooker Hall too," he reminded me. I was happy to see them go. I was even planning to take a new name. Chuck. My middle name is Charles. What better way to start a new life than with a snappy new name like Chuck. I'd been so unhappy with the old one.

Henry and I nodded to each other. We were both dark-haired, crew-cut, and a tiny bit pudgy. He smiled more than I did. No, we were both big smilers. Too many people to please. I thought he was sort of cute.

We were both younger sons, and we both had fathers who hadn't amounted to much. Henry's father was a barber in the small New Hampshire town of Dowling, site of Paulson, the famous prep school. Henry'd gone to Paulson as the barber's son, the son of the man who cut all the boys' hair, all those kids from Park Avenue and Greenwich. He didn't live in a cramped apartment in Masturbov Gardens, but his house was small, a tiny house on a tiny hill on the other side of town. His brother had gone to state college because he wasn't as smart and his folks saved all their money for Henry, the one they were counting on. My brother had graduated just last June from Yaddah and he'd accumulated so many honors, friends, trophies, varsity letters, and elected offices that when people heard my last name they always asked, "You Seth's brother?" Was changing my name going to be enough?

"Your dad's a barber?" I asked Henry as we sat on the steps of Hooker Hall smoking cigarettes. Hooker Hall is one of those great dark nineteenth-century castles of rough-hewn stone that seem impregnable and eternal and righteous and *there*. I'm sure I sounded rude asking Henry about his father, but I was ashamed of my own. Like every other father in Masturbov Gardens, he worked for the government, but he knew and we knew that what he was doing was beneath him and not what Yaddah said he should be doing. He never talked about it except to say how tired he was every day when he came home from work.

"Yes, he is," Henry answered, smiling and dragging on his Chesterfield; but I could see that under all that noble bravura was shame equal to my own. I wondered if Henry had ever said out loud what I had: "I hate Pop." I'd said it to Algonqua for the first time when I was six. "Oh, don't say things like that, dear," she said, very matter-of-factly.

I'd wanted to go to Paulson. I'd come across an announcement of their summer school in my high school library. It looked so impressive, so welcoming. I knew Lester wouldn't pay the tuition, so without telling him I applied for a scholarship and I won. I still needed two hundred dollars more. But he wouldn't pay for that, either.

"But it's for Paulson! I thought you'd be so proud."

"It's just a summer school. You don't have to go to summer school. You'll get into Yaddah without Paulson. Hell, you'll get into Yaddah because I went there and Seth is finishing there and your uncle Murray and my brother Sam. And that cousin, Morton. It was a big deal then, Jews going to Yaddah."

"But it's just two hundred dollars and I'll impress them so much, I'll win a full scholarship for my senior year and you won't have to pay a penny." I wanted so badly to get out of where we lived.

"Paulson was great," Henry said to me as we moved into our dorm, Punic Hall. "We have sixty-two guys from my class here."

I asked him why he wasn't rooming with any of them.

"I wanted to meet new people," he said, frowning. Like me, I'll bet he didn't have any other choices.

Our other new roommates arrived. Henry and I had already staked out the twin beds, side by side. Pablo was Puerto Rican, but he'd been to Naughton, Paulson's rival, on a full scholarship provided by a rich neighbor back home. Tom, from St. Xavier's Prep, was repeating freshman year. They shared the other bedroom, with the double-decker beds. Tom asked for the bottom because he said he'd be bringing home a lot of girls.

At the last minute they stuck another guy in with us. Saville was very sophisticated. He wore an expensive tweed jacket, casually, as if he wore one every day, which it turned out he did. He was from Santa Barbara, but he'd gone to some school in Switzerland. He was tall and blond and he spoke with some sort of imprecise accent, maybe a combination of Switzerland and Santa Barbara, I figured. He said he was going to become a drama critic, and that he was a homosexual, although he wouldn't be in a few years, when he intended to marry. He said he didn't mind sleeping in the living room of our suite because he'd be spending a lot of time with his sister in New York, "to go to all the theater."

Everyone pretended not to notice what had just been said. Tom and Pablo looked at each other and shrugged. I looked at Henry. Henry didn't look at anyone.

I guess Chuck wasn't going to be protected here from that word either.

I'd been trying. I kissed Vivian Mesiroff and Nancy Winkelman and Rebecca Rudolph on their front doorsteps when I took them home. I'd touched the breasts of Marjorie Epstein and Lillian . . . I can't remember Lillian's last name, but I do remember the uncomfortable experience, Bernie Taubtuscher and Mariamne Teitel's younger sister in the front seat necking away like crazy, and Lillian and me in back, me trying to do whatever was expected, get that hand up under that cashmere, kiss those lips still tasting of pizza, keep up with Bernie, boy, keep up. No wonder I can't remember Lillian's last name.

Early in December, just before exams, Henry and I went to New York. Saville had got us free tickets to a show. The week before, Henry had decided to become a doctor and we were going to celebrate. We wore our gray flannels and blue blazers and button-down shirts and rep ties, our one good set of clothes because that's all our parents could afford. I watched Algonqua write out the check when she bought them for me at Garfinkel's. It hurt me to see that. I felt guilty. I wasn't worth it. She told me it was two months' salary but "it's worth it, darling." As the train pulled into Grand Central, an old lady sitting across the aisle smiled and said how nice we looked.

"I just know I'll be a good doctor," Henry said as we walked quickly up Manhattan's streets, braving the cold air of the big city without the camel's hair overcoats sported by all the Paulson and Naughton guys who weren't on scholarships.

"You decided to become a doctor just from reading *Not as a Stranger*?"

"I've read *Arrowsmith*, too."

Saville's sister turned out to live in her very own town house in the East Sixties between Madison and Park, which I could tell was a good place to be. Standing outside, I felt a tingling of anticipation all over my skin. What was I expecting? I'd been to plenty of expensive houses in Washington.

Henry pushed the buzzer and the door clicked open and we went in. Everything was beyond what I'd ever seen in Washington. The foyer was marble squares of black and white, the living room was endless and gilded and glistening with crystal lamps and chandeliers and paintings in ornate frames and real flowers in urns so big you could bathe in them. Long corridors seemed to go off everywhere. Henry and I wandered around like two openmouthed kids left alone overnight in Versailles.

"Some Paulson kids are really rich, but this takes the cake," Henry said.

"You can say that again. I wonder what Saville's father does?"

"Oil. He's president of Royal Dutch Shell. Or else he owns it. One or the other."

We pressed onward, into the interior. Would we find a mass murderer's pile of bodies that would stun the tabloids? An orgy of dancing girls veiled in opium clouds? How did I know to worry about either of these things? Where was Saville, our roommate, our host?

There he was, in a big wicker laundry basket turned on its side, spilling out sheets and Saville, naked except for his white athletic socks and his Shetland sweater over his button-down shirt, his penis dangling down the side of one thigh, white drops of semen congealing on his cock. He must have passed out reaching for the buzzer above him and fallen out of the basket, or into it. We were in a kitchen straight from a Dutch painting, Delft blue and white, hutch cabinets with lined-up plates, pitchers erupting sprays of dried weeds and willows. And Saville on the floor. Who would notice both décor and Saville? I would. Saville, certainly from the waist down, was very handsome. His skin was smooth and tan, and he had no fat on his belly, like a statue of a Greek athlete. His penis was beautiful, and so was the blond hair gently surrounding it. I didn't know I knew what a perfect penis with perfect pubic hair looked like, but I knew I was looking at it. I'd have to pay more attention in Punic Hall when Saville went to take a shower, so I could join him.

And then we looked beyond him to what must have been a maid's room, where a naked young man lay spread-eagled on the bed, his bottom glistening with semen.

I could tell that Henry was nervous. In fact, he was having a hard time trying to turn his attention to checking out the interior decoration when the young man in the maid's room, just a few steps away, groaned and rolled over, displaying his own dripping cock. It, too, was perfect and lovely. I was about to step closer to get a better look—after all, maybe there was something wrong with him and he needed help—when Henry grabbed my hand and started running to the front door, yanking it open to the cold December air that blew sharply in our faces. It would blow what we'd seen all away. That's what I thought Henry wanted as he smiled at me almost as if in relief. I noticed I had an erection. It had all been very exciting and I realized I was reluctant to leave. But the cold air calmed all of me down.

We went to a Broadway musical pretending to laugh and enjoy it, and then we returned to Yaddah and exams and books. When we saw Saville on Monday morning, we ate breakfast with him in Commons as if nothing had happened.

I couldn't get the image of Saville in that basket out of my mind. I'd seen naked guys before in gym, I'd played my share of forbidden games, but the look on Saville's face and the sound of the other kid's groan told me they'd been in heaven. I didn't know where heaven was, but I wanted to get there. Saville reminded me that whatever I thought I'd left for good in Masturbov Gardens (Pop always urging me to keep my eyes out for a rich girl: "it's just as easy to fall in love with a rich one as a poor one") was still waiting for me, like that appointment in Samarra (I was reading books of portentous influence).

A mysterious cough came next to hector me, a tickle in the far reaches of my throat that got worse and worse until it kept me up most of the night, hacking and barking so loudly that our freshman counselor sent me to the infirmary. Swabs and tests administered by doctors and nurses produced no cause and the cough endured. I must have whooping cough, they said, but they weren't sure. They didn't know what to prescribe beyond continued bed rest and that red cherry syrupy stuff they give to kids. But how was I to rest, missing so much of my coursework in which I wasn't that up to speed to begin with?

The cough dwindled and disappeared as mysteriously as it began. I was allowed to return to Punic and an even higher stack of books I had to crack fast, or else.

Henry and Tom were buddies now. Tom was on the verge of failing again, and Henry was helping Tom with his work. Saville and Tom were suddenly close too. One of the local girls Tom brought back had touched Saville's heart, and he was now involved in a romance with her that Henry and I observed with interest. Pablo was preparing for final exams "in the way we do back home," by steadily downing gallon jugs of "the cheapest sherry I can find."

No one took much interest in me. Only Henry had come to visit me in the infirmary, and he only once. I'd asked him if he and Saville had exchanged any words about New York.

"No, of course not!" he snapped.

I swallowed three hundred aspirin on a day in late February after I'd returned from a visit home to Masturbov Gardens. What was I doing there again, I wondered, in a place I didn't want to be? But there I was. I'd looked forward to midterm, going home with hope, until the instant of my arrival, when Algonqua opened the door and I entered the apartment of my youth, and I was swept into that treacherous current where I felt so helpless and unloved. Why in the world did I come back? To this scene of such a lonely and unhappy childhood. How could I think anything might have changed? And that miraculously I might be happier here with them than I was at Yaddah, where I was increasingly lonely and miserable and flunking out? I looked at my mother looking at me. She didn't want me here at all. I could hear her thinking, We just took you up there, what are you doing back already? Three weeks of this? How would I live through them? She closed the door behind me. I was home.

Neither one of my parents wanted me here. I suddenly realized that I was familiar with this feeling. What a dumb kid I must have been not to have known it then. Oh, I knew it all right.

Lester surfaced from listening to a ball game. A fat, heavy, lethargic man, he sweated a lot, no matter what the season. Algonqua said, "Say hello to him, Lester," and he grunted his greeting so as not to disturb Milton Berle, now coming on the new TV. I was back in prison. Even Yaddah suddenly looked good.

I looked in the mirror over my bureau. I resemble Lester. I have the big head, the big ears that jut out, the protruding jaw, and the same unhappy, dissatisfied eyes. I had fought so long not to be like him, to outrun the genes of failure passed along like this old bureau and this peeling mirror. Now here I was, just like him, doing poorly. What was there to return to Yaddah for? More of the same. What was there here in Masturbov Gardens? More of the same.

I began to have nights of sleeplessness. At 3 a.m. I'd go out and walk in the black cold night through the empty streets, through this bleak warren of my childhood. I felt like a fugitive looking for a safe place to hide, what with Mom and Pop still yelling all the time, my departure not having removed their favorite target, each other. At dawn I returned home exhausted, my head still vibrating with fears, some more identifiable than others. I fell asleep only to be shortly awakened by the noises of their own unhappinesses, doors closed sharply, voices raised in disharmony. Sleeping late in this household had never been an option.

Almost to the finish line. If I could only last two more days, then one more, I'd be able to go back to Yaddah, now the clear winner as the lesser evil. Algonqua finally noticed my sorry state. She came into my room in her nightgown and sat down on my bed, none too carefully protecting her body from a son's eyes. She took my hand and clasped it tightly as she asked if anything was troubling me. I knew this confidential pose of hers: she'd struck it many times. Once again she was going to make me feel guilty for something I didn't do in the first place, whatever it was. Her favorite was trying to get me "to apologize, for always yelling back at your father who works so hard to [take your pick:] feed you, clothe you, send you to Yaddah," a place I never wanted to go to. I always found it uncomfortable, this implication that some special bond between us should procreate confession when she desired it. I saw in her expression, in the rejected sag of her body, her message that if I didn't tell her something, anything, some private bit of evidence that she could call her own, then it meant I didn't love her. But could that really have been news to her? I didn't want to be here, I don't want to go back there. What was I going to do? Physical torture couldn't have extracted words from my mouth right now, even if I could have found words for any of my current feelings.

Then once again she tried to ask me: "Are you sad because of a girlfriend who isn't working out?"

And when I didn't answer and her body had sagged, she'd sighed: "Would you like some aspirin, dear? They often make me feel much better."

I remained silent and she let go my hand, which was sore because she'd been clutching it so hard, and she left me there.

Of course Lester never noticed a thing.

I got myself back to Yaddah. I hadn't written the term papers I'd planned to over my vacation. They were way overdue now, one of them hanging over from my hospital stay. I hadn't prepared for the exams coming up next week. There was no euphoria of return. I was right back where I started, no matter where I was.

The notification from the Dean's Office was on my desk. Henry had put it there. It had been slipped under the door. I was flunking out officially. Unless I improved my grades I'd be joining Tom, whose baggage was already gone. I looked at his bare mattress. At least he'd fucked. At least he'd had some intimacy. I wondered what he'd do with his life now that he'd flunked out of Yaddah twice.

As Henry and I tossed in our beds that night he asked me if I'd had a good vacation.

"It was awful."

"So was mine. What did the dean say?"

"I'm . . . I have to do better."

"I'm sorry."

"I don't know how I lived there so many years."

There was such a long silence I thought Henry might have fallen asleep.

"Chuck . . . ?" He started to ask me something. I know he did.

When he didn't finish, something lay in the air. I waited a bit more before asking him, "What?"

"Nothing," he said softly.

"What were you going to ask me?"

"Nothing. Really. I wasn't going to ask you anything."

There was another long pause.

"Henry . . . ?" My voice was barely a whisper. "Would you come into bed with me?"

He didn't answer for the longest time. Finally he said decisively, "It's against God's way."

I saw him turn over to face the wall. I heard him fall asleep. I heard the birds announce the beginning of the new day.

My brother got married a month before I took the aspirin. Her name was Jean and she lived on East Seventy-first Street, between Madison and Fifth. She was a Smith graduate and she worked for the Institute of High Art, as assistant to the curator of the entire collection. When Seth asked what I thought of her, I told him how much I liked her. I didn't know why he bothered to ask. I'd never disapproved of anything he'd done in his entire life. I stayed with her in New York one weekend, I came back early when I thought they'd be out and they were making love half-naked on the living room floor. We were all very embarrassed as they scrambled for their clothing.

The wedding was at the country club across the street from the old colonial house where she grew up in West Charity. Her father was a federal judge covering all of New England. Everyone made a fuss over him, but I thought he was unkind and demanding. Her mother was quiet and sad and waited on him hand and foot. I danced the Charleston like crazy with Jean's sister, who was my age, and stuffed myself with food from the buffet and drank too much champagne. Lots of people pinched my cheek and said, "I'll bet you can't wait until it's your turn to get married!" I walked around the golf course and finally puked my brains out.

I sat on the manicured turf or whatever it's called and yanked my new tie up over my head as if I were hanging myself. The salesman at J. Squeeze had assured me it was the latest, as was the rest of the clothing he sold me. I'd charged it all. A couple of thousand bucks by now. I had no idea how I was going to pay for it. Lester only gave me fifty bucks a month for an allowance. But I had to look nice for Seth's wedding, didn't I? I wanted him and Jean's world to be admiring and accepting of me.

"Where did you get all those new clothes?" Lester asked me when he saw me all dressed up for the wedding.

"I won them in a contest." That's what came into my head. "They had this contest. You had to write an essay, 'What Freshman Year Means to Me.' I won and this was the prize."

"As long as I don't have to pay for 'em," he said. He didn't congratulate me for winning or tell me how handsome I looked.

I was the best man, which was nice of Seth, because I wasn't his best friend. I didn't lose the ring. I managed to offer it at the proper moment. I got tears in my eyes when the vows were exchanged. They seemed so courageous and hopeful and final, all mixed together. "Please, God, let life be good for them," I said to myself. I wished them well. I really did.

After the wedding they went to Europe for a three-week honeymoon.

I was scheduled to take four make-up exams that would wipe out all my accumulated failures, if I passed them. I'd wipe the slate clean all in one blow. It would be like taking a new name all over again. I'd tried to study. I sat there in our room with the striped chintz edging on the curtains Algonqua had made and the matching bedspreads Henry's mother had made, trying to store up information for the tests, but my brain had no ability to absorb. I'd stare at the printed page and think of Australia, another place like Canada where I thought that I'd be safe. No one would miss me.

My cough came back. I was serving food in the dining hall as part of my scholarship, and the lady in charge of the steam table told me not to cough on the vegetables. The next day the dietitian told me I'd have to stay away until I stopped coughing and I'd have to make up my lost hours before she'd credit my scholarship. I went back to my room and tried to study some more. Henry tried to help me, but I didn't know how to tell him what I needed. How do you explain that you can't make your eyes read? Pablo was having one of his heavy Mission Bell sherry nights and playing mournful Spanish music on his phonograph. I knew Seth and Jean were back. Had they had any fights? Were they still together? Was it going to work? What was sex like for them? I went to sleep with tears in my eyes. I was flunking four courses. I didn't have a girlfriend. I couldn't pay for my clothes. I couldn't stop coughing. And I certainly didn't want to go back home to Masturbov Gardens.

I took the three hundred aspirin at noon the next day, Saturday, while everyone was out. My reasoning was that I needed to sleep. If I could only sleep I'd be able to study when I woke up. I only wanted to sleep till Tuesday. The exams were on Monday. On Tuesday I'd wake refreshed and explain that I'd been sick but now I was better and could I take the tests next month? Ten aspirin should get me through the day, and then another fifty through the night, and another fifty through the next day. Oh, why not take them all? That'll do it till Tuesday sure. I shoveled them into my mouth by the handful. Three bottles. I watched myself in the bathroom mirror and I looked calm enough. I'd never heard such quiet. The water I cupped up in my palm was cold and refreshing. I didn't even use a glass.

I lay down on my bed waiting for all that aspirin to put me to sleep. But it didn't. My stomach cramped. I began to get scared I'd done something I shouldn't have. I called the campus cops and they took me to the emergency room, where doctors stuck a hose down my throat and pumped my stomach. It took a bunch of people to hold me down and I threw up all over them. I offered to pay their cleaning bills before I passed out.

When I woke up a young psychiatrist was sitting by my bed. "I am not going to leave this room until you tell me why you did it," he said. "Go fuck yourself," I said, and went back to sleep till Tuesday.

Seth was there when I woke up again. They made me give a next of kin before they would pump my stomach. I didn't want to put down anybody but the doctor said unless I did I would die and the longer I waited, the closer I would come. Seth was wonderful. He didn't ask me why I did it. He didn't blame me. He didn't bawl me out. He just sat there with me for a long time, even before I was fully conscious or able to talk. Then he said he was glad I'd failed, because he would have missed me. That alone made me want to get better.

Seth was a friend of the dean's, so I got to take the tests and stay. Daniel Jerusalem helped me study. I did just well enough. Usually Yaddah steered messed-up kids to the army, but I was allowed to stay if I saw a psychiatrist. Which I did, and we talked for three years until I graduated. He said I was a complicated young man. I learned that I hated my parents and I was a homosexual and I was afraid. Of success. Of doing what I wanted to, whatever it was, including being homosexual and being a writer and being in love. I told him I'd known all that before I took the aspirin, and he said I no doubt did.

Henry, who became a doctor, would have four mental breakdowns and hospitalizations before he committed suicide by sucking gas through a hose sitting in his car in his second ex-wife's garage when he was sixty. She had divorced him, as had his first wife, because he beat her up. We did have sex once, when we were fifty or so and had hardly seen each other since Yaddah. He just showed up at my New York apartment one night and I opened the door and I knew why he'd come and we went to bed together. It was okay. No, it was very sad, two pudgy middle-aged men holding on to each other briefly. I'd managed to get him to talk a bit before we started. He lived alone in New Hampshire. In fact, in his parents' old house. On his deathbed his father told him what a disappointment to him Henry had been. "You were supposed to take care of us," he said. Henry's medical practice was gone because he fell in love with his male clients and spent so much time with them that he went broke. He had to go to work in the emergency room of the small local hospital. He fell in love with a young man who was cruel to him. He bought a dog who chewed up all his furniture. That night, I tried to get him to stay, but he wouldn't. It was 3 a.m. when he left to drive back north. He'd done what he had to do, I guess. And then, a few years later, he did what he had to do, again.

•

One-arm is back. She comes back with a man. She went to parts of Africa where my history is buried. I am more scared.

DR. JACQUES PEPIN!

GRACE: Fuck fuck fuck fuck fuck, this time my fucks are happy fucks. I met the most extraordinary expert on dating the past. His name is Dr. Jacques Pepin. We have sworn each other to secrecy while we each finish fucking with the fucking discoveries that are pouring out of our continuing investigations into the Dark Continent. Until then, I talk only to you, my fucking lab notebook.

More anon anon.

•

JACQUES PEPIN: There is no doubt that The Underlying Condition was present in the Kongo in 1959.

•

BOSCO DRIPPER: In 1963 I was sent a *Pan trog.* from Africa.

THE PEN PALS MEET AGAIN

Fred Lemish and Daniel Jerusalem met up again. In the Yaddah hospital when Daniel was on duty.

"May I come in, Fred? Masturbov Gardens? I'm in the medical school here now and I saw your name on the hospital intake."

Yes, I remember him, each of them thought. Each of them also thought kindly thoughts about the other. Not bad-looking. He looks nice. He's grown up. That sort of thing.

"You don't have to talk if you don't want to. I just want you to know that I'd like to help you in any way I can. I'm sorry you felt so awful that you had to try something so extreme, although I very much understand where that can come from. And I am already saying more than I should be saying, professionally, I guess."

Fred managed to smile. Daniel managed to smile. They spent about fifteen minutes talking to each other. They talked about Masturbov Gardens, of course, and how much each hated it and couldn't wait to get out. And Fred said Daniel was lucky he knew what he wanted to be. And Daniel told him he didn't have to be in such a hurry, he was only a freshman, after all.

"I think I am the only gay man here. It scares me. I am very lonely."

"Now you know you're not the only one here," Daniel said.

Then Daniel sat down beside Fred on the hospital bed and held his hand. And Fred took the hand and kissed it and held it to his cheek. And Daniel bent down and kissed Fred on his lips. And they lay side by side until groggy Fred fell back asleep. There was still a ringing inside his head. But maybe it wasn't from too much salicylate, which is what a nurse said caused this, but from a bell going off because he'd found someone nice who liked him.

Yes, it was Daniel who helped Fred to study for his exams and pass them. He drilled him over and over again, and since he'd taken two of the courses himself and passed them with honors, he was just the teacher Fred needed. And during all this, each thought he might be falling in love.

They are very tentative lovers, fumbling and awkward, uncertain how to do what with what. Neither is experienced in love. Daniel, as we have seen, has certainly dipped his toe in Mordy and been dipped in himself by his wretched uncle Hyman. But as desperately as he wanted Mordy then, well, it is different now, the other person is available and also as alone as he'd been then, and, well, it is all too new and . . . and . . . and . . . And Fred . . . can't remember all he'd ever done besides a few ugly faces. Perhaps, Fred, you don't have to remember *everything* when you write a history.

But neither of them was really ready for love. Timing is so important. And a young man studying to be a doctor has so little time. At least that was Daniel's excuse. He also recognizes in Fred what he knows by now is in himself: that extreme need already mentioned, which can only get in the way. Best to turn everything toward being buddies. And so they do, without knowing quite how they do it, how fast the sparks of potential love turn into friendship and relief from pressures lifted.

No, no, no! Each had actually said to himself, I didn't want it to turn into sadness. I want someone to tell me how it's done. Please, how do homosexuals fall in love and live in this world, a world that doesn't want you around?

They won't see each other for a while, although each of them thought exactly the same thoughts. He liked me. We had nice sex. We learned something nice about homosexuality. It was not cataclysmically ecstatic, not that either would recognize that if it were. What's wrong with nice? Isn't nice enough? What went wrong? What was I afraid of? Because I was afraid. How did we come to each other and lose each other and and and not see each other after so many days and nights of study! I liked him!

Daniel left New Godding, to continue his education at Table Medical Center in New York. Fred visited him a few times, but it was obvious that he was in the way of Daniel's work, which took up so many hours of the day and night that when they tried to make love one night, Daniel fell asleep after telling him that a fellow intern was expelled for having sex with another man in their dorms; he'd been "turned in" by one of his straight roommates. And when, back in his room at Yaddah, Fred tried to masturbate thinking of Daniel, he couldn't keep his erection.

No, the time wasn't right. Each tried not to think about it, much.

Fred spends a lot of time walking around the Yaddah campus, looking on the sly at the faces of others. He doesn't so much know he's lost out on someone as he knows he's still searching for someone he hasn't found. He hates it here. He does indeed feel he's the only homosexual in all of Yaddah. Then he is willingly seduced by one of his professors, who gives him his first case of crabs. Several months later the professor tells him he'd best be tested for syphilis, which he himself had come down with. By the time he graduates he knows the names of everyone in his class from looking at their pictures so often in his class book. He knew who went where to prep school and what city they were from, but it didn't make him any new friends because he wasn't much good at saying hello, or even looking up from the ground. He went to his classes, wrote his papers, took his exams, saw his shrink, and somehow graduated from the fucking place, but only barely.

DAVID AT SAN FRANCISCO STATE UNIVERSITY

Somewhere along the line I stopped having sex. I'd seen such awful things connected with sex that when I had an orgasm I screamed so loud, I scared myself. It was as if I were being punished or reminded, same thing. It hurt too much.

I've read everything I can get my hands on about the many men like me. Men wanting other men, not knowing how to look or ask or love them if and when they found them. All the books say we're sick. One book tells me to read another, and I do. They all say the same thing.

I know I have been exposed to a great deal of experience and information. I don't know how it fits together. Why did my father treat me this way? Where was my twin? In every classic I study here there's a messenger of warning, of disease, of loneliness, of irresponsibility, of some coming plague, of some denial of humanity. Alone is the biggest group of people in history. Is my twin all alone now, too?

Have Philip and Amos Standing and Mr. Hoover ruined my life? Was I cooperating? Am I still? How? Shouldn't I be angry by now? I keep waiting to get angry. Daniel had a temper. Daniel could get furious at Philip and I'll bet Philip didn't do anything to him as bad as he did to me.

Do I hate my father for what he did to me? Do I want to bring about reconciliation with my twin? How do I find a world where humanity is my goal? I never knew such a place. Would I even recognize it?

Why do people need to do awful things? Why can't the world get to the other side of revenge? All these classic messengers I've been studying never answer this question. They just show that somewhere at the heart of it all is something awful.

This city is filled with handsome men. Many of them seem to have found another. I get cruised a lot. I'm not very good at saying hello. It still hurts too much.

DR. HERSCHEL VITABAUM

EXECUTIVE DIRECTOR, HEALTH OF THE WORLD (HOW)
GENEVA

Many things have been happening in Africa. I believe it started many years ago but no one was paying any attention. Very strange illnesses never seen before have been showing up. The Congo River brings from the interior many people including from Germany's Kamerun colony. I am told that loggers with chain saws are chopping down the forests and that much bush meat is being consumed. Léopoldville is the capital of what is now called Belgian Congo. In 1940 its population was forty-nine thousand. In less than twenty years it is four hundred thousand. Many people develop purple spots. The increase of these strange illnesses parallels the growth of the population. There is little establishment of anything medical or for disease, in any of this part of the world. There is no such thing as a doctor who has been educated decently. I write warnings to doctor contacts in all our participating countries and to my main benefactor, America's Center of Disease. I hear back from none of them. This is, tragically, not unusual.

Dr. Sister Grace Hooker and I meet and bond in Léopoldville. She is collecting samples of blood and of feces and urine, from both humans (prostitutes) and chimps. It is a bit difficult for her to get around easily. She is no longer a young woman. Her stalwart determination is inspirational to me. We are on the same what she calls "wavelength." I will write a report on my site visit and send it back home to COD.

By chance and good fortune Grace and I meet up with Dr. Jacques Pepin from Canada. He has been studying infectious diseases in sixteen African countries. I forgot that he has been one of HOW's consultants over the years. He is a microbiologist. He and Grace understand each other. She is overwhelmed with excitement at what he tells us.

•

Nothing to fear but fear itself, Franklin? What about me? You, personally, had me, you know. Not exactly me, but a cousin of mine, the distinguished M. Guillain-Barré, who found what he calls a syndrome. It fucks up your immune system just like I do. Franklin, you had a fucked-up immune system. Did anyone tell you that before you died? Your people don't even know what is an immune system.

BOSCO WEEPS

In the Everglades alligators eat some of my monkeys. Two alligators die. Three of my monkeys disappear. Three lost chimps and two dead alligators in two weeks. I am uncertain what if anything untoward is happening. There are very few vets smart enough for me to talk to. The Primate Society is going down the drain. Serves them right for kicking me out.

OOZE IS COMING OUT OF HIS MOUTH AND NOSE

"They helicoptered Olaf from Ocean City to some hospital in Baltimore. He had collapsed on the dance floor and we thought he was dead. There is no local ambulance and no hospital near here. He lay on the dance floor and we looked down on him and could still see what a beautiful man he was even though ooze is coming out of his mouth and nose. He's from Norway and was on vacation here. The DJ, they call him Terry DJ, was standing in his booth and looking at us looking down on Olaf. He didn't stop the music. The music played and played and nobody moved Olaf until the swoosh-swoosh-swoosh of the arriving helicopter was heard and it landed and some medical guys rushed in. Ooze was now coming out of Olaf's ears too. He is lying in a big puddle of his own ooze. It was ghastly, a dark yellow greenish color. I don't think I have ever used that word *ghastly* before. When the men in white came in with their bed on wheels everyone moved farther away automatically. Terry DJ finally stopped the music. As they wheeled Olaf out, you could hear people gasp and stifle cries of their own sudden fear, maybe even despair as in could this ever happen to me. I don't think I have ever used the word *despair* either. But what was this really handsome blond man from across the sea telling me? I had just danced with him for hours. We had made love last night and it was wonderful. I had met the man of my dreams. He died in the ambulance. I went with him and I was holding his hand. His oozing turned into some kind of major hemorrhage that the attendants couldn't stop, and the floor of the ambulance was swirling with this ooze that evidently was so full of some kind of poison that one of the attendants contracted something and died later that week. I wonder how long before this is me."

I sent this to *The Monument*, where I'm a stringer. But it didn't run. They said it was "too graphic." I said could they please reconsider because Olaf was going to move here and be my lover. They not only said no, they fired me. My editor said, "All you guys do is dance and fuck and you expect us to feel sorry for you?"

FRED WANDERS

I got hired so easily because representatives of the InterNational Press Association turned up at Yaddah just short of graduation, looking for "adventurous young writers." As Daily Themes was the one course I excelled at, and I didn't want to get drafted, I grabbed it. It sounded exciting.

At first I was a reporter on a newspaper in Riddle, Saskatchewan. It was freezing cold and not much happened to write about and the people weren't very friendly to Americans. I was sent to Alaska, which was worse. They hated everyone who came up from "the mainland." I got myself transferred, which sent me to a bunch of awful places, *The Natal Forward, The Abididan Networker, The Carinso Spear, The Vorwaarts Messenger, The Léopoldville News, The Nairobi News*—you've heard of none of them. They were tiny rags, published in English in countries where few understood it. The only thing they seemed to have in common was they were always at war with one place or other. Even though my country had not so long ago lived through one, I was amazed how brutal these local skirmishes could be. At first I thought these papers were to serve the few English-speaking inhabitants who found themselves in these distant outposts that were all connected to some mother European power. I wish I could say that writing for such and such a paper in such and such a painfully impoverished and bellicose part of the world was a challenge. It was not. I was not allowed to write about local or international politics or the poverty or anything critical about . . . well, anything. I could only write "happy stories about America," none of which I presently knew. I was more like a calendar of events transpiring that most of these populations couldn't attend or want to go to in the first place. And in each place I found that being a white man made me shunned and unwelcomed. I did not like that feeling.

Then I began to notice that my paychecks, albeit from a dozen different banks, came from similarly named accounts; apparently all these newspapers were owned or controlled by the same person or persons or corporation. We know now that they represented early overseas investments by our government's newly established Central Intelligence Agency. And that I was in that part of Africa where UC was growing at the same time. I sure was a lousy reporter to not pick up on anything about this. Just like my extreme isolation kept me from having any true notion of what was really going on back home.

I got tired of writing for shitty newspapers in the fleapits of the world. On a break I went to London. I saw a sign in Mayfair for Magna-American Motion Picture Enterprises. On a hunch I went inside and asked if I might speak with someone in charge. I asked the man who came out if he had any work for a smart on-the-ball experienced reporter and he hired me on the spot. My entry into the film industry was as easy as that. Moses Rattner liked me. I would discover that all film tycoons have names like Moses Rattner. It doesn't help to be gentile in the film industry.

My job was to comb books and manuscripts, galleys, scripts, articles, anything with plot or story that could serve as the basis for a movie as long as it wasn't based on a current event or the truth. Because the address appealed to me, I rented a tiny house off Fleet Street, barely more than a room and a bath, on one of London's oldest streets, Jews Yard.

I thought I'd be happy now but I wasn't and it got worse. My Yaddah shrink Dr. Rivtov, to whom I'd written, wrote back, "Just call Anna Freud. She's listed in the phone book." And so I undertook what would turn out to be a psychoanalysis with one of Dr. Sigmund Freud's students, Dr. William Gillespie, to improve my rotten sense of self. He was evidently sympathetic toward homosexuals and was even president of their International Society of Shrinks. "You're rotten to the core, Maude, rotten to the core," was an old Noel Coward song that Beatrice Lillie made famous. There will come to be a crackpot theory that UC is really caused by a bad self-image. I know it's crackpot and everyone with half a brain knows it's crackpot, but it persists to this day. "Internalized homophobia" is cheap-shot jargon used by amateur and quite a few professional "arbiters" of what's "really" wrong with us. Dear Dr. Gillespie would have none of this. And, unlike Rivtov, he did not believe in changing us to straights.

The English were still getting over the war. It bothered me that people educated at Oxford and Cambridge were forced to live in tacky bedsitters and feed coins into meters to keep warm or have a hot bath. What kind of government allowed people to so stew in such postwar juices? I didn't have many English friends beyond a trail of pasty lads who wanted me to fuck them and fall in love with them and take them with me back to the States.

London was filled with blacklisted American screenwriters who'd come up against Congress, Vurd and Roy Cohn and Sam Sport. (Dereck Dumster was with Roy but no one was paying him any attention yet.) They envied my job and I was able to hire a few of them. It was hard for me to fully comprehend why my own country had exiled them, had taken away their ability to make a living. As I was learning how to write for a living myself, I couldn't conceive of being denied the right to do so by my very own people. I was so far from home as to be unaware of all the social upheavals going on over there, particularly among homosexuals. We were legal at last in England, so the Brits, like *The New York Truth*, weren't writing about gay problems anywhere.

Moses Rattner soon offered me the chance to write screenplays and I was to draw on various realms of terror I'd covered roaming the world; many of these awful places were exceptionally cheap to film in, which was Moses's "Bottom Line." When I described my screenplays and their subject matter rather disparagingly to Dr. Gillespie during my psychoanalysis (yes, five times a week on the couch), he said it sounded like a good opportunity to bear witness. And that this was the true calling of a writer. As he rarely said anything, much less anything of a complimentary nature, I felt I'd been knighted by the Queen. So I was meant to be a writer? This corny shit I was churning out was writing? I must confess that in all this I was finding out that I enjoyed writing even if it was shit. I loved words and language and discovery.

My house on Jews Yard was my only safe place. As my depression continued, I hardly would leave it. I didn't need to go into an office to write the stuff I was writing. The actors we employed spoke little English, so too many words of more than two syllables were useless. One day I heard a gurgling in my basement and found behind an old nonfunctioning water heater a cache of papers that turned out to be the love longings of a long-dead homosexual American playwright. I started to dream of William the playwright and his younger lover, whom he seems to have somehow lost. I came to feel their presence, for I summoned the young lover back for him as I lay on my mattress masturbating while I pictured them making love in this same place a few centuries ago. Thad sounded to be a most sweet young man. I'm overcome with the realization that I'm still looking for what they were looking for then. St. Arbuthom? I still can find no reference to this name in either England or Holland.

I slept with a lot of men. It was the easiest way to lasso loneliness. Nights were long in London. I was always cold. Usually no guy my age had a decent flat or seemed to bathe regularly or could afford to do something about his teeth, still rotten from the bad nutrition of war. London still had many scars from the war. No one made much money, and I picked up a lot of checks.

I was trying my best to figure out what "bearing witness" amounted to. My current slate of screenplays included alligators in Haiti, a teenage interfaith love story in Ireland/Northern Ireland, a teenage interracial love story in Cape Town (being shot at the same time and with the same cast and crew as an interracial western), and a murder on the moors. Moses wouldn't go for anything "too classy" and he definitely vetoed any sort of "message." I sensed it was time for me to father something more serious. But since a Freudian psychoanalysis takes a long time, there wasn't any challenge in being in too much of a hurry.

I found myself thinking of Daniel a lot. He seemed to be the last man, maybe the only one, I remember holding fondly. I missed America, and he came to embody that. I knew he was a doctor practicing in Washington. I often jerked off thinking of him.

Then one day Moses told me he was sending me to Hollywood. I was going to write a Rust Legend Production! I was going to be paid a quarter of a million dollars! I was to adapt *Bleak House* by Charles Dickens. As a musical! It was going to be a piece of shit. There was no way it could not be a piece of shit because Rust Legend only made pieces of shit. The good doctor and I agreed it wasn't a bad moment to investigate a more remunerative life back in my homeland.

FRED GOES TO HOLLYWOOD

Rust Legend.

He came west from Tarpoo, Nebraska, "plum spot on," he liked to tell you, "in the dead center of the heart of this country, where I was born as Graham Puss. My students—I was a sixth-grade schoolteacher—were constantly telling me how handsome I was. 'You ought to be a movie star, Mr. Puss,' they constantly said to me. 'You're so very very handsome.' Behind my back they entered my photograph in a talent contest and the judge from MGM came right to my door in Tarpoo and knocked and I said, 'Who is it, please?' and he said, 'A very good fairy,' and I opened the door and without even waiting for me to pack—'You won't need your old clothes,' he said; 'we're going to give you brand-new ones!'—this nice sweet man whisked me to Hollywood, where I immediately started my training to become a movie star."

What would Dickens have done with Rust Legend? What would I do?

"I was assigned to my first movie and you'll never guess who was its star! Cary Grant! Cary took one look at me and said, 'I must have you for my very own immediately!' and he took me back to his apartment, he lived in an apartment in those days, on Fountain (way before he and Randolph Scott had their ocean love nest in Santa Monica), and he locked me up. That's what he did. He wouldn't let me out! I was locked up in Cary Grant's apartment, never to see so much as the lights of Beverly Hills. 'I don't want anybody to meet you! You are so very handsome they will want you too,' he said. I had to find a way to break out! I had to run away from Cary Grant! He had guards watching me every minute he wasn't there! His chauffeur, his doormen, his maids, his secretary, everyone was warned by Cary not to let me out 'under pain of exile from my kingdom should my divine morsel who is so very very handsome get out of my apartment!' His voice, that beautiful mellow voice, could turn ugly. He wasn't all smiles and charm by a long shot. 'You are the most handsome young man in the whole wide world,' he said to me each night as he tried to cuddle me in bed. I was afraid he would stick that thing into me yet again, or worse want me to stick mine into him. He was insatiable. This was not a life I wanted to live. It was not the life of an MGM starlet. And I had no way even to get a message to Mr. Mayer! Mr. Louis B. Mayer. The head of the MGM studio himself. The very man who was responsible for my being whisked out here from Tarpoo. I wasn't allowed to use the phone! Each day there was a new biddy standing over me, sterner and more threatening, and taller, than the last. I don't know how he found so many big tall strong forbidding women. They all had arms like Tarzan. I learned later he got them all from Central Casting. What actress wouldn't do anything for Cary Grant? The cheapskate didn't pay them a dime. They all thought they were auditioning and I was grading them. No wonder they acted with such determination. I still have black-and-blue marks from some of those Ten Ton Tessies. But I found a way! You cannot outfox foxy Rusty. One of the biddies was smaller than the others. She said she was a stand-in. Vilma Villa Lobos, the Brazilian matadoress, couldn't come. She'd been gored to death on the set the day before. Let me tell you, I jumped her stand-in fast! I got her arm around her back and she screamed uncle and I escaped wearing her clothes, which were just my size. Cary was very angry. He didn't speak to me for years. By then I realized that acting was not for me. I had to be Number One. I had to become the great and popular and enormously successful movie producer I am today. And so I have, so I have. I have worked my ass off but I am here. You are here. We are making this great great movie. I have lived to see it all come true, day after day, movie after movie. Star after star. Oh, I am so tired today. Nancy wanted me to fuck her so badly last night but I said, 'Nancy, I'm so tired, we'll do it tomorrow night. My boots ain't made for walking just right now.' That's a song she's going to record and it's going to be so big that Frank will want her back."

These autobiographical sexual updates were a regular part of our daily script conferences: I heard how Mitzi and Nancy and Carol and Helen and Virginia, the most favored of Rust's women friends, "my girls," a number of them old enough to be his grandmother, were all desperate for him to fuck them. I had to look him straight in the eye each time and say sharply, "Rust, this is me, Fred," to snap him out of wherever he was. And he would slap his forehead with his palm's heel. "Oh, yes, of course."

Well, at least I was in Hollywood. The months I'd spent writing a script for Rust called *Beyond the Mountains, Beyond the Stars*, had been no fun at all. Originally based on *Bleak House*, it was now set in a Tibetan monastery, high up in the Himalayas, "where Monsieur Benny Henri can design glorious wafting robes of gauze and tulle and net and chiffon, in all the colors of the cosmos, with the timelessness of the timeless." And: "So that Heinz-Herbert Montoya, Jr., can design sets of unsurpassable majesty and magic." In other words, not just any old monastery. But also, of course, with monks. "Avec monks," Rust would joke. *Bleak House* took on a new meaning.

I had made a certain English film for Moses, *Lest We Sleep Alone*, the first thing I wrote that Dr. Gillespie and I were proud of, that was distinguished in Rust's mind because it contained a good deal of what was then referred to as "full frontal nudity," male of course. He would often ask me shyly, almost blushing, "How did you have the courage to do that! I mean, you showed Oliver Reed's penis! And Alan Bates's penis! However did you get them to disrobe so . . . completely?" I explained that this scene was filmed exactly as written in the classic novel it was adapted from, which had been in print since 1930, so the censor finally allowed it. The actors were drunk and Oliver played with his cock just before the camera rolled so his looked much bigger on-screen, and hence for all time, than Alan's, which was not really the case. "Ooooh," Rust gurgled. "Imagine going to the set and being able to see all that!"

Someone had told him about *Bleak House*, with its lawsuit that is never resolved. Well, he'd been involved in any number of those. He'd also discovered an old novel about monks at the top of the world that appealed to him. And then, in speaking to Lollymae August, a Lovejoy Disciple, he secured the right to film his film in any Disciples of Lovejoy temple around the world that he chose. Why not bake all this into the same rich cake! "*Gone with the Wind* is about a lot of things." Many hours of "conferences" turned *Bleak House* into a Disciples of Lovejoy monastery, and all those wretched lawyers in Chancery became monks. In his high concern for an author's due, Rust looked around for the agent who represented "the Dickens estate" to make his deal with. "We don't want to make too many changes in the basic material if we don't have all the rights."

I had had absolutely no interest in writing this script. The more I had said no, the more Moses called me to announce further increments in Rust's offer. I wound up with that quarter of a million dollars. I figured, yes, I would sell my soul for that. Well, perhaps I could write the great Hollywood novel about Rust Legend. Take the money and run. Take the money and get outta town.

I had thought a lot about those monks. And my own life as a developing homosexual. I had accumulated plenty of evidence that homosexuals had an image problem and needed all the help we could get. I had learned enough from Moses how to publicize stuff, to get "causes" in the papers. Those interracial love stories had made a lot of money. They were only banned in the American South. I convinced myself that Rust could be useful. I would persuade him that we could make a great contribution to modern civilization if we dealt with the problems monks had in such isolation.

"What kind of problems?"

"Their attraction to each other."

"Attraction?"

"You know. They want to fuck with each other."

"You expect me to show that in a multimillion-dollar Rust Legend Production, nine of which are among the highest-grossing films of their year?" He was fond of uttering this phrase catechistically, often in concert with "I have the taste of The American People."

"Perhaps *Beyond the Mountains, Beyond the Stars* could become the highest-grossing film of all time! Controversy sells!"

"No, no, no! Do you think so? Let me think about this for a moment." He went into his toilet. He often did this in the middle of meetings. He went in there to masturbate. His half brother Andre, with whom he lived, told me that. "Everyone thinks Rusty pees a lot. Unh-unh. He jerks himself off. And by the time he finishes he's reached his decision."

Indeed, he did have America's taste. Nine of the highest-grossing films of these years were indeed Rust Legend Productions. Weepies, love comedies in which no one ever fucked, out-of-retirement reappearances by former goddesses with barely enough mileage still left in them, all "swathed" in what he called over and over and over "my gorgeous, gorgeous, gorgeous clothes." For him, women's clothing was the key to his success. That half brother of his supervised the costumes. He was a good copycat. Women in shopping malls longed to wear them. It's hard to work a huge and varied wardrobe into a monastery of monks, but Rust would manage it.

When he came out of his private toilet he said, "I cannot do anything like what you are suggesting. My monks, if anything, will be admiring of the famous love goddesses I shall have swathed in my gorgeous, gorgeous, gorgeous clothes."

"Wouldn't you like to do something positive for our people?"

"Our people? What people are you referring to? I am an American!"

"Rust, we are homosexuals."

"Young fellow, beware you do not go too far."

I tried to pursue my line of argument but he suddenly got up, pulled closed the blinds, pulled closed the drapes, sent Fat Pearl, his enormously overweight secretary, who sat outside his door on the tiniest of typing chairs to buzz people into Rust's locked office, out to an early lunch because she always overheard everything. Leading me to a sofa on the far side of his lair, he took my hand and held it throughout the following.

"Listen, Freddie, I am going to tell you the truth about Hollywood. It goes beyond Cary and Randolph Scott living together as lovers. Or Barbara Stanwyck marrying What's-his-name for a beard. Or George Cukor being fired from *Gone with the Wind* because Clark didn't want a fairy director. Or the many many many of us hiding as I must for fear of our lives and livelihood. Jimmy Dean, that gorgeous, gorgeous, gorgeous young man who died, was murdered by Jack Warner. That is correct. The Jack Warner who owns Warner Brothers studio. He was murdered, Jimmy was, because he was homosexual and because Jack, to whom Jimmy was under contract, hates homosexuals. Hates! He makes puking noises if the subject comes up. When I go there for dinner he looks at me and says, 'You are not one of those nelly fairies like Jimmy Dean, are you, Rust?' And then he makes the puking noises as if he's throwing up. He does this sitting at the head of his dinner table. Around this table are great great great stars, trying to eat. Bette Davis, Rosalind Russell, Humphrey Bogart, John Garfield, Jimmy Cagney—all of them are embarrassed for me and averting their eyes. Mr. Warner goes on: 'I used to love Jimmy until I found out he is a fairy. I loved him so much I took out a big insurance policy on his life in case anything happens to him. He's uncircumcised. Did you know that about Jimmy? My big young star on the rise is uncircumcised. He's a queer and he's uncircumcised and he's about to go to Metro to star in a film for them behind my back. What kind of gratitude is that? You tell me. Roz, you are a fair person. Tell me what kind of gratitude is that?' Everyone sat there like we were all encased in cement. Finally Bette spoke up. Brave Bette. No wonder our people, as you so sweetly call us, worship her. 'Jack, stop this immediately! You might show some gratitude if for no other reason than that he is making you more money loaning him out to Metro than you ever put into him. Now stop it and eat this marvelous dinner!' And then she turned to me: 'Rust, darling, ignore Jack. He can be a monster, as I well know.' That Bette, what a pal. What wasn't being said out loud was that Jimmy Dean hated Jews as much as Jack Warner hated homos. I mean our people. I mean your people. I don't know what I mean. Jimmy had been fucking with Sam Sport and learned that Meyer Lansky and Mickey Cohen and their Jewish mafia mobs were secretly investing huge sums of money in the Warner Brothers studio to save it. So Jimmy *really* had to be eliminated. Which he was. Jack had him bumped off in that car crash. And Jack sent a huge display of flowers to the funeral with 'Goodbye Jimmy you ungrateful uncut fairy' spelled out in red roses. Now you please tell me how I am going to make a movie in this town that portrays affectionate men. I can't even live with my lover without calling him my half brother! The very president of our biggest union, Peter Ruester, blabbed names of commies and fairies at those awful congressional hearings. The names he named will never work in this town again. So if you have any notions of bringing enlightenment for 'our people,' get over them. In fact, it might be safer if you left town. With your opinions you could easily be murdered too."

The huge failure of *Beyond the Mountains, Beyond the Stars* will put paid to Rust. Hollywood will send him out to pasture. He will continue to live with his "half brother with whom I was brought up with ever since he was found as a tiny foundling on our doorstep in Tarpoo." Very little will now be heard about him until his death.

The movie I wrote for him tanks, bombs, stinks, sinks, and deserves to. I was ashamed I'd written the (non)fucking thing. No, I didn't want to stay in this grotesque town or make another one.

The money, however, will prove quite useful when I start fighting for my people, Rust's and mine. Seth will increase it for me a great great great deal.

So I had learned that I did not want to write movies. Great writing about Hollywood is scarce for a reason. Great novels are not fashioned from the likes of Rust Legend, or should I be corny and say rusty legends. He was neither Mr. Micawber nor Mrs. Gamp. He wasn't anywhere near a Mrs. Proudie, and Monroe Stahr was above him by far. Neither he nor his work had redeeming qualities. The ability to like him was lacking in all that work he did.

No, I would have to look elsewhere for the "basic material" with which I'd try to bear witness to the world, and how it treats my people.

They say you must write about what you know. And that you must suffer before you do. Well, we're coming to that.

THE DECADES OF HOPE

That's what these postwar years will be called by historians. Steele, Comminger, Ginn, MacNeill, Morris, Jackson . . . All diseases will be eliminated. Polio will be gone. Enough food will be available for all. If a disease isn't eliminated, it's about to be . . .

In 1931, Dr. Israel Jerusalem had discovered a new disease that ate the flesh of people after they'd eaten the brains of each other. He won a Nobel Prize for it. He believed something inherent in his discovery could be effective against cancer. He never got the chance to find out because such research as would be required—the consumption of human bodily parts by other humans—would never be allowed in this country. Dr. Sister Grace tried again with Israel's samples, this time at Partekla. There is something about Israel's and Grace's work that interests Dr. Stuartgene Dye. From Partekla he checked with NITS to see if it knows anything about their work. He discovers that NITS owns it. Israel first discovered it while working on a government grant. He'd named it glause. He'd called it "a bodily poison." And he'd won that Nobel Prize.

Who's president? Americans rarely remember in what order their public servants serve them. They certainly give them names, like men naming their dicks. Fucker, Putz, and more often than not, Asshole. American presidents come and go and are rarely remembered. Each new president of course always promises that new day dawning tomorrow. Play it again, Sam. There will be no more disease. Hunger will be eliminated. Poverty will disappear. Everyone will have health insurance. Progress is our most important product. Yaddahyaddahyaddah.

•

Do you remember Miss Trudy McNab? She got some of me in her eyes when she fell in one of those bloodmobile things. Young Daniel was blamed for it. She has just died from me although you don't know me yet. It did take her a long time. Some people take longer than others.

VENUS RISING

Begin now the more fully blossoming *Sexopolis* years, the years of its wider-spread hold on the heterosexual world's erotic imagination. Increasingly men everywhere feel they have permission to perform as well as imagine. Whatever dark thoughts they've been harboring can now come into a brighter light. Mordy is hailed as a great man, the king of a mighty revolution. And so he is. It's hard to underestimate the importance of what's going on now with the penises of the American heterosexual male, the significance and relevance of what they're doing, these penises, these men, because of this magazine, because of Mordecai Masturbov, son of Abraham and Doris Hardware Masturbov, grandson of Herman and Yvonne Masturbov and of Horace Turvey, Jr., and whatever her name was, and cousin to Daniel and Lucas and Stephen and David Jerusalem. Anthony Comstock would turn over in his grave. But who the fuck remembers Anthony Comstock?

Mordy anthropomorphizes his subscribers. They are all living, breathing beings to him. He even talks to his own penis. Nothing new about this. But Mordy's penis talks back. *Sexopolis* has a column by Mordy's penis. "My Friend," he calls it. My Friend talks to his fellow travelers in direct, instructive ways. "It is more pleasurable to both your partner and yourself if you can locate those specific spots of her vaginal canal that bring on the fullest excitement for you both. Don't be selfish. Remember there are two of you. Write to this Box Number for our illustrated instructions." Sometimes the baton is passed to Witty Ora, My Friend's fellow columnist, a specialist on the intricacies of oral sex: "Honeys, listen to me. You got a mouth. You got a tongue. You even got teeth but you got to be careful with them. But God gave you all these things. So learn how to use them to their fullest, you hear! Write to this Box Number for our illustrated instructions." The sort of thing that had never legally found its way into print before is now being purveyed to a "mass market." Some subscribers have even been known to break legs rushing to their newsstands on publication day, or to sprain wrists reaching too quickly into RFD mailboxes. "Be careful how you use your hands," My Friend writes often. "Your hands are your conductors, for your own symphony orchestra. Cream them just like you cream me." It's no wonder each issue finds so many hundreds of thousands from across the globe joining "Our Box Numbers Master List. Welcome!" So it's no wonder Jerusalem & Sport, Mordy's law firm, as young and eager to grow as he, is hiring many a smart-ass horny associate to defend *Sexopolis* in courts of law.

Lucas is the only one who worries their success won't last indefinitely. His law firm with Stephen and Sam Sport is not only making them rich but making him uncomfortable. This ascension is not without a lot of fights. There are many in this country that don't want a *Sexopolis*, in any way, shape, or form. Stephen is in one court or another on a regular basis, as is Sam Sport in the higher courts, fighting against being classified as "pornography," such an ugly and derogatory word.

Lucas wonders if he knows his own brother anymore. Stephen is annoyed that he has to keep reassuring Lucas. "Listen, it'll take a long time to get judgments from local courts appealed up to the Supreme Court. *Sexopolis* already has more money to fight for its rights than most states have to fight us back, and each day we only get richer. You and me both, bro. We're getting fucking rich representing this magazine that's giving our country what it wants: fucking! How to do it! Why to do it! Permission to do it! America has been waiting almost two hundred years for this. America, *our* America, is not going to let it slip away. Can't you see that?" "You sound just like Mordy," Lucas says quietly. "What's wrong with that? What's fucking wrong with that?" Stephen replies. "The penis is mightier than any law," Stephen and Mordy yell at Lucas over and over. "You're not getting laid enough" usually ends all discussions.

And then there are the moments when Stephen takes Lucas aside and says softly to him, "Lucas, we're young. We're rich. We're getting richer. Enjoy it, will you, my brother I love?" And moments when Mordy has to be reassured himself, by, of all people, Jinx Seeley, who's become a buddy of sorts, hanging around the Sexopolis mansion, which is what Mordy's house is now called, with a growing group of girls with gorgeous everythings while waiting to be photographed or fucked. "There's not a man, woman, or child in these United States, perhaps the world, who hasn't been affected by you in one way or another," Jinx scolds him. "How many people can make that statement? Why is it that Jewish boys have such difficulty in enjoying a job well done?" She reminds him of this regularly.

Yes, by now everyone knows *Sexopolis*. Every full-blooded American Man knows *Sexopolis*. Your Friend is mine. Get with the program! Climb on broad, er, board.

It is his readers who are Mordecai Masturbov's family. They are all living, breathing people. He takes them all to bed with him. They do not leave him in the middle of the night. They wake up with him in the morning. He does not have to show them out the door. They do not leave him at the close of day. They love him as he loves them. Faithfully. As he's never loved or been loved before.

He will have everything but his Claudia.

By 1960, *Sexopolis* will be selling one million copies a month.

The population of the world had now reached three billion people.

THE ABOUT-TO-BECOME FIRST LADY (OF CALIFORNIA) HAS TO GET LAID

Purpura Ruester has to get laid. Why should she not have desires? Does not a First Lady (of California) have needs?

All those years Peter schlepped across America speaking out for Greeting, back and forth, back and forth, she never saw so many men in dark suits. Black and navy suits are the safest. They are usually worn by lawyers, and lawyers don't talk. She rarely sucked off a lawyer who couldn't get a big one up for her. She'd had to get laid quite a bit over the years in their travels. Why waste a dark blue suit?

Now that she and Peter are elected, she's forced to settle down in one of the ugliest state capitols in America. Foppy Schwartz, her mentor in matters of style and taste, advises her to relax. "I predict that you won't have to stay too long in that dull, dreary, bleak, unpleasant pit." The state mansion is actually falling down. They expect her to live in *this*? She knows she'll just have to get laid more than usual. A body's needs can get aggravated by geography and real estate. Carlotta Punic is also giving her lessons on how to dress. "We'll hide those piano legs, honey." She's always been self-conscious about her legs. Legs are so important to men. And skirts are shorter now. Between Foppy and Carlotta, Purpura will emerge stylistically triumphant. And dressed to kill.

Stay tuned. To be continued. Sacramento is simply too boring to spend too much time on or in, at this moment.

GOING FORWARD TO LOOK BACK

Terartunian Mdeske is a Haitian accountant working in the Democratic Republic of Congo as a tax collector in a country where it's hard to collect taxes. Belgian Congo is one of several central African countries where UC was unknowingly living around 1930, when it is thought to have jumped from chimp to man. As a public servant he's entitled to all sorts of perks, including especially his pick of any women and men from any tribe that catches his fancy. He is very handsome so there are many willing picks. He is a long way from home. Yes, he gets infected with what will be The Underlying Condition, for this is where it presumably came from, from all these poor starving people hunting monkeys for barter or eating them. Terartunian Mdeske travels often to neighboring Uganda, carrying letters of credit to that country, which he will deliver around 1965 to Maj. Gen. Idi Amin, right-hand man to another master-murderer Milton Obote, whom Amin shortly gets rid of. Here, too, Terartunian Mdeske is a hungry fucker of both sexes. He knows he's going home to Haiti, where it will never be as good as this.

So Terartunian Mdeske returns to Haiti carrying the deadly virus, just after Idi Amin begins his own ethnic cleansing, his army also mass raping and massacring women in Uganda and in Tanzania as well as in Congo itself, which had just been the setting for Lumumba (who was assassinated and his body completely dissolved in acid) and the monster Mobutu and the mad-dash exodus for freedom by hundreds of thousands of their civil servants, many of them Haitians. In fear, the entire non-African population—which for many decades served as civil servants in these countries—fled to the four corners of the globe, particularly Brazil, Asia, India, Haiti, and the United States, carrying you know what with them. And leaving behind hundreds of thousands of women who survived only by selling their bodies to various conquering armies. There was not one single medical doctor in the Congo in 1960.

And yes, Terartunian Mdeske, on his next assignment from Haiti to the United Nations in New York, brings the UC virus with him here too.

One thing about Canadians. We did keep good records of everything.

•

Yes, yes, that is a part of what happened! I am brought to your shores again, this time in 1969, more than a full decade before your public health "experts" realize they have an awful lot of me on their hands!

•

DAME LADY HERMIA: Grace confides in me that she is frightened. "Why do I fear for my own fucking life, dear cousin? What secret am I treading so close to? Someone is going to an awful lot of trouble to make me look guilty. Of what! Shitty-ass rat fuck!"

THEY DIDN'T TEACH ME ANYTHING LIKE THIS IN MED SCHOOL

DANIEL

My older brother Stephen is now also obsessed with sex. He credits Mordy for luring him in, slowly but surely, not only as his legal adviser and stockholder, but as participant in all that *Sexopolis* and "My Friend" define as "new and different." He is handsome. He is horny. He had learned how to tell when a girl was horny too. Sometimes in the nice weather they'd sleep out all night in Rock Creek Park. He found ways for them to sneak into all sorts of places. One night he and a cheerleader actually slept in the locker room at Griffith Stadium after the Redskins football team won the championship. He had more good-looking girls mothering him than he knew what to do with.

It's interesting how some kids can become adept at providing for their needs in spite of parental abuse, or lack of interest, or whatever you want to call Philip and Rivka not paying attention to us. Stephen had clap a few times and crabs a lot of times but he really sincerely genuinely loved fucking. It was magic to him. Magic he couldn't get enough of. He told me some of this. Claudia would tell me the rest. His grades weren't the greatest but he was smart enough to figure out how to get through college and law school. Through it all, the grip of sex grows stronger and stronger on this man who only a few years ago was straitlaced and easily shocked. It's surprising, though it shouldn't be, how many people have few memories of a past they don't desire to live with. He, like Mordy's growing army of readers, is both amazed and pleased that there are many a new "sexopolized" tool to make his old tool yesterday's model T. I could see all this happening as well with my gay patients. It was also a brave (not for me!) new world of physical adventure.

At Doris's, Stephen's discovered Claudia. In no time at all he becomes convinced that Claudia is the answer to all his needs. She treats him like she treated his young brother, me, like she treats all men, which makes him want her more. For the moment it's not a story ready for its telling. She hasn't changed much, except she's getting paid for it, and he's got plenty of money to pay. He's read a book on the subject of sexual satyriasis; to be so inclined, it appears, has less to do with appetite than with some dysfunction in the goals department. He no longer wants anything else badly enough. From poor boy to rich man to boredom! And still so young.

Yes, he's rich, and Lucas is, too, thanks to Mordy and *Sexopolis* and Sam. This has been said before but rich with what *Sexopolis* is providing them is *really* rich and deserves to be emphasized in a family history in which there doesn't seem much else but money to motivate. This source of wealth is different from owning land or real estate. My older two brothers' riches are from protecting physical passion. And from Sam Sport's finding illegal ways to challenge prohibitions via secret contacts that no tax or moral code has plugged up yet. There's a reason for the expression "living high off the hog."

This magazine and this owner are the clients any law firm longs for. While *Sexopolis* is always in trouble, *Sexopolis* is always profitable. Stephen is excellent at dealing with trouble. Sam is excellent at scaring people. All three partners are excellent at either defending against or threatening sexual improprieties, which Stephen now understands firsthand; and the very litigation he's usually involved in on behalf of *Sexopolis* serves the additional plus of turning him on.

He doesn't need a book to tell him that there must be complicated psychological reasons why he should have to jerk off in toilet stalls or visit Doris Hardware's so often to be with Claudia or go with Sam Sport to Stuartgene Dye's or Dereck Dumster's when some event is scheduled. (Yes, I'll find out about all this too.) He considers himself happy, perhaps even very happy. He can imagine no other occupation that would relieve his boredom so profitably. From the bottom drawer of his desk in his office in the Jersualem & Sport Building in the new downtown District of Columbia that he and Sam Sport and Lucas, and Mordy's father, Abe, have done so much to raise from the decaying ruins of the old Washington, he shows me a mail order catalogue that would bring to P.O. Box 123, Vienna, VA, one rectal vibrator ("a new way to mate your masturbations with the earthquake sensations from a vibrating anal device and its soft vibrating sleeve, both washable and reusable"), one Extasx ("introducing the world's first and only SUCK vibrator, a cunning device that moves up and down, extending and contracting

smoothly without a sound, lifting you to the highest level of sexual fulfillment in the privacy of your home or office or anywhere you wish to be stim-
ulated"), and one Super Pumpit ("the latest and most effective Pneumatic
Male Penis Enlargement Device to make your masculinity grow and bring
out the best in you, just insert your penis through the foam-rubber, flesh-like
collar attached to the ejaculation chamber . . ."). Mordy's Friend has tipped
him off to all of these. My Friend writes constantly about how everything can
always be better.

No, they don't teach any of this in med school. And quite frankly, my
entering this new world of burgeoning sexual revolution without my older
brothers to teach me, along with what Fred is writing about from New York,
is filling me with growing apprehension.

GRACE HAD WRITTEN TO DAME LADY HERMIA

"YOU ARE THE ONLY FUCKING RELATIVE I HAVE LEFT IN
THIS FUCKING WORLD!"

MORDY TELLS DR. KORAH LUDENS, HIS SHRINK, ABOUT VELVALEE PELTZ

An exceptionally beautiful woman by the extraordinary name of Velvalee
Peltz, who was from Fille de Maison, in Franeeda County, but much farther out than Masturbov Gardens, came to Washington with the goal of
becoming a serious model. By *serious*, she meant that sex would have no part
of it. Because she was both exceptionally beautiful and from a small town,
she knew that sex was a part of everything. She also felt that she was strong-
willed enough to utilize her beauty to get her own way.

Yes, I know I'm sounding as if I'm writing this up for my magazine.

She wanted to be on the cover of women's magazines and in the style
pages of the newspapers but she most emphatically did not wish to appear
nude or in *Sexopolis*. Since she was not only lovely, but the proper height, coloring, and attitude, there appeared to be no obstacle to prevent her fulfilling
this dream of hers.

She didn't want to go to New York. She didn't want to become a movie
star. She only wanted to make enough money to buy a nice home in D.C.

and stay pretty much to herself. She didn't enjoy the company of others. Most men wanted her in bed and most women were jealous of her beauty. It was an old story. Nothing new about either occurrence. Long ago she'd learned it was safer just to stay indoors and read a book. Beautiful women aren't supposed to be capable of intelligence. That's the only thing she wanted, to be smarter. I wanted her even more.

No sooner had she arrived than the leading modeling agency took her on immediately and without her even having a portfolio. Mindy Bruner, who runs Lovely to Look At, takes one look at Velvalee and knows that this woman has a remunerative future. Velvalee is sent out immediately on calls and within her first weeks she's achieved sufficient bookings to rent her own apartment and begin to be talked about, in those circles where models, photographers, advertising agencies, and representatives of various things that have to be bought and sold talk about beauty as the product that will do it. Her face, particularly, begins to appear on local television and in print commercials.

So it isn't long before she comes to my attention.

I'd been looking for a particular woman, a very particular woman, with whom and through whom I could increase the scope of my magazine. She would personify class. Most women I used didn't and couldn't do that. Sexual mores are beginning ever so slightly to shift from the bacchanalian toward more individualized, one-on-one pursuits. The pendulum always swings. The damn thing never stops swinging. I'd caught it as it went up and wanted to survive if it's going down or sideways. Best, always, to greet change, which is inevitable. Hence my search for the Classy and Elegant New Woman.

She'd be like owning the *Mona Lisa* or *Venus de Milo*. She'd look gorgeous on our cover, completely clothed. In Chanel.

Very much against her will, a meeting was arranged between us.

I become businesslike. Yeah, she's gorgeous but there's never been a gorgeousness I couldn't seduce, journalistically, financially, or sexually. I'd seen her pictures, so I knew she was physically perfect, in the way America likes its female flesh: natural, long blond hair, tall but not too tall, willowy, long daffodil legs, hazy green eyes, inquisitive without being intrusive, aloof without being withdrawn. Oh, and perfect teeth. Very white. No stains. No jaw filled with oversized overbites. Americans demand perfect teeth.

But, shit, I couldn't get away from it. I wanted her. And Mordecai Masturbov is going to have her. She sees it immediately. She sees I'm not going to take no for an answer. It's going to be everything awful she had known it would be. She thinks of leaving without even opening her mouth. I saw this look cross her face and I frowned. She realizes we're all alone and that I could stop her physically. She decides to just start talking.

"It may sound stupid but my biggest ambition in life is to become like the Cosmo Girl. I know there are many other girls I could become. I cut cabbage for coleslaw in the back of Deltoid's Barbecue way out Bladensburg Road Extended and I looked at this big blow-up from some New York newspaper stuck up on the wall by some girl who'd worked there before me. I can still recite its words. This beautiful girl, beautiful hair mussed up just right, looked straight out at me for months and months, until the grease from the griddle spotted her up too much, I could still read, 'I can earn as much money as my darling Robert. My favorite magazine says part of the glory of being a woman now, this moment, is being allowed to live up to every ounce of my perfection and my potentiality. I am allowed to go where my beauty takes me, and letting other people, including male people, live or not live up to their perfection and their potentiality, which is not my problem. God bless me because I'm a Cosmo girl.' Isn't that the most selfish shit you ever heard?"

"Then why are your ambitions still limited to becoming the Cosmo girl?" I realized these were practically the first real words I was saying to her, after only nodding hello, and being so struck by the necessity of having her in my life, and I was already noting everything in reference to her, historically: this is what I wore; this is what she wore; this is what I said; this is how I felt. My body feels too inferior to give to her. No, I couldn't let her know that. I like to tell my readers how I feel about everything, all my innermost thoughts and emotions and fears and hopes and dreams. It didn't make any difference if I never saw the girl again. Only now it does.

"I don't want to hear anything about *Sexopolis*" is her answer. "You sent me that roomful of roses. Listen, back home roses grow wild and don't have much value as tokens of anything much. Please, I don't want to be in your magazine. *Sexopolis* is real sex and *Cosmo* is fake glamour and I don't want to be a sexual symbol. Please. Please don't pursue me. Please leave me alone. Please."

"You sound like a virgin desirous of sex but protesting for propriety's sake."

"That's an awful and untrue thing to say. You don't understand me at all."

"I'm sorry." I had never meant to apologize. It is not my style. It has never been my style.

"I just know you're not going to take no and I've had a lifetime of defending myself against . . . oh, I don't want to accuse you, but you must know what I mean and what I want and how I feel and men look at me and want me and it takes so much energy just fighting each day."

"I'm sorry you're saying what you're saying. I feel good about you. The way you look out at me so. I know you think I'm this guy whose first, middle, last name is dirty sex. I'm sorry you think of sex that way. I think I've been a hero. I took sex out of the dark closet, out of the dark bedroom, and I'm proud of that. Even if some people hate it and me, I know that this time and this place we're at, well, we wouldn't be here without what I've done to bring relaxation of rigid standards and enlightenment to what were the dark ages."

"I don't want relaxation of standards, and what enlightens you does not enlighten me."

Now it's my turn to talk.

"Well, things are going to change, are in the process of changing, are already changing. I guess we're all freed up, Americans, and I don't want to tucker them out. I'm afraid men can only fuck so much. I may be showing the American Male as many naked ladies as any imagination can possibly absorb. Fantasies, too. A lot of them have come true for a lot of horny buggers. Because men now have the wherewithal—by which I mean the courage, the guts, the ability to overcome possible rejection—to bring fantasies into action. I helped make all that happen and I'm damn proud. But what's the next step? I think the men of America are telling me that they're ready for something new, that it's time to move on to something new. I don't mean to sound like I'm going to desert the men who have been so loyal and faithful. But I want to find something new. All life is the search for something new, or should be. But I think that the progress that has to be made now isn't with men. Those pieces in the puzzle have been set in place. No, the next step is with women. It's their turn now. Your turn. Perhaps it's given to us, the chance to do some exploration. All life is exploration, or should be."

She interrupts: "All those layouts of naked women, they weren't for women, they were to excite men." Her voice bristled.

"To relax them. In the face of voluptuous strangeness. To give the traveler a map."

"You're not going to put out a magazine filled with pictures of naked me, to give anyone a map!"

"No, that isn't what I have in mind. Although the principle isn't so far off the mark. What I want to do now is re-create my magazine so it's directed to men *and* women. I mean a mature appraisal of where women are today and how to capitalize on these gains and become stronger and stronger, both as a group and as individuals, and both intellectually and sexually. Women are now more than ever aware of their bodies, aware of their physical and emotional, spiritual, and yes, their intellectual needs."

Somewhere about halfway through my words she senses that I'm winging it, making it up as I'm going along.

"And I want Velvalee Peltz to be there at my side helping me!" I lost a bit of my cool saying this. "I want to make you the New Modern Woman!"

She was afraid of me. And we were alone. I could see her thinking, What can I say that can get me out of here safely? "Will you let me think about it? Would you call Mindy and I'll talk to her and it's been very nice meeting you, I'll just slip out now because I have a booking and it's clear on the other side of the city in ten minutes . . ."

She ran, she ran, oh, did she run. She didn't want to see me ever again. She makes me feel dirty.

KORAH WRITES HER SIDE OF THINGS

A CASE HISTORY

Somehow Mordecai courts, follows, pursues, tracks, overwhelms Velvalee Peltz to such a degree that there is no place in the entire Washington metropolitan and suburban area she can escape from some reminder of his presence. She sees his limousine following her, waiting outside her apartment in the Dorchester Arms on Sixteenth Street, a big doorman building that was meant to provide security. There is not a day that does not bring her overwhelming explosions of flowers, bursts of blooms she's never seen before. Clothes and jewelry she leaves in boxes in the mailroom. She will not take them in. So they pile up there until garbagemen or neighbors remove them. "Don't you want this brooch?" "Don't you want this heavenly coat?" "You must be crazy." She becomes so embarrassed that she moves, not once but several times. But he always finds her. Why doesn't she go to the police? She asks a lawyer, who tells her: "But he isn't doing anything illegal."

She receives a letter from him one day that is strangely different from the rest, which have all been solicitations for meetings, for acknowledgments of an interest she simply doesn't share. This one offers a conference "with a wise woman, a psychoanalyst whose name, Dr. Korah Ludens, you can check out with anybody, who will tell you she's the best. She's offered to meet you, with me, without me, both, I hope, and you can talk and say whatever you want to."

I am unprepared for the touching beauty of Velvalee when she finally comes. But then I have been unprepared for much of what Mordecai has talked me into over the years of his analysis. He is among the strangest of many men I have taken on as clients, either here in Washington or in New York at the institute I finally started there. No, that is not correct. Dr. Stuartgene Dye is no picnic. But Stuartgene is not strange. Stuartgene is deeply disturbed, beyond strange. I try to think of him as little as possible, as if he might go away and I would not have to deal with him. And I can handle Mordy. Besides, it is fascinating to analyze the man who has changed the sex lives of the world. He has now arrived.

"I don't know why I am here," Velvalee says immediately as Mordecai enters my office. She is very nervous, walking around, touching things here and there, not for any reason, but perhaps just to touch something, a piled-high stack of journals, a small pile of rubber bands and paper clips in a mound on my desk, unemptied ashtrays from earlier sessions today, the chewed-up toys of the my small golden cocker spaniel who's called Ranger, and who plays quietly at his mistress's feet. "This man wants an involvement, a relationship, and I don't, and I told him so from day one, from the very first minute, God I've told him so so many times I don't know what there is left to say! Why doesn't he take no for an answer!" She's hardly paused to breathe and there's desperation to her immediate assumption of Dr. Korah Ludens as her ally that I find moves me deeply. "He sent me your books. I read your books. You are brilliant! You are a brilliant woman who has achieved mightily in your world. How did you do it? How do you stand up to men? Please tell me how. That is why I agreed to come."

I find myself asking too directly, perhaps even too soon.

"So, Mordecai, why have you brought this charming young woman here? If she's been saying these things to you, why haven't you been listening?"

He looks at me with huge eyes filled with his sense of having been betrayed by his best friend. "I am paying you eighty-five dollars an hour! Please tell her how wonderful I am and how she must stop being so frightened of me and running away! She doesn't even know me. I want her to at least try to get to know me."

Velvalee, who is still standing, never looks at him, never looks at anything but my face and eyes. "He keeps writing me these notes telling me I'm running away. He uses the same word over and over again: *relationship*. Well, I don't want one of those. Why does he keep telling me that I'm frightened and running away and why can't he understand that whatever it is he wants in or out of bed I don't want it with *him*?"

The rejection, repeated again and over and over, makes him wince more than he thought he would have to. He knew it would be painful, though he'd been willing to take the chance. But now he finds himself like a lawyer in court, his arms outstretched to the judge and jury, as if he's caught the witness in an inconsistency.

"You see. You see!" he bellows. "First she says she doesn't want a relationship with anyone, not especially just not with me, and then she says she doesn't want one with me, specifically me. That isn't very consistent. That isn't very open-minded. We can't get anywhere with her acting like that, saying things like that."

And then he sits down in the big leather armchair with the arms that had bits of leather picked off by years of nervous patients, and he says very softly, to nobody really, just out loud: "I am a very nice man."

"What am I doing here what am I doing here what am I doing here," Velvalee keeps mumbling. Why does she feel she is losing ground that she never inhabited anyway? She is unaccustomed to discussing personal matters, that's for certain, and certainly not so endlessly and in such great detail as she's discovering is asked for here.

"Look! I refuse to be made *wrong* in this situation!"

Hearing her talk like this makes Mordecai want her even more. He had no idea she could speak with such grown-up terminology. He gets up to rush to her, but she runs for cover to stand behind me and he stops dead in his tracks. His mouth sputters out words that his brain is not hearing. "What's the use. Nobody loves me. What's the use? Goodbye."

But he doesn't turn to leave. He falls to the floor, upon his knees, in front of her, in the classic position of suitors.

"I think about you all the time and all I can say is that I hope you will reconsider and please know that whenever you want to you'll find me here waiting. I could love you."

He raises himself from the floor and, evidently liking the sound of what he's just said, says it again, softly. "Just *know* that I could love you." He wants to say it a third time, so much does he like the sound of his voicing of these words, the feelings of this feeling, and this situation, all rolled together into such a nice little emotional scene, as if his whole life is meant for the voicing of these words, the validation of himself. "Just know that I could love you," he does say again, softly, before at last turning away and leaving.

I ask Velvalee if she would like to sit down, or have some tea, or tell me what she is thinking.

"What am I thinking? I am thinking that I should like to go and live in a whorehouse where I can get my own back against men by not letting them touch me. Or live in a nunnery except that I could never believe in God. Men are pigs. I feel sorry for every woman. I'd like to help all of us, somehow."

AND SO IT GOES

Bohunk Vernissage, a little-known subsidiary of Greeting Pharmaceuticals, further improves cryoprecipitate, thus making possible the world's first commercial freeze-dried blood-clotting concentrate for hemophiliacs. It is not heat-treated. Von Greeting knows it is not heat-treated. But it will now be possible to market a product for a growing market fueled by the anger of helpless parents at our government for so long ignoring this condition. It will be called BaxxterDridge Factor VIII. This product will be made from blood pooled from thousands, eventually tens of thousands, of donors.

AND SO IT GOES . . .

Dr. Stuartgene Dye doesn't like to lie down, so they sit face-to-face.

"Arnold just watched last night. I invited him to join us. Claudia was strangely passive. She hates Ethan Zimmer. Which makes it more exciting when he's with us. Although I tied Nellie up. She performed only adequately. It wasn't good for me. It made me want another woman. Perhaps Jinx. Although this isn't really Jinx. Plus Claudia watching, of course. I phoned down to Doris but there was no one who would come to me. Doris said she's trying to cut out 'all your kind of crap.' I told her that would put her out of business. Every time she says that I tell her that actualizing fantasies is the most important progressive step she can take and that she should read *Sexopolis* to keep up with the times. So Nellie receives the brunt of my anger, of course. Does all this shock you? Or have you heard it too many times?"

"No, it always shocks me," Korah Ludens answers.

"Ah, your moralizing tone."

"Yes."

"At moments like this you wonder why you've devoted your life to this. And what has happened to turn our world into such a universe."

"You are imagining for me again. We are here to talk about you, not me."

"'I have imagined everything conceivable, but I have certainly not done, and certainly never will, all that I've imagined.' De Sade. I think I know myself inside out by now."

"I know you think you do."

"Ah. The innuendo."

"More specific than innuendo."

Korah wants to say, "You have almost killed Nellie several times." Instead, she listens as he says, "Arnold and I have to finish with Ethan Zimmer."

"What are you going to do with Ethan Zimmer?" She should not be asking direct questions.

"You know I can't tell you that. You'll excuse me this slight . . . repression."

She doesn't respond.

After a moment, he says, "I'm courting death. I know that. It's an old Native American tradition. Perhaps it won't be long in coming." He looks at his watch. "Our time is up for today. You're still a wonderful analyst."

"You make me feel helpless," she says, knowing such a thought voiced out loud is not recommended.

"I merge vengeance with transgression and transform transgression into glory. Another Native American belief."

"That is intellectual bullshit!" Another something she should certainly not have said out loud to him.

He jumps up suddenly, causing Ranger to bark. Stuartgene smiles as he leaves. She sits there, numb. Even when the dog jumps into her lap and she automatically rubs him behind his ears, her eyes can't focus. Oh, yes, she does know everything about Dr. Stuartgene Dye that any analyst needs to know including the fact that he is high up in dealing with the health of The American People and she is helpless to help him, or, come to think of it, in this case, them.

•

She goes back to Rivtov, back to her training analyst at Yaddah. She'd been his prize student. He'd also voted to have her thrown out of the society. Some thirty-odd years ago, all of this was. She used to know the dates.

"Get rid of him. That's still my advice to you." He's now white-haired, his glasses thicker, but still waving his clubfoot as he talks to you, the leg with this clubfoot crossed over his good leg, the clubfoot in its space shoe dangling, misshapen, almost flaunted for inspection by an incumbent patient's eyes. "You have let yourself become too involved in Dr. Dye's case, allowing everything to advance too far. He is not a patient with whom you should allow yourself to be affiliated. From the very beginning you must have sensed that. How could you not? You should have realized that there is nothing you can do to help this sort of patient. He is an embarrassment. A danger. An obtusity. I believe I have told you all this before."

"Obtuseness," she corrects him.

"Dr. Ludens, please get rid of him. Again, you have overstepped the guidelines that we set up long ago for our own protection. You simply always go too far. Did your failure to raise the place of women not convince you of the harsh difficulties, nay impossibility, of changing certain immutable things?"

She wants to say, "I hate you." She wearily stands up and looks at him. The argument that comes from her heart and soul is the argument that also came out some thirty-odd years ago when they expelled her, as it has also been the argument upon which she's based her life.

"I can only go where the patient takes me," she says with all the force she can muster. "I cannot stop the direction of his unconscious will. Nor would I want to, even if I knew where it was heading. Isn't that like a kind of abortion, Reiner Rivtov? I know you are not against abortion."

"Now I am for it."

"Perhaps that is an inept analogy, then."

"It is a sign of the impossible situation you have put yourself in that you so confuse your metaphors that they no longer coincide with your own personal safety."

AND SO IT GOES...?

"What did you say, Mickey?" Fred asks his old friend, Dr. Mickey Marcus. Fred is in New York, in Greenwich Village, in his own apartment overlooking Washington Square and seeking a next outlet for his energies. He's known Mickey since as a med school student he'd come to meet Fred in London, where they'd tricked. That was years ago but they've stayed in touch.

"It's in the *Journal of Death*. Put out by COD. There's a puzzling appearance of *Pneumocystis carinii* pneumonia in gay men. Pewkin at COD told me when I called to request information about the only medicine for it. They have embargoed it for some reason, I can't imagine why. Aerosolized pentamidine. It's been around forever. No drug company makes it because there's no profit in it, it's so cheap to make."

"Do you die from it?" Fred asks.

"Yes. If left untreated."

"What do you think is happening?"

"I don't know but I'll write about it in my health column in *The Prick*."

"Is this the next thing we have to worry about from having so much sex?" He remembers his own bouts with VD, hep. B, amoebas . . .

"I can't say that!"

"Maybe put in a cautionary note? Be careful."

"Pewkin won't release any of the med. That's what's really puzzling."

"Be sure and write about that, too."

"You're such a troublemaker! Isn't writing that novel about us enough to calm you down?"

"Better safe than sorry, no?"

"I don't want to lose my license. Remember I work for the city."

DEAR GOVERNOR RUESTER

I am working on a liquid that when drunk will kill its imbiber in one minute's time. I plan to take a large supply and pass it out at those secret meetings of the fairies in the Redwoods that I've heard about. I hate fairies and I hope you do too. I'm glad you're running for president so you can start killing them all before it's too late.

DAME LADY HERMIA'S HISTORY OF EVIL

It is generous of Fred to include me in his research into what he calls "the real and honest history of our country." As a truly educated woman in a world that allows us scant attention of any significant nature, I come more and more to acknowledge that we like-mindeds must join together and fight in every way we can. I have looked forward to further installments as the monsters he is so carefully observing move closer to Ground Zero. I continue to be increasingly agog, which is what good history should arouse in one! My own work is not yet nearly "agog" enough!

Let me enter here this maxim of a brilliant chum, Hannah Arendt, to engrave upon our hearts and minds: "The destruction of a man's rights is a prerequisite for dominating him entirely."

Arendt has of course written about the camps. "The most essential function of camps is their role as major killing centers *'in the larger terror apparatus.'*" Well, your history has described several of America's early camps in operation. What we have all been rather lackluster in attending to is this query that I now wish to raise: What really *is* this larger terror apparatus now? Discovering Partekla and researching NITS, I wonder.

One of the most difficult of tasks is discerning the line that divides evil from other man-made happenings. For me evil requires a certain conscious intentionality. I have decided this will be my yardstick, so to speak, and I shall stick to it as we continue to explore America's sordid history of this plague.

The arrival at NITS of one Dr. Jerrold Omicidio has not even been noted. He is sneaky that way. Now you'll see him, now you won't. I hope our attempt to unravel and understand his actions shall form a major portion of our history of evil. And of poor Sister Grace, whatever she is so frightened of now.

"There are many ways to kill people in large numbers," Omicidio said in his text, *Today's Bible of Infectious Diseases*, which will become the largest textbook on this subject ever published. Would Hannah identify and include NITS as one of her major killing centers, one of the world's largest?

"WE'RE HERE, WE'RE QUEER! GET USED TO IT!"

In 1969 a bunch of drag queens fought back like tigers when a parcel of cops raided their bar in Greenwich Village called Stonewall. The cops had never confronted such resistance from the fairies and overextended their brutal response. This escalated out to the streets and before you knew it a full-scale revolt materialized as gays from anywhere nearby came to join in. It was a couple of weeks before it sort of calmed down.

Something historic had happened. Gays had fought back with other gays and got the courage to continue doing so.

There had been over the years a number of small and powerless groups organized to bring gays out into the open. Nothing had worked. A few guys and women picketing in front of the White House wasn't doing it. Starting with Stonewall, groups got bigger and if not yet angry enough at least more visible and volubly louder in their demands for equality. Some kind of historical line had been confronted, breached, and crossed by a number of people. It would start to slowly change things for the better, at least for a little while.

By no means was it the organized movement that was certainly required. Gays had never been good at organizing and really fighting back. The early movement activists and the heroic band of Stonewall protestors were numerically small compared with the crowds that will be coming with the disco era, dancing and drugging in the hope that their newly perking acceptance will be waiting for them with open arms.

It will be the bars and the discos, presumed to be their ticket to ride, that will also serve to lead them to their continuing entrapment.

Neither Fred nor Daniel is on the scene for Stonewall. Fred's winding up a movie somewhere far away and Daniel in Washington is still living in never-never land.

Who is on the scene observing what is happening are Roy Cohn, Sam Sport, and their tagalong monster-in-training Dereck Dumster. Roy is teaching them that the first requirement for any behavior or action is always: "NEVER APOLOGIZE, NEVER EXPLAIN."

ANOTHER DEAD BOY

Murphy Evers, age sixteen, student at Michigan Mountain Day School, Ann Arbor Village, Michigan. Died Sept. 18, 1970, while participating in soccer practice after school. He was the team captain. He had not been in bodily contact with any other player. He had no ailments that his doctor knew about. His teammates said "he just turned purple and collapsed." Evidently he was in every conceivable way a healthy normal American teenager. His death was registered as "from unknown causes." His father, returning from a business trip to Haiti, collects his son's body from St. Purdah's, where Dr. Alvaar Heidrich had asked to study it.

—PJ

You will not be able to know for another eighteen years that this is a death from me, when Murphy's body will be dug up by his grieving parents, who are trying, like you, to put pieces together. Murphy's boyfriend had been a hemophiliac taking BaxxterDridge, one of those Factor VIII thingies. Don't know how they got hold of this thingie so early, and in Michigan. I hadn't been in Michigan yet. His folks must have had what you call connections.

VON GREETING MEETS WITH
DR. STUARTGENE DYE

I was looking at a photo in *The Washington Monument* of these people marching in a parade past the White House. I realized that the time is approaching wherein they could be eliminated forever. Once and for all we could get rid of homosexuals. Words like *pansy* and *fairy* are not nice. *Homosexual* is awful enough but it's what they're officially called. In science I know you respect names. Taxonomy, I believe it's called.

The salient point is not what they're called but that they shouldn't be here. They get in the way of orderly progress. Now there are so many of them I worry it might be too late. I'm not certain why they want to show themselves so aggressively but they seem to be doing so more and more. You'd think they'd know that they were safer when they were secret and invisible.

I am being pestered about the release to regurgiacs of our first batch of our alpha. I am told by your people that it's still too early. "You don't have your ducks all in line yet." Our alpha is from batches of donor blood from all over the world and combined together and processed down into single injections. Both of us know it's not clean and that I shouldn't be distributing it until we know how to clean it. We all know it can't officially be approved by FADS until then. But more people will get sick and die if I don't distribute it, which is the convenient threat I'll use unless you approve of releasing it before it's clean. I figure we've got one year, two tops, to get this stuff out there into gay bloodstreams before that door will be closed by some newly discovered technique that will clean alpha up and out. The window of opportunity to mass-infect an entire population will be cut short. Partekla says there are more gay hemophiliacs out there than we think, all waiting to further infect each other with whatever their nasty habits are giving them.

GAAAH, ETC.

Grossie Wildeschone, Pubie Grotty, Cocker Rutt, Babs Gershowitz, and Muxter Questlos—these names enter themselves in the pages of this history as their owners summon themselves to the halls of New Jersey's School of Continuing Dentistry to found the Gay Association of Academic Alliances of Homosexuals and Lesbians (GAAAGAAHL, though soon to be short-ened to just plain GAAAH). Within months of word getting around they are joined by several dozen others, men and women, academics all, who de-sire to be recognized for who they are in their academic environments, that is, as full-frontal homosexuals and lesbians. It is time for gay teachers to stand taller in the groves of academe. The movement is slow to grow but these few are fervent.

What means this word *gay* that is more and more heard in the land? Gay? In what sense? Is there dancing in the streets when those so named decide to get together? Nothing but smiles? Frolics and tra-la-la-ing? The origin of this word, as it applies to homosexuals, is imprecisely known, much like *hushmarked* had been for previous centuries. What is known is that for whatever reasons the word *homosexual* sits unhappily on tongues and shoul-ders as too clinical and harsh, too limiting, too *medical*, as precise taxonomy is apt to so be.

Grossie, of course, is the famous lesbian scholar of ancient Greece and Rome. She it is who wrote the book on what it means to be a dyke, in psy-chosocial terms, just as Dr. Muxter Questlos did for homosexual men. Their "definitive" tomes are long and virtually incomprehensible, hopelessly caught up in the growing linguistic spiderwebs of "queer theory" and "gender stud-ies," now beginning to be spun. *Gay* will soon not be good enough for this lot, who will start calling *everything* "queer," it occurring to none of them that *queer* is also a revolting and demeaning word and still abhorrent for many who recall it from being stoned with it in their youth.

The defining of gay groups by their members has never been an easy matter. "Queers have been here since the beginning," they state in its sim-plicity, which of course is true, that homosexuals have been here since the beginning. But "the beginning of what?" is the question that sends every-thing off the track. The word *homosexual* did not exist until 1864, so to these new queer theorists, homosexuals did not exist before then, so that another all-encompassing "timeless" word is thus required for today. This nonsense is another nail in the coffin of gay people ever locating their history, ever defining precisely who lived it, ever agreeing on a history at all.

The groups that were forming up, GAAAH, GAA, GFA, GLOW, HLF, started multiplying before and after Stonewall. They were all liberal and progressive, of course. What they weren't was unified in their goals. Always, though, the question "What will our movement be all about?" is not only asked but answered, in varying degrees of impossible impossibilities before a minimally acceptable notion will surface, more or less. Another nail coming up and going in.

What it all eventually boils down to is this:

"We want sexual freedom, to do whatever we want with whomever we want whenever and wherever we want." It is curiously parsimonious, this stingy description that excludes so much more than it includes or dares to dream. Why does it all boil down to sex? Why does no one dare to go further in outlining a vision for a future that includes *all* rights denied, of which there are too many thousands to count? The reasoning behind this is also imprecisely known. For one thing, so few are speaking for so many. Where are these many and why do they allow so few to speak for them? *Allow* is as imprecise a word as all the others. To some gays Pubie Grottie's famous cry, "We Shall Fuck in the Bushes and on the Streets!" has had a mobilizing effect on those who thought only of this and, hearing support from their friends, believed they were speaking for the many. Whose is the loudest voice in this alliance? God knows, no dyke wants to fuck in the bushes. So Grossie was overruled, hence sending her into the already overflowing number of women who tried to fight for their rights, only to disappear for fear of the men.

But this small isolated cocky proclamation is the entire tit that this invigorated gay movement sucks on. "We want to live our own *Sexopolis*!" is heard from more and more. Whatever new organizational entities burp forth during the coming years, they will proclaim only this paltry hedonistic wish, continuing unchanged, unaltered, and sworn to in fealty until it will be too late. The damage will be done. The world will think gays, at the least, perverse. This is a movement founded on wanting too little, dreaming too small. It will prove to be the death of an awful lot of people. And of course it will be the men who rule the roost. Lesbians determinably now tend to their needs more quietly. Grossie Wildeschone and Babs Gershowitz, in fact, will not be heard from again.

To a later historically famous meeting Pubie Grotty, Cocker Rutt, and Muxter Questlos will invite the famous French Futurist Jean-Paul Fatoottst, who is to play such a pivotal role in fashioning the text for future male "queer bonding." He formulates most of it on this very trip to America after a visit to the Pit of Hell, a New York S&M bar where he's so thoroughly punished by absolutely everyone that he goes home to Paris and creates his historic "A Philosophy of Participatory Incarceration," which, should you really be able to parse it, glorifies the pleasure and entitlement of the most extreme of sexual acts. Academics, particularly, love him, no doubt because his queer prose is so incomprehensibly dense. But his message of the glory in being pissed on appears to fulfill an academic and scholarly need.

YOU GO TO MY HEAD

Since back in America, Fred's learned to dance. With so many new friends, Fred's danced and danced. He'd been to Fire Island. He loved the new discos. He was even a card-carrying member of Capriccio, a hard-to-get-into place. On lower West Broadway near Canal, on a second floor above a Chase, in a hangar as large and twisted as Saarinen's at Kennedy, the cavernous Versailles that was Capriccio, all high gray-flanneled walls and the widest field of shining waxed wood on which to move and glide and shake and boogie and sweat and show the muscles (he'd even joined a gym!), wiggle the ass, bump the crotch, say goodbye to all cares, with all our brothers, everything bathed in light and sound, the legendary sound!, which Juanito, Puerto Rican handsome, English not so good, in his control room turned all into greatness as he placed his Vlandor Arm with its Nefisto cartridge on its Zee-able turntable, thus activating speakers and woofers and super tweeters, the resultant decibelacular sound engorging all of the above, Hot Men!, Dancing!, Love!, Friendship!, this legendary spot of Heaven on Earth, our very own beloved exclusive club, Capriccio!

And the Lights! A cacophony of multicolors, flashing waves and arcs, electronics of incredible wizardry, channels for Spin and Normal, Invert and Pause, Advance and Throb, button after button touched to program mood after mood, synergistically Siamese-twinned to songs and shoutings and mind-expanding Joy.

And the Clothes! Tight tees and tight jeans and old boots and bare chests, or the finery of show-off: costumes of delicate frippery or outlandish look-at-me.

And the Men! Have you ever seen so many Hot Men! Gloried, storied, muscled, fatless, mustached, youthful, smiling, sexy MEN!

Fred had never seen anything like it. What has happened to his country since he went away? It was like dancing exuberantly in his bedroom in Masturbov Gardens, only now he was doing it out in the open and for real.

And the Drugs!

Tonight everyone was high on a snort of Magic by midnight, to be followed by a tab of Glycn at 2:00, a half of Nyll at 3:00, and a hit of Blotter by 4:00, acid not usually ingested so late, but a long night was wanted, tomorrow was way off, with so many more events to follow after that. Sleep was for lazies, dropouts, unconcerneds, incompetents, misser-outers.

The music was in high gear, songs intertwining, a low feed-in of the theme from *Cobra Woman*, played on the theremin by the composer himself, audible beneath the overriding blanket of "Honey, Where's Our Love Gone," the tensions of many thousand bodies minutely matched to the music's every whim and the evening's drugs, all this amplified, innuendoed, transmogrified beyond anybody's pure cognition, the smashing of the brain!, all it felt was GOOD!, this place can really show us how to play!

And to forget!

Fred took no drugs. He'd tried them but found no answers, and he was on a pilgrimage for answers. Isn't that what writers bearing witness must do? He had to be clearheaded for that!

As they all dance Fred thinks that in this mélange of sound he's heard the theme music from his own hit movie *Lest We Sleep Alone*.

THE AVOCADO

The Divine Bella, *The Avocado*'s gossip columnist and man in the East, attends a shitting weekend at the Putnam County mansion of Moud Soud, a Saudi prince enamored of the many new things he's learning from The American People. Forty-three young handsome men shit on each other, or are shat upon, or walk in it barefoot, or give each other shitpacks in the many-hissing-spigots steam room. Bella's column, which he composes in his head almost on any spot, pausing only to give himself his shot of BaxxterPlusOneAlpha, tells it like it is, even if *The Avocado*'s current editor, Skolnick Jameson, thinks it's a bit too much. "Bella, it's a bit too much. Make up something else."

The state of the gay press at this moment in time is in dire straits. Well, it's always been in dire straits. There's never been a time when it hasn't been in dire straits. *The Avocado*, out of lazy Los Angeles, rules the roost by default and the generous pocket of Dranch Nuckel, a short, overweight, intense pseudo-intellectual homosexual whose fortune comes from selling insurance to the indigent and then foreclosing. He is fond of editorializing about "Our day will come!" and "Brother must meet brother in fraternal love and honor." That he is without love, or indeed many friends, does not bother him. He pays for them both and is thus surrounded by each. The magazine is profitable by dint of its many pages of classified ads of those men looking for what most gay men are looking for, and hence widely subscribed to and passed around. *The Avocado* fears no competition. *The Prick* is too invisible and Orvid too eccentric. That this is the best the gay world can put forth to communicate with each other coast-to-coast, keeping everyone up to date, is sad, and when UC arrives, will be, along with so many other items, tragic.

The Divine Bella's name is Bertram Bellberg. He, too, is overweight but jovial and never-endingly full of enthusiasm for the audience he visualizes writing for. He bounces, literally, from event to event, always wearing his signature outfit, a worker's uniform of some kind or other. He has an endless wardrobe of them, which he wears buttoned open to his navel or one overall strap casually askew, his hairy chest of Brillo pridefully displayed. If one can overlook the shitty subtext of his life, Bella is a loving, lovable, well-meaning fellow.

A CLEAN BILL OF HEALTH?

In 1973, the American Psychoanalytic Association removes homosexuality from its book of sicknesses. This has been a long fight and it is far from over.

Based on the evidence they have gathered, or rather the growing pressure that's been brought by an increasing number of closeted gay members, the Committee on Nomenclature recommends delisting homosexuality as a mental disorder and sends its recommendation up through the APA bureaucracy—the Council on Research and Development, the Assembly of District Branches, the Reference Committee, the Executive Tandem. Eventually it reaches the APA Board of Trustees, which in December 1973 casts thirteen votes in favor of the change, with two abstentions and four members absent. Both Shmuel Derektor and Korah Ludens vote in favor. Dr. Aalvaar Heidrich votes against.

Cure-therapists, mostly psychoanalysts such as Irving Bieber and the zealously homophobic Charles Socarides (whose son will turn out to be openly gay and work for President Boy Vertle), are furious and begin gathering signatures demanding a referendum to overturn the board's decision.

The referendum is held. Of ten thousand psychiatrists voting, 51 percent support the board's decision, 47 percent oppose it, and 2 percent abstain. With that vote the issue is settled and the APA finally acknowledges that millions of gay Americans are not, after all, mentally ill.

This decision does not go down well with that 47 percent, and, as will continue to be seen, with an almost overwhelming number of other groups and organizations and politicians and presidents and shrinks and just plain ol' folks and your next-door neighbors, all of whom and which refuse to accept this sort of thing.

FAREWELL TO ALL WHAT?

The little cottage in Hykoryville sits alone no longer. The neighborhood is all built up. Other little cottages crowd in upon it. You can see in everyone's windows as you walk down the street. Rivka Jerusalem now has the beat-up Dodge, which she drives here from Masturbov Gardens and parks in the narrow driveway, so she can't even see Mrs. Lemish on the bus to ask about her own sons, who must be quite grown-up by now. She wonders if her blood organization still even employs her. It seems that the world is closing itself off more and more, especially in small towns like this one. Yes, she recalls that what Verdingy did was secret and that being not seen was an issue, but really, way out here in the sticks, it's been hard to take any of that seriously, though of course she worries about it down deep, like so many things that seem too complicated or too uncomfortable—oh, what's the difference. For years now she's just spent the day in an office where no mail comes and no phones ring. She sits at her desk and stares, or sometimes she goes to the stack of old magazines piled on a neighbor's curb awaiting the trash collector's biweekly visit, and brazenly plucks a few (once upon a time she would have considered such an act undignified) and takes them back to this cottage empty of the needy clients she so enjoyed helping who used to line up on busy days during wartime, to aimlessly thumb through them. Where did all the people disappear to who needed her help, the destitute families and lost servicemen or their wives missing monthly allowances the government hadn't sent? She's no dummy. She reads the local papers. She knows there are still problems

ARB would ordinarily routinely handle. Fires, for instance. There have been houses burning down more frequently now as the population grows poorer. But she receives no summonses for help. Who isn't telling her what? The silence is killing her. This was the one place where she could be useful.

For a while she tries to write her autobiography. For six months she writes each day, beginning with her birth, scribbling on the backs of outdated forms with now useless rerouting numbers, getting down everything she can remember. A few weeks into month six she realizes she's making it all sound nicer and more romantic than it was. She is writing the life she wishes she'd lived. She's writing lies. So she stops. She realizes, and it stuns her, that she does not want to write the truth. She does wonder why they closed down the Hykoryville office after all those poor little boys were murdered, but why did they reopen it again a few years later, and transfer her back here from the District office, where she thought she was still doing important work? Was it because she'd asked a few innocent questions about all those mysterious packages going in and out of someplace called Partekla? She still gets her check every two weeks in the mail like the old days. Once or twice over the years she even got a little raise in salary. Miss von Lutz has long since disappeared from the main office, and no one seems to know anything about her, or even that ARB has an office in Hykoryville. "Where is Hykoryville?" the girls on the phone downtown always ask. "It's true we're experiencing a difficulty in volunteer recruitment now that there are no more wars," one woman admits. Rivka's past the usual retirement age by five years or so, and she fears that if she pushes too much she'll lose her check. She doesn't want that. Then she'll have to stay home all day with Philip, who's been ready to retire and claims he's only waiting for her.

One morning a young woman arrives in a limousine with the ARB emblem and driven by a uniformed driver. She wears an expensive two-piece tweed outfit, with an overcoat and bag made of the same material, and a little hat too. She is very much of a muchness, Rivka thinks, noticing a tiny gold pin with the ARB emblem on the woman's lapel. Rivka had never seen the pin and wonders why she was never given one.

"Hello, Mrs. Jerusalem, my name is Junilla Almong and I am from Home Office and I have come to tell you that we are closing down this branch, which cannot be much of a surprise to you. We should have done it years ago but quite frankly no one even knew it was here until last week. You have been an exceptionally faithful and loyal employee and so in addition to your pension and health insurance we are giving you this lovely watch.

What's a retirement without a watch, eh?" She hands Rivka a little box. The watch is so small that Rivka knows her eyesight will not work well with it. "Your employment with American Red Blood is officially terminated, or will be when you sign these forms."

This woman with the strange name takes a manila envelope from her tweed bag and removes several pieces of paper, which Rivka dutifully signs where indicated. The woman leaves before Rivka realizes she hadn't said a word or offered a cup of tea. For some time now she's recognized such symptoms in herself as those of depression. She's read a book from the local library after seeing an item in *The Monument* about its author, who says that many aging women suffer greatly from depression. Well, why shouldn't she be depressed? She lives with a man she hardly speaks to. She has four sons she never sees or hears from. Indeed, the one who was away so awfully long has gone away again. Now it turns out she's spent her adult life doing a job that has come to nothing. Everything, it now appears, is and has been an unanswered question.

Philip's job with the government has been over for several years. He sits at home as helpless and disengaged as she does here. When he speaks he only says things like "I want to live someplace warm," or "I want to live someplace where I don't have to move." Once she asked him what not having to move meant. "I want to sit in one place and look at something pretty and not move," he said. "Forever?" she asked him. "We have so much time left to use words like that?" he answered. She remembers being struck by the poetry of that sentence and wondering again if perhaps her husband harbored talents he'd never shown her. Now she finds herself strangely touched from his saying, "I want to retire to that hotel in Miami Beach where we went on our honeymoon."

Rivka walks around the cottage for the last time. She goes upstairs to bedrooms that have never been used except for file storage, and downstairs to the basement, where huge refrigerators are still rumbling, gobbling up electricity, with no more blood inside to keep cold until it's collected. She was told—how long ago?—not to turn them off, just in case. There is nothing here of value to take home. The typewriter is ancient and every ream of paper yellowing. There's a little money in petty cash and a little in the local bank. Presumably the house is worth something if it is to be sold. The price of places in this neighborhood had "held firm," as the local free weekly newspaper recently reported, although Rivka can see the neighborhood's turning black. Would Miss Tweed Outfit be interested in any of this?

She doesn't know what to do about locking up for good. Take the key and turn it in the lock and then do what with the key? Throw it back through the mail slot? She decides to take it with her. If anyone wants it or wants any further information from her, they must know how to find her. Surely her home phone number, utilized so many many times during the war when "emergency shipments" were due, is in a file somewhere. Maybe not. She doesn't care.

What has she learned in all her years here? she asks herself as she closes the last window, the one in her own office, a dining room once upon a time, with a few framed frayed photos of her family dusty on her desktop. She throws them in her wastebasket. Then she bends to retrieve them and rips them into pieces, lest some enemy discover them, and laughs out loud. She sits down, winded by this act's impertinent and inherent demoralizing effect. She feels degraded. All those names that had sounded so mighty. Puttsig. Von Lutz. Tolson. Brinestalker. Grodzo. Or romantic: Oderstrasse. Port-au-Prince, Kinshasa. And of course Partekla.

I have learned that Amos Standing loved Philip Jerusalem and that because of it my son David was taken away from me when he was less than six years old. I have even learned that he was at that Partekla and that he, like his twin, like their father, is a homosexual. He came home, all right. But he went away again. He was only home for what now seems five minutes. How time flies. No. It really doesn't. Some things last forever. What is this thing that gobbled up all my men?

She gets up from her chair and locks the door and throws the key through the mail slot after all. She gets into her old car and drives back to Masturbov Gardens. She guesses she now will have to go to Miami and sit with Philip looking for something pretty, never moving until there is nothing left to look at.

DR. SISTER GRACE'S NOTEBOOK

This world war almost thirty years ago took 80 million dead of which 55 million were civilians. The NITS Committee of Statistical Intervention has *finally* released these figures. NITS is a fucking blight on the world of scientific information.

One of my patients at Partekla—he was actually one of the soldiers imprisoned for being gay—died from something strange. I sent some of his blood to Pewkin at COD, not an intelligent man but that was the chain of command dictated for such as this. He did not respond. The soldier had been stationed in Africa, so I sent his blood to Pepin, who suggested I go there. Vitabaum would not pay for my trip so I paid for it myself.

Pepin took me through jungles and I stood underneath collecting what monkeys in the trees shat and pissed into the buckets we were holding.

Shit has been causing deaths since Christianity threw out the rigid commandments Jews demanded for cleanliness. I guess Jesus didn't wash his hands before he sat down for that Last Supper. Christians blamed plagues on the use of bathhouses!

Our fucking Center of Disease wasn't even founded until 1946. Not to take care of disease but to investigate biological warfare.

I am getting closer. To something.

•

She is. I must get rid of her.

DISTRACTIONS OF ACTIONS NOT TO COME

Once upon a time, in the poorest neighborhood of the District, there lived a boy named Sammy Sircus. His father was long dead and his mother made what pennies she could to feed her young son by repairing bras and girdles. Those were the days when women still wore these and were considered slutty if they didn't. Each and every day of his boyhood, Sammy looked around his impoverished world, and across town at the other world, and vowed to himself, "Fuck this cunt shit. I am going to be one of the richest men in that other world. I coulda shoulda be able to fucking do that!" It was a rough neighborhood and they spoke like this. And you got beat up less for being a sissy if you said words like *fuck* and *cunt* a lot.

Many children make vows like this. Most of them never come true. Sammy Sircus's vow will come true. He will be a billionaire. Since he's a gay man, he will thus also be a gay billionaire, perhaps one of the first known publicly as such. Sammy Sircus will be very powerful in all the fields of media. He is reasonably attractive, reasonably intelligent, exceptionally lucky, and a long way from the corsets of his childhood.

Sammy's childhood was rife with clues to his future prominence. That he will support a cause or two—can this not be traced to all those girdles?

That he will so unvaryingly identify with women performers and make the world pay attention to them—must this not come from helping his mother with her bras? "Ma, why is this one so much bigger?" "Ma, why is this one all spotted with funny-colored ook?" "Ma, I'm sure glad I don't need these." Years later, when interviewed by a biographer, he says, "As long as I didn't have to come anywhere near her tits, I knew how to present a woman to her best advantage."

Why will Sammy Sircus be important in our history and our country and our plague? Well, actually he won't be. But because he has so much money, he coulda shoulda been. What will he do with all his money and influence to help his dying gay brothers? Not much. Why not? Why did American Jews help to murder German Jews? *Wer weiss?* Who knows? as his own mother answered difficult childhood questions. "If God wanted me to uplift the world in more useful ways than bras, He would have summoned me. 'Billie,' He would say, 'find more uplifting work.' But He didn't. And maybe He's right. Boobies well placed can make a man happy. A happy man makes a happy woman. Happy men make a better America. I look upon my work as a necessary calling, like a rabbi or a nurse." Sammy learned this lesson in charitable self-interest from his mother. When she died, she left half a million dollars, just from bras and girdles for the shiksas in Northwest Washington. She'd penny-pinched all her life and never gave away a dime.

Trafe Elohenu is what Rabbi Chesterfield's nephew Ralph now calls himself. He hates being a Jew so much that he gives himself this sacrilegious name and announces to his uncle that he's a fegalah. Not another one, the rabbi thinks to himself. What is God telling me? Trafe knows Sammy because Trafe came with his mother from the Northwest for her fittings. The two boys stared at each other knowingly. They somehow knew they were meant to be in each other's lives just as Billie Sircus knew she was meant to be in tits.

Kipper Gross is a third lad out of Washington who bonds with Sammy and Trafe. Kipper meets Sammy when he comes to "apprentice" with Billie. "Can I help it if this fine young man wants to learn all about brassieres? That he has heard I have the magic fingers," his mother demands when her son inquires why cute Kipper is suddenly there. "I want to be the most successful women's wear designer in the entire world," Kipper says practically every day to Sammy. "How do you know this so early?" Sammy asks him. "I have known it since I was a little boy. I can feel it in my fingers." At least Kipper knows how he wants to make his millions. Sammy's path is not so precisely set.

In the end Sammy Sircus will be the richest. Kipper Gross will be more world famous. Trafe Elohenu will be the tagalong. He'll be very rich too, but he doesn't want fame the way the other two do. He'll make his riches representing all the famous performers with big tits that Sammy will discover and Kipper will dress, all three turning them into the biggest and most remunerative of stars.

Actually, they are not three, they are four: we must not forget to include in their bonding, their pact of everlasting friendship, Randy Dildough, a bit more of a loner than the others, and who doesn't smile as much, perhaps because his own path is still not satisfyingly set, even after all the success that's come to him by the time of the plague. That he will even marry the famous women's fashion designer Dordogna del Dongo is as good an example as any that he's troubled in his focus and his deepest desires. But together they'll find their billion, one way or another, multifactorially.

It is interesting that none of these great American gay men, upon reaching middle age, will have found love. Their true longings will remain unfulfilled.

Certain industries in America are more important than others. Media is on its way to becoming the most important of all. Media, which includes movies, TV, computers, rock music, publishing, and fashion, is the most important because media is messages everyone will hear and see. These four American gay men by the time of the plague's arrival will be more important in our country's heterosexual social fabric than anyone imagines.

The straight world's had its Rockefeller, Astor, Morgan, Harriman ad infinitum, who, even though they were big-time crooks, lent their names to mammoth improvements to America and for The American People. What will these four build for their own people, people they fucked with for so many years? How will they say thank you to their gay brothers? As with Horatio Dridge and Clarence Meekley, that the filthy rich include these gay fellows escapes true scholarly attention to the history of homosexuality.

At this still-preplague moment Randy is chairman of a major motion picture studio, Kipper head of his fashion empire, and Sammy Sircus is closing in on that first billion, acquired from buying and selling record companies and movie studios and talent agencies and acquiring a burgeoning collection of the world's most valuable art. Trafe, who's lately been spending more of his spare time with his new hobby, interior decorating, has decided to become, after all, a serious Jew. So he stays home a lot studying Hebrew and the Talmud while choosing from swatches of samples to tastefully cover some rich yenta's sofas and chairs, not to mention curtains and drapes.

When our coming plague reaches new peaks of its destruction, these four will be well on their way to controlling some twenty-plus billion dollars.

SAM SPORT

Sam Sport is a big shit. One of the biggest The American People's ever produced. He ran his office in New York but a really smart shit was more and more needed in Washington. Roy Cohn's got New York covered. So Sam is the man who is Lucas and Stephen Jerusalem's partner in Jerusalem & Sport. This was a marriage arranged by Abe Masturbov, a longtime client of Sam's. Abe wants Doris to have the best protection that money can buy. Sam is that, and Doris remains in business. Sam Sport has played upon the stages of history before, learning how to be a shit from the best of them. He was assistant to Roy and to Sen. Vurd in their infamous notorious postwar blacklisting trials against faggots and commies that put thousands out of work or into jail or out of the country. That's where and when Sam became chums with Peter and Purpura Ruester, soon to be living a few blocks away. If doing evil deeds shows up on your face, Sam Sport is sinisterly handsome. There are few practical gifts God hasn't given Sam Sport except decency. Like all big shits he doesn't give a shit. Sam Sport doesn't look his age, whatever it is. Age is one of the many things he lies about. He keeps his body, which is short and thin and extremely agile, well tailored so he doesn't look old at all. For sex he works hard to keep it this way. His face is ashen and expressionless, with deep-set eyes that see everything and show nothing. His whole package is like some doormat of harsh cocoa matting bristlingly embossed with "Don't Tread on Me." Those that pay attention to such things suppose that Sam Sport is homosexual. He is. On other days he's also other things to other people. Some days he is Italian for his Mafia clients and some days he's a Catholic for the cardinal. His laws, or rather the laws he fights against, or defends, all of which he treats proprietorially, like his desires, are as changeable as a jukebox. Sam allows all rumors to flourish. "There is no truth" is of course too simplistic. So, for Sam, is perversity. His sexual fantasies are neither of men or women. They are of self-glorification. When he fucks guys, or preferably is fucked by them, it is not because he's a homosexual but because it's perverse to be a homosexual when everyone around him, every figure of power he represents or associates with, and all of whom need him and his legendary ability to get you off free from almost anything, is on record as full of hatred for the queers, and that's a turn-on. That gets him hot. That makes him come. To have the cardinal suck his cock knowing he's violating two thousand years of his religion's condemnation is a very potent aphrodisiac. "Never go where you're not wanted" had been his poor and dreary father's failure. "Always go where you're not wanted" has made Sam Sport powerful and rich.

Sam is always dapper: jaunty, perky, nattily (another archaic word) dressed in the stuff younger guys wear: gabardine, tweed, corduroy, oxford cloth, repp, cordovan, loafers, button-downs, and always the "intellectual" spectacles, a college kid's wire-rimmed glasses. He must be sixty now and still he looks like a boy, thin, with all his hair, his face somehow still unlined, unless you stand up close, when you can see he's not a kid at all. He's hard and wrinkled, like a shattered windshield with a cobweb of almost invisible fractures. Daniel knows he's gay, but Sam denies it daily and constantly, so Lucas won't allow his brother Daniel to talk about it.

Daniel once asked Lucas why Sam Sport is a partner in his firm. Lucas got very defensive.

"It's important to remember the concept that everyone, no matter who, is entitled to good legal representation. He saved my life once when a contract was put out on me by the Mob when I lost my first case and our client had to go to jail. We started this firm together, just the three of us, in one room across from the Archives Building, with a secretary and an empty file. Now we have three hundred and seven lawyers and we own this building and fill up its seven floors. That's not bad for two poor brothers from Masturbov Gardens. The first time I saw one of his Mafia clients pull out a gun in the middle of a deposition when he didn't like the cross-examination, and I looked over at Sam and Sam was smiling . . . I knew I'd have to make some major decisions. I still know I have to make some decisions. In the meantime . . ."

It was, for Lucas, a very long answer, and nervously spoken, which is unlike him, and of course the subtext is that he loves Sam and that Sam is a shit, and what do you do when the shit you love is your partner and friend and can reach everyone powerful anywhere in the entire world and has made you and your brother as rich as *Sexopolis* has made Mordy?

A RUDE AWAKENING

Fred had recently studied his Seven Star Mini Diary, which had revealed:

Dates leading to orgasm: 57 (counting street tricks, the tubs, and Fire
    Island, but definitely not counting the Meat Rack)
Dates interesting enough to want to see again: 2
Dates seen again: 23
Tubs attended how many times: 24
Discos danced at how many nights: 37 (not counting Fire Island).

He had been dismayed at how many of the faces he no longer remembered. He'd spent all this time with a faceless group of sex objects. Talk about sexist! Talk about using the body as a thing!

Why hasn't he been writing anything about all this?

PROTESTERS THROW HUMAN EXCREMENT
AT GAYS

Fristberg, North Carolina, December 8, 1975.

Hundreds of angry protesters gathered at the Fristberg Gay Community Center building site at Ridgemont and Central Avenues in downtown Fristberg where several hundred others, gay men and women, were celebrating the completion of a fund-raising campaign to pay for their community center they plan to start building on this site on January 2, 1976.

"I was hit by a bag of s—t and I had to go home and wash up," said the Rev. Maria Torrero of the Gay Community Church.

"I was covered with it from head to foot. It was quite smelly," said Anderson Vibro, who works for the First Fristberg Bank at 17 Corners.

Human excrement, eggs and rotten food were flung. Anyone who looked gay was liable to a pelting.

"Despite our requests for police protection, no police arrived to protect us," said Marvin Wilson, a bartender at Nestor's Bar and Grill at 1773 Nemoy Street. "These people are Nazis."

The protesters, who call their group "No Way," claim, "We are a highly organized alliance of Christian fundamentalists," said Fulton Bianchu, of Bianchu and Son Landscaping, 2000 Col. Hiram Herbert Highway, East Fristberg. "We do not welcome this building or these people in our town. We see documentaries on CBS and PBS about them. Nasty!"

"We cannot allow people who are unacceptable to a large part of America," said 18-year-old Tricia Cocks of the University of North Carolina at Chapel Hill. "We study them at school and that's what statistics tell us."

Mayor Kathy Sullivan-Feinstein called the attempt "by those people to put up their own building right in the middle of our lovely town" "a desecration, a provocation and a contamination. Of course people beat them up," she said.

—*Reported by Roy Turbelow,* Calhoun County (NC) Patriot

IT'S A HELLUVA TOWN

FRED TRIES TO CAPTURE THE MOMENT NOW THAT, PER DR. GILLESPIE'S INSIGHT AND ENCOURAGEMENT, HE IS AT LAST CHOOSING TO BEAR WITNESS IN HIS NOVEL *FAGGOTS*

The last orgy of the spring season before decampment to Fire Island was held at the home of Garfield Toye, a closeted member of the New York office of the law firm Jerusalem & Sport, who was not expecting to hold it. He had a free evening on his hands. He considered going to the baths, but what was the point of having a Central Park West penthouse in the sky if not to stay at home, make a few phone calls, and ask some friends to drop in for a quiet evening chez moi. Word would be passed around with speed and by nine, ten at the latest, he would have an apartment full of humpy numbers. Garfield just loved being a faggot in New York. You could get things done so quickly here.

Winnie Heinz came, bringing a Florsheim shopping bag that he said contained just a few old sneakers, and Troy Mommser, who was Winnie's creative director at Heiserdiener-Punic-Slough, came with several other models from the Hans Zoroaster Agency, and Maxine came alone—"I don't know where Patty is, he said he'd meet me here"—and Sammy Sircus came, too, though Garfield wondered who'd called that cunt, unkind and ungenerous as the day is long (Garfield was a lawyer for Sammy's expanding media agglomeration, already in trouble with the SEC).

A call to One Touch of Penis produced Vladek, Cully, and Midnight Cowboy, Penis's top three in billings, all for free, they must want to get in shape now that summer's coming. They brought three youngsters, including that Paulie whom Garfield had paid fifty to only just last week, he sure is looking pale and run-down, and also including one of the most beautiful morsels Garfield had ever seen, he thought he heard his name as Timmy, and one look at that Junior Adonis and Garfield knew he wouldn't be at One Touch of Penis for long. The three kids went off into a corner with Troy Mommser, always a quick worker passing the early grass for the evening, plus a little angel dust, judging from the smell of things. Garfield watched as Timmy Gorgeous inhaled on—could it be his first encounter with the weed? I wonder how old he is, his mind then automatically reminding him: corruption of the morals of a minor—ten to fifty . . . then eyed Maxine and hoped that tonight he wouldn't change into drag.

The black contingent arrived, headed by Morrison van Gelding and Hubie Stint, both hulking figures you'd cross the street to avoid if you didn't know them but Garfield did and knew that both were pussycats. And, at the sight of so much black flesh, he practically expired in the excitement of his own anticipation. Morrison and Hubie each had a cute little white boy in tow, like prize pugs on leashes: Morry's was Wilder and Hubie's was called Slim, who was evidently just in from the Coast, where he was a math teacher, and he'd met Hubie and Hubie's eleven-inch wonderful instrument while cruising Central Park. Morry said he'd informed a few of his black friends at Legal Aid about the event and Garfield might have some additional dark meat soon.

So all in all, what with the ones he'd called and the ones they'd called, Garfield knew his doorman would clock about eighty single gentlemen in before (a new record) nine-thirty. Through the portals came, among others, five attorneys, three art directors, seven models, ten would-be models, twelve said-they-were-models, five journalists (including *The Avocado*'s Divine Bella, and Blaze Sorority, who writes about the White House for *The New Gotham*), three hairdressers (one who only does coloring), two antiques deal-ers, one typewriter repairman, one manager of a Holiday Inn, one garbage collector, two construction workers, one toll collector from the Verrazano-Narrows Bridge, three policemen, two firemen (one from out of state), seven hustlers, one elevator operator (Garfield's landlord's son), one bass player, five doctors, twelve students, one ethnic dancer, a couple of writers for *The New York Truth*, two restaurateurs (one gourmet, one shit food), one judge (rather old, but Garfield had to think of business), one newscaster, one sportscaster, one weatherman, two football players, one folk singer, four truck drivers, twenty-nine on unemployment, eleven unidentifieds, and the new assistant rabbi for an Orthodox congregation on Long Island. And these were just the early birds. The evening had all the earmarks of an eventful one, and Garfield was already busy in the maid's room with a Puerto Rican efficiency expert when Winnie Heinz from across a crowded room fell in love with Timmy Purvis.

Timmy did not know that anyone was looking at him. His head was beginning to have the light buzz he'd been told to expect by Troy, who kept injecting the thin cigarette into Timmy's mouth and telling him to "suck, suck, you gorgeous number, suck, and hold it in like this," and then expanding like a peacock to illustrate. Troy was old enough to be Timmy's father, if only his father had had the sense to be as attractive and worldly and well-dressed and to smell of nice cologne and just-brushed teeth, and Timmy was a bit surprised to discover that a tingly feeling was appearing not only in his head and arms but also in his crotch. He found himself relaxing into Troy Mommser's warm, enveloping arms.

"Oh, you little darling," Troy sighed as he nibbled at Timmy's ear and then kissed him warmly on the lips. It was Timmy's first true kiss from another man on a nonfamilial level. It wasn't bad. And in such a nice, comfortable, homelike apartment, too. And the man being old enough to be his father made it even more cozy and safe. He was going to love New York.

"Come on, you beautiful thing," Troy said, practically picking up the young package and carting him into one of Garfield's homelike bedrooms.

Winnie watched all this and his heart sank. Why was he not in the right place at the right time when it mattered? Why had he not brought his own dope and dust this evening? He could have turned the kid on. Oh, he was beautiful, and his heart wanted to hold him, no, he wouldn't have this one walk on him, he just wanted to hold him and kiss and cuddle and go for weekends in the country and swims in St. Bart's and make a life together—my goodness, the entire gamut of a fantasy future was jelling before him. What is happening to me? I'm not like this. I've always played the field. And I don't even know his name. And he doesn't look Jewish. Oh, well, Troy's a nice man, my friend. The kid'll be bored to death with a nice guy like Troy. So, swallowing his impatience, he joined a cozy corner foursome that included a black kid wearing a Star of David around his neck, to kill the time until the moment when his cutie would be free.

In the dim-lit bedroom, drapes to match the walls, four inches of Bigelow underfoot, Timmy was naked in Troy's arms on the king-sized walnut four-poster. Troy's big strong barrel chest, warm with soft hair, was something he wanted to curl up against forever. It was safe, he just knew it—was this what it was all about?—and he wanted it to go on and on and on and on. They both tried to pretend there was no one else in the room, not too easy a task when there were twenty or so, each busy in his own way. But if one could ignore the grunts, the smells, the slurps, all your usual sounds of foreplay suckings, the patches of sheets beginning to get damp from sweat, the three hustlers, Vladek, Cully, and Midnight Cowboy, practicing a synchronized muscle-flexing gymnastic arrangement by the headboard, the three models, Carlty, Lork, Yo-Yo, forming an observing triptych at the foot, yes, models all, uptown and downtown versions but all paid for essentially the same thing, plus a busy Paulie, who should be home resting for his big scene tomorrow, darting about looking for his own future, plus Maxine sticking his head into groupings, searching for Patty and wondering if it might not soon be time to change, then one could more or less imagine that one was more or less alone.

"You sweet little thing," Troy mumbled, and heaved his big self up and reversed positions so that he could suck young Timmy's young cock while placing his own huge thing close enough to the lad's mouth so that it might get the same idea. Troy was certainly enjoying himself—young flesh was always a treat—but he did wish the handsome thing were a wee bit more experienced and didn't just lie there and would the Gnome be here tonight, because his supply of drugs was running low. The pretty ones are always bores in bed, Troy thought, and as creative director for Heiserdiener-Punic-Slough, America's butchest agency, he was certainly in a position to know. Every gorgeous male model had passed through his portals.

Troy sucked on, vaguely aware that Timmy was having trouble encompassing as much food as he was offering, but at least the lad was trying, bless his heart. Suddenly, before Troy could wedge his nourishment a little farther into Timmy's perfect if still inexperienced mouth, Timmy's perfectly inexperienced cock began to emit his little load and Troy, the perfect gentleman, concentrated less on himself and more on keeping up the lad's excitement to the last second.

"How was that, you little pumpkin?" Troy asked Timmy after a suitable pause, as the lad lay against his chest again and they both tried to ignore the hovering presence of the thirty or so others who had gathered around to watch with relish.

"Mmmm," Timmy mumbled. It had been nice. Should he admit that it was his first time? "It . . . you were my first."

"Holy shit," somebody muttered in the dark.

"A virgin," sputtered another.

"I didn't know they still made them."

"He just did."

"Fucking Troy, he's done it again."

"Don't pay any attention," Troy whispered to Timmy, patting the lad's head. "I loved every minute of it. How do you feel? No guilt?"

"Unh-unh."

"That's a relief."

"What's gilt?"

Troy smiled. One certainly didn't need an upset violated virgin on one's hands. Then, patting the firm white tush, he said, "I'm flying to Tokyo in the morning, but perhaps I'll see you when I get back."

Winnie, who had just concluded a deal with the Gnome for a gram and a half of Best Angel Dust, sampled, purchased, delivered on the spot, was doubly pleased when he saw Troy come back into the living room, fully clothed and alone.

"Where's the beauty?" Winnie asked him.

"I think he fell asleep."

"How was he?"

"I was his first. I feel one hundred and five. I didn't even come."

"You were his first?" Winnie felt hugely despondent. How could he have missed out so outrageously?

"He's beautiful. So are you. Go take a look." Troy caressed Winnie's cheek as he thought to himself, About to be unemployed, poor baby, I'm glad I arranged a shoot in Tokyo so I don't have to tell you. "See you in the factory."

Winnie watched Troy leave. He was glad to have such a fine old friend. Then he went into the bedroom to look for the kid.

Timmy was not asleep. Ten men were devouring him. Two held his hands and played with his fingers. Another sucked his toes. One, of course, was sucking his front thing while another, of course, had a finger up his back thing. Another naturally played with his young marbles and one more sucked each of his titlets. Another man had his fingers in Timmy's ears, and several others massaged his stomach, touched his teenaged skin, touched him all over, wherever prior prospectors had not staked their claims. Timmy was being worshipped like a god. If this was New York, then he wished to live enthroned here forever.

Suddenly activity ceased. Timmy opened his eyes and looked up. Someone was standing over him, was standing up tall on the mattress with one leg on each side of him. Suddenly no one else was on the bed or in the room or in the world.

It was the Winston Man. He knew it. The whole world knew the Winston Man. Timmy had masturbated over the Winston Man, taking his father's *American Legionnaire* magazine into the bathroom and jerking off with the faucet running, wondering how one ever became as handsome as the Winston Man, wondering down deep if it would ever be possible to meet someone so perfectly handsome, so perfectly the perfection of one's dreams. Seeing him there, Timmy winced. He winced at first because he thought he might be hallucinating from the drugs. He winced at second because he was a little frightened to have yet another dream turn into reality—too many dreams were coming true too quickly today in New York, things he hadn't even known he was dreaming about. And he winced at third because he didn't know what to say. Whatever he said to such Perfected Beauty he felt would be not good enough.

The Winston Man spoke first: "Hi. My name is Winnie."

"I . . . I know."

"Now how do you know? We're just meeting for the first time."

"You . . . you're the Winston Man."

"That's right. And who are you?"

"Tim. Tim Purvis."

"Hello, Tim Purvis. Would you like to come home with me?"

Winnie helped Timmy find his clothes, scattered to the four corners of the room, and helped him dress, pushing away other hands which, Laocoön-like, wished to impede, and then dressed himself. All was silence. Something in the room was ending, phase one of the evening perhaps, and with the departure of Adonis, Junior and Senior, something would be drained away, some of the energy, some of that ideal physical fuel necessary to heat the rest of the night. Winnie felt this tangible atmosphere and knew that he and Timmy were responsible for it. Still no one spoke.

Instead, two arms reached up and pulled Winnie down and pinned him to the bed. Since these arms belonged to Vladek, the Hungarian hustler, thick, hairy, and overbeefed in biceps and wrist, Winnie could not resist. Another two arms began to unbutton his shirt, another set to extricate him from his trousers. Others attended to Timmy, like handmaidens to the princess in some movie about ancient Egypt, pulling him down and back, removing his raiment. Soon the two naked beauties were laid out side by side on center stage, the edges of the wide expanse of king-sized bed now packed with spectators, each watching the animal of his choice, as if two cocks were pitted in the arena, which, in truth, they were.

Winnie and Timmy, mesmerized by the moment, by their naked exposure, by the sheer exultant glory and joy of being so visibly, forcefully worshipped by fifteen pairs of eyes, now growing to twenty, thirty, thirty-five, as word spread around the apartment: "the hot stuff's in the master bedroom," "which one's the Master's bedroom?," and other rooms evacuated swiftly, as naked bodies, forty-seven flavors of manpower, fought to witness beauty meet perfection meet beauty, these naked witnesses now coalesced into one huge grabbing organism, with undulations of its own, as a group and not as individuals, all swaying, holding, watching, breathing, wishing, empathizing, Stanislavskians all, as Winnie and Timmy kissed, two long planes of flesh layered together like some delectable French pastry, then began to twine and intertwine, into cruller or Danish, receiving pleasure from each other's movements, from the touchings each to each, each growing hard, Timmy still too young to know that this, his additional coming within one hour, would be a record many of them, try as they might, could not emulate, Timmy learning how to experiment with his tongue and fingers, learning how to duplicate the movements perpetrated upon him by Winnie's tongue and fingers, Timmy, being Crisco-ed anally by a strange hand reaching from ringside, Timmy, on his back, receiving from Winnie, for the first time a man's cock up his ass, so this is how they do it!, his own legs grabbing around that famous narrow waist, wanting to cry out in pain, the virgin on her wedding night, her hymen pierced, he thought of that, of reading *23 Ways to a Sexually Fulfilling Marriage* in a plain brown wrapper, hidden in an old suitcase under his parents' bed, expecting pain, but no, there is no pain, for Winnie is deep inside him, up, he thinks, to just beneath his heart, he feels his heart massaged, he feels the love within it, imprisoned within it all his lifetime up till now, begin to explode out toward Winnie like a life handed over, take my life, Winston Man, take all of me because you are the most beautiful human being I have ever known and felt and I want to spend the rest of my life with you, just like this.

"Fuck him, fuck him . . ." There they go again, soft chantings from the witnesses, "Fuck his tight young pussy . . ." Shut up, Timmy tries to call out, if he only could speak, don't ruin it all with those ugly words . . . "Fuck him, fuck him . . ." and Winnie fucks this virgin chicken, excited in a way that he hasn't been since little Bernie Rosen at Hill School in Pottstown, Pennsylvania, and getting pleasure from a fuck, no boots, not even a Jewish boy, no extra paraphernalia necessary, though he wished the lad were circumcised, well, perhaps this was nice for a change, the beginning of a new era, feeling his own love grow as he comes closer and closer, no, hold it back, make this time last, uncircumcised only requires extra cleanliness, extra attention to smegma, hold it back, hold it back, make it last, wanting to cry out: I love you, you little fucker, but not doing so, never say "love"—what is happening to me?, it must be the audience, it must be the angel dust, why am I turned on so?, Jesus God, it never felt like this, his little ass is squirming for more, wriggling about wanting me to fuck it, look, no don't look, at the drops of blood on Garfield's Bill Blass sheets, Christ, he really is a virgin, "Oh my Christ I'm going to come!" and damn it, come he does, and, would you believe it, at precisely this same moment, always a good omen, Tim shoots all that's still left inside him, up and into the air to stick to Winnie's stomach like squirt against the ceiling, and Winnie falls on top of Tim and the two adhere together, clutching each other, holding tight to prolong the moment, unconscious, oblivious to the fact that around them sixty, no maybe only fifty-five other orgasms have been reached with such intensity that this night, Garfield will be proud to remember, will go down in history, and he will go down as the Perle Mesta of the Orgy Circuit, Garfield's future as a primo New York party thrower assured.

Winnie's eyes opened and looked down at Timmy's, looking up at him. The Winston Man spoke first. "I think I'm falling in love with you."

And Timmy answered, "I love you, too."

And they held each other tightly, and each began, unseen by the other, to cry. If this was love, this was wonderful, and the moment must last forever, and each tried to memorize the feeling so that, in years to come, when they remember this, and they must remember this, they would be able to summon up at will just what this historic moment brought them. They were still holding on to each other, neither knowing how to get the hell out of here before it's too late, not knowing that it is now about to be too late . . .

A NAME BY ANY OTHER NAME

Isidore Schmuck Medical Center is renamed Isidore Peace Medical Center. It had been impossible to break the old man's ironclad will legally, so it is done illegally. A long-lost cousin presents to the Washington District Court in Punic Center a piece of paper saying that Isidore Schmuck, on his deathbed, had given her permission to allow a name change whenever she saw fit. No one believes either her or her piece of paper, but so many people are so tired of driving past so many signs in their neighborhood saying, THIS WAY TO SCHMUCK, including the judge, Everett Tuschey, who has his own problems with last names, that his ruling in favor of the change is allowed to stand.

Isidore Peace it is to this day, though not so peaceful as its new name would have one hope.

AMOS WANDERS

How do you end a life you decide to end? I don't mean by what means. Where I grew up, gentlemen used pistols for that. Yes, I have my pistol, my ever-faithful companion, my Averva pistol. It's accompanied me around the world a number of times on my assignments carrying out my government's nefarious instructions. Have I actually used it to shoot anyone? What self-respecting spy would ever tell you? Yes, I have used it to shoot at people. I cannot say my aim was always successful. However did they come to choose me as a spy, I used to wonder. All the shit I've shoveled for Uncle Sam! What could possibly have been on my record that encouraged my Yaddah professors who enlisted me to offer me up to such unseemly tasks? "You are being chosen for great things! You and a number of your brothers in Toad and Frog." Hitler, the OSS, the CIA, Partekla, it was one big never-ending vaudeville show of juggling false information and tossing bodies in the air to be shot down somewhere by someone. Spying is like that. It has very bad manners. I have never had a thank-you note from anyone. When I retired I just left my office. There wasn't anyone left from the old days in the entire building anyway. Why did I stay there for so long? The turnover became so substantial, I couldn't tell you who was in charge of what. They're so disorganized down there now that I'll bet they think I'm still sitting in that office. Yes, it became an embarrassment to work for them, not that I had anyone to tell this to but myself. The first Standings were in the Revolutionary War.

And in that French and Indian one. No one else knows that now but me. All things come to an end. The brothers Dulles long gone and James Jesus growing into a paranoid aging crone, naming the names of practically every leader in the world as being under Communist control. By now there's such an entrenched rivalry between the CIA and the FBI that if one doesn't get you, the other is sure to. And I definitely do not like the growing smell from old spy-in-arms Bill Casey now more and more sniffing his crooked nose into and around a growing number of "things." Get out while the getting is good.

No, I mean how do you end it in your head? That what you've done hasn't been decent. I am not feeling sorry for myself. I loved the immorality and danger of it. It was no small thrill going into the studio every day knowing Adolf Hitler's your boss and you'll talk to him a number of times each day about making his movies. Partekla is germ warfare contrived by Edna Hoover to beat the Japs and Germans at whatever James Jesus and Kim Philby and others said that they were up to. Partekla was, and still is, about beating all "thems" at manufacturing epidemics first. It is successful, as the world will shortly discover. Yes, how do you leave this world with all this upstairs in the back rooms of your mind? I've ignored it all for years. Why not now? I have no guilt and I don't want to have any. Guilt doesn't exist for Standings, or for spies. It just doesn't.

What I do care about right now is that I have remained unloved. No one has loved me. But knowing it doesn't make getting old alone a posting an aging spy wants to say yes to.

I left that office, and I left the agency, and I got in my car and started driving north. I realized I was headed for New Godding and I knew that I wanted to see where Philip and I met and fell in love. I have not seen him for many years. Men need something to believe in and hold on to when nearing death. That is my current state. I resort to the only person I ever loved. Once a gambler, always a gambler. You either survive or you don't. You either use your gun or you don't. Spies don't think like other people.

I loved them all, unlikely as that sounds, Philip and Rivka and young David and even Brinestalker doing whatever stupid things he was doing. Brinestalker was a big spoiled child with a peculiar charm when he got all excited about whatever was exciting him. He bubbled over like champagne and it was fun to watch him. He believed so much in IBM and that Hollerith machine that he sold a million of them. My father's brother, Owen Standing III, was like that, always finding some modus operandi he was going to change the world with. My father always called him a fool.

Hell, when I got out of Cincinnati and got to Yaddah it was fun to watch anyone get excited about anything, but especially cocks. There wasn't much excitement in my life until I met Brinestalker and Philip. Very rich Wasps whose family built the ships that sailed down the Ohio, and the Mississippi, and built the canals that made the city become America's first inland boom-town, and then built the railroads, and then built the streetcars, the Stand-ings were very big on transplanting people on our way to making so much money that we became straitlaced and humorless and determined to not only stay that way but not let anyone from any outside get anywhere near us. Every great fortune's like this. You think it's worth it.

Philip took my mind off everything. He was the first Jew I knew. He was like some rare poison I had to take. I had to beat the shit out of him. The way he looked at me, the way he looked at everybody, the way he lived in the world, just made me want to slap him silly. When I did that it gave me a hard-on and gave him one too, as if he was saying—shit, he *was* saying—More! More! More! I'd never done anything like that. And he hadn't either. I was the first wealthy Wasp that he was friends with. I wonder if each of us was punishing the other. We certainly weren't the lover we could take home to mother. Or in my case, Aunt Margot Charlotte, the doyenne of the Stand-ing dynasty. Longfellow called Cincinnati "the Queen of the West." That was really Aunt Margot Charlotte. She wanted me to go to England and marry someone royal. They did things like that in those days. Lady Astor was just a rich American gal from Virginny.

Yes, I hired Philip. NITS must still have his reports—going back to the '40s, when he started to work for me, at first in Berlin and eventually in Wash-ington tallying case histories on how many people died at NITS and Partekla (which become the same entity), and, as much as possible, getting them to sign over their estates to us. That's how Partekla continued to be financed off the government's official books. It was all Hoover's idea. He took a cut of all that Philip's work extracted. At some point I stopped seeing Philip. I became concerned I would go too far. He understood intellectually that I was right, but he was too weak to accept it and he would come begging, phoning in the middle of the night or pounding on my door. It was a mistake for me to move back here after the war. But James Jesus Angleton dangled fascinating assignments in front of me, "that only someone who worked with Hitler would appreciate." That of course was getting Partekla up and running, and that was preceded with another bit of juicy government back-room concern, who was JFK fucking and what did she know because of it. Right at the end of the war I'd been offered a posting to England to live at Farm Hall with all the German atomic scientists whom we and the Brits had rounded up and put under house arrest, recording every word in their completely wire-tapped existence. "Hitler's Uranium Club," it was called. James Jesus's boys are said to have made personal fortunes out of that one. But I'd had enough of Germans. Besides, I wanted to work more closely with Hoover. He fascinated me. I suspected in advance that from Hitler to Hoover wasn't much of a stretch and I wanted to see this borne out. So I went to Partekla, where I learned once again how powerful forces, this time our very own homegrown ones, could alter a world totally ignorant of what was going on.

Philip and I hadn't had sex in many years, and he didn't want to see me. Through my work with blood I came to see Rivka again. I hadn't seen her since their wedding. She was surprised to see me and not very friendly, which meant that she knew.

As I was driving I remembered the first time I saw her. She was very pretty, not much over twenty, always smiling and trying to please and be interested and attentive. Philip brought her up from Washington for a winter-weekend carnival at Yaddah, an annual event with lots of parties and dances. I gave him the money to do so. He said he'd dated her in Washington and their families both owned grocery stores. I was very drawn to her and danced with her a lot, which of course annoyed Philip, which of course was the reason I was doing it. But I found I genuinely was attracted to her. This pleased me, that there was another quiver in my arsenal of arrows. Nothing much came of it, of course, but back in Washington after all these years of our living our lives I could see that Philip had ruined hers. And that I had been a big part of that. For a while that just made me want to beat the shit out of him even harder when we finally had sex again, especially when he told me that David had come home and run away. "How could you have allowed that!" I actually raised my voice in anger as I kicked him silly. "You don't know how much trouble had to be gone through to get him back to you who had left him!" It was then that I finally asked myself what the fuck was I doing, and then my cock wouldn't go up for him anymore. End of story. Or so you would think. Or so I certainly thought.

The OSS had seemed romantic (yes, running Hitler's film studio was romantic, at least in OSS terms—think Orson Welles and Graham Greene and *The Third Man*), but when the CIA was born out of its cocoon, I could tell right off it was going to be nasty and stink to high heaven, and that James Jesus, whose OSS cock I'd diddled with on many a long winter's night, was, now that it was a CIA one, out to screw everyone the whole world over. He needed a ripsnorter of a supportive president to allow this to happen, and we had a string of them. Subversive was the CIA's middle name from the get-go. The OSS had been gentlemen. Now a bunch of would-be Nazis were plopped into place in the CIA organizational chart to somehow keep that ball rolling. Real Nazis I'd reported on to FDR as of great danger to world peace. I didn't want to work alongside these born-agains, but it wasn't the sort of thing I could complain about out loud. After all, I'd been Hitler's PR man. And I'd loaned my name to a very peculiar camp in Idaho after Brinestalker and Hoover talked me into it, a camp that was supposed to make homosexuals more masculine but wound up, so far as I could discover, killing most of them just like Grodzo and Mengele did at Mungel. So after dealing with the mess of the murder of Mary Meyer, who was indeed JFK's mistress for quite some time and did indeed stuff him full of LSD and a number of others with them on their trips, and then finishing up my last case, which was routing out a mole named Drinnell Torpor who was working on chimpanzee shit and piss—a most peculiar and expensive endeavor he was covertly sharing with Russia—at our new germ warfare operation at Fort Detrick, a new part of Partekla, all of which was now a part of NITS, where I knew Philip was still working at its St. Purdah's, I decided it was time to retire. Whew! In that one paragraph alone resides the whole Cold War.

Except I had some years left of my life to live and I didn't know what to do with them. I can't say that my conscience was clean at this point. But I'd never thought in terms of conscience. I'd been too much the rich Wasp playboy during most of my life to think like that. But here I am, going on seventy years old. Something was at last frightening me. Concerning me, I should say.

To clear my head, I went to a small town in rural Maine, on a lake. It was calm and picturesque. I was contemplating buying the pleasant cottage by the water's edge that I'd rented for two weeks, when a homosexual man was thrown off a bridge in nearby Camden to his death. He was a professor of literature in Washington and it was he who'd suggested I might enjoy living here near his own place. "Nothing much happens, the people are decent, and we can make fires and cook dinner for each other." The murderers were found soon enough. They were young men, out of work, angry, powerless, with a need for some visible proof of their manhood. I'd encountered enough like these over the years. One of the guilty lads said to the press, "Does this mean I'm going to the chair? I hope so. I don't want to live anymore." It touched me, these words and the picture of him in the local paper. A very handsome young man. Would that I had been able to teach him—and David as well wherever he was—how to appreciate his beauty and live more fully because of it. How do you teach that to handsome young men without being murdered yourself or sent to jail? Maybe that's why Brinestalker changed, having failed so miserably in his own attempt at something like this. His Greek Warriors either escaped or were eliminated somehow. Well, I don't know how to change, at least not that. I may not be "getting any," as they say, but you live with that fact, as most of the world does.

I began to notice the local people staring at me in an odd way. Were they warning me to leave before something happened to another homosexual man? Evidently they were. My rental cottage overlooking the lake was torched in broad daylight while I was out stocking up on groceries for my intended retreat. I had brought little of value with me beyond the few dreams I was nurturing for what I was finally courageous enough to call my declining years. Just some books and a portable typewriter. It's time to write that book! Isn't that what so many people of a certain intelligence and achievement finally retreat to?

I had gone to Maine to consider this subject: Who is Amos Standing? Has his usefulness expired? I returned to this journey. I had a suitcase that had escaped the torch only because it was still in my trunk along with my typewriter. I left the pressing of any charges to the owner of the cottage. The police were reluctant to allow me to leave, but I told them that two attacks on single men in such a short time did not encourage anything but a hasty exit. I gave them the name of my lawyer in Cincinnati if they needed to locate me. Gottschalk is accustomed to getting me out of awkward situations. When I asked the police chief if he didn't think these acts were despicable, he shrugged and said, "Maine has never been friendly to homos." How had I not known that, who knew so much else about the location of our world's hatreds?

It was while driving south through Massachusetts that I began thinking of Philip. I thought of him more and more the closer I got to Connecticut. I arrived in New Godding and checked into a hotel and went to bed thinking of him. An erection appeared, an occurrence I could no longer count on. I quickly attempted to take advantage of it but it didn't last. Still, my sleep was sound for the first time in many nights. Walking around the glorious campus the next morning cheered me even more. Perhaps I should think of living here. This is where Philip and I fell in love. I could teach here. Old spies were teaching all over the place. Several Yaddah presidents had even been OSS/CIA operatives during the Cold War years.

Yaddah was still gorgeous. Much donor money had made it even more resplendent. I lived for four years in this town and I have not been back since we graduated. The Three Comrades. Philip and Amos and Brinestalker. Did I move back to Washington to be near Philip? I once tried to marry Rivka, thinking I could love her to be near him. I wonder how many lives I have hurt because of Philip. Rivka, the twins? Philip? Myself? There must be others. He had two older sons as well.

Brinestalker and I of course no longer talked. He is still involved in turncoat activities of the most perverse kind. How does a mind turn on itself so completely? Quite frankly, I was worried about something like this happening in myself. Philip does not respond to my letters, even my reply to the passionate one I received from him out of the blue, but a phone call to Miami Beach resulted in his hanging up when he heard my voice.

My ancestors built ships and fleets and died doing so with their boots on. What else have I got to do with my boots on? I want one more thing to be proud of before I die, assuming that serving my country has been noble. Gottschalk had already been instructed to locate David and give him a healthy amount. The rest of my inheritance will go to Rivka and her old friend Gertrude.

Edgar's funeral was not what it seemed to the world and the press. Oh, the emissaries of the world's leaders and countries attended him with tribute, but the real man is not in that coffin. Who were these many young "agents," lined up in black, their faces hard with that cold impassivity drilled into them? What did they know? What did anyone there know? Except Clyde. What will anyone else ever know? This man who controlled the free world more than any other ruler has ever done died knowing more about America and the world than anyone before or since, or ever will. For another thing, it was *the* love story. Johnny and Clyde were lovers in the truest sense of that misused word. In Sickness and Health. These were strong, tough, disciplined G-men. Look at the photos of the handsome young square-jawed Clyde. He was the model for Dick Tracy. He worshipped Johnny and Johnny worshipped him back. When Johnny up and suddenly died, Clyde was devastated. Johnny had always been there. Clyde had only a couple of weeks as acting director to burn all the evidence and protect his beloved. That accomplished, he never left Johnny's house except to visit his grave. In visiting him, I had never before seen such a face of grief as when this strong man cried because he'd lost his beloved. Such was the roaring voice of their silent love. Edgar left Clyde forty large sterling silver napkin rings. Clyde collected napkin rings. J. Edgar Hoover left Clyde Tolson everything, but it was these extra-large napkin rings that Clyde cherished the most. They had called each other Edna and Tilly as they played house.

I wanted one of those true love stories. I'd always had everything I wanted but I'd never had one of those. Yes, I felt sorry for myself and was now shedding tears to prove it. I had never shed a tear before.

I thought of that as I stood in front of Hooker Hall and Standing College, the two dormitory buildings we lived in and loved in. Yes, Standing is named after my family. I was surrounded by a sea of youth rushing by me as if I weren't here. That I had lived here once and rushed around as they were doing now was of no interest to them, and why should it be? Still and all, they made me feel old, and I did not like the feeling one bit. These handsome young men were longingly attractive to me. It made me feel young just to look at them, until I pictured what they would see if they looked back, which of course they did not. I hated the thought I might be considered a dirty old man.

Philip had never been good-looking. What was his attraction for me? He was short and stubby and pale, with a hairy chest and a hairless body. His face was soft, with fleshy cheeks and a bit of an Adam's apple under his chin. The hair on his head was almost gone. He had big ears and a largish nose. What comparison did he bear to any of the attractive young men around us when we lived here? None. Still I cannot picture myself fucking any of these youngsters, even if I were their age, but fucking Philip was always exciting to me. Tying him up was exciting to me. Making him wear leather was exciting to me. Making him obey my orders was exciting to me. Making him crawl naked across a room to suck my erect cock was exciting to me. I can't even fantasize making one of these lads do anything like this. They're too wholesome, too clean-cut. I can picture watching them have sex with each other. I certainly had my fill of this at Partekla, whatever that place was really about, something I now refuse to allow myself to remember in much detail, but of which I do recall there was a great amount to forget. That's spy talk for you.

Our entryway to Standing College had been conveniently vacated for repairs, so I was able to locate our rooms on the third floor. I went in and closed the door behind me. The view from the windows, looking out at the towers and turrets of this handsome and stalwart university, was still thrilling, the elms and maples and oaks even more grandly healthy and beautiful now.

The suite still had two bedrooms and a living room. One bedroom still had a double bed in it. It was inconceivable that it would be the same bed, although it looked like it. Could two men be sleeping in it still? The walls were scruffy and colorless as ever. We used to call the shade vomit green; now it was more like pale piss. I lay down on the bed and fell asleep in Philip's arms.

I don't know if he enjoyed any aspect of his servitude but did it because I told him to. I never discerned any true displeasure on his part. I thought he enjoyed everything we did together. If he hadn't, would I have felt the reciprocity that motivated me? I was thinking all this now as I lay on this bed from our past.

The single room was Brinestalker's. He'd painted it all black and hung maroon drapes over the windows. He had lamps, but the place was dark as a dungeon, and not a dungeon of fun, just a truly depressing monastic cell. Neither Philip nor I enjoyed "visiting" him in it. Perhaps that was the beginning of his drifting away from us, not that I would have noticed, because of my growing obsession with Philip. We had occasional threesomes of course in our double bed and let him go on his way when he didn't wish to join us. How did I remain friends with Brinestalker for so long, and partners with him as well in that nefarious project? I sometimes think we were out of our minds. Perhaps it was Philip's passivity in our midst that kept us together and perhaps I'd like a little of that now. It's a nice thought. I can only say that those crazy projects didn't seem crazy at the time. Brinestalker and I thought we were revolutionaries. We were committed to new ways of living, to new ways of being homosexual. Kim and the rest of the Cambridge spies thought the same way.

I left my bed, crossed the campus, and walked to a rougher section of town, which in New Godding was still not very far. I located the gay bar I remembered from my youth. It was still here! A burly young man who appeared out of nowhere followed me in. He tried to strike up a conversation with me, tried to buy me a drink, blocked me when I tried to walk away, which I did several times. I finished my beer and went to the men's room to pee. I didn't look at him or his cock. When I turned to leave a policeman snapped handcuffs on my wrists and said I was under arrest for soliciting sex from a minor. I said he was not a minor and I was not soliciting, to which the officer replied, "Resisting arrest, additional charge," or some such. I was taken in handcuffs to the station, where I was treated equally harshly, if expeditiously. "Why don't you old geezers stay out of New Godding? You think you'll get into some kid's pants? You've been under observation for the past day. You have two hours to get out of town."

I would say that the experience surprised me but it did not. I have been arrested for one thing or another not unlike this, traveling around the world and this country many times. For this I have not tasted a single cock or felt another's flesh. All I've tasted is the bitter hate of this world for the homosexual male. In the past I had papers of identification that would set me free. I no longer have these.

I finally drove to Miami Beach. By the time I got there Philip could hardly move his arms and legs. "My boy has still not come back to me. My wife no longer talks to me. My other sons are uninterested in me. What did I do to deserve all this? What's this?"

"A sterling silver napkin ring. Mr. Hoover left many like this to Clyde. I thought it might amuse you. They loved each other very much."

I waited for an answer. He stared at me for a very long time without speaking. And then in my arms he died.

I was too late. I had gathered him up into my arms as best I could. I kissed his lips. I wished him well. I said, "I'll see you on the other side." And then I left. I did not wish to face Rivka when she returned.

I called Gottschalk in Cincinnati. It is time to execute the other half of my plan, I told him.

I now could reach finally for my answer. My ever-faithful companion that I knew would never let me down would take me there. I will not tell you where you'll find me. That's spy talk too.

DR. EKBERT NOSTRILL VISITS NORTHAMPTON, MASSACHUSETTS, WHERE JONATHAN EDWARDS BEGAN HIS GREAT AWAKENING CRUSADE IN 1734, AND READS TO THE LARGE ASSEMBLY FROM ROMANS 1:27

"And likewise also the men, leaving the natural use of the woman, burned in their lust one toward another; men with men working that which is unseemly, and receiving in themselves that recompense of their error which was meet. And even as they did not like to retain God in their knowledge, God gave them over to a reprobate mind, to do those things which are not convenient: being filled with all unrighteousness, fornication, wickedness, covetousness, maliciousness; full of envy, murder, debate, deceit, malignity; whisperers, Backbiters, haters of God, despiteful, proud, boasters, inventors of evil things, disobedient to parents, without understanding, covenant breakers, without natural affection, implacable, unmerciful: Who knowing the judgment of God, that they which commit such things are worthy of death."

SHITTY POO POO ASSHOLE BALLS TWATS CUNTS PRICK FUCK

I am thinking that women's reproductive systems hold an unexplored potential clue to what I am looking for in my blood and piss samples. Congress forbids NITS from following through on my superb suggestion. Women's bodies are a no-no. Shit on Dr. Stuartgene Dye for ignoring someone much smarter than he. He of course blames Congress. Why do we constantly dispose of placentas after birth? What secrets are we flushing down toilets with these? Fetuses shed little pieces of DNA into the bloodstreams of mothers-to-be. What shit from the fucking male was she thus carrying on with?

WHAT TO DO? WHAT TO DO?

So Fred Lemish writes a novel about gay life and where it wasn't going. It was not well received. In fact it made many angry. For what seems an unending time, he will not be much fun, which is why everyone will be avoiding him. He will go out rarely, not even to a gym, and what friends remain will be so bored with hearing about his concerns that they no longer inquire, "How are you?" for fear he'll tell them, again. You would think that at his age he'd be better at accepting rejection, but his novel is certainly being rejected and his hurting lonesome would-be creative heart doesn't seem to repair itself. He is blue. He is depressed. He will wonder, How am I going to live the rest of my life like this? "A day at a time, please," Dr. Homer will remind him, citing the age-old advice of shrinks and the many programs of self-help.

Yes, another analyst will be sought and found, a nice elderly gay man with the remarkable name of Dr. Odysseus Homer, who will work mightily to reinstill in a not-getting-any-younger would-be hero a modicum of courage. Fred can be very stubborn. He does not let go easily. Also, writers are a gnarly bunch. Just like Jonathan Swift, the more he dislikes the world he dislikes himself or anyone in it. Will he be of any use to his people in this time of approaching plague?

Who will be?

Fred doesn't know that he's already been exposed to The Underlying Condition.

•

No comment.

DR. MUXTER QUESTLOS

Fred has been totally ignorant of what gay politics was doing or trying to do. Our forces were so tiny and absent from the white-bread mainstream that he lived in. He had never been black, poor, a female, or trans, he had no unusual sexual peccadillos, nor had he given any of these issues much thought. That's why a lot of us at first paid him no attention and then, when it was obvious he wasn't going to shut up, turned against him. He was truly a one-issue loudmouth.

Gay left, gay right, who knew how best to define our movement? One thing we all were was radical. We wanted things and we resented things and we wanted to change things. But one guy's "normal" appetite was another guy's fetish and it was hard reconciling such divergences into a movement. One set wanted marriage and complete assimilation, and another wanted to expand the range of sexual expression for and to everyone and everything. Which of us were actual revolutionaries? There was GLF, whose mission was to challenge and change heterosexual "norms," and they rejected all efforts to acknowledge our differences. All groups refused to accept heterosexual definitions of what is good and bad. When gay male sexuality is attacked as sick and degenerate, no one should apologize; we should rejoice in what our homosexuality bestows. Gay people were not like everybody else! And society must be transformed to admit it. We've developed—necessarily in self-defense—our own set of values and perspectives. If the straight "mainstream" doesn't want to hear it, we don't care. We don't want to be like you anyway.

As Fred will find out, there aren't many in any of the radical groups, all of which give up just prior to Stonewall anyway, to be replaced by the much more limited GAA, whose single goal was to get civil liberties for gay people. Nothing radical in that.

GAA wanted to win their place in society as it is. Stonewall wasn't bringing many out of the closet. It was evident that too many wanted to live within a society defined by the way things are rather than work toward what it might be.

It was all much more complicated than this, of course. The gay movement as it's come to be known had a lot more and a lot less than can be argued about here. Cocker Rutt maintains that the reason the movement was soon reduced to only fighting for sex is because that was the only issue everyone, one way or another, would support. It allowed for no discussion of just what in our sexual lives we were talking about. Drag queens, bears, S&M activists all had their champions and their detractors. Try making a political movement out of all this! GLF and GAA bite the dust with no resolution to the never-ending question of how we present ourselves to both the mainstream and each other when making any demands. Take them on a tour of the Pines or the Mine Shaft or the Toilet Bowl? Fred has just done that and exiled himself to Siberia.

So our "movement" becomes single-issue, catering solely to our own primary concern, first, last, and foremost of which is sex, in any way, shape, or form.

I write the above with sadness, which I will come to share with Fred. I return myself to Yaddah, where my English Lit department has just fired two of my faculty. For being gay. And rejected my course on Walt Whitman if I made him gay. So I told Yaddah to stuff it and went off to New York, where I started my own institute.

BELLA GOES TO PRESS

This is the Divine Bella reporting to my legion of fans all over the globe. I am here, still and yet and may it last forever, on our beloved Isle de Feu, where frankly I have not been feeling so well. Memories are so painful. They make us want to run back so furiously to embrace the past. I am alone, as dear Greta always said. I do not vant to be alone. I walk these sands, now gray and hardening as winter comes. Why did I not, as with all my friends, rush my return to the mainland? To the fashions of the fall? I cannot tell you. I can only say that when it came time for me to leave this year, I could not. I simply could not. For the memories, the passions, the adorations, the arrivals of this past summer, when all of us reached Heaven at last, could not be jettisoned so swiftly. I needed Time!

Those who know their Bella know I like to muse. Have we not been living the Summers of Our Lives! Our just desserts! After so many eons of pain and suffering, of rejection, of hatred, have we not arrived! Yes, it's so hard to leave.

I sigh. Bella Bellberg, your Divine Bella, has excreted his column only monthly in a biweekly *Avocado* that *still* hasn't the courage to put itself out every single week of our important lives, for are we not each and every week embracing from sea to shining sea even greater gobs of glory, goodness, and gorgeousness than the very week before? Magnificence must be recorded! Each single minute demands reportage to and about the ever-increasing millions of us now joined *visibly* in a stunning ever-apparent army of beauty, arms locked as we kick-step toward our future. Let the whole wide world know so many of us are here! We're here! We love and love and love and love each other at last! And Freedom is ours! Here, now, waiting, reach out and touch it, it's *there*, it's almost here, it's almost ours, CAN WE WAIT UNTIL NEXT SUMMER?

Can we wait for our next summer of Gaydom! Of Faggotry Triumphant! Of Pansies and Penises! Of Fairies Flitting Furiously and Fashionably and Flagrantly and Famously! Not a day goes by in which another famous faggot doesn't come out of the hated closet. Why, it will only be a Matter of Moments before presidents will be gay!

I bring you news. The opening soiree of next summer's season will be held at the oceanfront home of Heerkie Odongo (Heerkimer Odongo IV). At his palatial opalescence, Fort Tie-Condor-Ogre. He has bought an entire tract of land on the ocean. He has torn down the ancient adjoining shacks and built his palace, his Shangri-La, his Xanadu, his Taj Mahal. It will be ready for our viewing come next Memorial Day! Can you not wait! Bella knows he can't!

•

How long can I write this stuff? I am so tired.

When the Oil of Turtleshit didn't take away his bothersome blemishes that just don't seem to go away, Bella dragged himself back to the mainland to see Hokie Benois-Frucht, dermatologist to the stars.

"Hokie, tell me what this is, I'm scared."

"It's serious, Bella."

"Serious to die or serious I can't afford it because I have no health insurance or serious like in chemotherapy and I'll lose the rest of my hair?"

"I think it could be serious all three."

Bella takes Hokie's hand in his examining room at Table Medical and gets down on his knees before his doctor in an impetrating fashion.

"Save me, Hokie. Please keep me alive. I feel so awful. And if it's awful please don't tell anybody. My empire will crumble. How much money do you need to start looking for the cure for whatever it is I've got? I have so many, so very many of the richest of rich readers!"

And then, almost in passing, it occurs to him.

"Has anyone else got it too?"

AN EARLY CASE? IF SO, OF WHAT? IF SO, SO WHAT?

Josie McGluck was a short guy, a little over five feet tall, and very likable and popular. Josie's lover was Dom Dom, who was as tall as Josie was short. Fred knew them both on Fire Island. They were quite a pair seen side by side. Mutt and Jeff, if anyone remembers those comic strip characters. Dom Dom was called "the Nazi," which drove him nuts because he quite rightly didn't think this funny because he was half German, tall and blond and buzz-cut like in a war movie. But he was also very persistent, always demanding his own way, another reason for his nickname. They were a very popular couple on Fire Island and in the Village. They had a share in the house in the Pines with gorgeous Bruce Niles, who was an old friend of Fred's, his neighbor in the city.

When Josie came down with a mysterious something that made him so weak he couldn't stand up, Dom Dom carried him in his arms from doctor's office to doctor's office. He went to anyone and anyplace that would let him in a door. He would take Josie in his arms and offer him up for observation for some clue to what's going wrong. He didn't care that everyone stared at them and moved out of their way fast when they saw that Josie was very sick-looking and Dom Dom was heading toward them. When he had seen maybe a couple dozen doctors in New York, he went to Philadelphia because he'd heard there was someone down there who might help, and then to Baltimore because their hospital was so famous. In each place, when guards tried to stop him in a hallway or entrance, he would hold up Josie's body, which was runny and smelly, and say, "Get out of my way!" and they usually did. Doctors were terrified when he stalked into their offices and practically rammed Josie's body in their faces. Everywhere he went, no one knew what was wrong.

Finally he heard about Dr. George Gist at NITS. In all America, NITS was the place to go, and Dr. George Gist was in charge of infectious stuff there. So he carted Josie to NITS, arriving, as everywhere else, unannounced and without an appointment. They'd had to drive there in a borrowed heap from New York and get there early on a Sunday so the NITS campus, where Gist lived in one of those ivy-covered director's houses, would be sleepy enough that they could slip through. Dom Dom had done his research. His mom was a nurse who knew a nurse down here. There wasn't much in the way of security anyway. By the time they got to the NITS campus Josie had thrown up a few times and shit and pissed on himself too. Dom Dom was out of clean stuff to change him into.

Dr. Gist was not pleased. He was a stern-faced man, about sixty, and in his bathrobe and pajamas and slippers. There was another man, half his age, hovering in the background, also in pj's and robe. They both stared at the strange couple that had accosted their house and their sleep.

"I do not see patients without referrals. Who referred you? Why are you carrying that young man? Put him down immediately. Come in, come in, before someone sees you. Put him down! He is blue. Why are you blue, young man? Don't just stand there. Take his clothes off. He has a nice face. Is he a kind person? Are you a kind person? How did you get onto our campus? Dr. Herky, help this tall young man undress this youngster. I think I must put on a pair of gloves. Dr. Herky, get me some gloves and find a pair for you. No, there aren't any gloves here. This is my home. Well, we will try to be careful. He is covered with spots. Those are cancers. I have not seen this kind in a long time. He is boiling hot. I would suspect pneumonia. Let me see his records. You have brought me his medical records? Let me see them. You have certainly been to a great many doctors. You are certainly a desperate man. You must love him very much. I do not think I have witnessed such public devotion between two men before. Have you, Dr. Herky? No, of course you haven't. What is this diagnosis from Dr. . . . at St. Hollyhawk's in . . . Sayville, Long Island? Cat scratch fever? What a lovely penis. Dr. Herky, note the lovely penis. I think it is true that short men often have extra endowments. You are so tall that yours is probably short. Is that so? Is your own penis short? I ask only because if you are fucking him that might be important to know. Not that it is short but that you are fucking him. He'll be dead very soon. Do you have a cat? You both certainly smell."

"He has three. He's dying from cats?"

"It's very rare. Something peculiar is obviously going on. You just can't say it's from cats. That's not very scientific. I wouldn't respect a scientist who diagnosed a death from cats."

"But if that's what it is . . ."

"Well, of course, it could be and it couldn't be."

"Half of New York has cats." Dom Dom was now crying. He'd started dressing Josie because his friend was shivering. Dr. Herky had stepped forward to help, nervously, though also unable to keep his eyes off Josie's lovely penis.

"Cats carry diseases," Dr. Gist said.

"His cats are very clean!" Dom Dom was now bawling.

"You must keep a hold on yourself, young man. Did you boys in fact practice anal intercourse?"

"Half of New York practices anal intercourse."

The doctor sighed. "I guess that's not very scientific either." Then he warned, "But I predict if Paulus Pewkin and his idiots at COD are heard from they'll use anal intercourse to string you up. Do you want me to look at your body too?"

Dom Dom picked up Josie, who felt lighter than ever. He wanted to slug this creep with a stinging retort but all he could think to say was "So Josie's dying from taking it up the ass from cats?"

"Initial visit and consultation one hundred dollars," said Dr. Herky uncertainly. "Where shall we send the bill?"

"That's a bit much."

"Yes, it is," the young man agreed. "Dr. Gist is the best."

Dom Dom stared at him. "Did I fuck you or did you fuck me?"

"You fucked me."

"Then you're going to die," said Dom Dom, leaving the small house. Poor Josie's body was not going to live through many more doctors.

Josie died that very morning. Somewhere between the NITS campus and St. Catheter's Medical Center in Northeast Washington. In Dom Dom's arms. As Dom Dom was still hoping to find a doctor who could give him a sensible explanation of what was happening to his beloved. Dom Dom himself died a few months later back in New York, not long after he told Fred all of this.

Dom Dom had carried Josie in his arms to see Fred, too. As noted earlier, matters had not been comfortable for Fred Lemish. Since the appearance of that book in which gay life was so front and center, many did not wish his friendship. You're giving away our secrets was a constant charge. The gay press had crucified both author and work. So had *The New York Truth*. People he knew crossed the street to avoid him. No, Fred had not been treated well since that book appeared.

"You seemed to know everything in that book," Josie had said, almost accusing him of being ignorant after all. Boo Boo Bronstein had called Fred as well. "I am not feeling well and no one understands why. Do you understand why? You always were Mr. Know-It-All." And Bella called to tell him that Timmy Purvis was not well. "And neither is yours truly."

At least Dr. Homer had Fred up and back on his feet.

THE NEXT PERSON I KILL IS THEO

He is in much pain. I go into his room at the clinic and he's looking straight at me. Even though he isn't. His eyes are focused on the door like he's waiting for death to come in. The doctor says he can see. "He just doesn't want to see." This is a stupid thing for a doctor to say. Of course he wants to see. How could he not want to see? Nobody would not want to see. The doctor is the one who doesn't want to see. They are all assholes, doctors. They are all blind. I should kill the doctor while I am at it. He won't give Theo anything for his pain. He says it's against the law and if Theo doesn't like it he should write to the president. So that is three people I have to kill. My Theo and the stupid doctor and me.

CIRCULAR POSTED IN BRISTOL (CT) POST OFFICE

Three male bodies, one crudely butchered to death and two dead from consumption of lye, have been found in a patient's room at the Gardener Clinic, a small facility outside Bristol that serves the small Native American population in this rural area of northern Connecticut. The butchered body was that of Dr. Raygood Brimpton, an attending physician. The young patient, Theodore Scales, and the third body, also of a young man, so far unidentified, consumed the lye. Anyone with information that might prove helpful is requested to contact the Police Department.

AN ADDRESS TO THE KINSEY INSTITUTE

DR. VENTNER O'BURGEREE, A PROCTOLOGIST

We basically defined the polymicrobial etiology of gastrointestinal infections in gay men. What we found was a Pandora's box. They had everything. They had shigella, salmonella, they had campylobacter, they had herpes, they had chlamydia, they had gonorrhea, they had syphilis, they had warts—and I could go on and on. They had *Entamoeba histolytica, Giardia lamblia,* and other types of parasites. There was everything in there because of the sexual practices they were engaging in. Large numbers of people were having multiple sex partners and they did not use condoms. It was not uncommon to find a man who had had uncounted numerous sex partners in the previous week. Unbelievable. Never saw anything like it. Turned my stomach, actually. Thought of looking for another job, if this is my future. And it was anonymous sex half the time. That was what was going on in San Francisco and in New York. I was not alone in doing these investigations. Others were also reporting epidemics of intestinal infections in gay men. What are the anal-rectal infections in gay men? Gay men engage in anal-rectal sex, oral-anal sex, and they get contaminated with these fecal organisms, organisms from the intestinal bowel. We are calling it "gay bowel syndrome." Dr. Pewkin at COD did not believe me when I submitted this report. Yaddah Med did not prepare any of us for this.

MORE SKINNY FROM ANN FETTNER

PART TWO

(Long, but riveting, Ann Fettner, Fred's expert on viruses, wrote this for The New York Prick. *Orvid Guptl said that even edited, it would be the longest piece he'd ever published and* The Prick *couldn't afford so many pages. So in fact this*

never appeared. Part One of Ann's "skinny" as well as her personal story appears in Volume 1 of The American People.)

THE FIRST ROLLOUT

Okay, Fred, here's more stuff for you from Ann.

In 1968 the German drug maker Hohenzollernwerke AG figures out how to pasteurize blood to remove poisons interfering with its clotting factors. Germans are good at finding out stuff like this.

[DAME LADY HERMIA: Also in 1968, Dredd Trish, Jr., graduates from Yaddah along with his "boyfriend" since youth, "Pinky" Birch.]

Dr. Gordon Grodzo, at Partekla, in 1970, views this German advance. "It will be not difficult to get around Hohenzollern's patent," he informs his co-worker at Partekla, Dr. Sister Grace Hooker, whom I personally know to be a selfish uncooperative cunt who won't share her data with anyone. Boy, did our government get a bargain when they bought a mind like Grodzo's from the Nazis. Well, it's now 1971 and still no one has taken up Hohenzollern-werke's offer of sharing its discovery, i.e., financial partnership of some sort. No one wants to go into partnership with a starving former Nazi company. Greeting-Dridge gets in on this; to this day I cannot discover who did what, but it is apparent that G-D was calling the shots and even had a secret sub-sidiary (Hohenzollern?). No one at today's Greeting is able, or willing, to talk about these early years of the development and release of "their" product. This product to treat hemophilia that will be called Factor VIII.

With, it will later be discovered, 90 percent of its many millions of mem-bers already *unknowingly* infected with whatever it is that is shortly to come gushing down the pike, the World Federation of Bleeding Men and Women (BMW)—hemophilia rarely affects women, but they can be carriers and transmit it to their male offspring—puts out rather tepid requests that all manufacturers of what is now called DridgePlusOne (has anyone ever no-ticed that Greeting names all its questionable products after poor old Horatio Dridge?), that these pharms make all efforts to ascertain if their product is clean and has been carefully studied and all possible poisons have been killed. BMW is a chickenshit organization out of Chicago that is afraid of offend-ing anyone even though most hemophiliacs already have been infected with hepatitis B (which was discovered and identified in 1967), from taking earlier versions of Greeting's previous factormetric, called BaxxterDridgePlusOne. By 1972 Von Greeting (Von's his nickname, short for Vonce), the suddenly appearing new president, is ready to roll his newly renamed crap out into the world.

BaxxterDridge, the subsidiary Von Greeting had set up to make this crap, was the only factormetricator operating in America at this time. No other drug company wants to come near this with a barge pole. Factormetricating involves collecting blood gathered from all over the world and then spinning it and partitioning and reconstituting it into Factor VIII, a clotting factor necessary to hemophiliacs so they won't bleed to death if they in any way get bruised, etc. We know *now* that D-G knew *then* that the blood they had collected from all over the world and were using to manufacture their new product and then exporting same all over the world was indeed *poisoned by something*. I often wonder if the sudden appearance of Von Greeting had anything to do with any of this.

How could it not be poisoned? This product was manufactured from blood pooled from thousands, eventually from two thousand to twenty-five thousand donors per vat of blood plasma also from all over the world, including most notably from Haiti, where gangsters were exporting six thousand liters each month to the United States. *The New York Truth* actually did write about this:

> PORT-AU-PRINCE, Haiti, Jan. 26, 1972—Hemo Caribbean, an American-owned company here, is buying blood plasma from impoverished Haitians who need the money and exporting 5,000 to 6,000 liters of it every month to the United States.

Collectors hired by G-D had long been circling the globe to buy this blood, particularly in places dense with poverty. People rush to sell blood when they are hungry. Brazil, South America in general. India. The Middle East. Africa, it's a long list. In Haiti you only have to pay them pennies. And also in our country, from prisons. Every major lab has always had contracts with prisons for testing something or other. One doctor in Oklahoma contracts with a number of prisons throughout the south and Midwest for exclusive rights to collect their blood. Greeting was his biggest customer. In San Francisco's Haight-Ashbury "flower children" had become huge "donors." In the United States alone millions of pints of infected blood are being collected, bought, and sold.

And so some ten thousand hemophiliacs have unknowingly become infected with the still unidentified UC from taking Greeting's DridgePlusOneAlpha Factor VIII.

Von Greeting must have known all this.

Hell, Boris Baxxter Greeting himself must have known, before he suddenly and mysteriously disappeared from the scene (Laddy, we hardly knew thee) and the place was turned over lock, stock, and poison to Von Greeting, presumably a relative. What is going on here? It is 1973.

What proof do we have that the blood being used to manufacture DridgePlusOneAlpha was poisoned?

We know because one hundred and fifty young men hailing from Partekla, Idaho, and calling themselves "Greek Warriors," all dropped dead from something after receiving at Partekla an injection of "something or other" before somehow escaping and selling their blood at a local storefront for buying same. By the way, in 1973 a law was passed to subsidize the distribution of blood-clotting factors to hemophiliacs. Knowing that this blood had to be tainted because of where it came from, our own government, without demanding that the blood be tested and monitored further, colluded with the thoroughly corrupt blood product industry, and BaxxterGreeting was seeing to it that all hemophiliacs were, in effect, consigned to death. Who got that law passed? You don't keep pumping blood back into the pipeline when it's come from such sources. You just don't. But somebody has.

"The" announcement by COD in 1981 of what will become UC via our pals at the Science Department of *The New York Truth* labeled this new outbreak of death as caused and spread by homosexuals. I don't want to get into this now but between 1975 and 1978 Dr. Dale Mulch, then at NY Harriman Oval (now at NITS), discovered that five *women* were infected, and for various unknown reasons his research findings were not published then, when he made his discovery and wrote it up and submitted it here and there and around and about and it was totally ignored, indeed not published until a year *after* the *Truth* article about the homosexual cases, which will of course be in July 1981. (Mulch now claims his cases were in men!)

Please pause to think about this for a moment: had Dr. Mulch's article been published in 1978, or 1979, or 1980, or even the first part of 1981, this plague would not be known irrevocably and so incredibly damagingly (too many adverbs!) as a gay disease. Nor was there any information available here yet of what was going on in Africa, where in Kinshasa, the Congo, in 1929, a black man died of what would eventually be mistakenly thought of as the first case of what would come to be called UC. Or, indeed, in Paris and Brussels, where cases of what would be UC in black women had been seen many years before any American case. What is going on here, again and indeed? Intentional? Bad luck? Dale is a shy guy and he isn't very precise in detailing what happened, but all evidence points to him being a decent person; he just should have opened his mouth about his discovery of these women. But he didn't. Why not? Doctors don't open their mouths much. Why not? G-D meanwhile was on its way to becoming the largest pharmaceutical company in the world. Maybe it already was.

DR. DALE MULCH: No! No! I made a mistake. They were male.

GRACE: How can you mistake a woman for a man! What really happened, Dale? You had eleven infected patients by 1981, half of whom were heterosexual or drug injectors. I cannot locate any official announcement by you of these.

DridgePlusOne is also shortly to be released into worldwide distribution by its foreign manufacturers and licensees: SeineLouvre in France, HeisslicheFrankfortKlippen in Germany, and TwinkelPurple in Japan. These companies are the chief international dealers of blood products for the world at this time. They work with the local Red Crosses and Red Bloods and Stars and Crescents and International Banks for Blood to get the blood out there where and when it's needed, which is more and more everywhere and all the time. DridgePlusOne will then be sublicensed by Greeting to a bevy of American business beauties, among them Cutter, Hyland, Baxter, and Armour, which was owned by Bayer, all of which are ready and waiting to sell it. It is 1973.

Since the end of World War II, blood is more and more an international daily necessity. Populations are exploding. More bodies are falling apart everywhere on a second-by-second basis. There are, and have been since the end of World War II, a number of things you can do to clean the blood, but no one wants to do them. What if, in doing such and such, you also did such and such that made it even worse? That's the argument, anyway, exposing laziness and reluctance (dare one label it inhumanity? Why not; I hereby so label it) to do anything. But even with all the bleeders in the world, this isn't thought to be a large enough market to be profitable to get so frightened and/or greedy and/or protective about. In fact, nobody really knows how many hemophiliacs there are. BMW (the org. of Bleeders, remember?), like your gay organizations, is not very good at gathering numbers to put forth. (We still don't know how many gay people there are, and that, in my opinion, is wrongheaded and actually quite tragic.)

It's very un-American to criticize American Blood. It's been a long time since Clara Barton and Florence Nightingale and gals like that, even Daniel's valiant mother, Rivka Jerusalem, with her bloodmobile. It is 1974.

Word is already out about that newest DridgePlusOne, subname Alpha. A number of bleeders have been and still are in clinical trials for the stuff. It works on them, and nobody so far has come down with anything visible. There is much excitement. For the first time in history hemophiliacs will have a blood-clotting medicine that will save their lives, maybe indefinitely. For the first time in their lives hemophiliacs will be able to leave their homes and not be afraid they'll bump into something and bleed to death internally or externally before they get to a hospital. They can now lead a normal life. Hemophiliacs used to die by the time they were eleven years old. Von Greeting is interviewed on *60 Minutes* and his face is on the cover of *Time*. *The New Gotham* profiles him with an Avedon photo of him.

Dr. Stewwinger Foss at Yaddah Medical School, the world expert in hematology, and Dr. Caudilla Hoare of the Association of Red Bloods, have said, "Nonsense," more or less in unison, when the safety of the blood supply is questioned by anyone. Nobody dares to disagree with Stewwie Foss; he is like some ancient patriarch in the world of blood. He's royalty when it comes to hematology. If he says the blood supply is safe, it's safe, even when, as now, it isn't. I wonder who got to him. He's too decent a man to lie. So somehow he must believe it. How could he believe it?

The folks at G-D take a different course. They claim loud and clear that the risk of contracting the suddenly mushrooming cases of hepatitis (which, unknowingly, almost all hemophiliacs already have from earlier infected plasma) is the price hemophiliacs pay to live a longer life. No drug company has ever said anything like this out loud. Von Greeting is obviously a case to be reckoned with. Employees at one of his subsidiaries actually die from what will be called UC from inhaling the vapors emanating from the boiling vats of purchased blood that they are supervising. What kind of man are we dealing with here, this Von Greeting person?

So, no company in any part of the world is willing to prove this product safe, this product they are getting ready to pump into the veins of hemophiliacs all over the world. But then, no drug company is ever willing to guarantee *any* product safe. Isn't that what FADS is for? FADS is supposed to be the main official USA watchdog over anything and everything The American People put into themselves. But Dr. Ekbert Nostrill (another bloody Lovejoy!), for some reason now the acting head of FADS, had in fact already given G-D approval to market DridgePlusOne. So now it can be called DridgePlusOne. "Alpha," which indicates it is still in an experimental trial and unapproved, is no longer necessary to declare on its label. BMW of course and quite rightly doesn't trust FADS either. The previous "lifesaver" for bleeders, something that came to be called, would you believe, Away We Go, had been approved after the Second World War; and it knocked off about ten thousand before it was pulled from the shelves. But that was before FADS. Or was it? Who remembers? Who even remembers what Greeting was named then? Because Away We Go was put out by Dridge too. They seem to have changed their name with peculiar regularity. Do companies change their names like some people do, to get away from something uncomfortable, like murder? Ten thousand dead is not an easy past to bury, but they did it and no one was the worse for wear. Except for those ten thousand dead hemophiliacs.

Anyway, does any endangered population ever try to get to the root of who, by name, has been fucking them over? "Take it [whatever 'it' is, or was] at your own peril" has always certainly been de rigueur among the bleeders. "What else can we do?"

Besides, the product is ready to roll out. The latest. The newest. DridgePlusOne-no-longer-Alpha. It is 1975 . . .

FADS is not admitting something. To give Fullest Approval (they have only granted Full—not Fullest—Approval) would require going through all that expensive and complicated animal-model-monkey stuff. "We shall have the anti-fur-coat crowd picketing our headquarters, *encore*," Seine-Louvre's *directrice des rapports communitaires*, Marguerite-Brigitte Bourgeois, tells Obissa Voltune of *The International Herald-Tribune*. Nor is anyone acknowledging that for some reason monkeys suddenly appear in very short supply—everywhere. Bosco Dripper throws his hands up in despair, knowing this is true. And there is now an organized religious opposition too, emanating from Utah and Rome. Suddenly, according to Netroit Farty at FADS's own Bureau of Community Relations, "We is [*sic*] inundated with requests from every sect you all can think of to immediately prohibit using living things for experiments of any kind. God don't like ugly."

Besides, and anyway, and of course, the product is ready to roll out. Hemophiliacs have been waiting a long time. By now there are even more mommies crying publicly about their bleeding sons, demanding its release. Drug companies are not happy when mommies cry to the press about sons dead because their drug isn't out there yet.

Who is it, exactly, who wants gay men dead?

Stop, stop, stop, nobody is yelling out, Stop! Don't release this shit as a cure for this shit!

Since it's still officially nameless, that's what UC is unofficially called, "this shit."

But the product is out there. On the market. For sale.

It is about to be discovered though not admitted that gay hemophiliacs given DridgePlusOne in its current form will be perfect transmitters of "this shit" to homosexuals, who we know are fucking each other like crazy all over the globe.

Even after overcoming this cleansing barrier (which was not so difficult to do), even when it is overcome (which will be fully achieved by 1983), all these companies will continue to distribute untreated Factor VIII for two, for three, for four, sometimes for five more years. What is going on here? That's what's going on here. These companies led by Von Greeting are and will be getting away with murder. Old stock has to be cleared from the shelves, you know, before the new stuff can be produced in bulk. Talk about a criminal act. Did no one ever hear of just throwing shit in the toilet and flushing it? And why did it take so long to refine the heating techniques that were first used by Army scientists on the battlefields in the 1940s and were first announced in *The Journal of the AMA* in July 1945? That's how long heating blood has been around, to get rid of hepatitis from donated blood. What is this delay all about? Who's calling the shots? Where is our country's official overseer on this particular product?

It will not be until 1987 that Factor VIII will be completely cleared of poisons. By then most of the gay population, certainly in New York, will be infected with the UC virus. Indeed, by the time the population of the world has reached five billion people, indeed, by the time the UC virus is actually identified, which is earlier, on the eve of 1985, almost every gay man in America who's had sex will have been exposed to it or to someone who has been exposed to it. Just as all it took was only one donor infected with UC to fuck up the entire batch of a pool of collected blood from all over the world from which Alpha was made, all it will take is one thus newly infected gay hemophiliac to get it out into the gay population, partying as ever in never-never land. Dr. Rebby Itsenfelder's screaming about Dridgies and their derivatives and knockoffs will shortly be almost (but not quite) beside the point, they having been joined by infected DridgePlusOne, Partekla and its tentacles, and, of course, NITS, as leading tributaries feeding into the roaring river of what's to come. The gay world, and hence and thereafter the rest of the world, will never stand a chance.

It's 1975. And we haven't even come to ZAP.

Back to you, Fred.

DANCING IN THE DARK

In the effervescing 1970s, Greeting's bestselling product has been Dridgies. Dridgies are everywhere. They seem better than ever. Are they the real Dridgies?

America is soon flooded with many kinds of "poppers." Many kinds of Dridgies. Many kinds of Dridge Ampules. The real, the fake, the beautiful, the damned. In ten minutes there is not a sex store anywhere in the world that does not sell a knock-off version, made who knows where and from who knows what. Fuck your brains out, dears and dearies. You go to my head!

FRED WASN'T THERE

Fred tried a couple of times to get into Ruby's 69 but they wouldn't let him in. Ruby's was the hottest place anywhere in the world. You had to be gorgeous, rich, famous, powerful, at least one of these things. People lined up for blocks and waited hours to work their way toward bozo bouncers selecting which ones could be passed through the ropes. There some gay guy he knew from somewhere would give an almost imperceptible nod of his head to admit the chosen ones. When he finally made it this far one night he realized this guy was someone who hated his book. So he never made it inside this holy temple. He was pushed to the side. He stood there and watched as Sammy and Kipper and Trafe and Randy and Dordogna and Andy and Mick and Sam Sport and Roy Cohn and Junior Trish and Dereck Dumster and Liza and Halston all went toddling in. They all seemed drugged out of their fucking minds. He recognized them all except for Dumster, who would one day attempt to destroy his people.

THE WEAPONIZATION OF VONCE GREETING

Von's notebooks are in the Greeting Library in London, but not available to the public. It is noteworthy that almost everything you need to prove a hideous case of anything is available somewhere or other, most often under lock and key. And it is remarkable that much material that you'd think would have been destroyed by somebody was not destroyed by anybody. The best record-keepers of all were, ironically, the Nazis themselves. They must have known they were making history.

Von knows he is trying to make history. What is the point of living otherwise?

Von writes in a notebook: "I am proud to be an American. I am proud of my success, of my Yaddah education. I am particularly proud that I was captain of an all-Ivy football team, to show—well, to show that I'm a true man. My desires and goals are worthy."

Von is still a handsome man, over six feet tall, with all his hair, with the disciplined body of the athlete, the football player, the shot-putter; also the Yaddah scholar (with good grades garnered by a successful ability to cheat). No one would think he is gay.

He's read deeply into what he calls the Supreme Haters. Barbie, Schellenberg, Merwin Hart, Gerald L. K. Smith, Heusinger, Gehlen the great, Skorenzy, von Bolschwing, Kremer, Antonescu, Trifa, Malaxa. And of their Supreme Facilitators: Ford, Rockefeller, Allen Dulles, John Foster Dulles, Huey Long, Father Coughlin, IBM's Watson, Harriman, Wainscott Trish. And of course Hitler. Lumped all together he calls them the Great Exterminators.

He wants to be one of them.

Von wrote: "There is much to be learned from all these gents."

John Foster Dulles had said, "For us there are two sorts of people in the world: there are those who are Christians and support free enterprise and there are the others." He became Ike's secretary of state. President Eisenhower fired every gay government employee shortly after his election. Brinestalker and the Dulles brothers provided him with the names.

Von had worked under Allen Dulles at the OSS and CIA. Allen Dulles was so eager to negotiate with the Nazis at the war's end, if not before, that he masterminded a scheme "to recruit large numbers of SS officers for Cold War service" (writes Doug Henwood in "Spooks in Blue," a 1988 article in *Grand Street*, also drawing on Robin Winks's *Cloak and Gown: Scholars in the*

Secret War 1939–1961). Allen Dulles wanted them over here in America and, "with the assistance of the Vatican, engineered the 'escape' of thousands of Gestapo and SS officers." Among these were Josef Mengele, Klaus Barbie, and Adolf Eichmann. Exfiltrated Nazis were free to offer their services to Latin American dictators and drug traffickers as well as the CIA and NITS and, of course, Big Pharma.

Von wrote in his notebook: "H. L. Hunt will help me. He has three hundred radio stations and $50 million a year of income on his fortune of billions. And there are many other names on the Powell Memorandum list. Coors. Scaife. Koch. McKenna. Olin. Bradley. Richardson. Earhart. Mellon.

"You've got to hand it to the Jews. If it weren't for the yids, there wouldn't be all this useful hate of fairies. Hitler also put fags front and center on the map of Unwanteds. He threw them in hand in hand with the kikes. It's an interesting thought. I'll have one of my PR boys write an anonymous pamphlet about it. 'The Bonus of the Ovens: How the Jews Facilitated the Mass Extermination of Homosexuals.' Thomas Paine was big into pamphlets and he's still famous to this day. I studied him at Yaddah with Tom Jones and James Jesus.

"Yes, I want to be a Great Exterminator too.

"And I have the weapon to accomplish it. I will weaponize it to kill as many queers as possible. With a bunch of hymies thrown in for good measure."

THE DIVINE BELLA SETS SAIL

There is little agreement on the importance of Bertram Bellberg's last acts. He'd administered to himself his daily shot of DridgePlusOne and changed into his leather policeman's outfit of chaps and vest and boots. He feels the need to be humiliated and he knows where he can go. He leaves Herbie's house-sitting chores and hops the ferry and train from the Island to the city and heads to the Wise Old Owl, a club that caters primarily to straights, but in the dark shadows a whip is a whip, piss is piss, shit is shit, and there are always a few desperate gays like Bella who need a quick fix. An active imagination—and who here doesn't have one of those?—can even believe for the moment that some hefty lump is not a babe with tits but a man with pecs. Groveling on the ground disguises a multitude of shortcomings. And so he goes here, and he satisfies his needs, and he leaves a little bit of himself scattered around and about.

Did any heterosexual customer of the Wise Old Owl contract an illness from contact with Bella/Bert? All that shit and piss and gism on the cement floor, it's hard to know.

Our Divine Bella, Bertram Bellberg, then catches his ferry in time and returns to a very empty Fire Island, to walk along its abandoned shoreline, carrying his boots as he walks barefoot in the sand once again to Herbie's elaborate villa on the ocean that he's still house-sitting. A few hundred feet from its regal stairway that from the sand leads up to the cascading series of verandas and various porches and lookouts from which you can wave hello to the world, the Divine Bella collapses to the ground and dies. It will be several days before a representative from Ocean Trash discovers him on his weekly removal rounds.

BANNER MOMENT!

BaxxterPlusOne (as it is finally named for the moment) is now in the veins, the bodies, the blood of The American People. It has been for some six months since July 3, 1975, when Von Greeting at Greeting-Dridge and Dr. Ekbert Nostrill and Dr. Stuartgene Dye at Partekla/NITS pushed the GO button. It's now out there for real. Signed (by FADS), sealed (by NITS), de-livered (by G-D).

This moment in the history of gay punishment is another milestone in the continuing evolution of its current chief manipulator, Vonce Greeting. He had supervised every moment of the development, release, and rollout of this "treatment." Not a bip or bleep or pimple had escaped his attention before his permission was granted to proceed. He had been the creative force that brought his Mona Lisa into being. Deals have been cut with each of his foreign distributors to allow him to speak for all (and to funnel all profits out of America). They all were on fake Bohunk Vernissage's fake books as "sup-pliers and manufacturers," a device to avoid not only taxation in America but also any further FADS approval. Had anyone raised a cry of alarm, he had only to say, "We're making our marbles in France, Germany, and Japan," which meant "Shut up or it will be smuggled into this country" (which some of it already has been anyway).

But a stark realization now smacks him in his face: his own company re-ports that his poisoned Mona Lisas aren't infecting enough men fast enough. He's monitoring these new numbers like a man who's not going to leave the

Vegas craps tables until he hits a big enough killing. Yes, statistics are dribbling in, particularly from New York and San Francisco, but not at a rate sufficient to indicate infecting a big enough "patient load" of gay men.

He didn't want them dead at first. He just wanted them very very sick. If there are as many of them as the overwhelmingly successful market for his Dridgies indicates, this is a huge untapped market for newer and newer drugs to keep them breathing. That's how giant pharmaceutical fortunes are made, via million-dollar drugs like his BaxxterDridgePlusOne followed by whatever can be whipped up after it ad infinitum as "new" or "improved." If we're lucky, maybe a billion! His scouts have already found some cockamamie new drug in, of all places, Czechoslovakia.

What would the Nazis have done in a situation like this?

Done? Shit, I'm doing it.

What would Edgar Hoover have done?

We're doing it! What do you think Partekla's all about?

He must tell Brinestalker and Dye to work that place faster.

FROM THE LAB NOTEBOOK OF
DR. STUARTGENE DYE

I want to cry.

I am almost there.

I have disposed of most of my Donalds successfully. Doc Rebbish would be proud of me. From Doc's thick book of knowledge in that big green trunk filled with possible cures and combinations from traveling native Seneck medicine men I have fiddled and tinkered and revised and broken through to this.

A few more trials will perfect it.

According to the Nazi defectors, the Russians now have means to totally disable a victim, making a man completely subservient to their will. But only temporarily. Their nerve gas isn't the right path. They are ruthless but don't know what the next step should be.

I knew what they were doing wouldn't work in the end. It is my discovery that will totally and permanently disintegrate a body into nothingness.

I am giving birth to one of the most ingenious weapons ever made.

Germ warfare is taking place all over the world. My Partekla will surpass any germ warfare center anywhere. My friend Sir Roy at Porton Down wants to partner with me in anything I choose to do. Not this, Sir Roy. Not this.

And fuck the Russians. We'll fuck them before they fuck us.

And it will all be because of me.

And Doc Rebbish, of course. Doc would have had a ball at Partekla. What goes around comes around, these white people say.

THE KAFFEEKLATSCH

WHEREIN WE MEET SOME MEN BEHIND THE MAN
THEY WANT TO MAKE OUR PRESIDENT
BY JOSEPH KIDNEY

(Joe Kidney has a couple of Pulitzers and many other top journalist awards. He writes a weekly column for the Washington Monument/New York Truth *Syndicate. His column is circulated all over the world until he will write his great book about the Ruesters,* A Very Bad Dream. *The number of his subscribers will then fall from many hundreds to half a dozen.)*

•

Sometime in advance of every election any serious candidate for political office gathers not only his thoughts, if he has any, but accrues to himself the people who can get him elected. In the case of Peter Ruester this transpired over many years before succeeding. He was ready and waiting way before he ran. No one had taken him seriously for the longest time. But he had. And so had Purpura, his wife.

So he was ready when, finally, "they" were ready. "They" are the people Peter Ruester, and more important, Purpura, the only person he trusts or talks to, have had gathered to them as hatchet men, his Kaffeeklatschers. Good choices are those with lots of money and the ability to get plenty more. These men—they are always men—are of course looking around for their own hatchet to back, some appealing guy who can speak nice and smile nice and who of course can be bought and reduce all their taxes to a pittance. And to make America strong again: it's never strong enough for guys like this seeking more power over all and sundry. They thought they'd been on their way with Nixon but boy did he screw up. So they have been waiting around just as long for a Peter Ruester as Peter Ruester has been waiting around for them.

They all sit around in one of their mansions in Palm Springs or Beverly Hills (they try to live where it's warm) to determine how to divvy up the spoils. There are always spoils. In the entire history of presidencies there have been spoils. Everything everywhere is always getting more expensive and only high-stakes players need think of anteing up. This Monopoly is big-time.

Then they figure out what their political philosophy "for the good of The American People" will be. It must be different from whatever any other opponent's political philosophy of what is good for The American People is said to be, and of course isn't, so they can criticize the hell out of it. And then they get The American People to elect their new president. That's all there is to it. That's how it's done. As old as America itself.

I sure never thought Peter Ruester stood a chance. I have to say that up front. I wrote many columns saying as much. Not only that, I had never heard of any of the bozos gathered around him. Every one of them looked like they had bought themselves out of some kind of trouble and were still doing so.

When the candidate is as unlikely, and as unacceptable, as Peter Ruester appeared to be, it is best to have your Kaffeeklatsch all bagged and tied way, way, way in advance. The more unelectable the candidate, the tougher the bunch of baggers required, and the more time and money they'll need. (Who ever heard of Jimmy Peanut or Boy Vertle until they were practically in the White House? They were ready and waiting for a long time too.)

Peter Ruester had been a washed-up actor reduced to making his living as a TV host and star of *The Greeting Half-Hour Hall of Fame (of Tales That Made This Country Great)*. One week he was a cowboy with a dying herd of cattle and the next week he was captain of a Mississippi riverboat hijacked by gamblers and then he was an Indian brave running for mayor in a colonial New Hampshire village who saved a drowning blind white girl whose father had taught the Indian English. Stuff like that. He was always the hero, so he sort of had a sort-of hero image to throw into any sort-of kitty. The series was never very popular. It appeared only in "scattered situations," as TV folks call the sticks. It is pretty fair to say that Peter Ruester as a serious candidate for president of the United States was something few of The American People took seriously. Why, he didn't even have an hour-long program. Let's face it: when he started running he was a joke.

But a few people believed in him. Beginning in the early 1960s Peter

Ruester constantly traveled around America making speeches to whoever would listen. He was the national spokesperson for Greeting Pharmaceuticals, and they really worked him off the beaten track, where no amount of advertising for their products could reach. I guess that if you speak to enough people—and Peter Ruester spoke and spoke and then spoke some more—a few are going to listen. That's often all you need to start with. A few people.

What had he told them all, in all those "scattered situations"? He told them America was the greatest country ever and they weren't getting their share by our government. He didn't say it with anger, but with the most disarming smile that any actor ever had. He promised them that if he were elected he'd see to it that they were all taken care of, "and about time, too!"

Peter Ruester is then elected governor of California by that state's "scattered situations."

His Kaffeeklatschers saw all this and now were ready. Now they have their man. They are greedier than ever for what they believe this country owes them. All leaders and their Kaffeeklatschers believe fervently that they're overdue for payment on *something*. The more they already possess, the more they believe they're still owed. I never met a billionaire who thought he had enough and wasn't damn certain he'd been robbed somewhere along the way by "the government." Peter Ruester would take care of them.

Now, how to get enough of The American People to fall in love with Peter Ruester? No one knew he was an ice cube frozen in some unknowable place unreachable to all. The Kaffeeklatschers pumped in a lot of money, no question. Information on just how much, and from whom specifically, has been impossible to determine. It's amazingly easy to hide money in America. But we are not about to meet a bunch of humanitarians who want the world to know all the good they're doing with their fortunes. You do not get rich from helping people. And you get less rich by talking about it. In fact, we're not going to see much of any of them individually, except for Buster Punic, whom they elect the front man willing to show his face in public. By their own choice they're going to stay hidden. They're going to do everything off-stage. No fools they.

They are all generic rich types or prototypes or stereotypes and they'll all react pretty much as expected. Used cars. Chains of 7-Elevens. Soap opera and TV guides. Savings-and-loan banks. Networks of cut-rate drugstores. Loan sharks. Slum landlords. Scrap merchants. Liquor distributors. Bars all over the country. Loaded wastrels. If I listed their names you wouldn't remember them or tell one from another.

Each is rich and each is harsh and they stick together like glue because they have learned the Lewis Powell lessons by heart. Stay in touch. Stick together. These Kaffeeklatschers are going to get a hold on things, the "things" being America, and they are not going to let go. To look at them, and study them, and try to analyze them, you have to say to yourself, these are not top-drawer folks. These are not gentlemen you would be proud to know or even to hang out with. And these are not guys you want to mess with your country. It should be of never-ending amazement what a long run they're going to pull off. Interestingly, Peter Ruester owed them everything and thanked none of them. Purpura wouldn't even invite most of them to the White House for dinner.

In your search for "evil" in the history of this plague, Fred and Hermia, just know that Evil is a tricky and elusive thing. It doesn't want to stay put in just one place. Now you see it; now you don't.

Ten years before Peter Ruester was elected, the Lewis Powell I refer to, a Virginia lawyer, was secretly commissioned, in 1971, by the U.S. Chamber of Commerce, an independent organization whose mission is to fight for business and free enterprise, to write a confidential plan on how to take back America for "the free enterprise system." Not democracy. Free enterprise. Nixon was about to tank. Goldwater already had. The women's movement, black civil rights, student protests, antiwar protests, protests for or against everything "certain people" believed in: abortion, gay rights, equal rights, troublesome unions that never learned their place, everything certain people can think of, was happening all over the country and once and for all had to be stopped. And a group of very rich men had had enough. Nine especially rich families and their foundations started to fight back in a big way, under the insistent goading of Joseph Coors. The Bradley Foundation. The Smith Richardson Foundation. Four Scaife (Mellon) Foundations. The John M. Olin Foundation. Three Koch Family Foundations. The Earhart Foundation. The JM Foundation. The Philip M. McKenna Foundation. A few more of the Coorses. Foundations are great places for rich people to hide their money and from which to spend it.

I call all these guys a cabal, a group of powerful men working secretly to get their way any way they can. America has made them all immensely rich. So they feel entitled. They will be joined by many more people in business, in industry, and particularly in religion. Every single one of them will feel entitled too.

This is what Lewis Powell wrote in his famous Memorandum: "Strength lies in organization, in careful long-range planning, in consistency of action over an indefinite period of years, in the scale of financing only available through joint effort and in the political power available only through united action." These guys got the message from the get-go. Peter Ruester will be the first real beneficiary of this cabal's growing strength, power, wealth, and cohesiveness. They're learning to fight together, no easy feat among so many strong individualists. For instance, just when your plague will be truly springing out of control, this cabal alone would contribute some $650 million to their conservative message campaign against homosexuals. These guys all know each other. This crowd always manages to know each other. Hate, and let's not kid ourselves, it is hate, hatred of everything they're not and don't want to be and don't want anyone near them to be, is a mighty strong glue. Democracy is not their bag. Yes, the Kaffeeklatschers and the Lewis Powell disciples like what they see in Peter Ruester. As I say, he'll be their first big test.

As Bill Moyers will write: "This whole bunch will very successfully take the richest and most liberal nation in the history of civilization and turn it hard right into a classist, racist, homophobic, imperial army of pirates." Money does buy everything, just like Santa says.

Lewis Powell, by the way, as his reward, got appointed by Nixon to the Supreme Court, where of course he voted, big-time, against blacks and gays.

Jules Stein had put together all the Kaffeeklatschers. Peter Ruester was a client of Jules's. Jules Stein had been an eye doctor in Chicago. An eye doctor. Like that guy in *The Great Gatsby* whose big eyeglasses sign hung swinging unmolested while Jay Gatsby's world crumbled to bits, Jules had his eyes on lots of prizes and knew how to get them all. Dr. Jules Stein had started out by befriending Al Capone and becoming his buddy. When he went west like Horace Greeley advised everyone to do, he started what became the biggest talent and movie and TV operation in the world. Hitler paid close attention to movie studios. Nobody's really written about the importance in history of movie studios and their powerful moguls. And how they shaped history, how they affected the way people wanted things. If you did it right, you could actually change how people thought. Nobody's really written deeply and perceptively about Jules either. Hospitals are named after him. Medical centers. Educational stuff. Noble things. He bought his way into heaven. Jules the Jew, he was called, behind his back, of course. Better be careful talking about him, though, or else old Al's buddies could still get you plugged. Jules didn't think much of anything was funny. He was not known as a smiler. Like the Kaffeeklatschers, Jules Stein preferred not to be seen.

And if Jules asembled these guys together for Peter, it was Lew Wasserman, who worked for Stein, whom Stein had made his chief agent against a world they jointly wanted to rule, own, control, using, of all things, the entertainment industry to do so, and with huge success, who put Peter on his feet to walk the walk. This most powerful agent in Hollywood turned one of his floundering boyish untalented good-looking actors into the governor of California, a very eccentric state, and held his hand all the way to the White House.

You think all the names you read in the papers of the guys running the world are the guys running the world?

It will be difficult to hide Buster Punic. His family's too old and rich and has been around too long. He's a big show-off. And he wants something out of Peter's presidency. Buster's going to be a handful even for the satanic Manny Moose, who will be attorney general, the visible guy who's running Peter's show. Manny, by the way, and you'll be happy to hear it, is aiming to rid the world of *Sexopolis* magazine, which will shortly be banned for sale from all those 7-Elevens and drugstores. And you'll be happy to hear that he is also going to eliminate the faggots, "once and for all." Manny actually said that to me, winking. He didn't know that my own son is gay, like his own. To "consult" on faggot elimination, Manny's located this very strange man named Brinestalker, who says he has a way of doing it. I think Manny's the scum of the earth.

Peter Ruester wasn't a completely blank piece of paper. He never said anything he didn't believe. His message pure and simple and out front and never varying was: "I love America. America is the greatest country there has ever been in all of history." And they loved him, America did. He wasn't such a two-bit actor after all.

And with and after him the deluge.

He, under whose reign your plague begins, will pass it—the Presidency and the Plague—along in the healthiest of states. But we are getting way ahead of where you are, Fred. Just couldn't resist.

I have left one chap out, an unofficial Kaffeeklatscher. The multimillionaire J. Peter Grace. He was involved in Operation Paperclip—a postwar CIA arrangement to remove classified information from dossiers so that former SS members and nine-hundred-plus Nazi scientists could emigrate to the United States. Hundreds of war criminals would find employment within government agencies and at companies such as W. R. Grace's chemical company, whose president was J. Peter Grace.

According to Simon Wiesenthal, whose life has been devoted to knowing stuff like this, there will be, by 1984, ninety thousand SS war criminals still alive. That's quite a few.

And quite a few will be in America.

JUNIOR'S LAST DANCE . . . WITH ME

DAILY THEMES 101
YADDAH UNIVERSITY
PERKY WEINSTEIN

Junior Ruester and I go dancing at the Cock Ring, a cute gay bar across the street from the Ramrod, another gay bar that's not so cute, around the corner from Christopher Street, Main Street in the New York gay world, on West Street facing the Hudson River, in Greenwich Village in New York City, in the very same United States that Junior's father is running to be president of. In front of the Ramrod, on November 20, 1979, a crazy man by the name of Ronald Crumpley, a minister's son with a submachine gun, fired forty rounds into the crowds of gays, shooting eight and killing two, one of whom was the organist and choirmaster of the local Catholic church. Crumpley was a retired police officer who yelled: "I'll kill them all—the gays—they ruin everything." On this very night that Junior and I are dancing, it has been retrospectively determined that Ronald Crumpley was prowling this very vicinity with a loaded gun in his pocket. He even looked in the window of the Cock Ring. Well, this is the neighborhood to do it in—shoot us up, I mean. Gay men are everywhere. Especially very late at night, like right now. Two federal agents already assigned to Junior wait in cars outside, and two are stationed inside watching the dance floor, and for all of them the novelty of guarding this "twerp of a fairy" is already wearing thin. "I thought it would be a hoot," one says to the other so Junior and I can overhear. "All it is is lotsa late hours and enough smoke to kill ya." We all laugh. Then one of the feds says, "Well, maybe his pop'll tell him he shouldn't do shit like this no more and we can steer clear of this shit."

Junior doesn't call himself Peter Ruester, Jr. That would be too bold, too show-offy, too look-at-me, too uppity, too full of hubris (if he knew what *hubris* meant, but he didn't take Greek Tragedy, where Professor Knox taught us about it). He's shy. That's why I love him. I like shy guys. Who are cute. Junior is cute. There's a difference between good-looking and cute. Junior is not good-looking. Most gay guys at Yaddah don't go for cute, which is maybe why Junior's unhappy here. Right now he needs people to think he's good-looking, not cute, because *cute* means "gay" and the last thing he needs right now is for people to think he's gay. He's taking a ballet class, and that's not going to help either, especially with that father.

Junior doesn't know how to talk about any of this, and he still doesn't know what he wants to be when he grows up, but he knows he's not only timid and without ambition but relatively talentless. "I can't do anything, Perky!" He's smart enough to know that. Like so many gays, all he has is taste. He can move a chair and make a room. He can lengthen a skirt and make up his mom. But nothing is satisfying him. He doesn't even want to have sex with me anymore. "I am going to have to stop because I'm about to be in the spotlight," he said on our way down here tonight when I suggested we cap off these last days of freedom by having one final fuck for old times' sake, followed by a last dance somewhere hot. He finally agreed to the dance, because he loves to dance. "We'll just dance in a gay bar. We won't be gay in a gay bar." Somehow he can separate out things into compartments. He says he got it from watching his mom. "I don't think I'm going to be able to have sex with anybody for the rest of my life."

Yes, he's tied in knots, which makes him even sweeter. Although such a confusion, it occurs to me later, is not so dissimilar to the one helping Ronald Crumpley act out his own crossed wires. Junior could never do anything like that, of course. But Junior will wind up putting himself in the same kind of prison for the rest of his life as Ronald Crumpley is going to live in. Well, not quite, but you know what I mean. You can tell I'm writing my thesis on Greek tragedy.

But at this moment, at least, Junior twirls and jumps and splits to not a little applause. ("Is that who I think it is?"). Another twirl and jump and split. ("No, it can't really be who we think he is.") "Having a faggot son annoys my father very very very much." He's not only cute and confused, he's sad, which makes me love him even more.

"Be careful one of these days you don't go too far," his only female friend, Ursula Ule, had warned him. She's an older woman who he thinks may come in handy. He's told her to sit tight just in case. Gossip columns are already zeroing in. Marriage to Ursula Ule? His mother says reporters are forever under your bed. "I just wanted to do it all before I got caught!" he moaned as I tried to hold him close at the end of the set. The Secret Service men watch him closely. "I've gotta admit the kid's got guts," they say so we can hear this too. I think it's against the law or something for them to actually say anything personal to him directly.

Here's what he wrote for Creative Writing 101, Daily Themes. He was thinking, I might try and be a writer.

Junior Ruester was not ready to become a president's son, nor was he particularly interested, nor did he either admire or love his father with any conviction. If he thinks of him for too long, he gets frightened. He breaks into a sweat. He sees visions of his father's long, rope-like penis, which has haunted him since he was a tiny tot. Yes, he thinks too much about his father and he is frightened of him. And of that rope-like penis. Which Peter let him play with when he was that tot and they took showers together or went swimming together naked in their pool. And which scared Junior shitless. Because he didn't have one like that. And still doesn't.

So most of the time he's still scared shitless. There's no hope.

He can pretend to love his pop. He's good at it by now. He can show affection and concern in public. It's one of the first lessons he learned from his parents about politics: always show public love and affection and concern for your family. And always smile. And he does. Even as a baby. God knows how he learned such a lesson so early. "Pop tickled my pee-pee."

Junior has known he's homosexual for as long as he can remember. The first naked body he responded to was his father's, not in the flesh, but in an old film he saw when he was three. His father, in the film, was in his twenties, and his chest was smooth and strong, and he was tall, and his hair was plentiful and styled and glistened from some beautician's goo, much as it still looks today, so many years later and still the same shade and still smelling of the same goo. Junior's three-year-old dingle tingled. He made his parents run that movie for him all the time, for years, and they thought it was so cute that he was so interested in seeing his naked pop in a pool with lots of other naked men in the background.

Then one day his pop took him into a locker room because he felt Junior should get used to being with the boys, being one of the boys, listening to the talk about getting laid. In the locker room he could really see the cock of the man who might become president of the United States.

Is it a federal offense to describe the cock of the man who might become the president of the United States?

His cock is like a rope. It's long and floppy and it sort of coils up when he sits down on the wooden bench in the locker room, and it coils around and settles notably in the mesh pouch when he puts on bathing shorts. But I liked it best when we took showers together when I was just a youngster and I stood beside him and my face was at the same height as his cock. It swayed back and forth right in front of me like the pendulum of his grandfather clock, back and forth, under the shower, back and forth, side to side, and when he lathered it up with soap all the bubbles and foam made it slippery against my body, and I had to hold on to his leg or slip and fall down. He would laugh and soap me all up too, and we would slip and slide together. He never fell down, of course, but I did, and then he would bend over to help me up, and that rope would flip-flop in the air, bending over me too, and as he pulled me up I could almost taste it in my mouth, my mouth would be open, almost automatically, like I was going to be fed, like some food I needed to stay alive. Like babies suck their mommy's tits.

Then his cock became like a thick stick. I didn't know what that meant. When it got that way Pop would immediately turn off the shower, grab huge towels for himself and me, and scoot us out. Our warm and soapy time together was over. This is all stuff I dredged up when I got into therapy and lay down on the couch of Dr. Rivtov at Yaddah.

"I can't turn this in for Daily Themes!" he yelled when I told him it was great. "I can never write anything at all forever because all I have to write about is my life, which is what Daily Themes is teaching us is what every writer has to write about, his life. There's no hope."

I hug him close and of course he pulls away.

He refuses to see me anymore.

He broke my heart.

People always ask me if Junior was gay. Of course he was gay. But what good is saying that when he ran away from the only world he really wanted to live in.

•

I am happening so quickly that I cannot keep up with me! I am now on my way to touching every single gay man in America.

BUSTER STARTS TO SENSE HIS SHITTY SITUATION

Buster Punic doesn't like it that his visibility is being curtailed even before Peter's sworn in and he himself will officially get to work. Buster Punic and Manny Moose were meant to be Ruester's two personal chief hatchet men, and Buster was going around trying to talk Peter up when all of a sudden Manny forbids Buster from talking to the press. "In fact, to anyone." Buster knew that Purpura didn't like him, trust him, or want him around. She would have canned him except that his wife, Carlotta, is Purpura's best friend. Carlotta had begged Purpura to find something, anything, to get Buster out of the house. Purpura owes her one for her sublime taste in making Purpura over, not an easy task.

Buster didn't come to Washington to shut up. He even bought a fancy house in Rock Creek Park. He wonders if it was a mistake to arrive so early from Beverly Hills and set himself up for a scene that is not quite ready to shoot. He makes a bigger mistake when he meets Claudia at Doris Hardware's. And starts going there every night and a few afternoons as well. He doesn't have anything else to do. He has too much time on his hands. Idle hands are the devil's workshop. He is falling in love with Claudia. Not good. He wants Peter to appoint him an ambassador to Britain or France. He's too spoiled to know this is not the way to get it. The Punics have always gotten what they wanted, ever since the American Revolution, or was it the *Mayflower*? There are a lot of old families now. All here a long time. All very rich. "Old blood" doesn't mean much anymore and Buster doesn't know that either. Dumbo is Buster's nickname for Peter Ruester. Would that it had been his nickname for himself. If it had been, a few people might still be alive.

Buster felt sorry for Peter. Peter needed all the help he could get. Buster knew what it felt like to be married to a bitch. Carlotta had put him in a closet the day after they were married—the morning after their wedding night on which he fucked her for the first, only, and last time. He had an enormous penis and she couldn't take it, and she told him so to his face: "You are never going to stick that thing into me again." Buster had told this story many times because he thought it reflected well on his manhood. He can't remember why he'd wanted to marry her. As a Catholic, she had extracted many guarantees from him before they married, like his converting, which he still felt guilty about. The Punics never liked Catholics. Back in the late 1960s he and Peter partied around together. Peter liked to watch Buster use his enormous penis on hookers. Somehow in the course of their activities Buster sensed Peter's coming rendezvous with destiny and told him about it more and more. Peter enjoyed hearing about his rendezvous with destiny. He certainly wasn't hearing it from anyone else. Except Purpura, but she was his wife. Carlotta wasn't telling Buster about his rendezvous with anything. But she was Purpura's best friend. That was why he married her. He knew Peter was going to be somebody. And he needed a somebody if he wasn't going to stay an anybody.

Buster had recognized that Peter had been a poor candidate (meaning he didn't have any money); but he didn't recognize that when you are a poor candidate, and what candidate for president is not poor in some way, that's when others are paying for your ride and you can't complain about the fare.

It wasn't long before Buster was left alone with his big penis. Manny tells him to his face that Buster's around only because Carlotta begged Purpura for this one favor, get her sex-starved husband off her back. (Literally. When she wouldn't take him in front he had attempted rear entry.) Purpura was grateful that her own biggest bonus in marrying Peter was how undersexed he was, so she felt free to have sex anywhere she wanted. Peter had a pornography collection. It was a secret hobby that only Buster knew about. Whenever Peter and Buster did get together now, all Peter talked about was what it had been like to be a movie star. Finally Buster knew enough to say, as he did to Claudia, Boy, is Dumbo going to be one dumbo of a president. Now that he is exiled before he began, he'll have to find a way to show the world that Buster Punic was worth having around. Or else. With all he knew about "those two," he figured he should be able to come out an ambassador.

No one wanted to know about Buster Punic and his messing around with Claudia Webb. Manny Moose had the media in his pocket. He'd raised a lot of money to play with, Manny had. But that wasn't the only factor. Nobody wanted to know about it because it was so tacky and trashy and disgusting and The American People will want to give their president-to-be the benefit of any doubt so early in his new reign. Buster's messing with Claudia should have been major front-page dirt for just about everything now being trumpeted as "The New Agenda for the New America," which is what Manny is launching as "Our Thrust."

"God, it is such a good story," Anne-Marie Wallende will write in her *The Punic Scandal: My Biggest Story Never Told*. "Who are my sources? I've really got to reveal them? Well, for starters, Claudia told Daniel and Daniel told old Washington royalty Ianthe Adams Strode and Ianthe told yours truly. I will have said much of this (except for naming my sources), and a lot more, in my article in *Vanity's All*, which was expanded into a book nobody paid any attention to, either the article or the book. So what good are 'sources'? At least I beat Kitty Kelley out on this one."

What good are books? What good are readers? He really will be Teflon, that Ruester.

A BRIEF INTERNATIONAL TREMBLE

In Geneva, Dr. Herschel Vitabaum, American representative to and president of Health of the World (HOW), the international organization of nations united for protection against infections, looks at his pile of accumulating daily teletypes and at the pins sticking in his wall map of the world and acknowledges to himself that yes, he is seeing at least five hundred new infections of unknown origin and that most of these pins are stuck in the Especially Poor Places (EPPs). These new infections can't all be the same thing, can they? Sure, some of them could be from the growing amount of syphilis since the war. Fucking hookers are everywhere now. But he has multiplied the common vector $(.023)$ by the overall poverty surge (123.45654) and divided it by the number of countries he supervises that do not have running water (107) and divided this by the number of medical centers that actually have a full-time doctor or nurse on staff (120) and then factored in the number of Adult Potentials (APs) in millions $(111,879)$ and realized that no matter which way you fuck up the math it can only be a plague. He peers into the future and he trembles. He has trembled mightily for quite a few of the years he has been headquartered here in Geneva, which is twenty-six. He has seen epidemics come and go. One plague at a time. No, that's not true. There are usually a couple of them running at the same time. Over the years he's trembled so much and alerted so much and complained so much that he finally decided to shut up and wait and see what the Americans do. Which is never very much. The American political hierarchy is never interested in world health. This guy who's been running for president is already threatening to withdraw from HOW. "We are not in the business of being doctor to the world," he had announced somewhere on his campaign trail, "and the world better get used to it." Tremble tremble. There goes our future. There goes the Health of the World. Up until now, America's been the only member country that has dutifully paid their share of HOW's upkeep.

So if whatever he sees is now happening, the rest of the world is not going to know it for a while. If ever there was an international humanitarian organization more hamstrung than even its EPPs, it's HOW. If ever there was a bureaucrat so weighed down with the problems of the world that not only can't he stand tall, he can't even look anyone in the eye, at any conference, in any country, or in any language, it is Herschel Vitabaum, M.D. Herschel is a bent-over man, both physically and emotionally. The childhood scatosis that gave him a curvature of the spine has been partly eradicated, even (thanks to him) in the EPPs, but that just makes him feel awful when he sees little black babies in deepest Ethiopia and Somalia who still have it. He really shouldn't be head of HOW anymore, but that's true of a lot of the bureaucrats in world health. After a while you just go numb to tragedy, there's so much of it that no one cares about, and it's harder to keep your sanity. But as always when his term of office is up and it's time for a new election, no one anywhere, in any country that belongs to HOW, wants the job, so he's reelected by acclamation and it's four more years of Vitabaum. And he really doesn't have it in his heart to leave all his EPPs with their unknown or unrecognized diseases and epidemics and plagues. After all, *vitabaum* means "tree of life." He feels the weight of his obligation, if nobody else does.

Whom should he notify, anyway, about his exploding pins? The United Nations Ministry for the Eradication of All Illnesses is worse than even HOW. They can't agree on anything. For every country that supports someone or something there's a country that hates the same. The Geneva Conference for World Blood, Sweat and Tears (originally financed by the music industry to deal with drug problems among their membership)? Worse still. There are many organizations concerned with world health and he knows that none of them is any good. None. Tremble tremble tremble. "Fools! They are all run by fools! I shall sit down and compose a report on my findings and send it to that soon-to-be president and his fine soon-to-be First Lady back home where I never can seem to get reassigned and perhaps I'll receive a nice plane ticket to meet with them and their now-being-handpicked administrators to discuss my daily mounting pins. Perhaps my assessment will worry them as it worries me."

That's what he tells himself and that's what he does, send out his alert. He's that desperate and naïve to actually think someone will do something, like answer him, which would be a first. *Plague* is not a word that HOW likes to use. Nor does HAD. Or NITS. Or FADS. Or COD. It scares people. You say "small outbreak," or maybe, if you have to, "epidemic." Best is "a few cases." As long as he's been in public health Dr. Vitabaum's never seen the word *plague* used, even when that's what it is. Maybe *pandemic*. That's a useful word that no one understands. But all these pins look to already be much more than that. How can you call a plague of wall pins an ice cream cone? Well, you can't. And he knows it. It will have to be described in just this fashion, i.e., not really described at all. And he knows it. Childhood dreams of being a doctor to the world have long since been retired, as he so longs also to be.

Herschel had degrees in all this. From Harvard. And from Johns Hopkins. What has he learned? That no one ever learns. He trembles yet again. This new one sure smells plaguey, and it doesn't take a big Jewish nose to catch the whiff of stink. He writes his thoughts in his *Your Medical Diary for This Year* sent to him annually by one of the pharmaceutical companies that are always trying to get him to buy lifesaving medicines he can't afford. Tremble, tremble, tremble, tremble.

Receiving no answer in many months from his new about-to-be-inaugurated president et al., Dr. Vitabaum resubmits his report. Within weeks Dr. Vitabaum receives a letter from a Mr. Linus Gobbel, chief of staff for he who is coming, reassigning him to a post in the Mestazia Peninsula of Lower East (Former) Borneo, in charge of nasal hernias, a local problem in no danger of spreading anywhere.

Tremble, tremble, tremble, tremble, tremble.

Dr. Herschel Vitabaum decides to take the remaining money from petty cash and go to Washington. Nasal hernia indeed.

IN WHICH DAME LADY HERMIA OFFERS A FEW WORDS ABOUT HISTORY AND EVIL

The introduction and arrival of new emerging strains of history are as vital to investigate as they are troublesome to pin down.

CORAGGIO!

Are we all able to keep everything, if I may say so, straight?

WE MUST NOT FALTER!

(Fred, you should be telling us this!)

Your great gay writer Melville said, "It is not down in any map, true places never are."

Thus we must strive even harder in our study of evil not to take no for an answer.

For, as your Myra Breckinridge might have said, "If one is right, the unsayable must be said."

What is history?

What historian does not ask this question daily?

Hegel thought that history was not meaningless chance, that it was a rational process, what he called the realization of freedom.

Nothing rational is going on here.

And who has freedom?

Livy, Thucydides, Herodotus, Gibbon, Tacitus, all were motivated to write their histories by despair.

Despair!

Hobbes, on translating Thucydides, used the word *silly*. "He made me realize how silly is democracy."

Let me update my growing view of evil thusly:

I believe that the acts that most radically alter the course of history are evil deeds perpetrated on others intentionally, and that these perpetrators and these deeds force history to become what it should be recorded as: a narrative of evil deeds.

Your Dame Lady Hermia Bledd-Wrench joins Livy, Thucydides, Herodotus, Gibbon, and Tacitus in their shared motivation for writing: despair.

The plague of The Underlying Condition is upon us.

We are entering the Ruester Years.

Truman, Eisenhower, Nixon, Ford, Kennedy, Johnson, Carter. What did they really do? Do you remember? Truman dropped bombs. Eisenhower kept a mistress, his wife was a lush, and he fired ten thousand gay employees. Nixon told lies. Kennedy got murdered. Ford played golf; his wife drank too much too. Johnson mired the world in Vietnam. Carter grew peanuts and believed too much in God.

What really changes history?

It's not what history thinks it is.

Peter Ruester will be responsible for more deaths than Adolf Hitler. You do remember Adolf Hitler? In fact Peter Ruester will be responsible for more deaths than Joseph Stalin. Did you even know Stalin murdered more people than Hitler?

As Edward Gibbon said, "History is indeed little more than the register of the crimes, follies, and misfortunes of mankind."

Read on, Fred's American People, read on and weep. The era of your greatest heartbreak is about to begin.

Fred, come back! We must continue to more precisely define and elucidate the particular evil we are dealing with here.

We need you and your bouncing ball.

Will I—or will Fred—be of any use in this era of plague?

THE RUESTERS ARE COMING!
THE RUESTERS ARE HERE!

BY FELIX TURNER, STYLE REPORTER, *THE NEW YORK TRUTH*

. . . Purpura Ruester has brought along her California decorator, Swish Turtell, and "my best boy chum," Foppy Schwartz, "both possessors of sublime taste," who, with Purpura's best girl chum, Carlotta Punic, whose taste is also better than hers ("almost everybody's taste is thought to be better than hers," according to *Women's Wonderful*), comprise "my own cabinet of advisers." She goes on laughingly: "Swish is my Secretary of the Interior and Carlotta is my Secretary of Human Services and Foppy is Secretary of Everything Else, which therefore must be State. How can I go wrong?" She laughs again. From Day One, does our new First Lady desire to be such a hoot?

It is suddenly now fashionable to write about the Ruesters and their circle. "That guy who owns *TV Guidebook* wants to become ambassador to Britain! Yes, it all becomes more and more a hoot," Old Washingtonian Ianthe Adams Strode told this reporter.

There is no denying this town is overflowing with new light and life. A new set of faces, most of which have never been seen in Washington before, have taken center stage overnight. Mrs. Ruester has surrounded herself with her special court that dances to her every dream. She has parties scheduled a year in advance. She has new gowns from Estrez Ovida arriving daily. Houses and apartments are gobbled up so fast real estate agents retire. Old-time Washingtonians marvel at how fast they are dropped from every list as if they've never lived here all their lives.

It is she and her women friends who already set the tone—Purpura and Carlotta and Carolina and Mica and Chesty and Judy and Nan, all on the arms of their Foppy, their names like a string of valuable-enough pearls. It is their first names only that *Women's Wonderful* already is emblazoning in its pages, accompanied by glamorous photos of this handsome proud arrival of strong females dressed to the hilt around the clock. Even Jackie is popping back, so fallen from grace with "that Greek ocean liner," and she's actually welcomed by this crowd, which understands her better. Again I quote the inimitable Ms. Strode.

Your Style Section predicts there never will be a reign—for that is what's transpiring in this town—like the one that's now revved up for action. Washington has never been a city in its soul. It remains a town, and for these women now embarked upon their adventure of living here, it is so much easier to live in a town. Our Town, they already call it.

And indeed for them it is and will be.

DR. DANIEL JERUSALEM

I've lived in D.C. all my life and I've never seen anything like this. Washington's always been an indecent place to live. Centuries go by and no president changes the poverty of this place in which they live. I help to supervise a clinic at Mea Montezuma for the indigent. We process five thousand to eight thousand patients a *week*. That's unheard-of for a hospital in a town.

JANUARY 20, 1981

PETER RUESTER IS INAUGURATED AS PRESIDENT OF THE AMERICAN PEOPLE

If one is to pinpoint a moment in time when the shit in the closet starts hitting the fan and extruding itself into our plague, there are some who will always believe it coincides with the arrival on the Washington scene of Purpura Ruester and her Peter.

•

INT. VARIOUS BALLROOMS. WASHINGTON. NIGHT.
Montage of shots as Peter in elaborate formal attire and Purpura in various gorgeous designer gowns dance at one celebratory ball after another. Everyone roars and cheers.

STATE OF THE UNION

Upon the assumption, by Peter Ruester, of his presidency, an assessment of the economy finds this country to be in "a more severe depression than anyone thought possible under my predecessor," a Democrat. Since the new president made much campaign fodder out of how badly all his predecessors going back to Franklin Roosevelt had depleted the resources of The American People, this situation must be rectified as quickly as possible. Still awaiting the appointment of various economic advisers (so far no one approached can understand the jargon they are being asked to support, prepared by an unknown young man named Stockman), Attorney General Manny Moose releases the following to the financial press:

> It is not the best of times. The National Abundance Ratio (NAR) is $459 trillion. This is very bad. The Triculosis Factor (TF) is less than minus .07. This is also very bad. The Bohunk Institute, the most reliable of market forecasters not funded by a specific industry, now predicts a price-earnings-wage-ratio-cum-salvage factor of 2–1, the lowest since the Great Depression. This is exceptionally worrisome. A new scale produced for your new President by the highly respected Nimkins-Strato-Perdist Group tells us that not one single state in the entire Union can claim phangel results that are not inferior to any posted in the last four years. This is a terrible indicator we must immediately attend to.
>
> All budgets and expenses except for the military must therefore be reduced immediately and accordingly.
>
> We have inherited all of this. We must not forget this. We must prepare ourselves so that this state of affairs never happens again.
>
> So President Ruester has his work cut out for him. He pledged to deliver to you his and your economic revolution.

He has asked his newly appointed Chief of Staff, Linus Gobbel, to personally supervise this revolution.

The President asked me to deliver this message to you:

"I pledge to The American People that I will deliver on my promises. I promised you I would make America great again. I know you will join me as we now fight together to make our country great again. So great that it will be morning again in America. Together we will make it so. God bless America."

To begin to rectify as much of this situation as quickly as possible, the new president of The American People proposes to the Congress of The American People a new Desed-Offal Bill that will allow the Treasury to exceed all former debt limits by up to 5,000 percent. "This will be a splendid antinecrosis factor!" Ruester beams his now-famous smile as he presents his plan to Congress.

The new Congress, in love with its new president, overwhelmingly approves the measure immediately. The honeymoon is on. Mr. Stockman gets to work. The first thing he must do is lower taxes on the rich to start paying off the Kaffeeklatschers, an ever-growing group.

There are a few personnel announcements. Dr. Stuartgene Dye has been appointed as Ruester's director of NITS, and henceforth "he will be responsible for the health of The American People." Do we remember Stuartgene, whose hobby, nay obsession, is to perfect the complete evaporation of the human body? For the good of humanity, of course. He had run Partekla. Do you remember Partekla? It's still there and quite busy. (No one knows Dye was in charge of it. Or that he has a collection of Picassos.)

DR. STUARTGENE DYE

Ah, yes, my Picassos. I cherish them. It was Doc Rebbish who taught me how much beauty can come from pain. He gave me my first Picasso, a lithograph of a gored bull being mourned by a lovely girl. He'd received it as a gift of thanks from a dying Seneck chief. "For a life devoted to the care of our people through your search for knowledge" is written on its back, I believe in the chief's own blood, above his seal of office. Picasso himself said, "Art is an offensive and defensive weapon against the enemy." I identify with that. I am an artist too. I create with chemicals. They are my paint.

HOPE!

As always, there are medical realities that should be sobering. COD identifies the first case of "this shit" in a hemophiliac. It is announced in *The
Journal of Death*. Dr. Paulus Pewkin is quoted: "I wonder what this means?"
An inquiry to Drs. Dye and Omicidio at NITS receives no response. *The
New England Journal of Spots* and *The New England Journal of Blood* reject,
i.e., refuse to publish, letters submitted by concerned doctors, which detail
transfusion (i.e., ostensibly non-gay) cases of "strange" and "very strange"
and "weird" and "unaccountable" and "troubling" blood infections in several
large medical centers and in rural areas. Dr. Emma Brookner of New York's
Table Medical Center writes a particularly alarming one.

Nevertheless, our Washington newcomers bring hope! All new administrations bring hope. This one will sustain it longer than most. As long as the
right people become richer, and they will, all will be well. And hopeful. You
bet. You'll see. It will be a hoot.

NOTES TOWARD UNDERSTANDING
THE NEW FIRST LADY

VIA IANTHE ADAMS STRODE

Why am I introducing this? One of my burdens has always been to know
all the First Ladies. One of my oldest friends is Purpura Ruester's secretary,
Patti Montgomery. I've known her since she worked for Pat Nixon, not an
easy gig. She's worked for Purpura Ruester forever. They are very intimate friends, she and her boss who quite obviously revels in telling her
all, indeed in acting it out in her retelling of it to her longtime assistant.
So Patti knows where all the bodies are buried. There are always plenty of
bodies. Some people like me believe fervently they must be exhumed. For
the good of The American People. So does Patti, whose words these are.
(You can tell she's been thinking about this for a long long time and taken
voluminous notes.)

PATTI 1

Pat Nixon was easy and straightforward. She hated her husband and stayed all day in her rooms. The new First Lady must get laid regularly. She thought she could hold out longer than one day after her husband's inauguration. She can't. You'd think she'd be exhausted from dancing at all the inaugural balls. We all watched her endlessly on television. She looked like a queen. You can see she now thinks she is one. And that royalty will get what it requires. Yes, you can see that from day one. This queen was destined to rule a country.

As long as I've known her, despite all she's constantly told me, she is still a mystery to me. I could tell you what she does but in the end I still can't tell you why. I know this country would not tolerate her life, should they know about it. For instance, this on our answering machine:

"This is Mrs. April. Is this my rare book dealer?"

"What do you want?" he whispers hoarsely.

"I want you. Fuck the code words."

He responds immediately. "I'm sitting here naked thinking of you. My dick is in my hand and it's thick. Do you remember how thick?"

"I remember!"

"It wants you to come and sit on it. Say, 'My cunt is wet with great need for your cock.'"

"My cunt is wet with need for your cock."

"You left out *great*. Great need for your cock."

"The greatest need for your cock."

She met him a few years ago flying to Cleveland. They were sitting side by side in first class. He looks too old for her, though she can see he's in decent-enough shape. He takes her hand and places it on his crotch. Just like that. She can tell he is enormous. So the first time the First Lady sucks his enormous cock she isn't the First Lady. They're in the airplane's toilet, just like Jack fucked Marilyn. Then Purpura meets him again that very evening, at cocktails for Major Cleveland Benefactors. It is at a time when nobody thinks Ruester can get elected. Purpura feels less constrained realizing that obviously high-class types like he appears to be are on their side so early. He knows Peter will be elected. He says so. He has an enormous tongue. In her room during the fund-raiser he eats her out like she has never been eaten out before. She gives him another blow job. She is amazed he can maintain such an erection for so long. And at his age. He is on VAM, he tells her. "You're not!" she exclaims. "However did you get it already?" She wants to try it too and will. When she and Peter arrive in Washington, this man will be convenient. His name is Brinestalker. He tells her he is a lawyer. That's all she has to hear.

He has a furry body. Daddy is hairless. Daddy is boring in every conceivable physical way. He doesn't even kiss with his lips open. Peter's just acres of arid white skin like the desert. Who wants to sleep in the desert? That's why she calls him Daddy. She started calling him Daddy before they even had kids.

"Would you marry me, if ever Daddy died?" she likes to ask this guy Brinestalker after he's ejaculated and she's untangling the knots of his pubic hair. He has followed her across the country, more or less. She is impressed. What woman wouldn't welcome such attention in middle age from a furry man with a very large cock as a therapeutic aphrodisiac?

"No."

"Good. I wouldn't marry you either."

"He's a tasteless boor," Foppy Schwartz tells her. "How could he say anything like that to you?"

She usually gets laid at Foppy's apartment in New York. Nobody in New York cares what you do. But she can't get to New York so easily now.

"He's huge." She loves to talk dirty with Foppy. He is such a useful friend.

"Ah," Foppy sighs.

"Someday your prince will come."

"It is highly unlikely. Not because of my age, which is deterrent enough, but because I suspect that deep within me I desire too much. I have contented myself with less."

"What do you do when you get horny?"

"I utilize my right hand while standing erect over my toilet, you nosy tart. Or I listen to Stuartgene tell me about his activities."

"Oh, tell me more! Who is this Stuartgene?"

"He hung someone in his shower last week and went off to a medical conference in Austin, completely forgetting to let the lad off the hook. He's my doctor and you won't find anyone better. He knows all kinds of ancient American remedies."

Foppy loves to tell stories like this.

"I hear there are penis operations in India if you're small," she says.

"I would prefer staying small to going to India."

"I didn't know you were small."

"Only from disuse. It's lying in waiting."

"I'm glad." The First Lady loves Foppy.

She gets laid a lot and she sucks a lot of dick years before she is elected First Lady. She loves the taste of semen in her mouth and the feel of it as it trickles down her throat. It's evidently not easy to be a good cocksucker unless you really like it. You gag and choke a lot. It takes a lot of practice before you stop gagging and choking. Purpura's a pro. Purpura hasn't gagged or choked in years. Her father had abandoned her when she was a kid and it's as if she's been searching for another one ever since. That's one reason older men appeal.

Her first career, as an actress, coincides with the decline of the heyday of the great Hollywood stars. She sucks many famous cocks. The two most famous cocks she sucks belong to Clark Gable and Spencer Tracy. The most powerful cock she sucks belongs to Benjamin Thau. Benny is the head of film production at Metro-Goldwyn-Mayer, still a famous studio. Everyone knew Benny couldn't keep his hands to himself. Benny invented the Casting Couch. You want a part at Metro, you suck Benny's cock. He doesn't want to fuck you. That's too risky. He might get VD. At noon every Saturday Purpura sucks Benny Thau's cock, one of Hollywood's most important heads. When she finishes him, she throws the rubber down his toilet. The secretary always notices on Monday that the toilet's clogged. Benny arranges for her to service Clark and Spencer. Benny knows a good blow job and passes it on, like the generous man he's said to be, to Gable, despondent after the death of Carole Lombard, and to Tracy, a heavy drinker married to a Catholic woman who won't divorce him. Spencer has a hard time staying hard. Spencer is also a homosexual, but that doesn't come out until many years later when Katharine Hepburn is his beard, as he is hers.

Purpura is not an equal recipient of Benny's generosity. For all her hard work, her career at MGM does not flourish. Benny knows she's a lousy actress standing up. Neither Spence nor Clark wants to see her face with his on the screen. Some actors make love to the camera and the camera loves them back. She is not one of these.

One day she meets Peter Ruester. He's been divorced from a star much bigger and getting bigger still. Who is also a lesbian, this star Peter got married to. The studio measures an actor's worth by how many fan letters are received. The dyke receives far more letters than he does. The notion of her in bed with another woman's exciting. A lot of good it does him. He was said to have dallied homosexually himself.

Why does Peter marry Purpura? Her reputation must have been known. A life like hers is not kept secret in Hollywood. His own career as an actor is still promising. True, he wants A roles and is only given Bs. But he's given Bs with regularity. Nobody ever whispers anything about Peter Ruester. Long before Teflon he is Teflon.

He knows what it means to suck dick too. And to be available for gentlemen callers. These facts are generally unknown. Or, because he's so boring, hard to believe. But when he was just getting started in movies, he lived dangerously. He's passed around among certain sets. In these days no one frowns when boys will be boys. These are considered larks. For laughs. Not to be taken seriously. Actors have to do many things to get ahead.

He loves being worshipped. The dyke never adored him. These guys get down on their knees and lap him up. To clear his conscience, he does it for money. He is, after all, an actor. Actors often don't have much sense of an identity. Actors pretend. Letting men worship his body is a good early example of how well Peter can pretend.

After the dyke divorces him he's wretchedly lonely. Even a lesbian's better than no one. Oh, he goes out. Starlets and singers and big blondes and outdoor types fond of hounds and horses. Lots of rich women kept horses then. It's good practice for him for when he must do those westerns. He busies himself as best any beleaguered out-of-a-home-ex-husband can.

And so, finally, he dates Purpura seriously. God knows she's been pushy and forward, never leaving him alone after their initial introduction. She's getting older. Very quickly she wants to be serious and he won't talk about it. Then she decides not to push. She has few options. She's not being courted or pursued. Her career, on-screen and off, is in the toilet. After two years of dating a marriage is arranged at last.

It is Purpura who gifts him with a return of that potency the dyke's rejection so disturbed, one that left him fearful he'd never perform again. How had that fine actress, who won an Oscar playing a deaf-mute the very year of their own child's birth, torn his potency from him? She is to say publicly, "He was about as good in bed as he was on the screen."

By the time he's president he has, even for a president, an extra-large pornography collection. He started amassing it before he married the lesbian. All these years he's had his pictures. He learns quickly of Purpura's need for constant sexual servicing and of his own inability to constantly oblige. He decides to display what will be one of his earliest examples of good sense: Let her take care of her own needs. Manny and Buster bring him new pictures. Eventually Purpura will provide him with a few. Then he can squeeze his rope. That's what he calls it. His rope. What cowboy doesn't have a rope?

What does Peter see in Purpura or sense in her or know about her that makes him not only marry her but allow her such freedom? Does he know then she'll be what he requires? Is she already satisfying him in other ways? What are these other ways? Does he have any sense of his destiny? He will always be expert at keeping himself to himself.

And what does she believe she's getting? Has she any notion of what he'll turn out to be? Even then, is her sense of her powers so strong that she knows she'll make him into something? Surely neither of them at this juncture is thinking president. That would be delusional.

Often into a man's life a woman comes along to make him great. Does she or he think that she's this woman?

How come he marries her?

If he hasn't heard about her skills originally, how can he not have heard about them latterly?

Does he know and it doesn't bother him? Or he gets a kick out of it? Or they may both get off on it? To thumb your nose at the world is an exciting sport, if that's what they think they're doing.

Or does he have some secret of his own? Do they trade like kids with baseball cards? I'll give you one of this if you'll give me one of that. He'd practically raped a woman on their very wedding day. Is there more dirt under the covers like that? He was tired of sex and she'd be a relief?

He dated every girlfriend he ever had for years and never touched them. *Touched* them, as in kisses; forget the fucks. If Purpura likes to do it and Peter likes to look at pictures, they don't appear to be such a hot fit.

Do they grab each other to save themselves? From what? Shared secrets bind people together in tormented pacts. His lack of interest in intercourse would have been acceptable to a lesbian and would explain his great depression when that marriage ended. For the next one he'd have to perform. Perhaps not, if she's already got such a thriving business door to door.

Does he feel sorry for Purpura? Did he feel sorry for the dyke? Does Purpura feel sorry for Peter? Peter believes in smiling whatever the hardship. His family on the plains wasn't really drunks who never worked. They were noble Americans beset with adversity. Yes, he knows how to rise from ashes. They both know.

Why does he need such a *large* pornography collection? We are not talking about a few little dirty pictures and a couple of dog-eared books. We are talking about the equivalent of a philatelist with a major collection of stamps. If he gets little sex and gives little sex, does he just jerk off over dirty pictures? If she hardened Spencer Tracy, is this something she does for her Peter? As Wallis Simpson does for her duke. A gift is a gift. God doesn't discriminate whose hands are laying on whose.

Is he marrying Purpura, the cocksucker, his very own live-in dirty-mouthed pornographic semen swallower? Is she marrying Peter Ruester, the dirty-minded collector of smut? A family that plays together stays together? All of this is a stretch. But then so is his election to his presidency.

Does guilt have anything to do with anything?

It is said, by Anne Edwards, the eminent biographer of both of them, that Ruester was a deeply religious man from childhood on. If he thinks he's a washed-up sinner, then perhaps another washed-up sinner is what this exercise is about.

How can any history of the Ruester years be true without any exploration of all this?

After his marriage his career goes further on the skids. The studio won't turn him into an Errol Flynn or a James Cagney or even a George Brent. Only Mr. Nice Boy, Mr. Boy Next Door for Pete. At first he considers this unfortunate.

When does it occur to him—or them, he and his fine new wife—that this is the part he is born to play? That playing this part of the Common Man will turn him into God? Does he make some Faustian bargain with his God?

Peter brings with him to the governorship one Manny Moose.

Peter brings with him to the White House one Manny Moose.

One day Manny Moose is just there.

One day Buster Punic is just there.

One day those Kaffeeklatschers are just there.

It isn't all that long after he's governor that Peter Ruester is president of the United States, an eccentric country.

So the man with the huge pornography collection and the woman who gives the best of blow jobs are now the president and First Lady of the United States of America, now an even more eccentric country.

"I'm a cocksucker. You like dirty pictures. Let's rule this country."

"Why not the world?"

They've stayed together and wished upon a star.

PATTI 2

Ours is a greedy, hungry country that's learned how to meet all needs. There are special places to cruise for lawyers, as there are for homos and hookers. There are plenty of lawyers if you know where to find them. She can walk into a conference or bar or restaurant and spot the one she wants. They wear suits that fit them differently, and their ties, no one else wears ties like lawyers, and their shoes, you can always tell a lawyer's shoes. Yes, lawyers are boring, but boring men can be great fucks, I gather. Partners in law firms are the most boring, safest fucks. They've got the most at stake. Soon she's only fucking the partners. Many of them will be helpful to her for years.

The only men who aren't boring to her are homosexuals. Swish and Foppy are gay. She's had rollicking fun and laughs with gays for as long as she can remember. Her mother's closest friends were lesbians. She figures her mother was one too. Her mother's best friend was Zasu Pitts, a movie star of sorts and a dyke. Mom was friendly with Mary Martin, another dyke, who cast young Purpura in one of her musicals on Broadway. In the old days, when gay men or women gave the only parties she was invited to, she was grateful to them. They kept her from being too lonesome. Gay men helped her dress better and did things with her hair and makeup. Hers is not an easy face. Small. Squooshy. And she's got those legs that belong on a piano. When gay men tell her their problems—their romantic problems are evidently always so complicated, and usually involve more than a cast of two—she gives them advice. That's how she learns she's practical. "Queers always come back for more. They need constant tending and reassurance. They cave in so quickly." Her advice is never to cave in. Such wonderful practical experience, running lives. When one died years ago—"what was his name?"—from old age, she actually cried for him. She was surprised to realize she missed him, but she was running a state by then, so we couldn't send flowers.

It's easy to get laid quietly in New York. There are millions of people to hide you. You can get lost in half a tick. You wear sunglasses, a wig, and a big hat. You can even walk. It's not easy to get laid in Washington. There's always "some spic maid who can't keep her mouth shut or some schwartze chauffeur who likes to brag." You can't even take a cab. All the drivers think they're about to get arrested or are being followed by Secret Service men with guns, which they probably are. It doesn't help to play Big Deal. It makes cocks go limp. Cocks tend to get a bit dangly in D.C.

But she'll find a way, now that she's reached the big top. Why, she might even get her dream, Frank Sinatra. He'd snubbed her many times in L.A.

From the day of their inauguration—because she's anointed queen as much as he's made king—America's on a love fest with Peter and Purpura Ruester. No one *dares* to criticize them. Funny how it would be so easy to make fun of them, yet no one does. Felix Turner tries to write amusingly about her in *The New York Truth*, but Manny's put a stop to that.

Why and how will they get away with so many extracurricular activities?

And I haven't begun to tell you the half of it!

Purpura and Peter know that their son is gay. And there is something out there infecting and killing gay men.

FROM THE NOTEBOOKS OF JAMES JESUS ANGLETON

CODE NAME: MOTHER

So Patti is blabbing again. She continues to be most helpful to me.

It's a good thing I keep notebooks. All the best of us do. If only for our own salvation—to save our own necks when someone comes after us, as someone always will.

Laws have to be broken if the rewards look substantial. All lies are told for a reason. I have intelligence files on large numbers of people. I have an army of spies under my personal control. I enjoy manipulating my boys and girls.

I always assume the worst. My definition of both counterspy and counterespionage is that one is overt, the other is covert, but it boils down to the same and together they form Counterintelligence, and that is what I am in charge of. CIA Counterintelligence is mine!

Drastic remedies are often called for. I learned that from Tom Jones at Yaddah. It's interesting how many of the best of us were from Yaddah. We had a nice meeting before he died, Tom and I.

My enemies think I am going too far, bringing on a police state, a Gestapo. But it's they who will bring this about. Someone has started a typhoon against me, claiming I brought in Nazis to reinforce my troops. What nonsense. I need no one to help me call my shots.

I must know everything that's going on. It is sex that creates, rules, and ruins history. The Ruesters are incorrigible. With lots of new idiots ruling the roost since Nixon, I am constantly sending in my own Deep Throat to keep me apprised. It's not only my own skin that I am saving.

CHICAGO

On March 3, 1981, Tidgy Schmidge and Kristos Rosenkavalier threw their two adopted twin baby boys out of their eighty-first-floor apartment on Lake Michigan and jumped after them. It was an exceptionally windy day so the bodies flew all the way to Michigan Avenue before they landed and went splat into millions of pieces. Still, it could be seen that all four bodies were covered with purple spots. Tidgy had had a brief affairlet with Fred Lemish, whose hairy ass Tidgy maintained turned him on. Fred was not aware his ass was hairy but Tidgy was a nice man anyway. "You have just a little but it's hairy enough for me," Tidgy told him. Kristos and Fred had been dancing partners many Tea Dance afternoons ago at Fire Island. Fred gave him this name when they were cuddling one evening listening to this opera and Kristos was holding a rose.

RARE CANCER SEEN IN 41 HOMOSEXUALS

THE NEW YORK TRUTH, JULY 3, 1981. PAGE A31
BY DEARIE FAULT, M.D.

Doctors in New York City have diagnosed among homosexual men 41 cases of a rare and often rapidly fatal form of cancer. Eight of the victims died less than 24 months after the diagnosis was made. The cause of the outbreak is unknown.

The announcement was made by Drs. Hoakus Benois-Frucht and Emma Brookner of New York's Table Medical Center. Dr. Benois-Frucht classified their findings as "utterly devastating." He said that these cases had all involved his homosexual patients who have had multiple and frequent sexual encounters with different partners, "as many as 10 sexual encounters each night up to four times a week."

Many of these patients have also been treated for viral infections such as herpes and hepatitis, as well as parasitic infections such as amoebiasis and giardiasis. Many also reported using drugs and "inhalants" such as Dridgies, manufactured by the Greeting-Dridge pharmaceutical giant, to heighten sexual pleasure.

Dr. Paulus Pewkin of the Federal Center of Disease said there was no apparent danger to non-homosexuals from contagion. "The best evidence against contagion is that no cases have been reported outside the male homosexual community or in women," Dr. Pewkin said.

Dr. Benois-Frucht said he had tested nine of the victims and found severe defects in their immunological systems. The patients had serious malfunctions of two types of cells called n-3c and 729.

He also emphasized, "It is impossible to tell yet whether the immunological defects are in fact the underlying problem, or whether something has developed secondarily to the infections, or from drug use, or from the inordinate amount of sexual activity. I believe we're only seeing the tip of the iceberg."

The Center of Disease officially reported the cases in their weekly publication, *The Journal of Death*.

SHIT!

That does it for Fred. He gets frightened. He gets frightened enough to stop being such a zombie. He instantly knew that Josie and Dom Dom were in these statistics. And who else that he knew? Well, he'd better start finding out a lot of things. Starting with how *The New York Truth*, the most important newspaper anywhere in the world, then, now, still, and continuing, and known by every gay person as exceedingly unfriendly to anything gay, had arrived at the "information" it was peddling in this article. Boo Boo Bronstein's father, for whom he'd written a screenplay (Fred had fallen a bit for Boo Boo, Fred being the first man who ever fucked him, or so Boo had said), called to tell him Boo had died. Now his friend and Village neighbor Bruce Niles has just called to tell him that his lover Craig died. Fred had had an affairlet with Craig, too; Fred ended it when Craig told Fred he loved him and wanted to get serious. Not long after, Craig and Bruce met and bonded. It had been going along quite nicely. Four friends in two weeks. What the fuck was happening? Who'd be next? Why and how did he assume somebody would be next? He just knew.

THE SCIENCE DEPARTMENT OF
THE NEW YORK TRUTH

Yes, on July 3, 1981, first word "officially" reaches The American People about what will, in a few years' time, become the plague of The Underlying Condition. The article is hidden on an inside page of *The New York Truth*. Something is killing gay men. The announcement, which originally appeared in the pages of COD's *Journal of Death* only a week before, is made by Dr. Hoakus Benois-Frucht of Table Medical Center, where he is chairperson of skin, and Dr. Emma Brookner, a hematologist there. Dr. Benois-Frucht is trying to beat to the punch Dr. Egypt Poo of Invincible Crewd-Harbinger, where *he* is chairperson of skin and with whom he's shared similar findings. Dr. Poo, who is indeed an Egyptian, would have made the announcement to *The Truth* first, because in fact he saw his First Case a day before Hokie saw *his* First Case, but for the unwritten and unspoken and never-violated rule at Invincible Crewd-Harbinger: "The Institution may be mentioned to the press, but not the Self." So Dr. Poo sees his First Case, knows he is seeing something special, knows he should report it, and senses that by not doing so he may be excluding himself from certain recognition, but with three kids at Dalton, a co-op almost on Gracie Square, and a wife with Grand Ambitions, the immediate present shuts him up.

Table, Jewish as against Invincible's gentile bent, has no such qualms. Jewish doctors love to see their names in the papers. Table specialists are on a first-name basis with Velma Dimley, Dr. Dearie Fault, Manny Shmutz, Rodney Pilts, and Ricky Twaddle, the science staff at *The Truth*, so of course Dr. Benois-Frucht answers Velma Dimley's call and Table takes this opening trick. Not that there is, or will be, another hospital or medical center in the entire country that would want it.

Velma Dimley, who today is doing the legwork for Dr. Dearie Fault, who as the only M.D. among them will get the byline, jots down Hokie's answers to her questions. She recognizes, for a change, the worth of what he tells her, as "hot stuff," if not as science, with which she has less familiarity, and bangs it into *Truth*ful shape. She runs her short article by her editor, Ricky Twaddle, a transplanted Englishperson still suffering from a childhood filled with unkind references to his lack of masculinity when in fact he was, and is, a heterosexual. Before turning it over to Dearie for the final polish that will give it his special authoritative voice, Ricky queries Velma on Hokie's warning: "We are seeing only the tip of the iceberg." "The tip of the iceberg," a favorite phrase, appears in nine out of ten of Velma's stories, about anything. She is invariably offended when questioned. "That is what he said and he's a doctor" is, as always, her defense. Ricky and all his staff have been at *The Truth* a long time: there is no higher place to go in writing about science than *The Truth*. Velma's article is approved by Ricky, as is Dearie's rewrite by Rodney, who as the longest-lived as well as suffering, is last in line in double-checking his associates. (Manny Shmutz is on vacation.) Rodney deletes the tip-of-the-iceberg stuff. Dearie restores it and initials his final approval and sends it off into the world.

As noted, these First Cases have already been officially reported in *The Journal of Death* (*JOD*). That is the law of the land. Provision 2B of the Heimat-Dingus Hate Protection Bill mandates (a favorite Washington verb) that deaths from Anything Unusual must be reported to the Department of Health and Disease (HAD), and to the Center of Disease (COD), which is in Natchez under the direction of Dr. Paulus Pewkin, and to the National Institute of Tumor Sciences (NITS), in Franeeda, now run by Dr. Stuartgene Dye. HAD, also in suburban Maryland, is now run, and very badly, by its new cabinet secretary, Hoidene Swilkers. While it is NITS that Congress, in 1912, chartered and charged "to look after the health of the American people," it is HAD that is America's overall umbrella agency for anything to do with— well, health and disease. If HAD is the top of the pyramid, then Hoidene, with her retinue of several hundred wigs, will be its tippy-top. COD's, and hence HAD's, *Journal of Death* is sent free of charge weekly to anyone who wants it, which at this time is some twenty-three thousand persons, who may or may not be doctors or connected to public health or medical or scientific reporters or just creeps who get off on reading about the ghoulish and macabre, with which its several poorly printed pages are routinely filled. It is seen by few and read by fewer, and Velma is to be congratulated for her eagle eye.

A few First Cases of whatever this might be had also cropped up inconveniently in San Francisco and Los Angeles; *The Truth* prefers New York locales so doesn't mention them. Five of them were indeed reported in *JOD* on June 5, 1981, and *JOD* will claim years later that *these* are the first reported cases of UC in America. But no one paid any attention to them because it takes *The Truth* to stir up the pot and Velma had ignored these "first" cases in *JOD*. Doctors on the West Coast, unlike Jews in the East, also prefer anonymity, even if it means breaking the law. To be mentioned in *The Journal of Death*, which is published in Milwaukee, is a surefire way for a West Coast doctor to lose half his practice. And *The Truth*, where a mention is worth at least a dozen new patients to a New York doctor, is little read in the West and thus a negligible commodity there. To be written up in Dr. Arden Morron's *New England Journal of Spots* (*NEJS*), which of course is published in Boston, is worth at the very least a couple of dozen new clients anywhere in the country. But *NEJS* will not write about this, whatever it is, for quite a while. *NEJS* and *JOD* do not suffer each other gladly, each aiming for the scoop. *JOD* broke this one, so *NEJS* will punish all by not writing more fully about this for another three and a half years. Also, Arden does not trust Hokie, who once, when they were students at a postgraduate seminar in Switzerland, made a rejected pass at him on the slopes, no easy trick, causing Arden to break his leg and limp badly for the rest of his life. Had Emma Brookner been the sole reporting doctor, *NEJS* might have picked up on this story right away. Arden relates to her, she being confined to a wheelchair.

A nervous man, with a twitch in his left eyebrow and a tremor in his right hand so pervasive that it is difficult for him either to type upon his computer or to see with clarity what he's written, *The Truth*'s Dr. Dearie Fault once worked for COD, an institution with fascinating if still murky early years that dribble back a long long time. Since the end of the nineteenth century intrepid heroes have manned its desks and laboratories, its microscopes, test tubes, and decompression chambers, and trod its bleak hallways. But over these many decades the once so highly flown banners of epidemiology have sagged and COD's weekly tally of America's Most Morbid is not much noticed except by Velma, and by Dr. Fault, whose heart, truth to tell, is still in Natchez, and who constantly chronicles his former employer's doings for *The Truth* as if it were the only government agency involved in saving The American People. COD can do no wrong in *The New York Truth* even when it does, which it will now commence to do with increasing fevered regularity. "As officially reported by the Federal Center of Disease in Natchez" appears in nine out of ten of Dearie's stories.

If Velma's heart is a wayward and unfocused one, Dearie is a fluffer of facts. It is always safer to be imprecise when dealing with disease for so many millions of readers lest they catch you out in some way, and there are always many who try. The unspecified number of early cases reported by *JOD* ("early reports have not been confirmed as of yet as to the exact number") and headlined as forty-one by Dearie's report in *The Truth* of Velma's revision, could not be said, as Dearie did say (or was it really Velma?), to be a true indication of what was out there. Hokie had said, "I'd estimate there are already thousands!" and Velma, accustomed to readjusting the hyperbole of ambitious doctors, had written "in the hundreds," and Rodney, whose eyesight is also dreadful, for some reason saw, or wrote, fifty-one, and Dearie reduced it to forty-one.

So *The Truth* headlined forty-one cases (it is now known that there were more than four thousand) and Ricky removed "presumably all" from Velma's "in presumably all gay men." ("Who told *anyone* that?" Hokie Benois-Frucht screamed into Velma's answering machine after this added bit of information appeared; he had said his cases shared a similar symptom profile with some of his gay patients.) And in later editions, where the cancer was actually introduced more fully, Rodney smoothed out Velma's "cancerous manifestations" into outright "cancer"—Hokie had identified it as a "skin cancer" (after all, he is a dermatologist)—and Velma had changed this to "body blemishes" and Dearie had whipped it into "cancerous-like skin growths" and Ricky had clarified this to "apparently malignant cancer-like bumps on the skin" and Velma made one last pitch for glory with "purple lesions embossed upon the flesh," which in fact did make it into print, though only in some editions. Further, according to Rodney, who, along with Ricky, is vitriolically homophobic, as is Dearie, although less vitriolically, this disease imparts— and he literally makes this symptom up—"a repellent odor to the victim's smegma." Smegma is an accumulation of excretions that gathers under the foreskins of the uncircumcised, and this is certainly the first time the word has come anywhere near to appearing in *The Truth*. Fortunately Adolph Arthur "Pish" Dunkelheim, who is son to Adolph Arthur "Push" and Clytemnestra Dunkelheim and grandson to Mesopotamia Starker Dunkelheim, daughter to the world-famous Conservative Jewish Rabbi Herkules Starker, who will shortly be heard from herself, and is currently being groomed to take over *The Truth* one day—Pish, that is—queries both the germaneness and validity of the smegma attribution, so that Ricky, who had sneaked it up to Pish in his usual ass-kissing way, smells a not-right-time to take a stand; otherwise this new disease might have been launched into the belief system of The American People as a cancer of the smegmatized and uncircumcised.

Rodney Pilts, in his own bylined report on WRAH, *The Truth*'s radio station, claims outright, along with Velma, no bones about it, that "this new cancer occurs only in homosexuals because of their sexual practices." Note that he does not make any distinction between homosexual acts and homosexual people, between which, as any expert on etymology or logic will tell you if he or she is unbiased, which he or she is usually not, there is a world of difference. Note too that already there's not a scintilla of "alleged" or "suspected," no linguistic softeners *just in case* this truth might not be so truthful.

This new Whatever-It-Is is thus set in concrete before it's even got a base to stand on. This baby has *happened*. It's launched. It's out there. So sayeth *The New York Truth*.

Well, it's always better to err on the side of bigotry and bias, lest *The Truth*'s legendary reputation for correctness be in jeopardy under its editor in chief, Jakie Flourtower, with his tendency to see a Communist plot for world domination under the ass of every East European diplomat as well as every New Yorker living on the Upper West Side (while he lasciviously eyes every full-bosomed woman not his wife in the same neighborhoods and naturally on the job). Jakie, feared by one and all who daily write *The Truth*, is ignorant, as most Jewish heterosexual men are, of smegma, but with it or without it, he's certainly happy with this article and its subtle subtexts. He hates pansies the most, and since he's the boss, the most effectively. If Dr. Dearie Fault and the gang had not included as much antihomosexual innuendo as they did, Jakie would have demanded a rewrite. *The Truth* is not a place where gay people remain employed.

So Ricky Twaddle, as supervising editor in charge of Science, by initialing Dearie's final initialed draft, launches into *The New York Truth* the first worldwide story about what, a few years hence, will be named The Underlying Condition. Faggots are dying from a fatal cancer. Hokie, a tasteful closeted fairy who collects good art and has never been to Fire Island, much less its Meat Rack, or attended anything remotely resembling an orgy, is immediately accused by GAAAH's (Gay Association of Academic Alliances of Homosexuals) spokespersons Cocker Rutt and Muxter Questlos along with Pubie Grotty of *The Village Vice* of being self-loathing, antisex, and puritanical about Dridgies. "Dridgies? I never talked to Velma about Dridgies! What in God's name are Dridgies?"

The Truth's subtext, of course, is that it's contagious. "Each of the victims who have died of this rare cancer has a long history of other venereal and sexually transmitted diseases," Rodney maintains (speaking from certain dungeon clubs along various stretches of waterfront where he vents his misogyny on petite women he ties up and harshly whips before fucking them in front of the crowd). Rodney should know a case of clap when he has one.

There's something else. The tone of *The Truth*'s prose is that of a man holding a stink bomb in one hand and with the other a clothespin on his nose. It conveys, and this will become a plague propelled less by text than subtext, "These filthy homosexuals do unpleasant things to each other and the worst is finally happening to them and we really don't like writing about any of this in a Family Newspaper."

So sayeth *The Truth*.

And while no one is saying outright, "And they're spreading it to Us!," from this moment on everyone across the globe, as fast as reading Dearie, Rodney, Ricky, dear Velma (who by the way lusts unrequitedly for Jakie Flourtower, for whom she's not nearly buxom enough), and Manny (when he comes back from vacationing in Thailand, for the prepubescent girls) allows that everyone under variously located full moons will think it, and will be thinking it, and won't stop thinking it.

So much for *The Truth*.

CLYTEMNESTRA DUNKELHEIM ERUPTS

This is our America! This is what my ancestors slaved for! This is what my beloved father, the great Rabbi Herkules Schwartzer Starker, prays and worships for! It is for this that my beloved husband, Adolf Arthur Dunkelheim, publishes each and every day our greatest newspaper in the entire world! So that homosexuals and their diseases can be paraded for all the world to see!

Already several dear friends have called to say, "Clytemnestra Dunkelheim, what is this in your newspaper today!" I am the proud daughter of Mesopotamia Schwartzer Starker, whose great-grandmother founded the Daughters of the Other Confederacy while still in high school to shame Jefferson Davis. That is my proud heritage!

How dare Dearie Fault, my lovely old friend, write such as this? Someone else must have done it and only used his name. I want all details of how such a story got into my paper! I want the name of every single person on my payroll who contributed to writing this disgusting filth about disgusting fairies and their disgusting habits on my pages of my greatest newspaper the whole wide world has ever seen!

•

Clytemnestra Dunkelheim is no passive anything-goes woman or just any majority stockholder or wife or mother or Jew or American. She will tell you, "I am *The Truth*," of course meaning, "I am the truth."

Yes, she is also the daughter of the famous Rabbi Herkules Schwartzer Starker, who is also an outspoken critic of homosexuality, "a repellant aberration that does not occur in Jewish people." He is so famous that some people think he isn't even Jewish. A Jew could never have such fame that gets him invited, president after president, to the White House. How many other Jews can make that statement?

Jakie Flourtower, who edits her paper, is a balm for Clyt (the nickname by which she's known) and her husband, Push (that's what Adolf Arthur is called), who runs their paper. Jakie can calm Clyt down. Since subscriptions are at an all-time high, she allows his ministrations. Flourtower is fat, obstreperous, ambitious, a swell dresser but still slovenly. He is a survivor of Wienerblut, a concentration camp on the Austrian-Swiss border much hushed up because of the widespread belief in its Swiss neutrality. Though so many German Jews, including the Dunkelheims, claimed Swiss origins for their imagined safety and, yes, the racial purity such a "heritage" imparts, *The Truth* and its owners are still perceived as putting out "a Jewish paper." You spend so many generations cleaning up your act only to fear someone will smear the same Scheisse all over you once more. For this reason, Rabbi Herkules Schwartzer Starker, Clyt's own father, is as well-kept a secret as such a great and famous rabbi can be kept. You will never find his name in the religious columns of *The Truth*.

It is interesting to search in all of this for any reality. This lot really does believe the world now thinks of them as, if not gentile, no longer Jews. A non-Jew called Dunkelheim. You want to yell at them, Get Real. But of course no one does. Clytemnestra and Flourtower are vicious payer-backers of all slights, imagined or otherwise.

Clytemnestra continues to go on. "I never want to see the word *homosexual* in my paper again! Perversions and perpetrators! I want them all expunged! All! We are not amused!"

A notice appears that afternoon on the bulletin board in the main newsroom of *The Truth*.

Attention all reporters. From this moment on there will be no further use of the word "homosexual" in Our Beloved Newspaper of Record without clearance from the undersigned.

—Flourtower, Editor in Chief

The immediate effect of this dictum is that there will be no further mention of or information about the fast-festering plague of what is not yet ready to be called The Underlying Condition in the world's most important newspaper until further notice. And when such information does appear, several years hence, it will be so stingy and mingy and cringy as to be hardly visible at all. When the truth doesn't want to be told, well, there's no one better than *The Truth* at not telling it.

Other newspapers across America, indeed all over the world, follow suit. What's good enough for *The Truth* is good enough not only for New York, not only for America, but for the whole wide stupid undereducated and fucking world.

Yes, *The Truth* so sayeth.

VITAL STATISTICS

February 1982. COD reports 252 cases, 99 dead. In March there will be 285, located in seven states.

•

Wrong.

COMMUNIQUE TO FRED

MICHELANGELO SIGNORILE

The UC plague arose within a period of time in which Jacob Flourtower had created such a chill throughout the newspaper around the issue of homosexuality that it had become institutionalized. Flourtower just had grade-A anti-gay, over-the-top homophobic sentiments. He came back from overseas sometime in the '60s and was suddenly running the Metro desk, and it was a new New York. He looked out and he saw homosexuals on the streets, holding hands. It scared the daylights out of him. He assigned one of the most homophobic stories *The New York Truth* had ever written, a story that ran on the front page in 1963. It was all about this rise of homosexuality in New York and its visibility on the streets. He headlined it "Growth of Overt Homosexuality in City Provokes Wide Concern." *On the front page.* That says it all, about Jakie, about *The Truth*, about what's going to happen to us. And then came the Stonewall riots, and the 1960s led into the 1970s. Yes, we were scaring him to death.

•

INT. DR. EMMA BROOKNER'S EXAMINING ROOM.
TABLE MEDICAL CENTER. DAY.

EMMA: Who are you?

FRED: I spoke to you after the article in *The Truth*.

EMMA: You're the writer fellow who's scared. I'm scared too. Take
    your clothes off.

I hear you've got a big mouth.

*She is in an electric wheelchair. She is a small and pretty woman of
thirty-four. She dresses beautifully, with long skirts that cover her legs.*

FRED: Is big mouth a symptom?

EMMA: No, a cure. Take your clothes off.

FRED: I only came to ask some questions.

EMMA: You're gay, aren't you?

FRED: Yes.

EMMA: Then take your clothes off.

(As he hesitates:)

Don't be nervous. I've seen more men than you have.

CUT TO:

*Fred stands naked before Emma. She is examining him. First with
stethoscope to his chest. Buzzy, her cute nurse assistant, is taking some
blood. When Emma isn't looking he winks at Fred.*

FRED: Hi, Buzzy. Didn't know you worked here.

EMMA: To answer your questions, I don't know. Not even any good
    clues yet. Whatever it is, it stinks, and it's scary as hell. Never
    seen or heard of anything like it. And I think we're only seeing
    the tip of the iceberg. And I'm afraid it's on the rampage.

FRED *(to Buzzy, who is still drawing blood)*: You opening a store?

(Buzzy finishes.)

EMMA *(listens to his back)*: It takes years to find out how to pre-
    vent and cure anything. Turn around. *(She lifts his testicles with a
    throat stick, taking him by surprise.)* Easy.

*She pats the examining table. He jumps up on it. She grabs his foot and
starts inspecting between his toes, carefully.*

EMMA: I'm afraid nobody important is going to give a damn. Right
    now it only seems to be happening to gay men. Who cares if a
    faggot dies? If we don't stop it early it will be too late. The cat will

be out of the bag. It may be out already. Does it occur to you to do anything about it? Personally? Buzzy says you're well known in the gay world and not afraid to say what you think. I can't find any gay leaders. I call gay organizations. No one ever calls me back.

FRED: None of them are any good.

EMMA: Have you had any of the symptoms?

FRED: Yes.

EMMA: Which ones?

FRED: Most of the shit *The Truth* said.

EMMA: Which ones!

FRED: Amoebas. Syphilis. Gonorrhea. Hepatitis . . . You don't know what it's been like since the sexual revolution. It's been crazy, gay or straight.

EMMA: What makes you think I don't know? Any fever? Night sweats. Diarrhea. White patches in your mouth. Loss of energy. Shortness of breath. Chronic cough. Weight loss.

FRED: Don't I wish. No. But they could happen with lots of things . . .

EMMA: And purple lesions. Sometimes. Open your mouth. *(Looks down there, in his ears, up his nose.)* It's a rare cancer. There's a strange reaction in the immune system. It's collapsed. Won't fight. Which is what it's supposed to do. So most of the diseases my guys are coming down with—and there are some very strange ones—are caused by germs that wouldn't hurt a baby, not a baby in New York City anyway. And the immune system is the system we know least about. So where is this big mouth I hear you've got?

FRED: Dr. Brookner, no one with half a brain gets involved with gay politics. Anyway, what I think is politically incorrect.

EMMA: Why?

FRED: Gay is good to that crowd, no matter what. There's no room for criticism, for looking at ourselves critically.

EMMA: What's your criticism?

FRED: I hate how we play victim when many of us, most of us don't have to.

EMMA: Then you're exactly what's needed now.

FRED: I tell you, nobody will listen! This group does not know how to play follow the leader!

EMMA: Maybe they're just waiting for somebody to lead them.

FRED: I don't want to lead them! Wouldn't it be better coming from you?

EMMA: Doctors are unfortunately conservative. When you make too much noise you get treated like a nutcase just when you're needed most. Don't you know that yet?

FRED: Needed? Needed for what? What exactly are you trying to get me to do?

EMMA: Tell gay men to stop having sex.

FRED: What?

EMMA: Someone has to. Why not you? It only sounds harsh now. Wait a few more years, it won't sound so harsh.

FRED: Do you realize that you are talking about millions of men who have singled out promiscuity as their principal political agenda, the one they'd die before abandoning? How do you deal with that?

EMMA: Tell them they may die. Are you saying you can't relate in a nonsexual way?

FRED: It's more complicated! They think sex is all we have. We're not exactly allowed to live out in the open like human beings. You want me to tell every gay man in New York to stop having sex?

EMMA: Who said anything about just New York?

FRED: You want me to tell every gay man in America . . .

EMMA: In the entire world! That's the only way this disease will stop spreading.

FRED: Dr. Brookner, isn't that just a tiny bit unrealistic?

EMMA: Mr. Lemish, if having sex can kill you, doesn't anyone with half a brain stop fucking? But perhaps you've never lost anything. You can get dressed. I can't find what I'm looking for. Goodbye.

FRED: Is it contagious?

EMMA: I think so.

FRED: Then how come you haven't come down with it?

EMMA: Because it seems to have a very long incubation period and require close intimacy.

FRED: It's like some sort of plague.

EMMA: There's always a plague. Of one kind or another. I've had mine since I was a kid.

THE MAYOR OF NEW YORK CITY
IS A CLOSETED GAY

FRED AND HERMIA TELL US HOW NEW YORK CITY
GOT ITS USELESS HEALTH COMMISSIONER

"I don't want to know about it" will be Kermit Goins's favorite expression. He's the mayor of New York City and has been since I moved here. He's not making any statement on behalf of gays, or what is happening to us, and apparently, he isn't going to. I've tried to contact him a number of times, telling his secretary I'm the "award-winning filmmaker," and drop in names like Sammy Sircus and Randy Dildough as if they were my buddies, just like Moses Rattner taught me to be pushy. No dice. That pisses me off. I've supervised movies that have cost millions of dollars and I'm not used to not being able to get big-deals on the phone.

I know Kermit Goins is gay. I know members of his staff. I'd been to bed with one of them who had dinner with him every week. I don't like getting treated like shit.

I was losing a friend or two each week and hearing about a couple others. A guy named Leo, from Montreal, just called me from there to tell me about the time we made love under the stars at Fire Island and he loved me then and loves me now but it was too late. He was rattling out his words with increasing incomprehensibility when the phone dropped and was picked up by his father, who said I was the only man his son had ever loved and what was this he just died from that turned him all purple blotches.

It's scary. It's increasingly scary. I'm scared. No mayor, no president, no *New York Truth*, no gay leaders, no anything. Except dying friends.

I realize Kermit Goins is the reason this shit is becoming so bad in New York City. Did he call and ask the president or anyone else for help? Did he put out a health warning to all his constituents? I've never hated anyone but I now begin to hate him big-time. Dr. Herta Glanz told me every time he tries to talk to the mayor he says, "I don't want to know about it!"

Kermit Goins has appointed Dr. Herta Glanz to be this city's health commissioner. Why did Kermit Goins do this? Dr. Herta Glanz is a medical idiot.

DAME LADY HERMIA RESPONDS

My dear Freddy Fredchen, New York City's health commissioner, Dr. Herta Glanz, will hear these words of denial many times from his boss. Dr. Herta Glanz himself will eventually go on record that your mayor is "a beast of self-ishness and there is little I am able to do about it. When he sees me coming he heads the other way. Mr. Orvid Guptl writes in his newspaper *The New York Prick* that I don't know how to fight back, and that I am a born victim. I have been in the Public Health Service a long time and that charge comes with the territory. People get sick and die. I am not God. I cannot save them by myself."

In his years in public health, Dr. Herta Glanz has failed upward, each step taking him one step further into hell. His career is part of this chapter about your mayor in my history of evil. Backstories are so important. In fact all history is backstory of one thing or another.

Dr. Herta Glanz (the name, both first and last, is Obsidian, as in some Baltic island I cannot locate, and his medical degree is from some university there) first encountered COD recognition and promotion as a young man (you say he now looks one hundred and is counting the days until his retire-ment and pension), when a contagious and often fatal illness then known as "the nigger problem" was dumped in his ambitious lap. Negroes, "well, there are simply too many of them and the best way to get rid of anything you've got too much of is to kill 'em off, and since this here is a country that has laws against doing acts like this too openly blatant we just try to figure out a way to do it less so." The speaker was a Southerner who was Franklin Roosevelt's health commissioner for the underprivileged. It should be inconceivable to us today that such a high government official (his name was Dr. Elphonse J. Richardson II: Roosevelt had a way of slotting into his government men he thought to be of "his own kind," as not a few of his biographers concede) could speak this way but that is the way things were. It should also be incon-ceivable that scientific experiments were undertaken by the United States government utilizing an entire unknowing population that was—*for the next forty years*—systematically allowed to suffer and die from syphilis without any treatment at all. That was the study Dr. Elphonse J. Richardson II was talking about. Its code name was "Fetchit."

How many of the chief perpetrators of this mini-mass-murder-cum-tragedy-cum-farce can be identified now? Troublesome names and records always, *always*, conveniently disappear. All that's left is a bunch of old lackeys who ran things, many, sadly, black themselves, too accustomed to the weekly bribes their salaries amounted to, which had caused them to turn on their own and keep them quiet over all these years. But at some point in the latter years of this "study" (1968 or so), Dr. Herta Glanz managed to eliminate from all files all references to himself as a vital participant.

But Fetchit was not to be the only scandal in his career. No sooner had Fetchit sunk in the south than the SLAKE flu suddenly presented itself as a "National Disaster" farther north.

I cannot tell you how long it has taken me to unravel all these tributaries, to sort out the relevant paperwork, its trails, its false trails, all its roads to nowhere. The imagination involved in getting this following story "lost" is most impressive. I have yet been unable to locate who was calling the shots.

Epidemiologists on the staff of COD under the supervision of Dr. Herta Glanz come forth with the information that all the flu that is suddenly occurring at Washington's Mea Montezuma Hospital portends awful things, indeed a possible plague. "These are among the worst sets of sputum slides I have ever seen," said Dr. Trace Understeer of the National Society of Sinus Specialists to *The New England Journal* of same. Dr. Understeer named the flu strain SLAKE. No one now has any notion why, or why he put it in all caps. He is not heard from again. But enough is out there publicly for Senator Paul "Porky" Pollen of Mississippi to send out emergency reports underlining Dr. Herta Glanz's warning. There are more citizens from Mississippi in Mea Montezuma than from any other state, and while Mea Montezuma was a wretched hospital for patients and doctors alike, as we all know it remains, it was better by far than anything in Mississippi. Sick people actually migrated like the sharecroppers and underground railroaders of old to Washington, figuring that Uncle Sam as a last resort would help with whatever it was that was making them feel so awful. Suddenly all of Washington was in an uproar over these sputum studies, which were on everybody's desks, and everybody was petrified that in no time flat whatever was in that sputum was going to get into the system of The American People. Senator Paul "Porky" Pollen orchestrated all this with his well-known bureaucratic sleight of hand. Mississippi's budget left him no other choice: the feds demanded each state pay for its own illnesses, and to pay for this spreading SLAKE Porky would have to stop building all those casinos on the Gulf.

Senator Paul "Porky" Pollen knew what to do when government interference from HAD and NITS said to him, "Aren't you overreacting?" Locate an expert. Calling Dr. Glanz. As fate would have it, he's free. Fate has made him available. Can we swiftly arrange his transfer onto this problem full-time? Call Dr. Nostrill at HAD. Dr. Ekbert Nostrill, newly under the tight reins of Manny Moose and his draconian budgets (all those dire Perdist Poll predictions must be rigidly righted), prohibits spending any money on anything, and this SLAKE could be expensive. Chevvy Slyme, Ruester's assistant, doesn't allow expensive anything. Nostrill issues a directive ordering Glanz to "somehow" get rid of this SLAKE. Senator Paul "Porky" Pollen scores again. Both he and Nostrill are Brothers of Lovejoy.

COD's Dr. Pewkin is now warning Glanz that if he didn't get to work posthaste to keep The American People from dying he'd never keep this reassignment, "which is so vital to COD's historic reputation as *the* disease warriors of the free world."

Manny Moose decided to make use of all this growing grumbling and spend a few bucks to build his new president into *the* champion of public health. "It will be well spent," he told his ol' (read "new") "Jew buddy" Jakie Flourtower, who then wrote the now infamous *New York Truth* editorial "We Are 100% Behind President Ruester on SLAKE. Thank you and God bless you, Mr. President."

Word of course was out in Spanish that there was free medical care courtesy of Uncle Sam, and Mea Montezuma was now overloaded with various hideous immigrant ailments from "all those spics using that shithole as a free hotel." (This was a Senator Vurd.) Evidently medical centers around the country, because they received only $0.97 per patient per day supplemental governmental funding (as against $4.10 in D.C.) under the McCarren-Frail Act of 1947 (rev. 1967), would be forced to fork out their own money for their own "spic welfare," should all this SLAKE take firm hold anywhere out of the District of Columbia, which was what "all the experts" were beginning to fear. Their response is the shipping out to D.C. of everyone sick on welfare. I hope you're beginning to see how complicated your "public health" can be.

How to get Glanz going? Doing what? Puff and Porky knew Dr. Glanz could not stand up to the barrage of high-powered phone calls that Puff and Porky "request" top board members and rich powerful patients made on the behalf of SLAKE flu and the Ultimate Danger (read "Death") it presented to The American People. When one of these calls came from Dr. Stuart-gene Dye himself, Dr. Glanz immediately knew that he was cornered before he began. Great Humanitarian World Doctor descriptions of him were not presently in the cards. He must get his own plan going. After some forty years in the Public Health Service, he knew: always be ready with a plan.

What was the poor man thinking? He was probably already on his way to losing his marbles. The trouble with marble losing is that it's hard to notice in doctors. They're usually so quiet.

So Dr. Herta Glanz invented the SLAKE Flu Serial Shots. The entire country would be inoculated with .47 cc of inert *Vertibronsky focum* (IVF), manufactured by Greeting-Dridge's German Bohunk Vernissage. Harmless stuff, and actually used in place of cod liver oil among the Eskimo children, or so it is stated in a study in *The New England Journal of Eskimos*, your useful yardstick of northern North American health. President Ruester now ordered SLAKE flu serials for all The American People. So SLAKE flu serials all The American People would have. No one had told your citizenry this could cost $4.5 billion. There is no record of Stockman's response.

A Bohunk factory in Meddling, Mississippi (where else?), was turned over to emergency manufacture of inert focum (G-D had the patent on ert focum, so it wasn't hard to reverse all the machinery to make ert inert) and in no time at all every doctor's office and every pharmacy in the entire country was swimming in SLAKE flu serials. People lined up everywhere for the shots: free in clinics and emergency rooms, five dollars a set everywhere else. Tens of thousands were quickly inoculated.

Then a few people suddenly die. Five hundred and twenty-four (it is reported in *The Truth*), and they apparently die without reason except they've all been injected with SLAKE. Several thousand more become dizzy or show minor symptoms of discomfort. Seventy-seven suddenly can't use their left arms, for anything. (Shades of whatever happened to Dr. Sister Grace?) These left arms (interesting it is never right arms) suddenly just hang there, swinging in the breeze. And one hundred and ten men become impotent, or claim they do. No one knows how to dispute them. But the number is not "statistically significant" enough to make courts of law believe them, as six of them discover when they unsuccessfully try to sue Uncle Sam. When a few hundred more people die, Ekbert Nostrill, now in full charge at HAD, calls the whole show off. "Did you have to do it so soon?" Manny Moose yells over his secret Code Red phone. (Records still exist of all Code Red calls.) He'd loved his notion of making Ruester a health hero. Ekbert doesn't hear him because he's so terrified when the Code Red phone rings that he immediately evacuates his entire building, including himself. (*The Washington Monument* has a lovely wide picture spread of all HAD's employees out in the street.)

The total damages the government is forced to pay out to the dead and the dizzy and the swinging-limbed amount to $184.9 million (not counting the amount to G-D for its manufacture), and Dr. Herta Glanz is up for reassignment in the Public Health Service. (Public health officers can't be fired.) He becomes known as "the doctor who created the epidemic that never was."

This flu strain of course by now had passed into oblivion as most flu strains are wont to do.

But no good deed goes unrewarded, as we know. For reasons unfathomable to anyone with any functioning thinking mechanism, Dr. Herta Glanz, by now considered a true medical moron, is hired in 1981 as health commissioner of New York City by your mayor, Kermit Goins.

There. Phew.

It scares me, too. And I worry about you muchly. Please take care. As we Brits say: Good luck and God bless. Glad to have you back on our case.

THANKS, HERMIA. HERE'S SOME MORE.

There are a lot of reasons why I think Kermit the shithead kept his mouth shut. He had to protect the tourist industry. No one would come here if they thought the city was sick. He was also in hock to the real estate powers that put him in office. Real estate powers don't like faggots. We've gobbled up too many of the city's rent-controlled apartments. So he had a city to safeguard, which could only be done by someone lying. He already smelled "this shit" about to burst into full and stinking and puking bloom, and so he needed somebody to be the fall guy to take the blame. SLAKE flu was an epidemic that never was, and the plague of "this shit" looked sure as shooting on its way to mowing us down one by one. Get the biggest schmuck in the field of public health and see if he can fuck this one up too, and Kermit can blame the feds and their stinking Public Health Service.

I think Kermit Goins appointed Herta because Kermit Goins is a closeted gay man and he knew this shit was hitting gay men and he was scared shitless that

(1) he would catch it; and/or

(2) it would force him out of the closet; and/or

(3) he needed a fall guy to make a truly great fuckup of everything so Kermit could look blameless for not doing anything (and he planned on not doing anything; how could he, it would nail him as gay for sure if he did anything); and/or

(4) he needed a dumb asshole who could see to it that his former boyfriend, a twerp named Nathan Perch, who has come down with something strange,

would die from it in Crewd-Harbinger before he could announce to the world that he had been Kermit's sweetie, which Nathan Perch was coming close to announcing to the world because of one Fred Lemish, who was looking for someone to announce publicly that Mayor Kermit Goins is a closeted gay and helping to murder his gay brothers.

All of the above, which of course are all the same thing.

Kermit Goins is more frightened of being identified as gay than he is of what is still called "this shit." Kermit Goins is the really sick man here. And if UC continues to grow, sicko Mayor Kermit Goins will be looking even sicker.

•

I sure hope so.

MORE OF JOE KIDNEY'S VERY BAD DREAM

Finally, someone was located to become President Ruester's secretary of Health and Disease (HAD). Arrived in Washington was one Hoidene Swilkers, along with her husband, Roddy, both from Pulce, Nebraska. In return for a $57,000 contribution to President Ruester's campaign fund, Hoidene has been appointed secretary of HAD. Roddy brokers wheat, flour, and pigs. Hoidene has never been to Washington, never worked in medicine, public health, government, or a bureaucracy, indeed has never held a job or employed more than household staff of half a dozen. When her predecessor at HAD, who spent four years trying desperately to do good deeds, and who knows a good deed, meets and talks with this person who will replace him in charge of America's health, he actually throws a book at her, the *Federal Register of Offices and Their Holders*. Hoidene had stopped by for "a peek-a-boo howdy."

"I could not believe anyone in their right mind would put her in charge of the health of The American People," he is to write in his memoirs, which of course he will be unable to get published.

Candidates for President Ruester's cabinet have been hard for Manny Moose to find. Peter has not come to Washington welcomed by that class of public servants usually available to work for the good of their country. Hoidene Swilkers will be the first of Ruester's four secretaries of HAD. Unfortunately, she will be the best.

To be in the kitchen with Roddy when he had his hands up Hoidene's maid Pansi's skirt as he was describing to me the auction when he bought his latest prize set of matched Salinas sows threw me for a loop. No one would believe any of this, I said to myself. They'd think I made it up.

FRED GETS CREAMED FOR WRITING THIS IN *THE NEW YORK PRICK*

The men who have been stricken don't appear to have done anything that many New York gay men haven't done at one time or another. We're appalled that this is happening to them and terrified that it could happen to us. It's easy to become frightened that one of the many things we've done or taken over the past years may be all that it takes for a tiny something or other to get into us who knows when from doing who knows what. In the past we have been a divided and invisible community. I hope we can all get together on this emergency, undivided, and with all the strength our numbers in so many ways possess. We must take care of each other and ourselves.

DR. DANIEL JERUSALEM VISITS DR. HOAKUS BENOIS-FRUCHT

Dr. Daniel Jerusalem. It is a mighty-sounding name, isn't it? It sounds like it should summon its bearer to perform courageous feats. My internship and residency in infectious diseases was done at the renowned Rubinsky (now Table) Medical Center in New York. Washington never having been any good for either the study or the successful treatment of infectious anything, I thought it would be the place where I could be most useful. At the commencement of this mess, I am almost fifty years old. Half a century of faithful service. To what? In all efforts to become the hero of my life I have so far failed. (I am sounding like Philip and I must stop it!) I did well at Rubinsky. I believe I am a good doctor. I am also an intelligent man who is not blind.

If something fatal is being spread sexually there will be no way to stop it short of universal chastity or an immediate cure. I am sufficiently familiar with the world of medical research to know that the latter is unlikely, and with human nature to know that the former is impossible. That seems obvious to me, and I assume that others smell millions of dead bodies too. How can there not be others blessed with this modicum of insight?

I make an appointment to come to New York to see Dr. Hoakus Benois-Frucht, one of my faculty supervisors when I was at Table, nee Rubinsky. (The Table Brothers paid Dean Grafft $10 million to break the ancient Rubinsky will.) Hokie had seen the first cases. What could he tell me?

To walk into Table Medical Center is to walk into what is perhaps one of the best medical centers in the world. Every white-coated body you pass in a corridor is without doubt an expert in his or her field. Patients pour in from everywhere for treatment. There is certainly nothing near to touching Table in Washington, certainly not at NITS, where the fact that doctors work for the government and are civil servants seems in the end to defeat its own purpose. Yes, I come back here and walk Table's halls with awe. It's not that I'm filled with pride in being a graduate; it's more like I'm aware that since leaving here I've let them down. If you haven't succeeded in the outside world, a walk down these halls seems to be saying, it's your own fucking fault. We gave you everything we knew.

Over the years, Dr. Benois-Frucht has made the Skin Department one of the world's best. Skin is often a medical center's stepchild: everyone has it, but nobody pays it much attention beyond the cosmetic, which makes it slightly disdained. But since there are more vain people than sick ones, Skin is also a medical center's most profitable division, particularly since dermatologists have learned to charge many times more than what other "specialists" get away with for the same few minutes. He is a prissy man, Benois-Frucht, and a proud one: his name, he says, is a compound of two ancient families, one Dutch, one French, both American from an early date. He's a chatty man. His eyes light up when he hears or relays any gossip. I like him because of his idiosyncrasies as well as his brain. Everyone in Washington seems boring compared with a Benois-Frucht.

"Precisely why I left there!" he exclaims when I tell him I'm bored in D.C. "I had a fellowship at NITS during the early Gist years. Talk about a silly, useless old queen!"

He is responsible for developing the Benois-Frucht Test for the analysis of urine in Third World countries. His test has allowed, for the first time, verification of the fact that Third World diets are remarkably deficient in certain vitamins. It will eventually prove a cheap means of testing for UC there, too, perhaps the only cheap thing that will appear on the benighted landscape of this oncoming plague. While it will become more than obvious to the naked eye who's sick from this shit and who isn't, it is unfortunately the requirement of scientific research to require verification. You cannot just call a red dress red. You must prove that the red is not maroon, whatever maroon is, or lavender or pink or vermilion or fire engine, which is not so easy, or so useful, as most scientists and researchers insist upon insisting. All of Hokie's famous research (he will become an important investigator of nimroid, discovering it has a life of its own) has always been funded, to the tune of many millions, by the Sherman Stumpf Foundation. Shermie Stumpf is an old boyfriend of Hokie's. They had crushes on each other as rich kids in New York. Both men, in their late sixties, are in the closet. Shermie once propositioned me at a bar, and Hokie gave me an A in skin when I allowed him a blow job, both these interactions occurring during my first year as a Rubinsky intern. I needed that A desperately to keep up my average and maintain my scholarship. He has a nice smile, Hokie does, so the deed wasn't as arduous as the motivation was tacky. It just happened, in his office, while we were going over my final paper, and he had his hand on my knee, and it sort of felt nice, and—well, when he finished he just wrote a nice big A on my paper. I have no idea what came over me. But to this day Hokie looks me in the eye and maintains he's straight. I will never understand how a man so many people know is gay the minute he opens his mouth can maintain in all seriousness the fiction that he's a heterosexual.

Hokie orders me to take my clothes off. "You're here, so let me look at you. I'm the expert on this stuff, remember. You are sexually active, even in the District? I had no sex life when I was at NITS. Sexless place. Hateful. We must talk about it. I hear Gist is on his way out finally."

He is paying particular attention to my testicles. "A lot of fibrous tissue here."

"Is that bad?"

"I don't know."

"Isn't it the way I always was?"

"How would I know?"

"You sucked my cock."

"I most certainly did not. And that in no way would have given me an opportunity to examine your testicles professionally."

"Oh, Hokie."

Still holding on to my balls, he looks at me. "A lot of your friends are going to die. Thousands. Tens of thousands. Perhaps millions. Perhaps tens of millions. Perhaps hundreds of millions. Perhaps a billion. Anyway, a lot. Not that even one or two wouldn't be too many. But you get my drift. You certainly do have very large balls. I've never been certain what large balls means. It must mean something. George Washington had very large balls. Did you know that? Look at all those famous paintings of him in his tight britches. What a basket! Perhaps it's a genetic sign of leadership. Do you believe in signs? Go out and tell them to stop fucking. Then they won't spread this. My, how low your scrotum hangs. You must sit down more often. Unless, of course, you want a long scrotum. Some people do. I find it unappetizing. A lot of death down the road. Tip of the iceberg. Lots of men are going to jump off the cliff, to use Dr. Brookner's quaint expression. Young men. They won't get sick if they stop fucking. A lot of fibrous tissue around your balls."

He gives my testicles a final rub-together with his thumb and fingers, like some Indian fakir with his metal marbles. Then he pats them paternally and lets them go. "Keep your eyes open."

"For what?"

"I don't know yet."

"What's going on?"

"If I knew, I could get the Herkimer. There's a Herkimer Prize in all this. I want one. Don't know how to get it. Virus probably. It's always a virus probably. Easiest convincing answer is always a virus probably. I'm not a virus man. I'm a skin man. Surface. On the nose, not in it. There goes my Herkimer. No skin man ever won a Herkimer. That's why we don't feel guilty charging so much. Pity. I saw the damn thing first. That Nazi Greptz is going to say he saw it first. Mark my words. But he didn't. I did. Greptz is an infectious-disease expert. A Herkimer's possible for an infectious-disease man. No, I don't know what's going on. *The Truth* said I said it's spread by sex. That isn't exactly what I told that Dimley woman, but it is. Spread by common, dirty, little old sex. Weenies up the asshole. Tongues up the asshole. Fists up the asshole. Your boys have gone too far. Tell them all to stop. Nothing to do but stop. You're still in good shape." He takes some skin cream and starts massaging it into my testicles. "For the fibrous tissue. Deep penetrating action. Soothing."

"Hokie!"

"Made from the same ingredients as Helena Rubinstein. Would you believe it? Smart woman, Helena Rubinstein. Started out in Australia. Old family recipe. Why don't you go on and get an erection? It's all right with Hokie. You have a nice cock. You have no idea how many not-nice cocks I look at every day. People simply do not take good care of their skin. Past a certain age the skin requires constant care. It dries out. It sags. It becomes quite unpleasant to the touch. You're becoming an old man. You can't even get an erection. Oh, get dressed. It probably wasn't such a good idea. It isn't that I want to masturbate you. That would be an unprofessional act. I want a sample of your semen. Something going wrong in the semen is my current considered professional opinion. If there is something untoward in the semen, then when this semen is inserted in bodily cavities—rectum or mouth—horrid things will happen. You have no idea what I'm seeing in mouths. And up assholes. That's usually not my territory, belongs to Howie Horewits in Gastro-Ent. But now I'm called in to consult. Hideous. Purple scabs. Scabrous purple sores. Monstrous skin eruptions. Wretched. Putrid. Runny. And *smelly*. Looks like a vel reaction. Vel's not my territory either. Belongs to Grace Hooker. You remember Grace Hooker? Used to lecture here. Used to be a nun. Probably still is. One leg. Or is it arm? There's something in saliva, too, I'll bet my Herkimer. The sores are less runny if they're in the mouth. Interesting. Spit and shit. Spit belongs to . . . I don't think anyone's cornered spit yet. But they will. Probably a Herkimer in spit. I could be wrong about spit. Spit might be a red herring. The race is always to the swiftest. They're going to come out of the woodwork. It's got nothing to do with intelligence. Just luck. There's an old Dutch saying: He who is lucky is unlucky. Do you think you could go into the little boys' room and jerk off into a cup? Think dirty thoughts. Pretend I'm massaging your cock with the deep penetrating action of Helena Rubinstein. Pretend you're a policeman and I'm a bad young truant. Isn't life sad? No, I didn't tell *The Truth* it's only caused by sex. What serious scientist would say anything as specific as that on Day One? That Velma Dimley is a stupid woman. As dumb as that stupid Arden Morron, who runs *Spots*. We'll pay a price for their stupidity. Mark my words. On this I bet a Herkimer. Velma Dimley is a stupid cunt."

I dress, walk down the hallway, go into the little boys' room, enter a stall, and do as Hokie asks. Why? Because he may not sound like it but he's very smart. He has fourteen Mendlestick Prizes, which is some kind of record, certainly for anyone in Skin. He has a Forwards. He has a Needler. Yes, every time he opens his mouth something unexpected comes out. The papers he writes for the journals are always of astounding perception and brilliance. The trudgeon. Hokie discovered it. You can't be in practice today without utilizing a trudgeon to test for skin cancer. Foresnaps. Same thing. Retina globular ointment tinctured with okly *does* cure warts. Skin dermal abrasions *can* be caused by hyperdrangia. So I jerk off into his cup and return to present it to his nurse. Maybe my gism will help. Every interaction with Hokie is always a mass of contradictions.

I'd like to interject a theory I will see played out over the coming years. My theory involves what the Greeks called "the tragic flaw." Everyone who could have been important, who should have been able to contribute something major to stop this epidemic from becoming a plague, was prevented from being important because of some personal trait that had nothing to do with medicine or science. Hokie sounds silly. Even with all his prizes, even now, when he's been proved right so many times, no one listens to Dr. Hoakus Benois-Frucht. He is the first person to see what's happening and nobody listens to him because he often comes across as a silly, flighty man and that is that.

And now that I have the advantage of hindsight, and am able to piece together many disparate strands, I can see my own tragic flaw, my inability to act in the face of mounting evidence, or in the case of my own brother, guilt.

"Go back to Washington. My regards to the First Lady. I once removed a fenal wart from her . . . never mind. Oh, what do I care? I'm not going to win a Herkimer. From the tip of her tongue. Most unusual wart. You don't usually find fenal warts on tongues. Too much moisture inside a mouth. She must have been doing something major with that licker to dry it out so. When you're in town again come to dinner. I have nice balls too. I'll show them to you. We can play with each other's balls. Balls are safe. As long as you don't draw blood. Try not to draw blood. Blood is where the trouble is. Come to think of it, while you're here, let me draw some blood."

And so my blood was drawn too. Which is why I know now that in 1981 my semen was rein-free and my blood was low in blodes. Most peculiar. But I had normal vel. All this knowledge today tells us a lot. It explains why I'm still alive. It still doesn't tell us how. Hokie says one of these days it will.

"Tell you something else I'm thinking," he says to me as I'm leaving. "Something funny going on here. Nothing going on now hasn't been going on since time began. Up the ass, down the throat, we've all been there before, without chagrin. Something too neat and tidy going on. Got to be a virus. Got to be. Only thing is, no virus knows how to be so picky and choosy. No, sir. No virus is that smart. Why, it's acting just like some bigoted human being knowing exactly who he's going to hate."

When I return to Washington my scrotum still feels warm. It feels warm for several days and nights, as if Hokie's massage had irradiated it with the chemotherapy of Mission. Everyone I know has had every possible transmissible venereal disease for the past decade, at least. Everyone I know, including myself, has fucked and been fucked and interacted in every conceivable anatomical position from blowing in ears to sucking toes—for at least a full ten of these drug and disco years, and for many much longer. If anything is going to spread itself around, it's got many a welcoming host. If it's not already being passed around. *Sexopolis* couldn't have got the message around any faster.

As if to bear me out I discover upon my return that three more of my patients have died from what the attendings at Isidore Peace classify as Unknown Causes. This is happening too quickly.

Hokie's right. Why now?

I call a number of my fellow gay doctors. In each instance I'm told that I'm an alarmist and that a few cases do not an epidemic make. My protestations of "But indeed they do! And are!" elicit responses along the lines of "You're such a worrier. It will go away. Be patient. Gist even said so in his text about it. 'This too will pass.'" It reminds me of when I was a little boy and knew I was seeing things that nobody else did. While I waited for Uncle Hyman to canvass his route I met a crazy gypsy fortune-teller in her tacky storefront on Ninth Street. I'd given her some of my candy to hear her prediction that I would have "a long and eventful life, but those around you will be sad." I nodded, fully comprehending life's sadness even then.

One of these days I must get back in touch with Fred. I've read how hard he's fighting.

•

INT. CITY HALL. DAY.
A rotunda reception area. Various bureaucrats are milling around. A banner reading: DEPARTMENT OF CULTURAL AFFAIRS. A big cake iced GOOD LUCK HENRY. Henry and Fred talking at the side.
FRED: So I just go over and say hello. Henry, he doesn't know I hate him?
HENRY: I told him I invited you, that we went to Yaddah together.
    This is my farewell party. What's he going to do? Let's go.
They start walking to the group surrounding the mayor, Kermit Goins. Bodyguards move in closer to the mayor.
GUARD *(to Henry)*: His Honor would like your friend to disappear.
FRED *(jumps into action quickly, pushing toward Goins)*: Mr. Mayor,

you've got to help us. There's this new disease. You must know about it! We need help. Bad . . . Badly . . . Bad . . .

The whole thing quickly becomes a mess. The closer Fred gets to Goins, the harsher the guards' treatment of Fred is. Three guards corner him, twist his arm behind him, and start pushing him quickly away.

FRED *(contd)*: We're dying! What are you doing! Stop it, you pigs! This is America! Help! Henry, help!

Fred is quickly silenced and out of sight.

The music is upped in volume.

HENRY *(to Goins)*: Shit, Kermit. You didn't have to do that.

MAYOR: Henry, I told you a dozen times. Don't mix politics and friends.

Fred, leaving, is stopped by a tired-looking older man, Dr. Glanz.

DR. GLANZ: Mr. Weeks, I think you must have the general idea by now. I would leave but for my pension.

And he walks away. He is a beaten man. Fred watches him.

FRED WASN'T EXPECTING THIS

That little warning letter I wrote in *The Prick*, that I thought of as a heads-up kind of thing? Seventeen columns of hateful invective were the response. Orvid said they'd never received so much hate mail. The featured letter was from a guy who had come to interview me, followed by a fuck, decent enough, not special enough to want to do it with him again, but he wanted to, and when I wouldn't (why are you even fucking at all, Fred! after your warning to all the others! You think you're immune or something?), this is what he wrote:

I think the concealed meaning in Lemish's emotionalism is the triumph of guilt: that gay men *deserve* to die for their promiscuity. In that novel he wrote he told us that sex is dirty and that we ought not to be doing what we're doing. Now, with this stuff attacking gay men, he assumes he knows the cause. His *real* emotion is a sense of having been vindicated, though tragically: he told us so, but we didn't listen to him; nooo—we had to learn the hard way, and now we're dying.

Read anything by him closely. I think you'll find that the subtext is always: the wages of gay sin are death. I ask you to look closely because I think it's important for gay people to know whether or not they agree with him. I am not downplaying the seriousness of the current illness. But something else is happening here, which is also serious: internalized homophobia and anti-eroticism.

Among other correspondents also throwing major shit in my face were Pubie Grotty, Cocker Rutt, Muxter Questlos, and now Jervis Pail. By now they'd all gone on record with how much they hated me because my novel about our lives said stuff they didn't think should be said. "He's giving away all our secrets," Pubie wrote in the *Vice*. Jervis also diagnosed me as "suffering from a major rampant case of galloping internalized homophobia." That means they think that I hate myself for being gay. How do you fight back against this one? Cocker Rutt was a "scholar" over in New Jersey teaching about "genders" and Jervis was "our leading writer," according to Pubie, who was "our leading journalist" at *The Village Vice*. Muxter had been a "Distinguished Scholar in Literature" at Yaddah, I'm sorry to say. I hadn't yet had the pleasure of meeting any of them. We'd never moved in the same circles. I hadn't worried about encountering circles.

The four of them co-signed this letter: "Who is this strange moron appearing out of the depths of nowhere to tell us how to live, we who have forged this movement out of our very bowels to give our people pride?" They are just warming up. "Out of his own self-loathing this crazy man Lemish continues on his unrelenting mission to brand us hateful sinners."

Sin? I'm an atheist! Don't you have to believe in God to believe in sin? I don't believe in God! I don't like the feel of any of this at all. If this was some sort of baptism by fire, I wanted to run away.

To Dr. Homer I run, of course.

I cry out plaintively. "I wonder if this disease will just be a continuation of the disease that's been my life. I am going to die because homosexuals hate each other?"

"This is a strong insight and conclusion to reach from these accusations," Dr. Homer says. Of all things, he encourages me to explore this new and fertile territory. Shades of Dr. Gillespie. "You must bear witness, no?" Yes, Dr. Homer also encourages me to fight back, "since you seem so angry, of course."

Dr. Homer is always saying, "Nothing wrong with anger."

WHATEVER HAPPENED TO WHAT-WAS-HIS-NAME?

Faggots everywhere are saddened to read the following in *The Avocado* of March 1982:

> Timmy Purvis, that beautiful morsel, is our first famous person who dies from this something. We noticed and watched and wondered. Why is he going outdoors looking like that? He's our most exceptionally handsome model. We have been in awe of his beauty through his meteoric rise to international fame. We all know many beauties that become bigheaded the moment they're clicked by someone paid to take their picture. That was not our Timmy.
>
> The great Dr. Hokie Benois-Frucht himself took care of Timmy, which was sadly for a very short time.
>
> Timothy Peter Purvis gets sick right in front of us.
>
> Timothy Peter Purvis dies right in front of us.
>
> Timothy Peter Purvis is taken from us, this beautiful dream.
>
> His beauty had broken our hearts and now his death will do the same.
>
> What did he die from!
>
> Oh, what is happening to us?
>
> What is happening to us!
>
> Timothy Peter Purvis, our Timmy, is scattered into the Hudson, "never to be forgotten," say one and all.

The Divine Bella obviously filed the story before he himself died, though *The Avocado*, as with everything connected with this plague, neglected to inform its readers in a timely fashion.

•

EMMA'S VOICE: Mr. Lemish, what have you been doing since we met? I haven't heard from you . . . Mr. Lemish, are you there?

INT. FRED'S LOFT. NIGHT.
Very large and high-tech. Walls overflowing with books. Dr. Emma Brookner is speaking to a group of about seventy-five guys, sitting and standing all over the place. The room is hot and everyone is sweating. Fred, holding his dog, Sam, looks around at all the reactions, from

fear to sleep. Bruce, Mickey Marcus, exceedingly intense and caring,
Tommy Boatwright, a tall Southerner, Pubie Grotty, Morton, a
handsome serious Texan in glasses, etc. . . . Morton and Pubie are
already hammering at Emma. Sam now scurries about happily. Fred,
Bruce, and Mickey are paying particular attention to the reactions.

EMMA: I think you are all going to infect each other. Now only a few of you have. Unfortunately we can't tell yet which ones.

PUBIE *(interrupting)*: You make all your assumptions on the basis of fifty-six cases!

EMMA: I made my decision on the basis of half a dozen. I now have ninety-three.

MORTON: Six people and every gay man in the world has to give up sex? I don't think so, Doctor.

PUBIE: You sound like some born-again. *(Morton and Pubie nod to each other.)*

EMMA: Long before we isolated the hepatitis viruses, we knew about the diseases they caused and how they got around. I think I'm right about this.

MORTON: "Think" is not enough, Doctor. "Know" is what we require.

EMMA: That will prove to be very foolish. By then you will have all infected each other!

RAYMOND: Why are we only hearing about this from you?

EMMA: I sent my first reports to the medical journals over a year ago.

PRISSY MAN: I am certain I've never done whatever it is she's going on about.

MAN IN LEATHER: I'm certain you've never done it too.

PUBIE: But they haven't published them?

EMMA: No, they haven't.

MILTON: How do you know what to look for when you don't know what you're looking for?

HERB: That makes sense.

EMMA: Yes, it could take a long time to locate the virus.

DECENT SORT *(frustrated)*: But don't you understand? You're not telling us enough!

EMMA: But don't you understand, there's not much more to tell you. Doesn't common sense tell you to cool it for a while?

DIEGO: Not much to look forward to.

MORTON: What if it turns out you're wrong?

EMMA: Then the worst thing that will have happened is that you will have cooled it for a while.

MICKEY: No, that's not all that will have happened. Guys will have become frightened of sex, guys will have lost their gay self-respect, so long fought for, we'll be scapegoated worse than ever, the world will think we're carriers, the Moral Majority will have even more of a field day . . .

HERB: Fred, Pubie's right. We have to think everything through very carefully before we do anything.

Emma senses the crowd is getting restless. A few people are even leaving.

EMMA: Wait! Come back! I am seeing more cases each week than the week before. Half of all my patients die. What's wrong with you!

GUY IN LEATHER: I hope she winds it up. I've got a tiny little orgy on the Upper West Side.

KID NEXT TO HIM: So far?

PUBIE: You can't even give me enough hard facts to write about this in *The Village Vice.*

TOMMY: And we all know how many hard facts the *Vice* needs to write about anything.

ANOTHER GUY: Oh, I like their personals!

A VOICE FROM THE BACK: Where's the mayor? Where's the Health Department?

EMMA: They . . . We . . . I'll tell you if you'll be quiet for a minute. The mayor—

GRAHAM: You don't really expect the mayor to do anything for us, do you? He's just like the president.

TERRY: This mayor has done more for us than any other mayor.

TAYLOR: If you believe that, you'll believe the tooth fairy. The mayor is not gay.

TOMMY: Oh, come on, Blanche!

TERRY: I think it's tasteless when gay men make fairy jokes.

BUZZY: Get real, girl.

SERIOUS GUY IN GLASSES *(gets up to leave)*: This is just like every other stupid gay meeting.

More people are leaving, waving goodbye to others, blowing a kiss or two.

EMMA: Please wait! Listen to me, please! Most of you are going to die!

Others are leaving. She is so furious, she turns and plows her way through the crowd to the door.

EMMA: Get out of my way, you stupid people! Open the door!

Fred has been watching her. He has been very moved by her.

FRED *(to the guy next to him, who is Tommy)*: She's going to be right, you know.

Tommy nods. Fred runs out after Emma.

Fred tries to catch Emma before elevator leaves.

FRED *(shouting after her)*: Welcome to gay politics!

Elevator door closes in his face.

INT. FRED'S LOFT. NIGHT.

FRED *(returning and trying to stop people from leaving)*: Wait! Don't go yet! Bruce and Mickey and I, we want to help Dr. Brookner. Anybody interested in forming some sort of group or organization, hang around, okay?

MORTON: What do you want to do?

BRUCE: Spread information. Raise some money. Craig didn't have any insurance. For instance.

The room is almost empty. A dozen people have remained, including Tommy.

TOMMY: I can start a hotline for help and information, I'm a hospital administrator. *(To Fred:)* You doing anything for dinner, you handsome man?

BRUCE *(whispering to Fred)*: Who's he?

TOMMY: Oh, he does not know who I am. My name is Tommy Boatwright and I'm a southern bitch.

FRED: Thanks. I'm busy.

TOMMY: Forever? We'll just have to see about that.

DIEGO *(sees some kid admiring him and Pierre; they're holding hands)*: It gets better as you get older, just like your momma told you.

WALTER: My momma left my father after six months.

CHRISTOPHER *(holding up a few checks in a baseball cap)*: We actually got a few checks. Total: twelve thousand dollars.

BRUCE: Holy shit.

FRED: So why did they all leave?

RAYMOND *(talking quietly to Christopher)*: Sammy Redburn. And Monty Epispo.

CHRISTOPHER: I hadn't heard about Monty.

FRED *(to Bruce)*: I' m sorry about Craig. Want to take in a movie or something?

BRUCE: Actually, I've been seeing . . . you know Albert? I don't like living alone.

MICKEY: I thought she was very impressive. I'll write about what she said in my next column. She's the only important person who's had the guts to say all this out loud.

FRED *(to the few guys left)*: Are we going to meet next week, or what?

Bruce, Mickey, and Tommy and a few others . . .

Fred's voice: And so was unofficially born what I came to think of as my first child. GMPA. Gay Men Pay Attention.

EXT. BOARDWALK. FIRE ISLAND PINES. DAY.
A gorgeous day. Hordes of bathing-suited men walking back and forth. Mickey, Tommy, Fred, and Bruce are handing out copies of Mickey's article in The Prick, *entitled "Cancer in the Gay Community." Guys who take copies glance at them and then throw them in a trash barrel.*

FRED AND REBBY AT A PISS PARTY

"How is your new organization going?" Rebby is asking me.

We are sitting in the glass-walled observatory overlooking the dance floor in the old Balalaika disco rented for the evening by Garfield Toye and Marvin Moon for a "Piss Party."

Believe it or not, it had seemed like a decent idea to support. Contributions would be collected for GMPA. I wasn't in favor of it but Bruce and Tommy were. "It provides a good example of the . . . what can I call them? The ironies of our growing predicament," Tommy said as he took off for a much-needed vacation. Bruce bowed out too. He's not looking so hot. So it was left to me to show up representing GMPA.

The event was billed as a Piss Party more as a joke. Piss was very '70s. Garfield and Marvin decided that everyone needed something to cheer everyone up. "A remembrance of things pissed," Marvin quipped. Guys are getting sick, etc. So many friends . . . just disappearing. Etc. That is correct: disappearing. More people are getting scared. Not enough of them, true, but it seems to be building. So Garfield and Marvin decide to invite all their friends and the invitation reads: "PISS PARTY PISS PARTY PISS PARTY! You must strip down to your nakedness. You must check all your clothes at the door. You can wear jockstraps only if you must. It will be just like the old days. We can see each other again in our entire splendor. But we just won't touch. No, we can touch. We just won't swallow. Or receive. Or give. LIFE IS HELL!" It is the sort of thing the Divine Bella would have written. But of course the Divine Bella, Bertram Bellberg, is dead. His spirit is here, though.

The few hundred here pretend they're not lost in a space that once held many thousands. The mirrored ball still works. Jacente is the DJ. Everyone had loved Juanito. Juanito is one of the ones who disappeared. Jacente was his assistant. He, too, has the gift. He can take the kids up and bring them down. And since it is dark in his DJ's booth, no one can see he's not looking well at all. "He is not well," Rebby tells me. "He is my patient. Jacente is a nice boy. Indeed, half of this room are my patients. That is why I am here. The other half are probably Emma Brookner's."

We watch all the pretty young boys frolic past us, naked, without jockstraps, obviously so not-yet-closed-for-business that it makes one sad. They are all adorable.

"You don't remember once I played with your nice cock in the Everhard Baths. Before it was burned down, of course," Rebby says to me.

"You did?" I smile politely. It must have been very dark for me to have let Rebby play with my cock.

Dr. Rebby Itsenfelder is like some prophet from an earlier, ancient time, to whom no one listens and who is forced to wander the earth endlessly ignored when he is right, or right enough. He suffers mightily for being unable to convince others. I don't think I've seen anyone who suffers so agonizingly for the causes he believes in and his failing to deliver on them. His distress is visible, from his face to his walk to the sound of his voice, which is almost pleading, Please listen to me. Please! This is serious!

He is haunted by the question, what could possibly be going on? I identify with the growing obsession this question is also making of my life. By now we have both seen too many young men who are not well in strange and differing ways. This one has pus, this one has scabs, this one has lesions, this one has nodes on the lungs, this one's lost too much weight, this one coughs so hard he can't talk, this one's turning purple, this one's . . . "There is no discernible pattern. It is as if each is suffering from a different disease," Rebby says. "Even blood tests are perverse. Vel, blodes, even forzicht ratios, a favorite diagnostic tool of mine from my interning days in South Africa and my lab work at Cambridge."

So why and how are they all connected?

"Because they are all happening at once and only to gay men." He is by the way the only gay doctor who allows himself to be visible and identifiable as a gay doctor, something that is beginning to really bug me.

He has hesitated to talk to the only person he believes might be interested and able to help. Dr. Monserrat Krank is a formidable presence—regal, buxom, her blond hair knotted as if she's some Scandinavian goddess of wheat or knowledge or virtue, and he's already been through numerous complicated wars with her. Rebby knows Monserrat is bored. Since being asked to leave Invincible Crewd-Harbinger for receiving too much personal publicity, she has little to do. And her husband, Binky, is playing Washington this year. He's decided he wants to more effectively influence the way of the world. So much money, such an important lawyer, so many vital contacts in the highest seats of power around the globe must be put to better use to make said world a better place. For a while he thought making movies could change bad ways of thinking. He even bought a film studio. He was wrong. Westerns in which the villain doesn't get caught make more money than the ones where he does. So Oliver Wendell "Binky" Krank takes trips to Washington. Like Bernard Baruch, he sits on park benches and advises important people. And they listen to him because he is famously smart. "He has won more important legal cases establishing new and vital precedents that have brought the law into the modern age than any other living lawyer," *The Truth*'s legal correspondent, Ethan Allen Tubster, has written. "If this were the golden age of ancient Greece or Rome surely he would be chief tribune of the forum." To avoid making yet more millions handling the divorce of one more buxom babe from one more horny aging billionaire, he has taken to sitting on a park bench in Washington's Lafayette Square. And here they come, presidents and kings. Leaving Monserrat sitting on Sutton Place desperately seeking something to do.

I should interject that I worked for Binky Krank at First American Films when Moses Rattner brought me there. I was one of Binky's assistants. It was an honor to sit in on his meetings while he brilliantly pieced together complicated deals that somehow satisfied everyone, greedy producers and greedier stars, while still leaving plenty for First American. They financed my film of *Sleep*, from which I actually made some money because of the way Binky set me up. I still get invited to dinner once in a while. I have heard Monserrat speak fondly of Rebby. In fact, I was there when their organization sprang into being.

He had finally worked up his courage. "Monserrat," Rebby begins, barely inside the handsome living room of their town house, then stops. He's nervous again, she realizes, and says nothing while waiting for him to go on. He won't sit down. She looks up at him expectantly. She is very fond of this infuriating man. She once thought him a genius. Matters have not turned out well for either of them. She was once thought a genius too. Science is so very fickle.

"Monserrat, we have both in our lives seen a great deal that is awful. This is more awful than anything we have seen. The jungle ditropa we worked together to eliminate in North Africa was benign compared to what I see is happening."

"What do you think is happening?" Her voice is soft and guttural, still with cadences of some foreign land. She always says it's Switzerland, but then do not they all, those for whom German is a first tongue? In her case it is impossible to question her political bona fides. As a mere teenage girl she went to Israel. She, a Christian, had somehow fallen in love with the notion of this young country fighting to exist and so she went there to live and fight with them. She fell in love with a Jew and married him. They fought side by side in the Irgun, the armed terrorist organization. She fired rifles and threw grenades. She became a doctor there. By the time she was noticed once again by Oliver Wendell Krank, who'd first spied her on a previous trip, she'd already divorced her young Israeli husband. She did not want to marry Binky. She did not want to leave Israel, which she felt needed her. She did not want to come to America, which she knew did not. But Binky is very insistent. He was ready at last to marry after years of playing New York's most eligible bachelor and now he had found his wife. It's actually a very touching story. That's why the media loves her. That's why she got all the publicity at Invincible that sealed her doom there. But I knew Binky had little sympathy for the homosexual.

"Plague," Rebby answers her simply.

She nods. She knows his great tendency to over-worry has previously been more or less partnered with fact.

When he tells her what he's seen, she immediately realizes she's found a full and fine, indeed noble occupation for herself. Inside her there is sympathy for these present-day gay sufferers. Many more Israeli young men were gay than her country will admit. She had been in love with not a few of them. She described all this to me when I came to interview her for our GMPA newsletter. Noble is very important to her. She and Rebby had almost been a great partnership several times in the past, with other potentially noble enterprises. She immediately starts noodling around in her brain for possible names they might call their organization, which of course they must immediately commence to establish. She will call hers the American Foundation for . . . Well, perhaps it is a mite too early; this disease does not appear to have a name yet. But she will be executive director. She will give Rebby some sort of title, of course, like medical director. Yes, she is very fond of Rebby but he is very sloppy, very messy, very unkempt, and must be kept away from the fund-raising parties. That he is a homosexual and that this appears to be a homosexual disease do not bother her. In fact, this touches her. Rebby touches her. He so wears his heart on his sleeve. He is incapable of disguising his feelings, which are always strong and emotional and fervent. She now, too, is a Jew. Jews are so committed to the weal of the world. She is proud of that fact. It is one of the things that drew her to Israel from dreary Switzerland and one of the things that drew her to Rebby when they were both working on that lifesaving project at Cambridge that didn't save anyone. Now that they're both in America she'll find a way to work with him that will be more satisfactory. They are both very smart scientists who respect each other.

His many patients flock to him because they know he cares for them as if they were his children. If you have no money or insurance he treats you for free. This is rare among doctors, particularly in New York. She knows he has no money, and she has given him some.

He will prove to be one of the very first doctors of homosexual men to sense that something awful is coming on, and that, unhappily, they are partners to their new diseases, although in fact he will also believe it started long before anyone else will think it did. He remembers seeing strange stuff in Africa, his homeland. "Men butchered monkeys there and ate them" was what he thought at the time might be the cause of whatever was killing people there. Of course no one believed him. Africans had been eating monkeys for centuries. He, with Dr. Emma Brookner, will say that this awful something is spread by having sex. And that the only way to stop it happening is to stop having sex. Which is an impossibility. So whatever it is that's happening can only continue to happen. Martyrs have been crucified for saying less.

How can he fashion an alternate route, a higher road, another ticket to ride? How do you make unsafe sex into safe sex? It is not a concept that has been so on the table before. He knows in advance it will not go down well. It will not go down at all.

Of course no one listens. Dr. Rebby Itsenfelder will have his failures to contend with all his days. When Daniel and I come to talk to each other again we'll find ourselves both using that sad description of "tragic flaw" as certainly defining Rebby.

Rebby has just been served by his building's co-op board to vacate his rental office, "because of your predominantly homosexual patient population, which, according to everything we have been able to determine, are now contagious individuals entering and leaving our building and hence endangering the health and the lives of our shareholders."

"Tommy Boatwright has assembled a group of lawyers at GMPA," I tell him. "They will help you."

"They are calling themselves Gay Men Pay Attention," Rebby had told Monserrat, to which she replied: "I wonder if it is wise, hitting the nail so on the head? Whose idea was that?"

"I believe it is Fred Lemish who came up with the name."

"That explains it."

Rebby shares this with me and we smile.

Then he suddenly throws up his arms. The gesture coincides with an upswing of musical volume from the DJ and screams from the floor.

Rebby is unaware of this. He is lost in perplexity.

"I got a letter this morning with a xerox photo of somebody's penis with a butcher's knife drawn over it, chopping it off. And my name is attached to this hand that is holding the knife," he yells over the music.

"You saw all the letters attacking my articles in *The Prick*?" I yell back.

Rebby nods. The music fades down. "Has the mayor put a price on your head?"

"It was like this after my book came out. Friends just suddenly stopped being friends. I'm trying to learn how not to let it bother me."

"When you learn how, teach it to me." He clasps my hand and gives it a squeeze. "Patient after patient looks at me so puzzled. 'You didn't warn me that this was coming,' a few of them have said. Now it's my fault!"

Below us a few hundred naked guys are trying not to jerk off. It is like Fire Island Pines but indoors and in the winter of our next big discontent.

I change the subject. "Where did the name Rebby come from? I assume it has something to do with rabbi?"

"I am the most irreligious man in the world. And I am stuck with this name, which actually is Rabbi. Can you believe parents would do that to a child?"

"Rebby, if it isn't just one thing, what is it?"

"The evidence simply isn't there for just one cause."

"Why? Why isn't the evidence there?"

"Because whatever it is isn't very strong, if you can believe that. Vel tests tell us that it constructs a weak blode. And a weaker neutra. It throws out a pathetically impotent fulce. How could any of this make so many of us die? I don't care if the n-3cs are not protective enough. I have patients with no n-3cs. Or no 729/s. I just don't think these are good enough surrogate markers for an epidemic. I do think there might be something else that could ignite some fuse. I just don't know what it is. And I don't have any money to investigate it."

And then he looks out into space before continuing in his tone of despair.

"And when and if there is money for research, I guarantee they will research the wrong things. They will look first for the causative agent instead of at all the infections that are killing my boys. This is putting the cart before the horse and it is always the way science is done, putting people last. It would be far easier to find cures for the infections than to find this virus, which it undoubtedly is, and which will take forever to locate."

He looks back at me. "*The New England Journal of Spots* and *The New England Journal of Blood* are both refusing to report this worsening symptomatology, claiming that it's still 'anecdotal.' Fred, it is going to be truly awful."

He sags visibly, a body wounded by years of being denied the means of verifying the truths he identifies. "Greeting is making so much money from Dridgies that its British chairman, Newnham Treadway, was knighted and then made a lord. Sir Newnham is now Lord Farst. I played with Newnham's cock too, in a Bayswater sauna. I am still a British subject, you know."

"How did you meet Monserrat?"

"We were both young scientists working on Radiant Opthamole at Cambridge. You probably don't even remember Opthamole, radiant or even lambent. Well, for ten seconds it was going to change the world. It was going to cure all ailments and illnesses and maladies, cancer included. Cancer especially. The wonder drug to end them all. It was even on the front page of *The Truth*. We discovered it in the Greeting Labs at Cambridge. It was flushed down the toilets of American Greeting. The results that Monserrat and I obtained could not be duplicated elsewhere. I still suspect there was a little industrial espionage going on, although I don't know what kind or by whom, or why. Opthamole had promise. I suspect someone will resurrect it someday. No drug company ever completely throws anything away. If it can't be used to cure your arthritis it will surface to cure your gout. For my sins I came to America to work at NITS, which for me was a mistake, and Monserrat went on to marry one of America's richest men. And now she is very grand. Try as we might, we were not able to put our knowledge together. Perhaps with our new organization. I asked you how yours is coming along."

As if to answer for me, Jacente brings the music up to its most crashing crescendo, turns on the mirrored ball, and the dancing dervishes below us all start screaming and yelling and, yes, pissing on each other.

"1,112" AND COUNTING

BY FRED LEMISH
THE NEW YORK PRICK

If this article doesn't scare the shit out of you we're in real trouble. If this article doesn't rouse you to anger, fury, rage, and action, gay men may have no future on this earth. Our continued existence depends on just how angry you can get. In all the history of homosexuality we have never been so close to death and extinction before. Many of us are dying or already dead.

There are now 1,112 "official" COD-defined cases of what is happening to us. When I first became worried, there were only 41. There have been 195 dead in New York City from among 526 victims.

But these numbers do not include the uncounted number of us walking around with swollen lymph glands, pneumonia, purple skin lesions, and fatigue.

The rise in numbers is terrifying. Whatever is spreading is now spreading faster as more and more people come down with this stuff.

Leading doctors and researchers are admitting they don't know what's going on. I find this as terrifying as the alarming rise in numbers. Doctors are saying out loud and up front, "I don't know."

Suicides are now being reported of men who would rather die than face such medical uncertainty, no therapies, rotten hospital treatment, rejected insurance claims, and the appalling statistic that 86 percent of all cases die so quickly.

If all of this had been happening to any other community, there would have been such an outcry from that community and all its members that the government of this city and this country would not know what had hit them.

Why isn't every gay man in this city so scared shitless that he is screaming for action? Does every gay man *want* to die?

No matter what you've heard, there is no single profile for all victims. There are drug users and non–drug users. There are the truly promiscuous and the almost monogamous. There are reported cases in men who claim to be abstinent.

There have been no confirmed cases in straight, white, middle-class Americans.

Hospital staffs are so badly educated about us that they believe we're all contagious. Our patients are often treated like lepers. Food trays are left outside their doors. The few hospitals willing to take us have long waiting lists, no matter how sick you are.

If this were occurring in straights, instead of in gay men, you can bet all hospitals and their staffs would know what's happening. And it would be this city's Health Department that would be telling them. New York City's Health Department might just as well not exist for us.

There are increasing numbers of men unable to work. There are increasing numbers of men unable to pay their rent, men thrown out on the street with nowhere to live and no money to live with, and men who have been asked by roommates, and even their lovers, to leave. And men with visible symptoms are more and more being fired from their jobs.

Our closeted mayor, Kermit Goins, appears to have chosen not to allow himself to be perceived by the non-gay world as visibly helping us in this emergency. No *human* being could continue to be so useless to his suffering constituents.

Repeated requests to meet with him, or with his health commissioner, Dr. Herta Glanz, or with his openly gay assistant, Hiram Keebler, have been denied us. Repeated attempts to have Goins make a very necessary public announcement about this crisis and public health emergency have been refused by his staff.

With his silence the mayor of New York is helping to kill us. Has he even bothered to call our president, whose attorney general has announced: "the president is irrevocably and unalterably opposed to homosexuality"?

I am sick of our electing officials who in no way represent us.

I am sick of closeted gay doctors who won't come out to help us fight.

I am sick of *The Avocado* and *The Village Vice*, which refuse to write about this, not to mention the virulently homophobic *New York Truth*.

I am sick of gays who won't support gay causes.

I am sick of closeted gays. It's 1983 already, guys. By 1984 you could be dead.

I am sick of guys who moan that giving up careless sex until this blows over is worse than death. How can they value life so little and cocks and asses so much? Come with me, guys, while I visit a few of our friends in Intensive Care at Table Medical. They'd give up sex forever if you could promise them life.

I am sick of guys who can only think with their cocks.

I am sick of everyone who tells me to stop creating a panic. I don't want to die. I can only assume that you don't want to die either.

I am angry and frustrated. My sleep is tormented by nightmares, and visions of lost friends and the tears of funerals and memorial services.

How many of us must die before *all* of we the living fight back?

I know that unless I fight with every ounce of my energy I will hate myself. I hope, I pray, I implore you to feel the same.

Here is a list of twenty recently dead men that I knew:

Harry Blumenthal
Richard Bronstein
Robert Christian
Ron Doud

Winthrop Heinz
Leon Hudsons-Bay
David Jackson
Kristos Kostos
Karl Krintzman
Michael Maletta
Timothy Peter Purvis
Jerry Rappa
Nick Withers
Stephen Sperry
Pierre Steinhardt
Robin Swindon
Vladek Tortorelli
Carlton Wiegand
Craig Valenti
Bertram Bellberg

And one more, who will be dead by the time these words appear in print.

Can we fight together?

A bunch of us have formed GMPA for GAY MEN PAY ATTENTION. We meet at the Center every Monday night at 7 p.m.

Come fight with us! Please! I beg you.

If we don't all fight back immediately we face our approaching doom.

•

1,112! Who is doing your counting, you dumb fellow. I am by now up and running in many hundreds of thousands of you at least, and not only in your country.

PUMP UP THE VOLUME!

I had sweated the piece. I had been pent up for so long, with whatever—anger, fury, which I guess are the same. Or they were coming to be. It all seemed so *wrong*. Being treated like shit every place we turned.

On that list of dead men, I had had sex with Harry, Boo Boo Bronstein, Ron, Leon, Kristos, Jerry, and Robbie.

Robbie Swindon. He of the handsome gymnast's body. He whom I lusted for and bedded down for . . . how many days or hours? I thought I had really found a nice man to love at last. Two days was all it turned out to be. He left our burgeoning bliss when his lover suddenly died in an airplane. "I can't see you again! I feel too guilty! He was on the plane at the same time we were . . ." and he collapsed in tears and grief.

I could tell you stories about all of them. I wondered if I had anything to do with . . . These kinds of thoughts were creeping into my consciousness little by little.

Everything had exploded after a session with Dr. Homer, who said, "Fight for what you believe in! If you think something is wrong, then fight to right it!" It seems simple and obvious, that advice, but you have to be in a place to listen to it, and I guess he worked me up to being in that place. So I wrote the above "1,112 and Counting," and Orvid Guptl published it in *The Prick*, and then something like two dozen other gay rags across the country ran it. So it got around. People talked about it, thank God. People began getting frightened, thank God. I hadn't intended that, but I was to discover that fear is the best motivator, bar none. Not enough people were getting frightened yet, but they would. They would. They must!

I realized soon enough that one puny article in *The Prick* wasn't going to be enough. For one thing, not many read *The Prick*. Not like they read *The New York Truth*. For another, the mayor still hadn't said anything, *The New York Truth* still hadn't said anything further, the president still hadn't said anything publicly at all, and each day I heard about a few more dead friends. Once there were five in one day. How do you deal with that? Which monster do you go after first? And I was realizing that so far I was one of only a few bellying up to the bar to fight. I couldn't be the only one losing friends. I wasn't, of course. As much as I found these deaths hard to take, that so few of us were reacting visibly and audibly to the deaths of *their* friends was coming to be just as hard on me. All this, all of this, was new to me. It was a long way from writing shitty screenplays about mixed marriages in Outer Mongolia.

They were still coming after me, those that considered me some sort of Antichrist, like Pubie and Jervis Pail, both particularly persistently hateful. But just knowing that my article, *mirabile dictu*, was being passed around all over the country made my mouth open up and I began working it all over the place. It was like I discovered I had a new organ. Woe to anyone who stopped me in the street and asked, "How are you?" I let them know in no uncertain terms what I was doing and what I thought they should be doing too. People thought I was crazy, again and/or still. GMPA was slowly growing as more people knew more dead friends, but our president, Bruce Niles, was definitely opposed to my big mouth and its association with this organization we had founded together. If I heard one more time that "honey gets more than vinegar" I think I'd slug the speaker (not Bruce, of course). But Bruce was handsome and popular, a gay icon. I was the crazy person. Except for Tommy, GMPA was in Bruce's corner. And he was in the closet.

I could see soon enough this growing number of GMPA volunteers weren't fighters. They were like church parishioners, quiet do-gooders, and we certainly had much for them to attend to, even quietly and invisibly as was their style.

I had never thought much about closets and what they meant. Now I could see—clear as day—all of us flushing our dead selves down the toilet without a peep from our gay mayor or our president with his gay son. God knows how many other closeted gays in high places were just like this.

I only knew how to write. What could I write? Novels take too long and I'd already written one. Plays? The only one I'd written had closed on opening night. That left movies. I could write screenplays in my sleep. And had. I still had a few contacts in that business. And I had crossed paths with a few gay moguls along the way. Randy Dildough, of course. I'd made a pass at him once in Hollywood. Sammy Sircus and Trafe Elohenu were his good friends, as powerful in the film industry as Randy. I knew them all, sort of, from my Hollywood days with Rust Legend. Publications in "the mainstream" would not name names for fear of being sued. We were still a few years away from throwing out the old hoary traditions of not yanking our own out of the closet. I wondered how useful these three would be anyway. I knew the answer but went into my own denial. I would beg them for their support! I would get down on my hands and knees and beg them. That's what I would do! Randy and Sammy and Trafe, you can see what's happening. It could happen to you. You have to help your brothers. You have to help your people. You are each exceedingly rich and powerful. If you were Jewish—which, actually, all of you are—you would be major donors with your names on bronze tablets in the temple. Your mothers would be proud of you. Aren't we all in this together? Aren't we all—somehow—brothers? I was beginning to talk of "us" like that. My brothers. My people. Film my fucking movie script!

My people. Are we a people? The first time I called my people my people, the audience of gay men I was trying to rev up at one of the many gay organizations I went to plead with started giggling, then laughing, then laughing harder and not stopping. It made me want to hide. When I was in junior high school I was in a pageant about the Declaration of Independence, the actual document, on a train ride across America. I came out onstage and proclaimed, "The Freedom Train is coming to your city!" The audience went into convulsions of laughter. The kids wouldn't stop laughing. While I stood up there marooned on the stage, a shit-eating grin on my face, waiting for quiet so I could continue my speech, a plea to them to go and visit this fucking train ferrying the Constitution and Declaration at Union Station. I got through the performance somehow. Then I retreated, mortified. Lester had named me a sissy and here was yet another example of it. No, I do not like to be laughed at. And my people didn't want to be called my people yet. Just like my people didn't want to know about this shit.

Had I really thought this "people" stuff out carefully? Probably not. I was now punting from the gut, to use butch football terminology. What do I know about football? Football was Seth's game. Seth. My brother Seth, the jock, the honor student, the football player, the boxer, the tennis star, the stud, the rich white straight man.

How interesting that suddenly I was thinking of myself as part of a bigger something or other. Now I just had to figure out what it was. And I had other, more pressing issues. It did not occur to me that these two issues— our sense of ourselves as a people and this new disease itself—could be and should be and must be combined. It was my people who were coming down with it. True to the history of all peoples, our heads were still in the sand. Sooner or later something was going to have to give. Somehow. Wouldn't it? This shit could not take over the world. God, what an awful thought.

And good old Dr. Homer was pumping me up every day. I was back to going five times a week. I had not had that kind of weekly workout since my days in London with Dr. Gillespie or my days with Rivtov at Yaddah, or with Shmuel here in the city. Hurling words like *responsibility* at me, Odysseus really rode my ass.

There were many more men I slept with during this year. Yes, I had sex with other men. That was what we still did. Before we were forced to acknowledge that the law of averages we were counting on could no longer protect us. How long did it take before it sank into my own thick head, as thick as everyone else's, that we couldn't do what and when we wanted to do just because we wanted to do it? Many of these faces are in front of me still, before my eyes, evidently not to be lost. Good. I want to remember them. They are a part of me. I have the semen of some of them inside me. If not their semen, then the saliva of their kisses. And they had my semen inside them. And my kisses. I was always a big kisser.

These thoughts. All these thoughts.

•

You are getting so far off the track that my heart beats with joy. You still know nothing about me, where I am from, how long I have struggled, where I have visited, indeed what I truly look like. My future is assured.

DR. BOSCO DRIPPER, DVM

Today Veronica, one of my young chimps, died. She had been sent to me by the Washington Zoo.

DR. SISTER GRACE HOOKER

I have confirmed "this shit" in the vaginal discharges of five women in Partekla. Fucking A!

In my female patients at Partekla I verified my earlier instincts. Many of them were secreting large amounts of vaginal discharge with similar blood impurities. Dr. Dye is not interested in my pursuing this either, even though I also discovered these women were contagious, that this discharge was hence a sexually transmitted disease akin to syphilis and gonorrhea. Women patients were sneaking off and fucking in corners with men, health-care workers on staff, who promptly came down with whatever this fucking shit is that we are seeking. I have just been suddenly personally called by the White House, a Mr. Gree Bohunk (boy, does he sound like a piece of fucking work), who more or less ordered me to "cease any investigations involving women." Ruester does not want the country or the world to know that there are any sick women among The American People, "and I would watch my step, young [hah!] lady, if I were you." You see, Hermia, why I am becoming frightened. I know too much. I first put out my report on all my various suspicions in 1969.

Vitabaum at HOW said then he had no money and had more pressing worries. How and why is the White House taking this stand now? And in this obnoxious and insulting and fuck-you fashion?

A WEDDING CELEBRATION

There is no question that the Jerusalem brothers have been falling apart as brothers. Daniel saw and spoke little to Lucas, whom he grew up worshipping and who is now particularly withdrawn, and he had no contact with Stephen, who has no interest in anyone. And all three are still ignoring David's existence, almost dutifully, as if he had been a genetic malfunction in the family. (Shades of Rivka living all those years with Philip, knowing all that she did.)

And Sara, Stephen's wife, has always seemed to Daniel aloof and high-and-mighty. She never invites him to dinner or talked to him when there was one of the law firm picnics Daniel used to go to.

Sara's story begins, or rather ends, at a party given by her uncle by marriage, Israel Jerusalem, whom she adores. His last son from his Nobel wanderings is getting married. She is talking to her husband, to whom she often doesn't. They are in their Jaguar nearing Israel's house when she decides to bring up what's on her mind.

"Why are you fucking *her*?" At last she confronts her husband. She knows it can only be a fruitless conversation, getting her nowhere (where does she really wish to go?), only revealing her own hand, only hurting herself.

"Who says I am?"

"Why have you been fucking her for so long?" She feels very small. All these years and so little fighting back. "Don't you ever get tired of her?"

"I won't dignify that by responding," he says.

"You were fucking her the night your son was born. You didn't even come to the hospital."

"That's not true!" He is thrown by this accusation so late in the game. Their son is in his teens, he thinks. He pulls up in front of the house and relinquishes his Jag to a valet.

She looks for the host, his uncle, her beloved uncle who insisted on not canceling this party because of all these strange new cases from fucking that keep him so busy at Isadore Peace. "But I have much to celebrate. The last of my unmarried adopted children."

Her husband can talk to anyone here. He has enough clients to say hello to that he won't feel stranded. She on the other hand, who rarely goes out, who rarely socializes with him, is a stranger here and enjoys her anonymity.

These days he doesn't even have his breakfast coffee at home.

The day before yesterday, Sara Jerusalem turned forty-two years old. Around her was a crowd of varying degrees of closeness who brought her gifts and best wishes. She'd studied the mountain of generous gifts, most of which she'll return or give away because she knows they'll be tasteless junk from the privileged investors Stephen allows to participate in his Masturbov syndicates, tokens that shout, Remember me next time you need a few million. Everyone wants to be remembered. Everyone knows his partner is the creepy, repellent, and powerful Sam Sport. Sara feels contaminated every time Sam's in her house. She never wanted the party. Stephen just threw it, as he'd always done for her birthday, a strange activity from a husband who finds few other ways to stay at home.

A live string quartet commandingly knifes into her self-pity with the opening cries of its adaptation of the last Beethoven piano sonata. Only Uncle Israel would have them play such a selection. Thomas Mann wrote movingly about this sonata, so misunderstood for so long, he said in *Doctor Faustus*. She tries to remember what he had said exactly. She can only remember that he said the sonata was misunderstood. For a long time. So now we can all appreciate it properly. If we read *Doctor Faustus*. She'd enjoyed *Doctor Faustus*. But wasn't the last Beethoven sonata really *not* the last sonata, only the last to be published? She'd read that somewhere too. Mann was no doubt dead when this was discovered. Man is always dead by the time many facts about his life's obsessions are at last discovered. She reads too much. Books are her only friends.

She'd been in England last summer and she'd found an old paperback about the Profumo Affair. How fascinating! A woman's vagina brought down an entire government. She had read about men who have such lusts that they go to extraordinary lengths to satisfy, that this applies to men in positions of power particularly, that whatever a man's tastes there is always somebody willing to supply his indulgence . . . that deep within most men there lurks a response of fierce joy to the shame and pain of others . . . She thinks she's recounted accurately and with justice what some Jew who wrote this book had said. His name was Levin. Like in *Anna Karenina*. Was Levin in *Anna Karenina* Jewish? Do Jews understand sex better? The man who has broken my heart is a Jew. I have ruined my life because of a goddamn Jew.

Sara Jerusalem, the day before yesterday, was forty-two. Upstairs—the mansion they live in is on Kalorama Road, across from the French Embassy—her husband slept soundly and untroubled, as far as she could tell, having come home long after midnight, dashing out after her birthday party was over, his cock now no doubt tired from being with Claudia. He had been fucking Claudia for twenty years, why hadn't he married *her*! Their son, Stephen Jr. (called Stevie), nineteen years old and a day student at George Washington, who she found out after the fact has already done an injury to his penis, necessitating some kind of reparative surgery, claiming, "I just hurt it in football scrimmage, Mom, jeez, you never believe me when I tell the truth," slept also. Why does he prefer to live at home? He has a trust fund of gigantic proportions; he could build a dormitory for himself and all his friends; he could build a housing development; he could retire some Third World country's debt. College is for getting away and trying new things, but perhaps, with his endowment, both between his legs and in his trust fund, it's better that he lives at home. Stephen once alluded to bodyguards hiding in the shadows and she thought he was joking but perhaps not. She has a sense of how truly rich he is. She is married to a man who is exceptionally rich, and who long ago gave her a large bank account in her own name, but who has not given her, at least for the last nineteen years, any physical enjoyment in any tactile way. She was twenty-five years old the last time she felt his penis inside her. In her bed she choked on tears in honor of the barren intervening years, and her sadness, and her inability to confront him with her sadness, and her loss, and his.

Mr. Bernard Levin's Profumo book concluded with: "Yet healing is impossible without the lancing of the boil."

Somewhere inside her she believes she is courageous. Where? How so?

How long ago was it that she found her husband's smallish dark purple lizard notebook. She'd thumbed through it. It was filled with Stephen's minute calligraphically precise script, and she closed her eyes, for there was Claudia's name, over and over again. Do this for Claudia. Go there with Claudia. Claudia wants . . . Buy for Claudia . . . Claudia and I did this . . . Oh, she had known it but now she knew it. She had clamped her eyes closed that night too. I thought I knew who I was. I haven't found out anything at all. If one summons up the image of old Lev Tolstoy, pushing crazily through the winter's night-cold darkness, away from his Yasnaya Polyana estate, his home for so many, *many* years, to find peace at the age of eighty-two and a half only through expiration and death in the waiting room of the train station at

Astapovo, one can more or less see that this search is rarely successful. Not to mention Virginia in her River Ouse.

So the first infidelity Sara Jerusalem commits in her marriage of more than twenty years occurs in the master bedroom of her uncle Israel's house on Managua Road while his lavish celebration is transpiring on the ground floor and in the back garden, to the zippy tunes of Beethoven's last sonata. So much fine food, so many distinguished people! She can hear Israel addressing them all in the garden on a public address system replete with some static. He hopes everyone honors this ceremony by examining their deeds and stays on the lookout to turn away from all evil, for there is greater need of repentance for the sins of which one is uncertain than for sins of obvious certainty. "Now, what in the world does all that double-talk mean?" Mordy Masturbov laughs out loud protestingly. Mordy has begun to appear at family gatherings, at Abe's request. Mordy is an enigma to Sara, as is his magazine, as is his mother, as is her whorehouse. Israel is always surprising anyone who will listen by quoting interminable passages from one thing or another, not necessarily germane to the moment. He is now talking about his son just married. "I brought five Iwacky boys home with me from the Andes. I educated them and turned them into good Jewish boys, all of whom have pleased their father by becoming doctors. Jacob is the last of my children who have brought me much joy. Please, I ask of you, join with me in enjoying this special day."

Her first infidelitor (Sara thinks this rather a charming term), in the master bedroom of the house of her uncle Israel, says he is (he is not) an assistant secretary of state. He calls himself Ronald, which she thinks rather bland, though apt for him (I'm starting off easy, no challenge here) because he is, well, bland: his skin is pasty, his clothes fit badly and are made from awful-feeling material, and additionally, his breath smells of the salami he's eaten downstairs. Not an auspicious debut. Why is this woman so suddenly intent on fucking herself silly all over this house? Oh, there are too many questions for this poor woman. No! I am not poor. Don't make me a victim! Her conscience always works so very hard.

"I am in a division responsible for funding worthy black enterprises in Africa, you know, the Third World," he is saying as she notes that her hand is rubbing his crotch. She has never done anything like this in her life. Why am I being so cheap? You fucking wretched husband! How dare you parade your cock all over town!

"How interesting," she says to Mr. Bland. "Are the people in Africa better for having you around?"

"I try to pretend we are not too late," he seriously replies.

Am I vengeful? Do I really want to be doing any of this?

The eternal plaints of women in bondage since the beginning of time.

"I deal with many black men who come from other black countries which cannot take care of them." He is mumbling now because he has a pretty good idea what is on her mind and what is on his cock's mind. How unexpected. Such an unlikely setting, this room, its walls covered with old framed photographs of the Holy Land, Palestine, Jerusalem, all from an era so long ago. He hopes she will not ask him what in the world he's mumbling about, because if queried too closely he will prove inept at remembering all the new black countries' names.

Sara interprets the mumbling as some boyish discomfort in him, which makes him appear all the safer to her, as if he is living his name, Ronald, safe, pale, button-downed Ronald, an easy conquest—no test here!—like Jell-O. She is amazed at her growing courage and proficiency. He moves away from her hungry hand and closes the door. She had actually left the door open. He says, for some reason, that he's been divorced for fifteen years after only one year of marriage. Is this a declaration of his availability as husband material or an alibi in advance in case he disappoints her sexually?

He sits down on the bed, next to her, on some sort of old-fashioned hand-made quilt. He says it's not been an easy week for him. Why does he have to go into this? She stands up, placing herself in front of him, and performs the most unromantic act: she touches her own crotch. He looks past me, beyond the window, outside, into the space between this house and the one next door (far enough away), and quickly, nervously, he sticks his finger up under my skirt (from Bendel's, Jean Muir) and under my panties (pale gray, Marks & Spencer) and . . . into me, and I sit on his lap, on his finger, and push myself back and forth, he who groans in much too short a space of time, poor lad, poor bland Ronald, that the tawdriness of this brief fingering should be erotically satisfying for him so quickly, and his penis still within his trousers, now resplendently wet, a growing, ever-increasing stain on his early-season seersucker. He jumps up, extricating his finger and holding it up in the air like it's covered with shit and in immediate need of cleansing, and excuses himself as he rushes into the toilet across the room. I believe I hear him throwing up.

Should I pause now to explore my feelings or continue with My Day (as I believe Eleanor Roosevelt documented her daily activities for all her avid audience so many years ago)? I smoothe my wrinkled British garments and go to join he who might be a possibility for my second conquest—why, they are simply walking around this house looking for me, word must have gotten around there's an easy lay upstairs, or do women in heat send out messages like Western Union? I believe I heard him say he was also a government official, upon our introduction downstairs earlier, near the roast sliced turkey and various salads, I believe he said something about price controls, or the possibility of, the study of, their invocation by the new president, not, he said, that he had actually met the new president, but there was a meeting scheduled soon, although he thought the new president not intelligent enough to truly understand his specialty. Now they view some etchings on the corridor walls, also of the Holy Land, and make some small talk, and she flirts a bit more and coyly walks away. He's too boring, even for me.

She had heard the shower still running in the bathroom inhabited by he with the dirty finger. Why does she return there? Ronald is standing naked in the narrow shower stall, soaping himself up, particularly his finger, which, like the hand of Lady Macbeth, troubles him greatly. He stands in puddles of soap bubbles. Immediately when he sees her, he starts babbling of a wife and eight children, all of whom are under college age and all enrolled in different parochial boarding schools so that they will not be placed in a position of having to compete in situ. I am hungry, goddammit. I take my clothes off and slither in beside him and stick that thing that's hard again inside me and we rumba together sufficiently and I feel my own tremors, feeble though they are under such circumstances, and I pull away as he squirts a few more drops into space. I move him back under the water again, reversing our positions, like I'm taking a package that's in the wrong place and putting it somewhere else. I have yet to be truly aroused, beyond a cursory intellectual interest. I step out and dry myself with what I notice is a Minnie Mouse towel. It is next to a Mickey Mouse towel. Hers and His begin so young. Does Uncle Israel actually wipe himself with Minnie and Mickey? I replace the towel and dress. He is still in the shower, still washing his hands and, of course, his cock.

I check my makeup and touch up my hair in the mirror, and I go out into the hallway. I ascend one flight of stairs, where I find my next conquest. This one surely will bring me some relief: Isn't that what they say about black men—that they fuck white women well and good? He is less black than swarthy, someone of mixed identities. Do you now detect a certain bravura brazenness in my voice? His clothes, which are very good quality, very well made, are nevertheless a bit too tight on him, so that everything is bulging out, which I believe is the intention. He is very handsome and I want to joke out loud to him with much devil-may-care and joie de vivre that as far as I'm concerned he can bulge out all he wants to. I close a door behind us, and I lock it. We are in a children's nursery! There is a lovely antique rocking horse. There are two beds, one a crib and another full length alongside it. I ask him where he's from. He answers: "Here. But I grew up in Havre de Grace. I work for NITS in Franeeda County."

I believe that he is honest. Oh, daring Sara! I kneel on the floor before him and bury my face in his crotch. The mountain beneath my cheeks is touching to me in a way that is more maternal than sexual. I will protect you because you are almost a Negro or what they are now calling a Native American. He pulls me up and lays me back and carefully raises my skirt, as if he's opening a special present, and gently pulls down my panties and . . . I open my eyes. He is staring down at my vagina. His enormous cock is sticking out of his fly. Suddenly he pounds himself into the entrance. It hurts me. Stephen has a large penis too, and when he did use it on me he didn't know how to use it on me. Or so I thought. Or so I think now as this dark man uses his large penis on me, thicker too than Stephen's, he is much less slurpy than Stephen, at least as I recall Stephen, there is no sound of slurp or suction, but no, this one knows not how to give pleasure either, now he's performing with the same sort of regimental pumping as her husband, *that* she recalls, her bravura exercise in antidiscrimination revealing that all men are brothers, performing as they exercise in a gym, a certain set contains a certain number of repetitions that are checked off one by one until a total's achieved that preferably tallies or surpasses some goal set in a previous workout. He appears to come in buckets. I wonder if some men store up semen like camels store water. He does not move, he is still hard, I should pump myself to climax on his still-hard cock. Why don't I? I am conscious of a terrible silence. Not even grunts. No, I believe I've heard a few grunts. The leaves are going to fall late this year. But they're going to fall. All Profumo did was fuck a high-class hooker. How does one bring down a government? For that is what he and his women did. How amazing. How does one become that powerful? This man, who still has his clothes on, is still hard and he isn't moving and I feel light and giddy as I reenter this fray and we're soon enough both sweating buckets and we're drenched from each other.

She thinks, I am tired of feeling safe. There is absolutely no safety, and a great deal of danger, in feeling safe; and even if she wanted to, safety was taken out of her hands by the discovery of a little purple book. And I always found such safety in books! They have always been my only friends. I thought all the knowledge in the world could be found in books. And now I'm proved right. The weeping willow bloomed late this year. Yes, the seasons are late. They can't handle us, they can't handle us, and they don't know what to do. She giggles to herself, causing the current occupant to pull his hose out of her abruptly with a loud pop that elicits more giggles from her. One government official and one semi-schwartze. She is taking a survey: Have I passed the rigors of test marketing? How can I live? How can I live? How can I live? And I am a woman, the giver of life and death, the original power, the original imagination. Who says! I have let my life be taken away from me. I want it back. The new man, in his pool of sweat, has fallen asleep. Perhaps he's dreaming of a new kind of mattress made of women. I want to talk and talk. There is so much I want to tell somebody. Who is there to tell? Who is there to listen? I want my Stephen. No. I do not.

I feel like Virginia Woolf again, wading into the river, never to return. I am naked. Virginia had sense enough to drown with her clothes on. He wakes and lifts me up and carries me into the small nursery shower, and I notice the walls papered with Donald Ducks. The water coughing out is rusty, but warm enough. He removes his clothing. He leans me against the wall of this tiny space while he pays particular attention to soaping his pubic area. I am pleasing him enough to nurture renewed growth. The tomatoes are coming in sweet this year. With new courage from my journeyings, I run my palms up and down his smooth flat body; he feels like stones from some creek that have lain there forever. Oh dear, this rusty water is making us both slimy. His body appears to me suddenly quite repulsive, this flat, smooth, hairless, thin, upright body of—is it suntanned?—flesh with its now enormous erectile projectile . . . Unh. He hurts. The thuds of it and him . . . I push him away and quickly take some grungy soap and lather his erection. It's like holding a piece of rusty hot pipe. He says nothing. I vaguely discern his disappointment, perhaps even anger at me for denying him continued entrance, but now come his tremors; he's shaking all over, his penis spouts semen like a fire hose gushing the volumes still inside of him, it never seems to stop, it's all over me, his stuff; he rubs it into my skin, over, all over, like I lavish my skin with emollients before I go to sleep. It's not unpleasant . . . Now he, too, is fingering me. He has one finger inside me and his hand over my mouth . . . The finger inside me is now much more than a finger. The hand over my mouth now covers my nose. I can't breathe and I can't move against the power of his fist that pinions me to the wall . . . I can't breathe . . .

No, there is no such thing as safety. Intellectually I know that it is unreasonable to require safety via the conduit of another person. That's all a load of shit, that safety within another's arms is as essential to a person's well-being as the search for knowledge and the seeking, as Chekhov put it, after life as it ought to be as against life as it is.

I can't breathe . . .

Stephen, I am dying. Where are you?

I am dead. Everything is yesterday's cold leftover pizza. One must not be boring. The ultimate sin and crime is to be boring. I was boring. So I move on. Courage is all. I am now courageous.

•

Is Sara really dead? Well, Stephen will think so when he's called upstairs to view her clothing on the floor along with her earrings, her bracelets, her watch, her rings, including her wedding band. It is as if she'd been decomposed and this is all that's left. He had hoped for so long that something would happen to get her out of his life. He had ignored her for so long, hoping she would just go away. Well, she has gone away. Her body is not here. Nor will she be found. He is sensitive enough to know that he has done this to her.

•

No, I did not do this one. Not my style. Impressive. I wonder how he does it.

•

EXT. CENTER OF DISEASE. DAY.

INT. AUDITORIUM. DAY.

A sign. OUR VISITOR TODAY IS: DR. LEMISH. GMPA. NYC.

FRED stands on a platform, alone. He looks out at the audience.

There are maybe six or seven in this huge place. One woman, Dr.

Fester, has an enormous crucifix; one man, Dr. Moskowitz, has on a

yarmulke; one blond guy, Dr. Harrow, could be a Nazi. Dr. Paulus

Pewkin is the boss. He sits stone-faced.

DR. MOSKOWITZ: A question I have. Why you guys don't get
        married? If you were married this wouldn't happen.

FRED: We're not allowed to get married.

DR. MOSKOWITZ: This cannot be so! Everyone is allowed to get married.

FRED: Two men? Tell me where and I'm moving there.

DR. MOSKOWITZ: Oh, I don't mean two men. Why don't you marry women?

FRED: Excuse me, but is this your entire staff?

DR. HARROW (*the Nazi*): It doesn't make any difference.

He presses a button. A very complicated slide comes on filled with names and arrows from one to the other.

DR. HARROW (*contd*): We've discovered the Chattanooga County Cluster!

FRED: Yes?

DR. HARROW: I have personally interviewed all of these arrows and discovered they are . . . interconnected.

FRED: Yes?

DR. FESTER: We discovered a high incidence of . . . between and among . . . anal intercourses.

FRED: Must be a lot of new terms hard for you people. Are you saying you think anal intercourse is the cause of this?

DR. FESTER: Well, it would certainly make sense!

FRED: I know guys who are dead who never got fucked.

Dr. Fester winces at the word fucked.

DR. HARROW: Can you prove that?

FRED: Can you disprove it?

DR. MOSKOWITZ: We are only looking at the gayish lifestyle.

FRED: I don't know what that is.

DR. MOSKOWITZ: You have sex every night!

FRED: Sometimes twice!

DR. BOOEY: Whoopee! I'll buy that!

This from a tiny gnome of a man not noticed.

DR. FESTER: We are considering your promiscuity.

FRED: Doctors are now reporting cases of single-contact infection. That's not promiscuity, that's bad luck!

DR. PEWKIN: Dr. Lemming, could I speak with you privately for a moment?

CUT TO:

The back row of the auditorium. Pewkin and Fred sit side by side. The others have left. On a chair beside Dr. Pewkin is a stack of New York Pricks *with Fred's articles.*

DR. PEWKIN: I think you should know that we have other diseases that are of more concern to The American People. I wanted to meet you because of an article you wrote. In it you condemn us for intentionally not treating Negro people who had syphilis, and state that we are undertaking a similar tactic in dealing with homosexual men. The Public Health Service is one of the noblest institutions in the history of our great country. I am honored to have devoted my entire career to it. I will in no way allow you to tarnish us for your own salvation and I wanted to tell this to you personally. I wanted to tell you also that you are despicable in my religion, which is also the religion of my superiors—the surgeon general, the assistant secretary, indeed many people who run America's health-care system. You are all despicable to all of us. Now perhaps you can find your own way out.

He gets up and leaves. Fred is alone in this great auditorium. Slowly he gets up and walks down to and up on the platform. He pulls out some notes.

FRED: Thank you very much for coming today. The great Dr. Alfred Kinsey has written that one out of every ten men in this country is gay. He has taught us that only fifty percent of all men are exclusively heterosexual throughout their lives. He has taught us that one out of every two men you meet responds sexually to another man at some time during his life. He has taught us that only four percent of all men are exclusively gay. He has taught us that forty-six percent of all men are neither exclusively straight nor exclusively gay. He has taught us that thirty-seven percent of all men will have sexual relations with another man that results in orgasm. It may only happen once in a while but at any given point in time thirty-seven percent of the adult male population of our great country has done it or is doing it with another man. This is more than one-third of our country's men. For our government to confine its definition of this growing plague to a homosexual problem shall prove to be a great tragedy, perhaps one of the greatest this world will ever know. This is not a gay problem any more than it is a gay country. We are a country where men, just like women, love, admire, respect, and need each other more than we are willing to acknowledge. I want to thank you all for coming here today and listening to me. I would be grateful if you could pass along all the information I have just related to you to all your companions in arms in your Public Health Service.

He places his notes in his briefcase and picks up his coat and walks out of this enormous auditorium.

"THIS SHIT" FINALLY GETS A NAME

JOE KIDNEY CONTINUES HIS VALIANT ATTEMPT "TO GET THIS ADMINISTRATION, LIKE NO OTHER, DOWN ON PAPER"

It was true that many have referred to whatever is happening to gay men as "this shit." Even Secretary Hoidene Swilkers of the Department of Health and Disease (HAD) is known to do so. Finding it increasingly necessary to refer to it in public less offensively, she convenes an emergency council "to come up with a better name for this shit than 'this shit.'"

"When in doubt, summon an emergency council" is the advice passed on to her by nine out of the ten cabinet members and department heads with whom she consults, choosing only ones that she considers less hostile. She has correctly noted that all are generally a suspicious lot in Washington. She has not been received with open arms. They know she's in way over her head. (Hoidene in her short term in office will summon seventy-three emergency councils.) "Be careful The American People won't come to think you can't make your mind up about anything," the secretary of the Bureau of Budget Adjustment (BOBA), Newder Phlue, an economist once on the faculty of the University of Benares (Moose thought it was in California when he approved the appointment), where he taught the Law of Diminishing Returns, advises her in their first meeting. "That happened to me when I first came here from India. Indians love bureaucrats who cannot make up their minds. Americans don't. Indecision scares Americans. I had to learn to appear as if I had made up my mind, when of course I hadn't."

But Halacia Sanders, the secretary of HAD's Division of Census, Polls, and Standards, advises her, "Don't worry about a worry that isn't a secure worry. The American People like it when you're not a hundred percent sure and you admit it." And then she speaks softly. "Don't listen to Phlue. He's an Indian. From India."

So, with no consensus, Hoidene summons her first emergency council of the Department of Health and Happiness (HAH-EC1) (at Purpura's sudden "suggestion," Health and Disease, HAD, has been renamed HAH), which votes unanimously to officially name "this shit" The Underlying Condition (UC). Fairy Flu and Gay Cancer are ruled out, though not before discussion. An Unidentified Fatal Male Malady (AUFMM) is thought imprecise. "'I'm suffering from AUFMM' would also be a mouthful," one of the participants points out. "Homosexuals Oppressed Per Example" (HOPE), although a nice acronym, is believed to be too positive. It's agreed, finally, "The Underlying Condition" has, in the words of Dr. Roscoe Middleditch from NITS, "a neuter sound." "In the absence of a consistent symptom to identify it by, what else could this shit be called?" this last from Arturo Ferri, from the Government Printing Office, where he is billed as "Supervising Director of Typesetting."

As with so many historically important milestones, no one quite remembers from whose mouth this wording sprang. Who said what first? Who or what inspired whom so that three words, "The," "Underlying," and "Condition," could be pieced together as the summation of this afternoon of work and its entry into medical history, and the world's.

"Doesn't it sound nicely mysterious and reminiscent of something pastoral, from Wordsworth?" Dr. Caudilla Hoare muses.

Dr. Middleditch tries to sum it up. "It seems harmless enough. It seems nonspecific enough. It seems inoffensive enough." He is thought to be a useful mediator to have on your side.

"That's what we want," Hoidene says. And then, after a moment's pause, "Isn't it?"

Dr. Rebby Itsenfelder, brooding and looking concerned, turns on Dr. Hoare. "Wordsworth? You are mentally deficient. We are talking about dying men."

Dr. Hoare smiles icily. "It is always so disappointing when one's cohorts have no feel for poetry. Rupert Brooke, then. At least he was one of your poofters."

"I would like to change my vote," Rebby says.

Dr. Monserrat Krank, who has come down from New York with Itsenfelder "for this important meeting," says, "You cannot change your vote, Rebby. The vote has been tallied and approved."

"What difference does that make? Since when is good science so rigid? If this rude and inept woman is for it then I am against it. In fact, the more I hear this new and stupid name, the more I am against it. And I do not think that gays will like it either."

"Do we really have to worry about what they think?" Dr. Nostrill asks. He has just been officially reappointed the head of HAH and is speaking up more forcefully. Evidently many don't like this reassignment. "Now he's really over us. Everyone has to report to HAH." "I thought Swilkers was the head of HAH." "No, she's the secretary. She is higher. She's in charge." These two speakers decline to give me their names for attribution. "Are you kidding?" one of them says. "In this place? No way."

Dr. Dye is smiling and Dr. Dodo Geiseric is nodding off. He lost interest when they wouldn't name this shit DG-101 after him. He actually suggested it. "After all, I will be its principal discoverer at NITS." This is obviously news to everyone in the room.

Dr. Dye stops to speak with Dr. Itsenfelder on their way out. "I just love it when you call doctors inept and rude. Please don't stop. What did you say your name is?" He makes no attempt to read Rebby's badge.

Rebby blushes. Obviously no one in this place has ever asked him his name. Hoidene beams. The director is speaking to one of her boys. She must rehire him immediately.

Later I wondered why no one at HAH was filled with a sense of excitement: here was a new disease. Was this not a challenge? Did it not instill a tiny bit of ambition in anyone? After all, doctors are supposed to be on the lookout for new stuff that could make them famous. The well-known illnesses are woefully overcrowded with scientists to study them and doctors to treat them. Until you've latched on to something new no one knows who you are. You don't want to go into anything too crowded. You want a new baby. This one sure looked like it qualified. But, no, not this illness and not this crowd. I constantly hear the whispers. "Faggots. Yuck." Tom Boatwright of GMPA, a gay man, actually said it out loud. "Gay sex is already known as 'the Ick Factor,'" he told everyone, hoping for some understanding. I'm evidently to know GMPA stands for GAY MEN PAY ATTENTION. They certainly seem to be preparing for the worst.

I say to Hoidene, "I guess you'll have to try and figure out which ones are the jerk-offs and which ones are the just plain bigots." She answers, "Isn't there anything in between?"

Dr. Krank, to her credit, did go up to Dr. Hoare. "*Poofters* is such an old-fashioned word, Doctor. I'm sure you would like to appear more *au courant*." And she regally walks away.

Later that afternoon Hoidene receives a call from the White House. "They love our new name for this shit!" She calls me often to tell me things like this. "You are just so sympathetic," she says. "I recognized a kindred spirit the minute I saw you." It turns out she says that to a lot of people. She feels very insecure and she has good reason to. Everyone here has good reason to, but she doesn't know that.

I feel compelled to point out that Hoidene leaves all her meetings at least three times and returns shortly wearing a new wig, each more fetching than the last. With each reentry, she smiles in pride at her achievement. Every now and then she gets some applause, which makes her smile even bigger and she gives a little curtsy.

At her first most-ballyhooed press conference (Manny wants to show her off), and brandishing a copy of the latest issue of *The New England Journal of Spots*, she stands with its editor, Dr. Arnold Morron, Dr. Stuartgene Dye and Dr. Dodo Geiseric of NITS, and Dr. Megace Frolik of COD, Dr. Euterpa Vondel of FADS, and Dr. Nostrill. Hoidene announces, "We don't know what's going on but at least now we have a name for it. We have decided to call it The Underlying Condition."

"What does that mean?" come the clamors from the press for further clarification.

Dr. Geiseric steps forward.

"It means simply that something is happening in the body that upsets the equilibrium of the immune system. Whatever it is that is so upsetting, it is an underlying condition to something else that is going on above it (or perhaps below it for that matter), not only in the frontal system but in the body as a whole. My experiments in my lab reveal beyond any shadow of a doubt that if we can isolate what is happening to the frontal system then we will be able to attack what is destroying, certainly injuring irreparably, the body whole."

"What in hell is the frontal system?" a white-coated young doctor yells out.

"That will be all the questions for today," Hoidene announces. She'd thought more attention would be focused on her. "I had not expected Dr. Geiseric to talk so long. Not that anyone understood a word he said."

I believe I have got all this down right. More and more I am confronted by the harsh reality that this is not my beat. It should be but no one will believe it.

At the announcement, a Dr. Benois-Frucht confronted Velma Dimley. "It may have a name but that's all it has. Has any budget been increased? No. Has any budget in fact been drawn up? Not according to my contacts. Has any real research begun? No. Has *The Truth* lifted its prohibition on writing about it? No. Is *anyone* out there sounding a warning, behavioral or otherwise? No. Will President Ruester say this new name out loud?" He said all this right to Velma's face.

Jakie Flourtower was there with Velma, and rather attentively so.

"Shucks, what a shame. So many fegala dyin' like fairies and nobody's flappin' their wings," Jakie said to B-F after B-F yelled at Velma.

I have no idea why these *Truth* people came down from New York for this. I would say they could have read about it in *The Truth* except that no coverage of the event appears in *The Truth*.

•

I like my new name also. It makes me sound so . . . mysterious. And relevant. And universal.

FROM DAME LADY HERMIA'S EVIL NOTEBOOK

Few constituencies are reacting to what is happening. Both *The Truth* and *The Monument* editorialize, briefly, "on behalf of all perplexed citizens: What does 'Underlying Condition' mean?" (*The Truth*.) "Does it mean we all have it—whatever it is—inside of us in some underlying form or other?" (*The Monument*.) At a meeting in the Oval Office, Linus Gobbel asks: "Is someone trying to tell heterosexuals we can get it?" "Well, theoretically we can all get everything, even rich" is Dr. Dye's amused response to *The Monument*'s Science, Technology, Computers, and Automotive columnist, Horenda Tybalt. That paper's rabidly right-wing columnist Beaufort St. James editorializes: "If someone is trying to tell heterosexuals we are all potential homosexuals, nothing turns voters into Republicans faster than fear of faggotry. The more they show themselves, the more they can be hated."

"This new emergency council summoned by Swilkers has seen too many horror movies produced by Dr. Krank's husband. What is Dr. Krank doing on a government commission anyway?" asks Dr. Nesta Trout in a letter to the new editor in chief of *The New England Journal of Spots*, Dervis Tuttle. Nesta was once an associate of Dr. Krank's at Invincible Crewd-Harbinger where Monserrat had made another blemish on her record promoting that Ingaardium-X, some concoction from Paraguay thought to be a cure for cancer. No one lost their lives, exactly. Several people in Paraguay just no longer walk. This is not to be confused with the Radiant Opthamole that Monserrat and Rebby worked on at Cambridge when they were younger. I believe a number of patients on those trials were lost. Monserrat is now acting like a good film executive's wife, still looking for what I believe is called a hit. *NEJS* actually publishes Nesta's letter. One wonders whom she's diddling with. And why.

FRED'S JOURNAL

THOUGHTS ON PEOPLEHOOD

No one could think of a better name than UC. Most of those suggested are nasty and fill the gutter press. This continues on the TV talk shows and as fodder for late-night comedians. And then the whole name issue disappears. A good name is always hard to find.

The gay population, which might be thought to like the name for the very reason that others don't, hates it the most. At least in New York. As with so much concerned with our well-being, gays in the rest of the country are voiceless. Not that they are so rah-rah help us! in New York, but here a certain number of them, at least, talk about matters in a vaguely public fashion, and worry about themselves in a slightly more audible manner. If this sounds confusing, it's just that *activism* is an unfamiliar, uncomfortable, disagreeable, and totally unfamiliar word. Nobody wants to be called an activist. It's always been a disparaged activity. Those few who felt compelled to speak out on our behalf in the past were considered drips. Of the first water. Everyone knew this. I certainly did. And. Guys are crossing the street when they see me coming. I am not getting good (gay) press. Even though GMPA is growing bigger, no one likes what I am saying so publicly, most particularly Bruce.

Oh, a number of meetings are convened by the unusual assortment of social organizations that fall within the homosexual rubric of gay men, lesbians, and transsexuals/trangendereds (we are having trouble distinguishing between the two, should there be a distinction). Tommy and I try and go to as many as we can locate, to plead.

These are what we have to work with:

Soul Sisters, Drag Queens of Coarse, Drag Queens Über Alles, Black S&M Activists, White S&M Activists, Black & White Brothers Who Are Not into S&M, Black & White Sisters Who Are into S&M Lightly and Amusingly, Lesbian AA Below the Bowery, Gay Men AA Above the Bowery, Harlem Whites Against Gay Racists, Lesbians Alone United, Gay Men for All Seasons, Marimba Marching Men, Dykes on Bikes, Lesbian & Gay Truckers, Pink Pussy Patrol, Butch Men for Jesus, Lesbian & Gay Jews in Opposition, Gay Gals & Guys Who Square Dance Together—all groups of gay thises and thats looking for something to get behind or on top of, or at least onboard with, anything to while away rainy days and lonelynights. Has something appeared that just might get all of these off their Buts? Are there suddenly Gay Guys & Gals Who Care that their fellows are getting sick and dying? Can we start making T-shirts emblazoned with HELP! We all know how much we love our T-shirts.

The painful fact emerges. There are many groups. Each group has few members. There are few if any alliances. Why work with another group when yours hardly functions? They're just like everyone else. Why should they be different? Particularly when so many of them spend so much time trying to be like everyone else. Gay doctors in Queens don't talk to lesbian doctors in Queens, if indeed there are any lesbian doctors in Queens, or gay ones either, which of course there are. It's like this across the board, across the country, across the world, as will increasingly be obvious in these upcoming years. We are people but we are not a People. We're going to die because of it, but we don't know that yet. I must try to make them see this. I must. I must. I must.

It is actually an exciting prospect.

It is!

YOU FUCKERS! WE ARE A PEOPLE!

More and more I am trying to say this out loud.

"Why do you think," Pubie Grotty muses in his weekly column in *The Village Vice*, "that gays are so opposed to this new disease being called The Underlying Condition? Because once again we're the scapegoat. Because once again we're being blamed for something we're not responsible for. Can't you see? 'Underlying Condition' is just a metaphor for homosexuality." Once again Pubie Grotty assumes the role of automatic spokesperson for everyone gay.

Pubie, as often, has a good point, but just as often he twists it around to point the dagger into his own heart. If there is an "Underlying Condition" of homosexuality, then can't this be made into something positive? That all The American People have homosexuality in us, the idea Linus Gobbel pooh-poohed? Using this disease as a vector to make this case could be a useful tool. No one would buy it, of course.

Gay men are feeling very guilty very quickly. You can be in denial, but you can only deny so much as more and more friends fall by the wayside. Sex drops off fast and furiously. At first. For some. More or less. Sort of. States of denial don't last long. Denial denies even itself. Guys actually move to states where there are no cases, as if to some magic never-never land. Or countries. Many rush to get their passports in order. A few are already living in Canada.

"To be both a possible carrier and a card-carrying homo is a heavy trip for too many," Bella had defensively answered when I asked him in Hokie's office before he died why *The Avocado* wasn't writing about what was happening. "I think that means don't write about it." Bella couldn't remember his editor in chief's name at the moment, who'd ordered this. There had been several recently. Bella had looked awful, thinner, terribly frightened. I was reaching a point where everything was looking bleak, without differentiation. Even the sun didn't shine on the days it was shining.

"Doesn't your editor know what's going on?" I pressed Bella further.

"Oh, Fred! What *is* going on!" Bella started crying. I tried to embrace him, which he allowed for only a second. "I don't want to know!" And he ran out into the hallway of Table and that was the last time I saw him.

•

INT. GMPA OFFICE. DAY.
A very small space. It's a madhouse. People in and out. Everyone on never-stopping-ringing phones. Mickey is going crazy on several of them. Tommy with a couple more. Phil, who is black, is trying to direct Grady and Lenny, two young volunteers. Estelle, an older woman, also taking calls. Emmett and Lee, now an item.
ESTELLE: GMPA. Estelle speaking. How may I assist you?
(To Grady): Well, aren't you some hunk!
(To the room): Someone needs a will.
PHIL: Give him this number.
LEE: Where's the patients' group meet?
PHIL: Tonight. Here's the address.
EMMETT: Is there a parents' group?
Bruce comes in from the street in a suit, with attaché case.

TOMMY: Not yet. But I'm working on it.

GRADY *(picking up ringing phone)*: GMPA.

LENNY *(picking up ringing phone)*: GMPA.

GRADY: Hey, they've got their first case in Moscow.

LEE *(picking up ringing phone)*: Oh, hi, Mom.

GRADY *(to Estelle)*: Thanks. I joined to find a boyfriend.

TOMMY: Graciella, City Hall is an equal opportunity employer, doesn't that mean you all have to learn English? *(Slams down phone; into another)*:

Don't move! I'm sending a crisis counselor.

(Dials another number.)

BRUCE *(putting down a phone)*: San Francisco's mayor just gave their organization four million dollars. Mickey, why aren't you in Rio?

PHIL: I put the phone on service. You guys should get some rest. We don't want any burnout.

TOMMY: Good night, Phil. Thanks.

(Phil leaves.)

Phil got diagnosed today.

BRUCE: No!

TOMMY: Richie Faro just died.

MICKEY: Richie!

BRUCE: Mickey, why aren't you on vacation in Rio?

MICKEY: I was in Rio. Gregory and I, we just got there, day before yesterday, I get a phone call, from Glanz's office, I'm told to be in his office, right away, this morning . . .

BRUCE: From Rio? What kind of meeting? Why didn't you call me?

MICKEY: Because unfortunately you are not my boss!

BRUCE: What kind of meeting?

TOMMY: Take it slowly.

MICKEY: I get to City Hall, Herta keeps me waiting forever, finally he comes out and says the mayor doesn't want to see me any-more. I wanted to scream, I haven't slept in two days, you dumb fuck! but I didn't. Instead I said, please sir, then why did he make me come all the way back from Rio? He says, "I'm afraid he didn't take me into his confidence," and he walks away.

(Waving a copy of The Prick*)*

Fred's article attacking our gay mayor and his gay assistant my boss Hiram Keebler just came out!

Fred, having entered, is seen standing on the side, listening.

FRED: What about it, Mick?

MICKEY: You keep trying to get us to say things we don't want to say! And I don't think we can afford to make so many enemies before we have enough friends.

FRED: We'll never have enough friends.

MICKEY: We can't like magic all turn into nuns!

FRED: A Canadian nun in Haiti just died after making love only once in her life. Ray Schwartz just died. Terry Spalding is calling all his friends from under his oxygen tent to say goodbye. Tibby Maurer took an overdose. Hal Schecter has stumps for feet. Frannie Santuzza has lost his mind.

MICKEY: What if it turns out not to be spread by having sex?

FRED: Then we won't have to cool it anymore.

MICKEY: STOP IT!

TOMMY: Mickey, are you all right?

MICKEY: I don't think so.

TOMMY: Tell Tommy.

MICKEY: Why can't they find the virus?

TOMMY: It takes time.

MICKEY *(going through a stack of* Pricks*)*: I've written about every single theory in my health column in the *Prick*. Repeated infection by a virus. New appearance by a dormant virus. Single virus. New virus. Old virus. Multivirus. Partial virus. Latent virus. Mutant virus. Retro virus. Animal virus.

TOMMY: Take it easy, honey.

MICKEY: And we mustn't forget fucking, sucking, kissing, blood, voodoo, drugs, Dridgies, needles, Africa, Haiti, Cuba, blacks, pigs, mosquitoes, monkeys—what if it isn't any of them!

TOMMY: I don't know.

MICKEY: And our own government! COD says it's fluoride in the water, HAH says it's a fungus, FADS says it's rough sex upsetting the body's equilibrium! The Great Plague of London was caused by drinking water from a pump nobody noticed. I don't know what to tell anybody. And everybody asks me! They're calling me from all over the world! I don't know—who's right? I don't know—who's wrong? I feel so inadequate. How can we tell people to stop when it might be caused by—I DON'T KNOW!

BRUCE: That's exactly how I feel.

MICKEY: But maybe he's right! And that scares me, too. Freddie—you scare me!

TOMMY: Easy, Mick.

MICKEY: Do you think the president really wants this to happen? Do you think the CIA really has unleashed germ warfare to kill off all the queers Senator Vurd doesn't want?

FRED: Mickey, try and hold on.

MICKEY: To what? I used to love my country. *The Prick* received an anonymous letter describing top-secret experiments at Fort Detrick, Maryland, that have produced a virus that can destroy the immune system. Its code name is Firm Hand. They started testing it in 1975—on a group of gays. I never used to believe shit like this. They are going to persecute us! Cancel our health insurance. Stone us in the streets. Quarantine us. Put us in camps. And you think I am killing people.

FRED: That is not what I said!

MICKEY: You did, you did, I know you did! I've spent fifteen years of my life fighting for our right to be free and make love wherever, whenever . . . and you're telling me that all those years of what being gay stood for is wrong—and I'm a murderer. We have been so lonely and oppressed! And one day we found the arms of another man, and another, and another, and we thought at last we'd found freedom! And heaven! I worship men! I don't think Fred does. I don't think Fred likes himself very much!

FRED (*through gritted teeth*): Fred likes himself just fine.

MICKEY: Can't you see how important it is for us to love openly, without hiding, without guilt? Can't you see that? Can't you?

BRUCE: I can.

MICKEY: I went to the top of the Empire State Building . . .

TOMMY: Mickey, come on. I'm taking you home.

MICKEY: . . . to see if you can jump off when no one is looking.

TOMMY: Let's go home.

MICKEY: Fred, I'm not a murderer. All my life I've been hated. For being gay. For being short. For being Jewish. Fred . . . someday someone is going to come along and stick the knife in you and tell you everything you fought for all your life is SHIT!

Mickey lunges furiously for Fred, only to be caught in time by Tommy and Bruce.

TOMMY *(cradling him)*: Tommy is here. It's all right. I'm taking you home.

MICKEY: Take me to St. Vincent's. I don't want to go home.

TOMMY *(comforting Mickey in his arms)*: We're all real tired. We got ourselves a lot of bereavement overload.

(Snatching coats, Bruce hands him one.)

MICKEY: We're the fighters, aren't we?

TOMMY: You bet, sweetness. And you're a hero. Whether you know it or not. You're our first hero.

Tommy takes Mickey out.

Fred and Bruce are alone.

FRED: I wonder if we're all going to go crazy, living this plague every single minute, while all the rest of the world goes on as if nothing is happening, going on with their own lives and not knowing what it's like, what we're going through. We're living through war, but where everyone else is living it's peacetime, and we're all in the same country.

Suddenly he gives a big smile. Felix Turner, a very handsome man, has been in the back listening.

Let's go home, honey.

MORE SKINNY ACCORDING TO ANN FETTNER

PART THREE

Okay, Fred, here's where we are, research-wise. The crazies are coming out of the woodwork. God help us:

UNDERLYING CONDITION: the illness, the disease, the epidemic now manifesting itself, which seems to challenge the system and which for reasons still not fully comprehended is capable of shutting the system down. What is the system? Indeed. You would think it is the body, or rather, the body as composed of all *its* various systems: respiratory, digestive, immune, etc. But with UC it is possible to observe—Dr. Stuartgene Dye is maintaining this (though it's rumored his experiments, which he has not shared, have been extreme)—that the system can be shut down even if all or most of its component parts are operating normally. As Dr. Sheldon Grebstyne of NITS has reported in *The New England Journal of Vel* (*NEJV*), it is also possible to have a vel count of zero and still feel and look fine, with full energy. Vel has been considered the gold standard for measuring the body's health ever since Dr. Sister Grace Hooker discovered it in 1951 (and received her Nobel for it in 1956). Nothing in the intervening years has replaced vel as the yardstick for measurement of the body's current situation. Dr. Sister Grace Hooker does not fight for her discovery's place in the sun so much as demand it and disappear when challenged. Now we are seeing people with no vel who feel fine. This hadn't been observed before. And now we are also seeing people with no vel who are dying, as the expression goes, like flies. So the first thing one might think by way of explanation is that maybe vel is worthless, or not the right yardstick to measure strength and health. But no one allows themselves to think this way. One can't. Vel has been the only measurement. There isn't any other measurement. If vel wasn't used, then how could anything be measured? Just about every experiment and God knows how many medicines for many ailments are based on the results of vel counts. So either vel is right and we still haven't found out what's going on, or vel is wrong, which might explain . . . what? We have not seen enough of anything yet to make such a blanket statement; the longer a disease hangs around, the more time for mutant something or others to show up. So it's possible to have UC and have a perfectly normal vel, if anyone knew what a perfectly normal vel count is: One thousand? Ten thousand? One million? Ten million? (Would that Dr. Sister Grace responded to the pleas for help.) There are UC cases from each of these numerical categories walking the streets feeling fine. Or sick. You can feel awful with twelve hundred and fine with ten. Which makes you wonder. Or should. But wonder *what* precisely? Besides, of course, why this whole thing is so lacking in sanity.

Which leads to the logical next question. Can there be *another* system at work here? Dr. Itsenfelder now believes this is the avenue down which success lies. More and more he is using the word *multifactorial*, which automatically places him at the top of the "crazies" list. "Whoever heard of such nonsense!" cry not a few famous scientists. Nobody pays attention to Rebby Itsenfelder (although his patients are reputed to live longer). His medical degree is from South Africa.

One thing that can be said about this UC: a lot of "facts" that were taken for granted before it, in every field you can imagine—immunology, pathology, infectious disease, certainly hematology, even biology—are now going to be up for grabs. It will be interesting to watch, should this scramble for newer, "higher" ground show up. But don't hold your breath.

Dr. Jerrold Omicidio, one of the few meant to be smart enough to realize that no one is making any sense, nevertheless appears to have become fiercely motivated by some patriotic conviction that as the government's top UC man (so far—who knows what President Ruester will do to him if and when President Ruester realizes what's going on) he must not be perceived as wrong and that he must also be the one who finds the cure (that's right: THE cure). Obviously this is a very ambitious man. There is nothing wrong with that. So many others unfortunately are hiding for some reason, possibly because their hands are empty and they're ashamed that after three years they have no idea what's going on and are afraid to say so. Omicidio sits on the sidelines, saying nothing but sitting tall though he is a short man, eyes front and center, waiting for his chance to jump in. One has yet to discern if he'll have the necessary luck, for if there is one obvious fact in scientific life at NITS it's that brains and abilities are not sufficient to make dreams come true. So as a deposit against that great future deed he's preparing to take credit for when and if it happens, Omicidio declares up front that at the moment we just have not figured out how all the pieces fit together. This is hardly news, but he is the only official to say so bluntly. Most doctors listen to Omicidio. It is simply safer to do so. He has emerged, somehow, and somewhat mysteriously (in that it's happened before our eyes and no one knows why and/or how), as the government's chief, and only, spokesperson on UC, not that he's saying anything (for want of a better word) definitive (read "helpful"). Drs. Dye and Gist and Middleditch and Grebstyne are not saying anything at all. So for a sane person, and of course there must be one somewhere in all this, though which one, or ones, will only be known after these early shakedowns (if even then), Omicidio is all there is to bet on, mainly because he's publicly saying that he's not really saying anything, for there is nothing to be said. Congress loves his double-talk. The White House and its inhabitants appear never to have heard of him. My Deep Throat buddy at NITS is keeping me abreast.

If ever a plague wasn't talked about among those charged with its supervision, this is that plague. It's because of President Ruester and the entire stigma his stance and his staff have about showing any interest in UC at all. He's already said, or Moose said for him, that he's "unalterably and irrevocably not interested in homosexuality." This country, since its founding in 1776, has held on for dear life to an aversion to dealing with the truth when it's unpleasant. So much for Public Health and the glory of serving it. When, as now, it can't be—well, not much gets done. This can only augur bad things. And lots of name-calling.

Everything in math, in economics, in the determination of what's happening to populations that are getting sick, the testing of almost anything, must be partnered with numbers, so an artificial determination of the definition of UC has, out of the blue, been "set" by the Center of Disease (COD): a vel count of two hundred or less is bad. It will mean you have UC *officially*. Until last year it was a vel count of three hundred or less. But now there are so many UC cases that COD was ordered by Dr. Ekbert Nostrill (everyone is under HAH) to somehow lower the number of UC cases, and the obvious way to do so was to decrease the "official" definition of who is considered "infected," if that's what's happening, and if vel is accurately responsible for the measuring, neither of which it should be clear is clear. President Peter Ruester is also said to not want it known that America's such a sick country. Apparently no one has told him that, UC or no UC, it's already too late to worry about that. It's also said that the president doesn't even know about UC.

No official will take the responsibility of classifying UC as a plague. It is difficult to comprehend the reluctance of the American government to speak out on this matter. Dr. Grodzo says that German officials leaped at this kind of "wonderful opportunity" to inform people that they were facing danger and possible death. "The very *Krankhaftigkeit*—you say, I think, *morbidity*—of this opportunity was very appealing to German sensibility. We have a distinguished heritage of dealing with such symbolic morality tales, from Lembeck through Goethe to Wagner and Nietzsche and Mann to Hitler."

If you think water is being treaded, you're right. In government it's usually important that one is thought to be slogging the good slog.

It ain't happening here.

•

INT. CORRIDOR. ST. VINCENT'S HOSPITAL. DAY.
Fred walks down a hallway with a bouquet, looking for a room.
Gregory is sitting outside Mickey's room.
FRED: Hello, Gregory. How's Mickey?
GREGORY: He's very sedated. I hate you.
FRED: I'm sorry to hear that.
GREGORY: Don't you ever consider the effect you have on people?

FRED: Me? I don't believe anybody hears a word I say.

GREGORY: I find that hard to believe. You terrorize people. You're a monster.

INT. HOSPITAL ROOM. DAY.

Mickey is in bed. Fred hands him the flowers.

GREGORY: Fred, go away somewhere and leave us alone.

MICKEY: You disgust me. I'm ashamed we ever were friends.

FRED: Bruce looks bad. They need you. They need a board member to speak for them.

GREGORY: You're taking away our lives. And you're giving my lover a nervous breakdown.

MICKEY: I've known you since I was in med school. You were living in London and I was there for a summer program. We went to bed once. Do you remember?

FRED: Yes.

MICKEY: Why are you saying what you're saying?

FRED: Why aren't you saying it, too? We *are* infecting each other.

MICKEY: We don't know that yet! We can't say that yet! I am not going to write and say that. You're as bad as Bruce being in the closet.

INT. FRED'S LOFT. NIGHT.

Fred and Felix Turner are naked, having made love. The walls are filled with bookshelves.

FELIX: That was very nice.

FRED: Yes. It was.

FELIX: You know my fantasy has always been to go away and live by the ocean and write twenty-four novels, living with someone just like you, with all these books, beside me writing your own twenty-four novels.

FRED: If you really feel that way how come you write all that society and party and fancy ball-gown bullshit for *The Truth*?

FELIX: Don't you gobble it up every day?

FRED: I do. I also know a lot of people who have died.

FELIX: I'm sorry. I don't write much about parties now. Mrs. Ruester has made me off-limits. She didn't like what I wrote about her.

FRED: When I came to your office at *The Truth* it was only a few.

FELIX: Is that why you agreed to our date?

FRED: Do you know that when Hitler's Final Solution to eliminate the Polish Jews was first mentioned in *The Truth* it was on page 28? And on page 6 of *The Washington Monument*? And both papers are owned by Jews. The American Jews would not help the German Jews get out! Their very own people. Jewish leaders were totally ineffective, Jewish organizations constantly fighting among themselves, unable to cooperate even in the face of death, Zionists vs. Non-Zionists, Rabbi Wise vs. Rabbi Silver . . .

FELIX: Am I at last seeing in action the real Fred Lemish I've heard about?

FRED: Aren't there moral obligations, moral commandments to try everything possible? Where were the Christian churches, the Pope, Churchill, Roosevelt! A few strong words from any of them would have put Hitler on notice. Dachau was opened in 1933. Where the fuck was everybody for eleven years? And then it was too late.

FELIX: Look, I told you this when you attacked me in my office. Flourtower would fire me on the spot, so I'm not going to tell *The New York Truth* I'm gay and could I write about these cases of a mysterious disease that seems to be in the way of our fucking again even though there must be half a million gay men in this city who are fine and healthy. And this is not World War Two. And all analogies to the Holocaust are tired, overworked, boring, and a major turnoff.

FRED: Are they?

FELIX: Boy, I have found myself a real live weird one. I just called you weird.

FRED: You are not the first.

(Fred suddenly grabs Felix and kisses him. The kiss becomes quite intense; Fred jumps up.)

FRED: The American Jews knew exactly what was happening. But everything was downplayed and stifled. Everybody had a million reasons for not getting involved. Can you imagine if every Jew had marched on Washington? Proudly! Huh?!

FELIX: Jews, Dachau, Final Solution, what kind of crazy date is this? Fred, you don't remember me, do you? We've been in bed together. We made love. We talked. We kissed. We cuddled. We made love again. I keep waiting for you to remember something, anything. But you don't.

FRED: How could I not remember you?

FELIX: I do not know.

(Felix shakes his head with sadness.)

It was at the baths a few years ago. You were busy cruising some blond number and I stood outside your door waiting for you to come back and when you did you gave me such an inspection up and down you would have thought I was applying for the CIA.

FRED: And then what?

FELIX: I just told you. We made love. Twice. I thought it was lovely. I asked what you did and you answered something like you'd tried a number of things, and I asked if that had included love, which was when you said you had to get up early in the morning. That's when I left. But I tossed you my favorite go-fuck-yourself when you told me, "I really am not in the market for a lover": men do not just naturally not love, they learn not to. And I think you're a bluffer. Your novel was all about a man desperate for love and a relationship in a world filled with nothing but casual sex.

FRED: Do you think we could start over?

(They return to their lovemaking.)

FELIX: We have.

CUT TO:

They are still naked, lit by the moonlight. Fred touches his finger to a spot of liquid on Felix's chest. He holds up the finger and they both stare at it.

FRED: Yours or mine?

FELIX: If I had it would you still see me?

FRED: Sure. Would you if I did?

FELIX: When we first met, why didn't you tell me you were a writer?

FRED: Why didn't you tell me you worked at *The Truth*? That, I would have remembered.

FELIX: If I had told you that, you would have seen me again?

FRED: Absolutely.

FELIX: You hustler-slut.

FRED: Hustler-slut! *(This breaks them up.)*

FELIX: It's sad how much time we lost.

FRED: Felix, we just weren't ready then. *(Realizing it:)* I've wanted a lover like you my whole life and you haven't showed up till now and I'm scared shitless I'll do something to fuck it up. *(Pause.)* Do you really think I'm crazy?

FELIX: I certainly do. That's why I'm here.

FRED: My fucking board. Two solid hours they all yelled at me the other night. I'm creating a panic. I'm making myself into a celebrity. Not one of them will be interviewed or appear on TV, so I do it all by default.

FELIX: And you love to fight.

FRED: I love to fight. Moi?

FELIX: And you're having a great time.

FRED: Yes, I am.

INT. DISCO. NIGHT.

A huge dancing crowd. The place is mobbed and decorated beautifully. Everybody is very up. Music: Gloria Gaynor, "I Will Survive." A big banner: GAY MEN PAY ATTENTION.

CUT TO:

Bruce delivering a speech to the crowd.

BRUCE: We sure are glad you all showed up! We kind of feel this gives us a mandate to carry on doing what we're doing.

(Loud cheers.)

And in the way we're doing it.

(More cheers.)

Tonight we're proving we have more than looks, brains, talent, and heart. Tonight we've raised more money than any gay organization has ever raised in this city before.

(Fred hands him a card.)

Fifty-three thousand dollars!

Huge cheers. Fred and Bruce embrace. Morton, Dick, Tommy come up to join them.

CUT TO:

New York City Gay Men's Chorus singing "The Man I Love."

CUT TO:

Fred and Felix in a corner making funny faces at each other, then giving each other a big kiss.

CUT TO:

Everyone on the floor is kissing each other as the chorus crescendos. It is an amazingly wonderful sight. Even Emma, with several of her sick patients, does a sort of dance.

FRED: Would you like to move in with me?

Felix nods. Fred starts to dance like a crazy person.

INT. FRED ON TV.

Being interviewed by a woman, SaraBeth Clare.

FRED: What do I think? I *know* that the government is intentionally ignoring this epidemic.

SARABETH: You're accusing the government of the United States of a conspiracy to murder all gay men?

Lettering appears under Fred: FRED LEMISH, CO-FOUNDER, GAY MEN PAY ATTENTION.

FRED: Yes. Yes, SaraBeth, I am. Yes.

INT. BOARDROOM. DICK'S LAW OFFICE. NIGHT.

Walls shelved with law books. Several new faces, including Joey, a young Hispanic. Bruce presiding. Fred in the hot seat. Mickey is visibly upset by the fight going on and glaring at Fred. Morton smirking. Tommy looking glacially into space.

BRUCE: You can't go on national TV and accuse the government of murder!

FRED: Why not?

BRUCE: One of these days they're going to give us money, research, grants . . .

FRED: Ruester still hasn't said the word in public! Congress still hasn't appropriated a dime. *The Truth* still hasn't . . . The mayor still hasn't . . .

DICK: Fred, when you go public, you have no right to speak for this organization unless we have approved what you say in advance. In point of fact, you are not even an officer of this organization and shouldn't be speaking for us at all.

FRED: Thank you for letting us meet in your office, Dick.

(Walks out.)

INT. FRED ON TV.

The interviewer this time is a man, Malcolm Murphy.

MALCOLM: Why do you think New York City is being so slow to acknowledge and recognize this emergency?

Lettering under Fred: "Fred Lemish, Gay Activist."

FRED: You're implying that the city *has* recognized and acknowledged this emergency, Malcolm. It has not.

MALCOLM: Why not, do you think?

FRED *(after a beat)*: Because the mayor is gay and scared out of his panties that it'll blow his cover.

INT. BOARDROOM. NIGHT.

Fred in the hot seat again. Very heated. Similar expressions on faces. Mickey is upset by yet another fight. Another new face, Dan, a schoolteacher.

FRED: You can't tell me what to say when I'm speaking for myself.

BRUCE: Everyone knows you're one of us!

FRED: You can't have it both ways!

DICK: No, *you* cannot have it both ways!

MORTON: It is totally and politically incorrect to call people gay who do not self-identify as being gay!

FRED *(working this out and saying it for the first time)*: I know it's been that way forever. But something different is going on now. We're dying. I don't want to die because another gay man is too ashamed of himself to help us stay alive. I am not going to let him kill us because he's ashamed of what I'm proudest of. If it's been commanded by the gay "movement" to protect such people, then it's wrong. *(To Dick:)* The mayor—he's your personal friend. You want him to appoint you as a judge. Do you have a little conflict of interest going on here?

DICK: I told you. I sent him a memo.

FRED: When?

DICK: Through channels.

FRED: When!

DICK: He'll answer me.

FRED: When!

DICK: Three, four . . . months.

FRED: There were three hundred, four hundred new cases in those three, four months!

He looks at Bruce, who has his head down between his legs.

FRED *(contd)*: Do I embarrass you?

BRUCE: Yes, you do.

JOEY: You get more with honey than with vinegar.

FRED: I've never heard that one, Joey.

DAN: No, obviously he hasn't.

FRED *(in Joey's face)*: The squeaky wheel gets the most grease. Ever hear that one, Joey? Dan?

BRUCE: If we get too political we lose our tax-exempt status. That's what Harvey in your own brother's law firm advised us. We got more than we can handle just trying to help patients.

(To Tommy:) Give your report.

TOMMY *(consulting notes)*: We have trained forty-five crisis counselors to help the newly diagnosed in whatever needs they might have. We have twelve group leaders who meet with these counselors at least once a week to go over all their clients. There are now seventeen volunteer social workers, psychologists, and/or psychiatrists. I can call on five lawyers. We helped draw up seventy-five wills last month—

FRED *(interrupting)*: You think the Catholic Church, Jerry Falwell, the Salvation Army, the Red Cross, aren't putting political pressure on somebody somewhere for money and help? Bruce—you were a fighter once. Did you like being a Green Beret?

BRUCE: I loved it.

FRED: So why did you quit?

BRUCE: I didn't quit! I was gay. I had to choose.

FRED: Have you completely forgotten how to fight?

BRUCE: Don't you fucking talk to me about fighting! I just fight different from you!

FRED: I haven't seen your way yet. Bruce—your Albert may be dying.

BRUCE: Shut up! Just you shut up about Albert!

FRED *(to Dick)*: And you have no right being on this board unless you pressure your friend the mayor. That's why I asked you to join us in the first place. And you know it.

Dick and Fred stare at each other.

INT. FRED ON THE *DONAHUE* SHOW. DAY.

WOMAN IN AUDIENCE: What you do and say are against the Bible, against God, against Jesus . . .

FRED: How do you know? Were you there? Jesus was a single gentleman.

Gasps from audience. Fred suddenly stands up and walks among the audience. They look at him like he's the enemy.

FRED *(contd)*: Don't you understand? We can't change. Just like you can't change. You can't become gay and I can't become straight. So what do you want us all to do? Take poison? Jump off buildings? Slash our wrists? Die?! Do you want to put us in ovens? What would your Jesus say about that? You want us all to lead normal lives, but you won't give us any legal or theological ways to do so. Why are you punishing us so? We are your sons and brothers! And husbands! We are your children! This plague isn't the wrath of God—it's the wrath of you!

INT. SUBWAY. DAY.

An older man, Arthur, stops Fred.

FRED: Arthur, how are . . .

ARTHUR: I think what you're doing is awful.

FRED: What am I doing, Arthur?

ARTHUR: You're destroying all our progress. You're painting us as sick. It's not going to happen to me—do you hear me? It's not going to happen to me or to most of us and you should keep your mouth shut! You're destroying homosexuality forever!

Arthur gets so worked up that, in his fury, he starts pummeling Fred. Fred disentangles himself and Arthur runs off. Fred stands there unbelievingly.

DORIS HARDWARE'S REMARKS AT AN INTERNATIONAL CONFERENCE OF MADAMS

AMSTERDAM

I am often asked to describe my customers. I don't know if you share similar descriptions. Please know of course that I mean no insult to any countries' manhood.

The British in Washington have always been among my best customers. The Brits have the most fucked-up of all sex lives. The Japanese are the most childish and come the quickest. I have my biggest profit margin on the Japs. Except they won't use condoms and now I am more and more insisting on condoms. There's less profit in Germans. Germans take forever to come. They say they're enjoying themselves longer, but Germans don't understand enjoyment. The French—there's no rule of thumb with the French. One does not generalize about the French. They really are more inscrutable than the Chinese. The Chinese are only inscrutable because their language is incomprehensible, both visually and aurally. The French are inscrutable even if you speak or read French quite well. The French couldn't care less whether anyone understands them or not, whereas it's very important to the Chinese that you don't understand them, that they remain incomprehensible to you, because we are the West and they are not. The French try for elegance and style, which are so important to the French. Elegance, of course, masks truth. The French are not very honest. South Americans, Spaniards, and Mexicans scream and make a lot of noise when they have their orgasms. No one has ever been able to explain to me why they are noisier than, say, the Portuguese. It seems to be a point of particular pride among some Hispanic men to scream when they come. Or perhaps they are just surprised at their achievement. I put them in the farthest rooms. Australians are very well behaved, but not too highly sexed, I think because they are the most attractive physically. I wouldn't mind catering to Aussies exclusively. No fuss, no bother, nothing too out of the ordinary. But there would have to be more of them. I couldn't make a living on the few who come to America. Which leaves my beloved countrymen.

The American male. What about him? He can be everything, anything, and nothing. He can be rude, polite, charming, destructive, and physically cruel. That sounds like the French. But Frenchmen have no eyes. You can't see inside a Frenchman. You can see an American man lie right down to his toes. Since they lie even to themselves, they're completely predictable. America can be read in her men's eyes. All the lies. All the I'm sorrys and You won't believe this buts . . . Our men are the weakest, least trustworthy, most cowardly. And ironically the most appealing. Their insecurities propel them into trying to seduce you into loving them, a rather deceitful way of having sex that most women fall for.

And would you believe Republicans and Democrats really *are* different? Republicans fuck less, enjoy it less, and feel guiltier afterward. Democrats are more randy, tip better, are more decent to women—Republicans still treat us like servants; God, how I hate Republicans—but Democrats are slobs, they bathe less, slobber more when they kiss, dress with less taste, a lot less taste, have poor teeth, bad breath, and they want to shoot again after they rest up, not because they have a new and refreshed desire but because they're certain they didn't get their money's worth yet. Democrats have much more energy. The GOP has much more cunning. My biggest customer base is Republican.

Of late there have been customers from Africa. So many revolutions over there that I can't keep the names of their countries straight. Since a growing number has inquired for black women, I have taken on a few of these who are surprisingly increasingly in demand. I brought two of them over from Léopoldville in what I believe is now called the Belgian Congo. They were highly recommended to me by Madame Rose, whose house there has been protected by their government as a service to returning soldiers from one of their never-ending wars. Would that my government be so considerate! I met Rose at an international conference of us organized by the Health of the World organization in Geneva. We had a wonderful time. I was amazed and pleased by how many sterling, stalwart, hugely intelligent, strong women I met there and see among us now. The two girls from Rose that I brought over—Brazzi and Kinni, named for the towns they hail from—are touchingly sweet as they learn English from their favorite customers. They say that in much of Africa many girls service a thousand or more clients each year in search of a better life. There are five men to every woman in Léopoldville. They are called "free women." Imagine that. Velvalee, one of my staff, has taken them particularly under her wing. She is very moved by all our new girls. She has become sort of the den mother of us all, untouchable herself but exemplary to all. She helps me run my business now. I would be lost without her, as I grow older. I urge all of you to find yourself a Velvalee.

The world of course is getting rougher. Male machismo is getting markedly out of control. Politics have become increasingly nasty and untrustworthy. My client base reflects this increasingly nasty development in world events. *Gentleman* is not a word one can utilize much anymore.

I'm certain you're all familiar with much of what I've spoken about. How we can bring harmony to our calling and legal respect for our girls is still way beyond our reach. Perhaps at one of our smaller workshops we can brainstorm about this problem.

•

Very interesting. I have been to many of those countries. I will soon enough reach the others. I am going to live forever. I am. I am. I keep telling you and you keep not listening.

ANN FETTNER

More crazies are showing up. American scientific research is based on the most absurd of notions. You do not tell scientists what to research. You wait until somebody decides to look into this or that. Scientists are not a bunch who can be ordered what to do, as it was in Germany. It's one reason why everything takes so long. One must wait for the prima ballerinas to go en pointe in ballets of their own choreography. The Germans over here cannot believe how much freedom is allowed the individual scientist to research whatever he wants. Even Grodzo has said, "Hitler would never have happened with this much *freiheit*."

There are an increasing number of ridiculous statements about what should be researched and how. The "world-famous" hematologist Dr. Nelson Golly comes from Oxford to Harvard to make the case for Sals Particularity as the cure for UC. Harvard gave him a Distinguished Scholar Fellowship to pay for this research, something Oxford (and English law) found unsavory. But Harvard then advised him to go to NITS. "They're not doing anything there."

I am reminded of a radio program from my childhood, *Can You Top This?*

DR. NELSON GOLLY ON SALS PARTICULARITY

Sals means "salt." A particular salt. No one knows where the term comes from. Salt has been in use culinarily as far back as ancient Rome, and medicinally for just as long. Paracelsus, the great Swiss sixteenth-century physician, asserted that "the elements of all things are salt, sulfur, and mercury," and that "salt added to any extract increases its strength," and that "whatever purges, does so by reason of the salt in it." Have you taken your particular salt? My colleagues in ancient medicine agree that the term appears more Roman than Greek.

But *sals* can also mean, medically (see Novotrott's standard text, *Medicine of the Ancient World*), "a not-quite-particular-enough salt." In other words, a sort of ambivalent salt, although Novotrott does not elaborate. My article in *The New England Journal of Salts* makes a case for this ambivalence, sort of the bisexuality of salts. This goes a bit too far, some think, because Sals, alone, by itself, is not ert. It is not living, and no one expects it to get it up. But according to me, that's precisely because it is not quite "particular" enough. If the salt were more *formed*, more *specific*, it would produce an effect other than the effect it produces *as is*. Anyone who puts salt on food can understand this. There are different kinds of salt—regular, rock, seasoned, Jerusalem, Accent, kosher, herb, Krazy Jane's, Lawry's, Marks & Sparks, even from Madagascar—and each gives the food it's sprinkled on a different taste. Think of it this way: the salt is serving to mask the true flavor of the food it's sprinkled on. It's putting a *protective sheath* over it. It's not accentuating the vegetable's flavor, it's masking it. The real essence of asparagus, like semen sheathed by a condom, can't get through.

A few years ago, when a rush of cancer of the nose was in the air, I spent a lot of time and money trying unsuccessfully to develop a "denser" salt. A Dr. Goetzee from India had suggested that a dense salt should be sniffed up a cancerous nose; he had seen it work in his country, where this cancer is common. He suggests that Sals Particularity is not dense enough on its own against this Underlying Condition. He says that my salt's ranshees are probably too weak and free-floating.

It is a difficult task to muck around with salt. According to Dr. Goetzee all you have to do to get a denser salt is to blanch in more ranshees. He sent an up-to-date recipe on how to do this.

Unfortunately, I then discovered that ranshees don't get along with pus. I discovered this by using the pus slides from those six dead nuns at Mater Nostra Dolorosa. Pus is now top of the hit parade of possible causes of this shit. Nimroids, which I named after the famous Greek surgeon, exude poisonous pus. Ransheed pus produces only a terrible body rash that is also quite malodorous.

Dr. Horace Vetch, a plastic surgeon at Princeton, claims patients can die instantaneously from exposure to this pus. That was the first anyone had heard of such a speedy demise. His work is considered "Fringe, on the borderline of crackpot," according to the pioneer eugenicist Jeremiah Brinestalker in New Godding, who is evidently internationally famous for his horses. Dr. Vetch claims to have infected a horse with nimroid pus, "cleansed" it via plasmapheresis of its blood before returning it to the animal, and then entering it in "a thoroughbred race, which it won."

Experiments have been done on monkeys. This is always the Proof thrown in the face of the Unbeliever: "But experiments have been done on monkeys." It's always the "monkeys." So much so that Dr. Dripper is facing a shortage of them. It's never "But experiments have been done on mice." Or "chickens." Or even "amoebas." (Although we have just seen a horse.) And of course it's never—*never*—"But experiments have been done on patients." (Which is why these charges against Dr. Sister Grace Hooker are so threatening. Much too much was "learned" at Nuremberg about fostering quick results.) Anyway, Dr. Dripper's monkeys appear remarkably unaffected by my denser salt.

I am now trying to find out how to make ultra-ransheed salt get along with pus. My work is of particular interest to Middleditch (misidentified somewhere by that Lemish character as Middlemarch), whose star scientist, that nitwit Geiseric, evidently now feels threated by my work, which he is unable to take and run with. Dr. Middleditch must protect him and the glory of NITS.

I start injecting denser salts into sick young men to see if they remain alive longer. So far the results are inconclusive. Goetzee claims that the tolerated dosage hasn't been reached. That is always what's said when the results are inconclusive (i.e., patients keep dying). My studies are now under way involving the injection of gradually increased doses of ultra-ransheed salt directly into bloodstreams. Patients report that everything they eat now tastes of salt. They are also always very thirsty. Both good signs, says Goetzee.

This is proving a most laborious process, working with a body that is simultaneously succumbing to the ravages of this shit and dying of thirst.

DR. REBBY ITSENFELDER

Salt is salt. It is about as particular as it's going to get. These theories are so ridiculous as to make one gasp for breath. Salt, no salt, better salt, different salt, denser salt, weak salt, strong salt! Ranshees! Gollys! PUS! God help us. Why can't we just admit we don't know anything about what causes this shit? If there even *is* an Underlying Condition. I cannot get back to New York fast enough. NITS! NITS is full of nits!

DR. BOSCO DRIPPER

Dr. Lucien Van Hoof's son in Antwerp forwarded to me some newly discovered last reports written by his great father just before he died. Lucien had been concerned about strange deaths in western Africa of *Pan troglodytes troglodytes* and sooty mangabeys and "even some gorillas." Like niggers, *Pan trogs* take such godawful care of their environments. But these various primate types do not infect each other. It is not in their mechanisms. *Pan trogs* fuck only with other *Pan trogs*. What were *Pan trogs* eating? Lucien died in 1948.

•

Yes. That is correct. I was there. I didn't like it much. You're right about a nasty environment! What is an Antwerp? Have I been there yet? I am finding so many places to go. What please is a nigger?

•

INT. GMPA OFFICE. NIGHT.
It's nighttime. Fred and Bruce are doing paperwork. Fred looks at Bruce and realizes he's been crying.
BRUCE: Albert is dead.
FRED: Oh, no.
BRUCE: What's today?
FRED: Wednesday.
BRUCE: He's been dead a week.
FRED: I didn't know he was so close.
BRUCE: No one did. He wouldn't tell anyone. You know why? Because of me. Because he knows I'm so scared I'm some sort of carrier. This makes three people I've been with who are dead. Albert, I think I loved him best of all, and he went so fast. His mother wanted him back in Phoenix before he died, this was last week when it was obvious, so I get permission from Emma and bundle him all up and take him to the plane in an ambulance. The pilot wouldn't take off and I refused to leave the plane—you would have been proud of me—so finally they get another pilot. Then, after we take off, Albert loses his mind, not recognizing me, not knowing where he is or that he's going home, and then, right there, on the plane, he becomes . . . incontinent. He starts doing it in his pants and all over the seat; shit,

piss, everything. I pull down my suitcase and yank out whatever
clothes are in there and I start cleaning him up as best I can,
and all these people are staring at us and moving away in droves
and . . . and I sit there holding his hand, saying, "Albert, please,
no more, hold it in, man, I beg you, just for us, for Bruce and
Albert." And when we get to Phoenix, there's a police van waiting for us and all the police are in complete protective rubber
clothing, they looked like fucking astronauts, and by the time
we got to the hospital, where his mother had fixed up his room
real nice, Albert was dead.

(Fred starts toward him.)

Wait. It gets worse. The hospital doctors refused to examine
him to put a cause of death on the death certificate, and without a death certificate the undertakers wouldn't take him away,
and neither would the police. Finally, some orderly comes in and
stuffs Albert in a heavy-duty Glad bag and motions us with his
finger to follow and he puts him out in the back alley with the
garbage. He says, "Hey, man. See what a big favor I've done for
you, I got him out, I want fifty bucks." I paid him! Then his
mother and I carried the bag to her car and we finally found a
black undertaker who cremated him for a thousand dollars, no
questions asked.

*(Fred crosses to Bruce and embraces him; Bruce puts his arms around
Fred.)*

BRUCE: Would you and Felix mind if I spent a few nights on your
sofa? I don't want to go home.

DEEP THROAT

You're in big big trouble, Fred. Your guys just don't know how big.

•

EXT. BEACH AT FIRE ISLAND. DAY.
*A bleak day. The beach is deserted. A big photograph of Albert held
aloft. About twenty guys. Fred, Felix, Mickey, Gregory, Christopher
now with Herb, Pierre, Nick, Morton, Buzzy, a few others who are
recognizable. A man with a minister's collar hands Bruce a small box,*

*then gives him a hug. Bruce, in his Green Beret uniform, starts to
scatter Albert's ashes over the water and then, even though he is clothed,
wades into the water, scattering more, walking out farther and farther.*

EXT. FIRE ISLAND PINES. NIGHT.
*A mammoth beach party is in progress. The beach is crowded with
dancers. The music is intense. Fred stands with Felix, over to the side,
taking it all in.*

EXT. WEST SIDE HIGHWAY AND CHRISTOPHER
STREET. DAY.
*Emma arrives there with Ned. The area is mobbed. A sea of men on
a warm sunny Sunday afternoon. She glares at him. He stands there
helplessly. Her eyes start to fill with tears. She suddenly takes off in her
wheelchair. As she can't get through the crowds of men she heads out to
the highway itself, zooming alongside the traffic. Fred runs after her.*
FRED *(calling)*: Emma! Come back! Please wait for me!
*He finally catches up with her and places himself in her path so she has to
stop. Traffic is forced to stop and go around them. Lots of honking horns.*
FRED *(kneeling)*: Please tell me!
EMMA: All those men! Fred. All those men out there! They don't
    know anything!

INTRODUCING DEEP THROAT

I have asked you not to use my real name, Fred. I intend to tell you the truth
as I know and find it. For now, let me just say that I run the pathology labs at
NITS. Ann Fettner put us together. She recognized birds of a feather. More
important, you should know others know about you, too, and want me to
keep them updated. "There is much rot in Denmark," I say enigmatically. If
you are sharing this with others, please honor my anonymity.

I was most impressed with your letters to Omicidio that were published.
I am worried that your principal contact at NITS, Dr. Daniel Jerusalem, is less
than what is needed. He appears to me so far as just another cog in the wheel.

Today I was standing at the Army's Walter Reed National Military
Medical Center watching a Change of Command ceremony. I am here to
represent NITS. Army labs are meant to be supervised by NITS.

The Army has lots of ceremonies for lots of reasons. They all seem united in a theme I once heard said of the British Army, that they confuse sentiment with ceremony, so instead of embracing a colleague and expressing their sorrow at parting, they assemble buglers, trumpeters, drummers, and colleagues in foppish adornment to avoid expressing that sorrow. The expression of emotion is not only a sign of weakness in the military, it might suggest graver symptoms. There are barracks of enlisted men brokenhearted at the reassignment or death of dear friends, and too brokenhearted to confess this love or to cry. And enlisted men don't even have departure ceremonies or Change of Command ceremonies the way officers do. For either, behavior that will not result in visible emotions is required.

As I stand in the hot sun and watch this ceremony, I puzzle over the strange reports I've been reading in *The Journal of Death*. I read this wrinkled quarto avidly; it's important to stay up to date on the stuff they cover. Reports about a new disease. A killer disease. A disease that so far has killed only known homosexual men. As I watch the parade of young men assembled to pay homage to the departure of some incompetent bureaucrat who was commander of an incompetent battalion, I wonder how many of his men might die. Will lesbians sicken as well? It occurs to me that I don't really know much about homosexuals. I've been told that since *Sexopolis* and the sexual revolution gave free license to sexuality for everyone, homosexuals have engaged in extraordinary feats of activity. I know that the Capitol men's toilets have been a favorite trysting ground for congressmen. I have heard about "T rooms," public toilets where men engage in anonymous sexual encounters lasting only long enough for ejaculation. But I don't know much. I'm not sure what rimming is. Fisting is totally foreign. I don't know how they do it. The idea that a Dr. Golly might ascribe this new illness to bad dope, he who only recently was betting on ransheed salt, seems to require a lot more exotic dope than I ever tried. To produce a full-fledged immune collapse would require monster doses of something that makes chemical sense. I can't see how the many homosexuals so far affected could possibly have taken that much dope in so coordinated a manner that they all got sick at once. Assume that the amyl or butyl nitrite, the main ingredient in the Dridgies that *JOD* said all the boys are taking, was contaminated with some deadly poison. Amyl nitrite from the worst sources is at least 95 percent pure, and it would take about 95 milligrams to send somebody on the point of orgasm totally over the moon. That leaves 5 milligrams of bad stuff in the rest of the popper. It seems unlikely that these 5 milligrams could contain more than 1 milligram of really new chemicals likely to poison the immune system, which means that a substance had to be active at one part in 50 million. Assuming a functioning liver, it seems very unlikely that such a small dose could be diluted in the body and still remain active long enough to produce the types of lesions that occur. This Dr. Itsenfelder, the proponent of the Dridgies as cause, does not know his chemistry.

This was what I was thinking about as I stood and watched the Change of Command ceremony. I didn't think about the money these things cost. A year ago, one of the buffoons at the Armed Forces Institute of Pathology had a model airplane built big enough for him to sit in while having his picture taken. The entire carpentry shop worked for four months on that one.

I was still smarting about having called a reporter at *The Washington Monument* to draw his attention to the *JOD* article about the "Gay Plague" and hearing him respond, "So what?" (Jerry is to criticize me for this interaction). From what I have read, the disease was characterized by *Pneumocystis carinii* pneumonia. A bit later, Kaposi's sarcoma was reported. Poor old Kaposi. He was a pathologist who described two diseases that bear his name (about the only way for us pathologists to become immortal is through eponymous naming of diseases), and one of them is Kaposi's sarcoma. Sarcomas are a type of cancer. Strictly speaking, sarcomas are true malignant tumors that not only invade but spread to other parts of the body. Kaposi's doesn't do this. Pathologists have tried to think up terms such as "tumor-like" or "Kaposi's lymphoderma perniciosa" to keep from calling it a cancer. Until the "Gay Plague," Kaposi's sarcoma was only an interesting skin disease. Patients rarely died of it. Blacks in Africa got KS and lived with multiple spots on their legs or arms for years. Blacks in America almost never get KS. It is found in white men fifteen times oftener than in females. In Europe it is a disease of old men, in whom Kaposi first described it in 1872. Until the reports from New York and San Francisco about nimroids, which turn out to be Kaposi's lesions, we thought KS was an exotic disease that would rarely cross our lives.

The other tip-off in the reports was the coupling of *Pneumocystis carinii* pneumonia with this Kaposi thing. PCP was a lost disease, found in the most amazing circumstances. Like KS, PCP was first described many years ago. Its discoverers thought it was a form of sleeping sickness rampant in South America and Africa. There were sporadic reports of the disease in rats and guinea pigs for some years, and then it dropped completely out of sight until the aftermath of World War II. Central Europe was devastated and the very

young and the very old suffered most. In the orphans' homes of Czechoslovakia and Belgium babies died of a terrible pneumonia that turned their lungs
into a kind of soggy sponge cake and their wasting bodies blue. Two bright
Czech pathologists hypothesized that the pneumonia seemed to be caused by
the parasite found in rats some thirty years before. They failed to establish a
therapy. The disease lapsed into obscurity again as nutrition in Europe improved and babies got better care.

Beginning in the 1960s, crusading cancer specialists started treating
their patients with a whole collection of agents, first based on war gases and
antibiotics, but later on custom-tailored molecules that could poison cancer
cells preferentially. As the toxic drugs killed cells in the immune system, people became deathly ill from diseases that would never have affected them if
they were not taking the drugs. The mysterious pneumonia that appeared
baffled the oncologists, and specialists in obscure diseases were called in. One
of them was Dr. Israel Jerusalem, who had won a Nobel for his work on an
obscure disease in cannibals in the Andes and elsewhere, who was able to
identify PCP as a major complication in patients undergoing chemotherapy.
A leader in the next step was NITS's Roscoe Middleditch, soon to cause me
so much sadness. Middleditch recognized, by way of Israel's discovery, that
the connections among the effects of PCP, the use of chemotherapy, and a
disintegrating immune system cause the last to be further compromised by
the arrival on the scene of an increasing number of Opportunistic Infections
(also noticed by Itsenfelder). Cease the chemotherapy and a few of the other
OIs disappeared, which unfortunately wasn't enough. Middleditch, perhaps
one of the better oncologists around, recognized that treating cancer with
chemotherapy and radiation is a juggling act. The physician must bring the
patient near to death, using every skill to keep infections at bay until the
treatment has progressed enough to destroy the cancer cells. Middleditch experienced a tragic example of these types of patients when his own son developed an irreversible blood disorder that left him without a proper immune
system, so that the kid spent the last years of his life living in a bubble house
of plastic to protect him from infections. Is it a small blessing that the child
survived the immune deficiency only to die like that?

As our current tragedy unfolds, it is evident that we are dealing with
a new disease. As I stood outside Walter Reed and squinted at the jackass
general in his space cadet suit, with row upon row of ribbons representing
his years of excellence as a faithful bureaucrat, the puzzle of these seemingly
unrelated occurrences eluded me. Previously healthy homosexuals dying at

an early age without evident alcoholism or consistent IV drug use. Death from a parasite that crawls around inside the lungs of rats, guinea pigs, and men. I was hearing on the grapevine that not-dissimilar occurrences were appearing in southwestern Africa.

I went by the Officers' Club to cash a check. It had the musty smell of everything to do with today's Army. Stale food smells and crumbling remains of a time when America cared for its army, before Vietnam. Being an officer in the United States Army is now neither an honor nor a privilege. The enlisted men have about bottomed out and a significant number of volunteers for our armed forces are certifiably mentally retarded. Shoving the cash in my pocket, I paused to look at the photographs in the entrance from a time of greater splendor. There sat Walter Reed himself, staring back with his baleful eyes. "What would you do, young Walter?" I wondered aloud to the amazement of two women officers. Poor Walter, brilliant scientist, perhaps a thief of the discoveries of others, died as a result of attempting to second-guess his own appendix, which ruptured while he temporized and killed him horribly with peritonitis.

Then an idea hit me. Shades of Walter Reed! I should start a collection! Get docs to establish a central repository of information about this disease of young men. *JOD* certainly wasn't providing that service, nor was *NEJS*. And certainly not at our labs at NITS. We knew fuck-all about this. COD had never even bothered to inform us in the first place. And what better place to affiliate with than the Armed Forces Institute of Pathology, where the records of decades and specimen remains of thousands of young men who died untimely deaths were kept. Surely the Army would want to keep tabs on this new disease. Surely the Navy would be interested too. What a great idea! What we might learn! Mother would appreciate it.

The pathology of humans is a curious science. Recognizing that diseases are the result of changes in tissues was a major discovery that took most of human history. In the briefest of slivers of geological time, it became apparent that human tissue, as a part of human beings, become diseased from causes. In the 1850s a towering genius named Rudolf Virchow proposed the theory that all cells come from other cells, but more important, that all diseases have causes. This was the limit of medical rationalism. Thanks to autopsy and pathological methods laid out by Virchow and perfected by several generations of morbid anatomists, it became possible for even the least gifted healing artist to dissect out the cause of death from corpses who'd had far more time on the far side of the mortal veil than one would imagine possible.

The autopsy ritual is an ancient one. As a visiting student traveling about, I had first seen it in the autopsy theater in ancient Krakow unfolding before tiers of onlookers, the pale yellow light streaming down from the skylight, the surgeons intent on the waxy remains of an aged crone, long dead of cancer. The sounds of the Virchow chisel being struck to open the cranium brought back the image of the soft-boiled egg I decapitated in the Hotel Francuski for breakfast. The autopsy room in the famous General Hospital in Malmo, Sweden, where 70 percent of the deaths of the city's inhabitants are autopsied and the autopsy rooms are as clean and modern as the operating room for the living patients, lives with me as well. My journeys taught me this first principle of the science of pathology: Death has a Cause and the Cause can be found by examining the remains of the person, first by eye, then by knife, finally by probing with the extension of sight, the microscope.

I am always amazed by autopsies. Amazed at the intricacies of the body, the subtle or grotesque changes that transform and compromise the organs, the surprises brought by careful dissection, the finger probing the windpipe or the unfolding of the gut to reveal the ghastly cancer perforating the tubes. My repugnance at death is overcome by the miracle of the human body and the mystery that causes death.

After the sexual liberation of the 1960s homosexuals evidently became more open in their promiscuity and it accelerated both in degree and in the nature of the acts. I plow through some of the reports and I learn about homosexuals who have a thousand sexual contacts a year and who have all the "classic" venereal diseases. The details are tragic. Intimacy as the result of compulsion and degradation instead of affection seems to mark many of these homosexual characters. If gay lifestyles really do include all the events I read about in the medical journals, it is no surprise that a new disease has appeared. Immune exhaustion seems far more likely as an explanation of what is causing this UC.

Immunology has been as a fog to me. It all seems so ill defined. The body's domination of evil entities such as bacteria or foreign proteins should occur with transfers of energy. Immunologists, though, do not have this simplistic view of the matter. They seem to believe that any problem can be solved with an antibody, a "receptor," and a "model" to study the problem. That they would have us believe we live in such an uncomplicated relationship with all the forces that would or could destroy us in no way has cleared this fog.

A lot has happened in the field of immunology. A bewildering variety of cell types have been identified in humans as well as in animals. Blood or immune cells can now be fractionated by dozens of exotic methods. Lymphocytes can be grown in the laboratory, and to some extent Martin Arrowsmith's dream of artificially making antibodies has come true. My intransigence in keeping up with immunology had been leaving me feeling superannuated, or like I was the new kid in the neighborhood. Well, in this case, that's not a bad thing. There should never be such a thing as certainty. Pathology had taught me that.

Jerry Omicidio is an immunologist.

The Old General to whom I presented my Great New Idea had his latest joke ready for me, about the queer congressman who bought the new car: "The first thing he did was blow its horn." Suddenly I knew what would happen. The Ruester administration would clam up about the problem of the "Gay Plague." It would be relegated to the dirty jokes told by Americans who would never understand. I knew then that would happen.

It seems there is a patient at Franeeda Navy who is exceptionally ill. The patient was known to be effeminate and has a peculiar set of symptoms. He is demented with strange mental lapses, has constant diarrhea, and has suddenly gone blind. Blind? The ophthalmologist was brought in for a consult. The guy had wispy little cotton-like stuff in his eyes and was blind as a stump. Yes, he does have some funny bruises on his legs, but they may be due to a vitamin deficiency since the guy has had the shits for months. Yes, it does seem like the guy won't make it, and no, they didn't call across the street to NITS for a consultation since we are civilians over here. The guy can't be queer, though, because he swore that he wasn't when he enlisted in the United States Navy, and the lawyer with the judge advocate (called in by the Navy attending physician) asked him right out if he's queer. The patient denies ever being homosexual. This is a secret more likely than most to be carried to the grave. Blind! Oh shit, the queers are going blind and crazy!

On Monday I call the Navy. The National Naval Medical Center is a national tragedy. The military has two major health centers in Washington, one for the Army at Walter Reed, the other for the Navy at Franeeda. The Navy hospital is supposed to serve the catchment of most of the mid-Atlantic region; in addition, it has the responsibility of providing health care and hospitalization for the president and other functionaries of the U.S. and foreign governments. The Navy is ill suited to care for such eminent and highly visible patients. The hospital has recently been rocked by a major scandal concerning a surgeon who was both physically and professionally incapable of performing the heart surgery he insisted on doing. It has been under the direction of a series of incompetent admirals drawn from the ranks of the Navy's Medical Service Corps, who have, among other things, neglected to determine the credentials of physicians practicing in the hospital. A "new" hospital had to be remodeled out of an old annex because it was discovered that the "Tower" on the old hospital was a firetrap. A succession of presidents have been victims of hasty and slipshod health care provided by the Navy here. The lifesaving treatment that Peter Ruester will receive at George Washington University Hospital after the assassination attempt by a demented sexual pervert armed with explosive bullets would have been more problematic if he had been taken to the Navy. He'd probably be (fortunately) dead.

My friend and a most respected fellow pathologist, Jay Truslove, who is at Navy, was dealing with the case of the blind Navy sailor. The kid had been taken to the intensive care unit and should make it into the autopsy suite within the week. Nobody is certain whether this man has anything in common with the California or New York cases, but he has had a strange history of skin lesions that "look" like Kaposi's and, because of that stupid British asshole Nelson Golly, were still being called nimroids. In addition to being blind from cytomegalovirus retinitis, he has been out of his head for two months and now has an interstitial pneumonia. Fascinating.

On Wednesday Truslove calls. The guy died at six in the morning and the autopsy will be at ten or so. He'd like me to help him and suggested, "You should even bring your boss so he can see what he's going to be up against." I pour some preservatives for electron microscopy and light microscopy and leave with my box of dissection tools. Jerry comes with me along with his assistant, one Daniel Jerusalem. (The autopsy room at Navy is in somewhat better order than the one at Walter Reed, where there was blood on the doorknob the last time I was in it.) Truslove is ready to start when we get there. The corpse is on the gurney covered by sheets. I quickly change into the disposable paper scrub suit in the locker room. The technician has moved the gurney alongside the autopsy table. The body is still covered.

When the sheets are drawn back I get my first look at the specter that will haunt me for the rest of my life. My first inside look at UC. Jerry and Daniel are riveted as well. The body is grotesque. He was twenty-eight years old and about five feet ten. He is so wasted he looks like one of the corpses from Belsen or Auschwitz. His cheeks are so sunken that his face looks like a skull. The eyes, still open, stare into a void. The wasted body with the points of the pelvis like crags above the shrunken abdomen looks more horrible than the hundreds of cancer patients I have seen on autopsy tables. His hair has the scruffy look of chronic disease. The genitals lie like an afterthought attached to the distorted pelvis. His circumcised penis has a large purple spot on the glans, and there are other purple blotches on his knees, lower legs, and ankles. There are white flecks at the corners of his mouth, as though he'd been eating chalk as he died.

Jay seems as fascinated as I. The kid had been a clerk-typist at the Washington Navy Yard. Gossip says that he was a raging faggot who provided blow jobs or his behind to any and all. No doubt he had officially denied being homosexual since it would compromise his care, cause the revoking of his medical benefits, not to mention a dishonorable discharge.

The autopsy proceeded. I was content to watch as Jay made the Y-shaped cuts across the chest and down to the pubis. I was getting my vials and dissecting dishes ready when "Jesus Christ! Look at this!" broke into my preparation. Jay had opened the chest, and the lungs were sodden masses. The kid, Paul, had been a smoker, so the color was a mottled red and black, but the normally air-filled lungs were rock-hard solid. I took several pieces from both lungs for my dissecting dishes. Some I cut into tiny cubes for electron microscopy. The larger pieces I would look at later with the light microscope at NITS.

The organs came and went, liver, kidneys, heart, adrenals, pancreas, finally testicles. Testicles are difficult to dissect: when the capsule-like membrane of the testicle is cut, the tubules where the sperm is made unravel like yarn from a skein. By the time we were finished and Paul was ready to go to the undertaker I had assembled some forty vials of tissues in addition to samples for the Navy's autopsy report identifying some cause of death. From the anatomical part of the autopsy we knew Paul had died from a whole string of diseases. In short, Paul was a train wreck. Every single one of his organs was malformed beyond belief. Even Jerry was shaking his head unbelievingly. After a while he and Daniel took off.

It was nearly four when we finished. Jesus! What a mess!

In the locker room Jay and I are alone. He is talking animatedly. I toss my old shoes into the trash and strip off to my skivvies. My locker is next to his and I become aware of a presence in the cramped quarters. He is looking me in the eyes and suddenly an amazing thing happens. He expands! He puffs up and seems to be twice as big as he was a few seconds ago. He stands before me with flashing eyes and flexed chest. I am startled to numbness. I look away to avoid his gaze. I catch a glimpse of his crotch and realize the guy has a hard-on. Jay is coming on to me! Jay is queer! What does he want to do with me here in the locker room of the Navy hospital morgue?

I panic. I mumble incoherently and grab my clothes from the locker. I dress as fast as I can while avoiding his eyes. Sensing my alarm, he seems to shrug and goes into the cramped toilet-shower next door. The shower starts just as I finish dressing. I step to the door and yell more loudly than necessary, "I'll call you as soon as I know anything, Jay." He replies indistinctly and I leave, marveling at the entire experience.

Setting up the specimens for processing takes until after nine. Still shaken, I walk home in the dark.

Two days later I get a call from the Old General at Walter Reed. He is an Army general of little distinction other than getting a medical degree from a Corn Belt land-grant college while in an ROTC program. The Army has been good to him, giving him a job, an identity, and now, as a final reward, the directorship that will allow him to retire to the private sector and be paid five times what he's worth, consulting to impressed clients. Sadly, malpractice lawyers have not discovered the vulnerability of aging, so this bozo will get away with the myth of his competency.

He wastes no time. He plunges right in.

"Hell no, Dr. Doctor, hell no! We don't want people . . . no, we don't want the Congress to think we got queers in the military! I don't want to see yours or anyone else's report of what's happening."

And that was the end of that.

Except that the person who puts the kibosh on any part of my Great Idea, I am to discover, is Jerry Omicidio. Why in the world would he care?

Garrie Nasturtium of Ruester's staff actually looks me up and pulls me aside. "Are you crazy? You expect taxpayer money to pay for a study of faggots? You're as bad as that nun pestering Dye about placentas."

And I say, "Garrie, all these centuries of fellows fucking each other, and no one's so much as looked up a rectum or followed a seminal vesicle. In the end it's going to cost much less, starting now, and not waiting for what's undoubtedly going to happen. There are important mechanisms, engines, which are working overtime to do something that's killing so many."

Then I threw in this kicker. "This applies to women as well. What happens inside her organs or indeed her vagina and rectum when this shit gets into them? No one's ever gone in to look there, either." Garrie almost choked to death.

Dr. Jerrold Omicidio, my titular boss, was not pleased to hear about this conversation either.

•

INT. FRED'S BEDROOM. NIGHT.

Fred and Felix have been making love.

FELIX: If I had it, would you leave me?

FRED: You already asked me that. No, I would not leave you.

FELIX: How can you be so certain?

FRED: I just know. My mother was a social worker. I'm not programmed any other way.

FELIX: I have something to tell you.

FRED: You're finally pregnant.

FELIX: Well, I was married once.

FRED: You never told me that.

FELIX: I thought I was programmed to be straight. She said I'd been unfair to her, which I had been. I have a son. She won't let me see him.

FRED: You can't see your own son? But didn't you fight? That means you're ashamed. So he will be, too.

FELIX: That's why I didn't tell you! Who says I didn't fight? Fred— what happens to people who can't be as strong as you want them to be?

FRED: Felix, weakness scares the shit out of me. My father was weak and I'm afraid I'll be like him. His life didn't stand for anything and then it was over. So I fight. Constantly. And if I can do it, I can't understand why everybody else can't do it, too. Okay?

FELIX: Okay.

Felix gets up and goes out of the room.

FRED: Where are you going?

Fred looks in various parts of the apartment.

FRED *(contd)*: Hey, you okay? I didn't mean anything . . . Felix? I'm really scared of lots of things. Really. Heights! I never told you. I'm terrified of heights. I can't go above the third floor or I get really scared . . .

INT. FRED'S BATHROOM.

He finds Felix sitting on the floor naked, in a pool of his shit and piss and vomit, his clothes having been ripped off and tossed to the side. He looks terrified. Fred immediately grabs towels and pulls him up from

the floor and they hold each other tightly. Then Felix shows him the
purple lesion on his foot.

INT. EMMA BROOKNER'S OFFICE. DAY.

Emma is confronting Fred. Felix can be seen in the adjoining room
standing naked.

EMMA: You've taken a lover!

FRED: What are we supposed to do—be with nobody ever?! Well,
   it's not as easy as you might think! Oh, Emma, I'm sorry.

EMMA: Don't be. Polio was a virus, too. I caught it three months
   before the Salk vaccine was announced. Nobody gets polio anymore. *(Looking toward Felix:)* I'll put him on some chemo. A
   couple of chemos. My own recipe. We'll hit it hard.

FRED: Thank you.

EMMA: Yeah. Fred, your organization is worthless.

EXT. WASHINGTON. ESTABLISHING SHOT. DAY.

EXT. WHITE HOUSE. DAY.

Fred at the gate, having his ID checked. He looks up at the place. He
takes a deep breath and strides confidently forward.

INT. OFFICE OF CHEVVY SLYME. DAY.

A sign on his desk: CHEVVY SLYME, DOMESTIC POLICY ADVISER TO THE
PRESIDENT. *It's obvious he does not want this meeting. He is tiny,*
red-flushed, beady-eyed.

FRED: Just so I understand. What exactly does your title mean? In
   terms of our plague?

SLYME: We prefer not to use negative terms. It only scares people.

FRED: Well, there's 3,339 dead cases so far. Sounds like a plague to
   me. I'm scared. Aren't you? What does your title mean?

SLYME: I come up with ideas for the president about what to do
   about what's going on.

FRED: Okay, good. We're desperately looking for someone to be in
   charge of this. Sort of a czar. Could you get the president to appoint one?

SLYME: We look upon the president as the czar.

FRED: So the money's there, then, right? It just hasn't been spent. So there's this new drug in France. Could you get the president as the czar to get NITS to study it? I mean, what I want . . . what we want . . . what we desperately need is for somebody to help us cut through all this red tape.

SLYME: I can assure you that not a week goes by that I don't bring new information and reports to the president. I'm told the progress that's been made on this disease is unprecedented . . .

FRED: Excuse me, sir, but what progress are you referring to?

SLYME: Tell me again who you knew to get in here?

FRED: The editor of *Newsday* and I went to Yaddah together.

SLYME: Who's the editor of *Newsday*? It doesn't make any difference. Answer me one question. This shit, can hookers get it and give it to their . . . clients?

FRED: Of course.

SLYME: I was told no.

FRED: You were told wrong.

(Slyme makes a note.)

But it's contagious! Can't you see! Because it's contagious you have to work faster! And you're not doing anything!

SLYME: Do you really believe that anybody in a serious public policy position, in their heart of hearts, or even in their most closeted meetings, says to each other, "Hey, guys, let's not get too upset about this."

FRED: Your boss still hasn't even said the word out loud.

SLYME *(gets up and closes door to his office)*: Answer me one question. Um. This shit, can you *prove* that hookers can get it? Or someone who had a one-night stand?

FRED: It's a virus. It doesn't discriminate.

SLYME: You can't prove that. I mean, from what I understand, from what I've read, female-to-male transmission through normal vaginal intercourse does not seem to be . . .

FRED: It's contagious. Sir, it's contagious.

SLYME: Yes, but it's very difficult, isn't it? It's impossible for a straight, you know, regular heterosexual guy to get it, am I right?

FRED: I'm sorry.

SLYME: There're no documented cases, am I right? There's not a single documented case of a heterosexual man getting it. Not from fucking or a blow job . . .

FRED: We don't know that.

SLYME: Great, that's what I thought. Thanks. *(Gives him his card.)* Call me anytime.

(A buzzer rings loudly on his desk. Slyme immediately rushes out through another door.)

FRED: Wait!

(He furiously rushes to follow him.)

(Screaming into the hallway:) A million people are going to die! It was in the London *Observer*!! President Ruester, my new lover is dying! Help! Please help!

(An alarm goes off. Guards rush in and haul him out.)

SMELLS LIKE A BIG ONE

Dr. Ekbert Nostrill is a Furstwasserian Brother of Lovejoy. Ekbert is one of many Furstwasserians placed in Washington's high strategic places by the Vestry. "That's how we get things done our way," First Father Herod could still and always be heard whispering into the ears of all his placements. Ekbert belongs to the Second Tier of the Vestry, which is the next-to-highest secret part of this religion. Indeed, when he was placed here he had received a mandate from the Vestry, First Tier. See that no activities transpire which deal with homosexuality. Homosexuality is to be ignored as if it were not around. Make certain as little as possible is done to stop any behavior causing any illness among homosexuals. Ekbert is troubled by these instructions. Surely they are un-Christian. On the other hand, his predecessor had left him notes on lots of files of unfinished business "that quite frankly I did not know how to finish. I do not know how to say 'don't lick your partner's asshole' or 'suck my peter' in a way that would be acceptable to us."

Purpura questioned Manny Moose about Nostrill's suitability for his special job as she envisioned it. While she knows that Manny is selling off key positions like they are pieces of land, she's worried whether enough of them are decent acceptables to join her new home team. It's always been a smart Republican tactic, layering the government forever with right-wing civil service appointees who by law can't be fired. Furstwasserian Lovejoys have been especially good customers for Manny's bounty. It's been a tough haul for Manny. Peter Ruester had not been an easy sell. Purpura was not happy with Manny's excuses and not a few of his choices.

That the world as we know it will end is the goal for many of today's religions. And so it is with Lovejoys and Furstwasserians, whose vision of the end is catastrophic. All the Herods and Ezras and Brighams and Josephs and Hesiods have talked about this with fevered fervor for over a century. They have been increasingly concerned with more precisely defining how to go out with a bang and not with a whimper. But there are now more liberal Brothers of Lovejoy who don't want to go out either way. It is still a young-ish religion and Ekbert wonders if this particular thorny theological aspect of their joint future can somehow be manipulated in a more life-affirming, positive way. Getting rid of homosexuals once and for all would certainly be a step in the right direction. Both conservative and liberal Lovejoys would be in favor of such a clean sweep. Then they could live forever and not have to worry about it. There are few religions in America that did not and do not exhibit similar behavior.

Ekbert's HAH job description calls for him to track down the root of whatever evil lurks in the bodies of men. More or less. That's how he reads it. Smells like a big one.

Will this big one make him happy or sad? Sometimes diseases come along that make him happy. They kill off poor people who have no money to eat and never will. Ekbert thinks then that this is God's way of calling His children home to Him. I will feed you now, He seems to be saying. This here new one that smells so big is different. Homosexuals aren't poor, at least not that he's heard of. He knows they're different. He knows they put their little dickies in places where he doesn't. This doesn't sound like something God would call His children home to give a home to. What would the Original First Father Herod say as he led his people across the swamps of Naugatauk? "Get rid of the fairies" comes immediately to mind.

"So what do you think?" Ekbert quietly asks Dr. Paulus Pewkin at an all-department meeting at HAH.

"The fairies?"

Ekbert nods.

"Smells like a big one."

"My very words."

"What do we do?"

"Smells like a big one."

"Nothing?"

"Smells like a big one."

Dr. Nostrill nods and starts to leave, feeling filled with empowerment.

"And, oh, Doctor Nostrill . . ."

"Yes, sir?"

"This illness is a gift to our people."

THE WHITE HOUSE

OFFICE OF THE PRESS SECRETARY
PRESS BRIEFING BY LARRY SPEAKES

Q: Larry, does the president have any reaction to the announcement from the Center of Disease that there is now an epidemic of some sort, hundreds of cases?

MR. SPEAKES: What's some sort?

Q: It's known as "gay plague." *(Laughter.)* No, it is. I mean it's a pretty serious thing that one in every three people that get this have died. And I wondered if the president is aware of it.

MR. SPEAKES: I don't have it. Do you? *(Laughter.)*

Q: No, I don't.

MR. SPEAKES: You didn't answer my question.

Q: Well, I just wondered does the president . . .

MR. SPEAKES: How do you know? *(Laughter.)*

Q: In other words, the White House looks on this as a great joke?

MR. SPEAKES: No, I don't know anything about this, Lester.

Q: Does the president, does anybody in the White House, know about this epidemic, Larry?

MR. SPEAKES: I don't think so. I don't think there's been any—

Q: Nobody knows?

MR. SPEAKES: There has been no personal experience here, Lester.

Q: No, I mean, I thought you were keeping—

MR. SPEAKES: I checked thoroughly with the president's personal physician this morning and he's had no—*(laughter)*—no patients suffering from whatever it is.

Q: The president doesn't have gay plague, is that what you're saying or what?

MR. SPEAKES: No, I didn't say that.

Q: Didn't say what?

MR. SPEAKES: I thought I heard you were in the State Department over there. Why didn't you stay there? *(Laughter.)*

Q: Because I love you, Larry, that's why. *(Laughter.)*

MR. SPEAKES: Oh, I see. Just don't put it in those terms, Lester. *(Laughter.)*

Q: Okay, I retract that.

MR. SPEAKES: I hope so.

Q: It's too late. *(Laughter.)*

•

Why is everyone making fun of me? I am in so many of you now that you would think I'd be taken seriously. Of course, I am thankful that you're not. It just tells me what kind of people you are.

•

EXT. EMERGENCY ROOM. NYU MEDICAL CENTER. NIGHT.

Fred and Tommy help Felix get out of a cab. Emma is there to meet them. Felix is wrapped in a blanket so we hardly see his face.

INT. INTENSIVE CARE. DAY.

Felix is connected to many devices. He is holding Fred's hand.

FELIX: You want me to get better and I'm not getting better and I feel so fucking guilty.

FRED: You're going to get better.

FELIX: Fred, let me die.

FRED: I can't do that.

FELIX: Please learn how to. I'm so tired. *(Fred holds him tightly.)* You are such a bunny tiger. Please, God, give us one more year. I promise I'll eat my spinach.

TALLULA AND THE FOOD HANDLERS

Tallula Giardino is a tall and breasty and bossy lesbian, with long ballerina's legs that make her look top-heavy. She is lovingly intimidating, in that she speaks her mind, and how, though you don't feel threatened by her. Fred, who adores her, wonders how she will be handling this one. How will she get her constituency to listen, the people she cares so much for? She makes them listen, she's that convincing, and she's particularly good at getting rich gay men to part with a few bucks for her organization, the Lesbian and

Gay Union (LAGU), though never nearly enough, no, never enough. She is passionately committed to the rights of gay people and can make you feel ashamed when you aren't too. She's a good leader of her small group of volunteers. In the straight world she'd be getting paid. When people say there are no gay leaders, they should know that it's hard to get good people to work for nothing. Tallula works for nothing.

"The blood supply. We're here tonight to speak about the blood supply. What are we going to do about it?" She's a forceful speaker. She gets invited to speak all over the country. There are a few gay groups out there, struggling themselves, wanting, needing to be inspired by her energy and presence. How many other gays are willing to go out there and speak forcefully and pointedly to their own? Quite frankly, none. "I am tragically before our time has come," she jokes, "I am pathetically against the tide," only half-joking, following up with "And our time will come!" which of course is what her listeners want to hear as they erupt in spontaneous applause. "Someday maybe they'll put me up at a decent hotel. I can't tell you how often I have to sleep in the guest bedroom with a dog or a cat. Maybe both. I like dogs but I'm allergic to cats." It's hard to get elected anything as a lesbian. She refuses to get elected to anything by not being a lesbian. A gutsy lady. "America is so awful to its disenfranchised," she tries to remind people every chance she gets. "We can't even pay for our very own salvation." These are not arguments many understand.

Fred loves the way she can parry and thrust, knocking down fools without them feeling they've been anything but vital to the cause. He wishes he had that gift. His gift, he's beginning to see, is "I get angry. I give good anger. Can't do what Tallula does. Can't not litter the ground with blood." Which is how he now thinks we should be playing this one.

"We have to consider the food handlers." What's Tallula talking about? "They will lose their jobs." What are food handlers anyway? "People who prepare, cook, serve, buy, sell, and deal with the food of our city, the food of our country, represent a large number of our gay brothers and sisters. We are very heavily invested in this field. And think of how many gay waiters there are!"

Fred's losing her. Food handlers doesn't top his list of what we're heavily invested in. What a peculiar cornerstone.

"Let's choose something straight people will sit up and pay attention to," she tells him.

He thinks there's something ass-backward about to happen. Why are

we protecting potentially sick people's jobs when they may in fact be infecting others, and not fighting to protect their lives before they do?

And so the first ad hoc meeting composed of some hundred gay men and
lesbians who do not belong to GMPA, and who will have nothing to do with
those elitists, votes this early morning to tell gay blood donors to continue to
give blood.

There are one or two who believe this is strategically and morally wrong.
"We must take the offensive, not the defensive," they argue. "Tell gay men
to stop giving blood immediately! Take our marbles and stay home. They'll
miss our blood donors soon enough. And at least we won't be killing people."

"Oh, stop talking like Fred Lemish! You're assuming that we are trans-
mitting something to each other."

Fred's pariah-dom is continuing to extend its reach.

"WHAT THE FUCK DO YOU THINK WE ARE DOING!" shouts
Fred Lemish himself at this very meeting, shocking Tallula and others.

Fred, who came for help, finds himself loaded for bear.

He does not like arguing with Talllula, who is his friend. But here he is
arguing, mightily, with Tallula.

"You all are crazy!" Fred continues. "Food handlers! This is what you
choose for your first Waterloo!"

The meeting is over. The group disperses. Tallula Giardino flips Fred
Lemish the finger as she walks out, saying, "Kisses."

WE KNOW WHO WE ARE

"Those of us who have lived a life of excessive promiscuity on the urban gay
circuit of bathhouses, backrooms, balconies, sex clubs, meat racks, and tea-
rooms know who we are . . . Those of us who have been promiscuous have
sat on the sidelines and by our silence have tacitly encouraged wild specula-
tion about a new, mutant, Andromeda-strain virus. We have remained silent
because we have been unwilling to accept responsibility for the role that our
own excessiveness has played in our present health crisis. But, deep down, we
know who we are, and we know why we're sick."

So wrote Michael Callen and Richard Berkowitz in *The Prick*. It is an
astounding, brave, and unexpected public confession that you'd think would
shake up lots of things in all worlds, gay, straight, public health, government
circles in general . . .

It didn't. It was as if it hadn't been written. Rebby was their doctor. "At least I am proud of you," he said.

DR. DANIEL JERUSALEM BREAKS DOWN

Francis is dead on my floor.

I am waiting for the undertaker.

I'd had a good night's sleep. There was no horror show of dreams. Each day and night I fear for the worst and wonder when the next one will come and the flood will take control.

I went into medicine to help people. I think most doctors do. Too, because I loved men, my mission was even more resplendent. I don't mean in any salacious way, although there are certainly pleasures in handling, so to speak, one's own kind. Indeed, there are more men in medicine to touch the ladies than anyone would believe. Most doctors have difficulties in personal relationships, difficulties with words, sentences, talking out loud. It's no wonder that the calling to medicine, to bodies, to investigations, can be so appealing to the socially maladapted. And I just mean that one is doubly blessed not only to be able to help people but also to help those people one instinctively loves the most.

I fall in love with my patients all the time. Oh, nothing ever happens and they don't even know it. These are my silly romantic fantasies. They hurt no one except perhaps myself, for I've had precious little of anything permanent. I assume this must be the way I've wanted it, that I've discovered I'm relatively shy, and this shyness, more than anything, makes me live alone, even though unwillingly. I think it must be hard to overcome shyness successfully. We keep so much inside ourselves, doctors. And the fantasies get worse, not better. When nothing comes along to take their place, the prospect of love becomes an even greater goal, further from possibility. No! It still can happen!

I fell in love with Francis, who is dead on my floor. Not that I would have said to him, "I love you," even if I'd had the chance. I fell in love with him as he was dying. I diagnosed him with this new thing when he showed his body to me, hardly a few months ago. I can sense now when someone has it. It's got to do with the look of the skin. There's some sort of light purple glow, almost invisible, as if it's radiating from deep inside. This is not an easy burden for the body or mind or soul of either patient or doctor to bear. Francis is the seventeenth death in my own practice with this.

His skin, now, is burnished bronze. My theory about this has to do with that hazy, almost imperceptible purple interior luminosity, which I think is caused by pigmentation gone awry that can coalesce the melanin, upon approaching death, into this healthy suntanned glow. His skin was naturally dark anyway, so he looks even more stunning. His lovely Northern Italian genes passed on blond hair and dark skin, and the feel of it, smooth, slightly brushed with fine golden wisps of hair on his chest and his strong legs, which are, *were*, long and pliant, like a swimmer's or a dancer's—oh, stop it!

He kissed me this morning.

I was up. I'd had my coffee. I'd glanced at the boring *Monument*, which reports what's happening not at all. I was dressed for office hours. The bell rang early. It was Francis.

"I didn't sleep so well. I'm feeling awful. I'm burning up. I'm sicker than ever. I just know it. I'm sorry for coming over so early without calling. I didn't know what else to do or where to go. I don't want to go to a hospital! Please don't send me to a hospital!"

Going to the hospital already means *sequestering*, which is another word for being quarantined, which is being talked of as a possibility. As if locking up all the cases will make any difference. Even if anyone could identify all the cases.

I examined him immediately.

He stood in front of me, naked. I found swollen glands everywhere. Under his arms. In his groin. In his neck. My hands darted softly, exploring for more signs that could only tell me the worst. I was crying inside. Death was raging inside this beautiful young man. And my penis was hard, so I was bending forward awkwardly, trying not to look foolish. At moments like this (the sentence of death, not the sexual arousal, though that too), doctors never know what to do.

"I'm really sick, aren't I? I'm such a chatterbox. I can find words for all occasions. I've fucked with guys all my life, guys my own age. You're old enough to be my father. Right now I'd give anything to live the rest of my life with someone like you. But it's too late, isn't it?"

And that's when he leaned forward to meet my leaning forward, and he kissed me. I held him tightly in my arms. I ached to protect him from all harm. And my erection went down as I could feel his rising up.

"Well, look at that," he said, smiling down, completely unselfconscious, as only the young and the beautiful can be about their bodies, which haven't been their enemies, as they are for the rest of us. "I watched this movie on

TV with Cary Grant and a tiger or a lion, and he reminded me of you. You wear the same kind of glasses."

I wanted to say, I have longed to kiss you and hold you from the very first moment you walked into this office several years ago, fresh from Michigan, where, yes, you had been on the swim team. I was on a swim team once, at Yaddah, before you were born, but not for very long. I wasn't good enough.

"Can you save me for a little longer?" He clapped his hand over my mouth. "I don't want to hear your answer. Just do your best."

I held his hand to my mouth. I kissed it and then I just held it to my face. I think my tears came before his. But his came too. And we stood there, awkwardly, looking into each other's eyes and crying.

"You don't know how handsome you are," he said.

"Come, put on your clothes" was all I could say as I tried to help him dress.

"No, come here. Beside me." He sat down on the cold floor of my office with its threadbare oriental whose dark browns I once thought bookish, way overdue for changing, along with my desire to be viewed as bookish myself. He pulled me down beside him. I could see that his hand, which I was still holding, was turning the blazing red we would soon enough learn signifies final consumption by sarcomas as they usher the blood on its final journey from heart to brain; and the blotches and spots on his face were now merging into one great splotch. I touched this face. "Oh, my Francis." I wanted to say . . . what? Oh, my Francis, I love you? Oh, my Francis, I am so sorry? Oh, my Francis, we have been so foolish in this world to believe we are wanted and loved, and it is in another world that we shall hold each other, never to be so naïve, never to let go, never to waste so much time. I lay down beside him and we held each other. I felt so clumsy. I felt so old, so very old. And most of all, so useless. He was burning hot. He was trying to pull my clothes off, my thick tweed armor. He was kissing me, but his kisses flew to the air. He was thrashing so hard from the fever erupting in him that he had no control over the sudden jolts tossing him this way and that. He was like a criminal being electrocuted.

"I can't stand up!" These were his last words on earth. He was in fact trying to stand up. In the seconds since I'd last seen his face, his skin had gone from red to purple, as if in some horror movie with special effects scaring the bejesus out of you.

Then it happened, of course. Impious me begged a god I never knew to save this boy, to give him just a little more time—to get him cooled down, to get him to a bed, to get him a shot of Faranx (which doesn't really help, though we give it anyway because we have nothing else to give; you buy it at a camera store; it's used to develop X-rays, another of Golly's follies), to grant me just a second extra to say I love you, I think of you all the time, I worry about you, what are you doing for dinner, I apologize for this awful rug, I've wished as long as I can remember for someone to share this house . . . oh, all these silly thoughts of a lonely man who could and should have had love but for whatever reasons—mine, the world's—has not. I was holding his hands so tightly and he was looking up at me with eyes so filled with questions: Why? Why me? Why now? Perhaps: Isn't there even time for another hug?

And then he lay dead in my arms.

Francis is dead in my arms.

So now I sit and wait for the men from the morgue. They are already wearing protective clothing so thick they could survive Hiroshima. Francis. Diagnosed with the nimroid and dead from The Underlying Condition and incinerated into ashes in a little over an hour. The law will shortly say that all UC deaths must be incinerated swiftly. Burial is forbidden. When I phone his parents and when they hear the diagnosis and recall the article from *The New York Truth*, they refuse to claim him. Send them the bill. There are no siblings who wish to come forward, or so the parents say. Is there a lover? A what? they ask. They hang up before I can answer. Diagnosed and dead and incinerated and disowned in a little over an hour. My God.

I hear the mail come through the slot. I fetch it by force of habit.

There is a letter from Francis:

Dear Dr. Jerusalem, I love you. I want you to hold me and kiss me and make love to me. All this time we've wasted. I haven't had the courage to tell you my feelings. All this time neither have you. I can tell the way you touch me and look at me, wanting to kiss me and hold me and let me kiss and hold you back. But afraid. Like we're all afraid. Why are people always afraid?

Francis is dead on my floor and there are stains in my trousers from love unshared. How much time is left? To do what?

My eyes fill with tears. My tears turn to sobs.

I believe my country is allowing this to continue.

I cry. And then I cry some more.

If I silently witness something evil, am I then an evil man?

•

EXT. LENOX HILL HOSPITAL. DAY.

Pouring rain. TV camera covering a few pickets, Fred and about ten others. We see the signs: OUR BACHELOR MAYOR LETS GAY MEN DIE! COME OUT OF THE CLOSET, MAYOR, AND SAVE YOUR DYING BROTHERS! *Fred is photographed holding this last sign.*

INT. NEW GMPA OFFICE. DAY.

A raw space, empty. The board is all here, trying not to look at Fred, who stands apart.

BRUCE *(entering)*: This is perfect for our new offices.

DICK *(to Fred)*: You organized that picketing of the mayor?

(Fred nods.)

And those signs?

FRED *(nodding)*: He *is* a heartless, selfish son of a bitch.

DICK: Your next play is about a First Lady who gave the best blow jobs in Hollywood?

FRED *(nodding)*: And her gay ballet dancer son.

BRUCE: You got into the White House and they had to throw you out?

(Fred nods.)

BRUCE: You tried to organize our over six hundred volunteers to go down to Washington to storm NITS?

(Fred nods, grinning.)

BRUCE: You scared them all to death. You're circulating a flyer calling Dr. Omicidio a murderer?

(Fred nods with a bigger grin.)

(Sounds from outside, down on the street.)

EXT. STREET. DAY.

People of all ages, carrying signs: KEEP YOUR DISEASE OUT OF OUR NEIGHBORHOOD. COCKSUCKERS DESERVE TO DIE. I THANK THE LORD EVERY TIME HE KILLS ONE OF YOU. I HOPE THEY NEVER FIND A CURE. GOD LOVES YOU. *Tommy comes hurrying toward the building. One of the picketers tries to prevent him entering. Tommy hauls off and decks him.*

INT. NEW OFFICE. DAY.

As Tommy enters.

FRED: The mayor has four more hours before we carry out our threat of civil disobedience if he doesn't meet with us. Don't worry, a bunch of us are doing this on our own.

BRUCE: Tommy got the call.

FRED: Why didn't you tell me? You see, it works! What time?

BRUCE: We can only bring two people.

FRED: What time!

BRUCE: Tommy is the executive director.

FRED: I'm going.

BRUCE: I polled the board.

FRED: I'm on the board. You didn't poll me. I wrote that letter to the mayor. I got sixty gay organizations to sign it. I organized the picketing when the prick didn't respond. That meeting is mine! It took me twenty-one months to get it and goddammit I am going to go to it representing this organization that I have spent every minute of my life fighting for and that was started in my living room or I quit.

(No response. Dawns on him.)

You'd let me quit? Just when you need me most? The mayor is the one person most responsible for ignoring this epidemic in our city and allowing it to grow into a plague, and now you're going to kiss his ass?

BRUCE *(takes out a letter and reads it to Fred)*: The board wanted me to read you this. "We are circulating this letter widely. We take this action to try to combat your damage, wrought, so far as we can see, by your having no scruples whatever. You are on a colossal ego trip we must curtail. To manipulate fear, as you have done repeatedly in your 'merchandising' of this epidemic, is to us the gesture of barbarism. To exploit the deaths of gay men, as you have done on television and in publications all over America, is to us an act of inexcusable vandalism. And, after years of liberation, you have helped make sex dirty again for us—terrible and forbidden. We think you want to lead us all. Well, we do not want you to. In accordance with our bylaws as drawn up by Lemish, Frankel, Levinstein, Mr. Fred Lemish is hereby removed as a board member of Gay Men Pay Attention. We beg that you leave us quietly and not destroy us and what good work we manage despite your disapproval."

(During the above we notice that Morton's and Dick's lips are moving as Bruce reads. They are the writers of this letter.)

INT. GMPA OLD OFFICE. DAY.
Fred is clearing out stuff from his cubbyhole corner. Some volunteers watch nervously. Fred is pushing Tommy away. More volunteers will come in as the scene builds, until by the end the room is filled with people staring at Fred.

TOMMY: The executive director isn't on the board. I didn't have a vote! What could I have done?

FRED *(screaming with fury and rage)*: You didn't support me! You're all nothing but undertakers! This organization is a funeral parlor! All you do is take care of the dying! Who's fighting so the living can go on living? History is worth shit. We're becoming our own murderers. Is this how so many people just walked into the gas chambers?

(He comes across an almanac of famous gay people. Everyone watches him going crazy. Bruce enters.)

FRED *(contd)*: I belong to a culture that includes Marcel Proust, Walt Whitman, Tennessee Williams, James Baldwin, Herman Melville, Thornton Wilder, Brahms, Cary Grant, Tchaikovsky, Auden, Forster, Byron, Plato, Socrates, Henry James, Aristotle, Alexander the Great, Cole Porter, Michelangelo, Leonardo da Vinci, so many popes and cardinals you wouldn't believe, King James and his Bible . . .

(Grabs Bruce.)

Hey, Mr. Green Beret, did you know it was an openly gay Englishman who was responsible for winning the Second World War? His name was Alan Turing and he cracked the Germans' Enigma code. After the war was over he committed suicide, he was so hounded for being gay. When are they going to start teaching any of this in the schools? A GAY MAN WAS RESPONSIBLE FOR WINNING WORLD WAR TWO! If they did, maybe he wouldn't have killed himself and you wouldn't be so terrified of who you are. That's how I want to be remembered—as one of the men who won the war. Being defined only by our cocks is literally killing us . . . Bruce, I know I'm an asshole. But, please, don't shut me out.

(Bruce walks out followed by everyone else. Everybody's walked out, although Tommy has tried to catch his eye until Bruce pulls him with him. Fred's all alone.)

•

HERMIA: Fredchen, my dearest one, I am so sad for you. Everything that I am discovering is immensely sad.

You are trying to do too much! You are trying to tell us too much all at once. Your beloved organization, your first child, disinherits you. Your beloved new lover is dying. The history of this wretched plague that grows more complicated whether you go back or go forward. Your hateful country hates you. You need as much help as you can get! Did you know that lovely Ann Fettner has died? Middleditch couldn't get all the cancer out of her lungs. She was preparing for you her thoughts and feelings about this Omicidio, which I sense will prove most uncomplimentary. She has turned these over to me and I shall continue this investigation to help move you along. I smell much more evil coming. With such ancestry, how could it not be so.

Just know that I adore you more and more each day. Your own, your one and only, Hermia.

•

INT. HOSPITAL CORRIDOR. DAY.
Fred, dressed in a suit and tie, hurries down the hall.

INT. FELIX'S HOSPITAL ROOM. DAY.
Curtains drawn so light is dim. Felix is almost dead. Fred comes in.
FELIX: I should be wearing something white.
FRED: You are.
FELIX: It should be something Calvin Klein ran up for me personally.
FRED: What am I ever going to do without you?
FELIX: Don't stop writing. Okay?
FRED: Okay.
FELIX: Promise?
FRED: I promise.
FELIX: It better be good. Fred, don't stop fighting. Don't lose your anger. Just have a little more patience and forgiveness, for yourself as well.

Emma comes in with Tommy.

FELIX *(contd)*: Emma, could we start, please?

EMMA *(taking Felix's hand)*: We are gathered here in the sight of God
to join together these two men. They love each other very much
and want to be married before Felix dies. I can see no objection.
This hospital is my church. Do you, Felix Turner, take Fred
Lemish . . . to be your . . . ?

FELIX: My husband. I do.

FRED: I do.

*Felix is dead. Emma leaves. Orderlies come in and put a screen around
him. Fred tries to go to him, but one of the orderlies gently prevents him.*

FRED: Why didn't I fight harder! Or go on a hunger strike? Or
picket the White House all by myself if nobody would come?

TOMMY: We will, sugar. We will.

A SAFE HOUSE?

GARRIE NASTURTIUM

I live in what's called a safe house. Purpura insisted on it. She had it found for
me and then came and checked it out. I'm too valuable to her, she said. What
are you afraid of, I asked. You never know, she said. She had Patti help me
furnish it. Even Mr. Schwartz came to say hello.

She trusts me. She doesn't trust anyone else. I try to present her to the
world as she wants to be seen. It isn't easy. She knows that. She's grateful
to me. She is always thanking me profusely when anything complimentary
about her appears. She can smell trouble coming faster than anyone I ever
worked for. When UC was secretly described to us by Slyme, long before
The Truth, she knew right away what was going to happen, way before that
Lemish guy. Her main concern is keeping it as quiet as we can. "We must
at all costs prevent the world from knowing that this is happening in Peter's
and my country."

She's always saying she loves me a lot, that she couldn't do without me.
"We are on a secret mission together," she tells me more than once. More and
more she's running the country. She's a busy girl, no doubt about it. When
I compliment her telling her this, she answers, "Let's keep that our secret,
shall we."

•

INT. CREMATORIUM OFFICE. DAY.

A clerk approaches a counter with two cardboard boxes. Fred is there, as is another gay man, Edward.

CLERK: Let's see. Fred Lemish, for Felix Turner?

FRED: That's me.

He takes the box. He is crying. Edward, who's taken the other box, sees this.

EDWARD: I'm so sorry. *(He gives Fred a hug.)* My name is Edward Alsop. I know who you are. I've got a car outside. I'll drive you home.

FRED: Thank you. I'm so sorry for your loss too.

INT: CHAPEL. DAY.

The urn with Felix's ashes. A small crowd for a memorial to Felix. Emma, NYT staff, Felix's wife and son with a minister. Tommy is holding the huge blown-up photo of Felix while Fred talks. Other photos hanging. Felix stands to the side, looking on. We see that Edward is also here.

FRED: Felix Turner and I loved each other very very much. Thank you for coming to remember him.

MINISTER *(wearing collar, southern accent; stands up)*: Felix Turner was a sinner, and his wife and son, Felix Jr., and I have come from Tulsa to join with you in praying for the salvation of his soul. Let us all rise and pray for the soul of Felix Turner, who sinned himself to death.

No one moves.

FRED: Felix Turner was a fine, noble, smart, adorable, beautiful person. I am grateful that he graced my life. How dare you come and spoil his day?

The pastor and Mrs. Turner, well and expensively dressed, have their eyes closed as their lips move in prayer.

TOMMY: Don't let it get to you, sugar. It's what I grew up with too.

FELIX JR. *(about eleven years old)*: Mommy, can I take that picture of Daddy?

CUT TO:

Felix looking at his son.

FELIX'S VOICE: It's the first time I've seen him in years. He's grown so.

FRED *(giving the boy a photo)*: Your father was a wonderful man and he wanted to love you very much.

Mrs. Turner snatches the photo from Felix Jr. and starts ripping it to pieces.

MRS. TURNER: I hate you. I hate you for ruining our lives. *(Turning to the audience.)* I hate all of you for what you are doing to our country. *(Grabs Felix Jr. and starts to pull him out. Then she rushes over and grabs the urn of Felix's ashes and starts out with them.)*

TOMMY: Here now, ma'am. Let me take this from you.

He takes the urn. Mrs. Turner is sobbing. She allows Tommy's embrace. Fred takes the urn and gives it to Felix Jr.

FRED: Here. I know your father would want his son to have him.

INT. FRED'S BEDROOM. NIGHT.

Fred is lying facedown on his bed, shaking with tears. Tommy sits beside him trying to comfort him.

CUT TO:

Fred and Tommy still in street clothes, lying next to each other. Fred is asleep but Tommy is staring at the ceiling. He is by now very much in love with Fred. Fred suddenly shoots up from a nightmare.

FRED *(screaming)*: Help!

Tommy takes him in his arms and they both start crying.

FRED: I wonder how long any of us has. I wonder it every single moment of every single day. I feel so dreadfully lonely.

TOMMY: Oh, sugar, me too.

INT. FRED'S LIVING AREA. NIGHT.

Fred and Tommy, their eyes still filled with tears. They've been eating Chinese takeout. There is a big blow-up photo of Felix, so that Fred can talk to it.

FRED *(kisses Felix)*: Felix, why are they letting us die? Someone is letting this happen.

TOMMY: Bruce is in Invincible. My own brother's sick now. Why did you go to Dachau? To see how awful everything was?

FRED: Something just said, Go look. I'd been thrown out by my friends. I was looking for something. I needed to fight.

TOMMY: You still do.

Fred is looking at Felix, who shakes his head in agreement and blows him a kiss.

FELIX: Yes, you still do. You promised me.

FRED: How did you become a hospital administrator?

TOMMY: I was a Navy SEAL. I ran the propulsion plant, the nuclear reactor, on a fast-attack submarine up under the North Pole for six months at a time. I swam underwater missions into Russia. A couple of times. I learned how to kill on cue without batting an eye. My reward was they sent me to college to learn how to administer hospitals. They made us look at films of Dachau. God, what evil.

FRED: That's what's happening to us. Evil. I want an army. We need to start a new organization devoted to political action, to fighting back.

FELIX AND TOMMY: YES. YES. YES.

FELIX: Fred, start your army. Make another speech! You promised me to not stop fighting.

FRED: Who would show up now to hear anything I said? No one talks to me. They cross the street when they see me coming.

TOMMY: You'd be surprised. More and more people are more and more frightened than when you started GMPA. They're asking me where you are, why you aren't there.

IN WHICH FRED HEARS FROM DR. DANIEL JERUSALEM

"WELCOME, DOCTOR. I HAVE MISSED YOU. I REMEMBER NICE TIMES IN YOUR ARMS."

Dear Fred,

What are we to do? I have read your novel. I have read what you are writing in *The Prick*. I know about GMPA and salute you. I support what you're trying to say and do. I'm writing because I'd like to help. Awful things are happening here, too, of course.

Where have I been all these years? In so many ways one attempts to set out on a life, and to achieve a belated independence from that which chained you: a family, myriad unhappinesses, an adolescence that tortures the self more than physical changes can ever straighten out, but most particularly that family, that body of flesh and blood which eats at the same table as you, always. (I know you are familiar with much of this yourself.) God, how I wanted to get away from them. I hated Washington. I still do, now more than ever, which is why I'm happy to work with you in whatever way I can. I agree that we must bear witness.

Yes, I have become the doctor you saw me preparing to be. It just seemed the right thing to do. And I do it. I'm good at it. Does that mean I like it, being a doctor? I don't think I want to know the answer. You have a lot of time to ask yourself that question as you sweat through all the years it takes to become one. It's not about "like." It's about "have to." My conscience is riddled, like some bulletproof vest that should but doesn't protect me, by "responsibility." That word stabs me all the time. It has a lot to do with my patients dying before I can help them. I suspect it all has a lot to do with David as well. I know it does. I never stop seeing his back, all scarred with the mysteries of his being. I don't know if you remember my twin. Whatever happened to him, could it have been because of me? I now think the main reason I can't leave Washington is that I'm waiting for him to come back. How would he find me otherwise? And I have been unable to locate him. I know this sounds too mysterious for words. It is for me as well. I know little about what happened to him beyond the fact that he was imprisoned in a German concentration camp during the war when he was still a kid. I believe this camp was for homosexuals, and that our father, who was evidently homosexual himself, had something to do with it. I guess this is all shocking to lay out in a letter. I'll tell you more the next time we're in bed!

So I never left town. I spent years saying I couldn't wait to get out of here, but I was back in Washington from Yaddah Medical School (where I studied and we fucked), and from Table Medical Center (where I interned and we fucked, I think), as soon as I was fully credentialed. I rented my own first apartment, overlooking a relatively pretty bend of the Potomac from a Georgetown hill where George Washington is said to have looked over to Virginia and declared, "I shall build my home over *there*." George is said to have stood everywhere in Washington and looked out over everywhere and declared ownership from every perch and balcony. I'd never had my own place to live, one where I bought everything for it. Now I do. The apartment led to a comfortable house in Georgetown where I live and work part-time.

I opened my own office. I see mostly gay men. I was a success fairly quickly. There are few gay doctors who admit to being gay, and guys are increasingly wanting that. So yes, I saw early cases of what's happening. I wanted to do something. I didn't know what to do. I felt utterly hopeless. So I applied for and was granted a Goffman Visiting Fellowship at the National Institute of Tumor Sciences.

The NITS wilderness of our childhood is now a large federal bureaucracy of more than fifteen thousand employees and hospital inmates comprising some two dozen individual medical centers and a large hospital, the Hogarth Hooker Clinic, where admission is based solely on a case's applicability to specific research that one of the thousand or so doctors on staff is pursuing. There's so much here that I've not been able to take it all in. I doubt many who work here have! America is getting sicker by the moment, not only with our stuff. You can feel this expansion of America's illnesses, and from here at least, it's meant to feel challenging. Dr. Stuartgene Dye claims to have ambitions and goals, although he seems a very strange man. He walks around the place as if he's preparing for something. He announces coolly that we must be prepared for the "treatment" of hundreds and thousands of patients who will be "the guinea pigs for the future health of the world." Please parse that for me, will you?

The two men I am assigned to are Drs. Middleditch and Omicidio, the former rather stately and intellectual and the latter scrappy and handsome, to me at least. He was evidently quite the ladies' man. He told me that "you guys" don't like him. Middleditch is some sort of stealthy leavening force who keeps a low profile and tries to keep things running smoothly. He's in charge of Cancer. It's by far the biggest section of NITS and it's where this shit we've been living with should be housed when they stop ignoring it. That's right. There is nothing being done at all. I thought maybe that's why they assigned me to NITS, to work on this. But after my initial inquiries produced only vague answers, I've stopped asking. There is an enormous cast of characters, both here and connected to here, and I assume, and hope, we will all be meeting each other about this soon. There's been more than enough to keep me busy just looking. I guess that sounds weird, doing nothing but looking. But I think most people here are doing the same thing. It's a big ocean and I'm trying not to drown; perhaps we all are. I keep looking for ways to live in a new country that I can't seem to locate. This does not auger well for us, but I'm still trying to withhold judgment.

Omicidio has obviously been waiting for something to happen, something to pounce on, something he can call his own. He's hungry, as some doctors are, for something to ride to the moon. You can see his impatience. He's always looking around, eyes darting everywhere even while you're talking with him. It's not unlike being in a gay bar and talking to someone while trying to see who might be looking at you from across the room. Ostensibly he's researching some rare blood disease that maybe ten people a year come down with. "At least I've got no competition," he said to me, not smiling, although I took it for a joke. "UC is going to be a tricky hard sell," he said. "Too many who'd rather hate than help."

Unusually, I'm also permitted to continue to see my own patients in my Georgetown office, I guess (or hope!) because it's recognized how little NITS knows about gay men's health, even though not that much is changing because of this realization, meaning that I don't see gay patients being studied here. Too long a sentence to describe a big empty hole! I don't see any gay doctors either. I think why I got accepted is because of my uncle Israel Jerusalem, who has a Nobel and did a lot of his early work on NITS grants.

I've been required to become an officer of the Public Health Service and to swear to more oaths of allegiance than I feel comfortable with. Once a month I have to wear a uniform, not unlike a naval officer's. I've been told I look cute in it.

The reputation of NITS, of both the sum and its parts, has been considered incontestably fine. Or so I thought, which is why my inquiry to you out of the blue comes at this moment in my own perplexed observations of what is and is not going on here.

To both borrow and paraphrase the work of the late Professor Erving Goffman of the University of Pennsylvania (after whom my appointment is named), which he set down in his classic study *Asylums*, it was his belief that any group of persons—doctors, scientists, academics, patients, support staff, prisoners (there is even a hospital here filled with prisoners, under lock and key, who happen to suffer from illnesses of interest)—develops a life of its own that becomes, once you get close to it, a disabling social structure enfeebling those entrusted to its custody. And that a good way to learn about this world is to submit oneself to the company of the members therein residing and to the daily round of contingencies, petty and otherwise, to which they are subject or in which they choose to become engaged, if contingencies can be said to become engaging, which in terms of a bureaucracy they certainly should but often aren't. That is another long-winded sentence that I guess translates into my wanting to try and find out why gay men as a group are so disregarded because of their health, and if this has something to do with our health-care delivery system. In Washington we tend to view everything in terms of "systems." You always hear, "If it ain't broke, don't fix it." And we know that broken things rarely get fixed. All this interested me, intellectually, at least until my patients began dying, when I started being interested in it emotionally. Am I making any sense?

Anyway, for a short while after I entered NITS I felt safer inside this place than in my own office in Georgetown. It's just so big here, with so many impressively credentialed docs and researchers that initially I wanted to just talk to as many of them as I could, only to discover that most of them aren't very talkative. They all—and I mean it seemed like every single one of them—sensed I was gay, and they definitely didn't want to talk about UC. If this is how bureaucracies exist and thrive, and if they're so safe, why can't people grow within this place discussing anything and everything? I'm coming to sense that isn't possible, certainly not about people like us. How are we to take care of each other, we "homosexuals"? As I write these words I see, as Goffman said I would, or should, how naïve I've been, how sheltered and protected you can become with Yaddah and Table degrees, etc., etc. Did my own family not teach me all that I needed to know about fear and distrust and I want to say hatred but I won't . . . yet? (Someday I'll fill you in on all that as well!) Is this the world Goffman went on about? Is this place I am at "a disabling social structure"?

There are no studies here into homosexuality. NITS is prohibited by law from funding anything so controversial. Ruester's Congress has silently seen to it. So it would never even occur to anyone to study it and us. To be forbidden from doing so now with the arrival of UC is utterly disabling.

You would probably say that I was beginning, as you certainly already have, to develop a sense that I belong to a people. I don't give myself that pat on the back yet. Gay people are hard people to belong to, to be a part of. Although you and I were briefly lovers, we didn't continue that closeness. We didn't continue to see each other. What does that say about us, as a people? We are strangers to each other and ourselves.

I sensed that you, too, had an obsessive interest in what was going on. We have this in common, and why it hasn't thrown us into each other's arms again is as good a question as any for which both of us should be seeking answers. More and more as each day passes I see how sad so many gay people are and probably always have been, and certainly will now be in increasing numbers. Like I say, how do we take care of them and their health, particularly when we've so failed at looking after our own emotional needs? I see this in your writings too, you who survived your own attempt to take your own life.

I have learned that for certain causes and cures, goals are too threatening. This has shocked me—that research is not responsive to demands. So how in the world are causes and cures discovered? Who or what is preventing this work from being done? I certainly did not think, going in, that the answer to this last question would be, as you are beginning to write: the president, and those around him running our country.

P.S. It's sad we lost touch with each other for such a long time. I have remembered your skin. And that you kissed wonderfully. I've seen photos of you in newspapers and gay magazines. You appear to have held up quite well. I think I'm rather uninteresting to look at, an aging doctor with graying hair and glasses, but it's an image I cultivate to make my patients feel more comfortable with me, and I with them. I'm almost fifty and I hope I don't look it. I'm lonely. I admit it. I fall in love with my patients all the time!

Dare I ask about you?

P.P.S. Did you ever complete the purchase of that turquoise Estabrook fountain pen?

•

HERMIA: Where is our dear Grace? A Dr. Schwitz Oderstrasse is beginning to be quite voluble publicly with his accusations about Grace and her activities at that Partekla place. She's usually not one to let a cat get her tongue. It has been a while since she was at Partekla. But there is never an end to things, and she knows it.

DR. SISTER GRACE'S WAR: I AM UP SHIT'S CREEK

OKAY, IF THIS GLORIOUS CUNT IS GOING DOWN, SHE'S GOING DOWN FIGHTING HER FUCKING GORGEOUS ASS OFF

No one is going to listen to Dr. Sister Grace. I can see it happening. I can feel it. I recognize it. The fartfinks are closing in on me.

By now I know that everyone dealing with this shit is a fucking clinch-poop grade-A idiot.

I give the following information for safekeeping to my only living relative, Hermia. It is important. It will save our people, all people, all our all-over-the-world people. I give it before the crapulent assholes get me. The assholes usually win in the end. You must have it in case I am eliminated. I have left further instructions in my will, which Lucas Jerusalem has prepared for me. I will not go down having kept my mouth shut.

No one will talk about shit. The kind we shit all day. No one is talking about assholes, rectums, vaginas, penises, semen, what happens when fellows stick their wangers up assholes or into cunts. No one is talking about placentas or reproductive organs.

I have discovered that a certain type of vaginal bacteria causes a thirteen-fold higher likelihood of becoming infected with UC. Nasturtium shat in his pants when someone told him this. (Who?!) He definitely does not want anyone to know it. What is wrong with those White House assholes? How can you embargo an important discovery like this!

NITS refuses to study any of this, citing a law passed in 1923 that prohibits "the use of any human waste as a medical nutrient." (Code$w32#, Section: Annals of Int. Med., NITS Archives, Bk 20872347.) In 1923! A law passed in 1923 is *still* followed to a T, this stupid grubby obtuse fucking law. It is against the law to research "anything connected to the human reproductive and ancillary systems." "Ancillary" in 1923 included everything from the breasts to the knees.

The Vurd Act has been amended to bring earlier terminology more up to date, pointedly excluding homosexuals.

I went to Dye. I hauled this old bag of bones down there and said to him, something is going on here that involves shit and sex. (Shades of Hermatros!) That nimroid pus smells like shit for a reason. I cannot get one single dollar to investigate this from any source and I want to know why, with so many dead kids and more dying every day. He looked at me and took my hand in his— I hate when they do that—and he said, "Sister, there is not one religion in our great country, there is not one politician in our great country, which and/or who would stand up and publicly support such research. Find me another way to study this." To which I replied, "Shit is shit. Sex is sex. And we haven't talked about cunts and placentas." And he asked me how old I was now and didn't I think it was time to "pack it in." I told him he was rude and I hoped I'd last longer on this earth than he would at NITS. And that I was already more famous in the history of medicine than he could ever hope for. He literally showed me the door. And of course the following week I received word that a couple of my requests for authorization for NITS grants were "suspended pending investigation." It's a good thing I'm so fucking ass-kissing rich, although using private funds for government research is another big no-no.

Of course I went to Omicidio. He's the new boy on the block. He basically kicked me out of his office too. Well, I've got his number, which is that he doesn't have a number. Mr. No-Show. What did the world do to give us the likes of him!

It's just so snotty how these crock-of-shitters treat women. There's not a one of us on Omicidio's staff. One of his kiddie interns shook my hand, "honored to meet a Nobel Prize winner." Rudely, Jerry-O said disdainfully, "You've won a Nobel Prize? Is that how you got the money to do your work?"

Nobody knows shit's secrets. After all these centuries. Dr. Ventner O'Burgeree at St. Luke's in New York, an important shit doctor, is now more famous for being the primary care physician of an impressive list of cock- and cunt-sucking celebrities. "Shit is just my sideline," he demurs. I'm told he exhales a sort of cackling glee when sticking his finger up your ass to test for parasites. A modern-day Hermatros? Hardly. He calls what he's doing "tropical medicine." I offered that nomenclature to Dr. Minge-Nipple Dye as our possible decoy and he just roared. "Congress will think we're getting free trips to Miami!" Lucky Vent. It's not every doctor who can stick his finger up the ass of Leonard Bernstein and Greta Garbo and get paid for it.

Israel and I are talking again. Neither of us can remember which of us was at fault, so we kissed and made up. But he calls what's going on "glause," and this and he are not helpful because he can't recall all the details of "what I discovered."

Believe it or not, one of the many things I learned at Partekla is that the best antidote to the pain from early nimroid is drinking one's own urine. The Indians taught us that, remember? How neat of nature to come full circle and so dug-sucking majestically. Piss on the shit! At Partekla I got them to give me urine samples. Those basket cases Schwitz accuses me of murdering? It wasn't me. Someone got there after me, big time, and they all died in one fell swoop. That's the clue that proves I didn't do it. Pissing on shit isn't *that* effective. Whatever "they" were doing was. No, it was some other doctor's experiments; my throbbing armless arm tells me that it was good old Dr. Dye.

What were they really doing at Partekla? It's called germ warfare. All the best cesspool countries never stop doing it. Who's the first goober grabber who can develop a plague that can get rid of everyone else?

Where the fuck have I been?

I have been to Africa. This UC family can be traced there from 1901. Scummy sleazy slutty 1901. Since then each generation of UC has become more lethal than the one before. They gather fury as they age and multiply, turning into even more hungry, rabid muckmouthed killers. And Bosco's monkeys, whether they ate each other or man ate them, are the killing field so many are refusing to explore.

And it's not just what pricks are doing inside men; it's what they're doing inside us all.

UC must have killed people here in the past several hundred years and was no doubt the cause of many "deaths from unknown causes" that muddy the cheesy statistics in COD's *Almanac of American Mortalities of Past Centuries.*

We should look again at discoveries and exhumations like those at Fruit Island and Dickson Mounds and Staten Island and New Bliss, but the Dyes and Vurds of this world will never give us permission to do so.

I know what Schwitz is up to and I don't like it one twatworthy bit. It's as if somebody doesn't want my new knowledge out there and is out to get me before I deliver it. Or the reverse, that somebody is so glad I'm saying this that they want me besmirched because that also makes it look like what I'm saying might be true. Either way I smell like shit.

Here is what I discovered at Partekla and have been refining ever since. Bear with me because it's messy, it stinks, and no one will want to know a shitcrapping suckhole about any of it.

Minute organisms of poison live in our bodies and in our shit, just like those parasites the great American Indian vestal virgin Hermatros catalogued. I hope you remember Hermatros and all I told you about him once upon a hornswoggle time ago. These parasites multiply and mutate and stay one step ahead of anything devised to kill them.

What Schwitz's blubbermouthing presages is vexing. Why is he, of all our cast of dicksucking cuntcrackers, after me, and any of this?

I was trying to finalize my thoughts about these vultures when Schwitz criticized my research to Omicidio and the new head of FADS, some fucking bilious Navy doctor who's an expert on whales and flying fishes. Marine biology is all the buggerfucker knows and marine biology is not what this Sister of Motherloving Mary's about. Partekla was a great place to work on shit, indeed the perfect place, which is why I went there. Basket-case patients at death's door, why not put them to use? That's what we were invited there by Brinestalker and Aalvaar and, yes, Stuartgene Dye, to do: "A quiet haven for confidential investigations." I could not work on this within the safety of Mater Nostra's protective walls. Mother Superior saw to it that any church participation in work on feces was gone with the wind.

I just about had my proof that something's definitely rotten in Denmark when Omicidio pulled my plug.

Kiddie, your old babysitter is boxed in in a hundred different ways.

Linus Gobbel, another germ from the White House, informs me that Omicidio informs him that I am working with "fecal matter," and "the president will not condone such usage of the valuable hard-earned money of The American People on *that*."

So now even Schwitz Oderstrasse believes he's contributing to the health of The American People by finally tattling on Grace. "You cannot Scheisse on us with your Scheisse," he had the nerve to say to me, to *me*, she whom he wouldn't be here save for my signing on as his sponsor. He desperately wishes to prove to America that our purchase of him from the Nazis only minutes before his execution has proved a good bargain. He comes now to tell me that he had some of "your poisoned blood" at Partekla injected into patients (i.e., those near-death basket cases) and it killed them. "Your input has done this! And you will make it patent and get richer even than you are richer now."

I had discovered at Partekla that poisoned blood was being "created" by taking it from all sorts of sick people and then injecting it into other people. That's *really* what Partekla is all about. Chemical warfare! It sounds horrible when you put it this way, that these dying guys were, in their own way, being gifted not to medical science but to political warfare. I used to read in the files at the Vatican how plagues all through the ages found church doctors and scientists doing the same goddamned thing. It's always a race to see who could find out something from the dying before they died themselves. Now this miserable piece of Scheisse has started a campaign that I am "the murderer of Partekla."

Oh, I also find supportive relevance in Aalvaar's maintaining that gay men's very own assholes are a major conveyance mechanism of UC or whatever is killing you: this is a fucking monumentally important world-changing suspicion I have had myself. He says he "discovered" this at Partekla. That's what he was using his prisoners for.

Shitty Schwitzy, by the way, has just been awarded a NITS "genius" grant "for imaginative thinking." No, none of this augurs well.

No one will want to know a shitcrapping suckhole about any of this.

I am an old lady. I am weary. I am not so certain, my darling Fred, how much I have left in me to continue fighting this fight. An old lady should not have to constantly defend her mettle.

I won't get through this.

Or I will.

•

I knew this woman was dangerous. She is what you call a major stirrer-upper. How can I shut her up for good? She is getting too close to me.

WHY IN FUCKING HELL WERE WE NOT TOLD ANY OF THIS?

GRACE CONTINUING . . .

What is worse, or just as bad, is what I am about to tell you, my Fred, my Hermia.

Who embargoed the truth so that Felix and all your friends are allowed to die? Because somebody did. Somebody allowed UC to happen.

Intentionally.

Where have I been?

I have been in Africa. I have met Dr. Jacques Pepin.

This shit has been around, as I have said, since 1901.

I have now learned what was going on that we knew nothing about, and that no fucking health honcho told anyone about. While we have been force-fed by stickpussy "experts" that UC is a new gay plague that gay men are perpetrating and escalating, some seventy-five years of UC had been happening in Africa that somehow escaped any snot-tinged acknowledgment of same. For seventy-five years, godawful very long years! Wrap your head around that grungy pissbottle of a scenario for one of your movies.

Countries of central Africa—the two Congos, Cameroon, Gabon, the Central African Republic, and Equatorial Guinea—are home to the *Pan troglodytes troglodytes* ape, the only species to carry this shit out into the world, via humans and prostitution and unclean needles. As I say, a first ape case was noted in 1901.

Pan trog is some four hundred and forty thousand years old. Humans in central Africa have been in contact with *Pan trog* for at least two thousand years. The first lethal encounter between a *Pan trog* chimp and a human can be traced to 1908 in southeastern German Kamerun. (Wouldn't you know there'd be fucking Germans.) In 1960 there were one million chimps of all species. They have a life of about fifty years. Six different males fuck the same female in just ten minutes. The modes of transmission are the same for chimps and us.

My chum Laurie Garrett explained to me how all these dipshit pipsqueak African countries were constantly at war with each other. Vampire dictators came and went, their populations decimated by each other. What kept some sort of order going were the civil servants, hired mostly from Haiti. When it all got really too muckfucked and out of control, these Haitians, to save their own lives, rushed back home to Haiti.

•

BOSCO: In 1963 a *Pan trog* was sent to me from Africa. She was infected. It was her blood that Dr. Sister Grace was also exploring in those secret labs at Partekla. I gave it to her. Yes, chimps are very promiscuous. I have one male who since puberty has mated at least 335 times with twenty-five different females. One of my females copulated fifty times within a twenty-four-hour period. If I had known my life's work would involve living things with such disgusting habits, I would have concentrated on taking care of people.

•

DR. SISTER GRACE: That's fucking right. Haiti. The gay watering hole incarnate. *Pan trogs* were the only chimps that carried this shit to people. We still don't know why it discriminated so. Yes, that palooka Bosco Dripper gave me that fuckawful blood. It scared the bejesus out of my nookie. It is what took me to Africa and to Dr. Pepin.

Prostitution. Over three and one half centuries some 10.3 million wretched slaves were shipped from Africa to hither and yon. They did not all come to America like we are selfishly taught to believe. Many of these slaves came from central Africa and were sold to other parts of the continent. By the nineteenth century the European powers were all fighting for more and more parts of Africa, particularly the French, Germans, and Belgians (the biggest fucker-overs) but also the Spanish, Dutch, and even the Danes. All these sleazy carpetbaggers would wind up with too much turf to mine, plunder, and thus they populated it with armies of cunt-starved beyond-horny laborers seeking the only available entertainment, a cunt. Those female slaves sure became handy. Population outposts became villages and towns and small cities. Several of them were in areas that shared home base with the *Pan trogs*, particularly the Belgian Congo, with its Léopoldville and Brazzaville, and the German Kamerun, soon to be Cameroun Français. Early records for much of this were kept by a Frenchman, Pierre Brazza, in the late 1880s.

What led me to all of this? Amazingly, these records were located at Harvard by the greatest of genius figure-outers, a totally unequivocal hero, the Canadian microbiologist Jacques Pepin, who personally escorted me through much of this fetid domain and all its putrid history.

Eighty adults living in central Africa in 1921 had been exposed to blood containing simian UC from cutting up a *Pan trog* and/or eating it.

One thousand and fucking nine hundred and twenty-one! Pepin showed me an ancient death tally he located in Brussels.

It would take a Frenchman, Dr. Leon Pales, arriving in Brazzaville in 1931 to discover in a patient a syndrome certainly suggestive of UC. This in effect would be the first patient zero. It was calculated that this syndrome had lived in him and others from at least 1915. From this would come the plague that will infect many millions around the whole wide fucking world and that gays are being blamed for. The strain the *Pan trogs* were carrying existed several hundred years before this crossover to humans. Maybe even longer. Eons!

Which brings us to all those poor sweeties who had no other way to feed their starving bodies.

Three-quarters of all men infected in this area will become infected from prostitutes or, as the more independent women called themselves, "free women." In 1933 Belgium opened a first clinic for sexually transmitted diseases in Brazzaville. In the midst of World War II officially authorized brothels were opened to cater to soldiers waiting to be sent to the Libyan front line. The best known was owned by a Madame Rose. She and her house and her girls were quite famous.

What has never been mentioned is that some fifteen years prior to the various African revolutions in 1960, during World War II American troops had been stationed in the Congo, including Léopoldville, to beef up the colony's defenses. They were known to be frequent customers of the prostitutes and "free women." What the fuck else is new? Men everywhere can never be trusted to keep it in their pants.

Beginning in 1920 and continuing pretty much to the present day, the largest number of transmissions of UC virus to humans has been via improperly sterilized needles and syringes. Transmission of UC is ten times more effective through the sharing of needles and syringes than via sexual intercourse. By 1979 one-third of all addicts in New York were infected with UC and were forbidden by law from partaking of any clean needle exchange program. Once again we prove to be a fucking country that doesn't know what it's fucking doing. Except that a number of certain fart-faced chaps did know and wanted it to happen. Like almost every elected official from the birdbrain bottom to the bootlicking top. Don't get rid of the fucking junkies.

A first small lab had been set up in Léopoldville in 1899! Before then there was not a single trained medical worker in this entire part of this continent. Those turdy turf-stealers back home in Europe couldn't care a crock of shit about the heathens in the jungle who were only good for digging all the gold and other negotiable shit from the earth. Eventually a few other labs with trained staff poked up, run by people trying to do some good. By 1950, some one hundred and fifty thousand injections had been administered for one thing or another. By 1960, prostitutes in Léopoldville were each servicing some thousand clients per year. Many cases of nimroid were seen. (Where was COD? Where was *JOD*? Where was HAH? Where was FADS? Where was NITS? Where was HOW?) Many cases, too, of tuberculosis. TB and nimroid are now known to facilitate UC transmission. Being uncircumcised, as most men were, also hastens transmission. UC was introduced into both Haiti and the United States by the end of the 1960s, having been introduced into Haitian bodies while in the Congo working for one dictator or another.

Imagine the tenacity and ingenuity of glorious, gorgeous, divine Dr. Pepin in locating statistics confirming all the above!

Haiti was thus to become the next stepping-stone for the export of UC to America. Reports by local social workers call attention to the growing gay interactions between locals and American tourists becoming obvious by the late 1940s. Indeed, a widely attended international gay convention was held in Port-au-Prince in 1979. Nimroids were diagnosed in 1979. You know what kind of conference that was.

Air Haiti carried blood plasma that was sold to American companies: Armour Pharmaceuticals, Cutter Laboratories, Dow Chemical, Baxxter-Greeting among others. Shipments of blood were sold by Haitian bloodletters and sent to customers all over the globe.

A respected French company began extracting and exporting plasma from placentas. HOW, in 1975, condemned this and attached fines, which nobody paid, against the disobedient.

By the 1970s, because this virus had so extensively and relentlessly gone from Africa to Haiti and then America, a global epidemic became unavoidable. By 1978, 6 percent of the gay men in San Francisco were infected. Each infected person would infect at least one other person.

And now, like the old lady twitchingly poking wisps of stray hair back in place after removing her too-tight hairnet, I've got to take a rest. I'm pooped from this unloading. I'm pooped from worrying they will really put paid to me, whoever they are. No one here in our entire ruling class wants anyone to know about any of this. There is not one single person in our entire Public Health Service who would want any of this known.

There is a lot of blame to go around. As with the Holocaust, too many people had to know what was going on!

What did people know and when did they know it and why weren't we told and if they didn't know it why didn't they know it!

Yes, I am afraid, for me, and for you, and for all of us. This is no idle plague that is plaguing us.

Why in fucking hell were we not told any of this!

As Dr. Pepin said to me: "It was all there to be known." He is writing a book, God love him.

PURPURA RUESTER

A First Lady always finds time for the important things. That's what I get laid for.

AMAZING GRACE, HOW SWEET WAS HER SOUND

Fred will never receive any of the above from Dr. Sister Grace. Sadly, she will be found dead in her bed at her beloved Mater Nostra Dolorosa. "Old age" and "bad heart" are among the "learned" opinions put forth by various investigators. Her papers? They are rendered in such foul language that Archbishop Buggaro demanded that her quarters be cleared and fumigated and all its contents, including Grace, be cremated. Is this to be the end of her great usefulness to humanity, to The American People? Hooker contributions had been nonstop since before the American Revolution.

HERBIE IN BIRMINGHAM, ALABAMA

I want to cry so much. I feel so funny. I shake so, I can hardly write my name. My stomach bloats like a big balloon. I fart and want to fart and can't fart and then I shit in my pants when I am not anywhere near a toilet. You'd think in a town this size someone would know what's wrong with me. No one knows what's wrong with me. I know what's wrong with me. There's something wrong with me! That's what's wrong with me. I want to cry and cry. A new doctor takes a lot of my blood. He sees I want to cry. He holds my hand. "It's all right to cry," he said. "I am doing it a lot lately myself. Strange things are happening in our city." He says he wrote to our congressman but didn't get an answer. I told him our congressman is my father and he hates what I am. I also told him, "And he hates you, too, because to him you're a nigger."

•

INT: EMMA'S APARTMENT. DAY.
She is making Fred brunch. She is wearing her braces and moves awkwardly but effectively around her apartment.
EMMA: How you doing?
He doesn't answer because he can't.
EMMA: What have you been doing?
Fred sort of shrugs.
EMMA: You've got to do something. They need you.
FRED: Oh, yeah.
EMMA: Yeah. Stop feeling sorry for yourself. I know you miss him and I know they threw you out and Buzzy tells me you aren't very popular.
FRED: Old friends cross to the other side of the street.
EMMA: Guess they weren't very good friends. Why do you give a flying fuck?
FRED: Were you in an iron lung?
EMMA: I was.
FRED: For how long?
EMMA: Long.
FRED: And then what?
EMMA: Then I was in bed at home. I was connected to my classroom by a little loudspeaker. All the kids would be required to come and visit me. We'd say hello and then not know what to say next. "Oh, I recognize you by your voice." "Oh, me, too." They were terrified of me. Still are. I scare the shit out of people. The holy terror in the wheelchair. But I graduated first in my class at college and med school.
FRED: You're amazing.
EMMA: No, I'm not.

FRED (*eyeing the food she's laid out*): Do you think that being Jewish
   makes you always hungry?

EMMA: I don't know. I'm not Jewish.

FRED: You're not?

EMMA: I'm German.

FRED: Everyone thinks you're Jewish.

EMMA: I know. In medicine that helps. Get to work.

FROM THE POCAHANTI ARCHIVES

ANOTHER ANNUAL MEETING
FLADD DAJUSTE, RECORDING SECRETARY

It is sad where we are and what we are going through and what we must
now do to stay alive.

We need new blood!

We are still the Pocahanti. There are still a few noble Americans left
proud to be connected to those who were here first.

But what can we do, we hundred men of blue blood? We are running
out of steam. We are not strutting our stuff sufficiently. We are meant to be
a visible symbol of Our Country's Valor and Victory and Vibrancy. I love the
letter V. It is so American.

Trace Vanden Schuville makes many an address to us about our torpor.
"Get off your duffel bags" has been his charming way of challenging us.
Age has always been a problem. All of us qualify as old farts. Such are the
rules of admission that by the time a man has been qualified for membership
to replace a fallen—i.e., dead—Pocahanti, he is often close to being a dead
Pocahanti himself.

"But a number of us want to do something before it is too late," says old
(eighty-seven) Basil Rummigen, without inserting any specific details into his
very long (forty-seven minutes) speech of encouragement. Everyone nodded
in agreement, that is, those who weren't asleep.

We at present have among us twenty justices of the Supreme Court,
forty-three officers of major Fortune 500 corporations, and many assorted
others who helped to run and fuel our country. We should be accomplishing
something! We must reconnect ourselves to the seats of power. Each year

there are fewer descendants of George Washington we can draw upon. The only way out is to change our definition of what it requires to become a secret Pocahanti. We have a new president, Peter Ruester. Our board has already, in secret chambers, elected Attorney General Moose to the office of our 293rd chief Corn-Gatherer. He gratefully consented. He sees in us something useful for the president's vision of America. Quite right! Ruester stands for the same ideals as we do. Was not his campaign promise "I'll put America back in America"?

The secret word went out to our board, the one dozen Decision Makers. "Come to the clubhouse tonight at midnight. We have important matters to introduce."

"I am getting too old for midnight meetings," a few of us were heard to mutter.

"Don't be an old codger." I believe that was Cadwallader Rampage Trumpith. And then he added to those complaining, "Take a longer nap beforehand."

Manny Moose calls this, his first, meeting to order. He is a fine-looking American. He looks most resplendent in his robe of office, a long carapace made, of course, of corncobs, quite heavy, and so he's sitting down on his throne. This throne, woven from stalks, is prone to invasions by rodents but the exterminator stopped by today.

It is true that Chief Corn-Gatherer Moose is not in fact a Pocahanti, in that he has no ties to either George or Martha. But if we don't do something we'll die out like the Shakers. Our average age is eighty-eight and a half years. "What you stand for must not be killed off," Moose said to us. "You just need new blood!" My very words! Already he's seen to it that we've had an infusion of new capital "from like-thinking friends." Tonight he's meant to offer his plans for our new future.

"I call this meeting, the 29,456th out of camera and the 378th held in secret even from our brothers, to order." Moose is a big man even without his robe of office. Our investigations revealed that he is spiteful, vindictive, determined, unceasingly ambitious, dishonest, hypocritical, known to be all these things, and for Ruester's administration the perfect attorney general. Well, they said many of these same things about our Founding Fathers. America, as Ruester himself tells us in his special mailing, is "heading into decline unless we extricate it ourselves." If you were such a doddering ancient organization, wouldn't you put the president's chief judge in charge if you could? (I address this question also to our posterity that one day will read these minutes.) I am merely calling a spade a spade. I shall be the lifesaver of the Pocahanti! I believe I am the only one without a pacemaker or a hearing aid.

I note Buster Punic sitting nervously at the far end of our ancient table, this huge piece of tree from just that spot on the bank of the Delaware where George crossed over to the other side. Although Buster has been an automatic member since his birth (the first Punic arrived, we must not forget, and we have, in Easthampton in 1644), it's only with Moose shaking us up that Buster has finally come around to putting on his tribal robe and taking his rightful seat in our midst. Because his lineage is not only ancient but can actually be traced, Buster is entitled not only to Pocahantidom but to Decision Maker status. To keep to our limit of a dozen we had to chop off some Ear of Corn to fudge Moose's elevation. It was estimated that Supreme Court Justice Northrop Droppsie would be dead within the week. And he was.

A tall and distinguished old man steps forward. His Ear of Corn reads: Brent Fairfax. I hardly recognize him. His ancestor . . . well, it is beginning to come out now, that unfortunate story. Fairfax, Virginia, was once their land. George was diddled by that original old Fairfax, who was such a poofter he was ordered by the king to get out of England. I wager more and more tidbits like this are going to be discovered in the hands of these wretched revisionist new historians. They will be calling all of us fairies if we don't watch out.

"The chief Corn-Gatherer has asked me to introduce several outsiders who have Precious Corn to place before us. I ask the Decision Makers of the Pocahanti to invite inside those who await outside." Ah, yes, Mr. Fairfax is a friend of the new chief Corn-Gatherer.

"Permission is hereby granted," Chief Corn-Gatherer Moose replies.

It was Fairfax who saved us in the Hoover years. His "friend" Edgar threatened to expose us for being "a hotbed of homosexuals unless you let us in." So we let in Edgar and dear Clyde. They were active and distinguished Corn-Gatherers for quite some time. We gave them good value, access to a world they never knew or could otherwise know. And Edgar protected any of us who got in trouble.

Fairfax manages to lead in three blindfolded (as tradition dictates) men, each of them (as tradition also dictates) carrying an ear of dried corn. Each is guided to place his ear of dried corn on the table and is then allowed to remove his blindfold.

"Dr. Vonce Greeting. Mr. Arnold Botts. Mr. Linus Gobbel." Reading from a card, Decision Maker Fairfax intones the names, and they almost sound well-born enough.

Fairfax continues: "Dr. Greeting is head of the largest pharmaceutical company in the world. Mr. Botts is his assistant and is preparing to launch his own manufacture of lifesaving drugs. Mr. Gobbel is President Ruester's right hand, and he has just been appointed, as well, the director of LOTS, that brand-new branch of our government that polices Law, Order, Theft, and Sex Crimes, the latter now coming under scrutiny at last. Now I think I have read all this correctly."

Murmurings of "Hear, hear" are heard, along with a round of soft hands clapping. (Or is it "here, here"? I have never known.)

"I believe Mr. Gobbel wishes to say a few words," Moose says.

"Thank you. Corn-Gatherers, I am honored to be here tonight and to become a member of your historic organization. The president and I would be honored if the Pocahanti would take under their personal attention our new division of LOTS, which is going to be called the Tricia Institute, and is being spun off as something private and independent. It will be solely devoted to, shall I say, looking into certain things, meaning things pertaining to the wretched stain of homosexuality, which must be expunged before it devours our people."

Let it be noted that there follows a lesser number of "Hear, Hear"s, along with much clearing of throats.

Linus Gobbel then says: "We also intend to reestablish that greatest example of America's fight for independence, the Minutemen from the days of our Revolution and birth. Our president is already at this very moment converting our many state-by-state National Guards into Minutemen. I shall be in charge of them. I will name them Special Forces. Every country has them."

At this point Chief Corn-Gatherer Moose suddenly announces, "Will the recording secretary hereby cease his notation, acknowledging for the minutes that our decision-making is begun, so that we may all now proceed, in the secretive manner prescribed for us by our ancestors, to discuss how to effect the calling for which we now are being called."

I hereby attest to the accuracy and veracity of the above minutes.

•

INT. MEETING ROOM. HEALTH DEPARTMENT. DAY.
A big tacky room. Health Commissioner Glanz sits facing an audience of a dozen or so scattered attendees. A few familiar GMPA faces, Lee, Herb, Morton, busy making notes. Away from them all, Fred, with Tommy, is sitting bored out of his mind, with his eyes closed.

GLANZ: I have been assured by the Center of Disease and by Food and Drug Supervision that this has not entered the general population of The American People . . .

Fred's eyes open suddenly and he will now go ballistic. He grabs a newspaper out of his attaché case.

FRED: Dr. Commissioner Glanz, you have just uttered one fat fucking lie. And you know it! I hold up evidence to present to this stupid useless Inter-Agency Task Force the mayor has called into being to show the city that he is doing something, this copy of the London *Observer* newspaper, which has the following headline, and I quote, "One million people will become infected. Including heterosexuals."

He runs through the aisles shoving The Observer *in front of everyone's faces.*

Straight people. Men and women who fuck with each other. *(Drawing out this word:)* Het-er-o-sex-uals. Cocks into cunts. Infecting each other. Dr. Commissioner Glanz, have you talked to your friends in London? In Washington? Oh, I forgot. You haven't got any friends in Washington. They killed you in Washington. How many gay blacks were in your syphilis study that murdered so many? Where is your conscience, our commissioner of health! Isn't there some oath you swear in medical school? Or has someone sworn you to secrecy? The White House? Which secretary of what department? Our putrid mayor?

He rams the paper into Glanz's face and leaves. After he's gone a second, he comes back in.

By the way, Doc. I like to think I am part of the general population. An awful lot of us do. You might want to make a note of that.

He grabs the newspaper back. Tommy follows him out. In the back of the room observing all of this has been Arnold Botts, who's been making notes.

INT. CORRIDOR. HEALTH DEPARTMENT. DAY.
Fred collapses into Tommy's arms.

FRED: We're not getting anywhere. There's got to be a better way to make people pay attention. We need a fucking army.

INT. FRED'S LOFT. NIGHT.
Fred is staring at the large photograph of Felix. Tommy is with him.
FRED: I want so much for us to be better than straight people. Where is everyone?

RIVKA JERUSALEM IS FINALLY REWARDED

Rivka Jerusalem realized she had no place to turn for help but to Gertrude Jewsbury in Palm Beach.

When Philip finally died they'd been married fifty years. So now she lived alone in the tiny room in the Hotel Eden in Miami Beach.

He'd told her many times over many years that he was waiting to die. Indeed, each day he waited for it and each night he went to sleep hoping for it and each morning he was disappointed when he woke up still here. Sometimes she thought Philip had been waiting to die for as long as she'd known him. Indeed, he had been.

Clearing out his belongings she had found a letter to her. "Dear Rivka, my Rivka," it said, "I am sorry I did not give you a better life. I am sorry it took so long for me to die. I am sorry that I often did not know what to do and did things I did not understand. Many times I thought I might be losing my mind. There is not a day I can remember when I did not feel sick to my stomach and wanted to end all this pain. I am sorry I never knew what to do with you. You were so beautiful I could not understand why you would have me. I often wished you would go away and leave me like your own grandmother had three times divorced the men in her life who she said treated her 'rotten.' I am sorry that because of me we have four sons who have not been good to us because I have not been good to them or you. I am sorry. I am sorry. I am sorry. I am sorry. I am sorry. I say this five times, one for each of you. I go to someplace where I hope you will forgive me."

She was not going to allow herself to think about any of this.

Rivka hadn't seen Gertrude since 1925. That was the year Amos Standing married Gertrude after one last time trying to convince Rivka to marry him. But Rivka married Philip Jerusalem, Amos went away, and Gertrude departed for what would become decades of world travel: postcards came to Rivka from farther and farther away until they came no longer. Yes, Rivka had turned Amos down time after time and finally married Philip, his best friend. Amos was a Christian, so she could never marry him even if she found him attractive, which she did not, and even though he had a great deal of money, which Philip certainly did not, and even though her own father, who was tired of being poor, suggested she might do her parents a favor anyway by marring the rich goy.

Many times over the years Philip also told Rivka, "When I die, you won't have enough money to live on. Find Amos Standing. Tell him I'm dead."

Rivka was running out of money. Gertrude must have all that money Amos had settled on her, money that would have been Rivka's if Rivka had been Amos's bride. Rivka only had two thousand dollars left in the bank. Philip's benefits from his pension from working for the United States government since World War II would now be halved, and they'd hardly been enough as it was, even with her peanuts from her tiny pension from American Red Blood. She couldn't afford to stay at the Hotel Eden anymore. She couldn't afford to go anywhere she could think of that was remotely pleasant. She had long ago lost touch with whatever friends might still be alive and in any position to help her because she had always been so ashamed of her awful marriage. Yes, Amos's money would take care of Rivka, as he himself had wanted to do so long ago, something she had never told Philip.

She didn't know how to find either Amos or Gertrude until she saw the photograph in the Miami newspaper of the Palm Beach charity ball. There she was, identified as Mrs. Gertrude Jewsbury of the Breakers. Rivka would have recognized her anywhere, even if she hadn't changed back to her distinctive maiden name. There she was, looking very Gertrude, very grand, very haughty, very beautiful. How could her old friend not want to help her?

The Hotel Eden was completed in 1930 and the Jerusalems came here that year on their honeymoon; they were the first guests to stay in this very room, not having seen it or Florida ever since. Philip wouldn't listen when, in Masturbov Gardens, she tried to read him the newspaper reports of riots and bad times here. "Then the Hotel Eden will be cheaper" was his answer. He was going to retire there, and that was that. Decisive he seldom was, and impetuous rarely: she never understood why this place had so delighted him. For most of their early years here guests couldn't even go out at night for fear of street gangs and muggings, and even during the daytime it was necessary to walk to the grocery in a group or take your chances. But now things were changing. Preservationists. The neighborhood and the Hotel Eden and its three-story pink stucco art deco refinements were of great interest to preservationists. Architects and designers and real estate people were always sticking their noses into lobbies and corridors and admiring essentials inhabitants had given up praying would be updated by the landlord.

As soon as they moved into the Hotel Eden, on February 12, 1970, which was not only Lincoln's birthday but Philip's, Philip had a stroke. He became numb in his left leg. The doctor said he was okay and must not let it get him down. Philip rarely left this room again. The Jerusalems' nineteen-by-nineteen third-floor room had been a tough fit for two. Until his second heart attack he watched the television, sitting in the middle of the sea-green plush sofa, which also had art deco curvatures, and which had developed a sag where he and all his predecessors had sat. The TV had been playing. The Mills Brothers were singing "Be my life's companion and you'll never grow old." Old songs were always being played in Miami Beach.

For the first time in her marriage she had had a fine night's sleep. The mattress no longer tilted in his favor.

•

She set out to find Gertrude Jewsbury. She'd called the Breakers hotel and left a message that she would be arriving and could they meet. She put on her best outfit, which she knew to be unfashionable and no longer flattering. She caught the bus to the north. She realized that she was already enjoying herself.

The bus was whizzing by so many expensive places to live! Such a proliferating repetition of elaborate high-rise hotels and evocatively themed motels impressed her. She felt she'd not been properly prepared for Eldorado, Versailles, Tiffany, Park Avenue, Monte Carlo, Hollywood, the Riviera, as replicated in oceanfront towers in an unbroken line. So much had certainly been happening in the outside world. She imagined Gertrude would certainly be living so grandly.

I want to love you.

Those had been Norman's words.

"I want to love you."

The rabbi had said them to her at the beginning of the one and only week they were to have together after the embrace in the Miami Beach temple's library where she volunteered and before his death. (He tripped and fell down the two steps into his sunken living room on Indian Creek Drive, hit his head and had a stroke and died—all on the same day.)

He was holding her hand under the table, at their first luncheon.

"I want to love you, but you are not letting me."

She said nothing.

"If I rented a room somewhere, would you come with me?"

"No!" she said too loudly.

"Why not?"

"What could possibly be gained by two such old bodies getting into bed together?"

"You're shy."

"Of course I'm shy," she said, accepting his excuse. And leaving him to go back to Philip in the Hotel Eden.

When she hadn't accepted his first invitation, the rabbi said to her, "We are just like the Jewish people. Our timing is always a little bit off. At another time, perhaps God will let His daughter out of His house of bondage."

She would not think of how she and Rabbi Chesterfield, who did not remember her from her years of teaching at his Washington Jewish Sunday school, spent one night together tenderly cuddling in a secret motel, the night before he had that fall and died. Something else not to let herself think about.

Rivka followed the arrows toward 1012. The Breakers was the most magnificent hotel she'd ever been in. The hallway reminded her of Philip's descriptions of the hotels he'd visited with his mother on the grand tour of Germany Zilka took him on after his graduation from Yaddah. It had been Philip's tales of this trip that made her reconsider him as a potential husband. His descriptive powers were so magical then! He wove captivating stories about that trip, and Rivka longed to travel. Today her fingers, like a little girl's, were trailing along the embossed wallpaper and reaching up toward the height of the chandeliers, and she was trying not to look at her impoverished reflection in the gilt-framed mirrors hanging everywhere. Rivka Wishenwart, for one second in time, was a young woman walking down the hall of some fancy foreign rich hotel Philip Jerusalem hadn't taken her to at all.

"Here I am!"

And there she was, Gertrude Jewsbury, staring at Rivka, waiting for Rivka, standing there regally outside her room. You look so dignified, Rivka thought. You're not in a wheelchair like so many here and at the Hotel Eden.

Rivka, who knew she'd been studied from head to toe as well, and found wanting, gallantly kept on her smile. "And here I am."

They did not throw themselves into each other's arms. They did not hug or kiss or embrace. Neither knew yet what to do with the other. So for this moment they did nothing. Then Gertrude stood back and allowed Rivka to enter her suite before her and closed the door behind them. They were in a vestibule, then into the huge room beyond, each hardly breathing, each shyly and slyly looking the other over, these two friends from long ago, wondering what changes time and fate had wrought.

"Life has been good to you. But then I knew it would be," Rivka exclaimed. "I am so happy for you."

The first time Rivka saw Gertrude Jewsbury was the day Gertrude married Amos Standing. It was in 1924, at the Wardman Park Hotel, and Rivka was relieved that this beautiful woman had come from across the sea to marry the pest so that she wouldn't have to. It was a very lavish wedding, because Gertrude was one thing Amos wanted to show off big. He was now living in Washington full-time and, judging by the number of guests invited, he knew many people, although there appeared to be no good friend but Philip, his Yaddah roommate and his best man.

Amos and Gertrude moved into an enormous house near Dupont Circle and Rivka became her best friend. Every day the two women walked, past the big mansions in one neighborhood after another in the Northwest, holding hands like schoolgirls, planning imaginary trips around the world. Gertrude's car would pick Rivka up in the Northeast, where she and Philip were living with Zilka, over her store, and Rivka would show her a new neighborhood. The chauffeur followed in the car until they got tired. Gertrude had much to learn about America, and Rivka, ever the teacher, was happy to impart whatever she could.

One day shortly after his wedding, Amos asked Rivka to walk with him around the bleak Northeast neighborhood. He apologized for behaving so shockingly the last time they'd been alone, and since he seemed sad and subdued, Rivka felt sorry for him and agreed to the walk. He told her the story of Gertrude's past, which was not nearly so fancy as he'd led everyone to believe.

"She was just a poor girl, like you. She worked in a dress shop in Mayfair. Her parents are dead. She had no one and nothing. I have transformed her. I have given *her* a new life."

Rivka waited for more, but Amos just looked at her, like a petulant child who wants something his mommy won't give him. She realized the implications of his words. When would he leave her alone? She ran from him before their walk went any further. But he caught up with her and grabbed her wrist and held on to it tightly. "You are the only woman I ever wanted, and since you won't have me, you'll be punished."

Within two years Gertrude bore three sons. Each of them died not long after birth. Gertrude became very depressed, and then she became a recluse. Finally, she left Washington and disappeared, without even saying goodbye to Rivka. Once a bolt of delicate lace arrived from Barcelona, with a note, "Until we meet again, my dear friend"—but there was no return address, as there was none on the occasional postcard that arrived from abroad. By then Amos had been transferred somewhere overseas for work.

"Rivka, do you think fate has sent you to me just at this particular moment as an omen?" Gertrude pulled the collar of her Chanel jacket tight around her neck, as if she were suddenly cold. "You do know, don't you, that you are the person I've known longest in the world? Does someone from the first part arrive at the end? Some attempt at order and structure after all? Save room for dessert at dinner. The desserts are the only good things they do." They were having tea and biscuits.

"Amos has taken good care of you." Rivka was looking at the far end of her room, where there was an entire window banked with fresh flowers.

"Amos? Amos does not take care of me."

Rivka was uncertain she had heard correctly. "He doesn't?" She was feeling more uncomfortable than she'd bargained for. Was she on the wrong track? "Why . . . why did you change your name back? If you don't mind my asking."

"Mrs. Jewsbury shocks the pants off everybody. Which amuses me."

"Where does it come from?"

"It's a very common Yorkshire name. Jewsbury. Dewsbury. It can be spelled half a dozen ways. And it was what I was born with. I did not want to carry any more traces of *him*."

"I read somewhere there's a Jewtown, Georgia. Isn't that awful?"

"Why? Why is it? It's not dissimilar to Jewsbury, Yorkshire."

"It's not the same at all! It's much more . . . hateful."

"We Yorkshire people are filled with a great deal of common sense," Gertrude was continuing. "Not religion. Just common sense. Religion does so get in the way of common sense."

"Philip told me Amos was worth over fifty million dollars and would take care of me after Philip died."

"My goodness! Why do you think Philip said that?" Gertrude was looking at her very attentively, and Rivka felt her hands beginning to shake. She let her words come tumbling out. "Because Amos wanted me to marry him and I wouldn't. I thought you knew all this. He told me he told you. When I turned him down he went on that trip to London and that's where he met you working in a shop and he brought you to America and just before the ceremony he asked me again and I said no again and he married you. And after he married you he . . . came back again. And before I married Philip he tried one last time. And when I got married he said he would never let me forget him." She'd wanted the words to come out in a calmer, more orderly fashion, and instead they'd rushed out, as in some child's game, ready or not, here I come.

"Why didn't you marry him?"

"I . . . I don't know. His breath always smelled. Why did you? For his money? He made you very rich."

"Yes, his breath always smelled."

"Did you feel guilty you married him for his money?"

"He discarded me! I must tell you something, Rivka. His entire settlement upon me amounted to one hundred thousand dollars. Twenty-five thousand dollars for each dead son, he said. I am worth far, far more than that, but not because of Amos."

Questions were coming to Rivka too quickly. She did not like asking questions. "That's all he gave you? Did you know Philip would always be poor?"

"Of course."

"How did you know?"

"One senses these things."

"You could have told me. We were best friends."

"Well, I only . . . surmised."

"I surmised too."

Then she said everything out loud that she'd said to herself in the Hotel Eden in Miami Beach.

"If I had married Amos you wouldn't be here and now I don't have anything and Philip said Amos would always take care of me after he died, Philip died, and I don't know how to get in touch with Amos and I thought you could tell him Philip's dead and could he please take care of me now." There were tears in her eyes. "I'm ready now."

"Amos is dead."

"Amos is dead?"

"He died a number of years ago. He took his own life. Or someone murdered him. I have never known which. He was involved in some top-secret work for your government. His obituary called him a 'diplomat.' I remember laughing and thinking, Oh, is that what he was."

There was a long silence before Gertrude spoke again.

"Amos was not in love with you. Nor was he in love with me. He was in love with Philip. I found them in bed with each other several times. When I confronted him, he made no secret of it. That is why he purchased me in Mayfair. Because my circumstances, which were not dissimilar to yours at present, necessitated that I be for sale. These things—all of these things—happen."

Rivka wanted to cover her ears forever. "He badgered me to marry him! Over and over and over! He wouldn't leave me alone!" Falteringly, trying to speak words she was not accustomed to speaking, much less thinking, she told Gertrude about the awful experience, the sight of Amos waving his erect penis in her face, crying out, "Take me! Mine is much bigger!"

Gertrude's eyes closed momentarily, and her hands became small fists. "It sounds a most desperate act," she finally said.

Then she continued. "Amos was a tortured man. He scared me to death too, many times." Then she stopped, and she took both of Rivka's hands. "Philip rejected Amos. Philip told him he would marry you. Amos then convinced himself that capturing you was the only way that he could have Philip. Do you understand any of this? He used me to make Philip jealous. That did not work. He had brought me back to parade before his entire town. Philip would still not go away with him or live with him."

"So Philip did not love him!" She was about to say, Because he loved me!

"Love? You lived with him. Do you think Philip Jerusalem was capable of love? He married you to hide what he was."

"But Amos could have taken care of him on the grandest scale . . . What am I saying?" She understood none of this. A man taking care of a man? A man caring for another man as would a wife? Tending and cooking and mending and shopping and buying the fruit from the cheapest market?

"Jewish boys did not run off with other boys and have sex with each other in those days! My dear Rivka, he married you to escape these feelings, and to hope for the best."

There was another silence before Gertrude spoke again. "I must also tell you that yes, I know if you had not been so unavailable, I would not have been purchased and we would not be here."

Rivka said softly, "I don't want to know any more."

"But there is more."

"I have heard too much already."

"It was not over between them, even after both of our marriages. They continued to meet here and there. Amos would call Philip at his office and they would meet somewhere, and yes, Philip would call Amos. I would hold my hand over the receiver and listen. 'I need to see you right away,' I would hear Philip say. It was like he was in some sort of pain and Amos was the doctor with the medicine to make him feel better."

"Why didn't you tell me any of this! We were like sisters!"

"How could I tell you any of this? It is hard for me to tell you even now, so many years later! 'My husband is sleeping with your husband.' How could I tell you this when we and the world both seemed so young? I was a poor girl who'd been given some outlandish opportunity to come to a new country and earn money for her future. What if there were strings attached? There are always strings attached!"

"Did Philip push me into finding you—to discover all of this? What a very vengeful man I married. Why didn't Amos leave some of his money to Philip?"

Gertrude suddenly grabbed Rivka's hand and took her out on her balcony with its magnificent view of the ocean.

"I want to make you understand something and I don't know how to do it. I hope my words will lead toward some safe harbor.

"Amos located me before he killed himself. I was living in Paris. He said he had had enough of pain and disappointment and loneliness. He said there were events in his past that he was now too ashamed to bear. I thought this was Amos the actor again, playing out another drama to get sympathy. He told me he wished to leave his estate to Philip's son David, and that if I could find David, he would reward me as well. I located David in San Francisco, rather down on his luck. As was I. My money had run out. I had traveled too far and too wide and too long. Amos did leave David several million dollars, and he appointed me the executor of them. We all had misguided notions of how wealthy he ever really was. David and I traveled at first. He was a shy young man, with little knowledge of the world beyond its pain. I don't believe you know the full story of what he had endured, and I shall not be the one to tell you. He felt exceedingly unloved, and I believe I was able somehow to help him rise above self-pity. We made each other laugh. For myself—well, I discovered I had a great deal of pent-up motherhood within me, just waiting for release. In Paris, he convinced me we should take Amos's money and buy an old hotel on the Left Bank that required extensive renovation. It became popular, and profitable, quite swiftly. He had much imagination. So we went on from there. We bought a much larger one in Rome. We performed the same renovation and achieved the same rewards. I was, to my surprise, quite good at business. We rescued ten old buildings, each one larger and grander than the one before. We became, and I hesitate to say this, millionaires many times over ourselves. I wanted to locate you, to share some of our good fortune. But . . . he forbade me. He is sick now, from a disease no one can identify or cure, and he has disappeared. Amos took his own life when Philip had his stroke. Did you know that? Amos came to Miami Beach to see Philip, and Philip would not talk to him. David and I pieced all this together. Amos left him some papers and diaries. Philip wrote Amos love letters full of tantalizing ardor he could not deliver in real life. Indeed, he wrote one from Miami Beach. I have been wanting you to know all this, Rivka! Please believe that. Each day I wake up and play out scenes in my head of how I would come to Miami and tell you. David only disappeared quite recently. I should have told you. But how could I tell you! How could I tell you all of *this?*"

"My baby is very sick?"

Gertrude nodded. "By now I suspect he may have died."

"He felt we never loved him?" She had tears, yes, but she realized she didn't know which son she was crying for. "What's the use," she said. "If I cry for one I cry for all and mostly for myself. I will not cry for myself." And she wiped her eyes dry with her hands.

Gertrude said nothing at first. Then she said, softly, almost whispering: "I hope you realize that now, Rivka, we both are . . . free."

"Yes!" Rivka suddenly exclaimed excitedly. "Yes, Gertrude, we are free!"

"So here we are, my dear Rivka, two old ladies, unloved all our lives, scorned by men who couldn't love each other, sitting together by a mighty ocean. Can you not see that the rest of our lives are not very long at all?"

Then, like a siren heard only dimly through the fog and from a distance, or like a high-pitched croon from some animal Rivka herself had certainly never seen or heard or known, some animal or bird or mate suddenly set free from captivity and understanding it not a whit, she laughingly celebrated her availability out into the wind with a mighty guffaw. The new nighttime answered her at first with only silence, not even a rustle of a breeze from the ocean, not even a distant hint of a tune from an orchestra gathered in some far-off ballroom, playing for the old-timers.

Then Gertrude embraced her. She took Rivka in her arms and Rivka's head fell upon her shoulder. They held each other tightly. Gertrude kissed Rivka's forehead as Rivka smoothed the other woman's hair.

Stories like this are never over. There is always a future to be haunted by a ghost or two. Did Rivka stay with Gertrude? Did the two old ladies finally and at last have some kind of happy ending, now that the Jew between them had been led out of the house of bondage?

Yes, she did, and they did.

DANIEL THE SPY

It was good to hear from you, Fred, at last. I am so sad and sorry about your Felix. You are forgiven for not answering sooner.

As I am more and more hurting for my missing brother, I understand how one can miss someone more and more as time goes on.

Now that I know how I can help from this end—well, that is what I will do. And now I feel like a spy in a movie and I love it. *Daniel the NITS Spy!*

There is much to fill you in on to get you up to speed. Perhaps you know some of it.

First and foremost, you must know by now that Ruester is completely out to lunch for us. No one can get anywhere near him. He's guarded and protected and shielded and hidden and spoken for by these men: Manny Moose, Chevvy Slyme, Gree Bohunk, Garrie Nasturtium, and Linus Gobbel, who is rumored to be the "hidden force." Slyme you've met. Garrie was All-American something or other, I think football. He's knockout handsome without being sexy in the least. He's ambitious but he looks like he's missed a few career steps on his way and knows it. Gobbel and Bohunk are both killers and seem to work as a team. There's not a first-class mind among them. They are all connivers. It's said that Purpura wants it this way. It's no secret that she's calling all of Old Peter's shots. That's what Ruester's called by many of those around him. Old Peter.

This is the group of bozos who are making all the decisions for The American People.

Garrie Nasturtium says all the time to Jerry—they appear to be friends from somewhere (I'm allowed to listen in on the phone)—that "Old Peter" hates fairies the most. He said Purpura said to Old Peter, "You can't call them fairies in public," and Old Peter answered, "If I did, I'd get reelected by the biggest majority anyone's ever won." Garrie and Moose and Peter go way back. Garrie got caught at some kind of midnight orgy in Sacramento. One of my patients who was there said it was all gay. Garrie couldn't run for president after that. But the ultraconservatives love him and so he nourishes hope. Moose and Slyme have revived the old Office of Unnatural Acts. Moose renamed it the Tricia Institute after one of the Nixon daughters. And stuck it under Linus. It's meant to gather information about gay people, including our names and where we live and work. I asked Jerry what he thought about this and he said, "Welcome to Washington." When I told him I'd lived here all my life, he answered, "No, you haven't. Not really."

After three very long years of UC an all-staff meeting is finally convened by Dr. Dye.

"I'm perplexed not all of you know each other. It's sad when the people who should don't. How can you work in such similar fields and in the same buildings and in some cases practically on top of each other and be such strangers?"

I wonder (and I wonder if anyone else is wondering) why he's talking like this. He sounds like Mr. Nice Guy, reasonable. Did somebody bawl him out? Is he covering some tracks of his own? Is he admitting he needs help? He doesn't know a single one of us himself.

In the NITS conference room (109AH7 on the map I sent you) are, for starters, Dr. Nostrill from HAH, Dr. Pewkin from COD, a couple of strangers from FADS, Drs. Oderstrasse and Maudilla Chanel-Bosch from Blood of All Nations, Vonce Greeting (whom Dye introduced as "my old friend"), Dr. Caudilla Hoare from American Red Blood, and of course Omicidio. Oh, and Dr. Middleditch. And Dodo Geiseric, who still doesn't recognize me or my name. That's your first clue to what a jerk he still is. There are a lot of others (the room is packed, a couple hundred), but they have that blank, nonparticipatory look of bureaucrats that I've come to recognize on far too many. And yes, Gobbel and Bohunk, Purpura's boys. And the laugh-a-minute Hoidene Swilkers, secretary of HAH, who tries to call the meeting to order but Dye tells her coldly to sit down: "I called this meeting." She takes this personally and huffs herself out of the room.

He continues in his nice vein. "Let us claim this day as when we officially begin our counterattack in earnest, our defensive full-frontal counterattack so the world can see us. It's a nice fall day. Why, it's almost Thanksgiving. We must give the country something to be thankful for at last." Hmmm. He's willing to admit that we're this far behind?

Dodo has been here at NITS all his working life, as has Jerry; both are in their mid-forties. They're not particularly cordial to each other. Dodo already has a Needler and a Vorsicht and will no doubt win many more upper-tier awards. He's smart but, like I say, a drip. He knows he's smart and is very narcissistic about it. As the saying goes, it's his way or the highway. Middleditch, who is chief scientist and who's very smart, knows Dodo's smarter and tries to protect him like the only precious cargo that's going to bring glory to NITS. Middleditch, who must be over sixty, is just finishing his Faust daVinci Fellowship, some sort of recognition given to long-termers who've never been given anything else. "Dodo's the brightest I have ever come across since Israel

Jerusalem." He said that to me. Indeed, I wonder what's happened to Israel Jerusalem. All I know about my cousin is that no one ever talks about him.

Dr. Dye continues. "It's been brought to our attention by Dr. Poo of Invincible, and Drs. Benois-Frucht and Brookner of Table, that something's begun to happen. I gather that no one has any notion what's going on or how to go about finding out."

"Not true! I am quite far along in my research!" Geiseric says, standing up abruptly as if he's prepared to launch into a description of what he's doing.

"Kelvin?" Dye turns to Geiseric.

"Nobody calls me Kelvin!" Dodo explodes in laughter. "Most of the time I forget that's my real name. I've been called Dodo since I was a mad kid scientist with my chemistry set in our attic. I blew the place up once and set it on fire a couple of times. I've never been called anything else since."

"Isn't that interesting," Dye says.

"You know that I am quite far along in my research?" Dodo tries again. The audience is riveted in attention. This is big-time Big Stuff talkers talking.

"Well, let us keep it our little secret," Dye mock whispers. "We don't want to give too much of it away yet."

"Just like a spy movie," Dodo actually squeals, like an excited kid.

"Exactly," Dye replies.

"Goody-goody," Dodo also actually says. "That's what Mr. Slyme said we must be like. I talk too much for Mr. Slyme."

"So he has told me."

"Not you, too!"

"Yes!"

Dodo now grins like a boy just caught stealing something. This is the man Middleditch thinks is going to save the world from our plague. Indeed, Middleditch is giving Dodo a shut-up-already stare and Dodo shuts up and sits down.

I think Omicidio is exceptionally handsome, full of beans, also very full of himself. I've been assigned to him full-time now. Dr. Gist is on his way out. He predicted this shit was going away. "The theory of the herd," he calls his theory in his required textbook on infectious diseases. Once it passes through everyone it will then pass out of existence. Did you ever hear such bullshit? Gist's actually being moved on because Dye discovered he lives with his boyfriend who's also his assistant.

Dye said to Jerry, "When I saw you I immediately thought: I need someone attractive to be the spokesman for our institute. To the media, the

TV cameras, to the reporters, to the world itself. I do not wish to speak to anyone. I want you to be our star pitchman, Jerrold. I want the world and Congress to know how important we are and give us some money for this shit."

Is it interesting that no one here has been particularly friendly with anyone else? I find that all over the place. Dye and Middleditch and Gist must have been—I don't know what to call them: passive? out to lunch? uncaring? homophobic? frightened or nervous about something? to have fertilized such an atmosphere. Or is it just endemic to scientists and research? I keep wanting to ask, wouldn't it be better if we all could be buddies?

"You will be my Big Three." Dr. Dye has his arms somehow around Dodo, Jerry, and Middleditch.

Then, changing the subject and opening up his smile, and his arms, to the whole room, he says, "We must all assure our country that the blood supply is safe." What a funny item to throw out to us. Especially since we have no idea if this is true. And he knows it. In fact, he must know the blood supply is filthy as shit.

"Oh, God, that's true," Maudilla says. "Dr. Stewwie Foss, who is not only on my BOAN board but is chair of Hematology at Yaddah Medical School, says that the blood supply is completely and utterly safe and I am sick of people scattering idle chatter otherwise!" Everyone's impressed she takes such a tone with Dye. But then BOAN's an independent entity, reporting to no one. I make a mental note to try and find out where their money comes from.

"How has Dr. Stewwie Foss arrived at his clean bill of health?" Dye asks.

"He's asked me to submit this report." Maudilla hands him over a few pages. "It presents statistical calculations that show it's not possible and confirms his opinion that whatever's happening isn't blood-borne."

"But dat iss ridiculous," Dr. Oderstrasse sputters. "Dr. Stewwie-Foss is wrong. This is his last name, Stewwie-Foss? You did not tell me this!" He's talking to his boss and she's not answering him.

"Dr. Foss is also honorary chairperson of American Red Blood," Caudilla Hoare of American Red Blood pipes up, protectively. She wears a flowery ensemble with a big bow at her throat. She also wears clumpy shoes. If the blood is puky, American Red Blood is in deep shit.

Good, good. Stuartgene nods and smiles. It would seem as if he was enjoying the infighting.

Von Greeting also nods quietly to himself. He looks like an old movie star, tall, black hair probably dyed, certainly slicked down with something to keep it in place, great tailoring. I'd swear he's gay, even though he wears a wedding band. But then, everyone in this town wears wedding bands. He has that forward-pelvic-thrust posture when he's upright that I notice in my patients who get fucked a lot. Greeting may be an ancient company with a long history, but no one knows much about this Von.

Dr. Dye acknowledges him. "Mr. Greeting, as you must know, owns and runs the largest pharmaceutical company in the world." Von beams, and I almost expect him to stand up and take a bow. "And of course we all have high hopes for their newest drug, which I understand is now named Regurgia-Plus, to provide a higher standard of life and living for the world's hemophiliacs." Greeting now raises his arms like a prizefighter, his palms together in a clasp of victory. "Let us hope, Von, that Greeting will also deliver to us a protective medicine to help us against UC. That's why I've asked him to join our little chats."

"Boss, anything you want to do collaboratively, this Greeting and all the other little Greetings are here for you ten thousand percent." The voice is prideful and mellifluous in the extreme. Oderstrasse's nose is wrinkling.

"Wat does all dat mean?" he asks. He is not answered.

Von then gets serious. "Actually, I do know what to go after, guys. Stay tuned." Everyone in the room starts exchanging looks and shrugging shoulders. You certainly don't admit publicly you have secrets you're not going to share.

I'm still not aware of any direction, any leadership, and certainly no sense of urgency. I realize no director from FADS has showed up. FADS is under HAH although FADS thinks and acts like it's over everybody. Well, there's no one here from FADS. Guess they figure there's nothing for them to approve yet.

"So no one is going to demand that precautions be put in place?" I venture to say.

"Absolutely not!" Maudilla says.

"And destroy the confidence of The American People in all the work of American Red Blood?" Caudilla says.

They are said to be competitors. Couldn't prove it today.

Schwitz is silenced by Maudilla's staring at him. Shut up, her stare says. If you know what's good for you. Blood people are said to be difficult people. Blood is so tricky. My mother always said so. Indeed, I will never forget my own childhood experience on that bloodmobile.

"Dr. Nostrill?"

"Yes, Dr. Dye?" He sounds nervous that he's been singled out. HAH is over NITS, so why is he nervous?

"What are your thoughts about all of this?" Dye asks.

"Smells like a big one."

"It does, doesn't it. That is all you have to say?"

"Not much more to say at this point, is there?"

And that was that.

I am now spending more time sitting in on discussions with Jerry and Howie Hube and Debbi Driver and an assortment of potential "investigators" who come and go, discussions about what we can actually start doing when some sort of go-ahead is given. This is pretty daring of Jerry, because he's not officially authorized for any of this yet.

"Greeting wasn't at that meeting for nothing," Jerry says. "He's got something."

I already think Howie Hube is a drag, but he managed to pull a NITS study of childhood whooping cough together quickly with reasonable results. When we get something to test he's going to be in charge of getting UC clinical trials on their feet, over gung-ho Debbi, who's only a nurse practitioner, but who's evidently run successful NITS trials all over the country. She already hates Howie, which I'd say is good taste if I thought Debbi was so great. Fred, they are both just so second-rate. I boldly asked Jerry if he didn't see that. "I see a lot of things. Seeing them and doing something about them are two different matters." Then he clapped me on the back and went into his john to change into his jogging gear. I look at him with insuppressible interest when he emerges in his shorts and T-shirt. I do, I do. He likes it too. He winks at me.

At the next meeting: Drs. Dye, Omicidio, Middleditch, Grodzo, Nostrill. Secretary Swilkers, dumb as a doozy, today in a wig of red hair that makes her look like a lollipop. Theoretically she's over everything and is the most senior person in this room. And a Dr. Nutrobe, the new head of FADS, the whale and fishes doc (and a retired admiral!). There are now even more observers from different agencies who walk in and out as if they're auditing a class. Again the room is full. I'd say a hundred. Also here, in that the White House rarely sends anyone to a meeting like this, is Chevvy Slyme. Also from Congress, Representative Something-or-Other Dingus. Middle-aged and mean. Dr. Garth Buffalo from Harvard, also a nonsmiler but better-looking and much better dressed; he's married to some heiress and he's got a Nobel. Dodo again, friend from our youth. Dr. Buffalo and Dodo don't like each other. The competition between them is tangible. Dr. Buffalo doesn't waste one second before he says, as has Dodo, "I can cure this shit. I know how to do it." He turns to Rep. Dingus. "I need a lot of money but it will save you money in the long run." Dr. Buffalo has that Nobel, so he's used to being taken seriously. But Dingus is chair of a powerful committee that investigates anything it wants to. How's that for power. "I do not like your approach," he says flat-out to Buffalo. "There are proper channels and you are welcome to go through them." "You want answers now. Your channels take longer than World War Two," Buffalo replies, obviously annoyed. Dingus ignores him from that moment on. "Pretentious creeps, scientists who claim they can cure. Pompous perverts playing God," he says so everyone can hear him. "I don't think Dr. Buffalo is gay," Dr. Middleditch says, surprisingly. "Irrelevant," Dingus says. "I will find a way to put him out of business." Buffalo of course has heard all this. Dingus trips over the sleeping Dodo on his way to his exit. "Is this what we pay you for?" he yells, by now truly incensed. He grabs Dodo's name tag on his white coat, ripping it almost off. "Geiseric! I will find a way to put you out of business too." He leaves us, mercifully. All six foot plus hulking bit of him.

Slyme clears his throat. No one knows who he is and he's annoyed. Dr. Dye starts to speak. Slyme dives right in: "The president wants you to know—" he starts out in his high squeaky voice, but several voices interrupt him to get their own items on an agenda that Grebstyne is preparing. Grebstyne's sort of a jolly-looking neater version of Rebby Itsenfelder. Jewish brain (from the Bronx) but said to be mean as a snake. He wants Dye out of the way so he can take over NITS. But that's a presidential appointment, so he's screwed because he's a Jew.

Again, no one's really in charge of this meeting. Dye is just sort of a presence, but he's not directing us to anything. That's the way of most meetings. A dozen or more other divisions and their heads could be right here in this room for all I know. And they never meet with each other!

Omicidio sits on the edge of his seat, not wanting to miss a trick. I love looking at him and trying to imagine what his neat compact body looks like naked. Jerry's taken over from Gist officially. Gist was caught sucking off one of his interns, and Jerry's appointment finally got Moose's (i.e., the president's) approval. Gist's labs had long since fallen apart and are not worth running as is and I know that appeals to Jerry.

Dr. Dye is cold to everyone. But then, so is Omicidio. Come to think of it, almost everyone is cold to someone or other. I can't imagine what in the history of this place made it into this.

I notice that a Dr. Grodzo is looking at me intently. He suddenly gets up and leaves. I don't know much about him.

"The president wants you to know—" Slyme starts up again.

Dr. Dye cuts him off again and announces the following. "You tell the president and his Mr. Moose that I was not amused by his treatment of me and we're going to get nowhere attending to the health of this country if I am to be treated in such a fashion. I called Ruester personally to tell him about this shit when it first broke, so he would hear it from me first if he had any questions. He grunted and hung up. Almost immediately Moose called me back. 'I think it wise, the president thinks it best, to let this one follow its own course. Perhaps it will just burn out.' 'There is no way it can burn itself out,' I replied firmly. 'Well, let's just see what happens, shall we? And by the way, there is a chain of command here and the president does not like to be confronted directly.' 'This *is* a Chain Blue emergency,' I said, 'which allows me to call the president.' 'I am not familiar with that.' And he hung up."

"I am here today to further this discussion," says Slyme. Everyone now turns to him. His eyes are bulging even more. Slyme—well, you've met him—in his scrunched-up body he looks like a dwarf and you just know he was called a sissy when he was a kid and he's out to pay us back for it now, big time. He starts to stutter and cough. We wait. Hoidene gives him a glass of water. He finally manages to scream it out in his high-pitched voice. "The president is in no way interested in anything whatsoever that pertains to homosexuals! Do not call us again about this shit!" And he bolts up and leaves.

"Lady and gentlemen, the meeting is adjourned," says Stuartgene, and everyone gets up and gets out fast. But not before Omicidio comes into Dye's line of sight. "And when are you going to say something out loud?" Not to be outdone, Omicidio snaps back, "When I have something intelligent to say."

Meanwhile, over at the White House Stockman and Gobbel and Moose are cutting everybody's budget in the entire government. Pewkin's COD has been really slashed after that Chattanooga "choo-choo" stuff. COD now has a ton of vacancies in every single lab and division. The White House definitely doesn't want anyone to know about this shit.

When I point this out to Jerry, I get his increasingly all-purpose "That's not our department."

"How can you say that?" I ask him.

"Got anything better for me to say?" He winks and grins.

Not good. Any of it. Three years going on four.

I have left the best part until the end. Dr. Middleditch brought around a Dr. Dash Snicker to meet with Jerry, Hube, Debbi, and yours truly. He's with Greeting and yes, they have a drug and Stuartgene's already given the go-ahead to test it in trials without telling or asking anyone. It's called ZAP.

We're not supposed to talk about it because you're not allowed to test a drug for something (virus?) that you're still officially looking for and haven't sufficiently identified. Except that, in certain desperate situations, you can. It's under the Wartime Emergency Powers Act, or something like that. I haven't the vaguest idea how G-D and Dye got approval from FADS. Maybe they didn't. The jerk Nutrobe who runs it has already said: no virus, no causative agent, no clinical trials. Maybe that's why nobody talks to each other. They'd all kick each other in their balls.

Okay. Now we're up to date.

HOME ON THE RANGE

PURPURA: I found a note in Junior's wastebasket.

FOPPY: You read his basket?

PURPURA: It said, "I'm going out into the world to dance, you bitch." What do you think it means?

FOPPY: First Mommy Mary's son, Jesus, also spoke in parables.

PURPURA: Foppy Schwartz, answer me, is Junior a confirmed fairy?

FOPPY: Confirmed in the sense of accepted into the faith? Bar mitzvahed?

PURPURA: Answer me!

FOPPY: As Tallulah Bankhead once said, "Well, darling, he's not sucked my cock."

PURPURA: Are you telling me Junior hasn't quite found himself yet?

FOPPY: Am I telling you that? Yes. Why not?

PURPURA: I tried to explain to him that running a country is more important than flapping around the White House like a fairy in *Swan Lake*.

FOPPY: There are no fairies in *Swan Lake*.

PURPURA: There aren't?

FOPPY: Swans. There are swans in *Swan Lake*. We were flappers once. Don't you remember?

PURPURA: Junior has quit Yaddah and is going to ballet school!

FOPPY: There are numerous ballet dancers who are not homosexual men, although I can't think of any at the moment. *(To himself, aside:)* Junior, my young sweet friend, at the rate we are going we shall be shot at dawn.

DANIEL AND JERRY

Jerry says, "I guarantee I am the only one who wants to take this piece-of-shit division and work on this piece-of-shit new disease and make the whole thing work."

"Why do you tell me everything?" I ask him.

This catches him off guard, as I wanted it to.

"I got no one else to talk to. And you can't hurt me. And I need a witness for whatever I do from now on. Besides, you're cute."

This makes him laugh out loud like he'd told a hilarious joke.

"That's what you wanted to hear, right? You don't have to answer that."

I asked Jerry how anyone could ignore what was obviously happening to us. Jerry didn't answer me for a while. Then he replied, "Do you think anyone cares?"

I hope it doesn't shock you that I'm sexually attracted to Dr. Jerrold Omicidio. There's no question he shows warmth toward me that he doesn't show to anyone else. I wonder if he has anything he doesn't want to talk about? Maybe if we went to bed together I could find out. Only joking. I wonder if I should ask his help in finding David.

FRED TO DANIEL

DON'T YOU DARE FALL FOR OMICIDIO! REBBY ITSENFELDER AND DEEP THROAT AND MONSERRAT KRANK AND BENOIS-FRUCHT AND DR. SISTER GRACE HAVE ALL SAID HE'S NOT TO BE TRUSTED!

DEEP THROAT

You're not learning fast enough, Daniel. You're too naïve and innocent. NITS is a cesspool of suspicion. Always has been. Since this place was only bungalows. There are plenty of docs and nurses still here from earlier years. They get to wear gold pins so you can identify them. But you can tell them by their sour pusses.

Finally, a first patient with UC was admitted yesterday. Jerry didn't tell you that? This is more than three years since the *JOD* and *N.Y. Truth* articles.

Jerry and Grebstyne don masks and gloves and poke at the poor guy. Jerry calls me over and I can tell from his look he wants me to "refresh" him about what he's looking at again. Without mask or gloves I point out everything that this kid is manifesting. The whole menu of shit. The kid is terrified. I'm naming all this stuff out loud and by now other docs have come closer but not too close. I caress the kid's cheek to comfort him. When I touch him, you can hear the group to a man sucking in the breath of fear.

Daniel, this is not the real world in any way, shape, or form. I think your Mr. Goffman was barking up the wrong tree trying to find out what human monkeys are like in captivity. This is Stephen King material!

DANIEL THE SPY

Dr. Sister Grace has died. It was quite some time before this was announced. No one knows how. A fire destroyed her wing at Mater Nostra. Her body was not found, nor her research. Boy, has that all been hushed up. Not even an obituary anywhere placed by someone. Deep Throat told me that she was onto something. He said that she'd been picking his brains about shit. "Shit *can* be used as a surrogate marker for certain kinds of illnesses," she told him, which made him happy to hear acknowleged by a Nobel laureate. She reminded him that polio was carried in feces. "Feces and vaginal bacteria can harbor an illness and carry it through the body via the rectum or the urethra or the penis or the placenta." He was so fucking happy, he said. "This is what we had to find out!" And then he said: "Big-time shitstorm ahead, young Jerusalem and Lemish. Grace also said that Factor Eight was killing homosexuals. And that Von Greeting knew it."

DAME LADY HERMIA SENDS FRED A BOOK

I am enclosing a most instructive volume for your perusal, M. Scott Peck's *People of the Lie*. I particularly commend to your attention this passage: "Those who are evil are masters of disguise; they are not apt to wittingly disclose their true colors, either to others or to themselves."

Does our new "spy," Dr. Daniel Jerusalem, whose reports you have been sending me are so riveting, realize he is in a swamp and in danger of being sucked in? Medical bureaucracies are like that, you must know by now. Beyond a certain point, there is no escape. He is in a heart of darkness. It is this heart that I believe has murdered our Grace.

I do not wish to discuss Grace. I am in deep mourning.

GREETING PRODUCTION REPORT

Von Greeting orders the production of Dridgies tripled. Factor VIII sales figures are disappointing. He then travels to New Godding to be sworn in at Yaddah as one of its board of directors. It's a great honor.

WHAT IS DAVID JERUSALEM UP TO AND WHERE IS HE?

I'm interested in spies. I'm reading everything I can find about a lot of names I want to know more about. I was used as a spy. Mr. Hoover was a spy. He spied on the whole world. Mr. Hoover was gay. I am too. Are many spies gay? Why would a gay man want to spy? British spies appear to be more famous than ours. Burgess and Maclean and Kim Philby each knew each other since they went to Cambridge University. They seem gay to me, but I can't find anyone who's written about this as being important. These guys all worked in Washington. Mr. Hoover must have known them. I'll bet Mr. Hoover stayed in touch with them like he stayed in touch with me. After all, they each share the other's biggest secret, don't they?

There was an obituary in the San Francisco newspaper for a guy named Garrie Nasturtium. He was found in the woods of Rock Creek Park. They said he committed suicide. They said he was very important to Mrs. Ruester. I recognize him as one of my clients at Mr. Hoover's whorehouse. Is that why he killed himself? Or did somebody else do it for him? Does that mean that someone will be coming after me because of all I know? I've seen a lot of famous men's faces in the newspapers that I recognize from the whorehouse.

I do not have any friends. I don't trust anyone. They could never understand what I have been through and I don't want to tell them when they see my body.

I bought a car. I've learned to drive! It's exciting. It's great having so much money!

I miss Gertrude. I got sick and I didn't want to burden her. But then I got better. I should go back to my twin brother at last. I am still angry with my whole family for abandoning me. What is wrong with me that I still live in such a prison?

VON GREETING AND ARNOLD BOTTS ARE IN BED TOGETHER

"It's interesting, is it not, how little attention there's been in the press about Nasturtium?" Von said.

"Who cares if faggots die," Arnold replied.

"Or Dr. Sister Grace's 'disappearance.'"

"She was a faggot too, you know."

"I didn't know that. You're overdue for a major punishment."

"Not tonight."

"Stuartgene wanted you particularly."

"Yeah? Well, he's really sick when he gets going."

"People with great power exude great energy to get what they want. What are you doing with that drug I gave you?"

"I found a partner. Knows his way around. Tell me again why you gave it to me. Isn't it any good?"

"I need a dummy front to disguise what else we're doing. Who knows if it's any good. You and your partner will find out. My scout bought it in Czechoslovakia. Who's this partner?"

"One of those Nazis at Partekla."

"Be careful."

"He has a couple drugs of his own too and is looking for a setup. And Sam Sport is our lawyer. You must know him."

"I'm impressed," Von said.

"Unusual for you to be impressed."

"I have Nutrobe in my pocket. Gobbel's ordered him to behave or else."

"I'm impressed," Arnold said.

"Ruester came to town with a shitload of expert behind-the-scenes terror mongers."

"All the great presidents do."

"Well, I wasn't a hundred percent certain about Old Peter. Now I'm certain."

"Anything you want to share with me?"

"Not yet. It's best that you not know yet."

They both said that.

Von said, "You look real cute tonight. Give me a kiss at least."

•

Arnold Botts is employed by G-D. Working with the men he has, he's become fascinated by their methods of control and domination to get what they want. With promotions at Greeting-Dridge he was given power to do certain things. He and Von will have only so much time to get away with them. Someone honest might actually get elected, although he's learned enough to doubt this. He sees the path his country is hell-bent on taking. It pleases him a lot. Could anyone who knew him growing up in Masturbov Gardens have seen this survivor coming out of that childhood?

How can Arnold have known Old Peter? Well, if Ruester was G-D's public pitchman for so many years, he and Manny and those Kaffeeklatschers would come to know Arnold Botts really well.

A SCENE IN THE COUNTRY

It looks like a full moon, Arnold thought, as they tried to walk to the cabin over the debris-littered field without getting their polished shoes filthy. Each was walking forward with different memories. Arnold's contained visions of pleasurably torturing his boss Von, and Mount Vernon Pugh's of how Sam Sport had so pleasurably allowed him to fuck him. Mt. Vernon, still in his twenties, is compact and cute and dresses like he still lived in England.

"Okay, now what do you want to tell me?" Arnold said almost immediately after stepping out of his sporty little MG, which he parked behind the now-boarded-up Deltoid's barbecue. Once upon a time he thought he'd fallen in love with the babe who worked here, name of Velvalee. She ditched him and he still hates her for it wherever she is.

"Listen to me. I got only peculiar things to say," Mount Vernon said as they entered a back door that went into the basement. "We discovered a new poison in blood. We didn't do it on purpose. I mean it presented itself to us unasked for. Two little girls out Littham Grove way. They died. Pathologist said it was because they'd had shots from our whooping cough serum. Whooping cough serum contains one iota persumatin, which has maybe got a touch of plasmatene in it, one tiny speck so microscopic it wouldn't hardly be known to be there if it weren't known to be there."

"How did you get through science in school, the way you talk?"

"I didn't get through science in school. I'm the boss's cousin, remember? My English grandma was a Greeting. They had to put me in charge of something. I own too much stock. I built the whooping cough division, one thousand, one hundred and ten percentage. People didn't know their cough was whooping until BaxxterDridgeGreeting convinced them it was not just an ordinary cough. You know our commercial. 'Not just an ordinary cough.' Scared everybody to death."

Yes, Arnold knew it. He got Velvalee to make it.

"What about the poisoned blood?"

"What about it? This seems different from the shit we had in that Factor Eight Alpha. The shit you told me about."

"You mean this is new shit?"

"I guess."

"Jesus, don't you know? Did you get rid of the old shit?"

"Of course not. You ordered me not to."

Then Arnold took Mount Vernon into the secret room in this hidden cabin, where he punished the kid real good.

•

INT. FORT DETRICK OFFICES/LABS. VARIOUS. DAY.

MICKEY'S VOICE (*screaming*): . . . top-secret experiments at Fort Detrick, Maryland, that have produced a virus that can destroy the immune system. Its code name is Firm Hand. They started testing it in 1978—on a group of gays!

MONTAGE:

Fred visits several offices and several people, all of whom seem decent enough. They will look at him pleasantly and they will shake their heads pleasantly, or come back pleasantly from a search empty-handed. Finally he will be taken to an enormous storage warehouse where shelving loaded down with decades of files seems to reach up to the sky. No one is in this huge place except Fred and the employee who will ride him around on a cart as he investigates various locales.

DRIVER: Anything really important, you won't find here.

FRED: Where would I look?

DRIVER: Nowhere. They'd all be burned up.

DEEP THROAT *(v.o.)*: If it is true and you get anywhere near to finding anything, which I doubt, did it occur to you that you could be killed?

FRED *(v.o.)*: You're serious?

DEEP THROAT *(v.o.)*: Congress appropriated one billion dollars for biological warfare last year and the Pentagon doesn't have to say where it went. We are spending more money developing germs than we are to stop them.

FRED *(v.o.)*: What does Omicidio say about any of this?

Deep Throat just lets out a big, loud laugh.

WHO'S TALKING?

There is now an office of the Tricia Institute in every major city. Each month new tallys are reported to me of the number of homosexuals it has located. The numbers continue to rise. While none of us is certain what we are to do with this information, I am instructed its time will soon come.

DR. MONSERRAT KRANK

The reactions I am hearing from many of my heterosexual friends remind me of the stories I heard about Jews during the war, that homosexuals were dirty and evil and deserved to die. I am determined to prevent my gay friends being treated this way. Fortunately, my heterosexual friends are rich and are grateful to Binky for something or other, so it's been easy to shame them into contributions for my organization with Rebby. Sadly, Binky is not very supportive. It is his movie star clients I'm going after.

DAME LADY HERMIA

Where are you, my Freddie? I await your further contributions to my ongoing history of evil, you who are hurling "Hitler" and "Holocaust" with increasing regularity. Are you aware that as we spread our wings Jewish scholars now condemn us for "sullying" their own precious Holocaust? They argue harshly that "their" ur-text is the only Original Holocaust, and we are forcing it to lose its "necessary bold-face currency as the only currency, lest it be cheapened"? Indeed, one camp survivor has written me, "If so many see evil lurking now everywhere behind every tree and in every nook and cranny, how can the world be expected to remember the real thing?" We must teach them that evil is evil, in any time and every place, and if "they" don't like it, so what, so (as you and dear lost Grace would most certainly say) fucking what. Goodness, listen to me.

And listen to this:

"Every able-bodied man they could find was put to work in three shifts: writing file cards for an enormous circular card file, several yards in diameter, which a man sitting on a piano stool could operate and find any card he wanted thanks to a system of punch holes. All information important . . . was entered on these cards. The data was taken from annual reports, handbooks, the newspapers of all the political parties, membership files; in short, of everything imaginable. Each card carried name, address, party membership, whether Jew, Freemason, or practicing Catholic or Protestant, gypsy, homosexual; whether politically active, whether this or whether that."

These are the words of Adolph Eichmann as published in *Eichmann Interrogated: Transcripts from the Archives of the Israeli Police*, edited by Jochen von Lang and translated by Ralph Manheim. This book has created a bit of a stir. Questions are raised about the accuracy of the translation—ridiculous since Manheim is an award-winning translator of great standing. The inclusion of the words *gypsy* and *homosexual* is questioned. The book sells well, particularly in the Washington area.

THE WHITE HOUSE

OFFICE OF THE PRESS SECRETARY
PRESS BRIEFING BY LARRY SPEAKES

June 13, 1983

Q: Larry, does the president think that it might help if he suggested that the gays cut down on their "cruising"? *(Laughter.)* What? I didn't hear your answer, Larry.

MR. SPEAKES: I just was acknowledging your interest—

Q: You were acknowledging but—

MR. SPEAKES:—interest in this subject.

Q:—you don't think that it would help if the gays cut down on their cruising—it would help this . . . thing?

MR. SPEAKES: We are researching it. If we come up with any research that sheds some light on whether gays should cruise or not cruise, we'll make it available to you. (*Laughter.*)

Q: Back to fairy tales.

VITAL STATISTICS

COD reports 2,259 cases, with 917 dead.

•

Insulting.

DANIEL TO FRED

Gobbel has just appointed as "Adviser to the President" a man named Brinestalker. Therein lies another whole history that I don't have the stomach to go into today, but my father worked for a Brinestalker and I'll bet he knows something about David. Word is that he's advising the administration on homosexuality. I tried to locate Brinestalker. I left my name at his office downtown three or four times and he's not calling me back. I have this creepy feeling he'll tell me David is dead.

DANIEL THE SPY

The bloodies *finally* meet. It's taken them this long. NITS, HAH, FADS, COD, ARB, BOAN, Army, Navy, etc. It's mayhem. Even Representative Dingus showed up; he's known to appear only when he smells something for him to expose.

COD and NITS are each convinced that the other is invading its turf and trying to purloin money from the other's budget, which is pretty puny to begin with. And hemophiliacs are terrified that Factor VIII will be taken away from them because they're being linked with homosexuals. Various Red Crosses and Bloods are afraid of being attacked for some fuckup or other as blood is obviously getting more infected. The pediatricians are screaming, "My little babies did not get this from having sex!" And the revered head honcho of all blood, Dr. Stewwinger Foss of Yaddah—you remember all those photographs we had to have taken of us naked freshman year, to test our "posture"? Foss was in charge of that. It was his idea. I wonder where all those photos are? And what his rationale really was, to photograph every freshman naked; how did he get Yaddah's president to go along with that?—he keeps announcing over and over like a mantra, "The blood supply is safe, the blood supply is safe," as if his own life depended on it. He's giving himself absolutely no wiggle room, which I've learned in D.C. is something you just don't do.

Interesting how there are all-institute top-level meetings for blood, but nothing for research or for that funny word *cure*. Dye says, "I am not interested in other divisions' opinions." "Other divisions"! What's his opinion on what we should be doing if not this?

Monserrat and Rebby, also here, realize it's been way over three years with no research, no plan, no coordinator, no prevention methods, no official guidelines or health recommendations from anyone, concerning blood or anything else.

And Jerry has just testified to Congress that no further money is needed: "We have all we need." This is an outright lie but it's the mantra he's ordered to repeat by Gree Bohunk and Linus Gobbel, who have whispered to him they'll find him a few bucks behind Stockman's back if he keeps his mouth shut. A few bucks!

How could there not be a plan, any intelligent person would ask. Well, this intelligent person is wondering if perhaps the plan is that there is no plan. Monserrat discusses this possibility with Binky, who's had much experience interacting with presidents. "This present lot, I fear, is scum." She quotes him in Jerry's office. She's come to bawl him out "for your total lackluster behavior," she announces regally. She next goes to Sec. Swilkers to ream out Hoidene, who has no idea who she is. "Nasturtium won't return my calls," Monserrat tells me. "It's very dispiriting." She didn't know Garrie's dead and now they don't think it was suicide.

Paulus of COD came in looking white as a sheet. He's learned that "it can take anywhere from five to eleven years for this UC shit" to bloom inside us into full-blown activity. This is terrifying news. It means that the government can continue to ignore it because it will remain relatively no problem, or not enough of a problem, for many years to come. How can that be? The answer is it can't.

Paulus made this discovery in his own lab, and Dodo heard about it, and Paulus's lab was briefly shut down. Dodo screams out at Stuartgene's meeting, "I will not be trumped! I will not compete with incompetence! Dodo's lab must reign supreme!" Middleditch calms him down.

And COD's budget is cut some more.

VITAL STATISTICS

Cases reported in thirty-nine states, as well as D.C. and Puerto Rico, and twenty foreign countries.

•

Wrong. Wrong. Wrong. Wrong. Wrong. I giggle with glee.

ONE LAST TOUCH OF PENIS

The One Touch of Penis agency, R. Allan Pooker proprietor, is as busy as ever. If there is trouble ahead, R. Allan's clients aren't thinking about it. R. Allan, however, is a mite concerned. Several of his boys have quietly died, several more are not well, and one of them, that cute fresh kid named Durwood, disappeared and the word is that he passed away on the job somewhere.

R. Allan is filming a few of his still living beauties, Cully, Midnight Cowboy, and a couple of new ones whose names he already can't remember. R. Allan fills his boys' noses full of Dridgies, he still has some original Dridgies left in the original orange packaging. They don't age, they're worth a fortune, the boys can't wait to have them, he's got hot music on the speakers, the lighting is perfect, he's rolling his cameras, he's got two going, running back and forth from one to the other because his regular cameraman is dead . . .

No one can get it up.

R. Allan makes an appointment with Mordy Masturbov to discuss matters with him, really to try to sell him One Touch of Penis. "But I have never partaken of your kind of business," Mordy says dismissively. "That's not what I heard," R. Allan says. "In any event, that is not to argue. We've both been responsible for encouraging whatever's happening to happen. Don't you think we should discuss our future? That is, if we're to have one?" Since R. Allan's business is quickly disappearing and Mordy's isn't—*Sexopolis* is healthier than ever—Mordy doesn't give R. Allan's words a second thought, even when he receives an invitation a few months later to a memorial service in R. Allan's honor, after his death from "pneumonia." Funny thing to die from, Mordy remembers thinking. In this day and age.

MAYOR KERMIT GOINS'S LOVER NATHAN PERCH IS SICK IN AN UNDISCLOSED CLINIC IN CALIFORNIA

He was after me, after my body, after my brains, after my mouth, after my life, I couldn't take it anymore, he was driving me nuts, he said he loved me, he said he hated me, he said he's going to pay me off with contracts and send me to the Coast or else he's going to encase me in cement . . . So here I am on the Coast.

When we first met he looked deep into my eyes and said, "I want to spend the rest of my life in your arms," and he found me a rent-controlled apartment and he got me a job in his Department of Sex and Germs. Just to be near him. He liked to be sucked off under the desk in his office. "You won't have to do a thing, just come when I whistle," he'd said, and he whistled every Wednesday night, we ordered in, neither of us could cook . . . I had the most famous lover in the city!

He told the world he loved Donny M. and then he said Donny M. was a pig and then Donny M. killed himself. He told the world he loved Stanley F. and then Stanley F. got indicted and sent to prison. He told the world he loved Bessie M. but she became a lying shoplifter and no longer any good as his beard so he couldn't pretend he was going to marry her. And then Mario B. got indicted, and then Dereck D. started saying nasty things about us unless he was given lots of West Side real estate, and then Geoffrey L. turned into a stoolie. And Bessie M. became a lesbian and told the press she couldn't marry him anyway. And then Herb R. and Dan W., who owned *The Village Vice*, talked to him . . .

. . . and then the latest polls showed that less than 30 percent wanted him reelected, and then he came every other Wednesday, and then he came one Wednesday a month, and then he came every other month, and then he stopped . . . paying my rent, and then in my job at Germs I learned all about the growing plague and he said, "Shut up, you goniff twit, it's a secret, haven't I taught you anything about secrets," and then a huge Italian man with a big big gun came and gave me money and told me to keep my mouth shut and get out of town fast, don't even pack, or the ripple of destruction and the swirl of death would drown me in the Hudson in that cement.

So I came west to be among my brothers. I thought I'd be safe here. But then the gay leaders discovered all about us, and they found me and came after me to publicly blab the truth, they are ceaseless in their tenacious fixation to destroy him for destroying them, but they're coming after me, I'm caught in the middle, so all of this—all all all of this!—has brought me closer to death because he's coming after me because I know too much and he knows I know too much and he knows what I know could . . . He's running for a fourth term!

VITAL STATISTICS

January 1984. COD reports three thousand cases of UC, with 1,283 deaths.

•

This is getting ridiculous. But I keep forgetting none of you can count.
You have achieved little in the way of progress, America. You're
not smart enough to figure me out. Thank goodness.

THE HOLY TERROR IN THE WHEELCHAIR CALLS
THE HEAD OF TABLE MEDICAL CENTER

"Dr. Grafft, this is Dr. Emma Brookner, in Hematology/Oncology. I'm the doctor in the wheelchair you had to build all those ramps for. Yes, that holy terror in the wheelchair. I didn't expect you to remember every woman doctor's name on your staff—there are only a dozen of us—but I thought you might remember mine since I cost you twenty-seven million dollars. Well, I'm having a little trouble with your latest letter to the staff. 'Please try to curb your admissions of UC lest Table become known as the exclusive hospital for this growing epidemic.' As I am the prime overadmitter, I thought I'd ask you just how many you'd allow me to admit. I have, let's see, thirty-three in right now. I had thirty-seven yesterday, but four died. I give you a fast turnover. Yes, I think thirty-three is excessive too. Where would you like me to admit the twenty-four I expect to need beds for in the next few days? I only have a one-bedroom apartment."

FRED CONTINUES TO FLIP HIS DAILY LID ON THE COUCH OF DR. ODYSSEUS HOMER

A creep is now saying, "I saw my first case in 1976"! And then other creeps start being interviewed and, boing, plop, into the historical record go doctors and scientists who saw this shit going back into the 1970s, earlier even, there are a few edging up to claiming they'd seen this shit in the 1960s. And I am saying, fuck you all, you are liars and opportunists. And if you were seeing stuff that scared the shit out of you so much that you didn't know what to do, what kind of fucking doctor were you, are you, what do you mean you didn't know what to do! You sound the alarm! That's what you fucking do. And nobody sounded any alarms, anywhere. The silence among docs everywhere was deafening, all the way from Gretta Lell in Miami, who now says she was keeping mum because her sick Haitian patients were putting curses on her, invoking voodoo rituals, to Dr. Paulus Pewkin, who when Gretta told him about her earliest cases, responded, "I am very skeptical about what you are saying," she said he said, and that, taken with the Haitians calling her names and other black doctors treating her as a "rich white racist," which of course is exactly what we all are . . . And also she claimed that COD very reluctantly went down to Florida to interview her patients, "and they totally insulted them, and tried to pin homosexuality on them, and said, 'Are you sure you didn't get sick not from voodoo but from cock up the doo-doo?,' which did not go down well." "What year are you claiming for your first ones, Gretta?," someone tried to pin her down. "I think it was 1979, 1980." "You don't know? You don't have records to double-check your memory?" "Get off my fucking back! You think you were the only one around worried about what was happening! What ego! What pomposity! You're full of shit."

That New Jersey doctor who claims he saw cases in kids in 1980, well, at least he has proof that he sent reports to several journals and to *The Journal of Death* and he was turned down everywhere. COD and *JOD* would not publish his paper, which *NEJS* had turned down too, until now, 1984. I actually saw a letter from somebody at COD, "How could such a filthy disease happen in children?" By 1984, *which is now*, some five thousand cases have been reported to COD, with over two thousand dead. It took three years for the first five thousand cases to be reported to COD and ten months for the second five thousand cases . . .

Grace is gone now.

I feel shitty, shitty ass ratfucking awful.

I feel, I sense, I'm now losing Daniel as well.

DANIEL

Fred, Jerry got $12 million from Congress. Don't yell. It's a start.

DEEP THROAT REPORTS TO MOTHER

You're right. Of course he will win again. You and I both know that Ruester is more popular than ever. And anyway, it's all been planned. And Dredd Trish is there for after Peter Ruester, not instead of.

The cadre of Homo Haters that enunciate on Peter's behalf protects him. "Homosexuals are never numbered among The American People for the simple reason that The American People doesn't have any," Linus Gobbel writes in *Capital Hill Jesus*. There's no one on staff that's a Homo Friend.

It's finally being asked, how can so many dead bodies remain hidden from sight?

Well, they are.

His Homo Haters know this. You and I both know that all the best presidents have them.

They know they're successful in what they're doing. When you aren't besieged by a multitude of calls, letters, and criticism in the media objecting to your actions, as you know that's like money in the bank.

You know Washington is now *the* place to be. Swarms of worker bees continually arrive to join Ruester's efforts in one office or department or division. You can just feel the almost tangible electricity. They have a leader they can follow. They now can believe openly that what they are doing is for the health and good of America and The American People. What they are doing is the will of God. Homosexuality is a crime and a sin. This becomes an established ideology. It's worse than what you warned me about.

It's being called in certain circles the Grand Elimination.
And hanky-panky is brewing among several of the pharms.
Stay tuned.

•

INT. OLD BELLEVUE HOSPITAL MEDICAL
AMPHITHEATER. DAY.
*A huge, ancient amphitheater once used for med school lectures. It
is quite beautiful. Emma is making a presentation to Dr. Omicidio
and other officials. She's been coughing and wheezing and will use
a nebulizer to control it. Various slides of incomprehensible data are
flicking on the large screen overhead. The hall is filled with observers:
some we have seen before at NITS and COD; some are staff from the
hospital and medical center, of course, but also a large group of Emma's
patients, in various stages of health, sitting up front with Buzzy and
Fred and Tommy. Daniel Jerusalem is also present in a far corner at
the back. Mickey and Bruce also sit removed from Fred. Bruce looks
terrible.*

EMMA: We have more data of every kind, and, I humbly submit,
    more experience. I am confident that our persistence and enthu-
    siasm will yield results.

*Emma finishes her remarks, smiles, and nods to Omicidio. There is
wild applause from her patients.*
CUT TO:
Omicidio and his group have been studying some papers.

OMICIDIO *(looking up finally)*: Dr. Brookner, the government's po-
    sition is this. There are five million dollars in the pipeline, for
    which we've received over fifty-five million dollars' worth of
    requests.

EMMA: Five million doesn't seem quite right for some two thousand
    cases. The government spent seven million investigating seven
    deaths from Tylenol. We are entering the third year . . .

OMICIDIO: President Ruester has indicated he will veto . . .

EMMA: It looks like we continue to have a pretty successful stalemate.

OMICIDIO: Well, that is not what we're here to discuss, is it?

EMMA *(sensing what's coming)*: Go ahead. At your own peril.

OMICIDIO: We have voted to reject your application for funding.

EMMA: Oh? I would like to hear your reasons.

OMICIDIO: The direction of the research you're suggesting is imprecise and unfocused.

EMMA: Oh, it is, is it? You don't know what's going on any more than I do. My guess is as good as anybody's. Why are you blocking my efforts?

OMICIDIO: Dr. Brookner, there are now other investigators. It's no longer just your disease, though you seem to think it is.

EMMA: Oh, I do, do I? And you're here to take it away from me, is that it? Well, I'll let you in on a little secret, Doctor. You can have it. I didn't want it in the first place. You think it's a privilege to watch young men die? Oh, what am I arguing with you for? You don't know enough to study boiled water. How dare you come and judge me!

OMICIDIO: We only serve on this peer review panel at the behest of Dr. Dye.

EMMA: Another idiot. And by the way, a closeted pervert doing everything in his power to sweep this under the rug. And I vowed I'd never say something like that in public. How does it always happen that all the idiots are always on your team? I am taking care of more victims of this plague than anyone else in the world. How can you not fund my research or invite me to participate in yours? Your NITS received my first request for money over two years ago. It took you one year just to print up application forms. It's taken you three years from my first reported case just to show up here for a look. The paltry amount of money you are forcing us to beg for, from the four billion dollars NITS receives each and every year to protect the health of all The American People, won't come to anyone until only God knows when. A promising virus has been rumored, in France. Why are you refusing to cooperate with the French? Why are we told not to cooperate with the French? Just so you can steal a Nobel Prize? While something is being passed around that causes death! Women have been discovered to have it in Africa—where it is clearly transmitted heterosexually. It is only a question of time. We could all be dead before you do anything! You want my data?

(Hurls out files.)

You want my ideas?

(Hurls out more files.)

You want my patients?

(Hurls out more files.)

> Take them! TAKE THEM! Just do something with them! You're fucking right, I am imprecise and unfocused. And you are all idiots!

She has hurled masses of papers and files out into space, toward the doctors. She rises from her wheelchair, only to fall on the floor. Omicidio tries to help her.

EMMA: Don't you dare touch me!

Fred and Buzzy and Tommy run to gather her up. She is sobbing.

THE FIRST LADY TALKING TO AND ABOUT HER HUSBAND

"Yes, Mommy will be home to shoot you up again and dress you for tonight's performance. Yes, it's a new costume. Yes, the Marine Band will play you in. Yes, there's a long long long red carpet. Yes, you'll be on during prime time. If the media asks about anything, just play dumb like you do so well on Iran. Then you can play with your dirty pictures. Yes, Mommy is still going to fire . . . Now, don't cry. Stop it! Remember, you must say directly to the camera that you believe it is a tragic illness but yes you still believe they should remain illegal. And never ever say the letters *UC* or the word *homosexual*! Now go upstairs and watch *General Hospital*. Yes, I'm still at Uncle Foppy's. No! No, listen to me! I've been a good girl since . . . Kiss-kiss, Pootie Pie."

She disconnects. "Oh, God, I need it. Can you see how passionate I feel?"

"Yes. I do," responds her Foppy.

"Do you know what it's like to really need it?"

"Yes, I do."

"The latest problem is he mixes up his movies with real life. He plays with his footballs in his bathtub and wakes up in the middle of the night to see if his leg is still there. His leg! The hardest thing I've had to deal with in over thirty years of marriage is his leg!"

"That is exceedingly desperate."

"Every time he passes an American flag he salutes it. Do you know how many American flags there are in the White House? Seven hundred and twelve.

"I don't know why everyone thinks this job is so much fun. Everyone thinks it's all free dishes. Everyone thinks it's all mink coats and Russian presidents' wives. Everyone thinks it's all Frank Sinatra for long private lunches upstairs with my door locked. Everyone thinks it's all parties parties parties and balls balls balls. Well, it is. He said all he wants now is to live the quiet life again. Horse shit on the hacienda at our ranch high up in the middle of nowhere. Our mingy two-bedroom split-level featuring furniture from his childhood back home again in Indiana. Or was it Illinois. Carlotta Punic throwing it up to me on every phone call, 'I have a hundred million dollars, how much do you have?' The sacrifices I've made to go into public service! But I'm making the best of it! Lady Bird planted her pansies on the highways. Eleanor Roosevelt was a lesbian with bad teeth. Mamie was a lush. Betty Ford was such a mess she opened her own cure. Rosalynn was Attila the Hun. Pat Nixon pleaded a bad heart and she certainly had one. Who even remembers Bess Truman? All she was was just a wife and mother. I'm better than all of them! Mrs. Wilson ran the country, so can I! Why don't I get as good press as Jackie? I dress better and my husband is faithful! Should I run for reelection? You bet your fucking ass!"

TESTIMONY BY
BRADEN BENNETT, M.D., PHARM. PH.D.

CONGRESSIONAL ADVISORY COMMITTEE CHAIRED
BY REP. HENRY WAXMAN (CA)

In science, you need never be wrong. That's why there's never a real "cure" for anything. Because there really are no true absolutes in scientific research. Every scientist wants you to think there are, but there aren't. All there are are various degrees of possibility. And, also, you can never admit you wasted so much money finding anything. Yes, of course you have to attempt to justify your work's efficacy, no matter how rotten the shit is. But most times, you really can't. In the end you are going on hunches, and some sort-of-interesting, often half-baked research done by lab interns who oftentimes don't even speak English. So a lot of lying goes on. And most of it passes by unnoticed, unattended to, mostly because everyone knows it's going on. Oh, once in a rare while FADS gets into the act, or is forced to get into the act. I was on many a FADS committee where an "approved" drug got caught with its ineffective pants down killing a few folks and the attitude was "Oh, shit, do we have to deal with this old turkey again!" Instead of "Oh my, someone has died; what can we do to make the product safer?" Safety is not the name of the game in the manufacture of pharmaceuticals. I wish the world would know that and stop being naïve. People want "cures" and "relief," etc. These do not come unalloyed without the odd nightmare. They just do not. That is life. On the whole, until recently, the pharms have had a fair record of the occasional amazing result. Those days are not gone, by and large; they are just increasingly hard to bring off. People want too much assurance. They don't want to face up to the fact that it's all a craps game, what we do. And rule number one in the drug-manufacturing business is never admit you're wrong. That way lies bankruptcy. And we want to make money more than we want you to get better and live. But that is capitalism. And until the government is in charge of all this, and really takes charge of the health of its people, it is going to happen that every major pharm will have, every once in a while, something that turns into poison for them, and of course for those who take it.

And the pharms demand their payoff, or else they won't do anything. They'll just keep churning out new kinds of aspirin if they don't get their payoff. That's all you really need to keep the stockholders happy, another "improved" aspirin. No problem advertising it. No side effects. No R&D costs. No royalties to divvy up.

Payoffs usually lead to drug approvals from FADS. From, currently, Dr. Heiney Halfender, formerly the CEO of Acme Trucking Company (the "Dr." turned out to be from a business school). Payoffs mean tacit agreement to an article in *The New England Journal of Spots* that says the new shit was tested on 356 patients at the University of Coconut Grove Medical Center by Dr. Gretta Lell and that, lo and behold, thank you, Jesus, all 356 got up and walked. So gimme the fucking license because, don'tcha know, Greeting-Dridge spent $120 million of its very own money researching and developing this shit for twenty years at least. And they have a hundred lobbyists to convince every official that this is all true.

The pharms don't think of anybody or anything but the pharms. They certainly don't think of the sick, and they don't consider anyone's pocketbooks. All these guys—and the pharms are always guys—ever think about is WINNING. The insurers will pick up the tab, if you can only get the shit to market, approved by FADS.

Sooner or later some square peg is going to fit in some round hole. These guys work on the law of averages. Spend a hundred million bucks, a few million on a hundred different possibilities. One of them has to hit. Figure out the highest possible amount of dosage the body can humanly tolerate each day without keeling over. This is how chemotherapy was developed. Every cancer is treated with some kind of combo that, by itself, didn't work for squat in the beginning. There probably never has been a chemo since time began that's worked on its own the first time around. Before any results are ever found it's got to be administered in voluminous amounts and in combinations with something else.

That's what will probably happen with UC. We just need a couple of things to pump into the patient. On their own each can be shit. But together they are less shitty. That's what medicating people is all about. Finding the less shitty. NITS has never actually found a cure, a real cure, a total cure, for anything. But you didn't know that. Nobody seems to.

Combo. Combos. Voluminous amounts. If the right shit is pumped in, it might only need to be minute amounts of whatever will do the trick. But pharms secretly know that their patented chemicals work much better in smaller doses than voluminous amounts. But chintzy "humanitarians," which is what every pharm advertises itself to death to be, know there ain't no money in small doses. You can reason that more people living on smaller doses bring in more money than fewer people keeling over after voluminous amounts. But statistics prove this isn't so. Actuarial tables indicate that while it's a long time dying from small amounts, if you calculate the cost of money and interest, it's not that much less of a long time to the payoff of a lesser number dying from voluminous amounts. Go for the gold. What's a few more dead bodies? Cancer is *supposed* to kill you.

Statistics can say anything you want them to.

Thus you never are wrong.

Do I think the present system works? Of course not. Do I think it should be replaced? You bet. Do I know how to do it? Nope. And neither does anyone else.

Not anyone that I trust, anyway. Not that trust plays much of a part in anything. Luck is what plays a part in everything.

What was that last question again, Senator? Do I believe we can find a cure for UC? Well, as I've said, and I hope you were listening, *cure* is a funny word. It means a lot of things to a lot of people. I wager that not a few of you here secretly hope and think that the best cure for UC is no cure for UC. I suspect that what with one thing or another this is what we are going to see for a long time. So do I believe we'll find one? No.

Now, I've heard scuttlebutt that Dr. Geiseric has said that he has found a putative virus that probably is the cause of this shit. Forgive me, we have been calling it "this shit" for so long it has become a habit. For The Underlying Condition. As I understand it, NITS, with some twelve thousand employees, has had only one lab actively working on this for the past four years, that of Dr. Geiseric. That is not a way to cure a plague. And as I also believe, there is not much interest among scientists or pharms in researching UC. If it is this viral agent causing UC, as most expect it to be, that only makes matters worse, since it will be poison and fearful to handle. And, most important, drug companies consider the potential market for any treatment of this population to be a small one.

I am going to predict something else, if I may. Despite all the putative "knowledge" that Dr. Geiseric is intimating is so, the fact remains that there will be increasing worldwide disagreements as to who did what and when. And these are going to wind up in courts, in lawyers' offices all over the globe. Knowledge is never free. And I do not see the current purveyors of putative knowledge, like their heroic forebears, such scientists as the Curies, or pharmaceutical giants such as George Merck, who provided the results of their discoveries for free for the good of humanity, doing any such thing here. In fact, I predict that each of our current crop will become so selfish and greedy and determined to own the legal outcomes as their own that absolutely nothing will be done for years until this is all resolved. Lots more dead bodies while they work it out.

I work for one of them, so I know.

Thanks for the use of your hall.

DANIEL THE SPY

For some reason, Dodo blabs to *The New York Prick*.

"Of course anybody can get UC! Anal intercourse is probably the most effective way to catch it. And of course straight women already have it. I'm working on it. Stay tuned."

One wonders why Dodo chose this paper to say all this. "They asked me questions and I answered them" is his defense, when confronted (see below) by Slyme et al. "I'm told nobody reads it anyway."

Dingus and Slyme, with big tough bozo Gobbel, showed up at our morning meeting today. In front of all of us, Gobbel took Dodo by his necktie and yanked him up out of his chair and said he was going to see him hanged if he publicly said the things he said in the *Prick*. It's nice to know that they're reading *The Prick* up there in the White House. "I will see personally that you are hanged by the neck until you are dead if I see one more reference to the very idea that anybody except fags and niggers and junkies can get this shit. There is not one woman in our wonderful United States who has it or will have it. Do you hear me?" Dodo just stared at Linus, whose face was in his face. Then Dodo said, "You are crazier than I am, and that is saying a lot."

Rep. Dingus just beamed. For whatever reason he has the hates for Dodo. He now confronts Dodo: "I am preparing an investigation into your work and your laboratory and your staff and anything about you that I can investigate, including the size of your cock, because I hear you are fucking certain persons not your wife in your lab, which is government property. I need not remind you—well, perhaps I need to remind you—that fucking other women not your wife, shit, fucking anybody on government property is against the rules and you know it, sir, and if you don't know it, sir, you better know it now, sir." And Slyme and Gobbel marched out. There was even some applause for the performances. We're getting to be *the* hot ticket. People come to our meetings just to catch the fireworks. "Best show in town."

Slyme, of course, popped his head and self back in and screamed: "And we don't ever want to see those words *anal intercourse* again!"

Dingus remained and, staring still at Dodo, announced very loudly: "And where is your esteemed director, Dr. Dye? His attendance record has become quite spotty. As has yours." Why Dingus, who is a Democrat, is against whatever Dodo is doing is one of those good questions, the increasing number of which in this history is reaching uncontrollable proportions. Like why was Dr. Garth Buffalo excommunicated and sent out into some wilderness? He's got a Nobel and says he has an idea how to tackle UC. I've asked around for any gossip, but my greedy hands remain empty. Buffalo was fired from Harvard, where he'd been picketed by a group calling themselves the Minutemen.

Jerry said to Dingus, loudly, "Dr. Dye and I are still waiting for some money."

Dingus exited with the growing-too-familiar curtain line: "That's not my committee." Then he, too, popped back in to go and take a look at Jerry's name card. "What kind of name is that! Too long to write down." And he's off.

•

INT. FRED'S LOFT. NEW YORK. NIGHT.

Fred and Tommy, their eyes filled with tears. There is still a big blow-up photo of Felix. By now Tommy is even more in love with Fred.

TOMMY: My brother's sick now. Emma took Bruce out of Invincible and put him into Table. She hates Invincible, calls them butchers. She hates Dr. Poo. She calls him a charlatan quack.

FRED *(kisses the blow-up)*: Felix, why are they letting us die? Someone's letting all this happen, Tommy, and it isn't God. I wonder how long any of us has. I wonder it every single moment of every single day.

CUT TO:

Fred and Tommy still in street clothes, asleep next to each other. Fred suddenly shoots up from a nightmare.

FRED *(screaming)*: Help!

Tommy is awake and looking down at him. Then they hug and start crying again.

THE WHITE HOUSE

OFFICE OF THE PRESS SECRETARY
PRESS BRIEFING BY LARRY SPEAKES

MR. SPEAKES: Lester's beginning to circle now. He's moving in front. *(Laughter.)* Go ahead.

Q: Since the Center of Disease *(laughter)* reports—

MR. SPEAKES: This is going to be a sex question.

Q:—that an estimated—

MR. SPEAKES: You were close.

Q: Well, look, could I ask the question, Larry?

MR. SPEAKES: You were close.

Q: An estimated three hundred thousand people have been exposed to this, which can be transmitted through saliva. Will the president, as commander in chief, take steps to protect the armed forces' food and medical services from these patients or those who run the risk of spreading it in the same manner that they forbid typhoid fever people from being involved in the health or food services?

MR. SPEAKES: I don't know.

Q: Could you—is the president concerned about this subject, Larry—

MR. SPEAKES: I haven't heard him express—

Q:—that seems to have evoked so much jocular—

MR. SPEAKES:—concern. It isn't only the jokes, Lester.

Q: Has he sworn off water faucets? No, but I mean, is he going to do anything, Larry?

MR. SPEAKES: Lester, I have not heard him express anything on it. Sorry.

Q: You mean he has no—expressed no opinion about this epidemic?

MR. SPEAKES: No, but I must confess I haven't asked him about it. *(Laughter.)*

Q: Would you ask him, Larry?

MR. SPEAKES: Have you been checked? *(Laughter.)*

OUR FIRST FAMILY

"Foppy, you were the first person I told I was gay. You told me I wasn't sick and to keep my mouth shut. Well, I want to open my mouth. I keep wanting to come out of the closet and you keep pushing me back in. As a public personality I have a responsibility to my people. Our people! I want to be a contender!"

"My thinner Marlon Brando, my shorter Tommy Tune, your father does not like us."

"But all you do is go to parties with Ma's Dragon Ladies."

"This makes me privy to much useful information."

"Such as."

"She looks good in red."

"She must know you're gay."

"We do not discuss it."

"Why not?"

"Why not, why not, youth wants to know? Because Mommy and Daddy are rulers of more than two hundred million people who look on us as freaks."

"You deny your true feelings."

"Better that than she deny me all her parties. One makes choices."

"The Supreme Court makes its choice today. You want to bet we're going to be officially declared null, void, and illegal?"

"The Supreme Court is voting today?"

"You can be locked up for making love in your own bedroom. I'll black-mail him! I'll tell the world about me. I am going to New York to dance with Robert."

"Robert has just died from this plague."

"Oh, no! It's getting worse and worse and it's my own father's fault. How dare he! And you! With all you know, what are you doing to help? You have known her since she was a girl. Help us, Foppy!" They hug each other. "When Uncle Rock was in that Paris hospital and they found out with what, they wouldn't call him back."

"She told me she called him every day."

"Foppy, you've got to wake up."

"Your father was a cheerleader in college."

"A cheerleader?"

"With pom-poms. And tight sweaters and white duck pants that . . . ac-centuated . . . the positive. In his early starlet days he would emerge naked from the ocean at Santa Monica looking like an Adonis. He was always ex-posing his . . . He was very popular . . . among certain sets."

"Pop?"

"A little diddle now and then. One had a career to further."

"Pop?"

"Everybody did it. Cary Grant and Randolph Scott and Tyrone Power and Errol Flynn. Well, Errol would do it with anything that moved. It was a different world then. Occasional transgressions did not require bombing Libya."

"So why does he hate us?"

"Those who hate are usually guilty of what they hate."

"Are you sure this isn't only gossip?"

"Gossip! Gossip! Gossip is life! And death."

"So these are the facts of life. What else? What else do you know about her?"

"In for a penny, in for a pound."

"I knew you knew more."

"There once was a man named Benny Thau. No, I cannot. We have known each other too long. I adore her. She adores me. Why, we are so close we know each other's very thoughts." The red phone rings. Foppy almost collapses on the floor. "Never underestimate the power of a queen." He answers. "My Lady Macbeth, what is this surprise package I hear will be un-wrapped at the Supreme Court?"

Junior claps his hands in silent glee. "Way to go, Fopp!"

His mother is heard on the speakerphone. "It has happened. The vote was five to four. Tough break. You are now and still illegal."

"But I . . . we had so hoped." Foppy's voice cracks a bit.

"One of the justices was on the fence. But he fell off. Be careful, Fopp. Friends are one thing, politics another. History is what we make it."

Foppy mimicks her. "History is what we make it." He hangs up on her. "Which of us has a past that's passed, my Mommy Dearest!" He picks up the phone. "Operator, I need a number in Pasadena. Is there an old farts' home, folks' home, for movie old-timers, you know, alta cockers . . . My dear, thank you. Don't let anyone ever tell you again that your service stinks." He dials and turns on a tape recorder. "Make way, Kitty Kelley, here comes Foppy! . . . Hello? Mr. Benny Thau, please . . . Well, don't they have phones in Intensive Care? . . . Well, hold the phone up to the respirator! . . . Hello? Benny? . . . Benny! *Was machst du?* It's Foppy Schwartz, First Mommy's best friend. You remember us from the old days? I'm so glad you're still alive. What? You were just on your way to meet your Maker? Well, I know you want to go and meet him with a clear conscience. Listen, what do you remember about First Mommy? You know, the real dish." He starts making notes furiously. "I know that. Something better . . . Not bad . . . A little better. Now you're cooking! Go for broke, baby. It's your last chance . . . No fucking shit! Benny, I love you, Benny. Yes, I know you're not a fairy. But you are, Benny. You are. You're the good fairy." He hangs up the phone and shows the tape to Junior. "Our redeemer liveth. Although he didn't sound so hot."

Purpura appears.

"My Capital Concubine . . ." Foppy begins.

"Yes, my oldest friend, First Fopp . . ."

". . . you have always surrounded yourself with the sensitive, the gifted, the amusing. You have even allowed yours truly to be among your most trusted confidants . . . You do remember your dear mother's dear lesbian friend Zasu Pitts who was so helpful to you? Your Broadway career—such as it was—thanks to lesbian Mary Martin . . ."

"Such as it was!'"

"Oh, my Supreme Dictator of Right and Wrong, I have been thinking of how happy we were in those old days when we were young and carefree, swinging along Hollywood and Vine, gallivanting at homes and studios, with powerful moguls like Benny Thau . . ."

"Benny Thau?"

"MGM's studio head has nominated yours as the best blow job he ever had."

"My Beatrice Lillie, will there be fairies at the bottom of my garden?"

"You were a very ambitious starlet, my Eve Harrington."

"'Were,' my Addison DeWitless?"

"Yes, it's always been mandatory for you to get ahead. Soon, perhaps, historians will have the balls to fill in the blank with: whose?"

"You are treading on very tender toes."

"You were kneeling on the most active of knees."

"Since when have you become so interested in the politics of power, my Benedict Arnold?"

"Since you became so interested in fucking my people, my Linda Lovelace."

"Then be careful you don't go too far, my Alger Hiss."

"I go too far? From your very first . . . screen tests . . . arranged by Benny with Spencer Tracy and Clark Gable—"

"Spencer Tracy was a drunken faggot who couldn't get it up."

"As was said of your husband and why he married you."

"Now you go too far. Do you know that the penalty for exposing official secrets about officials is death!"

"My Ilse Koch, I have located dear Benny." He happily waves the tape of their conversation.

"So you, too, are into tapes, my Tricky Dicky?"

"Let us try not to allow history to punish us so much."

"Do I sense a negotiation about to transpire?"

"You do. Filled with junk bonds, my Drexel Burnham. Daddy has ignored all action on UC. It appears he cannot even form the letters with his lips. With three official commissions on this deadly matter, is it not time you taught him not only to read them but how to say our name out loud? Indeed, with your own son at such peril—"

"So you are going to tell the whole world about my Junior?"

Junior speaks up. "Junior is going to tell the world about Junior!"

"So everybody will know!"

"Aw, come on, Ma. Everybody knows. And I was born this way."

"You were not born this way! You were just too young when I took you to see *The Red Shoes*."

"And I also want First Daddy to propose legislation prohibiting discrimination on the basis of sexual orientation—"

"And don't forget: Mom, men are going to marry men and women women!"

Foppy says, "As long as we are negotiating, my Sandra Day O'Connor, Daddy must also petition the Supreme Court to rehear that wretched wrongful case that has made your own son and your oldest friend illegal."

"Oh, Uncle Foppy, I'm so proud of you! I can't thank you enough. Our brothers and sisters can't thank you enough!"

"Oh, no, you don't! It is not too late to marry you off to an understanding older woman or a dyke! In the old days all the dykes made movies. Now they play tennis. Junior, your mother is going to buy you a tennis player!"

Electra, the black maid, appears. "You have the highest disapproval rating of any First Mommy ever," she says courageously.

"Be quiet, Electrolux, or I'll take your drugs away."

"Glory, hallelujah, it's about time!"

"Not those drugs. Take all those drugs you want. I mean health care, medicine, education—that's a drug for you people—and abortion! I've already taken away all your abortions. So you can never get out of your filthy rut, with your voracious appetite for sex and children and sex and more children and more sex—"

"Really, this is your Mad Scene, my Lucia. Is it not time to make your exit now and steal home to advise Daddy to—"

"Home! Home! I've swallowed enough. What do faggots know of home? You don't have children. We won't let you have children. We won't let you get married. Unless you marry one of us and have our children. You call yourselves gay but you're not happy. How could you be happy with all the laws we pass to make certain that you can't be. Tell the world? You think the world cares? You think the world wants to know that my son is gay? That my daughter is a drugged-out hippie? That my husband's children by another marriage are of little interest to us? That Benny Thau blabs how many times I got down on my knees and opened my mouth? All my people care about is that I'm a married woman and a mother whose husband is the most powerful potentate since Jesus. No one wants to believe anything juicy about Jesus!"

"Dishonor is the bitter part of squalor. But I have yet to play my ace for the world."

"Your ace? That ridiculous tape of your alleged conversation with Benny

Thau? No one will believe you. And no, Junior, you will not tell the world. No, you will not become a dancer. You will get married. To a woman. Lest your people be quarantined, put into camps after mandatory testing, with no research or treatments or insurance or jobs, and allowed to die. You think the United States of America has time for your people?"

"But soon there will be . . ." Junior seeks help from Electra.

"One billion . . ."

". . . people infected all over the world. Mommy, please don't do this to us. To me! I don't want to pretend forever."

"Why not? I have. After a while you can't tell the difference."

"I will never speak to you again!"

"I have to get us reelected! I have to untangle Iran! I have to win the Cold War! I have to end the arms race! I must sort out Israel and Russia and I don't have time to end your filthy plague! You think the world cares if I sucked every dick in America? They're amused perhaps, but The American People know that a person's sex life is his own business. I have a man to rule! I have a country to run!" She dials a number on her portable phone. "Pootie Pie, it's done. I've saved our reign for history. Now run along to the camera. Kiss-kiss."

"Turn on the television set, Electrolux," First Mommy commands.

"Turn the fucker on yourself," Electra answers.

First Mommy raises her hand to strike Electra, but Junior stands in her way. He switches on the set. First Mommy comes and puts her arms through his and Foppy's as they watch together.

"My fellow Americans. It's been nearly three years since I first spoke to you from this room. Together we've faced many difficult problems and I've come to feel a special bond of kinship with each one of you. Tonight I've come here for a different reason. I've come to a difficult personal decision as to whether or not I should seek reelection. Vice President Trish and I would like to have your continued support and cooperation in completing what we began three years ago. I am therefore announcing that I am a candidate and will seek reelection to the office I presently hold. Thank you for the trust you've placed in me. God bless The American People and good night."

NOVEMBER 6, 1984

PETER RUESTER, PRESIDENT OF THE AMERICAN PEOPLE, IS REELECTED WITH THE BIGGEST ELECTORAL LANDSLIDE IN ALMOST FIFTY YEARS

THE REELECTION OF PETER RUESTER

IANTHE KEEPS US UP TO DATE

Yes, dear Fred, unfortunately we shall have four more years of Purpura to live through. She has proved herself indefatigable in every imaginable way. She is never out of sight, with him, without him. Her power daily extrudes more and more throughout the land from the White House, where she reigns supreme and where they are scared shitless of her. Polls indicate she is not liked. This doesn't bother her. She even jokes about it. "They'll accuse me of stealing all my dresses again," she laughed. Of course she doesn't pay for them. "The idea that I should pay to dress up for The American People when The American People want me to be dressed up!" Is she still giving blow jobs? You know, I don't know. Patti doesn't think so.

"She knows she now has more important things to do with the big boys. They are all certainly frightened of her, which is a new role for her, to have *this* much power and sway and authority. I've seen it coming of course, this unmitigated power, for many years, rising up slowly at first but firmly until now it is truly throbbing. What need now of blow jobs indeed! She is blow-jobbing the country—the biggest cock in the world."

The second inauguration was as lavish as the first, with celebrities gushing like oil wells. She has learned how to look lovely. Her knobby piano legs have somehow been disappeared. Her hair is immaculate. Her makeup is excellent. She has perfected the role of devoted partner, two steps behind unless he's holding her hand, which mostly he is. He can't get along without her. Some of us can see that now. We forgot he was an actor. He was not a good actor. Now he is a good actor. The scripts are still as crummy as ever, but he long ago learned how to surmount mere words with his confident smile. Do I think she's making policy? You bet. Do I think she's running things? You bet. Do I think she's heartless and bold, pragmatic and fully skilled at keeping her eye on the prizes of Fame and Posterity and making him into a Great Man? Dumb questions, all.

Her children, one and all, keep their distance. She has ruined Junior's life. I wish he had inherited her balls, or at least one of them. The girls are crazy in their own ways. The other son is a joke. It's the most dysfunctional of families; the amazing thing is how off-limits this is in the press. She has managed to create just the images she wants, and off with the head of whoever veers from her course of action. Even I am impressed. Hell, your Ianthe owns to never having seen the likes of it. In all this she has her henchman; now that Garrie's mysteriously gone, her handpicked axe wielder is Linus Gobbel, the house Nazi. It is he who conveys to the press that unless they behave there will be no access to the crowing Ruester. Strangely enough, they behave. It's distressing how well they behave. They're learning it's a mistake not to take her seriously.

Isn't it interesting that in summing up his first term, their first term, I've spoken only of her? Peter has been receding more and more each day. Purpura and her Bohunk and her Gobbel and her Slyme are keeping him busy so he appears to be doing all sorts of governmenty things and can constantly be photographed signing something or other with his huge, contagious grin. I doubt any historian will ever write the true history of his era, because if it is to be honest—and what is these days?—it will all have to be about her.

In this town the filthier the life, the safer.

Patti tells me Purpura's busyings are increasingly about missile shields and things Soviet, matters she had never found riveting. But as we are seeing, she's a quick study.

I save the saddest for last. Patti also tells me that Junior comes often to cry on her shoulder, literally. He says he has somehow miraculously escaped UC and he is "torn in a thousand pieces between gratitude and guilt and indecision and shame and fear and trembling and duty, but to what and whom?" I could not put it more succinctly or movingly, so I won't try.

He now knows, as very few know, that the UC policy, or nonpolicy, starts right there in the White House at his own mommy's desk. "No son of mine is going to be a fucking fairy ballet dancer," she gritted through her teeth when I asked what she thought of his burgeoning career. And we all thought it was Peter who would put paid to that. "Tough love," she said, "and that's all I am going to say about that!"

PISS ON THE PRESIDENT

IN WHICH DARCUS CHARLES GRAVES DOES JUST THAT

Darcus Charles Graves watched as workmen constructed the enormous viewing stand for the president's second inauguration. Sam Sport is in New York, so Darcus has a day off and has decided to walk around Capitol Hill. Darcus remembers this area from his boyhood as a place of shitty slums, and while he's watched it change into something cleaner, with escalating property values, it's not his people who are benefiting. "Our slums just moved farther out. We still live in shit," he said to his wife. He nods to some black construction workers hammering nails to keep the planking up long enough to hold this president with his heavy crowd, and they nod back. He likes to watch workers doing tough stuff, but he's glad he doesn't have to do shit like that. No one seems to care much as Darcus goes to stand under the spot where he imagines Peter will swear his oath on the old Ruester family Bible. His own papa, Felindus Max Graves, swore in a president once. Darcus couldn't tell you which one, and Felindus Max is hidden away in some home somewhere, nutty as a loon, so never able to be trotted out to testify that he once did something so grand and patriotic.

Darcus pulls out his enormously long penis and urinates on the ground and on the wooden supports and metal piping, and, holding it like a hose, he washes down a little of this part of the Capitol building's base. Then he squirts upward directly under the president's podium, smiling as a bit of his urine rains back on him. He laughs softly. "Here's piss in your eye, Mr. President. Mine, too. It's for good luck. A big black nigger cock is good luck, man." With his cock still hanging out, he's spotted by a group of tourists from Georgia wearing large pins that say, "We are the Georgia Klan." He wishes he had more urine inside him to hose them down too, but he waves his penis at them anyway. They scream and run, falling in line behind a leader carrying a big placard lettered in silver and gold: THE KKK CELE-BRATES THE REELECTION OF PRESIDENT PETER RUESTER AND THE CONTINUING BIRTH OF THE NEW ERA. Again Darcus laughs, louder this time. It's not a mean laugh; it's the laugh of a man with little to laugh about. He's taken it upon himself—in his new program of self-realization, education, and betterment—to understand all he can about "Black Suffering!" as spelled out by the big letters on the wall of the small room in the basement of his father's church. He wonders if the president will discuss in his speech from this podium any of the subheadings listed under "Black Suffering!" on that basement wall: "Black Invisibility!" "Black Sadness!" "Black Misery!" "Black Death!" He pulls out the extra-large handkerchief he's taken to carrying since he started sweating so much and he wipes his face and under his arms and sticks it down in his crotch. He wonders why he's dripping so much as to seep through the tailored shirts and suits Sam buys for him. He doesn't have much to do until he picks Sam up tomorrow and brings him right back here. Sam has front-row seats. Sam is buddies with the First Lady. Darcus has no place to sleep since he and his wife are having another fight. He'll sleep in the backseat of Sam's very big Mercedes that's parked in Sam's garage. Sam says he can stay in his guest room full-time if he wants to. He has a key. But he doesn't want to stay inside Sam's. Sam pays him to keep himself free. Darcus would prefer if he had something to keep him occupied. He thinks of too many things he would like to do, like this pissing on the president and strangling white kids. Sam is going to all the inaugural balls and parties, so Darcus will be busy. He wonders if he could actually get inside the White House grounds and what he could do if he did. Sam has been saying more and more that he wants more of his big black nigger cock to fuck him. Darcus does not know how to process shit like this.

He is tired of what white men are doing to his people. He is tired of what white men are not doing for his people. He is tired of Sam Sport fucking him so much. It disgusts him more and more to have that white man's cock inside him.

•

I would be less than honest if I did not confess to my growing realization that of all the weapons this country and this plague are providing me to work with and to move forward with, nothing is so effective as its hatred of homosexuals.

IT IS NOT SO PEACEFUL AT ISIDORE PEACE

The board of directors of the Isidore Peace Medical Center meets to listen to a report from Dr. Israel Jerusalem, a staff specialist. In the Great Hall, overlooking the Mathilde Eiker Schmuck Memorial Gardens, one dozen Important People wish they were somewhere else. Dr. Jerusalem, who is seventy-three and has been on staff since Schmuck's opening day, in 1933, is and has always been an unpopular doctor, rarely listened to or believed. ("Staff specialist" is an uncomplimentary title reserved for those who have not achieved as expected at a Jewish hospital.) Dr. Jersualem reports on his resighting of a troublesome organism that he once called glause. He first named it glause in 1935. Now glause is evidently fatal. When will it stop? Does he not think that the brains in our heads have a statute of limitations? Those several members of the board who are as old as Israel, and were in this very room when he reported many other meshugas to them over fifty years, exchange covert glances. The crazy is at it again. As is his way in time of stressful confrontation, when not supported by his fellow doctors, he stomps out. Where has Grace gone? She would have understood.

With the unpopular doctor gone, the board now listens to the Committee for Decisions. Should they or should they not be the first hospital in the city to officially put a quota on the UC patients it admits?

"Why is NITS not advising us on what to do?" asks the chairman, Dr. Meyerwitz.

"I believe that they don't know themselves," Dr. Schwartz responds.

"Quotas are embarrassing," says Dr. Morganthau.

"We've got to give them *something*." This from Dr. Fester. "We can't just turn them away."

"Why not?" says Dr. Dressy.

"This illness is pure poison," says Dr. Schwartz, "at the rate it's going."

"Good. Maybe it'll kill them off faster." This from Dr. Moses.

"It could bankrupt us. They're already taking up so many beds!" This from Dr. Sonnenschein.

"I couldn't get my own mother in last week." This from Dr. Mommser.

The entire board votes unanimously to turn off the UC tap.

"After all, we don't want to be known as the local UC hospital like Table in New York," says Dr. Fink.

Israel sends word he will not comply with "such inhumane treatment to fellow human beings. Need I remind the board of their own heritage of tsuris their mischbocha suffered and most likely did not survive?"

MORTON DIES

FRED

I'm with Morton in Mount Ostroff when he dies. He's the guy from GMPA who rewrote all my stuff for our newsletter behind my back. And wrote that letter Bruce read, kicking me out. We went roller-skating once, Morton and I, in nineteen seventy-something, and later in his apartment I tried to kiss him. "You have too much need," he said. "I can feel it." He'd been handsome, with intellectual glasses, and I always felt warm toward him, which I guess is why it's me he came back to.

He was a rich Texan Protestant, and, at thirty-five, still had never told his ma and pa he was to the penis attracted. He was particularly fond of exceptionally large dildoes. He went home when he got sick without saying what he was sick from but assuming it was more or less obvious—I mean everyone watches the evening news (and his pa owned all the TV stations as well as the bank and newspaper)—and that they'd take care of him. They knew and they did not like what they knew and so Morton's dad told Morton to leave. Just threw him out. Just like that.

Morton came back practically dead from what I'm about to describe. Somehow he'd found his way to my apartment, and the doorman called me from the lobby and said I'd better come right down "because this one ain't going to get himself up to you." I had to take him to Mount Ostroff because Table and Invincible and a few others I also lugged him to wouldn't take him. The only way I could get him into Mount Ostroff was by threatening them: "He was your patient and you let him out before you should have! And that's grounds for a lawsuit." Something like that.

After being thrown out by his folks Morton had then gone to stay at a pigeon farm run by an old geometry teacher he'd had in prep school who'd made a pass at him when he was in eighth grade. He felt so weak he knew he was going to collapse. He was afraid of another hospital. Ostroff had been awful. He discovered fast enough that Texas doesn't have any hospital health care for the indigent. He had no car and he had no money and he was walking down the highway and where he collapsed was by Homer Thrall's pigeon farm and Homer remembered him as a kid and cared for him until an ambulance came and took him to Dr. Prespice in Houston, more than four hundred miles away and a place that some new experimental treatment for UC called Adnover was available. Adnover was some crud from Israel made from margarine and soy and it smelled and tasted awful. He got a little better and made it back here to New York and I got him as I said back into Ostroff, which by chance is the only hospital in town licensed by Mortimer Pharms to administer Adnover (of course you need a license to administer a treatment, even when the patient's dying: NITS regulation 107984b6c,1934). Morton, who isn't circumcised, was almost denied admission, or readmission, because some Hasidic emergency room worker admitting that day said to him, "I'm sick and tired of all you faggot goyim being sick in our hospital." Morton fainted, vomited, and shat all at the same time, which is what got him the private room, only it was one with bars on the windows, and he woke up facing a psychiatrist with a yarmulke on, Dr. Korp, standing in front of him, staring at him, waiting for him to wake up. He'd been asleep or out of it or away from consciousness for about a week, and more than anything Ostroff wanted their private room back. I'd already warned them that if they threw him out, well, I was getting where I could threaten with great authority.

"So!" this Dr. Korp starts, rather emphatically.

"So what?" Morton said back, hating him on sight and trying to be just as emphatic and not doing such a bad job of it, all things considered.

"Why did you do it?"

"Do what? Suck cock?" Then he thought of an even better one. "Take giant black dildoes up my ass?"

His mother had a hard time with this one. I should mention that his mother, Carisse, was now here. At this point she excused herself to go to a restroom. She dropped his hand, which she'd been holding. Interesting she knew what a dildo was.

It's really hard being with anyone dying when a mother is around. Not that it's so easy when she's not. Some guys want them around. Some don't. It was just so awfully hard for this son to acknowledge that, really, his mother wanted out. Morton's ma is scared shitless of his illness. She knows he's sick with something awful and she hadn't wanted to come and she particularly hadn't wanted to come when she heard the hospital was Jewish. "Everyone here is tough as nails," she offered in a rare moment of chatter. To her credit, she cried a lot. And my goodness, she was well dressed and all turned out.

Dr. Korp continued: "Why did you leave your beloved parents, who brought you into this world and cared for you and spared no expense to educate you and give you the very best and still you become something they deplore, but that is now beside the point, my question to you here and now is: Why did you run away from them when they so wished to offer you succor and comfort in their Texas home? You cannot expect charity from this hospital when such an alternative for you exists."

Well, this is the first Morton hears this version of his departure from Prairie Gulch. He also wonders how come this Dr. Korp knows so much. Morton had a way of snorting when something outrageous landed in front of him to deal with. It was one of his endearing qualities. I haven't strewn in here facts from our own relationship, all our fights at GMPA mainly. I caused Morton many a snort. But we somehow stayed friends.

Morton summons every ounce of the strength that Adnover was giving him (it turned out that this shit had a high amount of caffeine) and pulled himself up and spat out the words, "Get the fuck out of my room before I vomit on you!"

When Dr. Korp just smiles at him benignly, Morton pulls himself up and jumps off the bed with his various IVs and Dr. Korp sees that the threat is about to be father to the deed so he runs from the room, heavily, because he's a corpulent man. ("Although this in no way interferes with my making love to my wife, which we do most enjoyably and often," he said out of nowhere one day to me when I was visiting another friend and Korp and I were washing our hands in a men's room.) Today he is screaming out as he runs, "You will never leave this hospital, where I am chief of psychiatry and you are in a locked room, until you talk honestly to me, and kindly." The episode was very macabre, particularly with Ostroff wanting Morton out and all that.

I was still in the room with Morton when his mother, Carisse came back from the john. She looked even more beautiful, the expensive clothes and jewelry that wasn't showy but wasn't fake. She was very quiet, as a type, as is Morton, so they just looked at each other for a long while. I started to go, but Morton wouldn't let me.

"I don't want you to go. You're my friend. She's not my friend. She wasn't there when I needed her. Now I know the truth for gay people and that is that our friends are our family."

The word *gay* made her wince. But she said, "I'm sorry about what happened."

Morton snorted loudly. Then he went "Hee-Haw!" like he was back in Texas.

"I'm glad Morton has had one friend through all of this."

"Why were you so cruel to him back in Texas?" I am never one to waste time in getting to what I want to know, really.

Her pride and gentility didn't allow her to respond to me. She looked at her son, who waited for an answer too. No longer any Texas boy, he. He always said Jewish boys were too pushy, and I smiled at him, to welcome him to this side of the fence. He smiled back. She started to cry, feeling, I guess, shut out.

"Oh, Momma, don't cry," he said.

"Oh, son, what's happened to us all?"

I'm happy to say she wanted to be hugged and went to him, her son, and he hugged her and she allowed it and her unblemished clothing got a mite wrinkled. I cried, too.

"Why did you have to be homosexual, and why must you die for it?"

He let go of her on this and pulled himself back. His breathing was very labored all of a sudden, the racking sobs caused by their reunion escalating into gasps as less and less air came into his lungs to cry with. In a moment he collapsed back into her arms and she held on, hard, because she knew before I did that he was now dead.

MY BEST FRIEND TOMMY

We had had a tough time of it for a while. But it was very moving he was there for me so when Felix died. We started hanging out all the time, even though that annoyed Bruce too much, that Tommy might be telling me secrets. He lost his lease so I let him move in with me. We tried sex a few times. I could see how much he was in love with me so I tried. But it didn't work out, the sex, nor of course the timing. I just wanted to say now that little by little Tommy (that is his given name, Tommy, not Tom or Thomas) Boatwright and I have somehow remained the best of friends.

Neither of us had any other real friends and we had gone through sad times together and even our own little affairlet, that stupid word, during the production of my play—mercy fucks, they're called, those gropings for other bodies in the dark, if only to keep warm, to be less afraid—well, I could see there was nothing I could do that would put him off me. He liked me too much. And God knows, no one else did. He even *admired* me. He just thought I was the best. He was GMPA's first official full-time executive director to whom we paid actual money, and what the organization became, a group of UC nurses' aides I insulted for being "candy stripers" and not warriors out there on the barricades, was largely his doing. He had worked in hospitals, a lot of them, and had his emergency medicine down pat. That's what he figured we needed most, and besides, as he pointed out, "Honey, these guys who are turning up to volunteer are not activist material. Just look at them. They are sweet little momma's boys and we have to make use of them for that." To this day, that's what they still are, if they're still alive, that is. Good little boys and girls grown up into decent good little men and women. If this sounds condescending, I'm afraid that's what I mean. And my best friend, because that's what Tommy is now, took them all in and gave them succor and substance to operate this way, and so GMPA, my beloved first child, is a bastard I want to disown half the time. But they'll help you draw up a will and get your dog walked and feed you if you're hungry and of course assign you a trained caregiver to visit you in the hospital. But effect public policy? Forget it. Bruce and the board won't even allow Tommy to go on TV.

In my furious race to put things right, to figure things out, I'm also learning some stuff about myself. I brook no interference and suffer fools badly. I never knew I possessed either of these traits. They both take anger and, dare I say it, guts, and I also never knew that I had either. Is that why I have no lover, yet and still? Guts? I don't think I have any guts at all.

He's very tall, Tommy is, and lanky, all bones, with cute little jug ears that cup out quite remarkably. I sort of think he looks a little like the young Abe Lincoln, who was also tall and cute and with those ears. Sex with him was difficult for me because he was so big and tall and I'm not and I didn't know what to do with all that body—we just didn't fit right. After a few months of actually living together I finally had to take him out to dinner at a Chinese restaurant and tell him it wasn't working. This from the man whose hand he held constantly in public and was holding under the table at this moment. "Let them come at me!" he'd say defiantly from his height above us when we walked on crowded streets. He stared down anyone who stared unkindly at us. He loved to read. And I who buy and still own more books than most bookstores have on their shelves am moved by this habit; I buy them and read them only delicately, rarely fully, seldom to completion; I am so impatient when they don't, for some reason, possess me. So little of anything does these days, I realize.

Tommy Boatwright will be by my side from now on throughout these continuing wars. I've been told by various mutual friends that I broke his heart over that Chinese dinner and wounded him irrevocably, in that he's never had another love again as deep as the one he felt for me and continues to show me every day.

Anyway, I come to love him very much. I don't think I ever had a best friend before.

His brother is dying now from UC. So it's important for me to be with him when it happens, as he was for me with Felix.

THREE OLD JEWS ON THE BEACH OF FIRE ISLAND PINES

Monroe Abst, Jeffrey Curling, and Hy Evermore sit on a blanket late in the season. It's the Jewish holy days so there's still a somewhat crowd to attend services at Maury Diskind's. Also, the sun is suddenly and miraculously out and warming.

Their bodies are old but their eyes are young, and until now their thoughts and imaginations have been younger still. They wear brightly colored billowing long-sleeved shirts to cover their bodies, but the sadness in their eyes is harder to cover, as is their fear.

"Did you notice the drop-off during the summer?" Monroe asks. "I have been thinking that this shit is a prophecy of what lies ahead of us. Do you not think it is a prophecy of a bleak fate?"

Hy says, "Usually I think that you are such a pessimist, Monroe, but the memories this is already stirring up for me condemn me to agree with you."

"I, also," Jeffrey says.

"I am afraid," says Monroe.

"I am afraid," says Jeffrey,

"I am afraid," says Hy.

Yes, each says, one after the other, that he is afraid.

"My father got us out of Berlin just in time," says Jeffrey.

Monroe says the dreaded word first. "This is our Holocaust."

The other two nod their heads.

"Did you read Dr. Geiseric in *The Prick*?" Monroe asks. Neither of the others have.

"You don't read that rag?" Hy asks.

Jeffrey reminds Hy that they have both used *The Prick*'s personals, "for laughs only, of course. That dishy little kid from Haiti, Ernesto Jean-Paul, remember, we all three had a taste of him? We found him through *The Prick*."

"Stop!" says Jeffrey.

"Stop!" says Hy.

"What are we to do?"

"Where are we to go?"

"We must not lose our balance just because we are old Jews who remember when no one paid attention."

"We must not overreact."

"Perhaps it is not overreacting."

"Canada."

Later, no one recalls who said "Canada."

"I will look into it," says Monroe, who has a travel agency.

"We are being silly, silly, silly," says Jeffrey, shaking his head as if to get bad thoughts out of it. "Let us all go in for a swim. There are few days left when the ocean will be as warm as today."

And he leads the way, stripping off his billowing long-sleeved shirt of many colors, and dabbing some sun oil on his crinkled chest and arms and face, and then running into the ocean, followed by his two old friends, though one limps from a hip replacement and the other is out of breath just from standing up too quickly. They have shared this house in the Pines since 1965. And each and every summer weekend over all these years they have sat on their blanket on this beach in their billowing long-sleeved flowered shirts, under their protective overarching umbrella, and looked at all the beautiful young men who seem to get younger and more beautiful with each passing year. That this might be coming to an end, that they might be approaching their own Kristallnacht, is almost more than they can bear to think about. Their mishpocha escaped the first one. A second time might not be so lucky. Do you think that they are not still sexually active? Why do you assume that? *Sexopolis* is always running features on sex among the aging. It is one of Mordy Masturbov's continuing crusades.

Each of these men will die within the next three years.

"SPICE PINCHED FROM SPELLMAN BIO"

A biography of Francis Cardinal Spellman that states that the late prelate led an active gay sex life which was embarrassing to the church will be toned down somewhat before its publication. John Cooney, author of *The American Pope: The Life and Times of Francis Cardinal Spellman*, told *The Prick* he will rewrite the pages of the book dealing with Spellman's "alleged seductions" of altar boys and others while spiritual leader of the New York Catholic Arch-diocese from 1939 until his death in 1967.

Avocado Books, the publisher of the biography, was questioned about whether Cooney's information was adequately substantiated, according to an August 2 report in *The New York Truth* ("Publisher Wants Proof Cardinal Spellman Was Homosexual"). After meeting with their lawyers, Cooney said he would rewrite the portion of his book dealing with Spellman's sexu-ality along the lines of "many people say Spellman was homosexual, priests all took it for granted, but who knows what takes place in a bedroom?" Such a change would be a significant alteration of Cooney's original text, which included details of a purported 1942 liaison with a chorus boy supplied by a leading sex researcher and author, and accounts of gay parties attended by the cardinal. Other sources quoted on the matter of Spellman's sexuality included a former seminarian who served as one of Spellman's altar boys and the owner of a bar popular with gay men during the 1940s and '50s.

"I have no doubt in my mind that the cardinal was gay," Cooney told *The Prick*. He maintains that revealing the cardinal's sexuality was important. The biography is not a flattering portrait, Cooney readily admits; the author sees the cardinal as a "first-line candidate to illustrate the use and abuse of political power. He was such a moral hypocrite. I don't think he even be-lieved in God."

Cooney worked eleven years as a writer for *The Wall Street Journal* before leaving three years ago to pursue freelance writing full time. *The American Pope* is his second book. His first, *The Punic Legacy*, was a study of a family's attempt at "changing dirty money into clean power."

TOUGH LUCK

An aging Sen. O'Trackney Vurd sees to it that legislation is renewed, and rather overwhelmingly it is too, that prohibits federal money to any program or organization or entity utilizing educational or therapeutic material that contains the word *homosexual*, now expanded to include such words as *sexual* and *intercourse*, those for various "personal body parts," and yes, "the under-lying condition," which words, without capitals, slip through without protest. This legislation effectively prohibits any material from being disseminated by the government that might help educate and curtail UC. This prohibition will not be overturned by a federal judge for many years.

•

New York Truth headline: "ROUTINE CONTACT CAN SPREAD THE DISEASE, SAYS NITS'S DR. GEISERIC."

DEEP THROAT AND BIG PHARMA

The head of Big Pharma is Tolly McGuire, the typical Washington lobbyist, hale-fellow-well-met, who slaps you on your back every other sentence with a beaming smile while he says, "I doubt my boys and girls will go for this." We've known each other for too long. He's a cruel and heartless and greedy bastard. That's why he's always reappointed as this inhuman industry's spokesperson.

"No," he continues, "I've heard no buzz on this one." Then he said, before I could answer, "I state that emphatically. And there's no money in this. It doesn't constitute a big enough market."

"Oh, it will be a big market. And getting bigger every day. It looks like it's going to be a major public health emergency."

"Well, now, public health is not our bag, is it?"

"It was, once upon a time when we were young."

"Look, how many ways do I have to say this. You always were a stubborn cuss paying no attention to reality. I have never seen less interest in an illness than I'm seeing in this shit. Sure, we talk about it, we even sponsored a confidential sort of conference on it, where we could sort of brainstorm. The big guys all came, Rolf Voss from Heissliche, Frankfurt from KlipperInterswiss, Talbott Prenderghast from Dinkens-Savoy-Trailheim, Barney Osterveld from Prinkus Maxwell, Diane Globbenger from InterAmerican, this rich new bunch from something they're going to be calling Presidium, and of course, how could I forget, Dash Snicker from Greeting. Dash was particularly against 'entering this field,' as he put it. Oh, and Molly Trachtbart from *NEJS*. She wanted to cover the conference but she had another engagement."

"Isn't it *NEJS*'s job to report what's going on?"

"Get on track, will you. Listen, you and I have known each other a long time. Read my lips: nobody wants to touch this shit with a barge pole. How many ways can I say this? There's still no hundred percent yet confirmed definitive causative anything found yet, and this Dodo as far as pharms are concerned is a dodo, announcing one bullshit thing after another, with, I might add, no clue as to what he's thinking that could give us a head start on a Help Out, and the infected population means we'll have a lot of trouble convincing our scientists to go anywhere near this. You get the picture? Nobody likes faggots. Period. Especially stockholders."

I nodded. "What happened to the 'for the good of humanity' stuff?"

Now he nodded. "You're still such a fucking troublemaker. Is Uncle Jerry willing to throw in any grants for us to jointly start the 'for the good of humanity' stuff?"

I knew Uncle Jerry was not. When I relayed to him the above he said, "They know I've been turned down by Vurd and HAH for support."

"What about the president?" I asked Tolly.

"You should pardon the expression but you've got to be joking" was his answer.

I shall report all of this to Mother.

MOTHER

Good work, Deep Throat. It is just as I expected. NITS is simply not doing its job.

"LET THEM EAT SHIT"

I was trying to write a book about my love for Junior Ruester. It was painful trying to do this, and when I got sick I put it aside. He knew I was sick and he never even called. He has refused to keep in touch with me. He didn't invite me to his wedding, of course. On our last time together, after the last time we made love, he said, "I know someday you will violate our sacred trust. Farewell, forever." And he got up and got dressed and he didn't even kiss me goodbye. Anyway, here's what I wrote about when he asked me to take him to Dr. Horace Vetch. Out of the blue he called me up and said, "Perky, I'm on my secret phone. I'm in trouble. I need you to take me someplace." I feared the worst because the worst was already starting to happen to me.

We arrive at a top-secret location, a treatment center far out in West Virginia. He says his Secret Service men are probably frantic. This time they don't know where he is. It's just as well.

He's referred to as Patient X. In other rooms there are seven Patient Xs and five Patient Ys also receiving this secret experimental treatment.

At 8:22 a.m. Peter Ruester, Jr., called Junior, the son of the just reelected president of the United States, is connected to the Neutralitron. I smuggled him here. He has come down with ridilinitis. His nimroid factor is high. Rebby said to me, "The ridilinitis, ironically—for it is usually a fatal syndrome on its own—can in the smallest number of cases mediate with UC, keeping each at bay . . . but for how long is still unknown. It is only known that there is a 'window of opportunity' during which this interference might operate successfully. Your 'secret friend' might, just might, be okay. Ridilinitis is not necessarily UC."

It's all mumbo-jumbo to me.

Dr. Horace Vetch sounds like the name of a quack, and I'll bet he is. I guess there comes a time when you have to go along with blind faith, and this is such a time. Guys are dying like flies. Seven guys from our class at Yaddah so far.

Dr. Horace Vetch appeared from out of nowhere with a treatment that utilizes shit. "Cultivated human intestinal bacteria, including *Streptococcus faecalis*," to quote the *New Statesman*, which headlined its report on this treatment "Let Them Eat Shit." Copies of this article are in Vetch's waiting room.

Your shit is dried at temperatures high enough to turn it into a fine pulverized ash. This ash is combined with your blood, which is irradiated with fluorescent something or other. Dr. Vetch claims that his treatment raises the vel level and that after monthly treatments, the 729/s will increase and the system will slowly reconstitute itself. I ask him if it melts the muscles, which I've heard happened to some poor guy. He ignores me.

It all seems pretty absurd, except that Dr. Vetch has produced, in living suntanned flesh, five UC patients who have been treated with their irradiated shit, a procedure he's patented and calls V-200. And they are very handsome. They bounce around in bathing suits at medical presentations, where they parade before any interested doctors. They wear those Speedos. Even Rebby has to admit these guys look and act terrific.

Rebby says there are many such shows these days—doctors suddenly appearing from out of nowhere with alleged cures and cavorting muscular suntanned showboys to promote them. "We must not allow them any validity," he warns me. "But you just did," I point out to him. He blushes. "Did I? I guess I did. I was carried away by the beauty of them in their bathing suits."

The son has not been unmindful of his place in history. During the early days of this plague, as all around him friends and fuck buddies and fellow Yaddahs fall dead by the side of the road, Junior begins to have gnawing pangs of conscience. I just knew it! And now he's finally telling me about it. On our trip to West Virginia he tells me how he wakes up in the middle of the night and vomits. "I know that my father is the only person in this country who has the power to help me and my friends like you and assure the salvation of our homosexuality." I never heard him come anywhere near to talking like this. Maybe he could be our hero after all. "I'm also scared shitless of my mother, who thinks I must get married. Which I said I will. So I'm safe. For the moment." So much for the heroic. Where and how he finds safety in all this . . . Well, you have to know Junior.

Even in the waiting room, even on the trip home, he still won't tell me how he really felt about the two of us. Or if maybe now he feels it again. A little bit, maybe . . .

Of course, Junior Ruester is not considering these personal issues as he is wheeled into Dr. Vetch's presence and strapped down under the Neutral-itron, a heavy machine like an iron lung I saw in some movie about polio. Vetch is very ordinary-looking. You'd lose him in a crowd. He inserts tubes into Junior's arms and into his chest. One is funneled through his throat into a lung, I guess so he can breathe. And another tube is stuck up his ass. He's conscious because Dr. Vetch said consciousness is necessary for V-200's best results. The look in Junior's eyes is pure terror. I know he has all his fingers crossed as best he can. We both stare wide-eyed as we watch the path of his blood going through yards of tubing out of him and into a big vat.

This vat is filled with boiling water, and the irradiated powder made from his last shit that he brought in a container is dumped and sprinkled into it lovingly by Dr. V. before he switches a switch and it's pumped back into Junior. "A 'fewtra' of hot shit is being administered every ten seconds," Vetch proudly tells us. It's very painful and Junior screams as best he can. I wish I could be holding his hand.

The process in its entirety takes some four hours plus. Junior's terror does not leave his eyes for one single moment. I know in his heart he knows that Vetch and his shit are a load of shit, but he's trying valiantly to believe that the handsome men dancing around in those Speedos whom Vetch had running around even here to show us before he started that "cure is just around the corner!" might indeed be a prelude to Junior's own return to dancing. With his new wife, unfortunately.

So the pathetic young son of the just reelected monster president and his awful wife is lying under what looks like a flying saucer and dried shit is being pumped into his body at an undisclosed location in the middle of nowhere by a quack who says he's discovered a cure for The Underlying Condition. And this use of shit has been talked about in the *New Statesman* magazine in Britain.

It didn't work, of course. Forty-nine guys died. There were fifty who got his treatment. Someone in the White House had heard about Vetch and his Neutralitron and saw to it that FADS gave permission for as many cases as Vetch could perform. Junior was number fifty. I wonder if he knows how lucky he is to still be alive. When *The Prick* wrote about all this (not incuding Junior, of course), Horace Vetch left the country real fast and with his ill-gotten gains he set up a clinic just south of the border in Huarales, Mexico. Guys are still going there. I forgot to mention that each treatment cost $25,000 cash. I loaned Junior the money and I don't expect to ever get it back. He says he's not allowed to have any money of his own.

I just wish that somewhere along our way he'd said thank you. The whole thing is just pathetic. Or did I already say that?

DANIEL WITNESSES HIS FIRST DEMONSTRATION

It is not too long after Dodo's "hopeful" comments in *The Prick* before the NITS campus is quietly invaded with groups of young men who come and sit quietly outside Building 12, where his lab is, waiting for him to appear. When he does, they rush to touch him, to get near him, to hold on to him, to beg out loud and plaintively, "Save me! Save me! Save me!" The first time this happened, it is said that Dodo broke down and wept. Contingents from foreign countries soon join, carrying their flags with signs: BRITAIN'S UC'S BEG DR. GEISERIC FOR HELP! FRANCE IMPLORES DODO! Much of this sort of thing. After a few days of them congregating, even when they're removed at the close of day, and their reappearing the next morning, Middleditch instructs the NITS police to keep them out, period. There is no press. Dodo proclaims surprisingly, "When I scream and yell it's usually on the evening news!"

Middleditch asks me to meet with the group, which has now requested a meeting with "someone, anyone, who will listen to us." And so I come to meet my first "angry activists," as they are rather dismissively called by the *NITSY Transit*, our house organ. There are more than a dozen of them, all as presentable and well-spoken as you could wish, albeit frightened. And with good reason. Just looking at them I could see the various permutations of what I'm seeing in my sick patients. I asked them where you were. (This is when you went to Auschwitz.) They said they didn't know and anyway were angry with you for abandoning them. I asked them to identify themselves.

"Sir, my name is Simon Watchtower originally from Britain."

"And I am Marcus Dobkin from New York."

"And I am Siebert Anthony, once from Denmark."

"And I am Drouet Vivier from Paris."

"And I am Matty Milano, also from New York."

"And I am François Delamain from Haiti, from Port-au-Prince."

It went on like this for many minutes, for as soon as the twenty or so that had been admitted had finished identifying themselves, more appeared, evidently having pushed themselves past guards and inside this soon very crowded meeting room. As moving and painful as all this was, it was scary, because I could see that crowds like this will scare the shit out of anyone at NITS, anyone anywhere working on UC. They all stood quietly after identifying themselves. They expected me to say something. I could see Stuartgene now standing in the back, the unsmiling one, as I have come to view him, frowning his discomfort over why all this is happening in his hallowed scientific temple. Since he barely ever acknowledges me, I figure he disapproves of me, but no, everyone says he's this way all the time. Whichever, he was waiting for me to speak, too.

"First, let me apologize. I am sorry that your actions have made you unwelcome here. You must understand, or perhaps it is we who must understand, that science has not been accustomed to having our worst nightmares made so plain and obvious and visible. We know you are not well and we know you need help. That is for certain. And we want you to know this." I was vamping and lying already, and I knew it. What did I want them to know? That nothing much was happening here, and that we were waiting for Dodo, too?

At this point Dr. Omicidio marched in, ramrod straight and officious in a way I hadn't seen in him before. The crowd could tell he's important. They started to chant, "Save me! Save me!" I could tell Jerry wasn't having any of this and I hated him for it.

"I am Dr. Omicidio. UC falls under my supervision. I will not tolerate this kind of behavior in our environment. We work here. You are not welcome here. When we have something to impart to the world, then the world will hear about it. Please leave before more police are called in to escort you out!" And he turned and started out.

"Hey, wait a minute, buster! You can't talk like that to us. We are taxpay-ers and this is a taxpayer-supported institution and we are permitted access and the right of observation! So cool it and tell us what the fuck is going on here or you will find yourselves with a little demonstration right here on your sacred premises." This was the Dobkin guy from New York. He was tall with lots of very black hair and he spoke like an angry lawyer, which he evidently is.

Jerry continued his exit, summoning me aside when we reached the empty corridor. He spoke to me coldly and imperiously.

"You have been assigned to me full-time for a reason. I need you to front for me with these people, to keep them at arm's length without letting them feel as if we are shutting them out, which is what we must do." And then he said very quietly, looking deep into my eyes in a way I had not experienced from him before, "You must not forget that while you are one of them, you are also one of us. I trust you can manage this."

Then he pinched my cheek, slapped my back, and said, "You'll do just fine."

And so came the "little demonstration." The police marched in, several dozen of them, and started literally hauling the guys out, all of them, placing restraint bands around their wrists behind them if they protested, which they all did, kicking and screaming. That Dobkin guy yelled out as a cop was putting him in handcuffs, "We haven't done anything, you pricks," which got him a punch in his crotch.

Several of them yelled at me as they were carried past me. One guy I recognized as one of my earliest patients yelled out: "You're one of us! What kind of a faggot are you?"

Fred, this was all quite amazing for me. I know you have regaled me about demonstrations, which sounded exciting. They are still exciting! I must just learn how to handle them when they occur where I work and in front of the people I work with and they are attacking me, quite rightly, as well. And I hate myself for saying this.

I wish I could say that this little portent of things to come registered in some sort of positive way on any of my fellow workers. At our next meeting it was not even referred to. As Dodo himself didn't show up, we couldn't even hear a progress report from him, not that we had come to rely upon him saying anything specific. The etiquette of this place does not allow for us to push or even request, but to wait. "Good science cannot be hurried," Middleditch said to me in a hallway. "Try to put those young men out of your mind, touching as their plight might be to you."

"Is it not to you?" I dared to ask.

"I have been here a number of years, and I have witnessed many . . . issues, including, I might add, protesters that included my wife and daughters."

"But we aren't going to be able to shut them out forever."

"Be that as it may, we cannot be threatened. That is simply not allowed." And he walked off.

•

Where am I hiding? You still don't know where I'm hiding. You can't get rid of me until you can find out where I'm hiding. And if I've been here for 60 million years, I'd say I'm doing a pretty good job of it. And you're not. And I shall live forever!

PATIENT NOTE TO HIS JUST EX-LOVER BEFORE LEAVING HIS ROOM AT PRESBY AND JUMPING OFF THE GEORGE WASHINGTON BRIDGE:

"I never imagined I would have UC and be left all alone to die."

WHAT IS HAPPENING TO DAVID

A man knocked at my door. He was tall and stern and handsome. He showed me his badge. He was from the FBI and could he talk to me. We sat down and he showed me some photos. One was of that Garrie Nasturtium. Did I know him or anything about him, he asked.

"I knew him," I answered.

From where and how, he wanted to know.

I said that I had been a good friend of Mr. Hoover's.

"What has that got to do with it?"

I guess he didn't know about Mr. Hoover's whorehouse.

"How did you find me," I asked him.

"We can find anybody. You appear to have a pretty thick file already. Did you meet Nasturtium in the whorehouse you worked at?"

I told him I had seen him there a number of times. And that's all I knew about him.

"Who else did you know there?"

When I didn't answer, he showed me a photo of the major who had loved me. I started to cry.

"Why are you doing this to me and so many years later?" I asked.

Then he showed me another photo, of an old and sad-looking man. I shook my head no.

"His name was Dr. Herschel Vitabaum. He was head of Health of the World in Geneva. He came to Washington to give our government important information. His body was found buried near to where Nasturtium was found dead. Then, a bit farther on, your Major O'Lesky's body was found buried. They were all in the backyard of Nasturtium's house."

He finally left, after showing me lots of pictures of men I'd never seen and giving me his card "in case you remember anything."

I don't know how, as they say, to process any of this.

THERE ARE MANY STUDIES DONE MANY YEARS AGO INVOLVING MANY HOMOSEXUALS

"The history of blood donation is the history of the highest calling for men and women. Tradition is so important in our world of blood." This from Dr. Caudilla Hoare of BOAN, Blood of All Nations. One wonders if she knows much about the father of blood donations, the guy who started all the Red Bloods after the Crimean War in 1856. He was disappeared because he was a homosexual. His board found out and got rid of him fast. They did things like that then, too. No matter how marvelous the achievement, get rid of the poofter queen.

Caudilla doesn't want to share anything BOAN has to share. Old records. Data. Study results. All the stuff that people who do studies are usually happy to share. Or at least begrudgingly willing. Or at least a deal can be made. Over the years BOAN and ARB have taken blood from many—many with regurgia when it was still called that, many with hepatitis, and most recently many hemophiliacs, now at last classified as such. The gay community was always asked to generously cooperate. It was for a good cause, unnamed. It will turn out that gay blood included one thousand regurgiacs. The results of this last were . . . well, at the time, the mid-1970s, nobody knew what that meant. In fact, no one knew precisely why Caudilla was doing studies. The results of all these studies told how much of whatever was at that moment out there in "the gay community." Important stuff. Thousands upon thousands of frozen blood samples. A veritable history of the blood of decades of New York homosexuals. Stored away? Unwilling to be shared? Most peculiar. What historian, medical or otherwise, would not long to get a gander?

Of course, this is not quite the whole story. All the studies were of possible interest and usefulness to the pharms. So information from these studies that sounded innocent enough is worth money. It won't be the first time gays have been unknowingly spied on for the economic benefits of others. But some participants included hemophiliacs, who were the early participants in the "trial" of G-D's Factor VIII. Who was paying how much to whom? Is this where and how BOAN gets it money?

Since every gay man was urged to participate in ARB/BOAN studies, total ownership of the results is not so cut and dried as any release each participant was asked to sign. "They are the property of Blood of All Nations. BOAN is a private organization," Caudilla stated. "But you are sitting on information that might tell us something that could save time and lives," Tommy answered. "Perhaps they could. Perhaps they couldn't. But they are none of anybody's business. Ask your lawyer."

Within these frozen samples is the only evidence that they've been exposed to poisoned blood. How much is this worth to whom to expose to the world? Or to keep it from the world?

Is Caudilla evil, or is she just a selfish bitch? That's what Tommy has come to call her. But then Tommy is coming to call lots of folks selfish bitches whether they're female or not. Just to me, mind you. He's still being polite to the outside world.

Tommy wants to see Caudilla's studies because so many GMPA clients took part in them. And many of these clients are now dead. Caudilla's "studies" might tell us just how long gay men in New York had been sick, when they came down with whatever is revealed in their blood, now frozen away in this selfish bitch's vaults, and provide damning evidence to put G-D out of business for peddling Factor VIII.

So you could make a case for Caudilla being evil in not releasing this information. But *evil* is a word you've rarely heard in this history so far except from Dame Lady Hermia.

•

INT. JOHNNY'S APARTMENT. DAY.
The door breaks open and Tommy and Emma, with Buzzy and Fred, come rushing in. Johnny, Tommy's brother, is lying on the bed. An open

bottle of ZAP is lying on his stomach. Buzzy pushes Emma quickly to him.

EMMA *(with stethoscope)*: Your brother dove over the cliff. Sorry, Tommy. *(She starts making notes about Johnny's body, aided by Buzzy.)*

(Tommy is sitting by his brother, holding his hand and teary-eyed.)

TOMMY: We had a wretched childhood but his was worse because he was younger and our bitch of a mother was a real pro by then. She'd been a World War Two flight instructor and would punish Johnny and me by holding our heads underwater or slapping our faces until we could take it without whimpering. We grabbed our ankles while she beat our behinds as hard as she could with a three-foot length of one-inch black rubber hose. Then she would sit on the toilet seat while she painted our naked bodies with witch hazel while she cried, "What have I done to make you a fairy?" Another set of unhappy parents who shouldn't have married each other and had so many kids. We—I—have two born-again brothers. I never told you about them. They're a trip. One's a major general in the air force. He prays for me and Johnny all the time. Thanks for the house call, Emma. You're a peach. *(He lays his head on Johnny's chest.)* Goodbye, bro. Brave bro. *(Taking the bottle of ZAP. To Fred:)* Do you want us to shoot our murderers? We'll be guerrillas.

FRED: I don't know how to shoot a gun.

TOMMY: You can learn. I can teach you.

FRED: I'd be afraid I'd turn it on me.

EMMA: I did not hear all that. How do you want your brother disposed of?

EXT. HUDSON RIVER. DAY.

Tommy with Fred sprinkles Johnny's ashes in the upper Hudson where the water's edge laps your feet. They have taken off their shoes and socks, rolled up their pants, and waded in.

TOMMY: This is where he wanted to be buried. He would sing "Ol' Man River." *(Singing:)* "He just keeps rolling along."

DANIEL THE TROUBLED FRIEND

Why am I having such a difficult time relaying a certain part of my history, Fred? You will think I'm one negligent participant for not speaking up to tell you everything I know.

You may wonder, as do I, why after I saw Gordon Grodzo staring at me at that Dye meeting, and then found out that he'd been a Nazi, I did not get to work, *right away*, instantaneously, to excavate information from him about my brother.

I've known that David, my long-lost and by then (I must be honest here) not-so-missed twin, was taken off to Berlin and had somehow wound up in a German concentration camp. I'd seen his back, scarred badly, when he briefly returned to Masturbov Gardens. I'd tried to hug him and get him to tell me what happened, but he wouldn't say one single word to me, his own twin brother, even as I begged for information. And then he disappeared. I was pissed off by his behavior, which I didn't understand. Which I still don't understand. Okay, he went through hell, I'm sure, but it was as if he was punishing me for it, as if I'd had something to do with what happened to him. I assume he's still alive somewhere and that if he wants to get in touch with me, he knows how. I've stayed in D.C., though I would have preferred to practice in New York. But I figured he might have an easier time locating me if I stuck around here. Our folks moved to Miami and I assume they've died. One day Mom just stopped contacting us, so I don't know whether she's alive or dead, and neither do Lucas and Stephen. We were never fond of her, so it's not so much that we cut her off as out of sight, out of mind, and we figured she felt the same. We hadn't been good sons, but we all felt she hadn't been a good mother. Lucas particularly still has very angry feelings about her for not being home when he was a kid. Just writing this all down makes me see how totally fucked up our family was, and why I don't like to think about it. Dysfunctional, they call us now. I have no idea how much our parents knew about David or what he knew about them.

Anyway, I'm stalling again. I did talk to Grodzo. I found his office after that meeting—I apologize for not telling you—and I said, "My name is Daniel Jerusalem. I have a twin brother, David, and I believe he was in a concentration camp in Germany. Might you know anything about him, or how I can find out about him? I know the war is long over, but he did come back and now he's disappeared."

He was silent for the longest time. He probably wasn't used to this kind of confrontation now that he was in the good old safe USA.

Finally he held his hand out. I didn't want to offer mine but found it impossible not to.

"Dr. Jerusalem. Yes, I knew your brother. I am happy to hear he got back to this country alive. I will be honest with you. During my long silence before answering, I was thinking that I would deny any knowledge. That would certainly be more safe for you and for me, and it was quite some time ago and old men do not remember so well, except that in this case I do. It is a horrible story, the Mungel concentration camp, where we both lived, your brother and I, in a sort of . . . barracks. He was not in danger. He was there safely. I do not know the details of why he was there. We all learned not to ask questions, about anyone or his situation. We all had different rules to live by that kept us alive. I believe he was hidden away there by somebody for the duration of the war, out of harm's way, you call it. Outside was much worse than inside for many of us, if you can allow that."

I followed up with a barrage of questions. He pleaded ignorance, but I could tell he wasn't ignorant about this at all. He just wasn't going to say any more. I asked how long they had shared their "barracks." He looked at me silently before he finally said, "It was a long time and we became good friends. When David came to Berlin he was a boy, and he was not released from Mungel until the last minute of the war, in 1945, when he was already a young man. Now you must forgive me. I have already said more than I am allowed to say under the terms of my permission to live in your country. I signed many papers to live here with you. I am not permitted to talk about the old days."

"Who was your sponsor?"

"I am not permitted to tell you."

"What kind of science are you involved in that America guaranteed you such safety? No, I know the answer. You are not allowed to answer that either. I didn't know that NITS was involved in such top-secret work, but that's probably naïve of me."

"Yes, I am afraid it is."

I just turned and left. I didn't say goodbye or thank you or see you around. I was at a loss for words of any kind. Shaking and sweating, I walked out of his building. Here was a person who had the information I valued most. I couldn't find out what Grodzo was doing at NITS. Even Omicidio wouldn't tell me. I could usually get him to tell me things. Or rather, he said he didn't know about any of this but he said it in a way that I didn't believe him. Well, I realized that I now wanted my brother back.

The next time I went to find him, Grodzo's building had been declared off-limits to unauthorized personnel and I didn't have the right kind of ID to get in. And he no longer came to Dye's weekly meetings.

This has obviously been haunting me and I don't know what to do about it.

ADREENA SCHNEEWEISS!

I, little Fred Lemish, who still might be found dancing around his bedroom to her recordings, spoke to Adreena Schneeweiss for two hours on the phone!

When my agent told me to expect her call while he was taking me to lunch, I lay down on the floor of the restaurant and jiggled all over in excitement and glee! The most wonderful singer and . . . actress (?) and director (?) and personality in the world, the gay man's idol, wants to make a movie of my movie of my play about Felix and GMPA and Emma and Tommy and our plague and gays being treated like shit!

I am so excited! If she makes this movie then EVERYBODY in the whole wide world will see it. They will see two men in love. They will see two men kissing each other. They will see two men living together and in bed together like in all those heterosexual movies gays are condemned to watch where straight people do all this, feh!

Question: Is she any good as a director? Answer: Who knows, and if she fucks it up and makes a gookie movie, who cares, because if she makes it then EVERYBODY in the whole wide world will see it anyway. And all my messages about our plague will get out.

Question: How do you feel when you talk to her about gay sex and photographing it for a Major Motion Picture for the first time and she says she's not sure she wants to show all that, feh! She said "Feh." And then when we meet and I give her a very artistic book of photographs of men making love, this time she says FEH! FEH! POOH! And she throws the book down on the floor from the sofa where we sit looking at the pictures. I am in her house in Malibu. I am sitting next to her. Her skin is so beautiful. Fred, get real. She has just thrown down on the floor (maybe it slipped from the sofa) this beautiful picture book of men making love that you brought her from New York, saying, Feh! Feh! Pooh! And her own son is gay! Why didn't you say:

Adreena, but this is what your son does when he is in love! I did say that. And she answered, "But he has never been in love, or so he tells me."

Answer: I will convince her gay sex is just as romantic as straight sex and show her how to film it beautifully. I will write her a screenplay that will delicately outline and describe for her how to light the scene and move the camera and place the actors, a star playing Fred, a star playing Felix, two stars for the first time playing gay men in love! How can she say Feh! Feh! Pooh! about the sex her own son enjoys, if only once in a while? I'll bet he says Feh! Feh! Pooh! about the sex she has. Or had. And wants to have again. She says she's looking for a boyfriend too.

But why do I feel that I am a whore here?

Adreena said to me: "When are you free to start work on the script?"

I guess I should stick in here somewhere that my play is running in New York and it has been running for this past year or so, and if I have not sounded like I've been doing much it's because I have been tied up down there, at the Public Theater, where I go and watch my being thrown out of GMPA acted out for me. It often makes me cry because, well, that is why I wrote it, to make people cry, and I guess I succeeded. It is fun to watch when Fred kisses Felix for the first time. You can hear the proverbial pin drop. People are often taken aback. But by the end of the play, when Felix dies, they are very moved. Every single performance is sold out and receives a standing ovation, and if I have not been filling you in on every iota of UC dish, this is probably why. Although I think I have not been doing so badly, filling you in. But I do need to do something less heartbreaking than sit around making long endless lists of all who have died for this new book I'm writing.

THE CONTINUING HISTORY OF ZAP

In the citation for her Nobel Prize for vel, Dr. Sister Grace Hooker had been additionally commended for "the participatory inclusion in the genealogy of this discovery, the heretofore unknown protein, Zinander Alpha Periculosa (ZAP)." This would be the primary ingredient for G-D's first drug to fight The Underlying Condition, which Von names ZAP. Orvid put a large mock bottle of ZAP with a big bow on the front page of *The Prick*. "OUR TIME TO LIVE OR OUR TIME TO DIE?"

Through her lawyer, Lucas Jerusalem, Grace was about to challenge

G-D's right to release this medicine, a by-product of her Nobel Prize. She knew it wasn't ready. She'd seen Oderstrasse's warnings.

Then Dr. Schwitz Oderstrasse released his bombshell. He publicly accused Dr. Sister Grace Hooker of "murdering" patients while doing research work at Partekla, some twenty-five years ago.

"This drug will not cure or even stop UC," Grace had told Lucas. "Talk about murdering!"

"Then best to ride this out and see," Lucas had advised. "If you say that now it will only look like sour grapes."

"But it's only going to give a lot of people false hope! At the most! Just like garbage-shit Geiseric and his phony cockteasing innuendoes. It will . . . kill . . . a lot of them. I hate to say these frigging words. I hate to be frigging Cassandra."

She hated Dodo. *He* was the liar and the murderer. Why isn't Oderstrasse out to silence him?

Dr. Sheldon Grebstyne stepped into the fray, defending G-D, and defending ZAP as a product owned by the United States government and developed with taxpayer money by Dr. Arthur Kittering, who worked at NITS in 1950.

Speaking for G-D was its vice president, Dr. Dash Snicker, the supervising executive for upcoming clinical trials of ZAP on "desperately needy victims of this wretched new disease. Nothing must stand in the way of this humanitarian challenge to it that G-D is providing." His mission, and his determination, to dictate and control every aspect of ZAP's birthing are sounding dictatorial already.

The news about ZAP's forthcoming debut is in *The Truth, The Monument,* and the press of the world. Almost overnight huge waiting lists clamor to get on it—at NITS and at first six but then fourteen other sites around the country where Jerry will place his principal investigators (P.I.)

Grace had asked Lucas how one fights back against all of this. "Her" ZAP would now be accused of "murdering" a lot of UC patients. Getting old is awful. She thought she'd earned a better old age than this.

Well, now she's dead and few people know it.

In case you've not kept counting, this makes three unexplained dead people from our current cast of important characters, Garrie Nasturtium, Herschel Vitabaum, and dear Dr. Sister Grace.

•

DAME LADY HERMIA: I am investigating this! Through my tears.

DEEP THROAT CONTINUES THIS HISTORY

As with Greeting's, ZAP's history has been only somewhat told.

Every scientific lab, every pharm, every medical center, every university must deal at some time with the troubles inherent in the launching of new products. Bottles and powders and formulas and frozen test tubes of stuff from the beginning of time—no one dares to throw anything away for one reason only: somebody may own it and lawyers are known to suddenly appear with demands. Medicine and medicines are a most litigious part of life. You can't just say that it was one of those things found on the shelf. Which in this case it was, or at least seems to have been.

G-D is now fighting for its turf. There are already problems crying out for possible litigation. One of ZAP's patents is in the name of Dr. Sister Grace Hooker, from its association with her Nobel Prize.

Yes, you could say that the genetic predecessors of ZAP evolved from, say, Fruit Island. You could even say it came from the ancient world, Abyssinia, Egypt, mummies in their tombs. Who really knows where aspirin came from? Or who owns it? Mr. Bayer? Mr. Anacin? Dr. Middleditch had claimed Dr. Joseph Apfelfinger was the discoverer of ZAP. Who is Joseph Apfelfinger? Well, his name was on the bottle in the closet. Because Middleditch found some ZAP in a NITS closet, its formula, which, when fed into his new computer, as he was doing with the several thousand formulas he also found in all the NITS closets, which as you can imagine is a lot of closets, actually shows some effectiveness against cohorts of this "thing" that Dodo is currently claiming is "the cause of UC." What is Dodo claiming this week? He is not permitted to tell. Middleditch, rather swiftly, gives ZAP— yes, *gives* it, for free—to Von Greeting with the proviso that he gets it out there "swift as lightning! ZAP's analogues and Dodo's dirms match up!" Who was Joseph Apfelfinger? Dr. Middleditch had filled a name in where a name was needed.

Middleditch was like a nervous father of the bride. He told Von and Dash Snicker, "Test it on patients fast! You're famous for your fast-tracking. Omicidio and Debbi Driver and Hube will get us plenty of patients for the trials. I have chosen G-D because you are mean and nasty enough to get this out there fast no matter what." Was he finally receiving pressure from someone to get his ass in gear? "I am not at liberty to discuss that." Five thousand COD-counted cases can do that.

In almost every sentence of the above resides a lawsuit coming down the pike, and if not a legal obstruction, then certainly a public relations night-mare. I'll wager dollars to donuts that ZAP will become one of the most hated, nay loathed, feared, and mishandled medicines to ever come down that pike.

Deep Throat is telling you all this. You heard it here first.

THE AWAKENING OF DARCUS CHARLES GRAVES?

"Some eighty-nine percent of all people of color believe UC is something the white man invented to get rid of us. Most of those didn't know what UC is or meant but if it means something bad it was invented by the white man."

When Darcus Charles Graves hears a Dr. Abernathy say the above to a group of blacks, Darcus gets up and yells, "Makes sense! Doctor, you make sense!"

He's so overcome by his explosion that he collapses to his seat. But he's covered with people in an instant, black people, all clapping him on the back. He starts to laugh, very happily.

"You're right, brother, you're right. Makes sense! Makes sense! Makes sense!"

He is at a Brotherhood for Black Men support group that Maureen, his wife, told him about. He didn't want to go. But since Felindus Max died, all kinds of voices telling him all sorts of things haunt him. "Get your act together." He hears that voice a lot. That seems to be the dominant theme. Dr. Abernathy had said, "Our brothers, we must never forget that these are our brothers!" Darcus had brothers (he guesses he probably still has them somewhere) but they never made him feel anything but inferior because they'd worked so hard to please Felindus, which none of them had anyway. The one sister, Alethea, said, "Not a one of them has amounted to much, Darcus Charles. What about you? I run my own little business where I run up sweet dresses for young ladies. What do you do?"

He had to tell her that he was a chauffeur to a very rich and important white man but that the man was evil, and he had to find something else. "I been to an Abernathy meeting that changed my life."

"How so?"

"It makes me want to do something to help our people."

"Uh-oh," she said. "I hear the ghost of our pappy in those words. Be careful. Helping people gets you in trouble."

"How so?" it was now his turn to ask.

"People don't want to be helped, it's been my experience. Nobody trusts a free meal. Something always comes along with a free meal that doesn't go down right."

"How do you know this?"

"Because I tried, too. I joined the Sisters of Abernathy."

"The preacher who is so good with words?"

"That's him. I had two abortions because he's so good with words. So it's just me and my Singer sewing machine at present. He gave me that, at least. Good to hear from you. Let me know what you figure out, if you figure it out."

"Don't you want to see me?"

"No. I don't want to see you. You will make me cry for what might have been. I have been working on trying not to do that anymore. I blow you a kiss, though."

He heard the kiss and he heard the hang-up.

The medicine Sam got for Darcus is making him feel strong. Sam wasn't feeling or looking so good, though. He was taking this medicine too. It was sent over by special messenger from the White House.

Darcus often found Sam spread out unconscious on the floor. Sam won't even leave his house to go to the office. He doesn't know what he'll do without Sam, but Maureen says, "It's the best thing that could happen to you." He was back at home and they were living together and yes, she knew he was sick and he was very touched how considerate this made her toward him. He actually liked living at home with her now.

"What are you going to do with all of this?" she asked him.

He nodded, but no words came out.

DAVID REVISITS "SCENES FROM THE CRIME, MY LIFE"

Someone is watching me. I wondered how long it would take before this would happen. I still remember what it feels like, being watched by the unknown. Someone is there now.

I earned a degree in chemistry. As I said, my Mungel teachers instructed me well. I also studied history. And law. I am now a lawyer. It is as if I can't take enough courses! There is so much to learn and I want to learn it all.

I am fifty years old now. I think.

Grodzo is seventy years old. He's lived in America since 1945. He has more than eight hundred patents listed in his name and in the name of the places he's worked for, Greeting-Dridge, and BaxxterGreetingDridge, and now NITS. Some of these patents are in partnership with a Dr. Stuartgene Dye and a Dr. Jerrold Omicidio and a Dr. Sister Grace Hooker. I recall her name as a babysitter we had in Masturbov Gardens.

I have seen photos of Brinestalker and Grodzo in the newspapers. They are written about as if they are important people.

I went back to Berlin. I wanted to see where Amos Standing, my father's lover who came both to Mungel and to Partekla, had set me free. I couldn't find Mungel. It's disappeared. No one knows anything about it when I ask. It's just like no one knows where Hitler's bunker was. Before he put me on that plane back to America, Amos took me to a place called Einstein's Tower on the outskirts of Berlin, near his UFA studio. Here he made love to me, the son of his own lover, my father, in this weird twisting modern building full of holes in its walls for windows. We could hear the Nazis outside calling to each other. I held on to him tightly. For those moments deep in those woods full of soldiers running away themselves and the awful sounds of bombs and rifles shooting and the sky bright with fire, I was helplessly in love with him. I have read a lot about the love of young boys for older men and the reverse. It is much more common than is generally known. I still can get an erection thinking of Grodzo. Einstein's Tower is still there, as is UFA, which is now a huge movie studio where they make lots of movies and TV.

I flew back to America via Florida. I wanted to see Gertrude Jewsbury again. Gertrude was in a nursing home, blind and almost deaf. I could still see in her face how beautiful she was. She had been so kind to me. She clutched my hand, so grateful that I had come. She kissed me and kissed me. She told me that I was soon to be her heir as well and to do something with the money for the good of the world. "You will now be a very rich man indeed!" she said. We both cried and hugged goodbye, this time for good.

I came back and I managed, finally, to start to write the section, David's War, that Fred has included in this history. It was an arduous and painful task and it did not free me up one bit.

I am still trying to rise up from my ashes.

Someone is still following me.

WHAT IS HAPPENING TO US?

Frederick? Daniel? I hear from no one.

I wish to shame you for faltering in your participation in our noble endeavor, but I sense instead that one by one you are becoming overburdened for the most sad and valid of reasons.

We are grappling with one of the greatest existential dilemmas of all time, an unresolvable turmoil of murderous indecencies.

Corragio!

FRED IN THE DUMPS AGAIN

I still miss GMPA too much. I failed at what I wanted it to do and I've still got nothing to take its place. After such a long period of furious activity, constantly ringing phones, a mountain of daily problems waiting for my input, and the sustaining closeness—indeed comradeship of a sort I'd never known or felt—of so many devoted fellow workers as we all aspired to make something happen, for several years now I have found myself alone, with nothing to do, bereft . . . God, such melodramatic words for loneliness, for inactivity, for self-flagellation, for the conviction that one is right and no one can see that. I feel like a pariah again. Feel, fuck, I *am* a pariah again.

In all my *Prick* articles and in my play, I never put out *specific* suggestions on what we should do to fight back. It's one thing to scream we must fight for our lives, *but how*! And I certainly haven't come up with any suggestions to me, myself, and I on what I should do to not feel so fucking empty and useless. I go to Dr. Homer. I don't go to Dr. Homer. I go back to Shmuel, another old shrink, whom I left when I realized the Orthodox Jew in him couldn't really connect with homosexuality. I go to that dyke shrinkette who helped me "get over" Felix. I've had so much therapy over the years! You'd think I could get up and walk. Shmuel used to make me feel that I was one of the most important people in the world. How did he do that? How can I get through what I must get through? He'd shrugged his shoulders enigmatically. "No loss ever goes away, if it's been that meaningful," he said.

There's a benefit tea dance for GMPA at Boy Boy. I go. I know I'm not welcome. The place is packed. Nobody talks to me. By now my fights with the GMPA board are pretty well known. I wonder how Bruce and Joey and Dick and Dan and Mickey and . . . explained my absence. Fred's gone crazy.

Fred's become a total loony useless schizophrenic psychopathic self-obsessed idiot. How can I sit here and accept such ignominy? Hi! Hello, there! At last somebody nods.

"Hello, Gabriel."

He turns around and walks away. Gabriel. How long have I known you, Gabriel? Fred, they don't want you here. Gabriel doesn't look well. Dick doesn't look well. Dan doesn't look well. Bruce doesn't look well. And another of his lovers has died, but I hear he has a new one.

"Hi, Jay."

"Who's that?"

"He can't see you," Jay's companion says. "He went blind last week. I guess you can't tell in the dark. I guess you can't see a lot of things in your own blindness."

"Who are you?"

"Oh, you wouldn't remember me. We fucked when I was twenty-one. I thought you were quite a man."

I slept with this guy once?

"Fred? Is that you, Fred?"

"Hi, Jay. I'm sorry to hear about your eyesight."

"Yeah. It's awful. There isn't anything for it, you know."

"I know. What about that ZAP stuff from Greeting? Are you eligible to sign up for a trial?"

"Not yet. And it doesn't work for this."

It's hard to look at him. He must have lost fifty pounds. He was a lawyer, a good lawyer. Very smart. I sent Robbie Swindon to him to sort out his dead lover's will.

"You heard about Robbie?"

"Yes," I answer. "Of course."

"You don't even remember me, do you?" the fuck from long ago asks.

"Fred—" Jay is still talking.

But I've left them. I've been watching the DJ booth. The loud music's taking a break and so is the DJ. I know him, Bobby, Joey, something. I walk over to his glass wall and wave. He waves back. I motion for him to let me in and he does.

"Hi!" I say enthusiastically, using our embrace to smother the fact that I can't remember his name.

"What's up?" he asks me.

"Not much. How about you?"

"Nothing much. Life's okay."

"Still never seeing the light of day?"

"I'd shrivel up and die."

"Hey, can I use the mike to make an announcement?"

"Sure. You guys are sure doing great work. Here."

And he shoves the mike into my hand. What am I going to say?

"Hello! Testing, testing. Can you hear me? This is Fred Lemish coming to you from the DJ booth. I have something to say to you. You belong to an organization run by a board of murderers! They refuse to fight to keep you alive. All they do is help you die. Tell them they must fight for you! Tell them they must fight and not be so timid and not be so afraid. Tell them they were wrong to throw me off of the board. Tell them . . . oh, tell them we created something wonderful and they need me back!"

This is not what I'd wanted to say. I wanted to rev them up to be fighting troops. To get them angry, but not at me! All I was venting was my never-ending hurts and pains and kvetches. Why can't I let them go?

By now there's a crowd outside the booth, on the other side of the glass wall, staring at me as if I'm crazy. I don't even look at the DJ as I hand back his mike and open the door and return to the room where the music suddenly goes on again, loudly.

Five guys, ten guys, a hundred guys, two hundred guys, I don't know how many, but I'm surrounded and pummeled and poked and yanked.

"You're trying to destroy us!"

"Shut your fucking hole!"

"Go live in another country!"

"You're trying to destroy your very own child!"

That hits home. I start to run. Once again I realize I can't criticize this group without hurting it and this group is all there is. What am I doing? When am I going to learn . . . what?

I hit the cold air outside and I keep running. I hear someone running after me. The once twenty-one-year-old long-ago fuck. He comes home with me and holds me as I cry my frustration. He wants to stay the night. I don't want him to stay the night. I send him away. I want to be miserable all alone. I wonder how Daniel is. Daniel's been sad and strange lately himself. I wonder if he and I should try to make love again. We're both a mess. A great recipe for beginning "a relationship."

I look up. Tommy's let himself in with his old key.

"Sugar, are you all right?" He rushes to take me in his arms.

I don't know words to use. I hang my head and shudder no.

He comforts me. He spends the night beside me. He tells me the names of at least a dozen more who've died. "Somebody died on the dance floor after you left." Throughout the night I awake to cry and Tommy is there sobbing with me.

●

To:
Sir Polkham Treadway
Director
Sir John Greeting Institute of Worldwide Medical Knowledge of All Peoples
London
From:
Vonce Greeting
President
Greeting Pharmaceutical Company
Washington, D.C.
My dear Sir Polkham,

I have been fascinated to read of the remarkable exhibition you have mounted at the Institute, "The Asylum and Beyond: Aspects of Treating the Mentally Ill Since the Thirteenth Century." You have certainly extracted much of great interest from the far-flung collections assembled by our joint original progenitor, Lord Greeting. I'd heard he was passionate about so many things, but electric machines emitting voltage into the brain, portraits and etchings of patients being whipped and chained and put into Bedlam, detailed early directions for cranial surgery, the list goes on, was certainly ahead of its time. It is no wonder that one review I read complimented you for putting on "the creepiest show in London."

I was particularly struck by the work of the Hungarian psychiatrist Leopold Szondi, who in the 1930s maintained that he could tell a patient's illness by examing their reactions to photos of, for suspected homosexuals, homosexuals. I would be grateful if you could send me more detailed information about this doctor and his experiments, should you have any to hand.

I should also like to explore the possibility of your transferring this exhibition to America under our joint auspices. Washington's primary repository for the mentally ill, St. Purdah's, has been shut down. Easily a hundred years of records of the sort you are exhibiting cannot, for some reason, be located anywhere. I believe I can interest Yaddah University, where I have recently been honored to serve on their Board of Overseers, to join with us in presenting to America the records you have been able to salvage.

I commend you for your remarkable entrepreneurship!

Yours in brotherhood,

Von

A REPORT FROM LITTLE ROCK

Bob Saliccia was arrested parking his car behind the one gay bar in town, The Mystic Eagle. He was arrested because he had a suitcase containing a woman's blond wig and a matching gown and pumps in shocking pink. Officer Bud Bracken, who said Arkansas did not tolerate "this sort of thing," had hauled him out of his ancient Plymouth two-door. Asked by the judge what "this sort of thing" meant exactly, Bracken said, "He also got falsies and a big brassiere." The judge pressed him further. "He also got big purple spots on his dick." The judge asked him how he came to see the suspect's penis, much less the contents of his suitcase. Bracken answered, "Because he was waving it at me in the parking lot." Bob Saliccia was then questioned. "He took out his gun, Judge, and said, 'Let me see what you got.' When I did, he said, 'You expect me to let you suck my dick when you so diseased and with all them ladies' clothes?' Then he said, 'You want to work again in your drag you gotta give me the names of a dozen of your friends who come to this bar from over the state line.' That's when I got back in my car fast and started my engine and tried to drive away, but he called more cops who cornered me and beat me up and—well, Judge, here I am." "You ain't gonna believe some sicko person like this, Judge, against the word of an officer who worked faithful for this city and state for fourteen years?" "Young man," the judge, an elderly gray-haired unsmiling woman, said to Bob Saliccia, "I don't like cases in my court like this one here. I suggest you take a powder, maybe move to another state, and never let me see the likes of you again. As for that spotted penis, I am sentencing you to a visit to the emergency room at that hospital down the road. If you got what I hear is going 'round then I don't want it going 'round any faster because of you being in my state. Come to think of it, maybe they can cut it off. I believe we still have some laws on the books from the good old days when we did such things. I'll have my clerk check and phone the emergency room. Officer Bracken, please escort him there. And stay with him until he crosses the state line."

BRINESTALKER TO SLYME

Yes, I did tell you that I could change homos to heteros. It is a further extension of the groundbreaking work I undertook at Partekla, which I also told the First Lady about. I started out as a homosexual myself, but because of the pathetic obsession my best friend of that time had for a weak and pathetic lover of his, I determined that if this was what "gay" love was all about, it made me puke. My pivotal Partekla work had to do with turning prissy sissies who liked to get fucked into men who did the fucking. It was my first step out of bondage.

I am sorry to hear about her son. Unfortunately, I no longer have my office and staff to deal with his case. However, I recommend that someone get in touch with Dr. Charles Socarides in New York and make an appointment for the young man. Charles has had extraordinary success in this field. He and I were once students in Vienna together. I will notify him to expect to hear from you.

Here are a few words of Charles's wisdom: "Over the years, I found that those of my patients who really wanted to change could do so."

I hope this will be the case for her son.

Of course I will keep this confidential! You need not have asked.

In the meantime, may I thank you yet again for your support for our efforts, yours and mine, and for your latest contribution of names for our growing list at the Tricia Institute.

My best regards to the First Lady.

FRED GOES TO DENVER,
AND THE DENVER PRINCIPLES

The Denver Concordia Protocol Initiative was actually called into being by Dr. Kiefer Kreditz of the New York Association of Gay Doctors, a drip of the tallest order, who invited me and COD's Dr. Paulus Pewkin because, as Kiefer said, "It is time for us all to convene and listen to each other." Pewkin and I shared a room at this conference. I remembered him from my journey to COD and him telling me to get lost and I delivered my Kinsey speech to an empty auditorium. Now he's saying, "I hope to overcome some of your skepticism about COD and our intent and competence." I didn't want to room with him, and told him so, because I still thought his organization was awful, which I also told him, but there were no other rooms. Paulus had already been featured on *The Prick*'s cover, with that swastika overlaid on his face. I asked him why he was here, had he come to spy on us?

I tried to talk to him about syphilis. I'd heard he was a leading player in this field and had majored in sexually transmitted diseases at Harvard. "Is there any connection," I asked him, "between UC and syphilis?" The answer is he was not answering.

"Why do you guys, by which I mean doctors working for the government, have such difficulty responding to direct questions with direct answers?"

"I guess we're afraid to be wrong. You don't know what a disaster life in government service can be if you're wrong."

I think that was the only sympathetic thing I ever heard him say.

Out of the blue, a ragtag group of men with UC had decided to piggyback this scheduled "national" meeting of this existing meek organization of gay doctors and health-care professionals presumably interested in their health. Its spokesperson was Michael Callen, who had himself become a pariah for courageously admitting publicly that he knew he was sick because he'd been out there fucking the world. Not only, as I well knew, did no gay man want to hear this, but no gay doctor did either because it marked them as irresponsible for not saying so too. Few doctors were willing to be openly interested in gay anything. They thought they were courageous just showing up here, but I was coming to distrust the lot of them. They claimed to represent a huge group of gay doctors, but they obviously couldn't get most of them to meetings like this.

More notably, this wimp Kiefer Kreditz had tried to hijack GMPA in a sleazy way. When we were starting up, we needed a tax-exempt organization to use for our first fund-raiser, the April Showers dance, where we made our first real batch of money. This gay docs group loaned us their tax-exempt number but then they tried to hold us up for some $25,000 of the $50,000 we raised. Fortunately I'd had all the checks mailed to me and I deposited them in our account and I never gave the creeps a dime. Kiefer Kreditz was still antagonistic toward me. "You promised my group money, Lemish, and I'm still waiting for it." And then he said, "I'm sorry we agreed to let you speak. I hope you're not going to tell us all to tell our patients to stop fucking." Well, if our own doctors are talking this way, you can see that the battle is long and the night is dark and the mountain is high.

"Don't you think you have a responsibility to convey the thought that this is spread sexually?"

Kiefer walked away. Throughout the following two days of the conference I was approached by a half dozen of "our" doctors, all pleading, "Don't cause alarm, don't cause panic."

So why did you invite me, fellas?

The hotel refused to post the name of this meeting on their bulletin board of daily events, that word *gay* again, so the guys with UC went berserk—an early example of the kind of activism I dreamed of—and threatened to do damage unless they gave us our proper billing. The hotel countered by limiting the number of rooms we were stashed in, hence my sharing with Paulus Pewkin. Bruce Niles was here and that would have been nicer. Bruce and I were still friends then. Sort of. No, we weren't, but I still would have liked to room with him. He brought Tommy, which means Tommy and I couldn't be seen together. Bruce kept him on that short a leash of distrust. I was the enemy still.

There were maybe fifty closeted gay docs present and twenty very uncloseted sick men. More and more, guys were showing their symptoms in public. It was no longer just a few guys passing you on the street looking downtrodden and disfigured. Now it was hard-to-look-at people. Spots were breaking out all over the place. Terrible wastings, terrible blotched faces and arms, teeth beginning to fall out, sometimes in the middle of sentences (it was that dramatic). Fingernails so yellow and warped they belonged in a horror movie. Pus exuding from open sores. It was hard to smile and say hi, and to ask "How are you?" was embarassing. So this was our future. The growing brutality of fact.

But these sick guys were getting themselves together. They were learning to fight back a bit while they still lived. Under Michael they had actually caucused and come up with a manifesto for the group he was starting, the National Association of People with The Underlying Condition (NAPWUC). This manifesto became known as the Denver Principles. The first principle was and remains: "We condemn attempts to label us as 'victims,' a term which implies defeat, and we are only occasional 'patients,' a term which implies passivity, helplessness, and dependence upon the care of others. We are 'People with UC.'" They went on from there. They demanded to be treated decently in all ways and laid out compassionate specifics. They would not be scapegoated. They would not be fired from their jobs. They were to be included in all levels of decision-making. They would live—and die—in dignity. It was an impressive and moving list. They had made themselves a big banner from some of the Holiday Inn's sheets, and they stormed the closing session of the conference to present their demands. One after another physically wasted Person with UC declaimed each of their new principles. There was not a dry eye in the house.

My speech was rescheduled opposite a "keynote" speech to the doctors by Kiefer Kreditz so my audience was a scattering of NAPWUCs. Even Bruce, with Tommy, went to the doctors' session. Bruce said, "It was disgusting. And they don't like us, that's for sure. Why did we come here, to be treated like shit?"

"It was meant to be a conference of togetherness," Tommy said. "But they're burned at not successfully screwing us out of that twenty-five thousand bucks."

I thought the whole meeting was weird. Breaches of unity were appearing everywhere, not only NAPWUC vs. Everyone, but doctors feeling so overwhelmed with what was obviously the heavy-duty shit ahead that they were already preparing to abdicate right and left, scattering their good intentions like dying autumn leaves. Many of them couldn't wait to get back to good old anonymous New York and their closets. "Lemish, you are a dishonest crook," some creep named Martin Paleski yelled at me at one point. And another guy, this one a Hispanic patient, yelled out that GMPA was now so rich it didn't have to pay any attention to anyone except rich white men. To which the annoyed doctors, for some reason, cheered. To which of course Bruce had to get up to reply to the doctors, who now booed him, something new for him. For some reason I cried out, "The pot is calling the kettle black." To which a black guy with UC got up and yelled, "Hey, Lemish, watch out what you say about blacks!"

Dr. Kiefer Kreditz disappeared. I was told he was sick. I know Martin Paleski died, because he got an obit in *The Truth*. They had started out as a social organization, no doubt to meet others like themselves who might be date bait; but now physical interactivity was becoming a lot of those autumn leaves. The first national gay and lesbian organization devoted to gay and lesbian health, which was what this was meant to be all about, had gotten off to a lousy start. It was proceeding as every other gay group always proceeded, to make itself irrelevant.

EQUAL TO MURDERERS

To:
Mr. Punch Dunkelheim, *The New York Truth*
Dr. Dearie Fault, *The New York Truth*
Mr. Jacob Flourtower, *The New York Truth*

Ms. Velma Dimley, *The New York Truth*
Judge Richard Gasp, Gay Men Pay Attention
Mr. Tommy Boatwright, Gay Men Pay Attention
Mr. Bruce Niles, Gay Men Pay Attention
Ms. Tallula Giardino, Lesbian and Gay Union
Dr. Herta Glanz, NYC Commissioner of Health
Mayor Kermit Goins, City of New York
Mr. Hiram Keebler, Mayor's Liaison to the Gay Community
From:
Fred Lemish, writer/activist

I am attaching an article from last Friday's *Washington Monument* entitled "Epidemic Is Expanding, Not Shrinking, Experts Say." As you can see, this was a main, featured article, appearing on page A-3.

Why hasn't this information been conveyed to people in New York?

Why is there so little information passed on to the New York gay community about the appalling continuation, the march of this epidemic? After all, New York is still the worst hit, but you would not know it from reading *The New York Truth*, or any of the blather put out by any of the above. The worst epidemic known to modern man is happening right here in this very city, and it is one of the best-kept secrets around.

That all of you listed above continue to refuse to transmit to the public the facts and figures of what is happening *daily* makes you, in my mind, equal to murderers, with blood on your hands just as if you had used knives or bullets or poison. Because you continue to refuse to inform New York's population, the perception by the average gay man is that this epidemic has disappeared or leveled off or improved or never been heard about in the first place. Because *The New York Truth* is not reporting any vital news, because the city's Department of Health is not releasing cautionary recommendations, because the gay community's own organizations are too cowardly to speak out and speak up—all of this perpetuates the widespread ignorance that can only make for continued contagion, infection, and death. The average gay man is living with his head in the sand.

In the name of God, Christ, Moses, whatever impels you to, at last, perform acts of humanity, when will you address this issue with the courage it demands?

•

My use of "equal to murderers" in attacking my own people, some of my once best friends, is not new. I had called them the same when I was thrice rejected for reinstatement to the GMPA board. My reputation by now is that of a crazy man. I am already being dubbed "the angriest gay man in the world." Me?

BRINESTALKER MARCHES ON

The next step, or the continuing step, or the step that was my intention all along, is to find out how many homosexuals we are presently talking about, how many are going to get sick, how many we can make sick, how long this will take, and how much we have to budget for it. The problem of staff continues to be a major one. There is this special sales task force out there pushing DridgePlusOne, and shortly, they shall have ZAP, but their distribution of both will of necessity be confined to just that, selling these products.

The partner to this next step, of course, once we have numbers on a wide-enough scale, is to isolate their locales and habitations (of course, I mean, "where they live") so that we can concentrate on further infecting them in situ. It is our good fortune that they are already cooperating with us to some extent. For instance, they choose, indeed they prefer, to live and play among themselves. And, wonder of wonders, I hear that the infected are enthusiastic about participating in anything that might portend a "cure." Our friends inside NITS indicate there's a mad rush of inquiries about enrollment and slots are filling up quickly.

It is all proving easier than anticipated. I am wondering if we can further co-opt their population to participate in the calculations of their numbers, of both infecteds and healthies. They now have in existence in all major cities organizations pledged to care for victims of this disease, New York's GMPA being a good case in point. I understand they are exceptionally committed individuals. They believe accurately that our government is intentionally ignoring them. So this very fear can be made to serve as an incentive for them to do this work for us, by coming out of their closets so to speak and becoming visible. I will forward you a list of all these organizations. As I say, I believe these groups are covering more and more of the country and are in contact with each other. No doubt it will not be long before they open an office in Washington. That would be most helpful to us indeed. I plan to encourage this with a grant or two.

I wanted to discuss all this with Slyme, but it appears that he's been fired. Gobbel and Bohunk now jump to Purpura's desires.

Regarding Botts's earlier original suggestion of "neighborhooding" our efforts, I think that's what we're putting into motion. Our continuing "targeted" outreach to their organizations is our most effective tool for obtaining the most accurate data. We have already had on-site visits to specific enclaves of homosexuals, such as Greenwich Village in New York and the Castro neighborhood in San Francisco. COD's Dr. Gibbard has sent in full reports on his interviews with many victims in both of these places. What is particularly fascinating is how many men are so desperate to participate in the activities "our government" is planning, which Gibbard sketched in for them (more or less), including our taking a census of them, their symptoms, their partners, their sexual activities, all, of course, on the premise that knowledge is power and will lead to helping them. Gibbard assures me that it went down well. "There is absolutely no sense among them that such a census could in any way be harmful to them." I think he is overoptimistic in this assumption, but our overcoming any resistance will be a key to our success.

We have just received a fuller report from our agents in San Francisco. The amount of data they have already collected in such a short period is spectacular. God bless the new models of handheld IBM Hollerith computers. Old Thomas Watson, who ran IBM, totally screwed Herman Hollerith out of a fortune. I was there and thank God I bought a lot of stock. Watson screwed a lot of people out of a lot of fortunes. But that is another story from our earlier history. All IBM files on this part of their history were long ago embargoed from view.

Our office has already cross-referenced some seventy-six thousand cases. Yes, seventy-six thousand more names and addresses. Yes, this figure is light-years ahead of the paltry number COD is putting out. (I don't know what the problem is with those guys. Perhaps you can look into this.) But far, far less than the Germans were able to calculate with their IBM Hollerith machines by 1938, when Himmler claimed there were one million four hundred thousand homosexuals in his country. We should have a hundred thousand by next month.

Gobbel and Moose are tickled pink that things are going along so well and we are moving into higher gear.

In closing, your suggestion of bonuses for our staff to insure fidelity to our work has been approved in the amounts you laid out for us at our last meeting.

I hope you are as overcome as I am with the goodness of our hopes and goals and deeds. After a very long life of searching for a life of meaning, I have finally found it.

By the way, I love the new name they've given us. The Tricia Institute. So, I gather, does the First Lady.

HERMIA

I have received a last note from our beloved Dr. Sister Grace. It is mangled and ripped and shredded and postmarked like it, too, has been through the wars.

"Is it worth all the energy it's going to take to make any of this clear to the putrid male-dominated world that will decide my fate? I am genuinely tired. Must I wait for Schwitz to blacken my name for all of medical history?"

•

The one-armed lady from Africa is dead! Thank you to your Jesus.

TO FRED FROM HIS FRIEND ROBERT COUTOURIER

You have to read the adventures of Gilgamesh and Enkidu. Both were mythical heroes of the Sumerian civilization, the first culture to invent writing, accounting, the hoe, pottery, etc., and our direct ancestors, since Abraham was from Haran, one of the Sumerian towns. Anyway, these two heroes had an obvious homosexual relationship, and when Enkidu died Gilgamesh said the most tender and moving words. All that more than five thousand years ago!

I was thinking about the whole Sumerian thing and the story of Sodom and Gomorrah. What God was against was not sodomy but inhospitality; you don't go rape some total strangers asking for your hospitality. It's not the sexual act itself God opposes, just the violence. That fit better with the times, four thousand years ago when love as shown in all works of art did not distinguish among men to men, men to women, or women to women, but just the act of love. So much more sensible, no?

I am in Kazakhstan, or is it Uzbekistan? It's very dark and scary. My client is a Russian Jew who is so frightened of being murdered now that he's exceptionally rich that he's guarded every moment of his life. And I as his potential decorator am as well. He has an enormous plot of earth on the edge of the Caspian Sea. It's very ugly because it's so flat, but he wants high walls around his house, so I guess it makes no difference. His guards all look like

Mongols, dark-skinned and all in fur pelts and, I am certain, high on drugs. Some of their faces are splotched with UC, I am also certain. My "client" does not understand what I'm talking about. "All the young men have these spots now," he said to me. "I thought it was some sort of fad from America."

Keep up the good work. Do not flag or falter!

I DIDN'T KNOW HOW ELSE TO DO THIS

RAYMOND LOPEZ, GMPA VOLUNTEER SUPERVISOR

My stomach hurts so much that I don't know what to do. My legs hurt so much, and my feet, that it's hard to walk and to come to work. All my doctors say they don't know what to do and I must learn to live with it and be grateful I'm still alive. I'm not very good anymore with "learning to live" with things. When I don't feel well it makes me mean and rude and turns me into a person nobody likes and I don't like. Gordy and Frank and Trevor all say the same. This is the worst pain we have ever had, from anything. Trevor is on so many painkillers that he can't talk sense or walk upright. "I don't know how to escape this pain except by killing myself," he said. As our physical discomfort increases day by day, we sit around and discuss how we'd do it. Yesterday was worse than the day before and today is worse than yesterday, so our conversations about this subject have become increasingly intense. Drugs like marijuana and speed that I take to feel better don't make me feel better. Tappy gave me some MDAF and I vomited all night. Heller James gave me some Hound's Tooth and I vomited all another night. Everyone I know and half the volunteers I'm supposed to be in charge of are on something. I don't hear from any of them that they've found a way to feel better. I am afraid now. I hadn't been afraid before now. I am also afraid of killing myself. I make lists of possibilities. Jumping from high places. (This seems horrible, the wait between cause and effect.) Jumping in front of fast-moving vehicles. (This seems like it might be the fastest but I don't want to kill the driver.) Taking poison. (This might take too long and I would change my mind the minute I did it.) I need something that works real fast. I don't know how to buy a gun but that doesn't seem to be an insurmountable possibility. Forgive me. Please tell Fred to murder the mayor and the president.

•

TOMMY: Fred, Raymond blew his brains out in his cubicle at the office. His blood and brains were all over everything. I had to find some cleaning service that deals with human poisons. It wasn't easy. The only thing without blood on it was the letter above that he left with your name and mine on it. We closed the office down for a few days, of course. Bruce doesn't want anyone to know about this. As if you could keep something like this a secret. Raymond was one of our very first full-time volunteers. He had a rich boyfriend, Hector, who had died.

FROM *THE BOOK OF THE DEAD*

Herbert Ruler, Norbert Haas, Rob Daniele, Andrew Weissman, Fergus Alcorn, Alan Weints, Terry Fulcrum, Daniele Torronella, Fill Schwarts, Abernought Ficks, O'Hern Philpotts, Trent Delwits, Butts Fassenden, Hal Adonowiller, Oscar Phail, Nils Swedenborg, Gus St. Alban, Ted Witt, Noel Fish, Tom Donatt, Nestor Alhambra, Irving Slough, Hubie Stint, O'Donahue Morrisey, Rich Alexander, Leonard Rappsteiner, Furden Blye, Nick Spadafury, Paulo Rudolpho, Gianni Starchi, Jude Wrenner, Neil Warrenburst, Richard Allan Notum, Whipp Thresher, Louie Westerngartner, Ahasuerus Farouker, Lester Vann, Tom Dorr, Grant Griller, Loyal Trow, Peril Fort, Sam Simmser, Sam O'Harris, Sam Natale, Adam Schwartzkopf, Bobby Bulew, Tersh Teller, Boy Tallahassee, Buntrum Salsy, Vic Burns, Michael Callen, Nirv Vatter, Nobby Franjuro, Al Hassen, Peter Verduro, Saul Pinner, Alexander Durant, Makos Georgos, Makos Allesandri, Nirvos Trotta, Dick Netesso, Philip Riddil, Norton Newsome, Oden Ushervov, Tim Tripplehorn, Arthur Andrew Talc, Talbot Fuchs, Render Mylo, Phelps Drunenberg, Roger Realston, Roger Van Dycken, Tiny Fewshis, Cordon Trumbull, Luke Newton, Samuel D. V. P. Granite IV, Luis Secundos, Bob Marshall, Tulsa, Babe Harley, Marshall Potash, Harry Wyanat, Tiger Vettle, Narwood Vane, Liam O'Malley, Aleichem Singer, Toots Beyzar, Al Hoydenberger, Ray Knight, Bobby Borley, Clay Esterhaus, Joe Pearl, Felix Turner . . .

Felix Turner. Felix Turner. Felix Turner. I type the name and stare at it.

•

The numbers released are stupid. I personally have infected some half a million people in the last two months alone. Again I wonder what advantage anyone feels is received by such what you call lowballing.

You do not know that in Uganda the people I am infecting lose so much weight they are said to be suffering from the "slim disease." Isn't that amusing?

A NEW VOICE IS HEARD IN THE LAND

Dear Mr. Lemish,

I cannot tell you how gratified all Muslims and our comrades in arms are with the lack of success for your endeavors, now manifesting itself with increasing visibility. It is not often that our religious dictates reap such tangible support in the West.

Equally pleasurable to us is the obvious tacit approval your own country displays as your labors lead to your much-deserved bad fortune.

Muhammad blesses all these endeavors, most obviously, for no success comes without the blessings of Allah.

It is now impossible to dispute this fact: even should some cure be found (we shall continue our attempts to see that this remains highly unlikely), entire unreplaceable generations are being destroyed. As with the Jews during the world's recent holocaust of them, you and your people will not get back on your feet.

It is against our religion to be a homosexual. Such a crime is punishable by death. We stone and shoot and kill and hang and decapitate homosexual men and women. Because you are not interested in us, you do not hear this in your country. But it is so, and true, and right. And it will continue, as will our efforts in your country.

Keep up your cooperation!

C. George Aziz
President and Convener
The Muslim Confederation Against the Homosexual Scourge

DEEP THROAT LECTURES FRED

Why has this poison only now begun to knock your people off en masse? You haven't figured this out yet? Because up until recently there simply hasn't existed a population large enough for this underlying poison to "contage," i.e., be spread around with enough generosity to keep it alive before it dies from lack of what is called "cuddling," to use the technical term.

A population, to "extinct" itself, must engage in nonstop lethal interactions, over and over, day after day, around the clock, for an extended period of time. Otherwise the poison can't spread. It will die out in its group of hosts and be unable to continue on its journey. It is very "site-specific." Grace told me it started with one kind of monkey. It didn't like other kinds of monkeys. Now it apparently likes human beings. Lurking here is the reason its targeted victims are so specific. It isn't so much that it's gay men who are the central core of victims. It's that they are *a specific community*. A population, if you will. All doing the same things to and with each other. Yes, straight men are going to get this. Because Kinsey told us there's no such thing as a totally straight man. You know that.

You are being extincted.

My boss points out to me there was and still is much bad feeling between the FBI and the CIA, each fearing destruction by the other. Each has been and still is involved in many "extinctions."

BEST BE ON YOUR GUARD!

HERMIA

I have been in touch with an old chum from Cambridge, the renowned hematologist Dr. Abraham Karpas, who has this to say about your Dr. Dodo Geiseric: "Dr. Geiseric is a crook, a charlatan of the most heinous order. Best be on your guard!"*

The nooses are tightening. Forces are continuing to make you disappear!
The passivity of your people continues.
Where is every gay person's determination to stay alive!

---

* Dr. Karpas will be the first to provide confirmation of the French discovery that the causative agent of UC is a distinct virus and not, as Dodo will claim, his KGLV.

I know Fred will cry out in despair, "How many ways can you say, get off your fucking asses or you are going to die," to quote his recent article in *The Prick*.

I put to my old chum Abe Karpas the information in Grace's letters as well as Fred's. He was aghast. He could not speak for several minutes. "Are we still connected, Abe?" I had to ask several times before he responded.

"I fear this plague will never end," he answered.

BOSCO DRIPPER IS DEAD

He is found dead on his monkey farm in the Everglades, where his arching negritas are dead as well. He had crawled out to join his monkeys because he knew he was dying. He had gone to sleep with his monkeys, all of which were dead by his side, having starved to death for lack of food and supervision. They had evidently tried to stay alive by eating parts of him. It was not a pretty sight.

He'd learned that his monkeys were no long needed by NITS. A friend from France said, "This is a retrovirus, not a virus we are dealing with." And therefore Koch's Postulates, the bible of whether a disease is contagious or not, don't apply without complications. Animal models will evidently no longer be necessary for this coming plague he'd hoped to figure in so importantly, so front and center, so worth the long wait for his day in the sun.

An anthropologist at HOW in Geneva, Melanie Poussin Abstruse, had sent him a copy of her report on a recent trip to Africa. There is no question, she claims, that "the current plague of The Underlying Condition stems from Africans eating 'bush meat,' including chimps. I do not know why this information is not being promulgated throughout the world. Dr. Vitabaum was taking this information to the home office in Washington but he appears to have mysteriously disappeared and has not yet been replaced."

Abstruse is never heard from again.

Bosco wrote on the cover of Abstruse's report, "I no longer want to live if my chimps are responsible for this plague. Whoever finds this, please know that I have lived my life for nothing, that I have loved in vain and lost, and that I no longer wish to live."

AND THIS IS JUST THE *READER'S DIGEST* VERSION

We can't do anything until we find the virus, right? Well, the answer to that question, which will take over three more unnecessary years to disentangle and be approved, is embedded in what follows. And this is just the *Reader's Digest* version:

DANIEL THE SPY LAUNCHES US INTO DODOGATE

At our next meeting, house overflowing as usual, in front of all of us Mid-dleditch tells Dodo to "cut the crap and get to work on UC. Get to work! That's an order! You are meant to be a genius. Prove it!" Roscoe Middleditch really thinks Dodo is a genius, which is why he puts up with such a strange, cantankerous man. Dodo knows that Middleditch doesn't usually talk this commandingly. He also knows Roscoe hasn't anyone else to assign to this. On the one hand, that's a compliment, meaning he's the smartest guy at NITS, which he certainly believes. On the other hand, it's an insult. I suspect he doesn't really want to do it, and nobody asked him about that. Either he's a good Catholic boy uncomfortable with homosexuals or he's a good Catholic boy all too familiar with homosexuals. The few hints he's dropped here and in *The Prick* about "stay tuned" are lies to protect him should any competition show up. Whichever it is, he does not like to be a loser.

Grebstyne comes to me. Sherwin Grebstyne is now Roscoe's executive coordinator of infectious diseases. "You and me," Sherwin says to me, "we're the two Jewboy outsiders here. We got to keep our eyes on Dodo."

Jerry laughs out loud when I relate this to him. "Dodo isn't our department. I'll tell Roscoe."

"I hear Roscoe's on his way out."

"You what? He's got seniority. They can't fire him."

"He's been caught manipulating stock."

"What the fuck? Roscoe Middleditch's ass is cleaner than the Ivory baby. Where did you hear that? Manipulating how?"

"He's being charged with profiteering on the stock market. Insider trading with Greeting stock."

"Jesus, Jerusalem, how do you know all this?"

"I can't tell you." Actually, my brother Lucas is representing Roscoe— I put them together when Roscoe came to me in a panic and had read about my tough brother's firm—and Lucas wants me to "see what you can sweat out up there."

A young man named Mount Vernon Pugh, who is some cousin to Sir Norman Treadway, whose wife is a British Greeting, was found dead and with his balls cut off out in some gulch in Fille de Maison. It wasn't reported anywhere. Some lab reports indicating that Greeting's Childhood Cough Syrup is poisoned were found on him. Roscoe signed these reports. It's even more complicated. Howie Hube had been in charge of those childhood whooping cough trials for Roscoe at NITS. By all accounts Howie had done a decent job, which is why Jerry is using him with Debbi to set up a system of clinical trials for us, to be ready if and when. But the report in Mount Vernon's pocket indicated that Greeting's kiddy cough syrup, well, two young girls in Lithamgrove have died from it, while taking it on one of Hube's trials. Jerry frowns but doesn't reply.

In the late '70s, Dodo made two "discoveries" in his lab, only to have both be, he says, "sabotaged"—once by a refrigerator being turned off for an entire weekend, thus killing "important assays" that for whatever reason could then not be regrown, and once by actual culture dishes being contaminated with various monkey viruses appearing, it would seem, from out of nowhere. Dodo asked Middleditch and was turned down for a permanent guard for protection. A few years later a flight to London he was booked on but did not fly on blew up from a bomb and crashed into the ocean. It had been announced that he was flying on that plane and that he was going to make an important announcement. Dodo is always making important announcements. He loves to see his name in the papers and his face on TV. Dodo is now maintaining that "someone was and continues to be out to get me," and that any work he was and will ever be doing will bring the wrath of someone down upon him. Lucas was the lawyer for the plane victims' families and got a monster settlement for them, which brought him to the attention of Roscoe.

It's even more complicated. This kid Mount Vernon also had a summons in his pocket to appear before the Tricia Institute. This is the renamed Office of Unnatural Acts. They're giving summonses now. (How can they do that?) The summons was to come for "an interview about your activities while on government time. You are suspected to be homosexual. You face possible arrest." This is scary. (Who authorizes the dispatch of threats like this?)

Arnold Botts slips Poopsie, who runs Dodo's lab and hardly speaks English, money to tell him what's going on in their lab. And Poopsie slipped

Mount Vernon money to tell him what he finds out from Arnold about what G-D is up to. Mount Vernon also makes money giving blow jobs, evidently to Arnold and Poopsie. I guess the Tricia Institute got wind of this. Minna Trooble, a girl I used to know in the Jew Tank and in high school, is my source on this dish.

Greeting stock lost a bundle when the whooping cough deaths leaked out.

Roscoe Middleditch is accused of insider trading of Greeting stock.

Grebstyne's now in charge of Dodo.

Howie Hube should have been fired but wasn't.

Who murdered Mount Vernon Pugh?

What did Poopsie find out from Arnold to tell Dodo?

•

DEEP THROAT: Nobody in America knows that throughout laboratories in and around Paris, Drs. Gaston Nappe, Astolphe Bordeaux, Jacqueline Françoise, and Franc Giblette, along with their associates, had started immediately in 1981 to biopsy lymph nodes of sick men they're seeing in increasing numbers, all of them gay. (No one in America had thought to biopsy anyone. Biopsy? Biopsy who and for what and why?) Lymph nodes clog French worktables, in their bottles, petri dishes, refrigerators, freezers. Day by day all findings are meticulously recorded in all workbooks. My friend Marcel Schwartz-Levinsky has a go at writing an article about these explorations, which he submits to Dr. Nutrician Valmont Peersie, the editor of *Medicin et Action* (*M&A*), who rejects it even though his publication usually has the guts to publish "cutting-edge" ("à l'avant-garde") submissions in France. Although Gaston Nappe tries to keep an eye on everything that goes on in his lab at Centre Curie-Cassatt (CCC), he is not an able man, in either medicine or administration, or in public relations, but he has learned how to "fake it," as he's heard we Americans say. Keep your eye on Jacquie, his instinct tells him. She is the cleverest, and the least likely to raise objection when, as head of the lab, he gets his name first on any discovery. She is meek and quiet, a good Catholic girl from the provinces. She also seems to know a lot of gay young men who are sick and can convince them to "come in and give me one of your nodes." French boys aren't frightened yet. "Yes, they're still having naked orgies in discos on weekends," a French journalist friend of Fred's, Didier Lestrade, told him. They are evidently more sexually sophisticated than American disco dancers, if you call disco orgies sophisticated. Well, the French boys think they are. Your popular gay writer Jervis Pail has affectionately written about this "touching remembrance of things past" in Philippine *Vogue* in one of his "Letters to America from Abroad." My wife read it to me from under the dryer at her hairdresser's.

No one in America knows about anything remotely scientifically interesting that's going on in Paris, and that's the way Gaston wants it until he's ready. As does the White House. And good old boy Von Greeting. You heard me correctly.

And the CIA. Linus Gobbel. Let's backtrack to about 1960 before we can go forward.

Before I wound up here, I studied and learned and taught pathology in many places that excited something in me that said, "Let's go there and take a look." I'd been in Iceland diving into the innards of some mighty strange sheep I'd heard about, all dying from unknown causes. Sure enough, I found the culprit for them, a virus of sorts. Since there was no cure for it, and since it was obviously transmittable, the entire sheep population of Iceland was put down and they started anew with "clean" sheep from Greenland. Dr. Lief Ovo, Iceland's chief pathologist, told me some interesting things about what he'd heard about the Belgian Congo, so it's there that I decided to go to continue my education. It was not a safe place for anyone. The Belgians had raped the country in every conceivable way. When Léopold II began lopping off the hands of every worker for not producing enough raw rubber, revolutions started to occur, bloody ones. The Belgians bailed in 1960, taking everything with them that they could. The CIA had jumped in before the Belgians left. The U.S. Army was called in to run some "peacekeeping" missions as cover. The spook in charge was Linus Gobbel, currently a powerful resident in Peter Ruester's White House. The CIA had helped build the Belgians an air force and then provisioned the various combatants. It participated in the grisly killing of Patrice Lumumba. I had discovered that apes were dying, *Pan troglodytes schweinfurthii* chimps from Mombasa and *Pan troglodytes* chimps from Cameroon and Gabon, about a thousand miles to the west. The Pasteur Institute in Paris had even written about this. I had to get out of the Congo pronto or I would have been butchered, along with all their civil servants dashing to return to the safety of their homeland, Haiti. Gobbel got me on a U.S. Army plane back to the States. (Actually, Mother got me on that plane. He hates Linus Gobbel.) I did manage to take some samples of the apes' blood. They didn't make any sense to me until UC came along and I shared my samples with Grace.

Jerry, of course, didn't want to know about this. "It's not our department."

And Gist was still saying that whatever it was would soon fly away. Jerry said to me, and I quote, "You're a real troublemaker, aren't you?" He didn't mean it as a compliment.

I suppose in a place like this I am weird. I'm a romantic. The sudden appearance of UC is a drama and a cause I can now understand. Its complexities are unknown and arcane. It's an intellectual challenge. I want to know its structure, its culture, its history. I want to find it in the bodies of the Pauls and Kevins who are beginning to appear in our clinics with Kaposi's sarcoma devouring their skin and guts. To do this, I'm once again serving a kind of apprenticeship, learning about the down-and-dirty of molecular biology and immunology while we await Dodo's "discovery." And just as the White House and the Congress cast exceptionally longer and more menacing shadows. As does Jerry.

•

DANIEL: Roscoe Middleditch recognized in Dodo the ambitious pain in the ass I hear he once was himself. That's how he became chief of Cancer. As he quieted down he thinks he lost his touch, which he probably has. I'm beginning to see how full this place is of once-geniuses who have lost their touch. You can see it in their faces, and how they walk the corridors, less and less proudly the older they get. He compensated for this by backing winners. He's good at this, so good that Cancer at NITS has a pretty good reputation. Not as great as Hopkins or Cambridge, but this is not a top-drawer posting, which I'd also been surprised to learn. And no one talks about all the vacancies that the Ruester cutbacks prevent from being filled. You come here to work if you want security, not to work with "the great ones," because most of them are somewhere else. I can't remember if Goffman noted anything like this in that *Asylums* book of his.

UC didn't have to be discovered for the smart ones to know it would be a virus. Dodo knew. Roscoe knew. Your Dr. Brookner knew. Grace knew. Rebby knew. Hokie Benois-Frucht knew. They all just *knew*. Jerry, who is an immunologist, didn't know, and wasn't going to back any horse so specifically yet. Deep Throat calls him a "fence-sitter." Immunology is one of those newish specialties where, for those not in it, it's hard to understand what's going on. To the outsider it doesn't seem to have much to do with viruses. At first Stuartgene wanted to assign UC to Roscoe instead of Jerry. Jerry got very pissed off. "'My' division is meant to be in charge of *all* infectious diseases." Jerry won that one. But only, I think, because Stuartgene isn't around here very much. He's taken a bigger interest in Alzheimer's and Congress is backing him up for it. Anyway, Middleditch will be out of the loop soon.

•

DEEP THROAT: At NITS viruses and cancer are not dissimilar but they are not the same, and though they cross over, everything in nature crosses over, and it is up to the clever ones to know where to draw the line, or rather where the invisible line is drawn, and then to respect the boundaries and somehow still come up with something. The subtext of this is that this place is as regimented as all hell and this kind of puts a damper on all-out enthusiasm. You can get yourself knifed in the back in many professional ways. Cooperation is no one's middle name. Stuartgene encourages all this because he belongs to another school, which is to pit all the bulls against each other and the devil take the hindmost. That there has never been a cure for any major anything that has come out of NITS is a fact to which no one pays any attention, including Congress, which understands NITS about as well as it understands everything else it funds.

•

DANIEL: Dodo believes everyone is out to get him because they are. I've never seen a more unpopular guy. I gather that's been useful in the past to get his juices going, the fuck-you, I'll show you mentality. He's made major discoveries. He's written important papers. The trouble is that now more people are seeing that he's an asshole. Roscoe knows that he'd best scare Dodo into a higher gear pronto. "I don't feel and hear your heart in this, Dodo. You're relying too much on Poopsie. I don't smell the Dodo touch yet. You spend too much time talking to reporters. Stop all that shit and really get to work. You know what I'm talking about." All this before another packed auditorium. Attendance at our now irregular meetings is still standing room only.

"I am offended, Roscoe. I am dumbstruck that you are downplaying my great discoveries. I've already discovered UC's analogues and dredge participants and its vectors—I have discovered its vectors!"

Middleditch continues. "Okay. So let's just say, what if you have discovered a viral cause of this?"

"What if! I am offended again, Roscoe. I *have* discovered the viral cause of this." This isn't true, but no one knows this. Dodo is vamping, with his "made-up" vocabulary of scientific terms, which many of these guys tend to do. "Dredge participants"? What the fuck are they?

"Then why haven't you shared your dredge participants with us? Where is your paper on them? Where is your paper on your viral analogues? You're usually into the journals faster than anyone. On their own, these new 'discoveries' do not sound like they amount to a full virus and therefore don't amount to shit in moving us forward. And you know it. We're all sitting here, waiting for you. I've watched you for years, Dr. Dodo Geiseric, and the only time you discover anything is when I see smoke coming from the top of your head. I am not seeing any smoke." And he turns and leaves. He walks out of the meeting. Dodo doesn't like this. He sees that Roscoe Middleditch, whom he has looked upon as his father and protector, is now all of a sudden not acting very paternal or protective. He doesn't know that his safekeeper is not going to be around much longer.

Dodo had only Poopsie and a couple of others in his lab. Middleditch had given him three dozen more, including a young smart one, Flo Hung Nu, Jr. Twenty-five years ago when he was a student winner of the Westinghouse Science Competition for high school kids and got to work at NITS for the summer, Dodo fucked her mother on this same lab floor, and this one's his daughter, whether either one of them knows all this or not. (Thank you, Hermia, for digging this up. And Minna for confirming it.)

Now we are beginning to hear that something of more than routine interest is going on in Paris, among several people Dodo knows and even worked with. He'd asked for and received their isolates. In science one never refuses a fellow scientist's request for isolates, for that's how progress is made.

•

DEEP THROAT: It's also how credit can be manipulated, and dare one even think so, stolen.

•

FRED: As has been mentioned, this is the *Reader's Digest* version. A lot will be written about how Dr. Dodo Geiseric stole or did not steal the credit for *the* "discovery" of the UC virus from the Drs. Français. It is a nasty story, an unkind, selfish, inhumane story, no matter which way it's told. Just know that from here on in manipulations that would do Nixon, Kissinger, and Tony Soprano proud will transpire. This will not result in progress. It will result in deadly delays. It will result in the loss of yet more precious *years* and the concomitant deaths of many thousands of people who might have been saved if Dodo had responded in a dignified and humane fashion. Dodo is not that man.

•

HERMIA: Dr. Kelvin "Dodo" Geiseric is an evil man. I am featuring him prominently in *my* history of evil.

•

FRED: There's growing belief by such as Rebby Itsenfelder that Dodo stole "his" isolates from that blood sent over by Gaston Nappe at CCC, who himself is now rumored to be fighting his own battles with Astolphe Bordeaux over who is closer to Jacquie. No more than two people can win a Nobel for the same discovery. Yes, that noble word *Nobel* is starting to be heard. The French have evidently never come up against the brute force that Americans can display in science. I am now learning firsthand: Where the fuck have I been, or was I when I was a journalist and then a screenwriter schlepping through Africa and other places populated by the French?

•

DANIEL: Dodo's increasingly shorter fuse turns him beet red if anyone refers to "Jacquie's discovery." Everyone at NITS has seen her work by now and it looks irrefutably convincing. Even Jerry's impressed. "Looks like bingo to me," he tells me.

•

DEEP THROAT: What remains is for Jacquie—or someone—to duplicate her discovery by proving it can actually cause UC. NITS no longer has any monkeys, and it's against the law for Dodo's isolates to go straight into humans. Dodo's determined to prevent her proof from being proved. He's the one who's going to prove it. I know the type. I can see it in his eyes. All I can see in Jerry's eyes is someone who'll be here until he dies.

•

DANIEL: I'm learning that science is all about backing horses, and Dodo has been considered a better scientist by far than Jerry. No one takes Jerrold Omicidio seriously as the scientist he so wants to be taken. Nobody suspects that Dodo is stuck in a rut, except Dodo and that Flo Hung Nu, Jr. (he's indeed now fucking her on his lab floor, it's no secret), and Jerry, and of course Deep Throat.

It's getting messier, sadder, and dare I say farcical.

Hey, I'm getting pretty good at this spy shit, no?

What happens next is that Dodo "proves" that Jacquie's isolates do indeed isolate UC. Only he'll claim that she's discovered this with *his* isolates, when in fact they'll be the ones she sent him.

Oh, Middleditch suddenly isn't here anymore. Lucas won't tell me what's happening.

•

REBBY: I do not approve of it, of course, the stupidity of shots in the dark, but I do not completely disdain it either, because there are too many instances when stupidity has been partnered with genuine genius. We must be free to fall on our asses. It takes courageous scientists to confront the world with ideas that are off the wall. But none of this applies here. Theft is not science.

•

DANIEL: "I have my own clues to this new plague's residence in the body and I honestly believe I'm winning." Dodo actually announces this on ABC Television's *International Medical Journal*. Jerry's becoming more unpleasant. I actually am feeling sorry for him. I'd got him drunk over dinner at his favorite Italian restaurant and he said to me: "*I* want to discover the cure for this shit! I'm not going to leave here until I do."

"But you haven't started anything and we haven't any money! How are you going to discover dipshit!" I found myself saying. Must have been the wine. He didn't respond and he wouldn't look me in the eye. I suddenly don't feel sorry for him anymore.

Dodo then takes those isolates of his to Japan, where he somehow manages to infect several dozen people and, from there, announces his "major discovery" to the world, which he now names KDG-1, "the cause of UC."

And he also says: "It contraindicates what we are seeing from France, which is something else."

You would think that the bunch of them, Dodo, Jerry, Flo Jr., Poopsie, Stuartgene, even Hoidene as their boss, would be called to the White House for a meeting, a thank-you, at the very least a handshake. Does that mean no one believes him? Or doesn't want to?

•

DEEP THROAT: In one word: *lawyers*. Lawyers for any and all scientific researchers know what "Something Else" implies. It means that the primary
investigator of The Underlying Condition in America's premiere research
institution is saying, in essence: I'm going to tell you what I discovered but
since it's protected and copyrighted and patented and registered, you can't
steal it and claim it for yours. If you do, I'll sue the shit out of you. This process is one of the wonderments of Modern Scientific Research and is perhaps
the main reason why America is where it is, that is, light-years behind where
we could be, in this instance embracing and cooperating with France. This is
how teamwork is encouraged, under the guise of that great American suffo-
cating canopy of enforced competition. Another race to be won by the most
swift, most clever, most On the Ball, with side skills in deceit and chicanery,
and of course, it goes without saying, to the most crafty. Read: the biggest
thief. These NITS lawyers can now maintain that what Dodo had done was
very original indeed. The French will be suitably baffled or dare I say checkmated. They haven't even seen Dodo's paperwork from Japan and already
they're being accused of being thieves.

Always remember that in medicine, in science, as in all else, successful obsession is the name of the game. It is not always the calm, composed,
decent, fair, thorough, gracious, noble, generous, moral, upstanding, honest,
and undefiled person who claims the Answer. It is often the crank, the crazy,
the nutcase, the person no one can stand and many people hate. The loony in
the attic. The madman in the cellar. The screamer. The crook. The Dodo. I
believe Fred and Hermia have posited the very same.

Dodo's obsession respects no boundaries. You think that Dodo has discovered the virus? That's what he's more than intimated, and the world is
rushing to his door or his virus's door to hear all further details. What
everyone young and idealistic is going to find out, at NITS, at med schools,
in the labs, is that if you have an idea someone like Dodo will steal it from
you and make it his own. If he can get hold of it. Dodo has ahold of it. It is
called Jacquie's own isolates.

He will now lie and cheat and murder and kill. Well, no one is certain
about the murder and kill business (at least not yet), but anyone whose labs
deal with what is laughingly called "the slave trade," advertising in Japan
and the Third World for human volunteers for "official clinical studies by

America's foremost research institution by America's leading scientist," can reasonably be assumed to have lost a few. We have only to not forget Partekla. It comes with the territory. There's an old saying around every major lab in the world: "If you haven't killed anyone, you haven't been doing your work right." Try to get that truth in *The New York Truth.*

Dodo has learned that in medicine as in so much else in this country, celebrity is all. He doesn't know that shortly no one is going to pay any attention to him, except for Rep. Dingus, who's really out for his ass. And lots and lots of lawyers will soon be increasingly on call. Before he's yanked from center stage Dodo will cost NITS, and hence The American People, millions and millions in legal fees. Dingus will figure this out.

But at this precious moment, Dodo is now going to perform once more for the world.

FLING WIDE THE DODOGATE!

DANIEL: Dodo appears on another national news show, this time CBS Television's *World Medicine Today.* He says, "If my KDG-1 causes UC in the Orient it can happen in the Occident. Thank you, fine citizens of Japan. Thank you for helping me prove it."

This fucker is telling the world that his "discovery," which no one's seen, causes The Underlying Condition! How the fuck did he prove it? Who did he kill to find out? How many Japanese? *The Monument* runs an occasional column on Saturday entitled "My Latest Discovery." So many of these haven't panned out that when a few readers mention this, the column is retitled "What I Am Working On." (Another reader suggested it should be called "What I Did on My Summer Vacation.") Matura Nelson Swife, who edits both science and cooking, or cookery, as she prefers to call it, for both *The Monument* and "our sister" TV station, MONU-TV, has a soft spot for "really good, solid scientists and their really good recipes," so Dodo's been on her show a lot.

Dodo's next present to the world, via Matura, includes this announcement:

"I sincerely and sadly believe that anyone can be a carrier of The Underlying Condition. I know that most of the cases are in homosexuals and drug folks and a few women, although I am not supposed to say that out loud, about the women, I mean. Our president doesn't like it known that our fair ladies might not always be so fair, and I'm going to get into deep trouble for telling you this. But you got to know, fellas and gals. You got to know. So you tell your congressperson, Hey, guys, you give that Geiseric more money, you hear? He needs all the money he can get to refine his discovery. In the meantime, I want all the fellas to keep it in their pants a little while longer. Dodo will take care of you. And ladies, you make sure he does keep it in his pants, you hear?"

It doesn't make *The Monument* but it does make the noon news on MONU-TV, which is good enough. This is the first semi-sort-of-official word put out that women are at risk for UC. (Dr. Mulch's five women in 1978 never made a dent on anyone's consciousness because for some unknown reason no journal published it even after he changed their sex to male.) No journal publishes this new news from Dodo either but MONU-TV is better than any old journal and certainly better than *The Prick*, where his last announcement of this female infection was buried. There he said that anal intercourse was probably the most effective way to catch UC and that straight women already have it, both of which are probably true. Grace certainly thought so. Interesting how a truth can often come by way of the strangest journeys.

He quickly follows this up with Hoidene and another national TV announcement, another "historic breakthrough," another "landmark discovery in the history of American science and medicine," another "major, major discovery by America's leading scientific genius" (Hoidene is getting good at this), "the cause of The Underlying Condition, KDG-One!" (She will shortly be reassigned to our consulate in Northern Ireland.)

No meeting in the White House.

By the next day there have been so many damage-control press releases barrel-assing out of NITS and the White House press offices saying, Whoa, this guy is way off base, he's unloading unproven "cures" on The American People. Even Velma Dimley is commanded by Clytemnestra Dunkelheim to "expose this research for the sham it is!" In no time flat the spin on Dodo's story is that the government is trying to deny that this shit is only happening to fairies when in fact it's been saying all along that it's only been happening to fairies. That's quite a spin. Who's got this kind of reach? And of course it works, because no one is interested in fairies. Anything to do with fairies is a killer.

I must get down to Jerry's office. This is when he changes his clothes to go jogging and showering. Don't scold. It's the only honest fun I'm having these days.

•

DEEP THROAT: He'll get the money as long as he's willing to be made out by his government to look like a fool. Which of course he's prepared to do because he doesn't know any other way to appear. Even Mother has said to me: "I enjoy watching this asshole in action. Unfortunately, I am uncertain how to get involved in this. While I am accustomed to cesspools, I see no way how to muck this one out. We must continue to follow Mr. Lemish's bouncing ball."

•

DANIEL: By now everyone in every lab in the world has seen Jacquie's report of her great discovery, JFV-1. Poopsie has "discovered" that JFV-1 is real and well and alive and living in Paris, France, and also in his lab in Franeeda County, Maryland, where Dodo now demands that it live. "This is *mine*! Mine! Mine! *Mine!*" Dodo walks the halls muttering this. Poopsie is ordered to "lose" all earlier pieces of paper detailing his work. Destroy all evidence! Poopsie, in the manner of the old country, had written everything down on little pieces of paper, which he'd thrown into a drawer.

English is not Poopsie's mother tongue. He is Romanian or Hungarian or Albanian or one of those. He speaks pretty good French and he's fucked Jacquie at some international conference. She even came to Dodo's lab to learn certain tricks, like separation, and folding. Dodo wondered if he should screw her on his lab floor but decided she wasn't smart enough for him. Jerry got a kick out of telling me this. I wonder who told him.

What is a chief lab assistant without any legal status in this country and a wife and two kids here and another two kids back in Hungary or Albania whom he also feeds and whose English is rotten at best to do? Poopsie is getting very confused. Dodo has "leaked" his KDG-1 and it's been written up in *NEJS*. Poopsie knows he's bad with English. But show him a formula or any lab result and he can bake a cake out of its ingredients, so to speak. Dodo had found him in Czechoslovakia, where he'd seen his work and hired him on the spot. Now he's baked that cake with Jacquie's isolates. Dodo gave him a nice cashmere sweater. Poopsie understands this much English: the French lady Dodo didn't fuck but Poopsie did has beaten his boss to "this great discovery," which Dodo is claiming as his, and Poopsie knows he and his should take the first plane home if only he had enough money to pay for it and for their life there ever after.

Meanwhile America can't utilize Jacquie's virus (for that is what it's now being officially called in France), or use her blood test that she's made to test its presence in the blood and that thereby and therein and therewith could save an awful lot of lives. I ask my patient Joe Madison at Kohlhaus Drumm why the pharms aren't after Jacquie for her test, and he says, "Are you kidding? What do the words *lawsuit lawsuit lawsuit* mean to you?"

"Why?" I ask him.

"Because Dodo now has his own blood test and is going to sue if her work is recognized."

"How can he sue?"

"Grow up, Jerusalem. Aren't you learning anything at NITS?"

BACK AND FORTHING WITH MORE PIECES OF THE PUZZLE

FRED: Emma told me that she diagnosed seventeen women last month, although this has been vigorously denied by COD and doubted by Omicidio. Herta Glanz told me that Bohunk called Mayor Goins and yelled, "There are no infected women in New York City! Do you hear me!" And the mayor turned to Herta and said, "I think we better not know anything for a while longer."

Jeff Schmalz, who's closeted and getting sick and is Flourtower's pet reporter, told me that at *The Truth* board meeting Dearie Fault turned to Jakie and asked, "Fairies are walking time bombs. Can we write about them now?" And Flourtower said flat out, "No." And Push Dunkelheim, he's the father, shook his head in agreement, while Pish, the son and heir apparent, who is supposedly being groomed to take over, was about to disagree when Push adjourned the meeting.

I asked Velma Dimley why she hadn't written anything about infected Factor VIII from Greeting killing gay men. She laughed out loud.

"What's so funny?" I asked her.

"You guys come up with such ridiculous plots. You sure are paranoid. You think the whole world is against you."

•

DANIEL: I saw my first case of some new "opportunistic" infection today that doesn't even have a name yet. No one at Mea Montezuma had ever seen anything like it, and they shipped him over. Jerry took one look at him and left the room. It's really too painful to look at. Skin all stretched and blown up, like a balloon in a science fiction movie. The bulging eyes on this kid were terrified and terrifying, oozing pus that was scarlet red. I tried to hold his hand, but he pulled it back. "Don't," he said, "you don't want to touch me." By the time I got back to my office, there was a call from Dye that this patient must be sent to Miseraria and no other cases of whatever it is are to be admitted to NITS. Of course, the kid was dead before they could get him out of NITS. Dye ordered his room and the hallways all the way to the emergency entrance fumigated, along with all the folks who had come anywhere near him: nurses, doctors, ambulance personnel, the housekeeping and kitchen staff. Fumigated! Jerry laughed. "We don't even know what the kid's got, so how does Dye know which compound to clean up with?"

•

FRED: Claude, the blond Jewish model, is in Invincible. Egypt Poo says it won't be long. Claude was really handsome. I don't know why it's sadder when they're handsome, but it is. Beauty is some kind of truth to weak men like me. Beauty is a horny man's fantasy. I tricked with him a bunch of times when he first got here from Paris. "I didn't know Jews could be so handsome and blond like you," I said to him. I went to see him. I couldn't believe he's the same person. Not only is he physically a wreck, but he's lost his power of speech. A deaf-mute maid on staff wants to teach him sign language. Egypt brought Monserrat in to look at him. She ran out in the hall and started to cry. She looked up at me and Egypt and said, "It's too horrible. I will send Rebby up to look at him." Interesting that she has such trust in Rebby as a doctor when she's so mean to him. She's told him he can't be co-chair of "their" organization that he started because "you present such a sloppy and unkempt appearance. I do not wish to expose our rich contributors to you." What's Miseraria? I don't remember any hospital named Miseraria.

•

DANIEL: Miseraria, along with Mea Montezuma, is part of Mater Nostra Dolorosa Medical Center, in Northeast D.C. Dr. Sister Grace's hangout. It was Sibley Hospital when we grew up. The Catholics bought it when the city shut it down because it was so decrepit. The city thought that the Church would remodel. It didn't and won't. It's where they put the worst cases in isolation, the incurables, the lepers, so the nuns can take care of them. Only the nuns won't take care of them.

Jerry, when cornered, says he's surprised by all these new OI strains emerging so quickly. Not Rebby. He's not surprised at all and can't understand why these what are now officially called "opportunistic infections" weren't being studied immediately. "Infections can be cured! This is what my boys are dying from!" He stopped by to say goodbye, having packed up here to go back to New York "at last!" Jerry wouldn't see him. "He's a nutcase." "Why? Because he won't leave you alone?" "You're getting too big for your britches." We're bantering like this more and more.

Gretta Lell will be in charge of one of our trial units for this new Greeting drug they've been able to cobble after somehow getting a copy of Jacquie's virus. There will now be six divisions, at six medical centers across the country, this group Jerry's putting together. None of them are doctors I've heard great things about. I said so to Jerry and he nodded and replied, "I have registered your disappointment." Wait till you get a load of Gretta Lell. "The twat that stalks South Beach," the Haitians are calling her.

There's my phone . . .

Tristan, a patient, just died. I've got to go.

DEEP THROAT CONFRONTS DR. DALE MULCH

"Dr. Dale Mulch," I said to him, "if what I hear is true, you make me ashamed we work in the same place."

"Why are you going after me?" he whined. He's a small man, perfectly formed but small. I was checking out a rumor I'd heard.

"Because you changed women into men."

The earliest UC cases he saw at Cornell were in women. By the time his report was finally published by the *JOD* they'd somehow become men.

"I was ordered to by Gobbel. 'Society must show its disapproval of such behavior,' he yelled at me."

"Did Jerry know all this?"

"Of course! He's my boss! Yours, too. We were interns together. Best buddies. He brought me here!"

I sighed. I had first encountered Linus Gobbel when he worked as education secretary and was trying to fire my daughter, who was fighting to get gay sexuality taught in schools. "If we don't watch out, these people will demand that the government's responsibility is to cure them," he told her. When UC reared its ugly head, from the White House he said it again and to Jerry: "If we don't watch out these men will demand the government cure them. Therefore, we will go on letting them spread this as fast as they can." Jerry said to me, "We keep our mouths shut about this."

"Isn't it our duty to save people?" I asked him.

"There you go again being a troublemaker. If I've told you once, I've told you a bunch of times to keep your mouth shut. We're not politicians. We're scientists. This is politics. If I blabbed about this, I'd be fired on the spot."

"Everything is politics."

"Shut the fuck up."

•

CONNOR: I am taking care of thirty-five guys as a GMPA crisis counselor. It really sucks, what's happening to us. It's Tommy who keeps me and us going. Fred seems to have finked out.

FROM SISTER GRACE'S NOTEBOOK

(IN LUCAS'S SAFE)

Dr. Daniel Elleder of the Czech Academy of Sciences, who has been studying the origins of UC, now believes it can be traced as far back as 60 million years. Shit on a fucking stick.

FADS?

Fredchen, I am not hearing the word *FADS* from you! Are you aware that Dr. Norbert Nutrobe is too incompetent a person to hold the directorship of such an important stuck-cog in this wheel of murder? Marine biology! He is a marine biologist. He is a specialist in whales! He then went on to obtain a degree in veterinary medicine. Your lives are in the hands of an animal doctor! Where do they find these people!

FRED'S JOURNAL

I'm walking up Seventh Avenue when I'm stopped—actually, it's Sam who is stopped by a giant schnauzer—by someone I didn't know. The guy looks straight at me and without even an introduction, launches in. "I want you to know how angry I am with you. I've lost my best friends. Because of hearing you speak and reading your articles I counted on you to do something. You haven't and that makes me furious, you hypocritical Mr. Loudmouth." I suddenly shouted at him, "Did it ever occur to you to do something about this yourself?" "Go fuck yourself," he shouted back and walked off dragging his schnauzer, who was hitting it off with Sam, who doesn't usually take to larger dogs.

●

EXT. GMPA OFFICE. DAY.
A troupe of protesters are holding an enormous banner that reads:
THANK YOU FOR DYING. IT'S THE RIGHT THING FOR YOU TO DO. *Tommy and Fred stand there looking at them.*

INT. TOMMY'S OFFICE.
Very makeshift. Tommy is showing Fred a package that he's opened. It contains several turds of shit.
TOMMY: We get one or two of these a week now. How does it feel, being back here?
FRED'S VOICE: To work on writing this history each day is very painful and haunting. I desire only to live long enough to finish this.

●

Poor baby. You have lost. I have won. And I continue to win and win and win some more. There is not a place in this world where I have not left my mark.

MOTHER ASKS DEEP THROAT
SOME GOOD QUESTIONS

It is becoming a perfect counterterrorism case. Much has been proceeding on the part of many parties each evidently in possession of something that each believes is only his.

Let us try to piece together a timeline.

Middleditch and Grebstyne discover in a closet at NITS an old formula from the '60s that has components that match what dumb Dodo is now calling his.

Middleditch turns this formula over to Von Greeting at Greeting-Dridge to get whatever this is out there fast.

This young woman in France has already discovered the virus of The Underlying Condition.

Dodo disputes the French discovery, claiming that it's his.

But Von Greeting has been developing ZAP long before he'd seen Dodo's dirms from NITS. He had microscopy photos of the UC virus presumably discovered by the young woman in Paris.

How did Von Greeting get these photos so early?

And since you tell me ZAP is a piece of shit, why is Greeting now commencing to promote it? Surely Von must know of its deficiencies.

I have now lost a dozen of my best operatives. I am finding this not only sad, but painful. I was very fond of several of them. As I am of you as well.

What do you think might be coming next?

Are we prepared for it?

PEOPLE WHO NEED PEOPLE

Adreena Schneeweiss called me!

"When are you free to start work on my script?"

Oh, Adreena, Adreena, may we make the bestest movie ever made!

We will get this awful and sad and tragic story out there quickly! You will be my conduit to the world. At last our story will be told! If you make it, every one of your zillion fans will see it, which means the whole wide world.

I've forgiven her for wasting the years since she bought my play while she made an awful movie about whores.

DODOGATE CONTINUING

DANIEL: Dodo is not shy about accusing Jacquie. "Jacqueline Françoise worked in my lab and she stole my shit and took it back to France and now she calls it hers! I taught her how to do it! I taught her how to make the fuckers fuck!" Gaston Nappe tries to cooperate every stage of the way, or so he tirelessly maintains, "but your Dodo is a big-time cheater." No journal in America will publish the French studies, or the letter from Gaston claiming "foul play." Yet all journals are competing to publish Dodo. The longer this unresolved resolution of ownership goes on, the more determined each side is to WIN. Forget the saving of lives. All these delaying tactics—and others about to commence—can only take a long time.

At our next mass meeting Dr. Dye announces, "I am pleased with the progress of this plague," which is a strange way of describing things. He was called to a special meeting in the White House with Ruester and Manny Moose and Dr. Nutrobe. No one knows what they talked about.

Dye announces that he's decided to immediately launch drug trials that will revolutionize the treatment of this serious illness, "and may this be the first of many successful trials that NITS and Dr. Omicidio will supervise, beginning with this most promising ZAP from Greeting." Von, of course, is in attendance; it's been a while since we've seen him here. He's beaming and gives us that old clasped hand above the head prizefighter pose. Grodzo is not here.

I can see that Jerry doesn't appear happy. I asked him why he wasn't brimming over with happiness now that he was officially in charge of NITS. "You're a Jew. You should understand. It's tempting fate. Catholics worry about that too."

Sure enough, the next day *The Monument* and the wire services have headlines about "NITS forging ahead on UC treatment front," with a quote from Manny Moose "wishing them well." I forgot to mention—it's proving harder for me to get all the step-by-steps in coherent order—that it has now been definitely "proved" that Dodo's "virus" and Jacquie's virus are indeed one and the same (thank you, Rebby), and Dodo has denied this vehemently in every outlet that comes to him, which are quite a few. He's not being hailed as a hero, but he certainly is still a celebrity. And we're not allowed to talk about this! This from our attorney general, Mr. Moose. Each side blaming the other for why this might or might not be so and to claim that the American lab was contaminated by the French isolates or for the French to maintain the reverse . . . well, Deep Throat "guarantees this fight is going to prove endless." "Lawsuits, lawsuits, lawsuits," as my friend Joe Madison prophesied.

And the testing of ZAP before it's settled is really not very kosher. Even I know that. The more I'm learning, the less I'm liking.

But here comes the whopper. Monserrat Krank got her Binky to negotiate with the presidents of both France and the United States to sign an agreement that the UC virus was a joint discovery, just so that at last work could be started testing people to see if they're infected. Gree Bohunk convinced Purpura to get Junior tested, just in case, to make sure . . . (Ianthe found this out.) She used Jacquie's test. Three years this all took. More than three. Three-plus years wasted from when Jacquie first made her discovery. It turns out she'd prepared her test then as well, waiting and ready to go! But nothing's been signed yet. Dodo won't sign over any of "his" royalties for "his" test.

Those two words, *blood test*, will still take at least another year to be more than words. Both Dodo and Jacquie demand that, signed international agreement or not, only their test be recognized and used. There will be a fortune to be made in royalties from this test, and everyone on both sides knows this. Enter more armies of lawyers. Well, they've never actually been away. But at least we have a drug to test on sick people. No one knows much about this ZAP.

WARD F

DANIEL: Jerry took me, or rather he marched ahead and sort of allowed me to follow him, into the NITS UC ward, Ward F. It requires going through several locked doors and guarded passageways. I wonder why there are guards now, particularly since this remote place appears to be so empty of activity. It's in a wing most people here don't even know exists. This doesn't mean anything. NITS is very big and winding and full of corridors with nothing but letters and numbers to identify them. When you consider how many hundreds of doctors there are here, maybe thousands, and how many illnesses are meant to be of interest, ignorance of so much of what's going on isn't surprising. It's not like a university where at least at your indoctrination you're given a tour and map. I've talked to nurses who have never seen any part of NITS but the stations they work at.

Jerry unlocked the last door. Ward F has thirty private rooms. Every one is empty. In a *Monument* story this morning, and on the Sunday morning TV talk shows, Jerry is saying, "I have been studying UC in patients since before 1981." That's an outright lie.

Jerry takes me to a large double-door refrigerator and opens it. Its shelves are stacked with bottles of ZAP. "These are for the trials Dr. Dye referred to. Just so you know, this stuff is shit. And we have to give it to guys to prove statistically how it works. We need a baseline entry-level drug to build on, to work from when a new one comes along to combine it with. I need someone honest like you around. We're going to have to make a lot up as we go along. I hope you're up to it.

"But in the meantime we can't start our trials until we know if all the applicants are not only UC-positive but healthy as well. G-D won't allow any sick people to be on any ZAP trial."

"We're really going to learn a lot from that. How do you know ZAP is shit?"

"First drugs always are."

"Don't you not like the smell of all this? You won't be able to say 'it's not my department.'"

"That's what I've got you for."

"What's that mean? To lie for you or to cover up for you, or what?"

"A day at a time."

WHITE HOUSE MEETING

(THE RUESTER LIBRARY: TOP-SECRET/CLASSIFIED/ EMBARGOED DIVISION)

In attendance:
President Ruester
Mrs. Ruester
Mr. Manny Moose
Mr. Linus Gobbel
Dr. Stuartgene Dye

Redacted by:
Patti Montgomery
Sec. to Mrs. Ruester

Mr. Moose asked Dr. Dye, "I ask you once again. What is taking so long?"

Dr. Dye: "What?"

Mr. Moose: "For more people to come down with this shit."

Mr. Gobbel: "When I was in Africa twenty-odd years ago they were falling dead all over the place. I was told it was only a question of time before it spread all over the world."

Dr. Dye: "Told by whom?"

Mr. Gobbel: "That's none of your business."

Mr. Moose: "I ask again. Why is it taking so long?"

Dr. Dye: "I ask again. Why is *what* taking so long?"

Mrs. Ruester: "For all the sick fairies to die from this . . . shit!"

Dr. Dye: "I would say they are doing a pretty good job of it. On a day-to-day and month-to-month basis. *(To Mr. Gobbel:)* Why wasn't America told about what was happening in Africa?"

Mr. Gobbel: "That's none of your business either. Anyway, that was Nasturtium's bailiwick, and as you know, he's dead."

Dr. Dye: "It just could have helped us get our ducks in order much earlier."

President Ruester: "Ducks? What about ducks? I used to hunt ducks with great pleasure when I was a boy."

Dr. Dye: "You know we're starting trials on a first potential treatment? You gave us your permission to commence, overriding a thus far lack of approval from FADS."

Mr. Gobbel: "You led us to believe this treatment wouldn't work and would make them die faster while making us look on the ball."

Dr. Dye: "Dr. Omicidio, who is in charge of these trials, is doing his best to get them up and running. We could accomplish this with more dispatch if we had some money from Congress. They're pretty much starving us to death."

Mr. Moose: "Patti, send me a memo to speak to our friends in Congress."

Mrs. Ruester: "Everything's taking too f'ing long!"

Dr. Dye: "I'll bear that in mind."

President Ruester: "Can I go now?"

Mrs. Ruester: "Sweetums, you know I only bother you when it's important."

Mr. Moose: "Okay, meeting adjourned. Keep us posted, Dr. Dye."

Mr. Gobbel: "Yes, keep us posted."

Dr. Dye: "Slyme had been doing that before he was fired. He came to our meetings to convey the president's wishes. He got a bit overexcited and I questioned his usefulness."

Mrs. Ruester: "I said Manny Slyme was a drip. I'm glad I got rid of him."

President Ruester: "I liked Chevvy. He makes me laugh."

Mrs. Ruester: "Well, you're wrong. Listen to Mommy."

Mr. Moose: "Once again, this meeting's adjourned."

President Ruester: "If we give them free treatment they will fuck more."

Mrs. Ruester: "Half a tick. Your trials must not include any women."

Dr. Dye: "Trials rarely include women."

Mrs. Ruester: "I will not have the women of my country besmirched."

Dr. Dye: "Yes. I mean no."

Mrs. Ruester: "Confine it to the fairies. Shut that Dr. Dodo up. My friend Bill Buckley is going to announce that all the sick fairies should be tattooed."

President Ruester: "How are Bill and Pat Buckley? Give them my love."
Mrs. Ruester: "Have we made ourselves clear?"
Dr. Dye: "Couldn't be clearer."
Mrs. Ruester: "Now this meeting is adjourned."
President Ruester: "The way to stop crime is to just go out there and stop it."
December 17, 1985

DO YOU REMEMBER
REBEKKAH REGINA PLOTNICK?

In her room at Doris Hardware's, Jinx Seeley sits down on the middle of the rug she made when she was at Tripp Lake Camp for rich Jewish girls. Maine was deserted then. It was an extraordinary experience to go somewhere so beautiful and so far away and so empty of adults. The rug is long and oval, fully fifteen feet long and adeptly made, nothing to be ashamed of. It was bigger by far than any girl had ever made at Tripp Lake, and the other girls made fun of her and her big rug, taunting her that she'd never finish it by the end of the season. The mad Russian lady who was the arts-and-crafts counselor, Madame Vera, said it could be done but nobody listened to her except Jinx, or Becky as she was then. Rebekkah Regina Plotnick. Of the Washington Plotnicks. Her father had made an awful lot of money selling expensive fur coats. She found Madame Vera's voice intoxicating, like the sounds of the trains in Union Station that said, I'm going far away. Yes, the rug is still with Jinx, but who knows where Madame Vera is, or any of those other Tripp Lake girls who were so haughty. Or the kids from her druggie period when she called herself Mary Jane. Once in a while she used to call Fifi Nordlinger, because Fifi was still a real person in the outside world to her, to ask what had happened to all the others, and Fifi would give her a rundown on Heidi and Marianne and Susu and the others, and wind up pointedly with "And where are *you*?" (She doesn't know that Fifi is dead now.) They all sounded like girls still, with so little to be proud of. Once they were proud of their poppas' money and their big homes with recreation rooms, rich Jewish girls ready to marry rich Jewish boys or Jewish boys who would become rich if you guessed right. On one end of the rug stands a king-sized bed without legs, its box spring just plopped down on the floor, and beside it a hard-backed wooden chair, and a few books, and a solitary floor lamp with a lovely white glass bowl of a shade and a base of solid pine that she'd cut and fashioned from the tree outside her cabin at Tripp Lake because she knew that in some way she'd been happy at Tripp Lake in Maine and when she left she'd never come back to the world of girls' camps, or at least not that kind of girls' camp, or been so more or less happy. Now this is her room, her cabin bunk, and she wonders when it will be time to leave here, too, knowing she'll never come back. She wonders only for a second when that might be.

There is a knock on the door and Claudia comes in. The two of them sit on the bed, on the Amish quilt. Claudia takes Jinx's hand and both hold on tightly.

"We can find a way to stay safe," they both seem to say to each other.

So far they've felt safe at Doris's. Claudia said that would change when they'd been here long enough.

Now Jinx confides in Claudia, her best and only friend.

"Mordy Masturbov has asked me to marry him."

IN WHICH WE LEARN OF THE DEATH OF CLAUDIA, AMONG OTHER THINGS

It's Peter Ruester's second term and Buster Punic is still not ambassador to Anywhere.

A woman's body is found under heaps of leaves, both leaves and body beginning to smell of moldering. In her faille navy purse, which her fingers clutch, is more than $500,000 in large bills, thousands and ten thousands, and she wears expensive pearls and diamond clips on her torn dress, a famous French designer's, and beside her is a mink coat—this lady was rich. On this beautiful afternoon, the cool crisp air after days of gray brings out strollers and kids playing football, two of whom, locked in a tight embrace not dissimilar to physical passion, both cradling the football as if it's something important, worth fighting for, roll over and over in the rotting leaves, and soon there are three, though one of them is dead.

There is much commotion and policemen are quickly in evidence, many of them, because police are cheap in Washington, as plentiful as the daily murders and the unraked leaves in this park, which is called Rock Creek and usurps huge portions of expensive real estate that Buster Punic, on happier days, along with other rich men like Abe Masturbov, would prefer was not a part of the public sector. He, like these many others in this town, is already prospering even more mightily because of Peter Ruester. Gobbel has told *The Wall Street Journal* that the economy is worse than ever, opening the way to tax raises for the poor and reductions for the rich. Buster has always been rich beyond any imagination's greed. Peter Ruester promised to make all his faithful friends even richer. He is keeping his promise, in spades. The Ruesters have made Washington the social place to be. It is impossible to find a suitable place to live. Rock Creek Park is a waste of good land. Any good Republican will tell you that.

He is terrified, Buster is, that his semen is inside the dead woman. He knows that recent semen is not so difficult to detect inside a dead woman as once upon a time. Isn't there a test available? Isn't there now always a test available when you don't want one? He stands in the woods adjoining this high and level spot, watching from his hiding place. How long has he been here? He knows he must be out of his mind to be anywhere near here now. But this murderer cannot leave the scene of his crime.

Buster has many connections with policemen, with these policemen and their superiors and their superiors, right on up to God. There isn't anyone Buster can't get to. He hides and watches these cops playing policemen in Rock Creek Park, holding diamond clips up to the light to see if they sparkle, if they're real, discerning correctly that the answer to both is yes. Buster watches them as his dog, a huge Alpine savior who knows how to direct drool the way a human can spit, lies at his feet, his own heart heaving in labor because he loves his master and knows his master's upset. Though this is a lovely park and usually filled with people enjoying it, something about what's going on right now says, Go Away, Go Home. Now Dobermans and German shepherds are arriving, the cops have called for dogs, and also men in rubber suits with masks and tanks of chemicals to spray on everything to seal in the truth. To get out of here Buster must break cover, he must pretend he's walking his dog, holding the leash firmly lest confrontations between rival breeds occur. So he walks away, down a path, though he will turn back up where it joins another walkway, one that will return him to a perimeter where he still can see her from another part of this forest.

These policemen know that Buster Punic is close to High Places. While attending to the duties of uncovering and studying and photographing and removing the body of this beautiful dead woman they do not look at Buster; they just note that he's there, knowing who he is and that he's connected and that he'll have all the alibis in the world, should he be "involved." Most of all, they know that he's dangerous. And that if Buster and his connections want it to be, it will be, and whatever it is they uncover and photograph will be irrelevant.

"Dangerous," in white Washington, has different connotations than in cities like New York and Chicago and Los Angeles, where guns and torture—the more visible expressions of danger—prevail. Danger in those other places is violent. Bodies are found in rivers and stuffed down chutes for laundry or garbage; they are hurled from roofs, dismembered, pumped full of drugs; they are found at the bottom of bodies of water, weighted down by cement, or lying in alleyways. Danger, in white Washington, among those in high places, is more banal. Rarely are people shot or killed or murdered, although in recent years there have been several "unsolved" very upmarket exceptions. Who remembers Anna Undershaft? Polly van Euhling? Mary Pinchot Meyer? It's the women who remain unsolved. Where did they go? Sometimes a body is found, as in Meyer's case. Or in Marilyn Monroe's, if we dare to throw in her mysterious demise far from Washington, but not really so far at all. Men tend to be disappeared to another country, but they are usually dispatched alive. They may be exiled from the kingdom, but their mouths stay shut . . . at least for a while; and after a while revelations make no difference; no one is interested in last week's heinous deeds, for they have been supplanted by more capital cavortings. Whittaker Chambers got away with it and Alger Hiss went to jail. If Hiss had been a woman he would have been executed like Ethel Rosenberg. Anyway, no one in Washington believes anything anymore. Or rather, they believe it all and find it unbelievable. The result is that so few believe *in* anything, really. In the end, though, it is just as dangerous to tell the truth here as anywhere else.

So white people have to be extra-special careful in white Washington. If you are important but not that important you will only lose your job, which is invariably connected to pensions and health insurance, bonuses and stock options; or your promised promotion is denied and you find yourself selling your house in Virginia and moving farther out, West Virginia perhaps (the state, not the avenue). But they have to find you first!

Most dangerous white people in high places who've done something wrong are rarely found out. And everyone knows that.

Buster watches several of the cops pocket diamond brooches. Only one of six—they were a set of six from Bulgari and he'd bought them for her in Rome—remains on that part of her dress that both suppressed and raised her breasts—they were lovely breasts. The officer in charge, a captain (how did they know to send so high-ranking an investigator, and so quickly?

Buster worries), even caresses them not so accidentally as he takes off her pearls, and holds them dramatically (the pearls, not the breasts, though he licks his lips unconsciously, like a dog wanting a treat) so that everyone can see him drop them into an official envelope. At this moment, Buster's Alpine mini-bear breaks loose and runs for the mink coat and buries his face in it, rolling his head from side to side, caressing the mink coat with his huge head and snout as if it is the face of a lover, emitting little short whines of pain.

Destroy evidence—or don't leave any around to begin with. Important people in Washington know to do this. (Important people everywhere since time began know to do this.) Investigators of scandal spend more time trying to unravel false defenses than they spend calculating the damages or estimating the fallout from the crimes. There is always someone to grab at a soapbox opportunity to preach about Right and Wrong instead of just being practical. Actual accusations are rarely made in Washington, and then very carefully because it is a vindictive town. Even 100 percent certitude is not good enough. Do you really want to open yourself up to charges and threats from who knows where and when and forever? Not in this town, you don't. The government of The American People is here.

The police captain tries to put himself in the place of the murderer. Of course it was murder. She's all in one piece. Must be poison. Could be suicide. In high heels in Rock Creek Park? He knows her face. Beautiful face. One of Doris's girls, he wagers. Cold as ice, they say. There have got to be lots of big guys who want this one dead. Handle the evidence carefully. Handle the report of the evidence even more carefully. Don't say anything too definite. Leave holes for alibis to crawl through. Every dumbah cop knows that. What's around? Diamonds. Pearls. Mink. Can't make it look like a robbery. His instincts tell him this is going to be a juicy one. In all the papers. Lots of TV. He straightens his tie. New mayor's black and under pressure from his people not to let the white guys get away with everything. He may be forced to solve this one. Find the killer. Find the motive. Shit. Such a task once filled him with eagerness. Fucking shit. He already knows the outcome. This town will close its mouth in unison. Big-time Washington scandal, everyone gets lockjaw. He remembers Mary Meyer. James Jesus assigned him to that one too. Half the women in Georgetown knew about Mary Pinchot Meyer and how she was feeding Jack Kennedy LSD that she got personally from Timothy Leary himself up in Millbrook, New York. Mary was going to turn world leaders on and overthrow the whole warfare system. "Make love, not war, Jack," she is said to have begged him in her own drug-induced state. That was her mission. She was found dead on a towpath in George-town. Her diary was located and burned on the spot by James Jesus Angle-ton, head of a new CIA division (or was it still the OSS? who remembers?), and a closet homosexual, which in this case meant . . . what, exactly? The captain knew Mother was gay because Angleton propositioned him. He was amazed how often men in government suits propositioned him. That Mary Meyer lady, he went over her garage with a fine-tooth comb. She wanted the whole world to be happy. Garage filled with every book on enlightenment and peace through chemicals you could find. And Angleton was her father-in-law, and he was in the garage together with him. They were on all fours pulling more books on getting high out from under old cars and shit, and Angleton, clumsy bastard, just grabbed him to him and tried to kiss him. It was all very sad because he himself was gay and knew what the man must be going through. He figured Angleton knew about him. Didn't the CIA know everything? "Please, sir, I am happily married," he said, which was true, sort of. The CIA knew more about LSD than anyone. They helped develop it, though he wasn't sure why. They say JFK was about to dismantle the CIA. Hoover was facing retirement and knew he had to find a big issue to avoid this. So Edgar and James Jesus both wanted JFK dead. Some in the CIA always said Lyndon Johnson was behind Kennedy's assassination. He won-ders if this lady here with the diamonds fits in . . . where? You think things all fit together in D.C., in one gigantic puzzle of a million little pieces? They probably do, but we'll never find out.

Well, Mr. Big Cop Captain will see who calls in. How many telephone messages from unlikely callers will be waiting on his desk to tell him whether he has to solve this case or bury it?

Buster watches them heave her body onto a stretcher and realizes, as the dress rises up in the wind, that her sweet pussy is staring at him for the last time, a fleeting glance at longing unfulfilled, like all of the other times he wanted her and she wouldn't comply, and he wants her now so much his balls hurt, yes, he'd fuck her dead, like he finally fucked her last night, his greedy appetite at last fulfilled. When once she called him a pig he swatted her hard across those breasts and bruised them, and she punished him good for that, no pussy period, yes, he'd fucked her dead right on this heath, and he has tears in his eyes as they take her away, and Bismarck, his dog, whines loudly as his master grabs his choke collar and pulls hard to shut up the whine.

After the police and their entourage leave, a few civilians mill around; a few kick the leaves for possible further diamond droppings.

"Why are you crying? Did you know her? She was very beautiful," a little girl holding a teddy bear says to Buster. "If you knew her, shouldn't you go with her and tell the policemen what you know? That's what always happens on TV." Her father takes her hand to lead her away. "I'm sorry," he mumbles to Buster. "But Daddy, he knows something and he's going to get away free."

Buster lumbers down the hill. Buster is burly and bull-like and usually he walks tall. He's proud that he's so rich, that he's Peter Ruester's best friend, that his wife, Carlotta, is Purpura's best friend. They are, the four of them, best friends, oldest chums. They have a lock on this town, this country, this world. He thinks of his cock. He has a huge cock. This town is full of huge cocks and huge fortunes, and behind thick walls of expensive homes with tiny windows curtained thick, how great to have both. His penis terrifies Carlotta. She only saw it once, on their wedding night. It's one of those famous D.C. stories told over and over at D.C. men's locker rooms. "You think you're going to put that in me?" She laughed that first and only time she saw it. They had their two kids by artificial insemination. For a few years she was the only person in the world he wanted to put it in. He hadn't been ashamed of being Jewish, or at least he hadn't thought he'd been—his ancestors, after all, were among the first Jews to settle in New England—but when he married the Catholic Carlotta, he converted for her and his Jewish roots were never mentioned again. He was happy to ditch them, even if he couldn't ditch the big nose, big ears, cut cock, all the fingerprints that gentiles use to nail Jews.

He's hard in his pants now, thinking of her, dead or not, thinking of her. He walks faster through the woods, stumbling down the hill toward the main road below. Claudia thought he was handsome. You are a handsome man. He would take her to foreign films starring men who she said looked like him: big hulking blond bears, a kind of actor more popular abroad. American male movie stars are all small, or perhaps *short* is the better word when talking only of height. Peter was tall, and he once confided in Buster that he'd not become a really big star because he wasn't short enough for all the actresses. Along with Manny and Purpura, Carlotta was furious when she heard he'd been seen publicly with Claudia. That was the only time he found Carlotta remotely interesting: when she was furious. Sometimes he hit her to shut her up. Once he slipped her a mickey and fucked her up her ass. She liked it! When the mickey wore off she kept screaming at him. God, could she scream! "Get that goddamned pipe away from me!" she screamed that it scared her to think anything so big and alive could be inside her. Why do we get ourselves into marriages like this? Why do we get married at all? If he were only younger, he wouldn't have to get married. It was okay not to get married now. He could have had even more of Claudia. His cock gets harder and harder until it's painful to walk. Get home. Get home fast.

His house isn't far from the park. It's her house, really. The house he bought for her that she refused to live in. She always went back to Doris's. Somehow, running and stumbling, he gets himself to the front door and finds a key, his hands trembling. He enters. Carlotta would have brushed the burrs from his tweeds, made him wipe his feet. "Did you have a nice walk in the park, dear?" She wouldn't care about the blood on his underpants. She'd be happy if he were dead. She'd be the richest widow in Washington whose husband got his dong bloody from jerking off too passionately over a hooker who'd also slept with Jerusalems, Lucas and Stephen and . . . Only Doris knows for sure who else, but the who elses are no doubt a Who's Who in D.C. His cock is harder than ever and his eyes are pouring tears and the strange combination of sex and sorrow makes him churn inside. He finds himself in a dark corner, and he cries standing up, facing the wall, like a bad boy.

And there he whips out his huge cock still sore and bloody from using it and he pulls at it, jerks it off again so brutally that it will hurt for days, jerks it and tugs it and punishes it, pretending she's down there on the floor, lying down under him, looking up at him, still with him, never leaving him, I will always remember you! I will always love you! AAAACH! He collapses in his own come, mixed with the blood of his cruel ministrations and that last tortured, torturing orgasm with Claudia last night. It was his birthday and she finally let him inside her.

Bismarck comes in and stands beside him, coughing and drooling and finally spitting out a diamond clip for his master. On the back is engraved the date they first made love, if love you could call it (that's what he calls it now), if what bonded them could ever be called love. Yes, that's what he calls it now, and will always call it as long as he lives. Yes, I loved her! Goddammit, I loved her! I would have married her if Carlotta hadn't . . . He'd married Carlotta in California: the wife gets half of everything. Half of Buster is half more than Buster is willing to relinquish. No! I would have married Claudia! We didn't need my money to be happy. We had love! God, how fast myths begin. Love? Before now he called his obsession with her torture, agony. I can't get rid of her. She's worse than crack. She'd let him love her. An ice queen bestowing knighthood on the morganatic. He knew she fucked with many others; she was a hooker, for Christ's sake. "Do you enjoy it with me?" he once asked her. "Of course not" was the answer they both knew she would give. And she gave it.

Buster briefly wonders if he should inform the White House. Purpura won't like it. Dredd Trish, the snotty vice president, hates him as only a rich well-born gentile snob can hate a richer well-born Jew. The vice president's father and grandfather had worked for the Nazis. Brinestalker, who'd worked in Berlin, had confirmed it, "for a fact."

Buster rushes to Doris Hardware's. He cried in his house, and now he cries driving to Doris's. This is the time of day when he would have been with Claudia and tried to have sex with her. He's got a gaping hole inside him. He'd thought he'd be relieved of it. But he's never missed anyone before. The feeling surprises him. He's overwhelmed by the notion that he's crying. There's not a human being he's ever cried for. Carlotta the unfuckable? That's every marriage he knows. All the jokes in all the locker rooms aren't about wives but other women. You find yourself a Claudia only if you're lucky. Otherwise jerk off alone. Rent porn films and jerk off alone or stop and let it shrivel into old age like Peter.

He's terrified of his future.

Claudia always asked him, If you're so uncomfortable with Carlotta, why do you persist? Then marry me, Buster begged. Don't be silly. Her favorite expression. And then she'd touch his face softly. No, he can't understand why he stays with Carlotta, who gives him no joy whatsoever. Men think Carlotta gives him joy because she keeps a lavish house superbly well. And Carlotta is Purpura's best friend. Which means a lot of invitations to the White House and everywhere else. But Purpura is a bitch and Peter is stupid and their parties are boring because everybody kisses so much ass, pretending they're all good enough to run the world. He knows that he's just a billionaire who wants to spend all his time with a hooker in a whorehouse. He never considered that pretending at all.

Only now the hooker's dead.

Buster hopes like hell the tape is still in her rooms. He's on that tape.

Eating out Claudia. It was sort of awkward watching his naked bulky body lapping her up, but it's a precious memento, this tape, because it's all he'll have of her now. He can count on one hand the number of times she let him inside her in all these years. And he tried not to look at the attorney general, also on the tape. Who is fucking someone. And there were other fucks going on, several members of the White House staff fucking several women Claudia brought in for the night, a couple of them black. For these, the attorney general thanked Buster especially. What a joke. Moose couldn't keep it up and couldn't keep it in. It kept plopping out.

Why had they made the tape? Why had they done that? Buster doesn't want to think about it. Manny made it for the president!

What if it falls into the wrong hands? How many copies did Manny Moose make? It could destroy a lot of people, like an atomic bomb.

Doris keeps a safe house. No one gets anything on Doris. But this tape was filmed at some house in the woods.

"And they won't!" Doris said when he told her about it. "I've got something on every one of them, or on somebody related to every one of them. It's a small town. It's a small country. Hell, it's a small world. The people who actually *do* things aren't that many. They all know each other. One way or another they're connected, like the Mississippi and its tributaries. Yes, I'm a completely safe woman. There aren't many of us. Jackie Kennedy was safe, before she married Onassis, after which nobody cared. She'd achieved the ultimate sellout. Madame Chiang Kai-shek, I think perhaps she was safe, though it's difficult to tell with Oriental women. There's always the chance of inscrutable danger, like in those Anna May Wong movies. Anyway, nobody remembers Madame Chiang Kai-shek. She was very important in this town once. I guess Lucille Ball is safe. At least she's funny. God, how I wish I were funny. Purpura is not funny. Why am I thinking of Lucille Ball?"

She is babbling on. And she knows it. She's an old lady now. She didn't need all this as a capstone for her great and profitable career. They are sitting in her living room. She's trying not to talk about what happened, what's in the air of this house, along the garden pathways, in the bedrooms and suites of the other women. She's redone her living room, using Swish Turtell, who specializes in chintz and overstuffed furniture and big-based lamps with huge shades. "It's known as the British Style." She sighs and plumps up the pillows behind her on some enormously long and flowery chaise; she sighs and wipes tears from her red haggard eyes. She fears that whatever the reason for this death, somewhere, in the heart of something—this house, this calling, Doris herself—there is some due cause that might implicate her in guilt. She's never killed off anyone before. Even the African girls from Madame Rose were nipped in the bud by being married off.

"The British Style. The British in Washington have always been among my best customers. The Brits have the most fucked-up of all sex lives . . ." And she's off. Buster sits there. Shut up, he wants to say to her, stop yakking. "The French—there's no rule of thumb with the French. One does not generalize about the French . . . Yes, that must be the point."

Buster waits to see if she will finally say, okay, let's talk about her. But she isn't allowing it, though her voice is now harsher, the eyes more red than wet. "I wouldn't mind catering to Aussies exclusively. No fuss, no bother, nothing too out of the ordinary . . . Which leaves our beloved countrymen." Now she is crying again. Doris is not the kind of woman one expects to cry. Ordinarily she can be counted on to be the brick who keeps everything from getting messy.

"The American male. What about him? He can be everything, anything, and nothing. Our men are the weakest, least trustworthy, most cowardly.

"BUSTER!"

Finally she's run out of steam and screamed his name and he feels pain everywhere inside him. They rush to embrace each other.

"I want to go to her room," he says. "It's a demand, not a request. You stay here."

She watches him go. She's been through Claudia's rooms carefully. Her cop contacts called as soon as Claudia's body was found. Claudia was here for seventeen years. Claudia came here like a girl goes into a nunnery. She just wanted to get away from the world. That was my reason, too. It doesn't make sense to everyone but it makes sense to some. Claudia understood exactly what she understood. Claudia understood it all.

In Claudia's suite Buster starts to cry again. He knows its feel and smell and he can walk around it in the dark without bumping into things. He knows the patterns of the flowers on all the chintz as if he planted them. He gets down on his knees, tears running down his cheeks uncontrollably, and pulls open the bottom drawer of her biggest bureau and starts crudely yanking soft clothing items aside.

"Buster, if you're looking for a souvenir, tell me what you want and I'll give it to you. But don't muss." Doris is there bending down beside him, then both of them sitting on the floor, she wiping his cheeks dry with her tiny handkerchief, then she crying too, then both of them holding each other tightly for a moment or two.

"I was only looking to see if there's anything that might lead the suspicious to me."

"I've been through everything. There are only some clothes, some underwear, some shoes. There's nothing else."

"Have the police been here?"

"Yes, but I wouldn't let them come in here. I showed them another room."

She leaves him alone again. He looks everywhere and finds nothing. He throws himself on her bed. He buries his face and nose and tongue and teeth in the pillows. He pretends she is there. He tosses and turns and tears off his clothes and holds the pillows to his naked body as if they are her, rolling around and practically strangling himself in her sheets, pumping and pumping his already woefully manhandled member until he has the most painfully erotic orgasm of his life. He gasps for breath. "Don't leave me!" He screams so loudly that the whole house must have heard him.

In several weeks, Buster is appointed ambassador to Great Britain.

THAT TAPE

The tape starring Buster Punic and Claudia Webb and Manny Moose and an astounding assortment of supporting players cavorting through imaginative scenes in delicious costumes is being lapped up by the president of the United States, Peter Ruester, who is sitting in his rocking chair in his darkened office (there is never any work that takes much time; his "team" already knows he does nothing but nap), leaning back, rocking, holding his long rope of a flaccid cock in his hand, still hoping he can get it up again, Please God, one more time before I die.

But this is really too funny. Manny Moose under a girl in leather! Manny!

Peter hoots so loudly his secretary outside can't imagine what in the world's so funny.

Manny has just signed an ordinance prohibiting the public sale of pornography. No more *Sexopolis*. No more *Playboy* and *Screw* and *Hustler*. The world will be a cleaner place.

Manny turns around and watches as that young Dumster fucks the ass of some voluptuously tushied bimbo. He looks at the camera and gives a lascivious wink as if to say to Old Peter, Remember when we could do that, too?

This makes the president a little harder. His hand swings into immediate action. So rarely does the blood reach his cock these days that when a driblet of it does, he knows he has work to do. His eyes stay glued on Manny Moose and Manny watching Dumster's huge cock, and the memories of the president of the United States go back to their young days out west together, when Peter was running for his first office and Jules Stein—the Big Jew, Peter calls him now that he's president and Jules is dead—sent him Manny Moose to manage everything and Peter Ruester and Manny Moose fell in love and became lovers for a few days and fucked their young asses off—goodness, we were handsome young men!—and whoops, I've just climaxed, and look, I even have a few drops of gism still in me. Manny, I love you still.

He pulls out his handkerchief and wipes the few drops away and sticks his old cock back in his presidential jeans and pulls his cardigan closer around his body. He is still chortling with pleasure. He goes to the phone at his huge clean uncluttered desk and presses the button for the attorney general.

"Manny, I just did it again!"

"Did what?" The squeaky voice of Manny Moose pierces the air with a worried sound. "You haven't gone and done anything half-cocked?"

"No, I did this one full-cocked."

"Petie, what are you talking about?"

"I just got my first boner in years and I jerked off and I even came a few drops and it was all because of you. You can still do it to me. Yes, you really can." He shakes his head from side to side with that disarming grin of mock disbelief that has won his country's heart.

"You got a boner? I'm so glad!" The voice has lowered substantially, but its enthusiasm is real. "I'm sorry I wasn't there." It is a sweet admission.

"Yes, and I got it looking at you in some sex orgy. They all seem to be heteros. Manny, what were you doing with them?"

Now the voice is back to its hysterical high. "Sweetie, I want you to listen to me carefully. That tape is very dangerous and extremely valuable and it could destroy your reputation for all time. Keep it hidden where only you know where it is and I'll be there immediately! Do you hear me?"

"I love it when you order me around. I'll be here, sweetie. Hurry, hurry. I love it when you call me Petie."

•

DANIEL: Do you remember Arnold Botts from Masturbov Gardens?
FRED: Vaguely. Wasn't he the creep?
DANIEL: The dangerous creep. He's become a very important person. He's starting up a pharm.

TIME, GENTLEMEN, TIME

Doris allowed herself to feel and show her terror. She trembled uncontrollably.

She'd been unable to locate the tape Claudia told her was hidden in the special compartment under her rug. It was empty. Did her murder have anything to do with this theft?

She went to her own special hiding place, which is not under her rug but in the base of a Chinese porcelain lamp. She took out a key and used it to unlock a panel in her wall. She reached in to press a button, and the entrance to a hidden office slid open. Here were all her files, years and years of them, not only on personnel but on customers. These files could bring down governments, a feast for historians of any era. She had also kept an ongoing ledger of the activities of her house day by day, a ledger that would do the best bookkeepers proud. Now she entered the office to find Claudia's file. She wanted to know if there were any next of kin who should be contacted.

Claudia's file was missing.

All the files were missing. The shelves were bare.

A large drawer was still open—the drawer that contained the most recent records. This drawer was completely empty too. Every single customer's account, his name and proclivities, was now out of her house and into the world.

The possibilities for damage of all sorts are enormous. Blackmail, murder, war. At one time or another over these years the world's most important men in any and every field had come to her house, this house, to fuck. They thought they were safe. She always had prided herself on keeping a safe house. Sam and Abe helped keep it safe. There was no way anyone could know how to get into this room. It has no entrance other than the one she'd just used.

How long would it be before she started to hear of the damage? Perhaps someone will contact her for some sort of ransom. No, that's unlikely. This isn't about money. This is about power or revenge. Everything in Washington is about one of these or the other. Or both.

How long did she have?

She went to her room and watched herself do what she was doing from somewhere outside of herself. She pulled the alarm. All over the house, the former house of somebody's God, clangings and sirens erupted as a loudly amplified impersonal bass voice commanded, "This is an emergency. Please evacuate immediately. This is an emergency. Evacuate immediately." Voices were heard, questionings, hastenings, curses. She pulled another alarm. Again the urgent impersonal voice, amplified even louder: "Attention. You must evacuate immediately. This is a fire alarm. There is a fire. Attention, attention. You have no time. Evacuate immediately."

The noises of alarms and fleeing inhabitants began to coalesce in her ears. She lay down on her bed. She wished Abe were here beside her so they could die like Romeo and Juliet. That would be a fitting ending, since that's how they began. We were so young, Abe. If we'd waited longer, would it have been better? Poppa, I tried. I carried your tradition as far as I could carry it. The family name. Whatever it was. She fumbled for the button behind her and pushed it. Amazing! So this is what it sounds like. Whooshes everywhere, the whoosh of igniting fuel combusting with age. She has set her house on fire. She hopes everyone's safely out. If you're not, you've been warned and you want to die as much as I do.

Outside, her many girls stand watching like white ghosts attending their former lives. A few hold hands with their evening booking, that is, the few remaining as even they peel off to protect their own safety, leaving the women holding on to each other. They are a beautiful group of women; a hundred years ago, in their flimsy gowns, they could have been at Vassar preparing to play nymphs in pageants, around maypoles, each holding a brightly colored streamer as they wove themselves into one. Buster Punic stands there, too. Doris had let him spend one last night in Claudia's bed. His face is hideously contorted, as if something of him is going up in flames along with the house. When sirens come from every direction, Buster turns and runs. The firemen have arrived. The police have arrived. He still has enough instinctive sense of self-preservation to live a little longer. Fear, at last somehow reaching him, can make an old man run fast. Or is it just his good old American white heterosexual Jewish stock?

Another old man is running not away from the house but into it. It's Abe, the richest Jew in Washington for certain, probably the whole East Coast, perhaps even in all America. He runs right into the fire. He runs into the house and through its cascading timbers and its drapes of flame. It's nothing to such an experienced fireman. He'd been here too many times before. He grew up in a house of fires. Yes, he knows his way around and he knows what to do. He parts the sheets of fire like Moses parting the Red Sea, away, away, get out of my way. Her room is there, though the wall is melting. He sees her on her bed, an island still unconsumed. Like an Olympic diver he springs forward, up, and through, to land beside her. He has her. He has her in his arms. He finally has her in his arms. "My beloved. My dearest Doris. Come. We're together forever at last."

It was Abe who motivated and orchestrated this alarm and fire. The only other possessor of a key to Doris's secrets had cleared all her secrets out. Claudia's murder had made up his mind. He was tired of all this whoring. He would find a way to transport the greatest love of his life forever into the eternity for which he determined they are finally ready.

Mordecai Masturbov watched his father run into the flames. He's lost both parents. And his Velvalee, who evidently had no desire to escape the safety his mother had provided her from him. But Jinx is in his arms and comforting him.

THE REAL STUFF

Sex scandals and plagues represent the time and place and era and ethos and vernacular and fabric and even the philosophy and religion of the world that they upstage. They and this are the real stuff of history, of war and peace.

I look out my window at Washington Square and my thoughts go back in time to people I loved. I realize I am alone and infected and my days are numbered, and I feel sad, for I know more each day that life is sad for almost everyone that I know, and I don't remember at this moment when I last felt happy.

I feel an abject utter failure.

I want to run out to the street and collar any gay man I see and ask him: How can you be happy? At this juncture of your life that is now? When we are more abandoned and alone and needier and under attack than ever?

THIS IS WHAT DANIEL SAW

I don't wish to be callous about the disappearance of my sister-in-law Sara Jerusalem and the murder of my childhood sweetheart, if you will, Claudia Webb. Coming at this moment in the escalation of the plague of UC, I can't get my grief around them: my arms only have room to embrace our side.

I didn't know that Stephen, my own brother, had been so involved with Claudia that her death caused him some sort of nervous collapse which sent him away for a while. Claudia's murder didn't get any press. No doubt someone was seeing that nothing was reported after the initial surge of the "Unidentified Woman Found Dead in Rock Creek Park" stuff. Doris Hardware's name was never mentioned either, in print, anywhere. Abe's death in the fire, "with his beloved wife of many years beside him," was of course news in the way obituaries of the very rich are news. We all dutifully went to their elaborate funeral. Since there was nothing but ashes from a house burned to cinders, those were what Mordy scattered to the wind at a private ceremony on his Sexopolis estate. He invited me and I went, full of memories of young Claudia and Daniel and Mordy wandering underground in those tunnels of Masturbov Gardens that his grandfather was only just building. He bawled now like a baby and tried to embrace me forcefully, as if holding on to something from an earlier and perhaps less troublesome era would somehow restore him to a reality he wasn't living at this moment of such unexpected grief. He really wailed and moaned and at one point threw himself on the earth after he'd poured out more ashes and pounded it with his fists. There was a rabbi in attendance briefly; I didn't catch his name. Mordy dismissed him about ten minutes into his service. "You did not know my father and my mother and my beloved Claudia, and your attempt to summon them up is horrible to me. Get out!" Oh, and Nate Bulb was in attendance too. He was there in his own urn. Evidently Abe had kept it in his downtown office and Mordy now summoned it to mourn with him.

And he pulled Jinx beside him and proclaimed to us that he would build a new and grander Sexopolis mansion in memory of his dear mother.

And . . . and . . .

And this is what I saw the one time I visited Doris Hardware's, from inside a closet Claudia put me into, "so you can finally see." I had finally gone to see her.

I saw Claudia whip the living shit out of Sam Sport, so hard his back was striped with bloody lash marks. It reminded me of David's back. And she was doing it with a smile on her face of total triumph.

I saw my brother Stephen watching this and jerking off, making it last so that he didn't come until Sam passed out.

I saw Claudia and Stephen then make love passionately on the floor beside Sam's body. I name it passion because they made love as if they were in love, as if they were making love for the last time before they would be taken off and shot, as if they had to grab what time was left to them before the end of life itself. I shudder to make the comparison that you would have no trouble making, but as if they were the last two about to be carted off to a gas oven during a holocaust, that's how they were making love. They had to feel it all before it was too late.

Watching it all was Dereck Dumster, that protegee of Sam's. Claudia had told me he's dangerous.

THIS IS WHAT FRED WROTE

If, as Tolstoy said, every unhappy family is unhappy in its own way, Tolstoy's not the right guy to reach for now. This is nothing like anything Tolstoy or most other keepers of the cultural historical torches would ever write about.

When I finish reading Daniel's words, I go to my bookshelves and take down *Dr. Faustus* by Thomas Mann, another gay writer who didn't know how to handle it.

"The section just concluded also swelled much too much for my taste, and it would seem only too advisable for me to ask myself whether the reader's patience is holding out. Every word I write here is of searing interest to me, but I must be very much on guard against thinking that that is any guarantee of sympathy on the part of the unresolved reader. Although I should not forget, either, that I am writing not for the moment, nor for readers who as yet know nothing at all about Leverkuhn and so could have no desire to learn more about him, but that I am preparing this account for a time when conditions for public response will be quite different—and with certainty one can say much more favorable—when the demands of this disturbing life, however adeptly or unadeptly presented, will be both less selective and more urgent."

To which pursuit I must now return. Fred, *pace* Faust and Mann, wants to know what's holding his world together at this moment.

STATE OF THE UNION

State of the Union. What union?

STATE OF THE PLAGUE

Jacquie had delayed approval of her test for use in France or the United States because Dodo had delayed approval for the use of his test in either country.

Not one major scientist, or representative of big Pharma, or PI (for Principal Investigator) of the forthcoming clinical trials, is noticeably audible in response to this heartbreaking roadblock.

The state of UC research is increasingly considered to be so shoddy as to curtail new scientists willing to enter the field. It had all sounded exciting and adventurous, but that was years ago, when we were young.

Included in some last-minute appropriations is an extra $8.5 million for FADS to rush the approval of Dodo's UC test. He has, at last, been successful in holding the world up for ransom and is now guaranteed his half share of all worldwide royalties. Now Jacquie is able to give her permission to pump her test out fast as well. The Ruester administration, however, decides it will use only $475,000 of the funds for the blood test, allowing the rest of the money to revert back to the treasury.

So once again a test to determine if blood is infected with UC remains unavailable in the United States. Infected blood is now infecting the entire country.

Statistics, numbers, hard facts about the state of this plague from any government agency continue to be unavailable. If they were, we'd see how they contradict each other.

"It is like a Watergate cover-up," said Dr. Philo Schwartzenbaum in Munich. "It all started with a theft by your Dodo. Doctors everywhere lose faith in American science."

Finally AudaciaUSA funds Dodo's blood test, and FADS approves its use. This is more than four years after this test could have been available in France, where Audacia et Cie was able to put out Jacquie's test. Few know yet how unreliable Dodo's test will prove to be. One wonders how FADS tested it, much less approved it. One wonders how AudaciaUSA can put it out. More than half the people who take the test are told they're infected when they're not. False positives, they're called. Pregnant women have immediate abortions. People commit suicide. People of all colors and interests are ignorant about this. No one writes about this.

The New York Truth still won't write about UC. Gertie (Mrs. Jacob) Flourtower, in her cups on one of those many weekends when her husband's away, commiserates with several of her gay friends in an East Side bar: "Yes, Jakie fires any faggot Johnny on the spot. 'I got to fire every poofter I can sniff and smell,' he says. 'This UC shit proves I'm right.' He practically had a heart attack when his sweet favorite reporter Jeffrey Schmaltz collapsed in front of him. Now, which of you real men will buy me another vodka stinger?"

And how could we have overlooked what's called the "Treaty of Franeeda," allowing Jerry to be in complete charge of the UC clinical trials. Grebstyne and Middleditch had established a workable system going back many years, of conducting clinical trials. Jerry's never done one and is staffing up with has-beens. What this portends, clear as a lesion on any gay man's body, is a lot more unnecessary deaths. It will take Jerry too many years to build a new system up from scratch. Jerry must have known this would happen. Is it arrogance or intentional?

DEEP THROAT

The "act of giving" in legal terminology is meant to extend for the entire life of the gift, *in activo res*, as an active thing. This is an important concept in disease as well. Even though the virility of a pathogen may decline, it's still considered to be "given for good." The establishment of a home in the host is thus factually protected, in legal and in medical terms.

•

Such a nice gesture in my behalf! Thanks so very very much.

AN ARMY OF LOVERS MUST NOT DIE

FRED CONTINUES COMPILING HIS LIST

Ed DiPasquale, Matt Schutz X, Brett Adams, Carmen Allesio, Brandy Alexander, Justin Alexander, Rev. Charles Angel, Way Bandy, Jim Beck, Michael Bennett, Jim Boatwright, Mel Boozer,

Bobby Borland, Arthur Bresson, Michael Brody, Roscoe Browne, Alan Buchsbaum, Jody Callahan, Bobbi Campbell, Lynne Carter, Henry Chenoff, Tony Clavely (Alessandro Abrizzi's lover) X, Ben Codispoti, John Congers,——Coppola (Vinnie Coppola of *Newsweek*'s brother), Jesue Corkes, Terry Costello, Richmond Crinkley, Jeffrey Croland, Joel Crothers, Cal Culver (aka Casey Donovan), Curt Dawson X, Larry Deason. Steve Del Re, Robert Denning, Harry Diaz, Ron Doud X, Angelo Donghia, Dr. Larry Downs, Robert Drivas, John Duka X, Donald Driver, Richard Dulong, Alan Dumont (lover of Bruce Kaye), Perry Ellis, Bill Elliott X, Kelly English, Nathan Fain, Mel Fante, Artie Felson, Robert Ferro X, Ron Field, Gary Fifield, Peter Fonseca, Bob Forcina, Ray Ford, Michel Foucault, Xavier Fourcade, Brad Frandsen, Stan Freeman, Carlton Fuller, Herb Gaines, Armando Galvez (Flamingo DJ), Ken Gaston (bar owner), Mort Gindi, Larry Goldberg, Bob Golden (Bruce Niles's roommate), Lee Goodman, Herb Gower, Paul Graham, Tolin Greene, Michael Greer, Richard Greene X, Peter Grimes, Michael Grumley, Sam Haddad, Jack Hedaya, Jack Hefton, Larry Henry (lover of Rick Janson, already dead), Emery Hetrick, Colin Higgins, Kevin Higgins, Anthony Holland, Fritz Holt, Roger Horwitz (Paul Monette's lover), Peter Hujar, David Jackson, Paul Jacobs (concert pianist), Steve Jacobs (Alice's hairdresser), Robin Jacobsen X, Rick Janson X, Tom Jefferson, Robert Joffrey, Tom Johnson, Harry Kalkanis (John-David Wilder's lover), Jim Kamel (Billy Bernardo's lover), Stan Kamen (Adreena's agent), Bruce Kaye, Ed Knudsen (architect of new GMPA office), Bill Kraus, Donald Krintzman, Barry Laine, Leon Lambert X, Ralph Landis, Phil Lanzaretta, Robert La Tourneaux, Steve Lax, Wilford Leech, Jean Leger, Bob Lemond, Ron Lohse X, Larry Londino X, Diego Lopez, Charles Ludlum, Jim McCabe (lawyer for Paul Weiss), Joe McDonald, Phil Magdaleny, Michael Maletta, Phil Mandelker. Royal Marks, Leonard Matlovich, Court Miller, Ed Moore (fireman, Norm Rathweg's friend), John Myers, Paul Myers, Jack Nau, Max Navarre, Hugo Niehaus X, Frank O'Dowd, Larry Okin, Don Otto, Kevin Patterson, Phil Patrick, Joe Peckerman, Glenn Person, Michael Pitkin X, David Poole, Deyan Popavik (gold speculator friend of Val's), Reuven Proctor-Levi (Tarsh's old boyfriend), Shelley, Paul Rapoport, Tony Rappa X, Norman Rathweg, Stephen Richards, Jim Reissar

(Dora Dull), Michael Riley, Michael Rock, Nick Rock, Ed Roginski (Sue Barton's boss at Universal), Bertram Belberg (the Divine Bella), Bernie Rubinstein, Harvey Sakofsky, Jonathan Sand, Luis Sanjuro X, Paul Sansone X, Neil Sansted (Channel 13 art dept., friend of Harvey Marks), Stash Santoro, Bruce Savan X, Michael Sklar, Carroll Sledz (Bob Alfandre's lover), Douglas Smith (Yaddah Gala), Justin Smith X, Willi Smith, Ray Spellman X, Charlie Springman X, David Summers, Michael Taylor, Carl Thomas, Bruce Thompson, Jacques Tiffeau X, David Towt, Bill Touw (Tom Hatcher's old lover), Orsi Ullman (Feffer da Roma's best friend), Richard Umans X, Richard "Boo Boo" Bronstein, Tom Victor, Peter Vogel, Dr. Tom Waddell, Sam Wagstaff, Bill Whitehead, Lou Walker X, Cade Ware, Steven Webb, Bruce Weintraub, Rick Wellikoff, Ron Wilson (decorator, L.A.), Steve Wolin, Lee Wright, Howard Brookner, Tom Victor, Tony Lambert, Rick Horton X, Dr. Barry Gingell, Peter Evans, Perky Feinstein . . .

An "X" after the names above means I had sex with them at some point in time. Or went to bed with them. Or made love with them. We who had once been called hushmarkeds still don't know what to call what we've been doing.

STATE OF THE FRED

I wrote my book and articles. I helped start GMPA. I wrote my movie. I wrote my play. I write another play. I had my first emergency hospitalization. My liver is trying to tell me something. I was pissing blood. I'd even gone to Auschwitz looking for . . . what?

Do I sound like I'm losing it? Some days I just can't tell.

Get off your fucking ass!

A CATHOLIC VISIT

At the Mercy of Mary Hospital out on Long Island, Mother Bertha, the matron in charge, said to me, "So you are what a healthy homosexual looks like. All my boys here are sick, and they deny they are homosexuals. 'What are you, then?' I ask them in my best Mother Superior manner. 'Jesus knows, so why not fess up?' This does not go down well, and I suspect I am doing more harm than good by invoking Jesus as a way to get them to tell the truth. I beg you, Mr. Lemish, tell me if I am wrong. Would not more honesty be better for all concerned? I have had a number of strange suicides of—I hesitate to put it this way—of a particularly religious Catholic nature." She then showed me photographs of various hideous self-inflicted acts: immolations, burned bodies, charred bones and unrecognizable faces; hangings, with hands still clutching dangling crucifixes; slit wrists, several emasculations, also self-inflicted according to Mother Bertha; two boys who ODed on sleeping pills who had laid themselves down in their own decorated coffin, again holding crucifixes and each other's hands. "It is amazing how your religion has so permeated their beings, even unto death," I ventured. She answered, "Is this not as it should be? Is it not the way we have lived for thousands of years? I am told these clothes they wore in their coffin were their confirmation suits. I suppose they had lost so much weight that they still could fit." Before I left she took my hand and said, "We are not the most progressive community, but then I doubt there are many places that are, with this ailment, or can be, given our vows. Needless to say, there is no one in authority in our diocese who is competent to deal with this. Our priests are particularly speechless. Messages to Rome have been useless. Perhaps I should not reveal any of this. Perhaps I should not even be talking to you. It is almost biblical, the tests we are being put to, do you not agree? Even though you are obviously a Hebrew."

•

INT. CONGRESSIONAL HEARING. DAY.
Dr. Omicidio is being questioned by Rep. Ted Weiss (D. NY); Fred in audience with Tommy and Dr. Monserrat Krank.

REP. WEISS: Dr. Omicidio, your drug selection committee has named twenty-four drugs for investigation. Why the delays?

REP. NANCY PELOSI: Assume that you have UC. You know the NITS delays and that patients are finding black market ways to try anything on the streets. What would you do?

OMICIDIO: Congresswoman Pelosi, I probably would go with what would be available to me, be it on the street, or what have you. I do not believe anything on that list is worthy of testing with the small amount of money I've been allotted.

CUT TO:

Same room. Another hearing. Dr. Monserrat Krank is questioning Jerry.
As with all who testify, she has an identifying plaque by her microphone.

MONSERRAT: So, what is happening? We got you money for research. I personally appealed to Senator Kennedy. Where is the
research? Where is anything?

OMICIDIO: I don't have sufficient staff, Dr. Krank.

MONSERRAT: How can that be?

OMICIDIO: Your research money does not allow for staff, Dr. Krank.

MONSERRAT: Why have you said nothing?

A JEWISH VISIT

In Boro Park, New York, the Moses Adonai Medical Center was ghastly.
"Jewish boys do not get sick with this, Mr. Lemish. Jewish boys are never homosexuals. Jewish men do not perform anal intercourse. Rectums are not kosher. They are used only for dirty pooh-poohs. Jewish boys are never fegalim.
Homosexuals are big pooh-poohs."

Who talks like this in this day and age?

Well, this guy does. Rabbi Dr. Goldenrod. A rabbi and an M.D. all
rolled into one. Goody.

At their temple avec conference center, the 5,904th Conference of Rabbis
Who Care is transpiring. It has been billed as an "International Conference."
I was asked to come and speak here, following Rabbi Schwartzer Starker's
keynote address to some five hundred rabbis, which is entitled "Jews Do Not
Get The Underlying Condition." It is a horrible speech. "Those so afflicted
have been punished by G-d and quite evidently they must die for their sins.
G-d is speaking very plainly and clearly and distinctly and loudly." Five
hundred bearded rabbis, all in black, wearing tiny caps unattractively out
of scale with the dandruffed scalps they rest on, listen to hours of speeches
just like Starker's in this large new edifice adjoining their Temple Bathsheba
Rehavotna. After several hours the hall reeks of the body odor of five hundred sweating rabbis. They have placed me last on the program. And I have
sat here for these hours. Someone speaks in hateful tones; then they pray;
then they stand up and pray; then they sit down and pray; then someone
else speaks another hateful version of the same. I think I sat there because I
couldn't believe there was so much hate in one place.

Rabbi Starker finally acknowledges me from the podium. I can see the hate in all the eyes staring at me. I could walk across the stage and say a few words. There is silence while they wait. I see a door. I walk to that door. I open that door. I leave by that door.

I hear someone call me as the door closes behind me.

Shmuel Derektor is here. Another analyst I started seeing after I tried to kill myself at Yaddah. He is very old now. "You look older," I say to him. We are standing in a vestibule. Over the years, he's been helpful to me.

"Who does not get older?" He is here as an observer only, he says. "I only consult now. I come and listen to the meshugas. They too are my clients. They too need help." Then he gives me his look, that knowing nod of his head.

"I am truly sorry things go poorly for you, Fred. This is not the place where you will find help for your cause, however. You are right to leave. The Orthodox are nothing if not . . . orthodox. Business for me is good. These men here believe that you will destroy the world. That what you represent will set fire to all the good they have done for many centuries. They look upon gays as Hitler looked upon Jews."

"Hitler looked upon gays in the same way."

"There you have it, then. I rest my case. You do not know you have been chosen to advocate for the despised. I do not think you know this."

He's slipped a lot into those last sentences. He did that a lot in our sessions, as I now remember. Out of nowhere, he slips something in.

He continues: "Why else am I here but to point this out to you?"

From inside the conference hall, as if on cue, comes a resounding hallelu-jah or trumpet voluntary, or perhaps both, to end the session with a crescendo.

"You see," Shmuel says. "Even the heavenly choir knows what I'm talking about." Then his smile turns serious.

"Please, I beg of you. Be the fierce and, yes, avenging angel. We deserve it. The Jewish people deserve it. They have forgotten already. Stand on their ramparts of hate. You will be good at it. Come talk to me whenever you like. I miss you. We can plan and plot."

●

INT. CONGRESSIONAL HEARING. DAY.
Another hearing. Monserrat is questioning Jerry. Fred and Tommy are here.
MONSERRAT: So, what is happening? Where is anything?
OMICIDIO: Your grant does not include labs and desks. I don't have enough space for the workers I hired with the money.

MONSERRAT: Again, you said nothing? Your inability or unwilling-
ness to tell anyone what you need is inexcusable.
Fred is fuming. Tommy calms him down.

EXT. HEARINGS. DAY.
*Monserrat and Rebby, Fred and Tommy are exiting the building with
others. A man in a minister's collar and with a* GOD HATES FAIRIES
crudely executed poster is speaking on a portable mike.
MINISTER: Save your money. I have discovered the cure for UC. Here
it is: 'If a man also lie with mankind as he lieth with a woman,
both of them have committed an abomination: they shall surely
be put to death.' And that, my friends, is the cure for UC. It was
right there in the Bible all along. Leviticus 20:13. We can have a
UC-free world tomorrow.

DAME LADY HERMIA IS WAITING

Fred Lemish, you are taking too long. Fred, you need to be more consistently
and visibly angry! I have read all you have done so far. Your center does not
hold. In fact, I cannot locate your center at all. And neither can you. It is all
a bit, how shall I call it, neither here nor there. Grace said that you were very
shy as a child. Is it not time for you to grow up and focus!

AN OPEN LETTER TO DR. JERROLD OMICIDIO
FROM FRED LEMISH

THE SAN FRANCISCO CHRONICLE AND THE VILLAGE VICE

Dear Dr. Death:
I write to you yet again.
It's imperative to have a top NITS scientist to properly shepherd the gov-
ernment's research process against UC. You're supposed to be that person.
You fucking son of a bitch of a dumb idiot, you expect us to buy your garbage
bag of excuses for what you are not doing and why! Your National Institute
of Tumor Sciences is an Animal House of Horrors.
I call the decisions you are not making acts of murder.

At recent congressional hearings, after almost eight years of the worst epidemic in modern history, perhaps to be the worst in all history, you were pummeled into admitting publicly what some have been suspecting since you officially took over three-plus years ago.

You admitted that you are an incompetent idiot.

Over these years $374 million has finally been allocated for UC treatment research. You are in charge of spending this money. It doesn't take a genius to set up a nationwide network of testing sites, name a principal investigator, commence a small number of moderately sized treatment efficacy tests on a population desperate to participate in them, import any and all possibly interesting drugs (now numbering approximately two hundred) from around the world for inclusion in these tests at these sites, and swiftly get into circulation anything that *remotely* passes muster. Yet you have established only a system of inactivity, chaos, and uselessness.

And four years later you are forced to admit you've barely begun.

It doesn't take a genius to request, as you did, 126 new staff persons, receive only 11, *and then keep your mouth shut about it.*

It takes an incompetent idiot!

To quote Rep. Henry Waxman, who asked you again at a hearing: "As best I can tell, six of these drugs have been waiting for six months to more than a year for you to test them. I understand the need to do what you call 'setting priorities,' but it appears even with your own scientists' choices, the trials are not going on. Why the delays?"

Your defense? "There are just confounding delays that no one can help . . . We are responsible as investigators to make sure that in our zeal to go quickly, we do the clinical study correctly, that it's planned correctly and executed correctly, rather than just having the drug distributed . . ."

Are you sure you're the right person for your job?

You had come bawling to Congress that you don't have enough staff, office space, lab space, secretaries, computer operators, lab technicians, file clerks, janitors, toilet paper; and that's why the drugs aren't being tested and the treatment centers aren't up and running and drug protocols aren't in place. You expect us to buy your bullshit and feel sorry for you?

YOU FUCKING SON OF A BITCH OF A DUMB IDIOT, YOU HAVE HAD $374 MILLION AND YOU EXPECT US TO BUY THIS GARBAGE BAG OF EXCUSES!

For agonizing years you have refused to go public with what was happening (correction: *not* happening), and because you wouldn't speak up until you were asked pointedly and under oath by a congressional committee, we lie down and die and our bodies pile up higher and higher in hospitals and homes and hospices and doorways and, yes, in the streets.

Meanwhile, drugs we have been *begging* that you test remain untested. The list of promising untested drugs is now so endless, and the pipeline is so clogged with NITS and FADS bureaucratic lies, that there is no Roto-Rooter that will ever be able to muck them out.

You whine you are short of staff. You don't need staff to set up hospital treatment centers around the country. The hospitals are already there. They hire their own staff. They only need money. You have money. YOU HAVE 374 MILLION FUCKING DOLLARS, FOR CHRIST'S SAKE!

The gay community has, *for five years*, told you what drugs to test because of what we hear from our own contacts. You couldn't care less what we say. You won't answer our phone calls or letters or listen to or meet with anyone in our community. What tragic pomposity!

To quote Rep. Waxman again: "Aerosolized pentamidine was named High Priority and there are still no people in trials."

How many years ago did we tell you about aerosol pentamidine, Jerry? That this stuff saves lives, and deaths from that pneumonia which is our worst killer opportunistic infection. And we discovered it ourselves. We came to you, bearing this great news on a silver platter as a gift, begging you: Can we get it officially tested, can we get it approved by you so that insurance companies and Medicaid will pay for it as a routine treatment?

You are a heartless murdering monster.

We tell you what the good drugs are, you don't test them, then YOU TELL US TO GET THEM ON THE STREETS! You continue to pass down word from On High that you don't like this drug or that drug— WHEN YOU HAVEN'T EVEN TESTED THEM! You pass down word from On High that you don't want "to endanger the life of the patient."

THERE ARE MORE UC PATIENTS DEAD BECAUSE YOU DIDN'T TEST DRUGS ON THEM THAN BECAUSE YOU DID!

The cries of genocide from this Cassandra continue to remain unheard. And my noble but enfeebled community of the weak, the dying, and the dead will continue to grow and grow—until you and your system diminish us out of existence.

DEEP THROAT TELLS FRED ABOUT THE PRINCIPLE OF THE PRINCIPAL INVESTIGATOR

Hello, Fred. I'm glad you reached out to me confidentially on Jerry-built matters, as Ann Fettner hoped you would. I wish your friend, Dr. Daniel Jerusalem, were as open to my thoughts. He is suspicious of me, as he becomes too close to Jerry to be objective.

Jerry could not tell the hearings that he's revving up for testing ZAP. Remember, ZAP itself has not yet been seen or approved by FADS. In other words, he's breaking the law. I have no idea why, although I suspect Greeting has something to do with it.

Farrell Obernought, Gretta Lell, Pansy Merridew, Tyrone Coffin, Max Blatz. PIs and blowhards all. Interested in only one thing: themselves. Howie Hube is already hostile to them. He thought he would be in charge of them, but they all outrank him and certainly aren't going to respond to him. Not that Hubie's any wunderkind, but Jerry's put him in charge of this network of UC clinical trials that he is finally setting up. That only these five have surfaced to be PIs is scary. It's not as if PI positions are in great demand. So how did these five show up? They're certainly all "distinguished," in that they're well known in their fields and neighborhoods. I'm not saying these are a bad lot of choices. I am just saying they've appeared out of nowhere. I am of course suspicious of things that appear out of nowhere. I suspect each of them has a strong affiliation with a major pharmaceutical house. That is increasingly the way of the world. I'll bet every one of them is too chummy with G-D. In other words, they too are breaking the law.

PIs usually get slots because each is able to convince the provider (in this case G-D's crafty Dr. Dash Snicker) that they personally have a large enough acceptable patient population to fill all the slots in their trials. Most doctors don't want to provide patients for trials. It's too tricky. What if they die? These Joe Blows obviously don't give a shit whether their patients live or die. Gretta Lell told me to "go stuff it" when I queried her interest. They want in for the same reason Jerry does. This is hot stuff, which only a few smart ones smell at present. They'll be in on the ground floor of what they already see—each has a lot of sick patients. They're ambitious. Believe it or not, most docs are not ambitious. And since they're already "owned" by a drug company, having worked with many of them in a "cooperative" fashion, they don't need to be. G-D will run them like slaves on its plantation but pay them for it.

In case you didn't notice, this virus wasn't all that hard to find. Jacquie found it in a matter of months very early on. Then Pewkin's COD discovered one. Then so did Chuck Salmon, a private doc with a gay practice in San Francisco. What's delayed NITS is their difficulty with dumb Dodo. He's worshipped like some Mother Teresa at Lourdes. They don't want to do anything to offend him until he fixes up his goddamn test and it can be used to enroll candidates pure enough to please Dash Snicker. His champion, Roscoe Middleditch, has been disappeared, as they put it. Too bad. I liked him. Seemed like an honest guy.

Under Ruester the various secretaries of HAH and COD and FADS are coming and going like a game of musical chairs. As Joe Kidney has written, nobody wants to work for Old Peter. Swilkers, Mason, Dietrikson, Ahearne, Noblonski, Velery, Bowen, it's always a potpourri of nullities running these loony bins.

Daniel doesn't grasp the effectiveness of this tactic of constantly changing "officials." Without continuity in an agency's leadership, no one's in place long enough to fight for anything, particularly money. Every Request for Funding automatically gets tabled, denied, or lost in the mail. Prepare your buddies to die, my friend. You're one less problem for the White House.

Okay. Jerry is about to launch his first big trial. Jerry's young and handsome, which should help make him a good leader. He is a bitch to work for. I say that even though I just know he'll find a way to get rid of me even though I'm meant to be protected here for life and he's not my boss. I worshipped him at first. I'm not certain why anymore. I like to worship whom I work with. I've worked side by side with a few of the great ones. I may have mentioned them to Daniel elsewhere.

I am smarter than anyone here and I know it and Jerry knows it. It does not pay to be smarter than anyone at a place like this, especially the man in charge.

I don't think anyone has any idea what it's like for scientists who don't know what to do while their boss is out jogging. Well, no one here knows what to do. Can't say this enough. Just can't. "Just test anything! Test aspirin, for Christ's sake," Dr. Fellow said, and he was not alone. He was doing his own research, it turned out, that Jerry agreed to co-author, which would result in an actual peer-reviewed article getting itself into *NEJS* claiming UC was, get this, a fungus. He actually asked Jerry to co-announce this and Jerry fell for it. Arden Morron fell for it. Fellow didn't last long. Jerry was ruthless about getting rid of Fellow fast. They still make jokes about "Jerry's fallow Fellow fungus."

A hundred years ago, when I came back from Africa, I was told by Dye to oversee what still are called "ancillary pathological studies." The announcement of my appointment was heralded in *NEJS*. When Jerry came on a few years later *The Prick* wished me luck, "because we sense Dr. Omicidio is a manipulative charlatan." They were onto him right away. "He is too cute to be a decent scientist," they added. You guys evidently have radar for things like this.

Remember, Jacqueline's virus, Dodo's virus, Paulus's virus, Chuck Salmon's virus, Jesus Christ's virus, not a one of them has yet received the Good Housekeeping Seal. No journal has given it a blessing. No one is using the words "*THE* virus." Amazing to see how much time was wasted while Dodo checkmated Jacqueline's work, supported by Middleditch, Nostrill, Grebstyne, Dye, et al. Time goes awfully fast, except when it goes too awfully slowly. The lawyers are still in here going through every lab's haystack.

"Well, fellows and gals," Leisha McGonigle starts each of the Jerry daily meetings jauntily, "where do we begin today?" Chief Nurse Leisha is very officious. "Someone's got to be," she says right to anyone's face. "I'm attractive enough to get away with it, but not so attractive as to make them want to fuck me," she told me. Good old Leisha. We've been through a few wars together and she's the real thing. Jerry's lucky to have her. Not that he knows it. Not that he knows he's lucky to have me, too.

Gretta is the first to get herself chosen a PI. She used to be prettier. She's a tough cookie. It's a good thing I never fucked her. I couldn't have kept it up for her, and she's the kind of broad who would happily pass that kind of info around. She's also the kind of gal who, when she passes you by, says something cute and snappy like "How they hanging?" Dash Snicker is not happy with her patient population. "I mean, they don't even speak English." She snaps back, "I do, and that's all you have to worry about."

Dash not only doesn't like her patient population, he decides they're all too sick, with indications of illness, so he announces, "I have said I will not allow any entrants into any Greeting trial who evince any sign of anything. And I mean it. Period." Dash knows in advance what he wants the results to be. They just have to be "official," meaning that the government is paying for them and G-D can't be accused of juggling the data. Ha ha.

So that's how we started in on our ZAP clinical trials. And each of those

PIs is starting a similar study in their own medical centers across the land. Two hundred and fifty patients in each.

"Stop the presses! Hold everything!" Dash Snicker isn't ready again.

Now he only wants to do two test arms. One in Miami with Gretta and the other in San Francisco with Farrell Obernought.

Jerry has told me he doesn't like me "being so constantly negative. Go cut up another body."

To be continued . . .

SAM SPORT TALKS TO HIMSELF

They are all fuckers. The whole fucking world. But I can fuck them all. I'll find a law anyone's breaking so I have them over a barrel. Otherwise they'll go to prison. No one treats Sam Sport in any way he doesn't want to be treated.

My clients control 34 gay bars in Washington, 134 in New York City. I get paid for every drink every faggot drinks. We own the bathhouses. What gay power I have! I enjoy thinking about this. I enjoy being the most powerful prick in their lives. Nasturtium had to be put down for telling Purpura all this about her buddy Sam, his old fuck buddy. I've got plenty of shit on her including her being a cocksucker with a dyke mother. But now she's shitting too far and wide. God only knows what she'll do next. Moose is a shithead who can't be trusted. He'd have me debarred in a minute if it weren't for my friendship with Purpura. Edgar warned me about him. Edgar was always right. Roy said always listen to Edgar. So does James Jesus.

Moose wants to be cut in on ZAP and G-D. He's looking for something to do after he leaves the White House. He ordered me to arrange a meeting with Snicker and Greeting. First of all, I don't take orders from anyone. Second of all, my Mob clients are already into G-D. They see how much my faggot brothers and sisters drink up in their bars. They see them beginning to not look so healthy and the bar business slipping away. We have to keep them boozing and fucking! Sex, drugs, and rock and roll! Give them more of what they want!

I trust my Mob friends more than I trust my president and his fucking first lady. As that good old honest blowhard Joe Kidney's been trying to tell us, Ruester's not the one who's running this country.

Dereck, I got to give Dereck more lessons. I recognize the real snakes when I see them. He's going to be king of the heap. He wants to learn all my tricks. He begs me. I sure would like him to fuck me. He won't, and his orgies are all filled with big-titted cunts.

ARE YOU FOLLOWING THE BOUNCING BALL?

You close your eyes and you can have too many memories, as Fred does. The scenes of sex that were so touching and felt so good. This is the history that made us, these memories, these experiences, into what we are today. They are the foundation stones, the building blocks on which we all stand. These memories are not just wisps of remembrance; they are poured into the concrete of the plinths of our lives. They're as firm as the facts in any history. Supporting evidence, Fred calls them.

Hateful and vengeful and angry memories, why should they be less plinthful, to coin an ugly word to hold them?

We're arriving at the moment in our history when the whole crude scientific apparatus around UC, the corset, is being created, more concrete's being poured. PIs up the ass are suddenly visible and audible. PIs will become more and more competitive, particularly when a rival pharm's drug being tested leaps a few steps ahead of the one you're working on, particularly when that other pharm was one you worked for, or who fired you. There is no love lost in this rat race, no matter which side. Fred hadn't seen that coming—that it would be a rat race. Fred really thought people would care and help. "I really thought people would join together to fight, like a band of brothers. I still have a lot to learn. Only yesterday no one wanted to touch this shit. But now strange men are coming closer!" And as they do, conflicts of interest start plopping out of assholes like rotten tomatoes from an overflowing overturned wheelbarrow. That, in the history of drug trials, is evidently "the way it's always been." Who knew? PIs plopping their contributions into the concrete plinth of drug testing are our next destructive guarantor of getting nowhere. Principal Investigators, a.k.a. People without Principles.

DEEP THROAT

PIs are going to eat Jerry Omicidio for breakfast, lunch, and dinner. And Jerry's going to let them. This is our leader. The PIs take one look at him and know they can take over.

Why didn't Jerry try to gather the best around him? Did Dash insist on *these* PIs? But since when is the pharm allowed to control the clinical trials of its own product? Dumb Anyone who asks this question. If the pharm's going to contribute for free the drugs being tested, disagree with anything they insist on and you're going to have to pay for them yourself. G-D is simply not giving its approval to go forward with anything they don't like.

Dash is one rude bastard. He is riding herd on everything as he studies the lists of all the potential trial entrants from each center, those hundreds and hundreds waiting impatiently in the wings all over the country. If all the entrants must be healthy, the results are going to be for shit. Well, all the entrants are going to have to be healthy to be accepted. This is allowed to pass. As Jerry's never run clinical trials before, he's not going to listen to the likes of Deep Throat, who more and more is getting on Jerry's nerves. Jerry calls around and discovers that this is how it is, and that G-D is known to be the worst.

"And what did Jerry do today?" Fred's always asking Daniel. Fred just knows Jerry isn't doing anything. He gives lots of interviews. *Lots* of them. "How can he be doing anything when he gives so many interviews?" Fred asked Daniel. "I thought he takes care of patients. I thought he was looking for a cure. I thought he was in charge of this shit!" What Fred is convinced Jerry is not doing drives Fred nuts. "Well, Jerry plays lots of stuff very close to his chest," Daniel tells him. "He used to answer his red phone when I was in the office. Now he asks me to leave." "What does that mean!" Fred asks. "How the fuck am I supposed to know what that means!" Daniel snaps back and hangs up. No, Fred and Daniel are not getting on.

THE MARCH TO ZAP

TOMMY: A new wrinkle. There is opposition to even taking Dodo's test. Question of civil liberties and confidentiality. You test positive for UC, who gets that info? It will be like a roll call of gays. Employers will love that. Gay lawyers at GMPA are objecting, led by yours truly: before this test can be administered, confidentiality must be guaranteed. This won't be easy. Senator Vurd's already thrilled, and his minions are ready to jot down every name they can get. On the other side of the fence, it's being pointed out by Fred and others that until there's a useful drug there's no point in getting a useless test anyway. "Frankly, I'd rather not know" is heard a lot. "Just as long as you're being careful and using a condom," I'm still not allowed to officially say. GMPA is not allowed to make any kind of behavioral or therapeutic recommendation.

·

DANIEL: Stuartgene turned on me at our next group Do Nothing. "You are our token gay. You are going to convince the entire gay world that they must take this test." And I am suddenly wondering if that's what's really wanted . . . by someone. For everyone to take a test that's inaccurate in the extreme.

"I don't think I can do that, Dr. Dye."

"Why?"

"Dodo's test provokes too many false results. I've reported on that to you and Dr. Omicidio. Our only recourse is to get Dr. Geiseric to finally do some readjusting. The only one he listened to was Dr. Middleditch, who's no longer here."

He looked at me for a long moment of silence before just turning around and leaving.

·

FRED: A doctor in Paris is claiming he's got a drug that stops the virus. Just word of that sends hundreds of guys stampeding to Paris. Rock Hudson is rushed to Paris on a private plane. The lines outside the Pasteur Institute go for blocks. Guys rush directly from the airport to the Pasteur and sleep on the streets. They don't even check into their hotels. Hell, most of them can't afford a hotel. Guys keeps running into friends they know from Fire Island or their gyms or the waiting rooms of their doctor's office. I was in France and England to set up productions of my play. I visited the site. I ran into a guy I went to Sunday school with at Rabbi Chesterfield's, who reminds me of Tibby, the rabbi's son. Tibby would have caught this shit for sure. What a dick he had. Too bad he didn't live to enjoy it at least for a little while.

·

DANIEL: Slowly and secretly ZAP is going into a few bodies. Grebstyne announces the results of a six-week study nobody knew was happening. ZAP kept the virus from replicating in fifteen of nineteen patients, raising their T cells, now the official barometer of improvement since Grace and her vel count have bitten the dust. It took sixteen months to do this six-week study.

NITS biostatisticians have somehow interpolated that 70 percent, maybe up to 100 percent, of gay men might already be infected. Just like Emma Brookner predicted. Who's ready for this? Why isn't Jerry making this known? I ask him, of course. "It's just statistal bullshit. Statistics are whipped cream. Pumped full of hot air."

"So what?"

"So I'm not ready to be crucified for creating a media tornado. You keep your mouth shut too."

Maggie Fuldy has the first major fuckup on a PI trial. Several of her guys had taken their ZAP immediately to a chemist and stopped taking them if they were the placebo. Dash blames her noisily for "not maintaining sufficient personal contact" with her enrollees. "Am I supposed to be in their bathrooms when they take their meds!" she asked him testily. She's taken off the trial, which is then combined with one of Debbi's. This is not kosher, but who's to know. The guys taking the placebo were told to get lost. Actually, they were told more than that. Dash reamed them out for being selfish and inconsiderate and irresponsible, "and how do you expect us to get data that will help everyone when you pull shit like this." One of them spoke up. "Sargent Pepper died on this dose." Sargent was a guy named Sparks Puffington's lover. Sparks is not happy about this loss and comes up to Dash and says to his face, "You're a murderer. Fifteen hundred milligrams is poison and you know it." Sparks is small in size and Dash isn't. Dash picks Sparks up and carries him to the door and puts him out in the hallway. Debbi doesn't like the way Dash was rude to Maggie and tells him so. He takes her off the trial too, combining her already combined trial with that of old Leisha's. After twenty years of doing trials for NITS, Debbi is furious. Jerry transfers her to another PI, forcing her to move to San Francisco to work with Farrell Obernought. Leisha's section is then unblinded. Her guys got varying doses with no placebo. Here it's apparent, more or less, that while everyone in her trial will eventually die, the lower the dose, the longer before they do so.

But G-D absolutely will not lower the "recommended dose." No money in that. "The patient population has to be broken in to the higher dosage, more slowly perhaps, but our testing indicates that the system can tolerate it eventually." Dash says this to Thelma Adroit of *Time*. Word's leaking out about the ZAP trials. No trial is producing results good enough for what everyone's been hoping. In all the PI-supervised trials all over America, those enrolled start taking matters into their own hands, dosing themselves up as they see fit—more for the days they feel good and less or none for those days they don't. "We've been had once again!" Orvid trumpets in *The Prick*.

"*The Prick* told you so!" Fewer people are willing to enroll in 1500 mg trials. Dash, who has oversold his product's benefits and oversupervised everything, reluctantly adjusts the "recommended dosage" to 1000 mg daily. Even this is hard for many people to handle. From one dosage or another everyone has a stomach pockmarked by indigestion and diarrhea. The more fastidious now wear Pampers or always stay home.

But then Gretta's and Farrell's trials are unblinded. It would appear that 1500 mg wins the day. Even though they may die on 1000 mg they die having felt better getting there, but on 1500 mg you will feel as awful as you've ever felt but you live a little while longer. But since Gretta's and Farrell's patients look so good (remember they were healthy going in and they were on the drug for only six months), even Pansy Merridew in Palo Alto, the most negative PI, proclaims, "the results look pretty good to me and it would be unethical not to start our trials in all centers," as he testifies at a secret FADS meeting recommending same. So another announcement is made by another secretary of Health and Disease, or I guess it's Health and Happiness now, and Jerry and yes, even Dodo are put out for show, and of course Von and Dash, praising "the progress of American research, and medicine, and science in delivering us this excellent new drug." G-D is even given a Presidential Citation for Excellence in Industry.

And that "free" ZAP Dash promised all trial entrants when their studies were unblinded? Forget it. "You cheated on your dosages, so why should I reward you?" is his rationale. Von Greeting actually says he's sad his company couldn't keep its promise. Hermia says he must want more gays to die. And I hear Von's gay himself. Go figure.

And so ZAP goes out to all the PIs and their centers. "The benefits in very sick patients outweigh the serious toxic side effects" is heard like some mantra of permission and recommendation.

Some thirty thousand people are entered in these trials. Almost immediately four out of five 1500 mg patients die. The 1000 mg fellows seem to be hanging on. But it's just the beginning. This "controlled clinical trial" is scheduled to last at least a year. The gay population is going nuts waiting for ZAP's official approval. It's already rumored to be going to cost $10,000 a year, which is more than any company has ever charged for a drug before. Dash is very eager to join the Billion Dollar Sales club. Dash et al. had finally rounded up ten thousand acceptable entrants. There is of course not one single woman enrolled. Women don't get UC, you know. Maybe the ladies were lucky. Let's wait and see. It's going to take a while. It's a double-blind placebo-controlled study (don't ask) and, well, it takes a while. Or should. If it's being conducted correctly. According to the law. Which Deep Throat says is full of shit. And isn't being adhered to anyway.

REBBY

"To rely solely on official institutions for our information and help is a form of suicide," Rebby writes in some unread newsletter or other.

PEARLY SNOW KILLED HIS DOG FIRST

There are twelve guys waiting for him at Pedro's apartment on the Lower East Side. It's a sixth-floor walk-up. It's a tough climb and all of them are really sick. The plan is that once they get up there they'll stay up there and take some poisoned Kool-Aid like those Jim Jones people and hold on to each other and, well, die. Word got out and a couple more guys want to join and are coming. Pedro says it's going to be a little crowded. It's a tiny apartment. Pedro is an expert on Jim Jones and Jonestown. His mother was one of the ones who drank the stuff, so he's excited about doing it too, and joining her. He got a doctor to get the poison and mix it all up right. She's an expert on poisons for the city, Pedro says.

Pearly Snow thought it all sounded very creepy when Pedro and then Xavier, his boyfriend, started talking about it, but he doesn't find it so creepy now. He finds the way he has to live creepy. Anyway, he has to go through with it now because he's already poisoned Ferdinand, his black lab, who's lying dead in his kitchenette, so there's nothing to go back home for. He used some rat poison and mixed it in his Alpo. Besides, he is really tired of living in Jersey. It's just too tough a commute to get his ZAP at the hospital and the doctors, just to stay alive. Anyway, Pearly is ready to go. Most guys say they're ready to go. They're all on ZAP in Dr. Poo's trial. The Kool-Aid exit sounds great. "How many ways do you spell *relief*?" they joke with each other. He's come to realize that what he's doing is kind of gutsy. He was always a nervy kid, thank goodness. He figures that's where he's getting the courage to head into heaven this way.

Pearly Snow is also a patient of Dr. Ginny's, a really nice therapist affiliated with GMPA and Table Medical. These kids break her heart, and she sees them for free. There are so many of them that she's taken to seeing them in groups of half a dozen or so at a time, but she usually winds up speaking quietly to each one alone in a corner or in the hallway or even in the toilet. She can give each of them maybe five or six good minutes before the kid is usually heaving sobs and tears. She wonders if she's doing more harm than good. The business with the poisoned Kool-Aid has her freaked. She doesn't know how to deal with it. What her patients tell her is meant to be confidential. She's been in similar circumstances maybe a dozen times already, where she's been informed in advance of awful things that have come to pass. She wonders when one of them is going to boomerang back in her face, and the city, which is paying for part of her contract for so many hours each month, will have her on the carpet and up on charges and it will be in *The Truth* where all their awful "human interest" stories appear. Now a bunch of six or seven or eight Hispanic guys are going to drink Kool-Aid this afternoon at five o'clock. She looks at her watch. It's six o'clock. She wonders if they did it. It's better if she doesn't know. It's also better if they did it, she finds herself thinking. It's a very inventive way to die. Just like Pearly Snow was a pretty inventive name. "I made it up myself," he'd told her. "It doesn't mean anything. Just like life." She wonders how long she can stand taking care of cases like this.

Pearly and the boys don't show for their next session.

DEEP THROAT ON (IM)MOR(T)ALITY

I didn't say, Fred, that the law is full of shit. It's the system that's full of shit. Alas, there is no reliable guiding light to decide how much or how little shit (in this case ZAP) should be administered. Trials have always been built on the principle of escalating to as much as you can until the patient croaks and trying to stop just short of it. And alas, Jerry is not a decision maker. Alas, Jerry is a consensus builder. Good science is not built on consensus. Scott-Joynt in Glasgow and Nelson Golly in London have formed a surprising alliance to claim that America is doing everything wrong and that it's time for America to "give over in your complete domination of and dictatorship over worldwide medical emergencies." Dodo and his mishmash of mixed signals have become an international laughingstock, not that you would know it in Franeeda. Golly thinks he knows a fake when he sees one. Wait until they get an even bigger load of Jerry. I guess you could say that things are "hotting up," as Bledd-Wrench stated it to me, except that nothing will come of it, which I told her.

Word of Bosco's death has finally reached us. He left a paper for publication in the *NEJMonkeys* that was heartbreaking. He titled it "Hail and Farewell, Noble Friends." Too bad. We could use him now. The animal model will always be needed, especially when you can't locate any monkeys and animal activists are winning and chimp research becomes a no-no. Word of Dr. Sister Grace's suicide is also leaking out. Hers is a great loss. Everyone badmouths her now, of course, which is usually the clue to a greatness of historic proportions. Hermia showed me the note she batted out to you and Daniel, riddled with typos among her tears. She also showed me a report that verified Grace's discoveries. "Her Nobel for vel has been acknowledged for the great discovery it was." The good Dame says she's not feeling all that warm toward you. She says she feels abandoned, "but via that route can only lead me toward unquenchable strength."

It should be very difficult to get a human being to take a drug that a sick monkey failed on. That's what a trial used to be all about. You win some, you lose some. People die on trials because of this truth. PIs are very selfish with the truth. They have to be. You want to know why doctors never talk much? Yes, there's something very immoral lurking here. But there are only so many ways we can find out some things. That's why pharma scientists will pump anything into you they can get away with. That's why they'd rather do so many trials abroad. They don't have to use monkeys over there. Well, we won't be using them here, either.

It's a complicated issue. Pharmaceutical company ovens the world over are stuffed with the ashes of drugs that had "animal toxicities" that actually wouldn't have bothered humans or, more sadly, might have saved them, if the monkey hadn't had its FADS-induced departure. But if something doesn't work for a variety of reasons, into the oven it goes. Ovens, as Hitler taught us, are not only for baking cakes. They are for destroying evidence. A pharmaceutical company does not want you to know what it has failed at. It doesn't want you to know the whole story of what it's succeeded at either. It's not a "whole story" kind of business, making medicines for our bodies. And no company has a very long run before it gets dethroned.

We're coming up to another . . . I hesitate to call it a milestone; let's just call it another chance. Here we've got this plague of UC and with the "success" of ZAP—because that's what Dash is peddling, big-time—all the pharms will soon be sniffing around, getting hotter pants each passing day.

Such a constellation of possibilities doesn't come up all that often: growing plague, growing numbers of desperate dying people, drug companies with access to a LOT of money, more than ever in their histories, really; no drug company before, during, or after the war (where they'd made fortunes selling stuff on black markets) had treasuries like the current bunch has accumulated in their greed. They also have smarter people working for them. I say this with no trepidation, which perhaps I should because young scientists these days with their unbridled ambitions are not overburdened with the milk of human kindness. And cretins run all the companies now. No George Mercks or Henry Klines, Charlie Lederle, Eli Lilly, the founding fathers.

So what does one do with crappy ZAPpy?

One gives it to people, of course. What else is one to do? That is why we have our FADS, not to shelter us from harm as they would have us believe, but really to legally usher us as close to the vicinity of an oven as they can. And we thought they were here to look after our health. Oh, dear God, it's all such a crap game, can't you see? Just like old Democracy itself.

HERMIA AND GRACE'S SUICIDE NOTE

"My dear freddy and danil iis my sad duty to tell you your grace committs suiciede. I tell mother superior and lucas j I named Hermai my enxt f kin."

We have lived in this same city for some twenty-five years and never visited each other or so much as dialed each other on a telephone. From certain papers that she left for me I don't think she performed her exit willingly, but out of desperation and great sadness. It will be my task to try to find out why.

•

INT. EMMA'S OFFICE. DAY.
Buzzy, Emma's nurse, has handed her some papers. She looks at them sadly. She looks up at Fred. Tommy is here with him.
EMMA: Your liver is tanking. *(Hands them the report.)*
FRED: What's that mean?
EMMA: If these numbers keep going down it means . . . your time is running out.
FRED: How long?
EMMA: I don't know. Livers are very tricky.
FRED: What about ZAP?

EMMA: I can't give it to anyone in good conscience. I'll cobble something else to try.

FRED: What happened to all those lesions everybody got?

EMMA: Nobody knows. They just disappeared. *(Screaming at him:)* WHY AREN'T YOU STILL NOT TELLING THEM TO STOP FUCKING!

FRED: I TOLD THEM AND THEY STOPPED TALKING TO ME! WHY AREN'T YOU TELLING THEM YOURSELF AT LAST?

They suddenly hug on to each other, joined by Tommy, then by Buzzy.

EXT. NYU MEDICAL CENTER. DAY.
Fred and Tommy are walking from Emma's office. Fred stops suddenly and just stands there looking into space. Then he takes the medical report Emma had given him of his lab numbers and stuffs it in his pocket. He tries to stand tall and strong as he marches forward.

INT. FRED'S LOFT. DAY.
Fred is staring into space. Tommy is observing him to see how he is.
TOMMY *(finally)*: How are you taking this?
FRED *(finally)*: I am not going to die.
TOMMY: Good man.

LAURIE GARRETT, PULITZER-WINNING SCIENCE REPORTER, WRITES TO FRED

The bottom line for me is that the gay community is taking the rap on this.

But by keeping records sealed from sight, governments and pharmaceutical manufacturers continue to endanger lives. My attempts to write all this have met with lack of interest and total rejection at my every attempt, even by the publisher of my book, *The Coming Plague*.

A very large lawsuit against Greeting was filed in the USA on behalf of the nation's hemophiliacs. But as part of whatever settlement, Greeting demanded and received a court order to seal all the records. I have unsuccessfully tried various legal maneuvers to get the seals broken, but I fear the truth is lost to science. My info from litigants indicates Greeting knew about hepatitis contamination in the 1960s and did nothing about it when releasing their Factor VIII. That they're fighting so hard to keep the deposition hidden should tell us all something.

THE ROAD TO ZAP

DEBBI DRIVER, R.N., DOES NOT LIKE FARRELL OBERNOUGHT, M.D., AND HERE ARE SOME REASONS WHY

Oh, I didn't mind being transferred out here. I couldn't take another day of Dr. Jerrold Omicidio. What a tight-ass. Besides I'm needed here, much more than in D.C., where the NITS ZAP trial is tiny compared with the mammoth one that must be done here in San Francisco. This town is death city. I have never seen so many sick and dying men in my life. This is new stuff. Boy, is it new stuff. It's historic what we have to do here. It's like climbing mountains! This is what I trained for, what I've wanted ever since I saw my first nurse's uniform in some movie and asked my mommy, "What's that she's wearing? Why is she wearing that? What's she going to do in it? I want to do it too."

Having said all these worthy things, I am reduced to working for another jerk. Who is Farrell Obernought and why am I thinking unkind things about him? Because he's very important and I'm trying to understand him, which is not an easy thing to do. Because Farrell Obernought is in charge of San Francisco and that means he's in charge of me.

I am frightened. I am not a person who gets frightened. I have worked in every shithole since Vietnam. I have 2,500 people in our trial, and Farrell Obernought, just like Jerry Omicidio, hasn't got a compassionate bone in his body.

Farrell Obernought is tall and handsome. This is a man who graduated from Yaddah Med and even went to Cambridge. At Cambridge, I believe, he learned to dress so well. Tweeds look good on tall men with broad shoulders and nice-proportioned feet for their brogues. Hair, I forgot the hair. He has good hair, dark and wavy, and it sits in place naturally so that the waves stay put without goo. You don't see many aging heads of hair these days that stay put without goo. It's sort of a freaky feat, this, like President Ruester's hair always being black with no gray or goo. Almost in his grave and he's never had a gray hair. How can you trust a man like that? Exactly! Now here we have another goo-less hairy leader who's keeping his mouth shut, afraid to let anyone know that he doesn't know what the fuck we're seeing while he acts as if he does! Just like our dear president. And Dr. O. Nobody cares that a 1500 mg daily dose of ZAP is knocking them dead from coast to coast.

Every patient wishes Dr. Farrell Obernought were gay because he's every patient's dream come true. But he isn't gay, so when they find out, then he isn't every patient's dream come true. Then he's a dream deferred, which is to say he isn't a dream at all. This is no way to feel when you're walking toward your death. And your doctor exudes, yes that's the word, *exudes*, reeks so much charisma that he doesn't give a shit about you. Gay guys pick up on this quickly about their docs. If they sense one iota of, what do I call it, not homophobia exactly, but *discomfort*, that word will do for now, the doctor-patient relationship is on a whole different footing, and one that I don't think is all that healthy or conducive to success in the work we're trying to do. Whatever it is. Right now it's still mainly about ramming 1500 mg a day down everyone's throat. Guys in the ward vomit 1500 mg. Farrell won't come anywhere near them if they're covered with vomit. This clue to his soul is just for starters.

Straight doctors are uncomfortable examining the private parts of a gay male's body. They're particularly uncomfortable anywhere near the rectum. I've already had to deal with a number of cases of rectal cancer because Dr. Farrell Obernought and his group of straight associates don't go there as a matter of course, which they must, given what's going on now. Dr. Lell even posted my memo about this in the PI network newsletter. All these straight docs won't look up an asshole or even under a testicle. They don't want to touch any private part of gay patients!

I've asked each of them, "What's it like having pretty much an all-gay-male practice?" and "What's it like when they come on to you?" Each blushed. "Why are you blushing?" I asked each and every one of them, which only made each do so, only more so. Give me the Jewish schmucks any day. "This is awful" is how the Jew docs are reacting as they reach for their stethoscopes, and I for one thank God for it. I brought this up at a meeting: "How are we supposed to deal with the fact that everything is so awful and you guys won't lay a hand on your patients?" I brazenly asked. Silence. Finally everyone looked to Farrell, our new leader. "Um, well, I think we must not be there for that. Rise above it. We're not their shrinks, for Christ's sake." Andy Goldstein from St. Louis General said, "Oh, come off it, Farrell. You sound like a fucking Nazi." Andy Goldstein was removed as a PI and St. Louis was removed as an official site. No kidding. Just like that. Next time I saw Farrell I asked him what happened to Dr. Goldstein and St. Louis. He gave me a sharp look and walked on. Later he stopped me and said, "Don't you think I am a compassionate man?" Okay, mister, I think to myself, if that's what that brain of yours is stewing on. "No," I answered. "I think most straight docs have trouble dealing with gay patients." He gave me another of those sharp looks. "You put it right out there, don't you?" "You bet," I answered. "And any time you want to get me transferred out like Andy Goldstein, be my guest."

Then I said to him: "I don't trust doctors who are cold as ice."

Then I said to him: "I don't trust doctors who treat nurses like servants."

Then I said to him: "You don't like gays, do you?"

"It's about time the fairies got their due, don't you think? They're certainly making a mess of my city."

I relayed every word of this to Jerry and Daniel.

I was of course reassigned back to Jerry. He showed me what Dr. Farrell Obernought had placed in my permanent record:

"Boy, she was one troublemaking bitch. Why she had it out for me I have no idea. I never said the things she said I said. It just gave me, fast and up front and right away, a taste of the kind of attitudes I was going to have to deal with."

PICTURES FROM AN EXHIBITION

FRED: Doc Stiles of UCLA Medical Center has a nervous breakdown. M.D. breakdowns are happening all over the place. Emma Brookner's cry of "I'm smart, goddammit, smart as they come, and I can't make these guys well!" is increasingly heard.

Stiles is truly convinced he's really found the cure. He's cried for his dead ones. He cradles his near-dead ones. He nourishes his still-living ones in any way he can. He took care of me when I was out there with Adreena. I really like him.

PetruV. No one knows where it comes from, but there it is, with endorsements from credible doctors and patients who are taking it. My friend Marty in San Francisco said it is worth a try, and Marty is someone I and everyone respect a lot. Guys who are taking it are okay, which in and of itself is an endorsement of sorts. I even make an announcement about it myself, which I shouldn't, in some appearance I make somewhere. I speak out in favor of giving PetruV a chance. I get a lot of shit for doing this. But guys need hope. Desperation makes for great hungers (mine included). But one patient dies, Gus Vamusky, in Marty's group as a matter of fact. News of this one death hits the gay papers and before you know it Velma Dimley is writing a blistering attack on Marty and me for not dumping on this "wretched unproven compound that has led to death." Interesting to note how some people, like Velma, are so quick to jump on one single death in a patient whose body was already falling apart from a dozen different OIs and blame it on an untested drug that might indeed be useful. Kipper Gross is reputed to be on it. He's looked so awful for so long, people think he's not long for this world, and now he's looking healthy.

I wonder how Purpura found out Junior was on it and on Vetch's Neutralitron. Rumor has it that PetruV was Stiles's stuff. And that Jerry had crapped all over it. Which he did. And whoever told Purpura, she killed it, getting FADS to declare it a federal offense to touch it. We'll never know if it's any good, except that Junior's still alive.

Whatever Stiles's "cure" is, he needs money for it and he's a reputable doc. But no one will fund him because he won't reveal what his cure is. He then starts standing outside various locales in Los Angeles with a tin cup, begging for contributions, "for my cure for UC. I've found the cure for UC. Don't you want a cure for UC?" Then he just disappears.

Some people still taking PetruV are fine. It's made of lots of harmless herbs and plants. Hog Hooker would have recognized most of their names. He grew most of them in his garden in Ontuit.

After about six months Doc Stiles reappears back in town, reopens his office, and carries on quietly.

•

DANIEL: Omicidio's face graces the front page of *The Prick*, again. Orvid doesn't give him the Nazi treatment this time but the photo makes him look twelve years old and very bewildered. He's headlined "This Little Piggy." Jerry has gone on record as in favor of Dodo's test. I want to choke him. Dodo is only paying any attention to clearing his name of the growing number of charges Dingus continues to rack up against him. So his test is not THE TEST we need, are waiting for, and for which we will now be required to wait at least another year or two. Or three. I literally beg Jerry to put some pressure on Dodo. Then in unison he and I both answer, "It's not my department."

•

TOMMY: Fred and I go down to D.C. to speak. Ten people show up. Washington is too full of Dumb Doras. Daniel said they can't be located beyond the bar scenes on weekends. Most of them work for the government and are terrified of losing their jobs, and with good reason, because some are beginning to lose their jobs.

Fred throws a drink in the face of this guy Terry Dolan at a gay cocktail party in Georgetown we go to. He yells at him in front of the fifty or so other guys there: "How dare you come to a gay party, and take pleasure from our life, when what you do is raise money for all our enemies to kill us." He runs a Conservative Political Action Committee and has raised millions that are turned into shit patties to hurl at us. There was an article about him in *The Truth* last week listing all his "accomplishments." Terry is fucking with Harold Millbank, a friend of Fred's. The other guys in the room stay away from us as if we've got the plague. Once again I hear someone saying, "Lemish is going crazy."

Daniel was too busy to get together. He says it wouldn't serve us well to be seen together. It's too bad because I'd like to meet him finally. I think Fred and he are having a little tiff. I wonder if he knows about the state of Fred's health.

•

DANIEL: Jerry is becoming a media whore. He will go on anything or speak to anyone and his face is becoming identified with UC and America's doctor for same. He obviously loves it. A car and driver have materialized as part of his job and he uses them daily to make his rounds downtown, going to Capitol Hill now, "checking in," as he puts it.

Guys no longer want to enroll in our studies. They're awaiting better results from *any* PI study. I point it out to Jerry, of course, after he's faced Dash's fury for "not minding your store!" So he says something to me like "Deal with it." Which brings Dash rushing back yelling at me, "You keep your fucking hands off my trial."

•

DANIEL: How did I know that Stuartgene was having "scenes" with Arnold Botts? Arnold came to me with a ripped anus, badly infected. He stripped down immediately without my asking him. I could actually remember what his body looked like. Pale skin. Even the same smell, like milk that's sour. Mad, crazy eyes that dart all over the place. How he'd risen to hold the jobs he has, both in our government and at Greeting and now at this Presidium, I have no idea.

He couldn't stop talking, as if he was on drugs, which his eyes told me he is. If my ass was ripped open like that, I'd be on drugs too.

"I can't find any doctor who can take care of this. I mean, I can't go to any doctor I know. If you know what I mean. You got this reputation as the gay doc. Do I know you from somewhere? Is whatever you're going to do going to put my asshole back together? I mean, I would be grateful at this point just to be able to crap without pain. Getting that other shit stuck up there, God knows how I got into it. You take enough of something, you can do anything. I was always one to respond to the dare. You know, the challenge of it all. When I was a kid I got pissed on by the other guys. I vowed I'd never let anyone piss on me again. You want to stick a piece of lumber up my ass, you have to pay me good. That's how you rise to the top in this town, putting out for big bucks from the big boys. The bigger the big boy, the bigger the bucks. You don't get to the top in this town unless you got hefty amounts of desires and of strangeness in your belly and brain. I got this one guy who's the biggest scientist at NITS. He's the one who stuck the tree trunk up my ass. You know, take enough shit and it actually feels good for a while. I got another guy owns a big drug company, he likes to watch us. Then he wants me to lock him in a closet. I hate faggots. I got a girlfriend more beautiful than life itself. She won't talk to me. But she will . . . She will . . ."

At this point he passes out. I had to get him to Montezuma fast. He was losing blood from his rectum. I got Jack Dorkin to sew him up. "I've never seen anything like this," Jack said. "And you say he isn't gay?"

"I don't think so. He hates gays. Go figure."

"What do we do with him when he wakes up? He's going to be in excruciating pain and there's only so much pain shit I can legally dispense."

"I have a feeling he'll be able to locate more. I'm turning him over to you. I can't see him again. Personal reasons too complicated to go into."

Jack threw me a strange look.

"Don't worry. My ass is clean as a whistle. We grew up together and he doesn't remember me. And I don't want him to."

•

IANTHE: "It has to do with the silent, invisible mob in men's minds and hearts that is waiting to burst out into spiritual violence and sometimes physical violence."

Letter from your great lesbian southern writer, Lillian Smith, to our great lesbian First Lady, Eleanor Roosevelt, telling her about her new book. I just came across this and I thought it must fit into your "history" somewhere, no?

•

INT. NEW YORK CITY BALLET. NIGHT.

Emma in her wheelchair sitting on the aisle, her feet moving in time with the music and dancers as best she can. Fred and Tommy are with her.

FRED'S VOICE: You really love ballet.

EMMA'S VOICE: More than anything. I'm a season subscriber.

EXT. LINCOLN CENTER PLAZA. NIGHT.

Audience going home. Avram is holding a sign with gay pink triangle inverted that says SILENCE = DEATH. Fred, with Tommy and Emma, is talking to him.

AVRAM: A bunch of us take turns meeting in each other's apartments to make activist art. Good to see you, Fred. We miss you.

VINCENT *(joining with another poster)*: We sure do. You've got to make another speech.

FRED: No one will come. Everybody hates me.

ERIC *(joining with another poster)*: They'll come. Guys are getting more desperate now. We'll spread the word. They're ready.

TOMMY: I keep telling him that but he doesn't believe me. More and more people are more and more frightened and keep asking me where you are.

FRED *(to Eric)*: Eric, how's Marcus?

ERIC: Dead.

EMMA: Marcus Noble?

ERIC: Yes, ma'am. He committed suicide. I loved him a lot.

Eric's poster: RUESTER IS KILLING US.

EXT. BUS STOP. NIGHT.

Emma, Fred, and Tommy are waiting for a kneeling bus to arrive. The weather turns bad. Emma pulls out an umbrella, which Tommy takes and opens and holds over her. A bus appears but doesn't stop for Emma. She jots its number down.

EMMA: Our wonderful public service. Don't give a shit for the people they're meant to serve.

FRED: I want an army! A wonderful army. I want to start a new organization devoted to political action, to fighting back. It's time for us to really shake things up!

FRED'S APARTMENT.

FELIX AND TOMMY: YES. YES. YES.

"SEX ÜBER ALLES"

Cocker Rutt teaches and writes what he does with pride. He's a proud teacher at the New Jersey Institute of Organic Philosophy. "Unless philosophy's left unbridled, what field be left to graze?" is the school's motto, more or less, in Latin. It used to be a school of animal husbandry until New Jersey became so populated with humans that the animal population couldn't support that curriculum. That not too many of today's students enroll in his course The Pertinambulae of Queerdom from the Third Reich to Steve Reich doesn't prevent Dr. Rutt, as he's known at NJIOP, from proudly writing the many instructive treatises that can challenge young minds. There are a number of self-published academic and pseudo-academic (the dividing line is elusive) journals willing to publish such as Cocker. "The Arrival of the Homosexual Penis as the Logarithm of Male Dominance" was a recent Rutt that elicited several letters to the editor of *Achilles and Madonna: The Journal of Queer Iconography*. A recent issue of *QUEER PUBE* features Cocker's "The Thrill of Pursuing the Destruction of Anti-Anal Rectitude." This paper, a particularly challenging and dense one, has yet to elicit either student or reader response, but the new issue of *PUBERTY PLUS!* has yet another of his essays, "To Be or Not to Be," which, with its pointed reference to Hamlet as "a major Queer icon," will surely garner attention.

Cocker and *The Village Vice*'s Pubie Grotty have come to the lovely town of New Priss, New Jersey, to meet with the great gay author Jervis Pail, who has recently returned to America to be a full professor of English at New Priss University, with tenure. For the past number of years Jervis has lived in Manila, where he was guest editor for *Philippine Vogue*.

There are many in the gay world who said out loud and even in print that Jervis left America when and because UC arrived, so Jervis is nervous about his reentry, lest he have lost his unchallenged position as gay lit's brightest star. He's defended himself against those charges in many interviews in *The Avocado* and *The Prick*. "I had to keep the slate of my unconscious clean so I could write what I read on it" was one of his more memorable defenses of his move to Manila. Another was "The politics of The Underlying Condition were and are simply too exhausting. Who can deal with the likes of Fred Lemish? I wish someone would come along and put him out of our misery." Jervis smiles when he makes a verbal joke. He is clever with words.

Fred Lemish had written in *The Avocado*, "He ran away from the most important subject he could write about." Pail's last novel had been "out of touch," according to *The Walt Whitman Review of Books*. What's he going to write about now? He doesn't know anything about UC. Manila is certainly not a hotbed of medical information. Since his return he's been both impressed and depressed by how an obsession with knowledge about this disease is consuming everyone he knew. It must be said that everyone he knew is also sick with it or of it, or knows someone who has died, or is dead himself. Not a few times has he considered returning to the Philippines. The boys are certainly very sweet there, and already sending him letters about how much they miss him. It's a good thing he held on to his ourie, which is a little country cottage, a shack really, made of mud and ferns and palm leaves, in Verteetoo, the small village an hour east of Manila where sweet boys can be bought for only ten doo.

Cocker and Pubie are humble in Jervis's presence. Most gay writers are. Jervis had been there first with a good review in *The Truth* and a classy publisher, Alonso Knockwurst. Gay writers tend to tie themselves together, as if the protection of their fellows can help them overlook the fact that even as a group they don't have many readers, and aren't written about in the mainstream press, or don't have as much talent as they think they have. Of all the gay writers, though, Jervis is still written about the most. He's long made it a point to stay in touch with everyone famous he's ever met, and his contacts with *Vogue* have certainly helped, even though he can no longer remember whose dick he sucked or which people he invited to one of his soigné dinners with other important people he'd gathered along one roadway or another. Not in Manila, of course. No one came to Manila. Which was why, in the end, he really had no choice but to come home. He'd made a wrong turn when he upped and left and he'd best face up to it and rewrite his route back into the center-stage spotlight.

Fred has always thought Jervis was a phony. "He writes beautifully but he doesn't say anything useful," Fred said in his *Avocado* response to Jervis's unkind words about him. "All he writes about is sex, as if gay men have nothing else in their lives, as if all we have to think with and about are our dicks." This, written before UC when Jervis was still around, was of course not dissimilar to spitting on Jesus, and many gay writers not only don't talk to Fred, they won't even consider him a writer. The *Avocado* piece was one of Fred's earlier forays into the world of gay art and culture, and it was in response to an attack by Jervis, in the opening salvo of what would become a continuing bitchfest: "Where did this Fred Lemish come from that he considers himself a writer, worthy of inclusion among our immortals, Proust and Gide and Genet? He is talentless. Utterly talentless." This was after Fred's first play had opened and closed on opening night and he was feeling exceptionally fragile. He considered the attack by Jervis unkind. If he represented the world of gay writers, Fred would happily steer clear of it.

Jervis was a founder of the Purple Peculiars, the most exclusive group of a few gay male writers, "our very own Académie Française," Jervis called them. Once there had been a dozen Peculiars. Now there are only three. Persh died, and Drean, and Paul-Marshall, and Murkt and Tilley and Jason Robert (JR, as he didn't like to be called). How many is that? It's hard to recall all their names because—well, it's hard enough to remember the names of many gay writers. No one will admit that when you consider the long noble line of sublime gay writers including Melville and Proust, none of the Peculiars, including Jervis, was anywhere near to being comparable. Jervis's last book, which he wrote with Mussy, another Peculiar, was *One Hundred and Ninety-Eight Ways to Have Rectal Intercourse.* Somehow, he'd been elected to the Academy of American Artists and Writers, no doubt via another sucked dick or two, or a few of those soigné Jervis feeds before he went into Philippine exile.

Jervis, as the only Peculiar to get reviewed in *The Truth* (it helps when you've been to orgies with top editors from all over town, particularly when they're masters who like to piss on slaves—and what top editor does not like to do that?—unless they like to get pissed on themselves, and there are certainly major editors who like that, too), had written to each of the dying Peculiars on their deathbeds, "History will remember you. I promise." Sadly, History hasn't. Another reason Jervis came home. He could tell how many times his name was not appearing now in . . . well, anything, really. How had he ever talked himself into thinking that he could stay in touch from so far away? Well, he had been frightened. Nothing wrong in that. If only he had just admitted it. Well, now he has. More or less. He will not admit anything out loud, of course. And now, since almost everyone is frightened, no one will notice whether Jervis was, or isn't.

It should be noted that Jervis, at Fred's request, had joined him in starting GMPA. Fred was looking for a "famous gay name" to join him in launching it, and Kipper Gross and Randy Dildough and Sammy Sircus had declined the honor. Jervis is still listed as one of the six founders although he left for Manila shortly after the meeting in Fred's loft that brought this historic organization into being. Fred, whose own ego has its weak spots, gets annoyed when he sees Jervis described as "a founder of GMPA." So to the list of Jervis's failings, to his lack (for Fred) of talent, to his preoccupation with sex, and shortly, to his unending espousal of his joyful masochism, Fred has appended Jervis's cowardice in running away just when he might be truly useful.

Now that he's back, writers start begging Jervis to jump-start the Peculiars, to locate suitable replacements for the departed PPs. Cocker and Pubie would both die to be Peculiars, but one is an academic and the other is a journalist, so they don't really qualify. But that's not why they've come to Beer & Burger in New Priss to meet with Jervis Pail. They've come to brainstorm the future, a future now increasingly overwhelmed by the past and those who have passed. Jervis had this recognition quotient before he left, and they all feel—well, "who else is there to speak for us?" They all know the gay world is all but bereft of willing gay spokespersons.

"Hey, how are you, Jervis? You look great!" Pubie, short, squat, balding, bushy-bearded, and smiley-faced as ever, hugs Jervis, who is in fact looking quite fat, fatter even than on his last trip home when the interview he gave to *Town and Village* showed him joking about it by lounging on a chaise, belly up and protruding like Buddha's, but who is just as jolly as on that visit, when he was still diagramming on graph paper versions 195 and 196 and 197 of how to fuck and get fucked for his book with Milo Mussy, which turned out to sell very well indeed. "Put on a little more weight, did you?" Pubie, who is sensitive to issues of weight, wants desperately to ask Jervis how, in his condition, he lands as many boyfriends as he claims in all his novels.

"What's the difference? Fat or thin, no one wants to fuck me without being paid. Can I still call One Touch of Penis?"

"Be careful," Pubie warns. "R. Allen died and so did most of his boys and those kids left are all infected."

"So am I," Jervis tells them.

"I'm sorry to hear that," Pubie says, genuinely. He's never sure how to respond to this news. Of course he's sorry to hear it. But he is aware that he looks upon this admission as some sort of disloyalty on the confessor's part, a desertion of the team, so to speak, a traitor to the cause. With which opinion Cocker most certainly agrees. "How will the gay world continue on our mighty mission to teach the rest of the world how wonderful the utter abandonment to the pleasures of promiscuous sex can be if so many practitioners are dropping by the wayside or calling it quits?" There, Cocker has said it out loud and straight as an arrow.

"Is everyone infected?" Jervis apprehensively asks, after a suitable pause for reflection.

"Nobody knows," Cocker answers. "And there's no way of finding out except by getting sick."

"Surely there must be some source of . . . safety?"

"There is no question that some people get sick and some people don't," Pubie says in his best journalistic tone of summing up.

Cocker continues: "But some people can evidently do anything and not get sick and some people can't do anything without getting sick."

"Oh, I hadn't heard about the ones who can do anything and never get sick," Jervis says, wondering how you met them. "How do you meet them?"

"I told you, nobody knows." Cocker and Pubie exchange looks; they are wondering if Jervis, having been away for so long, is in a state of denial. So many guys are who haven't even left the country.

"There's a test but nobody trusts it and the word is we mustn't take it."

"Then we must fight for a test we can trust!" It all seemed clear enough to Jervis. "We mustn't miss the boat."

"Be very careful before you join any group that fights for anything," Cocker warns. "They're becoming both very political and increasingly powerful and Fred Lemish is their leader. He's going to be making a big speech, I hear, one of these days."

"Fred Lemish is popular?"

"I know it's hard to believe," Pubie says.

"When I left, Fred Lemish was a joke."

"I know it's hard to believe," Cocker agrees. "Fred Lemish is paid attention to now."

"So you indicated," Jervis exclaims, unsmiling. He wonders again if he might have to return to Manila. Maybe *Vogue* could assign him to a more mainline edition.

"Fred Lemish has been getting his name in the papers and his face on television as if he were the only gay man in America."

"The only one?" Jervis's voice sounds to have lost some heft.

"He's going around calling all his old friends murderers," Pubie says.

"Goodness," Jervis Pail says. Perhaps there is a reason for him to stay here after all. Not only to reestablish his residence and reclaim his literary preeminence but also to sweep Fred Lemish out of the way. He never liked Fred Lemish. Or if he did, he can't remember when, or why. Fred always seemed like such a prude, criticizing him "for writing about sex so much." Just remembering all this perks up Jervis's juices.

"I'm going to write my Gay Pride feature on what a monster Fred's become," Pubie continues. "*The Village Vice* is putting him on our cover."

"Exactly." Jervis actually claps his hands. "Give him a kick in the ass for me." And then he asks, "On your cover?" Jervis has never been on the *Vice*'s cover.

"Give him a kick in the ass for me too," Cocker says. He feels a lot better now that Jervis Pail is home. No one reads *The Village Vice* anymore, so Pubie Grotty's voice is negligible. But Jervis Pail is our Nabokov and our Foucault. Our Updike.

Cocker Rutt, full of pride, then tells them about the lollipop he's been contemplating. "I want to start a new organization devoted to reclaiming gay sex lives in *all* their fulfilling glory. I already have a name for it. Sex Über Alles. And a catchy mission: "We must continue to fight for and defend gay sex.""

"Oh, I like that!" Jervis claps his hands again. He sees a vital and necessary new book to write about just this. He will retain his preeminence. His many fans will certainly listen to him. His voice is too important to ignore.

EAT, MY SISTERS

Clytemnestra Dunkelheim confides to her friends: "First it was the fegalim, then it was the junkies, now it is some schwarzahs here and there, and of course the kurvas. We are safe. You and I and our beloved families are safe." Each mother present for monthly bridge at Clyt's expresses her continuing gratitude that *The Truth* does not report "this awful story."

Someone named Fred Lemish keeps sending her letters asking if she remembers Walter Duranty. "He was your liar, your apologist for Stalin. You are doing it again! All what truth that's fit to print?" Today she received from him a book: *Stalin's Apologist: Walter Duranty,* The New York Truth*'s Man in Moscow.* He denied there was a famine in 1932–1933 at the same time as Stalin was deliberately starving some 40 million people to death. "Russians hungry but not starving," he wrote. For this reporting he won the Pulitzer Prize. He kissed Stalin's ass in order to have access to him. There is lately mounting noise about rescinding Duranty's 1932 Pulitzer. Has something like this ever happened? Certainly not to *The Truth.* Clyt remembers Duranty as such a nice man, even if he only had one leg. Push told her Duranty was "very big with the ladies." She wondered with one leg how he did it. Not that Push was doing it with two. She wondered why Jews had such trouble with sex and one-legged goyim did not. Not that she wanted it. She just wondered. What in our history has made us so uncompromisingly unwelcome to sex? She thought briefly of asking her "sisters" if they might be interested in a colloquium on this subject but then thought, No, I am the person, remember, who forbids fegalim in my paper. She remembers she had a nice cousin who was a fegalim. She has heard he was killed by Hitler. She had been attracted to him. But her father had warned her. "I can tell a fegalim at a mile distance. A rabbi knows," he told her. There is so much she and her sisters could talk about. Over bridge, one or two have even intimated that their sons or daughters might be gay. "But how do you know for certain?" Molly Karpilow had asked, directing her question particularly toward Clyt. "Clyt, why does not your paper talk about this and give us guidance? I want more, not less, from your fine paper."

Thank you, Molly Karpilow.

AH, YES, ANOTHER CHURCH

Cardinal Bernard Buggaro, transferred by the Holy Father from Washington to Boston, walks beneath some olive trees donated by a Sicilian parishioner, trying to sort out un-sort-out-able things. Sicilian olive trees do not grow well in Boston, and these show it.

Thank God free speech is not something that accompanies any job description in our church, he thinks. This illness is a great embarrassment, he thinks. It embodies many things of which we disapprove, he thinks. My boys will keep their mouths shut, he thinks. Although today he heard about another one, a bishop in New Mexico who buggered (he *hates* that word) boys when he was young, and the story is surfacing in a local paper there some forty years later. I thought there was a statute of clerical limitations, he thinks. If we are going to be condemned eternally for every ding-dong, what's the point of trying to sell salvation? He's heard that even the New York City mayor's a fairy. As was my predecessor there, now called to . . . wherever fairy cardinals are called to when they . . . pass.

Boston is bound to be a test of tests. I can only assume the Holy Father in his Infinite Wisdom has called me here for a reason. The Holy Fucker is rotten about giving me signs. Yes, the cardinal is angry. He can't see any way out of this one. Every priest and cleric and father and brother has tasted somebody's penis at some time in his Catholic career. It comes with the territory. And more than any place, Boston is the posting everyone prays for.

Boston's always thought to be a safe diocese. The cardinal is from Boston. The pews and confession booths of Boston and its environs are stained with the semen of many decades of the love for Christ. We used to think there was safety in numbers, he thinks. We were wrong, he thinks. We were wrong, he knows. What does the Church do when it knows it's wrong? Apologies are only for mortal men to make.

But now some of his brothers are getting sick and dying. Is God finally catching up?

PARLEZ-VOUS

Dear Fred,

It is awful here in France. Hospitals are overflowing and the gay discos are more full of sex than even in America. In fact, the bars and discos are overflowing with Americans! Your old trick from Paris you told me about, Jacques T., the famous fashion designer, he is dead. He fucked with dozens of people on the night before he killed himself. "If I am dying, then I die in the arms of my beloved countrymen," he is said to have said. He threw himself from his balcony. Twelve stories. He landed in the Seine. He had dressed himself in one of his famous expensive ballgowns that were sold in your Bergdorf. What are we to do? Please tell us all! You are the only one anywhere who is saying anything. Even here in France, when I mention your name, they make faces. In France, every leader gets laughed at when they try to tell the truth. I thought you were the leader.

Love, Didier

P.S. Pierre Bergé and Yves S.L. give me money to keep our *Gai Pied* magazine going. What do your Kipper Gross and Sam Sircus do for you?

THE UC DENIALISTS

Why did it take so long? Dodo is full of shit. French scientists are full of shit. Dr. Anyone who claims that UC is the cause of UC is full of shit. Marty immediately christens them the UC Denialists. Fred asks Marty why he takes them so seriously, why he even dignifies them by acknowledging their existence.

Laurent Lascivio, Dr. Pascall Dumtrum, and Orvid Guptl. They don't know each other, but they all say the same thing. There is no such thing as UC. Orvid has suddenly decided it's caused by pigs. (Something is beginning to happen to Orvid.) Laurent thinks it's caused by Dridgies. Dr. Dumtrum thinks it's caused by syphilis. Dr. Dumtrum is a distinguished scientist, with tenure at Yaddah. He even has a Nobel. The White House awarded him this country's Medal of Freedom. President Ruester himself hung it around his neck.

Enter young, attractive, homespun Betsy Leadstrom. No one's heard of Betsy, and she's getting published in leading magazines like *Playboygirl* and *The New Gotham*. Who is she fucking to get into *The New Gotham*? Hadriana Totem? Betsy's heard about ZAP and says it won't work on UC because there's no such thing as UC.

ZAP is once again making its way out of the shadows into life, or death. The first two sets of trials were such a mess that new trials are set up. There must be a trial that will produce more favorable results. Von is losing patience with Dash. Betsy is not the only one who's calling ZAP poison. Michael Callan of NAPWUC is calling it poison. Even Fred, in one article, has been far from neutral: "I am only positing this as a possibility: this shit isn't good for you," even though, as he often makes a point of saying, "I try never to take a stand on anything medical." Dash and Debbi and Maggie and Hube and Von and Daniel and Jerry huddle, liaise, brainstorm, ignore each other, save for one overriding principle, to nip this bad publicity, including these denialists, in the bud before it's too late. The only way to do that is to present a united front that ZAP is good for you.

Up to now it hasn't been.

They're going to try again.

A LOVER'S LAMENT

How do I love you now, my sweetie? With your vomit and your blood and your shit so messily adhering us to each other. Our love was always messy, wasn't it? But not like this. It was messy because of sweat and semen, passion's fluids, not death's.

HUGS

"Still no reason for hysteria!" So proclaim headlines of the Brothers of Lovejoy press in their 242 newspapers across the country.

The writer of this, Ortus Grumpp, had a great-great-grandfather who came west with Herod from Fruit Island. Today's Grumpp is an Elder Ancient (EA) of the Church. So much of history is filling in the gaps. Gaps are holes left open on purpose so the Grumpps and Elder Ancients of this world can fill them in. All the best histories have them.

"In spite of fears that it's spreading to heterosexuals, it isn't. Jesus has told me. He actually hugged me, He was so very pleased and excited." It should be remembered that one of the tenets of this religion is the freedom to talk directly to God, to Jesus, to angels, to anyone of authority in Heaven.

An article in *The Truth* by Dr. Dearie Fault himself raises the issue.

"Is it possible that heterosexuals do not get The Underlying Condition?" *The Truth* is now giving Dearie more latitude. Ortus is pleased to see that that Dr. Jerrold Omicidio has this to say: "We continue to see cases in homosexual men and drug addicts and find little supporting evidence that the heterosexual population is adversely affected." Good for Omicidio, Ortus thinks. Guess my boys in D.C. got through to him.

Yes, Jerry did say that. Daniel watches him. "It breaks my heart," Daniel tells Fred. "He's no good at politics. I sense he wants me to hug him and make it right. He is a cold and protected man. We have to have hope."

Fred screams at Daniel: "You're a fucking dreamer!"

Daniel ignores him. They speak to each other; they don't speak to each other; each day brings a different act in their own drama.

"What are you doing!" Jerry said when Daniel did try to hug him after a particularly nasty swipe at him in *The Prick*. Daniel told him he needed a hug because he was taking so much shit, "It has to be hard on you." "Keep your hands off me!" was Jerry's reply.

Fred goes apoplectic. Something is happening to Daniel. It's like an exposure to UC itself, the way he's being poisoned by some infection. Fred wonders if he's already lost him. "Can't you see there are many ways to lie and this is one of them! Why is Jerry saying this? He's *very* good at politics! Hermia's discovered that his wife's brother is a rabid right-winger. What separates the great men from all the rest is that they make the right decisions. That's definitely not been Jerry. Oh, Daniel! I can just see it all playing out. Jerry is a lie, a lie to society, to dying people, a helpmate to continued dying and death. A great man would have chosen other great men to work with so they could challenge each other to find a cure. Jerry does not want to be challenged. He acts as if he wants us dead. We continue to be in even bigger trouble. Deep Throat agrees with me. Oi and double oi!"

Again, Daniel doesn't respond.

Fred is sort of pleased with this reading of his tea leaves. He'd not put a few pieces together in quite this way before. How can anyone find anything hopeful at present? The notes for his speech are getting longer. By now more are impatiently awaiting it. Eric promised he'd have a full house.

So what is he waiting for? The former moviemaker is still telling him the timing isn't quite right yet. But he thinks it may be getting closer. Fewer guys are saying nasty things about him. One old ex-friend even reached out to him on the street and silently gave him a hug.

DR. ISRAEL JERUSALEM IS ARRESTED AND SENT TO PRISON

He misses Grace terribly, to share this with, to hear her say, "Congratulations, you fucking old Jew. You carry on the great tradition. We all were once medicine men." He remembers the first feelings of excitement that came from scientific discovery, from being with the Iwacky, where he got his first inkling of UC. Israel can see it as he sees a dark cloud in a bright blue sky. His medicine man past is living with him today, as if they are one and the same. There is still time enough for him to make his name for history. He is preparing to announce his great news about its origin, to take that dark cloud away.

He had not paid enough attention to UC. There had been a war on. His practice was sick soldiers, and old people's ailments, arthritis, liver, indigestions. A steady flow of aging patients all with bad tummies is enough to keep a doctor too busy. He is now shaking with excitement. When Israel un-earthed his ancient lab notebooks of more than fifty years ago, he finds that he saw the same in the blood of Evvilleena Stadtdotter, Mercy Hooker, and now Darcus Charles Graves, that all match the blood of the Iwacky and the blood that Deep Throat brought back from Africa. The cancers of this world work this way! He will be a Nobel Prize winner for Isidore Schmuck yet!

But Israel is suddenly arrested by federal police and Minutemen from the Tricia Institute for having sex with minors while being employed under a United States government contract to research the Iwacky tribes in the upper Andes Mountains when he was nineteen years old. The statute of limitations doesn't exist if the "crime" happens while on a government grant. His diaries for those years, so beautifully written that Margaret Mead herself cited them as "among the most important and sensitive of anthropological documents," had just been uncovered in the Admiral Mason Iron Vaultum Library by a Lovejoy graduate student, Nestor Fetman. Fetman had been tipped off about them by one of the ten Iwacky children Israel had brought to this country and adopted and educated as if they were his own. Fetman passed these diaries on to the more rabid branch of Lovejoys, the Furstwasserians, who have quietly sucked up a great many positions in the Ruester adminis-tration. Attorney General Manny Moose signed the warrant and President Ruester himself made a point of publicly ridiculing Dr. Israel Jerusalem as "a shameful, sinful man who has besmirched the face of American science." Once upon a time when he was young, Israel wrote in his diaries about his feelings for the boys who were throwing themselves into his arms, as was the Iwacky custom (and still is, in the Andes and Africa), which still requires such "rites of passage for all young men" or ostracization, both for the recalcitrant youth and the unobliging adult who is found guilty of insulting their cul-ture. These young men, who so hungrily sought his body to give them theirs, touched his heart deeply. And he wrote about the experience in startlingly beautiful prose. And so now Israel Jerusalem, at seventy-seven years, is incar-cerated in a prison in Nome, Alaska. No one from the media would hear his side of the story. Dr. Geiseric, to his credit—"Why is it to my credit? Israel was my mentor!"—tries to arouse some scientific support for Israel's release. "The man is seventy-seven years old, for Christ's sake. Since when do we put people in jail when they are seventy-seven years old?" There will be a trial, perhaps, if Israel lives long enough, but let's not count on it. How long will he be in jail before they bring him to trial? No doubt, at his age, it will be for longer than he can live.

You have to wonder. Fred, the always suspicious, wonders. It all happened so fast, and just after Israel got so excited over his realization about glause. Israel had called to tell him about it, "since I know from Grace that you are involved in telling the truth." Both Fred and Israel are still reeling from what Hermia told them about what had happened to Grace after her work at Partekla. "Sooner or later they always get you," both Israel and Hermia had said to each other and Fred.

Like Grace, Israel had seen the face of UC and been silenced.

So much for his decades of work and discoveries, for all the patients and young men he saved, for all the life he gave to others.

ANOTHER PIECE OF AGING VURD

By a vote of 94–2 Congress passes a revised and more detailed amendment banning any funding of UC programs that "promote, encourage, condone or mention homosexual activities." Introducing the amendment, Sen. O'Trackney Vurd said, "We have got to call a spade a spade, and a perverted human being a perverted human being."

The distinction between fact and fiction, true and false, no longer exists.

PUBIE'S MANIFESTO

The important gay journalist Pubie Grotty is an unattractive package and he knows it. He is dumpy and sloppy and unkempt and happy about it, even though he knows that if he cleaned up his act he might like himself more. It's a perversion, he knows, to be so stubborn about remaining in such a state. But being an intentional slob gives him energy, wonderful gism for *the* crusading gay muckraker, as he sees himself. Why, if he were attractive he wouldn't be half so angry. He gets his best ideas and stories this way: he smiles at people and they believe his smile is beneficent. He smiles, people are charmed, they confide too much, and there it is, all quoted in *The Village Vice*. On such a rink has Pubie skated his way to a certain infamy. It extends throughout the Village. He thinks *The Village Vice* is the world.

He is not without a kind of honor. He is extraordinarily proud of being gay.

Long ago it had come to his attention that his gayness and some other people's gayness are not the same. Well, there was nothing he could do about that. But now more than ever he believes there can be only one gayness. His gayness is the right gayness. Now, with this UC this difference in gaynesses has tried to spread itself like spilled varnish oozing irremovably across a garage's cement floor, impossible to scrape off. (He does not have a garage, but he likes the simile.)

It's been no good his seeing that *The Vice* ignores UC as if it isn't happening. Fewer and fewer read *The Vice*, even in Greenwich Village, and fewer still read Pubie and those few are either on his side already or are only reading him because they're sitting on the toilet with nothing else to read.

Before UC, gays read him. He even won awards. Why should his philosophy of gayness be any different now? Because of some illness in "malfeasant gays"? HE IS NOT SICK! HIS GAYS ARE NOT SICK!

"This article is about Fred Lemish, who is gay and who has taken it upon himself to be our leader in the fight to call attention to an illness that's been affecting parts of our community. Because of his prior total absence in the world of gay politics he has alienated a great many who were not absent when the rules by which we live were agreed upon and ratified by generations of gay leaders and their constituents and constituencies ever since.

"What has troubled many has been Lemish's implication, nay assumption, that this illness is of gay men's own devising, that it's spread by 'our promiscuity,' and that in order for it to be expunged gay men must live a life devoid of sexual pleasure. Lemish would have us give up our history. Lemish would have us deny not only our heritage but what defines us and what we live for. Lemish would have us conceive of a future in which the most important parts of our lives are eviscerated from us . . ."

Out, out, damned Lemish!

He hates Fred Lemish. The prose he's written doesn't reek enough of this hate. It's too . . . too reasonable.

Fred Lemish must be stopped!

My name alone will stop him.

"We will not change! We will not bow down before our enemies who are trying to tell us we are sick! We will not be told what we can and cannot do! We will not be flagellated into submission to the lives that our enemies want us to live!"

The newsstand sales of this issue with Fred Lemish on the cover ("Is Fred Lemish Gays' Very Own Gay Enemy?") do not meet the editor's expectations. Pubie is given notice he's being terminated.

"You'd think with all the people we know," Cocker Rutt says to Pubie.

"You'd think with all your fans," Pubie says to Jervis.

"You'd think with all your students," Pubie says to Jervis and Cocker.

"You'd think with all the gay readers and subscribers to *The Village Vice*," Pubie says to them all.

It is agreed they must join in countering the growing visibility and audibility of the likes of Fred Lemish. This is how Sex Über Alles was further germinated into the world. They and it will stem the tide of people too panicked to have sex. By not mentioning UC, it will not exist. To talk about it or write about it is to advocate for it, why, even to promote it, and we can't have any of that!

Now all he needs is a job.

GOD NEEDS AMPLIFICATION

Dr. Oswald Botkin is the new head of HAH. He, too, is preparing a speech, to be delivered to youngsters back home in Indiana who are meant to be straying. He, too, believes in lists. He sits down to pluck from his master inventory of phrases and feelings. Stuff that hits him where he lives. Stuff that were he up on a pulpit, which of course he is, or will be when he delivers this, he could send sailing out into the farthest crypt of the Temple with a booming resonance. When you hate hard you have to scream hard. His childhood playmates had made fun of him because of his religion. They don't make fun of him now. Jesus has given him a lot. When you're plain and poor Jesus allows you to hate.

Today's Jesus and *Today's Trinity* are the two largest-circulation publications in the AAFF (All-American Fundamentalist Family) movement. Its division, Fundamentalist Families First for Victory (FFFV), has given Oswald visibility, given him TV guest appearances and radio interviews and plenty of being quoted in *The Monument* and *The Truth*. *Today's Jesus* and *Today's Trinity* are more powerful in every way than ever, particularly in the halls of Congress.

This is Oswald's stock boilerplate: "A virulent moral sickness is attacking The American People. Its name is unrestrained sex mania and its leading players are named homosexuals. They are trying to teach you young people to glory in and glorify all the forms of their sexual sins and perversions."

His fingers can't type fast enough.

"The long night of human barbarism is increasing." Always a good one.

"The Christian West in becoming pagan is headed for inevitable doom. There is little prospect of a sunrise." Too negative.

"To assume that an Anti-Christ culture will escape perdition is beyond lunacy." Too complicated.

"The enemy is gaining on all fronts. The hour is late. Christian civilization is in its death throes." Too dramatic.

"America is experiencing an epidemic—an epidemic of homosexuality." Too true.

"America is experiencing a plague—a plague of homosexuality." Better.

"The homosexual blitzkrieg has been better planned and better executed than Hitler's." Possible, but is it too controversial? Don't worry, no one remembers Hitler.

"It is now or never to take up arms for Jesus."

"They live in sin! The Bible says so!"

"They are masculinity out of control, aggressive, powerful, unrestrained, raucous, perverse, orgiastic." Too complimentary.

"The gay man embodies a hypermasculinity, a maleness so extreme it literally explodes in a paganistic savagery." Definitely too complimentary.

"They steal our children." This is always good.

"Have they themselves not written in their very own newspapers, 'We shall sodomize your sons. We shall seduce them in your schools, in your dormitories, in your gymnasiums, in your locker rooms, in your seminaries, in your youth groups, in your movie theater toilets, in your army bunkhouses, in your truck stops, wherever men are men together. They will come to crave and adore us.'" Where did I get this?

"Promiscuity, seduction, and disease are the definition of homosexuality. The Big Three." Hmm. "And homosexuals are both rich and powerful!" Expand on this.

"You, my young friends, must not succumb!"

"You must turn away from this dangerous deviance from God's plan." Good!

Always wind up with: "God's kingdom *will* be established on *all* of this earth! You must and will help make this so."

"The world will end in chaos but you as true believers will be raptured unto Heaven."

He feels better. He who dwells in the house of the president is blessed forever and ever.

He then proceeds to also prepare his article for *Today's Jesus*. He will include the following in this week's "Culture Shock" column:

Sodom-on-Potomac
WASHINGTON—Hundreds of men engaged in homosexual acts—including group sex—at a "leather" bar in the District of Columbia the night before the city's "Gay Pride" parade, an investigation by All-American Fundamentalist Family revealed.

AAFF president Peter LaBarbera witnessed these acts, which occurred at a "Dungeon Dance" party held June 6 at the Edge, one of several "gay" bars in southeast D.C. just blocks from the Capitol building. The Dungeon Dance was advertised heavily in the homosexual *Washington Sword* newspaper.

An officer with the D.C. Metropolitan Police Department responded that the department is aware that illegal open sex is occurring in the homosexual bars but is reluctant to make arrests because of criticism for alleged "civil rights" violations after raiding several homosexual bars last year.

According to LaBarbera, the group sex occurred in two corners of a "dungeon" room inside the Edge. The areas were set apart by large black tarps hanging from the ceiling. Throughout the night and into the morning, men would enter these areas and engage in various sexual acts in full view of other men, many engaging in sadomasochistic whippings.

Besides the illegal sex at the Edge, AAFF reports that lesbians marched topless in the District's "pride" parade—despite a pledge by Mayor Archie Pomplona to control public lewdness. AAFF had reported similar public nudity at last year's march.

•

INT. MINE SHAFT. NIGHT.
Fred and Tommy push Emma through the crowded bar. Many of the guys are naked and playing around with each other. Emma frowns, shaking her head no.
MACDONALD *(naked)*: Hi, Doc. Fancy meeting you here.
EMMA: Go home, MacDonald. You're already sick enough. *(To Fred*

and Tommy:) This is unacceptable. You're all assholes. You must stop fucking each other to death.

BURIED ALIVE

In two towns deep in the country, one in the Tennessee Ozarks and one in the Florida Everglades, people with UC are reportedly being buried alive by their families. "I seen a dozen people with my own eyes," said Mabel Adzen, a local health-care volunteer in Marble, Tennessee. "People don't know how to take care of them when they get real sick, so they just bury them. And since they got no money for undertaking and funerals and stuff, they bury them alive. 'They's almost dead anyway,' is what you hear." In Dresden, Florida, Shane Lockster, another person who describes himself as "a health-care volunteer," gave a different explanation for why these people were buried alive. "It is what the witches tell us to do." He was referring to local practitioners of witchcraft believed to exist in this part of the state, which is very remote.

—Ochonobee Drumbeat,
Serving the Very Rural South for Coming on 43 Years

A BROTHER'S LAMENT

He can't sleep, because he wakes up seeing his brother's face before him, his cheeks sunk, his unshaved skin, his eyes desperately pleading, Please help me. Night and day he sees that face and those eyes and hears that plea. It never goes away. It never goes away. It never goes away.

HIMMLER SAID MORE THAN ONE MILLION GAYS WERE EXTERMINATED

"Himmler said more than one million gays were exterminated." Brinestalker reads this sentence in one of his notebooks. He must get it to Linus Gobbel. He types it out on a plain piece of paper. Then he types it out in all capital letters. Then he types it out in all capital letters and boldface:

HIMMLER SAID MORE THAN ONE MILLION GAYS WERE EXTERMINATED.

He must talk to Linus and also to Dredd Trish.

He remembers his father telling him, "There were half a million Jews in Germany before the war. In a country of sixty-five million people. Every single day we published twenty million copies of hate-Jew stuff. That was maybe fifty copies per Jew."

How can we achieve such deep penetration against the queers here?

●

David Jerusalem reads this sentence too. He writes it out on a plain piece of paper. Then he types it out. Then he types it out in all capital letters. Then he types it out in all capital letters and boldface and folds the piece of paper and slides it into his wallet:

HIMMLER SAID MORE THAN ONE MILLION GAYS WERE EXTERMINATED.

GO HETS, GO!

In *Sexopolis*, Dr. Dorrida Mae Schwartz, their resident adviser on Sexual Matters, writes in her column: "I have many women who have intense vaginal intercourse almost daily, accompanied by intense kissing, and they are fine. Several even confide they enjoy rectal intercourse with their partner." Mordy approves. He is relieved. He tells Dorrida Mae to run more reassuring information like this.

At HAH, Dr. Oswald Botkin declares that a "Designated Investigation Unit" be established at NITS, under Omicidio, who would have it in his power, legally, to keep UC-infected patients incarcerated because they are "in advanced states of infection." The White House point man on this is Linus Gobbel (now Purpura's favorite), who announced on *60 Minutes* that "these men are potential terrorists and their regional and worldwide networks must be eradicated, a mission we will carry out with our freedom-loving partners, The American People." The moderator lets this pass.

•

MONTAGE:
Various churches and gay organizations to which Tommy and Fred appeal. End with black church. Tommy grows in intensity, to Fred's approval.

INT. MIDDLE-AGED WHITE GROUP.
FRED: We must work together to fight! To save your lovers and sons and fathers and friends.
The audience remains stone-faced.

INT. YOUNG STRAIGHT ORGANIZATION.
TOMMY: We must teach and preach and confront and raise hell in the streets until we are numb; then get up and do it again. They can't make us disappear unless we let them. The power is ours. If you care to use it to help your gay friends.

INT. MIXED BLACK AND WHITE.
TOMMY: But we sure as hell don't need twenty different boards, twenty executive directors and financial officers and program directors, twenty thises and thats.
FRED: I beg you and all your groups to all work together! The power is ours.

INT. BLACK CHURCH. NIGHT.
The audience looks at Tommy with stern disapproval.
BLACK WOMAN PARISHIONER: Our boys don't do things like that.
TOMMY: Some do, and I do, and did.
ANOTHER BLACK WOMAN PARISHIONER: My Hilton and my Newton don't do things like that.
Applause from congregation.
TOMMY: How touching and beautiful, your gay men of color suffer and die so nobly and quietly. But we must all force their lying murderers to disappear. The power is all of ours.
FRED *(later)*: Good job, Tom. It's like some Greek tragedy where all the mothers are moaning. They know. You're a hit.

DEEP THROAT ON A SITE VISIT TO
A CHICAGO HOSPITAL

The kid was black and handsome and had rings in both ears and bracelets on both wrists, so I now can know he was gay. The pathology doc who called NITS for help said they can't figure out what to do with the black bodies when they're at death's door and nameless. "It is increasingly hard to unload dead nameless black bodies. Emergency is supposed to take them. This is the biggest medical center in Chicago and thousands of black people come in and go out every day." He would call up the special number until someone finally answered and a pickup was arranged and then truck drivers with wheelbarrows would come, take one look at the dead black body, and then wouldn't take it. "Ordinarily, dead nameless bodies are taken to one of the old meatpacking plants, where they're physically heaved and dismembered and their ashes surreptiously tossed into Lake Michigan. Emergency doesn't want a part of any of this. They say let the niggers come and do their own dirty work.

"No newspaper, of course, writes up any of this. Lately Emergency isn't even waiting to be one hundred percent certain that these nameless cases *are* dead. If they looked dead and/or the pulse was erratic and they were covered with vomit-encrusted blood they just left them here. At one point I had a stack of forty-three bodies right where we're sitting now. Quite honestly, I don't know who finally took them or where."

Just as the truck drivers arrived for this new one with the bracelets and for three other black men as well, a bunch of screaming women barged in, crying out in agony, looking for their Nestor. He was being piled into a wheelbarrow. The biggest woman, maybe the mama, tall, tough, strong, fat, waddled over and yanked her Nestor out of the wheelbarrow, and he fell splat on the cement floor, where his head split open. The other women, three of them, screamed. The truck drivers beat a hasty retreat with the other deads and the pathologist who summoned me was left with the one awful-looking kid splattered all over the floor and the four women still screaming. Now the four women tried to stuff the kid's body into a big shopping bag from Marshall Field, which of course he wouldn't fit into. "Ladies, please," the pathologist tried to say. "White man killer murderer, you daid my son!" the mother screamed, lunging for him, but the daughters held her back. "Mom, he's just a doctor." "So what so what so WHAT, doctors meant to save not murder and maim! Oh my baby boy, my baby baby baby boy, you was so beautiful, you was so very beautiful, what happened what happened *what happened?*"

The kid's blood is now all over the four of them. The pathologist tries to tell them, "Ladies you must be careful, his blood is infected," but Mama is rubbing the kid's blood onto her body like it's some kind of holy water, rubbing it into her arms and face, even licking it. The women try to pull her away from the body and out of the lab but she's not going. They get her half-way to the door and she breaks loose and dives onto the boy's body, covering it with her own. It's a big mess.

It must be another half hour before Security comes in their protective clothing and separates mother and son and wraps up the body. The girls get their mother out of here, dripping blood on the floor as she leaves. Don, the pathologist, realizes he still doesn't have a name for the kid to put on his file. Since the file now has blood on it too, he throws it into the big garbage can. That's what they've been told to do for all the Nameless ones. "No point saving it. Been a lot of them lately. Amazing how many of them don't have names. No wonder we can never get an accurate count. I sure hope I won't have to die this way."

I'm supposed to check out the fourteen medical centers where Jerry's latest ZAP trials are going to be held. Thirteen more to go.

DANIEL THE SPY

Our Supreme Ruester told some assemblage of international reporters that "the general population" is not at risk, which prompted some brave man with dark skin to shout back, "I am the general population and I have it!" at which point he was ushered from the hall, as they say. In handcuffs. By four armed policemen. He was booked and jailed for several days before someone from his embassy came to get him. His green card was canceled and he was de-ported immediately back to Brazil. He had been a reporter here for the AP for sixteen years. He left an American wife and a few kids and he can't get back here and they don't want to go there. "What, and starve to death?" the wife said. She also said she hadn't known her husband was infected, "so good riddance to bad rubbish." She clutched her crucifix as she said this, with one baby in her arms and two toddlers hanging on her skirt, and she managed somehow, while the TV camera was square on her, to cross herself and cry at the same time.

A young man walked into Johns Hopkins hospital in Baltimore sick. He is transfused with twelve units of blood. He dies. He tested okay with Dodo's test, which is now in increasing if not FADS-approved use. His many organs and his eyes and his skin are transplanted quickly. The transplant recipients start to die. There will be fifty of them, for skin and all. The accurate French test is flown over secretly from Quebec and this is used to determine that the man was positive. All the transplanted people die, every one of them. Not a single one of them lives.

Ironically, both Jacquie's test and Dodo's test are manufactured by Audacia, the former by their French subsidiary. There are enough lawyers for all this running around here, too. To even suggest we use the French test, available in Canada, is tantamount to being an everywhichway kind of traitor.

PCP is one of those OIs that no one is talking about. Opportunistic Infections. It sounds like something on a job application. Please list your OIs. Well, there are more and more of them. At least three, maybe four dozen. New ones are added all the time by COD. Stuff that guys come down with that no one is researching or knows what to do with. Stuff that makes you go blind. Stuff that makes you die. Stuff with names you can never remember. Rebby constantly screams about them. "Why is there no research into the OIs?" he exclaims every chance he gets. He calls Jerry "a monster," because "all you are looking for is the cure and the cure is not tomorrow and these young men are dying today." He said this to his face at some conference. In front of a lot of people. More patients are dying from PCP pneumonia than any other OI. COD has a treatment for it, but it's still embargoed.

At that conference Monserrat suddenly gets up and yells at Rebby. "We haven't time to call each other names. This country must get started on something! Let us disprove later! That is why I give you money, to jump-start *something*!" I gather that only since coming to America has Monserrat acquired the skill of speaking with exclamation marks.

Deep Throat says all the research is in chaos, and with Jerry in charge of it bears out his sad prediction that we're all working for an idiot.

Gobbel orders Jerry to tell Dye to send word to all the blood organizations and to all hospitals performing surgeries to destroy their records so we can't be found liable when Dodo's blood test is revealed to be so unreliable.

THE WORMS OF TIME

Dr. Nelson Golly, now at Yaddah for a year or two, brings up the ancient possibility of the ingestion of worms, hookworms, and "let's have a look-see at the system then. Worms were used for centuries, all over the world, the Chinese, the Arabs, in Iceland, in Celtic Britain. Why, the Austrian psychiatrist Julius Wagner-Jauregg, who was a cousin on my late first wife's side, won the Nobel in 1927 for his treatment of syphilitic paralysis by inoculating with malaria coupled with worms. High fever produced by the malaria parasites killed the syphilitic bugs and cured the patient! Worms have not been used in America, to my knowledge. But now I submit it is time to try. Pray tell, who will help me to obtain some willing subjects? And of course some worms."

Dr. Warrem Trubeshott in South Dakota thinks it's an idea worth pursuing. He is a Native American. He has seen Native Americans eat worms and their ailments disappear. "Worms make the body fight the intrusion. They can be flushed out if they don't work. The trick is to find the right amount of the buggers to swallow. Too few and they're not effective, too many give you a really bad stomachache, and more than too many, well, they kill you. I got a few Indian docs out at a nearby reservation that I've consulted with before. I'll check it out. Tell Nelson Golly I'll collaborate with him. He's a big deal."

So seven Pronto-Iwacki Indians from a decrepit reservation in the Black Hills are located and enrolled by Warrem. They have UC, but since they are Native Americans on a Native American reservation, they haven't been tallied anywhere. "I coulda had two dozen, maybe three," Warrem says when Paulus Pewkin calls to inquire, "What the hell is this all about? Nobody told me about any fucking Indians. Did you run this worm idea shit by Marie Clayture at FADS? I can tell you now, she's not going to like it."

"I've already started on it," Warrem says. "I got seven Prontos with anywhere from ten to one hundred Pacific Coast hooked longworms inside of them."

Paulus hangs up.

Warrem then tries to talk to Jerry but only gets through to Daniel. "I sort of feel I'm operating on this without much support from home office. Is that you guys?"

"Yes, Jerry approved Dr. Golly's grant. Keep us up to date."

"Well, you should know that two Pronto-Iwackis died."

"Already?"

"I don't think it was from the worms. These two were on the lowest amount. I got something else to report. The other five want their stomachs cleaned. They want off the study."

"Then I guess you better clean their stomachs," Daniel answers.

"I'm not sure how, and Golly won't tell me. He yells at me: 'Keep those frigging worms in those frigging Indians' guts!' And then he hangs up. What's frigging?"

"He's very distinguished in Great Britain and I think he feels unappreciated over here," Daniel says. "Anyway, I'll have someone get back to you right away with the recipe for a stomach lavage. And I'll deal with Golly."

The other five Pronto-Iwackis are cleaned out. Golly has hysterics for other reasons and goes back to England. And that's the end of the worms episode. Only it's not the end. The families of those dead Pronto-Iwacki Indians get a lawyer and try to sue NITS but the case gets thrown out of court because the judge didn't believe them and Golly wouldn't come back to testify.

None of this stops Dr. Warrem Trubeshott from trying the experiment on himself when he comes down with UC. Maybe he had it all along. This time he uses Atlantic Coast hooked longworms. He gets very sick. He shits all the time. When he hears that Nelson Golly is now back at Yaddah, Warrem journeys to New Godding, finds Nelson's office with him sitting behind a brand-new desk, drops his pants, and shits all over it. "Don't you ever hang up on an American doctor again, you hear!" He then collapses in spasms on Golly's rug, in his own shit, and dies. Right there. Nelson has him biopsied from head to toe. He had everything, Warrem did, from dementia to no toenails. Nelson of course writes the case up for *NEJS*. A protest is registered against NITS and FADS and the government by the Pronto-Iwacki Reservation, claiming that before this study commenced no one on the reservation had UC and now some three hundred of those living there are infected. Some 110 of these commit suicide upon receiving notice of their infection after having been tested with Dodo's AudaciaUSA test.

Paul Bellhoppe, Ph.D., of the Bureau of Indian Affairs, sent to investigate matters, discovers that there is no Pronto-Iwacki Reservation and that there is no such thing as a Pronto-Iwacki American Indian. "The Iwacky lived in the Andes and Africa. I can't find out squat about any USA Pronto-Iwackis."

A Mrs. Wendy Trubeshott shows up to bring suit against the government, claiming to be Warrem's wife, although no record can be found of his ever having been married. She is UC-positive and also brings suit against his estate, which turns out to be worth several million dollars. She wins the suit, but before the estate can be transferred to her, a woman claiming to be Warrem's mother appears to demand the money, insisting that her son had never been married. She, too, claims to be UC-positive and to have been infected by

her son. The Albuquerque judge throws out her suit, reverses Wendy's ruling, and orders that the money be donated to a federation of Pronto-Iwacki
Native American charities, of which he is the chair. By the time it's discovered that there are no Pronto-Iwacki Native American charities both Wendy
and Mom will be dead from UC and the judge has moved to Brazil with
the several million bucks and Dr. Nelson Golly, now back home as a don at
Oxford, is still hoping to try the worms business again.

*(You think I'm making this up? Just wait until July 1, 2008, when you can
read about it in "The Worms Crawl In," in the Science section of* The New York
Truth. *YRH)*

SOME SEMI-FINAL THOUGHTS TOWARD FRED'S CONTEMPLATION OF THAT OTHER ORGANIZATION HE WANTS TO START

He keeps putting off his speech. He's made enough notes to write a book. He
now accepts that Tommy's right, that the time is right, that people are ready
to show up to hear him. He doesn't want to fuck this chance up. He's coming
back from exile, like some formerly elected official who lost the last election
and doesn't want to lose the next one. Why is he making such a big deal out
of this, dragging it out so? He knows who he is and what he wants to say and
that he only knows one way to say things now.

He wants to be one of the guys but he can't. He's too critical, so adept at
calling attention to all that he knows is wrong. They're frightened of him. He
intimidates them. He tries to point the way when they don't want to hear it.
He has seen this happening, over the years, from his self-imposed permanent
placement on the outside of things. All the noise he made was just another
nail in his ostracization. Most of the time he hadn't minded it. Some of the
time he does. Right now is one of the latter. This time it's the life or death
not only of his people but of himself. He had not worried about his own
death before. He may live on Washington Square in the heart of Greenwich
Village but he feels like he's living on some remote island in the north of
Norway. He damn well better shape up and come back to the mainland.

He sighs. He sighs a lot too. Little groans as he's sitting somewhere, like
on a bus, emitted automatically, so that the person sitting next to him looks
at him questioningly, only rarely asking, "Are you all right?" He wants to say
something dramatic like, I have been reviled and misunderstood by many

including myself and what is to be done about it? But he knows the other person, in New York City anyway, is likely to reply, "Welcome to the club."

When he was parted from GMPA, rumors circulated that he was writing a novel about his unrequited love for Bruce, or Christopher, or Kenny, or . . . or Mr. Right or Mr. Wrong; that he'd left because he couldn't stand Tel or Friff or Griff or Stiff; that he'd started the whole organization just to write about it, and them. Many thought he'd fucked with half of GMPA when he hadn't, not a one of them. He felt a certain pride and righteousness that this was not what leaders should do. Interesting that rumors once started never let up. There must be a lot of Pubies and Jervises and Cockers out there to keep them alive. What a boring life some gays must lead if their topic of conversation is dishing him.

Well, he can live with all this, as he's learned to live with everything else his existence provokes on days when his skin is thicker than others. He can live with all of this. Sure.

But it is often difficult, on late spring afternoons when the dipping light cries out for handholding or "Come and see what a beautiful sunset" might be called over to him by a friend, and there is no friend. No Felix. Or when groups gather together, always together, to go places, make visits, invite others to dinner, or just to make phone calls of "hello, how are you, just checking in . . ." These are harder tests of stamina, of doing without. Saturday nights, and Friday nights, alone at home are hard. Oh, and Sunday all day long as well.

Tomorrow he has another blood test. Dodo's test is finally working although Emma's long since told him the bad news. Today was Ken Wein's funeral. Yesterday he had brunch with Craig Rowland, who's a skeleton and doesn't expect to live much longer. He talks about the sadness of the death of desire, the death of hope that love will ever come to him. Oh, God! That was happening to him, too.

He writes to himself: "We all loved each other very much. Why we fucked with each other so much is because we loved each other so much. That is hard for Them to understand. We had this superabundance of love to share. Too much, it turned out. We still do, only it seems we can't use it so generously anymore. There shouldn't be such a thing as too much love. Anyway, we all loved each other and we all killed and are killing each other. And there shouldn't be such a thing as killing each other by loving each other too much." He read this to Tommy, who started to cry.

More than ever Fred Lemish wants there to be some sort of record that he'd tried, he'd really tried. For history, of course. So that when some "historian" writes something mean and nasty, inapt, inept, incorrect, and and and . . . But he still hasn't yet stormed the barricades of "historical truth" as needed to be successfully assaulted. Not yet.

There can't be any other plan. Isn't it your responsibility when one knows too much and even if it can kill you as it did dear Sister Grace? How many pages of homo-hating history must vomit out before everyone listens? And fights back? Hasn't he been left alive to effect just this?

He's got to give it another go. Is he really ready?

"I want to give myself something to be proud of. Before I die too."

JOE KIDNEY

FROM HIS BOOK *PETER RUESTER: A VERY BAD DREAM*

No, I don't think he hated homosexuals. His Hollywood experiences had certainly thrown him in among them. But like Purpura's determination that "I will not allow the women of my country to be besmirched," this is an oddly apt defensive stance from someone who certainly was also a great be-smircher. I can only assume his anti-gay public statements served the same psychic protection for self-defense.

He made decisions quickly and didn't second-guess them. But his hold on the reins was flaccid, at best. His biggest problem, and unknown to him, was that he didn't know how much he didn't know.

In the void that he created, his staff rushed in to compete for influence to advance their own agendas. They are all expert manipulators. And of course they are in league with Purpura. If she didn't like you or you wouldn't do her bidding, you weren't there for long. They all treat Peter as if he were a child monarch. Since he thought it his due to be so treated, he loved it. Did he know about Brinestalker and the Tricia Institute? Much too complicated. Did he know about Gobbel's National Guard? He thought they were the Marine Band come to salute him.

"You get the people that you believe in and that can do the things that I sincerely believe need doing," he explained more than once to The Ameri-can People. The big decisions, he added, "are mine, and I make them." Since all his policies were framed and trumpeted "to advance the cause of freedom"—a principle that could mean almost anything—he could be counted on to support whatever Moose or Gobbel put in front of him to sign.

Did he realize what UC was up to? She would have seen that no information about it would reach his eyes.

Thus Manny Moose and Linus Gobbel and Gree Bohunk functioned as de facto presidents—with greater (Gobbel) and lesser (Bohunk) degrees of success. Other "advisers" simply asserted that their actions were consistent with the president's goals when he said to them, "We're here to do whatever it takes." One is reminded of how Hitler's government worked. He never issued actual orders on pieces of paper. But everyone knew what he stood for and desired and they didn't have to be told how to work toward that goal.

Don't forget President Peter Ruester's optimistic belief that the progress he was delivering was an American birthright, an inevitability that he was personally singled out to deliver. And his radiant constant smile as he waved to us all was enormously, seductively winning.

WHAT ARE THESE FELLOWS UP TO?

Gree Bohunk prepares his list of health recommendations in the name of Dr. Dye on behalf of the president, to be decreed by that new secretary of HAH, Dr. J. Purnold Drydeck, recently having arrived from Utah per his large contribution via Manny Moose:

1. Fellatio does not give you The Underlying Condition.
2. Kissing or exchanging saliva will not infect you either.
3. The only way you can catch this is by getting a transfusion or by participating in anal intercourse.

He sits back to think for a minute. Is there any way he can recommend anal intercourse? That would include so many more of them. It's a pity to discourage them when they want to do it so much.

Gree had read this fortnight's *New York Prick*. Orvid Guptl doesn't like him. "Numerous incidents of sabotage by an unknown person or persons of UC research have been discovered at a COD lab in Chattanooga." Gree wonders: How the fuck does Guptl know about that?

But *The Prick* isn't alone. "There is sabotage. There is chaos," said Dr. Tom Lee Tom, a virologist who last month had run away from Chattanooga and taken his experiments to another COD office in an unnamed city in the far west where he refuses to "speak for attribution."

Gree locates him. "The lack of response to this plague from the White House has been extremely unhelpful," Tom Tom tells him. "Intentional tampering of laboratory equipment has occurred in every COD lab devoted to UC work."

"Is that so," Gree said, hanging up. He doesn't want it on the record to have heard any of this or to have even talked to this man.

No one criticizes the hiring of Dr. Volker Heimat to reorganize the laboratories that Dr. Tom Tom vacated. Dr. Heimat has no prior UC experience and has been described by several sources as "another bully from another country." No one calls anyone a Nazi anymore. Dr. Heimat is an expert on anal intercourse. "Of course it is good," he says on his first TV outing. "One feels *wunderbar*!" Perhaps he's not ready yet for prime time. Or perhaps this is just what Gobbel wants.

"It's like Russia down here," a disgruntled employee of the COD home office says to Theodore Butler on *The Chattanooga Evening News*. After pausing for thought, the disgruntled employee continues, "And I thought it was gross working for Drs. Dye and Omicidio at NITS. COD is worse than NITS." Then, after another pause, he corrects himself. "No, nothing is worse than NITS." Then he corrects himself again. "It's a toss-up. Pewkin is an asshole. But so is Omicidio." A version is printed. Theodore Butler is fired. Gree Bohunk calls Pewkin from the White House and congratulates him. "The president wants you to know that you're doing a simply wonderful job."

"The research is going much slower in our local COD branch than it should be," said Bobbie Robertson, R.N., to *The San Francisco Bridge*. "The working conditions are brutal, and feudal, and disorganized. One research doc actually brings a whip to work." This made it into print too, but Gree now knows that whips are no big deal in San Francisco.

In Chattanooga, cultures continue to be thrown in the garbage, or spat into, or removed from incubators. Educational materials meant for distribution to the country have been sabotaged, lest information about prevention become available. "Somebody in here doesn't want anybody out there to get anything but dead," said the remaining COD senior scientist, Dr. Al Albertson, who brazenly announces, to heck with his job, "I don't hear much talk about saving lives or being a big-deal role model like they used to hold up to us." It's the last time anyone will hear from him.

Sam Sport calls Arnold Botts. "What's really going on? Are we trying to dispose of COD and Pewkin?"

"Stay tuned," Arnold says, and then quite uncharacteristically he adds, "Be careful."

"Anal intercourse is acceptable under many circumstances" is added to Dr. Drydeck's list for the president. Dr. Volker Heimat said so.

Dr. Paulus Pewkin goes on one of those Sunday morning TV programs and announces "anal intercourse is not always a no-no." In the following weeks, guests on these programs (four out of five) say the words *anal intercourse*. It's noted fairly swiftly that newscasts in which someone says "anal intercourse" have higher ratings. Viewers tune into the programs they know will deliver an "anal intercourse" or two.

Orvid announces in a banner headline, WHITE HOUSE OKAYS TAKING IT UP THE BUTT. And in the following article, "Clinics across the country are announcing a record number of cases of rectal gonorrhea." And he quotes Fred: "I can't believe this is happening!" Fred didn't actually say that about rectal gonorrhea, but since he's said it about everything else, Orvid figures he's in the clear.

Senator Vurd smiles. He introduces another bill into Congress, entitled: "Concerning the expectoration upon the American Flag and various other unpatriotic matters." It doesn't quite spell out everything. "Anal intercourse" is hard to rephrase in bureaucratic lingo. But it's in there. Anal intercourse is not only unpatriotic, it's a punishable offense, just like in the old days. You can go directly to jail if caught doing it. In a matter of months, police in Dallas arrest two men "in flagrante anal intercourse" in the privacy of their own home.

DANIEL THE SPY

Dash absolutely refuses to change the dosage, which is obviously too high. We had 124 studies mounted to go all over the United States. Their total enrollment was to be fifteen thousand. That fifteen thousand figure was seventy-five thousand until it was discovered that many of the entrants who signed up received their ZAP and went home and broke them open and if it tasted like sugar they never showed up again. They still make placebos to taste like sugar pills! So all the figures were fucked a month after we started. We've started a latest study with fifty entrants. Twenty-three died the first month. Seventeen died the second month. Except they are entered in the trial reports as three died and the rest dead from "other causes unrelated to the drug." Which is a lie.

I would not take this drug and I am recommending my private patients not to take it. A couple of guys, it is true, are seeing slight rises in their 729/s. Three guys. Out of fifty. This is what Dash points to. "See! It can work! We are not running a beauty parlor here!"

One of my patients threw up on him.

FRED VISITS ANOTHER HOSPITAL

Beth Teresa is an amalgam of two very old awful hospitals into one smaller awful hospital. The names of hospitals have long since stopped conveying any clear heritage they once were meant to convey of long-ago hatreds when Jews and Catholics demanded separate places to die. Is this one Jewish? That used to signify excellence. Is this one Catholic? Ditto. So, no and no. There are no nuns running anything and there are no yarmulked doctors not working after sundown on Friday. Beth Teresa sits very far west in Hell's Kitchen, and you wouldn't be interested when passing it, so bleak is the exterior, with its barred windows more akin to a prison. The archdiocese refuses to run it, as do various Jewish boards, and so would the city were it not useful as a dumping ground for the mounting UC cases that have nowhere else to be dumped. I didn't know the place existed.

It is of course understaffed and underfunded. But so is every other hospital. Velma and everyone else knows there are bad hospitals in New York that you just don't and can't write about because too many rich people are on their boards, Metropolitan Mausoleum, Downtown Local, Vanderbilt Rich Bitch, Hospital for Special Nothing—they all have been given demeaning names, in most cases deservedly. New York is not a town where you go to a hospital if you are sick and want to get better. You come to New York to see Top Doctors, and they are here. And some of them are even good. But there is not a one of them that thinks their hospital is as good as they are, and they're right. An interesting dilemma.

I had done a Grand Rounds this day to the medical staff and students at Beth Teresa, all ten of them. As I'd been met at a special entrance and via a special hallway to a classroom, I was still in the dark about what was going on here. I'm still at the stage where I'll talk to anyone who asks me. I try to scare everyone with the awful facts of the truth. I am increasingly convinced that fear is the best motivator for getting anything done, etc., etc., etc.

Dr. Deena Tuttle is in charge of the place. She is big and tough and no-nonsense; I've met her at city UC meetings and I like her. She invited me to come and visit. After I finished speaking, she said, "You really wanna throw up, come with me."

When I hestitate, she challenges me, "Come on, Fred, you're my hero. That's why I invited you. If I can do it so can you. Norm, come on, show us in!" An armed guard appears from somewhere with his chain of keys and unlocks a couple of very thick doors and in we go. I can hear them clanking closed behind us. Very sinister. Dickensian. Deena has slapped a gown and mask into my hands and is putting her own on. "Get into these fast," she says, and I do.

The minute we're in, I'm horrified. It's a huge ex-gymnasium or some sort of once-great hall. A hundred guys are slithering about on the floor. There are no tables or chairs or cots or any kind of furniture. They look at us as if we're saviors and start lunging for us. Norm has his gun cocked, and when they come too close he actually fires a couple of shots at the ceiling, which I notice is pockmarked. This sends most of the guys scurrying back.

"Bet you never thought something like this goes on in a New York City hospital," Deena chortles.

"All these guys are prisoners and all these guys have UC?"

"You got it."

"Why? They haven't committed any crimes and we're not quarantining them yet."

"That's what you think. I got emergency powers when a public health emergency reaches unpardonable heights of danger. These are all guys who have dementia, or for whom we have no way of tracing next of kin, or guys the police picked up soliciting or fucking in Central Park without any ID, stuff like that. Get away!"

She actually kicks a young man reaching up to her for help. No, he's reaching up to me.

He stretches his hands, both of them, up toward my voice. I guess he can't stand up. The place stinks something awful, and it gets worse with every breath. The floor of this entire huge room is full of these slithering guys rolling around in this stink. It is the most grotesque sight I have ever seen. Nobody seems like their eyes can see. Nobody is not yelling or whimpering or bawling. No one wears anything remotely clean. Everyone is caked with crud. If I'm not throwing up—well, I don't know why I'm not throwing up.

"Fred . . . Fred . . . Fred, honey! I am so glad you found me! I've been praying that you could find me."

I don't recognize this wreck.

"It's your Bo Peep. Did you find a boyfriend yet? He'll find you, Fred. Your boyfriend will find you, just wait and see."

"Bo!"

"It's your Bo. Bo Peep." He's crying, shaking, unable to stop.

I hadn't heard of any of my Fire Island Pines housemates in Grey Gardens for years. I'd written about them in *Faggots*. I'd wondered what happened to the ones whose names aren't on any of my lists. Bo Peep had been a particularly sweet friend. Just like me he wanted everybody to be in love. I can't recall now his real name or why we called him Bo Peep except he was short and cute and very angelic.

"Fred, where am I? Why am I in Canada? Why would they send Bo to Canada? They said I have a Canadian passport and they had to deport me. I'm not Canadian. I don't have a Canadian passport. I'm an American citizen. I have an American passport. No one believes me. No one believes Bo is from Alabama. Anyone listening to me knows I'm from the South and not from Canada."

He suddenly touches Deena's skirt. "Ralph Lauren?"

"Why, yes," she answers.

"Where is Tarsh? Tarsh used to call me every single day. He was my only friend. I don't have any friends in Canada. Why am I in Canada? Can you help me get out of Canada?"

He starts weeping uncontrollably. I am down on the floor holding this man in my arms as he blubbers and sobs and drools and keeps saying "Canada" over and over. I am trying to caress his head with my gloved hand. I can see he's pissing from under his gown, his shrunken penis dribbling pee on the floor. He used to be so proud of his penis. It was a big one and his short frame made it look even bigger. He'd march naked around our living room in Grey Gardens singing "Dixie."

"I wouldn't get too intimate," Dr. Deena Tuttle is advising. She nods to Norm, the guard, who nods back and presses a few buttons. I can hear an alarm sounding somewhere and the clanging of doors being opened and slammed shut, and then a couple of cops come rushing over, one to pull Bo off me and the other to hold on to me, hard.

"Don't move, mister, please," he says to me.

Bo is squatting on the floor now. He is shitting. He is scooping up his shit and eating it, stuffing it into his mouth.

And yes, I'm throwing up.

"I told you you'd throw up," Dr. Deena Tuttle says.

Bo is screaming as two cops haul him away.

I see other men I recognize. Teeter from the Public Theater and Billy Drosskopf from walking our dogs and . . . shit, I think I see familiar faces all over the place. I think I'm having a nightmare and I am. Many of these faces just stare, with their mouths open. The faces look like that Edvard Munch painting, *The Scream*.

"Can I do something about getting my friend out of here?"

Dr. Deena says to me, "He's on high-dose ZAP. They're all on high-dose ZAP. High-dose ZAP is supposed to cross the brain barrier. It doesn't. High-dose ZAP is shit. Low-dose ZAP is shit. I have a policeman who'll drive you home so you can shower fast. I'll give you a protective coat to wear, then throw it down your incinerator."

Bo Peep died before I got home. Dr. Deena Tuttle called to tell me.

"Any time you want to come up, come on up. We should stay in touch."

"Can I write about this?"

"Of course I want you to write about it! No one will publish it. I've tried. I even brought Velma Dimley up here. She threw up too. Anyway, this lot is all going to be shipped out of here next week. Seventy-three of them. They are going to Canada. British Columbia. Did you know that British Columbia is home to the largest per capita concentration of organized crime syndicates in the world? I have no idea what this has to do with anything but I'll just bet it does."

•

I hadn't been in touch with Tarsh, another Fire Island housemate, since I can't remember when. I called to tell him about Bo. He started to cry and vowed to call me soon. A few days later he called back. He wanted to "catch up properly." He proceeded to tell me all about his sex life, the sex club he belongs to. I asked how he could do this now and he said, "I'm not going to let this stuff get me down." I asked him what exactly was going on out there in L.A. "Well, my particular club is certainly very busy. We belong to a chapter of Sex Über Alles." I asked again what went on. "Well, we strip down and we just sort of hang out in somebody's apartment. We take turns using each other's places. It's very laid-back. Yes, Fred, we're all stoned. We still do that, too." He was so in my face with all this, his tone, that it made me not like him, as if he was now another person when in fact he sounded just like the same old Tarsh I used to know. But that was then and now is now. How can he still be living like this? How can he and his sex club still be living like this? He didn't once mention Bo, who'd been his best friend.

WHAT IS JUNIOR UP TO?

Junior Ruester, in an appearance on *Saturday Night Live*, says to the audience and the camera, "Hey, guys, write to my father and tell him how you think he's doing." Many letters are received at the White House. Many new names are added to Brinestalker's list.

WHAT IS VON GREETING UP TO?

When Von is notified that gays are not infecting themselves with the rapidity that his master plan had . . . well, planned for, he again ups the production of Dridge Ampules and sees that they are distributed freely at the bars and discos.

In fact, Dridge Ampules have never been off the market. They've just been out there under various other names, Sweat! Hot Gym, Crotch Odor Plus, redolent names like that. You won't find these names in the G-D production reports (at the Yaddah School of Business Archives), but the references to "Product X" and "Product Y" and "Product Z" are telling enough. They've all been manufactured by G-D under one "licensee" or another.

This company is working it from both ends—killing gays with one product, ZAP, and revving them up with another one, Dridge Ampules, so they can get there faster. Not to mention Factor VIII. This should be a case study at Yaddah Business School.

THE HOUSE OF THE LIVING DEAD

GRODZO: Okay, I try to write here what our life is like now, the three of us. We live in Daniel's house. We take care of David. Out of nowhere he appeared collapsed at Daniel's front door. I have more time than Daniel, who has much to do, many commitments, many patients, working at NITS besides. David is now more out of comas than in them, which is progress. It is hard to tell, because when he is out of coma he does not talk. Daniel says he has been silent before. His system must be very strong. He does not like to talk, yet he is pleased that I am here. He holds on to my hand, a simple act that breaks my heart. He is not so good at eating either. We make him eat. Sometimes we have to hold open his mouth and spoon it in. I make puree of everything so he can swallow. His stools are very runny, which is not surprising. I have slides made of them, and they are filled with organisms the pathologist here has not seen before in feces. "Yes, they move," he says; "but they are still unfamiliar." I ask him do we try to get these out of his insides. He responds he is not so certain they are unhealthy. "Much of the world is filled inside with living microorganisms that free float inside us. The system accommodates. Where has he traveled to?" I have Daniel give the feces report to Omicidio, who is not interested because it is "not part of the big picture." What a ridiculous answer. Medicine in this country is very strange. Did you tell him he is your twin brother? I ask Daniel. I bet then he will be interested.

I sent some slides to the great Max Planck laboratories in Germany, in Freiberg. I am much impressed with what is happening there in many areas. There are many Max Planck Institutes now in Germany, everything there is called Max Planck this and Max Planck that. He would be pleased, old Max. I receive a warm reply from Dr. Karl Reichman, who was once my fellow student in Kiel. "I am glad you are still alive, my old comrade! Me, too! I am glad I am alive as well!" He tells me they are starting a division of "Developmental Immunology" that could be helpful to what we are trying to learn about David. "I must tell you that this UC in Deutschland, it is not here yet much so we are not too familiar. But we will be! We try to beat you this time!" So they make jokes now again! He, too, tells me he has never seen Scheisse like this but he sends some tablets, which we give David. His stool becomes not so runny and some color returns to his cheeks. I ask what is in these tablets. "It is nothing but an old Bavarian folk remedy, many centuries old," Dr. Karl wires back. It is too bad David is not well enough to travel to Freiberg. Karl says they are looking for UC patients. What an irony that would be! When I tell David about this he does not smile. He speaks. "I do not want to go back to Germany ever again, even if it saves my life." Then he commands, "Promise me!" I promise him. He still sleeps many hours. We take him for a drive on a sunny day and he seems to smile a bit. He holds our hands a lot. It is as if he must hold on to one of us all the time. Of course, I try to talk to him and he listens, but he rarely replies. Once he answered, "Later. Not now." One night he crawls into Daniel's bed and spends the night. I hear Daniel crying after David is asleep. They are big sobs and he is trying to hide them in his pillow. David cannot hear him because he is drugged to sleep. I look often at the boy's scars. He is no longer a boy, of course, only to me. I tell Daniel he did not get these patterns of scars in Germany, at Mungel. Your country gives him these scars. We have no idea why and how and where. The only other place, he says, could be at Partekla. I try to research Partekla data but it has been what they call "disappeared" from the data banks at NITS. I can see that David's scars will not go away or lessen. The ridges do not become softer and merge into the surrounding skin, even with constant salves and unguents. I thought they were scars from being whipped. Now I wonder if it was some kind of experiment. Another question for another day. There are many. I think now he may even live to someday answer them. This thought makes me happy. It has been a long time since I have been happy. That it should occur here, in this house, with these two brothers, is remarkable.

As I suspect, when Omicidio hears Daniel's identical twin brother is found, he prepares immediately for a bone marrow transplant. It must be done "on the quiet" because in no way could all the permissions from all the divisions and committees and supervisors and peer reviews required by NITS and FADS be granted easily. I talk with Omicidio about his plan. I am not impressed. He is putting a horse before his cart, you say. He assumes if he kills off the circulating lymphocytes and replaces them with fresh from a twin—but who says this virus lives only in lymphocytes? I think more it must also live in blood. Or in shit, as that Dr. Sister Grace Hooker maintained before she was murdered in her convent. Here, too, the murders of the scientists! But this Jerry moves on ahead. I ask for a conference with other doctors and am told to keep out of this. All this takes place in front of Daniel and David, here in our house. Jerry supervises many tests on both of them. He is in and out, often unexpectedly, as if this house is an extension of his wards. I believe that he is moved, that somehow this harsh man on the outside can see what love is transpiring among the three of us in this house. And that he does not have this love. I ask him if he has tried this transplant on other infected twins and what were the results. He does not answer, so I know his answer.

And so does David. During the night, somehow, once more, he disappears. He leaves us this letter.

"My dear and special family, I am strong enough to go out now for a

while. I thank you for making me this well again with your love. I cannot allow you to have on your conscience that you approved of this Jerry murdering
me. Because that is what he will do to me. I have seen and met many murderers. I know the look. You will hear from me. Your David. P.S. to Daniel:
I love being back in your arms where we belong. I am sorry we lost so much
time. I am sorry for so much that has happened in our lives. It is very sad,
don't you think? P.S. to Grodzo: Please watch out for Daniel, and yourself
until I can come home! P.S. I love you both."

•

DANIEL: Yes, we slept together, my twin and I. We made love to each other.
I understand this is not unusual with twins, although waiting for so long to
do it perhaps is.

What did we talk about? In words that each other could actually hear,
precious little. But I know each of us felt the heavy weight of a certain longing at last removed. When I would try to talk about it, he'd cover my mouth
with his hand and shake his head and then kiss me.

In the middle of the night we each woke up to find the other crying.

"Have you missed me?" he whispered hoarsely.

I had not but at this moment I realized how much I had, so I could whisper back honestly, "So very very much. Now we are back together again. You
must promise me to never leave me again."

"But am I not about to die?"

"Your Grodzo will find a way to save you."

"I don't think so. He has said this virus is so far too complicated to understand. Especially since my blood is different from other UC cases."

"Then we must be very strong together. Our love will give us this
strength."

"I have never seen love to work such miracles."

"JERRY IS NOT QUALIFIED TO DO ANY KIND OF TRANSPLANT!"

DEEP THROAT: You were lucky your David ran away. Jerry would have killed
him.

MERCY KILLING

This time it's the doctor who's dying. His name is Tim. He's had a hard time of it, struggling now just to breathe. He breathes for Craig, for Craig who loves him and won't let him stop, the breathing, the living, the loving. Yes, it's been a good ten years. They've had the best of it. That they know. That they've told each other every day. Only now he can't breathe and Craig can't inspire air into his lungs by pure devotion. The machines by his bed-side in this private room in his own hospital, St. Victim's, aren't helping any-more. Craig wishes his own breathing would stop. He knows he'll live and he knows that without Tim he doesn't want to. Oh, these are just romantic notions, of death and love. Too many movies. Too many bad TV dramas. Too many tears. Why is sentiment so out of fashion when it's what's needed most? He has these thoughts while his fingers fool with his tools. He won't look at his hands. He won't look at what they're holding. He looks only at Tim's heart. His chest is wet with sweat. He lies naked in the hospital bed, all shriveled up, all of him, from the locks of his hair all gunked together to his toenails now peculiarly warped and gray. The only flat smooth place, like some very old stone in a very old stream, is his chest. How Craig loved to kiss him all over that godlike chest, not at all like his own stubbly bumpy thing. Even now his hands want to run themselves across that last outpost of Tim's beauty, and feel the smoothness, still. But he denies himself that last pleasure. He has work to do and he'd best do it fast or it won't be done at all, at least not by this fraidycat whimpering uselessly. How dare I call myself a lover. Well, I do. Here, Tim. Here's how much I love you. I do.

Potassium, it's called. Tim named it for him and told him exactly how to do it. Potassium, it's called, and hypodermic, it's called, and strength of will and character and muscle, it's called, but only if it's called upon and done. Into Tim's lovely heart, on that Siberian outpost of a tiny island of such smooth beauty, that X-marks-the-spot on his chest, Craig injects the potassium directly into Tim's heart. Just as he's been told how to. He kills his beloved. As we have been killed for centuries, he thinks, and so I must do what's been done to us. Do unto others. I hate God. Tim dies fast and Craig leaves fast, as a murderer must do, before he gets caught.

To this we've come.

NEW YEAR'S EVE

I wander through the Village. New Year's Eve has always made me sad. Washington Square is this pukey color from some sort of not quite fog that exudes a yellow tinge, as if the Christmas tree under the arch and all its creepy yellow bulbs bleed this color out like pus from a wound. It makes me think of UC-infected skin. I'm working with an overactive imagination in many areas now. Overactive? Get real, Fred. The night air is eerie and you don't want to be home alone. You always feel awful on New Year's Eve. This year is just worse. You walk by building after building where someone you knew had lived and died.

The streets of the Village are empty. There are no crowds of guys rushing off to the discos, which I will be told tomorrow were "sort of packed but not like the old days." More and more talk about the old days.

And Adreena has gone off to make a movie about . . . oh, who the fuck knows. "It was a pay-for-play for my co-star Jeff What's-his-name so of course it has to be made now." Of course. I'd had a new draft screenplay to show her.

We just can't get our story out, no way.

UC MAY DWARF THE PLAGUE

is the SMALL headline that appears on Page A-24 (the real estate page) of *The Truth*.

BETTER LATE THAN NEVER?

Martin Richtig, the new editor in chief of *The New York Truth*, sends the following "authorizing memo" to his staff:

"Starting immediately, we will accept the word *gay*, as an adjective meaning 'homosexual,' in references to social or cultural patterns and political issues."

Note that the use of the word *gay* as a noun is not authorized.

Jacob Flourtower is retired as *The Truth*'s executive editor. He has reached the mandatory age. The relief that sweeps through the newsroom is "palpable, almost giddy." He is heralded far and wide for "seventeen years of record growth, modernization, and major journalistic change." Tell that to Gertie, still drinking vodka stingers in the old Colony gay bar on the Upper East Side.

NY UC PLAGUE—150,000 PERVERTS DOOMED!

screams the headline of *The Sphere*, the supermarket tabloid. "A worldwide death toll in the tens of millions a decade from now" is what a former secretary of Health and Happiness, Dr. Otid Bowbender, is predicting in *The Monument*. "One hundred million could be infected within five years" is the prediction of Dr. Halfdan Mahler, the new head of HOW, also in *The Monument*. The current issue of *The Atlantic*, a publication whose pages had not previously been sullied with our plague, says that for every reported case there are sixty unreported. Nice of someone to let us know.

FROM *THE BOOK OF THE DEAD*

Gordon Wellschaft, Monica Druse, Pablo Esco, Nedrick Castleford, Miles Forster, Drew Hampton, Allan Nokes, Michael Dribble, Harry Brimm, Ray Malfuzzi, Trevor Alan Balding, Allen Barnett, Trudy Menscher, Victor Vaga, Thomas Fiorentino, Myron Shenker, Alden White, Nonny Paul, Sam Shoe, Astride Oguno, Moe Alhambra, Norman Browne, Alex Alesandro Aguilla, Zack Daniels, Grosman Paul Schwartz, Jr., Drew Malone, Peter Eshman, Chick Soldheim, Marshall Bruckner, Harry Applebaum, Norman Gresham, Sam Smith, Ronald Starke, Teddy Neust, William Wolhheim, Hiram Vaughan, Pieter Samsung, Glo Wurttenberg, Miles Allenson, Tom Tom Fury, Fergus Marshallseigh, Martin O'Dempster, Sasha Feigenbaum, Natalie Strong, Eleanora Fawcett, Alana Reese-Enders, Galvan Deuter, Martin Federmann, Rojan Mahar, Basinger Ryce, Craig Nottel, Engin Vazar, Eugene Monckton, Giorgio LaSera, Bill Kelly, Jim Duranto, Philip Clive, Michael Edgerton, Toff Graham, Caldwell Rothman, Norman Lignor, Alberto Gonzalez, Alvin Guttman, Allen Marsh, Forrest Altman, Andy Rosco, Bob Bakemeier, Carroll Banner, Jon Barton, Carl Weede, Paul Cohen, Roger Bernstein, Alexander Rosenthal, David Andre Billingsworth, Ross Lord, St. John Bradbury, Marty, Brimmer, Scott Brock, Hugh Butler, Daniel Campbell, Chris Chan, George Chase II, Doug Shapiro, Carl Bornstein, Duane Drucker, Richard Engelstein, Sawyer Eskridge, Brooks Feingold, Charlie Fox, Gareth Gardener, George Goldberg, Gould Sherwin, John Hammer, Spencer Horowitz, Morgan Greenend, Jerry

Coleman, Erich Estava, Kenneth Kim, Corety Concellos, John David Katz, Frank Steinman, Bruce Kaufman, Jamie Klein, Mark Lake, Jules Lethbridge, Matt Stull, Federico Rondino, Laurence Marstan, Vincent McGrath, Jacob Meadow, Danny Meyerwitz, Charles Karpel, Jeffrey Moss, Seeley Smith, Philip Nichols, Antonino Sursone, Roscoe O'Brien, Burt Fogelstine, O'Mara Calvert, Gene Rendell, Hermann Benze . . .

•

I am learning yet again that I work much faster in many of your people than in others. And the part of me your scientists are now trying to destroy, which I must confess frightened me, is still working. I continue to multiply myself undisturbed by any experiments. I continue to lurk in the guts of your people's reservoir of me. Thank you for your continuing hospitality.

GET OFF YOUR ARSE!

HERMIA: When will you face up to the fact that all these histories you are relating are the result of evil, which is the word Hannah Arendt used in identifying how the world responded to the poisonous deeds of Hitler (and Stalin)! Well, can't you see that you have a Ruester, an Omicidio, a Geiseric, a Gobbel, a Greeting, a Goins . . . the list of your murderers is increasing with every passing day. As beloved Grace would say, "Get off your fucking ass!" In Great Britain we say "arse"!

READY, SET, GO

Okay, Lemish! Bear fucking witness!

PART II

THE BEGINNING OF FUQU

GAY AND LESBIAN CENTER, NEW YORK CITY

MARCH 10, 1987

EXT. GAY COMMUNITY CENTER. NIGHT.
Crowd building as more and more enter.

INT. GAY COMMUNITY CENTER. NIGHT.
Place is packed, settling in. Fred at front is pacing back and forth
nervously checking the crowd. Tommy is in the front row.
ERIC *(to Fred)*: I told you you'd get a full house.
PHOTIS *(young, rough, opinionated; he is talking into a tape re-*
corder): It was a Monday night. And more people by now really are kind of scared. And here's this crazy would-be messiah
come down from the mount to deliver his tablet . . . and you're
like—*I'm* like—scared and excited at the same time. There was
talk about quarantine. We could wind up in camps again. With
numbers tattooed on our arms. Here he goes!

FRED

Thank you all for coming. On March 14, 1983, almost four years ago to
this day, I wrote an article in *The New York Prick*. There were at that time
1,112 cases of UC nationwide. My article was entitled "1,112 and Counting,"
and it was reprinted in seventeen additional gay newspapers across our country. Here are a few of its opening sentences:

"If this article doesn't scare the shit out of you, we're in real trouble. If this
article doesn't rouse you to anger, fury, rage, and action, gay men may have no
future on this earth. Our continued existence on this earth depends on just how

angry you can get. Unless we fight for our lives, we shall die. In all the history of homosexuality we have never before been so close to death and extinction."

My God, how many people have shown up. It's standing room only. They remember me and what I did and said! They want to hear me again!

Predictions are now rising astronomically. We have not yet even begun to live through the true horror. The average incubation period is now thought to be five and a half years. The real tidal wave is yet to come. People who got infected starting in 1981. You had sex in 1981. I did too. And after.

Last week I had ten friends diagnosed. In one week. That's the most in the shortest period so far for me.

Look at them looking at me. There're so many of them and they're frightened and they don't know what to do. God, they're so young and so touching.

I would like everyone from this right-hand side aisle—would you all please stand up for a minute? Thank you. At the rate we're going, two-thirds of you could be dead in less than five years. You can sit down now.

I have never heard such silence.

Let me repeat my *Prick* article of 1983. If my speech tonight doesn't scare the shit out of you, we're in real trouble. If what you're hearing doesn't rouse you to anger, fury, rage, and action, gay men will have no future here on earth. How long will it take before you get angry and fight back?

I have never been able to understand why for six long years we have sat back and let ourselves be knocked off man by man—without fighting back.

I don't want to die. I cannot believe that you *want* to die.

But what are we doing, *really*, to save our own lives?

Two-thirds of you—I should say of *us*, because I'm in this too—could be dead within five years. Two-thirds of this room could be dead within five years.

What does it take for us to take responsibility for our own lives? Because we are not—we are not taking responsibility for our own lives.

You know, each step of this horror story we're living through we come up against an even bigger brick wall. First it was the city, then the state, then COD, then NITS. Now it's FADS, the Food and Drug Supervision bureaucracy. Ann Fettner wrote in *The Prick* about FADS: "It's a godawful mess, documents are likely to get lost in the mailroom, they aren't even computerized, which means that pharmaceutical talent diddles doing nothing while it waits for FADS's judgment and permission." A new drug can easily take ten years to get FADS's approval. Ten years! Two-thirds of us could be dead in less than five years.

Who the flying fuck is in charge?

Certainly not our president, who has yet to say the words *Underlying Condition* out loud.

The one drug that NITS is testing is already proving less effective than what we need to stay alive. Why do they insist on testing it over and over again? Why do they refuse to test any other new drugs and treatments that are brought to their attention? We're willing to be guinea pigs. But give us something real!

Find us those fucking drugs that work to keep us alive!

An unwilling and unsympathetic Congress is at last throwing a few million dollars at UC. But it's not buying anything that will save two-thirds of the people in this room. A college on Long Island has been awarded a $600,000 grant from the Center of Disease—another organization I have come to loathe because it refuses to pay attention to us—to study UC stress on college students. I can tell them right now and save the government $600,000. I know what it's like to be stressed. So do you. What downright bureaucratic stupidity is operating here?

I called up the offices of our elected officials and asked them to send someone here tonight. They treated me as if I were ungrateful. "You got some money. Leave us alone."

So, what are we going to do? Time and time again I have said—no one is going to do it for us but ourselves.

We have always been a particularly divisive community. We fight with each other too much, we're disorganized, we simply cannot get together. We've all insulted each other an awful lot of times. I'm as much at fault in this as anyone.

I called Bruce Niles. Those of you who are familiar with the history of GMPA will know of the fights that Bruce and I had and the estrangement of what had once been a close friendship. Bruce is in very bad shape now. He's in Invincible Crewd-Harbinger. He and I spoke for over an hour. It was like the early days of GMPA again and we were planning strategy for what had to be done. We didn't talk about the hurts we each had caused the other. He supported me in everything that I'm saying to you tonight, and that I've been writing about in *The Prick*. He asked me to say some things to you. "Tell them we have to make gay people all over the country cooperate. Tell them we have to establish some way to cut through all the red tape. We have to find a way to make GMPA and all the gay organizations stronger and more political." This wonderful man who had been so frightened of becoming too political is now begging us to become too political.

This morning's front page of *The New York Truth* has an article about two thousand Catholics marching through the halls of Albany. On the front page of *The Truth*. With their six bishops (including one we know is gay). Two thousand Catholics with their bishops marching through the halls of government with their demands. That's advocacy! Southern Methodist University gets on national television protesting something about their football team. Crowds of black people marched on Mayor Goins's apartment after assaults on black men by whites and a murder at Howard Beach, and everyone in this city saw it on the news. Why are we so invisible, constantly and forever! What does it take to get a few thousand gay people to stage a march and get on TV?

Some of them are looking away, either restless or guilty or what? I'm boring them. They're saying, Oh shit, is he just going to yell at us again?

We can no longer afford to live in never-never land. Without every one of us working together, we will get nowhere.

We must immediately rethink the structure of our community, and that is why I have invited you here tonight: to seek your input and advice, in the hope that we can come out of tonight with some definite and active ideas about how to go forward.

I want to talk about power. We are all in awe of power, of those who have it, and we always bemoan the fact that we don't. Power is the willingness to accept responsibility. But we live in a community where no one is willing to take any responsibility.

Every one of us here is capable of doing something. Of doing something strong. We have to go after FADS—fast. That means coordinated protests, pickets, arrests. Are you ashamed of being arrested? And NITS! NITS is full of nits! By not doing anything these people in these places are murdering us. Dr. Omicidio and his nits are murdering us! But no one knows it or admits it. Isn't it time someone told everyone that we are being murdered?

Look who is our friend: the surgeon general, Dr. Alphonse Garibaldi. A Christian fundamentalist is our friend. He said, "We have to embarrass the administration into bringing the resources that are necessary to deal with the epidemic forcefully." He said a meeting has been arranged with the president "a number of times," and each time this meeting has been canceled. President Ruester's own surgeon general is telling us that we have to embarrass President Ruester to get some attention to UC. Why didn't any straight paper across this country carry this news? You sure didn't see it in *The New York Truth*, all the truth that's fit to print. We're not fit for *The New York Truth* to write about!

What does it take for us to take responsibility for our own lives? Because we aren't—we are not taking responsibility for our own lives.

It's our own fault, boys and girls. Two thousand Catholics can march through the corridors of Albany. Dr. Monserrat Krank's UC organization has on its board Elizabeth Taylor, Warren Beatty, Woody Allen, Adreena Schneeweiss, a veritable Who's Who; why can't they get a meeting with the president? Why don't they even *try* to get a meeting with the president? And if they get turned down, why don't they try again? And again and again and again.

And why don't we!

I love being gay! I love gay people! I think in many ways we're better than straight people. We're more loving. We're better friends and better at friendship. We're kinder to each other. I think person for person we're more talented and creative and imaginative. I feel proud and grateful that I'm gay. I look upon it as a great gift. I do. I do. *(Slowly tears are coming into his eyes.)* I really do think all these things. And I try not to forget them.

But we are dying. Somebody is killing us off. And we're not fighting back. We are really bad at fights. *(Suddenly screaming out in agony.)* WHAT ARE WE GOING TO DO ABOUT IT! *(Audience is stunned by this explosion. He takes a deep breath and tries to get a hold on himself. Then, pleadingly:)* I DON'T WANT US TO DIE! *(Long pause of silence.)* We must find a way for all of us uniting to save our lives.

That's really why I have invited you here tonight.

I want to start a new UC organization devoted to political action, to really fighting back. Do you want to start something like this too?

(Cries of Yes! Yes! Yes!)

I want so much for us all to live!

Thank you. Thank you for coming.

Now let's talk!

Look at them! Look at their faces looking up at me. Look again how many showed up to hear me. Nobody walked out. Look how young most of them are. Look how handsome and sweet and innocent most of them are. They applaud and applaud. They're giving me a standing ovation! How interesting that it's young guys who showed; the older farts are sick of me. Or dead. Or so frightened that they're paralyzed. I recognize some of the faces. Thank you for coming to hear me. I want to say "An army of lovers cannot die." I can't get that sentence out of my head. I want to yell out to all of them, "AN ARMY OF LOVERS CANNOT DIE!"

FRED TO TOMMY

Does it look like we have our army? *(They hug.)*

DANIEL THE SPY

The ZAP trials have been stopped again. They were such a mess that Greeting wouldn't release the results. They've got yet another trial ready to go. Everybody now wants to be on it, figuring they must have learned something from the previous tries. There's a waiting list of 125,000 all over the country. Dash has said yet again that if he can't be told who's sick with an OI so he can turn them down in advance, he doesn't want them to "muddy my waters." He continues to refer to ZAP as "my baby." What a nightmare!

Half the patients receiving ZAP needed transfusions. Patients were stopping taking the drug. "You're crazy, you must carry on, this is routine stuff we must get past . . ." Dash is over the top in his anger. He threatens again that if the government wants G-D to continue to contribute free drugs, "You are going to have to take the G-D package, all of you!" He is yelling this at Jerry, who does nothing until he's called by both Nostrill at HAH and Gobbel at the White House saying the First Lady is asking what's taking so long.

•

INT. EMMA'S OFFICE. DAY.
She is supervising Buzzy, who's administering an IV to Fred. Tommy is with him.

TOMMY: How many times and how many ways can Greeting test the same shit?

EMMA: Until they find some itty-bitty speck of something they can manipulate and piggyback into a massive market for the desperate. Patients will die from a drug approved and provided to them by their own government.

TOMMY: Rebby thinks their Dridgies are poison too.

EMMA: We're dealing with a company that's using two drugs to kill you. Dridgies take you to heaven only to have ZAP throw you into hell.

TOMMY: Dash Snicker is a great carny pitchman. He came to sell GMPA on ZAP.

EMMA: We were in med school together. Mark my words, Dash Snicker will single-handedly make ZAP the greatest drug in Greeting's history, and one of the great moneymakers in the history of pharmaceuticals. Not bad for a drug that's shit. *(She builds herself into a fury.)* Someone is out there determined to specifically smear shit on someone or something. *Any* protocol should have produced *something* by now.

BUZZY: You think they want trials to fail?

EMMA: My gut tells me this all smells like a desperate exercise for Greeting to prove that the higher dose is required when they start their next fucking "official" trial. I feel so helpless. Where's this new organization you're starting?

INT. GAY CENTER. NIGHT.
Even more packed. On the blackboard is their name, which Avram is finishing writing:

FUQU

FED UP QUEERS UNITED

Cheers from the crowd. Then Avram and his group of artists unveil a big poster. It reads: SILENCE = DEATH. Louder cheers. Fred and Tommy sits to the side, smiling.

EXT. WALL STREET. DAY.
A huge crowd of activists is sitting in the intersection, backing up all the honking traffic. A dangling effigy of Dr. Omicidio is waving in the breeze. Next to him is an effigy of Peter Ruester. Posters: TIME ISN'T THE ONLY THING THAT NITS IS KILLING and NITS = NOT INTERESTED IN TALKING SERIOUSLY. A number of the many protestors are carrying SILENCE = DEATH signs. One by one police drag them off to a waiting paddy wagon. Tommy walks around surveying. Guys are passing out copies of Fred's op-ed piece to pedestrians.

Fred is being hauled away by several cops.

FRED *(to the cops lifting him up and toward the paddy wagon; he gives them copies of his column)*: Here. Read this. I wrote it. *The New York Truth.*

TOMMY *(to Fred as the cops are now carrying him)*: Your first arrest! Congratulations, honey. One hundred eleven arrests so far.

INT. INSIDE PADDY WAGON. DAY.

Tommy is comforting a very young and nervous kid.

TOMMY: Don't be frightened, sweetness.

YOUNGSTER: What will they do to us?

TOMMY: It'll just be in and out.

YOUNGSTER: Then why are they going to all this trouble?

TOMMY: Because we're faggots, hon! Where you been?

Sparks, very smart and not friendly, moves to Fred's side.

SPARKS: I want to stay by your side every single minute. You're smart. My name is Sparks. I went to Harvard. They didn't teach me anything like this. I've got to learn everything. I've got to save my best friend.

SCOTTY *(very cute and also smart; to Fred)*: My group is planning a way to break into a secret location. Want to come? My name is Scotty.

MAXINE *(retired dyke professor, real leftie)*: I have been involved with every movement my whole adult life and you guys are already forming groups to do undercover stuff. Don't you think the floor should vote on it? That's the method we approved.

SCOTTY: But affinity groups can do what they want to. Very cloak-and-dagger.

MAXINE *(to Fred)*: My name is Maxine. I'm organizing a dyke caucus.

FRED: Dykes are that interested in us?

MAXINE: Check your attitude. We get it too. I know half a dozen women up and down the coast who have it. And NITS won't include us in their definition. I hope that's part of our fight.

RON *(singing)*: "Everything's coming up roses!" Sing out, Maxine!

INT. CBS STUDIO. EVENING NEWS.

Dan Rather is in the middle of delivering when a few activists from FUQU pop up behind him and yell at the camera. FIGHT BACK!

*FIGHT UC! Fed Up Queers United! FUQU! They hold up a poster
with* FUQU *on it. Then another with* SILENCE = DEATH.

FRED EXULTS

It was a wonderful beginning. All of America saw us! Or a nice part of it,
anyway.

As for my op-ed piece, I still can't get over that *The Truth* actually allowed
these words of mine into print in their hallowed bloodless pages. Here is a
sample:

FADS'S CALLOUS RESPONSE TO UC

Many of us who live in daily terror because of the epidemic of The
Underlying Condition cannot understand why the National Institute
of Tumor Sciences has been so intransigent in the face of this monstrous tidal wave of death. Its response to what is plainly a national
emergency has been inadequate, its testing facilities inefficient, and
access to its staff and activities virtually impossible to gain.

There is no question on the part of anyone fighting UC that
NITS along with Food and Drug Supervision constitute the single most incomprehensible bottleneck in American bureaucratic
history—one that is actually prolonging this roll call of death. This
has been only further compounded by President Ruester, who has
yet to utter publicly the words "Underlying Condition" or put anyone in charge of the fight against it.

It's little wonder that NITS and FADS flounder so grotesquely.
From the first day of what now has become a national epidemic,
the uppermost levels of the federal and New York City governments
have chosen not to acknowledge UC. And when the histories of the
Goins and Ruester administrations are truthfully written, this scandal
will dwarf the political corruption in New York and the foreign-
policy blunders in Washington. We need humanitarianism from our
president . . .

LAST WILL AND TESTAMENT

Brinestalker has kept track of Fred Lemish's call to arms. What can an old man do for his last hurrahs? Lemish is Daniel Jerusalem's chum. Daniel is a son of Amos Standing's lover, Philip Jerusalem. Brinestalker, Amos, and Philip once called themselves the Big Three at Yaddah. Daniel's brothers are Sam Sport's partners. Fred Lemish must be nipped in the bud. Brinestalker's not dead yet. How cooperative is the human capacity for hatred. Americans have a hard time recognizing this, unlike the Germans from whom he'd learned this lesson. He must erase Fred Lemish and all he must know.

One of Tricia's operatives recently returned from a worldwide canvassing of the Far East, Southeast Asia, India, and even Russia. He reported how infected men by far outnumbered the women. He wonders what Angleton will do with this news. Things are still too slow on the home front.

Yes, he's an old man now, eighty-seven more or less. He's been back to Switzerland and Germany so many times to remake his body that he looks much younger to himself and his mirror. He mumbles to himself out loud quite often. "I wasted too much time. I barked up some wrong trees." Since the Ruesters will be leaving Washington shortly, his contacts in those corridors will become less useful. Dredd Trish's new world orders are of a different nature. His past is far more putrid than Purpura's. Nazis. Arabs. Purpura just sucked penises. Now the Trishes will slice them off wholesale via various Arab ventures. Exceedingly rich, Arabs. One has no idea how much they will terrorize everyone, including, thank goodness, each other, which will keep them busy for a while. Our big problem will be our inability to tell all their religious beliefs apart. They are awfully good haters of each other. Shovell told him Dredd will keep the Arabs in line. Bart Shovels, one of his best and nastiest Tricia operatives, is going to work for Dredd.

Brinestalker continues his mumbling as he walks on Connecticut Avenue on this lovely spring day. He thinks he sees Ianthe Strode, so he crosses the street to avoid her. Now *she* is looking old. He could have given her his Swiss doctors' names. He smiles, remembering the day he presented her with a leather-bound copy of volume XXX of his list of Washington fairies that included her husband, Strode. "I feel as if I'm carrying an American flag," he said to her. "It's now been officially published by our printing office," he boasted. He autographed it for her.

He decides to pop into the cathedral to receive a pep talk with "My Maker." He walks into one of the luxury shops on the Avenue and asks to be shown to his pew. The stroke immediately follows, and his death in a bed of women's hats that he's overturned. Of course his death goes unannounced. The last of the Big Three at Yaddah departs our history of The American People. He'd learned finally what happened to Amos. James Jesus told him that his remains had been found and identified, washed up somewhere far away on some unidentified foreign island's shore. And Sam Sport had told him that Philip died in Miami Beach. The secrets people take to their graves, Brinestalker thinks as his own heart gives out.

Brinestalker had almost brought off his last coup, delivering to his coveted old friend Purpura, with whom he'd fucked so many years ago, the information that when Peter was governor of California, Garrie Nasturtium had been part of that Midnight Massacre gay orgy and therefore knew too much about all who were there fucking with him. He was disappointed when she told him she already knew it. James Jesus and his CIA ops had beaten him to the punch. She no longer seemed interested. She's too busy getting all worked up about Russia. Peter's called it "the evil empire." Russia had never been of interest to Brinestalker. He can't understand why the Ruesters are so up in arms about it.

The Tricia Institute, though he'd preferred their old name of Unnatural Acts, has certainly come a long way under him. Now it's connected to first-level divisions of many agencies named just as mysteriously, wherein domestic and foreign scandalous behavior is telegraphed to interconnected missions at bureaus far and wide. Linus Gobbel had seen to that. Bart Shovels will continue it. Such expansions and their tributaries have blossomed everywhere in the turbulence following various postwar thises and thats. Few are those who can penetrate these labyrinthine gold mines. Brinestalker is proud to have been a part of this. Enough but never enough, he'd be the first to modestly tell you. He was also proud to learn this very morning that his men have been able to infiltrate little Freddy Lemish's organization. Fuck you, too, Freddy, in memory of Amos and Philip who abandoned me so.

Washington is such a small town.

THE HOUSE OF THE LIVING DEAD

Nasdean Masrullah, Pedro Ofennback, Laurent O'Brialy, Farrell Ostend, Gray Tiger, Aleen Horst, Gregory Samms, Corbitt Bronson, Samuel Adams Levy III, Sandor Odensee, Forsythe Pleasants,

Count Gerhard Leonhardt, Billy "Burp" Broadway, Blake Mistrall, Thomas Jose Santiago-Jones, Wolf Hester, Will Balloon, Andrew Oliphant, Crawford Vander, Lyn Hoffenshue, Norbert Rue, Billy Federickson, Gloria Schmiesshorn, Morton Veblen, Stormy Whether, Altrud Vinnegan, Janus Wysterdamm, Tim Ogun, Robert Jose Alton, Kiefer Kreditz, Calvin Arthur Jones, Markt Heisenberg, Julian Baksal, Giovanni Aranato, John Jacobson, Ivan Kellerman, Matt Luxe, Peter Pauleski, Lindsay Williamson, Gritty Burthem, Morris Jay Libby, Durston Holder IV, Ronnie Mayes, Trumbull Martinson, GoGo Gallery, Marty Fink, Dolphus Schweitzer, June Morganthal, Harold Von Maur, Norstein Theblen, Larry McGuire, Jim Kellyman, Hyman Grossbart, Muhammed Ali-Kver, Drover Kimmel, Rex-Claudette Joelle, Bennett Arthurman, Sheryl DeGiuseppi, Carlos Santa Maria, Barry Ginestra . . .

•

INT: GAY CENTER. NIGHT.
A long line of FUQU members are lined up to add names for above list on a big blackboard. Bradley, the new secretary, enters them in his notebook.

AN ARMY OF LOVERS . . .

Many will write their FUQU history. It was as if each one came to know they were now living and making history. Dominant voices will push their way forward, determined to be heard. That is the way the best histories are written. Isn't it? Sarah Schulman will supervise, mold, and archive a lot of it. Fred, Maxine, Scotty, Sparks, Ron, David F., so many others, will all have their versions. And of course Dame Lady Hermia and Dr. Sister Grace.

MELVIN

I have been elected treasurer!
I am sixty-seven years old. I am a successful accountant.
FUQU!
Fed Up Queers United!

Queer.

Queer? I'm actually calling myself queer?

The word had been taboo. For decades homosexuals had fought to ban that word from our lips. We are *homosexuals*! Then came *gay*! Just when *gay* was finally acceptable the kids decided to rehab *queer*. We must corral the language of our oppressors, they say. Why? To defuse it. Oh. How does using it defuse it? It makes everyone hear it and say it. That's defusing it? It makes it a less powerful word. Then why do you want to call yourself something that's less powerful? We'll make it powerful in a different way: it will be *ours*. Oh, yes. Of course. I must try not to be an old fuddy-duddy. Older gays don't understand very much about the younger generation. Most of FUQU is young. I always tried to act young for my age. I wore a wig for a while but my young showbiz clients said it was more butch to just shave my head. I would never have thought of that myself. I'm actually able to pick up guys now.

They are a big bunch of angry kids. Cute, though, even handsome. The look of heroes, I tell myself, as we all meet together to plan some sort of future. I'm glad there are so many of them. I'm glad they're angry. At last someone is angry along with me. Half of my clients have died. My biggest client, Michael, is dying. He directed *Chorus Line*. Do we all still remember *Chorus Line*? It made me rich. It made him rich. It made Joe Papp rich. How can we just lie down and die? We have lots to be angry about!

FUQU is so cute and hot that our meetings constantly fill up with even cuter and hotter newcomers. Going to FUQU meetings has replaced going to the bars. Now is not so hot for bars anyway. Go to a meeting. Do something useful. Get out of the house!

Down deep they're frightened. I can see that. Many of their friends are dead too. They come from coed colleges where men and women live together. They've grown up reading gay and lesbian novels and seen movies about them-selves and documentaries and reports in the press and actors portraying them on TV. Many of them even have parents who don't mind their kids are gay. It's a new world. Older guys mourn the death of the old world. Not me.

They wear black all the time. Black jeans and black work boots or black dress shoes and black shirts and black sweaters and black dungaree jackets. They have the shortest hair one week and the longest hair the next. Guys have sideburns sliced above the ear top one month and way beneath the lobe the next. Whoever is dictating fashion and style is unnamed and invisible but when a change is made it is made quickly and by all. No argument. It's amazing. They fight with each other very little and with the world a great deal. They are excellent. I just know it. I am in the right place. I just know that, too.

We can change the ways of the world.

FUQU, world!

I just love our name.

"Where are you off to tonight, Melvin?" my office staff asks.

"FUQU!"

They don't get it yet. But they will.

We started with a few hundred. We hit five hundred one week. Then we hit it every week. Now it's even more! I collect two dollars from each of them for our rent to the Center and for our expenses. We rent buses to go to D.C. and Albany and Chattanooga and for wherever we're planning to protest out of town. I've invested our funds in money market accounts to make us a few extra bucks. I don't tell them. I don't think they'd understand the principle of money market accounts.

Some say we're an army, growing and growing into a national army. The women members don't like that comparison. It's too *them*, meaning heterosexual. We do not in any way want to be like *them*! A creep compared us to Nazi storm troopers. That really freaked me out, as the kids say now. I was in Nazi Germany and I know what storm troopers were like and what they did. I was only a little boy, but I remember, and we got out in time, thank God, but the twerpy young man who made that remark, on the floor no less, so that all could hear his stupidity, received a major tongue lashing. By the time I was finished and Maxine was finished, Ralph was in tears, blubbering, "I'm sorry, I'm sorry, I didn't mean anything." At the end of my tirade, I bellowed, "We must be proud of who we are and what we are doing!" There was major applause and whistling and stomping on the floor, *with their boots*! And at that same meeting I was elected our treasurer, unanimously. I have never been elected anything in my life.

Right-wing zealots are convinced that gays have huge lobbying organizations with enormous power and funding flourishing everywhere, especially in Washington. Can you believe that? In *The Washington Monument* there was an op-ed from some right-winger warning the world to beware of "sick homosexuals." I thought *The Monument* was supposed to be a liberal paper. How can they print stuff like that? I put copies of this op-ed on the back table and Kevin made a motion that we should go down to Washington and picket *The Monument*. It would have passed but Avram, who is a sensible leftie, said, "Whoa! Let's do more shit in this town first." And he was seconded by Eric and Frank, who are already boyfriends. And then Gerri got up and said, "I think we should form a committee to brainstorm what we can do against the Catholic Church." And there were enormous cheers. We have a lot of Catholics. I forget we have all these Puerto Ricans too. Hispanics, I must call them. I am learning lots about political correctness. "Meet me in the far back corner after the meeting," Gerri says. And that's how things get started. Next week they'll come back with the action all planned out and everything. She's very respected, Gerri. Big butch dyke with the sweetest angelic face. She's a contractor. "I'll do your apartment," she said to me. "I hear you're moving. Me and my team are really good." Her brother died of UC. "My younger brother. It really broke me up. It still does."

The biggest FUQU demo we've had so far was maybe six hundred. With a million faggots in the New York City area, that's not very many. I'm talking like Fred now. We ran up some pretty big expenses with lawyers and court stuff from getting arrested at our demos, but Tommy Boatwright at GMPA covered them. "But don't tell anyone, especially my board. They hate Fred. And they don't trust me because Fred and I are friends." This fucking community! But FUQU will change all that! As long as we continue to grow at this rate, I'm not worried. We'll win. We'll lick this.

Now there are beginning to be inquiries about chapters in other cities. Out-of-towners come to our meetings to see what we're about. When our demos sound like fun, we get bigger crowds. Going after Pig Goins is fun and draws a bigger house, as we say in the theater. Going after the governor and schlepping up to Albany is like a matinee on Yom Kippur, no audience. Washington, too, is kind of far, but we might be able to do it every once in a while if the weather's nice and our treasury increases. Scotty gave us a thousand dollars. And David Hockney is giving us some of his art to auction. Keith Haring, too. Scotty is going to arrange a big art auction. He's a real organizer type. He was on Wall Street. They fired him when they found out he was positive for UC, and he sued them and won. He got some big settlement. I think he's the first one to do this and win. He's from the Main Line. Philadelphia. Rich and handsome. His brother has a yacht. Scotty took a bunch of us on a cruise for a few days. I never took my shirt off. I couldn't. They're all so gorgeous. I never had a social life like this.

I wish the media paid us more attention. Just like with GMPA and UC, they don't cover us. Michelangelo and Bordo and Gabe and Ann and the Blotch have formed a media committee. Ann used to work for CBS and Diane Sawyer. Ann gives little demonstrations for when the camera is on us and we have to utilize every second to get our message out fast. And so adept are the kids at being cute and handsome and smart and convincing that the media will come to love us, I'll just bet. We are told all the time that the reason they don't cover us much is because their bosses won't let them. Well, we'll just have to give them more dramatic stuff. And then the world's perception of us will be as a great and indomitable and ferocious army.

You bet.

Great!

FUQU!

DANIEL THE SPY

Almost all on ZAP trials have had a case of PCP pneumonia. COD's embargoed the treatment for it. There is no data to suggest that PCP prophylaxis is beneficial. According to Jerry, it may, in fact, be dangerous, which is another of his increasing number of dodges. He doesn't know what he's talking about. "Dr. Omicidio does not feel it's beneficial to remove this particular obstacle with this particular procedure" is what Jerry's report to the White House said. Yes, he's been to the White House and had his photo taken with the Ruesters.

Of course Rebby screams any chance he can get. "Why is there still no research into the OIs?" He calls Jerry "a monster," because "all these young men are dying today." He said this to his face at a meeting at NITS. In front of a lot of people. People are now seen at meeting after meeting. "My patients live longer than any others!" Rebby yells.

"Why, do you think?" some young doctor asks.

"I won't give them ZAP, for a start. And I put everyone on PCP prophylaxis even though it is not approved."

"Where do you get a treatment for it?"

"I order it from South Africa, where it is readily available. It is a simple antifungal spray you inhale that is used there for a number of things. It is an act of murder not to use it!"

He will not be allowed into a NITS meeting again. HAH has put his name on some list.

Dash Snicker says G-D has over half a billion dollars' worth of advance orders for ZAP already. Debbi Driver says there are a quarter of a million applications for the new PI ZAP trials.

FRANK TELLS ABOUT ZAPS

THE ACTIONS, NOT THE DRUG

I like to tell everyone I invented the zap. I didn't really, of course, zaps go back to Jesus, but I had to explain to Fred and the floor what a zap was. I said we have to do zaps, lots of zaps, zap zap zap, and they have to be fast, quick, in and out, not too many people, or you can have a lot of people, depends, but you have to catch them off guard, whatever them we're zapping. I explained that you kept your zaps a secret in your own special little individual cells and we didn't have to vote on it on the floor like a regular action required.

I went into FUQU because I found out I was UC-positive and there was no in-between, you were either positive and you had to stay alive or you weren't and you were probably a useless wuss. Although many of my friends who are positive have turned out to be wusses. Drives me nuts. I tell them and of course then they're not my friends anymore. "Don't bother me with your shit" is their response. FUQU is my only friends now.

My friend Adrian does a lot of Chinese medicine and acupuncture, and my friend Rick who ran for mayor of Columbus, South Carolina, is into homeopathy and macrobiotics. He wanted me to give up meat and ice cream and I told him he was out of his mind. I said meat and ice cream have kept me alive for all these years, they're going to keep me alive for the rest of them.

FUQU is slowly becoming more UC-savvy, questioning and researching everything we can. The shit we found and the shit we took! God, we were vomiting and hallucinating to beat the band. There was this stuff from— well, I don't remember where it was from, but you felt like you were the size of a molecule and falling through a sieve, and you woke up on the floor. I had this young friend who wasn't UC-positive who wanted me to give it to him because it sounded like fun. I was like, oh please, flush it down the toilet. Then I heard about this stuff in Japan. Guys were taking it there and crying hallelujah. I have friends touring there in some musical. And the company that makes the stuff won't send it here. What better place to zap than their New York offices, which are listed in the phone book. So we get maybe thirty or so and we barge in on their offices in the Empire State Building and immediately start chaining ourselves to the desks and chairs and to each other, yelling, "Your drug or our lives!" and all the employees are terrified and do not have any idea what we're talking about. The American office only deals with shoes the company also makes. Michelangelo and Blotch had notified the Japanese media, which shows up in droves. Gloria, who speaks a (very) few words of Japanese, sort of explains to the assembled staff what we're on about and now they're rooting for us, raising their arms like the prizefighters in *Rocky*, and I guess these were the photos that got into the Japanese press because within a week I swear we had a message from their home office that they were looking into the issue and would get back to us, which they actually did. A few months later they would sell us this drug, which was called dextran sulfate. It didn't work. But we had got it. The grungy *Truth*, of course, ignored us altogether. We will get back at them!

This was our first effective zap, and we got to work with each other smoothly and we all had a ball doing it, which of course is most important. The more we work together, the more we come to really bond and love each other.

Fred knows Hal Prince, the big Broadway producer, who has a contact in Tokyo, and his wife has a friend she loves a lot who is very sick, so Hal got his office to send us a load of some other Japanese stuff we heard about called Urdzu. Our Dr. Levi Narkey had it analyzed and said, "Well, it couldn't hurt. It seems to be composed of compressed dirt and herbs." So we started on our own little trial, using a lottery to parcel the stuff out to some sick guys and some well guys, and sat and waited for something to happen, which it didn't, except that Wallace died, he was the sickest of the bunch and was on his way out anyway. "Thanks, guys," he said to us in the hospital, "I really appreciate what you tried to do for me."

I was there with Eric, who always makes a big point of going to see anyone in the hospital, and it really brings it home to you and makes us want to fight even harder. We stayed with Wallace until he died. He was an old friend of Eric's and he had no one else with him while he was dying. Awful sad. Awful. He said the Urdzu made him feel better. Eric says it was probably only what he called the "placebo effect." Meaning you feel better because you want to feel better after you take something unidentified that is supposed to make you feel better. He's learning a lot of stuff like this.

We are going to be distributing this Urdzu stuff. We have this dynamic young girl, Claudette, she can't be more than about fifteen or sixteen. She's French. She's going to be in charge of selling it to whoever wants to try it. She'll also sell that lipid shit made from soy margarine. It really stinks. I mean the smell. Suzanne and Griff have learned how to rip it off. She's a doctor and is administering it to several of her patients. This shit comes from Israel, from the Weitzman Institute, "so it must be okay if the Jews take it," Suzanne says.

Did I mention that I'm falling in love with Eric? He's strong and silent and he gets things done. He doesn't talk nearly so much as I do. Eric and Fred are old friends from the Y. He really loves Fred. I think Eric would follow Fred to the end of the earth. Eric says Fred saved his life. He read all the stuff Fred wrote in *The Prick* and immediately stopped fucking around. "No one else was telling me to be careful. My doctor wasn't saying dipshit. And he's gay."

The first really good friend we made after we moved in together, Bernard, he died last night. We were up with him until he died at dawn. It's a weird and transforming experience, let me tell you. I never saw anyone die before Wallace and Bernard. Eric has seen it twelve times by now.

CLAUDETTE

I wasn't fifteen. I was seventeen. Almost. I had graduated from Brearley and I didn't want to go to college yet. I heard about FUQU and it sounded like just what I wanted to do. I'd read about Athenian democracy and I wanted to be a part of something like that. We have hundreds of people every week, trying to make the process more goal-oriented and specific. Spud and I became friends, investigating the same drugs and companies. He was cool. He had green hair one week and purple hair the next, so I did that too. It really turned the other women off, so I stopped it. I could tell some of them were interested in me and I didn't want to kibosh that. I was in my lesbian phase. Spud's parents had been in a concentration camp and he was UC-positive. He was cute and we hung together even though I was a lesbian. I had been both, back and forth, trying things out, and Spud thought that was cool. "Such extraordinary life lessons we are playing with," I happened to say to him. For some reason, that made him start to cry. "Oh, come on, I'll race you to the corner," I said. And we did, just like two kids. I let him win, of course.

GENEALOGIES

A FEW DAYS IN THE LIVES OF . . .

Scotty is in love with Perry and everyone is smitten with Adam, who is in love with himself. Jonnie is particularly in love with Adam. Adam disdains them all. Adam says he walks home and has sex with two or three or four good-looking guys on the way. It's his way of forgetting that he's not happy with his life or his career or where he's going or who he is. He has little respect for anyone who's after his body. His body is rock-hard and overmuscled and his small head looks out of proportion. He knows he is not as connected upstairs as he wants to be.

Fred worries that his children are too promiscuous and that not all that much has changed since the old days, not that the old days were all that old or long ago. He occasionally throws into conversations about who is seeing whom, "I hope you're using condoms," and Bart or Mart or Evan or Gladwin will snort something like, "You are such an old auntie!" "Well, you all just better be," he declares, and hears "Yes, Mom," or "Sure, Pop," in response.

In a more ordered and orderly world, Scotty and Perry should be lovers. They would be good for each other. Scotty is good with organization and Perry is good with details and they both are cute and verbal, so people look up to them. There is one fly in the ointment: they both like to get fucked. Although the terminology of earlier eras—top and bottom—has been more or less retired as more and more like to do both, there are fellows who prefer one over the other. So it's a problem when a bottom falls in love with a bottom. Scotty is so in love with Perry that he says he doesn't think about it: "I only like sex during courting anyway. After, I just want to cuddle and watch TV and sleep in someone's arms." And Perry says that's what he likes too. His beloved now dead Francis is and will be forever on his mind, so cuddling's just fine for the moment. For a while, this will work. Everyone watches and waits. All boyfriending in this place is highly visible and of great interest and is a constant flow. And everyone knows how Perry lost his lover and still has scars.

Perry's also a young Greek god. He doesn't know it like Adam knows it (and as Bruce Niles never knew it; Bruce, who has lesions now, and whose gorgeous model Albert died, and who has a new boyfriend named Turtle, who's sick now too). Or if Perry knows it, it doesn't do him any good. He's convinced his life is totally fucked up. He doesn't know what to do with it. He lost the only love of his young life, and since Francis's death he hasn't let himself love anyone else. He just won't! He liked Scotty fine when they were just friends, but when Scotty said he was in love with him, Perry was suddenly uncomfortable. Still, Perry is lonely enough in the big city that he just stays put for now.

Both Scotty and Perry test positive for The Underlying Condition. There is this test now. At last. Most guys won't take it. What's the point? There's no medicine that works. I'd just as soon not know, a lot of guys feel, but some want to know anyway. So now Scotty and Perry know they're going to die. Though they say, I'm going to live through this! Everyone comes to say that. I'm going to be the one who licks it. I know everyone says that, but I'll be the one. You'll see. Fred doesn't have a sick friend who hasn't said it.

"I loved Francis. Francis loved me back," Perry told Scotty.

"Francis is dead."

"*I know that!*"

Francis made all our decisions, he wants to tell him. He made me laugh, too. I don't laugh very much anymore. He tells Fred all of this and it breaks Fred's heart.

Perry had worked in Washington for Daniel but Daniel and Daniel's musty house were depressing. He was smart and all that, but he didn't have much sparkle and oomph. He also talked to Perry about Fred constantly, all Fred was doing and had started, etc., etc. It was Fred this and Fred said that, so after a while Perry had to leave him a nice note and get to New York and join FUQU and find Fred for himself. Fred turned out to be just as Perry knew he'd be. Doing something important. That's all that Perry wants now.

So he spends all his time going to all the meetings that FUQU is constantly having. No sooner does a problem present itself than a committee is formed on the spot and a meeting time established. Soon it's possible to go to a different meeting every night and over the weekend. He managed to be tired enough at the end of each day so all he had to do with Scotty is allow himself to be cuddled. He still had dreams about Francis and would often wake up in tears. Scotty wasn't very good with tears, so it wasn't long before he suggested it was time for Perry to bunk somewhere else. Good thing there is already a firm tradition in FUQU of bedding down on spare beds here and there. There's always a place to stay for however long it's needed. Charlie had an extra bedroom.

In a few months, Fred will fix Scotty up with Kevin and that will last for a short while too, until it turns out that they're both bottoms as well. Ah, the love complications of wartime.

When Fred found out he was positive he felt existentially that he'd reached the end of time and was walking around in a void. He'd been writing his play about the Ruesters, *Just Say No*, and had to have an emergency hernia and they'd given him the blood test, which they weren't supposed to do without his consent. The surgeon said, after Fred protested, "Oh, stop it, Mr. Lemish. What if I had cut myself while operating? You are lucky

I operated on you at all. Most surgeons at Table will not operate on anyone who has any indication of UC. Period. Any other questions? Your scar is healing very nicely. You're welcome."

Dodo's test is still going to be a big problem, loaded with curves and innuendoes.

THE ARRIVAL OF IRIS

An unsmiling straight woman scientist named Iris got up one evening and said to the crowded room, "You guys don't know dipsqueak about what you are fighting or should be fighting. If anyone is interested, I'll teach you." She'd been observed sitting silently at earlier meetings, sternly frowning. Some of the women wondered if she might be some sort of a plant. Infiltrators are already being feared, and while an announcement at each meeting's start encourages unknown strangers to identify themselves or leave, no one really believes that will work.

Fred realizes immediately that the appearance of Iris could be the beginning of something really important in FUQU's development and history, and in the history of UC, and indeed the history of The American People.

Iris gathered her group and they call themselves the Treatment+Data Committee. T+D. It's Sparks and Perry and Stephen and James and Scotty (who is also on Fund-Raising) and Suzanne, that straight doctor with her straight infected husband she shouldn't have to put up with "unless I weren't such a masochist, mea culpa, mea culpa." Kersh and Barry are interested in the Data part. And Eigo, Sparks, and Scotty and Fred of course are obsessed with finding a treatment. The assortment will grow. Power will come to them commensurate with the knowledge they now will gain with Iris.

Iris is a Queens housewife who is a biochemist Ph.D. and has worked for both industry and in the medical field. "They both are difficult places to work," she says. "You'll see. This is a corrupt system, our health-care system. It's hard to work in and hard to change." Doesn't smile much but she's secretly pleased that her group has attracted smart ones; she can tell.

She starts by teaching them about how NITS is in charge and how it operates, as well as FADS and COD and HAH. "They're different but they aren't so different. But they think they're different, which will make our job more difficult. I think our big advantage over them will be our learning how to work with each other. They don't." Then she says, emphatically,

"We are going to work *together*. You hear me?" She made it sound like a religious commandment.

Of course Fred joins this T+D committee. He is not naturally adept at navigating scientific stuff, like the others are already showing themselves to be. "I can't differentiate between an antibody and an anecdote," he jokes. Since he senses that this is the committee that will do the major important stuff, he thanks Iris publicly every chance he gets. He's already proud of her. Stephen, and then Perry after Stephen dies, writes up all their meetings and puts copies on the back table for the main meetings on Monday night to read, along with piles of stuff now appearing in ever-greater quantities, put out by all the committees, and individuals as well. Everyone is amazed by the quantity and the quality of the stuff people are locating and even getting duplicated in their own offices on the sly. There must be a dozen committees by now, though they fluctuate as people's interests change, or as members die or move away.

Soon Melvin has to arrange a lease on a copying machine and they have to rent a room to put it in. "Is this an office? Do we call this our first office?" Maxine and Tom C. want to know about the room way over on Tenth Avenue. "I don't think we should have an office," Maxine says. "We are a grassroots organization." As if that would explain it to everyone, like it did to Maxine, who remembers "every political movement from way back when. And the ones that last are the ones that do not have offices and Xerox machines."

But T+D especially needs the machine, so its acquisition is begrudgingly approved by the floor.

FRED AND MAXINE

Strangely, Fred and Maxine like each other. They are from entirely different . . . well, everything. She has seen it all, a Marxist, a Stalinist, a Hegelian, a Trotskyite. "Yes, I go back that far," she tells Fred, who is interested in learning what they all were. "No, there are still a few of each around." When she explains them to him, he can't keep them straight. He remembers when he was in London many of the young writers he hired were proud Marxists. To be caught up so fervently in a political dialogue of diatribes and dialectics was new to him then, and it still is. Fred will joke that he and Maxine are FUQU's momma and poppa. "I did not become an activist until UC came along," Fred almost boasts. And then he said in a phony English accent. "And I lived abroad, you know." Then, as if he is suddenly back then and there, reliving something or other, "An American accent got you better everything, service, tables, you could get away with almost anything being an American." Including the English young men, he's thinking, the cute guys with their smooth milky white skin who seemed to like older men, who liked to have sex with him and talk about coming to America, where they'd never been. He wonders what's happening now to the guys over there, in London, where he lived for a while a long time ago, where he was (more or less) happy, and made a good movie that he was (yes) proud of. Another lifetime ago, Fred. And he snaps out of then and comes back to now.

Maxine takes him aside. "I've been watching you. Whatever's on your mind, you're going to torture yourself to death. And it's going to marginalize your effectiveness, which can be mighty and useful. Stop it!" He smiles at her and they hug. It's good for everyone to see that they're friends. Maxine is a major power force from the very beginning. She is a take-charge kind of person. When she talks, people listen. As more women arrive, she immediately corrals them into their own dyke caucus and feeds them brunch on Saturday at her house in Brooklyn. Max is a retired professor at a city college. Along her route she married, had two daughters, discovered she was a lesbian, and got rid of the husband. In his diary, Fred writes, "I get too angry. Max doesn't get angry. Max stays cool. I must ask her how she does this with such apparent ease."

"Because I have been on too many front lines for too many years," she will answer him. "After a while all the fights are pretty much the same and all the cast of characters are types I know how to deal with by now." She taught psychology. "You're an artist. I'm not an artist. Artists are meant to get excited and lose their cool. Just try not to let your psyche get caught in the doorjamb too often as the door gets slammed and then slammed again in our faces."

The women, of course, adore her.

AND EVERYTHING CONTINUES TO GROW

FUQU!

And more people become infected. And get sick. And die. Since fear is around more tangibly, no one talks about this. Yes, fear moves right along. It's stopping for no one.

About half of everyone in FUQU has been tested and half of these are positive. Or have already buried a lover. Or a best friend. Or a roommate. Everyone knows someone now.

Perry's count is five hundred. Under five hundred is the beginning of trouble. Under five hundred means you are supposed to take ZAP, which some guys have been taking on yet another trial. He doesn't want to take ZAP. As far as he's concerned, ZAP sounds like poison. Most of T+D are in strong agreement. Dodo and Dash Snicker may be silenced for the moment. "But Jerry can't be trusted," Barry is saying already, seconded by Annmarie, who is particularly interested in Haiti. She went to Haiti before and during the period when Haiti was considered a launching pad for this plague. She loves Haiti and it continues to break her heart. She sees that they have taken themselves out of the limelight, the Haitians going extremely ballistic in denying responsibility for anything to do with UC, and they have been able through diplomatic pressures to get themselves removed from that stain of the list of the guilty, as well as removed from whatever help might have come to them via HOW had they only stood tall.

Blacks from anywhere, certainly American blacks, are furiously unwilling to come anywhere near UC discussions. The number of people of color who show up at FUQU, though it grows, is never as substantial as it should be. The same was the case at GMPA. Bruce and Fred and Tommy had gone to black churches and tried to get them unsuccessfully to come and show their faces and be heard.

How difficult it is to stay on track! There are so many shoots and offshoots, not only of UC, but now of FUQU itself. All the actions, the demos. They just happen, almost spontaneously. That there is so much unrelenting energy is very moving. Best just to let it find its way, Fred believes, not that there is any other way to handle it. Deal with the problems when they occur. This was pretty much the way GMPA had sprouted. People came along and said, I want to do this, I can do this, and Fred said, Go ahead. If Tommy hadn't come along to put some rigid armor on the process, GMPA might have been what FUQU looked to be becoming, what Fred had wanted in the first place. A fighting force. Fred prefers this unstructured way. He hates the "job descriptions" that Tommy rigidly imposed at GMPA. The two still fight about this. The wear and tear on Tommy running GMPA are manifestly visible, but Fred is insensitive to it. Fred can be blind to other people and their problems if they get in the way of what he thinks he wants, of what he thinks is needed, of what he thinks must be.

Here, at FUQU, amazingly, Fred sits to the side most of the time, watching to see where all the rivulets will coalesce. Oh, he has his blow-ups, and even a few threats of "If you don't do this, I am leaving," to which no one pays any attention. Almost everyone knows who Fred is and many of them are respectful of this, and what he has done. Many, however, do not and are not. This proves interesting to him, if to no one else. He claims he wants to know when he is criticized. "How else can I learn?" He sounds naïve. He sounds too self-important. To how many is he a peculiarity: the aging infected gay man?

•

Scotty's count is 250. It was 650 when Perry was willing to sleep with him. But after Perry left it had fallen, his vidge count, rapidly, to 250. He is feeling shitty. He quite casually says all the time that he expects to die from UC. Greeting-Dridge will be charging $25,000 for a year's worth of its poison ZAP capsules. No wonder insurance companies are getting angrier, refusing to insure UC patients. You'd think our very own government of our very own country would see to it that *no* medicine cost *anyone* $25,000 a year. Scotty and Sparks think revenge is in order against G-D. Scotty has a touch of the film director in him, whipping things up. Fred can already see him in boots, with a riding crop.

•

Dr. Monserrat Krank is now on TV trying to convey the message to America that this shit is actually happening to everyone, please to open your eyes, but she isn't having much success doing anything, even though she's rich and looks maternal, and of course is a heterosexual, and a well-connected one. Jonnie says he believes that in her heart of hearts Dr. Krank feels it's already too late. Fred is beginning to intimate as much too, to Tommy, who agrees with him, and that's very depressing to the few who overhear them. Cute Tony who has just tested positive wrote him a letter asking him to please stop saying these things "because I need your courage to keep me going." At every meeting guys come up to him to whisper and beg, "Have you heard about *anything good* that's coming along?" The sad way of the world. Fred sees this every single minute.

Jonnie, by the way, is preparing for Dr. Krank and Dr. Itsenfelder and their new UC consortium a directory of possible stuff out there that people might look into taking. But when you look at the items on the list, not so many people are rushing to get them. What are Virdiginess capsules, available "out of" Richmond, even if they are available from and administered by Dr. Ralph Phalanx, who is said to have a decent reputation down there? "I have to give my kids something," he tells *The Richmond–Chesapeake Bay Boys Reader*, a gay throwaway. "I went into my momma's old book of early Indian remedies and Virdiginess is one of them. It's made from a local bark. Lots of famous drugs that work are made from bark. It can't hurt." Trace Huvel and Robert Garcia went down to Richmond to get some of this stuff. Robert is looking terrible. Jonnie does say that Dr. Krank is nervous about including stuff like this in their treatment advisories but Dr. Itsenfelder also says "it can't hurt." Dacey Dienstag was going to go down with Robert and Trace but he died. Monserrat quietly asks Jonnie to tone down his "noble ideas." She has her own memories of her own dramas and near obliteration from "the scientific community" for her championing, with Rebby, of Irgardium-X. (Which, interestingly enough, someone is considering now trying out on one of the OIs.)

•

It is exceedingly moving to Fred to watch people in danger finally climbing on board. More people are frightened. Fear is the best motivator in the world. Along with anger, of course. Which, for him, means that it must be so for everyone. Whether they want it to be or not!

•

So, FUQU. A bunch of men and some women who are all terrific, some infected, all angry, many of them unrequitedly in love with someone else, few connecting with each other for very long. "A little love is better than no love," Carlisle Hopkins says to Norbert Sinclair when they decide their few-months affairlet was better than nothing and even better On Hold for the moment. Why? "Well, maybe we rushed into each other's arms too fast," Norbert hazards. He remembers some lyrics from when he was in a singing group at college. "We'll be together again," he sings to Carlisle when they bump into each other at meetings. "Oh, yeah, when?" Carlisle ripostes; he had not been so eager to be put on hold.

But there's so much else to do besides fall in love. Activism is about togetherness. They draw closer and closer together. FUQU FUQU FUQU. Young men who never felt comfortable displaying signs of emotion and affection in public now do so as a matter of course. Everyone kisses everyone hello and goodbye. Yes, it is all very moving.

Fred watches it all. He's still alone, of course. That's his genealogy.

Although he wonders how he got infected. Not that it makes any difference anymore. It is just that Fred, ever more the historian, worries about these things. Where did all this shit come from? And why?

FROM THE DIARIES OF DR. STUARTGENE DYE

It has been very tiring living for so long in the white man's world and denying my Native American heritage. At least I have been able to do good work in honoring my true people. I have been able to insure a bit of retribution against the white man for killing so many of us. Gay corpses will not be allowed to spread disease as they did in life. With incompetents like Geiseric, Grebstyne, Middleditch, and Omicidio I achieved this by just letting them do what they do, which I knew would escalate mortality. So, as with much of my Nobel research for "The Pathology of the Missing Enzymes," I have been able to keep what they call a "low profile." You will find little mention of me in any history of this plague, no black marks against my name in any history of NITS. Indeed, a new laboratory at NITS is being contemplated in my honor.

I look forward to researching the history of my own people, and my particular tribe of them now officially named by the Department of Indian Affairs as the Iwacki Dakotas. I want to locate them, perhaps live with them, certainly talk with them to hear all their agonizing stories of ill treatment at the hands of white men. Perhaps at last they will give me a people to believe in, to teach as Doc Rebbish taught me. Perhaps they have some deity I can at last pray to for an eternal respite from the life I was forced to live for my Nobel-winning discovery. In his last words to me, Doc Rebbish, who certainly had found a great deal, on his deathbed urged me to "seek and you shall continue to find."

DAME LADY HERMIA SNEAKS INTO FUQU

I decided it was time to see for myself. The hall is very crowded. I see Fred and he looks right past me. A woman keeps trying to invite me to Brooklyn to brunch.

I'd never seen such a stark demonstration of democracy in action that I knew was headed straight to its own destruction. I knew they could not last, certainly not at the pitch they were going, so fueled by an adrenaline that could only deplete them. But also because at that one meeting alone announcements were made of the deaths of at least two dozen of them. I was impressed how this made them even angrier. Anger like this to a Brit is an unknown language. We don't ever see it, or dine on it, or respond to it. You'd think such suppression would have destroyed us over the centuries, but it hasn't. In fact, it's what's kept us alive.

I did cry, though. I went back to my hotel, ordered up a bottle of gin, and swilled myself into a horrific state. I bawled and bawled. This hard old nut. My great-uncle Sir Silas Wrench-Fergit taught me about plagues. "They are what they are, my child."

I made it back to Washington and my empty flat. Thank God his Lordship is out there somewhere doing something for the Queen. That evening I hit the gin once again and bawled and bawled some more because I had seen last night that Fred could not be the leader he wants to be, and that is desperately needed, and that he didn't know this. Oh, he talked a good game. He surveyed the room filled with dying young men, but he did not enter it. He accepted their kisses and greetings and hugs and he returned them. That is not what I'm talking about. He is off in another world, thinking, all the time thinking, what to do with all this. But where he's living is a writer's location and not a leader's one. He lives in his head. And while he loves his brothers and sisters very much, I could see he only has his anger.

I pray it will keep him, at the very least, alive.

I realized I'd never recognized how very dear he's become to me.

"I came to one of your meetings," I finally write to him. "You were far too passive. You're sitting on an army waiting to be led. But they are leading you! Even after all these years I cannot fathom aspects of American 'democracy.' You must take charge! I do not want to see one more man in a dress facilitating a meeting unless he's concealing a secret weapon. Dredd Trish's shot-caller Bart Shovels will make Moose look like a morning glory. He is another nasty evil man. Your few hundreds must more fully comprehend that there is an inexhaustible supply of them and you are not ready."

My husband constantly berates me. "Americans are too incomprehensible for we poor Brits to ever understand."

MY CHILDREN

As with GMPA, guys say I started FUQU to get laid with the beauties. I didn't want people to say that was why I was doing all this. I didn't want that to be the case, that the founder fucked his children.

Of course, it's just the reverse with most of the FUQU guys. They are fucking like bunnies, "to spite the evil eye," as Goober said.

Yes, from our very beginning, everyone all around me is fucking with each other like crazy. I get a kick out of watching them at meetings, walking around, surveying the room even when they're sitting, looking for and often finding the spark to ignite and pair off with someone and, usually, soon enough falling apart and brooding and then finding another. I make it sound like the biggest gay bar in New York. Well, in some ways it is. Broken hearts repair themselves with facility and speed when you know you don't have all the time in the world. Except for me. I have been writing this book for what now seems a hundred years and I ignore the fact that time will not be so kind and generous indefinitely.

That's not true. I worry. I worry. I try not to think of dying.

More and more we are one huge family.

I feel increasingly protective of them. Yes, I think of them as my children. I am so fucking proud of this FUQU thing. It is far too territorial for me to think this way. FUQU is much too democratic to allow a father.

DAVID

Reading a book review in *The Monument*, I learn that new Holocaust camps are still being discovered. Old camp sites, that is. There were some 2,900 of them.

When I was with Grodzo at Mungel, I learned that camps were all over the place. What's new is what I'm reading now: "The camps were filled with gays as well as Jews." So they wanted to get rid of all the gays, too. Just like what's happening now. Why haven't I been murdered? I have lived in many camps.

THE ANIMAL MODEL

MAJOR GENERAL HORACE WIDDUMS, M.D.,
FRANEEDA NAVAL MEDICAL CENTER

It is important that there be *good* monkey doctors. If a monkey isn't used in
an experiment then a person has to be used, which is against the law. And if
living people aren't available to be administered an "experimental" anything,
then be grateful to the little monkey who's willing to stand in for you. If you
think all this talk about monkeys and monkey doctors is beside the point,
please pause to consider that not a day goes by wherein an important scientific experiment, the outcome of which might bear on whether you or your
loved ones live or die, is not conducted somewhere in our country by an idiot.
Be grateful for the monkey. (S)he is your friend. (S)he is willing to die for you
and your sins. Jesus may want you for a sunbeam but a monkey only wants
you for your nuts.

None of this levity is to imply that an "animal model" for a disease is
something to treat lightly. But science, which despite its desire to breach fron-
tiers, must also be facile at covering its ass. The Animal Model is one of the
great Ass Coverings in Modern Medicine.

The Dridge Diagnostic Directory of Doctors lists the most respected
monkey doctors today as Nobu Chin Chen at Stanford, Renata Heil and
Vorschluss Heimatt (yes, two now very old Nazis granted immunity by our
government at the close of World War II because of "previous superiority in
the burgeoning field of animal husbandry") at Idaho Iroquois Medical Center, Yours Truly, and Bosco Dripper, of Yaddah's Deacon & Caplan D&C/
NITS Primate Center at El Modesto Estancia, Florida, whom we now know
to be dead. Along with all his monkeys.

And now all monkeys have been embargoed for use by NITS and COD
and HAH. Not so long since an assassination attempt was made on our president. He was given an untested experimental treatment.

No Animal Model (NAM) in a practical sense means No Government
Funding (NGF). And No Pharmaceutical Interest (NPI). Hence, No Cure.

Why has HAH suddenly announced that monkeys are no longer available? The monkeys have been disappeared not only at El Modesto but at
every other government-funded primate center in the country. I cannot get
my hands on a one of them. What do I do if another president gets shot?

A judge advocate on my staff confided in me that Dr. Geiseric rarely changes his underpants and that filthy shit-encrusted same are often found in his trash, which is still being "sifted" by legal authorities, i.e., searching for "suspect" matériel. When confronted, Geiseric replied, "Thomas Edison didn't wash either. He believed that changing his underwear changed his body chemistry for the worse. I confirmed this myself with an animal model."

AN ARMY OF LOVERS

What about turning FUQU into a national army? There are chapters sprouting up across the country. Put them all together, Fred, they spell *army*! Hannah Arendt said that Jews should have had their own army!

Gustavus Entshul, Morris Dawes, Perry Allen Miller, Drew Overlander, Magnus Hill, Gretchen Vorwarts, Teddy Stendenhall, Laurent Fest, Norman Stumph, George Hartford, Isaac Garfield . . .

I thought you were stopping this list making!

Teddy was in my bunk at Camp Adventure, my first sleepaway camp. Morris was in my astronomy class at Yaddah (we both almost flunked), Isaac was the son of . . .

Oh, stop it!

TOUGH LUCK

Congress approves yet another Vurd Amendment, which extends the prohibition on funding any and all UC education efforts that use the word *homosexual*. Only two senators vote against it. From this date forth and through all succeeding presidents, and indeed into the next century, further implementation of various government regulations will continue to prohibit use of the word *homosexual* to such an extent that any grant application for UC research that contains this word is automatically denied. Coincidentally (if there is ever anything coincidental about this plague that is plowing right ahead), this bill is passed two days after the historic March on Washington by one million gays and lesbians. That event must have scared the shit out of all these legislators. "There can be no more brutal index of the depths of anti-gay prejudice than the direct governmental interference and censorship of effective research concerning gay men and women at the height of an epidemic," writes Simon Watney in *Taking Liberties*.

Furthermore, little by little, Republican administrations will fill all civil service positions as they become vacant with "friends of the family," so to speak. It will take decades for any administration to put this right. Civil servants can't be fired.

BART SHOVELS

My name is Shovels, not Shove or Shovel. Please tell your secretary to learn how to spell it properly. Quarantine and mandatory UC testing are viable policy options. Bill Buckley has said publicly that gay men should be tattooed on their ass. They are scared we're going to put them in internment camps. Good! The more we can scare them, the better. Civil rights ninnies can protest all they want to, the more of it, the better. No one wants these fairies in our country. Armed resistance to them would be a justifiable response in a time of quarantine.

I remember sending you a confidential memo that these are all justifiable means, plenty to think about, talk about, and put into the hopper. I await your instructions and approval.

WHAT WILL ARNOLD BOTTS DO NOW?

Arnold Botts is packing up his office at G-D. Von's not been seen or heard from in longer than usual. Arnold, suspecting the worst, considers this a bad omen.

Arnold had seen the ominous signs. Not every gay is becoming infected. This is unexpected. UC is also spreading around the globe, infecting more and more people who are not gay, including women, for whom not one of the original instigators had spared a thought. It was meant to be a homegrown all-American anti-gay-male crusade for the elimination of all-American queers. Something has obviously gone wrong with the master plan, wherever that stands. Where is that fucking Tricia Institute and the Sons of the Pocahanti? If anything should blow up, he wonders if he should get out of town while the getting's good. He wonders if "they" will come after him. An insecure psychopath like Arnold always fears that somebody will miss him. In partaking of the poisonous libations of so much heinous trickery, he's learned there's always a somebody who will come after you. Someone always knows when someone knows too much. Each of his mentors along his journey has taught him this. Von Greeting, Brinestalker, Stuartgene, Vurd,

Slyme, Moose, Buster Punic, all the president's men, he's been tossed from pillar to post, working for all of them, learning from all of them, and he can tell you where on each body a blemish resides. What can he do with everything he knows? How would he even locate the right person to tell it to if and when the time comes? None of these mentors ever teaches you how to paddle after you've been pissed on. A penis can take you only so far. He doesn't know how to plan ahead. He only knows how to hate. He learned that early and he learned it well. But what will he do when all his best customers will be leaving town? Dredd Trish is gathering up his own Kaffeeklatschers.

Dredd Trish's son, another Junior, is also a faggot and has been ever since he was a kid. Shit, Arnold let Trish Jr. suck his dick once in the balcony of Loew's Capitol. Dredd Trish, Jr., keeps his childhood boyfriend around so they can still play side by side. Dredd Trish, Sr., who is an upper-class snot, no doubt will be the next president, and Dredd Trish, Jr., is no doubt waiting in the wings. The Trish family is particularly popular in places that are big on hate. Arab places where they throw you off of rooftops if you're a fairy, after chopping off your head. Unless you're a president's son. Arnold would certainly have a problem if Junior wanted more and more of Arnold's cock. In the end, that's what usually happens. The stupid farts want more. Arnold still gets calls in the middle of the night from a drunk Junior Trish. "Come on over, babe. I'll send a limo." How does he know even now that Junior will one day be president? No one takes Junior seriously. The Arabs are very rich and want Trish the Father, and Trish the Father wants Trish the Son. That's the deal. Von explained it to him. It's a pretty nice cock, Junior Trish's cock. Those rich Wasps are all circumcised. So many cocks in Washington aren't. As if things aren't smelly enough in the games they're playing. Junior Trish always tried to get Arnold to suck his after he'd sucked Arnold's. Arnold wouldn't. He doesn't do things like that. He's not a fairy. He pauses a minute to remark to himself about the unusual coincidence of having the Juniors of two presidents running around with gay-hungry dicks.

He knows that Jerry and Dodo have royally fucked things up. Before he was murdered, Nasturtium had told him that Purpura knew this from the beginning and it was just what Ruester wanted. Jerry Omicidio coming up with nothing pleases the White House, according to Buster, who revealed all this to Arnold as Arnold was whipping the shit out of him way out in the countryside in Fille de Maison. Buster always wants to be "done to" somewhere far away. It's a long drive, back and forth. It was enjoyably painful for

Buster, driving back to the District. Since Claudia, he's had trouble finding a good whipper.

No matter, any of this, so far. No one is writing about it anyway, anywhere, certainly not with anything resembling the truth about what's really happening. No one is asking, "Is UC an intentional attempt to rid the world of homosexuals?" Now, if that would only appear in, say, *Foreign Affairs*, would it be taken seriously? The fact that it isn't proves no one wants to know, and so Arnold knows he's still safe and his coast is clear. For a while.

That drug that Von gave him? A new company called Presidium is running with it and Arnold will be a chief operating officer, and tough Linus Gobbel its head honcho, which pleased Wall Street and Arnold to no end. They don't come any nastier than Gobbel. Although he's been hearing even nastier stuff about this Bart Shovels.

So what the fuck is he worrying about? One thing he should have learned by now, in Washington fear comes with the territory.

Besides, he's got a new customer. Bart Shovels has heard about his skills.

FRED WONDERS: WHAT IS HAPPENING TO ORVID GUPTL?

Orvid is becoming stranger and more unpredictable. He makes up "facts" about the people he hates, to coincide with his hatreds. The latest is he's convinced everyone in the CIA and the right wing are going to lock up all gays if we persist in making waves and fighting UC as a gay illness. So he's manufactured a straight epidemic, the Chronic Exhaustion Epidemic (CEE), to get the right wing's attention focused elsewhere. He thinks I'm dangerous because I harp on the gay community and the UC issue. He really hates FUQU. He beseeches me to use my voice to trumpet CEE or Chronic Immune Deficiency Syndrome (CIDS), which it would appear he's made up as well, and which is what you come down with if you have CEE. "Both of these, only straights can get. Don't you see!" he yells at me. It's actually a very clever ploy, if he believes anyone is really paying any attention to him or *The Prick*, which, somewhere, maybe they are. "The Library of Congress still hasn't canceled its subscription," Orvid tells me.

"You just called me dangerous," I say to him. "After all we've been through together and how much you've supported me."

He holds up a copy of *The Prick*'s next front page, with a photo of Monserrat emblazoned with "*The Prick*'s Swastika Seal of Disapproval."

"Monserrat's a particularly big enemy—because she knows that UC is not the cause and isn't saying so. She wants 'behavior modification' of the gay world enforced."

"That's not true and you know it," I say.

I try to take him to lunch.

"I don't eat lunch. What do you want?"

"I want to know why you're doing what you're doing. We used to agree with each other. More or less."

"I don't have any use for you now."

"Well, that's certainly blunt and to the point. I'm sorry you feel that way. We were very useful to each other there for a while."

He doesn't say anything for a minute. Then he says, "I have to do it my way."

And then, for some reason, because it has occurred to me recently that I've never dealt with this information in any . . . I don't know what to call it, meaningful way, I hear myself saying, "Do you remember Masturbov Gardens?"

"How could you forget that place. Gross."

"Well, we grew up together there."

"I know."

"And Arnold Botts was there too."

"I know. Snotty snit!"

"You pissed on him."

"I did not."

"Yes, you did. I thought it was very gutsy. He's going to be the new CO of Presidium. The word is they've got some new treatment discovery. And the guy with Coke-bottle eyeglasses is . . ."

"Dodo Geiseric." He gives me a piercing and challenging stare. "I've been doing my bit. I've run my Dodo Nazi cover three times. I also had Dr. Sister Grace on the cover. She was my babysitter too."

"Why did you make her a Nazi cover?"

"You don't think there are Nazis running around? She's nuts."

"She's dead. And she was a friend, not an enemy. She worked hard to save us."

"Yeah, well, that's your opinion. She used to suck my dick. My four-, five-, six-year-old dick."

"I don't believe that. She was a lesbian."

He shrugged and stood up.

I shrugged and stood up.

I made one last attempt. "You had something really important going. The best gay newspaper in the world. Why are you sabotaging it?"

He didn't answer. He wasn't even looking at me anymore. His back was turned to me as he searched for something on a table on the other side of him. I waited a minute but he didn't turn around.

And that was that.

BART SHOVELS'S LIST

Dear Boss-to-Be:

1. The mass media, owned by big business and cowed by government intervention and right-wing attack, will help us to bury radical activism by ceasing to cover it.
2. Activists are ill-prepared for the struggles in which they find themselves.
3. Covert action enables us to exacerbate a movement's internal stresses until beleaguered activists turn on one another.
4. Manageable disagreements are inflamed until they erupt into hostile splits that shatter alliances, tear groups apart, and drive dedicated activists out of the movement.
5. All this is done without undermining the image of the United States as a democracy, with free speech and the rule of law.
6. You will want to break FADS's balls so drug companies can release anything and everything faster at any price they want to.

Just to keep you apprised of what we're looking forward to.

JERRY LIES

DANIEL

Omicidio is on one of those Sunday-morning-in-Washington TV talk shows and lies. He says everything is being done to fight UC that can be done. He says he has enough money to do anything he wants to do. He says it is not so long until a vaccine will protect the unprotected, and a cure, which will keep people alive. Does anyone sense, can anyone see, if Jerry is conscious that he's saying these words of untruth, to hope, for whatever this might be worth, that he's aware that another person is saying them, another Jerry? Or is that still wishful thinking on my part? Since all his TV questioners are equally ill-informed about UC, and most uncaring, there's not much "explain your-self" that ordinarily transpires, whatever issues are being discussed. The con-servative guests (four out of five) are more interested in saying the words *anal intercourse* on national television.

I ask him why he said the things he said.

He answered: "I'm calming the waters."

I have sat next to this man long enough now and he is still a cipher to me.

Deep Throat had told me: "The last government bureaucrat who told the truth on Sunday morning on national TV no longer holds his appoint-ment. He was called into the White House within hours of his truth-telling and relieved of his duties by some tenth-in-command."

Jerry stares at me. He doesn't blink an eye but his stare is boring right through me, which I believe is his intent.

He gets up to walk out of the office.

"Why don't you fire me?" I yell after him.

"I don't know! You're a very good doctor, an endangered species around here. Maybe you're my conscience." And the door slams closed really hard.

FRED

I don't believe he said that about you being his conscience! I think you are now hearing things! You are seeing, still, only what you want to see. And I am seeing less and less in you of what I want to see.

I write to understand and I don't understand Jerry, no matter how much I write about him. I've always come to some conclusion about everyone I've written about. T+D is also trying to figure out the best way to deal with him and with NITS, which, as Iris tells us, amount to the same thing. He is Mr. Creepola and we have put our bodies in his jerk-off hands. Daniel, how can you continue to believe in this evasive lying asshole!

SOME WOMEN OF FUQU

JILL

After another demo at City Hall, Arthur turned to me and said, "There have been hundreds of arrests this time. We have to go to the police station and see what happened to them." That's when I started doing my pro bono work to keep our kids out of jail.

One thing that distinguished FUQU from other organizations was, not passion, but the depth of passion, because it really was life and death and no doubt about it. A lot of these guys were going to die, and they knew they were going to die, and they were already dying, so arrest was nothing to them. Nothing. They were going to participate in any act of civil disobedience until they were carried off. Rafsky, so thin and near to death, and others out in the frigid winter, shackled themselves to the axles of the pharmaceutical delivery trucks leaving Muck or Greeting in New Jersey at dawn in the snow and ice. They were prepared to freeze to death.

I try to convey all this in my appeals to each judge. Your Honor, my clients are willing to endure harm, to endure police abuse, which is happening more and more. And I've learned through them something they never teach us in law school—that really it's the fight that is important. The courage they give me, Your Honor, these men who are dying. I am proud to be their lawyer, to represent them in your court.

How could I have any fear! It's changed how I practice law!

MARIA

We read this article in *Cosmopolitan* by this guy who said that the vagina was so resilient that if you had sex with a UC-positive man and he came inside you, oh, your vagina was so resilient that there was no way you were going to—this guy was insane. We can't even believe that they published this. Jean, myself, Rebecca, Maxine, Gerri, Ann, we looked this guy up in the phonebook, called him, and said we'd like to come and speak with him, we were part of the Women's Committee of this UC organization. He lived on the Upper East Side. He was a slight man. He had gray hair, and he was quite gracious, and then as soon as we all sat down (Jean was recording this on her little tape recorder) we began to challenge him—what was he talking about, that the vagina is resilient? Where did he get that research? "Well, I read it." Well, how could you read something that is not even corroborated scientifically and then put it in a magazine that millions of women read and allow them to feel safe when they have no reason to feel safe? We had a very specific goal. Dr. Gould, we would like you to write in *Cosmopolitan* and tell the public that you were completely wrong. And he refused to do it, and we were all hustled out very fast. We tried to have a normal conversation, we tried to treat him like an intelligent human being. He's not. What are we going to do about it?

MAXINE

We marched on *Cosmopolitan*. Police had already set up barricades. They heard FUQU was coming. They immediately started asking for IDs, would not let us inside, and then they started pushing us off the sidewalk. And then a few of us got arrested and I started poking a cop, saying, I'm taking down your name and number. The one thing we'd decided was that the only person who couldn't get arrested was Gerri, because her second brother who had UC was in the hospital. He needed a blood transfusion that day, and she needed to get there. She was going to just be marshaling so she wasn't doing anything. I asked the cop, again, for his name and number, and Gerri saw that he was going for a nightstick that was in his boot. So she put her arm around me, to get me away from him. The cops were very nervous, because we had all these women. They had a police wagon there. Gerri saw that he was going to go and hit me—he had got his stick out, to hit me—and so she put her arm around me and she said, You don't want to stand here, Max, you want to come with me, and she started walking me down the street. Well, they grabbed her, and they put her into the police van. And it was like all of us knew this was it. Maria climbed up on the hood of that police van. The rest of us surrounded it. Everyone was banging on its windows, screaming, Let that woman go! We were crazed. It was freezing. Jean with her camera was wearing the thinnest little shoes. It was five degrees. And we were all off the wall, shouting and banging. Then one of the cops said to his buddy, we better give these dames a warning ticket to get them out of here, because otherwise all hell is going to break loose. And so then they let her go. And Gerri came out. It was a wonderful end to our demo. This was the first women's demonstration that FUQU did. It put the Women's Committee on the map and made people in FUQU aware of us.

MARIA

I had to go to a temp job, and this girl walks by, and she has all this dry cleaning and she goes, Maria? Don't you remember me? We went to Smith together. And she was this girl who had taken the path that a lot of girls took. She'd gone to Wall Street, she'd become very successful. The dry cleaning was the thing that got me because I didn't own anything that could be dry-cleaned. I was still sleeping in the same clothes so I could just get up and go the next day to another of our actions, and she had dry cleaning. And she said, what are you doing? And I said, I'm in this protest group, here's our flyer. And she said, wow, I really envy you, you're doing something impor-tant. I had defaulted on my student loans. I never had enough money to pay my rent. I did not have a job or any kind of career path. But she thought I was doing something really important.

JEAN

Did I have sex with other women in FUQU?

Yeah, I did. Not enough, really not enough. But I did. The men were having sex with men, the women were having sex with women, men and women were having sex with each other, and there were people who were migrating back and forth. It boiled down to the Emma Goldman saying: "If I can't dance, I don't want your revolution." If we can't fuck, what are we doing here? Bordo and I have a long history of working together. We're very dear friends. But there was one time being on a subway platform with him when I really wanted to throw him on the tracks because I found out that he had basically slept with all the women I was attracted to.

REBECCA

FUQU was very sexy. Its lack of compromise was very sexy, at a time when some of us were still hovering around an attitude of does the gay community like us. And FUQU said, Well, so what? Why do we need to be liked? For a group that had so much sexual energy I think that's important to understand in context. Here were all these people coping with an illness that is transmit-ted sexually. So to be happily sexual in defiance of that was extremely bold. It was radical to say that you were still going to have safe sex and fuck and be a cocksucker and all these things when there was so much shame attached to the fact that this disease was sexually transmitted.

Every moment everyone felt fear.

Which made us love each other more.

REVENGE FOR WHAT?

At the next Issues Committee meeting, this guy Kenneth suddenly speaks out for the first time. "You know, I bet that Jerry Omicidio wants to kill us for revenge."

"For what?" The question immediately comes from several in the room. FUQU has its first office to be used for committee meetings. It's way over near the Hudson, a very inconvenient neighborhood. But cheap.

"Well, you know, revenge is a funny thing. It doesn't have to be for anything specific. It can be a 'just because.' A 'just because' doesn't have to have any basis in reality. He could just hate us. He could be a fervent right-wing Republican. Someone in his family could be dating faggots or be gay themselves. Maybe his wife's a lesbian. Maybe he's gay himself. I'm just saying all this because so much of our energy is going into wondering why he's behaving like he is, and I'm just saying"—and here he shrugs—"people are going to be what people are going to be. Why, somebody murdered somebody last week at this place I work at. And he's claiming to be not guilty."

"Actually murdered? In cold blood?" Sparks asks. "I've never worked at places where murders happen."

"Where do you think you're working now?"

"Good points, Kenneth," Scotty said. "Sparks doesn't live in the real world sometimes."

"Fuck you, Scotty."

"Fuck you, Sparks."

Kenneth now suddenly says, "Do you think we've been infiltrated by some spy who works for Jerry?"

Fred suddenly wonders if Jerry actually *wants* his kids murdered. That possibility hadn't occurred to him. Revenge for what? Daniel said, "God, it really is like some spy story. Maybe Russia has infiltrated some moles."

"Do you believe in revenge?" Fred asks.

Daniel answers, "I think by now not only would I believe anything, but

I wouldn't rule anything out. I'm tired of you calling me Mr. Pollyanna or Mr. Naïve."

Sparks and Scotty have each started thinking about that word, *revenge*. Each tried to discuss it with Ann, who'd been a big-deal TV news executive. "So what?" she answered each separately. "Hate is hate, and too many people hate us. Don't you listen to Fred? We have to hate back bigger than their hate of us. I don't see that happening yet."

"MY GOD, OUR GOD, MAY WE NOT HAVE FORSAKEN THEE"

This is a speech delivered in the Herodian Amphitheater carved into the mountains near Etalba, on the Utah-Colorado border, by Dr. Ekbert Nostrill of NITS, on the occasion of his being raised to the Ninth Level of Theodicy of the Disciples of the Brothers of Lovejoy Church. Dr. Nostrill is by now a four-star general of the U.S. Public Health Service. The audience is composed of ten thousand young people, evidently singled out somehow for their appropriateness to hear these words:

> I express my love and total respect to my young brothers and sisters struggling with same-gender attraction. You who are true to the faith and obedient to sacred covenants are not few in number. I commend you for your unshakable faith in the face of the unwanted feelings you did not choose to have. I commend you for never forgetting that God loves you and that you are His sons and daughters. I commend you for not forgetting your magnificent divine potential for resisting temptation and evil. Deviations from God's commandments in the use of sacred procreative powers are grave sins. Sexual sin is not new to the world.
>
> The Lord's law of moral conduct is abstinence outside of lawful marriage and fidelity within marriage. Sexual relations are proper and appropriately expressed only between husband and wife within the bonds of marriage. Any other sexual contact, including fornication, adultery, and homosexual and lesbian behavior, is sinful. Those who persist in such practices or who influence others to do so are subject to Church discipline. Immoral behaviors, regardless of their cause, can and should be overcome and sinful behavior eliminated.

I desire now to say with emphasis that our concern for the bitter fruit of sin is coupled with Christlike sympathy for its victims, innocent or culpable. Our unequivocal statements are not hateful. If certain behaviors are abominable sins in the sight of God, and they are, then the Church and its officers would be unloving were they not to sound the voice of warning, just as a loving mother warns and protects her small child from the terrible consequences of swallowing lye. The Church must label as wrong behavior that which impedes eternal progress. Failure to do so would be cowardly and unloving. The world, rejecting eternal values while focusing on the physical and carnal, labels the Church intolerant, judgmental, and mean. The opposite is true.

Satan passionately does not want us to follow the Heavenly Father's plan. Therefore, he formulates cunning imitations based on the principle of gratification and pleasure. Subtly, his devious detours draw some of us away from our divine destiny. Satan attempts to distort our vision and make us blind.

God's plan tells us that our place in an eternal blueprint didn't begin with our birth. Nor will it end with our death and burial. The plan of redemption helps us understand that without covenants made in holy temples, we will not in the eternities to come enjoy the companionship of father, mother, brothers, sister, wife, children, or grandchildren.

We are eternal beings participating in a critically important temporary experience. This fallen earth is not our home. We are being tested. The power of Satan is real. He seeks to make us eternally miserable by tempting us to misuse our sacred procreative power and by confusing what it means to be male and female.

Individuals with these disorders have choices to make. The straight and narrow path leads the right way, regardless of same-gender attraction's cause, or whether or not it can be cured. The ongoing debate about the cause of same-gender attraction and whether it can be cured is irrelevant in the context of true religion. The right way is very simple. You did not choose to have these feelings, but you can do something about them.

Homosexual or lesbian behavior is a serious sin, as is heterosexual fornication in adultery. It must be stopped! The claim "I was born that way" does not excuse actions or thoughts that fail to conform to the commandments of God. We must humble ourselves, count our Gospel blessings, and take the tough straight and narrow path that leads us to our eternal home and the fullness of the Heavenly Father.

In order to stop homosexual behavior one must comprehend the seriousness of the transgression, feel deeply repentant, and have a firm commitment to change. The best way is never to offend the Holy Ghost in the first place. Let the Holy Ghost be your constant companion. When we make bad choices we need to get the light of Christ back. The right course of action remains the same: control thoughts and never, never participate in homosexual or lesbian behavior. In the day of resurrection you will have normal affections and be attracted to the opposite sex.

God bless you, my beloved young friends, and be with you and give you the courage to admit and correct mistakes. Pray for strength to overcome. You will be given power through the Savior to overcome your burden. You will possess the power to control your thoughts and to restrain yourself from behaviors that destroy.

I promise you, your Church promises you, all Disciples of Lovejoy promise you, Jesus Christ promises you, that we shall all do everything in our power to fight this fight with you to condemn anything that keeps your own righteousness from being achieved.

May the Holy Ghost save us all!

TAKE ME OUT TO THE BALL GAME

MAXINE

I was having these dyke dinners. I couldn't work in an organization where I didn't feel connected to people. And especially in a large, male organization I wanted to get to know the women. When you sit in a group with all those men and it's not you that it's happening to, and you're trying to figure out what you're doing there, it's good to verbalize that to each other.

So, next the Women's Committee decided that we wanted to focus on the only group of people who had not been told that they should do something—straight men. What is a quintessential, straight-male place where we could do this kind of an action? And then, Kathy and Rebecca—both big baseball fans—Kathy said, A baseball game! And both of them got electrified. Maria nearly had a fit, because she was, like, what? She didn't know from baseball games. But everybody else was going, Yeah, a baseball game, a baseball game. So immediately, we called up and found out, believe it or not, that there was going to be a home game at Shea Stadium on the day we designated Women and UC Day—what luck. So we got up on the floor of FUQU, and I was the person who presented it. So I said, What we want to propose is an action for Women and UC Day at Shea Stadium. Dead silence in the room—absolutely dead silence, tense dead silence. And then somebody stood and said, You're crazy! We go to Shea Stadium, they're going kill us there! Those homophobes! And then other people started standing up and saying the same thing, and I was saying things like, It's the men in suits who are killing us. And then, Ron, God bless him, stood up and said, Okay, folks, let me just tell you that a lot of gay men go to baseball games, and I am one of them. And it was like he came out of the closet as a baseball nut, and as soon as he did that, another man said, I do too. Still, people were really scared, so we would bring really detailed descriptions like what to wear to a baseball game, how a baseball game is played, and when, exactly, we're going to do something. We decided to make banners. We came up with all these great slogans: UC IS NOT A BALL GAME, DON'T BALK AT SAFER SEX: STRIKE OUT UC. Our idea was to buy seats in three parts of the stadium—right field, left field, and center field—and it would be like call and response. One group would open their banner, and then the next and the next. So we had to buy tickets, but we didn't have a lot of money, we decided we would start by buying one bunch of tickets—like sixty—three rows of twenty—and then we'd sell those, and with the money, we'd get the next bunch. We had no idea that this was going to get to be a huge thing. And then we decided that actually what this was going to be was an educational action—that we weren't going to rush the field or anything, because it was going to be televised on ESPN and we could reach hundreds of thousands of people who would see these messages, and we would also give out stuff at the gate. Debbie, who was on our committee—she worked for Creative Time, which does all kinds of performance art stuff—was already meeting with the security at Shea Stadium about doing something in their parking lot. We had been trying to get in touch with the Mets, because we wanted them to proclaim it Women and UC Day, and we kept calling, and they were not calling us back. Debbie was at a meeting with the community police about how they were going to handle her event, and they didn't know she was in FUQU, and she heard one cop say to another, Did you hear? FUQU is going to storm the stadium. David France had written an article in *The Village Vice*—the first big article about FUQU—and he mentioned how we were going to do this action at Shea Stadium, and I guess some cop read it. So they were talking about how they had to get riot cops out, and we just didn't want this thing to escalate into that. Gerri called up the local precinct and said she was from FUQU, and that she just wanted them to know that we were coming down to the stadium to do an educational action and that we weren't going to rush the field, in case they were concerned. And by the time that night came, the head of the Mets met us, took our press packets and our leaflets, and gave them to everyone in the press box. They let us be at every single entrance. We gave out twenty thousand leaflets. It was a great leaflet. It said, Here's the score. It had a score card: Single—there hasn't been one single acknowledgment about women getting UC; Double—double the number of women have UC than last year. I forget what Triple was, and then it said, Home run—most men don't use condoms. And then, No Glove, No Love. It was in Spanish and English. And we gave out twenty thousand.

We wound up selling three sections of 60 seats each, which is 180, and we had these banners, and it worked out great.

We started opening up the banners, and everybody started swaying with the banners, and then the people across the way opened up their banners, and then their banners started swaying. And then the third group opened up their banners, and their banners started swaying. You could see them from anywhere. You could read them really, really clearly, big white letters on a black background in a night game with these big spotlights. And there were loads of young people—a lot of young kids come; this is where they hang out on Friday nights with their friends. We didn't have any bad experiences from anyone. And then the cops escorted us to the subways. It was such a creative action and it was really fun to do. It was a combination of serious politics and joyful living that was so different from the left, which basically believed that you couldn't smile until the revolution was over. We would do actions where we really put our bodies on the line, and then we'd go out and party all night. When you don't have time for that kind of stuff, you basically dehumanize a movement. A movement is about people. If you don't have a community of people who make you feel good about who you are and what you're doing, you're not going to stay in it. You need some life. Because it was sort of like as soon as you were getting over feeling that you could go on after somebody's death, somebody else would die. So it was hard for people. It wasn't an abstraction. It was people you were working with all the time, and being with all the time in a social situation as well.

AND BY THE WAY, DON'T CRY

MAGENTI

Nobody dealt with grief, because we kept ourselves very busy. You were always on to another action. And the tacit agreement people made was: And by the way, don't cry. Instead, the understanding was that you would take your grief and turn it into rage, and you would take that rage and do something with it.

MARSHALL

But grief is also sadness, and loss. And a lot of people had already experienced that, and did not want to feel those things, and were tired of feeling sad and alone and defeated. So it made sense that this was just the place for them to be.

GENEALOGIES

LAST WEEK

We've all been each other's lovers. That's among the most moving facts about this plague.

Do we all have some sort of genealogy of death?

History's not been very kind to sex. Sex has always been the embarrassment swept under the rugs of history. History's not been very kind to homosexuals either.

What a bang-up combo double whammy.

DARREN IN INVINCIBLE

Darren fucked with O'Donaghue last week and Egypt told me O'Donaghue has minpasmosis, evidently very rare. Egypt says no one he knows has ever seen it. He had to look it up in some ancient text. (Dr. Sister Grace was always rushing off to consult some ancient text. "There is nothing new under the sun, Freddie," she always said; "all this new shit is so perverse it can't be new, it must be something ancient coming back to haunt us." God, I miss her mightily.) This minpasmosis takes on average one day to catch, manifest itself, and kill you. That means O'Donaghue should be dead by now, which he obviously isn't. "Well, so much for that fucking ancient text," I can hear Grace saying. Darren has heard that O'Donaghue has the minnies (it's ten minutes before it has this nickname) and thus thinks his own days are numbered. Darren has never been sick in his whole life ("I still have my tonsils and appendix!"), and now here he is, on the brink of some ancient death.

O'Donaghue had never slept with anyone else but Darren. He was his first. He'd been a virgin. O'Donaghue was seventeen when they met, and he was nineteen now and about to be dead.

Darren himself then gets sick. He faints at Macy's while redoing one of the windows that faces Thirty-fourth Street. It's the night of his FUQU affinity group meeting. Somehow he manages to scribble down Bradley's phone number for the ambulance attendants before instructing them to get him to Invincible, to Dr. Egypt Poo, who immediately connects him to an assortment of tubes and wires. Bradley calls me and all the members of their group, which is called the Macy Monsters in honor of Darren, and a bunch of us all rush to Invincible, where none of us is allowed to see Darren.

Egypt lets me visit the next day. Darren is convinced he'll never get out of Invincible. Invincible Crewd-Harbinger is known as guinea pig hell. Tommy says Invincible is the richest and has all the latest wizardry. It all looks very last-ditch-standish, science-fictiony. Tommy hates this place. "They don't want us here any more than any other place does." Emma told me to tell guys not to go there. But Darren went because it was where O'Donaghue now had died and Darren wants to join him in the next world with as little delay as possible. "I figure his spirit is in this room, certainly on this floor, because this is where we're all kept, and I'll die and he'll come and take my hand real fast and lead me wherever he's hanging out and that way I guess it won't be so scary. I guess that sounds pretty weird." Nineteen-year-old kid talking this way.

Darren had come to some lecture I did at Columbia about what it was like to write movies about "real-world events." I only did a couple classes. Movies were a pile of shit compared with the reality of the world I was dealing with now. Look at how no one wants to make my play-movie, even with

Adreena. I keep writing new drafts for people, for free even, when they come along and say they want to make it. I've written seven drafts so far for her. Darren and the class, of course, wanted to hear all about her.

Darren cries when he sees me. "You came to visit me?" Felipe, his (uninfected) roommate, is with him, holding his hand; the devotion flowing between these kids is heartbreaking. If only the rest of the world knew how to love so. It tortures me that I can't honor any of this sufficiently with mere words. What is "this"? How can I make it clear? Just tell the facts, Fred; just tell the facts; that's all you can do. Don't embroider. Keep yourself out of it. I wish I could. No, I don't. We're all in this together.

THESE *ARE* THE FACTS!

The facts are that Darren suddenly bolts up from my arms, like he's been electrocuted, then falls back on the mattress, dead.

Now I hold Felipe in my arms.

"I've never loved anyone, ever, in the world, like I loved Darren! And he was just my roommate."

•

INT. THE CENTER. NIGHT.
Meeting of FUQU in packed room. Felipe writing names on blackboard: Darren Reynolds. Michael O'Donaghue. *Fred stands facing the group as Felipe finishes.*
FRED: They both came to us so young. Let's try not to forget them.
We see many of the crowd with tears in their eyes. Ron starts a chant, picked up by the crowd.
RON: Fight back! FUQU! Fight back!
Iris stands up to talk. She stands until the room is silent.
IRIS: I was sent this letter from a Mr. Dropkin.
DROPKIN *(tall, black hair, a troublemaker)*: That's me.
IRIS: You want to know why it's taking T and D so long to what you call "deliver."
DROPKIN: That's me and a lot of us, I'm sure.
IRIS: You have a lot to learn about what I'm trying to teach you.
DROPKIN: Such as?
IRIS: Such as immunology, virology, epidemiology, blood, molecular biology, pharmacology, toxicology, clinical medicine, how stuff gets funded, how NITS and FADS and COD work . . . Any other questions? Guys, stand up and answer anybody's questions.

A bunch stand up immediately. Sparks, Scotty, Claudette, Barry, Perry,
Eigo, Spencer, Spud, Rebecca, others. No questions come from the
floor. Iris smiles. Applause from the floor.

ONWARD!

We can't sit still! Right now I'm coasting along on a certain euphoria that
Fred Lemish is getting his dream organization.

But the Ruester is still not crowing. He still has not acknowledged we're
alive.

And we haven't faced up to moving on NITS yet.

But this is what we have been doing. It seems like an awful lot. It's not
enough, not even for a whole year:

We did twenty-five full demonstrations with the whole organization. We
did seventy-three zaps with affinity groups or individuals without the whole
organization. We protested on Wall Street; at the General Post Office on income tax deadline night; at the White House, where we also performed civil
disobedience (CD), meaning seventy-six of us got arrested (including me);
at the Third International UC Conference in Washington, where we booed
Vice President Dredd Trish after Ruester got shot; we had our Concentration
Camp float in the Gay Pride Parade; we picketed at Federal Plaza here in the
city and had CD (173 arrests); we did our famous five-day, twenty-four-hours-
a-day, round-the-clock picketing of Invincible Crewd-Harbinger that really
freaked them out, not because they were the worst but because they were
supposed to be doing research and practically nobody is in their various OI
and ZAP trials. There are supposed to be ten thousand people in trials across
America and there are eight hundred, *only eight hundred*, across the whole
country. Iris and Kersh and Gary and David G. are trying to figure out why
this NITS system isn't working. We did a little demo outside St. Putrid's to
protest Cardinal Buggaro being appointed to a third UC Commission; we
did phone ZAPs of Northwest Airlines, booking tickets worth hundreds of
thousands of dollars, for their refusal to carry a sick and dying patient; we
demo-ed in D.C. at the public hearing of that useless second Presidential
UC Commission; we demo-ed at the Supreme Court and at the United Nations and at City Hall against Goins; at an appearance of Pat Robertson in
Bed-Stuy; and we had a number of sit-ins in the office of the fink new NYC
health commissioner, Elliott Garbantz, for lowering the number of UC cases

in the city—just like that, poof, they're gone!—so they don't have to officially statistically claim them or pay them for disabilities; and in December we interrupted a forum of the presidential candidates at Javits Center. Not bad for such a young group. We'll do better next year.

Fred is excited. I am, I am.

RON

We also did Seven Days of Rage. Each day an action on a specific issue: homophobia (a thousand protestors march up Christopher Street with pink balloons and at Sheridan Square we hold a massive Kiss-In); People with UC (University Hospital, Newark) protesting that only four people are enrolled in New Jersey trials; People of Color (leafleting in Harlem); UC and Substance Users (NYC Department of Health); UC and Prisoners (Harlem State Office Building); UC and Women (Shea Stadium, which Max arranged brilliantly); Global UC (Rockefeller Center); Pediatric UC (protesting the placebo blind trials in children, a difficult issue to make clear, outside the FAO Schwarz toy store on Fifth Avenue, a pretty lame demo); National Day of Rage (back to Albany, Vito Russo makes his historic speech: "Someday you will remember this").

PERRY

Mister Always Supportive Sparks Puffington said: "The net effect so far is a frenzy of small actions diluted by the sheer volume of activity." He and Scotty were visibly unhappy, dissatisfied, lurking around, never smiling. I suddenly wondered if we could trust either of them.

We have two more demos outside Elliott Garbantz's office. We do not leave this creep alone. Resign! RESIGN! How dare he say there are fewer of us getting sick than he'd said were getting sick, even COD said we're getting sick, we *are* getting sick! Such a strange thing to fight about. Not only has he chopped the number of total cases by half but some mysterious force has also cut the total number of gay people in America by 90 percent. As if *anyone* knows how many of us there are! Something very fishy.

ENTER JIM EIGO

Eigo nails Elliott publicly: "Dr. Garbantz, your estimates are based on comparisons between the UC epidemics in San Francisco and New York. But in New York one-third of all cases in gay men are in black and Latino men. San Francisco's cases are 96 percent white. So isn't comparing New York's gay populations to San Francisco's both racist and homophobic?" The man did not know what Eigo was talking about. We are learning that we have to read the ruins. Garbantz doesn't answer Eigo. So we start up our chant: SILENCE EQUALS DEATH! We put out posters with pictures of Goins and Garbantz with THESE MEN HAVE BLOOD ON THEIR HANDS all over the city. We go after Goins now big time. SHAME! We've already gotten rid of one rotten heath commissioner, Herta Glanz, remember, that sad sack of shit. Where do they find these guys? Now when Goins appears anywhere in public we drown him out. SHAME! They say he's worried we'll give him a heart attack. On TV he says, "I'm not saying they're Nazis or fascists, just that they use Nazi and fascist tactics." Thanks, Kermit, that helps us focus. Nazi/Fascist it will be. Hannah Arendt, here we come!

BRADLEY

At the beginning of each and every meeting people get up and write on the blackboard: since last week, Dennis Savine died. Donny Hallam died. Chris Vatter died. Truman Alexander Martinson died. Driscoll Kandinsky died. Calhoun Bingman. Greevy Putnam. Travis Stutts . . . died. I then list them in our official minutes that I've been keeping.

Out-of-uniform cops start infiltrating our meetings. We don't recognize them until the following week, when we see *new* new faces instead of last week's new faces, who aren't here this week. You'd think they'd have sense enough to send the same faces. They never look gay. You'd think if they are going to go through the trouble they'd fag themselves up a bit.

Freddy O'Rourke died. Cops break into the apartment of the Action Committee chair, Steve Quester, at 6 a.m. and break his nose after we'd been particularly vocally obstreperous against Elliott Garbantz, calling his house in the middle of the night. Paul Martinson died. At demos policemen now rough us up more visibly. Steve's nose had a lot of stitches that now get infected. We have pledged nonviolence. But they sure haven't. Michael P. and

Jeff G. get hurt. Jeff's in the hospital for two days. He was injected by a cop with something or other. They are fighting dirtier. We send a message to the mayor to call off his thugs.

FRED

Shouting SHAME and RESIGN is not going to be enough, even if fucking shithead Goins has his heart attack. It's not getting us anywhere, all we are doing. We are not focused. We are not dealing with research and treatment. We don't know enough yet about either of these. We've got to teach our kids about these faster. Iris is doing her best. Sparks, Scotty, Eigo . . . Hurry, hurry . . . We have to identify and go after the center cesspools of power.

We send a busload to D.C. to protest a hearing of the latest presidential commission: one cardinal, Buggaro, one straight sex therapist who advertised she could change gay behavior, one admiral, all Republicans, fourteen right-wingers, no gays or UC patients; we break up the meeting by serenading them, singing "Send in the Clowns." We zap Goins at a ceremony honoring Gay Pride Month, causing a huge backlash from the gay "establishment," which accuses us of "trashing our own." You bet, guys. We surround City Hall with bedsheets, protesting the lack of hospital beds. On Gay Pride Day, FUQU's contingent is many blocks long. THIS CROWD CHEERS US! THEY APPROVE!

Zap here; zap there; court dates for those arrested at Wall Street, at City Hall, arrested here, arrested there. Jill and Katherine and all our other pro bono lawyers are keeping busy.

ANOTHER NEW YEAR'S DAY

Another sad walk around the city, passing places where so-and-so lived. This time I leave the Village and Tommy and I visit hospital waiting rooms. It seems to us as if all the hospitals have nothing but UC patients. We watch as friends and parents and lovers come and go. We recognize many faces, as they do ours. No one is beaming Happy New Year thoughts. Many are in tears. A few stop to hug us. "We're all in this together now, aren't we?" a black woman says to me, before rushing out of Metropolitan City, not wanting to hear my reply. St. Victim's, Invincible, Beth Sinus, Table Medical, Presby North and

South. We run into Perdita Pugh at several of them, on her rounds. Tommy gives her an especially big hug. She's all dressed up, more than ever, he says. Tommy compliments her big diamond brooch. "Christmas present from my lovely husband," she demurs. She has thirty-one visits to make today, she says. We run into Emma at Table. She looks terrible, exhausted and coughing. I give her a hug. "I'm glad you're finally doing what you're doing but nothing's happening. I've lost one hundred sixty-three guys who've dived off the cliff. The dean's ready to throw me out." In the waiting room of Presby North, Caspar Schmidt waves and rushes over. "Fred, I am developing a new plan! I am bringing it to the floor. I have determined that UC is a mass hallucination! And I have discovered the cure. We must build a radiant cocoon, a sphere in which the body is placed for the blood to be heated." Caspar is tall, blond, Teutonic-looking, with a big smile. He's from Iceland. He looks pretty healthy. He's a psychologist. He says he studies mass behavior. He's a member of T+D. His last year's insight into "the cure" was based on "my firm conviction that the people who get sick and die are the people who do not like themselves, who are ashamed of being gay. UC is caused by internalized homophobia. None of my patients who are accepting of their homosexuality are sick with UC! I believe that the irrational forces of the blood can conquer the intellectuality of the spirit!" A few months later at a meeting he pulled me aside to tell me, excitedly, "The epidemic is half over. When that happened with the Vietnam War, it was . . . half over." By the time I get home tonight Caspar will have left a message on my machine: "Fred, this time I really have it. Walking home after seeing you, I finally have the cure! I'll tell you at the next meeting." By the time of our next meeting, Caspar's died.

I was to have met Deep Throat in Table's waiting room at six. He said he would come up to me, that he knows what I look like. I wanted to meet him, of course, and I wanted to introduce him to Tommy. But he didn't show up.

THE STATE OF CERTAIN THINGS

(FORMERLY STATE OF THE UNION)

Gays can hardly call their increasingly unwelcoming country a union. What do gay people think about America's history? What do gay people think about their place in history? Tommy will have a survey taken, an in-depth survey conducted by professionals, and they will ask several thousand San Franciscans whom they perceive as being gay whether they identify themselves as homosexual, bisexual, or heterosexual. Almost 70 percent answer bisexual. It's an unsettling result that so many gay people refuse to self-identify as homosexuals. No heterosexual would not self-identify as heterosexual. There is a passion for entitlement that should be obvious and relevant now FUQU has chosen for its motto Silence = Death. Will it be enough to inspire those who live through UC—because this Fred is determined to do!—to emerge with a sense of accomplishment and pride?

Homosexuals are not listed in any historian's indexes. Historians from Herodotus and Thucydides to the twentieth century have overlooked our presence. With the steady growth of knowledge about the existence and acceptance of homosexuality in ancient Greece (see, most recently, the amazing *The Greeks and Greek Love* by James Davidson), it is obvious that Herodotus and Thucydides and their followers somehow still elected not to see us, not to see so many of us, not to see such an overwhelming number of us. There are now more homosexuals than there are Jews.

What does any of this say about where homosexuals find themselves in these years of this present plague? What a dumb question. Why keep harping on it?

Haven't enough people noticed that Peter Ruester stacked the deck in such a way as to make it impossible to rectify what's happening? No one is noting this sufficiently. It's proving to be a quiet revolution that he's leaving as his legacy.

Peter has been a much-loved president. This is difficult for some to comprehend or to square with the truth of things. Fred will write a "Hail and Farewell" obit for *The Avocado* when "this murderer" will die in 2003, in which he will compare Ruester with Hitler. "He has been responsible for more deaths than Adolf Hitler," Fred will write, which will be true, because by then there will be some 80 million cases of UC worldwide. It would have been nice if during his final days in office someone whispered into his good ear, Peter, old boy, why not go out on a cloud of compassion for *all* men. Unfortunately we know he hasn't had these kinds of whisperers around him, nor did he appear to want them or miss them, or even know he doesn't have them. Certainly his wretched Lady Macbeth is not this person. What *was* this woman all about?

What hideous bequests he's leaving us. How can any histories of the Ruester years be convincing and definitive? They can't and won't be.

•

Mordecai Masturbov, the man who changed the mores and the morals of this country, does see handwriting on the wall. What will he do about it? Nothing but to weather the UC storm. It will go away. People have to fuck. He commences wild parties at a new Sexopolis mansion in Hollywood. Invitations are coveted. There are always plenty of B-list players with nothing else to do but publicly preen half-naked. He's not unaware that Fred Lemish is accusing him and *Sexopolis* of "an active participation in the cause of this plague." What a small world. He waits to see if Fred's accusation will have any legs, if the media will pick it up and come to hound him, or if any of his subscribers will cite it when they cancel their subscriptions. He need not have worried. So much for Fred Lemish. Like Von Greeting unleashing into the world a larger supply of Dridge Ampules to bolster his sales of Factor VIII and ZAP, Mordy redoubles the number of his Sexopolis mansion orgies and the coverage of same in the pages of *Sexopolis*. He waits to see which way the wind blows. It does not blow at all. He zips up the titillation quotient of *Sexopolis*. For the first time naked penises are allowed. Dimly and artistically lit, of course. Why, some of them might even be erect! This is a first and this garners much publicity. Circulation and the sale of newsstand copies shoot up even higher. Various cries of alarm from opponents of visibly erect penises try to prohibit this new development from proceeding too far, until Sam Sport challenges this in the Supreme Court, and wins. So once again Mordy has broken a mold. He starts escorting his *Sexopolis* girls out publicly. His marriage to Jinx Seeley? Well, like Doris and Velvalee, she's become quite maternal, attending to all his playmates as if they were her children. If Mordy wants to fuck one of them, she gives him her blessing. He finds he actually enjoys this "new Mordy." He's turning out to be his own ideal reader. Once again, he's saluted as a "role model" for the men of the world.

•

Fred went out to Fire Island for the first time in a long time, accompanying a friend who was looking for a summer rental. It was a bright and sunny and cold day in April. Guys were actually living out there, hiding from the world with their walkers and lesions. ("How dare you come back here after what you wrote about us!" one of them said.) The broker said that young people can no longer afford to come here and they're thinking of enticements. "We'll establish scholarship funds, just like for prep school." Fred went walking down a few memory lanes. Most looked the same, although many smaller houses had been torn down and replaced with ones twice their size. It was amazing how many guys were there so early in the season. Fred passed some of them walking the boardwalks, each showing some visible sign of illness. New opportunistic infections always seem to crop up in the New York area first, as if New York is Genesis Book One Chapter One Verse One of The Underlying Condition. Losing one's eyesight. He saw a few of these, being led by friends. Losing control of one's bowels, so that, on these very boardwalks, one must take care to maneuver around the piles of shit dotting the path. He saw someone suddenly stop and squat, unable to hold it in. Fred wound up carrying Sam, who like most dogs has a propensity for sniffing shit. The beach itself was also not safe, and men lying on blankets fully clothed could be seen suddenly jumping up and squatting, then covering these accidents with sand. Fred inquired as to the health dangers of all this and Dru Del Monte, the broker, was offended. "I don't know what you are talking about! Shit! On the boardwalks! On the beach! You are out of your fucking mind. You learned nothing the last time we asked you to leave. When are you going to leave us alone?"

ANOTHER OPEN LETTER TO DR. JERROLD OMICIDIO

BY FRED LEMISH
SAN FRANCISCO EXAMINER

I have been screaming about your Animal House of Horrors since 1983. I called you monsters then, and I call you a monster and a murderer now.

After all this time, you have established only a system of waste, chaos, and uselessness.

You are an incompetent idiot!

The gay community has consistently told you that unless you move quickly your studies will be worthless because we are already taking drugs into our bodies that we locate all over the world in desperation (who can wait for you?!), and all your "scientific" protocols are stupidly based on utilizing guinea-pig bodies that are "clean." You wouldn't listen, and now you wonder why so few signed up for your earlier meager assortment of "scientific" protocols, which make such rigid demands for "purity" that no one can fulfill unless they lie.

FED UP QUEERS UNITED was formed to get experimental drugs into the bodies of patients. FUQU has tried every kind of protest known to man (short of putting bombs in your toilet or flames up your institute) to get some movement in this area. Our years of screaming, protesting, crying, cajoling, lobbying, threatening, imprecating, marching, testifying, hoping, wishing, praying has brought nothing. You don't listen. No one listens. No one has ears. Or hearts.

Whose ass have you been covering, Jerry? (Besides your own.) Is it the head of your Animal House, the invisible Dr. Stuartgene Dye, director of the National Institute of Tumor Sciences? Is it Dr. Kelvin Geiseric, another murderer who's letting you be his fall guy? Dr. Ekbert Nostrill, Dr. Paulus Pewkin, NITS is overrun with possibilities, as are Ruester's minions, Moose, Gobell, Bohunk, all purveying party-line bullshit that All Is Being Done That Can Be Done.

I don't know (though it wouldn't surprise me) if you kept quiet intentionally. I don't know (though it wouldn't surprise me) if you were ordered to keep quiet by Higher-Ups Somewhere and you are the good lieutenant, like Adolf Eichmann.

I do know that anyone who knows what you have known for years and done nothing about it for these years is a murderer, not dissimilar to the "good Germans" who claimed they didn't know what was happening.

Yes, the level of rhetoric gets higher, the pitch more shrill. It is a style I am perfecting. Daniel is not talking to me. "How can I talk to you and work for him?" he writes. "Have you now gone around the bend?"

I wonder: where have been the voices of Norman Mailer, Saul Bellow, George Steiner, Victor Navasky, Philip Roth, Arthur Miller, William Styron, Elizabeth Hardwick, John Updike, Toni Morrison—to name only a few I used to admire but never heard from re. this most crucial issue now facing modern man.

SPARKS PUFFINGTON

I believe that if we work hard enough, we'll uncover some sort of cure. I constantly make glossaries of all the new words we're learning, from *accrual* to *zidovudine*. Treatment+Data has a teach-in. The hall is packed. Everyone is hungry for information. I can see that most of them don't understand what Iris and Eigo are saying.

Why do I think Fred's trouble?

Harvard men have different ideas about how to change the world.

This Harvard man thinks this Yaddah man is a big waste of time.

GRODZO: THEY DO NOT TELL YOU WHY

I have to say that the longer I stay here, the more I find similarities in the two systems of, how do I say it, processing people. *Der Prozess, die Protokolle.* It always comes down to people becoming a herd of horses that you must some-how push through your system. In the end all systems are the same. Doctors and scientists are not so polite at the required pushing, not really. That is another skill entirely, and if one does not have it he acts like a monster: "You will do what I tell you to do, you hear me, or I will not pay any attention to you, or worse, I will see that no one else does either. I will enter into your record that you are not cooperating." I give you an example. Mungel and NITS and Partekla, all are frightening places involved in unspecified and uncoordinated agendas. The patient is not told anything. Give me your arm and pump pump pump, I come back tomorrow and pump pump pump. More and more shots of strange stuff. But tomorrow is often not the same face, not the same person who pump pump pumps. With Debbi Driver and that Leisha woman we supervise many nurses who pump arms of several hundred each week. Many young men cry. They are *verwirrt*, bewildered. Often they grab hold of Jerry and will not let go of him. So now he has a guard, an armed guard, who "removes" the frightened young men who cling to him. This young man he will no longer see again. I do not know where this young man goes, where they push him.

All of this gives me too many bad memories. David cried often at both Mungel and Partekla. His body was often pump pump pumped, more than I think he remembers. I do not know who Jerry takes his orders from, who is ordering him to push push push. Who assigned me here to work at NITS? We are herded, the doctors, just like the patients. I did not know who was over me in Mungel. They were never names. They were titles. Everyone seems to understand their place in line. It is not recommended that doctors talk and share. There is that other former Nazi doctor here, Oderstrasse. He will not talk to me. And when first we met he warned me not to talk to anyone. He named names of doctors who are no longer here because of some reason they had been bad. Patients also. "They do not tell you why," he told me. "One day here, next day not here." I tell myself, do not be ridiculous. In Germany patients are sent to ovens. But death is death, you know. Here patients are given shots or not given shots and they die too. What is in these shots? ZAP, it is called. Zap is what it does. Zap zap zap. I have seen the face and the eyes of that man from G-D with the peculiar name. Dash Snicker. He is around here all the time, supervising "his" drug. There is no question he is in charge. There is no question he is more important than Jerry. And Jerry allows this position. I do not trust Dash Snicker one minute. And I cannot talk to Jerry. Jerry does not like questions. He does not answer them. So I do not trust Jerry one minute either.

I did not think medicine in America was meant to be like this. If I had known, I would have said no when Brinestalker, how you say, recruited me in Berlin to come to America.

MOANIN' LOW

HUFF

Well, I wasn't a very good nurse, but yes, I was in his affinity group, Wave Seven. He lived downstairs from me in the storefront, and it was hard not to see through the window that he was dying. He wouldn't go into the hospital. He liked visitors and he left his door open, so a bunch of us who were with him in Wave Seven started taking care of him. How could you not? No one wanted to go into a hospital, because they couldn't do anything for you except ignore you. We never knew his full name. His last name was Winthrop, so we called him Winn. It wasn't even his pad; it belonged to his friend who'd died. Winn's parents were real pills. They didn't like our doing this but they didn't want to do it themselves. "So what do you suggest?" Bordo asked the father, who was a particular prick. "I won't go home!" Winn yelled when we called them. "They would never clean up my vomit. Hey, Ma, I vomit gallons. They don't vomit in Back Bay." They disappeared after a while, the parents. And Winn died. And then Jon and Robb and Claudette and Spud and Spencer, they came up with this idea of a public funeral. We built this coffin, all of us together, hammering in nails, each of us. This nail is for Omicidio, this nail is for Ruester, we were really stoned and it was a monumental feeling, making this coffin for him while he was lying propped up dead in his bed waiting for us. We carried him in the coffin to Tompkins Square Park. Word had got around, so lots of FUQU were there and lots of others, and some guy had a violin that he played really well and I started to sing "Moanin' Low." I came to the city to be a country-and-western singer and had sort of got off track, like all the rest of us. What the hell good was a track anymore anyway? We carried him around the square a bunch of times. There were maybe a few hundred of us by now. What happened? You guessed it. The cops came. They got wind of what was in that coffin and they took it away from us. Not without a big struggle, I might add, which required a lot of truncheons and nightsticks and sirens, and finally arrests. It's like we all wanted to get arrested for this one so we all did something obnoxious to a cop. All of us packed into jail was a ball. We sang sad songs and happy songs and went on not only all night but part of the next day, by which time they were sick of us and let us out. We went back to Tompkins Square Park because Smitty had made a memorial tombstone out of tiles. He was a tiler, or whatever they call someone who tiles things decoratively. The tombstone read, "Tomb of the Unknown Soldier." As I said, no one knew his whole name.

FRED TO HERMIA

I hate this country now. It's hard to be proud to be an American if you're gay. I said that in a speech I made at Boston's Faneuil Hall and it didn't go down very well. I could see that, and *that* made me mad, so I yelled at the audience, most of whom were there to learn about FUQU: "And what the fuck are you doing to help!" Oh, I went on a tirade. "We need all the help we can get! This is a plague! Why isn't everyone here fighting with us to save our brothers and sisters?" People actually tittered when I called them "brothers and sisters." Which made me scream even louder, "What the fuck do you find so fucking funny in any fucking thing I'm saying!" Grace would have been proud of my language. They wound up giving me a standing ovation. I don't understand gay men not fighting, every single one of us. And I certainly don't understand my country.

Tommy says we should get guns and shoot our enemies dead. He already knows how from being a Navy SEAL, but he says he can teach me. I know I couldn't do it. I'd put the gun to my own head and fire.

RON

We join with other gay groups for a candlelight vigil and rally in response to a recent surge in anti-gay violence—309 assaults in the last six months, including killings in Central Park and a murder by the cops of two gay men on 103rd Street. The rally culminates with 350-plus protesters, led by FUQU members, sitting down in the intersection of 100th and Broadway for a spontaneous CD action: 105 demonstrators are arrested. I get to test out the new chants I'd been practicing for us to protest with.

TRACY

I am telling you my phone is being tapped! And that I got a death-threat phone call from some guy who said we were as bad as Jews. And there are people coming to our meetings who are infiltrators. I don't know them and nobody I know knows them. I keep getting up at meetings every week and saying this, and everybody looks at me as if I'm crazy. I am not making any of this up! Now I am telling you more. This morning there was a swastika painted on my front door!

ANN

I agree with Tracy. I believe we are being infiltrated. Diane Sawyer taught me always to expect it when you're doing something important.

DUDLEY

The thing to remember about this organization is that it really isn't that altruistic. It was an emergency. I mean, it's a matter of, I wonder if we can stay alive. I wonder if I can keep George from going blind. Right this second, because he's going blind right now, he's dying right now, he's got PCP right now, and I have to get something right now and I'm going to do whatever the fuck it takes right now. It really concentrates the mind—to be in a constant state of real emergency. It is right this second, right now scary.

•

INT. EMMA'S OFFICE. DAY.

Fred in a hospital robe has been examined by Emma. Tommy holds his hand.

EMMA: Your liver functions are dangerously low.

FRED: What else is new?

EMMA: I'm going to drain out all the ascites that's accumulated in your gut. Let's see what happens with that.

FRED: Why have you been coughing so much?

EMMA: That's none of your business. You two make a nice couple. Are you a couple yet?

FRED: That's none of your business.

TOMMY: Thanks, though, for asking.

FUQU STORMS FADS

DANIEL THE SPY

My first action. Fred would have loved it. Jerry was looking out some office window with another Dr. Schmuck, who's acting head of FADS, staring down at us as if we're some strange animals in the jungle. There were hundreds and hundreds of us screaming and yelling and chanting, waving banners, carrying posters with Jerry's face and a Nazi swastika. There were armed policemen on horses stomping through our hordes, trying to herd us off the range, and dropping piles of shit all over. A kid went around shoveling it up and depositing it in the building's entrance so no one inside could get out without walking in it. A guy named Scotty managed to climb up on the roof of the entrance overhang and tape FUQU and Ruestergate posters on the building. The crowd went wild. Evidently there were some 1,500 protesters there from all over the country. Someone said 180 were already arrested. Isn't it interesting that Jerry came all the way over from NITS to watch us? It's a good thing I was wearing civvies, black boots, and a mask of Ruester.

After the activism comes the feeling of fraud when I take off the mask. Am I a hypocrite, one way or another, wearing the mask or not? After the excitement of marching, sometimes even running after a target appearing from out of an office building, packs of us, like the frightened humans we really are, dashing to frighten them, which indeed we do. What comes next? I'm aware that I find the fear in the eyes of my fellow bureaucrats strangely amusing. We're not out for their actual blood, but they don't know that. When I go home I wonder about the person, me, who became this Masked Activist screaming at those I work with. *Amusing? Fraud?* Why am I using words like this? I haven't felt so . . . vital since Philip was my enemy through that never-ending childhood I couldn't wait to escape. But Philip's eyes contained not a drop of terror. Once I heard him say to Rivka, "I don't know what to do with him," and his voice did sound sad, just that once, but certainly not enough to warrant the apology Rivka pressured me to perform. "Never!" I screamed at her, my mother. Funny, I can see his sad eyes now and hear that sad voice now. Gay Philip. Homosexual Philip. Jerry's eyes today on the other side of that window reminded me of Philip's sad eyes. Trapped. Jerry is a homosexual too. I know it. My instincts for this are, after so many years of dealing with so many patients, usually not far off. Is he as unhappy about it as Philip was? He must be. How could he not be affected, having to take care of dying gay men when he's a dead gay man himself? Will our demo right under his nose loosen him up? I never felt like a fraud fighting Philip in Masturbov Gardens the way I feel a fraud right now. Why do I use that word even after a day of running around FADS and then over to the NITS campus running after Omicidio, joining in screaming "Murderer!" at the top of our lungs when he got out of his limo, and then coming home to reread Fred's attacks on us, as if it will help me regain the euphoric righteousness I felt all afternoon? Jerry's eyes this afternoon were the eyes of the endangered small animal scurrying away from his awful pursuers. Who put Elliott Garbantz up to slashing the number of New York UC cases in half? Who slashed the total number of gays in America all of a sudden? I asked Jerry about this juggling and he wouldn't answer. "Who is after us?" I demanded, surprised by my tone. "Does he or she have a name of his or her very own?" He pulled away from me. "Why are you yelling at me? I am not your real enemy." He looked small and terribly rattled, as am I in a way. I can see that activism is not for the faint of heart. When I asked him, "Well, then, who is?" he shook his head as if to say the question is too beneath him to answer.

Ann, to whom I revealed myself because I knew Fred and she were close, tells me that activism is not about feeling guilty. Maxine, ditto, tells me that FUQU is something to be proud to belong to. I had an instructive and moving time today. I don't think I want to go on any more of these demos, though. They make me feel too rotten. You shouldn't have to do shit like this to be treated equally here. What is wrong with me! Of course you must. I miss Fred. I miss David. I miss a life. I miss a personal connection to a real life.

WHERE WAS FRED?

I was in Table recovering from a "procedure." I'd collapsed after a FUQU meeting and Tommy rushed me to Emma. I am sad not to be in Franeeda with my kids, but I am, one, now momentarily drained of some new kind of poison that is endangering my liver, and two, filled with the increasingly morbid feeling: I am wasting time. Four quarts of something has been drained from my stomach and is already starting to replenish itself. I am told again that the days of my liver are numbered. Which means that I am too. FUQU is wasting time too. We aren't getting anywhere. We joke how good our "shows" are. And they are. But as with touring companies of *Oklahoma!*, how many times can you perform them if you aren't getting rave reviews in *The Truth*? And gay people can't tell the truth in *The Truth*. So much for *The Truth*. So much for the truth.

•

Your boys and girls are certainly a mess of a mass. Or is it mass of a mess? They join with your Mr. President and your Dr. NITS for guaranteeing my eternal life. Thank you very much. Love from Mr. UC.

DEEP THROAT GETS THE AXE

This is how it happened.

Dr. Alphonse Garibaldi was a distinguished pediatric surgeon. He was famous for a number of breakthroughs, including separating conjoined twins. He was tall, handsome, with an impressively neatly trimmed beard and a persona that you knew had no patience for fools. Ruester appointed him to be surgeon general. Dr. Garibaldi wrote the official U.S. policy on The Underlying Condition and took the unprecedented action of mailing detailed information to every U.S. household. Many people are unhappy with the way in which he dealt with gay sex and the high risk of infection through anal intercourse. The White House goes ballistic. Garibaldi is unapologetic and explains his position: such activities entail risks several orders of magnitude greater than other means of transmission; hence The American People must be warned. Additionally, Dr. Garibaldi infuriates conservatives by insisting on sex education in schools, ideally as early as the third grade, including instruction regarding the proper use of condoms to combat the spread of UC. While straightforwardly and officially telling the public that this disease even exists is controversial in itself, Garibaldi is further criticized for causing a subtle shift in public consciousness. Previously, government health agencies were expected to develop cures and vaccines for diseases (although they rarely did). Under Garibaldi, this mandate was expanded to include a "duty to warn."

"This is not the government's responsibility" had been Purpura's commandment, now delivered via Vice President Dredd Trish to Garibaldi.

Garibaldi had been first put forward by Chevvy Slyme, who then put his name forward to Moose, who thought it a splendid idea as Garibaldi was on record as against abortion, which would be useful for the anti–*Roe v. Wade* crowd. Ruester agreed and Garibaldi was already appointed and in residence when it turned out that yes, he was against abortion as a personal moral decision but not against it as a medical one. He was ordered to amend this opinion, made in one of his earliest reports. He did not do so. Although he still had not met the president or the First Lady, that did in no way curtail his determination to constantly advise The American People about their health.

Garibaldi is again called on the carpet for having published a second Surgeon General's Report to The American People on UC without clearing it with the White House. Once again he had simply sent the document to the Government Printing Office with instructions to print it and send it to every mailbox in America. The good doctor now strongly urged all of The American People to please use condoms. The fact that the surgeon general even mentioned that obscene device a second time is further anathema to every right-thinking conservative. The White House blew up, of course. The SG is asked to retract his position on recommending condoms or at least to state the high failure rates of condoms. The problem is that condoms don't fail very often. Conservatives want to believe that condoms fail all the time. The SG won't budge an inch. He sits there, like a benign Buddha, being hauled over the coals by Bohunk, never in fact opening his mouth.

I don't know why I've been told all this. Purpura's taken a fancy to me. Mother told her about me. Manny Moose orders that Garibaldi is given the axe.

The surgeon general, a rank from another era, had been a political plum reserved for doctors adept at raising money for presidential campaigns. The idea originally was that there would be a Commissioned Corps and staff for the surgeon general of the Public Health Service just as there would be an Army for the Defense Department. The PHS had been a haven for draft dodgers in the Korean and Vietnamese wars and was a means today for lazy physicians to make a better salary while keeping banker's hours working for the federal government. The Army's job was to make noise and kill people in case of war. The job of the PHS was to constantly make war on disease with the Commissioned Corps as troops. The surgeon general was to command the PHS. However, the surgeon general was never given the actual authority to use any troops, or to command them to do anything. In sending out his Reports to The American People, Garibaldi was really performing a heroic act above and beyond any actual prose in his job description.

One of the several reasons Mother originally sent me to NITS was because of my expertise on infection from diseases, which of course includes condoms. The SG is being ordered to retract his position on condoms, which he's refused to do. Now he is forced to listen to the president's domestic policy adviser, Gree Bohunk, who knows as much about medicine as Al Capone. The SG said this was the second time he'd been in the White House; the first, when he was sworn in, was the only time he'd been within earshot of the president. Gree started right in yelling at him that he had no authority to issue such reports. I was pissed enough to tell Gree that Dr. G. was the nation's doctor and ethically bound to give all of us his best advice.

The White House has also sent along Penny. Penny is tall. Penny is a little long on the vine, but a younger Penny must have been devastating. Penny is blond, groomed, and has long beautiful fingers and large hands that are impeccably cared for. I am sitting beside her. She is smart, mean, and I would like to go to bed with her. She has small breasts and walks with an assertiveness that makes you think she always gets her way. Pushy. I can almost feel the force and juice of her as she sits beside me. She is really hot.

Penny leans forward toward the SG, her frock sliding along my right side in a silken whisper. I nearly shiver. "But Doctor, this pamphlet you wrote and already sent out without our permission is not an educational lesson that we want to represent the administration," she says with all the passion of Catherine De Medici offering someone a delicious garnish of arsenic. He smiles benignly, and finally explains quietly and once again that the surgeon general's report is what the surgeon general felt was obligatory to report. "But, Doctor, you can't send this out as an *educational* message!" I couldn't take it. "Penny, the surgeon general of the United States is not sending out an educational message. The surgeon general is a doctor, the doctor to The American People! He is giving them medical advice! Medical advice is different from educational advice." I guess I spoke a bit more strongly than these fools are used to. The surgeon general sort of winced but bore up pretty well. Penny doesn't stop. "Congressmen are also sending out this report to their constituents!" she yelps. "So what," I say, "what if they decide to send *Harrison's Textbook of Medicine* to their constituents? The message will be exactly the same." Big Gree looks as though his dyspepsia and hemorrhoids have just collided. Penny keeps boring in. "Well, change the part about condoms. Condoms fail and people should know it," she says with a smile of ingenious triumph, as though this is both true and profound and God has sanctioned it. "We know that scientists at FADS have proved that condoms fail fifty percent of the time and if people use them they will have a false sense of security." The "scientists" she referred to is a third-rate statistician employed by the Catholic Church, the Right to Lifers, and for all I know, the American Fascist Party, and who is both evil and stupid. His name is Dr. Ronald Bletsch, and his supposed calculations are based on ancient anecdotes from traveling salesmen in colonial days, and a complete misunderstanding of new condom technology and the data supporting it. I told her this. She was pissed. I loved it. The more pissed she got, the more inflamed my fantasy of her became. What kinds of orgasms did she have, I wondered. The SG was back to smiling like a benevolent Buddha. The babe made one last stab, rather peremptorily, at "demanding in the name of the president of the United States that you as his representative send out to every household in this country additional information edited 'clean' of all references to condoms and intercourse and anal intercourse and gay anything." She practically choked, poor dear, on that word, *anal*. Buddha just sat there with his lovely bearded smile.

I knew the meeting was over and that we had won a victory that was too decisive and too outspoken. I was meant to effect a compromise. Gree stalked his five-foot-three-plus elevators out the door. Penny, to her credit, did shake hands with a strong grasp that made me look at my hand later to see if she had left a permanent mark to go with her other impressions on me. Nostrill, whom I'd not noticed had taken a seat at the back, was looking at me as if I were a representative of Satan on earth. I keep forgetting this place is swimming in Lovejoys. I wonder how much Mother knows about that.

The fallout took a little time. I was called by Jerry to tell me I had been involuntarily retired from the Public Health Service for dereliction of duty. I went to Building 1 and was told that my performance ratings from Jerry and others did not merit my promotion to the next step. The "brilliant" performance ratings that dated from before I had moved over to Jerry, I was now told, were unjustified and conflicted with my new ratings. Jerry, who had just been informed of my lymphoid reservoir work, offered me a temporary contract at much less pay and no benefits. I had just lost my pension and retirement somewhere between his office and Building 1.

Mother had told me this would happen and that I should take the temp position. There was still stuff he wanted to know more about. He would supplement my income from one of his budgets. He also said he might be assigning me to the White House, details to follow later. I should "stay tuned."

I wanted to stick around until I was certain of this lymphoid reservoir work. I had done what I set out to do, report with Don Kotler that the location of the UC virus was in the gut, which explained the awful GI difficulties UC carriers experience. Jerry was in no way involved in my discovery. It was, of course, work that he should have done a long time ago. I had practically begged him to do it. My degrees from Hopkins, Yaddah, Cambridge, and Uppsala counted for naught with Dr. Jerrold Omicidio.

I have a personal note from the surgeon general of the United States of America framed over my desk, thanking me for my support.

There was a big book burning. Nobody knows about that. Most of the copies of the Surgeon General's Report to The American People never left the government printing office. They were trucked into the country and burned to ashes.

DR. DONALD KOTLER

I had blood and tissue samples preserved in various ways, from deep-freezing to electron microscopy fixatives. Deep Throat didn't like any of them, and insisted I look at the paraffin blocks that he had done. His work was beautiful. I had given him biopsies from as many activists as I could, including ones from Sparks Huffington and Fred Lemish.

DEEP THROAT

Don has underplayed how this evolved and his significant role. I became interested in the GI complications of UC and looked in the current literature, where I found some of Don's publications of work he did at St. Luke's in New York. Since I could get no help at NITS, I called Don out of the blue and told him what tools I had. We started to work together on biopsies from the gut, totally unknown to Jerry. I had started working on UC in the parotid in a patient with what was then called the Nector (by now we knew that nimroid was early Nector, which is now named UC), and my findings were published without Jerry. There followed a whole series of papers, some with Don, some with other collaborators, on UC in the lamina propria, on UC in esophageal ulcers, on the lymphoid reservoir of UC, on UC in the human gut, on the pathobiology of UC infection, on hidden lymphoid germinal centers as reservoirs of UC infection accounting for the apparent latency of infection. No Jerry on any of these.

After I left, Jerry, with Pantaleone, published essentially what I'd found. In all of these major discoveries, Jerry played no part. Mine were all published in peer-reviewed journals. I don't need to make claims or argue over who knew what when. Don knows a bit of the depression and paranoia that anybody who has to work around Jerry goes through. Jerry still takes awards and prizes for what others did. It is my and Don's work that will change the course of this plague, not his. We discovered the mother lode.

Had Jerry been willing to listen, the plague's progression would have been otherwise. There existed a place to start from. I gave him that and he could have proceeded with his work from that. He ignored it and another three years were lost. This is of no interest to a number of people in high places.

This is the man you're trying to understand?

DR. DONALD KOTLER

Our GI work indicated that the virus is in the gut in almost everyone. I speculated as much and found some evidence. DT proved it beyond a doubt. Now people know that the gut is the earliest and often the most affected organ. In practical terms this means that looking at cells from a blood sample does not give the full picture of what is going on. And for years, then and now, it is the blood sample that is the basis of all interest and study, in almost everything. Think about what I'm saying. Even in patients without detectable viral loads, there may be residual viral activity in the gut, and elsewhere.

Jerry tried to get the journals not to publish our work.

DEEP THROAT

I have never known Jerry Omicidio to have an unselfish thought. You were recently speculating about his sexual orientation. He can't be gay, or even in the closet. His problem is somewhere in the Marquis de Sade. Something to go along with being short. Great deceivers are often short, like Napoleon and Hitler.

MEANWHILE, BACK ON OUR RANCH

SPARKS

It was scary when we finally got inside and saw what we saw. It was a meeting where Jerry and his staff presented some more of their lousy ZAP data. It is hard to believe they are even still studying ZAP. Everyone all over the world knows what shit ZAP is. We weren't invited of course, their meetings are listed on the NITS calendar, which theoretically means anyone can go. We thought we'd give it a shot. What did we have to lose?

The first thing I realize is how dumb and rude everyone is. Jerry sits there stone-faced, not even saying so much as Hello and Welcome. The meeting is conducted by his chief nurse practitioner, Debbi Driver, along with Jerry's assistant, dumb-ass-looking Dr. Daniel Something-or-Other, who looks real uncomfortable but says nary a word. Since this is the first meeting on trials in a while, this conference room at NITS is half-full, which I'm told is "a pretty good crowd," by some doctor, who looks at me as if I'm from Mars when I ask this question.

Debbi Driver is a big woman, a large woman, tall, dark-haired, too large for a Debbi. She is now in full charge of Jerry's trials. A Leisha McGonigle had been in charge of them. She seems to have disappeared. Just as a Margaret Something-or-Other disappeared. Just as well. She was dumber. They were both dumber. We saw their reports and literally gasped. Eigo says there are enough holes in them to shoot deer. And it is very evident Debbi's no prize.

Not enough people are signing up for any trial. And of those who actually apply, some 98 percent of them are turned down, for one of two reasons, because they're too sick or because they're not healthy enough. If that makes any sense. Which it shouldn't. But that is Snicker talk. A Dash Snicker rule. One way to guarantee good outcomes is to have healthy patients from the get-go. Dash Snicker makes a statement to defend this nonsense. Dash Snicker is a snot. No getting away from it.

Fred warned us about all of this but Fred can overdramatize. Obviously not about this. He confided in me that he has a mole inside here, who might come and introduce himself. I said, Mole like in a spy movie? And he said, Correct. I'm flattered Fred confides in me. I'm impressed his information tentacles can reach into covert corners. No one's shown up to talk to me yet. Including Fred, who once again is somewhere else.

Debbi is stern. Debbi is unyielding. Debbi is completely unreasonable. Debbi rudely turns down sick people as if they are scum, thus pleasing Dash Snicker and G-D no end. "Entry criteria must be relaxed, not tightened," Eigo tries to explain to her, to which she doesn't respond. She doesn't know who Eigo of T+D is and she doesn't want to know. So he makes a point of introducing himself to her every time he stands up to question one of her "statements as fact," as he calls them.

Almost ten years now. Makes you want to throw up. Fred would say, Makes you want to kill. That's one of the differences between our styles.

"Don't tell me what to do, buster," Debbi says, jamming her forefinger fiercely into the chests of first Jim Eigo and then yours truly, Sparks Puffington, and repeating her action, Jim's chest, Sparks's chest, Debbi's forefinger, as if the very bravura of it all provides her with the energy to repeat herself: she's famous for this same digitalization of dialogue and muscular action as she's coasted through one inconclusive trial after another. You'd think she'd break that finger. "She likes to be in touch with her audience," some doctor tells me. She is not popular.

Dr. Levi Narkey, a gay doc who's come with us, actually begs for two drugs to be tested at once. "What is there to lose?" You would have thought he'd spit upon the Cross, which of course he has, the Holy Grail of the Clinical Trial as devised in the year 1800 B.C. The pharms sit back and watch and snort. Pharms are beginning to show up at conferences. They won't talk to us either. Or rather they talk to us like we really are from Mars. We are wearing our FUQU T-shirts. "And what are you doing here, pray tell?" sort of thing. You can tell they're pharms because they look like traveling salesmen. Debbi Girl is protecting them, they know, protecting them from us heathen activists and who knows how much else. Eigo stands up, introduces himself to her again, and asks if she might respond to Dr. Narkey's request. "And just what two drugs do you have in mind, mister?" she spits out at Eigo. "I got one drug. You want another drug, you go scream some more at FADS."

"We would," Eigo replies in his unshakable calm tone. "But Dr. Marie Clayture doesn't return calls, or answer letters either."

"What are you guys doing here anyway? This meeting isn't open to the public."

"Yes, it must be, by law," David G. answers her.

Debbi walks out. Everyone just sits there, including Jerry, who doesn't bat an eye.

A few minutes later six cops come and escort our gang out. David G. refuses to go. "It is the law of this country that these meetings, which are financed by taxpayer money, must be open to all!" he screams at the top of his lungs. He is handcuffed and lifted up and out, yelling even louder: "We are going to get into one of these meetings! You are breaking the law!" All the NITS people remaining look at David G. as if he's crazy. They have never seen activism or activists so up close before.

MORE SHIT

The Table Family and the Hooker Trust are among the most secretive fortunes in the world. If you recall, Table and Hooker money originated in shit. Years ago, Fate pointed a finger at an earlier Table and said "Shit." There is lots of money in shit. Yes, it smells. All of a sudden your nose is so fussy? No Table, down deep, is thrilled that their money started out as shit. This is not bandied about at family get-togethers or in the society columns where Joan Table cavorts with the likes of Perdita Pugh. The early Hookers also weren't going around bragging about Massachusetts Waste, their own fortune from shit. But then there aren't many of that old family of Hookers left, which has made Dr. Sister Grace even richer.

In Great Britain, the Purveyor of Toilets to the Royal Family is Thomas Crapper and Sons. They have big showrooms emblazoned with replicas of the Royal Crest and Warrant—the Queen herself shits in a Crapper. Who in America would lend such a name to such a daily convenience? Do you know the name of the maker of your toilet? Who is Mr. American Standard? The Tables named a New York hospital. Their company is called Table Holdings. Even Wall Street doesn't know what that means, nor does anyone else. Or the Hooker Trust either. (To this day we still don't know what's in the Masturbov Trust.)

Do you know what is done with what goes down a toilet? You think shit just goes down there and disappears somewhere forever? You are wrong. Shit is useful. It can be made into lots of other things. It's used in food. It's used in fertilizers. It's used in building materials. It's used in hospitals. It's used in medicine. It's also a conveyer of diseases like polio and UC and is hence a surrogate marker for UC, which Dr. Sister Grace tried to tell you about. Didn't you know all this? You weren't listening.

Then what? What comes between being flushed down the toilet and the pill that you are ordered to swallow?

Just as there are different kinds of people, there are different kinds of shit. There is a difference between French shit and American shit, between the shit of someone who eats a certain kind of diet and someone who eats another, between southern shit and northern shit, between shit culled from inhabitants of the desert and of the mountains, the colder climates and the torrid, and, yes between black and white, or, to be more ethnically precise, between Caucasian and African American.

America is queasy about its shit. Other countries don't mind as much. There are countries where people squat and shit in front of each other in open public toilets and little men come around and scoop it up while others are still doing it. Many such places are in tribal regions, usually temperate, swarming with flies and overrun with disease. This shit is filled with fruits, vines, raw meats, and is extremely vitamin-rich.

American shit is problematic. For one thing, the American diet is now so processed that much of its nutritional value is lost by the time it exits from the body, by which time it's all turned to bulk, fibrous roughage. While some American nutritional "experts" advise that fiber is imperative, remember that the paper you write on, the paper you read each day, the paper you wipe your ass with, is fiber. Your intestines are filled with the equivalent of your daily paper, or at least part of it. You are shitting out *The New York Truth*.

Let it be noted, as it will be by Rose George in her several articles in *The New York Truth*, that ". . . human excrement is a weapon of mass destruction. A gram of human feces can contain up to 10 million viruses. At least 50 communicable diseases . . . travel from host to host in human excrement . . . in numbers equivalent to a jumbo jet crashing every hour . . . Uncomposted human feces can carry diseases and extremely resilient worm eggs."

Yes, Dr. Sister Grace Hooker knew all this and was murdered because of it. That UC could be carried in shit, just like polio was—who would not want such information known? Who could not want it known so much that using UC-infected shit for developing a cure would get Grace murdered? Deep

Throat's autopsy of her ashes revealed that she had been poisoned. "But not from any poison that I can recognize," he reports.

VINCENT MAKES THIS MOVIE ABOUT HIS FRIEND LEATHER LOUIE AND HIS FUNERAL

"THE BALLAD OF LEATHER LOUIE"

INT. LEATHER LOUIE'S VILLAGE BOOT SHOP.
In the midst of shelves of leather boots, Louie, in top hat and tails, very Fred Astaire, is singing to the screen. Music and words: "Your pleasure requested this evening at seven," and into the words of the song.

INT. CONCERT HALL STAGE.
Louie in formal gear is playing a Steinway magnificently.

INT. A PITCH BLACK PLACE.
A spotlight goes on suddenly, revealing a fleet of motorcycles, all shined and with adornments, and lined up side by side.
Then another spotlight goes on, on an audience sitting on bleachers.
Everyone is in total leather, except for Fred and Tommy.
Finally, after a trumpet voluntary, a spotlight shows us Louie's face in close-up. He's gaunt, his sculpted beard makes him look like a devil, and as the camera pulls back we see he is wearing a black leather outfit that is so shined that it makes the light bounce off it. He is lying in a coffin. New music: something violently romantic played on a piano, Chopin, Rachmaninoff . . .
Projected is a video of Louie at the Steinway playing this music, in his top hat and tails . . . Superimposed on this is a photo of his Pulitzer Prize for Musical Composition.
The audience cheers.
The lights go off, the music continues building . . .
We hear the sounds of fountains . . .
We see the Fontana di Trevi in Rome . . .
We see the statues gushing their fountains into the pool below . . .
We see these fountains now are men, a circle of nude men encircling the coffin from on high, all goldened-up . . .

And all pissing on Louie in his coffin.
Quick shot of a cherry being popped on top of a sundae.
One of the golden men turns his ass to camera and unloads a perfect
turd in the coffin.
The crowd goes nuts.
You could even see Louie might be smiling.
At the piano, he gets up and bows to all.
The audience goes crazy. Except for Fred. Although he does shake his
head with a little smile of disbelief.

EXT. PIERS ALONG THE HUDSON. DAY.
The fleet of motorcycles, driven by those naked golden men, and
bearing Louie's coffin, comes into place by the water's edge.
The men disembark and take Louie's coffin onto their shoulders.
We see that their naked bodies are covered with lesions and are thin
from illness.
They take the coffin to the river's edge and slowly slide it into the water.
There are tears in everyone's eyes.
We see Fred, Tommy, Jean, Bordo, Maria, Blotch, others from FUQU
all wearing FUQU T-shirts, watching the coffin disappear.

HEIL TO THE CHIEF

On January 20, 1989, Dredd Trish is inaugurated as the forty-first president
of The American People.

HOW DREDD TRISH'S FATHER, PROCTOR TRISH, HELPED ENABLE HITLER'S RISE TO POWER

DAVID

I see that British newspapers are writing about this.

I knew this man, the father, Proctor Trish. He came to see Grodzo when
I was living with him in Mungel. The war was on, so I don't know how he
got there. Grodzo was very polite to him. He even made all of us dinner. I
was told not to say anything, as if I was German and couldn't understand.

They talked about Mr. Hitler's gold in some bank in Holland and how Mr. Hitler better get it out fast before the Americans seize it. The gold had come from big German industrialists like I.G. Farben. I remember the son of the head of I.G. Farben. I met him at that big strange party at the UFA studio. They and Mr. Trish and a Mr. Harriman all had shares in this bank with Hitler and Mr. Thyssen, another big industrialist. Mr. Trish gave Grodzo some papers to get to Mr. Hitler.

MOTHER'S NOTEBOOK

There were slaves at Mungel, and several managed to survive and sue Proctor, who they claimed made a lot of money selling them to German businesses during the war. This money is the basis of the Trish family fortune. The American firm Proctor worked for, Brown Brothers Harriman, then the world's largest investment bank, was the U.S. representative of Fritz Thyssen, who owned all the steel plants in Germany and who helped finance Hitler. The files of I.G. Farben and Thyssen verify all this. So did my reports back from Amos Standing. Proctor Trish worked with several German companies the whole time of the war, including I.G. Farben. Harriman and Proctor Trish secretly set up the Union Banking Corporation in Rotterdam for the Thyssens. Harriman was the son of the railroad tycoon whose wife and daughter were so obsessed with American racial purity and gave all those lunches Mrs. Strode described. Everyone was especially interested in ridding the world of homosexuals, as of course was Hitler.

The "owners" of UBC had provided the slaves laboring at Mungel and elsewhere. Our government seized its assets after the war. It could never be proven that Harriman and Proctor Trish were actual stockholders. It proved impossible to be certain that all records were located. It has now been reported by my British moles that Proctor Trish sold UBC shares for several million dollars. This was all a violation of America's Trading with the Enemy Act. Edgar had requested me to bury this information for the moment. It still remains in my archives at our headquarters here in Virginia.

The two Holocaust survivors on behalf of all remaining camp survivors sued Proctor Trish et al. for a total of $40 billion in compensation, claiming they materially benefited from Auschwitz and Mungel slave labor. Harriman and Trish were represented by the Wall Street law firm of Sullivan & Cromwell, where the partners included Allen and John Foster Dulles, both of whom would work for American presidents. Allen was a predecessor of mine at the CIA. And John Foster was Eisenhower's secretary of state.

Edgar Hoover traced millions of dollars' worth of gold, fuel, steel, coal, and U.S. treasury bonds shipped to Germany and financing Hitler's buildup to and running of the war. But he kept this information private, to use just in case he had to threaten a Trish.

If the U.S. Air Force had destroyed the camps at Mungel, Auschwitz, and others, some four hundred thousand deaths could have been prevented. Pressure from Hitler by way of Thyssen via Harriman and Sullivan and Cromwell saw to it that this bombing would not happen.

John Foster denied "all those slaves claims." In his defense of his clients he said: "Many of these so-called slave laborers were homosexuals and would present their own unwanted sociopathic problems to society were they allowed to live."

How did they all get away with it? My boys have yet to provide me with answers. I would come to know all of these men. But I was to be posted to South America to help in the search for Mengele.

Proctor Trish, once considered a potential presidential candidate himself, is on record as being virulently anti-Semitic and homophobic. He had requested that Hitler specifically speed up the murders of all gay people.

Proctor got his money out just in time, before he could be discovered helping the Germans. He'd bet on Hitler winning the war. Now his family's fortune was secure forever.

And his son Dredd Trish will now be the president of The American People.

I shall be kept very busy.

DAVID

I had sex with Dredd Trish, Jr. I know him from my days at Mr. Hoover's whorehouse.

Grodzo told me Mr. Brinestalker made a fortune in Germany, illegally selling IBM machines to the Nazis. And he and my father were friends from Yaddah with Amos Standing, who Gertrude told me had been a spy. All the Trishes went to Yaddah. So did my brother.

I know too much.

No wonder I am frightened someone is always following me.

I wonder if Daniel is being followed too.

FRED

How could such a cover-up have gone on so successfully for half a century? This was the way Hitler was funded to come to power. This was the way the Third Reich's defense industry was armed. This was the way Nazi profits were secretly paid to American owners. This was the way investigations into the financial money laundering of the Third Reich were covered up.

I'll bet this is not dissimilar to the UC mess going on today. Someone is making his fortune by secretly murdering lots of my people.

JUST YOUR AVERAGE FEW DAYS IN MARCH

Steve Z. was a videographer of the UC movement and was trying to set up a nationwide network of people doing similar work. I knew him from working out at the West Side Y. He's found murdered in his apartment. He was wearing a FUQU T-shirt and he'd been stabbed to death through its lettering. The police were useless and couldn't have cared less, according to Steve's father, who rushed up here from Florida. A week later five thousand from FUQU demonstrate at City Hall to protest Kermit Goins and his continuing negligence and manhandling of our lives and daring Dredd Trish to be better than Ruester. We shut down traffic in lower Manhattan in the morning rush hour. Two hundred of us are arrested. In jail the women are illegally strip-searched, which leads to a widely publicized police scandal and an out-of-court settlement. It's our anniversary and this is one of our largest demos yet. Many of us carry posters of Kermit on the front page of the *New York Post* with its headline proclaiming, "I'M NOT A HOMOSEXUAL!" together with our additions superimposed over his mouth, "AND I'M MARILYN MONROE" being a favorite. A reporter from Brazil comes up to me and says, "You call this a big demonstration? In my country when they raise the bus fares a hundred thousand people show up to be angry. And they blow up the buses." Ron leads us in a chant he whips up: "UC care is ineffectual, thanks to Goins the heterosexual." Too bad Steve, who was UC-positive, wasn't here to film it.

EIGO TO THE FLOOR OF FUQU

FADS, in the person of Dr. Marie Clayture, has told yours truly that personnel in their antiviral division are unsure what an efficacy trial is, unsure what constitutes efficacy data, so they're talking it over with their lawyers. If they don't know what such a trial is, how have they been judging trials all these years and what are we to make of the so-called Trish Initiative, which can allow for marketing approval after two rather than three phases of trials when no one knows what an efficacy trial is? Our initial charge against the Trish Initiative (it's a sham, it's murder) seems more frighteningly accurate by the day. For those of you who need more info, President Trish, as a thank-you to his rich supporters in the pharmaceutical industry and on Wall Street, gets a bill passed that provides for much faster FADS approval. It is historic, but that's not why we got it. It was passed because it's good for business to get expensive drugs, for anything, out there quicker. Mixed messages? You bet. Like Ruester, who named us as kin to "welfare queens," Dredd Trish has not said the words of UC out loud. He's appointed another bad joke to be head of NITS, Dr. Stanley Wishbone, if you can believe it.

IANTHE KNOWS HER FIRST LADIES

Trish has a mistress, you know. Jennifer Fitzgerald. She's no secret, not in this town. He is no more faithful to his wife than most of his predecessors. Well, if you were married to that large woman with her silly name, Taddy—no, it isn't silly, it's stupid—you'd want someone else for comfort too. By the way, Taddy is distantly related to Franklin Pierce, one of the gay presidents you mentioned, an alcoholic. I believe you also pointed out that he was Hawthorne's roommate at Bowdoin and they were in love with each other. Taddy didn't know any of this when I told her. Her response to me: "Dredd is going to ignore anything having to do with homosexuals. Just like President Ruester. Just like every right-thinking American." Dredd Trish is a consummate snob, but then so is Taddy. But his Bart Shovels is exceptionally adept at protecting them. He is an expert manipulator of everyone and everything, including, of course, the truth. He reminds me of those weasels who protected Hitler that Strode used to tell me about. Hell, I would see them all too. Weasels all look alike in every country.

Jennifer, by the way, is older, not pretty, and has been with Dredd wherever he was, from job to job. She almost gives Taddy a nervous break-down. While Dredd has had plenty of women over the years, Taddy allowed him that. Until Jennifer came along and had some sort of staying power. That's when depressed Taddy took her life in her hands, becoming the butch image that made her appealing, if not to her husband, then to every middle-aged white woman in our country. She really isn't a very nice person, but one can understand why. Does she have the power of Purpura? No other First Lady has ever had the power of Purpura.

REMEMBER PERKY FEINSTEIN?

Junior danced again tonight on *Saturday Night Live.* There he was, in his underpants, showing off his long, gorgeous legs, which he wrapped around my waist once or twice as I had my cock inside him. I think he's trying to show the world that he's okay, because there are rumors all over the place that he's got UC. I keep waiting to be summoned again, to another trip for another strange treatment, but he doesn't call. I see pictures in the papers of him and his wife too often, as if I'm being punished. She looks much older. He looks so dumb on this program. Why is he doing it? He is better than this! He is better than the life he's leading! Why is he leading it! Why do I continue to love him? He never writes. He never calls. I sound just like my mother. But my mother doesn't still owe me $25,000 for a blood changeover from a quack doctor, and Junior does.

DANIEL TO FRED

I'M SICK OF YOU CARRYING ON SO. YOU'D THINK YOU ARE THE ONLY PERSON WHO HAS DEAD FRIENDS.

I see patients twice over, at NITS and in my Georgetown office, and I hardly know who I am anymore. I can't name their names out loud like you can. I certainly love them just as much as you do. I can't take them into my arms either or call them my children. Doctors are meant to be dispassionate about everything it's hard to be dispassionate about. Everyone's looking for help and relief . . . including me. I told Jerry we, the doctors, should have some kind of therapy group with a shrink. He said, Do what you want to. Would you come? I asked him. What do you think, he asked me. I realize I don't know, I said. "You, mister, who thinks he knows so much about me?" he threw at me. "You, mister, look at me every minute." Then he actually sat down in a chair and hung his head down between his legs. Before I could get to him to offer some comfort physically, he jumped up like he'd been electrocuted. "No, don't touch me!" Then, and it was as if he were making some superhuman effort to say it, he said, "I'm sorry." And he ran out of his own office to get away from me. We both know I can't leave here now. We're chained together. I have more patients here than he does. In fact, he's stopped seeing patients at all. And we've got this big bunch of second-raters on staff now; that's all we can seem to get; no one wants to work here. Jerry takes it out on me and all of us. Grodzo wants to go back to Germany. They offered him a full professorship and to restore his pension and benefits, with interest for all his years away from home. David will be sad to hear this, that is, if David ever shows up again. I am angry now with David. Here today and gone tomorrow. I want him here! I don't want to see or hear you yell at me again. I need you now but you're always off on a snit of one kind or another that you take out on me. I can't believe we ever fucked so much.

LASAGNA, PIZZA, AND G-D

FRED

Eigo delivers two speeches before two congressional committees, the Lasagna Committee—that's his name, Rep. Lasagna—and one before a committee that we call the Pizza Committee because it's so without funds that it's forced to meet in a basement room under some pizza parlor.

Yes, we are somehow getting nearer and nearer inside. Today we're even in an auditorium on the NITS campus.

Eigo is nervous, and brilliant, an intense young man with black hair and eyes ("black Irish," he claims as his heritage). In real life (that's how I began to deal with so many kids: "What did you do in real life?" as if this life we are now living is no longer real, which in many ways it isn't) it turns out that he writes pornography for money. Straight porn. "I take care of my dying father. No one would pay anyone to write gay porn." He is impressive, not only in looks but in prose and speech. His words just march out of his mouth, almost Gibbon-like, as he lists for the Lasagna Committee an assortment of congresspersons who do not inspire hope, and dozens of stupid mistakes being made by people who just can't be that dumb but obviously are. Debbi, Jerry, placebos, PCP prophylaxis, ZAP, winding up with, "And we are learning everything faster than you are." When he finishes, he is cheered by his fellow members of T+D (including me), who have traveled down to Washington to hear his debut. Sparks and Rebecca and Claudette and Spud and Perry and David G. and Kersh and Scotty and Spencer and Barry and Kenny. Kenny is very thin now, and Spencer's face is covered in strange bumps. Rebby, who has come as well, and who takes care of both Kenny and Spencer, is perplexed unto fury, as always. "Why do you persist in your stinginess?" he cries out to the committees after Eigo's finished. "We are dying from a hundred different infections. It is much less expensive to treat an infection than to locate the cause for an entire plague!" Yes, he's using the *plague* word, along with me. Rebby's voice is always so filled with the pain and agony of his every living minute that it takes the committee by surprise. This is an open meeting, and they have to listen to people who've signed up in advance, usually an endless number of crazies. They've not experienced the likes of us before.

And then, perhaps prompted by Rebby's cry of anguish, Eigo turns his piercing black eyes directly on Rep. Lasagna and says:

"A government that neglects UC, and thus abets the slow bleed of a large minority of its citizens, has ignored its charge to provide for the common defense and forfeits its right to govern."

I love this man.

Then Iris, our Queens housewife, our Joan of Arc (well, not exactly, because Joan was a lesbian), gets up to speak. T+D has discovered that there are only eighty-four people in new UC trials in New York for ZAP, for reasons Jerry refuses to explain or defend. None of these are people of color or on disability, and none are women. Eigo chimes in: "Dr. Omicidio has testified before this committee about the great success of his UC Clinical Trials Group program. How can a program with so few patients be termed a success? We do not need trials with no patients, Dr. Omicidio. We have no other choice than to attribute the program's failure to a lack of leadership, to a rigid institutionalized system that absorbs all available funds and then affixes pharmaceutical dollar signs on people's lives. And by the way, I would be interested in Dr. Omicidio's definition of 'success.'"

Everyone's eyes are on Jerry. He sits there, dignified, as if they are talking about someone else.

Next up is Sparks, small, untidy, unkempt. He is obviously nervous—

they all are, this is like opening night on Broadway—but he offers something of enormous sense (for him): in essence, that we are here now, and they are here now, and it would save an awful lot of time and stress if we could work together jointly, but that in any event no solution is going to get anywhere without full participation by the affected communities. "People with UC and their advocates must be full voting members of every decision-making body related to UC clinical trials, including the PIs and the various NITS and FADS committees."

How about that!

Again all eyes turn to Jerry. He now looks even more tight-assed. He's averted his eyes from me for this entire meeting, although I caught him staring at me earlier.

Loudmouthed activists are the elephant in the room, and no Lasagna or anyone folded into his committee will even look at any of us, even when one of us is speaking.

As I write all this, as I try to enter our progress into a comprehensive chronology, I am pained again by how long it's taking for the enemy lines to be breached even after we did all our backbreaking homework. One year earlier we were all dummies; four months earlier we had to have fierce demonstrations and endless zaps to be noticed. Yes, we worked fast. But getting in is not getting there, I am now more and more seeing firsthand.

Outside on a break, Sparks looks up at the sky: "It's never going to be this pure and clean again," he says to Eigo and Iris and the rest of us. "We're getting inside now. It's like the age of innocence is passing."

"Please don't get satisfied about such a picayune advancement," I say to him.

The final speaker before the Lasagna Committee is the usually quiet Kersh. "We are here to tell you that UC activists will agitate relentlessly until there is a cure for UC. We will agitate until it becomes impossible for advisory committees to ignore us, committees whose members appear to have neither knowledge of nor sympathy for those people who live with UC daily. This is a war as real as any war. Give us the weapons so that we can defend ourselves! Or else."

On the way home Gregg, who's recently appeared from our Boston chapter to become Sparks's boyfriend, suddenly says, "Let's prepare a whole fucking treatment agenda *for* them! We can drown the Montreal conference in copies of it!"

Even Sparks thought this a good idea, even if it didn't come from him.

REP. LASAGNA

The activists came dressed any old way, almost proud of looking bizarre. About fifty of them showed up and took out their watches and dangled them to show that time was ticking away for them. I'd swear that they must have read everything I ever wrote. And quoted whatever served their purpose. It was quite an experience. Greeting's lobbyist stopped by and I told him about it after he gave me my honorarium.

POWER TOOLS

SCOTTY

It started with Sparks and me meeting with Dash Snicker at G-D headquarters in North Carolina. He actually showed us around. Fancy digs. We demanded a price decrease on ZAP, which they were going to price higher than any other drug on the market, $10,000 a year. We told him we would be gearing up for demonstrations if they didn't lower the price. When he and they ignored us I organized a small group of people to come back and invade their headquarters. There were about seven of us, and we even had our own media spokesperson who had a coat and tie on, so we got past security. We called our affinity group Power Tools, we had those battery-operated power drills and we sealed ourselves into an office with screws after convincing a woman to evacuate. It was all over the local news down there, with very sympathetic coverage. It was a story where people were on our side from the beginning. Everybody was offended by the $10,000 a year. After they had to blast us out of their offices, which by the way cost FUQU $10,000 in repair bills, they still ignored us. Snicker won't talk to us. His mistake. Greeting's big mistake.

GAY IDENTITY?

"Like helpless mice we have peremptorily, almost inexplicably, relinquished the one power we so long fought for in constructing our modern gay community: the power to determine our own gay identity. And to whom have we relinquished it? The very authority we wrested it from in a struggle that occupied us for more than a hundred years: the medical profession. And who has led us into this den of iniquity: Fred Lemish."

So writes Cocker Rutt in *The Village Vice* Gay Pride Issue, in which Fred is once again hung out to dry.

AT LAST

A FADS advisory committee approves aerosolized pentamidine. A small, quick community-based study under Rebby and Kotler and Armstrong from Invincible yielded very clear answers about its great success in treating PCP, enough to please Marie Clayture. Take that, Jerry Omicidio, you murderer, you. We could have had this four years ago if you had only listened to Rebby and Rep. Waxman and Michael Callen and had the guts to do the trial yourself. What FADS approval means is that insurance now has to pay for this shit and its administration, often requiring a nurse's supervision. To this day no one can understand Jerry's refusal to test it from his first day on his new job, now some six very long tragic years ago. Evil, evil, evil deed, Jerry. Forty thousand dead because of you, Jerry.

A week later FADS approves ganciclovir infusion for treatment of CMV retinal infections, which have caused blindness in many thousands. This is a big win for FUQU and T+D and young Claudette and Spud and their new Countdown 18 Months project to locate treatments for the most debilitating of the opportunistic infections. Stick this one up your ass, too, Jerry. Another of your evil oversights. That it takes two kids still not out of their teens to pressure and propel this treatment into the world is shockingly shameful on your part, Jerry, old buddy. They paraded six blind patients into Marie Clayture's front yard and six who could miraculously see again using some stuff Rebby imported from South Africa that FADS hadn't approved here. Our own gay doc, Dr. Levi Narkey, supervised this trial. He duplicated the South African stuff. This evidently wasn't very complicated. We couldn't understand why COD embargoed it from distribution. Anyway, Marie has a kid with Down's syndrome, who ran to a blind patient and tried to lead him into their house. Marie's a cold woman but she let down her guard as she caught the two kids in her arms and broke down and cried.

MONTREAL

I stayed at this fancy hotel. They let me keep Sam in my room. On the first night I was taking her out for a walk late at night and who should I run into but Jerry, taking his own walk with one of his gay assistants, I can never keep them straight, no pun intended, Drake Something-or-Other, who protected him, as Daniel said they all did, like he was the king of England. Drake took one look at me coming toward Jerry and tried to reroute his boss, but Jerry—and this would be an action of his that never varied—threw his arm around me in some sort of embrace as if we were old friends and not two blokes who hate each other and are alone with each other, here for the first time.

"Fred! Good to see you! How are you feeling?" All beams and bonhomie.

We started walking along, Drake falling a few steps behind. I'd made up my mind about something when I heard my kids speaking at the Lasagna hearing, and also when I took them to a meeting at Bowel-Muck-Shit about getting them to move faster on a drug they had, an analogue of ZAP, and discovered at Yaddah, and one of the doctors asked me as we were peeing in the men's room, "That Puffington young man, he is Dr. Puffington, isn't he?" Sparks had been brilliant, rattling off knowledge about their drug, how it was made, how it worked, how it was different from ZAP, how their studies should be set up. I had been looking for the moment to put my thoughts into action, and Jerry by my side was it.

In T+D we'd been discussing an idea called Parallel Track. I don't know who came up with the idea first, or if it had its origins in some arcane regulation someone had uncovered, but such a thing would allow very sick people access to unapproved but promising treatments that were still being tested in trials, and allow them to qualify for them because of the extent of their illness or their failure to meet study entry requirements, which were stringent and ridiculously discriminatory. Eigo, Sparks, Scotty, Kenny, Barry, Perry, Kersh, Claudette, and Spud, many of us, me—we'd talked about it at various places but got no response. How to push it to the next stage?

"Jerry, how can we get Parallel Track into operation?"

"Funny you should ask. I was thinking of the very same thing."

"This conference would be a great place to announce it."

"Whoa. Let's talk about it first."

"What are you doing for lunch tomorrow after the plenary? I'll round up my kids and we can all have lunch."

"Let's do it the day after. Tomorrow is pretty booked."

Indeed it is. Ten thousand copies of the FUQU/T+D Treatment Agenda are handed out to one and all. It is a revolutionary document and it will have revolutionary results. It details all the mistakes every division of the government dealing with UC is making, which are many, overwhelmingly many, and how to rectify them. It is the kind of report Jerry should have put out years ago. It is the kind of report *someone* in government should have put out years ago. Why wasn't it? Another unanswered mystery to still haunt me.

All hell then breaks loose. Some three hundred activists—from all over the world now; we've made the template; we've showed how to do it to a veritable international flood of UC activists—invade the stage before the plenary can begin, and we don't leave it for the remainder of this assembly. The noise is deafening, at first in support of us, and of the Montreal Manifesto of the International Rights of UC-Infected People, an expanded version of the Denver Principles and equally moving as they are enunciated by people of all colors, all very obviously sick. Gradually, as the audience of some ten thousand realizes we are not leaving, they are less supportive, less welcoming, so we sit down on the stage and around it and allow the proceedings to carry on. The speeches of course are awful, platitudinous piffle, and we hiss liberally when something particularly obnoxious is said. These people—and we now know what "these people" means—don't get it, don't understand what we are about. A particularly bland speech causes one of the young men from our Montreal chapter to stand and take off his shirt and trousers. His body is covered with purple lesions. He parades back and forth as if he's a model on a runway, chanting, "This is what it's all about. This is what it's all about." The rest of us pick up the chant, and dozens of other men remove their clothes to show their own scarred and emaciated bodies. FUQU members pass among the audience handing out Treatment Agendas to those who don't have them. I can hear a voice or two actually hawking them like hot dogs at a baseball game. "Get your red-hot FUQU Treatment Agenda here!"

A particularly spectacular display of effective activist disdain erupts when Dr. Elliott Garbantz, of all people, evidently still willing to show his face in public, makes a speech announcing his plan to institute name-reporting and contact tracing. He delivers his speech in both English and French, alternating sentences. I am happy to say that he doesn't finish. He is laughed off the stage. No one wants either contact tracing or name reporting. Both may be right for public health, but to downtrodden minorities—well, even the public health officials here know these are inhumane tactics to exercise on a patient population that has no rights of defense, no protection in employment, and often no insurance; their names on any list would spell great hardship for them. It may have extended this plague, no doubt it did, not to have this important information, but once again, that is the government's fault for not protecting all of The American People. Ron, of course, has a chant for us as Garbantz speaks.

"First he said we don't exist. Now he wants us on his list."

That night, when Sam and I take our walk, Jerry is walking alone, almost as if he's waiting for me.

"I'm looking forward to our lunch tomorrow," he says.

I proceed to characterize the dozen or so members I'll bring. He knows who most of them are already. One way or place or another he's been exposed to us.

When I call Daniel later in the evening, he can't believe it.

"Be careful. Don't fall for the charm. Remember, he needs you. In a million years he'll never admit it, but he needs your ideas. He doesn't have any of his own. None of his PIs have any of their own. He's also going to get into deep shit with every scientist in America for letting you guys in. You're in the process of showing them how empty their brains are. Fred?"

"Yes."

"I thought we weren't talking."

"I guess we forgot."

"Fred?"

"Yes?"

"David's still missing."

"I'm sorry. He'll turn up. Like before."

"Fred?"

"Yes?"

"Good work. Congratulations."

"Thank you, Daniel."

•

INT. MONTREAL MEETING ROOM. DAY.
*Jerry finishes reading the report. The smart guys waiting for his
reaction include Sparks, Gregg, Scotty, Barry, Perry, Eigo, Claudette,
Spencer, and a few other faces we've seen at FUQU meetings. Fred,
who's watching, is proud of these kids.*

OMICIDIO: Some of your ideas and suggestions for research and testing are interesting.

SPARKS: They're better than that.

FRED: And you know it.

SPARKS: Why didn't your doctors realize any of them?

CLAUDETTE: We think much of what you and yours are doing is wrong.

OMICIDIO: How old are you?

CLAUDETTE: Seventeen.

OMICIDIO: Where did you go to college?

PERRY: I never finished college.

SPARKS: I went to Harvard.

BARRY: You don't have to go to college to be good at something. I'm an actor.

CLAUDETTE: I'm going to Radcliffe in the fall. On full scholarship. Fred got me the interview with the woman who's in charge, an old friend of his. Were you first in your class?

OMICIDIO: As a matter of fact, I was. Both undergraduate and med school.

CLAUDETTE: Then why isn't what you are doing better and smarter?

FRED: And faster.

OMICIDIO: I thought this was a friendship meeting.

FRED: I got us in your door. You haven't anything better to do. In fact, you don't know what to do. My kids would be saving your ass. The next steps toward friendship are up to you. We're very greedy.

SPARKS: Yeah, we all are.

GREGG: Very. Exceptionally greedy.

OMICIDIO: You know my guys will eat you alive. I can't protect you.

GREGG: You mean you won't protect us.

FRED: You want to destroy us.

OMICIDIO: Here I thought we were going to be friends.

FRED: Put up or shut up.

OMICIDIO: No shit.

Much laughter.

•

We have our lunch. My kids are brilliant and Jerry is speechless. Jerry will announce "his" parallel track program by the end of the month.

ALL THE NEWS?

1110 Fifth Avenue is where Push and Clytemnestra Dunkelheim live. Some five hundred of us meet there to march to the *New York Truth* building on Truth Square to protest the never-ending silence on UC in their wretchedly world-famous and revered and respected rag. Of course 1110 is cordoned off by platoons of police, on foot, on horses, in their sirened cars; there's even a helicopter. Despite the size and length of the march, not one single mainstream media outlet covers this. Not one.

FRED CORNERS AN OLD CLASSMATE

I had a meeting with Dr. Abner Bumstead of Bumstead-Muck-Squish, which we call Bowel-Muck-Shit. I found out we were in the same class at Yaddah, where he didn't know who I was. The word *Yaddah* to his secretary got me the meeting with him now. I dropped a few subtle hints that "some of my people have been able to obtain your new drug DID that you are taking your fucking sweetass time getting out to us and we have found a way of duplicating it." This freaked him out. "Bye-bye," I said, as he looked speechless.

SCOTTY ON WALL STREET

The New York Stock Exchange in September was another push against ol' Greeting and ol' Dash Snicker. By now they were under tremendous public pressure to sort out their ZAP shit so we hoped this would push them over the edge.

We had a member of FUQU who worked as a trader on the Exchange and told us how lax the security actually was. There was this door right under the columns that you see in the famous picture of the Stock Exchange. It faces Broad Street, and right behind those columns is that big floor you see on the news. You go through that door and then there's three steps to your left, a little landing, and another three steps up and you're on the floor. It's that close to the street. There was just one security guard there, with no metal detectors, and when our guy told us about that door I started quietly putting a crew together, much of the same crew I had in North Carolina at G-D's home office.

First we needed to get these white trading badges, so a couple of us went down with video cameras and we stood outside the Stock Exchange acting like tourists during lunch, when many of the traders were standing outside smoking and what have you, and we zoomed in on one of these badges and then drew one up based on that design and took it to this kind of pawnshop in Greenwich Village that makes badges and things. We gave the guy a whole story that we were doing a skit for a holiday party and we needed these badges for the skit. And they're just these white plastic tags that had those big traders' numbers on them with the name of the firm underneath and a black line through the middle. They also had photo IDs, but our contact on the floor told us that everybody kept those in their wallets. Nobody had to show them to get in. If you had the white badge, that's all you needed. They looked great but we did a test run to make sure. The Tuesday before the action, which was on a Thursday, a few of us went in with the opening bell in trader drag, ties and shirts and badges, pretending to be traders—shit, I had been one and I knew what to do—and the security guard didn't bat an eye and all of a sudden we were on the floor of the New York Stock Exchange.

I wanted to figure out where to do the demonstration, so we're walking around, the bell is ringing, trading is starting, everybody is busy, we actually pulled out little pads of paper because that's what traders do, and we discovered this old VIP balcony that wasn't used anymore. It had a steep little staircase, and it was perfect because it had a big NYSE banner hanging over it, which would be a great backdrop for the photo. Since it was unused we wouldn't have to push anybody aside to get up there.

But then I got stopped on the trading floor. This old guy came up to me and said, "Hey, you're new!" And I'm like, "Ah, yeah!" I started to sweat. And he said, "Bear Stearns." I said, "Yeah, yeah." All our badges said "Bear Stearns"—we just picked a firm out of a hat. And he said, "That's weird, 3865"—my badge number. He said, "The highest number on the floor is sixteen hundred; there are only sixteen hundred traders here." And I said, "I don't know. This is the one they gave me." And I was starting to sweat more and he went, "I guess they're trying a new system. Well, welcome." And he shook my hand and that was it, he walked away, and I was like, Holy shit!

So we went back to the pawnshop and got them to make all new badges. We had like forty-eight hours before the demo would be happening.

We met at a McDonald's beforehand that morning on Nassau Street, nervous as all hell. There were seven of us, five who would go up to the balcony and two photographers, and the photographers were supposed to take our picture and get out right away, and hand the cameras over to runners who would take them up to the Associated Press. Each of us had stuff under our shirts. One person had a huge banner that was all folded up. He looked a little fat. I had a chain wrapped in a fanny belt for chaining ourselves to the banister so it would take them a while to pull us off the balcony. We all had handcuffs in our pockets. We all had little marine foghorns that were ear-piercing, and that's how we would announce our presence. And then, in honor of Abbie Hoffman, who was the first and only person to ever organize an action on the Stock Exchange in what was then the visitor's gallery, which is now walled off with glass because of him—in honor of Abbie, who threw down real dollar bills onto the floor of the Stock Exchange as a rant against how capitalism was funding the war, we had fake hundred-dollar bills made up that said on the back of them, "Fuck Your Profiteering, We Die While You Make Money. FUQU!"

So we all piled in at 9:25, walking right past security, and the five of us went up the stairs of the balcony and knelt down and pulled everything out from under our shirts and put the chain around the banister and hand-cuffed ourselves to a railing. We unrolled the whole banner, which said SELL GREETING. At 9:29 and 50 seconds we jumped up and put the banner over the rail and let off the foghorns, and you couldn't hear the opening bell—it was extraordinary. The place went dead quiet just for a second, except for the foghorns, as everybody tried to figure out what was going on. Then we showered them with our fake dollar bills and they started going into a rage as they realized what was happening. Our photographers took their pictures quietly and got out, handed the cameras off, but they saw that the crowd was beginning to throw wads of paper at us and getting very angry and they were concerned, so they foolishly went back in and quickly got nabbed. The traders were looking around for conspirators and our guys got real roughed up, shirt collars were ripped and stuff like that. But one of our photographers did get out.

And these traders were just raging at us, and I used to work with that testosterone, and it was—ah, it was really one of the most gratifying moments of my life. It was done. We had succeeded. The picture was taken, this was a gigantic news story. And they could scream all they wanted but we were going to be on the front page of *The Wall Street Journal* the next day.

It was while walking home that I conceived of what had to be done next. Actually, I'd been thinking of it for a while.

HAZEL

I am sick of Scotty. He thinks he runs us and we are his own private army to perform for him. He thinks he can do anything he wants to do. Yes, he raises lots of money for us. The T-shirt sales were his idea. We have this whole wardrobe of T-shirts, SILENCE = DEATH, RUESTERGATE, READ MY LIPS, they're all very cute. And they do make us tons of bread, but that doesn't give him the right to be so lordy-lordy.

EIGO CONFRONTS JERRY

In Montreal Jerry had agreed to come to a FUQU meeting at the Lesbian and Gay Center. Eigo confronts him there before a packed audience that includes Daniel.

•

Why don't all your committees, considering the gravity of the crisis, meet more than three times a year? Why aren't you focusing on treatments to cure OIs? Why must every committee meeting be in secret? Why are you neglecting people of color and women? Why are your grants for anything so small? Why don't you coordinate your work at NITS with work being done at other agencies and institutes? Why don't you speak out more force-fully when you don't receive what you need? Especially when understaffing delays critical trials for so long? NITS was instructed to publicize locations of all trials. You list only the *states* where they are sited, not the towns, not the hospitals. Why do you continue to do dumb stuff like this? Don't you and Marie Clayture talk every day? Put it this way, when was the last time you and Marie Clayture talked? And you wonder why the trials are under-enrolled. It's almost as if you don't want them filled up. Why does NITS decline all grant applications from our own community research initiatives, like Dr. Itsenfelder's and Dr. Krank's, and Boston's Fenway Initiative, and Washington's own Whitman-Walker Clinic, while funding such bozos and dumbbells as . . . well, let us just say all the ones you do fund, not one of which has demonstrated an iota of the ingenuity and usefulness of our own clinics? I should have hoped that you had long ago weeded homophobia out of your ranks. Obviously not. You're as negligent as this second president in a row. Is the White House dictating this silence?

Finally, why, since your agreement to allow activists into committee meetings, are many of us, including yours truly, still prevented bodily from entering?

Dr. Omicidio, you simply are not doing a good enough job. Nothing personal, mind you.

No, I take that back. Everything personal.

•

DANIEL: I was there and I couldn't take my eyes off Jerry as Eigo said all this to him. He'd brought an assistant, Poppy Salad, that was her name. Poppy was some proper Smith or Wellesley woman with a spotless career of being assistant this and that in many should-be-important health-type organizations. I never heard a word said against her, which indicates to me that she was pretty useless except as some sort of tidy front. Jerry would lean over after every accusation and mumble something to Poppy and she would write it down. When Eigo was finished, all eyes were on Jerry, who stood up and thanked everyone for inviting him here and said it had all been an interesting evening for him and he looked forward to working with us, etc., etc. He asked the floor if there were any questions, which I think took everyone by surprise. They didn't know that this was Jerry in action, dodging the issue, throwing the ball into the other court as fast as possible. When Sparks pressed him for "a response, any old response will do, as long as it's a response" to the charges perpetually laid on him, Jerry stood there for a very long moment before finally saying something. It was at this moment that the thought occurred to me that he was an actor in a role he was getting better at playing with each performance. His timing was improving and his reactions and body language were becoming very smooth in portraying this Very Important Man of Mystery and Power confronting the enemy and saying nothing. Whatever love or lust I had for him is gone.

What did he reply to Sparks? You know, I can't remember. Whatever he said, it was a string of words pronounced with seriousness, conveying nothing. I could see how he'd be in his job forever and that nothing would change. It was a painful realization and, like so many others I'd come to about him, I wonder why it took me so long.

It was as if he had watched and studied every bureaucrat who'd had to deal with a mess and realized that they'd never answered a question directly either. And they got away with it. The media never questions presidents about not answering any questions.

No, Fred, who was there, and I didn't speak to each other. We didn't want it seen that we knew each other.

WE SCORED!

FADS approves DID for "pre-approval distribution" under "Treatment IND." Mumbledygook that can be translated as "FUQU and T+D scored." BMS must have put the fear of threat into Marie Clayture, no easy task. My threat to Abner Bumstead worked! Now our own Dr. Levi Narkey can continue his little trial with his no-longer-purloined stash, and we wait and see, knowing that Levi is now not breaking the law. As if we care.

SCOTTY

We scored. We scored! We fucking scored. It's time to play TAG for real!

FRED TRIES TO PLAY WITH THE BIG BOYS

Why am I in L.A. again? I hate L.A. I'll tell you why I am in L.A. again. I've written twelve—count them, twelve—screenplays for Adreena Schneeweiss. This woman is famous for driving people crazy. I have been experiencing it firsthand. Of course, she says that I'm the one famous for driving people crazy and everyone's told her so. I guess you could say we have certain traits in common. She has owned the rights to my play about the early days of this plague since 1983. She says it is the most important thing in the world for her, to make a movie of it, yet each time it comes down to her actually committing to making it, she goes off to make something else, something crappy. "Stop telling me it's crappy!" she yells at me when I tell her it's crappy, whichever movie "it" is.

Anyway, here I am again. She has recently, behind my back, hired another writer to write her a script. Not allowed, Adreena, not allowed. My contract calls for me and me alone to be the sole writer. "I have never granted any writer such exclusivity in my entire career," she has told me too many times. "Well, this time you have or you would never have had this 'property' from me." I hate how everything in the film business is called a project or a property, neither of which connotes that an actual act of creation is re-quired. The screenplay by this other chap is really crappy. She of course has the chutzpah to give it to me. "Go sit by my pool and read it and tell me your reactions. I believe there's a typewriter down there for you." When I calm down I write a twenty-five-page letter telling her my reaction: it's a piece of shit. This other writer, "we worked so wonderfully closely," she cooed to me, insinuating that she and I hadn't, which I actually thought we had, I mean, she did send me flowers once or twice when she said she was pleased with our progress. This other writer has of course made Dr. Emma Brookner the leading character, who zips around in her wheelchair all over New York and Washington and a number of other more exotic locations, fighting all the fights that I fought but am not fighting in this version. "You can make any movie of my play you want to," I end my letter to her by saying. "Just buy it outright." (She only has an option.) "The price, as you know, is one million dollars. You have one million dollars, don't you?" The woman is said to have the first dollar she made. (I can attest to witnessing many examples of her legendary parsimoniousness, but not here.)

But my purpose here is not only to tell you yet again that Adreena Schneeweiss, grand diva-heroine assoluta to 20 million faggots, is not telling our sad and tragic story. It is to say that on this particular trip to Los Angeles I finally met Nathan Perch before he was murdered.

Nathan Perch had been Mayor Kermit Goins's boyfriend. He'd been paid off and told to get out of town fast and stay out. Tommy and I had been looking for him but hadn't been able to find him. And here, at a fund-raiser for some local gay politician running for an office he'd never win, this guy came up to me, a reasonably attractive fellow, and said, "Hi, I hear you're looking for me, my name is Nathan Perch."

Well, better late than never, fast-thinking me opines. Goins had just been defeated for a fourth term, so getting the old boyfriend-in-the-closet out in the open to confess, as we'd wanted him to do, was no longer the helpfully damaging ammunition against Goins we'd longed for. But there is always residual value in any major shit fight.

We went to some dark Chinese restaurant in the San Fernando Valley where we were the only customers ("I thought it was important to not be seen together," he said). It brought forth plenty of dish. It was both rivet-ing and sad, that each of these two human beings behaved so basely to each other, Kermit Goins, the mayor of New York, making Nathan Perch, his "executive assistant," grovel so (Nathan had to suck Kermit off while kneel-

THE BRUTALITY OF FACT 617

ing under his office desk), and Nathan doing it ("I really didn't like him very much. He was ugly and unkind but I was just so in awe of his power"). He appeared to have made a life for himself out here, selling, of all things, hospitals. In not too long a period of time he will be said to die from UC, although Deep Throat says he was actually murdered. His will set up a foundation to help gay men deal with their self-loathing. Could it be possible that Kermit carries the virus? Wouldn't that be justice? Well, so far Kermit's still walking and talking like the straightest of shits; no virus has visibly felled him beyond the bugs of arrogance and ignobility, not unfamiliar insects that consume not-nice persons whom nobody likes.

What Nathan did do for me at this dinner, in this knock-three-times-and-whisper-low dive in the Valley, was to restoke in me a particular fervor. As long as I'm out here, I must talk to the big boys. Gather them in a room and lay it all out for them. I knew Randy Dildough. I knew Sammy Sircus, Trafe Elohenu, Kipper Gross. I knew Derry Humpher, who offered to gather them in his office. None of them liked me, except maybe Derry, whom I had known in London. But I hoped that a request for a face-to-face meeting would flush them out, if only out of fear of what I might write about them if they didn't show. By now Mike S. (in charge of FUQU's media) and I were learning how to use our voices in more shall-we-say targeted ways.

I had tried to enlist Adreena's help. "These men, whom you know so well, must be made to participate responsibly in the fate of their brothers," I said to her. "Just like you are doing," I said to her, "for the sake of your infected son. And all the gay men who are your most devoted fans." Et cetera. She was not unfamiliar with my spiels. After all, they were embedded in many of her speeches, as Dr. Emma Brookner as written by me and even as rewritten by young Mr. No Talent.

She would have none of it.

"We don't work that way out here," she said. "You would be perceived as a threat. Adreena Schneeweiss does not threaten."

"How about throwing a little lunch and we get tipsy on champagne and dream dreams about what all your respective fortunes could buy to help get rid of UC," I suggested. "No threats. Just dreams. All your songs are about dreams."

"I am singing so well even I am amazed. I am preparing an international tour to sing in all the great cities one last time. I cannot believe my voice is still as good as it ever was." That was her idea of an answer.

"It will take at least a year. I can't possibly think of anything else for a year. I'm going to open in Las Vegas. On New Year's Eve."

Great. Now I had to wait for a year for her to tour the whole fucking world.

Sammy Sircus had bought the Jack Warner house. I wonder if Sammy knows how much Jack Warner hated fairies. Sammy is by now overwhelmingly rich. He can't decide which of his palaces to live in, on Fifth Avenue, or in L.A., or in the Hamptons, or on Fire Island. Everything he's touched in his business life has turned to gold. He fucks cute little hairless boys, thinks he's in love for a minute, and then dumps them. "All they're after is my money," he says as if this was a surprise.

"Don't tell me what to do with my money," Sammy says to me when we do get together in Derry Humpher's office. "You're worse than your Scotty What's-his-name in FUQU. He's always hitting me up for money. All your T-shirts, I staked him the up-front money to order them. Did you know that?" I didn't know that. "Cute little ass he's got. A lot of good it did me."

"Unh, well, thanks. I'm glad at least you got your money back. Sammy, we are dying like flies. You know that. No one is in charge. You know that. We have one administration after another that hates us. You know that. You are one of the richest men in the world. You know that. Don't you want to become a hero and a role model for twenty million gay people? You and Randy and Kipper and Trafe?"

The more they sit there immobile, the more impassioned I become. I give them a copy of my new book with my essays and speeches on the plague. They promise to read it. No, I make them promise to read it. "Yeah, sure," they all agree. Derry tells me they left their copies in his office.

Why go on? You get the picture.

I leave L.A. again defeated and depressed:

No movie. No support from rich gays. A second president who doesn't say the words *Underlying Condition*. A *New York Truth* that won't tell the truth.

I am the dreamer who still sings Adreena's songs in the shower.

At some benefit party over the Christmas holidays back in New York, the L.A. big boys all shun me mightily. Randy's beard, Dordogna del Dongo, now more involved in her Randy-Ran's life than ever, comes over to me with a huge smile.

"Darling. You are doing such great work. But you do not expect us to like you? After all, darling, you have written such nasty things about us. I personally have found them all amusing. But that is only me. Poor little Dordogna."

CONTINUING DIRTY DISH FROM DANIEL THE SPY

In November, on our NITS campus, occurs the first meeting of the entire UC Clinical Trials Group with all the scientists, all the principal investigators, and a lot of activists from FUQU. In a room of 820 scientists and staff, the activists cause panic. Each of them is smart and knows what's going on. Each of them also knows that we are years behind and (save for the FUQU contingent) hasn't a clue how to proceed.

I am suddenly aware that I want to use the words *we* and *us* to include yours truly, Daniel Jerusalem. Interesting. Am I tired of being the spy? I must fight against this feeling. I need to stay right where I am.

Everyone now knows that Jerry has given permission for FUQU to be here. Nevertheless, Howie Hube, the designated "contact" between NITS and the PIs, stands up to say bluntly to the packed room of "our side," as he points at the FUQU contingent, "They come uninvited." The room erupts in cheers. Then he points again to the several dozen from T+D in the back rows, and repeats so harshly that his voice cracks, "And they come uninvited!" Crowds at football games don't cheer any louder. You would think this would be a challenge to Jerry's power and he would rise up and defend us. But he doesn't. He just sits there.

Last night Jerry met with that executive gang of PIs. They were livid about *any* activists in attendance, who would thus be "privy to our actions and decisions and data." They're afraid it will be discovered how the UC Clinical Trials Group is run. Obernought and Lell are particularly upset, having done a ZAP study that Maxine and her dykes protested upon its release "for its lily-livered anti-feminist ass-dragging." When Farrell and Gretta see Max, well, as they say, if looks could kill. Gretta now claims to be the first to discover that UC happens in women, ignoring the scuttlebutt about Dale Mulch, but at this point that's irrelevant. The party line from the White House is still that women don't get UC, and Gretta's been silenced.

Once again David G. gets thrown out first. A bunch of NITS cops come in, pick him up, and carry him out. Now Hube asks everyone else from FUQU to leave. Another dozen cops have appeared and are roughly facilitating their doing so. Police are increasingly in evidence every time there's a UC gathering. It's a little scary, like we now have our own secret police. They report to Jerry, although he won't own up to it when I confront him. But I've seen the official memo from Shovels to Jerry outlining and approving "all oppositions necessary." The idea originated with Shovels after Dr. Sullivan started getting booed wherever he went. Sullivan replaced Dr. Garibaldi, now recognized by these kids as a martyr. Trish is replacing Dye with some airplane pilot named Wishbone who races cars as a hobby. "None of my boys will ever get treated like this again by any fairies," Trish is overheard saying by my old friend from the Jew Tank, Minna Trooble, whom I have just rediscovered. "He also says terrible things about Jews," she said, "not knowing that I am one and in his very own office."

The UCCTG system has come to a grinding halt. No one knows why, of course. God help the historians who will try to write honestly about this someday. Costing a fortune, enrolling few takers, obtaining no data, it's an unholy mess. And PIs refuse to acknowledge any part in this disaster.

The Gang of Five is the inside group of principal investigators who have somehow found each other and coagulated into the center of power for all of the dozens of UC ZAP trials NITS is ostensibly supervising around the country, of which, presumably, *officially*, Jerry is supposed to be in charge. It's FUQU that dubs them the Gang of Five. Jerry is letting this gang call the shots. I ask him why he's abdicating the position of being in charge here. His answer: "What makes you think I'm not in charge here?"

That only five PIs have surfaced as important is scary.

"This is all going to take forever," I mumble to Jerry.

"How many years you been here now?" This is his idea of a joke.

"Jerry, there simply has to be a way to make all this crew go faster!"

"You can't make science go any faster than it does."

"I don't believe that. And neither do you." I pause. "I hope."

"You sound like Fred. How is Fred? He's been quiet lately. Give him my regards."

Farrell Obernought obviously has problems with gays. Gretta we have met. One tough Florida cookie. Tyrone Coffin is from the Midwest. His medical center has responsibility for about ten major urban areas, which is ludicrous. The result is he goes to none of them and nobody knows who he is. Pansy and Maxwell are in bed together on some kind of attempt at making a vaccine. Maxwell, at Harvard, is a vet as well as an M.D., and Pansy, at Stanford, is a shrink as well as an M.D. "What they know about vaccines beats me," even Paulus says. "Any vaccine they could concoct would make people even sicker."

Greeting-Dridge is also financing Gretta and Coffin. Your classmate Bumstead is now a G-D subsidiary. As is Bohunk Vernissage. G-D now has a monopoly of all UC treatments anyone's discovered. Such commercial collaborations are against the rules and regulations not only of NITS but also of each of these educational institutions. This comes up before the board of Harvard, where Maxwell's a big deal. Maxwell wins. Maxwell is allowed to start his own company, partner with Pansy, and own stock in it without being asked to leave Harvard, a first. Von Greeting is on the board of Yaddah, where he set up a deal for one of their faculty to work with Dash Snicker.

There's a new company called Presidium that's trying to enter and challenge the UC market. Nobody knows anything about it except it's well-funded. The dish is one of its owners made a fortune making food for cows and pigs and wants to break into the people-product business. "Several drug companies are already being accused of manufacturing products that intentionally make people sick," Deep Throat says.

David Byar, from NITS, this big bear of a man with UC himself, is a genius statistician and has worked up figures to dispute everything dumb Debbi and Hube are doing on the few protocols already in operation or about to begin. He and Rebby have somehow met and he's been introduced to FUQU's rhetoric and he's in love with them. "You are so right, here, and here, and here . . ." as he plows through Eigo's speeches. "This is what you should do. You don't need so many patients to extract decent data. A dozen will do." This, of course, is blasphemy of the highest order and of course he can't get it published even though he's acknowledged to be the best in his business. It would certainly put all PI and drug company trials out of business. He and Rebby become dear friends and play classical duets together on the piano. He's dying and your Rebecca's watching over him, having announced she's going to become a doctor. How do I know all this? I'm David Byar's doctor. Jerry told him his "cockamamie idea" was "more statistical bullshit. You guys can make numbers say anything you want to. We do science here, not fairy tales."

Nevertheless, despite any of the above, the Gang of Five will control the trials, which of course are *still* on ZAP and not OIs. Worse, SECRECY is the name of the game. When David G. finally sits in on a small committee meeting, they cancel the meeting. It's becoming a war between the scientists and the activists. They are unwelcome because they can prove that they know more than we do. It's that obvious. Newt Grossvoll and Levi Narkey are your smart gay doctors who are able to take one look at how one of our clinical trials is to be set up and show in a few sentences why our way will not provide useful information and their way will. David Byar agrees.

I gather your Levi Narkey's work is going on right now as the "official"

DID and DOT and DIP trials are being prepared. These are the "D" drugs that mysteriously appeared. Much of their investigational research was done out of the country, so nobody's known anything about it. How do I know all this? Via Minna in Bart Shovels's office. How and why does Shovels know so much about the pharms and their drugs? Minna answered me bluntly: "Because he hates you."

I keep overlooking the fact that Dredd Trish had been head of the CIA.

Oh, I almost forgot. Deep Throat told me that Dereck Dumster's father died and left him a billion dollars, and James Jesus says they're a dangerous family to watch out for. "He's going to want to be president. I can smell it from here."

•

I cannot tell you in all honesty that I am having no concern. Someone somewhere has discovered what you call a chink in my armor. In certain people I feel less powerful, like I am sick in the heart of me. These people have been given something to fight me. In most people, thank goodness, I am still what you call alive and kicking. They have been given nothing yet or what they are given doesn't work in them. In many countries far away like Russia and Southeast Asia I am spreading like what you call wildfire. But these are not people whose company I enjoy. But more doctors in more countries are secretly rushing to beat each other in understanding all of me. They work for companies with funny-sounding names. They each have laboratories all over the world. So far only a small chink of me has been what they call isolated. These zaps and dots and dips make me uncomfortable. I seem unable to restore what little they are chinking out of me.

DEEP THROAT: HISTORY IS MADE IN THE DARK

By now you guys should have a pretty good idea of how many conflicting battle-grounds are standing in your way. Statisticians want certainty. Clinicians want patient improvement. Evil greedy pharms only want more profits and no liability. FADS demands "safety and efficacy" as if there were such things. Patients want something that works, demanding that the long-established bastions of mediocrity provide it, and if they don't, then the patients should disobey them and take whatever they want from wherever they can get it.

Regulators, pharmas, researchers, doctors, patients, politicians, activists all have different agendas. And you haven't learned anything about the spies in our very own government. How can a decent outcome emerge from all this?

You have your high hopes and I have my deep fears and I'm older than you. And Mother taught me everything I know.

HEADS UP

DAVID

Partekla was in northern Idaho. It is a government institution. I read in today's paper there are terrorist groups there that chop the heads off of homosexual men they capture. I did not know that when I was there.

BILL SNOW

It took us a bit of time to sort of catch on to the science at the level that it happens at science meetings. When you go to a scientific meeting, it's a very formalized dance, and the scientists basically make presentations to other scientists. And for a nonscientist, the only thing you can understand is the title, and maybe the conclusion, if you're lucky. So we went to more and more UC conferences and learned how to listen to those talks. And what it meant was us learning ass-backward the virology and immunology Iris is teaching us. We had started at the cutting edge without having any of the foundation. So we'd end up with notes that made no sense and a list of words that were repeated a lot of times, so we figured we'd better look them up. And that was sort of how a lot of us learned our science. And the great discovery is that this is not Chinese.

PERRY

ZAP clinical trials are treading water. No one knows why. D-drug trials have been slow to enroll because of bureaucratic delay. Now NITS needs six months to transfer their data from Chattanooga and Natchez to Boston. PIs blame everything on Parallel Track. OI committee has protocols ready to roll but PIs won't approve them. Velma Dimley writes an article exposing lack of people in trials and blames Parallel Track *and* us. Hube blames Marie Clayture and FADS and us. Sudden shit is brewing: Women's Committee opposing T+D's unauthorized strategy of "going inside."

Fred isn't looking so hot. He won't talk about it with me, though.

KAFKA LIVES!

TOMMY: Have you ever heard that Kafka was gay and closeted? Living with Mom and Dad and so neurotic? In *The Metamorphosis*, the son doesn't know how to act or manage his body in his regressed state; obsessed with his fragile sister's music lessons (so Tennessee Williams); father's trying to kill him; mother's an insipid mess; he must be kept secret from the neighbors; is fired by his employer and appalls the lodgers. If *The Metamorphosis* ain't about a very different kind of son, I don't know what it's about! Sounds gay to me. Just finishing one of those great-masters courses, reading things I've only heard about or didn't grasp the first time, my gaydar was set off over and over. What about Jack London? So gorgeous and tortured. And spent all his time running from/to something to such extreme lengths, and always, always in the company of men and always high. Like Fred says, they don't teach any of this in the schools.

MINNA TROOBLE TELLS FRED ABOUT BART SHOVELS

I had a mad crush on you in high school. All the girls in the Jew Tank did. You would sit and talk to us all the time! You didn't seem to have any boyfriends. You and I may have edited the school newspaper together but that was it. I went to Swarthmore and you went to Yaddah, and that was the last time I saw you until we ran into each other at our high school reunion.

I've worked for Bart Shovels since Dredd came in with Ruester. I went to Swarthmore with Bart's daughter. He is pure and simple and 100 percent a shit. I stay because it's so fascinating. I can't believe I'm seeing so much evil. I figure someday I'll write about it. But I don't. Everyone in this town writes a book and nobody believes them unless they're Woodward and Bernstein.

Bart's the power behind the throne. Every high official has one—the one who's really turning the evil deeds into action. The secret to success in this town is that no matter whenever anyone says anything negative about you, you call them a liar and a fake. Dredd Trish is too cold to care much about people as human beings. He'd been a CIA spy for long enough that I think his brain's been fried. Like Ruester, he looks good in a suit. And he, too, has a bitch of a wife who pushes him relentlessly. Bart makes Purpura and Moose and Bohunk and Gobbel and that gang look like the seven dwarfs. Gobbel and my boss are big buddies. They are plotting things all the time. They not only want to get rid of all the homosexuals, even though Dredd has a gay son and Bart has a gay daughter, but immigrants and poor people and anyone who's costing the government money. You name anything noble, decent, humanitarian and it's on their agenda for removal.

Bart Shovels manipulated the election to get Dredd elected. There's a lot of new Arab and old Nazi money at play here. I'd get murdered if they knew I said any of this. Thank God, Dredd thinks I'm cute. He pinches my ass every time he's near me. Even Taddy sees it, but she ignores it. They even invite me to dinner lots of times in the White House to celebrate "our new home."

Sit tight and stay tuned.

•

HERMIA: This woman is recognizing evil, Fred.

•

INT. BART SHOVELS'S OFFICE AT THE WHITE HOUSE. DAY.

Dr. Sullivan with Bart Shovels. To the side, taking notes, is Minna Trooble.

DR. SULLIVAN (*reading from a piece of paper; he is black*): "There are certain times in history, when the goals of science collide with moral and ethical judgment, when science has to take a backseat."

SHOVELS: Well, done, Lou. Keep it up! Write more shit like that. I'll have my office whip you up some longer versions for your forthcoming public appearances. I'm sending you out on the road. Keep your bags packed. Minna, get me the president and Dr. Omicidio on a three-way.

INT. HOSPITAL ROOM. TABLE MEDICAL. DAY.

Fred is being drained again. He's connected to various tubes and bags. He doesn't look so hot. Tommy is with him, holding his hand. Emma comes in with another woman, Dr. Falloon.

EMMA: This is Dr. Falloon. She works for NITS. They're enrolling . . . You tell him.

DR. FALLOON: A new company named Presidium is testing a new drug that Dr. Omicidio thinks might be helpful for your liver.

FRED: How does he know about my liver?

DR. FALLOON: I believe through Dr. Jerusalem on his staff.

FRED *(to Emma)*: Okay by you?

EMMA: There isn't anything else to try. All the other stuff we've tried isn't working.

FRED: You work for Jerry?

DR. FALLOON: We're in the same institute. But I've been working mainly on children's health. We've used this Presidium drug on kids, and it seems to be having some effect.

FRED: Why doesn't Jerry work faster on UC?

DR. FALLOON: You'll have to ask him that.

FRED: Don't think I haven't tried.

Dr. Falloon gives a package of drugs to Emma.

DR. FALLOON: Once a day with food.

EXT. DISCO. NIGHT.

Hordes of guys going in. A group from FUQU holding up signs: DREDD TRISH WANTS YOU DEAD. *The crowds don't want to see them.*

FRED'S REMEMBRANCE OF THINGS PAST AND THE HOPE OF THINGS TO COME

For these past few years FUQU's been my life. As in the early days of GMPA, there is such an abundance of visible, tangible love and cooperation among so many that it's almost total joy. Each week hundreds of men and women with a shared goal and much energy and determination to achieve it come together. Finally there is visible *anger*. And it seems to be growing little by little.

There are FUQU meetings every night, including weekends. There is never enough time and we are in such a hurry. We all identify with that! Planning meetings, meetings for painting and wheat-pasting posters, meetings for civil disobedience training, meetings to learn about science and treatments and how NITS works and should work and what all those other acronyms we now toss around so blithely mean and how they all operate, and chapter and verse on why they don't work and how they must be changed so that they might . . . Oh, it's all very heady stuff. Committees often meet in our first office so late into the early hours that the landlord asks us to move.

We all plan constantly for the day when we'll truly be listened to, when it will be *our* decisions that right the wrongs. Weekly meetings of often five hundred people grapple with the difficulties of controlling this while at the same time continuing to inspire many more into regular and reliable and decisive cohesiveness.

I kept telling myself that little by little something seemed to be working.

•

EXT. ENTRANCE TO HOLLAND TUNNEL. DAY.
FUQU members are lying on the roadway effectively blocking traffic and holding mock gravestones. Standing members hold signs: YOU DRIVE, WE DIE. RIOT—UC CRISIS. RUESTER KILLED ME. TRISH KILLS ME. *Other members hand out information flyers to drivers, all of whom are blowing their horns.*

THE SWIM TEAM

INT./EXT. MARIA'S APARTMENT IN THE EAST VILLAGE. NIGHT.
MARIA: After every successful demo, FUQU has a party. *They're all packed in like sardines in this tiny studio and tapping a keg for beer, which they're drinking in paper cups and managing to spill all over each other. It starts when Perry's beer tapping releases a stream of foam that scatters onto Maria and she blows it onto Adam, who takes his cup and pours it over the head of Jon, who turns and does the same thing to Brad and Art and Mart and Matt and Perry, and the rock music is pounding as they throw off their clothes except their underpants and form a conga line and wiggle out of the room*

and down the hall stairs and out the front door and across the street to
Tompkins Square Park, where they throw themselves into the fountain
and stand under the spray and start hurling gobs of water at each other
and taking water into their mouths and spouting it up and out at each
other like whales. Then they start ripping the undershorts off each other
as each tries to keep his on. By the time everyone is naked they all have
their arms around each other like the football team in a huddle to call
the next play. They start kissing each other, all of them, one after the
other, saying each to each, I love you, or congratulations, or happy to
make your acquaintance, or likewise I'm sure. Finally they fall all in a
heap on the ground, under the falling water, exhausted, the dripping
water on their cheeks that could be tears of joy.

MARIA'S VOICE: So that's how all the best-looking guys came to be
called the Swim Team. It was a great party. Like Fred and Maxine said, we needed to party. Come to think of it, where was
Fred? You know, I think he is still in the hospital.

FRED'S STATE OF THE PLAGUE

The secretary of Health and Happiness, Dr. Louis Sullivan, is a useless, faceless cipher. Dr. James Mason, his assistant secretary, is yet another Lovejoy
who hates homosexuals. There is no director at COD. Pewkin's gone into
academia. The co-director of FADS, Dr. Norman Joe Triffid, has been fired.
It will take at least six months before new FADS and COD directors are chosen and approved. There are now forty unfilled research slots at NITS. The
PIs who run the trials blame activists for their poor-to-no-patient enrollment;
few want to take such high doses of ZAP. NO NEW PROTOCOLS WILL
BE COMMENCED ANYWHERE because of that NITS decision to move
its database from one center to another. When the new center (in Cambridge)
is up and running, it will take another year to organize. The horrid possibility exists that the main reason for changing database centers is that the one
they have been using at Greeting-Dridge (in Research Triangle) has been
unable to adequately process or interpret (or reveal?) all the data collected so
far. This means that THERE IS A GOOD CHANCE THAT EVERY-
THING NITS AND THE PIs HAVE TOLD US ABOUT ALL THE
UNAPPROVED TREATMENTS THEY ARE FINALLY SHOVING

INTO OUR BODIES MAY BE BASED ON USELESS OR FLAWED DATA. Dodo's crappy blood test has contributed to this. This means that AFTER NINE YEARS OF A PLAGUE THEY KNOW ZILCH. PIs still don't like FUQU because they are jealous of our success in obtaining conversations with several pharmaceutical companies, which threaten their ivory tower where they play Frankenstein, still pumping ZAP down the throats of UC patients like they were Strasbourg geese being fattened for the kill. The murderous dosage of 1500 mg daily of ZAP has still not been reduced. Our Drs. Levi Narkey and Newt Grossvoll present Jerry with data they collected from their own patients that shows without any doubt that 500 mg of ZAP is much more effective than the 1500 mg Snicker is still demanding patients take, which continues to make them very sick. Dr. GARTH BUFFALO AND DR. DODO GEISERIC HAD EACH said UC can be cured. Yet every impediment imaginable is being placed in the way of our receiving this cure. WE MUST REFORM THE UCCTGs. They aren't working, we know how they can work (Tommy has been especially helpful in showing us how they could be effectively reorganized), and if they won't listen to us we must take our bodies away. Meanwhile, would you believe that as more people get sick, more people now suddenly clamor to get into a ZAP trial!

•

"Tough titty," I hear one person scream at another. What, please, is titty?

•

FRED'S VOICE (*over scene below*): But is yelling at people enough? Nobody high up is really afraid of us yet. What could we do that would really attract attention? FUQU had a lot of Catholic members who'd lived their entire lives being told they were shit. They finally got it together to fight back.

STOP THE CHURCH!

EXT. ST. PATRICK'S CATHEDRAL. DAY.
Big crowd, posters, Fred and Tommy dressed in suits and ties walking the periphery of the group, checking it out, greeting friends. Many posters held by many members: PUBLIC HEALTH MENACE—CARDINAL BUGGARO. STOP THE CHURCH. KNOW YOUR SCUMBAGS. STOP THIS MAN.

CURB YOUR DOGMA. PAPAL BULL. CARDINAL BUGGARO IS DEADLIER THAN THE VIRUS. And of course: SILENCE = DEATH. *Ray, thin and dying, dressed like Jesus in white shorts and with crown of thorns, carrying a wooden cross on his frail body, walks among the crowd, blessing them with his free hand.*

RON *(leading chant)*: "Suck my dick, lick my clit, Cardinal Buggaro's full of shit."

Then Fred and Tommy go into the church. Fred stumbles and Tommy steadies him.

INT. ST. PATRICK'S CATHEDRAL. DAY.

FUQU members have stationed themselves around the worshippers. Some are lying down in the aisles. During the service they start calling out from all directions, one at a time. The cardinal, on the dais, has his head bowed in prayer, with an expression of disbelief. Undercurrent heard from outside and in: FUQU FIGHT BACK FIGHT UC, FUQU, etc.

FOTIS *(stands up from a pew and screams)*: STOP KILLING US!

From various different places in the church come similar shouts: STOP THE MURDER!

At the front, communion wafers are being placed on worshippers' tongues. A priest holds up a wafer to the tongue of Patrick.

PRIEST: Body of Christ.

PATRICK *(nervously stuttering it out)*: May the Lord bless the man I love, who died a year ago today. *(He then spits the wafer out onto the floor. People move away from him.)*

Cops start hauling FUQU members out one at a time, up the aisles, which are soon clogged. More and more shouts of STOP KILLING US echo from various parts of the cathedral.

INT. FUQU MEETING. GAY COMMUNITY CENTER. NIGHT.

A madhouse. Much rancor and negative reaction to their St. Patrick's demo. Attendance is even more packed. A table selling FUQU T-shirts is doing big business, Scotty collecting the money. Ann and Donald are the two facilitators; Donald, handsome and butch, wears a skirt. We see more people at the blackboard writing names.

KELLY: We went too far!

KEIRAN: We'll make nothing but enemies!

O'MALLY: Every newspaper and TV crucified us.

TERENCE: This will be the end of us! We might as well pack it in.

GERRI: My mother saw me on TV and won't talk to me.

FRED: That demonstration . . .

SHEILA: Fred has not been recognized.

DONALD: Fred, you should know better by now . . .

RAFSKY: Even Dredd Trish said nasty things about us. It's the first time any president even acknowledged that we're alive.

FRED (*weak and trying to fight it*): This demonstration wasn't the death of us, it was the making of us! It will make us be seen as a threat. Now we'll be seen as warriors, an army in black boots and Levi's, and not the limp-wristed fairies they always show on TV. This is the beginning of our being taken seriously! Congratulations! (*Applause builds.*)

TONY (*sweet kid, pulls Fred aside*): Have you heard of anything to save my life? I don't think I have very long.

FRED (*giving him a hug*): Hang in there, Tony. We've got to have hope.

FOTIS: We're fucking warriors and we're going to scare the shit out of everyone we can!

ANN: Ladies and gentlemen, let's all come to order!

TONY: But what's next?

MARCUS: We have another party to celebrate another great demo!

EXT. TOMPKINS SQUARE PARK. DAY.
The Swim Team is celebrating in the fountain. Posters from the church demo are lying on the sidewalk along with their clothes. Among the onlookers are Fred, Tommy, Maxine, Maria, Gerri, Eigo, Ann, all cheering the team on as they start ripping off each other's underpants.

WE MUST REFORM THE UCCTG

From the Treatment+Data Committee of Fed Up Queers United to Dr. Gerrold Omicidio
Re: The UC Clinical Trials Group

We hereby submit the following standards of care that we are fighting you for:

Unless every arm of every clinical trial is a viable treatment option, that trial is fundamentally impractical and unethical and we will publicize same.

Unless a clinical trials program invites dissident scientific opinions into the process, it invites ultimate failure.

Unless a UC-related clinical trial obtains answers to its real-world questions in a short time, that trial is effectively failing us.

Unless a clinical trials program is responsible to the symptomatic people outside its trials, providing them investigational treatment as early in the process as possible, it commits malpractice.

Unless a clinical trials program invites community participation in every stage of its development, it will fail itself & those it's charged to serve.

Unless a clinical trials program eliminates internal impediments to equal access to its trials, it is fundamentally unjust.

Unless the leaders of a clinical trials program publicly address the inequities within the overall health-care system that contribute to their trials' inaccessibility, they collaborate in an injustice.

Unless clinical trials' investigators proceed as if they can treat (save) all participants in their trials, they also commit malpractice.

And we shall continue to publicize all of this.

You would think you would know all this. It all seems so obvious. But you don't.

We feel more than a little used by you.

FRED

Dr. Omicidio, what is it you do all day when you go into your office?

THE RETURN OF DEEP THROAT

James Jesus assigned me to my next adventure. "This UC plague is going to get much worse. It's slowly happening all over the world." He wanted to know what was going on in Trish's White House. "Dredd Trish is an old CIA buddy, not that I liked him very much. He was a wimp traipsing around with that unattractive biddy who wasn't his wife. But I fear he's a wimp no longer. He has Shovels to manufacture him into someone dangerous."

Mother doesn't want it known that he's interested in Trish. He told me that thanks to me he'd had enough of Jerry. "I get the picture," he said to me, as, certainly, had yours truly.

I cite but one example of my new assignment.

Via the White House, thanks to Gobell and Shovels, a Dr. Donnston Privvy is put in charge of UC "coordination." His office is "downtown," meaning away from the NITS Franeeda campus. There are now so many cases that someone decided it was time to open a separate administrative office for it to coordinate with what all the other nitpicking, bits-and-pieces, here-and-there offices and divisions and bureaus are also not doing or should be doing. So now we have sort of an interagency agency for UC. The government is filled with these. Presidents love them because now they don't have to answer anything. My office is now here.

The rationale always presented to the press is that such an arrangement "coordinates" all the wonderful efforts being expended on all fronts by so many courageous and sacrificing American people. What it really does is save putting anyone with any power in charge. No, instead of appointing someone with leadership qualities who might have a desire to do something egregiously right, some real second-rater like Donnston Privvy is easily found and since he's put at the same pay scale as all the other "coordinators" in all the other offices, no one has to make any major overriding decisions.

Donnston Privvy would never do anything so bold as making a decision. It's no secret that no one makes a decision when anything controversial is involved. If anyone should happen to make a decision about anything controversial and it got in the paper, then his or her coordinator would be in deep shit with his or her supervisor, who would be in deep shit with his or her coordinator—and on up the ladder to the White House, where the president is not making decisions about anything controversial himself. It's much more expensive, of course, to have so many offices and agencies, each doing more or less the same thing, which isn't much anyway, but bureaucracy doesn't think this way. And as everyone knows, who's to know? Who's to figure it out? By the time *The New York Truth* or *The Washington Monument* do find out and indulge in their moments of high dudgeon, another president's been elected.

The first time I figured all this out and ran to James Jesus to lay it all out on the table as if I were Columbus, he just looked at me, then grinned, then actually laughed, and finally slapped me on the back. "I'm assigning you to UC full-time," he said. "It's going to be a pisser. Lots of laughs."

It's been a Ruester-maneuvered—i.e., Gobbel—regulation that all UC deaths must be reported as quickly as possible. No one's paid much attention to this before the arrival of Trish and Shovels, because of the fact (there are others, like confidentiality, not the kind protected by law but the kind paid for by rich patients) that any doctor with UC cases has too many of them to report them right away. But someone at the White House was rumored to have died from UC and President Trish had been terrified he might have picked up the fatal It from being anywhere near him (like his son). So Code 45, Section IX, Subheading Q-23—known as Q-23—was drafted, submitted, passed in committee and on the floor, and put into effect so fast you would have thought the life and salvation of the entire universe depended on it. These guys always think everything can be changed by just passing a new law.

Under Bart Shovels, Q-23 is "firmed up": not reporting a case now is a federal offense. Before it was just another regulation. Now it's a decree.

At the citywide monthly meeting of all doctors treating UC cases (attendance is very slim when everyone knows some sort of shit's about to hit the fan. In this town you can smell shit coming before anyone even farts), Q-23.1 is introduced and everyone sort of titters when Privvy reads it aloud to his staff, raising his voice in trembling emphasis at the part stating that "failure to adhere to these requirements can lead to incarceration."

From Shovels to presidential proclamation to the first arrest doesn't take very long.

Harry Straddler at Montezuma will be the first arrest. Montezuma is this city's main shithole hospital. It's like being thrown into a dungeon. They do so much patching of the already brutalized that there's a permanent bunch of cops on staff. Harry's a good-enough doctor, not the most motivated, but taking care of the entire poor section of the Southwest, as Montezuma has to, must make it pretty hard to stay motivated on a daily basis. You're lucky if you don't succumb to despair and take an overdose or steal some money and run away to an island that doesn't extradite, which acts are also said to now be happening. Because Harry's a joking sort, very happy-go-lucky, and lays a lot of the nurses, who enjoy him just because they don't have to take him any more seriously than he takes himself, he's kept himself going somehow, surrounded by nothing but UC cases as he now is.

Wouldn't you know it, Dr. Donnston Privvy from downtown HQ is doing a look-see at Montezuma with yours truly and Senator Perz from the Subcommittee on Disease escorting a bunch of ladies from some Hispanic charity that pretends to look after the indigent and the near-dead (at Montezuma one and the same—Death stalks these corridors like reruns of Desi and Lucy on the ward TVs). A set of quints is about to be born, which is big news any day, and Donny hears the buzz and troops us all off to take a look at the cute tots-to-be. In the space of the twenty minutes or so that Donny is gowning and masking himself and his excited and similarly attired entourage before being admitted to Operating Room 12, where Harry's preparing to birth the babies, the Hispanic mama-to-be, an illegal alien, pregnant with those quintuplets, right here in the corridor on an approaching gurney, pops out three dead and two diseased wretched bambini and then pops off herself.

The cause of death is listed as UC (it could just as easily have been listed as childbirth) on a chart signed by the Montezuma joke doctor, one E. A. Poe, a name used by any and all when no one wants to take the rap and/ or no one knows who the hell the deceased is and/or how in hell to find out (this happens a lot at Montezuma, where patients just show up without ID, without money, not speaking English, with nada but their dying bodies), and ordinarily that would be the end of that. Senorita goes steerage to the morgue, and the infected twins, lucky girls, get to go and join a few hundred other foundering foundlings in the subbasement of Building G, all fighting for the same stingy tin cup of the milk of human kindness that might keep them alive past tomorrow.

Donny Privvy, a born-again, and also a member of the President's Committee for the Forging of Family Values (FFV), notices while perusing her file that the mother was not married. He hates it that our government's money is used to help these people. He notices that the admitting doctor was a Harry Straddler. Why is he even letting these people in the door? When Donny asks for some kind of explanation, he's informed by the chief nurse, a Ten-ton Tessie who happens to be male and still makes passes at me, that if he bothered to hang around here for any length of time, he'd be told "Death by UC" for just about everything. Donny Privvy looks at Senator Perz. "If she hadn't had UC, those poor five babies would be alive today."

Senator Perz, of course, is from Florida, where he represents a lot of Cubans. The Hispanic ladies cluck their hypocritical agreement: every one of them has at least six UC deaths among their own familia but no one is talking plain English.

The Dr. E. A. Poe who'd just signed the death certificate was a staff pathologist who did his training in mainland China and pretends not to speak much English because it's safer that way (and who was once my student). He is routinely wearing rubber gloves, which make it harder for him to fill out the forms, but fill them out he did, putting in UC as the cause of death over the signature "E. A. Poe, M.D." Having written down the truth, and hating himself for it, Dr. Poe wants out as fast as possible. In fact, Dr. Poe is so nervous, with Donnston and Perz and the Hispanic harpies, masked and gowned as they all are, breathing down his neck, that rushing off he accidentally kicks over the pail with the stillborn triplets (I told you this place was awful) and they spill over the floor and onto one of the committeewomen's open-toed pumps. She screams, then vomits, then shakes convulsively, emitting incomprehensible curses in torrential shrieks that are presumably meant to scare away the evil spirit and that reverberate down the long corridors so piercingly that all the Hispanic staff and patients on the floor rush into the corridor, crossing themselves in terror. Confronted by such an audience and having stepped out of her vomit-encrusted shoes, she stands tall as best she can and demands, in the name of all her people, action, recompense, and vengeance, though she would be hard-pressed to tell you what she considers the crime. She then threatens to call Manute Zapata Geraldo, the host of a Spanish-language afternoon talk show, who specializes in stories about dead babies of color spilling out of white men's baskets.

Privvy rushes back to UC Central and calls his new buddy, some new assistant surgeon general, that woman whose name no one ever can remember except that she's Hispanic too, and when she speaks in public, which her handlers try to prevent, she sounds like Carmen Miranda (if anyone remembers Carmen Miranda). She then immediately gets on her intercom to the nearest secretary of something (another incompetent idiot also with a name no one remembers, but who is unfortunately—in that it makes it impossible to criticize him without being called a racist—black), who brings it up at the daily cabinet meeting, which I've been monitoring.

President Trish is late, so an assistant secretary of defense, who once served under Ruester, regales everyone with anecdotes about how Peter would often spend entire cabinet meetings dispensing anecdotes about every TV episode he ever starred in that dealt with childbirth, replete with details of what was used for fake blood and birthing babies. Over the years this ran the gamut from diluted raspberry jam, seeded so it looked like bits of flesh, to watered-down ketchup, used in conjunction with everything from baby dolls to kitty cats in infant costumes. Peter told a particularly juicy story about some actress, most desirous of winning an Emmy, who stuffed a live kitten into a rubber baby and then inserted all this into her particularly wide vagina to "make it look real." "And she won her Emmy!" the Ruester would howl and cackle, slapping his huge gnarled palm down on a cabinet table that was once touched by the likes of Lincoln. It's evidently still a favorite story heard around here. Trish arrives just as everyone is roaring with laughter about Peter. When he realizes he's less loved, Dredd gets that icy-bitch look on his face like a weenie ignored in prep school circle jerk-offs after lights out who remembers it until he dies.

"I've been told that a case of UC has gone unreported," he says quietly.

"And you are required by law to pay attention to this," says his sinister creep of an assistant, Bart Shovels, to another assistant secretary of somewhere.

"Attention must be paid," says another asshole from HAH, an old theatergoer just rushing in.

So Harry's arrest and imprisonment are announced, complete with a picture from his medical school yearbook twenty years ago, and with a bold headline on page one that includes the words *criminal* and *Fort Leavenworth*, in both *The Monument* and *The Federal Daily Posture*. Suddenly doctors are calling each other all over the place. Can you believe this! Holy shit! I'm moving to Brazil. Stuff like that. Every UC doctor in town is guilty of the same thing. They all have unreported UC cases, drawers full of them, file boxes, enough unreported UC cases that, if shredded, would clog every toilet in the city. Often these cases are private cases, many of them well-known people—we're talking major celebs and politicos—certainly more problematic to report than an impoverished woman in the charity ward of Montezuma, although Montezuma is more or less *all* charity ward. I recently did a grand rounds there. It's truly close to hell.

And that's how Dr. Harry Straddler winds up in Leavenworth. I've discovered, when you get right down to it, that all stories in Washington are long, and just as innocuous on the surface and putrid underneath. Within two days (can't the White House work fast when it wants to?), Harry has lost his staff position at Montezuma, his associate professorship of indigent medicine at G.W., and is transferred from the 27th precinct (near Montezuma) to the 207th precinct (near Denver), where he now awaits "a trial by his peers." Like I was, Harry is a fucking PHS officer, which puts him not under the regular laws of our country but under those of our armed forces, which means Denver is one step toward the maximum: twenty years hard labor.

Thea Template, now more conservative than Herbert Hoover, has long ago forgotten that (1) her father, Eugene, started *The Monument* to be the liberal conscience of this city; and (2) people often get caught up in tragic happenings beyond their control, as witness the suicide, in despair, of her own husband. So *The Monument* didn't write about Harry Straddler being charged, Harry Straddler being imprisoned, Harry Straddler being court-martialed. Or Harry Straddler committing suicide. Or Harry Straddler leading to a possible national quarantine. Daniel says Thea was a member of the Jew Tank for a while. One day she stopped coming. The girls there broke the news. "Haven't you heard, Thea's become an Episcopalian."

But *The Monument* does report that the secretary of Health and Happiness goes on prime time and tells The American People that this "new" national health emergency requires stringent precautions of the most severe sort, and to this end Q-23.1 is only the first step in "bringing to justice those who bring disgrace and shame to the best health-care system in the free world." Since someone had thoughtfully seen to it that a TV was installed in Harry's cell, it was while watching this announcement that Harry checked himself out.

As if to tie everything together without you noticing, Dredd also announced via Bart Shovels, and Thea did report, that an additional bill was sent up to the Hill that can send you to prison for life for having unprotected sex. Dredd and Vurd and Bart and others think it's important to nip this UC in the bud. Gay and FUQU activists somehow manage to get this law overruled, not knowing that Dredd's got old CIA buddies at work to nip their own growing power in the bud (which is of special interest to Mother).

An obituary appears in *Government Workers Daily*, including the suicide. I call Donnston Privvy. I've neglected to mention that he'd come to me years ago to "quietly" cure a bad case of the clap he claimed he'd picked up from some portable toilet on a top-secret assignment in some jungle, a popular excuse in Washington government circles. His wife and I had been on a community panel for making our neighborhood playgrounds safe, and she'd remarked to him what a "particularly sensitive" man she'd thought me to be. He came to me for quite a number of other jungle problems over the years. So much for fucking family values (FFV). For a weenie he had a huge wiener, and I was sort of glad he was sticking it in more places than a look at his face led you to believe.

I called him.

"Donny, why did you have to make such an example out of Harry Straddler?"

"The president."

That's a sentence in Washington. A verb or modifiers aren't required.

"And you'll never guess what's next." Donnston talks like a prissy old lady.

"What's next?"

Washington is filled with Privvys—old sucked-out sponges that you would swear are gay but aren't, just repressed pulped tomatoes with caved-in cheeks and colorless hair and balls you just know are sweating. God knows what he does to women in bed. I can't even imagine.

"I've been asked by Representative Bob Barrett to commence a study, preparatory to his submitting a full recommendation, on"—he whispers the word—"quarantine."

"Quarantining whom for what?" I know what he'll answer. Every UC doctor in America has been waiting for another reign of horror to descend.

"UC doctors and UC cases and those who have come in contact with them."

"That sort of includes a growing chunk of the population of . . ."

"I'm afraid so."

Then I say it the way Peter Ruester and Dredd Trish always say it: ". . . of The American People."

"That's going a bit too far."

"Isn't it a wee bit late?"

"Better safe than sorry."

"You got room for all of us somewhere?"

"You don't see . . . *them?*"

"Donny, it's a jungle out there."

He coughs.

"You'll have to test every person in America."

"The president." He coughs again.

"They'll have to go through every doctor's office and patient's file in America."

He coughs yet again.

"It will cost a fucking fortune."

He whispers. "The president." He coughs again. In fact, he's now wheezing.

"Isn't it a bit impractical to quarantine so many millions of people?"

"The president." The wheeze.

"And expensive?"

"The president." The wheeze, followed by the cough.

"Does everyone get their own private room?"

"The president." Ditto.

"And bath? These guys need their own private bath."

"The president." Ditto.

"Or else they contage."

"The president." Ditto, yet again. His whisper is now almost inaudible.

"I'd watch that cough if I were you. Maybe you'd better come in for a checkup."

Thank God he finally hangs up.

This story *The Washington Monument* does run. "PRESIDENT RE-QUESTS REPORT ON QUARANTINE POSSIBILITY." Every doctor's suddenly got the runs. Passports everywhere are checked, as are liquid assets. Countries are double-checked to see if they still let Americans in. And *The Monument* says more than half of D.C. doctors have never seen a UC case. Thea, baby, listen up: *Every* doctor has seen UC. Even yours. Even your dead husband's.

Have you registered all this, Fred?

Mother told me he was very pleased with this information. He asked me, "What do you think this is all the cover-up for? Who are the persons moving the pawns? Find out and let me know."

EXECUTION OF A MURDERER

I murder him. My luck, he's in the men's room in Punic Center. I realize the outside foyers are empty. Even the guards went into the main hall. Everyone is rushing to get seats to listen to Dye's replacement. I realize there's no one in here with us.

I come and pretend to pee in the urinal next to Dr. Donnston Privvy.

He thinks I'm reaching for his cock and he wants it. He uses his hand to help me yank it out.

Noxotrane. A little pinprick.

He's dead on the floor. Noxotrane works that fast. I'd written this note in forced handwriting:

This pervert was murdered by all who are violently opposed to any form of quarantine. When compassion returns, all murders will cease.

I put the note over his exposed genitals, still leaking piss.

I get out of the men's room and out through a side entrance without being seen.

It is morning again in America.

DANIEL THE SPY

Half our patients receiving ZAP need transfusions. Patients again stop taking the drug or start fiddling with the dosage. "You must carry on! This is routine stuff we must get past! Otherwise I will not learn anything!" Dash is now over the top in his anger, protecting "my baby." "You must provide me with an obedient patient population! Where are your fucking PIs?" He is yelling this at Jerry, who certainly doesn't know where his fucking PIs are. He does know he can't change any of the FADS regulations governing patient enrollments. These FADS rules are prehistoric, the worst ones from the Kefauver-thalidomide era, which are rigid and specific, "iron corsets" they're called. They are meant to protect patients.

On another front, Shovels has Nostrill notify all blood organizations and hospitals receiving government money to destroy all their records from the years when Dodo's blood test was so flawed. How does Shovels even know about any of this? I ask Jerry, who's been going to the White House. "How should I know?"

Deep Throat says to me, "Omicidio as usual is an idiot who must be replaced." He's never been so precise in his condemnation before. "But," he added, "he never will be."

DEEP THROAT

I continued to try and impress on Mother my condemnation of what's going wrong. He reminded me that his CIA position does not allow him to operate effectively in America. He can only freely manipulate foreign affairs. I had forgotten that. "That's why I have operatives like you to keep me up to date."

And then he added with a twinkle in his eyes, "And that's how I manipulate in America."

SCENE FROM OUR PASSING PARADE

DEEP THROAT: There's been a suicide at NITS. A note was found. "I am not smart enough. Perhaps my suicide will help pressure someone somewhere to press for progress against this plague." Of course this is all hushed up along with Donnston Privvy. When I try to discuss this with Jerry I'm told it's all a fiction. "But I saw the note," I protest. "This guy who killed himself, Jim D'Estes, sent me a copy." D'Estes had been one of my pathology team.

•

CLAUDETTE: Spud and I traced the recent grant recipients at NITS, and Jerry's name is listed on all of them as "Primary Recipient." So he's got money and he's not spending it, or telling anyone about it.

•

FRED: Scotty and Sparks and Ken and Marshall and Stella and Dobbson and Lee and Donald and Perry and Tommy and I and a half-dozen others are invited to lunch by Bumstead. We go with great optimism that they at last have news about DID, the drug that T and D and Levi Narkey have been following. Some of our guys always look like they could use the free food. I hope their scientists are noticing how wasted they look.

•

INT. HOTEL MEETING ROOM. DAY.
FUQU members are seated eating with representatives of Bumstead.
A huge buffet table laden with food. Banner with BUMSTEAD BMS
PHARMACEUTICALS on it. Fred is talking to their Dr. Su. Tommy is with
them.
TOMMY *(to a doctor next to him)*: Why is Dr. Su shaking?
BMS DOCTOR: He is afraid of Mr. Lemish.
FRED: Dr. Su, you asked us to lunch. What's the good news? You're
　　finally announcing a release date for DID? Great!
DR. SU: We are here to apologize. We are not ready to release the
　　drug at this time.

FRED: But we don't have time. When?

DR. SU: Perhaps . . . perhaps next year.

FRED: But your boss promised us!

DOBBSON: Yeah, you promised us!

Dobbson, who has heard all this, stands up and starts to overturn the long buffet table loaded with food. The other members join the action. When it is all on the floor, they start chanting: FUQU fight back fight UC, as they rush out of the private dining room and into the street, still chanting. Tommy and Fred smile.

EXT. STREET. DAY.

The group runs into the street, cheering each other for their success.

EXT. TOMPKINS SQUARE FOUNTAIN. NIGHT.

Handsome men are cavorting naked and in celebration of their successful little action.

RON, ADAM, AND OTHERS: Fuck You, Bowel-Muck-Shit! FUQU says, Fuck You!

FRED'S VOICE-OVER: They were the best-looking guys we had. Most of them will be dead in a year.

MINNA TROOBLE: Dredd Trish fires COD's Dr. Perseus Wine-apple for supporting abortion and stem cell research into your UC virus.

FRED: *The New York Truth* and its Science Department don't deign to write about this.

FIGHTS ON OUR HOME FRONT

There were two fights on the floor tonight. Little ones. All between women and men. One between Maxine and Scotty about his meeting with pharmas without the permission of the floor. She'd heard about it from Claudette, who'd accompanied Scotty to a few of them. The other was between some-one named Harriett and Sparks about his doing the same. She'd heard about it from someone she knew at Presidium. In each case all parties were defen-sive, felt they had been "needlessly and cruelly" "attacked," "maligned," and "violated." None of them wanted the floor to vote on "decisions we are going to have to face sooner or later," according to yours truly, who weighed in on the matter, trying not to favor either side but asking for a calm discussion. Barry from T+D came over to me after. "Who the fuck are you, Fred?" he asked me. "I thought you were our leader. Why aren't you on our side? My side is your side, you know. I'm fighting to save your life as well as mine."

OUT WITH THE OLD?

On November 7 a black man, David Dinkins, becomes New York's mayor, replacing the hateful Kermit Goins. The hateful Dr. Elliott Garbantz is replaced as commissioner of health by some Midwestern bozo doctor whose first announcement is his plan to quarantine all the UC-infected. Activists unite as if our lives depend on it, which they do, and Dr. Bozo doesn't stand a chance. Is it not a note of interest how health commissioners, here, there, everywhere, always seem to be so second-rate and disappear into the mist of historical irrelevancy? I can't even remember this one's name.

VITAL STATISTICS

COD estimates that one in four young men in New York City are now infected with UC.

•

Only one in four? Is Mr. COD on my side? He certainly isn't telling you the truth about me.

"I THINK WE MUST LOOK UPON THESE STATISTICS AS A GIFT"

writes Rigard Noyes, Ph.D. Div., president and minister of Chicago's God Assembled Church in *American Focus on Families Newsletter.* "I think we must look upon these numbers as a gift from God. He has heard our prayers and imprecations to expunge from sight these heathens who have embarrassed us for so many centuries. If we don't get rid of them now there will be more of them than there are of us."

THE SECOND (OR IS IT THE THIRD) PRESIDENTIAL COMMISSION ON UC . . .

. . . issues a second (or is it the third?) hideous report: "This epidemic is like an orchestra without a conductor." Bart Shovels from the White House angrily defends it. "That we need a national plan is not to the point. Our plan always is to act. This administration is taking actions."

•

FRED: *The New York Truth* and its Science Department don't deign to write about this report, either. Velma Dimley is now their "official" reporter on UC. Dearie Fault has retired.

DREDD TRISH TELLS THE AMERICAN PEOPLE ON *SIXTY MINUTES*

"I wish somebody could convince me that if you could only spend a quarter of a billion dollars more, we would have the answer. I must say some of the excesses of those groups who shout so much do not help their cause. We had a lot of mail saying people are quite embarrassed by that."

TAKE THIS, YOU GROUP WHO SHOUT SO MUCH

Dr. Marie Clayture of FADS announces that all UC meds in development by every pharmaceutical company except Greeting-Dridge have been denied approval. "They just haven't provided us with sufficient data," she's quoted in a FADS press release. G-D's data on ZAP is considered sufficient?

•

FRED: *The New York Truth* and Velma Dimley don't deign to write about this, too.

•

BIG FUQU POSTER:
THE WHITE HOUSE WANTS YOU DEAD!

MORE PUBLICITY

John Leo, in *U.S. News and World Report*, describes FUQU as "the No. 1 loose cannon of local politics, now powerful and feared . . . 'Brownshirts' (à la Mussolini). Support for the dignity and freedom of gays does not automatically mean overlooking the threat to our freedom by gangster groups such as FUQU." Ray Kerrison's column in the *New York Post*: ". . . while reserving for themselves the right to use any defamation, insult, outrage, ridicule, or mockery . . ." Paula Span in *The Washington Monument*: ". . . disrupting meetings to scream at public officials, pelting opponents with condoms . . . leaving the chalked outlines of bodies on sidewalks and streets, plastering cities with 'bloody' red handprints, employing the whole panoply of loud and sometime illegal protest . . ."

Fred loves it all!

DAVID'S BACK

I was being followed. I recognized the feeling. Fear. I think this time it started with reading about the head chopping in Idaho at a place called the Kursie Foundation, a division of Partekla. I discover this by reading a British newspaper, about a scientist at Oxford who has uncovered this atrocity, "perpetuated as part of America's ongoing trials into germ warfare." Patients had been fed a drug to erase memories and feelings. It was a crystal meth developed by Hitler so his soldiers could win the war. It was developed by Dr. Muck and by Mr. Bayer, the same man who gave us aspirin. It brought back memories of what might have been done to me at Partekla, to me and my back. No wonder I had no memory of that. All I remember was an extreme euphoria. I had never felt so good. To read that now this crystal meth is being snorted by gays in America, "of a strength stronger than that used by Hitler," brings tears to my eyes.

Who do I think is following me now? I am getting very frightened.

What were they trying to learn from my back? Was it to see how much pain I could endure?

$$$SCOTTY$$$

I arrange the first FUQU Art Auction. I know a little bit about this world. My folks are collectors and benefactors of the Met. So I know how to get to prospective purchasers to both give and show up. I got stuff by David Hockney, Keith Haring, Annie Liebowitz, Andy Warhol, Julian Schnabel. I made us $500,000.

I wish I could say I heard any gratitude from the floor. To most of this group I'm the rich kid who takes cute members out on his brother's yacht. It even takes a while for me to find a boyfriend. I sure like to have a boyfriend to cuddle with and watch TV. Fred had fixed me up with cute Kevin, who actually wanted to meet me. Once again the big problem is that we both are bottoms! Working night and day on Wall Street, I'd not had much experience in the gay world. I never thought something like that would be a problem!

Oh, well. At least I got all of us a big wadge of cash to fight with. I just wish somebody had said, Thank you, Scotty, you did good.

A number of the pharm reps I invited came to the auction and a few even bought some stuff!

•

INT. BLOOMINGDALE'S. DAY.
Fred, Tommy, Mario, Moses, Spencer, Gerri, Maxine, Photis, Dobbson—all wearing SILENCE = DEATH *T-shirts—are covertly putting small stickers on various items of merchandise, including mattresses and expensive dresses. The stickers read:* VELMA DIMLEY OF THE NEW YORK TRUTH *IS THE WORST UC REPORTER IN THE WORLD.*
GERRI *(smacking down a sticker)*: And this is for my brother Terry, who died two weeks ago. *(Another smack of a sticker.)* From ZAP.
MARIO *(speedily smacking down one sticker after another)*: Best results come when you're less cautious.
A guard is heading toward them. They disperse in all directions.

EXT. *NEW YORK TRUTH* BUILDING. NIGHT.
Fred and Tommy and Perry are plastering the stickers on the building.
FRED: For Felix.
TOMMY: For my Bro.

PERRY: For Francis. *(To Fred:)* How are you feeling?
FRED: Fine.
PERRY: You don't look fine.

TONY'S LOVELY WOMEN

Around Manhattan perhaps ten, perhaps twenty-five, there is no way of telling, affinity groups of FUQU are meeting and executing awkward, obnoxious, disruptive, probably even illegal zaps to bring "uncomfortable attention to our hideous situation as total outcasts from our country's health-care system," as Tony S. liked to say, *total* being a favorite word of his, as in "total all-out war," and everyone knows what he means, in feeling if not specifics. That is one of the things about FUQU: we sit around brainstorming total feelings until total specifics eventually emerge. It is totally amazing, how well it works.

Tony S's group, Tony's Lovely Women, because he is the only male in the group, go to Bergdorf's, where the dozen women all try on very expensive designer dresses and pin to their innards notes that say things like, "Your son or husband could be infected with UC and you don't know it. FUQU." In *Women's Wear Daily*, Gretchen Himmelstein, the chief buyer, estimates that "over $500,000 of our most precious garments have been damaged." When Tony S. dies, his twelve lovelies won't let anyone else touch him. They bathe him and wrap him in a shroud of $500-a-yard Scalamandre silk from Brunschwig et Fils and take his body all beribboned with their sashes and tassels, also purloined by members who worked there, and in the middle of the night deliver it to Mrs. Jacqueline Kennedy on Fifth Avenue, with a note, "Please help us! Oh you who should have been mother of us all. Love from Fed Up Queers United." Tony S. had adored Jackie. The women stand vigil by the coffin outside her apartment building. The police would take it away but Jackie hears about it and insists that Tony be given a proper cremation, which she pays for. We are told his ashes were scattered in the ocean at her home in Martha's Vineyard. The twelve Lovely Women write a letter of "deep thanks and reverence," and Jackie acknowledges "your sadness, which I understand."

No media outlet picked up this "human interest" story.

How can it not occur to me more and more that we're not *really* getting anywhere!

HOORAY FOR HOLLYWOOD!

I am back in L.A. finishing yet another draft for Adreena in her very ultra-elaborate new Malibu estate. The woman has enough money to personally finance "our" film a thousand times over. She keeps telling me that all the studios have turned her down. "I couldn't do that," she responds to my repeated possible solution of financing it herself. "They must fight over me to get me. I need to be wanted." We've just had another fight over showing two men in love with each other having sex. "I couldn't do that either," she said, making that face again to convey her disgust at the very notion. What is it about this town? It doesn't seem to have changed much since Rust Legend and his tales about Jack Warner murdering James Dean.

In one of Adreena's many *many* toilets I find a copy of the current issue of *Sexopolis*. Dorita Helen Schwartz is advising "more than ever we must blaze new pathways in this increasingly complicated world." What the fuck does that mean? She certainly isn't talking about safe sex or mandating condoms. Mordy himself has grown into an international icon, always pictured, as here in my hands, with several big-breasted sexmates draping from him as they overlook madcap celebrations of the only partially clad. Doesn't he ever wear anything besides pajamas? This month's spread is of some holiday celebration at his new L.A. Sexopolis Palace, displaying "another of our vivid demonstrations of healthy heterosexual desire and lust and *possibility*." It's all decorated to a high pitch of excess, like Adreena's but without her better taste. It's obvious that his enormous readership has yet to detumesce. His sales figures certainly bear this out.

I decided to try to talk to him. He was a few years older, so I didn't play with him much growing up. When I tried to tag along with the older boys on one of their escapades I'd get shooed home. Once Grace Hooker babysat the three of us, Daniel, Mordy, and me, and took us all to the zoo. Also, Daniel had filled me in a bit about their own tortured interactions. In any event, it was time to talk to him and I wonder why it hadn't occurred to me before. So I leave a message at the magazine's office that "Fred Lemish of Masturbov Gardens would appreciate a return call at my hotel." Within hours a messenger delivers an invitation for me to come to a party this very evening.

Mordy greets me immediately, even kissing my cheeks in that effusive California fashion.

"So this is the famous Fred Lemish, loudmouthed gay and UC activist troublemaker."

"So this is the famous Mordecai Masturbov, head of the *Sexopolis* empire."

"Yes, I remember you from Masturbov Gardens."

"You are familiar with FUQU?"

He laughed and then I for some reason followed suit.

"Some of my girls think you're a very adventurous band. Like Robin Hood. I'm quite amazed that you and your merry band haven't picketed *Sexopolis*."

"We've been considering it, now that we have an L.A. chapter. I thought I'd talk with you first."

"I am relieved," Mordy says.

"Don't be. I believe that what you're doing is wrong and what you've done is wrong and what you've created in this world is very wrong."

"How so?"

"You have changed the morality of this country. That change has helped to violently overhaul the way Americans have sex and hence infect each other without responsibility. I've actually written an article about how Mordecai Masturbov is as much to blame for the cause and spread of The Underlying Condition as anyone in the world."

"I must have missed that. Where is Daniel Jerusalem?" Mordy suddenly asks.

"Daniel is a doctor in Washington, working at NITS, on UC clinical trials, for Omicidio," Fred answers.

"For Omicidio?" Mordy is impressed. "I saw this documentary about him on PBS. Daniel must be a very smart doctor, then."

"Omicidio is an evil prick."

"Ah, that I didn't know. He appears on TV so often. Here we think of NITS as Lourdes. I have my girls tested regularly."

I am older by the day, Fred thinks, much older than even one more yesterday would allow, and I am getting nowhere, while this man has conquered the world that he wished to conquer, and in so doing he's changed it.

"We should have been lovers," Fred says. "Daniel and I. We still should be."

"Then why aren't you?"

Fred shrugs. "The way of the world."

Mordy nods.

"You must help us now that you have made so much money from us," Fred says.

"Who is 'us' and why have I made money 'from' you? I don't like the language you use," Mordy says.

"Why do you, how can you, put out this stuff? Are you really interested in it at all?"

"Of course I am. I describe myself as a hopeless romantic looking for the perfect woman, which of course I know doesn't exist. I love to remind my readers how many beautiful women I've 'dated.' I try to be their role model. It makes me feel desired. I like the drama. It's a game. No different from betting on a stock or a horse. I bet on appetites being awakened because I couldn't get a hard-on much as a kid. Daniel will tell you that. I still can't much. My magazine is filled with articles of advice for people like me. I felt deprived. You would too if you couldn't have all the hot men you must have access to."

"I scare everyone away."

"Well, same here. All these beauties around me want something from me. That I will make them a star. When I was a kid it was just my father's fortune that scared people. I've thought about this from every angle, and I'm bored with the subject. Maybe this UC shit reflects that, reflects how people so don't care about the seriousness of sex that sex is striking back. Do me right or I'll punish you, it seems to be saying. Doing it right should of course entail love. *That* we don't write about. Anyway, it's thoughts like this that go through my head. What about you? Why do you care so much?"

"Don't you know anyone who's died?"

"No. Not that I know of. I don't have many friends."

"I find that hard to believe."

"I parade all my girls around to make it look like . . . That I'm busy. That I'm a stud. That I'm the role model for each average reader I send each issue to. I read every word. I write most of them."

"Haven't you ever been in love?"

"I started all this when I was . . . I never went to college. I thought I fell in love with . . . Do you remember Claudia Webb? But she went to work for my mother. You know about my mother?"

"Yes."

"Then I fell in love with Velvalee Peltz. She wouldn't give me the time of day. I made an asshole of myself over Velvalee Peltz for many years. Do you remember Arnold Botts?"

"The schmuck."

"I spent a lot of money suing him for trying to take Velvalee away from me. In the end the judge ruled I had to pay him a great deal of money. It's the last legal fight that I've lost."

"You must have a very good lawyer."

"Sam Sport. You must have heard of him."

"Millions of people are dying because you're helping them to fuck themselves to death. You're worse than I thought. I'm sorry."

"I married Jinx Seeley, one of my mother's girls. We watch a lot of old movies. We both love old Hollywood movies. Black and white. That's my sex life."

"Can you imagine Velvalee being dead from some dread disease?"

"She is dead."

"Most of my friends are dead. I read the columns you wrote about Korah Ludens. She's a big deal. I read her book about the neurotic personality. I think I underlined every sentence in it."

"She said I'm an asshole, wasting my time."

"Well, don't you have enough money to do whatever you want?"

"Yes, I do. I am doing what I want. What would you like me to do with it?"

"Would you do something substantive to help end this plague? That's what I want. More and more women are coming down with UC. That's why I'm here. I thought I could shock you into it, shame you."

"How can I help?"

"You want your sex lives back, then we have to end this plague. It's spreading all over the world. To both sexes and all colors. Go after the government, the evil Omicidio. Shame Trish for NITS dragging its ass. Coming from you, that would be a big deal. People would listen. They wouldn't expect it, coming from you. Korah Ludens would be proud of you. Could you do this? Any of this?"

"Of course not."

"It's the least you could do."

"After all I've done. There you go again."

"Yes."

"But I don't think I did anything bad or wrong or causative. My mother told me men just have to fuck. People do what people do, with or without *Sexopolis*."

"That's not true."

"No? This plague, as you call it, would have happened no matter what. It was only a question of when, where, and how. Like the Roman Empire had to fall. It's common sense. The human body can only take so much."

"How can you say that?"

"Because *Sexopolis* continues to grow and flourish."

"You realize this and yet you perpetuate it?"

"I'm not responsible for what mankind chooses to do."

"But I tell you that you are! And what you're doing is evil."

"There you go with that word again. You seem to throw it around like Silly Putty, hoping it will stick against the wall. Give my regards to Daniel. What I did with him was quite . . . precocious. Come, let me show you around."

For a gay man the Sexopolis Palace is quite preposterous. Many dozens of naked, very blond girls, huge boobs, shaved vaginas, nose jobs, all parading around looking for a husband among the throngs of B-list celebrities. It sort of reminds me of Fire Island. I talked to some of them. Some were quite intelligent. Many come from lives they were desperate to escape. Each has to sleep with Mordy at one time or another. As he comes really quickly, it's not that much of an ordeal. "It comes with the territory," I hear from many of them. They're all afraid of him. He punishes them if they get out of line. There are many rules to abide by. "But in the end it's very boring," one of them said. "There's nothing else to do here but wait to see if he'll choose you for a Sexopolis Girl photo layout. I'll probably be grilled for talking to you for so long. There's always a girl who will tattle. I'm up for a TV show about us. Wish me luck so I can get out of here. You seem real nice. Too bad you're a fairy."

Sexopolis will mount a huge campaign. "Let Us Dream for You!" Whatever that's meant to mean. It's a big success. New subscribers galore.

Mordy, Adreena, Rust Legend, Randy Dildough, Sammy Sircus, Jack Warner getting rid of James Dean: this town's constipated with a bunch of not very helpful people.

So it's back to New York and our plague and our continuing FUQU.

ONCE MORE INTO THE BREACH

And in Idaho, that blessed state of beauty, who meets there now in the vicinity of David's first American incarceration? And what is this convention of people, all wearing masks and hoods, their bodies and faces shielded from sight and view? They are of course Furstwasserians, Klansmen, Black Nights, Adelphia Warriors, Stalwart Children of God, Lionhearts, Holy Nation of Yahweh, Alliance of Supreme Whiteness, and others, so many others, newer names from newer corners of our land, all now growing together into this monumental group, their membership increaseth a thousand thousand-fold since that very first Herod not so long ago. Each week another group arrives to settle in. Each day more members move here permanently. Hate is even more enshrined here. Encore! Partekla Endures! Partekla Über Alles!

All these people hate us.

FREE GIVEAWAYS

Continuing a tradition begun in postwar Washington, flyers covered with the names of specific targets of this week's hate are distributed in the cafeterias of all government buildings. After the war it was "the commies" who were exposed, followed shortly by "the fairies." Soon the fairies took precedence, Communists having lost favor. Your historian apologizes for neglecting to keep you up to date on all these perambulations of enemies and hate. Just know that once a week, in every government cafeteria, lists of names are handed out by men in black suits and ties. These are Brinestalker men. Minna Trooble occasionally passes along to Fred "confidential" reports about "The Comings and Goings of Government Employees" put out by a new Shovels front, the Personnel Tracking Division of the Government Services Administration. "It never stops—these lists," she tells him, "immediately followed by the departure of a noticeable number of male employees, many in important positions. I wager there are very few homosexuals in government employment by now, after all these giveaway lists."

DR. SALK CALLS UC
"THE METAPHORIC DISEASE OF OUR TIME"

"I see people acting like retroviruses. You might think of the regulatory system as being overly protective and becoming the equivalent of an autoimmune disease." What is this once-great man talking about? He said he could do it a second time, rid the world of a scourge. He presents his theory at a conference where he's the surprise guest speaker, all eyes on him. But his theory of the cause of UC has feet of clay and facts of sand. His experiments can't be replicated by others. No one has the heart to tell him. Sad. Sad man. Sad end. Like Bosco's. Everything is so fucking sad.

SO WHAT ELSE IS NEW?

DANIEL THE SPY: Even more lawyers! Most insulting to the French is that the American patent office officially acknowledged Dodo's patent for his blood test and ignored Bordeaux, Nappe, Françoise, et al. When they complained by pointing out that their own application for Jacquie's test was submitted some three years ago, the patent office discovered that the French application indeed had been on someone's desk since its receipt. The French *finally* get really angry. The fight long squelched in French hearts is now beginning to erupt. Now so many new lawyers are turning up here that it's impossible to remember not only who's representing who but also for what, i.e., which part of which suit and countersuit. Ironically, both Jacquie's test and Dodo's test are manufactured by Audacia, the former by their French subsidiary. Lawyers for each are running around here. There appears to be bad blood between Audacia France and Audacia USA. To even suggest we use the "already accepted and approved" French test available out of Quebec, instead of the "new and improved" Dodo test, which we still know is neither, is tantamount to being an everywhichway kind of traitor. Jerry isn't interested in this issue. "This is Dodo's ball game," he tells me.

•

DUDLEY: Gretta Lell is the ZAP queen. She's one of Jerry's PIs. She's partnered on the biggest ZAP study with that big hunk from San Francisco . . . Obernought. She has a big gay practice in Miami. Jerry keeps funding more studies of ZAP. Why? Well, a lot of times someone would do a study because they needed to eat. Which is pathetic. Or they didn't have anything else to do and didn't want to look like they weren't doing anything. Which is more pathetic.

By now more of the scientists know about FUQU and they agree with what we're doing. FUQU is a good guy to them. We could scream about the study that was getting funded that shouldn't have been, and about the study that deserved to be that wasn't. And we didn't have to worry about stepping on someone's toes because, you know, that's exactly what we wanted to do.

Levi says he'll bet a million dollars Gretta's study will turn out to be full of shit. We won't find out for sure until Berlin.

DEAR PERDITA

Perdita Pugh is rich, old New England rich, Park Avenue rich, always dressed in jewels and designer clothes, her hair famous for its unwavering upsweep, her crowning glory. For some reason, and from its very beginning, UC touches her mightily. She not only joined Tommy at GMPA as a crisis counselor but soon she's in charge of all crisis counseling, devoting more time than most people who work for a living give to their jobs. As more and more of her clients die, her daily schedule now includes longer visits to their bedsides and attendance at their memorials. Though proud, inherently because of her Boston Brahmin background, she is modest and desperately wants to please her world, whatever she thinks it is. Her husband is also rich, though less so. I am in awe of her and she is frightened of me, I suspect because I'm one of those she wants to please but is terrified I might single her out for criticism, which I am now all too famous for providing in print. Perhaps this is too fancy a way of saying I think that anger terrifies her, and that is what I have to offer. Why am I in awe of her? Because I have never known any straight person so committed to helping sick gay people to die. It almost appears a perversion of sorts. GMPA by now has thousands of clients. She knows all the sick ones, most of whose counseling she's supervised, and that is a lot of the dying and the dead. I have no idea what propels her enormous energy for this task. I don't think anyone else does either. I know she's often the butt of jokes as the "Angel of Death." Occasionally I'll run into her in a hospital corridor just coming out of a patient's room. She will have stopped by a wall or a corner, taken out a lovely lace handkerchief, dabbed tears from both of her eyes, blown her nose delicately, tucked the hankie back up a sleeve of Chanel, waved to me with a beaming smile, and carried on on her rounds to other rooms down this very same hall.

Dear Perdita,

We are desperate now. I don't have to tell you how awful everything continues to be. This plague is becoming even more monstrous than all the monstrosities it's showed us so far—and we have both seen many of them, far too many for sane people to witness and endure.

Through these years you have been among the most courageous of all. You joined our fight when few others would. Your courage and your energy and your love have never faltered.

I am asking you—no, I am begging you, to lend your remarkable voice and personality to another challenging task.

The ignoring of this plague at the highest level must simply not be allowed to get any worse. You know, we all know, that no one is in charge.

It is time to use all our energies to pressure the White House and the president for a UC czar. We must at last have someone who is given emergency powers to cut through the red tape and attempt to put some order into dealing with UC.

It is impossible for most of us to get anywhere near the White House. Our voices in Washington are not heard, certainly not to the extent that our enemies, organized into a rigid army, are heard, and unfortunately listened to.

You are a woman of great social prominence. You have grown up in this world of the rich and famous and powerful and you are connected to many who inhabit it at the highest levels. If you don't personally know them, you know people who do. You know how to get to them.

I am begging you to use this power, this power that we don't have. We must start fighting UC in this way—going after the people on top to do their jobs. Could you in any way add this charge as your cause? We need you to do what perhaps is uncomfortable for you, but what you were born to do—use your name and prominence, and gather with you others like you, to get us where we've been unable to go. I think particularly of Joan Table, who is on the GMPA board with you and whose husband is on the president's cabinet and to whom I have written a similar letter.

I know that a desire to help right terrible wrongs is the motivation that drives so many of us in the fight against this awful scourge. But we must look for the ways we can be the most useful, even if those ways are uncomfortable to us. Believe it or not, I do not like my role of angry man or bully, but I discovered early that at least this way my voice gets heard.

Yes, I beg you to try a new role, perhaps one less suited to your personality but not, I hope, to your conscience. That you and your husband come from old American families makes your efforts in the direction I am begging you to aim for a continuing fulfillment of your heritage.

Could I share with you some of my ideas on how to do this?

Yours truly,

Fred

She never responds. Nor does Joan Table.

MICHELANGELO

We'd formed this Outreach Committee. We prepared this program to take to the schools, "What Didn't Your Child Learn in School Today?" *The Truth* hears about it and writes an *editorial* headlined: "Why Make UC Worse Than It Is?"

FRED WRITES ANOTHER LETTER

Dr. Omicidio, what does it feel like to have so many deaths on your hands? What's it like, Dr. Omicidio, when you talk with Gretta Lell, who has many hundreds on hers, and Obernought, with several thousand of his own? Do you all play Can You Top This? I've got more patients than you have! I've killed more people than you have! I've murdered more people than you have!

Dr. Omicidio, tell me what you do all day when you go to your office?

TOMMY REPORTS TO THE GMPA BOARD

You asked me to put down a few words about what I am feeling and seeing.

The sad passion of being around all these young men, each and all of us pining for answers. They want to love each other again. What is love all about now? It's about holding each other in the dark. It's about not being able to get an erection. Or not wanting to get an erection. Or being afraid to get an erection. It's about being afraid to kiss, lest saliva be poison. It's about being afraid to take another's cock in your mouth, or anywhere else. It's about being afraid even to hold someone in your arms. Imagine being afraid of holding someone in your arms.

This is love in the time of plague.

You continue to oppose our taking our struggle to a higher and more public level. We cannot continue to remain so closeted, just holding each other's hands.

We must be stronger than ever.

THE STORMING OF NITS

ANN: To make a long and painful story short, no one came to see us. There was a big fire in downtown D.C. and the media all rushed down there. The best demo we've ever had played to an empty house. Every one of us deserved an Academy Award, for acting, for scene design, for costumes, the nurses and doctors and patients and corpses we portrayed literally littering the pathways with death, with those fucking police horses clumping through us, crapping their shit all over the place. No TV trucks or roving reporters to get all the sound bites I'd taught everyone how to deliver. There wasn't anyone watching us except for some employees looking out their windows. Oh, well. Catherine and Bordo and Jean and Maria and their gang shot tons of footage, and it will wind up in some library, for the future, if we have one.

It was the Big Show that no one came to. Not even Fred, who was in the hospital again. But his friend Daniel, wearing a Dredd Trish mask, came.

Once again Scotty managed to get himself hauled up to the overhang above the entrance and wave our banner, so at least we had a bit of a charge.

•

Piercing sound of an ambulance siren.
INT. HOSPITAL ROOM. DAY.
Emma is in an iron lung. Only her head is completely visible. Her breathing is very strained, and her speech is guttural and filled with pauses and coughs. Buzzy sits with her, not knowing what to say or do. Fred and Tommy are standing beside her.
EMMA: Buzzy, come here.
BUZZY: Yes, ma'am.
He puts his head near hers.
EMMA: I think you may die before I get out of here. Your labs are very bad.
BUZZY: Oh, dear. You not expecting to get out of here?
EMMA: It could be a while. Thank you for everything. You were an excellent assistant.
BUZZY *(he kisses her)*: Thank you, too.
EMMA: This monster contraption was invented in 1927. Would you believe that because of two vacuum cleaners powering it I can breathe?
(Two doctors enter. Her voice becomes sharp and clear as she confronts them.)
I know more about what's happening to me than you do. So go away. When I need you I'll let out a piercing scream. You'll hear me.

(The doctors withdraw. When they leave, her cough and breathing become labored again.)

(To Fred:) Your liver numbers are getting too low. That NITS drug isn't going to save you. You need a new liver. No one's transplanting HIV cases. *(To Tommy:)* You keep an eye on him, you hear? *(She has a coughing fit.)*

BUZZY: She hasn't been in an iron lung since she was thirteen. She's forty-three. She went home to her house on Cape Cod about five or six months later. She was gardening. She loved to garden. She had a stroke and her mom found her sprawled out in her wildflowers. She loved her wildflowers. "They grow good in Cape soil," she said. She left me some money, "So you won't have to go into a nursing home. Stay home as long as you can with Wilber. He won't let you down like some boyfriends do." Trouble is, Wilber died. These two important people in my life, gone. I can't wait. I really can't.

FRED TO FRED

The tidal wave of what T+D is learning and saying and trying to act upon and against is causing internal breakdowns. The women feel left out, sold out while the men go inside to deal with other men at NITS and the pharmas. The women now attack all advances as crumbs from the tables of male power. T+D members are now castigated for having "sold out the ideals of our movement." Calls by Maxine and Harriett and Hettie and Tracy and now a Hester and others on the floor for a "moratorium on 'going inside'" begin to frighten T+D, particularly Sparks and Scotty. People of color likewise begin to feel sold out and enraged. We're not paying sufficient attention to UC among people of color. Once again I see gay people beginning (?), starting again (?), trying (?) to destroy each other. It's heartbreaking to watch, if anyone is even looking at what's really happening. Which right now I wasn't.

And where was I while my organization was beginning to fall apart? As I seemed to be perking along okay and my liver seemed to be holding out, I elected to use my energy for what I thought would be the best use of my time. Nineteen ninety is a year of some acceptance of me by those who had earlier shunned and ignored me as a nutcase. I am increasingly asked to lecture, at places like Amherst, NYU, Yaddah, Oberlin, even Miss Porter's. I give my Student Speech to seventeen different schools. *People* magazine does a spread. I get a few more op-eds published in *The Truth*. I'm now seen, by some, to be right, for a change. I'm trying still to get a film out of Adreena. My book of my reporting is out.

But it's one thing to be right and another thing to force the system to finally do what we're asking. We're still out on our own in the world, and I'd left the kids at home.

And they are falling apart. Or about to.

You could research everything until you are buried in it, and you could talk to everyone still alive, and you would never, could never, get right the history of what's happening right now. Is that the way with all history? Or just the history of wretched events? Which events aren't wretched? No meaningful historical event is not in some part wretched. Hermia certainly bugged me enough about that fact.

When I go back to our meetings I hear the rumblings of approaching disintegration. I try to make nice. I try to get the sides I see forming up to talk to the other sides I see forming up. I recognize the signs of what I am hearing. I have been down this road before. How does one prevent a collision?

As if I could have made a difference. As if I could have put things right.

David will be critical of my inadequate behavior when he finally arrives. Just as Tommy was. And is.

ZIP

PERRY

I am driven in my bewilderment to set down at whatever cost the growing history of this latest drama and my part in it. It's the least I can do for Francis and what Fred is beginning to call "our people."

I am sitting in a corner, taking notes. This group of men are sitting in a private room at the Waldorf. They have completed the launching of Presidium Ltd. on Wall Street. Dr. James Monroe is the big head honcho who called Presidium into being and is the major shareholder. He's meant to be very very rich from developing compounds and licensing them to pharmaceutical companies. A drug Greeting gave to some guy named Arnold Botts has turned out to have worthwhile potency against UC. Dr. Monroe evidently immediately recognized the profitable market for this compound and bought it from G-D, which was busy betting on ZAP.

Arnold Botts is scary. He was vice president of Greeting, where he worked to develop the drug Von Greeting said he acquired from Czechoslovakia. Botts and this Dr. Oderstrasse reformulated it to be fast-tracked as an inhibitor for the treatment of cancers, no mention of UC.

Dr. Schwitz Oderstrasse is Presidium's chief scientist. He was a graduate of the Max Planck Institute in Germany and a staff member of Blood of All Nations, before joining the Partekla Institute in Idaho, where he and Botts tested this Adelphi on patients there. He's scary, too. He then followed up these results with tests in both Germany and the Congo. He believes he has amassed sufficient convincing results to put it into human trials. A controlled clinical trial must somehow commence. FADS regulations of course require it.

Dr. Stuartgene Dye as Presidium's chief scientific adviser urges caution. The good results thus far have been achieved in a hardly kosher fashion. Dr. Dye is now a Nobel Prize winner for his discovery of the primary mechanism for gene eradication and is considered an expert big deal. I don't trust him either. He's the strong silent type. He stares at everyone with piercing eyes.

The co-chairman of Presidium's board is Linus Gobbel, late of the White House, another impressive name to bolster the new company's respectability. "Fuck caution," he says. "We know enough important people to skirt a few rules." Bart Shovels is on the board as well.

This is big-time heavy-hittersville. And they're all in this room.

Dr. James Monroe opens the door to an adjoining room. He looks like some TV star playing the head of the hospital, very trustworthy and noble. Waiting to enter are Scotty and Sparks, and Dr. Levi Narkey.

Monroe addresses his people. "Gentlemen, here is our next step."

Monroe ushers in the T+D group. "Come in, come in."

He then summons in a man pushing a table on which are stacked boxes of drugs.

"We are going to call it ZIP. It will zap the shit out of ZAP. Dr. Narkey will commence to continue your private clinical trial but now using the real McCoy and not your bootleg version. We shall provide our own data. Fuck FADS. In return for our supplying you with ZIP, we shall contribute fifty thousand dollars to your new organization."

He then hands a check to Scotty, who gives it to Sparks.

Scotty says, "We had suggested a larger amount."

Sparks says, "And to be consulted as equal partners in your research and plans for its testing and release."

Dr. Monroe says, "One step at a time. Take it or leave it."

Sparks folds up the check and pockets it.

A CALL TO RIOT

OUT AGE MAGAZINE
BY FRED LEMISH

With this article I am calling for a MASSIVE DISRUPTION of the Sixth International UC Conference that is being held in San Francisco, June 20–24.

Every human being who wants to end the UC epidemic must be in San Francisco, either inside or outside the Moscone Convention Center, or the Marriott Hotel, screaming, yelling, furiously angry, protesting, at this stupid conference.

Dredd Trish has refused to speak at the opening of this conference. Dredd Trish has been a fucking shithead about UC, ignoring it just as much as his doddering, imbecilic predecessor with his Machiavellian wife.

This conference is about as "International" as the Ku Klux Klan. Dredd's government now forbids anyone who has UC or is UC-positive from entering his wonderful country. Dredd is punishing us for having the naughty UC virus in our system.

We are being INTENTIONALLY ALLOWED TO DIE.

HOW MANY TIMES DO WE HAVE TO HEAR THIS BEFORE WE ALL RISE UP AGAINST IT!

THIS GOVERNMENT OF SHITHEADS WANTS US DEAD.

WHY CAN'T EVERY GAY MAN AND LESBIAN GET THAT THROUGH HIS/HER HEAD? DREDD AND TADDY WANT ALL FAGGOTS, NIGGERS, JUNKIES, SPICS, WHORES, UNMARRIEDS, AND THEIR BABIES DEAD.

HOW MUCH MORE EVIDENCE DO WE NEED? WE ARE LINED UP IN FRONT OF A FIRING SQUAD AND WE ARE NOT ALL FIGHTING BACK!

WE MUST RIOT! I AM CALLING FOR A FUCKING RIOT!

We must scream and fight for our research and our cure AND OUR VERY LIVES!

BE THERE!

LEAVE YOUR FARTS IN SAN FRANCISCO!

And this is a shortened version. One way or another my call for a riot is printed everywhere.

That this all coincides with a return of my own body's decline is ironically aggravating.

•

Dr. Gerta Helgobottom at this COD place now says there are fifty thousand cases of me, and Dr. Eugene Madagascar from your Harvard says there will be one billion of me before you know it.

FRED CHICKENS OUT

I didn't go to San Francisco.

I chickened out.

I hadn't given any thought to what I meant by *riot*. Or rather I knew what I meant but what others thought I meant and what the word means were construed very differently by many people. I just wanted a gigantic FUQU disturbance that would not allow the conference meetings to be held in their passive, unquestioning, business-as-usual, uncomplaining, never-ending denial of what was really happening. I didn't mean violence, though I can see where it's possible to read that into my text if you're prone to it, by all means . . .

All hell was breaking loose in San Francisco. This was one time when my hyperbole was taken for fact. San Francisco went nuts. The news programs were filled with stories about what awful things might happen. Police were given extra training. The conference center was cordoned off and security beefed up. Everyone was expecting bombs and guns. They should have known that gay people just don't do that sort of thing. I got so many interview requests that I whipped the frenzy up even more. It was almost funny to turn on the evening news in New York and see yet another step being taken to prepare against what Lemish was calling for in San Francisco. They were preparing for a massive riot! Barricades and expanded police and calling up the National Guard. One newscast showed the insides of the jail cell they were preparing for me.

I suddenly feel utterly powerless. I feel my liver dying inside me. I knew I wasn't going to go to San Francisco. My liver is . . . no, I will not use that as an excuse. For some reason I think a lot about David, about what he endured and survived. I wasn't in a Nazi concentration camp and yet this is how I feel. I try to calm myself by walking around all the time condemning Ruester and Trish and Omicidio and Geiseric for murdering me.

Yes, I chickened out of my own call to riot.

In the end, nothing much happened except that Scotty made a ringing speech, and a projection of Dredd Trish on the giant screen was ridiculed, and the surgeon general at HAH, Dr. Louis Sullivan, was booed so loudly that his words were completely drowned out, though he continued undaunted to the end of his speech. (The result was that Dr. Sullivan paid scant attention to UC throughout his entire tenure and made no bones about the fact that he was punishing us. A great attitude for a doctor to take, particularly one whose own population—Dr. Sullivan is a person of color—is particularly hard-hit by UC.)

No, I didn't go to San Francisco. I received a number of phone calls warning me I'd be arrested at the airport and incarcerated until the conference was over. It didn't occur to me to sneak in like a guerrilla and direct my troops from some secret hideout, or that I could have given some nifty press conferences from that jail cell. I caved. I am ashamed of myself. Some warrior, me.

I've often wondered why when we are most assuredly being murdered, someone among us doesn't start murdering back?

The San Francisco disruptions didn't occur. There were plenty of activists milling about, many thousands of them in fact registered for the conference. But by the end doctors and activists all marched in solidarity, led by Dr. Farrell Obernought! And Scotty! Arm in arm with Omicidio! With a bunch from T+D! I stared at them on my TV. I was in Table Medical having another procedure. I couldn't believe what I was watching.

DANIEL TO FRED

So neither you nor I made it to San Francisco. What kind of spies are we? I'm not allowed to go. Why? No reason, Jerry says.

"Oh," I respond.

Another interaction as nonspecific as this.

Our morgue's told us they can't handle as many as we're sending. We have to outsource our corpses! Seventeen patients died yesterday. Jerry watches as Deep Throat, who's been called in to help, and I check each one out. He's expressionless. Like the dealer in a high-stakes game of poker.

And he smiled, the fucker smiled. "That's why you're here, that's why I need you both here. To bear witness."

Even Deep Throat did a double take on this one. Doesn't Jerry remember cutting his balls off?

STEVEN'S SUICIDE

AVRAM: Steven committed suicide on the eve of the conference. We had our tickets to San Francisco and I thought he was looking forward to going. He'd been a presence and force in FUQU since our beginning. In a way, he helped to birth us, to form us, perhaps more than many others. He had studied political science at Ohio State and volunteered at our first meeting to draw up our charter, our rules and regulations, our Robert's Rules of Order, which we came to call Steven's Rules of Order. He came up with something that sounded just right for us, amazingly so. I want to say—and this is not meant to disparage his contribution but to give you an idea how gay men often operate, and FUQU was certainly no exception—that he was very handsome, Steven was, with a friendly kind of handsomeness, not snotty, as beauties often are, or visibly racked with insecurities, as many beauties also are. I think what I'm trying to say is that because Steven was so handsome (as well as smart), he got listened to more. You'd look at him talking in such an erudite fashion and be blown away. I was. We were lovers pretty quickly. I was intensely drawn to him and he responded. He had sandy wavy hair and a gorgeous body and I had a scrawny hairy one, and such a combo for a couple is unusual in the gay world. Steven was insecure, but he kept it to himself and no one would have believed him if he'd confessed it, just because he was so gorgeous and everyone wanted to sit beside him on the bus, say, when we traveled to out-of-town demos in Albany, say, where he was the first to force entry into the House chamber and lead the troops.

He didn't smile much. I would discover he had little to smile about. But as for so many of us, FUQU came to be his whole life, the outlet for his anger and frustration, and he threw himself into it from day one.

It was a love like I'd never known. He was so beautiful and it was so beautiful and I still cannot bear that it was over so fast.

•

FRED: Steven wanted very much to be a writer. He was already freelancing, for a medical encyclopedia, and the stuff he showed me was as clean and direct as the charter he drafted for us. I suggested him to Pubie Grotty of *The Village Vice*, now that even they were writing about UC, and Pubie met him and gave him an assignment to write a short piece about a health bill pending in Albany. Steven showed me what he wrote, and it sure looked good enough to me. When he turned it in, Pubie was exceptionally abusive to him, going so far as to say that Steven would never become a writer, he had no talent, and then wound up the meeting by ripping the pages to shreds. Pubie confirmed these actions of his to me almost proudly when I confronted him.

"Why did you treat him that way?" I asked sharply.

"Had to do it. That's how you learn what they're made of. Do it to all the tryouts I am considering for further work. Sounds like I was right. He doesn't have what it takes."

•

AVRAM: Because Grotty destroyed his dream of being a freelance writer, Steven had to go back to his old job of being a booking agent for a "modeling agency." He booked women hookers. He hated it. He thought he would never have to go back and do it again. "No one knew he was doing it," I was told by his roommate, Kerry, a doctor who was writing the medical stuff for Tommy at GMPA and who knew Steven was back at his old job and hated himself for it. Kerry also told me that Steven was being kept by "a creepy ugly middle-aged married man who lives in our building who pays him for letting him suck him off so he can pay me some rent. I kept telling him he didn't have to pay me any rent."

"And he tested positive for UC. He has nimroids up his rectum," Kerry said. "It's been a tough few weeks."

Then Kerry called me to say "Come over," that Steven was lying dead on the floor at the foot of his bed. He'd taken pills from Kerry's medical supplies. I went over and lay on top of him and beside him and kissed him everywhere. He was still warm. "Oh, please come back," I kept crying over and over.

I fell apart. I was inconsolable. Everything was going great. We were going to move in together. "I make enough for the two of us," I told him. "Let me help you get on your feet." He was afraid to trust people. After all, his own father threw him out of the house when he found out he was gay. "I don't know why you love me," he said every time after we made love.

You want to know how Daddy found out? He found Steven in bed in a deep embrace with Daddy's assistant football coach. Daddy was head football coach at Ohio, and Steven was having an affair with his assistant coach, who was Daddy's best friend ever since college.

It just goes on and on. When will we stop being hated so.

I tried to deliver the ashes to Steven's parents. I went to Ohio and located the house. Mommy and Daddy wouldn't let me in, just like they wouldn't talk to me on the phone when I called and identified myself. They hung up after I told them their son killed himself. They came out of their house to confront me. I tried to hand them the urn with the ashes. They wouldn't take them. Daddy was an older version of Steven, very handsome, wavy hair, muscles. Mommy looked pretty long-suffering. She didn't say much. I put the urn down on the ground in front of them and started to leave.

"Don't you leave those here!" Mommy screamed after me, choking back tears.

Daddy picked up the urn and rammed it into my hands and pushed me away from them and the house, yelling, "Go away, go away!"

I got really angry then. I shoved the bastard back. Then I ripped the top off the urn and started throwing the ashes all over the place, running around like a fairy distributing fairy dust. Mommy was moaning and Daddy—well, you wouldn't believe what Daddy was doing. He was lying with his face in some flowers the ashes had fallen on and he was crying out, "Oh, my son, my son, my precious son!" I knelt beside him to comfort him, and he jumped up and threw me down and screamed, "You get out of here, you dirty faggot, or I'll shoot you. Now get!"

I got.

WOULD THAT WE HAD

Tommy had been a Navy SEAL on submarines and all that high butch stuff. We'd sit around and talk about murdering our enemies. We would have an ultra-secret covert group, and just go out and shoot them dead. Who'd be expecting nice gay fairies to be so butch? I brought up the notion on the floor and those interested met secretly to discuss it. We had about two dozen or so. I began investigating the legalities of owning guns. It all became quite complicated too quickly. Unless we could find a way to steal them, there was no way we couldn't be traced. I chickened out on this, too. Even as I write this many years later I wish I'd been able to murder a few of our murderers.

I realize that writing this is my way of doing so.

A "MANHATTAN PROJECT" FOR UC

Yes, I got another op-ed into *The Truth*. I won't bore you with the whole thing because you've heard most of it from me already, but it's ironically interesting how much they allowed me to say. I have no idea why. And who let me.

Here are some snippets:

"I am so frightened that the war against UC has already been lost . . . Everyone presently infected can reasonably expect to die. So desperate is the situation that Dr. Garth Buffalo, president of Rockefeller University, has called for a 'Manhattan Project' for UC, an equivalent of the scientific effort that produced the atom bomb . . . President Trish has done as little about UC as President Ruester . . . Ten years into the plague, the Federal agencies dealing with UC are mired in such bureaucracy . . . Exchange of vital information is often nonexistent . . . NITS laboratories have twenty-seven vacancies . . . Huge areas of UC still aren't understood and are prohibited from being studied by new Congressional regulations . . . Anything less than an all-out effort by the Federal Government will condemn millions to death."

I'M REALLY FRIGHTENED

TRACY: I know there are people here that shouldn't be here. I walk around the room each meeting to look for faces I can't trust. There are always new faces. Every week. We're the hot and happening thing. We have six, seven hundred at each meeting. So it's hard to tell what everyone's motivation is. There are fewer new women, so I can pretty well tell that we're all okay. The guys, I come to see what new ones there are from week to week. I don't think anyone is paying any attention to this. I mention it to Fred and he nods. "Don't know what we can do about alleviating your fears, Trace. Get up and talk about it." So I got up and told the floor that I was frightened. There was another swastika painted on my front door, bright red paint, thick, hard to get off, scared the shit out of me. I'm not Jewish, why are they after me? I don't think the floor believes us, the bunch of us who week by week become the objects of attacks, Harriett and Marsie, Paul J., we all live near each other in Alphabet City. No, Paul lives on the Upper East Side. His phone and mine were connected to each other somehow so that we get each other's calls. The phone company says they don't know how that happened. "Someone's trying to tap your phone, miss," the phone person said. Harriett gets hate letters, dyke hate letters. "You lick poison pussy and are going to die." Fred got sent a box of dried turds with the return address of a fake pharmaceutical manufacturer in New Jersey. Jim F. got up and said, "We shouldn't be surprised. Whoever they are, they're after us. We have to get used to it and not let it tear us apart and start accusing each other. That's what someone is trying to make us do, rip ourselves apart. It always happens after a while when they see we've got so many members." And he cited a whole long list of gay organizations that were "destroyed by outside hate." He got a lot of applause for telling us to "hang tight." Paul J.'s written this song, "Last Dance, Last Chance for Love." He says he knows the Angel of Death is ready for him. I'm afraid I totally lost it at the end of my talking to the floor. I suddenly started to cry and I screamed out, "Who is doing this to me and to us!" There was dead silence. Then, thank God, Jim F. and others started applauding and somebody yelled out, "Yay, Tracy!" I broke out in a grin and they all applauded even more. I love this place. I really do.

IDIOTS' DELIGHT

MAXINE

My history of women and UC is a history of criminal neglect by a government and its agencies, including those charged with public health and treatment research. It's a history of unscientific and unethical behavior, of white male science, of indifference to women. It is a history of racism, sexism, classism, homophobia. Straight men are too stupid to understand our world or the choices we've been forced to make. The history of FUQU is about forcing people to look at what we know is here. Experts and politicians make all our decisions for us. We don't want them to. That's why I'm here.

Why are lesbians told we can't get UC and can't transmit it sexually to one another?

Researchers applying for grants to study UC in women are constantly refused any funding.

Men in FUQU now are meeting with NITS and pharma representatives.

In order for women UC activists just to get a meeting with NITS has taken us, so far, almost three years of constant pressuring: NITS, FORM A WOMEN'S COMMITTEE NOW!

Our women have demonstrated on trips to Chattanooga and Natchez to confront Pewkin in his COD offices, trying to convince him to include us in his official definition. It's incomprehensible to us why COD and NITS and HAH persist in stonewalling our existence. They know there are cases. How could they not? Omicidio and Pewkin are still insisting that the definition of UC can't be changed to include infections women get, because there isn't enough evidence.

We took a dozen UC-infected women to Pewkin's office and wouldn't leave until he looked at them. One woman after another stepped forward to give him evidence, telling them about their infections: cervical cancer, bacterial pneumonia, pelvic inflammatory disease, yeast infections, and passing out copies of their medical records as "evidence." They stripped down naked so he could see their nimroids. That scared him so much, he ran from his office and in five minutes the cops came to carry us out. The cops saw the sores on these poor women's bodies and they turned and ran too. I'd say it was a hoot but it really isn't. It's just awful.

So we finally got our meeting with monster Head Honcho Omicidio, who's supposed to be in charge of UC. A meeting room in Franeeda at NITS was packed with UC Women's Committee members, now from all over the country, plus just women who were sick and willing to pay their own fares to beg for help. On his side, they had all men. I mentioned that, so someone went out and brought back a poor black secretary who was so tired she fell asleep right after we started.

Here is a representative excerpt from the transcript that I recorded of our interactions:

OMICIDIO: Let me make some general points. Now, about your approach toward me and my institute, maybe it will serve as a basis for future interactions, if, in fact, there are future interactions, and that's one of the points I want to make. That is, I think, as is always the case, and has been the case with people who are activists and who are very dedicated, but have the disadvantage of not being in the field, even though you say women know women better than anyone else knows women—that's true but in the scientific, medical, physical problems there may be an area where it may not be that women know more about it, even though the women's appreciation has to be taken into account because I don't think . . . and I agree with you that one shouldn't make statements or policies regarding women unless you have both a solid scientific base wherever that comes from, a man or a woman, as well as the real input from women, be they straight women or lesbian women, okay? However, as has been the case before, when you put a menu of ten things, several of the things that are said are completely incorrect. And if I were to close my mind to them immediately, I wouldn't have heard a couple of what I think are good points you made that would probably be productive. You've got to be able to accept that, if we point out to you some of the things that are not so incorrect that you're stupid, but incorrect that I think you may be looking at from the wrong perspective, so that we can get to the things I think are really important. And again I'd like to have the time sometime to be able to go over some of the statements that were made that just factually, I could understand how you came to that conclusion but may not really be scientifically correct, although some of them really are quite correct.

MAXINE: Do you want to dialogue with us about women and UC?

OMICIDIO: Well, no, because I want to tell you the ground rules of how we interact, and if the ground rules aren't the right ground rules we're never going to talk about women and UC. That's something you have to understand, because that transcends everything we're talking about. We won't talk about women with anything unless you understand that. But you've got to cut the attitude that "we're going to get to you because we're gonna, you know, march around your buildings." That's the point I'm trying to make.

MAXINE: Well, the point we're trying to make is there is a supposition on your part that having dealt with certain people in FUQU specifically, which doesn't represent all the FUQU members around the country, and having dealt with a specific group of people according to some agreement you have with them, that we come with the same agreement, and frankly, you haven't proved anything to us. That the basis of trust that you say you have built up with them over time with those people has not been built up with this particular group of women, and, therefore, at the same time you are telling us what you expect of us, we are telling you we have no reason to trust you in terms of women's lives. So, let us talk about how coercive you are being. It is unethical and irresponsible for the head of a government agency that is responsible for the entire population to tell any specific group of women that you are not going to do anything about women and UC if they don't "act nice."

OMICIDIO: I never said that I won't do anything about women with UC unless you're nice, I said I will not deal with you unless you do it in a productive way.

MAXINE: We resent your tone, like you want us to demonstrate that we're trained pets or something.

OMICIDIO: If you are going to deal with me you are going to have to learn how it is to deal with me the way I would like to learn about what is the best way to deal with you. You could hate me, that's all right. But it will be better if we do it in a way that's—

MAXINE: We have no interest in hating you. We just want you to do your job.

OMICIDIO: I'm doing my job. I'm doing my job better than you can imagine.

Et cetera, und so weiter, yadda yadda . . .

It basically boiled down to this:

OMICIDIO: Like you said, you don't know how many UC-infected women there are . . . Well, that requires screening the whole population because a lot of the so-called infected women that are silent and don't know they're infected until they get a severe gynecological infection because nobody thought of the fact that they might be UC-positive, they may be going a long time without appropriate care, which has much more to do with the whole policies of screening and finding out what populations are infected than it does the biomedical research at NITS. So, although that is an excellent point it's something perhaps we can help by discussing it at levels that are responsible for it trickling down to whoever is supposed to be doing it, than it is for us to be arguing with you whether we should be doing it or not. It is very unlikely that we have any avenue to answer that question, although I think it is a very valid question.

This from the man who is meant to be in charge of this plague.

Changing the COD definition of UC to include women does not happen.

Who is behind this and why?

We're being treated like idiots. Once again.

ASSHOLES

PERRY: Omicidio summons a meeting for activists to pummel Howie Hube, to crucify Howie with questions about the UCCTG that he can't answer. I'm suspecting Jerry's trying to take the heat off Jerry. Jerry just sits there, stern-faced. Hube's revealed as the dumb asshole he is. It's a very painful meeting for Claudette. She hasn't seen Jerry in action before. "This is the man who's in charge of UC?" she said. "But he's an asshole." Then, when Hube is transferred somewhere else, far away, she says, "Jerry brought his lackey for us to tear down so he can go and fire him. He's a double asshole."

WHAT PERRY LEARNS ON THE
S.S. *SCOTTY'S BROTHER'S YACHT*

Scotty took a bunch of us down to the Caribbean for a week on his brother's yacht. Scotty wants to get started up again since neither one of us has found anyone else. As he whispers this while we're trying to sleep mashed together in this bunk bed with Barry and Gregg snoring in the berth below, I don't tell him No Way. (Melvyn has spent this entire trip trying to get his hands in everyone's pants. He's becoming quite obnoxious.) The next day when we're alone making salad for lunch, Scotty tells me "confidentially" that he's officially incorporated a group that he calls TAG, for Treatment Action Guerillas, and he wants to leave FUQU because he sees nothing but grief coming from the Women's Committee, and from the floor, which always gives T+D a hard time when we ask for money for trips. He says he wants to run it himself, with Sparks and Barry and anyone from T+D who wants to come, but no Fred Lemish. I tell him I love Fred too much to do this to him. Then I just look at him like I don't know what to say. "What are you thinking?" he asks. "I think I never knew you before," I answer.

I don't know what to do. Sparks already arranged me a paying job in this TAG, keeping a record of everything and putting it out in a newsletter. Scotty got that Presidium pharm to give TAG more money, enough to rent an office and pay salaries to a few people (not me!), including Sparks. Scotty's billionaire buddy Sammy Sircus makes a lot of passes at me on Fire Island, and on days when I am really hungry, I've come close to accepting. It's just that I know his record of bed tonight and gone tomorrow. My unemployment's run out and I'm tired of sleeping on other people's couches. Scotty says to keep everything secret until he announces to the floor about TAG. "And by the way," Scotty asks me, "what about my offer?" I guess that's one way to keep eating, but I'd rather go hungry.

No matter where I fall asleep I'm holding Francis in my arms. I miss him so. You'd think by now I could have found somebody. Oh, I have sex, but I close my eyes and it's always Francis I'm with. I talk to many guys who lost their lovers and everyone says the same thing. You either find another lover right away or you don't find one at all.

Tommy was in love with Fred something awful, he says, and it didn't work out like I know Scotty and me won't work out. Tommy's kept me going with jobs at GMPA since I got here but he can't do that anymore. He's got a "pissing board of directors who have to approve every time I go to the toilet. You know why, don't you? Because they know I'm still in love with Fred." But I told Tommy I think Fred never knows when someone's in love with him. I see how guys cruise him and he doesn't notice. What's wrong with his generation? I know what's wrong with mine. We're all scared to death. I guess his must be too.

FROM *THE BOOK OF THE DEAD*

FRED: Vito dies at 1:30 a.m. on November 7. I couldn't go to see him. I'd said my goodbyes to him on the phone. I couldn't go to see him so shriveled up and . . . When Vito was offered the morphine drip for the first time in the hospital, his great friend Arnie asked him, "You know what this is for?" Vito nodded yes. Then Arnie asked him, "Do you want it now or do you want to stay a little longer?" Vito somehow found strength to whisper back, "I want to stay a little longer."

At some point we're all going to face that question and we're all going to want to answer it with the same words. "I want to stay a little longer."

The next morning O'Trackney Vurd is reelected to a fourth term. And it's announced that fifty-five thousand people died this month. And that 35 percent of all black churchgoers believe UC is a form of genocide. One in ten believes UC was deliberately created in a laboratory in order to rid the world of black people.

Oliver Johnstone, Kevin Smith, Ray Navarro, Phil Zwickler, Terry Beirne, Tom Hannan, Ortez Alderson, David Liebhart, Parker Gunn, Paul Jabara, Alan Robinson, Lee Arsenault, David Lopes, David Byar, Jerry Jontz,

Trudy Nabb, Marshall Fosterman, Antony Grossbart, Laurent Michel-Gros, Rex Brown, Carter Trimmer, Alfred Hammer, Dennis Levin, Alvin Christianson, Albert Zipp, John Tripp, Gary Bass, Fred Berlin, Andre Blandford, Tony Allegritto, Louis Bruno, Vaughan Brooks, Scott Cannican, Charles Seymour III, Christopher Churcher, Alberto Alvarez, Derrick Luhrlong, Douglas Dobbs, Karl Robinson, Ector Fuchs, Parker Erlichman, Emmett Fischer, Leon Fisher, Vincent Fischer, Paddy Fisher, Corey Stoltz, Steven Adams . . .

TOMMY'S POLLS

Hunter College Poll of Lesbians, Gays, and Bisexuals finds that homosexuals do not bond with each other as a group. "Our study has found that many gays do not share a strong sense of shared fate with other LGBs or think that their membership in the LGB community is particularly important. Only 41 percent of LGBs agreed that their lives were affected by what happens to other LGBs in the United States, and only 29 percent said that membership in the LGB community was an important reflection of who they are. Furthermore, 57 percent agreed that their membership in the LGB community had very little to do with how they felt about themselves, and nearly half (47 percent) said that their LGB identity had little to do with how they vote."

I also had another study taken in which a group of homosexuals were asked whether they called themselves homosexuals, bisexuals, or heterosexuals, and a majority claimed to be bisexual. This is out-and-out lying and self-deception. It just goes to show how few of us self-identify first and foremost as gays. Like Fred keeps saying, none of this bodes well for us getting where we must get as a population; that is, if we are to stay alive and get anywhere.

FRED'S JOURNAL

I speak at a FUQU meeting in Washington. A hundred people. They look at me apprehensively as I speak, like little Bambis in the headlights' glare. They know, because I certainly tell them, that I want more of them than they are able to deliver in our nation's capital. They know, and I know, that they are not going to deliver it. And I know that they are not going to lose any sleep over it. The following week only ten people show up for their weekly meeting.

FUQU at Yaddah. A couple dozen of Yaddah's own FUQU chapter. I had no idea they had their own group. We make it impossible for Dr. Sullivan to speak at Battell Chapel. He has continued to block any progress out of vengeance for FUQU's screaming him off the stage in San Francisco. He's surprised to confront us again. He is a vengeful, stupid man punishing and murdering his own people. These Yaddah kids will get into trouble with Yaddah's president, Bentley Belly, to whom I write, trying to save them from the expulsion he's said is coming. He is a double asshole, Yaddah's president, to quote Claudette's now-famous description of Jerry.

Beautiful, wonderful, inspirational Leonard Bernstein is dead. Lennie, who tried to pick up young Fred in London a hundred years ago, a Fred too frightened to say yes. Lennie, who played Brahms for a bunch of activists from Monserrat's organization in his Dakota living room, saying, "Listen to this music. Johannes Brahms was a gay man. Listen to it! Can't you hear it! Can't you know it!" Lennie, who came to Madison Square Garden to lead the Ringling Brothers orchestra in "The Star-Spangled Banner" for the first GMPA benefit almost ten years ago now. Shmuel told me, "The one thing in the world most important to Lennie was to write his Holocaust opera before he died. He didn't get to write it. Let that be a lesson to you, Fred." Shmuel, my old shrink, now a famous expert on death and dying, came to Lennie's side these past months to help him die.

ALMA MATER INDEED

I went up to Yaddah to talk to the business school about the evil attitude of the pharmaceutical companies in ignoring us. Perhaps one is inextricably bound by some sort of blood ties to a place where one's attempted suicide. Call it love-hate, call it corny, call it Ahab, but I've never got over the place and probably never will. *The Truth* once photographed me outside the freshman room I chose for my attempt. I have that picture always inside me. That I tried to do something so decisive makes me always fearful I might try it again. Yes, there's a lot of Yaddah's history in these aging bones.

I visit the shrine. I stand outside Standing Hall and just look at it, at that left-hand set of windows on the ground floor. I hope you remember, though I suspect you don't. There's always too much to remember in histories.

Bentley Belly is Yaddah's current president. He is Yankee family rich. His daddy made a fortune doing something. I'm uncertain how Belly got to be president of Yaddah. I know his wife because she made a documentary about homosexuality for ABC that was awful and I told her so. She filmed me speaking somewhere. She'd asked me lots of questions about homosexuality, indicating to me how little she understood. That was in the days when we still had to be called sick on prime time.

Bentley Belly is about to expel those three gay kids from Yaddah for protesting with FUQU and me at that appearance by Dr. Sullivan. This is against the rules at Yaddah. Free speech must in no way be interfered with, and violators are punished by expulsion. Pretty strong stuff.

I had written an appeal on behalf of the Yaddah students—Patrick Greaney, Sam Zalutsky, and Eva Kolodner—who faced expulsion for joining with me to protest. I'd been in the vicinity coincidentally: Dr. Sullivan was just a bonus. I had no idea he'd be there or that there even was a Yaddah chapter of FUQU, and with so many vocal members. And they all wore our T-shirts and our caps, emblazoned with SILENCE = DEATH.

I wrote to Bentley Belly.

I don't understand a Yaddah that could do this to these three young people. I cannot believe that official university reactions are so extreme, against what we did and what we stood for and what we stand for and what we are trying, so desperately and feebly, as activists, to accomplish against a governmental bureaucracy that does nothing to save us. How could Yaddah and Bentley Belly, in such a haughty, condescending, condemning fashion, be so far away from the reality of the lives gay kids must live with now?

One of your professors wrote, anonymously of course, in *The Yaddah Daily News*, "Someone has figured out that it's cheaper to let these misfit perverts die rather than try to save them. I say a Nobel Prize to this person."

Do you have any idea what it must be like to never love again without this sword of Damocles over your head? To hold another person in your arms. To live in a relationship. To be free from the fear that death will come with each kiss. With each lovemaking. Can you possibly imagine what that is like? That you would never be able to kiss Nola. Or make love to her. Or be free from concern that some of your saliva or some of your semen or some blood in your mouth after you brushed your teeth might infect her with this deadly virus. Or your children. You would be afraid to kiss your children. Can you imagine any of this? Can you imagine all of this being dumped on your head when you were still a kid in college? Before your life has even started, before much of what you'd hoped would come to you no longer can.

I wrote all this to Bentley Belly.

Belly's response is terrifying. Words like *fact finder* make me tremble that the thought police are indeed taking over. Bentley has appointed a Fact Finder, the dean of one of the residential colleges.

The Fact Finder's Wife, Mrs. Lytton Goldsmith, asked an openly gay professor, Dr. Alvin Novick, if he knew the names of others involved in this protest. He said of course he did. She asked him to tell her husband these names. He said of course he would not. What kind of place has Yaddah become where professors are asked to name names and professors' wives become spies to help their "fact finder" husbands? These are the tactics of a right-wing-religious-fundamentalist institution. I have gay friends who were expelled from Lovejoy schools in Utah when they were fingered for being gay. But at Yaddah? All this got in my letter as well.

You have singled out three students for investigation. You have only been able to identify three and accuse them because their names were in the New Godding newspaper. Patrick was quoted in an article and Sam and Eva wrote and signed their names to an editorial. You are, in essence, punishing them for practicing *their* right to free speech. Had they not spoken to the press, you would have no names to send before your Executive Committee. There were some *fifty* protestors involved. But you have been able to identify only three. So you will pillory them anyway. I believe I was probably quite the noisiest protestor inside. As I was sitting beside Sheila Wellington, the secretary of Yaddah, she can certainly attest to this truth. Should Sheila Wellington have whispered into my ear, "Fred, you are going to get them in trouble"? That would have been a kindness for her to perform. But then perhaps she is a member of your Thought Police too.

Do you know that this Fact Finder, the Master of Jonathan Edwards, Dr. Lytton Goldsmith, invited the three youngsters to tea "to discuss" the protest, and they went with the hope they would be permitted some sort of audience, that they could somehow at least be heard, and he heard them not, he yelled and shamed them during their entire visit to him. This appears as just another in a growing list of examples of how a university cares so little about our deaths, about gay deaths, about black deaths. Did you know that the real Jonathan Edwards, one of the "founding fathers" of Yaddah, was one of early America's great slave owner-haters? Along with a few others of those after whom Yaddah residential colleges are named: Calhoun comes also to mind. These two men turn in their graves that here on earth black students sleep in "their" dorms.

The kids get off. Why? Because I sent a copy of my Bentley Belly letter to Bishop Paul Moore, a Yaddah trustee from way back, the much-loved Episcopal bishop of New York, a friend to GMPA, and, though it will be many years before it's known, a closeted homosexual his entire life but one who before his death somehow managed a few happy years with another man. He chaired Yaddah's Executive Committee, summoned to adjudge this mess.

I'm happy to say Bentley Belly didn't last long. He went off to rehabilitate America's educational system with the first of what became "charter schools." I believe he and his partners lost a fortune. I hope so. He does seem to have faded from view. I hope for that as well, although it's become my experience that you can't keep a bad man down.

When, if ever, am I going to have a satisfactory relationship with my alma mater, the mother to the education that put the cherry on top of the person who compiles this history of The American People? Why do I care for someone that doesn't care about me? Is that the true definition of being a son? They make you feel that way, you know. They inject Yaddah-love in you whether you want it in your veins or not. Why is that? How do they do that? Even my unloving father said, "Just get that diploma with Yaddah on it, boy. No one will ever care how well you did."

•

INT. TOMMY'S APARTMENT. DAY.
A West Side apartment Tommy once shared with his younger brother, Johnny Boatwright. Johnny is sick and looks terrible. A box labeled ZAP *is on a table by his bed. He has just thrown up and Tommy is cleaning his face. Fred watches.*

TOMMY: I found him sitting in a pool of vomit. Just staring into space and whistling "Dixie." It's time for your next dose.

JOHNNY: None of this shit, bro. No more ZAP.

TOMMY: This is all there is. Your brother is not going to sit and watch you take nothing.

JOHNNY: Well, your brother is just going to lie here until they find something that doesn't make me feel dead already. It's a good thing I've maxed out my credit cards. I saw Paris and Rome.

TOMMY *(to Fred)*: From as far back as I can remember, our mother, who had been a World War Two flight instructor, would punish Johnny and me by holding our heads under water or slapping our faces until we could take it without whimpering. We grabbed our ankles while she beat our behinds as hard as she could with a three-foot length of one-inch black rubber hose. Then she would sit on the toilet seat while she painted our naked butts with witch hazel while she cried, "What have I done to make you a fairy?"

Johnny starts whistling "Dixie." Then:

JOHNNY: The crazy bitch did me a favor. I learned how powerful people could murder me. *(He goes back to whistling "Dixie.")* They're the ones who make fairies tough. *(More "Dixie.")*

TOMMY *(taking Johnny in his arms, both of them crying)*: Oh, my dear darling brother!

Fred's eyes are filled with tears too.

MAN IS CHARGED IN ARSON AT ACTIVIST OFFICE

THE NEW YORK DAILY JUICE

A man with two prior arrests for arson was charged with setting the fire that caused more than $50,000 damage to the building where the gay-rights group, Fed Up Queers United, has its headquarters in West Chelsea.

The man, Esquino Facundo, twenty years old, who has no known address, had volunteered to do chores for the group, a member said. He was charged on Friday with arson and burglary for the September 21 blaze, said Bill Fincke, a fire marshal supervisor.

The blaze was set three days before the group, the prominent and militant advocacy group to combat UC, was to open its new headquarters.

"Esquino was someone who showed up at a couple meetings and then went up to the administrator and said, 'Can I help? I want to volunteer,'" said Frank Smithson, the group's coordinator. About fifty sets of keys to the new offices were made and Mr. Facundo apparently took one of them and let himself in to set the blaze, Mr. Smithson said.

"He came up and did dirty work, painting and sweeping and cleaning. We had no reason not to trust him," Mr. Smithson said.

Mr. Fincke said, "It is not being considered a bias crime."

Fed Up Queers United has demonstrated on Wall Street and has interrupted services at St. Patrick's Cathedral.

•

INT. BOARDROOM. PRESIDIUM PHARMACEUTICALS. DAY.

A group of stern-faced men, including Gobbel, Shovels, Dr. James Monroe, and Arnold are watching a TV. Eigo's face fills the screen. He is identified as "UC ACTIVIST." Minna Trooble is taking notes.

EIGO: So the answer to the first question of this session (who owns the product?) is this: since it's a health-care product, we the people do, as surely as we own the law or speech or the stuff of any basic right. And my answer to the second question (who controls the pricing?) is similar: we the people should.

This does not go down well with the viewers.

GOBBEL: I think we must call in auxiliary forces. Don't you agree? It's your money.

DR. MONROE: I'm only the brains behind the drug. You guys are the muscle.

Shovels turns to address Scotty and Sparks, who are sitting to the side with Perry.

SHOVELS: You're not going to get anywhere working with us if you don't shut up people like this.

SPARKS: He's not speaking for all of us. A bunch of us are taking power into our own hands.

SHOVELS: Ms. Trooble, are you getting all this down?

MINNA: Of course, Mr. Shovels.

GOBBEL: Be sure to get it to President Trish.

SHOVELS: And to our friends in Saudi Arabia to let them know we're watching out for them.

DEEP THROAT: TOP-SECRET TO FRED

You think your secret comrade and admirer has been completely excised from this wretched health-care system? You think Omicidio the Ogre has had me put out to pasture to graze too far away from him? Well, I had been put on duty at the White House.

Let me pause to say that, in addition to my growing depression, utter sadness, and despair, I am fed up, not only with myself but with you. I am sick and tired of your feeble "Reports on the State of this Plague." Do you know what the word *turgid* means? Swollen. Distended. Bloated. Full of shit. This disease is out of control. This country's attempt to deal with this engorgement is full of shit—a lot of idiots on board gleefully watching and helping the ship going down. That is the state of this plague. There is no upside. FUQU is turgid when it should be lean and mean.

There is, yet again, as you know, no head of FADS. What's-her-face resigned. You challenged her to put up or shut up and she chose the latter. That's fine but you did not get inside, as I did, to discover that her entire agency does not have one single computer. All reports must be written by hand. And you have wondered why its approvals take so long! We now have no official government agency to approve any trial, any treatment, any progress. Our chief turgid asshole, Dr. Jerrold Omicidio, and Linus Gobbel, and the departed Purpura Ruester, couldn't be happier. Wait until you watch Bart Shovels.

DOT and DIP flunked out. ZIP and ZOK are in the wings waiting. Jerry refuses to test them. You haven't heard of them. You haven't heard of Presidium or what they're up to. Pharmas who own anything are each determined to win a race that hasn't been sanctioned by FADS. I have seen both the D drugs and ZOK. Each is just another analogue of ZAP. But that makes ZIP a little safer because, with ZAP's half-baked personality, it's time for combo trials with *something*. Gobbel and Shovels and Greeting want things just as they are, retesting ZAP. No one is happy this country is spending so much moolah on the sissies. Whatever Purpura wanted and set in motion, Linus concurred, as does the latest idiot inhabitant, Dredd Trish.

I know all of this. All your energies are on behalf of drugs that are full of shit. I thought your T+D smarty panties were supposed to know more than I do.

There are some two dozen potential treatments for UC-related illnesses that won't be available because Jerry won't test them and there's no FADS to approve them. And they are all categorized as "Top-Secret" by HAH, the kiss of death. Gobbel and Shovels are this country's Public Health Service.

I must now confide in you with one last "state of the plague" lest I don't live long enough to tell you later. I have not requested you call me Deep Throat without having due reason.

Why was I at the White House for almost a year?

The Whore of Babylon did not want the world to get even a whiff of whatever her hubby's got. His country had seen very little of him. He never knew enough about anything except what Purpura whispered into his ear. His staff were too busy competing and manipulating each other over everything. They treated him like he's one of the cowboys or soldiers he's played in his movies. She refused to accept that it's Alzheimer's settling in. While she's been running the war against Iran.

As a famous pathologist I'd been summoned to come up with some other diagnosis. She wanted him tested every which way possible, even if it's invasive. Well, I was not going to cut into a president of the United States when it's so obvious to me what's happening to him. So I am called upon to dream up skin tests and blood tests and scrapings from under his finger- and toenails, testing his urine, testing his shit—the poor bloke does not know what to make of me. I went so far as to perform a colonoscopy, which brought a wisp of puzzled sadness to crease his enduringly smiling face. When I kept telling Purpura what she doesn't want to hear, she dismissed me as an incompetent, only to summon me back in a few days to try something else her astrologer recommended. Enemas with prune juice. Some herbs flown in overnight from Russia. Something called a brain massager, which I said I refused to mess around with.

She has now had me reassigned to her staff in Los Angeles. That is why you have not heard nor seen me. My charge is now to just keep the old Ruester crowing.

She continues to be in constant communication with Jerry. She is determined there be no UC treatments to protect her son and his friends.

I promise you that before I die—and my liver, like yours, is caving in—I will tell you more about my boss James Jesus Angleton and our own relationship.

WEST COAST EAST COAST

There is a rift between West Coast and East Coast UC treatment activist organizations.

Marty Delaney, the respected West Coast activist, has no doubt what he wants. He wants anything and everything and he wants it all approved quickly, particularly stuff only scantily available on Extended Access (a.k.a. Parallel Track). A number of Easterners (whose new spokesperson is Sparks Puffington, who certainly is a turncoat on this issue), announce they're increasingly less ready to gobble down just any (legally or otherwise) available anythings blindfolded, just as the West Coast seems prepared to swallow and/or inject anything at all.

Velma Dimley writes a nasty piece about us in *The Truth*, identifying FUQU and me as UC's chief troublemakers impeding progress, and praising Jerry for doing such a swell job.

I try to outline the complexity of this issue in a letter I circulate to Push and Pish Dunkelheim, Martin Richtig (*The Truth*'s new editor in chief, replacing Jakie Flourtower), Dearie Fault, Velma, Omicidio, to name but a few. Long ago I learned that cc'ing the world often gets to more people than you might think. I got invited on to the Charlie Rose show to debate Omicidio. I never let him get a word in. I practically yelled out every fact from every speech and op-ed and I didn't stop. He actually tried to hug me when it was over. What is it with this guy? I fucking creamed him. I was shaking. Daniel called me. "Fred, what's come over you?"

"Are we friends again?" I asked Daniel. "I've had enough of this a-tisket a-tasket."

"We were never not friends," he said. "You just demand unbending loyalty and eternal fealty."

"They're the same thing. And don't you forget it."

It seemed an unsatisfactory conversation and so I said good night. I had wanted to know the latest on David.

What very few know about Marty Delaney is that he and his group have a secret first-class hijacker who somehow manages to gain entry into any pharms factory and make off with bootleg supplies for their own secret trials. Our own Dr. Levi Narkey contacts Marty and gets some of their bootlegged drugs-in-the-making. Amazingly, not one of the raided pharms notices a thing.

FRED KISSES OFF ALL HIS STRAIGHT FRIENDS

TOMMY

I was with Fred when he decided to lay into his straight friends. We went to Christmas dinner at the home of his old Yaddah classmate and friend Buddy Tinker. Buddy prides himself on being funny, a humorist in the tradition of Mark Twain. He writes for *The New Gotham*. Fred and Buddy's wife, Beverly, are close. He's helped her through a couple of health scares by investigating research and directing her to the doctors and even to Shmuel because she was having a tough time of not only having survived cancer but also with Buddy. She'd told Fred, "I'm just not a person to him. I'm on some pedestal so he can worship me, and I'm tired." Fred had asked for Buddy's recommendation to get into some classy lit. org. he belonged to. Fred has a lot of trouble not being taken seriously as a writer by *The New Gotham* crowd. Buddy said, "I don't do things like that," or some such, and of course that was it for Fred as far as Buddy was concerned. Buddy had failed the loyalty test. This was to be the last Christmas dinner he'd have with this crowd, which included a load of *New Gotham* stars like Joan Didion and David Remnick. "And I looked around that table," Fred said to me, "and I knew there wasn't one of them I could count on, for anything. I suddenly felt like the token fag. I was that way for most of my straight friends. And I knew it wasn't going to change." He'd taken me and he had Sam, his dog, who was old and arthritic and doing nothing but just lying there when some straight woman arrived and started screaming, "I cannot be in the same room as a dog! It's either it or me," and when Fred could see that neither Tinker was saying anything, he got up, grabbed Sam in his arms, and announced in a very loud voice something along the lines of this: "I feel more and more estranged from my heterosexual friends. So many of you here have power, connections, media outlets, strong voices. Not one of you has used any of your gifts and connections during the long ten years of this plague to help stop the murdering of my and your gay friends. I have been your friend for many years. I don't want to be your token faggot anymore. So, so long. It was nice while it lasted." And he left and didn't come back, as everyone expected him to (not me), leaving me to make small talk with a lot of straight strangers. I could have killed him. But he was right. When this harpy inquired later, "And who was your rude friend?" I answered, "We've lost a great many friends. Perhaps you've heard of the UC plague?" She shot up from her chair as if I'd infected her. Which of course said it all.

So now Fred no longer talks to Buddy and Beverly, who were two of his oldest friends.

SAM

Sam died. She was the best dog. She was the perfect writer's dog. She followed me around wherever I walked in my apartment and she stayed by my feet when I was writing. I brought her to FUQU meetings all the time. Everybody loved her. I just knew she was in great pain. She looked up at me with her big eyes as if to say, Hey, Dad, I don't feel well. Can't we stop this? I had to wheel her in a little wagon because it hurt her too much to walk. Her vet wrote me this letter: "Dear Fred, What a personality Sam was. She lived a wonderful and long life and I always enjoyed seeing her. Even when she was sick, she was very stoic. I was very fond of her and I will miss her."

I tried to be a good father but I was very impatient with her sometimes. Felix loved her a lot. She still sleeps where he lay on our bed beside me.

PROGRESS?

"I have been allotted a place on the newly formed Community Constituency Group. Nineteen ninety brought us to a turning point in FUQU's history. Our long campaign to gain access to power with the federal UC research infrastructure is proving to be a success. We stood at the gates of a newly intensified involvement with, and responsibility for, clinical trials of drugs to treat UC and its complications."

That's what Sparks wrote in his memoirs. Perhaps he'd even convinced himself that such was the case. Of course he was dead wrong, emphasis on the *dead*. I do not like Sparks. I tried but I am not succeeding. I am discovering that some of my children are not nice persons. I got him a book deal to write these memoirs. The publisher found them too boring to publish. I found them upsetting. They were filled with a large number of unkind things . . . about me.

He also wrote that he and Scotty had been meeting with pharmas on the quiet for much longer than I or FUQU knew. Wait till Max and the women in FUQU learn about this.

SHITTING IN SOHO

TOMMY

She is in a store on Greene Street buying a cap that matches the rings and bracelets she wears to match her African headband. It is dripping down her inside right leg. She's looking down at the store's shiny black linoleum floor and she sees and I see there is brown shit in the heel of her flip-flop. She is standing in her own shit. She is going to have to leave here walking in her own shit. She looks around terrified. She grabs her Amex card back and gets out to the street, searching for a cab that will never be there in this Saturday afternoon rush hour, stopping only to grab a piece of newspaper from a corner bin to wipe her leg and flip-flop. Sort of. At this point something inside her explodes and she passes out before I can catch her. What is coming out of this poor kid's insides is all over the place, not only shit but blood from her mouth. I call one of my emergency numbers and direct people to walk around her, while I stand guard, taking her pulse, which thank God she still seems to have. Her wallet tells me about the NYU freshman year she's just starting, and various pieces of ID tell me she's a diplomat's kid from Saudi Arabia, she prepared at Exeter, and has various embassy contacts here in the city. My ambulance gets us to Table Emergency, where they certainly know me. I caution care in handling her, I give them various necessary bits of information, I go to call her embassy contact, I ask one of the interns who's a buddy if I can scrub clean somewhere fast and borrow any outfit he can lay his hands on that would get me home. Of course the kid's got UC. And she's dead before I get home. I live near to where she collapsed on the street, so I called the precinct, advising some sort of fumigating near that boutique, and I'm told that already a couple of dogs are dead from lapping up the shit. This is the first transmission to animals that I've heard of. What comes next? She was really a pretty young thing. I'd already in my mind lined up a few folks who could help introduce her to other young people with UC. Funny how I can read their futures so easily now. I feel so fucking goddamn useless. So does Fred. I wish we could hold on to each other more. I wish a lot of things. They ain't coming true.

DAY OF DESPERATION

FRED

I feel every day brings something closer that isn't good.

Since I feel every day is such a day, why not turn it into a specific action?

Throw everything into the hopper, the whole nine yards, Fibber Magee's closet . . . Go for broke! Because it's impossible for me not to accept that we aren't getting anywhere. With all our actions, all my speeches, and articles, and op-eds, all I'm getting is a reputation for being the angriest gay man in the world. If I don't call somebody "murderer!" people feel gypped. How long can things be held together? Let's give it what we've got, girls and boys. Let's outdo even ourselves.

That's what Fred said to himself as FUQU responded favorably to his challenge of such a full-plate Blue Ribbon special. Was there still enough hope around to override everyone's growing sense of despair?

Just visualize hundreds of people in little groups, many carrying coffins, all over the city, with gallons of fake blood dumped outside the World Trade Center, to tombstones lined up outside homeless shelters in Harlem, to the Citicorp atrium with bags of chicken bones covered in ketchup dumped down on the courtyard on people eating their lunch . . .

•

INT. CITIBANK LOBBY. DAY.
Members standing on balcony, throwing ashes down on the people eating lunch in the courtyard on the floor below.
ANN *(yelling and throwing)*: This is the body of someone who died from UC!
Other members are echoing the same.
DOBBSON: Ground-up chicken bones dyed red.
ANN: Be quiet, Dobbson. We don't want to give it away.
Crowd in lobby below jumps up and scatters out quickly.

o'MALLY *(announcing)*: This is the body of someone who died from UC! *(Hurls out some more of the concoction.)*

TRACY: It could be your brother or your husband or your son or your best friend . . . !

PHOTIS: Stop murdering us!

•

Every bridge and tunnel into and out of New York is shut down and plugged up with piles of coffins cops are afraid to touch. Flyers hurled out everywhere sending flurries of the outrageous facts out and down like rain. Little by little our groups coalesce as they move toward midtown, a bulging body blowing itself up bigger and bigger, dropping off an occasional coffin as a memento that we were here. From every direction our rivulets become streams and finally a river into Grand Central Station. Yes, we take it over. Every train and subway has been stopped.

•

INT. GRAND CENTRAL STATION.

A mob of FUQU is blocking stairways and entrances to tracks. Many carry the posters from various indictments through their history. Dobbson and Photis hold a long banner reading FUQU'S DAY OF DESPERATION. *Scotty, dressed like the Statue of Liberty, is standing on the clock. Mulligan and Dorothy set off foghorns as cops come in and start arresting members. Jill supervises the arresting. Mario is filming her. A police officer is checking her out. She holds an ID pass.*

JILL *(to the cop)*: I'm their dyke lawyer. They're more than willing to get arrested. They're going to die and know they're going to die. So arrest is nothing to them.

A huge number of purple balloons is released and float up. Many cheers. Suddenly something is happening:

EIGO: Body coming through! Spencer just collapsed. Tell the cops to get an ambulance.

Barnaby and Sheila and several new faces are carrying Spencer's body aloft as the crowd parts for them to get through. The police officer has left Jill to deal with Spencer.

POLICE OFFICER: Body coming through! Spencer . . . what's his last name? coming through.

Jill is talking to several cops.

JILL: I don't know what he does in the outside world.
She breaks with the cops to go with the group carrying Spencer.
Everyone is in a state of shock. A group releases more purple balloons,
which float up to the roof bearing a FUQU banner. Someone yells out:
"For Spencer!" The roar of the crowd is mighty.

FRED'S VOICE: And you won't read about it in tomorrow's *New York*
Truth. Everyone in the station is looking up at the balloons on
the ceiling. I am looking at the pile of coffins at the bottom of
the stairs that Frank and his team of carpenters are loading into
his truck. And at the cops in their protective clothing carrying
poor Spencer out. He'd stopped taking his ZAP. I hope this
doesn't mean he's going to die.

HOW DO YOU WANT TO DIE?

JOSEPH

We had been reading and talking about David Wojnarowicz's book *Close to
the Knives* and the passage in there that says, "Every time somebody dies of
UC, I think their lover, their friends, should drive with their bodies a hundred miles an hour down to the White House, and throw their body over
the White House fence." And we started thinking—goddamn right, that
sounds just about right to us. So we decided that that's what we were going
to do. We would carry out this mission.

More and more we are beginning to talk about how we wanted to die—
like, when we died, what we wanted to happen. Burning of bodies on pyres
was high on the list. To hear Tim and John and Mark, those closest to death,
talk about this, it was very serious, and you as a still healthy participant just
knew that whatever it was they wanted, that's what we were going to do. But
it wasn't just about them, it was about me and everybody else, too. That was
what made the dynamic in the group so amazing. We were very much there
for each other. No matter what.

It was like family, you know? We were very close to each other. It didn't
matter what you did in that outside world. We met people that we'd probably never
meet in our entire life under any other circumstance, and here we were—we got
very close, and that was it, for life, while planning our very own deaths.

It's overwhelming. It took your breath away.

KENNEBUNKPORT, MAINE

TOMMY

We and the masses of cops took up the whole town, which admittedly is pretty tiny, every street and artery that fed down to that monster mansion out there on this island, like some rock fortress we could never get anywhere near. The people who live in the town must have thought the world was coming to an end, or that the Russians were invading, because they went inside fast and locked their shutters and we could see kids peeking out through slats as we marched past. Sure, we all really got off on it, it was a lovely summer day, etc. And yes, Dredd and Taddy must have looked out their windows too. But like Fred, I wonder, we've done all this, over and over, what's the next step?

Perry somehow discovered that the president's house doesn't even have central heating. Can you believe it?

At least Fred and I walked down the main street holding hands. We went and stood opposite *the* house. Maybe someone was looking at us through binoculars.

TORTURE AND PUNISHMENT

SCHWITZ ODERSTRASSE: I learn most things in Germany, things science can do to human beings. Humanity is always second place to results. Mungel and Mengele and Grodzo, they push envelope is how you say it. Much interest is in Grodzo for trying to discover what is homosexuality at Mungel. Much the same for Mengele for trying to understand what means twins. They have not produced any important information for good of humanity. Probably, probably not, too early to tell even this late date, for much interesting work done in past. You never know when old work becomes foundation of new work. You see how difficult, philosophically, it can be to draw a line between what is acceptable in science and what not to be allowed.

What is acceptable, even if something important lies at other end of tunnel of ignorance all scientist always enters sometime or other?

One thing I can do is recognize infected blood, corrupt blood, blood that has been, how you say, fucked up. I saw no work going on at Partekla that is any good for humanity. Dr. Dye tells me I wrong. He committed to experiments stranger here than any we work on over there. And Grodzo, he is fairy, so why he so interested in finding out ways of how he made and not accept he is just made by God to be fairy?

Dr. Dye organized Partekla so that there are many patients available for, how you say, rent, although he does not charge. He offers these patients to outside doctors to come here and test on his many patients almost anything these doctors want research. This is godsend to almost any serious researcher in the world. It is hard to locate guinea pigs to do anything you want to on them without interference from outside, higher-ups, across the streets, wherever. Many doctors come to Partekla just for this. Loth Schline come all the way from Japan, for instance. (She in fact becomes he at Partekla, another branch of research going on.)

Dr. Sister Grace Hooker had rare disease called mismytosis. She want to find cure for mismytosis, even though so rare only few people get it. She prepared many different bloods in her own laboratories she wants to test here on people which is not legal in outside world.

Dr. Dye will take each of her patients and use his own experiments to dissolve their humanity into ashes, into nothing. I do not think this is right.

It is true I do not like fairies. They do not add to world any more of God's people necessary to keep us going. Stuartgene tells me his work will take care of much of this someday. There are many people in America who do not like fairies.

I have learned that what you are doing here is as bad as anything was done in Germany. People everywhere do terrible things to each other.

•

DEEP THROAT: I accepted my situation with Jerry in order to do my work as a pathologist and explore my ideas. One might say that Jerry provided me with shelter for my outrageous no-bullshit persona, but one might also say that the rent at NITS was pretty high. I was forced into premature retirement with no appeal. The only person who could have gotten me out of the pickle was an admiral in the Public Health Service. That admiral, Jerry Omicidio, M.D., chose to let me hang until you came to my rescue.

•

MOTHER: The torture and punishment every country perpetrates is not so very different from one place to another. Even "informed consent" on human experimentation is a load of crap, no matter the legal and constitutional "protections." That makes my work all the more important. Somehow I must ascertain who's doing what to whom and where and what's the least harmful to The American People. My job is to shape new ways to hold perpetrators accountable. I believe our Founding Fathers would be in total agreement. But none of this can be said out loud, of course. Spies are not meant to talk like this.

TEN YEARS OF P-L-A-G-U-E

It is a testament to how many of these diatribes Fred is churning out that he can't locate where, when, or how this appeared.

We have been fighting this plague for ten years.

In a recent press conference, restricted to reporters who write about religious matters, President Trish denounced FUQU. He called us "outrageous" and "counterproductive." He said: "It is an excess of free speech to use—to resort to some of the tactics these people use."

Talking to students at the University of Michigan, Trish continues his whining. Free speech, he said, is "under assault" throughout the land. The American Way is threatened when various minorities, in desperate and last-ditch-stand attempts to be heard, make so much noise. The downtrodden should be more polite. "Political extremists roam the land, abusing the privilege of free speech, setting citizens against one another on the basis of their class or race."

The president, a white, heterosexual, upper-class male, desires that everyone "use reason in settling disputes." "Crusades . . . demand correct behavior."

"Let's trust our friends," recommends Dredd, "to respond to reason."

Dredd Trish is not my friend. I hate his fucking guts. And I figure he sure as hell hates mine.

Mr. President, what else can we do when we've tried every polite tactic in the books and still people like you don't listen?

There are fifteen hundred new UC infections every twenty-four hours.

There is one UC death every nine minutes.

Four of every thousand college kids are now UC-positive.

There are 8 to 10 million UC-infected people worldwide.

The fastest-rising risk group in the major cities is now hetero-sexual women.

The first 100,000 American cases of full-blown UC took nine years. The next 100,000 will take two years (one year of which is gone).

One out of four households in America has now been somehow touched by UC.

5,815 health-care providers have full-blown UC, including 42 surgeons.

The UC research program at the National Institute of Tumor Sciences has been condemned as totally inadequate by the National Academy of Science.

Sixteen percent of the supervisory positions at NITS remain unfilled.

Three presidential reports and more than a hundred congres-sional oversight hearings have condemned the inadequacy, in every possible area and field, of Food and Drug Supervision.

The Center of Disease is in such bad shape that one of its top directors just resigned, claiming publicly that he could no longer en-dure working in and with such "decaying facilities." Twenty other top COD scientists preceded him in resigning in the past two years. Ten of these positions remain unfilled.

Ten million children will be UC-positive worldwide in the next ten years. Eighty percent of all UC infections will be heterosexually transmitted.

UC is a plague.

As I hate my president, I grieve for my country.

Dredd Trish—you are, pure and simple, a murderer, as was your predecessor.

But President Trish doesn't have to worry.

Because our ranks are being depleted faster than we can re-plenish them.

UC is a plague.

And it need not have happened.

Happy Tenth Anniversary of your plague, President Dredd Trish.

•

Frederick, Freddy, Fredchen, they don't care. Goody goody.

DAVID CONTACTS FRED

I have been following you. You will hear from me. I will find you when I am ready.

ANOTHER GAY SON!

WHEREIN WE LEARN SOME INFORMATION ABOUT THE SON OF THE MAN WHO'S NOW OUR PRESIDENT BY JOSEPH KIDNEY

In the voluminous diaries and correspondence housed in the Dredd Trish Memorial Library in Devotta, Texas, all in her own clear New England boarding school handwriting, Mrs. Dredd "Taddy" Trish records a remarkable number of entries concerning her son Dredd Jr. These are, of course, not open to the public. Only tired old muckrakers like me know how to get in for a good read. Of particular interest to your history are her diary entries from the pre-Ruester days:

"I told Daddy that I keep finding photos of naked young men with erections in Junior's room. He has never been neat. He has always been sloppy. They didn't teach him anything at Paulson. I know he takes drugs, because I find evidence of this too. Pills that Dr. Dan tells me are 'mood-altering, and dangerous.' Little tins of powder that Dr. Dan says is that cokane stuff that is even 'more dangerous.' I have confronted Junior. 'How do you know so much, Ma?' he asks me with that big open grin of his that is so hard to confront, much less surmount. I tell him what I have found. I urge his father to deal with him about the drugs and naked boys. I always thought that being a cheerleader at Paulson was a suspicious activity for a healthy young man to be involved in. I have also always suspected that hanging around constantly with that Pinky Birch could only lead to trouble. I will not detail the photos I found of them together.

"After repeated reminders, Daddy Trish tells me he has spoken to Junior Trish about the pictures of naked young men with erections. 'Yes, I told him what you told me. He said that all the young guys have such photos now. I told him I found this hard to believe. He told me that I am out to lunch and should "get with it." He said, in fact, "Get with the program, Pop." I asked him to elaborate on what this program entailed. He said he would take me to a place called Studio 54 in New York where they take these pills and smoke these "joints" and . . . "Pop, Pinky and I get sucked off in the upper balcony. It's really cool." . . . Taddy, that is what he said to me, word for word. Taddy, I don't know how to deal with all this. I told him these sounded like activities and friends that could ruin his future career, in anything, if he ever has one, which I sincerely doubt as you know. He certainly could never get elected to anything. Again he said something like, "Pop, you just don't get it." And I told him that indeed I did not, that I thought he should see a psychiatrist. He reminded me that he and we had already "gone down that road." I told him, and I tell you, Taddy, I don't want to have anything more to do with this young man. He appears a lost soul to me. What did we do to have such a son? He's never going to amount to anything.'"

And I thought Junior Ruester was an unbelievable problem.

My book about Ruester the father is coming along. Talk about unbelievable!

FRED'S JOURNAL

This weekend I had a secret meeting with several officials from the U.S. Department of Health and Happiness. All of them are concerned about UC. They asked for this meeting to be confidential. They came to me as the founder of FUQU. They came to me because they don't know what else to do. They told me horror story after horror story. How nothing can get done because they are not permitted to do it. So all the offices set up to deal with UC are not functioning. How inept many of those placed in charge are. It was terrifying to hear. Everything one suspected, of course, only worse. And they came up to New York on their own time and money to try and get us, the activist community, to do something!

Mysteriously, miraculously, my T cells have gone up! "You could get drafted with them," Dr. Greene says. What does this mean for my life now? I have been spared yet again. My liver is apparently coping. What should I do with this gift of time? Are you crazy? What kind of question is that? Get to work. You have your own Holocaust opera to write, you stupid person who does nothing but waste time.

Brad Davis, who played me in my play and did so heartbreakingly, called to say goodbye. He's going to kill himself tomorrow. He refuses to talk of new drugs. Tommy had sent him everything he could get his hands on, over and under any counter or from any country. ZAP made Brad really sick. He told me, "Please tell Tommy not to call me with any new experimentals." Next day Susan calls: Brad's dead. He got infected with UC heterosexually. Half the cast of a movie he was making were shooting up. I wonder how any of the rest of them are doing?

PERRY TELLS ABOUT THE BIGGEST CONDOM EVER MADE

I knew this was going to happen. I just knew it and it makes me sad. Charlie F. says I should stop worrying, Fred is a big boy and when things happen they happen for a reason. It won't be long before Fred finds out. I just know Fred is going to hate me and think I've gone over to the enemy. That's how he thinks. And I think that way, too. He's taught me so much, Fred has. Sparks is already bossier than ever. What else did I expect?

It's getting harder to be in this fight without . . . more fights. I don't like fighting my friends.

The latest of what's just happened is this:

Scotty had the idea of putting a giant condom over Senator O'Trackney Vurd's house in Arlington. The money to pay for the condom and this action came from Sammy Sircus. Sammy doesn't want it known that he handed Scotty a big wad of bills, three thousand dollars' worth, on the beach at the Pines. I was there with Scotty and saw it. (We fucked again that night, Scotty and I, and, well, it just isn't going to work, so I don't know why he's so insistent.)

There were a couple of dozen of us who did all this. All of us are from FUQU. And I guess all of us now are from TAG as well. Although Sparks and Scotty say they'll let us know when TAG can officially be said out loud. When he gets wind of the condom story Fred is thrilled because he thinks it's a FUQU action. He doesn't know about how far along TAG is already in its development behind his back. A confrontation has been avoided only by sheer luck. This action was to have been TAG's official media launching. Vurd has one powerful media network, which is heavy-duty controlling what's said about him. Like that he and Sam Sport are bosom buddies. As they both were with Senator Joe McCarthy, who was also gay. I heard this from Artie, someone I fucked with at Fire Island who's been a fuck buddy with Sam Sport.

We got a big U-Haul to transmit the condom, which is really huge and heavy and was made to order by some company that makes them for horses and I even think elephants. Its manufacturer said it was the biggest condom ever made. He wanted to submit it to the *Guinness Book of Records*. We knew Vurd's daily schedule, so he wasn't there. We set up a portable generator, climbed to the roof with the condom and a cold-air blower, set up a second blower on the ground to inflate it from the bottom, and that was it. Inflated, it went up like fifteen feet in the air and covered most of Vurd's house, which was one story and surprisingly modest. There was lettering laid on it at the factory, saying SEN. VURD, DEADLIER THAN THE VIRUS, and WE NEED PROTECTION AGAINST VURD'S HATE! and VURD MUST BE STOPPED! The cops were there in ten minutes. But we'd managed to get the whole thing on and it settled down by itself. Claudette and Spud filmed the whole thing. But no one in the media would touch it.

I'm relieved our condom story didn't make the news to launch TAG. But I know it's only a matter of time before Fred finds out.

LIKE FRED HAS NOTHING BETTER TO DO

The Editor
Dramatists' Guild Newsletter

I would like to register my distress over your publishing "Ten Golden Rules for Playwrights" by Marsha Norman in your October issue. Why do writers write stupid things like this, which can be so harmful and detrimental to beginning writers looking for help and grabbing for straws from any source? I cannot for the life of me understand what possessed Ms. Norman to compile this list, and I cannot for the life of me understand who at the Guild was foolish enough to think it contained anything of wisdom.

Rule 1. "Read four hours a day. A noble ideal but ignored by many." Georges Simenon prided himself on not reading while writing, fearing his mind would be cluttered up and his famous style unconsciously tampered with.

Rule 2. "Don't write about your present life." Then I never would have written *The Normal Heart* or *Faggots*. Or this history.

Rule 3. "Don't write in order to tell the audience how smart you are." Then Oscar Wilde never would have written. Or Proust. Or George Bernard Shaw. And *War and Peace* never would have seen the light of day.

Rule 4. "Cut out characters you cannot write fairly about." Dickens's novels are filled with characters he was out to get even with. Restoration comedies are filled with grudges repaid. Shakespeare's villains were often based on real people.

Rule 5. "There can only be one central character." Who's the one central character in *Long Day's Journey*? *Much Ado*? What about Ms. Norman's own *'Night, Mother*?

Rule 6. "You must tell the audience right away what's at stake in the evening." Tell that to Beckett, Pinter, Stoppard, Ionesco, Genet, Agatha Christie, Stephen Sondheim.

Rule 7. "Never consider your audience or friends while writing." Tell that to Noel Coward, who fashioned parts specifically for his friends.

Rule 8. "Don't talk about your play while writing it." Maybe. But sometimes I get my best ideas from discussing a problem with certain trusted and respected sounding boards.

Rule 9. "Keep pads of paper near all your chairs." Gee, I wish I'd thought of that.

Rule 10. "Never go to your typewriter until you know what your first sentence is, since it's unhealthy to sit in front of a silent typewriter." If writers followed this one, nothing would ever get written at all.

Well, as I say, and certainly must now say again, and very loudly, after reading Ms. Norman's useless list: RULES ARE MADE TO BE BROKEN.

When the above letter is not printed, Fred resigns from the Dramatists' Guild. He guesses that in the scheme of things his life is full enough now and that this is small potatoes, but it makes him feel better, telling this useless guild that doesn't even provide health insurance to its members to stuff it.

SHIT IN CINCINNATI

Manolo felt guilty. He felt guilty he was alive. Gil was dead, and he was alive. He'd made Gil have sex with him over and over because he loved him so much. He didn't want to be alive now. So he took a big kitchen butcher knife he stole from the restaurant where he worked and he fell on it. He'd seen that on TV. You hold the knife to your stomach and you fall on top of it. It worked on TV and it worked on him. The knife went through him and he was dead soon enough. His roommate Tino came in later and found him and called the police. The police wouldn't touch him so they called an ambulance. The ambulance guys wouldn't touch him so they called an undertaker.

All towns this size now know what kids with UC look like. "They got that look." Manolo was an illegal immigrant and Gil Standing was an assistant district attorney and Tino was an illegal immigrant too, so he left before the police came. But Manolo had no papers on him and the police found some card with Tino's name on it, and so they reported the dead man as Tino Marchesi, and when Mrs. Marchesi in Turin, Italy, heard about this from a cousin in Cincinnati who saw a story about the "hara-kiri suicide" on the evening news, she took an overdose of some pills she had, "to join my Tino in heaven." That assistant district attorney, Gil Standing, was related to one of the oldest and most famous families in this city, which was uncomfortable with you if you weren't straight Caucasian. The cops found Gil's dead body in a closet, covered with spots and vomit, his eyeballs all runny pus, with papers in his pockets that told exactly who he was: Gilbert Standing, assistant district attorney. Gil's body was delivered to his wife by a messenger. This wife of this assistant district attorney gathered up their eight-month-old baby and jumped from the roof of Procter & Gamble, which an ancestor had founded. Gil's boss, also a Standing, didn't want it known that someone on his staff was dead from this crud and was therefore a faggot. "I would lose my federal grants if it was discovered," he had told his wife. "You are a bigoted pig," this wife had said to him. "You are a shameful representative of our country." He swatted her hard across the mouth and she had to have a lot of stitches. Her daughter wouldn't talk to her. "Why you don't leave that pig, Ma? How many times I beg you?" And the daughter left home and went to another city a little bigger than Cincinnati. St. Louis. She didn't have any money and she hoped she would find a job so she wouldn't have to turn tricks to eat like one of her sisters had done in Cleveland and wound up dead from UC herself. The Standings of Cincinnati aren't what they used to be.

PERDITA

The GMPA board member Perdita Winthrop Pugh is married to Parkinson Pugh of the Boston Pughs. This lineage makes them very important. Perdita and Parkinson Pugh live on Fifth Avenue overlooking the Metropolitan Museum. She is very beautiful. She has gorgeous clothes and jewels and loves to wear them. She keeps a hairdresser on staff because she also has beautiful hair. She devotes all her energy to doing good deeds for GMPA.

Tonight is a good deed that doesn't sound much fun. "We know all of this.

Why are you allowing *him* to speak!" Parkinson asks as he helps her connect her Pugh diamonds around her neck.

"I have this hunchie it's going to be awful," she agrees. "But Tommy insisted."

Why is she doing what she is doing? Many of their friends have wondered. The very first day she heard about this dreadful disease killing gay men, Perdita joined the fight against it.

Other friends wondered if she is terrified her Sweets is going to get sick and she wants to be prepared to help him when he becomes skin, bones, pus-covered, and sore-encrusted. Well, there are worse motivations for the charitable life; this one, in fact, is quite touching.

"They're letting *him* speak in the cathedral?"

"Ummmm." She is applying lipstick. She blows him a kiss. They are safe here. "Thank you for being so understanding."

We are safe here, his blown kiss says back to her.

He finishes helping her screw the Pugh diamonds. He reminds himself how much better this is than the fate of the emaciated "Little Whispers," as she calls them, whom she visits morning, night, and noon.

"Frankie died today. Mushie will be dead by morning. I must pop 'round to Invincible on the way to the cathedral to say goodbye to Fritz. Taylor will die tomorrow morning at Adonai. Murray should go tomorrow afternoon at Holy Pope. Heinz in the evening at Our Mother of Munich. And, oh yes, Paltz on Sunday at Russia's Spirit. Busy, busy days and nights ahead." Folding back the Week-at-a-Glance page in her Filofax, she starts to cry. So many Little Whispers just disappearing! She is a good woman, a good person, and she is trying her best, which is more than anyone else she knows.

How did she know the instant she heard about what would become UC and GMPA that her calling had called? "Fate. Just fate." She answers her own question without questioning herself any further about her neverending vigil. Winthrops don't usually ask the reason why. Winthrops are the reason why. She is leading actually and absolutely the very life she wants to lead, that she was bred and brought up to lead. The Winthrops are one of New England's oldest families. Boston is filled with Winthrop achievements, huge piles of stone shielding many a worthy cause from the painful rigors of an alien outside world. No Boston Brahmin could ask for more.

Bruce Niles is very sick now. Fred is needed now at GMPA more than ever. He was voted out three times. Yes, she is frightened of him. She knows he wants more of her than she can give. Thank God that FUQU thing seems to be keeping him busy. Such a rude and awful name.

Miss Prissy and her Sweets, which is what they call each other, set forth into the winter night for GMPA's Gathering of Remembrances and Renewal. She wonders if Fred will behave in a religious setting. St. John the Divine is usually her favorite place to gather her thoughts. Well, perhaps not tonight. The cathedral will be packed.

She wonders if she should tell him that Dr. Omicidio has asked her to serve on an important peer review panel at NITS. She knows nothing about science. She would have to leave her Little Whispers. She would have to journey constantly to Franeeda. Fred might have some good pointers. Fred might help her to make up her mind. But she is frightened of Fred. He will want her to confront Purpura and Taddy, both women she abhors.

NO SENSE OF URGENCY

This is going to be a repetitive, one-note, offensive, repellent speech. It contains words that many will find unsuitable for a cathedral. It is filled with a wrath that many will find un-Christian. Well, I state up front that I don't believe in God. How could I after what is being done to our people?

It is very easy to be angry with the system and the bureaucracy, with those who hate us, with those who don't care about UC or saving us.

I look at the two organizations I helped to start, GMPA and FUQU—my children—and I ask myself: What have we accomplished?

And I am forced to answer: very little.

People are still dying like flies. The White House is still as inaccessible as the moon. We have been unable to make the world pay attention, much less care. We are still pariahs. We have not stopped this plague.

I believe we do not understand how this disease, in all ways, is spread. I don't believe the blood supply is safe. Only a short time ago four hundred thousand people in France were given infected blood because of stupid bureaucrats.

I don't believe much of what any government agency tells me about *anything*: UC, statistics, safety, sex, *anything*. If you'd spent as much time as I have these past ten years dealing with bureaucrats, you'd know how second-rate so many of them are, how mentally, intellectually, morally, and spiritually bankrupt so many of them are, how inexperienced, naïve, and badly educated in their fields so many of them are. How could anyone possibly trust a government that puts out a definition of UC that denies that women can get it?

So ten years into a plague, here we are. It is exceedingly weird to picture, ten years ago, the start of GMPA in my living room, and to be here with so many of you tonight in this cathedral, telling you that everything we have done and we are doing has been useless.

The only thing that is going to make this plague go away is a cure at the most and successful treatments at the least. And UC research is still in the Stone Age.

There is not one drug that is any good.

GMPA should have been in the forefront. Dr. Krank's UC Foundation should have been in the forefront, a dozen other gay and UC organizations should have been in the forefront, of being the furious watchdogs on UC research. It is painful for me personally but I must finally face up to the fact that someone as clever and well-connected and appealing as my friend Dr. Monserrat Krank, and her partner, Elizabeth Taylor, have proved little more than dilettantes. Did it never occur to Elizabeth Taylor, who has a daughter-in-law with UC, to have requested a meeting with her fellow actor Peter Ruester, who got us into this mess? I look at the long list of famous names on Monserrat's national council. I ask myself: What have any of these people done for UC? Woody Allen, Warren Beatty, Burt Bacharach, Rosalynn Carter, Douglas Fairbanks, Samuel Sircus, Marilyn Horne, Angela Lansbury, Lady Bird Johnson, Adreena Schneeweiss . . .

Every one of these people knows people in positions of great power. And not one of them will get on the phone and call these people up and say, "Let's all work together to demand and obtain help!"

Brooke Astor was quoted in the paper talking about the New York City fiscal crisis in the '70s and how New Yorkers from all walks of life banded together to fight for this city. "Labor unions, financiers, artists, writers," Mrs. Astor said. "One just doesn't see that kind of rallying together today. I don't really know why."

Two years of my begging GMPA board member Joan Table for a meeting with her husband, Bob, one of the richest and most powerful men in the world, who was on Ruester's cabinet, have resulted in nothing. Joan Table, I don't think you or your husband want to end this plague.

Why haven't Bob Table and Dr. Saul Farber, the head of your hospital, the Table Hospital, and Dr. David Rogers and Dr. David Ho and Dr. June Osborn and Dr. Monserrat Krank and Sammy Sircus and Dick Jenrette and Randy Dildough and Pat Buckley and Perdita Pugh and Michael Sovern and Barney Frank and Gerry Studds all talked to each other and gone as a group to tell Dredd Trish that because no one talks to anyone else and because no one is in charge of a plague, millions of people are going to die?

Shame on you, Bob Table. Shame on you, Joan Table. Shame on you, Monserrat Krank. Shame on you, Perdita Pugh. Shame on you, Sammy and Randy and Dick and Douglas and Elizabeth and Woody and all the rest of you. Good fortune has presented you with wealth and prominence and power and a platform and a voice and you refuse to use them to end this plague that I am certain has already murdered a number of your friends.

It's ten years since my living room and everyone still doesn't get it!

Everyone will call me nuts—boy, this time Fred's really gone too far and flipped his lid, now he's even biting all the hands that are giving us our only handouts.

There's got to be a higher vision for your reason for being! You've got to want to end this! Instead I see thousands of volunteers spending hours and days at endless meetings—just like all the bureaucrats in Washington—meetings that have nothing to do with ending this plague. Plus all those useless, well-meaning board members who have absolutely no sense of urgency, no sense of urgency, no sense of urgency, no sense of urgency, that 40 million people will die in a few short years' time.

I tell you, it would make not one single bit of difference to the progress of this plague if GMPA wasn't here, and Monserrat's organization wasn't here.

We suffer one defeat after another, one death after another, one monster in the White House after another, and we take it, we lie down and take it, and our boards of directors and our national councils go home to apartments on Park Avenue in their limousines instead of driving directly to the White House.

Dr. Omicidio, little Napoleon, the government's great apologist, now admits publicly that ZAP still isn't working and that ZOK and the D drugs are yesterday's rotten tomatoes. Muck just canceled their L drug. There is not one drug that is any good! I am telling you research on this disease is still in the Stone Age! Why? You think it's because science has to take its own time? Wrong! It's because nobody's in charge of anything! Nobody is watching the pot not boil. Nobody is sending the blokes into the lab with the marching orders: study this! We know what has to be studied. It isn't being studied. The full pathogenesis of this virus still hasn't been studied. Pathogenesis means what's really happening inside us that leads to disease. It's usually the first thing that's studied. Ten years—it still hasn't been studied. Researchers do not want to study the bodies of dying, infected, contagious faggots.

I go to NITS and one office doesn't know what the next office is doing. This complete and utter lack of communication exists from the highest to the lowest, from lab to lab, from sea to shining sea.

For years I have been calling, begging, pleading, for a Manhattan Project for UC. Why does every board and every organization ignore such an obvious suggestion? Why does no one join me in this call? Bob Table, if the value of your real estate is going down because of UC, and this city, of which you are unofficial mayor, is going down the toilet because of fearful tourists, and your hospital is so filled up we can't get into it, why don't you and Dr. Farber join me in this call for a Manhattan Project? Bob Table, I implore you from this pulpit in this house of God to call this meeting!

Let me try and put it one last way. If we spent half as much time, energy, and money fighting for a cure as we do fighting conservatives on mandatory testing and condoms and education and where should the next international conference be held and who can legally attend, we would have that cure by now and the science at NITS would be better than the food at Bob's Big Boy. We are fighting for everything *but* that cure, and we simply do not have time to fight all these lesser battles.

And you don't want to fight for that science and that research and those treatments and that vaccine and that cure. Because it requires a real shake-up of the political and the medical establishments, and you don't want to get your hands dirty. You only want to feel good and virtuous, which comes from attending events like this and writing a few checks.

I don't want your dollars to help me die! I want your brains to help me live! I don't want your dollars to build GMPA another building! I want your dollars to save my life and save the lives of 40 million other people, which you can do without buildings and a staff of hundreds. You can do it with ten, twenty, fifty important powerful board members who are willing, finally and at last, to open their mouths!

We can't expect the government to get its shit together if we can't get our shit together. And in ten years we have not got our shit together. The right wing and the religious right and the conservatives and all our enemies, they have got their shit together and they're not half as smart or as rich as we are. All the energy and creativity that goes into the UC walk and the UC dance and the UC this and that, that's not how you end a plague. That's how you bury people pretty. People who bury people pretty are not serious about ending a plague.

How do I give you the guts to be heroes and leaders? When are you all going to do that? When!

Well, now you can go home and say I heard Fred Lemish really going nuts, out of his mind, downright crazy and blaspheming one and all in a house of God. And you'll ignore me again until ten years from now, if a few of you are still alive, when you gather here for another one of these tender meetings of "Remember, Respond, Resolve," you'll say, "Oh, Fred Lemish, thank God he's gone and we don't have to listen to him anymore."

DAVID!

In the audience, in the crowd, watching Fred speaking and riveted by what he's hearing and seeing, is David Jerusalem. He is smiling.

AFTER CHURCH

Mike Grundy and Farley Falls and Melton O'Gresci had left the cathedral fast because Melton had fainted at the end of Fred's speech and they practically carried him to some restaurant to get some coffee into him.

Melton bawled. "I can't stand to hear Fred Lemish make one more speech. He depresses me and everything depresses me and all I want to do is die."

Mike Grundy, who is Melton's lover and very very rich, as is Melton, shook an antidepressant out of a Cartier vial full of them and gave it to his lover with a bottle of water. Melton grabbed the vial and the water and ran out into the street. It was snowing heavily and he managed to get away from his friends by dodging cars and taxis and buses quite adeptly for one who'd so recently collapsed. He ran back behind the cathedral and found a little nook and swallowed all the pills and was found dead in the morning covered in snow and ice.

Fred, who had a terrible cough and managed to make the speech all doped up on something or other that Rebby had given him to "squirt down your throat," went home with Tommy.

"You were brilliant, honey. One of your best. Did you see how they all stood up for you and cheered louder than I've ever heard before? A standing ovation in the Cathedral of St. John the Divine!"

"I don't want a standing ovation! I want them to listen to me and do as I say! And they don't. They fucking don't." He took a sleeping pill too, but only one and just to calm him down enough so he could sleep until tomorrow.

FROM THE NOTEBOOKS OF
JAMES JESUS ANGLETON

CODE NAME: MOTHER

So our leading characters are busy, which is what leading characters do or we wouldn't need them for leading characters. It pains me to know what's been happening and is going to happen.

I have seen power all my life. I have seen the mighty fall and the fallen rise and return to avenge. I have seen presidents too dumb to wipe their own asses. I have been called upon to save several of these.

There is not a person or place or drama (potential, incipient, on the verge of exploding) where I cannot summon a contact or expert or lackey. I have fashioned this world with my instincts and brain. I know I am the most powerful of men. I know I have saved my country more than once. And certainly more than my predecessors, for whom I have little if any respect.

I have never been afraid a day in my life. I was made for this. It came too naturally for it to have been a choice. I have loved every minute of it, challenging myself to sort out the impossible. If I fear anything, it's that I'll lose my protective cover because of those in power that I have saved. Loyalty is a nonexistent commodity in my line of work.

There is a plague. Until Deep Throat, I'd not paid sufficient attention to it. World peace, certainly this country's, had not been threatened enough by it to bring it to my attention. Purpura facilitated much of this plague. Another foolish but very adept person who kept the country going, her way. She and Sam Sport had spoken every day. They each knew there are more idiots than usual running this world and capitalized on it. Neither had warned me about UC. Now Sam Sport has died from it. He'd been a horrid and evil fool, but useful.

I have known many evil men. Dictators only want power, so they could be tricked and bought. They're usually dumb. Evil people are often but not always dumb. Through the war years there were enough educated men I could call on. I'd brought many of them along from Yaddah. For years Yaddahites provided the intellectual grease that oiled every trouble spot in the world as we saw it. Now there are fewer men willing and open to such patriotic devotion. Tom Jones had located all the brains from Yaddah to work for our organization. I miss Tom Jones. We hadn't been such good friends after Hoover made everyone sign his pledge of allegiance against the Communists. No, that hadn't been one of Edgar's best ideas. You can't win them all, and James Jesus Angleton has won most of them. Beauty, too, can be evil, as is often the case in a plague. Ezra Pound was evil. He wanted to destroy every artist's beauty but his own. I'd published him in my student literary magazine at Yaddah. I'd had to have him murdered at St. Purdah's. He'd gone insane and treasonous. Tom Jones was dead now too.

Dredd Trish ran the CIA. I knew him well. He was a lousy spymaster. He was a lousy vice president and is a lousy president. He's ignoring this plague too. He's got a gay son he's going to make president. That will prove very dumb. I have always smelled the stinkers coming. That's how I know this UC will be a worldwide plague. Yes, I miss Tom Jones. Homosexuals have certainly been a complicated puzzle for this country.

Deep Throat's suggestions are too expensive and controversial and hence difficult to execute. I fear it may be too late anyway. I'll see.

These gay UC warriors are a touching and I fear a pathetic bunch. They are fighting with all their might. They can't get near a president or any real seat of power. Between Ruester and Trish it's one long kick in their asses. These poor kids are hated indeed. But I shall see what I can see.

These notebooks must be my elevation to a realm of unchallenged reliability heretofore unknown to CIA directors. Hans Frank laid waste to most of Poland and detailed every bit of his hateful crimes in hundreds of daily notebooks. They were his attempt to ascend to the Olympian Parnassian heights of immortality. He'd be there right alongside his Hitler, who had ruled his world. Perversely, Hans thought his notebooks would save him when he came to trial at Nuremberg. Well, my notebooks will give me the benefit of truth. I know my enemies will want to put forth quite a different story.

I begged Edgar to do the same, to detail his many remarkable feats. But he had everything burned, and look what a shabby image now sticks to him for all time.

Peter Ruester was a very stupid and selfish man, never able to comprehend and absorb the entire floor plan of his country's intelligence operations. It was left to the idiots Gobbel and Moose to keep his mind occupied elsewhere. This allowed Purpura to run our country. Until Deep Throat filled me in, I'd no idea she was so determined to bury UC.

Now, where was I? I'm often amazed I can keep the shenanigans of all these assholes straight. Eisenhower, Nixon, Ford, Carter, our country has rarely been blessed. Ah, yes, Dredd Trish. The idiot who's been let loose upon us now. His main talent is that he employs his manipulative talents without leaving any fingerprints. No notebooks for him! His genial disposition disguises how cunning and devious he is. We were at Yaddah together. He gave me no notice because of my interest in artsy-craftsy things. He was in Skull and Bones, of course, as was his even more manipulative father, whom he worshipped and tried so hard to please, and as will be his extraordinarily wimpy homosexual son. Between Procter and Dredd, they know every important rich man in both our country and in the Arab world. Remember, the father was a partner in Brown Brothers Harriman, then the most important international money management nexus in the world and founded by one of his uncles. Procter, too, thought Hitler was going to win the war, and he and the rich sheiks invested accordingly, which made him very rich. The Trishes are still big with the Arabs. That's how Dredd got into the oil business that made him even richer.

He didn't want to run the CIA. The CIA was a mess in those days. Too many mistakes in Vietnam, for starters. We've been in one war or another ever since. Watergate did not help. Dredd worked for Nixon who sent him to run the CIA. Being the country's chief spy was thought to be a political plum. Dredd himself thought it was a trick to keep him out of the White House. Shovels had yet to arrive in his life to provide the spine of steel that's upholding this ninny.

I consider it weak to hide behind deceptions, at which he is most expert, gentleman to the outside world and vicious ambitious sneak "with clean hands" to others. I guess Bill Casey, my predecessor, loved him; you could never tell what Bill really thought about anything: he spoke so softly you could hardly hear him and he never wrote anything down. Casey got Ruester elected.

It is now obvious to me that about the time UC was taking root, everyone in D.C. was wound up with taking sides for either Iran or Iraq. Dredd was viciously pro-Iraq and defended Saddam Hussein to the max. This had much to do with keeping his rich Arab buddies pacified.

Yes, it is straight white men's wars that are responsible for gay men's deaths. With so many wars going on, and there will always be a number of them, American power is focused elsewhere. But hate is hate, whatever its source. In this particular case, it breaks my heart.

Deep Throat has told me that for some reason Dredd facilitated the transfer via COD to Hussein of a supply of viruses, retroviruses, bacteria, fungi, tissue that was infected with bubonic plague, as well as West Nile viruses and plague-infected mouse tissue smears. All this to Saddam Hussein. Dredd was that supportive of Iraq. Others around him favored Iran, and others said, let's keep out of this part of the world, it can only portend major warfare. I was one of these. I pointed out that Iraq was working on developing nuclear weapons. But then Dredd would not pay any attention to me. I had not been in Skull and Bones. Slowly Saddam was murdering more than one million of his fellow Arabs. His menu of torture methods was even to me quite appalling. The world has little idea of how many different kinds of Arabs there are and how hate and retribution are acceptable under certain circumstances according to their Koran.

I discovered that bin Laden family money—and it was an exceptionally large family—financed Dredd Trish's Texas oil company. Dredd didn't know squat about oil but Proctor told him to move to Texas.

The bin Ladens were, with the royal family, one of Saudi Arabia's most important powers. Both families had heads who fathered innumerable sons by vast numbers of wives. What Bill Casey and Moose and Gobbel and Shovels (each of whom have privately profited hugely from Saudi "generosity") did not understand about the innuendoes of this culture, which would cost America a fortune and a great number of dead sons!

No one was listening to the likes of me. Bill Casey and Gobbel with Ruester and Purpura were in power, and most of the rest of America and its bureaucrats could not tell the difference between Iran and Iraq, including Dredd, who could be heard mentioning one when he meant the other. (Believe it or not, Edgar Hoover and I had both been warning the Kennedy brothers to beware the Middle East and stop worrying so much about Russia, which did not possess sufficient cash resources.

By the time UC dared to appear and spread, the attention of Ruester, Trish, Hussein, and bin Laden was busy elsewhere. As America would ignore UC it would ignore the long-term implications of being in bed with an equally destructive network of fundamentalist rebels. Afghanistan took a lot of minds off a lot of other problems closer to home. Politicians always like when foreign affairs can be whipped up to disguise their more homespun chicaneries. (Foreign affairs have been my bailiwick.) Dredd Trish certainly was not going to give a tinker's damn, a flying fuck, about some fairy problem, even though he knew his son is one of them. Russia was what everyone else in Washington, including myself and all my best minds, was convinced was the enemy, but Dredd Trish was manufacturing another enemy with this Osama bin Laden. We were and are supporting this war centering in Afghanistan into what will be a nonstop existence. Trish visited Osama, bringing a check for some $70 million. After calling Russia "the evil empire," Peter Ruester was more and more out to lunch and Purpura really wasn't interested in any of this. Dredd had thought his ticket to ride was via Hussein and bin Laden. And Bill Casey convinced him that the war had crippled the Soviet Union.

I had not been the only one calling Dredd a wimp. The media was after him for befriending so many questionable Arabs. To turn that tide Dredd did what Dredd does best as he hid behind his apparent wimpiness. He turned on Iraq and Saddam Hussein, who had promised not to invade enemy Kuwait then promptly did so, threatening the entire world's oil supplies. Dredd sent every important diplomat all over the globe to bid them to join America in ridding the world of Saddam, including our own chief enemy Russia. And the most powerful PR firm in existence, Hill & Knowlton (run by a gay man, my friend Robert Gray), created the most imaginative horror propaganda involving Iraqi soldiers kidnapping Kuwaiti babies from out of their incubators and leaving them on the floor to die. A teenaged girl told this story in tears, and those tears lubricated an unwilling America into war. (She was actually some Arab diplomat's daughter and there were no incubators in any Kuwaiti hospitals.) Thus came and went the Gulf War with hundreds of thousands dead from many nations.

The Trishes will be responsible for these great wars, which are still ongoing, with the aid of their Saudi friends. Both Hussein and bin Laden will be murdered on orders from Trish.

Why were we here, so far from Valley Forge and Gettysburg? To this we've come. Is this how we make America great? To set up the very system of Islamic terrorism we'll soon be trying so hard to dismantle.

"The less anyone knows, the better." These words are the watch cry as

Washington life goes on. Deal and counterdeal, alliances of friends and foes, mysterious bank accounts all over the world in places heretofore never considered anything but podunks, untraceable only to expensive lawyers. It is so easy to hide anything and everything in this country, and this world, that it truly is ridiculous. Why bother with law and order? "Plausible deniability" is the name of every game. Well, I am expert in playing this game of hide-and-seek.

Spies most often come from hideous unhappy childhoods and backgrounds and long to be part of a stable and paternalistic home base. I am their mother and father. They feel safe with me. No one felt safe with Dulles or Trish or Wild Bill, or anyone really, until I came along. I have invented a new world my boys and girls can live in and actually believe in irrespective of all the available evidence. All the good ones have been able to think themselves into this other place. I believe I have trained them well.

I feel great sympathy for the young gay men who are suffering. I was once one of them myself, facing a world I did not think I'd survive in. The Trishes of Yaddah would destroy me.

I am called "the theorist." I understand the function of trivia, of miscellaneous information, and assimilate it into a coherent scenario others might miss. "The theoretician of American intelligence." This is what I am called by the Yaddah historian Robin Winks, in his treatise on the secret wars that brought us into existence. How to penetrate the enemy without the enemy knowing? I am thought to have the greatest penetration in counterintelligence. Penetration is the key to counterintelligence. I believe in the spy as a valid, necessary, even primary and, yes, noble defender of American values. "Secrecy, silence, cunning," as I believe James Joyce said. That's the name of our game too. One goes to school with the poets to learn the use of language, especially the use of ambiguity. I can remember my own lies, necessary for a successful spy, at the same time as I often have affection for many who have lied with and/or for me. The nature of civilization often necessitates people to lie in order to stay alive. This wilderness of mirrors reflects our moral meaning. I believe in the highest goals for our country and am more and more truly frightened that these ideals are being destroyed by my own country's fecklessness and we remain in a state of constant emergency.

It all boils down to this: anything man could conceive of, however evil, men could and most probably will do. That is the base of human nature. Tom Jones, the most devious of men and the best of teachers, first taught me this. Because of him I have become head of all CIA counterintelligence. The press loves to call me "America's legendary master spy." How would it know? But thank you very much.

I will continue to cultivate all my orchids, the one sustaining beauty in all my life. I'm going to die soon enough. I can smell that coming too. I will be taken down by one of my own. That is what usually happens to spies, particularly the good ones. Just like I know that UC is a plague and that Deep Throat's suggestions will never be executed. FUQU will not save us from this plague. The homosexual population of this world is being greatly diminished.

Should I devote some discussion of the mole hunt that Floyd Harmish is manufacturing to bring me down? He had to create his own new stories when his old truth was all used up.

Or are there certain matters that you take with you to the tomb?

But then, no case is ever dead. Even if we are.

Yes, I have always kept a diary. Day by day, year by year. That is how history will know what I did and why I did it. The best record keepers were the Nazis. Immaculate, their facts and figures and directives. Amazing, the high quality of their belief in what they were doing. They obviously wanted history to know what they did. Everyone important thinks they're right and everyone who disagrees with them is wrong. I have been right, of course.

Fundamentally we all are liars. The better you lie and the more you betray, the more likely you are to be promoted. My boys and girls attract and promote each other. The thing they have in common is a desire for power that is useful. I was part of it and I loved it. I taught them to consider their targets and believe they were dealing with a bunch of people who would deservedly go to hell.

We had to think the unthinkable. And fashion confusion for our opponents with cleverly packaged false information.

With my death will go most of America's secrets.

Hoover and I both used secrets to keep everyone in line.

That's how I got along with Allen Dulles. I promised him if he left me alone I'd keep quiet about his connections with Hitler.

Hoover, by the way, was the greatest spy in our history. He did much more for this country than he's given credit for. His flaw was that he enjoyed the limelight too much. He loved being famous. And he does not appear to have left any notebooks. His beloved Clyde burned everything. The two of them kept more of us alive than will ever be known.

I must make a note here to keep an eye out on young Dereck Dumster.

I can smell him coming too and I believe he may surpass all his predecessors in iniquity against America. Sadly, I fear I shall not be here.

THE SHIT HITS THE FAN

PERRY: The FUQU Women's Issues group proposes a six-month "moratorium on meetings with COD and NITS and anyone on the outside." This proposal would restrict FUQU strategy "vis-à-vis women's issues and all our other issues" to direct action only. It proves extremely controversial and is voted down at an April 8 meeting.

•

FRED: Here it is at last, bubbling up out of its cauldron of suppression, out of the women's continuing rejection by Omicidio, NITS, and COD, and taking this out on the men of FUQU who "go inside" and talk to the pharmas, which the women still cannot do, no matter how hard they've tried. Each day the chasm widens between the women of the Women's Committee and the men of T and D. Each side is convinced, and determined to believe, that the other is against them.

•

SPARKS: A small group of activists, many of them from the Women's Caucus, are undermining T and D, breaking down trust between FUQU and other community organizations, enraging communities of color, undercutting the achievements of treatment activism, and obstructing future progress. The end result of all this activity can only be the exodus of most of T and D into our new organization, TAG, and the growing irrelevance of the remaining shell of FUQU in the area in which it had made its greatest initial impact, UC research and treatment. I have tried to negotiate with the Women's Caucus in good faith to work things out, but I am unwilling to give up the still nascent access to various pharmas that we in T and D are so recently and arduously winning.

•

MAXINE: Bill M. tells me that T and D is meeting with pharmaceutical companies about taking money to conduct research in community-based environments. They had not talked to the floor, to tell us, to ask for FUQU's permission. More and more it is apparent T and D believe they can do anything they want to. Bill had wanted me to bring up a proposal that would not allow this to happen. We are not only talking about this betrayal of our principles. We simply do not take money from the enemy, and the drug companies are our enemy!

•

SCOTTY: We decided last August in T and D that we would seek a million dollars from pharmaceutical companies. Why not? Rebby's CRI community research initiative had gone belly-up. The reaction from the pharmas is actually pretty good. Fourteen of them came to our meeting to discuss this. A few want guarantees that if they fund us we would not picket them, and we turned them down flat on this. I gave them the example of our working with Starlight on their Gavcon formula during the day and picketing them in the evening over their ridiculous price for their Vent, for which I spent the night in jail. The floor is in an uproar when they hear about our meeting with the pharmas. "We've got to stop Sparks and Scotty!" Maxine is telling everyone. I am more and more amazed that there are so-called UC activists willing to expend so much energy to win a perceived power struggle with their very own.

•

MAXINE: Policy is made by the floor, not by individuals or a committee, no matter how "good" the idea is. I am neither psychologically nor personally terrorized by Sparks's name in large print at the top of his letter to us, nor by his attempt to paint himself as someone I am trying "to get." Scotty and Sparks, your arrogance and egotism are amazing—I would not waste my time trying to "get" you. That you think every issue has you, personally, at its center is your problem, not mine. And whether or not we ever get to discuss and vote on the particular issue of taking money from pharmaceutical companies, I will continue to raise these issues as long as I am a member of this organization.

•

FRED: There was a smoking gun. I had smelled the smoke. I didn't recognize that it stank as much as it did. I knew it meant trouble but I thought I could talk them out of it. But when I tried, they weren't listening. No one was listening, T and D kids especially. The floor of FUQU didn't care. "Let them go. Snits and snots, uppity beyond belief, let the selfish bastards go." There are a lot who feel this way. Oh, I'd sniffed discontent in the ranks—it would be hard not to in an organization this size—but in any case, my paternal feeling about FUQU wasn't acknowledged by a lot of them so it wasn't as if I could do much more than shouting FIRE! Of course I'm weaseling out here: I could have done something! I could have! I should have! As Tommy has told me more times than I care to hear, I'm a great idea man but shitty on the follow-through, the details. I don't have the patience for that. So now FUQU is dying. I call them all my children in my heart, and many of my favorite kids are leaving home.

•

PERRY: The background to all of this included that T and D, all white men, objected to the women, both white and of color, who objected to their not objecting that the UCCTG Trial Seventy-six endangered the lives of pregnant women. This trial gave ZAP to pregnant women to see if their babies would be born uninfected and, again, COD, FADS, and now TAG, ignored input from women. Women of color in many chapters get incensed. How dare a trial that endangers our lives be something that any part of FUQU can support! That is too much to ask pregnant mothers to do: to possibly sacrifice their newborn infants in this way! I don't care if the bastards leave, they said; let them go play tag with their tiny pee-pees somewhere else. But it got even more complicated. Women of color who weren't in FUQU and weren't activists started screaming that *all* of FUQU should keep their noses out of it—these women *wanted* the drug and were willing to gamble and told us to all go shove it and mind our own business. This was the first time anything like this happened, and there was far from any consensus on the floor or off it of what to do. T and D of course had helped set up the trial's parameters. I wrote an article for the first TAG newsletter pretty much like what I've written here, and Sparks killed it. He didn't think it was "politically appropriate" at this moment.

•

HETTIE: Harriett, like Tracy, truly believes people are still spying on us. And what Harriett believes, Hettie believes. Someone threw a brick through Rebecca P.'s window, and she lives in Washington Heights. Yes, the resolution was voted down, but not before the damage was done. Sparks, particularly, and Scotty, felt they could no longer put up with a situation "where paranoid dykes could get the floor to vote on destructive stuff."

•

ANN: I definitely believe the FBI is infiltrating us to hasten our decline. I also think Harriett and hence Hettie was planted in our midst to cause damage. Maxine agrees.

•

PERRY: We may never know whether the harassment of FUQU women was the work of the NYPD, the FBI, or another government agency, or some disturbed member of FUQU. There are more than enough potentially crazy people around. Harriett and Hettie said they received many hang-up calls. Then they said they began to get bizarre phone messages, some linked to a three-way calling system that had phone sex on the third line. Other women were linked to three-way calls to which Harriett was connected. She said she hadn't placed the calls. Then she said it wasn't a brick, it was a bullet that was fired through Rebecca P.'s apartment window in Washington Heights. Someone left a vial of poison by Saramae's door. Keri's mother was told she had died, when she was actually on her way to a zap in D.C. Needle Exchange member Jane A. found a used syringe taped to her door with a note saying, "Use this you bitch." Each week another woman tells of another incident.

•

SPARKS: I don't believe any of them.

•

SCOTTY: UC activism was my whole life, exhilarating. When it stopped being fun, and when it became painful, it was time to get out, for self-preservation.

•

FRED: Okay. Then get out. Get out. Get fucking out! But do you have to take our heart and soul and brains with you? That seems incredibly selfish and arrogant. The least, the very least you could have done is to allow us to discuss this before making it such a fait accompli. I went to a TAG meeting uninvited and said all this to them.

•

PERRY: TAG is afraid of Fred. They think he's too powerful and volatile. And they feel vulnerable, especially starting something new. Therefore

Sparks insists that Fred's kept in the dark about what they're intending to do, and when the split occurs Fred's not asked to join our new organization. Many in TAG continue in FUQU. Maxine is convinced they keep attending so they can vote against anything that would interfere with what TAG is now planning. It's all nasty. Fred makes any number of "appeals to reason" on the floor, imploring "everyone to come back, get word to your friends to come back." Maxine's prediction about "our new powerlessness"—well, we see it beginning to come true. "There are no more outside-inside teams to work both sides of the street," she warns TAG. "You will never have the power that you had in T and D, in FUQU," she warns Sparks.

•

FRED: Everyone will have a different view of what is happening. But Maxine and yours truly will be right. The crazies will take over FUQU and TAG will become another bureaucracy. Just you wait, Henry Higgins!

•

SCOTTY: I know there was a general sense that I was responsible for taking the organization in a more structured direction than people were comfortable with. And there was a definite backlash against both real and perceived ego and arrogance on my part, that and the fact that I was the media darling of the organization and had a lot of the limelight culminating in my speaking in San Francisco and being on TV all over the world.

I figure because of me we sold more than a million dollars' worth of FUQU merchandise around the country. I had quite a mail-order business going at one point. In the gay pride parades we would sell twenty thousand, thirty thousand dollars' worth of merchandise at a pop. The biggest seller was always "Read My Lips," two guys, or two girls kissing each other, even more than our SILENCE=DEATH T-shirt. I was definitely full of self-confidence and cocky, and I was arrogant as all hell too, to the point of being obnoxious. We had two art auctions I ran. The first made about three hunded thousand, and the second one more than a million. We had real money at last! I made us rich! When I look back on myself during those days I'm a bit uncomfortable. I could have definitely used some humility then.

Very quickly in FUQU it became very PC to sleep with somebody who was positive, as a way of saying, I'm not afraid of this, safe sex works—it was a political statement. And God bless 'em, because I was dying to get back into the ball game and all of a sudden I was in high demand and it was just fabulous. It was fun. It definitely had for me the added dynamic that I was very, very frightened of dying without a boyfriend taking care of me, so there were not many times when I did not have a boyfriend. I would latch on to whoever was showing interest at the time, whether it was a good match or not. There was desperation on my part, and I know I ruffled feathers as I sort of kept trading upward from Michael M. to Brian McN. to Carlton and a few others and eventually to Kevin and to Perry.

At the same time Iris was teaching us in T and D about this gigantic bureaucracy, FADS and NITS, that is preventing any lifesaving drugs from getting to us. The more we poked our noses into that world, the more there was a growing palpable fear of us. You could see it and sense it and feel it. Our threat was FUQU demonstrations. We were doing quite a job on certain senior people at FADS and NITS, putting their pictures on posters, almost like branding them Nazis. We hit hard in a very personal way. We had never been violent, but there was now fear from Pharma that we would turn violent, that they were next. Every member of T and D was assigned a pharmaceutical manufacturer to get to know and let them get to know us.

For me the cornerstone of FUQU was the fact that we were not willing to be wedged into one standard idea of what an activist movement is. We had this level of desperation that permitted us to try any and all techniques at the same time, that ultimately came down to this inside-versus-outside approach. You sit down with them, and the very next week you punch them in the face. Marie Clayture at FADS wasn't evil to me. She was just playing a very predictable role, and we had to tell her what we wanted from her and FADS in very clear terms and then apply the external pressure to make her do what we wanted. But we weren't going to get her to do exactly what we wanted unless we did both things—the external pressure and sitting down and talking it out with her, and making her realize that she was dealing with highly motivated, highly rational and intelligent people who had something to say, not some screaming raving idiots who were calling her a murderer and marching outside her front door, which of course was us, too. It was that combination that I thought was our power. Fred had explained very early to the floor how all the big movie companies he'd worked for did a version of this. Good cop, bad cop, it's called. Marie Clayture quit because of us.

T and D greased the wheels to make it so that drug development could happen more quickly, and even though FUQU was raking companies like Greeting over the coals until they were one of the most disrespected corporate names in the country, by the time the '90s came around there were two or three times the number of companies involved in UC research as there were in the beginning, which really goes to show you how practical our approach was coming along.

FUQU went from someplace that was my family, it was everything, to a place that was just very painful. There were these two gigantic camps. One that wanted the organization to be solely a traditional civil disobedience group, and one that wanted it to be both a civil disobedience and really smart lobbying group. And those two camps started really butting heads. And it got down to a point where FUQU was trying to cut off the inside work. T and D was definitely working very independently. We were acting very elitist. It was a fair criticism. We felt like we knew what we were doing. The debates we were getting involved with were very complex. (We were kind of our own little enterprise, but we weren't the only splinter group in FUQU acting independently, as became very apparent at the church action, which became a definitely unchoreographed-in-advance extravaganza.) Then Maxine proposed that we should no longer be able to meet with the government or pharmas. It didn't pass, it wasn't even close, but it was frightening and it was a defining moment for T and D.

A few years earlier I had filed papers, and now I was ready to put it out: the Treatment Action Guerrillas. Did I smell anything that early? I think what I smelled was something I could be in charge of. I just kept waiting for the rest of T and D to get to the emotional place where they were ready to walk away as well. We formally split. Sparks and Gregg and Melvin and Barbara and Claudette and Spud and Barry and of course Perry—it was originally about ten to fifteen of us, maybe more. In no time flat we had thirty, forty, fifty at meetings in Melvin's loft. It was all by invitation only. Eigo wouldn't come. Fred wanted to be part of it when he finally heard about us, but Sparks said no.

•

FRED: Scotty, you do know that you are murdering FUQU?
SCOTTY: Fred, you're full of shit.

•

MAXINE: Fuqu had been listened to because we have been smart and can call out hundreds, and sometimes thousands of people to back up our demands and ideas. If we do not find a way to continue to do that—in actuality and not only as a threat—we will soon find out that we have no clout, no matter how smart we are.

•

SPARKS: Knowingly they sought to divide us. Their function is as destructive as if they were provocateurs sent in from outside to weaken us and divert our energies away from our proper goals and into FUQU's growing division. Our critics refuse to let us develop our new methods, which they claim lack the ideological "purity" demanded of "the movement," but which stand in stark contrast to their repeated failure to budge NITS. FUQU's ability to influence the national debate on UC has now been eclipsed by FUQU's own internal paralysis. This proudest and once most effective UC organization now finds itself involved in vicious cycles of self-recrimination, periodic orgies of attacking its closest allies, leaving the true antagonists unscathed. FUQU is now so bitterly factionalized it rarely rises to the occasion to mount more ambitious campaigns. To make matters worse, those of us who actually continue to focus on UC work are regularly vilified and held up to collective abuse. I am not interested in belonging any longer to a frustrated legacy erected over a pile of our corpses so that lifelong movement parasites can deny my agenda. Adherence to collective procedures can, in the hands of a practiced crowd psychologist, be as crushingly oppressive as an old-style oligarchy, churning up a series of blatant lies, enthusiastically spread. FUQU must take its directions from people with UC, and not from these parasites whose primary stake is only in political agitation and often over specific non-UC issues. At its best FUQU moved from opposition to constructive involvement in changing things. At its worst, it has been reduced to negating itself with intrigue and infighting.

•

MAXINE: I do not recognize the organization Sparks lambasts so. Scotty and Sparks are succeeding in dividing the world into the infected vs. the uninfected, even though both TAG and FUQU are peopled with each, and into treatment activism vs. social activism, the latter anything to do with women or people of color or drug users. I believe they are so successful because anyone who disagrees with them is too afraid to speak out publicly. TAG members keep coming to FUQU and voting against anything that might be against their plans. It's all increasingly nasty and escalating. This group, our very comrades-in-arms! A coalition can't work if we don't admit that in every category the world uses to describe us and we use to describe ourselves (UC-positive, women, men, Afro-Americans, Latino/a, white, gay, lesbian, trans, straight, and so on), people within those categories do not always agree with each other. We have to get past the idea that things we disagree about can't be discussed, even when there are passionate feelings on all sides of an issue, a discussion that TAG is stonewalling. I did not propose the moratorium on women's issues re. meeting with the government and the drug companies. I did bring that proposal to the floor for discussion on behalf of the FUQU Network Women's Issues Committee, which was concerned because of all the rumors that were creating so much underground dissent. I thought it was important for it to be discussed and voted on in a timely fashion, and a lot of new points of view were raised. I have been a longtime activist because there has been longtime injustice in the world. I did not come to FUQU opportunistically or to preach any particular line. I came to FUQU because I am a lesbian and because people in one of my communities, the lesbian and gay community, are dying as a result of government homophobia and criminal neglect. In the course of being in FUQU I learned more about the crisis and became even more committed to doing the work to stop it. Like Eigo, I believe that FUQU is the only organization doing the work we do, and I worry about us not being around anymore in full force to do it. And like Eigo and Fred, I hope we can find ways to bring back those who have left and to keep new people coming to a welcoming environment where they will take initiative to work on any and all issues of concern to all of us and that will contribute to our goal of saving lives.

•

FRED (confronting Scotty and Sparks): YOU ARE MURDERING US!

SCOTTY: Stop saying that!

FRED: You are taking away our brains and leaving us with only our bodies.

SPARKS: Don't be such a drama queen.

FRED: You will never have as much power as you have here with us all working together.

SPARKS: Your buddy Maxine said the same thing. Well, you're both wrong and we'll prove it to you.

FRED: Yes, but at what great cost to us! Shame on the lot of you!

SHAME

Yet another heartbreaking scenario playing out on our field of battle, the number of them growing, lessening, then expanding, like an accordion trying to squeeze air into its lungs, but in the end collapsing in disjointed disharmony as all the players playing are canceling each other out. Can facts among this debris be accumulated, sifted, whatever it takes to overcome the shame of it?

Fred Lemish has been told many times that *shame* is a shameful word to use when talking to gay people, a hateful word associated with too many traumas that plague memory with dense layers of unremovable gunk. It's called plaque when it sticks to your teeth and it's called shit when it comes out of your gut and it's called a smelly mess after you've farted out clouds of it with your compacted stored-up gas. You never can shit it all out. Or forget. Well, more and more shame is beginning to run through FUQU's History of Unremovable Gunk as all the once mighty rivers in this world of ours engorge into one.

T and D is having especial success in its endeavors to break down walls and open doorways into a system that many other FUQU members, particularly the women and the very sick, have been powerless to breach. But the women have been unable to force an officialdom to change the definition of UC to state unequivocally that UC indeed infects women. Such a stupid and unnecessary fight, and it has gone on for so very long. Pewkin had given many reasons, including that it would be too expensive to change all the paperwork. Dr. Paulus Pewkin, then in charge of America's Center of Disease, actually said that. He did not mention that it would greatly increase the number of Official Cases of Record (OCR), thus upsetting insurance companies no end and increasing disability benefits and such. Dredd Trish, of course, hates us as much as Ruester did. He's even heard off camera referring to us as "those fairies." Omicidio was by his side. Jerry's often invited to the White House.

Maxine has her own fervid group of devoted acolytes who are as one with her and the philosophy that she has made her life, through all her years of activist experience with every possible path and byway with which the left has flirted. She has lived through it all, and she has seen that ruptures are usually inevitable. Deference is based on the respect most feel for her. She does not like to think she sees the beginning of FUQU's end, as Scotty and Sparks do and desire. Yes, a good case can be made that they actually desire it, and the quicker its demise, the better.

T and D is another country where the language has been difficult to learn. It is a different jargon. It is a different rap. Eigo's Reports to the Floor, brilliant in concept and content and prose, are Urdu to too many. Non-T+Ders sense they are being talked down to by a very elitist bunch. While Fred is implored weekly by a growing group of the desperate for any information on treatments—"When is something coming along to save me! I don't have much time left!"—too many with UC are not being attended to, anywhere at all. T and D's progress reports do not yet translate into action, much less hope. ZAP and combo trials are now fully enrolled by more and more desperate guinea pigs. Word is out that ZAP's a crap shoot. But nothing else is forthcoming.

Fred has recently been hauled over a few coals himself for his own "arrogance and righteousness, sounding like he's an official FUQU committee all his own," wrote Daughton Bates Wrist (gay journalists have always had their problems with Fred), who himself will die shortly in "a coma clouded by dementia," as his doctor told Fred, but not before posting in *The Prick* a "Last Will and Testament," listing all the people, including Fred, "in our community who have helped to murder me." A few months later came a similar attack in *The Prick* by Vartan Greggovakis, who, only six months earlier, had sent Fred a Valentine's Day card thanking him "for saving my life." Upon reaching Land's End Vartan saw fit "to second Daughton Bates Wrist's realization that Fred Lemish is to be condemned and not congratulated for all his shameful endeavors that have shortened my life."

At this point Scotty and Sparks get along. Neither has the vision to see that two dictators in one hegemony cannot last. Sparks will win because he is mean-spirited and arrogant and Scotty is only vain and arrogant. And Sparks is also smarter. Studying economics and history at Harvard is more useful training than studying music at Oberlin. Sparks is—well, Sparks. Fred has realized for some time that Sparks is not likable. He appears to have few friends, and those he has are minions. But Fred has always loved Scotty. He will have a difficult time, Fred will, reconciling this affection with his discovery that Scotty has turned into a turncoat shit.

Sparks also has his reasons for wanting to leave the roost: the likes of Maxine and her interfering women. Yes, the historic battleground of men vs. women, lesbians vs. gay men, why should it not flourish here? Indeed, that it has not until now is a miracle of sorts. Fred had been given to speaking glowingly of how "for the first time in a major gay organization, gay men and lesbians work in harmony!" Fred is as naïve as Sparks is mean-spirited and Scotty is vain. Perhaps Sparks will soften up. Handsome young Gregg from Boston has fallen so in love with Sparks that he has let himself become UC-positive to join him in living together.

Does any of this validate the destruction of home? For home it is to many of FUQU.

What's left are what Eric S. describes enthusiastically, and Sparks condemns disdainfully, as "social justice issues." What is left among this brotherhood and sisterhood of the dying and the dead will now be scared away by those screaming for Help the Starving Armenian kinds of causes. Where there is an instance of discrimination anywhere in the world, it is suddenly important to place it immediately on the agenda. It didn't have to be about UC; in fact, most of the new "This is a matter of life and death!" issues are not.

Where is Fred? Well, if you were to ask him, he would ask the very same. How can it be that the founder of this great thing might actually be sensing it going down the tubes and not doing enough about it? "It was something I could not own, no one could own, and no one could even speak for, as an individual. It belonged to all of them. It is democracy, but to a fault." As Fred condemns Jerry for not being in charge of NITS, Fred himself can equally be charged for not being in charge of FUQU. That each and both of these "leaders" are constitutionally unavailable for leadership occurs to no one.

Yes, Fred is naïve. He did not study economics and history at Yaddah. What indeed did he learn at Yaddah? He no longer remembers. And years of working in the movie business does not prepare one for the Real World. Remember, he made his nest egg by writing a screenplay about a paradise avec monks.

Are we getting too far ahead of ourselves again? Or just repeating ourselves? By now chronology is no longer attended to. Every day is a drama and every drama is hurtful to some part of this big body in pain.

Does destruction lie ahead indeed? Is the only question when?

Yes, it's all one big fucking shame.

MORE ASHES

DARREN: I guess we started repeating ourselves, but who knew and who cared? Or rather, some of us cared about the same thing over and over and over. It was hard not to. It's as if we have learned how to communicate telepathically through our shared pain. That's how many of us somehow knew someone else who wanted the same things. I had Ralph's ashes and I knew I wanted to throw them on the White House lawn. Correction: I knew I was going to throw them on the White House lawn. I don't think I told anyone this, but George S. asked me quietly one night if that's what I was going to do because he had his Monty's ashes and was going to do the same thing come hell or high water. I remember it was the night it was announced on the floor that TAG was splitting off. I actually started crying because it really felt like the end of something wonderful and the start of something mingy and mean, which is how many of us thought about some of the TAG guys who were always so fucking high-and-mighty, and this was proving us right. That's when I decided it was time to take Ralph to Washington. Mr. Smith goes to Washington. Ralph's last name was Smith and he loved that movie. I joined FUQU to save him. He was very sick when I went to my first meeting, and he never got any better. Each Monday night when I got home he asked me, "Any good news?" After a while he didn't have to say the words when I came through the door; his expression of pleading hope said it all. I will never forget that expression as long as I live. That and seeing his handsome body cold and dead on a trolley being prepared for his incineration. I wanted to trade my life for his. He had everything to live for. We all did. I wanted to jump on that trolley and be burned up with him. Everything is still impossible for me to comprehend or accept.

I thought there were only about a dozen of us who were to meet in Lafayette Square near the White House. When I got there, or rather when we got there—I had Ralph in the cardboard box from the undertaker—I could see there were maybe thirty or forty of us, all carrying the ashes of someone they loved in their knapsacks or in little plastic baggies they'd hid under their coats. A large contingent from FUQU had strategically placed themselves in various places along our route in D.C. to the White House, sort of like a combination of an honor guard and a cordon of protection against anyone who might try to get in our way. As we walked toward the high fence around the White House lawn I came to see how many of us there were. My eyes filled with tears that all these fellow fighters had done this, had arranged it without our even knowing about it, to be there for us. There had to be many hundreds of us, and the police saw us and realized something was up. But our marshals had things so well organized that our people were all linked up even though all these police were on horseback and they were coming closer. We had just enough time, all of us with our dead lovers, to take a position along that fence and throw our ashes, the urns, the baggies, whatever, over this black wrought-iron fence and onto that perfect lawn. People were not only crying, they were moaning. You could actually hear distinctly this loud moaning cry of agony releasing from all of us. It was like some Greek tragedy where all the mothers are in mourning for all those things that they moan about in Greek tragedies. I never heard a sound like it. The ashes on the lawn started to be whipped up by sudden breezes and they were blowing in our direction. When we saw that, when we felt that, many of us spread-eagled our bodies against the fence so as to be bathed in these ashes, reaching out to try to grab some and rub our faces and skin with them, and clutch them to us like we had them in our arms, which of course we did. By then the horses were almost upon us and the marshals were crying out the orders they'd given us from previous experiences to "SIT! SIT DOWN!" So we all sat down and the horses stopped in their tracks. This set us all off into mass hysterical laughter. We were all covered with ashes and tears and we fell into each other's arms in one huge big heap of sobs and hysterical giggles. I think we must have stayed like that for hours. It was as if we couldn't stand up again. We didn't want to leave this place where we'd buried our beloveds. I don't know if we were in trances or we actually fell asleep in exhaustion. I just remember after a while a kind voice said, "Sir, you have to get up now." I couldn't believe it was a cop, but it was, and he had tears in his eyes too. So we all got up and left our other halves there and made our way back to buses that the Coordinating Committee had thoughtfully arranged for us and we cried ourselves back home to New York.

A FUQU "MEMBER"

There is no question, we must punish you for your lives. Go right ahead, you deviants! Protest! Protest LOUDER and NONSTOP. You deviants just keep on going. Yeah!!!! The more you protest, the more you will be fought against by the likes of me. The louder you shout, the further you will be pushed back into hell. I have my master locksmith's license now. And many shades of lipstick. Releasing my hatred makes me feel warm and comfortable and ready. Thank you, FUQU. Being in your group has been good for me. I have friends who already are on the wanted list by that Southern Poverty Jew group who keep all the hate lists. It's been my ambition to be on their hate list too. Our leaders decided we don't have to go to any more FUQU meetings.

THE BRUTALITY OF FACT 729

We have turned them against each other and set them up for their fall. It's best we skedaddle before our luck runs out and we are uncovered. I'll miss some of them, though. We had some good times. But Jesus said get going, get a move on, shake your asses.

HI, MR. LEMMISH

We just came across a fifteen-year-old boy, unknown diagnosis and lost for care. I am UC site coordinator for this clinic. It just break my heart and make me very angry that this child been struggling and there is no plan. It is so fragmented the care, just documenting things not a real plan.

It is just not right that people has to wait long hours to see a doctor who have no time to speak with them. We are just following what insurance company wants. Sorry I just needed to ventilate.

Please come and talk to us at Montefiore! I can't get any doctors to do it.

—Diana Ramirez R.N.

P.S. I forgot to mention some man says he's a doctor comes to ask us to try out new treatment cure he has from checkoslovakia. He said it must be confidential. You know anything about this?

FRED ONCE LOVED HER BROTHER

In Globa, Utah, at another one of their "secret" repositories of "special" situations, Delia Montagg Swindon, a direct descendant of a founding Disciple of Lovejoy family, is, since the commencement of the UC plague, in charge of dealing with all the "unfortunate happenstances coming down that pike." The Disciples of the Brothers of Lovejoy accepts unto "our safekeeping" every body of a Disciple dead from "this destiny of sin." These bodies are embalmed and they are then wrapped in that same holy material utilized in many of their daily sacramental garments, like their underwear; and they are then stacked on shelves in climate-controlled underground vaults situated inside a hollowed-out mountain "for eternal safekeeping." Most important, in their eyes, is the fact that these bodies have not been blessed upon dying, as all "healthy" Brothers are so blessed that they may then enter heaven and join the rest of mankind. But Lovejoys are nevertheless determined somehow to catalogue everyone who's ever lived.

Delia Montagg Swindon is now unhappy with this decision. Originally she'd have burned the lot of these sinners from the get-go. That is, until one of them turns out to be her brother, Robby Swindon. He'd been a sinner, going off to the big city instead of remaining home to "give back" to his people for the great education in interior decorating that Herod Furstwasser University had given him. Her brother, "whom I know you knew and wrote about in some book he wouldn't let me read," she writes to Fred, well, she wanted Fred to know that she would not burn her brother or leave him inside the holy mountain unblessed. In fact, she has done so, blessed him, although strictly speaking, she's not been given this kind of ecclesiastical permission; no woman ever has. This annoys her too. To have reached her age and not been claimed as a wife to any Brother Disciple has also always annoyed her. It's not as if there were too many wives running around. Robby told her she was being wasted out here. She never gave it much thought until, on one of their tour visits, she met with members of that FUQU Women's Committee traveling around the country to raise support for including women in an official definition of UC. Maria and Maxine both told her she was a fool "taking so much shit from men and for so long." She'd never allowed herself to think this way. But then she'd never been out of Utah and wondered if the time's come that she should. Robby's and her favorite song never stops running through her head. "Time waits for no one. It passes you by." She wished she knew what she was waiting for. Going inside that mountain wasn't doing it for her. She told Fred all this, ending with a plaintive "Do you know what Robby would tell me to do?"

"I thought you said he told you to get out of there," Fred answered.

FROM HERMIA TO FRED

Wherever you are, God bless you. I can feel your stress. It radiates itself down the eastern seaboard night and day to yours truly, your Hermia.

FROM DANIEL TO FRED

Fred, I apologize for my silence. Each day is more a nightmare than the one before. Yesterday the combined number of deaths from UC at NITS and the Army wards at Walter Reed and the Navy ones at Franeeda and my own private practice totaled 1,512. In one day. No one bats an eye. Jerry isn't here. He's on one of his international jaunts, showing up at a number of conferences. Today he's in Buenos Aires, where the topic for consideration is malaria. I told him yesterday's numbers and he said, "Live with it," before hanging up. Our ZAP studies here still produce scary results. Deep Throat was fired because he sided with Garibaldi. Jerry's been invited yet again to the White House when he gets back. I understand it to be a top-secret discussion directly with Dredd Trish to which, of course, I am not invited. My own spies tell me it's again about somehow quarantining people with UC. Trish has heretofore evinced absolutely no interest in UC. He hates you and yours for so publicly shaming and constantly attacking him. My spy source says Trish said, "Fucking fairies won't get a dime out of my government. Period."

THE WHITE HOUSE

Dr. Omicidio is ushered into the inner sanctum. Dredd Trish invites him to sit down before him. There are half a dozen others in the room. They are all royalty from Saudi Arabia. Dr. O. is not introduced to them. Instead Dredd plunges right in. It is obvious that he wants these robed royals to witness this conversation.

"Dr. Omicidio, as one of our chief representatives in charge of the health care of our country, I am interested in hearing your declaration that this spreading thing called The Underlying Condition is limited to only certain American cities and presents no danger to our close friends and important allies in other nations. Ms. Trooble, are you getting all this down?"

"Of course, Mr. President."

"That is what statistics from COD would indicate, Mr. President," Dr. O. says.

"Come, Doctor, we must be told more forceful information than that." This comes from another man, sitting among the sheiks.

Trish says, "Dr. Omicidio, this is Floyd Harmish. Floyd and I were Bones at Yaddah and together at the CIA. I asked James Jesus to assign him to help us with this disease. He is particularly expert on the pharmaceutical industry. He will be working with you."

"I look forward to working with you, sir," Jerry says to Harmish.

"No," Harmish answers unemotionally. "I look forward to working with you. What is happening on the treatment front?"

Omicidio replies: "Nothing is really working. I believe there's some action in the pipelines."

Trish asks: "Is there anything our Arab friends could help facilitate?"

"That's not my department, sir. I would assume a number of the pharmaceutical manufacturers might not be averse to some financial stimulation."

Trish: "Look into that, Floyd, will you?"

MOTHER HAS JERRY'S PHONE LINE TAPPED AS HE'S TALKING TO HIS WIFE

"They think I'm the one in charge. They've figured out so fucking much, why can't they figure this out too? Why are they blaming me for absolutely everything? How can they know what I'm doing is wrong? Why do they think I'm in charge of everything! Why do they think it's all my fault? No one's in charge of everything. Goddammit! Tell your rich powerful Republican brother to get me out of this shit."

ANOTHER USELESS EDITOR PEDDLING *THE TRUTH*

Fred Lemish is having lunch with the new editor of *The New York Truth*!

The first thing I notice is that he's a drip. It's all over his face and posture that he's a schmuck. He knows very little about UC, even though his wife works at a UC clinic in Harlem. He doesn't want to know what his paper is *not* writing about because he believes if they are not writing about it then it must not be worth writing about, and in any event it would be a conflict of interest because of his wife in Harlem. Only a schmuck husband could maintain such an attitude. I wonder if she begs him at home to ante up. Somehow I rather doubt it. He asks me to send him a list of stories I think are important, ones they haven't dealt with. He is a rather subdued man, not a look-you-straight-in-the-eye type. I would say he's shy but for my sense that it's a deceptiveness more than a shyness. I guess you don't get to become the editor of *The Truth* without knowing how to be deceptive. I wonder, as I do when I meet "important" guys like this, if he ever has that guilty fear that he's putting something over on the world. Why have you never written about Omicidio? I ask him over and over again at lunch. This I particularly try to drill into him. Along with NITS, NITS, NITS! There has never been any investigative writing about NITS.

I send him a list. Perry and Gregg write a long report, "The Unwritten Stories about UC Research," to send to him. Not one story we suggest ever appears. I write him a follow-up letter. "Your wife runs a UC clinic in Harlem! How can you not write about UC in your newspaper!" When I write him yet another strong letter, he writes back, "Your tone is so mean and vindictive." Well, I'm glad he at least can recognize that.

WAR

SPENCER: The bitter divides have erupted like the atom bomb over Hiroshima. TAG is now actively campaigning against FUQU, telling people that the days of demonstrating are over, and FUQU is dead. And the people in FUQU are now the devil incarnate. It just breaks my heart. I stop going to TAG meetings. I know Scotty and Sparks. We had all lived and fought together like brothers. We'd hugged each other and kissed each other and gotten stoned with each other and for all I know we fucked with each other. We all had the same dream, to cure UC. We didn't have to destroy each other's dreams. There are still plenty of us left who still want to demonstrate. Maria and others say our demos are what keep them going. We will continue to make gay history! History should not be about fighting and shaming each other. I don't have much time left.

•

BILL SNOW: The rest of FUQU, which didn't want to go to TAG or wasn't welcome there, decides that our new project is to be like the Manhattan Project that Fred had already advocated for with an op-ed in *The Truth*. We went back to look at how it was possible for something so scientifically advanced to happen so quickly. We'd already studied HAH and FADS and NITS and COD. One of the things we isolated was that there were these systematic constraints on research, pressures that pushed research toward whatever was the fashionable thing being done at the moment. If you were a university researcher, you needed to get grants. And not only just personally for your own work, but also for your whole lab, your staff, and your grant's matching funds that went to your university. Your university was counting on you. So there's all this pressure on you. So you get steered toward whatever the mainstream thing is. The drug companies are looking for profits, so any of those things that don't have a high profit potential . . . forget it. And then you had—the ways in which scientists were—the jargon now is they're "working in silos." The virologists are all talking to virologists, and the immunologists, immunologists, and the people who do oncology, oncologists. And they don't have much interaction. And yet, when we were reading the accounts of the Manhattan Project, a lot of breakthroughs happened because they were sitting over lunch, because they were together so much of the time. And we'd already seen that at conferences, where a lot of the most important traction happened in the hallways between sessions. And one of the things we realized was, if—if—you had these scientists from all these different backgrounds, who had all the money and facilities they needed, and they weren't going to have to hustle to get the grant because they knew it was all there; and they're all interacting much of the time, from across all the disciplinary boundaries—when one of them spins out the idea, Oh, I've been really looking to do X, Y and Z, da da. And someone from another discipline says, Are you nuts? Don't you know that such—? Or, they say, Now wait a second! See, I've been looking at—you just exponentially speed up the cross-fertilization, the possibility for changing the way science is done. The problem is, the Manhattan Project had been something to create this weapon of mass destruction. So some of our group said we shouldn't call it that—and that was when I thought, oh, please. The Manhattan Project—people recognize what it means; you'll actually be able to sell this better. But whatever. We went with the McClintock Cure UC Project, because Barbara McClintock— eventually a Nobel Prize–winning geneticist—had been iced out by the men. That was one of the things that inspired us. She was studying the genetics of corn. And trying to figure out how genes are passed from one generation of corn to another. And one of the things she said was if you find on this ear of corn that there's one kernel that's discolored, you don't ignore that because it's an exception and just construct your theory based on the ones that all fit the mold. No, you try to figure out that one. Because if you can figure out the exceptions, you get the rest.

And so our whole thing was that we had to create a system that would allow people to study the exceptions, to study long-term nonprogressors, say; to study sick lovers whose partners were fine, say. At one meeting Maxine suddenly said, You know, what do we know about what happens when a penis ejaculates into a vagina or a rectum? Where does the UC virus go, and what does it do? And we find out that you can never get research money for anything that deals with our sexual organs, so no one is studying this whole area. TAG, of course, thinks we're crazy. TAG believes they are doing what's right. And they are willing to be really underhanded about it, not to let the two groups just be out there, coexisting in one organization, but to play hard-ball with another group of activists, who also think they're right and believe they too have the approach that worked. So it was arrogance. Because by now TAG had been so intensely involved in the design of individual OI drug trials, they couldn't see there's a need for more than one approach. When you go, as they did, from creating Parallel Track and Compassionate Use to being on institutional review boards, and being on various committees, and then critiquing trial after trial after trial—I think it was extraordinarily difficult for them to step outside of it and say, we may be putting this intense effort into something that is almost certain to give us more of the same. And they kept saying to us, well . . . that's pie in the sky, what you're talking about, it's pie in the sky. And we continue to make arguments that had been so key in FUQU, that if you actually can get enough people in the streets again, you can expand the bounds of what's possible. But TAG is saying the time for the street demonstrations is over. You boys and girls go home now. And to say FUQU is dead, which is what they're saying, more and more and over and over, is an indictment of all FUQU accomplished. Just as they felt that our not fully appreciating them was an indictment of their work. And when you forget that it needs to be that inside-outside thing, especially when you are there talking to Jerry Omicidio or some pharma . . . It's a very hard thing to face up to the fact that getting a seat at the table means, really, almost noth-ing. The reason you're given a seat at the table is to get you to stop pushing so hard and being so obnoxiously in-their-face.

I'm just, I'm sad that we—we can't find the way to work together.

We'd lost our integration. We were unable to sustain the things that we'd learned. I hope I'm wrong. But the worst horror stories are real. I find that I only have two emotions anymore. Grief or rage. I thought burying one lover at the White House would help. It didn't. And the new guy I'm seeing is suddenly sick now too.

Thank goodness, we still have Maxine. She keeps us going. She said she's not surprised what's happening. "Sooner or later it always turns into war."

GAY HISTORY WILL NOT BE TAUGHT!

FRED

Donald cried when he talks about how we're destroying each other. "And that we are doing this to each other," he kept mumbling over and over. I had become close to him because he wanted to teach gay history and had been unable to. He fell in love with gay literature at Princeton and then at Berkeley, where he got his Ph.D. in gay lit. of the eighteenth century. I had been having my own horror story up at Yaddah about gay history. My brother had given Yaddah $1 million to set up anything I wanted. I wanted gay history to be studied. Yaddah was terrified, not only of me, but of the subject, of the very word *gay*. This was the first time they had an actual big donor gift for something "gay." After too many turn-downs by too many deans and officials they finally agreed to setting up the Fred Lemish Initiative for Lesbian and Gay Studies and had actually employed somebody gay to run it. Well, he, Jonathan David Katz, a cool and very smart art historian who gave up tenure elsewhere to come join this crusading new thing at Yaddah, well, he had to get approval from one of these shitty second-class deans every time he wanted to go to the toilet. FLI went from bad to worse to worst. I discovered to my horror that what they were studying wasn't gay history but all this queer and gender shit, not a whiff of gay Abe Lincoln at all. Constructionists. That's what the gender studies folks are called. They had made up their own "discipline" that dealt with all the nonspecifics of gender and none of the specifics of identifying who we really were and are and what we did.

I started losing my cool. I am not known for having much cool, so it wasn't hard for me to lose it. It was not ten minutes before I told them that what they were teaching was bullshit and not what my brother's money was meant to pay for at all. We never got much further along than that. The Fred Lemish Initiative for Lesbian and Gay Studies at Yaddah, a part of the Women's and Gender Studies Department at Yaddah, was kaput and that was that. Yaddah closed it down. They would not allow Jonathan's exhibition of the love letters between Jasper Johns and Robert Rauschenberg to open. They would not allow Abraham Lincoln to be taught as a gay man. They were particularly incensed when we uncovered that Yaddah's primary benefactor, John Sterling, had been a gay man all his life. Our website disappeared overnight. I believe I now called the associate provost a shit. But Jonathan said it was the president himself, Bendon Noduell, whom I called a shit. Well, you get the picture. FLI and its founder were not wanted on another voyage.

I took it all very bad, really hard. A mini-nervous-breakdown sort of thing. (It still pains me to think about it because they still don't teach gay Abe Lincoln etc.) How was I ever going to be able to get the history of "my people" out there?

Donald was suffering the same problem. He couldn't get arrested teaching anything near gay history either. He wrote, in defending his Berkeley dissertation: "what we are forced to teach is awful; can't we move on to the full truth." Well, this is heresy, what he was saying, and what I was demanding. After finding gigs at a few second-rate schools, he gave up teaching. So much for the magna cum laudes from Princeton and Berkeley. Heartbreaking. So much of what gays care so deeply about is heartbreaking. If the TAG boys are not destroying the FUQUs, the Yaddahites are destroying the History of My People.

Same thing, really.

MOTHER'S NOTEBOOK

Intelligence is, of course, evaluated information. If a sequence of events is open to different interpretations, each will have its champion, and that co-existence can be destructive to the agency. Thus counterintelligence contains the seeds of its own contradictions and perhaps, were it not for the likes of me, its own destruction. Tom Jones taught us this. I guess Freud did as well. Did these poor FUQU kids Deep Throat keeps telling me about know they were courting their own destruction? It is as if they administered this fatal virus into their very own bloodstreams. Who and where is their effective Mother?

JOE KIDNEY HAD PUT HIS PIECES TOGETHER

There's no there there, as somebody clever once remarked about somebody or other. I finished my book about Ruester. There was no *there* there. That's the big secret I discovered about him and the big secret I wrote about in some thousand pages. It was not well received. It was faulted for being short on details and shy on specifics, as if I'd left many things out. I had broken my nuts trying to convey this point exactly. But I was to be made the fall guy. Papers syndicating my column are gone with the wind. Along with what had been a record publisher's advance. How dare I take so much and provide so little, I guess you could say was the charge against me. Of course, now that he has Alzheimer's in the eyes of his millions of die-hard believers, I'm really a shit. They should only know how he set in motion financial destruction by reapportioning the wealth of our country. I certainly included that. One day my book will appear prophetic. By then the rich will own us lock, stock, and everything else. Ruesteromics will lead to Trishomics will lead to . . . 3 percent of our world owning 97 percent of it.

COMBOS, COMBOS, WHO'S GOT THE COMBOS?

PERRY WRITES IN *THE TAG POV*

FADS approves DIP from Bumstead for Parallel Track, even though the trials revealed it's not much of anything great by itself, so we are pressing BMS that it be put in a combo trial with ZAP. Greeting-Dridge and Bumstead-Muck-Squish are of course violently opposed to their drug being "contaminated" by "the other company's product." "Let's look at this another way," our Dr. Levi Narkey says to Drs. Tallu Sve of Bumstead and good old Dash Snicker of G-D. "I now have sufficient supplies of both of these drugs to institute our own little combo trial. In fact, I have already started. Want to come on board, or continue to kvetch and oppose us?" In fact, bootleg DIP has been available. Levi had someone smuggle pills out of Bumstead's Mexican plant, "and it's taken me a while to get our stuff duplicated precisely right." Tallu Sve is beside himself. He didn't believe anyone could duplicate it. Now he knows we can destroy his market unless he gets his DIP out there fast. He agrees to work with Levi on setting up a combo trial with ZAP. And that's how our own Dr. Levi Narkey immediately gets fifty guys to go into an immediate under-the-radar trial out of his office. TAG's first two-drug combo trial. So far it hasn't done much except kill a few more people. You really shouldn't take ZAP with DIP, because each competes for the same target, so all you get is something too weak. At least we found that out. Dash is thrilled when he hears this news.

Then FADS out of the blue approves something called ZOK for "Treatment IND," for people who have failed ZAP and ZAP and DIP, which is now pretty much everybody who takes them. This pleases Interswiss Pinkus, of course, which makes ZOK, having copied it, more or less, from various analogues to ZAP and DIP. (You wonder when they are going to start suing each other for copycatting.) Interswiss Pinkus, however, also will not allow its ZOK to be used in any combination trial with any other company's product. They are then accused of working with another product of their own to combine it with, though they deny such chicanery. "You make us sound like monsters," says Dr. Fehrheit Pinkus at their Basel headquarters, "when in fact we are attempting to secure the validity of our product." Whatever that means. We have not been able to bootleg ZOK, so Levi and his team of guerrilla doctors are unable to combine ZOK with ZAP and DIP, but since ZAP and DIP trials are nothing to write home about, Bumstead is furious and Dr. Tallu Sve is transferred to another division. Nordlinger Astor, the new chair of Bumstead, orders an all-out assault on getting "that next thing in our pipeline up and at 'em ASAP." To which his scientists rub their heads in wonder: What next thing in our pipeline? Nordlinger himself is already retiring. He is said to have cancer and all of BMS's various anticancer drugs have been unhelpful.

Von Greeting is said to be sitting back patiently waiting to see the next one he's going to have to battle with. ZAP is still the only thing out there; unapproved officially beyond Investigational IND as it is, it is somehow available to be sold and it's been a big seller for G-D. It's priced now at $35,000 a bottle. Von is in no hurry.

Okay. Now Levi has ZAP and DIP and ZOK. I am helping Levi do a secret combo trial. Rebby is helping now too, after being a bit standoffish because what we are doing is not so kosher hot. It is like we are spies, sneaking around in raincoats and with slouch hats covering our eyes. We think the pharmas are spying on us, which of course they are. So we act more spylike than ever. Levi has contacts helping him in every pharm going. The good old gay grapevine!

Some guys get rises in T cells and lower viral loads on this triple-drug combo, but it doesn't last very long. So Levi and Rebby fiddle around with the dosages of each. Levi seems encouraged, even though some of the side effects are gross. "There will be side effects, from anything and everything," says Dr. James Monroe at Presidium, who then refuses to talk to us. They're upset their secret drug got lost in this mix. Bumstead needs stuff for its pipeline so it sells itself to Interswiss, such a safe and calming name. These places change names really fast. But ZOK is actually owned by Yaddah University (where a visiting Czech scientist is said to have developed it), which only licensed it to BMS. Yaddah had become unhappy with BMS and vice versa so ZOK was relicensed to Presidium. At least that's the gay grapevine's scenario of how Dr. James Monroe got his hooks into ZOK, which is not the scenario that Fred will discover to be the case.

Sparks hates it when I condemn the pharms. Suddenly they're our friends. Scotty claims he's got half a million dollars in commitments from two dozen pharms, including Presidium, which he says has increased its contribution to us now that Levi's started three-drug combos.

Rumor now has it that Presidium has something that will work. ZOK is meant to be some sort of camouflage hiding the "something" from view. I ask Scotty and Sparks which drug they slipped to us at our meeting with them and was told to shut up. Levi Narkey says he can't get anywhere near wherever it is they're producing it. "It must come from another country," he said. "Isn't Dr. James Monroe from someplace like Czechoslovakia?" And someone named Arnold Botts has actually threatened to have Levi arrested if he doesn't "cease and desist." One of Presidium's head honchos is Floyd Harmish, a buddy of Trish. Fred had been warned to be careful of him.

Meanwhile the PIs at all the UCCTGs haven't anything new to test. FADS has not officially approved anything. Leaving only ZAP, which plenty of guys are still taking and dying from, hoping against hope.

It all really is like some complicated spy thriller. I wonder where's the truth and where the red herrings.

•

SPARKS: Perry, I told you not to give so much away in our newsletter. You do it one more time and you're fired.

•

MELVIN: What nobody is noticing except me, an accountant with very rich clients, is that the stocks of the manufacturers of ZAP and DIP and ZOK and ZAG are going up and up. The guys on Wall Street that sell them are surprised. The rumor about DOT is sending Presidium stock way up and ZOK and DIP and ZAG aren't even out there yet, really. I mean officially. But Wall Street hears fast about our little trials. Guess we have more members who work on Wall Street than I knew. Can't hurt. The power we increasingly have is remarkable. Now, if only some shit would work. Yes, we have power. TAG has maybe a hundred of us in and out. I tell Sparks all the time to be careful, he's going to piss it all away with his arrogance. He's now saying trials have to be made longer, not shorter. That doesn't go down well with a lot of us. He and Scotty aren't talking again.

I allow the TAG meetings to take place in my loft. This old ugly Jew hosting all these hot young men. I want every one of them. I make a fool of myself over someone or other all the time. I asked Perry if they thought I was a joke. "You, Melvin?" he said. That's all he said. I made the mistake of taking Perry down to my place in Miami Beach. Even getting us both stoned didn't work. Melvin, he is twenty-eight years old and you are over seventy!

I don't think hosting the TAG meetings in my loft is working for me. I think maybe I will move down to Miami full-time at last. FUQU was fun when we were younger, all of us. Now I have trouble remembering the names of the kids and all those drugs in the pipeline.

•

INT. GMPA MEETING ROOM. DAY.
The judge and the board facing Tommy.
JUDGE: You were directed specifically not to befriend Fred Lemish or have any connection with FUQU.
TOMMY: You know, Judge, you really have to let me run GMPA the way I think is most effective. Otherwise, why am I here? Fred is not only my best friend, but he also still cares about this place and has many good ideas of how to proceed effectively.
JUDGE: Such as?
TOMMY: We go to every gay organization we can think of and beg them to all work together and not duplicate each other's efforts.
JUDGE: That's more FUQU than GMPA.
TOMMY: It really isn't. Do you know how many clients I am supervising? Ruester murdered more people than Hitler.
JUDGE: That's definitely more Fred Lemish.
TOMMY *(to the board)*: Who are all you new guys? What do you know about our history? Where we came from. How I fell in love with Fred and he couldn't love me back. Just like you and me. Forget it. It's very dispiriting. I think it's time for me to take a rest.
JUDGE: That will be all.

CLAUDETTE

A bunch of kids from TAG and what's left of T and D at FUQU were together on our own to start "Countdown" to set demands for meds for the five leading OIs affecting people with UC: CMV, histoplasmosis, PCP, toxoplasmosis, and MAC. It was nice being all together again while the big boys are still acting out. We even have our own little demo in D.C. when yet another "UC Official Commission Report" said Trish had failed to meet his responsibilities to the monumental suffering, etc. etc. We're all sick of him and glad to see him go. He did bugger all for us. He even tried to take away our health insurance.

BYE-BYE, DREDD

Dredd and Taddy Trish are seen waving goodbye as they board a plane. In view are some FUQU pickets with their signs: FUCK YOU FROM FUQU!; THANKS FOR NOTHING!; YOU WANTED US DEAD BUT WE'RE STILL HERE!

THE ARRIVAL OF ANOTHER BULLSHITTER AS PRESIDENT OF THE UNITED STATES

After being wooed by "gay leaders" like Randy Dildough and Sammy Sircus, the first official act of Boy Vertle as president of The American People is to make it complicated for closeted gays to serve "openly" in the armed forces. He had promised us otherwise. "The destruction of man's rights is a prerequisite for dominating him. Why do you and your chaps believe this one will be any better than his predecessors?" Hermia asks, citing her beloved Hannah Arendt. Boy also does not deliver the major UC policy speech he promised at a fund-raiser that Randy and Arteria Madeleine Dontz and her Human Universal Gay Groups (HUGG) throw for him, which raised some million dollars to hand over to him that very night. But he won't stop promising. At gay fund-raisers he promises a Manhattan Project for UC and the appointment of a UC czar. Yes, he is such a bullshitter, Boy is. And HUGG is a useless waste of time. All it's good at is ass-kissing in Washington.

The right-wing zealot Pat Buchanan is now declaring that because of gays "we are losing a war for the soul of America." Boy refuses to comment. "I just got here, for God's sake," he says to his wife, Maude. "Give me a break."

OH, DEAR

TOMMY

Nobody lives. In the end that is the short and simple. Nobody lives. Talbott is sick. Norman is sick. Cal is sick. Hobart is sick. Mark B. is sick. Randolph is sick. Manolo is sick. Frank is sick. Robert G. is sick. Ted is sick. Myron is sick. Alfred is sick. There are more, overwhelmingly more. I can't recall all their names. My memory is sick.

And now Fred is sick. Lab tests reveal there's renewed escalating trouble in his liver. Many more liters of ascites are drained out of him. Dr. Greene said there's more still in there but five is the limit he can take out safely.

Fred refuses to discuss any of this with me.

•

INT. ROOM AT TABLE MEDICAL. DAY.
Scotty is visiting Fred, who's connected to tubes and is being drained of ascites.
SCOTTY: I bought you some soup.
FRED: Thanks. Just what I need, a little more liquid. That's a joke.
SCOTTY: Do you really think I murdered FUQU? That really hurt me.
FRED: Well, it's still there. And I'll be back in a bit.
SCOTTY: Sparks and I aren't talking. He's such a pain in the ass. Do they know what's wrong with you yet?
FRED: I need a new liver and they've never transplanted UC-positives.
SCOTTY: A bummer.
Dr. Fung enters. He wears red cowboy boots. He notes Scotty's presence.
FRED: He can stay. Dr. Fung is the keeper of the livers.
DR. FUNG: The approval came through. They're starting a clinical trial of transplanting people with UC. I have approval to do a bunch of them. You qualify.
Fred is so excited that he tries to jump out of the bed. Dr. Fung restrains him.
DR. FUNG: Whoa! You should know that I've already transplanted seven and six of them died. Your friend Mr. Boatwright is afraid you might die too and is uncertain that as your executor he wants you to do it.

FRED: What have I got to lose! I'm going to die soon anyway. Number Seven is going to live!

DR. FUNG: Hold on. You'll probably be number thirteen or fourteen. You still have enough to hold on for a while. We'll let you know. *(He leaves.)*

FRED: Our secret. Okay?

SCOTTY: Scout's honor. *(He bends over and kisses Fred.)* I need a new boyfriend. You found me two.

DANIEL STILL SPYING

Jerry continues to hire gay assistants, or at least men like Bogart Neill, who is ostensibly straight, but with whom he also has a strange relationship. What do I mean by *strange*? Well, that they appear bonded in some way with him that I don't. In medieval times didn't men pledge their fealty to each other in some sort of transcendental way? Blood brotherhood, the Germans called it. I will take care of you if you will take care of me. Have I failed him and he's now reaching out to others? There is no question that Drew Newley is gay. He's jealous of me and obviously worried that I will harm Jerry, of whom he's increasingly and very visibly protective. Why does he think I might harm Jerry? How? What have I revealed that I don't know I'm showing? It's interesting that Jerry keeps us all apart. I'm the only one who works on Jerry's patient floor; Bogart works on Jerry's lab floor; and Drew in his administrative office. I'm the only one who sees the patients. Jerry won't go near one anymore. Jerry's domain is slowly expanding. Some grants seem to have been approved after Jerry wooed the necessary congressional support. Floyd Harmish is giving him instructions how to do this. This would be great, except he doesn't know what to do with the money. Monserrat keeps nailing him on this. Monday morning all-institute get-togethers have long since stopped, so we haven't talked about any of our failures, everyone else's failures, the studies, no postmortems on *anything* so we can learn, so it won't happen again.

SIRCUS-DILDOUGH-GROSS

These three richest-gays-in-America are richer than ever now.

ONCE MORE, ADREENA

Is it Draft Ten, or Twenty?

She *has* become a bore. This idol, this voice of a lifetime, this star who never failed to entertain me, no longer entertains me. She is a pain in my ass. She can't make up her mind about anything. I am summoned back to her lavish life to hear that the scenes that she loved when I left she now hates. She then insists on reading them out loud in a ponderous stentorian school-teachery way that is evidently how she thinks important messages must be proclaimed, and how Dr. Emma Brookner should sound. Once again, I don't know what this woman wants. I have worked with difficult directors but they can usually verbalize what they want or what they feel is missing, "a little bit more of—" such and such. She has every draft of my now numerous scripts in a vertical file cabinet by her elbow and she is most adept at plucking (with her glorious fingers and nails) from each one what she's suddenly thinking about. I am impressed that she's absorbed them so efficiently. She's known to be a perfectionist and a control freak (no news here), and why shouldn't she be? But it's painful to defend lines that are trying to convey complicated emotions. You know, the stuff of drama. "Whaddya mean here?"

I finish yet another draft for her and she goes off and makes another lousy movie of something else. "I *had* to do it! Jeff Bridges was on a pay-or-play!" I ran into Richard Dreyfuss, the male star to whom she's offered the part of playing me, and he said to me: "Have you read the newest script she had written? She has taken every major action and motivation for herself. There is no motivation for Ned Weeks to do anything. I repeat, *anything*. She is the hero of this movie. I can't play this." No, I am not angry with her. Nor will I be angry with her when she and I go through several repeat performances of the above. By the end, she will have had my play tied up for a dozen years and walked off at each draft's completion to make another stinker. No, I have never been angry with her, though many a person in and out of the business has said I should be. "How can you not be angry at her?" these friends have asked me. "She has silenced our message for how many years of your life?"

At mealtimes she picks from my plate the food I haven't eaten. She is lonely and speaks often of her longing for a fellow. She never once asks me a personal question about myself or my life or any life of any of the characters who populate my screenplay.

My hopes and dreams for the great Adreena Schneeweiss changing the course of our tragedy into worldwide anger and action lie scattered like rejected balled-up pages of my many draft screenplays in the wastebasket.

GUESS WHO'S IN CHARGE OF FINDING A VACCINE?

"The UC vaccine field suffers from disorganization, fractiousness, sleazy politics, sloppy science, a shaky marketplace, greed, unbridled ambition, and leaders with shockingly limited powers." So writes the award-winning reporter Jon Cohen in *Science*. In a personal communication, he conveyed to me that Dr. Jerrold Omicidio, putatively in charge of this search, is inept as a leader of men. "He believes in compromise. He refuses to take a stand."

KRAFKA SPEAKS!

Dear Asshole Lemish,

Before it's too late in your crappy uncharitable inconsequential hodge-podge of vituperative contributions that don't amount to a hill of sneezes, let me say a few words for your "history" that you blab about all over the place. After all, all sides must be heard. Your side should be flushed down the toilet. Along with its constipated "history."

In a few years' time, one two three, you ungrateful fucks are going to have not one, not two, but three proton-alphas to gobble down your gullets. Two years after that, the death toll will be diminished.

We discovered these PAs. Not you, you sex-crazed shits.

Which one of your little terrorists with his cock up his schnozzle worked around the clock in a lab anywhere? Which one of your muscular black-booted show-offs did one fucking thing beyond make our lives and our working conditions and our bosses tortured beyond belief? You think that it was you that whipped us into discovering this shit for your shit—which shit, I might add, you deserve—not our shit but your shit, your repellent lives of filth? You got it wrong, my buster-buddies, way, way wrong. We did it because we are good Christians and God-fearing and believe in helping our fellow man. The Hippocratic Oath and all that shit. The Lord's Prayer and all that shit. "My Country 'Tis of Thee," and "America the Beautiful," and the "Star-Spangled Banner" and "God Bless America" and all that shit. We believe it all and we didn't want you to suffer even though we felt in our heart of hearts that you deserve it.

So don't give me that not one treatment is out there that is not out there because of FUQU shit.

What will be out there will be because of me, Bernhardt Krafka, and all the many companies he had to work for because he kept getting fired before he could zero in on the magic bullet, which we finally did at Presidium. They won't be out there because of ZAP from Greeting-Dridge, or ZIP from Bumstead-Muck-Squish, or ZOK from Interswiss. They will be out there because of a hundred-plus virologists and molecular virologists and medicinal chemists and structural biologists who were all out there screening a million-plus compounds without success. They will be out there because the head of Squish said so many times "Our business is not about saving lives but making money" that one of his crazed overworked staff tried to murder Mrs. Squish to shut her husband up and got nine years. They will be out there because one of our own got blown up by a terrorist over Scotland carrying top-secret formulas that every lab in every pharm has now worked day and night to replicate in honor of him.

You are, however, right—and you can tell I don't like giving you credit for dipshit—that they are not out there because of any of the dumb assholes at NITS or because of cheesy Jerry, who takes credit for them when the NITS program is totally run by laggards as bad as the virus infecting the world. We started our work before they'd even gone to the toilet. We didn't need all their clinical no-show UCCTG trials. Omicidio Fraud. Geiseric Fraud. Ol' Jerry gets his puss on TV every ten minutes. You ain't seeing my face or Pizzutti's face or Dienstag's face or any of our Jap and Chink docs' faces, no sir. History always rewards the wrong shits.

We didn't need anything after Geiseric or Jacquie or Nappe or Pewkin or whoever the fuck *really* discovered the virus. Then we went to work on our own. We saw what it looked like and started to look for ways to disable it. You fuck-you guys crap all over all our progress. Yeah, it helped. It's hard to look at so many good-looking young dying perverts without it touching you a little. If you hadn't taken the engine out of my car I probably wouldn't have got angry enough to finally write this to you. I give you that.

My son dying from this shit got me off my ass. Nelly little FUQU fairy he was. I beat the shit out of him all his life. I miss him. I didn't save his life. We were too late for that. Just you and lots of his and your sissy friends will be helped. If you can hang on a little longer. I read somewhere that every family is going to be affected by this shit. I didn't believe it. I believe it now.

•

INT. GAY CENTER. NIGHT.
Attendance is getting sparse. Pile of copies on table at back of FUQU meeting: A LETTER TO ALL FUQU FROM FRED.

FRED'S VOICE: My comrades in activism. What once we were is tragically evaporating. We created the greatest gay organization ever
in gay history. I was given a gift. And it was *all* of you. What can
we do to save it while staying true to our democratic ideals that
bonded us for so long and successfully? Why aren't we trying
to save ourselves as well as those we have been fighting to make
well? Perhaps when we are completely crumbling you will come
to your senses. I hope it is not too late.

HERMIA TO FRED

Hadriana Totem at *The New Gotham* is euphoric with the material I am showing her, after all. "ALTHOUGH YOU ARE WAY BEHIND THE DUE DATE, DEAR HERMIA, THAT I HAD HOPED FOR." Quite frankly, I'd forgotten her and was surprised she still wanted it. "'OF COURSE, YOU SILLY BILLY, THIS IS THE PERFECT WAY FOR WE BRITS TO FINALLY SHOW UP THESE YANKS!" She has taken to writing in all caps, I suspect because no longer is anyone paying any attention to her in lowercase, or her magazine. It's beneficial she's so rich. She's taken to dropping pesky little questions of concern, unlike her, like "WHAT SHALL WE DO IF AFTER ALL OUR YEARS IN THIS COUNTRY NOTHING PANS OUT? MY HARRY'S ALL WASHED UP. I DON'T KNOW WHAT TO DO WITH HIM. NOBODY ON EITHER SIDE WANTS AN EIGHTY-FIVE-YEAR-OLD PRESS LORD. AND WHO IN HIS RIGHT MIND WOULD WANT TO GO BACK TO MERRIE OLDE ENGLAND."

I have felt so alone in my pursuit of our cause. I have been abandoned. No Grace. No Daniel. No Fred. You have left me with nothing else to do but to contemplate my own history of evil. I gave you the opportunity to get yours out first.

FRED TO HERMIA

The third president in a row is full of shit. None of his preelection promises has he kept. Anything, everything, I've written and said and done since 1981 might as well have been flushed down the toilet. *Toilet* has become the metaphor of our lives.

I do so want to have some love and recognition for my people before I die. And not from Hadriana. She's a cunt. I forgot the British slang for *cunt*.

HERMIA TO FRED

Stop feeling sorry for yourself! Why must you yanks always wear your hearts on your sleeves? This is no time for love, only for anger, retribution, and stark-naked honesty.

ALONG THE JOURNEY OF HATE

DANIEL THE SPY

A few more words about Dr. Garth Buffalo. Both he and Dodo have trickled away from our narrative as they frittered away their importance to this history of UC.

Looking back, studying the records, the various versions, I can say, in the case of Dodo, you were and are an evil manipulating monster.

God, I assume we have made that clear.

I know I am tardy in joining you to make this outright condemnation.

As to Buffalo, who knows what he might have discovered before so many journalists and a wretched congressman named John Dingus start crucifying him? No one remembers that this is a country that *invited* a known Nazi, Dr. Wernher von Braun, to come here to supervise our space program! Why am I dredging that one up? Because Wernher, no matter what was constantly being written about him in yet another exposé, was enabled to never stop working in our behalf. Indeed, he got us to the moon.

He was saved as my brother was being carved up.

Rep. Dingus has been front and center in also eliminating Dr. Buffalo, who is, like Dodo, also considered by many a genius, a proud man, pompous and definitely self-serving, also terrible at relating to others, particularly with the media, especially when they are attacking him with such hostility. Dr. Buffalo might have helped save us had Dingus not been so obsessed with putting him out of commission as he has with Dodo. Dr. Buffalo, already a Nobel Prize winner (for helping to discover the very reverse transcriptase that has turned out to play so important a part in understanding the UC virus), was, until Dingus got through with him, the president of Rockefeller University. A most distinguished scientist, he'd said publicly that he believes UC can be cured and that he has ideas on how to do it. You'd think this alone, with a man of this caliber, would make someone of importance—like, for instance, the president of the United States, or certainly a congressperson, or someone at NITS, like my boss Jerry—jump at the chance to put Dr. Buffalo in charge of *something*. Well, think again. Dingus, who has great power in Congress, would allow no such thing. It's difficult to believe that Dingus is a Democrat! (As is Boy Vertle!) Is his head screwed on straight? It's truly hard to figure this man out, joining a growing list of same.

Yes, Dodo is a guilty shit. Yes, Buffalo made a stupid call. But it will take hundreds of millions of dollars for the government to prove Dingus's charges against these men. (This figure comes from an assessment by *The American Lawyers Review*.) Jerry could staff an entire army of new scientists.

Buffalo's crime, in the face of a plague that is heading for a billion people (that prediction in *The Observer* of London, if you recall) is so puny and unimportant as almost to not bear elaboration. He defended one of his students who may or may not have fudged some data on her thesis. (The latest "evidence," I believe, is that she did not.) When confronted with this, Buffalo became stubborn and, like Geiseric, too much filled with hubris. Hubris makes congresspersons and the media go for the jugular. Dr. Buffalo's been fired by Rockefeller and, like Dodo, is looking in vain for a way to redeem himself, not easy for a prideful person. (Fortunately, he has a very rich wife.)

Dare one raise the possibility of a plague *against* us? A conspiracy of hate? Well, that is what this history should be telling us. Hermia, you have been telling us this all along.

The Journey of Hate. For your Journal of Evil, Hermia.

HAH's Office of Scientific Oversight has just announced its "finding." Dodo gets off scot-free from the charge of stealing the French virus. Buffalo is still unemployed.

It has been nearly ten years since the French discovered the UC virus. Seven years have passed since the Institut Curie filed its lawsuits. Five years since the settlement was celebrated in Paris. Three years since . . . The White House had changed hands three times, a president was almost assassinated, wars had been fought, the Berlin Wall had fallen . . .

And I have become even more of a helpless nit.

May David, my very own twin brother, forgive me, wherever he is. I have let him down.

I don't think I've ever been so honest as in what I've written above.

DONALD

The McClintock Project, or the CURE UC NOW Project (we cannot get consensus which to favor), is toddling along rather well, much to Max's and all of our surprise. We find a lot of support for our ideas and actually begin receiving inquiries from various legislators about it and what it is, and can it be useful to them. Actually, it is only one legislator, Rep. Jerrold Nadler, from New York, and of course we can be useful to him, he has a huge gay constituency. So we begin, with the help of aides on his staff, whipping this into a proper bill he can introduce on the floor of the House. We are so excited and we also swear each other to secrecy, the growing dozens or so of our group, especially since we know TAG is sniffing around Congress as well.

A WALK IN THE RAIN

PERRY'S VOICE: We've all been watching him lose weight before our eyes. I finally have the nerve to ask him. We're walking from what's left of a FUQU meeting when it starts to rain. We stand under an entrance to a pizza joint.

PERRY: There seem to be more people coming back.

FRED: Well, you were there again.

PERRY: What's wrong with you? We're all frightened for you. How much do you weigh?

FRED: One thirty.

PERRY: Are you sick?

FRED: It's okay. Don't cry. Come here and let me hug you. I've wanted to do this for a long time.

PERRY: Remember when we first met at a FUQU meeting and walked in the night talking and it started to rain and we stood under this awning in front of this very pizza place?

FRED: I do.

PERRY: I wanted so much for you to ask me to come home with you.

FRED: I wanted to ask you.

PERRY: Why didn't you?

FRED: I'm old enough to be your father. You were just off the bus from D.C., where your lover died on Daniel's floor.

PERRY: I guess.

FRED: You guess what?

PERRY: I guess those are good reasons. I guess you're right. But I wished it then.

FRED: We all have a lot of "thens" in our lives. What are Sparks and Scotty up to?

PERRY: I got fired. I wrote an attack on all the manufacturers of the D drugs, and Sparks said in his pissed-off high prissy voice, "I told you not to write stuff like this . . ." The only reason I went there was because he said I could write what I wanted to.

FRED: Please stop crying.

PERRY: Please, take me home with you. Please take me in your arms and kiss and hug me. I don't want you to die.

FRED: I guess that's one of the sweetest off-the-wall offers I've ever had. Do you want me to say something to Sparks? Did he give you some severance at least?

PERRY: No.

FRED: Well, he'll hear about this from me. How dare he not pay you severance?

PERRY: He fired Spencer last month. Spencer was only working there to get health insurance.

FRED: I'll definitely have words with Sparks.

PERRY: Spencer committed suicide because Sparks fired him.

FRED: I hadn't heard about Spencer. That's heartbreaking.

PERRY: He said he had no choice. He couldn't pay for his meds.

FRED: How come no one told me about it?

PERRY: He went home to his folks in Louisiana and did it there. Sparks refuses to let anyone talk about it.

FRED: He's turned into quite a monster. The rain's stopped. Which way are you walking?

PERRY: I've got my own little place now. Actually, you got it for me, don't you remember? Your friend who owned the disco . . . It's $157.50 a month rent controlled. This is where you live . . .

FRED: Good night. Thanks for the walk home. I love you, Perry.

PERRY: I love you, Fred.

FRED: I hope you find someone soon. What are you going to do for work?

PERRY: Tommy said he'd help.

FRED: Good. He will, too. Keep me posted. I'm tired. Good night again.

PERRY: Good night.

FRED: Now stop that crying immediately! I'm not dead yet.

PERRY: We have to find you a boyfriend quick to cheer you up!

AT LAST

He just shows up at a FUQU meeting. I don't notice him right away. We'd never actually met in Masturbov Gardens. It was his brother that I'd been in love with and was still connected to. I was talking to Perry when I suddenly realized that this guy looked just like Daniel. Then it hit me. This guy in front of me is *David*! I just threw my arms around him and hugged real tight. We both started to cry, right there in the midst of this diminishing group of my stalwart fellow warriors. We went outside immediately and started walking and talking endlessly and for hours. We could not stop talking. We just had to plow on through so many years and so much shit, asking and answering questions and telling each other stories only some of which we knew or suspected. We didn't even stop for dinner. We wound up down on the Christopher Street Piers just as the sun was coming up. We put our arms around each other and at the same moment we each reached out to the other and slowly and softly and tenderly began to kiss, again starting to cry. I asked him if he wanted to come home with me, and he nodded his head yes. The minute we entered my apartment we started kissing again, not just on our lips but slowly all over each other's fully clothed bodies. I reached out to help him remove his shirt, which I saw was awkward for him. Then I took my shirt off, revealing my getting-too-skinny body. When I turned to him he'd removed his shirt and had his back to me so I could see the reality of what the world had done to him. I began to kiss that back, all over it, with tears in my eyes. Then he turned to look at me. "Thank you," he said. "I didn't know if something like this could ever happen." I said something dumb like, "I am so very sad for your life." He said how he should have come earlier, that he'd followed my life and I was such a fighter. Again I said stuff like, "You have fought far more than I have. I can't conceive of what you've been through." He told me to shut up and could we please make love. Which we did. And it was the most beautiful thing that ever happened to me.

FRED

TO TOMMY

What am I doing! I'm on my way to dying. I haven't told him that. Surely he's been punished enough. I did tell him about Daniel. He laughed when I told him it never went anywhere. "He didn't have the courage he should have had, letting you slip through his fingers. I shall tell him to his face whenever we all see each other. And thank him for being so dumb!"

He said, "We are two wounded fellows. Why in the world has this happened to us?"

"I haven't been able to do much about what's happening to us," I reply.

"Do you really believe that?"

I didn't answer him.

He answered for us both: "I have yet to come to believe in anything."

So we have that quest in common.

Tommy, don't look so sad. Please be happy for us.

•

INT. FRED'S LOFT. NIGHT.
Fred is making dinner for David and Tommy.
TOMMY: You're making him very happy.
DAVID: We share a long history.

TOMMY: So I gather. I love him a lot.

DAVID: I can see that. I understand. Then we must be friends.

TOMMY: He taught me everything I know. I hope you'll be very happy together. *(He hugs David.)* Happy to make your acquaintance. *(We see that tears are streaming down his face. Fred comes and puts his arms around him and cradles his head.)* I love you so much. *(Pulls away.)* And I'm jealous. Jealous as all fucking hell!

This sounds so melodramatic that he and then they all start laughing.

INT. FRED'S BEDROOM. NIGHT.

David and Fred are naked in bed.

DAVID: For years I couldn't stay in one place for long. I must have driven in every state. I carry my scars every minute of every day, trying to figure out what was done to me. I can see what was done to me. I just have never understood why.

Is it strange to have a desperate need to get at some truth of something I'm afraid is unexplainable?

(Fred shakes his head no.)

Why did I think that crisscrossing this country where I was born and looking at those who live in it could in any way satisfy my longing for some sort of answers? Were all the men like the ones I had to deal with in Mr. Hoover's whorehouse? All the churches and cathedrals and temples I visited, all the books about Jesus and God and religion and philosophy and law that I studied in San Francisco, nothing comes close to really answering my questions. I looked at faces everywhere. I looked into eyes. I listened. Years of doing this and all I see are versions of the same thing. Over and over. The inability of fellow humans to deal decently with others as fellow humans.

I come to wonder if I'll know what I want when I find it, see it, hear it, perhaps even feel it.

Until I met you.

I went to law school. The law really doesn't protect the likes of me. Of us. Why not?

FRED: I think we're both looking for the same thing.

CUT TO:

Moonlight. Fred and David have been making love. Fred touches his finger to spots of liquid on each of their chests.

FRED: Is it yours or mine? Is it . . . poison?

DAVID: It's love. I love you.

FRED: I know. And I love you, too. I'm frightened for us.

DAVID: Do we have to give ourselves permission to just be in love?

FRED: Why are there so many murdering us? When you were in Berlin did you know your father and Amos and that what's-his-name were lovers and having sex?

DAVID: No. I was very young. It was all very jolly. Pillow fights in a heap of bodies on this enormous bed by a beautiful lake. I didn't find out about them until Gertrude told me in Florida. I haven't told you but I'm a very rich man. Both Amos and Gertrude left me their money. We can do anything we want to! Why are you so skinny?

FRED (after a very long pause): I haven't told you that I may not have much longer to live.

Fred, with his back to David, is crying. Fred's tears become sobs. David takes him in his arms. Fred's arms caress David's scarred back. Then David starts to cry too.

FRED'S VOICE: I realize that he'll be there for me for the rest of our lives. We make love, over and over, we make jokes, I want a house, we start planning a house. Soon we are living together. "You feel comfortable. I feel comfortable with you," he says. And we love each other more and more each day.

Which of us said this?

Both of us!

•

I hide in parts of your body that remain out of reach of any of your so-called anti-me treatments.

CHURCH CALLS FOR VIOLENCE AT UPCOMING GAY PRIDE PARADE

In New Trobe, North Carolina, Mayor Jordan Fandan refused to block a right-wing hate rally that the Smoky Mountain Church of the Mountains has again organized, which is to destroy the annual local Gay Pride parade. Last year marchers in the New Trobe and

Central North Carolina Gay Pride parade were brutally attacked and beaten in the street when walking home after the parade. The parade was also firebombed with homemade "Molotov cocktails." The leader of the church, Bishop Monte Fiore, urged everyone to "throw stones" at Pride participants and called for all politicians who support the parade "to be drowned in Lake Oligarchee with millstones tied around their necks."

"Stoning, firebombs, public drownings, sounds like it's from the Middle Ages, not the twentieth century," said Andre Banks, a director of the Raleigh, North Carolina, LGB rights movement.

Last year at this parade, fifty persons were hospitalized with serious injuries, one pregnant woman had a miscarriage, one elderly gentleman had a heart attack, and one person died from rocks that struck his head. One local elected official, Ms. Natalie Olmstead, a town clerk, was indeed drowned in the lake.

The national office of the church, Affiliated Fundamentals for Christ, in Saginaw, Michigan, refused to comment or condemn its member church in New Trobe.

—Central Valley (N.C.) News and Views

FROM THE NOTEBOOKS OF JAMES JESUS ANGLETON CODE NAME: MOTHER

It makes no difference, the party. I've worked for them both, or all of them, for there are others. Tricky keeping everything straight, not letting others know. That's the secret of this trade. That separates the men from the boys. It's about experience, learning how cold and impersonal you can be, not giving a damn and all that, "that" including administering poison and shooting and—well, all that. And I've learned all that about myself, that I could do anything.

Most of The American People were brought up in the bosom of a really wretched family, including me. Washington is full of people with wretched backgrounds. It's the men more than the women who are more . . . I hate to use words like *wounded* but all the presidents I ever knew were sick in some inside part of them. I am too, but I learned how to use it, how to turn it on those deserving of hate. Presidents don't have the latitude to hate so openly.

That's why I always have a job. There are always jobs for good uncomplicated all-out anti-haters.

It's the wives who usually are the pissers. Maude Vehemoth Vertle has said pretty much the same things to me that Purpura Ruester and Taddy Trish had. "Just try to do all that is not being done and can't be done by overt means." Maude is one tough cookie. So were the others going as far back as I can remember. But I smell that Maude's much tougher and going to be around for a while.

Tom Jones is the one who taught me the difference between "overt" and "covert." "Covert is when they can't see you and overt is when they can. There's a usefulness for both of them," he'd said. "The trick is knowing which and when." That's pretty straightforward, you would think, only it usually isn't, and Tom taught me that as well.

Interesting how it's always the First Ladies who are really the pricks. Well, nine out of ten of The American People approve of what their husbands are doing, and it's their wives who realize this fact and take it from there. Nine out of ten Americans hate homos. That's a tricky thing for me personally to deal with, overt or covert.

I remember when I was a kid my own father was chief of the XY Section, keeping tabs on the American First Nazi Party. *After* 1941. American First had more than seven hundred secret chapters there for a while. My old man figured out how Roosevelt got America to enter the war. Nine out of ten Americans don't want to go fight—against anything. He scared them into it. Portraying Nazis as a threat to the American way of life worked pretty much like what is put out about the Commies and now about UC and the fairies.

I remember when I was initiated into the CIA. "If our aim coincides with yours, you may enter our Brotherhood. We try to improve the whole human race by combating the evil that sways the world and that has come down to us from the remotest ages, even from the first man . . ." Famous writers wrote our history. I forgot which one wrote this. Whoever it was, I fell for it full force.

Deep Throat told me of some typical Lemish rhetoric about who was the more evil, Dodo or Jerry. You're way off track here, Freddy boy. Dodo and Jerry are small potatoes. They operate at the beck and call of others who *are* truly evil.

Mother has an army at his disposal now. Top-secret, to be sure. I have special groups concentrating on the trickier stuff. They meet regularly, we don't have uniforms, and have maneuvers far out in the countryside where they discuss our ideas on, say, how to protect homosexuals and hide them so as to prevent their complete devastation. This country has had no previous experiences with such specific targets of this sort. This is definitely a covert job. Mother mapped it all out. We'll see what happens. Usually I have to re-jiggle things around as centers of power shift and change.

I am threatened by this plague in more ways than one. Someone inside here with me is covertly raising the ridiculous notion that I am a gay Soviet mole and must be relieved of duty. I have no idea who this person is, but it is obviously someone who desires my job. Several of my agents have died from this UC. From what Deep Throat is telling me, many in the White House and Congress are more and more out to rid the world of the gay political power now emerging. Hoover could have told me how to deal with this one, as he so successfully protected himself and for so long, not that I agreed with his manner of doing so. He knew how dangerous Dredd Trish is. "He would eat you for lunch if he knew what you were," Edgar told me. Ruester asked me outright, "Can't we put them all in reservations like we did with the Japs and the Indians?" That's what I'm dealing with.

Boy Vertle is not going to be any better. He's too sex-crazed to be able to be much help to the gays. And like Ruester, Boy smiles too much. Never trust a constant smiler. Maude can only put so much of a hold on him.

Of course I keep notebooks such as this one. They will provide evidence to defend me after I'm gone.

WE GO AFTER BOY

RON

Membership is picking up, thank goodness. People like Maxine's new plan, the McClintock Project Working Group. We have a daylong series of actions confronting President Boy Vertle on his visit to the city. We disrupt his photo ops by waving our posters, we stop traffic in front of his motorcade, we interrupt his fund-raising speech, and we pass out flyers pledging such disruptions until he acts to end the UC crisis. In front of his hotel we unfurl our latest creation, a big blow-up of Boy as a baby in a diaper.

Randy Shilts, Jeffrey Schmalz, Derek Jarman, Aldyn McKean, Michael

Morrisey, David Roche, Michael Callen, Clint Smith, Robert Massa, Jim Ser-
afini all die.

And Rudy Doodie is elected mayor of New York.

*(As Ron lists the names, we see him writing them on the blackboard at a
meeting in the Gay Center. Fred and David are holding hands, very moved.)*

•

INT. CONNECTICUT LAKE. DAY.
*David is showing the land and view to Fred and Tommy. It's very
beautiful.*

FRED: A fortune-teller once told me I had to do two things. One was
   to always wear turquoise; it would look after my health. *(Holds
   up his arm with turquoise bracelets and rings.)* The other was to
   live by water; it would make me a better writer.

DAVID: Do you like this?

FRED *(to Tommy)*: It seems I've landed a very rich man. *(To David:)* I
   do. Especially when I know I am a dying man.

*Again, this last sentence sounds so pompous that they start laughing.
David puts his arm around Fred as they look out at the lake.*

INT. FRED'S APARTMENT. NIGHT.
A mixed group. Fred and David sitting together.

ANN: The Issues Committee will come to order. Thanks, Fred, for
   the use of the hall since we've been evicted from our new office.

AVRAM: It's come to pass that some of us want to talk more than ever
   about how we want to die.

MARIO: We should make a movie about us. *(He starts shooting the
   group with a movie camera.)*

BRADLEY: Not now, Mario. We're talking heavy-duty confidential.

MARIO *(turning off his camera)*: I definitely do not want to die in a
   hospital.

MOSES: I don't want to die period.

MEMBER: I want to be burned on a pyre.

ANOTHER MEMBER: What's a pyre?

EIGO: Enough of this death shit.

LIAM: Well, I don't want to die. There's too much left I want to learn.

DOROTHY: Like what, Liam?

LIAM: Why am I positive and so healthy and feel so great? *(Looks at*

Roberto, who looks close to death.) I'm sorry, Roberto. I mustn't brag. I went through a horrible bout that suddenly lessened and went away.

ROBERTO: I felt good. Then one day . . . I'm ready to die now. I choose sleeping pills. I've had enough. *(To Liam:)* Don't worry. You will be sick again soon enough.

David is very moved by what he's witnessing.

INT. FRED'S BEDROOM.

Fred and David are naked in bed.

DAVID: Everybody's dying. It's like Mungel all over again. At least you guys are fighting back.

FRED: Not enough. It's not getting us anywhere. I'm sorry you have to face so much death again.

DAVID: But somehow we're both still alive. Why, do you think?

FRED: A perverse kind of luck. It's got to run out soon. At least we have each other until . . .

David puts his hand over Fred's mouth.

DAVID: All the years, in Mungel, in Partekla, I never thought I'd die. Was that luck, too? Now death is the main thing we think about. We are lucky: we have each other. Most people don't have anyone. I did have love at Mungel. Grodzo loved me. A Nazi loved me. He probably saved my life when I was back with Daniel. My own brother couldn't save my life.

FRED: You're still angry about that, aren't you? We should all talk to Daniel.

DAVID: Not yet. I'm having too much fun with you! *(Suddenly thinking:)* You go after all our presidents. But this Omicidio, he sounds like a kind of Nazi to me. He tried to do experiments on me when I was at Daniel's that would have murdered me.

DANIEL THE SPY

The chief biostatistician of NITS (and my patient), Dr. David Byar, who was sick himself when he was brought into the fray by some FUQU members, looked at Levi Narkey's secret trial numbers and realized that there was "no statistical barrier to the simultaneous participation of all kinds of patients in multiple trials." He argued against excluding potential subjects simply because of results on their lab tests. "It is important to study patients with abnormal baseline values as well as ones with normal ones," Byar said. Of course, this pragmatic perspective makes sense to activists, if it doesn't to any pharma or to FADS. This is a big-deal statement from a world expert and Jerry won't go along with it. What Byar is saying is that clinical trials are experiments, but they are real-world experiments with real-world implications. "They should therefore be designed not to answer ivory-tower theoretical questions but to help doctors make meaningful treatment decisions." But NITS's UCCTG, FADS regulators, academic researchers, and researchers for drug companies have all been brainwashed to adhere to archaic rigidities because that's how they'd been educated and trained.

Brandishing Byar's analyses as published in *The New England Journal of Spots*, activists are now demanding major modifications in trial design, and announcing that they will protest until they see them implemented. "We are demanding the use of broader entry criteria of more diverse subject populations," your Eigo has written. What Dash Snicker had demanded is now considered murder. Jerry goes nuts. He won't tell me his reasons. Why should he care? He should be thrilled too. Snicker moves to Florida with a big payoff from Greeting-Dridge. Why was he rewarded? Word is out that the international ZAP trial is another inconclusive bust. We'll find out once and for all at the Berlin conference coming up.

Of all people, your Sparks Puffington goes nuts too. He writes an angry public letter saying that trials should be larger, longer, and more controlled than ever. "Do we want another ZAP carnival on our hands?"

Byar further said, after studying Levi's results, that they proved it was absolutely possible to obtain perfectly adequate conclusions from trials with far fewer enrolled in them, even half a dozen. *NEJS* refuses to publish this part.

STEPPING-STONES TO . . .

SPARKS: When I first met Fred he was screaming about studying the guys who were lovers of those first guys who were dying but who stayed healthy. That's when I liked Fred and wanted to be like him. I don't need to be like him anymore. He can no longer dictate our development. We'd have been much further along if it hadn't been for Fred, directing the arguments, trying to control . . . well, everything. He's one of the main reasons we broke off from FUQU to start TAG.

•

FRED: And then, out of nowhere, TAG succeeds in removing Jerry from being in charge of UC at NITS. This is a mighty accomplishment for a bunch of kids, to topple this man from his throne. Monserrat joined forces with them. They went to her friend Ted Kennedy and talked him into sponsoring a bill. Behind everyone's backs, a bill is passed in Congress that says Jerry is now forbidden to run both NITS and the UCCTG and his own research (such as it is), and to approve any expenditure of funds. As *Science*'s Jon Cohen put it, "The era of Omicidio, leader of the largest research program in the world, is coming to an end."

This bill takes away from Jerry any authority over any money. He can't spend a dime of what FUQU managed to shame out of Congress. He has no hiring authority anymore either. All that is left to him is his lab and his lab staff and their work in his lab. I wish this had happened years ago.

David says not to count our blessings yet. "It's never that easy to get rid of the 'death-bringers,'" as he calls them.

It must be noted sadly that this new bill has put paid to the Barbara McClintock CURE UC NOW project, into which Maxine and Donald and David G. and Doris and Suzanne and many others have poured so much energy and hope. One hundred thousand copies for this proposal to restructure the national UC research effort had been sent all over the world. They had lobbied Congress. Nadler introduced it on the floor of the House. But TAG has now beaten it all back and down. "It broke our hearts more than anything," cried Donald to the floor of an FUQU meeting. "TAG's really stuck the knife in all our backs once again. I hate them. We've got to fight back!"

•

DANIEL: I don't feel any sadness for Jerry. He's already pretending that this new law never happened, that he's still in charge. And there's no one to dispute him except a declining bunch of once noisy activists who've been against him all along. Jerry will be just fine.

•

FRED: With David and Tommy, I go to Washington with Charlene from FUQU. Charlene is one of the few still angry and active. She's a fighter and thrilled to do what I outline. She's over six feet tall and stacked, a gorgeous Hispanic. Boy Vertle's new head of HAH Donna Do-Nothing is speaking at a dinner for hundreds of big and important bureaucrats in a huge government hall restored to its post–Civil War glory. We stand beside Donna D-N, Charlene on her right, me on her left. And we hold up big signs, blow-ups of the flyer that has also been distributed to all the tables by several members of FUQU's Washington chapter, such as it is. Donna Do-Nothing ignores us. She speaks on and on about what she's doing, about what Boy Vertle is doing. How wonderful it all is, and Boy is. I know I look awful, which is a plus for this performance. I've been tapped too many times and none of my doctors want to do it anymore. I weigh one hundred twenty-five pounds. My new liver hasn't shown up. Because I am so happy with David and he is frightened for me I am trying to not think of death. Good for me. Whoopee for me. I am usually such a kvetch. Tommy and David have become friends with each other. If I'm going to die I feel much safer with them in my life. I'm actually not frightened. Me the constant kvetch is not frightened. David and Tommy are more frightened of my dying than I am.

•

INT. OLD POST OFFICE ATRIUM. DAY.
David gets up from a front-row seat and stands beside Fred confronting the crowd. At the very rear of the room, Daniel has been watching.
CUT TO:
The huge atrium is empty of its audience. Workers are cleaning up. At the end of one table, Fred, David, and Tommy are eating dinner. Fred looks up and sees Daniel standing there staring at David. Fred motions to Tommy to leave with him as Daniel approaches David.
DANIEL: Hello, David.
DAVID: Hello, Daniel.
DANIEL: It's good to see you again. You look well. I'm happy about that. I'm sorry about a lot of things I couldn't do for you.
DAVID: This building . . . It's quite magnificent in its restoration. What's its history, do you know?
DANIEL: I think it goes back to after the Civil War, a post office or something like that.
DAVID: The mail was treated so . . . preciously?
DANIEL: I don't think there was very much of it and it was all from one rich person to another who could afford it. Are you happy?

𝔇𝔬𝔫𝔫𝔞 𝔇𝔬-𝔑𝔬𝔱𝔥𝔦𝔫𝔤 WORKS FOR
Bill the Welsher

It has been six months since **Bill the Welsher** got elected. It has been five months since we heard **Donna Do-Nothing** would be Health Secretary. WHAT HAS SIX MONTHS BOUGHT US? **Bill the Welsher** has announced **no AIDS programs**, nor put in place **ANYTHING** that would change, end, alter the horrors of the last 12 years. **Bill the Welsher** has announced **no AIDS czar**. No one even knows what kind of AIDS czar they want. **Far _worse_,** there is **NO HEAD OF AIDS RESEARCH**. Stupid Ted Kennedy has pushed an **appallingly dumb plan** through Congress that establishes _another_ bureaucracy at NIH. When will everyone realize there has **never** been one single major illness cured by NIH? Why do we continue to put all our trust and hope in NIH? NIH is **incapable** of operating in time of crisis, emergency, or plague. But who listens to us— we who understand what's wrong with the AIDS research system <u>and have ideas how to make it work</u>? **Hillary, Bill the Welsher's Wife**, has placed on her Health Panel **NOT ONE SINGLE AIDS EXPERT**. Dr. Anthony Fauci, for better or worse the government's leading AIDS researcher, has, during these past six months, received not one single phone call or summons to a meeting from **Bill the Welsher, Hillary the Welsher's Wife**, Donna Do-Nothing, or any of her lackeys (Patsy, the patsy, Fleming; Kevin, the invisible, Thurm, Dr. Phil, the hatchet-man, Lee). This is **appalling**. Not one single person of importance at the White House or in HHS has cared enough to call Fauci and ask him: how's it going? what do you need? what can we do to help? This comes at a time when _**important scientific breakthroughs**_ are occuring that need to be pursued IMMEDIATELY. **Time is being pissed away!** Just like it was under ReaganBush! _**NOTHING IS ANY DIFFERENT!**_ What kind of inhumanity is this? **THIS IS YET ANOTHER PRESIDENT AND YET ANOTHER HEALTH SECRETARY WHO DO NOT CARE ABOUT AIDS!** _**WHY DO YOU NOT SEE THIS?**_ WHY ARE OUR SO-CALLED "LEADERS" KISSING THIS PRESIDENT'S ASS? HE MAY BE SAYING ALL THE RIGHT THINGS BUT HE ISN'T _DOING_ ANYTHING! While we are dying! Dr. Haseltine at Harvard now predicts **ONE BILLION people** will be HIV infected by the new century. How can we sit by so passively and wait so passively for **Bill the Welsher** and Donna Do-Nothing _to **DO** SOMETHING_? Where are your voices? Where is your anger? Has everyone turned into AIDS whores? (The longer this plague continues the longer you have a job.) THIS NEW PRESIDENT MADE US PROMISES AND HAS DONE NOTHING TO IMPLEMENT THESE PROMISES OR TO EVEN DISCUSS WITH US THE POSSIBILITIES OF IMPLEMENTING THESE PROMISES. WE HAVE BEEN COMPLETELY SHUT OUT FROM ANY DISCUSSIONS WHICH IS BAD ENOUGH UNTIL YOU REALIZE **THERE AREN'T EVEN ANY DISCUSSIONS GOING ON**! _WHY DO PEOPLE NEVER BELIEVE ME UNTIL IT'S TOO LATE?! WE ARE BEING INTENTIONALLY ALLOWED TO DIE!_

OH, MY BROTHERS AND SISTERS, I BEG YOU TO LISTEN TO ME.

Larry Kramer

DAVID: Yes. Fred makes me very happy. Are you?

DANIEL: No. Not really. It's hard to be a doctor today and happy.

DAVID: I'm sorry for that. I understand. I don't understand why no one in our family came to help me.

DANIEL: You ran away from me.

DAVID: But that was later. Our very own father put me in a concentration camp. Did you know that?

DANIEL: He and Amos were spies for the CIA. Did you know that?

DAVID: I was told after they were dead and I was infected. Were they responsible for that, too?

DANIEL: That I don't know. Lucas, Stephen, and I had very little use for Philip. What happened to your infection?

DAVID: Mr. Hoover saw to it that I was given lots of shots that I guess must have worked. How strange to hear his name. Philip. Philip and Rivka and J. Edgar Hoover.

DANIEL: That part I don't know about. You knew Hoover?

DAVID: He was very attentive to me. Like a father. Over many years. Affectionate. Caring. He was very grateful to Philip for the work he did, for our country, he said. He said he was educating me about the ways of the world. He put me to work in a male whorehouse.

DANIEL: I wish I could have known. Why didn't you tell me?

DAVID: You had already abandoned me. As had all the Jerusalems. And what I had to tell was too awful to tell. Even to those who had caused it, like our father.

DANIEL: You knew about what he did to you from the beginning?

DAVID: Amos told me as he rescued me from Berlin when it was being bombed.

DANIEL *(with tears as he reaches over and takes David's hand)*: I'm so sad and sorry for . . .

DAVID: Both of us?

DANIEL: Yes.

DAVID: How could you not have known some of it at least?

Daniel can't answer. Then:

DANIEL: There are too many cogs and wheels in our history. I think at some point I just . . . closed myself off. I have always felt quite . . . powerless to do much except what I've been told to do. Philip called me a sissy. Still am.

David reaches over and takes Daniel's other hand. At this moment Fred and Tommy return with a bottle of champagne, from which they all toast.

THIS IS WHAT IS HAPPENING TO VON GREETING

A senior trustee of Yaddah University who had been under pressure from students to step down after his company admitted cooperating with both an illegal Arab boycott of Israel and the construction of plants for the manufacture of heroin in Syria, has resigned from the university's governing body. The trustee, Vonce Greeting, a member of the Yaddah Corporation's board for 13 years, is the chairman of Greeting-Dridge International, one of the world's largest manufacturers of medical pharmaceuticals and supplies. In March, the company agreed to pay a $500,000 fine and $6 million in penalties for cooperating with the boycott of Israel. Greeting-Dridge also faces charges in France for knowingly selling their DridgePlusOne Factor VIII product for hemophilia that is infected with the UC virus. Greeting-Dridge also controls ZAP, the only UC treatment drug in circulation.

"This man Greeting was a role model of corruption," Alan M. Dershowitz, professor of law at Harvard, said. At Yaddah, its new president, Richard Levin, said, "I have not really had time to look in detail at the Greeting situation, so I haven't really formed an opinion. Von is a really great guy who has been most generous to us with his many financial gifts."

—*The New York Truth*

DANIEL THE SPY IN BERLIN

The TAG boys are here at this conference, the seventh or eighth of these things, and evidently TAG's debut in public as a separate entity. Nothing but bad news is expected. But TAG is celebrating, here in Berlin. "We pledge that we will see to it that progress is made forthwith," TAG's flyers announce. Like you, they have totally convinced themselves that Jerry has stood in the way of everything. Sparks Puffington is particularly pleased with himself, the expression "shit-eating grin" coming to mind. He in essence engineered the palace coup. Jerry lived in that palace. It doesn't occur to any of you that Jerry has no intention of moving out. He's still the director of NITS, with or without budget oversights, and has tenure in the Public Health Service. For all their bellyaching that he and we "don't get it," TAG don't get it themselves. Maxine, in her obvious despair about being so brutally hurled with her group into the ashes, sent out a memorandum that was picked up everywhere, including at this conference. It said, "Dear Sparks Puffington and TAG Associates, You will never again have the power you had while you were in FUQU." It means nothing to most of those here.

Reports at this Berlin conference are indeed, as rumored, uniformly awful. One after another scientist from all corners of the globe reports on research projects that haven't panned out, producing only more dead bodies. COD and NITS are yet to reveal our latest ZAP figures, no doubt under instructions from higher-ups somewhere. Jerry won't talk about it.

But it's their own achievement and new world order ahead that they're toasting, these TAG boys and girls, in a beer cellar off the Ku'damm. I'm sleeping with one of them, let's call him Patrick, and let's call him very sweet and very "into older men like you." I would never have noticed him if he hadn't practically jumped me when we were alone in an elevator at this hotel where we're all staying. It's been so long since I've slept with anyone, felt another body, felt kisses literally rained on me. It's a wonderful feeling. When I finally came, I ejaculated buckets, and Patrick said, "Wow, dude, when's the last time you had sex?" And I said, "Not for a very long time." And he said, "Boy, what a waste. You're hot!"

Well, isn't that nice to know.

So now, like Mata Hari, I have decent access to what TAG and Sparks are up to, more or less. It would appear they don't know what they're up to themselves. The Kennedy bill dictates there must be a new chief of something to be called the Office of the Underlying Condition (OUC), and we now know this will be Homer Herky, a decent-enough NITS scientist and a spineless drip. Homer has already announced "a total reassessment on where we are," and to this end has appointed Pip Mussellman of Princeton to chair this review board. I know Pip, too. He's a friend of my brother, Lucas, and he once invited me to Princeton to talk about UC. He chairs a department there, in bioradiology and associated high-tech medical Star Wars kinds of things, and he's heavily funded by an exceptionally rich man who's also from my Yaddah class and has made his fortune screwing America, I think in jet planes or aerodynamic something or other. I have already written to Pip, betting him that whatever his Mussellman Report comes up with, it will not be anything we don't know already, in either the NITS or FUQU communities—in other words, he's embarking upon a worthless exercise. Pip wrote back that I'm probably right but that's what some regulation requires. You, of course, would have immediately demanded of him, "Then why the fuck are you doing it?" I, of course, can't do such a thing. I overstepped my boundaries by sending him my prediction in the first place. Homer Herky has said that he won't entertain any suggestions until Pip submits his report and it's studied and vetted. That will take a year, Homer says. Another year lost! I wonder how Sparks & Co. are going to deal with this. They can't attack Jerry for this.

Swastikas on kids' T-shirts are everywhere in Berlin. I try to locate where Hitler's bunker was, which seems to be in some dispute. I try to locate where Mungel was, and that is a place no longer known. To ask any German a question about the past is a waste of time. I don't know how they live with the knowledge of what happened, and I guess this is their way of dealing with it: "I don't speak English" or "I never heard of it." I think of David all the time as I walk, looking for the places he and even our grandmother Sybil had spoken about. I took the boat to Wannsee to visit the inn where Philip slept with Brinestalker and Amos Standing in their threesome days, joined I now know by David. It's very weird trying to put together pieces of my own weird past, and in this city, while at the same time attending a conference that's telling me our professional future as doctors is turning out just as weirdly. I tried to get David to come here with me but he adamantly refused. At least it's thrilling for me to know he's back at last. Although I must confess to you that he's forcing me to confront much sadness.

The full details of the international Concorde study of ZAP are announced. They're awful and useless beyond emphasizing the danger of taking the stuff. It's better to wait before starting ZAP than to start on it. But waiting for what? It took them more than three years and several thousand patients to find out what FUQU knew in the beginning, and what Jerry (it turns out) knew in the beginning but seemed unable to say out loud in the face of Dash Snicker, who by the way isn't here to hear the results of his failure; no one from Greeting is here. Deep Throat warned me that we're still not allowed to voice our opinions out loud. Trish and Shovell and this Harmish guy passed on to Boy Vertle the necessity of keeping our mouths shut. So now I guess we'll be at the mercy of Sparks and TAG.

Audiences at every session fall into increasing despair as one hopeless presentation follows another. The whole "early intervention" program (Parallel Track) that Jerry and FUQU seeded some four years ago—can it have been that long?—still bears no fruit. It's all Jerry's fault, Sparks and his minions believe with a fervor that would be touching were he not so arrogant. It's so obvious what an ungracious winner Sparks is. Sparks is already castigating Jerry publicly, making fun of him to all the scientists he and his TAG troops are cornering here. This is certainly in keeping with the FUQU-type tactics that we've also been witnessing. Patrick told me, "There are FUQU members here who aren't in TAG but you couldn't tell who." I asked him what this meant and he said he hadn't figured it out yet. "It's hard to tell because everyone's still tricking with everyone." Patrick, by the way, is now a total wreck, having heard the Concorde results and he having been a part of it. He bawled in my arms, "What am I supposed to do now! Will you be able to save me?" Tears were shed by both of us.

Gretta Lell presents her arm of the Concorde study, ZAP and ZOK and ZIP in various combos. Deep Throat warned, "Her results could only be a pile of shit because the drugs are shit." However, she distorts data to show that it's okay to take this combo. Several of the T+D/FUQU/TAG team confront her in the Q&A after her presentation and criticize her in front of some four thousand attendees for her false data, which sticks out like a sore thumb. They're right, and no one else apparently noticed it, including me. So Sparks took the mike and said to Gretta Lell that her conclusion wasn't acceptable. She couldn't believe he'd said this in front of all these people. Then he asked her to defend her conclusions, and Gregg G. asked her specific questions rat-a-tat-tat one-two-three and she couldn't open her mouth, and your Barry held up his watch and said we haven't got time for this, Doctor, and . . . she broke down in racking heaving sobs. In this huge conference hall. Four thousand people. Then Sparks spoke loudly and very slowly into the microphone, "Dr. Omicidio, do you have any remarks you'd like to add? I believe you were overseeing this trial." Jerry sits there on the stage like he's made of stone.

Gretta couldn't stop crying. She can't move either, to get herself off the podium. She stands there rigidly, tears streaming down her cheeks, her arms immobile at her sides. It's an awful and pathetic sight. Finally, Farrell Obernought, her co-author of this study, comes up and puts his arm around her and leads her off, weeping on his shoulder. There's no shortcut out; they have to walk up the center aisle of this gigantic hall. You'd think someone might shout out, "Good try, Gretta!" followed by a hall erupting in supportive applause. It doesn't happen. She does not reappear. She flies home to Miami on the next available flight. Jerry asks me if he should send her a note of collegial consolation. But then that would reveal that he had supported her, so I know he won't do anything.

He's acting as if nothing's happened, as if he's still in charge, as if he's still the best scientist on the block, as if he's still the one who will find the cure. I know him well enough to know all this. Even if word's leaked internationally about this new bill and his demotion, everyone here can see that Jerry's still the same old Jerry, delivering his opinion on this and that. It's a gutsy performance, indeed one of his gutsiest. Even I'm impressed. Perhaps with this new anti-Jerry putsch he can acknowledge to himself, finally, that he needs me. They tried to lay me off as well. I can see the hands of Sparks in that, too. But evidently Monserrat defended me and I made the cut.

Everything is becoming more politicized in depressing ways. It's interesting that I'm thinking about this in the middle of Berlin. In D.C. I live in the capital of the politicization of everything. But the presentation of the results from the combo Concorde trials made very clear where we are not and made very unclear yet again how we as physicians are going to deal with this fact, for Concorde has made it a definite fact. Before Concorde it was just years of opinions. Dan Blatz from Israel and Sir Naughton were both at the conference, as were Grutzman from Bruges and Globberg from Milan, Emmanuel Derd from Switzerland, five of the more prominent foreign UC doctors treating patients. None of the foreign docs display the despair that fuels Americans. "We did not believe in much, so we did not expect much" is their protective shield. "And anyway, we are counting on America. Who else is there to count on?"

Patrick started to cry after we had sex for our last time in Berlin. "I wish I hadn't come here. I'm more scared to death than ever now. And seeing all these international docs, they look so out of it to me. They look like the bad guys in the westerns. I just know they aren't going to be the ones to save me." His body was hard and muscled, with the washboard stomach guys work so hard to get. It was covered with his own semen, as mine was with mine, or was it the reverse? I don't have that kind of stomach, of course, but I had a lot of Patrick and at least that was wonderful.

Oh, by the way, the head of this new Presidium, Dr. James Monroe, appears to be very buddy-buddy with Scotty and Sparks.

I've heard you aren't feeling so hot again. Please hang on for that new liver!

DR. EMMANUEL DERD AT THE BERLIN CONFERENCE

I've never been attacked before by patients. They came after me. I was never so frightened in my life. First while I was delivering my paper at the conference they started chanting, "Time, time, time," and they were holding up their watches and then they started marching around the room holding up their watches and one of them had a tray of Kool-Aid and they were saying, "Emmanuel Derd equals Jim Jones at Jonestown, ZAP equals poison Kool-Aid," and they were passing out these little cups of colored liquid to the audience, and it went on and on like this, the marching and the holding up the watches and the chanting and the Kool-Aid, and I don't know how I finished my presentation. The doctors in the hall couldn't believe it either. Some of them got up to leave, but most of us were just so stunned. We'd never witnessed anything like this. Rodney Bodenheim spoke next, and they called him a Nazi because he insisted on using a placebo in his trial, and he was an Orthodox Jew and this really tore him up. "The blood of nineteen is on your hands," they are yelling—that was the trial that had placebo controls and also had nineteen placebo patients who died. "Nazi, Nazi," they are chanting, and this is Berlin, which makes it even creepier, and then later on the radio in my room I'm listening to Fred Lemish being interviewed, and he's saying, "We asked nice. We picketed. We've yelled and screamed. Nobody's listened to us. What we need is a few assassinations and maybe they'll start listening." From that moment I was afraid to go to another UC conference and I couldn't wait to get out of Berlin and Germany because it was all just combining into the most awful nightmare, and I even questioned whether I should continue to take care of these guys, whether I even wanted to practice medicine anymore, because this represented some new world order. And that young Scotty who led us in joint chants in San Francisco, such a nice-looking young man, I thought then—well, no more—he was leading these chants of hate with the rest of them. And Jerry Omicidio was no help at all. He just stood there. Isn't he in charge of something?

FRED AT NITS HOSPITAL

I stayed in Jerry's ward at NITS for a couple of weeks. I slept and slept. I was fussed over by every expert in any and every disease or malfunction that might occur to my body. I feel awful. There is something about the famous doctor taking care of you and trying, it would now appear, to save your life, that I find myself questioning every awful thought and word I've had against him. Instead of continuing to blame him for my being here in the first place.

It was in this ward of Jerry's that I finally become really frightened of death. So many "experts" in all fields are weaving detailed elaborations of what might be going on inside me, from their specialty's point of view, that it's hard not to be.

The last day, Jerry comes in and takes my hand and says, "I must tell you I was concerned when I saw you in our last TV appearance and recommended you come here for a look at you. Now, after consultation with the group of doctors who have examined you, we've come up with a plan. There is a new drug, an experimental drug, that we now have in a clinical trial. It's called ADAP. It's manufactured by your friends at Greeting. You take one twice a day . . ."

At which point I started to cry, shaking and bawling so much that he took me in his arms and comforted me, saying, "Fred, stop crying and listen to me. You've been told by your doctors in New York that your liver is on its last legs. It is. And your transplant hasn't happened. ADAP may buy you time, but it won't buy you your life. You were told six months. My guys here agree. But take your medicine, eat right and put on some weight, go to the gym, and let's see what happens. You're due for a break. Maybe this will lead to it."

"What's it like," I ask him, "for a straight man to handle so many gay men's naked bodies?" He doesn't answer me. "I just wondered," I said.

David doesn't know I'm in here. I told him I was going to Berlin. He refused to go there with me.

"Over my dead body! I will never set foot in that country again!" he said to me.

THE LOVEJOYS ARE COMING. AGAIN!

HERMIA

The Disciples of Lovejoy had been seen as "the quintessential American faith" by that intellectual blowhard, Yaddah's feared and fearful Ben Ezra Plonk. He pointed out in one of his more than one hundred scholarly tomes that "this new American religion was dreamed and launched and fervently successfully established on U.S. soil. In its sacred text, the Book of Lovejoy,

Jesus whispered to Billy Lovejoy that Missouri was home to the Garden of Eden in the past and the New Jerusalem of his future. Jesus will meet him and his Disciples there and together they will build a brave new world. Even though it was in Missouri where Billy met his maker, the Brothers of Lovejoy moved on and have flourished and prospered mightily."

Plonk neglects to inform his readers that the first Furstwassers hated homosexuals, even though Billy Lovejoy had totally accepted them. This hate has never wavered for an instant over all these years. But as you boys start becoming more visible, more politically powerful, even demanding, and moving closer to achieving not only equality with other white people but also seeking to marry like them, it becomes too much for all Lovejoys. They are collecting millions of dollars to locate ways to expunge your growing menace. Ben Ezra now claims to be beside himself in frustration. "I can do nothing," he moaned to me in his slobbering way. "I am only an academic who was listened to when I had something positive to say." He is such a phony, Plonk. Several women I know studied with him and were sexually assaulted. He denies it, of course, and Yaddah refuses to pursue the issue.

If you'll recall—and there's no reason you should and every reason Plonk should—one of Billy Lovejoy's original decrees was that it was perfectly acceptable for brother to love brother, and to cohabit with brother, and to even marry brother. This got quickly discarded along the way from Missouri to Utah, and you'd be hard-pressed to locate any who recall these doctrinal planks from the original Book of Lovejoy. Yes, Jesus is complicated. He always was.

Who says that religion is not based on an unhealthy dose of vengeance is mine sayeth the Lord (and anyone else who wants to join in)?

But vengeance because of what?

Your increasing visibility is proving to be one of UC's great gifts to the Lovejoys. In showing you off it brought many more into the fight to eliminate you. Chief among these haters are the ever-populating Lovejoys.

What I am discovering will turn your hair. I hope you and your troops are up to it. I fear otherwise.

Hadriana has informed me that what I am writing is too controversial even for her! You were correct: she is a cunt, in any language!

•

I learn many of your songs. They make me happy. The Health of the World organization reports that my presence is now so firmly estab-

**lished in your world that I can never be completely eliminated. I won-
der if there is a happy song for this. "I'm Forever Blowing Bubbles"? I
wonder, what are bubbles?**

PHARMA, PHARMA, WHO'S GOT THE PHARMA?

FRED AND PERRY

Von Greeting was never unaware of the many deaths his company's products
are causing. There are always lawsuits pending, which never bother him. "In
today's markets, the number of threats against you is actually a decent yardstick of the historical changes we're trying to bring about," he said in an interview with *Pharma Plus*. G-D refuses, as indeed do all the pharmaceuticals,
to cave in to the increasing accusations of "when-are-you-going-to-get-your-
ass-in-gear." They all vigorously subscribe to the mantra of the ever-negative
Tolly McGuire, head of Big Pharma, their Washington lobbying group, that
"there's no money in this shit so please stop pestering us." Tolly's peddled this
line to Congress, to Jerry, to Homer Herky. The subtext of Tolly's "official"
attitude, of course, is that if you want action, ante up, Uncle Sam. Congress
has anted up timidly. Ironically, the amount was so little that it was left under
Jerry's control. Once again Jerry can still be faulted for his cautious—or as
Sparks calls it, "mingy"—response.

Presidium believes it has the ammunition ready to shoot.

But as we know, sometimes action in one place is not the action others
want someplace else. Complete portraits of the viral DNA now cover the
globe. We've already seen Dash Snicker in and out of action at G-D with
ZAP. Now more Dashers (and Donners and Blitzens) ride in with their slays.
Fehrheit Dienstag at Interswiss Pinkus is at work on what will be NOX.
Pecker Drum, Dinkens-Savoy-Trailheim, Talbott, Uriah, Audacia, Muck,
names that earlier spiced an occasional entry in this history, now enter it
again. Industrial espionage has not yet visibly entered this playing field, but
sure as shooting, it's going on. For now arrives the mighty giant of them all,
Greptz, just plain Greptz, which stands alone in the history of pharmaceutical manufacturing in America, in the world. The company, like so many of
its competitors, was founded in Germany. Sometime in the late 1700s the first
Gideon Greptz, a name that still graces the CEO, determined that Greptz
will always be first to birth the important drugs, such as Pervitin, the heroin

derivative that kept Nazi Germany on its toes. Of course the current Gideon Greptz wouldn't admit to such a past. As he says from his world headquarters now located in New Jersey, "Ich bin ein Americanisher."

Once Greptz enters the fray, the cat is out of the bag and it's now a race and money's no object. Everyone has now taken on board chemists to pore over Dodo's dirms and Jacquie's VLF-1 (for Vive la France). (There are a great number of each one's dirms, and they do appear to resemble each other . . .) They pay top dollar for top talent because now there's a growing gold-rush mentality, which is also why medicines wind up costing so much. Dash Snicker had not been silent about G-D's "great financial success" from still-not-FADS-approved ZAP. Despite Concorde's failure desperate people keep taking ZAP. ZAP and ZIP and ZOK are somehow already out there in one kind of combo or another. Dr. Levi Narkey is still secretly at work on his own cohort of gay patients, using more sophisticated unapproved combinations. No one else is as far along this trail as Levi, breaking the law again. Levi's trials bring better results, and sooner. He's already slashed Tallu Sve's eighteen-capsule daily dosage of ZIP down to two, causing Nordlinger Astor to have a minor stroke. "How will we make money on only two!" he screams. He fired Sve, who was prepared to quit anyway. Scientists at pharms are rarely treated with decency. "A shitty pox on your decency!" screams Nordlinger. "I pay you one hundred thousand dollars a year. I need medicine I can sell in big glass bottles, not teeny tiny plastic vials! I do not care if eighteen capsules kill them! Give me eighteen capsules that don't kill them!" Sve is immediately hired by Greptz. The round robin of bench scientists has certainly begun. When Gideon Greptz sees how much he must ante up to stay in the game, he calls in James Monroe, who tells him about Presidium.

Why doesn't Jerry feel this fog-enshrouded air still wafting from Berlin? He's still in charge of NITS.

"He is mingy," Sparks had said. "He has no courage of his convictions because he doesn't have any convictions. Once again and as always Jerry is only saving his ass by not doing anything. These actions by the pharmas are happening because of FUQU's nonstop screaming at one and all, now more than reinforced by TAG coming along. Our newfound power in actually getting our very own legislation passed by Congress—fucking faggots got a fucking bill passed by fucking Congress!—everyone is afraid of us, especially Jerry. The activists now have power!"

It turns out that no one out there really knows the difference between FUQU and TAG. All they know is that we're UC activists and we're getting it done. And there are a lot of us, as they finally notice because the pharmas have read the tea leaves. ZAP is making a shitload of money, for shit's sake. There's been nothing else out there for the desperate dying to take!

•

DAVID (*who has been listening to Fred and Perry read the above*): It's far too complicated to follow. Who can keep all those pharmas and their drugs straight? No wonder you don't get results.

ANOTHER SAD ENDING

Darcus Charles Graves and "a beautiful pregnant wife" are discovered in a double suicide pact inside a derelict abandoned church on the outskirts of Masturbov Gardens, where Fred grew up. Fred's bedroom in the Lemish apartment had been directly across the road.

Darcus had been to Africa. He'd actually been taken there by Dr. Sister Grace along with a bunch of students from the University of Southern Jewry, on the faculty of which had also been his poppy, Felindus Max, who wanted his son "to please go out and see the fucking goddamn world and do something useful, you wastrel!"

Autopsies of their bodies revealed abnormally high titers of ZAP. Sam Sport had gotten it for him via Purpura. Imagine taking an overdose of ZAP to commit suicide, and leaving a note for "Dear Poppy."

HERMIA FINDS THIS IN ONE OF GRACE'S NOTEBOOKS

"I have just received word from some contacts I made in Africa—you must excuse me for not remembering their names any longer; I barely remember my goddamn own—that confirms what I posited, that fucking semen in a fucking male infected with fucking syphilis contains more UC than the fucking semen in a male not infected with syphilis. This certainly bears out every goddamn thing I have said for shit-eating centuries. I said long ago that this is a fucking plague of syphilis and shit, amoebas and piss. For those hordes who refused to believe me, they have had what they deserved, though of course that is not what I mean in punishment terms, only intellectual ones.

They have been proved royally wrong, and there's nothing a true scientist loves more than to stick it up the ass of those who all along cried nay. My vel was the yardstick that they all laughed at. Fucking Greeting took it off the market. Let them all break their asses trying to fashion a drug that really will work without my vel test."

•

What Grace was referring to in the above note in her journal was a study she conducted at Partekla that was rejected for publication by *The New England Journal of Clappe and Chancre* (one of the oldest of the New England journals). What she isn't mentioning is that this syphilis study was conducted in Africa on black men because ever since that hideously inhumane syphilis study on your black men at Tuskegee, Alabama, there exist residual prohibitions against any study involving blacks and infectious diseases. It's now known that the African men were infected with UC through infected prostitutes. The men were paid modest pennies each time they came to the "boudah" (collection depot) to masturbate into a small glass bottle, which most of them complained were too narrow-necked to accommodate them and too tiny-bulbed to contain all their ejaculate, so that invariably they got messy. It is very difficult to do academic studies of any sort in Africa. While *Clappe and Chancre* is a publication adhering to the highest standards of peer review, it's doubtful that any of the "peers" knew much about customs in small native African villages so far away from northern Idaho and Partekla.

Oh, Grace, come back! I miss you so.

FROM *THE BOOK OF THE DEAD*

BRADLEY

Dreece died. And Harold died. And Morgan died. And Taylor died. All last week. CarolyAnn died. She's the first woman in FUQU who dies from this. Gerri tried to write her name on the FUQU blackboard. But our meetings are now so screwed up, deaths aren't acknowledged on the floor. We are forgetting what we are here for. Oh, my. At least I can include these names in our official minutes.

An old-timer, Ann, got up to "shame us for this omission." Some new chick got up and said something like, "It is time to stop dwelling on our deaths and concentrate on freedom for all peoples." There is a big round of applause for "freedom for all peoples."

Yes, the "crazies," as Fred calls them, are taking over. And we no longer have the ballast to stop them. Who is "we"? I no longer know.

•

EXT/INT. INVINCIBLE CREWD-HARBINGER OFFICE. DAY.

A FUQU picket line. Signs read: INVINCIBLE, WHERE IS YOUR UC RESEARCH! ALL YOUR BEDS ARE EMPTY! *Tommy and Jim Eigo and Mickey are looking out the window at this. They each wear Invincible lab coats. They see that Fred is marching with David and try to wave to them. Tommy turns to face Dr. Marks, the head of the hospital.*

DR. MARKS: Those are your people?

TOMMY: Yes, Dr. Marks.

DR. MARKS: They've been picketing us around the clock for three days and nights now.

TOMMY: I believe they're going to do it for a whole week.

DR. MARKS: I see.

TOMMY: Around the clock.

DR. MARKS: I see. The last time your folks did this it was more time-limited. Can't you do anything about it?

TOMMY: No, sir. It's an activist organization. Very democratic.

EIGO: Invincible has enough ZAP plus newer D drugs to test them on a two-hundred-person trial. Only twelve have been enrolled. That's what this FUQU picketing is about.

DR. MARKS: I see. You know our board chair, Mr. Belly?

Mr. Belly, very rich and contained, enters.

TOMMY: How do you do, sir. It's an honor to meet you at last after working here for a while. I believe our friend Fred Lemish met your son when he was president of Yaddah.

BELLY: Our board feels you are not quite the proper fit for Invincible.

TOMMY *(to Belly)*: Dr. Mickey Marcus and Eigo here and I created a city-funded program for you to educate New York about prevention. I fully staffed a city-funded program for you employing one hundred social workers. I put you on the map as the place to go to in every network that . . .

BELLY: Nevertheless our board feels . . .

CUT TO:

Tommy with Mickey alone.

MICKEY: You and Fred were absolutely right to summon us to organize and I was absolutely wrong not to have also warned us not
to fuck without a condom. Whew. I've wanted to say that for the
longest time. It was just bottled up inside me.

TOMMY: Thanks, Mickey. Why are you crying?

MICKEY: I just had to say that. Tell Fred. I'm sorry they kicked you
both out of GMPA.

TOMMY *(looks out at picket line; sadly)*: Our friends are being allowed
to die. And I'm out of another job.

INT. TOMMY'S APARTMENT. NIGHT.

*In his tiny apartment, Tommy is lying on his mattress smoking a joint
and looking out into space, thinking.*

INT. GAY CENTER.

*A reduced attendance. David is observing the room, sitting with Fred,
holding his hand. Tommy sits beside them. Camera pans around faces.
We recognize fewer of them.*

FRED: My comrades in activism. Why aren't we trying to save ourselves? *(Stands up and pleads with them)*: I was given a gift. And
it was *all* of you. I beg each of you to find each other again!

INT. TOMMY'S APARTMENT. NIGHT.

He has tears in his eyes.

INT. FRED'S BEDROOM. NIGHT.

*Fred and David are asleep in each other's arms. The phone rings. Fred
jumps up to answer it. He listens for a moment before giving whoops of joy.*

FRED READS TO DAVID SOME FINAL THOUGHTS BEFORE HE GOES UNDER THE KNIFE, PERHAPS NOT TO EMERGE ALIVE

It takes a certain ruthlessness to be a leader. To perform well.

I haven't been ruthless enough.

Pollyanna me, for the longest time, thought anything wrong could be put right. I wanted us to be an army, the kind of army Hannah Arendt blamed the Jews for not having always at the ready.

Have we seen the best of it, or just the worst?

I sound like I am writing about my own death.

Maybe I am.

Please stop crying, honey.

•

EXT. RURAL AIRPORT. DAY.
Fred, David, and Tommy are being bundled into a small emergency plane, which then takes off.

LIFE OR DEATH?

Fred is going to disappear for a while. He is having a liver transplant in Pittsburgh. It will save his life. Dr. Fung ("the minute I saw you walk in in your bright red cowboy boots, I knew you would be important in my life . . .") predicts "at least another twenty years of life. We got you just in time. Your liver was on its very last legs, the end. It was pitch-black and shriveled almost into nothingness. From here on in you will be as old as your new liver. The liver I have transplanted into you is from a forty-year-old man in excellent health who did not drink or take drugs. He died from an embolism. To my mind, it is an excellent liver. I hope you will be very happy together."

Fred had made David promise to be the first thing he sees if he opens his eyes. And when he does, there indeed is David, and Tommy, and Fred, even in his very doped-up state, wants to cry, does cry, and is of course euphoric, very euphoric with all drugs considered. He's lived through it! He's the fourteenth UC-positive and Hep. B patient to have received a liver transplant, and the third one to have lived through it. From this point on, it will not be so easy for doctors and medical centers to refuse to transplant UC-positive patients. Infected people who need transplants and are afraid to sign up for them can now look at Fred. Once again he's called a hero. What kind of hero? he says to David and Tommy. I was almost dead!

In fact, for a moment the world thought he was dead. AP and UP and Laurie Garrett announce his death. It's a few hours before this mistake is righted. How it happened in the first place, no one knows. David thinks "your enemies got to the wire services!"

David decides they must stay in Pittsburgh until every possible thing that could go wrong is seen not to have gone wrong. Fred is out of the hospital in eight days, but David's rented a furnished apartment. They are to stay here six months while Fred recovers. Fred sleeps massive numbers of hours with David beside him and slowly regains his strength. Never has Fred enjoyed such attention from a loved one. He does not think of UC, he does not think of FUQU, he does not know he's being screwed by Yaddah, he does not think of gay anything. He is not in touch with the Outside World at all.

•

TOMMY: Wait. Don't rush it! He almost fucking dies! From the dumbest reason. After the transplant the fucker wouldn't eat. Sometimes that happens after surgery. The patient has no appetite. But usually you can make them eat something. Not Fred. He just would not eat. I've seen behavior like this a number of times in survivors. Pittsburgh is the first place Fred's allowed himself to plop himself down, even though it's out of necessity. He's certainly never had such attention from anyone as David's been showing him on the whole lead-up to and into this transplant thing (and quite frankly as *I've* been showing him—neither one of them has a notion of all the paperwork and phone calls and locating who the fuck to talk to one step higher up the ladder when you've been turned down by insurance companies, and Fred was turned down, a lot). Now, here, having survived a procedure that quite frankly neither David nor I thought he'd survive, Fred's not eating. Finally, John Fung pulls David aside and tells him he is frightened. "If Fred doesn't start eating something fast, he's going to die." It was New Year's Eve. It was snowing outside. David had been all over town buying sweet stuff he knows Fred likes. He stomps into Fred's room at Presby, his coat and boots all caked in snow. Boots and all, he climbs up on Fred's bed and sits beside him and opens his gifts of goodies. He offers them one by one but Fred won't eat. "I'm not hungry" is all he finally says. David started to cry. Fred heard him say things like, "Honey, we haven't come this far in our lives together for you to die because you won't eat! Please eat!" The tears were running down his cheeks. "Please eat for me, for Fred and David, who are together finally and at last." And then he grabbed some hunk of chocolate cake and practically stuffed it down Fred's throat. Fred by now was crying too. Fred ate. I left them sleeping in each other's arms. David still had his boots on, so I took them off. He opened his eyes and winked at me before going back to sleep. His eyes were still full of tears and so were mine.

DAVID IN PITTSBURGH

While Fred was sleeping soaking up enough energy to start his life with his new liver I was thinking about something that's been occurring to me. Fred had been given a new life. I, too, had been spared. But at what cost? The lawyer in me was curious. Why are we not protected by law? My thoughts took me to one of Mr. Carnegie's libraries in this city his wealth created after doing who knows what crimes to acquire his fortune.

My thoughts of course led me back to Germany and this to curiosity about the Nuremberg Trials that had transpired a few years after I'd left Mungel to return to America.

Why were there no protections in existence that would have saved all of us in different countries with different laws but actually still a part of international humanity?

There was much fuss made at these trials about the use of the word *genocide*, as against the use of the words *crimes against humanity*. The reasoning went something like this: "if one emphasizes too much that it is a crime to kill a whole people, it may weaken the conviction that it is already a crime to kill one individual." There was also much made of whether the Nazis could be punished for acts committed before the actual and official start of the war. Crimes committed before the war were entirely ignored. Thus those individuals were now protected, and their state as a contributing entity was ignored.

Those condemned were convicted for committing crimes against humanity. None were found guilty of genocide. That word was discarded. This, then, became the definition to forthwith be used in international law— "crimes against humanity."

Answers and objections seem so obvious to Fred and me. Why weren't they obvious then? Or now?

Why was Grodzo purchased to come to America? In Mungel he'd been tasked with trying to discover the cause of homosexuality. Were we a crime against humanity? Or a target for genocide? Was that why someone here knew about him and wanted him here? Is this what he was doing at Partekla? He told me that it was there where I got all the scars on my back. Why don't I remember any of that?

•

INT. BATHROOM AND SHOWER. PITTSBURGH
APARTMENT. DAY.
*Fred is standing in the bathtub as David sponges him down, being
careful of all the stitches. David is naked too.*
DAVID: Now we both have scars.
Fred is tearing up again.
FRED: I cry when you take care of me.
DAVID: But I want to take care of you.
FRED: I should be taking care of you.
David stands up and kisses his eyes. They hug each other.

DANIEL WATCHES MORE OF HIS LIFE BURN UP

Miseraria's been set on fire.

The place is so awful now that no one much cares who might have done it and if he or she should even be thanked. Miseraria, part of Nostra Mater Dolorosa, was originally built for the rich Catholics. Now it's where they put the worst cases of everything, even worse than Nostra Mater, which now means all the last-stage UC patients, which means Nearer Thy God to Be. It's also where I spent part of my internship. The staff used to all be nuns. But the Church ran out of M.D. nuns about a decade ago. The nuns working in Miseraria now probably aren't even nurses. For all I know, they aren't even nuns. But women in black outfits run the place and when we have to go over there, which I still do, too many times, to certify deaths or observe a particularly new and wretched symptom, we try to deal with them whatever they are. They aren't friendly and who could blame them. The smell was so awful that you talked as little as possible, tried not to inhale deeply, and to get out fast. Most patients couldn't speak English. There is not a day I was in that place that I didn't come home and scrub myself hard with antiseptic soap. Finally UC got so bad there that these nuns now complain loudly and bitterly and in the press. No one at HAH or COD or PHS or NITS pays any attention.

Someone set it on fire, patients and all. You'd think such an ancient pile would burst into instant flames. But it didn't. It just smoldered and smoked and refused to truly ignite. Everyone is evacuated, though I guarantee no one knows how many patients were in there. Hard to locate the truly decrepit in big city hospitals. I hear that all the time from around the country.

With the first hint of fire, the Church Albigensian Commission, which hasn't been summoned officially in Washington for 127 years, calls itself into meeting and decides a sacrifice to Christ must be made immediately. Since this was announced publicly, crowds of the devout start coming to take a look. The Catholic Archdiocese also summons all the parishioners that it can. Evidently you want a crowd for this sort of thing.

Cardinal Buggaro, just back from the Vatican looking really hot stuff in his crimson outfit, is intoning an outdoor Mass in his obviously stumbling Latin, one that's evidently very black. Medieval. Patsy Dura, with whom I went to junior high and run into here, tells me this. She still lives in the neighborhood and goes to the local church. A large contingent of priests stands watching while seven more burn the seven covenants of the deed of transfer from the Vatican to the Washington archdiocese. Then a bishop asks all the Catholics to pitch into the pyre a few splinters shaved from the actual Cross itself (where and how do they still say they get these things?), which are passed out to the large audience hungry to touch and accept them. For the not-so-true believers there are big piles of old planking and cartons of old clothing and whatever stacked for everyone to have something to hurl into the flames. A black coffin appears that contains the remains of the most recent death in the hospital who'd been waiting for the undertaker. Since everyone knows that every patient in this place had UC, everyone stands back as if the devil is in that casket and it's not the symbolic offering it's meant to be.

City officials, summoned earlier to be johnnies on the spot, are handed tiny pails of ashes of the burned deed. The hospital is thereby symbolically returned to the city's books, causing the mayor, whatever his name is (Washington mayors come and go quickly; no one ever knows their names), to throw a fit.

"Another fucking Catholic fuckup," the mayor screams at the bishop. "What makes you think I want this fucking sewer back! This pile of shit is yours!" And he takes his bucket of ashes and thrusts it into this bishop's hand, who then hands it to the cardinal, who's just finishing rushing around igniting various spots with a long taper, and he hurls these ashes in as well.

At last a mighty whoosh deafens the air. The crowd falls back in fear. But no one turns their back. Because this is part of the Mass, remember. When it looks safe enough, people fall on their knees and recite along with Buggaro.

It's all an amazing sight. Soon enough there's a pitch-black pile of heavy ashes. These ashes for some reason don't blow away. They just sit there. They're very heavy. Soon firemen start shoveling them to neaten things up and you can sense how heavy they are. Patsy tells me that really serious Catholics who have lived in this neighborhood all their lives believe this is a sign that Jesus doesn't want this place to leave this earth. "So our wish must be coming true." How would I know that Patsy had become so devout? Eventually the ashes start hardening into a sort of huge big malformed rock. The mayor demands that the Archdiocese remove "that whole shitty shebang." All of Nostra Mater Dolorosa Medical Center is built on top of a holy grotto of something, and Catholics from all over the world have over the years made this a place of pilgrimage. I remember being taken on a school tour when I was a kid, down into that grotto, how scary it was.

People now start to help out by taking chunks of the rock for themselves. Yes, they believe it has holy healing powers. They start arriving with their own hammers and chisels and wheelbarrows.

Every week of my young life I passed by this place on my bus trip downtown to either work at the Jew Tank or to go to Washington Jewish, where Rivka taught Sunday school. The increasing darkness of tonight reminds me of that awful trip home when Rivka and I left Philip presumably almost dying in the hospital having told us we weren't Jerusalems, and we went back to our flooded apartment in Masturbov Gardens waiting for the phone to ring to tell us he was dead. It reminds me that I don't even know if my father finally revealed what we're to be called. I asked David when I was taking care of him if he ever wanted to see Philip again. For once, he answered quickly, "Not on your life." Washington Jewish isn't there anymore either. It didn't burn down, it just converted to another faith as their Jews moved to the suburbs and sold it to some Muslim sect. I've noted various obits for the Jew Tank girls, but I've never seen any of them and I wonder why. All those lost Jews. Did we find any of them? Feef Nordlinger. All these years I wanted to call her. She made me laugh. I heard she committed suicide. My life has been so bereft of friends.

In my determination to be a fine doctor, to disempower a past as I created a future, I sure had lost myself. And I think that's exactly what I wanted to do. How else do you face up to a history like ours? With that I'm in harmony with all these bereft Catholics. Their Miseraria's gone for good. I guess misery is supposed to do that. It's just that the city's now lost a couple hundred beds. Not so coincidentally, today I booked my five hundredth case, four hundred at NITS and one hundred in my private practice. As if in honor of this, this four hundredth case at NITS was completely covered with scabs from various layers of nimroid, hard as a rock, like he was wearing a suit of armor, as if he'd been infected and then reinfected on top of the original infections. Haven't seen one like this before, the layered look. Are guys now reinfecting themselves but with slightly different and escalating strains? This guy had been a Catholic wearing a huge crucifix.

Fred once said to me that he heard the voices of the dead always talking to him.

Dr. Sister Grace Hooker lived next door in Mater Nostra. Is anyone hearing her voice? Is she watching her neighbor going up in flames?

Mater Nostra itself still stands, though, like a fortress, on its plain, huge hunks of ancient masonry that from a distance—and no road comes too close—looks intact and sort of majestic, as old heaps from past eras can do when they're over there and you're over here, like the handsome old woman whose makeup gives her a burnished luster from fifty paces but only a wrinkled endurance when confronted close up.

Shit, she's still there, isn't she? Fighting, surviving, doing her damnedest to stay alive. Men fall apart, collapse, fart themselves into unpleasantness. No one calls an old man anything besides smelly old man, old fart, old geezer . . . There are no Brownie points for fellas who survive. But there's always a soft spot for an old dame still in the race on legs that hardly support her. She hasn't sunk from the weight of agonies endured in all of its buildings' bodies.

It's dark outside. There's Sister Mattie, with whom I've worked on many a case, who of course is not as old as her cloister here, but just as tired. I know, because she told me, how she wants very much to die. She is that tired of it all. I can see her looking out her window, in this wing she shares with twelve other women, each as old as she, each as tired as she, each as anxious as she to join their much missed dearly beloved Dr. Sister Grace to pass over to the other side they know is waiting (because they are people for whom religion and God are living presences, like brokers for bankers and bookies for bettors), and she wonders if the light that is just dim over the horizon, just coming up over Bunker Hill, will be the day that will free her from this earthly hell, God forgive her, God be praised.

Sister Mattie realizes that the light she is looking at is Miseraria, still on fire. "Look, Sisters. Miseraria is still alive and kicking," I'll bet she's saying.

"Thank the Lord," I can hear them all say in unison, no one I'll bet quite knowing why.

ON THE ROAD AGAIN

HAROLD

I live in Baltimore. I live in Columbus, I live in Little Rock, and Houston, I guess you could say I travel a lot and I don't call any one of these places a home. Not since Myron died. I still do all this shit, stuff I think should be done. Really for him. Myron would have been approving and supportive. And of course for FUQU. Except for Fred and Tommy, most members don't know about me. We had more chapters for a while. I think we had way more than a hundred, all over the world. We're really petering out. I used to go to the new places in the U.S. and help them get started. Each chapter is then on its own. We don't have a network where we're all plugged into each other. We should, but "we should be a lot of things," as Fred says. He's been out of commission for a while, so I've been acting on my own. But he checked back in with me a few days ago. He says he feels great.

We're not very complicated, how we operate, so it's not rocket science, as they say. I guess the work I do, which is the most noble and exciting to me, and I'll admit I'm . . . no, I won't admit it, but you'll think it, you'll think I'm wacko, a nutcase. But what I'm doing is something wonderful and noble, and I spend a lot of time crying about it. That's how I know what I'm doing is decent. Thank God, Myron left me well off. I go around and help bury guys. I help facilitate the public funerals, the political funerals, some chapters like New York call them. We want the world to see what's happening, don't we? Fred or Tommy would call me when something might happen, I mean inquiries about a new chapter, or who wanted to bury their dead. I then go to Akron or Austin or Milwaukee, Dubuque, and try to get things going. I offer my help in subdued ways, being more experienced and all that and from the big city where they think FUQU/NY is the cutting edge. They all had sick people and so I'd intimate there are many ways to die and go to heaven and I'd try to find out if there was a way to—I use the word *integrate*—to integrate the funeral shit into whatever local shit they had to deal with, inside their group or out of it. Dead UC bodies are not exactly welcome in the burbs and sticks. Undertakers don't want them for sure. Well, there are a lot more "public" funerals than anyone knows. Maria and Jean and Maxine, they didn't know about them. They only focused on New York. Maxine, she is a trip. I would watch her when she got up to speak, and man, she is a take-charge kind of dame. No nonsense. Easy to admire. Very on the nose. A lot of women like her out in the Midwest, where I mostly am. Maxine is sure a role model to more than she knows. I guess Fred told her about me because I just took care of an old friend of hers in Portland, Maine. First woman I did this with. Maxine said leave her outside City Hall. The men out of New York are such wimps. Out in the sticks the juice all comes from the women. There are more guys, sure, but they still cruise too much.

I usually just get a call. Somebody whispering, almost. We got a body . . . So I take a couple of my friends—by now I have a list of contacts for willing helpers everywhere, mostly guys I'd helped get their own lovers out there expeditiously—and we would pick up the body or the ashes or the coffin in my hearse. I have an old jalopy hearse that I actually live in, sleep in, when I'm on the road. And in the wee small hours we'd drive around Akron or Columbus or New Harmony or Buffalo or El Paso or Charlotte or Des Moines and look around for an interesting place to leave the body. I had this official-type letter that was Scotch-taped to the urn or coffin that said something like, The guy who was once living and is now inside this coffin is dead because of UC and because you who are finding him here didn't give a flying fuck to help save his life. Different versions of that. Sometimes, if the weather's nice, you know, a balmy night with stars and stuff, I'll open the casket and leave it open and put the letter in the corpse's hands. That was actually my preferred way of doing it. We'd drive around to look for an open place that made sense and no cops were around and we just left him there. Then I'd drive somewhere farther out and park and then walk back to watch what happened. Sometimes it was boring, like the cops would just get the coffin hauled away. But sometimes homeless people would discover it or drunk kids would open it up and toss the body on the ground and leave it there while they slept in the coffin or had sex in it. Sometimes animals would come and start to eat the body. Starting at first light people would see it and just be horrified. I forgot to mention that the coffin was always painted with DEAD FROM UC on it. This meant that removal teams had to dress up in all their stupid gear before they'd touch it, so it could be a while before it was taken away. In Oberlin, Ohio—I mean, you'd think with a famous college there they'd be smarter—the open casket stayed open with the body in full view for maybe two days. I kept waiting for TV to come and shoot it or the newspapers to write about it, or the radio, but, you know, that rarely happens. These were events that no one ever covered, which if you think about it is more weird than what I was doing.

Now Fred said to stop it. He actually called me from where he said he was recovering from his transplant and he said he'd been thinking about all this body stuff and he was beginning to think it was sort of disrespectful of the dead. "I having come so close to it, I don't want to be treated like this if I die. They die in this place every minute. I hear the helicopter land on the roof above my head and drop them off and take them away." And then there was a long pause on the other end before he said, "I want to get some nobility back for us. I don't know how yet. We got our dead bodies onto the White House lawn a couple of times, so we've done that. I'm home soon. I may call you. I got to go, Harold. Too tired. Thank you for everything. I love you." And he hung up.

I did a couple more myself after that, where I called the local papers and TV and tipped them off, "Dead body from UC in front of City Hall demands that you pay attention," stuff like that, or that line from *Death of a Salesman*, "Attention must be paid," trying to get something noble into it like Fred wanted. That didn't seem to do the trick either. Fred said all along how hard it is to get this shit publicized right, and it's true.

I will kind of miss doing this. It makes me feel I was really doing something for the cause. Creepy as you might think it is, I didn't think it was creepy. But I've come to agree with Fred. I feel less noble because there's still no public acknowledgment for this dead body or this disease or this coffin in their midst, which means we've failed. Funny, also, that gay newspapers, not a one of them, in any of these places, wrote about this. Go figure. These were not places where guys partied real hard after an action. Maria would not feel at home here.

Wichita and Tulsa, they were the last ones I did after Fred said to stop. The firemen in Tulsa took the body out of the coffin and set fire to it and stood around and watched it burn to ashes. They drank beers while they watched, and tossed the empties into the fire. In Wichita the cops got their big dogs to rip the body to shreds. Then the chief came and told his cops they had to shoot the dogs just in case they got infected too. So they shot their dogs. And they made the firemen put on all their protective clothing to cart the dead dogs away. God bless America.

CAN YOU BELIEVE IT?

Can it be possible? No one can believe it. Dodo is asked to leave NITS. Who asked him? Has he been judged guilty or innocent? What's he done with

Poopsie? The final Dingus Report has been released. Our greatest scientist? Our great discoverer? The man acclaimed by that lady of the wigs as "our great savior"? What's in that Dingus Report? It's marked "Top-Secret." You never see the names Moose or Bohunk or even O'Trackney Vurd anymore. What happened to Vurd? (He committed suicide by drinking himself to death, according to *The Life and Times of the Scoundrel Vurd* by Glypha Jones-Morton, Ph.D., State University of Wisconsin Press.) Where will Dodo go? Who would want him now? Soiled beyond repair? Scorned and ridiculed for being scorned and ridiculed? Dingus did that! Dingus, who dingled Dodo and Garth Buffalo, too. How fleeting is fame. How fleeting is infamy. What are we left with?

Nausea, facial wasting, kidney failure, mouth ulcers, hair loss, blindness, peripheral neuropathy, lymphoma, rage, insomnia, skyrocketing cholesterol, lumps of fat, erectile dysfunction, ingrown toenails, arthritis, constant fever, eczema, oozing pustules, muscle collapse, constant farting, psychosis, swollen pancreas, brittle bones, persistent diarrhea, bad breath, gas, body distortion, enlarged breasts, hallucinations, mental confusion, vomiting, dementia, paranoia, nightmares, severe depression, suicide, pancreatitis, kidney stones, liver disease, heart attacks, death.

•

Who am I to complain?

STATE OF THE PLAGUE

Still, no one has discovered anything really worthwhile. There are many rumors and innumerable secret trials in and out of this country but the number of deaths grows staggeringly higher, so high that even the statisticians are filled with fear that they can no longer predict when deaths will top out. The White House has forbidden admission into the United States by anyone infected. Next come prohibitions disallowing any government employee from here going over there, to any foreign shore. Jeffrey Mannheim of the Budget Office is quoted in *The Truth* as saying, "It's a waste of money, these overseas jaunts. America's just not getting its money's worth." Caught off guard by the issue, Drusilla Lotsee of the State Department is quoted in *The Monument* as saying, "Of course we'll still pay to send a spy or two. A president will always want to know a thing or two. This president wants everybody to know that . . . this president still wants to know . . . a thing or two." Who *is* the president now? In this isolated world of science, some people actually have to think twice. Presidents and scientists live in different countries. Iran? Iraq? Afghanistan? Syria? Yemen? Arkansas? What are you talking about?

Dodo had tried to announce that he desired the name of his discovery to be the Underlying Geiseric (UG), but that the government agency where all employee discoveries must be registered restrained him from such personal aggrandizement as being against some regulation or other.

He'd also tried to announce that The Underlying Condition *maintains* a decline in T-4 cells as to eventually result in morbid, finally fatal, disease particles and an *inability* of the formerly high T-8s to reproduce enough to fight back. This should have been more or less obvious but no one was certain what he was talking about. "The only place you can get healthy-enough vectors for studying this is from the tissue of unborn worms." This is crazy talk. Besides, the abortion issue being as divisive as it is, the use of unborn anything on government property is forbidden. Do not laugh or scoff. This is so. See Regulation XVIII29s, 2005, ext. 4. It does not seem to occur to anyone that if Dodo is correct and T cells are rearranging themselves so fast as to kill off, as of this moment, 270 Americans every 4.5 minutes, and 1,300 other human beings around the world in each segment of 5.3 Greenwich Meridian minutes, it would be more humane to use every unborn worm you can get your hands on, which in and of itself is not an easy feat, and fuck Uncle Sam, the pope, and Rep. Dingus.

"When the furnace goes out, it goes out. I have discovered this in my lab. It is my parting gift to you," he pronounces to the sparse crowd come to hear his farewell address.

"T-Fours, T-Eights, what is he talking about? I swear to God I don't understand what Dodo is saying. Is it whole cloth?" seems to be the general response. Besides, no one believes Dodo any longer. He's been besmirched. And there's something in the paper about Poopsie being indicted. Poopsie Popovich? Honestly! He's only a Hungarian. Certainly he didn't lie to our government office in charge of patents and procurements. He can hardly speak English. They probably just misunderstood him. With that thick accent. He's taking the rap for Dodo for stealing the virus?

•

T-4s. T-8s. Yes, I answer to these two things. They will study them forever before they learn they are barking up the wrong trees. One-

armed woman could have told them that. Two different parts of me can get together and make another new kind of me. It is like what you call having my cake and eating it too. No? This Dodo and his research only extended my existence more forever. In my life there is safety in numbers. I'll miss the old guy.

OWNERSHIP?

SPARKS

There will be a new drug shortly! So we can officially go on two-drug (plus or minus ZAP) combo trials. How dare Fred and Maxine say TAG will have no power! The new drug will be there because of us! And because of our scaling the Berlin Wall of Presidium and demanding release of their proton-alphas that they paid us to study. Fuck you, Jerry. Fuck you, Fred and Maxine. From day one Fred screamed for "drugs into bodies" but you couldn't deliver.

Well, now TAG will be delivering.

OWNERSHIP!

DR. JAMES MONROE

These smart-ass kids are bragging too much. Right now it doesn't bother me too much. Yet. But it will. I am setting our price at $40,000 for a year's supply. That will be a bargain when our successful results are released and visible, enabling me to raise the price again. Everyone will want Peturba, which is what I'm going to name it. Bart Shovels says it'll be a bargain at any price, although he's unhappy it will keep too many homosexuals alive. I told him he can't have it both ways. We are both greedy, but for different things. Well, he is my protection at the White House and at the CIA. I am assuming that in all of this we can each get away with murder.

My smart-ass kids were blissfully obnoxious in Berlin. When I described it all to Dereck he roared with laughter. He wants to hire them to make trouble for him. His father had bought him a chain of hotels and he wants to get rid of the tenants.

DERECK DUMSTER

My father did not buy me anything! I am a self-made billionaire! Me, myself, and I did it all by myself! And don't you ever forget it!

GOODBYE TO ALL THAT

There are those who question the total validity of the whole package of Underlying Condition assumptions that are now pretty much accepted by almost all scientists. Those disagreeing are pariahs, outcasts, the ones who do not mind being viewed as crazy, unlike those who have learned to keep their mouths shut since there is no profit in being a naysayer in this world of yeasayers. Two of these outcasts are sitting, not next to each other, because they hate each other's guts, but still close, near Dodo, whom they hate even more and who'd actually invited them to this farewell reception, where his wife served her special pasta.

These two most important Dodo naysayers—as differentiated from the Total Denialists, who insist that UC is not the cause of UC at all and really are crazy—are a scruffy lot. That makes for part of their problem—that those in disagreement should be so physically unappealing. It's really hard to take people seriously when they're so unkempt.

Why do these two cringe from Dodo's every word? Once upon a time, early in the history of The Underlying Condition, Dodo trumpeted that the Nector and the nimroid (or was it the nector and the Nimroid?) were one and the same, or somehow related, or at the very least best friends. Or was it mortal enemies? Dodo announced his "discoveries" for each. Now we know that nectors and nimroids were different and never got along with each other and that no one talks about them anymore. How could such things as nectors and nimroids disappear from the scene just like that? You could ask the same question about Dr. Rebby Itsenfelder and Orvid Guptl. They may be sitting near each other now, but shortly they will just be gone. Tomorrow, perhaps. Later this afternoon, perhaps. So fleeting is fame. Well, neither of them was particularly famous, even if they were important.

Rebby and Orvid hate Dodo because for many years Dodo owned this plague and they both knew Dodo was lying about much of his work. What is that stupid expression, ownership is nine-tenths of the law? You get written up enough times, the world thinks you must have done *something*. Media is so naïve and stupid, and *complicit*. Thus this stupid expression about "ownership" will continue to be true, and those who are foolish enough not to have friends, not to have made allies and forged alliances, not to have done much but hurl shit über alles, or almost alles, and most important, preferring to hide behind the only protection they've ever known, their unending paranoid fits of disenfranchisement, will have no choice but to pass into the missed of history.

So, so long, Rebby. So long, Orvid. There is no point in wasting any more time on either of you. You had your chance at bat. You didn't stick it out. Historians must often be as cruel as this, even when, as in the case of Rebby, much love for this man existed and still does. Your beliefs held certain truths your lack of social skills kept you from conveying. Monserrat has had enough of you.

Orvid, we've already lost in the murky shit of pigs. Swine flu. What a stupid escape hatch. Orvid, you too were on your way to making history and you blew it.

TALES OF THE VIRGINIA WOODS

Tolly McGuire summons his many members to one of those conference inns hidden in the Virginia woods for their annual spring get-together. A big crowd is invited and a bigger crowd shows up. Tolly realizes he doesn't recognize half of them and he left his glasses home so he can't read their name tags. Every fucking pharma in the world has a rep in D.C. now. He'd like to believe they all were one, working together to save the world. That's why he went into pharmacology. Ten minutes on the road and all these guys hate each other. They all started as sales reps, which is competitive as all hell and you only get paid on how much product you've unloaded. So you told lies about every other company's unloadings.

People are still arriving. Names and more names. Rolf Voss from Interswiss Pinkus, Margery Guest of Schwein-Audacia, Barney Osterveld from Prinkus Maxwell, Diane Globbenger from InterAmerican, Arnold Botts, Gobbel, Shovels and Monroe from Presidium, Farse-Fehl-Forgotson (Three Fs), Boozer Feltwass, Garbast-Stokes-Helsen, Packer Drum, Terpsus Finnegan, Uriah, Pfisterer-Pipette, Nordsee Ogunquit, Mistere Pfiaf, Salvatore Avventura, Santa Maria-Missione-Glunck, the mighty Greptz, oh, and Molly Trachtbart from *NEJS*. Time to start melding the journals into the drama. Yes, we're all in this together now.

"My people tell me there's enough to work with now."

"That's funny because mine don't."

Tolly raises the main issue: "Is the consensus that we work together or work apart?"

"Well, it's cheaper to work together when the alternative is taking a bath."

"Remember Invidia."

"Remember GallstonePlus."

"That was just such an awful name."

"I've been wanting to name a drug FAGPlus."

There's obviously much subtext in the room. Drug companies are ultra-suspicious of each other. Everyone's really spying on everyone else. They all want to cash in in the biggest possible way. The virus is out in the world now and they stand to make the most if they're the first to find the way to kill it. And if not kill it, then to disable it. They'd all settle for a big disability. That way they can add new drugs as they discover them. Better a continuation than a cure! They've been quite profitably able to not cure cancer for decades. Each person in this room is waiting for somebody to tip their hand and say, "Manny Grlic in my lab is interested in going after the proin or the pyrokine or the volblatt." But no one is giving anything away. This only makes them all more suspicious. It verifies what each suspected: they're all working on something secretly already. And they've all made progress of some sort.

Each notes with interest that participants haven't come alone. They're all accompanied by small groups of others. A good sign if these are salespersons, the power that keeps them all afloat. No doubt they've all done market research and discovered that the potential of the market now is HUGE. No one says, "How did it get so big already, so fast?" At least and at last some folks have figured out why.

More likely, Tolly knows, these extra blokes are their lawyers.

Because they don't speak English, a lot of Chinks and Japs, the smart scientists who sniff the earth, the soils and plants and oceans for newer ingredients from nature, sit to the side, better to hear their own interpreters.

Everyone in this room recognizes among all the faces people who have worked for him or with him, or have stolen from him or have been fired by him or the reverse of each of these interactions. This is not a collegial business, making medicines. These people are not humanitarians.

To take the earth and turn it into an active weapon targeted against specific molecules is a black art, to say the least. That it sometimes works is usually a surprise to he who observed it. Nothing is out of bounds. Everything's ripe for consideration. Even shit. Remember that fossilized ancient American shit that was found on Table hotel land on the Gulf of Mexico? With absolutely no doubt it'll be in one of these "new" discoveries. Arthur Table and Gideon Greptz are cousins.

There is no representative from any government agency in attendance. Nor is there anyone from the UC activist movement. "We're on our own now, baby," Phil Owens from Greptz says. "The NITS didn't welcome us before. We don't want them now."

The consensus Tolly hoped to bring forth remains stillborn.

DR. JAMES MONROE

Yes, I see them all here, all the crooks and Ponzi schemers I'd studied for years. I was a reputable scientist, in Berlin and Czechoslovakia, and I had worked for the biggest prick of all, Von Greeting. Everyone in this gathering is getting away with murder. I hate everyone here, every single shit-eating selfish one of them. I am going to screw each and every one of these bastards by beating them to the punch. Von Greeting taught me every trick in the book. Only he wanted everyone dead, killed of course by the meds he's developing to get rid of them. People don't believe drug companies kill them after they rob them blind. Gideon Greptz paid himself a salary last year of $75 million! Pinkus of Interswiss took a salary of $45 million. The Audacia blokes the same. Drug manufacturing has turned out to be the most profitable business in the world! I have the first drug I guarantee will stop UC. It will be out there before any of these jerk-offs get theirs out of their toilets.

I hit upon the way I can do what I want. It's called FUQU and their TAG. They and my shit-ass powerhouse board of monsters will make Presidium the biggest game in town. Correction: world. I will cure the world of this plague and I will, repeat will, be paid most handsomely for my humane generosity.

OUT, OUT, DAMNED SPOT

Good old Boy Vertle is "forced" to take action and fire his new surgeon general for advising America to teach masturbation to schoolchildren.

A SADDEST LOSS

TOMMY

Bruce Niles died. He was so tough. Anybody else would have been dead long ago. He was completely covered with scabs. His skin kept blistering and peeling off him. He couldn't even turn his head. He couldn't breathe without an oxygen mask. He just wouldn't let go. He held on to my hand and said to tell Fred we should never have stopped being friends. His last words to his attendant evidently were "Keep fighting."

I'm finally starting a new job that even Bruce would approve of. Here's hoping!

•

NEWSREEL FOOTAGE
The March on Washington brings half a million gays to parade through the city. The evening newscasts on all networks announce and show this.

EXT. WASHINGTON STREET. DAY.
The FUQU/TAG contingent is larger and marches all together. UCGATE *and* SILENCE = DEATH *posters, as well as posters attacking Ruester and Trish and Vertle. Also one that says,* THE GOVERNMENT HAS BLOOD ON ITS HANDS, *with red handprints. Fred and Tommy and David walk in front of the crowd, Fred's arms through each of them for support. This is his first reappearance in public, and lots of folks wave to him and blow him kisses.*

EXT. WHITE HOUSE. DAY.
A line of marchers picketing, being arrested one by one by policemen wearing protective yellow gloves. The posters are being taken away from them. Fred is there, with David and Tommy. They stand posing for Mario photographing them directly in front of the White House. Then Fred throws his cane away and grabs a cop for them to be photographed with the White House.
RON AND MEMBERS (*chanting, re. the cops*): Your gloves don't match your shoes. You'll see it on the news.

EXT. MALL. WASHINGTON. DAY.
A huge screen shows Fred speaking passionately to the enormous crowd that is spread out on the Mall as far as can be seen.

THREE DYKES

"Tommy was with Bruce when he died."

"Stop, Tallula! I don't want to hear any more death!" Viv holds her hands up to cover her ears. "We are here to celebrate. To show the bastards how many of us there are."

Tallula Giardino, Pam Able, and Viv Brody are three tough dykes. Each had wanted to change their world. Pam and Viv have come to Washington for this parade and to visit their buddy Tallula, who now works in the White House itself, one of the earliest "out" lesbians to do so. Boy Vertle has assigned her to Personnel, and the only out gay man on his staff to Forestry. So much for all Boy's promises of inclusion and participation. They are watching the parade from a bench on Pennsylvania Avenue.

"It's embarrassing seeing how few women we can muster up," Viv says. "This was to be for dykes, too. To also show ourselves to Boy and Maude. Particularly Maude. What do you mean you work in Personnel? If I want a job in the White House I call you?"

"It's been a disappointment," Tallula says. "But he gave me the choice, this or nothing."

Pam asks, "Do you really think he's our friend?"

"No straight man is our friend." Which one of them said this? They all believe it.

Tallula then says: "He's abusive to women. He fucks a lot of them when she's away. I don't think he's going to get away with it. His enemies are whispering about impeachment already."

"For screwing women in the White House? Nobody said boo when JFK was so . . . busy."

"I think Maude should be president. She's very smart," Viv says.

Pam says: "But she's a dyke!"

"She's got several gorgeous assistants and best friends," Tallu tells them. "A sex-obsessed hillbilly and a dyke, forget any attention to UC. I don't care what he promised."

"Where is our organization in Washington?" Viv asks. "All they do is kiss asses."

They haven't been with women, alone, for quite some time. Lesbians are different from gay men and they appreciate, cherish, and defend this difference, as they should. If they are to be lumped together taxonomically with "our own sex-crazed goofuses," as Pam, who is a stand-up comedienne and very funny, calls gay men, "endearingly, of course," then that is that. But few of them feel like Maxine that they have to stand up with and for the boys, especially now it's more widely known what awful things are happening to them because of sex.

"But we cannot continue to stand by doing nothing," Viv, the most maternal of the three, declares. "I must confess that after all these years, I'm beginning to feel guilty. I should not have left FUQU. I was there with Fred for the first meetings. I should have visited Bruce. Fred almost died from his transplant and I never even sent him a card."

"He made a good speech today. Amazing, after what he's been through," Tallula says. "The organizing committee refused to let him speak and he just went right up there, grabbed a mike, and did it. Same old, good old Fred. I hear he's finally found a lover."

Then she says to Viv, "May I remind you that I, too, was there with them from day one of this shit. I personally presided every single Friday morning at the UC Network meeting of diverse voices that felt uncomfortable with GMPA. I personally negotiated the salvation of jobs for our food handlers. If you recall."

"That was many years ago, Tallula," Viv responds. "Matters are much worse now, and lesbians still haven't moved nearly close enough to them in friendship and support. Is this proper behavior on our part?"

"Well, whatever we do, we must not chime in with 'We told you so,' which is what I find myself more and more wanting to do," Tallula, the most politically adept of the three, declares.

"Oh, I don't know. I've been dying to stick it to them, they're such assholes," Pam also declares. "With humor, compassion, and understanding, of course." Pam has a growing reputation for her take-no-prisoners comedy routine about "the gay lifestyle," whatever the fuck that means.

These years of UC have presented lesbians with enormous problems. UC has swept every other gay issue off the map. Women have been unable to insert their own special concerns into the national gay agenda. "If one could locate one," says Pam.

"And it is not as if we have received their support or they're asking us, 'What can I do to help you move forward on any of your own vital issues?'" Pam also reminds them, not that they need reminding.

"They still can't keep it in their pants," Pam contributes again, referring to some new numbers from COD attesting to same.

"Don't, won't, can't, mustn't, shouldn't—we must try not to be negative, as we tell them to stop it and grow up and behave or there won't be any of you left," says Viv. "Don't you think?"

"We are not talking constructively," Viv then says, no one having answered her question.

Tallula is looking at the Capitol. "This town is useless. We have no one here. We have no power. It makes me sick. The first time I came to Washington to protest was when Roosevelt was president. Where have we found ourselves after all these years? Right back where I started from when I first started growing my boobs."

"What do you think we should do, Tallula?" asks Pam. "Be specific. Now that you're so close to power."

"That fucking LAGU that I started in my backyard in Brooklyn has all that fucking money, and from fucking dykes, too. What's wrong with those girls?" Tallula is referring to the Lesbian and Gay Union, which now raises more than she ever was able to. It's now fashionable to hate LAGU "because they don't do anything to change our lives." Fred has been particularly critical of them on the UC issues, and has been since his days at GMPA. "I was out of a job because my own board couldn't raise my salary," Tallula is reminiscing. "Is that specific enough?" Tallu struggled valiantly for many years at LAGU, "while continuing to starve to death. Now I work in the White House and I'm fat as a horse."

"Who precisely is ever on our side?" asks Pam. "We always think we know and then we're disappointed when no one shows up . . . anywhere." She too has many memories of cries for help, all alas unanswered.

As do they all. As does every lesbian any of them knows.

Each has labored, one could almost say monstrously hard (yes, let us say monstrously hard), in the gay vineyards of hope and aspiration, only to suddenly stop, exhausted, when recognizing that no progress was being made and that not enough support for their efforts has been forthcoming. No one, and Fred has written about this, over and over, endlessly, ad nauseam, no one who has spent any time working for "the gay movement" has ever encountered anything but similar "get-losts."

"It makes you cry," each has said at one time or another, each of these three warrior women, correction, once warrior women, because each sits at this parade more as observer than participant. They had participated in many marches over their years.

Pam reminds them. "Another parade. Great. Everyone then goes home for another ten years."

"I take it back," Viv says, referring to an earlier inquiry. "I don't feel well at all. The minute some food goes down, the gas comes back." She no longer enjoys discussing community politics. "They're all jerks," she says now unwaveringly. She pops another Tums into her mouth. "Why can't we just have our own national dyke organization, period?"

"Because the only members we'd have are us," Tallula points out. "We have been here many times before, need I remind you. I am thinking of moving completely out of the city and into the country. Upstate. Way upstate. I will start a local dyke organization up there."

"What makes you think there are any dykes upstate?" asks Pam.

"We are everywhere," Tallula responds. "Or so it has been my experience."

"Well, when they pay your salary let me know and I'll move up there too."

"Why aren't we helping Fred in his FUQU thing? I hear it's falling apart. This must be breaking his heart." Which one of them cried which one of these sentences out loud? Each knows it doesn't make any difference. The three all sit in silence as each recalls earlier days of much the same.

"We were younger then," Tallula says.

"And I didn't have two kids," says Viv, "and a lover to support."

"Why doesn't Mary get a job?"

"She runs the house and our two kids, for God's sake. Lay off Mary."

Of course Fred had asked these three women to join him in FUQU. They are among the three most intelligent women he knows, dyke or non-dyke. Each had been by his side in the earlier years of this fight, at GMPA, now laughingly referred to as "the good old days." They may not have been mentioned in this chronicle but it's difficult to keep all in attendance in attendance. Along with everything else, gays are their own worst historians.

As the parade dithers to its close, dusk is falling on this city. But numbers of both women and men still roam the streets, looking for some place to rest themselves, but perhaps not. No one seems to want to sit down or go back to a hotel or home. Our three women have remained together, sitting and watching the marchers from the sidelines, waving to a few old friends, realizing how many women are younger and much more pretty, and of course, thinner, and how much older they have become. The parade has been longer than they thought.

And then there appears what none of them expected to see, a contingent of sick men marching as best they can or being pushed in wheelchairs, some carrying GMPA signs, some with FUQU. A big banner is carried that reads IN SUPPORT OF OUR LESBIAN SISTERS!

"It is a bag of blessings, today, to remind us," Viv says.

A group is now seen carrying another banner. It reads TARGET BOY VERTLE AND IMPEACH THE SEXPOT.

"I am readier for upstate than I thought," says Tallula, wiping some tears. "Girls! Snap out of it," says Pam. "We are alive!"

•

EXT. MASTURBOV GARDENS. DAY.
Fred and David are walking among the buildings, this enormous warren of garden apartments where each once lived.
FRED: There! That's where I lived. Forty-two twelve. Where was yours?
DAVID: There! Across the street. Until I was six years old.
FRED: How amazing. Both of us being here again after all these years.
DAVID: I hated it here so much.
FRED: So did I. So this is where Daniel grew up?
DAVID: And Lucas and Stephen, too.
FRED: They ran with an older gang, I think. There were lots of kids here then.
Fred takes David's hand as they continue on their walk.

EXT. MR. HOOVER'S WHOREHOUSE. DAY.
David and Fred looking at the now very elegant building.
DAVID: It's sure been gussied up. It used to be sort of hidden behind a lot of bushes and trees. And there was a big parking lot for the clients. And there was a special private space for Mr. Hoover and Clyde. I wonder who lives here now.
FRED: She's a rich heiress with a famous art collection. It's open to the public. It's very popular, listed in all the guidebooks.
DAVID: I wonder if she knew what she was buying. Maybe our spirits haunt the place.

FRED: What do you think really happened to you here?

DAVID: Besides fucking with all the strangers?

FRED: Yes. Looking back on it all, what do you think?

DAVID: I was another person. I was Mr. Hoover's person. I thought he was nice to me and I wanted to please him and he would . . . I don't know. Every teacher I'd ever had was . . . strange. So I guess I never questioned them. They kept me alive. I almost fell in love with one of my clients. He was a major in the Army and I was the first man he ever had sex with. Like you, he kissed my back all over. That had never happened to me before. He fell in love with me and wanted to take me far away so we could live in peace. He was found dead somewhere. Mr. Hoover knew all about it, which scared me. But he paid for me to go to college in San Francisco. He said I could further my education there.

FRED: I wonder if Hoover knew a virus was being spread in this house. Or in San Francisco.

DAVID: But he was gay! Did he want me dead too? They gave us lots of shots to protect ourselves.

A tour bus pulls up and disgorges a crowd of women who rush to go into the house.

ARKANSAS TRAVELER

There is a now-famous *Monument* op-ed piece by the late Sen. O'Trackney Vurd written just before he died that concludes with the challenging question: "Do you want to visualize your president masturbating in his toilet in the Oval Office," referring of course to President Boy Vertle's troubles with the voluptuous White House intern Tynada Day, young enough to be Boy's daughter, "because that is what he's doing?" It is unclear if Vurd is implying that because he himself doesn't jerk off nobody else should either, or he is just upset Boy's doing it on the job, and at taxpayers' expense (though who hasn't wanked off occasionally in an empty office or employee restroom when on a break?), or he's disgusted that "you" are even allowing yourself to visualize this act at all. No one's suggested that after a full day in that office from which he ran the world Boy still had enough energy left over for an orgasm, and that might be a good thing. No one was in any way happy that

Boy and Tynada were trysting while Maude Vehemoth Vertle, Ice Queen of the Ozarks, was off in arms of her own, those of Renna, the youngest daughter of Pugh Harnett, the seventh-richest man in America, which is probably not such a bad thing either because Maude had heretofore evinced little facility for either warmth or affection, and it might be a good thing for history if someone warmed her up a bit before she's launched onto stage center to attempt a more enduring role.

Get the picture? Boy Vertle does not have UC on his mind.

You want to know what genocide looks like? Come to New York. Ghost Town. Death City. And this president, whom gays helped put into office because he made them promises, has done *nothing* to honor a word he said.

Boy Vertle is no better at ending this plague than Peter Ruester and Dredd Trish.

And lest we forget, his very first kicks in gay asses came when Boy signed "Don't Ask, Don't Tell," after promising he would allow gay soldiers to openly serve their country.

Boy Vertle will smile his lovely smile and say, "Well, I tried, but 'The American People' won't let me." If this isn't another act of a slippery-slope president, what is?

Gays have helped to elect a coward who will say the right things and do none of them. Sound familiar?

ONE BILLION!

On the op-ed page of *The Truth*, Dr. William Haseltine of Harvard predicts there will be one billion UC-infected people by the new century.

Fred reads it. He just stares at it. David gets angry at him for just staring into space. Fung warned of the possibility of dementia after a transplant. David will have none of that. "Somebody put his mind to work!" Fung prescribed. "Doctor's orders!"

There's nothing wrong with Fred's mind. He's having another attack of overwhelming sadness about so many dead friends he's been unable to help save.

David finally picks up on it. "Survivor's guilt, it's called. I've had it since I was born. You're depressing the hell out of me, my honey bunny."

"Honey bunny" makes Fred laugh.

David says: "Tonight's Tommy's show."

Fred jumps up: "Let's go dancing!"

•

EXT. ROSELAND. NIGHT.
*An enormous line waiting to get in. Everyone very up and ready
for fun.*
*Tommy is greeting Fred and David and ushering them in. A huge
poster:* BROADWAY CARES PRESENTS BROADWAY BARES!

INT. ROSELAND. NIGHT.
*Tommy, Fred, and David are standing at the front of a balcony
looking down at a huge spectacle of hundreds of half-clad youngsters
performing a pageant for a huge cheering crowd all packed on the
dance floor. The music is deafening!*
TOMMY'S VOICE: They're all kids working in Broadway shows. They
   break my heart. Fred, I'm on my way to turning this organization into a huge moneymaker for a hundred different UC places
   desperate for funding. I've already raised a couple million with
   events like this.
DAVID'S VOICE: You really are excited. That's great!
CUT TO:
*Everyone is now dancing, including Fred and David, who are doing it
cheek to cheek. Tommy is looking down on them from the balcony.*

DANIEL THE SPY

Welcome back to the world of the living, Fred. Your article in *The Avocado*
was impressively and refreshingly full of your old vigor. Yes, I'm still hanging
in, trying to update whatever history's being made here. Tommy said he was
worried because you rarely smiled and cried a lot. Jerry says a transplant can
depress you but you should be strong enough . . .
   Jerry's not in day-to-day charge anymore. In the strange determination
of this place, this is considered a major promotion. "Of course we have studies of how to treat patients on antivirals!" Dr. Homer Herky, now appointed
the first director of DUC (of course everyone now calls us "duck," and I
mean the verb not the fowl), defensively maintains when pressed for an estimate of how long it will take these studies to yield data. If pressed further
Homer mumbles uncomprehendingly because he knows what I know. It will

be two to three years *after* the one year needed for planning and designing any study, plus the one year to honor the law's requirement that information be posted around the country so the contract can be bid on by anyone, plus the one year it takes to sift these bids, plus the one year it takes to obtain suitable candidates for the winning trials as judged by the peer reviewers, not one of whom knows their stuff enough to make such a judgment. It's just like that now famous rant by Emma Brookner a hundred years ago at that very first NITS site visit in New York. Yes, any UCCTG trial to obtain answers to what's a right combination can still take from five to seven years, by which time whatever's been learned is no longer of use because it's either already been learned by self-treating patients and/or because newer treatments have come along that should have been tested first.

Homer is a drip (originally Gist's gay ex-boyfriend), and I work beside him every day and even told Jerry that Homer is a drip, which only provoked, "So what? Do you know how many unfilled job slots we still have here? We're lucky I could sneak him through."

A strange doctor from India arrived unannounced and insisted on seeing me.

"G-D won't help. They want full price for ZAP. My country will have fifty-five million infections. You must help us." He was really hot under the collar, sweating, his eyes ready to pop out. I figured I wasn't the first place he'd come begging.

I protest that we can't even help our own people. "No, you'll find no help here in Washington," I told him when he said all his visits have been shunned.

"We have more than three hundred cities each with over one million population. We have almost one billion people. China will be just as hugely infected," he said. "And of course the Soviet Union."

I admit that I hadn't been thinking much about the cases so far away.

"Do you know why it is so bad in my country? Because we have more men than women. Women are murdered as infants because parents know a woman's lot in our country is so wretched. So, when the young men come to the city, there are only other men to have intercourse with. It is not homosexual; it is pragmatic."

He then told me about the male children singled out to become "not a man"—the sect of men who wear saris and go out to be fucked by other men to honor a religion or a goddess.

"It is a tribute to holinesses long forgotten and even longer not understood.

In your very city here of Washington there are a number of this sect as well. They are infecting each other here also. And no doubt infecting American men who pick them up by the river, where they gather dressed in their saris. Do you know that our clergy now want marriage sanctioned for a young girl at nine years old? The boy, of course, must be twenty. We have five million wandering monks. We have inquisitions everywhere and around every corner, persecutions of just about every religion we might turn up, and of course homosexuals are murdered everywhere, hung, poisoned, stoned, hurled off rooftops of big buildings. Not only in India but throughout the Subcontinent. I went to call upon several gay human rights organizations here, those that claim international atrocities as their purview, all to no avail. One chap actually said, 'We are not interested in your country. We are hardly able to be concerned enough for ours. And we would lose the little funding we have if it was known we were helping those outside this country.' This is no way to stop a plague. And so it will not be stopped. And it will be America's fault. Your fault. Your fault. Your fault! You have given UC to the world!"

He was screaming this as he backed out of my office and ran down the corridor, so that heads popped out of doors to see what was making such a ruckus.

"It's your fault! It's all your fault! It's all America's fault!"

And then, just before the elevator arrived, he turned back to all of us now looking at him. He was bawling. "You gave it to me, too. I came to America to find love and freedom. You infected me with your poison and I took it back to my beloved India and I gave it to them, too!" And just before the elevator doors close, he manages a roaring, "America is murdering the world!"

Yes, welcome back. You are needed as much as ever. Tell my brother hello. I am so glad and happy you have found each other!

ISRAEL IS STRICKEN, AGAIN

"A country ages and becomes more and more diseased and dies. Just as a body dies.

"Do I die having like Sabin discovered something and been given little credit for it? Or will I die unheralded altogether?

"I discovered UC, you know. I discovered glause.

"And I am still in prison for it."

"The loony is at it again, talking to himself," one guard says to another.

"You'd think they'd take him out of a locked cell and put him in the ward," the other guard says. "It's not as if he's going to run away. A couple nights I forgot to lock him in. In the morning, he thanked me and shook my hand. What's 'glaws,' do you think? I went to the library in Anchorage and they didn't know."

Israel is on his deathbed. The one doctor from Fairbanks came and authorized his removal to the infirmary. Israel talks to the doctor: "Hitler won, you know. He destroyed all of a certain kind of Jew, the Jew who had soul, who cared. Those who came to America, they no longer cared. Those who went to Israel became crazy and loony. Hitler murdered all the Jews with soul and taste and humor. The ones he didn't murder, the ones who made it to America, they got killed by the Americans."

"That so," the young doctor says. "Could be. I'm an Eskimo. You're the first Jew I ever met."

Israel recovers! In his illness, he'd been released from prison to go home to Washington, where someone else can pay for him. Under his wife's care, he rallies, even though it has been so long since he's seen her, he can't remember her name.

But then the hideous story repeats itself. Once again his journals are "discovered" in the Admiral Mason Iron Vaultum Library. Only this time his journals are more liberally quoted. His beautiful love letters to his many "sons" that he had sex with in the upper Andes Mountains as children and brought to America to live with him, as he educated them all and sent them all to college. The tabloids have a field day. Who released all this to the press? Which taunting spectral rememberer of things past has never gone away and released this to the press again? Why? Why do some never cease their hideous persecution of imagined wrongs? Israel had sex with boys while on a government grant. In 1926. This is against a federal law for which there is no statute of limitations. The FBI is ordered to find living proof that will reentrap him. They find a man who claims to have had sex with Israel in the Andes. In fact, he still lives there. The man is now seventy-five years old. He does not speak English. Somehow a phone connection is pieced together so that Israel and this man can talk to each other. The FBI records the conversation between Israel and this man, speaking Pisthtu, the language of the Iwacky. Israel, deep in memories as the man's voice rises in excited recognition, collapses. His wife summons an ambulance just as a dozen FBI agents and local police surround their house. Israel is sent to jail again. He is almost ninety years old. Once again he is disgraced before a world that doesn't even know who he is, and doesn't care.

Yes, he who discovered the origins of UC is once again being sent to jail for it. Even Rodney Pilts writes about it in *The New York Truth*. Israel had once written: "The love of these innocent children for me is exceedingly touching. That they offer me their bodies is the highest tribute their culture offers. It is considered a major insult to reject their offer. Their own fathers have been known to kill those who deny their young sons this ritual path to their maturity." Of course, Rodney is allowed to print only the bare essentials of the imprisonment.

First Lieutenant J. J. Nopps, Jr., is awarded a Distinguished Combat Citation for apprehending "this notorious criminal who attempted to evade the law yet again."

This time he is being sent down south, "so at least the old guy can keep warm," Dodo cries when he hears the news. He flies back to Washington to catch him before he's shipped out.

"You were a great man, Israel. I know. I know what it's like to be a great man no one appreciates."

Holding Dodo's hand in the police van, Israel bolts up.

"Evvilleena Stadtdotter must be the conduit from Germany!"

"That so?" Dodo says. "Who is Evvilleena?"

"She was my first patient."

"At Isidore Peace?"

"Isidore Schmuck! Schmuck!"

"Maybe they have your old records."

"Stadtdotter!"

"How you spell that? What's this got to do with Germany? You say UC came from Germany?"

"Why not? Why not? Why not?"

Goddamn Jews, Dodo thinks. They all believe Hitler started everything.

Dodo is holding Israel's hand as Israel suddenly seizes up and dies, until the small shiver comes that rustles him back to another world, to his earlier life where he now thinks he was happiest. These two men who have seen the worst America can do to its men hold hands, each lost in his dreams of what might have been.

DEEP THROAT

I am still taking care of him. Peter Ruester, retired in Beverly Hills, parades around his house in cowboy gear, playing General George Custer, which for some reason he believes was one of his great roles that got him an Oscar. Fred tells me, "Custer was gay. And his lover was an actor named Lawrence Barrett, who was the second most famous tragedian of his time. (The most famous, of course, was Edwin Booth.)" I miss Fred. God help me, I miss Washington. Would that my new controllers at X-Seven let me retire. What I tell them about Ruester and NITS is no longer politically useful to them, and Ruester playing Custer they really don't want to know about. Shovels told me it was too embarrassing even for them.

Mother is dead now. Floyd Harmish got rid of him to take his place. James Jesus knew it was coming. He was accused of being a gay Soviet mole, just as he predicted. I flew back for his funeral. Mother was all laid out in a coffin overflowing with his beloved orchids. Not many of we boys of his showed up. They're all too afraid to be seen with him now. Harmish was there, of course, along with his new buddy Dereck Dumster. I wonder what Mother did with all his notebooks. I hope in the end he didn't destroy them like Clyde did with Edgar's.

I hope I got it all down on paper, what I've discovered. Fred boy, it's up to you now.

•

INT. FRED'S LOFT. NIGHT.
Fred and David are watching TV. The program is the Miss Russia contest.
A lineful of very buxom babes in bathing suits is parading in front of the judges, one of whom is Dereck Dumster. His father, Earl Dumster, is standing just behind him.
ANNOUNCER'S VOICE (*he speaks in Russian with subtitles on the screen*):
    And the winner . . . Mr. Dumster?
He hands the envelope to Dereck Dumster, who rips it open.
DUMSTER: Svetlana Moi . . . (*He can't pronounce it.*) Selevits-
    nitskyavitch . . .
The sound of the big audience erupting in applause as Svetlana approaches Dumster, who puts a crown on her head. He gives her a big kiss and embraces one of her tits as he does so.

David suddenly jumps up.

DAVID: I know that man!

FRED: Dereck Dumster?

DAVID: No, that man behind him. Earl Dumster. He must be his father. When Gertrude and I made all those hotels in Europe . . .

FRED: I remember.

DAVID: We sold them all to him and his company. Gertrude made
him pay a fortune. It's money I've been living on all these years.
I remember he was always complaining about his son who was
out fucking every babe in Paris. He was actually pretty funny.
Like a Jewish mother. Except he wasn't Jewish. After he bought
all our hotels he wouldn't rent rooms to "kikes or niggers." He
was meant to be one of the richest men in America and a big
crook.

AT LAST?

Fred is in one piece. Being with David he's overcome the peculiar feeling of
being brought back from the dead, which had been freaking him out. "We're
both longtime survivors, honey bunny," David points out again.

Fred has always been such an absolutist. Facts are facts to him even when,
especially when, they aren't for anyone else. He takes down his book about
"the summer of our lives," as he can still hear the Divine Bella calling it.

He updates the closing list of the book that he'd written called *Faggots*,
which had upset so many people, his first exposure to being a pariah:

"Fred is here, and so is Mikie (dead) and Tarsh and Bo Peep (dead)
and Josie (dead) and Dom Dom (dead) and Frigger and Fallow (dead) and
Gatsby and Bella (dead) and Blaze (dead) and Sanford and his snake (dead)
and Laguna beauties (dead) and Dick and Dora Dull (both dead) and Bruce
Sex-toys (dead) and B.L.T. (dead) and Irving (dead) and Hans (dead) and
Timmy (dead) and Charlie and Alex and Tidgy Schmidge and Toney
(dead) and Olive (dead) and Dennis (dead) and Laverne (dead) and Robbie
(dead) and Morry (dead) and Hubie (dead) and Jefferson (dead) and Montoya (dead) and Lork (dead) and Carlty (dead) and Yo-Yo (dead) and Dawsie
(dead) and Pusher (dead) and Tom-Tom (dead) and Yootha (dead) and Rolla
and Feffer and Vladek (dead) and Cully (dead) and Midnight Cowboy

(dead) and Lovely Lee and Garfield and Wilder (dead) and Harold (dead) and Anthony and Wyatt and Boo Boo (dead) and R. Allan (dead) and Billy Boner (dead), and the ghosts of palest Paulie and Patty and his Juanito and remember Winnie Heinz (all dead), and Leather Louie (dead) and Lance Heather (?), Adriana, Dordogna, Randy Dildough, S.S. *Berliners* all (?), the Gnome (dead), Derry (?), Floyd (?), Sprinkle, Tad (?), Kristos Rosenkavalier (dead), Canadian Leon (dead), Pinky and his cymbalettes (dead) . . . and and and the group keeps growing, friends, and new friends, joining every moment . . ."

He now opens the datebooks, the years of Filofax pages, that had been waiting for him. They've been there on his desk for quite some time. Slowly he goes through each day and each night. A lot of the faces were still clear and he was glad for that. He often forgot faces and names because he was too wrapped up in himself.

He realizes that he is truly in love for the first time in his life. He also realizes that he's getting more and more depressed as each day passes and more people die because this country doesn't care.

Tommy had said to him: You owe it to your new liver to shape up! Otherwise it should have been given to somebody else more useful.

•

FRED'S THOUGHTS AS HE, DAVID, AND TOMMY GO TO A FUQU MEETING

It's pathetic. Now that TAG has depleted us and Sparks has put out that there's a great new drug coming, our numbers are diminishing even more. I don't recognize most of the faces. The discussions are about non-UC-related issues, all concerning social justice to be sure but not about UC and a cure for UC that really works, which is why I started FUQU. A few people who remember me come to tell me awful stories about the terrible stuff they're taking, "but TAG's putting an end to *that*!" "We miss you at our meetings," a few say. A few know I'd been sick. Eric had actually said to me before my transplant, "Fred, you look like you're dying." Eric isn't here. Maxine, Ann, Vincent, Maria, Gerri, Suzanne, Avram, Perry, the short list of the stalwarts is painful. I blame myself that I wasn't here to stem the tide. Tommy said as much. I took it as a criticism from him. "How could I be here? I was getting a fucking new liver!" David calms me down.

Tommy says, "I was just saying that without you constantly on top of things it couldn't be expected, all of this, to be such a surprise."

I am surprised to learn that Monserrat was partners with TAG in this dethroning of Jerry. Like GMPA had done to me, she'd also shut out her dear old friend and fellow scientist Rebby from the organization they'd both started. GMPA hadn't even sent me a card. I figured if Elton John himself could send me a bouquet of flowers every week for six months in Pittsburgh (and I don't even know him), GMPA (and Monserrat, come to think of it) could at least have sent a card.

The nonstop ganging up on Jerry has unfortunately dissipated. Sparks says, "We no longer give a shit about Jerry." Sparks is now the titled executive director of TAG and is paid rather surprisingly a lot. Yes, it's already being funded. A gift from Sammy Sircus is announced with much fanfare: this strange man (Why? Why is he strange? He just wanted to be rich and famous, and he is) is actually giving money to something gay. Sparks has a paying job for the first time in his life. "It is very easy for you who are independently wealthy to criticize," Sparks says to me. "I just said I don't think when you get paid you can call yourself an activist," I say back, echoing Maxine. I remind him that when we first met he said something like "I want to be your son. I want to be by your side every minute so I can learn from you."

"I think you must be thinking of some other guy," he says.

No one asks to see my scar. I have a gigantic scar. For some reason I thought folks might want to see it. Scars used to be a turn-on on the beach to some. Thinking this makes me giggle. Then, thinking of David's back, I stop.

I am looking better and younger. I can eat a quart of ice cream and a big chocolate cake and not gain an ounce. Fung can't figure this one out, or why the white hair on my chest has grown back the black of my youth. The wish I've had all my life, to be able to gorge and not get fat, has been granted. As with many wishes that come true, I'm not getting all that much pleasure from it. Except for David, of course. Without him eating the gallon of double chocolate fudge with me I don't know what I'd do for fun.

Got to finish this fucking book fast in case something happens to one of us.

Tommy and David have been incredible. The transplant brought into operation all Tommy's skills as care provider and nurse and hospital administrator. He dealt with all the mounds of paperwork and permissions for the whole ordeal, which in the end totaled $500,000!—I saw the final bill—and was paid for, every penny, by my insurance. Tommy is still worried that I won't survive, despite Fung's reassurances that "you are as old as your liver."

"You know you took a liver away from someone younger and . . ." Tommy's pointed out a few times.

"Are you trying to make me feel guilty?" I interrupt.

"You know, I don't know. I just know there are a lot of moral issues involved in getting an organ when tens of thousands of other people desperately need them too. And when once again you're not looking after your health. Have you been back to the gym, or met with your trainer, or talked to a nutritionist?" I remembered all the terrified and forlorn faces showing up at Fung's clinic, begging to be told something hopeful. "Our whole town pitched in to pay for mine," a decaying woman not doing well post-transplant said to me. "I simply must pull through!" She didn't. Then there was the Arab prince whose huge jet was parked at the airport and whose elaborately robed retinue of several dozen kept vigil day and night outside his hospital room until Dr. Fung made his determination. "He's not in good enough shape." Everyone expected the departing Arabs to blow up the hospital. I remembered all this and Tommy reminded me of all this and "all of this should have made you grateful."

I still feel guilty I've survived when all those men I've danced and fucked with haven't. I don't talk to Tommy and David about this.

As I was recovering in the intensive care unit of that medical center in Pittsburgh that gave me this new liver to live with I came to realize that completing this history is the thing that would provide me with the path back from the dead to the living. Along with David, of course. For as I lay there I'd not only thought I'd die but I heard all my dead friends beckoning me to visit them again. But I came to, almost ruefully, accepting that what I still had to do was stay alive because my people are still dying.

Of course I must live for David! He's working on developing something he won't tell me about.

Now, is FUQU resuscitable? Has UC activism really gone bye-bye?

Eric came back just as the meeting was ending.

"Look who's here!" he yelled out to the small crowd. "Our founder's been brought back from the dead!"

There was a small scattering of applause.

ROUND ONE

Fred went to his Yaddah reunion. His classmate Von Greeting was on a panel of successful classmates talking about their great careers. This was the only reason Fred came back to this damn thing, to publicly accuse Von of starting the worldwide plague of UC. That being head of the company that knowingly sold tainted blood products had started the plague in America, certainly and without a doubt. Von Greeting was a very popular classmate. He'd been football captain and Skull and Bones. After my standing up and making this accusation you could hear a pin drop. Von, looking very aged and tired, stumblingly defended himself poorly and inaudibly and disappeared immediately after my accusation and from New Godding. Fred, shaking that he'd actually done this, thought everyone would now exile him into purdah. But Von's own roommate, Phelps Rundle, now pretty bent over from Parkinson's, came over to him and thanked him. "Somebody finally went after the Golden Boy. All his life, and he still lives near me, Von has hated two things, Jews and homosexuals. He didn't think there was anything wrong with hate like that. I am married to a Jewess. He refused to be my best man. My best friend from childhood and prep school and Yaddah refused to be my best man because I was marrying a Jewess. I don't know if you remember, Fred, but Von wouldn't talk to you when we all lived in the same entryway in Standing. He said you were a queer even then. He used to joke he wished there were courses here that taught how to eliminate people like you. Yes, I thought he was joking. When he bought into G-D he told me that time had come. He felt as happy in anticipation as he was before any big game at Yaddah. 'You are all going to be dead,' he recently said to me before he was booted off Yaddah's board. I have no idea how he finally figured out that I am homosexual too. In his eyes I was the same as a Jew. He believed that many Jews were also homosexuals. He said things like, 'It's bad luck Hitler didn't finish his job.' And he'd roar with laughter. It never occurred to him that he was turning against the only person who ever really loved him. And that was me."

ROUND TWO

Herbert, Tusher, Albertino, Mucosi, about a dozen of them, are crazy. They're certifiable. Their brains are fried from drugs and dope and coke. They've broken off from FUQU/San Francisco. No, that's incorrect. They've hijacked FUQU/SF and stolen that name for their own, while FUQU/SF stood hopelessly by in the face of off-the-wall idiots, once their own brothers-in-arms. FUQU has never had a mechanism for expelling anyone, even members who steal money from it, as happened on several occasions in New York. Herbert and his buddies hate Fred Lemish for recommending ZAP, which isn't true. But it's always best, says Herbert, "to hate the leader; that's how you get attention." They also believe Fred's in bed with Jerry, which certainly isn't true. It's difficult to discern just what they're trying to achieve. They've opened stands all over the Castro to sell "medical marijuana" and they're cleaning up. When Fred accepts his next invitation to speak, this one from San Francisco Gay Pride, Herbert and Tusher storm in with shouts and whistles as Fred's building to his climax. Fred knows who they are. From the dais he furiously throws himself on top of Herbert and, quite respectably for an aging nonathlete who's recovering from a liver transplant, beats the shit out of him as best he can, "for destroying my organization!" He's amazed his rage can mutate into something so physical. He'd never beaten up anyone before. Of course, he was really punching back at Sparks and Scotty and Claudette and Spud and his once-considered-children now playing TAG, another hijacked organization of dissidents. Hotel security has the intruders out in no time and Fred gets a round of applause. David picks him up off the floor and gets him back to the microphone. "Honey bunny, be careful. This was meant to be an out-of-town tryout, not a closing night."

As chapters of FUQU start falling apart or closing up, Fred visits Shmuel, now an old man. They sit in Central Park near the Plaza. Fred won't go up to Shmuel's office, which is on the twenty-third floor. Fred is disconsolate: I've failed. I've failed my people. I can't save us. "And of course I'm not getting much help from my people either, saving themselves." Shmuel reminds him of the story of Exodus, and of Moses unable to lead his people to safety in the Promised Land. His people were awful to him "after all he'd done for them. You can imagine."

After the session Fred realizes he doesn't know what happened to Moses.

THE DEATH OF VON GREETING

Von Greeting is found dead by his cleaning lady in his apartment in Waldbaum Towers. Autopsy reveals he's been poisoned. By himself? By another? He'd been seen at Tolly's last "secret" meeting, watching, saying little, which is unusual for him. Of all the people there, he alone knew that the first drug coming that actually works, which sadly will not be one of his, now called a protease inhibitor, is shortly to be announced by Presidium, which tested it on cohorts in Outer Mongolia, in Timbuctoo. Do not laugh. A sophisticated-enough population lives there that's both infected and geographically available for a secret clinical trial.

Von's residence in Waldbaum Towers is put under lock and key until Arnold Botts can clean it out.

There are a number of notebooks. No one will read these notebooks. They're still there to be read, embargoed in the Greeting Foundation's cavernous archives in Malt-on-Rest. The news of his death is not announced, by order of Galworthy Jenkins, the new director of the U.S. Office of American Security (OAS). As with the mysterious disappearance and death of Garrie Nasturtium, also never officially announced, nor was Dr. Herschel Vitabaum's or Dr. Sister Grace Hooker's (announced but full of lies), we still don't know how and why.

In one notebook, Von had written: "I'm ready. I've done what I wanted to do. I've proved you can come out of the sticks and turn a piece-of-shit company into a billion dollars manufacturing poison they beg you to sell them. Greptz's protease will come out first but it won't be strong enough. Presidium's will be. So there's nothing left for me. I killed off as many of them as I could with ZAP. Too bad kikeface Lemish blew my cover about Factor VIII, but maybe no one will believe him. America's the greatest land of all!" He leaves his fortune to Cambridge University to administer as part of the Greeting Foundation. Arnold Botts goes to England to run it. Dash Snicker is left a number of what turn out to be exceptionally valuable patents for secret drugs in the G-D pipeline. Just when these start turning into multimillions, Dash dies from lung cancer. The patents return to the Greeting Foundation, now one of the richest foundations in the world. Just go to Cambridge and see how many buildings are named "Greeting," after Lord Von Greeting.

When his death is finally announced it's by a decrepit and raspy-voiced Sir Norman Treadway in London. Among other nuggets of new information about this mysterious man he reveals is this: "Lord Greeting is survived by Arnold Botts Greeting, the great-grandson of the world-renowned interior decorator, Lady Syrie Maugham, the wife of the famous writer."

TWO TIDBITS

Jon Cohen writes in *Science* magazine:

"There never is to be a Manhattan Project for UC. One had been promised by no less than a successful candidate for president of the United States. High-powered meetings with leading scientists, policy makers, and activists had been held to package it. The name had been changed repeatedly to make it more palatable. A respected congresswoman and the White House's own UC czarina tried to sell the idea. *The New York Truth* ran an op-ed by a famous UC activist that pleaded for it. Two congressional bills tried to legislate it. But a Manhattan Project for UC—no matter what it was called, no matter who sponsored it, no matter how it was packaged—is not to be."

John Mohr, age eighty-six, Hoover's "third man," dies. He "played a central role in the mysterious disappearance of Hoover's legendary files," according to one of Hoover's biographers. Hoover's office was sealed off when he died, but Mohr never mentioned that the director had eight other offices crammed with files. Helen Gandy, Hoover's longtime secretary, pored over them under Mohr's supervision as truckloads kept arriving. Were all of the files destroyed? Betcha not.

COLLOQUY

DAVID: Why did millions of human beings allow themselves to be marched unresistingly into the gas chambers? Is it significant that those facing death didn't attempt to take one of their executioners with them? Is that like what I did or didn't do? There were scarcely any serious revolts. They had no one like my honey, angry Fred.

•

FRED: They would have shot your honey, angry Fred, first thing because of his big mouth. No! I would have found a way to fight back. I wouldn't let them shut me up. And honey bunny yourself, give yourself some credit for still being here. Think about it, sweetness. Somehow you wouldn't let them get you.

•

HANNAH ARENDT: To destroy individuality is to destroy spontaneity, man's power to begin something new out of his own resources, something that cannot be explained on the basis of reactions to environment and events.

•

FRED: Our fight has destroyed the will of many of those still among the living.

•

HANNAH ARENDT: Hitler knew that the system which succeeds in destroying its victim before he mounts the scaffold is incomparably the best for keeping a whole people in slavery. In submission. Nothing is more terrifying than these processions of human beings walking like zombies to their death.

•

DAVID: Then the very existence of UC is essential for the functioning of a totalitarianism that allows "them" to maintain we're sick. It kills off our moral value and usefulness in our own minds and in the eyes of the world. It obliterates the consciences of those who should help us and don't, liquidates our individuality and spontaneity, our ability to fight back, to hold our oppressors to task. They want to make us superfluous. Enforced superfluousness is the essential tool for perpetuating what Arendt means by absolute or radical evil. God, she was a brilliant lady. Thank you for telling me to read her.

FRED: Thank yourself. You've certainly been doing a lot of figuring out. I love that.

DAVID: You're my inspiration.

FRED: And you are mine.

DAVID: We mustn't get too gloppy!

FRED: Why not!

•

DR. JAMES OLESKE: You've got to stay with it. You can't take the next job. I try to tell medical students, once you make a commitment to a community, if you're really going to be an effective person, you've got to stay there, you can't give up; that's why I don't believe in this burnout thing. Because patients can't say, "I'm poor. I don't want this disease, and I want to leave Newark." They can't take the bus and leave Newark and go someplace and be well and healthy. And I don't think as a health-care provider that you have the right to say, "Well, I've seen too many kids die. I've seen too many problems, I'm going to change my job." I don't think we have that privilege. I just think that UC was my problem and I was called to deal with it. Not called. I was sort of there when it happened. I was called to stay. *(Bayer and Oppenheimer's UC Doctors. Dr. Oleske is medical director of the Children's Hospital UC Program at the University of Medicine and Dentistry in New Jersey.)*

•

FRED: By now UC doctors are falling by the wayside everywhere. It has just been too much for many of them. Some have contemplated suicide, many have retired, many have turned to administration or even working for the pharms. For many of them, burying patients for more than a decade is more than they can bear.

•

DR. WILLIAM FERWILLIGER: The degree of human misery and suffering associated with The Underlying Condition far exceeds anything I have witnessed during my fifty-year professional lifetime. *(Dr. Ferwilliger is the chief doctor at Bethlehem Redistrict, the largest medical complex in east-central Pennsylvania.)*

•

DAVID: I'm told that when I was at Partekla they'd find me walking through the corridors in the middle of the night looking for a way to get out. I don't remember that. What did they really do to me there?

•

DANIEL: It's funny sitting in Punic Hall. Everyone working on UC was ordered here to "meet and greet" Fergus Frisby, the new deputy head of HAH, already acting like a pompous ass, as if he's the new Messiah and not just the acting one until a new permanent one is chosen by Boy Vertle and Donna Do-Nothing, who are definitely not in a hurry. Boy's been a real loser on UC issues, dethroning the notion that it's only Republicans who won't touch us with a barge pole. And now here comes the Democrat Boy Vertle to do just that. "My old buddy Fergus from the plains of Arkansas will now have his very own shop to call some shots that I know he's been wanting for ever so long," Boy drawls, in anointing this hillbilly who is ten degrees lower than Hoidene Swilkers. HAH's become a joke. The Department of Health and Happiness. Who thought that one up? Why does no one want HAH to do anything of major importance, like, for instance, maybe saving lives? This is the kind of question you're dead if you ask in Washington. Study after study "reports that" another awful result has been tallied. Infant deaths are up. Hospital failures are up. Early deaths in seventy-three major categories are up. Unfilled vacancies in every single department at HAH, at COD, at FADS, at DOD, at NITS are up. Employees hired with substandard educational résumés are up. Numbers of Americans without health insurance are up. Public apathy is way up. In 1982, Dodo announced he knew the cause of UC. In 1983, Dodo announced he'd discovered the cause of UC. In 1984, Dodo announced he'd discovered another cause of UC. In 1986, Dodo announced his first cause was the only cause. In 1988, Dodo announced he'd discovered the cure and would tell us shortly. In 1990, Dodo announced he'd discovered the cure and would tell us shortly. In 1992, Dodo announced he'd discovered the cure and would tell us shortly. In 1994, Dodo announced he'd discovered the cure and would tell us shortly. In 1995 there is no more Dodo. I look at my president introducing his new buddy Fergus, who speaks English that sounds like a yodel.

Why do we all continue to sit here and listen to such shit?

I open a desk drawer and reread from Francis's letter of so long ago:

Dear Dr. Jerusalem, I love you. I want you to hold me and kiss me and make love to me. All this time we've wasted. I haven't had the courage to tell you my feelings. All this time neither have you. Like we're both afraid. Why are people always afraid?

Starting with my parents, every minute of my life has been about people doing hateful things to each other. And David's now back to remind me of it. My twin. A much healthier David, thank God. We've talked a mighty amount. At last something feels right.

And he and Fred are in love and are living together.

I wonder if it's ever going to be my turn! What a schmuck I was to let Fred go.

BOY VERTLE IS IMPEACHED FOR GETTING BLOW JOBS FROM WHITE HOUSE INTERN

SEXOPOLIS

Sexopolis über alles!

EMILY LAUDA HANNIMAN OMICIDIO PUTS HER THOUGHTS DOWN ON PAPER

Daniel and Fred think they know a lot about Jerry. They don't.

My husband has just killed another young man. There's always a lot of killing going on at NITS. Medicine is about death as much as it's about life.

The young man is in Jerry's private ward. There are twenty beds. In each bed is a dead man covered with a sheet and waiting to be collected. Jerry's injected sufficient morphine commingled with his own mixture of various tinctures suggested by his pharmacist father. The young man is quickly dead. The young man is about twenty-five. The dead young man's legs are lovely legs. Jerry is a big runner. Jerry massages the dead calves, feeling the muscles that still feel alive.

Doctors are meant to bring mercy and surcease from suffering, even lapsed Catholic doctors taking care of fairies.

I can tell Jerry feels dead. It happened after the first couple hundred. For a couple years after he took over he was proud of what he was going to do.

Now he hates the White House and the men who command him from there, the Mooses and the Gobbels and the Shovells and and and . . .

Now he only feels alive with his dead bodies. They're his friends. They understand what he's going through. He talks to them more than he talks to me or Daniel or . . . anyone. He's got doctors on his staff he doesn't know their names. Here, in his ward of dying young men, and in his lab, where something so monumental is out there waiting to be discovered that if he could figure it out he would be the most famous doctor in the world, this is where he wants to be. He wants to be written down in the history books as a savior of men, a good Catholic, after all.

He doesn't want to know why he's being asked to do the things he's asked to do. If he knows too much, there'll be trouble. Then he'll have to lie more than he already has. If COD won't call a plague a plague, Dr. Omicidio's not permitted to do so either. Fred Lemish heckles him publicly for not doing so. He'd never been forced to work on so much that's meant to be secret.

When Dredd Trish offered him the job as Number One, replacing Stuartgene, he turned it down. "No," he says publicly, "I want to remain in my lab. I want to stay with my patients. I want to see this through."

Ordinarily this means finding a cure.

A cure for UC doesn't seem to want to be found.

He's known all along that Dodo is nuts and Stuartgene too . . . strange.

But if he tells, his happiness will be taken away from him.

He once loved being a doctor.

He fingers lots of dead penises. I have seen him do that. "The cock is still a little warm. Blood remains in it. Blood doesn't drain out of a cock so quickly, like it does from the brain," he said to me once.

He has also said to me: "I belong with all the dead guys in this ward."

He knows the story of Linwood Wallis, Lucky Lindy because he'd coattailed onto a Nobel Prize having done none of the work but all of the pretending. A most beautiful woman, the most beautiful Jerry had ever seen, stately and noble, with cascading black hair streaked with white, a Jewish woman with numbers from a camp tattooed on her arm, had been sent to NITS for observation for a rare viral fever, perhaps harbored still from the camp itself, so long ago. Lindy had his primary medical training in postwar Germany tending to victims. He believed he had blood on his hands he could never wash off. He was so overcome by her beauty and her existential situation that he came to her room in NITS and apologized to her for all that man had done to her and then he fucked her, telling her that he'd save her life. For a moment she believed him. Then her stomach hurt her. She tried to get word to Dye, the president, B'nai B'rith, the Jewish Refugee people; the more noise she made, the more she was ignored. She poisoned herself in her room. Many victims from the camps still carried pills like this, always expecting the worst. She was an Orthodox Jew and now felt "irrevocably soiled, forever." Lucky Lindy got transferred to Bosco's monkey farm in Florida. But only for a few months, when he got that Nobel for something or other, and he came back here on staff and was promoted to captain.

Just like Lucky Lindy, Jerry wants to jerk off his dead handsome young men and have semen come out of them to show that he's really still alive, that he can perform some miracle of bringing the dead back to life like Lindy caught kissing the dying woman over and over and fucking her to make them both feel alive.

You have to be a doctor to understand stories like this.

"I should have made him take an experimental. Which experimental? All of them are worth shit and I know it and I don't say so out loud. ZAP is shit, and I told everybody to take ZAP. The White House ordered me to do it."

He'd almost told Fred about Goose. They were alone here in this very ward, Jerry examining him and wanting to give him something to earn his friendship, to explain his position, his life living in a vise. He started to say, "Once I . . ." and that was all he said. But I could tell that Fred knew he was going to tell him something. I'm sure he'd been through dozens of confessions by straight men over the years that started just like this. I was at the nurse's station pretending to do something.

Goose was long ago. In boarding school every guy had a Goose.

Once when we were all drunk at a Christmas party, Jerry asked Dodo if he ever considered he was lying. Or faking it.

"No. No, man. Dodo really believes. I have to. I have to."

"How can you always be so certain, saying all the definite things you do?"

"The best scientists are always certain. The best ones don't give a shit if you agree."

Jerry faked ZAP data so G-D could get FADS approval.

He wakes up every once in a while in a hot sweat, dripping wet. It's one of the symptoms of UC, he knows, but he's tested himself enough times to know this sweat is from other fears. He pretty much always has the same dream.

"I go to the White House for one of those private briefings with Ruester or Trish or Vertle, and I say all the appeasing things I know they want to hear and will keep me in my job and my lab. And the three of them grab me and tie me to a table and . . . violate me. On my own lab table."

It's hard to be a good doctor and a good scientist and a good American in this place. They all conflict with each other.

"Can I go to jail for killing so many kids because I know the people who run this country don't want these guys saved?"

Since almost the very beginning Jerry knows and Stuartgene knows and Dodo knows and Paulus knows and Grebstyne and Middleditch and Manny know and Purpura knows and Dredd knows and every head of HAH knows, this is a plague. (Ruester wouldn't know his name if he saw it printed in the paper.) But nobody says anything about the plague out loud. America isn't to be told the truth.

Jerry picked up the phone and calls Removal. The line is always busy. He has to call an operator and ask for an interrupt. "Dr. Omicidio, I don't have anyone to send," a woman will tell him. "You're . . . seventeenth. We just don't have anyone." So the kid has to stay there a little longer.

Goose. This one looks just like the young Goose. It's nothing to do with right or wrong. It's just what is.

He looks up. How long have I been standing here? He thought he'd closed the door.

He smiles. I come to him and put my arms around him. "Another one?"
He nods.

"I don't know how you handle it. I don't know how any of us stands it." I hate myself for saying such stupid things over and over. I try to make a joke by slapping my mouth. "Oh, mouth, shut up!" I smile, or try to, and he does the same.

I know he loves me. I am always painfully honest. He calls me a saint. But such a saint that all his guilts are multiplied tenfold when I'm the first thing he sees each morning and the last each night. My unblemished belief in him gives him the worst dreams and makes him toss and turn even more in sweat.

I think he's a hero.

I don't see now the hero I wanted to marry. He was chief intern and I was one of his nurses. He was a catch. I am furious he keeps his mouth shut. Yes, we loved each other, two people drowning in deaths, trying to hold on to something, which in the end, and to the surprise of each, turned out to be each other. Together we've formed an alliance that keeps him going.

Yes, you're dead, and yes, my husband is attracted to you, but can't you see that it's only the dead ones he can touch? I want him to have some sort of physical pleasure with someone alive.

Yes, I am a saint.

I'm having a worse time than he is.

TAG keeps trying to murder him. Why does TAG hate him so?

Why does Fred hate him so?

He takes me in his arms and begins to kiss me everywhere, first my cheeks and lips and arms and neck, proceeding . . . proceeding to everywhere, everywhere he doesn't go in the privacy and comfort and safety of our own bedroom. He gets down on his knees in front of me, kissing my legs and going up under my skirt, kissing the insides of my thighs and then licking my vagina. I shiver. I fall to the floor, and his head pops out and his arms lay me back, taking off my clothes, then yanking off his own stuff and . . . his body is black with hair everywhere, he looks like an ape under his neat suits and ties and uniforms, once a month he must wear an officer's uniform, all NITS doctors are officially in the armed forces, yes, he looks like an ape under all of this, no one ever sees this forest of fur but me—and Goose—and I know he is ashamed of the fur. "I'm not such an animal as this makes me look like," he told me once, honestly, tenderly, allowing me to see a scratch of vulnerability beneath his polished, uniformed surface. I love it, his fur, his bearness, getting lost in the voluptuousness of his velvety, wiry texture, and he is entering me now, and I close my eyes, no longer seeing the dead body that hovers there still, levitating in the air above us, nor aware of the many other dead men in their beds in this same room, and I smile, actually smile, as I realize how often we make love in hospitals with dead bodies, never in our own bed, rarely in a bed at all.

I come and he comes and we both know that when he comes he comes and that's it and back to work we go. I've learned to leave quickly, before his brusqueness makes me ill. I peck him on the forehead and depart for the corridor to finish dressing more properly in an empty room. One thing about Jerry's UC wards, there's hardly ever anyone in them for very long.

COITUS INTERRUPTUS

DEEP THROAT

It's quite dramatic, what Emily wrote. Mother would never tell me where he got this. One time or another of all our years together I've been in dying wards with Jerry and witnessed a version of this scene. I'd be on the other side of the ward attending to someone and he'd be thinking he was alone and she'd come in having eyes only for him. You'd think a ward of dead guys would be private enough but it isn't, it really isn't, certainly not in a hospital the size of this one.

Here is one of the ones I saw myself. He didn't know I was in the ward, of course. Jerry is naked on the floor. He's fucked her and he's come and she's left and he still has a hard-on, and it's for him on the bed up there, the nameless one on the bed, the dead one, up there so far away but not so far. Jerry stands up with his penis sticking out like a compass needle and he jumps up on the bed and stands over the guy, looking down past his own erection. He is huge, this short, compact, exceptionally hairy man with the enormous uncircumcised penis. The few drops left in him fall on this handsome dead young man, down there, still dead, so far away, but not so far, and still dead. He, the living one, is crying.

Jerry falls on him and kisses him, all his for this moment only, in his arms, cradling him, kissing this floppy dead thing he couldn't save. Even I was moved, I must confess. Finally, he gets up. He wipes himself with paper towels from the toilet. He wipes his semen off the dead body. He dresses himself. He covers the body with a blanket.

Like all the men in this ward he is gay. Like all the men who work for him are gay. Only Fred somehow senses this. But then Fred says that everyone is gay. He's probably right. But because Fred says this about so many, no one believes him. Mother believed him, though. "I've been through many versions of the same situation," he confided in me enigmatically.

ANOTHER OPENING, ANOTHER SHOW

PERRY

Sparks spoke out too early with his promises. Protease, protease, we are still waiting for the protease. (Proton alphas, they'd been called.) Sparks was in charge of sitting on Presidium. Scotty had been in charge of getting more money out of them. "They will be our lifesavers!" Sparks had told everyone. "TAG can take credit for this!" Levi's trial of Presidium's proton alpha provided the best of anything out there, so Scotty uses this info to get even more money from James Monroe. "Something is working! Something must be working!" say Claudette and Spud. Levi says, "OIs are down in our trials! Deaths are even falling."

Enormous and very nasty rivalries have been escalating as each pharma fights to possess *the* drug. There's a lot of arm-twisting behind the scenes, "mostly by stockholders as greedy as the manufacturers," David G. says, "as they raise not only the dosage but the price—twice as much in some cases." Barbara reminds us that a Greptz drug is about to be launched. "Everybody I talk to is frightened of Greptz. They're so powerful. I'll bet that's why Presidium is holding its horses."

Insurance companies, smelling multiprofits in drug combos, had raised premiums. ZAP had cost "only" $10,000 a year. There would be more excitement on the patient front if any combo didn't have such uncomfortable side effects. Never plan a route without knowing where the toilets are. Never leave home not wearing a Depends. Social lives are so fucked up that adherence rates fall noticeably. Now it's Levi Narkey's turn to plead, "Guys, stay on our drug!" Our very own Dash Snicker is making the same appeal. But a number of trial participants aren't so concerned with this argument. "You try and live in shit all day!" Grosse Wildeschone says to Levi. The most popular over-the-counter item is still Imodium. A few guys try butt plugs, but boy, do they not work.

Then, then . . . Not one of the next-in-line five or six drugs still in combo testing, being tested on hundreds of people, is working for long enough. One by one their manufacturers pull their own plugs and unload the losers on the Third World, where they'll take anything. Last fall these were the golden hopes, now these are pieces of shit. So suddenly there's nothing actually out there on the table. So the dosages of all the losers are upped. "Yes, of course! Why didn't we think of that? Increase the dosage! Just in case!" Sparks says this with excitement. "Of which one?" I ask. Sparks answers, "All of them, you ninny! Do a trial! Do two! Do a dozen. Until we get Levi's final tallies."

So a bunch more tests get started. Even the PIs are listening to us.

But then suddenly—mutations! Working meds turn into no-longer-working meds. Why? What happened? What's a mutation? TAG doesn't have anyone sitting on mutations. Something's got bent out of shape. What? Quick. Develop a test to find out what our old friend UC is up to. Tests for mutations, please! The only one who knew how to make tests like this was Poopsie. Forty-three lawyers immediately say Poopsie is a no-no, even if they could find him. Another Rumanian immigrant who can't speak English who works for another genius somewhere whips up a test. Everyone must now absorb an entire new terminology.

"My Two, Thirty-six, and Eighty-seven have mutated."

"I hear Eighty-seven is a pisser. You don't want your Eighty-seven to mutate. The Two and the Thirty-six won't be covered."

Each manufacturer of the next-in-line proton alphas starts touting theirs as the most beneficial to take first, as against any of their competitors' PAs, each claiming their mutations are less dangerous than any of the others' mutations. It's actually quite funny, if a bit macabre, each bragging which danger is less dangerous. "My mutation is smaller than your mutation."

I'm the naysayer on all this. Sparks orders me to shut up "once and for all, this time I mean it, period."

There's no doubt that every pharma and every scientist is still in way over their heads. But you know, it's like settling the Wild West. Who's going to stake out their land grants first? There's no trepidation on what to take. Guys will take anything! Three proton alphas? Only three? Why not four! One worked for ten seconds. Two lasted maybe a month, maybe two. A woman patient who lived in Truth or Consequences, New Mexico, actually lived six months. Should we all move to Truth or Consequences? The obvious rejoinder is "we're there already." Some guys do move to Truth or Consequences, which actually has a gay population and a gay doctor who can count T cells and has some bootleg stuff. Some people will go anywhere to get the latest. They're called "trial junkies."

When four fades out, why, of course there are five, mix and match. Just like detergent manufacturers. New! Improved! *Fuori il grigio!* as the Italians say. Out with the dirt! The doctor in Truth or Consequences is from Naples.

Hasn't Jerry now said, "Healthy UC asymptomatics not currently on antiretroviral therapy may have additional treatment options a year from now"?

Jerry has actually made a major statement! Gee, thanks and no thanks. Another whole fucking year! Jerry baby, what the fuck is a healthy asymptomatic with UC?

Onward, Dripp! Onward, Pinkus! Onward, FFG! Audacia! Boozer Feltwass! P&U! And, of course, our Mother Church, dear G-D. Excuse me, Greptz G-D.

What? There is no more Greeting-Dridge? The G-D part of Greptz G-D was sold to Presidium? How did I miss that one? So fleeting is fame, as Fred says.

The pharmas are taking over the world and we are all holding hands. I was there when Sparks and Scotty took the payola from Presidium. But they aren't releasing it yet. The first protease inhibitor, which is what proton alphas are now being called, will be from the mighty Greptz. It's being called CRIX.

Oh, and the D drug that guy at Yaddah made has been sold to Greeting-Dridge, excuse me, the Greeting part of Greptz. Some guy named Arnold Botts Greeting owns it.

Oh, and Scotty told me that he's already collected $150,000 each from every pharm working on any of this shit. I had to go to bed with him to get this dish. I just knew something fishy was going on. Wait until Maxine hears about this!

I forgot to mention that the protease from Muck, which was released to great acclaim, has tanked. Too many damned mutations appeared, almost out of nowhere, which hadn't showed up in its first wide-open PI clinical trial by Farrell What's-his-name in San Francisco. Muck's a big German monster and it's not happy. The rumor is that Muck's chief scientist on this was murdered when the home office in Germany heard the bad news.

GASLIGHT

In an operating room at Isidore Peace, Dr. Halycion Vrobuck is attempting a drexylated infusion cum transplant cum excision. This is an experimental operation involving the thymus gland, tried without success in Japan and Belgium. It requires two patients, preferably twins. Suddenly air circulation is turned off, and gas is pumped in. Everyone in the entire operating room, including medical students, fellow surgeons, and visitors, is asphyxiated to death.

A note is found hanging from one of the disengaged valves: ALL FAGGOTS MUST DIE. GOD BLESS AMERICA.

OLD SOLDIERS ALWAYS DIE

A German publication disputes all the great contributions of Dr. Sister Grace Hooker, her vel particularly. That she was wrong. That all she stood for is incorrect. What with both Grace and Israel now ignominiously refuted or ignored or disappeared, neither of them here to defend themselves, how is what they discovered to be carried on? That's what happens to old scientists. Over and over again, ways are found to hate. Very few prominent members of The American People go to their graves unscarred.

MOON OVER MIAMI

The Tiara-on-the-Beach Ball. It could be Balalaika in 1979. Or the Toilet Bowl, same year. Now it needs no darkness, no mirrored spinning ball of twinkling lights. No, it takes place out in the open, under the Miami Beach sun, in broad daylight for all to see. The bodies doing these things are older, wizened even, spotted with this and that, their tans the wrong shade of honey, only emphasizing their age and not disguising it. It is as if some Important Power determined that this annual event must still be seen, borne witness to, in all its unimaginably imagined unflattering detail. Bear witness? A peculiar expression for such finery of sequin and feather and satin, leather and denim, and chains and whips certainly, too. You would have thought that rimming, "eating you out," i.e., sticking your tongue and mouth into a partner's asshole, i.e., rectum, would have gone with the wind, pun intended. It hasn't. You would have thought that cocksucking, without benefit of a condom, swallowing semen, straight, no pun intended, would have gone up the lazy river, metaphor intended. On all counts you would be off base. Orgies of all this on the beach, on the sands of this ocean, under this glorious sun, without benefit, again, of condom—this is more than tempting fate. This is saying Fuck You to life.

David finds it difficult to understand why men demand approval in the form of tacit uncritical acceptance for these activities. "We'll never get anywhere defending these activities. We just won't. We can never be taken seriously if we continue to act like this."

Fred smiles. "You're beginning to sound just like me."

Then David out of nowhere says: "Joseph Goebbels was the Nazi propaganda minister. He said this: 'Make the lie big, keep it simple, keep saying it again and again, and eventually they will believe it.'"

"Oh, honey," Tommy says. "It's getting harder and harder for a boy from Alabama to make sense of anything. What does Goebbels have to do with this?"

"I'm thinking about it. I'll let you know."

Fred's come to Miami with David and Tommy to make another speech. The men cheer him. "Thanks for telling it like it is, Fred. We'll see you at midnight at our Fontainebleau Fuckfest!"

Which indeed is more of the same, but under the stars and full moon the three friends do manage to dance and kiss and hug.

Great and obvious truths are still elusive. "People will be people" doesn't do the trick. Not for his gay people, who he desperately wants to believe are better than this.

He and David talk about this a lot. David's experiences of exposure to naked men in groups confuse rather than clarify anything for him.

DAVID'S VOICE

IN FRED'S ARMS IN BED

I have not known what to do with all the history that our bodies have witnessed and endured. But I think I am zeroing in on something.

PRESIDIUM!

The following press release appears from Presidium (formerly Greptz Greeting-Dridge Presidium) Pharmaceuticals:

> We pledge to adhere to the highest ethical standards. We have a commitment to supporting patients' access to our medicines. It is not true that rising prices have little to do with increased production costs. For many years the world has been waiting for an effective treatment against the ravages of UC. Presidium is proud to shortly be providing the first truly effective treatment to you. We have named it Peturba. We are not apologetic for the high price of $15,000 per month and quite frankly we expect gratitude for our patience, our ingenuity, and the highest quality of what our great scientists have brought forth. There will be more drugs forthcoming from us shortly, each one a little better than its predecessor. But let us take this one drug at a time. God bless Peturba and God bless America.
> Linus Gobbel
> President and CEO
> Bart Shovels
> Vice President
> James Monroe M.D., Ph.D.
> Founder
> Presidium Pharmaceuticals

•

INT. HOSPITAL. DAY.

Fred is hallucinating, with David holding his hand. Dr. Brown is now his doctor.

FRED: Testing testing phase one countdown countdown Central Heating? Steve was murdered. Send in the clowns. Phase Two. Phase Three. Where's David? I want my David.

DAVID: I'm here, honey bunny. *(To Dr. Brown:)* Why is he hallucinating?

DR. BROWN: He has some kind of infection. That's what I'm treating him for.

FRED: First they say we don't exist. Now they want us on their list.

DAVID: What's happening to him? I've taken him to every one of his doctors.

DR. BROWN: An infection can be a good sign too. It can protect the brain while it recovers.

DAVID: Recovers from what?

DR. BROWN: From whatever it is that's infecting him. Tests will tell. I think there are some residual reactions to that ADAP drug Omicidio gave him that Greeting was testing without approval.

FRED: Himmler said over one million gays were exterminated.

DR. BROWN: We're going to get you through this.

DAVID: Hear that, honey? You can do it.

CUT TO (night):

DAVID *(lying with Fred, who is sleeping, in hospital bed)*: Our lives have been so messy. But not like this. This is the dark night of our souls. I love you even more.

CUT TO (morning): Dr. Brown looking through open door and seeing Fred and David still asleep.

FRED *(waking up)*: Good morning.

DR.BROWN *(smiling)*: Your fever has broken. I was right. I told you I'd pull you through this. A few days and you can go home.

David and Fred hug each other.

DANIEL'S LIFE

How do you dispose of so many dead bodies all at once? All over America, death counts mount. It's a problem not discussed. NITS alone produces three hundred dead patients a day.

Three hundred sounds like a lot for one institution, doesn't it? Well, they don't all die on the premises. Many die at home, and their deaths aren't included in this figure. I'm in charge of Jerry's unit now. I don't have much time to spare. I barely sleep enough, or eat properly, or even have time to cry. I've finally, somehow, learned how to let loose with tears and cry. If you think about having to deal with three hundred patient files a week . . .

TWO MORE

Arnold Botts Greeting was sent to Omicidio via emergency ambulance by James Monroe from Presidium's headquarters in Arlington. He passed out in the middle of a meeting. As his face was bursting out in purple patches, Monroe had a notion of what might be happening. Omicidio wouldn't go near him and it fell to Daniel Jerusalem to deal with him. As Deep Throat was visiting, he called him in to help. Arnold's clothes were cut from him and his naked body revealed that Arnold was pretty far along in UC deterioration. Deep Throat was gently pricking his skin for scrapings when Arnold opened his eyes. The first thing he saw was Daniel Jerusalem. "I know you!" he said, spitting and screaming out the words and jumping up. "You pissed on me in Masturbov Gardens and ruined my life." He grabbed Deep Throat's scalpel and slashed it across Daniel's face and rammed it into his heart before convulsing himself and choking to death. Daniel was dead on the floor. There was nothing Deep Throat could do to save either of them.

FRED'S LIFE

The murder of Daniel is a huge burden on the overburdened shoulders of David, and of Lucas. Fred feels like a witness from the sidelines. His own wretched family's past had offered him scant solace to share. He'd tried over the years to think of it as little as possible. But this is different. His husband's twin murdered is as if they all have been struck down. The plague's coming too close for comfort, not that it wasn't before.

David is not as inconsolable as Fred thought he might be. "It's all just part of our same story," David had said. "It's no better or worse than what we've lived through. I know you've longed for some happy ending. Well, this is not there. Except for you and me."

Fred has been sensing that some people think the plague's over, that the tide is stealthily ebbing back to pre-plague shorelines. Even though there are growing rumors that various ZAP and bootleg combo trials are only providing a certain diminution, what *appears* to be happening is a lessening of the virus's virility, provided that the drugs will be rigidly adhered to. For some, this works. For most, it doesn't.

Levi Narkey said: "We ain't out of the woods yet by any means and I worry about Sparks going crazy. It's amazing how much bootleg crap is out there, and he's determined for TAG to take credit for this new Presidium drug Peturba now that *our* bootleg trials of it have been promising and it's officially being released to the UCCTG for trials. It's almost some point of pride for Sparks that TAG's right and FUQU wasn't. It's like some sort of vengeance."

Perry says Sparks is drinking too much. And that he and Scotty are no longer talking.

And for most of the rest of the world, which is pretty much all of it, life goes dangerously on. Until everyone in the world is tested, which of course will never happen, there is no way either to know how large is the population of infecteds or how to curtail the present danger. "Present danger"? Already this sounds so . . . yesterday. And yesterday he had Daniel the Spy to help him fill in the State of the Plague. Now he has no one on the inside full-time.

How could anyone in his right mind think this plague is over? Peturba or no Peturba.

A "cure" cannot really be claimed to be on its way, as Sparks is now announcing publicly. "Well, nothing is ever going to be one hundred percent." That's heard a lot, as if an acceptance of some status quo is already setting in. Even though San Francisco has already figured out that their bootleg protease inhibitor didn't work on 35 percent of people there.

"People are tired," Tommy says. "I sure am."

Toward the end of her life, Hannah Arendt said that what she admires in Socrates is his capacity to provoke thinking by infecting others with the perplexities that she felt herself.

Dearest Hannah, it isn't working. What am I still doing wrong?

David is now reading his way through all of Hannah. That's one major task! "I didn't know anyone could be so smart!" he said. "To think we were both in Berlin at the same time. And come to think of it, fighting to save my life, too. And come to think of it again, I live now with another one trying to do the same."

Needless to say, this cheers me up. Come to think of it.

VIRUSES HAVE SEX TOO

A book by the important Dutch scientist Jaap Goudsmit comes out in which he discusses the danger of viral mutations. "Viruses can reproduce sexually—that is, by the mating of two nonidentical viruses with enough genetic overlap to allow cross-information. The UC viruses are past masters at such exchanges, meaning that within a matter of thirty minutes, two different strains of virus can swap parts of their physical makeup. It is a little like sexual partners swapping personalities so as to create an entirely novel offspring: a new virus, carrying the potential of a new threat."

•

You make me sound like boys' night out at your bathhouses, exchanging me all over the place. I love it. Now you know how I can keep my hard-on for so many millions of years without losing my power.

HIGHWAY ROBBERY

BARRY

In law school they did not give us case studies like this one.

Fifty million dollars is missing from the UC balance sheet at NITS. It is Spud from TAG, with his Navajo haircut now purple after a siege of chartreuse, who discovers this. It's $50 million that was given by Congress to NITS c/o Dr. Sheldon Grebstyne to devote solely to UC research. But Shelley isn't here anymore. It probably should have been earmarked just to NITS, but because Congress was worried about the excommunication of Dodo and Jerry, it came to NITS via Shelley, and so be it, who knows why or where or when and never look a gift horse, etc. Shelley's now a bitter man not prone to talking to anyone from NITS, filled as he is with the "go fuck yourself" attitude so characteristic of ex-employees. The thing is Spud can't find any vouchers or clues affixed to this grant file since its receipt and he can't locate the $50 million either. In Walla Walla, Dodo is still pursued by seventeen different courts and a hundred different lawyers, so his memory's been shut down too. So who else is there to query? Jerry certainly refuses to discuss anything pertaining to money as our TAG-inspired legislation now dictates he mustn't. Anyway, he would now have this 50 million bucks, not that he necessarily knows that it's missing.

Spud has been poring over all the books of the various divisions of NITS, looking for just such shit as this. The kid is a wiz, a marvel at spotting chicanery, legerdemain, the cooking up of the books. Wasn't his grandfather a top accountant in Germany, hauled off to the ovens when the war started "for being a rich Jew"? "He taught my pop, who taught me everything about how to hide stuff in the ledgers," Spud bragged to me. "Before he was hauled off to the ovens as well."

"Your father was also burned up in the Holocaust?" I said, sad and impressed. I've never known anyone who had experienced that horror so closely, even though I'm a Jew.

"I just told you," Spud says. "And my grandfather and grandmother. And my mother was killed in a Russian camp."

"Your father and your mother!" I said, even more startled by the news out of this kid's mouth. How could he even have been born by then, and old enough to learn all the stuff from his father about cooking books?

Spud seemed ready for this unvoiced question. "My father taught his brother, my uncle. He wasn't as good at it himself. He's in Leavenworth for not getting away with it somewhere. I thought you and I were going to have a date and you were going to teach me how to have anal sex."

"I did say that, didn't I?" I dimly recalled some such thing, although I can't recall why I offered. Spud's not really my type, and anal sex these days, well . . .

"Anal sex isn't so kosher these days," I said. "I assume your family kept an Orthodox home."

"I just told you I don't have any family left. They all got murdered by the Nazis during the war and the Russians after it. That was my mother's side of the family. She escaped to Russia, where she met the man who became my father, before they were both sent to a gulag by Dmitri Norbtrekno. Did you ever hear of him?"

"I don't think so, no. Who was he?"

"He was trained by Stalin to be a monster murderer. His gulag was the worst gulag."

"That's pretty bad, from what I know."

"You said it. Will you teach me how to kiss, at least?"

"You don't know how to kiss? What do you know?"

Spud began to cry. When I tried to take him in my arms, Spud broke away and ran off.

He wrote his report about the missing $50 million from the NITS coffers a week later. He put it out on the back tables at FUQU and TAG meetings, and what with one thing or another it must have made its way somehow into the wider world, because Dr. Sheldon Grebstyne's suicide at his new position in Arizona, "under unexplained circumstances," according to Velmy Dimley, happens maybe two weeks later.

I send Spud congratulatory flowers "for your really great and heroic work, and also because I really would like to go out with you and teach you whatever I can that you want to know." I do wonder how this really smart kid can also be so dumb. Sex is so perplexing now. Guess he knows that.

A few weeks later Spud sends me a thank-you note, also saying, "It was just as well you didn't fuck me and we didn't kiss. I am positive for UC, which I didn't tell you. I have become a much better Jew because of it. I go to temple all the time now and I'm learning Hebrew. Do you go to temple? Which one? Perhaps we could go together and hold hands."

A few weeks later, Claudette, who's changed from being a lesbian to not being a lesbian, runs into Spud at a coffee bar. He tells her that everything he had told me, and that he knows I told Gregg and Scotty and Sparks in our support group, and that hence made its way to Claudette, was untrue.

"About the Jews and about the Holocaust and about my accountant father, and, well . . . everything."

"You're not even Jewish?" Claudette asks.

"No."

"Why did you say all that? You're not even positive for UC?"

"No."

"Why did you say all that!"

"It all seemed to fit right in with the drama we're living."

Maxine's response to Spud's lies was very Maxine. "Some gentiles often feel so white-bread that they need to be Jewified."

I allowed that I'd never heard of that one.

The $50 million? Spud located it in Grebstyne's bank account in Switzerland. Jerry had to deal with it.

Sparks immediately called Jerry and demanded he now pay for more trials. Or he'd sic FUQU on him. As if FUQU would do anything for Sparks and TAG.

When I looked for Spud at one of our meetings I was told he'd moved out of town somewhere.

HOME ON THE RANGE

A Midwestern radio personality known as Smacker reads out on his show the names of all the sex offenders rounded up in his part of the woods. Another radio commentator, Pooh-Bah, this one gay, warns his audience to stay away from those parts of the country where Smacker is known to be operating, traveling a lot as he does, the better to pop in and surprise men in toilets, making an entrance with his camera already rolling and pointed toward a urinal. Laws against such sexual behavior in public places are widespread, and Pooh-Bah, who is the gay commentator, likes to warn his audience "to keep safe and out of harm's way, and if you have to do this, try and listen in to Pooh-Bah first to see if your area is high and dry. You may think what you're doing is normal, but others don't. You do know that, don't you? By now? After all this time?" He wonders why he goes to all this trouble to protect these laggards, except that when he drops the "Pooh-Bah's No-No Road Map" section of his program his ratings plummet. And he knows he is losing the ratings race with another gay commentator, Dangerous Dan, who "will be constantly interviewing lawyers from the ACLU about our legal rights to be in parks and other such public facilities. Remember, the next time you want to give money to any gay organization ask them their stand on sexual issues. If they refuse to support cocksuckers (don't mince words!), save your money."

•

A map of the United States is captioned ACTIVE HATE GROUPS. *It is covered with a blinding number of indicators of where these groups are located.*

•

INT. FRED'S LOFT.

David is showing this map to Fred.

DAVID: Look how many anti-gay ones there are. That's a lot of hate.
    Is it genocide or a crime against humanity?

FRED: What's the difference? Or why can't it be both?

DAVID: That's what I'm trying to figure out. In legal terminology
    they can't be both. Just one or the other.

ORAL HISTORY

DONALD: When I came back to FUQU after Warren died, almost everyone
I knew had died now too. I wanted to hug everybody and be hugged back. I
couldn't believe the fights and nasty letters. Nobody trusted anyone else. I'd
needed FUQU to vent my rage and sadness. TAG would no longer talk to
FUQU. Everyone hated each other on some subject or other. We were now
all becoming like monsters in some deep ocean when no one could really
swim. We had all been fighters together, side by side, once. There were no
demos to go to anymore. After a while, I went back home to Podunk. I don't
know why it suddenly felt more safe. I need someplace safe to cry.

•

DUDLEY: Too many of us are still dying. No new stuff is good enough yet.
The pharmas that make them all hate each other. Presidium's shit will now
cost $25,000 "a sequence," whatever that means and whenever we can get it.
And even more FUQU members are drifting away—partly in despair, and
partly because they couldn't take the fighting. Nothing was working. What
else is new?

MEANWHILE...

At a meeting at the White House with President Boy Vertle, a Lovejoy representative is reporting to Gobbel, Shovels, Dereck Dumster, Floyd Harmish,
and Omicidio. Minna Trooble is transcribing.

    "I am here to report that I believe we are most successfully demoralizing the gay population. More of them are dead. Fewer of the living are activists. All of the living will be offered a Presidium drug that is priced beyond their means, meaning they will have insufficient funds to keep on living."

"What about your list?" Gobbel asks.

"Longer by the minute. Any time you're ready to send out the troops."

"I'm not sending out any more troops," Boy says. "The faggots already hate me enough."

Harmish says: "I think it best you continue to leave that with us."

Dumster says: "Count me in."

"Don't I have any say in this?" Boy asks rather petulantly.

Shovell answers him: "Not when you've been impeached."

"What do I do if they come after me?"

Dumster answers him: "Deny everything. Never apologize. When someone punches, punch back ten times harder. Attack the messenger. Muddy the water. Accuse others of what you're accused of. Win at all costs." To Harmish: "Roy and Sam Sport taught me this."

FRED TRIES A GOLDEN OLDIE

HE WRITES TO DR. GARTH BUFFALO

You once announced publicly that you believed UC could be cured and you had ideas on how to do it.

You are back on your feet again, in charge of yet another major research institution.

I'd wondered if you were irreparably wounded by the Dingus mess. It would certainly be understandable if you were.

I hoped, with your obviously good sense of self, of who you are, you would not have been wounded, and you would have emerged angry, and eager to stick it to all your critics in the form of renewed overwhelming presence in a field in which you are once again and still top dog.

Instead I see you as having retreated into some ivory tower of safety, your mouth sealed shut, your brain idling on some sort of peculiar hold.

I never see your name in the paper in any forceful way—that is, forcefully useful in the way a name like yours can be useful in the time of a worldwide plague.

It always amazes me how people who have power often refuse to use it. I never understand why.

You know our government is failing us, our politicians are a sick joke as they sit watching millions die, and that the pharmaceutical manufacturers are woefully and greedily behind.

You have this opportunity to at last pursue your original inspiration.

Why are you dithering so?

Or have you lost your belief that UC can be cured and no longer have ideas on how to do it?

Dr. Buffalo doesn't respond.

THE NEW YORK TRUTH

UC 100,000 ARE DEAD
UC Now Seen as a Worldwide Health Problem.
Cases now reported in 33 countries and all inhabited continents.

•

Truth? You mean *The New York Lies*.

•

INT. MONSERRAT'S LIVING ROOM. DAY.
A very rich person's town house.
FRED: Monserrat, I thought you started an organization to fight for
   what we all believe.
TOMMY: Easy, sugar.
MONSERRAT: Elizabeth and I are doing that. But there are certain
   things I cannot bring myself to publicly discuss. *(Holds up a poster.)*
MEN USE CONDOMS OR BEAT IT. *(Poster is very graphic, showing an erect
penis half covered with a condom.)*
REBBY'S VOICE: Monserrat would not let "her" foundation support
   my insistence re advising safe sex and using condoms. In Britain

the women newscasters went on the air, on the BBC itself, to demonstrate how to put a condom on a banana. She was not amused. She was offended that we used words like *rimming, sucking, coming*, and, horror of horrors, *rectum* and *anal intercourse*. She said using such unspeakable words was bad for her fund-raising, which is geared toward straight people.

THIS SHOULD NOT BE NEWS

FRED: It's now "discovered" that drug-resistant strains of the virus are being spread from cock to asshole. Who's the stupid doctor who figured this one out. Guys on various bootleg combinations who have reached the state of being drug-resistant (as noted: certain drugs only last so long) are fucking and infecting guys who are not drug-resistant. This should not be news to anyone. More guys now have no recourse to any trial, official or bootleg. Bootleg drugs are appearing, stolen from a pharm and knocked off or imported from places like Mexico and China. "Studies" are going on in all kinds of crazy places all over the world by an unheard-of cast of characters. Jon wants to list all the rumors in Monserrat's directory "as a heads-up warning if nothing else," but she won't let him.

•

PERRY: Sparks pooh-poohs drug resistance as "just a phase we'll grow out of," and Scotty refuses to criticize any sexual act. He has come to jokingly calling all the fellows who are still orgying, including himself, "sluts." I don't know why I ever found him sexy. Few in either of our organizations want to confront or object to or even just discuss anything sexual. "Would you send your dying baby to Dr. Puffington?" is the kind of headline Orvid would have put on the front page of the gone and forgotten *New York Prick*.

•

DAVID: Tina Rosenberg wrote in *The Haunted Land* that any country that did not write an official accounting of its holocaust was doomed to fall back into terror and chaos. That maybe sounds a little over the top. But what are you supposed to do when what you know *is* over the top?

•

INT. T+D MEETING ROOM.

The group is all ears. Sparks is holding a magnum of champagne.

SPARKS: We did it! FADS has finally approved Presidium's protease inhibitor!

He pops the cork.

CLAUDETTE *(Her hair is now dyed turquoise)*: Taken with a combo.

SPARKS: Shut up. That's not true. *(Toasting:)* Here's to Peturba!

SCOTTY: We have a drug that works! We did it. We got it. Our meetings with all the pharms worked. *(Toasting:)* To Presidium and Peturba!

CLAUDETTE: It didn't save Spencer.

EIGO: It didn't save a bunch of people in Levi's trial.

PERRY: It didn't save a lot of people.

SCOTTY: Stop it! It's enough to keep guys alive.

EIGO: We don't know that yet for sure. And it's only a treatment. We don't have a cure.

SPARKS: TAG's gamble paid off. Fuck you, FUQU. Thank you, God. *(He takes a huge drink from the champagne.)*

EIGO: Sounds like another royal pain in the ass in the pipeline. And we don't have enough FUQU to protest with when something goes wrong. Which it will. I don't trust Presidium.

NIGHTMARES

INT. FRED'S BEDROOM. NIGHT.

Fred and David are naked in bed. Fred is asleep, rather restlessly. David is holding some pages, which he's just finished reading. He looks down at Fred. Fred opens his eyes. He sees what David is holding and tries to grab them away from him. David pushes him away and starts to read them aloud. Fred buries his head under his pillow. David yanks the pillow away and continues to read.

DAVID: "He began having nightmares about David's back. Not only could he not save his friends or himself, but he could not save this new great love of his life who had suffered so mightily. He would punish himself instead. He would jump from their roof. One night he could hardly sleep for fear the suicidal feeling stirring inside him would return again and pick him up out of their bed and take him to the hall and to the elevator and up to the roof and throw himself into space to punish himself for his failures. It was the Yaddah freshman fear returning to claim him at last and finish the job off once and for all. NO! He mustn't disappoint David! How could he abandon David! To leave him suffering on his own! David's already more than paid his dues in the tortured department. It doesn't make any sense, any of this. Why is self-punishment in order? Why is his own pain so unrelenting? He was afraid to discuss all this with David, who anyway is busy supervising the building of their new home. He longs to kiss David's wounded back. He must stop crybabying. He is so unused to actually being loved by a wonderful man that he can't see how selfish he's acting. He had to make both their lives worthy of saving, worthy of honoring what they've been through. That is what he must do before he jumps off a roof. He must stay alive long enough to lasso the answers and pass them on to history. He'd always wanted to be famous for something. He wants David to be proud of him."

(Both have tears in their eyes.)

We must never, never leave each other. Do you hear me? Do you promise me?

They are in each other's arms and shaking with tears.

THE WORKINGS OF THE SCIENTIFIC MIND ARE MANY

Dodo addresses the Walla Walla Medical School faculty. Way out west they think he's great. He draws crowds to his new institute. They don't understand a word he's saying. Here is what he's saying: Shit doesn't work (at least not yet) but piss does. Piss does *something*. Pregnant women's piss, to be precise. Pregnant women's piss from the first trimester. In other words, *specific* piss. If this specific piss is taken at a specific time and introduced into the UC lesions, the purple becomes less purple. How he discovered this, and what the mechanism at work is, are not revealed. Why the first trimester? Why not the second? Or third? He has Poopsie working on this.

ORAL HISTORY

SARAH SCHULMAN INTERVIEWING FOR
FUQU'S ARCHIVES

Sarah is interviewing Kersh. They are being filmed by Jim.

•

SARAH: The thing that I'm not understanding is, here you are, you helped start the T and D Committee, you were fundamental in getting the government to pay attention to really important issues that have changed UC and history. Suddenly, a disruptive FUQU group with not your kind of history and legitimacy is opposing you and . . . and I don't really understand what changed . . . that would create . . . it's just that it seems unfortunate that you felt you had to leave FUQU at that time because a group of people were harassing you on some level or disrupting your work.

KERSH: I didn't think I could be effective anymore.

SS: So, you just stopped going?

KERSH: I just stopped going.

SS: And what was that like?

KERSH: It was hard. Because I thought I'd given a lot and I enjoyed it a lot and was doing good a lot.

SS: And you had been there for how many years?

KERSH: Seven years.

SS: And how many days a week of those seven years were you spending on FUQU?

KERSH: Probably most of them.

SS: Were most of your important friendships inside FUQU?

KERSH: A major portion of them, yeah. Pretty much all of them.

SS: So, did you just have to walk away from your life there? You felt like you had no choice?

KERSH: Yeah.

SS: So how did you adjust? Did you stay involved in UC on any front after that?

KERSH: I became really close with Rebby. I attempted to do a couple of research projects with him. And then he walked away from everything.

SS: Tell me about it.

CUT TO:
Sarah interviewing Matt E.

MATT E.: I remember the first time I walked into Capriccio, I thought I'd died and gone to heaven. It was the most beautiful assortment of amazing-looking men I'd ever seen in one place. I had never seen anything like it in my life. I was, I was eighteen. I'm like, whoa, this is overkill. And then—I don't know. The dance floor, it was the perfect symbol of the FUQU crisis. Because gradually and little by little, it just thinned out and thinned out and thinned out, and soon it was next to nothing. Nobody was dancing at Capriccio. I'm sick now too. And the Greptz protease isn't working fast enough to save me.
SS: And what are you going to do now to fight? With whom?
MATT E.: I . . . I don't know. I . . . I'm scared.

DANIEL HAD DISCOVERED THE TRUTH ABOUT ISRAEL

Daniel had written this for Dr. Sister Grace and for Fred. David discovered it among his brother's papers:

> I couldn't remember the last time I saw him. I heard he was dying, so I went to see him. But I didn't get to him in time.
> He was, after all, my cousin in a strange family of unhappy men and women, not counting myself, of course, who's escaped being crazy only by being boring. The more I look around me as I age in my profession, the more I see that most doctors are boring. Israel wasn't boring. That I knew from hearing about him from friends at Schmuck, and that's why I stayed away from him. He was a crazy recluse, they said, distinctly unfriendly, and "sour," which they would further define as "like someone who's been overlooked so long that he's turned sour." Dodo is now being heard calling Israel "my hero" and "my role model" and "perhaps the real co-discoverer of UC." Israel always appeared to me as more modest than anything, shuffling around medical meetings. He would wave and smile and say things like "Hi, cuz," but he never came closer, so neither did I. It must be genetic in the Jerusalem family.

I'd heard Israel made major discoveries early in life. I decided to investigate what they might be.

I went to Admiral Mason Iron Vaultum and found his study of the Iwacky children:

"I discovered that these young people had participated in what were called 'mortuary feasts,' before missionaries suppressed this ancient tribal custom. The victims descended into trembling madness before they died. These young boys and young men had all exposed themselves to the brains of their ancestors as a sign of respect for the dead, for these ancestors, for those whom they loved who had come and gone before them. It was a cultural custom, and quite touching, albeit an exceptionally dangerous one. They had cooked and eaten the bodies and brains of tribe members who had died, including their feces. At autopsy, I found their own brains to be shot through with spongy holes. The killing virus in these spongy brains had overtaken them and plunged them into orgies of sex and more sex. At death their bodies were encased in purple scabs."

The stuff about the spongy brain virus won him a Nobel Prize. I wonder why he never spoke of it.

He named it glause. Yes, the mechanism of what was going on was not dissimilar to various mutations of The Underlying Condition.

Strangely, he saw himself as an anthropologist. "My biggest contribution was showing that you could take someone born in a Stone Age and bring them to this country. Someone could jump through five thousand years of human society in one lifetime. That is what my sons did. That is what I did for my sons." He had brought some dozen young men to America. I wonder where they are, what happened to them, why no Jerusalem ever knew or talked about them.

"*The Truth* comes to interview me," he wrote. "Some man asks if I repent my sexual relationships with my Iwacky sons. I tell him that America and Americans are too prudish to hear that sex with young men was normal in the cultures I studied, all the way back to classic ancient Greece, which is the foundation of Western Civilization. What has America given the world to match the gift of ancient Greece? They taught men to love each other, and we have destroyed that love."

A MESSAGE TO DAVID

Your Grodzo writes to you from his homeland to tell you that he thinks of you often and misses you. But it has been good for me to be back home. I think sometimes I beg you come back to Germany and we live together but I respect your wish voiced to me that you would never come back here.

I write to tell you things you do not know. I tell them now to you because much is being written in Deutschland about Mungel, about Hitler, what was happening. There are fewer secrets as we grow older, me, Germany. Much of this will become known. It is best you hear from me before the Oxford and Cambridge chaps get their own histories of us out and into . . . circulation. Already a German scholar, Norman Ohler, has written a book that is attracting great praise and attention.

Hitler—he had difficulty urinating and had frequent infections in his bladder. We know now he had an abnormal urethra. He washed his hands a lot and it was thought had difficulties with anything sexual. He had inflammation in his arteries, which is an autoimmune disease, as is UC, which could explain many of the maladies of which he always complained. We thought he was a hypochondriac but perhaps he had a genuine affliction, causing his endless headaches and troubles with his body and organs and digestion. He was convinced his father was Jewish and had died of syphilis, which he believed he inherited. He always called it "the Jew disease." He believed it was this syphilis that caused him such difficulty to urinate. I found an old gypsy who instructed him to take a bath in his own urine, to prevent his syphilis from becoming active, which many gypsies believe. I gave him such a bath, several times. I could never locate his syphilis. But even with the abnormal urethra and something inherited called spina bifida occulta that can cause many things, that plus constipation and the fact that he was always farting (but who wasn't then?), these don't necessarily add him up to such a monstrous murderer.

Yes, I consulted on his case, both at Mungel and in his final bunker. You did not know this and I have not told anyone. Who wants to admit this willingly? He took my hand when I examined him. It was a gesture, I believe, of his fear, for his health, for his mortality. Terrified patients often do this, reaching for some sort of special connection with their doctor, as if this could save them.

I was not his only doctor, of course. There was much fighting and disagreements with all the doctors who attended him, each with differing diagnoses and treatments of him. By the time I was summoned he was frail and wasting and the faithful doctor he had trusted had been banished.

I could have killed him easily. I injected him many times with various things. Our famous pharmaceutical companies were constantly inventing many new things. It would have been simple to substitute a poison and no one would have known. He had almost died several times from one thing or another. His health was that weak. When I bathed him in that tub with his urine I could have held his head down to drown. There was no point to it by then. On his own he would never leave this bunker alive.

Yes, I thought about doing this. I could have earned a prominent place in history. By the end whoever did this would have got away with it. But I did not do anything. I wanted to see what the ending would be like. Because it was obvious the ending was near. I wanted to witness this.

I could have been a hero to the world or a disgrace to my people. I chose only to be a witness.

You know, it was Hitler who gave us our freedom at the end. He released those of us from Mungel, including you, when he knew the end had finally arrived. He sent us his thanks for what we were attempting to achieve for him, and in his gratitude he wished to reward us with our freedom. He did not want to die before any witnesses.

There is more I wish to tell you because its discovery will be a revelation to you and explain some things that I know have puzzled you. And this is the origin of the scars upon your back. I had told you they did not look like German scars, as I could recognize our own by instinct. Now has come word from Dr. Oderstrasse that verifies what I suspected: that the cause of these scars was something performed on you at Partekla. You remember little of Partekla because you were much of the time drugged and were unconscious when experiments were done on your back. They had samples of your skin and the skin of others. Who ordered all of this? And why? The drugs you were given were German, though. They were the same as were used on Hitler. They were administered to you by a Dr. Schline, who was in charge of the Partekla/NITS experiments in germ warfare. His method of stitching up skin was that of someone educated in the Far East.

You were being tested to see how much pain your body could endure. As you can remember none of it, I tell you now: evidently quite a bit.

There will be more to come . . .

MORE COLLOQUY

SPARKS: Yes, I know Jerry's just won a Nerdlinger. And a Leibniz. So he's in total denial about his position. Jerry is never going to have to admit he's wrong.

FRED: Did it never occur to you to admit that TAG is selfish, only thinking of your own agenda, killing off FUQU? I can't believe I gave birth to you!

SPARKS: I refuse to discuss this with you. You're not rational about this. You hate TAG.

FRED: I hear you're drunk a lot, always drinking. I thought you were so fucking happy and satisfied.

DAVID: Fred, you're not eating again. I leave you eggs every day! Protein! You must finish your book! So what if TAG turned into a big disappointment for you. So what if FUQU is self-destructing. We must move forward! And you must eat!

FRED: As William Burroughs said, "Paranoia is having all the facts."

DAVID: The fact is that it is impossible not to believe that everything connected with UC is a giant plot against those who are exposed to it, a plot whose intent is that it should *never* be cured. No wonder you look for the masterminds. No wonder you believe quite easily in paranoid scenarios. No wonder you believe in intentional genocide. I do too!

FRED *(hugging him)*: Listen to you!

•

INT. GAY CENTER.

FUQU meeting only half full.

SPARKS: Yes, we got ten pharmaceutical companies to give us money.

Boos from the floor.

MAXINE: The floor was not consulted. Again! It was not voted upon! Again! And you've destroyed us. I've had enough of this.

She gets up and walks out. Several women join her.

SCOTTY: But we've got our first drug! We've come to tell you about it.

PHOTIS *(into tape recorder)*: And it came to pass that our drugs were released.

He gets up and walks out followed by others.

CUT TO:

Less-attended meeting. New faces.

MEMBER: We've got a drug. What do we need FUQU for?

Gets up and walks out.

CUT TO:

Even less-attended meeting.

MEMBER: Now I can go fuck anyone and live.

Gets up and walks out.

CUT TO:

Practically empty room. Maybe a dozen strangers scattered in this big hall.

CUT TO:

The room is now empty. Camera pans the familiar space. Many of the handsome posters we've seen are dangling on the wall and are beginning to come loose and fall down. Avram collects them all like his wounded children.

Fred, Tommy, and David sit in the empty huge hall. A last poster falls from the wall to the floor. It reads: SILENCE=DEATH.

AVRAM *(clutching the poster to him)*: This room pulsed like a nightclub, blaring with ideas instead of music. It was an ever-expanding life raft for the disinherited, a dating service, an employment office, a health-care facility, comedy club, performance space, research institute, company store, a tutorial in world-making. It was not for the fainthearted, but every one of us knew what was waiting outside these doors. So we clung to each other as we chanted our hymn, "We'll never be silent again! FUQU!" *(He runs out.)*

DAVID *(to Fred)*: I have something to tell you.

FRED: You're leaving me too.

DAVID: Guess again.

FRED: You've met somebody.

DAVID: I love you.

FRED: What? I love you, too.

DAVID: No, I mean it. I love you. And our house is almost ready.

EXT. VILLAGE STREETS. DAY.

Fred and David carrying crudely lettered posters: WE NOW HAVE A DRUG THAT YOU THINK ALLOWS YOU TO LIVE THE KIND OF LIFE THAT GOT US INTO TROUBLE IN THE FIRST PLACE. BE CAREFUL!

BAD NEWS

At the new rather-well-furnished office of TAG, the core group is studying official documents. The expressions on their faces show their disappointment.

"The Greptz drug is shit. The Muck drug was only marginally better. What do we do now without a decent combo drug?" Perry asks forlornly.

Peturba is not going to work for everyone indefinitely without a decent combo drug.

Taking a swig out of a small bottle of liquor, Sparks answers the question. "We test them all together!"

"But Greptz and Muck hate each other!" Perry reminds him.

"Didn't I fire you once?" Sparks says.

"You asked me to come back."

"My mistake."

"Sparks, lay off Perry," Scotty says gruffly. "We get Levi to test Peturba with ZAP!"

Sparks turns to Perry. "Get out of here for good. You inhibit my creativity."

And that's the last anyone saw of Perry. He did write to Fred, though. "Thank you for teaching me and loving me. I think I'm going back home to Ohio. But I'm not certain. You taught me so much I have to think about."

DEEP THROAT SAYS GOODBYE

What did I expect? Mother had promised me so many things. I even allowed myself to have dreams of being his replacement, although of course I was too old by now and my contacts in high places were fewer and farther afield. Mrs. Ruester had made promises as well but she left few friends.

Mother was kiboshed, destroyed by his own. Floyd Harmish was a prick of the highest order. James Jesus had fallen for his charms and ass-kissing. Harmish got rid of me, too. He claimed I was gay and lovers with James Jesus. Rumors like this are impossible to erase in Washington.

I cannot bring myself to say goodbye to those I have worked with most touchingly. I want to warn them about James Monroe, and the Dumster family. They will see to it that whatever drugs come out of Presidium will not come without a large price to pay. They are not out to cure any gay person. Simple as that.

But perhaps it's best not to tell you goodbye. There will be nothing you can do to stem any power now that your own dissolution has taken away your piss and vinegar. This is a lesson you will finally have to learn for yourselves. I have learned my lesson the hard way too. On-the-job training, as they say in the military. Time to pack it in. It's been an interesting and unsatisfactory journey.

•

INT. ROSELAND.

Loud celebratory show business music. The kids are putting on a show, A BENEFIT FOR BROADWAY CARES. The audience pushes close to the performers, all wearing tight shorts, and sticking bills in their crotches. Tommy, looking down on them, raises his arms above him like a winning fighter. But his eyes are filled with tears.

TOMMY *(to Mickey)*: Most of these children won't live through this. I cry for them all the time. Five hundred of them have died since our last event. It just breaks my heart no one's come to save us.

On the dance floor, Fred and David are kissing. Tommy watches them kissing. Tommy waves and throws them kisses.

SCREEN GOES DARK. SUDDENLY:

SOUND OF A RIFLE SHOT.

EXT. TRUTH OR CONSEQUENCES, NEW MEXICO. DESERT. DAY.

At the top of a hill, Tommy has committed suicide. He lies out neatly on a tarpaulin, his rifle lying across him. A cop and an undertaker look down at him. Fred and David.

COP: I never saw it so neatly done. He even left instructions. His gun license. His marksman graduation . . . *(Showing pieces of paper.)* You're his next of kin. What do you want us to do with him?

UNDERTAKER: He paid me in advance three weeks ago for his cremation.

TOMMY'S VOICE *(we hear him)*: You were the love of my life. The power had been ours. We couldn't save them. The drugs won't save us. We will never have a cure.

FRED: When we first met, he had such a boyish face. I told him he reminded me of the young Abe Lincoln, with those cute little jug ears that stick out from his head.

David and Fred hold each other as Tommy's body is carried away.

FLASHBACK:
INT. FRED'S LOFT. NIGHT.
Bruce and Fred and Tommy are sitting on the floor eating Chinese takeout. They've consumed a bottle of wine. A GMPA banner is strung across a wall.

BRUCE: After they find a cure, I have this dream for us.

FRED: What is it?

BRUCE: We'll turn ourselves into a big health plan for gays. Maybe even have our own hospital. That way they can't treat us like they are.

FRED: That's a lovely dream.

TOMMY: We can make it happen!

DODO IS INTERVIEWED BY DRESHA BANDITT OF *THE WALLA WALLA ECHO*

"Do you think," she asks him, "that your being, as it were, out of action and way out here, The Underlying Condition has been allowed to get even more out of hand? Do you feel humbled by this thought?"

"No, no, no, no, no. You get too humble, you lose all your confidence. The humble don't think about science. I think only of science. Science doesn't want me to be humble! Fuck humble! What are you talking about? What do you mean, out of action? Get outta here!"

He will shortly be put in charge of a fully taxpayer-funded new research institute in Atlantic City. He'll have a lot of money for him and Poopsie to play with. His board members will include Junior Trish and Dereck Dumster. Dumster owns the building and will take a $160 million tax deduction on it.

•

EXT. HUDSON RIVER. DAY.
Tommy's ashes being scattered into the water by Fred and David at approximately the same place where he'd scattered his brother Johnny.

We see Tommy watching the scattering of his ashes.

TOMMY'S VOICE: I'm sorry, honey. I hope you and David will find
   some peace and contentment.

FRED: Goodbye, sweet man.

STATE OF THE UNION

HEADING FOR THE LAST ROUND-UP

At the start of the plague, The American People number 250,832,030 breeders, 7,987,456 kikes, and 10,490,321 faggots. There were 16,093,325 faggots before the plague, as there were 12,987,456 kikes before the Holocaust. Kikes have replaced their diminished numbers by dint of breeding and conversion. Faggots didn't and have to wait for breeders to bring them into the world again. "Breeders" is defined as straight, white, heterosexual, and not a faggot or a kike. While this history includes a few niggers, spics, and whatever you want to call Native Americans, it's primarily concerned with breeders including niggers, kikes, spics, and faggots.

In our world's scheme of things, much has happened: 9/11, the global world wars of the closeted homosexual Dredd Trish, Jr. (and Shovels), resulting in the deaths of 60 million people (and still counting), soldiers and displaced refugees, Dredd Junior now being labeled by Maureen Dowd of *The New York Truth* as "the real American psycho, a professional assassin," the continuing damage Junior's done in his father's footsteps to our country's economy and declining place in the world, the predictable bureaucratic cipher TAG's become—the perfect name for an also-ran organization—the election of both the best (a person of color who helped enable legal gay marriage) and the worst (the monster Dereck Dumster) of presidents, and of course the state of today's gays, which remains, along with all of this, sad and fearful to witness. It's been and is continuing to be quite a record of one thing after another. Why, even Coco Chanel has now been revealed as a Jew-hating lesbian and a spy for the Nazis. And Sigmund Freud considered Woodrow Wilson a homosexual. History can tell you almost everything if you wait long enough.

Of course, while all this has been going on, UC has covered the entire globe and that one-billion-dead figure is proving spot-on.

David and I go out to Fire Island. They still dance till dawn and fuck in the Meat Rack night and day, the only difference being there are bags of condoms hanging on the trees. The Pines has aged, the houses more weather-beaten, like their inhabitants. The crowds are not all beauties, the bodies not all pumped up, the age range more noticeable. It remains a place to escape to, a beautiful ocean and beach. The orgies still go on, house by house. Boys will still be boys.

Yes, I am sad we still haven't amounted to more.

I keep waiting. Surely surviving a plague should inspire more motivated gratitude. We are an ungrateful lot. We are still leaderless and bereft of most rights. I am not bitter, I am older and my health is declining, as it comes to all, and I must attend more now to my exit, my last years with David. I see each day that he's more frightened of not only losing me but also of being alone, going through this ordeal of losing our freedoms a second time with this new president, who should be impeached for his nonstop mouthfuls of hates.

A recent unexpected bout requiring an emergency scanning of a bulging stomach brought both of us back into that most haunted of locales, the emergency room. Why did I blow up, just like Felix used to do? No more Emma to talk to me about seesaws. David and I live only because of Presidiums I, II, and III, which cost each of our insurance companies $100,000 per drug per year. The scan revealed I was taking too much of it all and my dosage was recalibrated. Our new president threatens to cancel health insurance to those with The Underlying Condition, as well as our now legal marriages. Yes, David and I are married. We sleep legally in each other's arms each night, which I must confess is heaven.

I must finish this book, and I shall. It's been a long history, hasn't it? How enlightened do you feel? Do you hear the voices of the dead as I still do? A nurse at Table actually remembered me and talked about Bruce and Craig and others from those early days. And Dr. Donald Kotler offered this opinion of the Riddle of Jerrold Omicidio. I asked him, "Why did Deep Throat hate Jerry so?" And he answered, simply and logically, "DT got fired because he had Jerry's number. I'm sorry to hear that he died." Deep Throat's real name was Dr. Cecil Fox, and much of what I've told you I learned from him. He wound up almost penniless teaching at some Podunk school in Nebraska. James Jesus wasn't around to take care of him. Mother himself was thrown out of the CIA, accused of being that homosexual Soviet mole. Floyd Harmish was responsible for getting rid of him so he could become the new director, which he is.

Time, as it grows shorter, provokes more questions from me. "Jerry, what does your last name mean?" I asked him once. Long pause. "Omicidio is an old Sicilian name. It means I could either kill you or be killed by you. A very archaic word. Take your pick."

State of the Union? State of my Union? Smithereens. Still and continuing. By 1992 we had hit rock bottom. In 2008 the Nobel Prize goes to Jacqueline Françoise and Gaston Nappe for the discovery of the UC virus. Dodo will be purposely and intentionally passed over.

The facts remain these: that so far millions of Americans, human beings, were helplessly dragged to their deaths. The method employed was that of accumulated terror. "We hate you." "We have no cure for you." "You go to hell." First came calculated neglect, deprivation, and shame, when the few weak early birds died together. Second came outright ostracization as people died by the tens of thousands. Last came the death factories, that moment of "hope" when "cures" were pumped into us—and we all died together, the young and the old, the weak and the strong, the sick and the healthy; not as people, not as men and women, children and adults, boys and girls, not as good and bad, beautiful and ugly—but as detritus brought down to the lowest common denominator, plunged into the darkest and deepest abyss of primal inequality, like things that had neither body nor soul, just piles of medicated corpses who'd all been given drugs that didn't work. Seventy thick FBI files are finally cleared for eyes to see how the Ruesters' hatred of us started this. Purpura had us infiltrated by Hoover's paid informants. He, old noble Pete, had once named the names of seventy of his best friends as Communists and destroyed their lives. He was their president then, of the Screen Actors' Guild. The San Francisco reporter Seth Rosenfeld successfully fought an FBI that spent $1 million to prevent the release of these damning files. It was always believed that what Ruester said was true, that he never turned anyone in. Rosenfeld calls him "a Hollywood informer." FUQU was visited by informers. Almost from our very beginning there was someone or other sending in reports. It's amazing we were able to accomplish so much while being so interfered with. There's a memo in a Dredd Trish folder that says, "Cut back on the moles. They will murder each other on their own." Shovels referred to us as his "mass indoctrination program." There are many bits and pieces, half letters, like this from Purpura to someone: "I very much appreciate the help of yourself and your associates in providing the true facts in this matter of the perverts." And this from Dredd Trish, Jr.: "I wish I could keep them in my sight."

It almost seems too late to learn. The damage has been done and there's no visible impetus for how to repair it. Next weekend gay men of San Francisco will march around the Castro naked with their cock rings and leather outfits on display for . . . what? The controversy brewing locally is whether cock rings can be displayed so blatantly. Boys will be boys who play with each other. And monsters will be monsters who forbid it. It is in this inequality without humanity that we see the image of our continuing hell. March on, you cock-ringed warriors. Eighty-six countries have laws punishing gay sex with jail, and seven of them allow the death penalty.

A hundred million cases of gonorrhea are estimated worldwide, of a disease that has been known since antiquity. Cases are now reported that are resistant to all known treatments, and this superbug is growing rapidly all over the globe. It is being spread primarily by oral sex, which has become, by default, the "safe sex" of choice." Mordy, Mordy, where are you, Mordy? Are you in despair yet about your contribution to the spread of UC? What will you ever do to help us? He shows up at Masturbov Gardens with busloads of *Sexopolis* girls. "This is where it all started. This is where my fortune came from!" He builds a huge tent for the mightiest photo shoot in its history. *Sexopolis* girls through the years. From barely exposed tits to gaping cunt holes, he acts like Mr. Ziegfeld presenting his Follies. Then he burns down Masturbov Gardens. Yes, another fire! Everyone dear to him has been consumed by fire. His parents. His grandfather. The brother he never had. Claudia. Velvalee. It is almost as if this trait of pyromania is inherited.

Jerry's ward is pretty empty these days. Cases don't wind up in the hospital. Jerry had sat down on dead Daniel's bed. He is so tired he falls asleep taking his pulse. Daniel had caressed his forehead with his last bit of life. Jerry snapped to attention. Then he reaches out, Jerry does, as if to say to Daniel, I want your hand too. But Daniel is dead now. Jerry jumps up and starts to bawl. "You were not meant to die on me! Not yet."

And *The New York Truth* has actually printed a piece by some bozo that insists that UC really does not happen to heterosexuals.

Hermia says, "I think it is time for this old Dame to return to England. What use are all my answers here? America doesn't want another Hannah Arendt. Awfully sad and sorry, old chaps. I was onto something!" She retires to a comfortable adult residence in St. Simon's on the Wharf. "The neighborhood's become quite fashionable now. I shall have nothing else to do but to contemplate evil. It's a never-ending tale to tell. And something quite spectacularly important might yet emerge to further enlarge my view of history. Always observant, Dame Lady Hermia Bledd-Wrench is ready."

I wanted, somehow, to be a hero. I failed. Artists are meant to create with the intention of ennobling the human condition. I can't do that. I think the human condition isn't noble at all. I had hope once. Up until 1981, when hope was slowly taken away from us.

•

INT. FUNERAL PARLOR. DAY.
Daniel is laid out in a coffin. David and Fred, holding hands, look down at him. Lucas joins them. David takes Lucas's hand.

DAVID HAS A MEMORY

DAVID: Mommy. RIVKA: My God, it cannot be, is this at last my David? Let me feel you. I cannot see. DAVID: I am happy that you found a comfortable resting place at last. RIVKA: Yes, Gertrude has been very good to me. As your father told me she would be, perhaps one of the few truths he ever uttered. Why is your back so rough, just as Gertrude described you? Oh, who did that to you, my son? Did that man that I married do this to you, our son? I have been waiting for you to come before I can leave this wretched earth. Your twin? Your brothers? You have seen them? Tell me, why have you all ignored me so? DAVID: I look for similar answers to unanswerable questions, too. I think we are all put here to suffer in our own ways. RIVKA: It should not be like this. DAVID: Would you like to come back and live with me? RIVKA: Thank you for your offer. No, I'm ready to die now, and I'll stay here and be buried beside Gertrude, the only true friend I ever had. It won't be long now. Just give me a big hug and kiss and say goodbye. More words will only bring on more memories I've tried hard to forget. DAVID: Goodbye, Mommy. RIVKA: That's a good boy. I never should have married your father. I never loved him. Your father was very cruel to both of us. Amos told Gertrude that Philip was a spy for Mr. Hoover. Imagine that. I can't.

THE LAST NOTEBOOK OF JAMES JESUS ANGLETON

Why did Mother become a spy? Because like all those Brit spies, I loved other men and my country would have punished me for that love. I had to find a way to protect myself and my fellow beloveds, for I knew there were many of us who would be unable to defend themselves. The rules and laws of The American People demand unlimited hypocrisies just to stay alive. Counter-intelligence at its best understands hypocrisy. Edgar was only interested in protecting his own skin and that of Clyde. It was quite selfish of him. I like to think that my motives and actions were humanitarian. I wanted all of The American People to flourish.

FRED AND HIS FUCKING BOOK

I've worked on this fucking book for many years. It's a mess and I know it's a mess. As I got older and learned more and more it's grown harder to handle. Like life itself. But I'm almost there. And I know I have written what I wanted to write. I hope it lives after me. I'd once figured I'd finish the last page and keel over dead. Like Proust. More than forty years ago I wrote another history called *Faggots* in which my attempts to deal satirically about gay life in Manhattan were still hot on my fingertips and tongue. And then, before anyone knew it, came the fucking plague. It's painful when the good times decide not to hang around. One, two, three, five, ten, twenty, a hundred, a thousand, a million, and now of course many many many millions, all around us, everywhere, the world over, have died and will die from UC. Crazy madcap lives can appear funny and silly and in the end they're easy to write about. Plagues are just depressing. It is very difficult to write about a plague. I hear too many voices fighting to be heard. Then, somehow, I think rather miraculously, but then David says I'm much too sentimental (he who cries at weepy movies and TV shows), he and I came together. And now we live in the country house with the white picket fence overlooking the lake in colonial Connecticut, every single bit of the fantasy I'd had. We ask each other all the time, "Why am I alive?" Or we make it a statement: "I don't know why I'm alive." And of course we don't know why, either one of us. Just being infected was supposed to be the certain sign of death. Just having unprotected sex with someone who was infected was supposed to be a certain path to death. It still can be. Yes, "God knows why or how we're still alive," we say, especially when we're holding each other at night in bed in each other's arms. I know I sound like a kid when I talk about him. Curmudgeons like I'm thought to be aren't meant to mellow so. I like to believe in powerful spells between us. I like to think that he and I are special and have been since the first moment we saw each other, in another lifetime, on a day hundreds of years ago, even though it wasn't and I can see it as if it were yesterday. He's still trying to teach me to not only talk about love but to feel it on a more universal basis. I tell him we are brothers in a great brotherhood of gay men who have existed since the beginning of time. They are in our blood. They are why we are able to love each other. I didn't think it was ever going to happen, happiness. It almost didn't . . .

•

Fred enters, exhausted, and rushes toward the bedroom . . .

FRED'S VOICE: Once upon a time there was a little boy who always wanted to love another little boy. All his life that's all he wanted.

INT. BEDROOM. NIGHT.

David enters. We see what he sees: Fred has lost control of his bowels. A trail of diarrhea heads to the bathroom.

INT. BATHROOM. NIGHT.

David runs in, Fred is half sitting on the toilet still shitting and half vomiting into the sink. David grabs him before he falls over.

FRED'S VOICE: He's supposed to use gloves. He's not supposed to do this. He's supposed to not kiss me. *(They kiss.)*

FRED: The newest fucking greedy 150,000-dollar Presidium drug has too many side effects!

David leans Fred into his body, grabs some toilet tissue, wipes Fred's ass. He then grabs a washcloth and wipes Fred's face. Cleanup done, David tenderly kisses the top of Fred's head and hauls him to a standing position . . .

FRED'S VOICE: I remember when I had to do this for Felix.

INT. BEDROOM. NIGHT.

Fred is in bed. His eyes are filled with terror. He never takes his eyes off David. Suddenly Fred does a projectile vomit, so that the wall is spattered with it.

CUT TO:

David wiping and washing down the wall. Fred watches from his bed, tears in his eyes.

FRED: I know five guys who left their sick lovers last week. Just walked out on them.

DAVID: I hate them for that.

FRED: You can leave me. You have my permission. You're still handsome and could find someone.

DAVID: I don't want to find someone. I found you. Shut up.

INT. LIVING ROOM. NIGHT.
*David and Fred in pajamas watch an old movie, eating ice cream from
cartons. Fred turns to silently look at David.*

DAVID: I told you—never for one second do I think of leaving you.
Please believe me.

INT. SHOWER. NIGHT.
*David is giving Fred a shower. We see the wreck and tragedy that is his
body now, from head to toe, as he sees David's back. Fred starts to sob.
David holds him, sobbing too.*

FRED'S VOICE: You cry and you cry until you think you can't cry any
more and then you cry some more.

INT. BEDROOM. NIGHT.
David crawls into bed and holds Fred.

FRED: Dr. Brown said you saved my life.

DAVID *(yelling)*: You are not ready to die! Besides, I am going to have
a big surprise for you.

FRED: What?

DAVID: I'm not quite ready yet. The mark of the good historian is
a deep curiosity about the world outside your head. I read that
somewhere. That's what I'm working at.

FRED: So we have another historian in the family. And here I thought
you were just a lawyer.

DAVID: Same thing, really. Or so I am discovering and out to prove.

FRED: Okay. Whenever you're ready.

WHAT IS THIS HISTORY ALL ABOUT . . . ?

All of us are made up of history and few of us are likely to study it nearly
enough. I sometimes think, so anxious are we to move ahead with everything, "to get on with it," as the English say, that we are, also as the English

say, hoisted with our own petards. Even now, as too many think the worst is over, I am still making notes, knowing that it's not.

There are many ways to relate a history, to organize and structure the information a foolish man labels "the facts" his research has "discovered." History is never so neat and compliant as to allow itself to be rendered that coherently. I am trying to finalize what you've read. I have included a goodly portion of my own history, not because I have had such a noteworthy life but because I still hear voices. I can't get them out of my head. Dead lovers. Dead friends. The murderers. Lots of murderers. I write our history because it is an obligation I owe to myself, my past, my people, my husband, David. There was never a day when I wavered from this decision.

The people who have written most histories must be dreamers. They look for sense where there is none. They look for patterns. They look for hope, which isn't there either. Hope is the thing with feathers, Emily Dickinson said. I have been a dreamer to believe it could be otherwise. And, yes, I am still a dreamer. It's all either right or wrong. It's all there in black and white.

The real truth about all my people's never-ending horrors? The consortium of people, through the ages, that met and intentionally willed, called for, and arranged the past and continuing deaths of everyone gay? The way of life as solidly seeded into our earth at Sagg, Fruit Island, New Bliss, Abbator, Nantoo, Mungel, Partekla, and NITS, that goes on and on, traditionally? Be it Furstwasser, be it Dye, be it Omicidio and Geiseric, be it Botts, be it Greeting, be it Greptz and Presidium, be it all the suppliers of tainted blood, be it Ruester, be it Trishes big and small, be it the most evil and wretched Dereck Dumster, and on and on? Have I got it all? How could any historian get it all?

Today's NITS comprises thirty component institutes, employs more than thirty thousand physicians and scientists and support staff, has one 317-acre and twenty satellite campuses around the world, provides more than 40 percent of all money allotted for the support of health research and development in the United States and nearly 70 percent of the total federal funds expended for support of medical research in universities. Except for homosexuals. Vurd's Law still prevents federal funding for anything to do with homosexuals, and year after year, president after president and Congress after Congress decline to reverse this.

So the plague hasn't gone away, of course. People may not all be dying like flies in this country but they certainly are in the rest of the world. So there's no glory in any contentment. If you're infected you never forget that death still has a hand out that can grab you at any minute. When I think about this out loud, David yells at me yet again: "You are not ready to die!" Yes, he took the look of fear out of my eyes. Love and hope can do that if you're lucky.

I am finally lucky.

DAVID'S WAR

I have been slowly putting pieces of my case together.

•

The Founding Fathers wanted religion to have no part in their government. It was Benjamin Franklin who said, "Lighthouses are more useful than churches." John Adams said, "This would be the best of all possible worlds if there were no religion in it." And "Christianity is the most perverted system that ever shone on man" was said by Thomas Jefferson. George Orwell, who died at forty-six, said this: "If you want a vision of the future, imagine a boot stamping on a human face—forever."

•

These are thoughts that echoed in my head as I wandered haphazardly around America. Where was this God so feared by our Founding Fathers? Where was the deadly disease predicted by our enemy Russia?

•

I checked the many notes I made from my years of wandering in hope of finding something to belong to. From Tarpon Springs to Manusha Falls to O'Keefe Center to Marigold Farms to Detroit to St. Rudolph's to Little Ogunquit to Marine Harbor to Mount Rainier to the Abadibgee Reservation . . . looking, talking, asking, trying to absorb some insight from all these people who have settled in these uncomfortable places. Why do you stay here? I continue to ask this question even when I learn the response is predictable and dispiriting. "Where else could I go? God must want me to stay here." In every place they stayed there was a different God they believed in.

•

Beginning after World War II (ironically, not long after I had been set free of Hitler), Russian counterintelligence by way of their Stasi forces in East Germany commenced a disinformation campaign to convince the world that the United States was waging germ warfare with a biological weapon it had created to infect the entire world. Russians had experience with covert campaigns like this. Their modus operandi was always the same: identify where local strife was occurring, point to inconsistencies and ambiguities in the news reporting, fill these cracks with "meaning," and repeat, repeat, repeat. From an article planted in a little newspaper in West Africa, which was not so coincidentally secretly financed by the CIA, it was not long before this first "official" warning was picked up all over the world. This campaign aimed, according to the Kremlin's chief of disinformation Dmitri Norbtrekno, to generate "a warning to other countries that this biological weapon is the result of out-of-control secret experiments by U.S. scientists and the Pentagon involving new types of deadly diseases aimed at targeted populations."

•

In my life there is safety in numbers. We don't kill each other off. We manufacture many more of ourselves. By now there are more of us alive than can ever be destroyed. So we have saved ourselves, certainly long enough to create more of our "perverted" selves. Have not you learned this by now from me, you how you say, dumb dodos?

FRED'S BOOK

I always thought that what would motivate me to set down everything I knew and had seen would be that I owed it to all the dead, not only the ones I'd had sex with but those yet to come. It's the least I could do for all the hordes of friends and acquaintances from our crowd and the hundreds of thousands of guys from our kind of person, which is gay men, and the millions of people around the globe who joined us in getting UC.

Responsibility to the dead, and the obligation to tell the truth, that's all very high-and-mighty sounding. But on a practical level it's hard to get up every morning to write of death and try to honor it. You kind of want to slit your wrists a little too often and end it all for yourself once and for all.

The push that finally did it was something more specific.

I went through all those boxes and all those clippings and all my diaries and datebooks and notebooks. Those places where you write down every-thing you've done and everyone you've seen. I've kept them dutifully since I left Yaddah.

I made a list of all the men I had sex with in the years just before *The New York Truth* announcement, those early years before the discovery of the virus, which are the years when presumably I became infected.

So far as I could decipher all my notes and scribbles, I believe there are twenty-four friends I had sex with during those years who I know are dead. It is said that anal intercourse was and is the favored means of entry of this plague's cause. Well, I put my penis in the rectums of many of those twenty-four men and my semen went into them. I can remember what many of these men looked like. I can even sort of remember how they felt in bed.

Then I made a list of all the men I had sex with over this same period whose faces and names I could not remember, even though I had written them down. There were fifty men who I knew had died who were on this list.

Then I made my last list. I put down the names of all the men I had sex with after Emma said we should stop, before any official causative agent was discovered. There are twenty-six men's names on that list that I know are dead.

One hundred dead men. One hundred dead men I might have killed.

I wrote "killed" but I deleted "murdered."

I can't stop thinking I murdered them.

I can't stop thinking I certainly murdered some of them.

I certainly murdered the ones I fucked with after we were told some-thing out there was happening.

This history is for all of them.

This history is written by a murderer.

I'm sorry. I'm sorry. That I murdered you.

WHAT THIS HISTORY IS NOT ABOUT

There is a chronicle from the Middle Ages that narrates: "After this, when the plague, the flagellant pilgrimages, the appeals to God and Christ and Rome, and the slaughtering of Jews and the free minded were over, the world once more began to live, and joy returned to it, and men began to make new clothes."

STATE OF THE PLAGUE

EXT. FRED AND DAVID'S HOUSE IN THE COUNTRY.
DAY.
*They are sitting next to each other on a porch swing looking out over a
lovely lake.*
FRED: There were only forty-one cases when I started GMPA.
DAVID: They still won't call it a plague.
FRED: We're beginning to sound like each other.
DAVID: All the best marriages do, I'm told.
FRED: Who told you?
DAVID *(kissing him)*: I have never seen such wrongs as this plague
    says about us all. At least we have each other. Our work isn't
    over.
FRED: Thank you for our house. It's beautiful and I love it too.
DAVID: You're welcome. I'm going to court next week. My turn at
    bat has arrived, the secret project I wouldn't tell you about. You
    were its inspiration.

DAVID'S PUNIC TRIALS

I had decided it's time to do another Nuremberg Trials. At law school I
studied the Nuremberg Trials. These had been the first time in history that
leaders were put on trial before an international court for crimes against humanity and/or genocide, each before then not considered as valid legal categories. I've been researching how to do this in America. It is essential that
The American People face up to this great mass murder, and all gays learn
about it so they might take more responsibility for each other. I said this over
and over to myself, and of course to Fred, over our years of trying to figure
out how this might be accomplished. His book will certainly address this.
But his charges won't be legally enforceable.

Every survivor needs to confront the past. Inequality leads to terrible
things. That lesson we both have learned.

It wasn't easy to locate a specific and recognized and accepted legal category to cover what I want to achieve. Poorly structured legal arguments and
presentations can have unintended consequences, provoking the very wrongs
they're meant to prevent.

I realized it all boiled down to this question: How could there be a law to punish mass killing?

And what was the definition of mass killing?

As successful as the trials in Nuremberg were in condemning to death some Nazi murderers, the outcome bought us nothing sustainable in the form of an effective all-encompassing law. They were willing to classify "crimes against humanity" as something an individual could be charged with, but they balked at the use of "genocide" as being too inclusive, that is, not specific enough. That is the most that the lawyers and jurors there could agree upon.

Thus, how does one prove intent to destroy a population? It's not enough to just say, as was said at Nuremberg, that those acts on trial were "obviously committed by crafty desperate men." The notebooks of Hans Frank (which Angleton went on so about), who laid waste to much of Poland at the behest of Hitler, were certainly enough to hang Hans Frank from the gallows; but they weren't enough to kill most of his additional cohorts who were his equal in craft and deed. I admire enormously the great Hannah Arendt and her historic report on the trial of Adolph Eichmann in Jerusalem. But, again, he was only one of many just as evil who got off scot-free. In our case, it is not enough for Dr. Monserrat Krank to state emphatically, as she has in my deposition of her, "This is a historic plague that need not have happened. It could and should have been prevented." And she has certainly witnessed much evil in history. Where are her names of the guilty? She is too polite to share them.

International criminal justice? Ways are still needed to hold all perpetrators of murders anywhere to be accountable to the same law. Torture and murder are universal occurrences. Judges, prosecutors, and defense attorneys, all from different cultures and legal traditions, do not inspire agreements or definitions to be arrived at easily if at all. An effective worldwide criminal court is still a nightmare when it should be a dream come true. One has only to witness the folly that is the United Nations to witness how difficult it is to fashion worldwide agreements. America is quite bad in this area. Special human rights monitors are, depending on who's in the White House, appointed or deemed "no longer necessary." The first International Criminal Court in the Hague was not created until 1998 and did not open until 2002. And it has become bureaucratized and largely unsuccessful and will remain this way as long as such powerful countries as China, Russia, and America refuse to acknowledge or support it.

So how to locate protection against the extermination of entire groups? How to punish for participating in genocide?

Whether, from the outcome of either Fred's history or my trial before the district court located at Punic Center, anything gets accomplished—a guilty verdict, a verdict at all, additional charges, a revolution, change—well, one can only hope. I've more than discovered that hope is one of man's great forms of denial. When you hope, blame is usually tossed out the window. The question of responsibility should constantly haunt any trial that is attempting to apportion blame. But it is not. *Responsibility* is a dirty word and relatively nonexistent in legal terminology.

So I fear there will be a dispute whether such a trial as I'm embarking upon is even legal.

And, since a number of the guilty malefactors are now deceased, how does one nevertheless get to the portal vein that fueled their engines of hate and still does? Herein again I fear is where this trial can be thrown out in advance as not being legal. Is a person liable after a war is over? Or before it officially began? Is a person liable after his or her death? Many Nazis with blood on their hands were released into freedom simply because the war was over.

The case I am attempting is itself, as a matter of law, a peculiar one. It is not exactly a Nuremberg Trials kind of case, where there was worldwide opinion raging against a group of obviously guilty murderers, and it was just a question of presenting the evidence that visibly existed for their fates to be sealed. Also, mine is not exactly an Eichmann in Jerusalem kind of case, where there were enough people who remembered him and his deeds and these deeds were self-explanatorily horrendous enough to condemn him personally. In the case of the plague of The Underlying Condition, while there are plenty of witnesses to deeds, and perpetrators of them, and evidence of them, they do not jibe together into neat joists that can securely support a case that can stand up against any laws as they currently exist. And (although it comes closest to this) it is not exactly a class-action-suit kind of case, wherein a large number of aggrieved are permitted to band together to sue, as one entity, the object of their aggravation. This is more because the afflicted populations are leaderless, disorganized, and not, as a whole, anywhere near to being angry enough. This has been particularly painful for Fred to deal with.

How can I locate ammunition sufficient to deal with all of this, aiming for satisfactory permanent legislation and punishment?

•

I have discovered something called the Black and White Act.

Because Washington, D.C., is not a state and also has codes of law of its own, I discovered on its books that there has existed from its founding in 1800 an act known as the Black and White Act. Alexander Hamilton created it just before he died to protect "the little man of no importance in the eyes of naught save God." Mr. Black or Mr. White, "with nary a penny in his pocket," is entitled to "champion his beliefs against the mightiest of his caretakers should there be evidence to question the wisdom of those charged with his care and safety sufficient as to seek recompense and retribution as determined by the laws of our land." That is all it says, no more, no less. Citizens are entitled to protection, is what it says. There are no codicils or addenda, no footnotes or wherewithals. There are no suggestions of what fines or punishment the accused, if found guilty, should endure. There are no suggestions of what rights of appeal exist, for either side. Hence, since its obvious intention is no different from many a more complicated law passed since then, it would seem a useless instrument, a vestigial one like our appendix. So far as I can locate, it has never been summoned into action on its own. Which I believe is what must happen.

From reading Fred's book, I discovered a possible reason why the act was never called upon or invoked. Washington, being a southern city, objected to the name Mr. Black. The prime objector was Thomas Jefferson, who owned many slaves. And he also hated Alexander Hamilton, his rival for George Washington's attention. As Fred has written in *The American People*, Alex was a homosexual. He was also from the West Indies, where he was brought up and educated by two native gentlemen who recognized his great potential and sent him to America to study at what is now Columbia University. Obviously he was comfortable with people of color. Could he not have framed this new law to protect both homosexuals and blacks?

To this day the Black and White Act remains on the books of the District of Columbia. While it does not appear to have ever been invoked, it also has never been removed.

I have invoked it in my first foray into this lion's den.

With the help of my brother, Lucas Jerusalem, a Washington attorney with much experience maneuvering through this town, I issued charges of genocide against the following:

Kermit Goins
Peter Ruester
Purpura Ruester

Dr. Jerrold Omicidio
Chevvy Slyme
Manny Moose
Gree Bohunk
Dr. Stuartgene Dye
Dr. Ekbert Nostrill
Herod Furstwasser XX
Dredd Trish
Linus Gobbel
Bart Shovels
Mr. Brinestalker
Dredd Trish, Jr.
Mordecai Masturbov
Greeting Pharmaceuticals
Vonce Greeting
Presidium Pharmaceuticals
Dr. James Monroe
Boy Vertle
Dereck Dumster
Cardinal Alphonse Buggaro
Dr. Gordon Grodzo

And the following from *The New York Truth*, entrusted with honesty in reporting the matter:

Dr. Dearie Fault, Rodney Pilts, Ricky Twaddle, Manny Schmutz, Velma Dimley, Richard Flaste, Erik Eckholm, Dr. Lawrence Altman, Nicholas Wade, Philip Boffey, Gina Kolata, Philip Hilts, Jacob Flourtower, and Dunkelheims mother, son, and grandson.

I have already deposed Dr. Krank, Grodzo, and Dye, all of whom have since died.

Even Fred was shocked when I showed him Dye's deposition:

They said I committed thousands of patients to various clinics under my control where I had them killed in great numbers through overdoses of tranquilizers and amphetamines. They said I organized the murder of thousands of patients and inmates who were suffering from major depressions I myself was responsible for inducing. They said I mutilated all their penises, cutting them off, stuffing them and hanging them like trophies on my wall. They said I strung up young boys in closets and left them there without food or water for days. They said I extracted gallons of infected men's blood and reinjected it into healthy people. They said I had intercourse with every male patient who came into my personal laboratory. They said I killed them after or I killed them during or I killed them before if they wouldn't . . . whatever. They said I was responsible for murdering bureaucrats who were in opposition to my programs. They said I photographed and filmed and recorded everything, that my archives are huge and filled with only the most hideous and unimaginable stuff of acts made flesh made real. They said I was responsible for the plague in the first place because it was I, Dr. Stuartgene Dye, who saw to it that the tainted blood that made its way around the world was released during my tenure at NITS with my authorization that it could be administered to one and all. They said I got presidents to sign authorizations for the disposal of persons with an incurable illness and therefore unworthy of living. They said so many things and they still do and they always will. I now fear there is no way in heaven or hell that I can ever have a life wherein I am considered worthy and reliable, a scientist who fought so that others might live. A doctor. A scientist with a Nobel Prize.

This is but one example of the fertile territory I must legally explore.

Here is one more, from my once-loved friend Dr. Gordon Grodzo:

I told you there would be more from me. This is more complicated and upsetting. It involves much history you would not know or were in no condition to remember. I try to make it clear. It does not speak well for my country or your old friend Grodzo.

First I must tell you that by the time you read this I shall be dead.

I am relieved to finally get all this off my conscience.

Germany was the home that gave birth to the amphetamine, the morphine, opium, heroin, and all its derivatives that would both relieve and obscure pain but also elevate behavior to such a high level of energy and euphoria that even an injured soldier could stay attentive at his post for a number of days without sleep or pain.

We owe most of these derivatives to the pharmaceutical companies of Greeting, Gideon Greptz, Muck, Monroe, and Bayer and to their products developed going back to the last century. Greptz's cocaine was thought to be the best product ever made. No one recalls anymore that Germany was home to many great chemists, educated in what was then the best education system in the world. Each of these companies comes into its major fortunes with its own version combining much of the above.

Your friend Dr. Gordon Grodzo knew about all these tablets and injections, having for years prescribed them to his own practice of wealthy Berliners, many of whom of course were Jews. Hitler believed that the Jews were poisoning the soul of the German people. Many of these pharmaceutical manufacturers and their staff were Jewish. Many of these then went to America, establishing their old companies there for safety.

Temmler, a German company, had discovered that Benzedrine could be fashioned into something stronger. Temmler synthesized methamphetamine and patented Pervitin, perhaps the most important drug in history. Temmler, as a Jew, would disappear, but no matter. He had sold his company to James Monroe, who was not Jewish. He was not American or British either. He chooses this name to protect him in America, where he knows he must go. Monroe's crystal meth, which has become such an epidemic in America, is an only slightly less strong version of Pervitin.

Next came Eukodal, an opioid synthesized from opium with a higher response than heroin and fewer side effects. Eukodal was manufactured by Muck, which also makes cocaine. Bayer had its own version but its effects were of shorter duration.

Soon there were cocktails of several and all: morphine, Pervitin, Eukodal, opium, plus massive amounts of vitamins and even the blood and livers of various animals. I administered to Hitler many of these cocktails. Officials and officers were ordering any tablet they could by the tens of millions.

It would not be long before soldiers themselves were prescribed one or the other pill by their officers before being deployed on another of Hitler's wars to take over the world. They came to depend on the drugs, which led to constant victories. The officers of Hitler's forces were ecstatic. A couple of Pervitin a day for all the victorious fighting forces confirmed the Führer's unshaking belief in Germany's destiny. No one had told him the real reason. He prided himself on being abstemious, even though he was by now unknowingly addicted by Dr. Grodzo, so successfully attending to his leader's extreme hypochondria. For the first time in Hitler's life his body and its aches and pains were not his enemy. Grodzo was there with another tablet or a shot to return him to the forceful presence that his people expected and to which they responded with faithful devotion.

Your Grodzo, of course, was by now briefly addicted himself.

At this time I was looking after you at Mungel. Many of the marks on your body were administered or authorized by me in my ceaseless determination to uncover the secret of homosexuality. You would not remember some of this because I was also trying out various versions of Pervitin.

Today more than 100 million people consume various recipes that might include Pervitin and methamphetamine. It is called crystal meth. It is called OxyContin. It is called a number of things. But it is all based on the same original German recipe. It is this that killed Hitler and his National Socialism. Germany, land of much scientific genius, found the way to destroy its world. It was speed that had won his early battles, and it was speed that destroyed everything when too much of it was taken for too long and too many overdosed and collapsed and were killed in action.

It was the crystal meth that was given to you by your Grodzo that allowed them to scar your back at both Mungel and Partekla. This crystal meth is still manufactured by both Muck and Greptz and sold under the name Pervitin. Greeting, too, has a version.

But now it is most successfully manufactured in their own new doctored version by Presidium. Including an extract from a proton alpha, it is all now reformulated and sold as Peturba, a "cure" for UC. Your TAG has facilitated the great success of this Peturba. Presidium's Peturba and OxyContin and your TAG are turning America into a country of addicts.

James Monroe is not only hugely rich but hugely homophobic. His own son had been fucked to death by a fellow faggot.

I am the "fellow faggot" who fucked his son.

I am also the doctor at Partekla who administered Monroe's

drug to you. That is the reason you recall so little, and perhaps why you are still alive. I am grateful you did not become addicted.

As I said, I am grateful to get this off my chest. I am grateful that we had a chance to become, for a while, friends.

I say goodbye to you now, with love.

•

These listed are the main strange bedfellows I accuse of participation in causing, so far, some billion deaths. Of course, the validity of this number, indeed all numbers, has already been questioned. As Fred has taught me, every step forward in the progress of homosexual acceptance has been checkmated for as long as possible by our enemies.

Now, of course, this Black and White Act is not being allowed to cooperate.

In the five years since I uncovered this law and the two years since I officially sued for its application, the Black and White Act has come to represent something else. Civil War historians point out the act was created only to protect the slave against his master. Legal scholars are responding that if this were so, that if the act was on the books, and known to be on the books, then the Civil War was, in essence, illegal. It shouldn't have been allowed to happen. Somehow our judicial system fucked up royally. If Mr. Black (or Mr. White) didn't want to be a slave, which would most certainly have been the case, according to the Black and White Act he couldn't be forced to be one. And anyone who tried to make him one would be in violation of the law. And presumably open to punishment. Somewhere along these centuries the Black and White Act was silenced.

Legal scholars are also asking: Are these just a few words accidentally found, or left, on the statute books, ones that somehow weren't excised completely for one reason or another, quite possibly because of their evident uselessness due to the numerous revisions of the Legal Code of the District of Columbia carried out over two hundred years since? It had, as Justice Punic said, "been on the books forever if anyone had ever bothered to look at the books."

And gay rights advocates, in the person of yours truly, are maintaining that the Black and White Act was meant to mean something very specific: it was meant to protect a minority against a majority, many of whom were against this protection. The Negro might be the obvious original beneficiary of the act, but it need not be just the Negro. It can be any minority. Like a poor white man. Why, it can even be the homosexual.

•

The question I then raised is this: If there is a plague that wipes out generations of gay people (as well as many others), and the government and others can be proved to have not done their utmost to protect the gay population against this plague, both before and during it, then said government and others are as guilty of genocide of homosexuals just as they were of the Negro at the time of the Civil War, when the Negro was at the mercy of slave owners who no longer wanted them around having exploited them near to death. The Black and White Act certainly allows this interpretation.

But homosexuals were "not known, recognized, not in existence at the time of the passing of this bill," as Aluto Allelelujah, a justice of the Supreme Court, immediately rules, in disallowing my argument to come forward for adjudication before this court. "And anyway, too many of your cast of characters have died."

Thus much confusion has reigned since my suit was brought in law courts right up to the Supreme one, which finally ruled that the law stood on the books as read, but only if proof would be forthcoming about when it was drafted and passed, etc.; and only then could it be sought for safety by the "current aggrieved." (Fred's Volume 1 attempted to prove that homosexuality certainly existed in 1800.) If it is a fake, in that it was interposed on the books by forgery, then someone will have to prove that, and if there indeed was homosexuality at that time, someone beyond Fred will have to prove that, and to this end the Brothers of Lovejoy have set to work delving into their archives, reputed (by them) to go back to the beginning of the Christian era. They have thus requested "a pause in the proceedings" to allow for this investigation to be "thorough and fair." This investigation will be supervised by one Delia Montagg Swindon, in partnership with Cardinal Blissful of the Vatican.

But as the plague reaches heights of almost unparalleled morbidity, a number of homosexuals, those worst stricken, citing the Black and White Act, have finally been granted legal permission by the federal district court to immediately bring suit against the United States government and Greeting and Presidium Pharmaceutical companies, both entities as joint representatives of the long list of others, dead and living, for alleged genocide, and for an unspecified amount of damages. "How do you put a price on a billion dead?" the chief lawyer for the accusers, Lucas Jerusalem, quite logically asked D.C. Chief Justice Detroika Flingge, who presided over this decision, assisted by her two associate justices, Verdant Rhue and Harry Lynn Thyme.

If any of the living defendants are actually found guilty of genocidal crimes against humanity, would they be allowed to walk away from the Punic Trials free? Or would they go to jail? Or be condemned to death? Could those alleged perpetrators who have died be condemned in absentia? These are not idle questions. Chief Justice Flingge's decision "leaves many points unclear, while allowing me to proceed, with trepidation, I might add," she wrote in her decision.

It must also be pointed out that there is still no ruling on any terminology necessary for differentiating between "genocide" and "crimes against humanity"—terms that remained purposely undefined or differentiated at Nuremberg itself.

So now I await a court date from D.C.'s court, with its Republican majority, after which I shall again appeal to the Supreme Court, also stacked with Republicans because of years of monsters running our country, Dereck Dumster being the most recent and hateful: the justices he's appointed have proven to be horror shows and are filled with hatred for almost everything.

So now, as with so many of the world's tragedies, we wait to see if justice continues to remain unavailable even if and especially when it's granted by a law that is hundreds of years old.

WRINKLES

The wrinkles are discomforting to look at, particularly the ones hanging from my tush. They look like bad drapery, hanging poorly, made of cheap, rough stuff. Attractiveness, if not beauty, if not perfection, has always been so important in the gay mystique. All people, to be sure, suffer aesthetic distress with aging. Still, it is uncomfortable to confront the mirror's inevitability.

Love has become something different. It is no longer physical as in other days. David and I go seriously to a gym each day and work out as strenuously as we can. He's over seventy (and I'm over eighty), but his body is quite a bit younger. He says mine doesn't bother him, but I know he's worried for me. We hug, we peck our kisses of greeting. I know he loves me as he knows that I love him. To say this after all we have been through should proclaim a certain triumph. As noted, we are even legally married. How did that sneak its way in? And how long before they take it away? Why after all these years are we still feeling so shy with each other? He is very happy. I can see that. He is a workaholic with much to work on as his case wends its way painfully slowly through the courts. He doesn't like to sit still. Even when he comes home to our house in the country, my once fantasy now made beautifully real, he is too busy to relax much. To be grateful I am alive, as everyone seems to think one is or should be every day upon arising, has never been a part of my genetic makeup, I am sorry to confess, no matter the transplant, no matter the "life-saving" meds, no matter the return of David, who saved my life not once but three different times, certainly surpassing any of my doctors.

He says to stop worrying. "Don't worry!" I often find on little Post-it notes he puts on my desk when he leaves early in the morning for another task, and I am alone to revise my book with finality for submission to my editor. "I love you," they say. "Write well."

Yes, I believe him.

How lucky we did not murder each other.

How excellent that we at last found love.

•

And we can all live happily ever after. Like in all the best, how you call them? Fairy tales.

•

INT. SUPREME COURT. DAY.
The courtroom is packed. David and Lucas sit up front awaiting the arrival of the justices. Fred sits along the aisle beside them.
CLERK: All rise for the justices of the Supreme Court of the United States of America!
Everyone stands as the justices enter and take their seats on the dais.
CHIEF JUSTICE: Mr. Jerusalem, are you ready to present your case?
DAVID: I am, Chief Justice.
CHIEF JUSTICE: You may proceed.
Suddenly a man in the audience stands up and shoots David Jerusalem. Fred rushes to cradle David in his arms. But David is already dead. The assailant has disappeared. Fred buries his head in David's body.

•

Yes, we can all live happily ever after. Like in all the best fairy tales.

ACKNOWLEDGMENTS

This has been my history of the plague I lived through, a brutality few ever dreamed of.

I do not pretend to have given an inclusive picture. There is no one who could give an all-embracing recital. I hope this book will encourage others to add their own experiences and histories so that the world will never forget.

While it is my story, my history, I am grateful to many others who contributed their voices and experiences to it. To particularly: Dame Lady Hermia Bledd-Wrench, Daniel Jerusalem, Dr. Sister Grace Hooker, Ianthe Adams Strode, Patti Montgomery, Sarah Schulman (The ACTUP Oral History Project [www .actuporalhistory.org] by Jim Hubbard and Sarah Schulman), Minna Trooble, Ann Fettner, Maxine Wolfe, Joy Johannessen, Laurie Garrett, Hannah Arendt (how many of them are women!), Craig Lucas, Rodger McFarlane, Dr. Cecil Fox, Jon Cohen, Norman Ohler, Dr. Jacques Pepin, Will Schwalbe, the inestimable Alex Star, Jonathan Galassi, George Sheanshang, Ryan Murphy, Peter Staley, Ron Goldberg, Edward Alsop, Jim Eigo, FUQU Brothers and Sisters all, and of course the memories of so many dead friends. I have been cared for by too many doctors to name. And I have been particularly cared for by my beloved husband, David Webster, whom I have loved for many years, and who has literally saved my life a number of times.

A NOTE ABOUT THE AUTHOR

Larry Kramer is a writer and an activist. After graduating from Yale College, he worked in the film industry and received an Oscar nomination for his screenplay adaptation of D. H. Lawrence's *Women in Love*. In 1981, he and five friends founded Gay Men's Health Crisis, and in 1987 he founded the AIDS Coalition to Unleash Power (ACT UP). His writings include the novel *Faggots*; the plays *The Normal Heart*, *The Destiny of Me*, and *Just Say No*; and the political works *Reports from the Holocaust* and *The Tragedy of Today's Gays*. He has received two Tony Awards, an Emmy Award, a Lucille Lortel Award, a PEN America Award, an Arts and Letters Award in Literature from the American Academy of Arts and Letters, and an honorary doctorate of humane letters from Yale University. In 2019 he was inducted into the New York State Writers Hall of Fame. He and his husband, the architect and interior designer David Webster, live in New York City and Connecticut.

A NOTE ABOUT THE AUTHOR

ALSO BY LARRY KRAMER

FICTION

Faggots

The American People, Volume I: Search for My Heart

NONFICTION

The Tragedy of Today's Gays

Reports from the Holocaust: The Story of an AIDS Activist

DRAMA

Women in Love and Other Dramatic Writings
(Sissies' Scrapbook, A Minor Dark Age, Just Say No)

The Destiny of Me

The Normal Heart